WOMEN CELEBRATING THE LOVE
BETWEEN WOMEN

Two Friends by MARY E. WILKINS (FREEMAN)
This collection's exquisitely written title story brings to life the decades-long, passionate relationship of two nineteenth-century women as death threatens to part them and reveal a secret hidden for forty years.

Max—Or His Picture
by OCTAVE THANET (ALICE FRENCH)
Alice French's "coded" story was written at a time when love relationships between women were pathologized. In it a woman never removes the ring that everyone assumes her husband gave her, but that, as we learn, symbolizes another, more powerful love.

The Falling in Love of Fedora by KATE CHOPIN
Part of a collection of unusual stories of passion rejected for publication following the furor over Chopin's *The Awakening*, this small gem was far ahead of its time in style and theme as a self-possessed woman of thirty falls unexpectedly in love.

There and Here by ALICE BROWN
Anyone who loves a ghost story will savor this tale of a love between women strong enough to conquer death, by New Englander Alice Brown, who was a member of the literary circle surrounding Sarah Orne Jewett and her partner in their "Boston marriage," Annie Adams Fields.

SUSAN KOPPELMAN is a prize-winning literary historian and the editor of *The Signet Classic Book of Southern Short Stories* and *"May Your Days Be Merry and Bright"*: *Christmas Stories by Women* (Mentor). She lives in Tucson, Arizona.

EDITED AND WITH AN INTRODUCTION BY
SUSAN KOPPELMAN

TWO FRIENDS

*and Other Nineteenth-Century
Lesbian Stories by American
Women Writers*

A MERIDIAN BOOK

MERIDIAN

Published by the Penguin Group
Penguin Books USA Inc., 375 Hudson Street, New York, New York 10014, U.S.A.
Penguin Books Ltd, 27 Wrights Lane, London W8 5TZ, England
Penguin Books Australia Ltd, Ringwood, Victoria, Australia
Penguin Books Canada Ltd, 10 Alcorn Avenue, Toronto, Ontario, Canada M4V 3B2
Penguin Books (N.Z.) Ltd, 182–190 Wairau Road, Auckland 10, New Zealand

Penguin Books Ltd, Registered Offices:
Harmondsworth, Middlesex, England

Published by Meridian,
an imprint of Dutton Signet,
a division of Penguin Books USA Inc.

First Printing, August, 1994
1 3 5 7 9 10 8 6 4 2

 REGISTERED TRADEMARK — MARCA REGISTRADA

Library of Congress Cataloging-in-Publication Data
Two friends and other nineteenth-century lesbian stories by American
women writers / edited and with an introduction by Susan Koppelman.
p. cm.
Contents: Introduction—My visitation / by Rose Terry—Since I
died / by Elizabeth Stuart Phelps—Felipa / by Constance Fenimore
Woolson—My Lorelei / by Octave Thanet (Alice French)—Miss
Grief / by Constance Fenimore Woolson—Two friends / by Mary E.
Wilkins (Freeman)—The long arm / by Mary E. Wilkins (Freeman)—
The falling in love of Fedora / by Kate Chopin—There and here /
by Alice Brown—Martha's lady / by Sarah Orne Jewett—Max—or his
picture / by Octave Thanet (Alice French)—A note on the text.
ISBN 0-452-01119-1
1. Lesbians—Fiction. 2. Lesbians' writings, American. 3. Erotic
stories, American—Women authors. I. Koppelman, Susan.
PS648.L47T86 1994
813'.4080353—dc20
94-3896
CIP

Printed in the United States of America

THIS BOOK IS DEDICATED TO JOANNA RUSS.

JOANNA RUSS, great feminist, great writer, and my beloved friend for twenty-two years, always more than a thousand miles away, always near and close, always generous in every way, always receptive, sharer of the sentence of lives of pain and weariness, inspiration, influence, support, and, now, my neighbor.

CONTENTS

TWO FRIENDS

PREFACE

With the publication of *Surpassing the Love of Men: Romantic Friendship and Love between Women from the Renaissance to the Present* (1977), Lillian Faderman established as a fact that women loving each other has a history and a culture. Lesbian cultural theorist Judy Grahn demonstrated in *Another Mother Tongue: Gay Words, Gay Worlds* (1984) a way of unearthing that history through linguistic detective work. Other scholars have worked to make available to readers various cultural artifacts and interpretations of that history. This book is a collection of short stories by nineteenth-century U.S. women writers who were elemental in the creation of a lesbian tradition in literature in that period, in this place.

Can a person living in the late twentieth century know what it was like to be a person living in the middle or late nineteenth century? *Even if the nineteenth-century person had a lot of the same attributes that you have*—sex, race, religion, a good ear for music, a passion for reading stories, similar appearance—*doesn't the fact that almost everything else was different*—technology including everything from food preservation to modes of communication to ways of killing other people, the scientific understanding of the way the physical world works, commonly accepted beliefs about the nature of a human being—*mean that we can't imagine what it was like?*

Our sense of the past changes as we are exposed to increasingly sophisticated or at least *different* portrayals of the past. Our understanding of relationships between people who lived in earlier times changes, too.

Even though the stories were set in the nineteenth century and things were *very different* in the nineteenth century, if we read about a man and woman loving each other in the way, for instance, that Abby loves Sarah in "Two Friends" or Martha loves Helena in "Martha's Lady," we would not wonder what the story was about or quarrel about how to label the relationship. We would know.

When we read the lesbian historical novels written in the last twenty years, we recognize the love relationships, the sexual attractions, between women as *lesbian*. (See, for instance, *Patience and Sarah* by Isabel Miller or *Avalon* by Mary J. Jones.) There is often explicit genital sexual activity between the women, and the women frequently declare their love to each other in contemporary terms. We can say that the vocabulary is anachronistic, but as for the sexual activity and the emotions—we cannot know that they aren't authentic. Certainly sexual love between women was neither unknown nor unremarked by the end of the nineteenth century, when most of these stories were written. In Carl Degler's *At Odds: Women and the Family in America from the Revolution to the Present* (1980), he quotes a report delivered to the American Medical Association in 1899 warning against the dangers of young women going to college:

> The young girls, thus thrown together manifest an increasing affection by the usual tokens: They kiss each other fondly on every occasion. They embrace each other with mutual satisfaction. It is most natural, in the interchange of visits for them to sleep together. They learn the pleasure of direct contact, and in the course of their fondling they resort to cunni-linguistic practices . . . after this the normal sex act fails to satisfy her. (P. 157)

I could adduce evidence to "prove" that these nineteenth-century stories are "lesbian" stories; I could invoke the work of contemporary historians (herstorians), literary scholars, political scientists, and sociologists (Blanche Wiesen Cook, Carroll Smith-Rosenberg, Gloria Hull, Lillian Faderman, Julia Penelope, Joyce Trebilcot, Sheila Jeffreys, Margaret Cruikshank, Barbara Smith, Bonnie Zimmerman) to support my contention that these are "lesbian" stories. I could detail point-by-point comparisons between contemporary lesbian fiction and these nineteenth-century stories. But this is not the place for such arguments. And besides, for every argument, there is a counterargument if someone is inclined to argue. Instead, I will say that these stories *feel* like lesbian stories to me.

These stories *feel* like lesbian stories to me in the same way that stories like O. Henry's "Gift of the Magi," Arna Bontemps' "A Summer Tragedy," and Kate Chopin's "The Storm" or Zora Neale Hurston's description of the relationship between Janie Crawford and Teacake in *Their Eyes Were Watching God feel* like heterosexual stories.

I have been reading short stories written by U.S. women writers of the nineteenth and twentieth centuries as a literary scholar, archaeologist, and historian for more than twenty years now. I did not start with any ideas about what I would find other than the belief that women's stories were there, somewhere, and I would be able to find them. But I didn't assume I knew what they would be about. And it wasn't until I had been reading widely and deeply, until I had read at least one story per day for ten years, that I began to feel that I had read enough to assert that I was beginning to know what women's stories are about.

At least half of the stories I have read have turned out to be stories about relationships between women. All kinds of relationships between all kinds of women. Stories about mothers and daughters. Stories about the relationships between women who discover that they are each in love with the same man and that he's messing with both of them. Stories about women who forge bonds of friendships that sustain them. And stories about women who *love* each other. The mothers and daughters usually love each other. The women who are being deceived by the same man almost always grow to respect each other, and, sometimes, to care for each other. The friendships always involve reciprocity, caring, and love. But the stories about women loving each other are different from all those other kinds of love.

I recognize these stories as stories about women loving women in the variety of romantic ways that we wouldn't even have to struggle to define if we were talking about men and women loving each other. We don't have to wonder about whether or not love between women exists. It does. It always has. And, in the nineteenth-century United States, after the Civil War, during the height of the struggle for Women's Rights, during the years in which were born the generation of women whose members had the highest percentage of never-married women in the history of this country, women began to write lesbian stories. Here are eleven of those stories.

ACKNOWLEDGMENTS

This book wouldn't have happened without the help and encouragement of many people. My deepest appreciation to Joanna Russ and Joyce Trebilcot for their perceptive readings of and writing about these stories; to Emily Toth both for drafting the Kate Chopin headnote and for sharing her unpublished work on Mary E. Wilkins Freeman; to Barbara Grier for early encouragement of this project and for information about contemporary lesbian historical novels; to Carole Appel for continuing encouragement of this project; to Jessica Amanda Salmonson for calling my attention to and providing a copy of "Since I Died"; to Carol Farley Kessler for helping me contextualize this Phelps story; to Blanche Wiesen Cook for talking with me about the ideas and stories in this book and for all the work she has done; to Pat Frazier Lamb for locating and sending me a copy of "The Long Arm" after my two years of trying to get a copy were unsuccessful; to Paula Bennett for discussing my questions about nineteenth-century symbolism. Thanks to Betty Burnett, Carolyn Karcher, and Annette Kolodny for advising me on textual questions, especially relating to "Martha's Lady." Thanks to Martha Baker for helping me think through some of the issues in "Martha's Lady."

I am grateful as always to Rudolph Clay of the Washington University Olin Library, to Bruce Collins and Linda Ballard of the University City Public Library, to Ron Allen and Kay Sheehan of the Olin Business School Library at Washington University, and to Herb Warner in the Economics Department at the University of Missouri, St. Louis, for help in understanding some of the economic issues of the period covered by this collection. I am also thankful to Meg Schoerke for her able and intelligent assistance during the final months of preparing this manuscript. Thanks also to the staff of Our World Too, the Lesbian and Gay Community Bookstore of St. Louis, who have always been generous with their time to answer all sorts of what must have sometimes seemed to be really strange questions. What they couldn't find for me, they found out or found out where I could find out.

I am grateful to my editor at Dutton/Signet, Rosemary Ahern, who has now seen me through two books with never-failing kindness, patience, and good humor. And more thanks go to my agent Beth Vesel at the Sanford Greenberg Agency. She has faith in me and that is both a pleasure and a comfort.

My continuing gratitude to Rebeccah Kiske of Tampa, Florida, whose work as a massage therapist made it possible for me to begin the return to my work, and to Terry Trushel and Barbara Eaton, Doctors of Chiropractic, and to Lori Hoffman, massage therapist and student at Logan College of Chiropractic, who continued Rebeccah's work in St. Louis. This book took six years longer to complete than I expected. As Barbara Hillyer has argued so movingly in the chapter "Productivity and Pace" in the book *Feminism and Disability*, chronic illness sets its own pace. It also gives our ideas time to ripen.

My abiding and immeasurable love to Frances Koppelman, Dennis Mills, Emily Toth, Martin Daniel Richardson, and Barbara Harman for their love, support, and patience through this book and all my work and life. Each of them read many drafts of many parts of this book. My mother, Frances Koppelman, worked with me to establish textual variations between the periodical first publications of each story and the later book publications. We read aloud to each other for hours. It was probably the most fun part of this whole project.

I quite simply could not work without a computer. And I

never would have dared come to computers without the help and encouragement of my beloved son, Edward Nathan Koppelman Cornillon. Thank you, Nathan, for making me safe in the world of computers. I've even begun to explore a little on my own, finally, knowing you will be there to right my mistakes.

I also want to thank the many dealers in antique jewelry along Royal Street in the French Quarter in New Orleans who took the time on Good Friday 1993 to read the section in "Max—Or His Picture" and tell me what they knew about the ring. I included the information that was confirmed by at least three of them in the second Thanet headnote. Only one of them was certain that in the late nineteenth century the sapphire was a stone that lesbians exchanged because of its associations with Sappho but since I could not otherwise confirm the information I have omitted it. (Except for sneaking it in right here!)

Riff-Raff IV, the only cat in our family of cats to survive the 1991 summer outbreak of feline leukemia virus in our home, did his part, too. Not many of us can write without at least one cat in the house. I'm glad I don't have to try. We continue to mourn Pizza, Bruce, Emily, Squeaker, and Jack. And we still miss Mrs. Cat, Raggedy Andy, Pepper, and Riff-Raffs I, II, and III.

Whenever I finish a book, I look up and around to see what's happening out in the world. As I completed these acknowledgments on this day, May 29, 1993, I looked up to see what seemed to be hundreds of women streaming in the direction of Washington University, carrying the familiar-to-me cases and gig bags with trumpets and trombones, euphoniums and French horns and tubas. Today is the second day of the First International Women's Brass Conference. On page two of the IWBC program I read "The first known mention of women brass players occurred in a treatise, written in 1564 by H. Bottrigari, in which it was reported that women were playing cornetti and trombones at the Convent San Vito in Ferrar. Even after nearly 400 years, the amount of information regarding women brass performers is still virtually nonexistent. As a result, women performers today are largely unaware of their ongoing contributions to music history." It is thrilling to see that yet another part of women's past is being recovered. I want to pay tribute to Susan Slaughter, the first woman ever to be named Principal Trumpet of a major symphony orchestra, the Saint Louis

Symphony Orchestra, a woman whom I have never met, who founded the International Women's Brass Conference and put this conference together. I'm looking forward to a wonderful time listening to women make music for five days. What a wonderful way to celebrate completing this book!

INTRODUCTION

Nineteenth-century writers and readers loved a good ghost story. Ghost stories, riddle stories, stories of mystery and illusion not only thrilled the reader's imagination, but freed the writer to explore ideas scented with the air of the forbidden, to hint at possibilities that weren't discussed openly in polite company. Underlying the excitement of the mysteries were intimations of the unspeakable.

Ghost stories, stories of dreams that appear to be reality until the last sentence, stories in which the central character solves problems as she walks in her sleep, stories told by a narrator who is revealed to be an inmate in an insane asylum, and riddle tales in which some crucial element to understanding the events or characters in the story is left to the imagination of the reader gave writers the opportunity to allude to the unsayable, or, perhaps, the unpublishable. Since the central theme, that is, the real subject, of the story was never spelled out, the stories couldn't be censored—or even criticized for their impropriety. After all, if it wasn't identified overtly, then perhaps it wasn't really intended. And if some reader "read" the unspeakable into the story, then might not what the reader "read" be a product of his or her own diseased imagination and not at all what the writer intended? And so the nineteenth-century stories that deal most obviously to the modern reader with a variety of deviations from explicit social norms are stories that never actually name the so-called deviation. Thus, we find stories about incest, infidelity, wife abuse, addiction, and rape. In this same category of stories female characters rebel against the patriarchy, pursue their personal ambitions, achieve success where they are forbidden to even enter, and love women more than they love men.

This collection of eleven stories about love between women might have been titled "Stories of Mystery, Illusion, Transformation, and Death." In most of them, there is a mystery, a death or both. In "My Visitation" a mysterious Presence haunts a woman until she identifies her lost love; "Since I Died" portrays what we now call a "near death" experience—although there is no reversal of the postmortem state in this story; "My Lorelei" tells of a strange and accursed prophesy fulfilled by the death of a beautiful woman; in "Miss Grief" a gifted woman dies before her gift is recognized; Abby tries to forestall the impending death of her beloved Sarah by creating an illusion in "Two Friends"; "The Long Arm" is an early classical locked-room murder mystery; a consoling ghostly visitation is the central event in "There and Here." That is seven of the eleven. "Felipa," "Fedora," "Max—Or His Picture," and "Martha's Lady" are stories of transformations in consciousness—a kind of emotional magic.

Each of the eight authors of these eleven elegantly crafted and exquisitely written nineteenth-century U.S. stories was recognized both in her own time and in ours as an important and accomplished writer. In her own time each had devoted readers, achieved a respected place in the professional literary world, and earned a comfortable income by exercise of her imagination and her pen. These writers helped shape American literature to their taste and in their image. Each of these women wrote about a wide range of subjects and characters with insight, beauty, and authority. These are their stories about women loving women. And these stories are the beginnings of lesbian literature in the United States.

We won't find the word "lesbian" in any of the stories in this collection. What, then, does it mean to call these stories written in the nineteenth century *lesbian* stories? These stories are about various aspects of romantic love: sexual love, partnership love, mated love, infatuated love, idealized love, lost love. All of these kinds of love are love between women.

There is sustained domestic commitment between Abby and Sarah in "Two Friends." Unrequited passion of one woman for a cruel, seemingly heartless other woman sets the tone of "My Visitation"; idealized and transfiguring love in "Martha's Lady" reminds us of medieval chivalric passion; and the confused, impossible, and misunderstood pubescent passion of "Felipa" is as heartbreaking as any contemporary love story. The love stories range from the ethereal in the anguished loss of a beloved in "There and Here" to the clearly carnal in the disinterested sexual experimentation of "Fedora." There is the intense romantic friendship between Constance and Undine in "My Lorelei" and the faithful remembrance of Elly by Margaret in "Max—Or His Picture." The grief of her surviving partner pulls the recently dead beloved in "Since I Died" back to the world she has so recently departed. Self-righteousness and jealousy result in murder in "The Long Arm." We so take for granted these kinds of romantic love between men and women that we qualify nonromantic love between men and women with its own special term: Platonic love. People are always wondering if it can *really* exist. The stories in this book are stories about non-Platonic love between women.

Two stories are simultaneously the center of this collection and its opposite poles. Published within seven years of each other ("Miss Grief" in 1880 and "Two Friends" in 1887), they each portray lesbian lives and sensibilities, one in a covert way ("Miss Grief") and the other quite openly ("Two Friends").

"Two Friends" illuminates the climate of the time and place in which lifelong partnerships between women were lived publicly and with community acceptance. The resolution of the story is one that reaffirms the strength of the connection between two women who have spent their lives loving each other. It portrays a domestic establishment that supports community values and a community status quo which includes devoted female couples.

"Two Friends" is only one of the nineteenth-century stories that help us re-create and understand a world in which this type of relationship was common enough and visible enough that it could be the background rather than the foreground of fiction. In the foreground of the stories are those themes and conflicts common to stories about consummated and publicly condoned love: illness, natural disasters, separations forced by circumstances beyond the control of the lovers, financial crises, misunderstandings, the temptations to infidelity, and so forth.

Ghost stories. There are three of them in here. In the first story, "My Visitation," the narrator is first conscious of "It" as she suffers from the ague, the chills and fever, of illness. And it is autumn, a time of year she characterizes as sad, as dominated by "the hush of decay." We later learn that "It" is the manifestation of the girl she fell in love with when she was sixteen. But since "It" appears first when the narrator is ill and might be delirious, we can't be certain that there really ever was a ghost. The ghost in "Since I Died" is the narrator herself. And we learn only at the end that the lover from whom she is parted is a "her." And even then, it's just possible that she is writing about—could it be a sister? Because she mentions "mother" as if the woman could be the mother of both of them. And yet, at the end, when she refers to "mother" again, this time it is "*my* mother," and not *our* mother. The intimations of lesbian love in this story come slowly, bit by tiny bit, and then still are subject to interpretation. Alice Brown's story "There and Here" also revolves around a thrilling, joy-filled visitation from a departed beloved. Three ghost stories.

And "My Lorelei" turns around ancient legends of supernatural women fatally dangerous either to themselves or to those who love them—and the fulfillment of a superstitious curse. Another supernatural phenomenon!

"Miss Grief" is a classic nineteenth-century riddle tale, the sort of allegory popular then which has, still, as its lingering effect an obsessive question. The question "Miss Grief" leaves the reader with is "What was it that the master editor couldn't 'cure' her writing of?"

The conceited male narrator of "Miss Grief" tells us that he himself has written a riddle tale, and that it is his favorite piece of his own writing. He admits that Aaronna Moncrief's interpretation of his "psychological riddle" is even deeper and more astute than his own understanding of it. His recognition of her ability to understand and interpret a riddle tale alerts us not only to the possibility, the likelihood, that "Miss Grief" is also a riddle tale, but suggests that perhaps Aaronna Moncrief's drama and stories are also riddle tales. If she can understand *his* riddle tales better than he can himself, then it is likely that he doesn't even recognize that *her* work is riddled. Or rather, he *does* think her work is riddled —as in: it is flawed; it has a fault running through it as serious as the New Madrid or San Andreas faults.

Because he recognizes her genius, her originality, and her "force," he assumes the job of trying to rid her work of its flaw. He rewrites and rewrites—and discovers that it cannot be done; the work cannot be separated from the fault that runs through it and remain "the work."

This story makes me wonder about what and how much about a piece of writing can be changed and have it still remain the same piece of writing. Is it the same story if I change the names of all the characters? Is it the same story if I set it in another country? Is it the same story if it happened fifty years ago instead of yesterday?

Willa Cather thought she could answer yes to the question: Could it still be the same story if you said that it happened between a man and a woman instead of between two women?

Sarah Orne Jewett, one of Cather's literary idols, wrote to Cather after reading her story "On the Gull's Road" and warned her that *it can't be done*:

> "The lover is as well done as he could be when a woman writes in the man's character,—it must always, I believe, be something of a masquerade . . ."*

Gertrude Stein wrote a story about a love triangle that was played out while she was on a cruise with two other women. She called the story "Quod Erad Demonstrandum (Things as They Are)." Later, she wrote what she thought was the same story, but this time the triangle consisted of two women and one man. This version of the story she called "Melanctha." Most of the attention paid to "Melanctha" by critics has been directed at the fact that the characters are black, but it is at least equally important that

---

* Quoted by Lillian Faderman in *Surpassing the Love of Men: Romantic Friendship and Love between Women from the Renaissance to the Present*, p. 202, from the *Letters of Sarah Orne Jewett*, ed. Annie Fields (Boston: Houghton Mifflin and Co., 1911), pp. 246–247.

they are heterosexual. Gertrude Stein thought she was writing the same story—but was she?

In Edith Wharton's autobiography *A Backward Glance*, she remembers her friend Walter Berry:

> . . . I was much helped by Walter Berry. No critic was ever severer, but none had more respect for the artist's liberty. He taught me never to be satisfied with my own work, but never to let my inward conviction as to the rightness of anything I had done be affected by outside opinion. I remember, after writing the first chapters of "The Valley of Decision," which I had begun in a burst of lyric rapture and didn't know how to go on with, confessing to him my difficulty and my discouragement. He looked through what I had written, handed it back, and said simply: "Don't worry about how you're to go on. Just write down everything you feel like telling." The advice freed me once for all from the incubus of an artificially pre-designed plan, and sent me rushing ahead with my task, letting each incident create the next, and keeping in sight only the novelist's essential sign-post; the inner significance of the "case" selected. Yet when the novel was done, I remember how meticulously he studied it from the point of view of language, marking down faulty syntax and false metaphors, smiling away over-emphasis and unnecessary repetitions, helping me patiently through the beginner's verbal perplexities, yet never laying hands on what he considered sacred: the *soul* of the novel, which is (or should be) the writer's own soul.

The narrator of "Miss Grief" tells us that the drama, "Armor," is Aaronna Moncrief's greatest work, the purest expression of her genius, but he doesn't tell us what it is about. The only story of her work that he tells us is her prose story, about which he says, "she was less fantastic . . . but hardly more reasonable" than in her drama.

And *that* story is the story he is telling us in "Miss Grief," the story that Constance Fenimore Woolson has written, the story of a handsome-faced, sweet-voiced but commonplace man who is mistakenly idealized by a pure but mistaken, dying girl. *He* is a commonplace man, weary of and bored by the role of mentor and advocate she has tried to propel him into. And she, Aaronna, is the pure but mistaken, dying girl.

Now, why do I call this a lesbian story? Because of that "fault" the narrator goes on and on about—without ever describing. Because this is a riddle tale and what can the riddle be if it is not "What was the 'fault' in Aaronna's writing?" And if we are to believe Edith Wharton, then the "fault" of the work must also be the "fault" of the woman, because it is clearly the "soul" of the work that cannot be revised out of it. And Wharton tells us that the soul of the work is the soul of the writer.

I think what the conceited narrator calls Aaronna's flaw is a lesbian/feminist/womanist vision—a vision of the world in which *either* the assumptions of the heterosexist patriarchy are exposed, described, laid bare, stripped of flattering pretenses and "scientific" rationalizations *or* she imagines a world in which the patriarchy is deposed, a lesbian/feminist utopia—something like Charlotte Perkins Gilman's *Herland* or Joanna Russ's *The Female Man*. Whatever "it" is, it is something that *he just doesn't get.*

That the other stories in this collection are lesbian stories has never been questioned by any of those who have read it in manuscript. And in those stories we find all sorts of "blatant" portrayals of lesbian love, lesbian passion, lesbian heartbreak, and lesbians living out their lives together as accepted members of their community. If, in the nineteenth-century United States, it was possible to publish stories as explicitly lesbian, as overtly about the subject of women loving women, as these other stories, then what might have been so daring, so deviant, so dangerous about "Miss Grief" 's vision that it had to be written as a riddle story, that it could only be inferred by a deviant reader, that it could be implied subtly enough that the author was safe from any accusation that she had actually written what we can read into the story?

That is the riddle. How daringly can we read this story, this lesbian riddle tale, in the context of all those other flagrantly lesbian stories? That all depends on what we dare. What we remember. What we wish for. What we are angry about.

EPIGRAPHS

*Because difference arouses fear and condemnation, there are seri-
ous methodological problems involved in writing about women
who, for political and economic reasons, kept their private lives as
secret as possible. . . . How then, male historians continually ask,
do you know these women were lesbians? . . . Women who love
women, who choose women to nurture and support and to create
a living environment in which to work creatively and independently, are lesbians.*

*It may seem elementary to state here that lesbians cannot
be defined simply as women who practice certain physical rites
together. Unfortunately, the heterosexist image—and sometimes
even the feminist image—of the lesbian is defined by sexual behavior alone, and sexual in the most limited sense. It therefore
seems important to reiterate that physical love between women is
one expression of a whole range of emotions and responses to each
other that involves all the mysteries of our human nature. Woman-
related women feel attraction, yearning, and excitement with
women. Nobody and no theory has yet explained why for some
women, despite all cultural conditioning and societal penalties,*

both intellectual and emotional excitement are aroused in response to women.

> "Female Support Networks and Political Activism: Lillian Wald, Crystal Eastman, Emma Goldman" by Blanche Wiesen Cook in *A Heritage of Her Own: Toward a New Social History of American Women* edited, with an introduction by Nancy F. Cott and Elizabeth H. Pleck, Simon and Schuster, 1979, pp. 419–420.

In the interstices of language lie powerful secrets of the culture.

> *Of Woman Born: Motherhood as Experience and Institution* by Adrienne Rich, Norton, 1976, p. 249.

. . . I did not want to mask the nature of the relationship nor to sanitize or homogenize it to make it easier for readers to accept. I do not know if they even slept together, nor do I think such intimate knowledge is necessarily central to our understanding of their relationship. We do not demand proof of sexual activity as a badge of heterosexuality.

> "Unlocking the Porter-Dewson Partnership: A Challenge for the Feminist Biographer" by Susan Ware in *The Challenge of Feminist Biography: Writing the Lives of Modern American Women* edited by Sara Alpern, Joyce Antler, Elisabeth Israels Perry, and Ingrid Winther Scobie, The University of Illinois Press, Urbana and Chicago, 1992, p. 59.

. . . we might expect that before the twentieth century, before love between women was counted among the diseases, women would have had little reason to disguise their emotional attachments; therefore, they should have left a record of their love of other women. And they did.

> "Who Hid Lesbian History?" by Lillian Faderman in *Lesbian Studies: Present and Future* edited by Margaret Cruikshank, The Feminist Press, 1982, p. 115.

*We are not free, nor will we be, until this silence at last is ended
and we are invisible no more.*
> Paula Bennett, "Dyke in Academe (II), in *Lesbian
> Studies: Present and Future*, edited by Margaret
> Cruikshank, The Feminist Press, 1982, p. 7.

*The word "Lesbian" must be affirmed because to discard it is to
collaborate with silence and lying about our very existence, the
closet-game, the creation of the UNSPEAKABLE.*
> "It is the Lesbian in Us" by Adrienne Rich, *Sin-
> ister Wisdom*, Spring, 1977, pp. 6–9.

*. . . in order to see lesbianism—and this is true regardless of one's
sexual orientation—one must develop clear vision. . . . I hope that
all feminists will read with lesbian sensibility, just as all white middle class women must read with a sensitivity to third world and
working class reality.*
> Bonnie Zimmerman, " 'What Has Never Been':
> Directions in Lesbian Feminist Literary Criti-
> cism," paper presented at NWSA, 1979.

*The essential question is not whether these women had genital con-
tact and can therefore be defined as heterosexual or homosexual.
The twentieth-century tendency to view human love and sexuality
within a dichotomized universe of deviance and normality, geni-
tality and platonic love, is alien to the emotions and attitudes of
the nineteenth century and fundamentally distorts the nature of
these women's emotional interaction.*
> Carroll Smith-Rosenberg, "The Female World of
> Love and Ritual: Relations between Women in
> Nineteenth-Century America," *Signs* I, no. 1,
> 1975, p. 8.

ROSE TERRY

If a man has a reputation as a writer, it does him great service; there are a few men in America who might write the wildest nonsense, and in their script and under their name no editor would dare to refuse it; but it is not so with women. . . . This is the sort of thing that befalls a woman who writes, and all she can do is to accept the situation.*

"My Visitation" was first published in *Harper's New Monthly Magazine* in July 1858 when Rose Terry was already a well-known and highly distinguished writer. The magazine, a subsidiary of the successful publishing house co-owned by the four wealthy Harper brothers and edited by one of them, Fletcher, declared in its initial issue in June 1850 its intention to "place within the reach of the great mass of the American people the unbounded treasures of the Periodical Literature of the present day." The editor of the maga-

---

* From "A Letter to Mary Ann." *Sunday Afternoon* 3 (Jan. 1879): 79–83, quoted in *"How Celia Changed Her Mind" & Selected Stories: Rose Terry Cooke* edited and with an introduction by Elizabeth Ammons, Rutgers University Press, New Brunswick, New Jersey, 1986.

zine counted on the writers he published to exercise moral self-censorship so that nothing in the magazine would "violate the house policy of printing only material that could be read aloud in any family circle." Even Thomas Hardy was forced both to rewrite and to submit to editorial rewriting of his work to avoid even a suggestion of vulgarity.

And yet, these policies did not result in the exclusion from *Harper's* of Rose Terry's story about the passionate love of one young woman for another. It was, evidently, not considered wild nonsense. Perhaps that is because, at the end of the story, this woman who so passionately loves another woman, is learning to love a man.

The story is written as a conventional ghost story in which "weird" happenings are "normal." Additionally, the story is written by a narrator who proclaims herself incoherent and reeling, who describes herself as "morbid, intense, and excitable . . . ," and who suffers repeated emotional collapses. All of these attributes render her version of events untrustworthy. Can we really believe what she writes when her state of mind is so troubled? But even with the double remove from the facts provided by a ghost story and an unreliable narrator, this story is clearly a lesbian love story. It is about a woman who "never could have loved any man as I did her," who "had but the lesser part of a heart to give any man," who "loved a woman too well to love or to marry," whose "one present and all-absorbing passion" was another woman, Eleanor —whose betrayal of the narrator was so horrible as to be, finally, unspeakable, and who could ask for forgiveness and declare her own love only after her own, unexplained death.

The most peculiar thing about the publication of "My Visitation" is that this story, which is clearly a Christmas story, obviously a story about forgiveness and redemption—"The Christmas bells pealed loud and clear for dawn, and my thoughts rung their own joy bells beside the steeple chimes"—was published in July. It may also be significant that the story was never collected in one of its author's volumes of short stories.

Rose Terry (Cooke) was born on February 17, 1827, in Wethersfield, Connecticut, the first child of Anne Wright Hurlbut and her husband Henry Wadsworth Terry. In her sixth year, she, along with her year-old sister Alice and their parents, moved to Hartford, Connecticut, to live in her father's mother's home. Although she recorded in letters and essays abundant memories of a happy childhood, in her Introduction to *"How Celia Changed Her Mind" & Selected Stories,* Elizabeth Ammons suggests that there was a much darker side to her childhood, one in which is rooted "the adult author's repeated dramatization of a man's power to terrify a dependent female into submission and silence." (P. xvi) Rose was graduated from the Hartford Female Seminary, the school founded by Catharine Beecher, at the age of sixteen. In this same year, she became an active member of the Congregational Church after a conversion experience. Her Calvinist religious ideas color many of her stories.

After several years away from home working as a teacher and governess, she inherited enough money to return in 1848 to her family, to a life of domestic and literary work that continued without much change until her marriage twenty-six years later. During these years she produced increasingly well-received stories. She was invited to contribute the leading story to the first issue of the *Atlantic Monthly* in 1857.

After her beloved mother's death in 1872—about whom she wrote "For myself, I owe whatever power of expression I have to the patient care of my mother, who educated me chiefly herself . . ." —she married Rollin H. Cooke, a widower sixteen years her junior with two daughters. His father's business failures and his own financial ineptitude drained her savings and she began to write more quickly than carefully to keep bread on the family table, draining not only her literary resources, but also her physical resources. Her health was always fragile, but under the strain of financial pressure, she became increasingly ill. Repeated episodes of pneumonia undermined her health further and she died in Pittsfield, Massachusetts, on July 18, 1892, after a series of bouts with influenza.

Rose Terry (Cooke) published nearly two hundred stories in various periodicals. Fewer than half of them were collected and published in book form in *Somebody's Neighbors* (1881), *Root-Bound and Other Sketches* (1885), *Sphinx's Children and Other People's* (1886), and *Huckleberries Gathered from New England*

Hills (1891). She is recognized as a major figure in late nineteenth-century American literature, one of the founders of the so-called school of "local color" or "regional" writing.

My Visitation

> "Is not this she of whom,
> When first she came, all flushed you said to me,
>
>   *   *   *   *   *   *   *
>
> Now could you share your thought; now should men see
> Two women faster welded in one love
> Than pairs of wedlock?"
>
> The Princess.

If this story is incoherent—arranged rather for the writer's thought than for the reader's eye—it is because the brain which dictated it reeled with the sharp assaults of memory, that living anguish that abides while earth passes away into silence; and because the hand that wrote it trembled with electric thrills from a past that can not die, forever fresh in the soul it tested and tortured—powerful after the flight of years as in its first agony, to fill the dim eye with tears, and throb the languid pulses with fresh fever and passion.

Take, then, the record as it stands, and ask not from a cry of mortal pain the liquid cadence and accurate noting of an operatic bravura.

The first time *It* came was in broad day. I was ill, unable to rise; the day was cold; autumnal sunshine, pure and still, streamed through the house and came in at both the south windows of my room, the curtains drawn wide to receive it, for the ague of sickness is worse to me than its pain, and not yet had my preparations for winter enabled me to have a fire. Every thing was clear and chill; Aunt Mary, down stairs in the parlor, sat and knitted, as it was her custom to do of an afternoon; Uncle Seth was not at home; the servant had gone to mass, for it was some feast-day of her Church—no sound or echo disturbed the solitude.

There is something peculiar in a silent day of autumn; melancholy pierces its fine sting through the rays of sunshine; sadness cries in the cricket's monotonous voice; separation and death symbolize in the slow leaves that quit the bough reluctantly, and lie down in dust to be over-trodden—to rot. I can endure any silence better than this hush of decay; it fills me with preternatural horror; it is as if a tomb opened and breathed out its dank, morbid breath across the murmur of life, to paralyze and to chill.

But that day I had taken refuge from the awe and foreboding, the ticking of the clock, the dust-motes floating on light, the startling crack that now and then a springing board or an ill-hung window made. I had taken a book. I was deep in Shirley; it excited, it affected me; it is always to me like a brief and voluntary brain-fever to read that book. Jane Eyre is insanity for the time. Villette is like the scarlet fever; it possesses, it chokes, flushes, racks you; it leaves you weak and in vague pain, apprehensive of some bad result; but it was Shirley I read, so forgetting every thing. I am not lonely usually, yet I know when I am alone; there is an indescribable freedom in the sense of solitude, no alien sphere crosses and disturbs mine, no intrusive influence distorts the orbit; I am myself—or I was, then. Presently, as I lay there, the clock struck three. I was to take some potion at that hour. I must rise and get it. I set one foot on the floor, and was putting a shoe upon the other cautiously, when it occurred to me, why was I so careful? and I remembered that it had seemed to me something was on the bed when I moved—my kitten perhaps. I looked, there was nothing there; but I was not alone in the room—there was something else I could not see. I did not hear, but I knew it.

A horror of flesh and sense crept over me; but I was ashamed; I treated it with contempt. Shivering, I walked to the shelf, reached the cup, swallowed my nauseous dose—now tasteless—and went back to bed. It is not worth denying that I trembled. I am a coward. I am always afraid, even when I face the fear; so, shaking, I lay down. My throat was parched, my lips beaded with a sweat of terror, but the consciousness of solitude returned in time to save me from faintness. *It* had gone. And that was the first time.

Here, perhaps, it is best to interpolate my own story, as much of it as is needful to the understanding of this visitation.

I was an orphan, living in the family of my guardian and uncle by marriage, Mr. Van Alstyne. I was not an orphan till fifteen years of happy life at home had fitted me to feel the whole force of such a bereavement. My parents had died within a year of each other, and at the time my story begins I had been ten years under my uncle's roof. He was kind, gentle, generous, and good; all that he could be, not being my father.

It is not necessary to say that I grieved long and deeply over my loss; my nature is intense as well as excitable, and I had no mother. What that brief sentence expresses many will feel; many, more blessed, can not imagine. It is to all meaning enough to define my longing for what I had not, my solitude in all that I had, my eager effort to escape from both longing and solitude.

After I had been a year under my guardian's care, Eleanor Wyse, a far-off cousin of Mr. Van Alstyne, came to board at the house and go to school with me. She was fifteen, I sixteen, but she was far the oldest. In the same family as we were, in the same classes, there were but two ways for us to take, either rivalry or friendship; between two girls of so much individuality there was no neutral ground, and within a month I had decided the matter by falling passionately in love with Eleanor Wyse.

I speak advisedly in the use of that term; no other phrase expresses the blind, irrational, all-enduring devotion I gave to her; no less vivid word belongs to that madness. If I had not been in love with her I should have seen her as I can now—as what she really was; for I believe in physiognomy. I believe that God writes the inner man upon the outer as a restraint upon society; what the moulding of feature lacks, expression, subtle traitor, supplies; and it is only years of repression, of training, of diplomacy, that put the flesh totally in the power of the spirit, and enable man or woman to seem what they are not, what they would be thought.

Eleanor's face was very beautiful; its Greek outline, straight and clear, cut to a perfect contour; the white brow; the long, melancholy eye, with curved, inky lashes; the statuesque head, its undulant, glittering hair bound in a knot of classic severity; the proud, serene mouth, full of carved beauty, opening its scarlet lips to reveal tiny pearl-grains of teeth of that rare delicacy and brilliance that carry a fatal warning; the soft, oval cheek, colorless but not pale, opaque and smooth, betraying Southern blood; the delicate throat, shown whiter under the sweeping shadow and coil of her black-brown tresses; the erect, stately, perfect figure, slight as be-

came her years, but full of strength and promise; all these capti-
vated my intense adoration of beauty. I did not see the label of the
sculptor; I did not perceive in that cold, strict chiseling the assertion
that its material was marble. I believed the interpretation of its
hieroglyphic legend would have run thus: "This is the head of
young Pallas; power, intellect, purity are her ægis; the daughter of
Jove has not yet tasted passion; virgin, stainless, strong for sacrifice
and victory, let the ardent and restless hearts of women seek her
to be calmed and taught. *Evoe Athena*!" Nor did I like to see the
goddess moved; expression did not become her; the soul that
pierced those deep eyes was eager, unquiet, despotic; nothing divine, indeed, yet, in my eyes, it was the unresting, hasting meteor
that flashed and faded through mists of earth toward its rest—
where I knew not, but its flickering seemed to me atmospheric, not
intrinsic.

I looked up to Eleanor with respect as well as fervor. She was
full of noble theories. To hear her speak you would have been
inwardly shamed by the great and pure thoughts she expressed, the
high standard by which she measured all. Truth, disinterestedness,
honor, purity, humility, found in her a priestess garmented in candor. If I thought an evil thought, I was thereafter ashamed to see
her; if I was indolent or selfish, her presence reproached me; her
will, irresistible and mighty, awoke me; if she was kind in speech
or act—if she spoke to me caressingly—if she put her warm lips
upon my cheek—I was thrilled with joy; her presence affected me,
as sunshine does, with a sense of warm life and delight; when we
rode, walked, or talked together, I wished the hour eternal; and
when she fell into some passion, and burned me with bitter words,
stinging me into retort by their injustice, their hard cruelty, it was
I who repented—I who humiliated myself—I who, with abundant
tears, asked her pardon, worked, plead, prayed to obtain it; and if
some spasmodic conscientiousness roused her to excuse herself—
to say she had been wrong—my hand closed her lips: I could not
hear that: the fault was mine, mine only. I was glad to be clay as
long as she was queen and deity.

I do not think this passion of mine moved Eleanor much. She
liked to talk with me; our minds mated, our tastes were alike. I
had no need to explain my phrases to her, or to do more than
indicate my thoughts; she was receptive and appreciative of

thought, not of emotion. Me she never knew. I had no reserve in my nature—none of what is commonly called pride; what I felt I said, to the startling of good usual persons; and because I said it, Eleanor did not think I felt it. To her organization utterance and simplicity were denied; she could not speak her emotions if she would; she would not if she could; and she had no faith in words from others. My demonstrations annoyed her; she could not return them; they could not be ignored; there was a certain spice of life and passion in them that asserted itself poignantly and disturbed her. My services she liked better; yet there was in her the masculine contempt for spaniels; she despised a creature that would endure a blow, mental or physical, without revenging itself; and from her I endured almost any repulse, and forgot it.

She was with us in the house three years, and in that time she learned to love me after a fashion of her own, and I, still blind, adored her more. She found in me a receptivity that suited her, and a useful power of patient endurance. Her will made me a potent instrument. What she wanted she must have, and her want was my law. No time, no pains, no patience were wanting in me to fulfill her ends. I served her truly, and I look back upon it with no regret; futile or fertile, such devotion widens and ripens the soul that it inhabits. No aftershock of anguish can contract the space or undo the maturity; and even in my deepest humiliation before her sublime theories and superhuman ideals I unconsciously grew better myself. A capacity for worship implies much, and results in much.

Yet I think I loved her without much selfishness. I desired nothing better than to see her appreciated and admired. It was inexplicable to me when she was not; and I charged the coolness with which she was spoken of, and the want of enthusiasm for her person and character in general society, to her own starry height above common people, and their infinite distance from her nature.

So these years passed by. We went to school; we finished our school-days; we came out into the world; for, in the mean time, her mother had died, and her father removed to Bangor. She liked the place as a residence, and it had become home to her of late. I hoped it was pleasanter for her to be near me. When Eleanor was about twenty a nephew of Uncle Van Alstyne's came to make us a visit; he was no new acquaintance; he had come often in his boyhood, but since we grew up he had been in college, at the seminary, last in Germany for two years' study, and we did not know him well in his maturer character until this time. Herman Van Alstyne was quiet and plain, but of great capacity; I saw him much, and liked him. Love did not look at us. I was absorbed in Eleanor; so was he; but to her he was of no interest. I think she respected him, but her manner was careless and cold, even neglectful. Herman perceived the repulsion. At first he had taken pains to interest her—to mould her traits—to develop some inner nature in which he had faith; but the stone was intractable; neither ductile nor docile was Pallas; her soul yielded no more to him than the strong sea yields place or submission to the winged wind that smites it in passing.

He was with us three months waiting for a call he said, but stricter chains held him till he broke them with one blow and went to a Western parish.

He had not offered himself to Eleanor and been refused. Wisely he refrained from bringing the matter to a foreknown crisis: he spared himself the pain and Eleanor the regret of a refusal that he regarded truly as certain. I was sorry for the whole affair, for I believed she would scarcely know a better man, but it passed away; I promised to write him when his mother found the correspondence wearying, and we interchanged a few letters at irregular intervals till we met again, letters into which Eleanor's name found no entrance.

Three years after he left I went, early in July, to spend some weeks at the sea-side, for I was not strong; in the last few years my health had failed slowly, but progressively, till I was alarmingly weak, and ordered to breathe salt air and use sea-bathing as the best hope of restoration. I do not know why I should reserve the cause of this long languor and sinking: it was nothing wrong in me that I owed it to the breaking of a brief engagement. A young girl, totally inexperienced, I had loved a man and been taught by himself to despise him—a tragedy both trite and sharp; one that is daily reacted, noted, and forgotten by observers, to find a cold record in marble or the catalogues of insane asylums, another perhaps in the eternal calendar of the heavens above. I was too strong in nature to grace either of these mortal lists, and I loved Eleanor too well. I had always loved her more than that man; and when the episode was over, I discovered in myself that I never could have loved any man as I did her, and I went out into the world in this conviction, finding that life had not lost all its charms—that so long as she lived for me I should neither die nor craze. But the shock and excitement of the affair shattered my nervous system and undermined my health, and the listless, aimless life of a young lady offered no reactive agency to help me: so I went from home to new scenes and fresh atmosphere.

The air of Gloucester Beach strengthened me day by day. The exquisite scenery was a pleasure endless and pure. I asked nothing better than to sit upon some tide-washed rock and watch the creeping waves slide back in half-articulate murmur from the repelling shore, or, eager with the strength of flood, fling themselves, in mock anger, against cliff and crag, only to break in wreaths of silver spray and foam-bells—to glitter and fall in a leap of futile mirth, then rustling in the shingle and sea-weed with vague whispers, that

"Song half asleep or speech half awake,"

which has lulled so many restless hearts to a momentary quiet, singing them the long lullaby that preludes a longer slumber.

It was excitement enough to walk alone upon the beach when a hot cloudy night drooped over land and sea; when the soft trance and enchantment of summer lulled cloud and wave into stillness absolute and cherishing, when the sole guide I had in that warm gloom was the white edge of surf, and the only sound that smote the quiet, the still-recurring, apprehensive dash, as wave after wave raced, leaped, panted, and hissed after its forerunner.

The Beach House was almost empty at that early season, and I enjoyed all this alone, not without constant yearnings for Eleanor; wanting her, even this scenery lost a charm, and I gave it but faint admiration since I could not see it with her eyes. It must be a very pure love of nature that can exist alone, and without flaw, in the absence of association. The austere soul of the great mother offers no sympathy to the petulant passion or irrational grief of her children. It is only to the heart that has proved itself strong and lofty that her potent and life-giving traits reveal themselves. In this love, as in all others, save only the love of God, the return that is yielded is measured by the power of the adorer, not his want. Truly,

> "Nature never did betray
> The heart that loved her";

but she has many and many a time betrayed the partial love—scoffed at the divided worship.

After I had been a fortnight at the Beach, I was joined by Herman Van Alstyne. He had come on from the West to recruit his own health, suffering from a long intermittent fever, by sea-air; and hearing I was at Gloucester, had come there, and asked my leave to remain, gladly accorded to him. We had always been good friends, and my unspoken sympathy with his liking for, and loss of, Eleanor had established a permanent bond between us. In the constant association into which we were now thrown I learned daily to like him better. He was very weak indeed, quite unable to walk or drive far, and the connection of our families was a sufficient excuse to others for our intimacy. I delighted to offer him any kindness or service in my power, and he repaid me well by the charm of his society.

We spent our mornings always together in some niche of the lofty cliff that towered from the tide below in bare grandeur, reflecting the sun from its abrupt brown crags till every fibre of grass rooted in their crevices grew blanched, and the solitary streamer of bramble or wild creeper became crisp long ere autumn. But this heat was my element; the slow blood quickened in my veins under its vital glow; I felt life stealing back to its deserted and chilly conduits; I basked like a cactus or a lizard into brighter tints and a gayer existence.

There we often sat till noon, talking or silent as we would; for though there was a peculiar charm in the appreciative, thoughtful conversation of Herman Van Alstyne, a better and a rarer trait he possessed in full measure—the power of "a thousand silences."

Or, perhaps, under the old cedars that shed aromatic scents upon the sun-thrilled air, and strewed bits of dry, sturdy leaves upon the short grass that carpeted the summit of the cliff, we preferred shadow to sunshine; and while I rested against some ragged bole, and inhaled all odor and health, he read to me some quaint

German story, some incredibly exquisite bit of Tennyson, some sensitively musical passage of Kingsley, or, better and more apt, a song or a poem of Shelley's—vivid, spiritual, supernatural; the ideal of poetry; the leaping flame-tongue of lonely genius hanging in mid-air, self-poised, self-containing, glorious, and unattainable.

I have never known so delicate an apprehension as Mr. Van Alstyne possessed; his nobler traits I was afterward to know—to feel; but now it suited me thoroughly to be so well understood—to feel that I might utter the wildest imagination, or the most unexpected peculiarity of opinion, and never once be asked to explain what I meant—to reduce into social formulas that which was not social but my own. If there is one rest above another to a weary mind it is this freedom from shackles, this consciousness of true response. Never did I perceive a charm in the landscape that he had not noticed before or simultaneously with me; the same felicity of diction or of thought in what we read struck us as with one stroke; we liked the same people, read the same books, agreed in opinion so far as to disagree on and discuss many points without a shadow of impatience or an uncandid expression. We talked together as few men talk—perhaps no women—

> "Talked at large of worldly fate,
> And drew truly every trait"

—but we never spoke of Eleanor.

And so the summer wore on. I perceived a gradual change creep over Herman's manner in its process; he watched me continually. I felt his eyes fixed on me whenever I sat sewing or reading; I never looked up without meeting them. He grew absent and fitful. I did not know what had happened. I accused myself of having pained him. I feared he was ill. I never once thought of the true trouble; and one day it came—he asked me to marry him.

Never was any woman more surprised. I had not thought of the thing. I could not speak at first. I drew from him the hand he attempted to grasp. I did not collect my stricken and ashamed thoughts till, looking up, I saw him perfectly pale, his eyes dark with emotion, waiting, in rigid self-control, for my answer.

I could not, in justice to him or to myself, be less than utterly candid. I told him how much I liked him; how grieved I was that I could have mistaken his feeling for me so entirely; and then I said what I then believed—that I could not marry him—for I had but the lesser part of a heart to give any man. I loved a woman too well to love or to marry. A deep flush of relief crossed his brow.

"Is that the only objection you offer to me?" asked he, calmly.

"It is enough," said I. "If you think that past misery of mine interferes against you, you are in the wrong. I know now that I never loved that man as a woman should love the man she marries, and had I done so, the utter want of respect or trust I feel for him now would have silenced the love forever."

"I did not think of that," said he. "I needed but one assurance—that, except for Miss Wyse, you might have loved me; is it so?"

I could not tell him—I did not know. The one present and all-absorbing passion of my soul was Eleanor; beside her, no rival could enter. I shuddered at the possibility of loving a man so utterly, and then placing myself at his mercy for life. I felt that my safety lay in my freedom from any such tie to Eleanor. She made me miserable often enough as it was; what might she not do were I in her power always? Yet this face of the subject I did not suggest to Mr. Van Alstyne; it was painful enough to be kept to myself. I told him plainly that I could not love another as I did her; that I would not if I could.

He looked at me, not all unmoved, though silently; a gentle shading of something like pity stole across his regard, fixed and keen at first. He neither implored nor deprecated, but lifted my hand reverently to his lips, and said, in a tone of supreme calmness, "I can wait."

I should have combated the hope implied in those words. I was afterward angry with myself for enduring them; but at the moment uncertainty, shaped out of instinct and apprehension, closed my lips; I could not speak, and he left me. I went to my room more moved than I liked to acknowledge; and when he went away the next morning, though I felt the natural relief from embarrassment—knowing that I should not meet him as before—I still missed him, as a part of my daily life.

A month longer at the Beach protracted my stay into autumn;

and then, with refreshed health and new strength, I returned home—home! whose chief charm lay in the prospect of seeing Eleanor.

It is true that this hope was not unalloyed. I am possessed of a nature singularly instinctive, and for some weeks past a certain shadow had crept into her letters that pained me. No word or phrase denoted change; but I perceived the uncertain aura, and was irrationally harassed by a trouble too vague for expression.

When I reached Bangor it lay waiting for me sufficiently tangible and legible in the shape of a note from Eleanor.

And here must I leave a blank. The forgiveness which stirs me to this record refuses to define for alien eyes what that trouble was. All that I can say to justify the extreme and piteous result which followed is, that Eleanor Wyse had utterly, cruelly, and deliberately deceived me; and when it was no longer possible to do so, had been obliged by circumstances to show me what she had done.

Of that day it is best to say but little: the world cracked and reeled under me; I returned from a brief stupor into one bitter, blind tempest of contempt; and in its strength I answered her note concisely and coldly. An hour's time brought me a rejoinder not worth answering, simply perfidious—a regret, "deep and true," that she had been compelled to grieve me, to "reserve" from me any thing.

True! I had believed in truth, in goodness, in disinterested love, in principle; where now were such faiths swept? Verily, over the cliff into the sea! I was morally destroyed; I made shipwreck of myself and my life; my whole soul was a salt raging wave, tideless and foaming, without rest, without intent, without faith or hope in God—for he who loses faith in man loses faith in man's Maker—and this had Eleanor Wyse done for me.

Doubtless, to many, this emotion of mine will seem exaggerated. Let them remember that it was the loss of all that bound to life a lonely, morbid, intense, and excitable woman. Need I say more? If, after many years, with the kind help of nobler men and women, and the great patience of God, I have worn my way, inch by inch, back to some foothold of belief, I feel even yet—in some recoils of memory, some recurring habit of my soul—the reflex influence of those wretched days, months, years, when I suspected every one—"hateful, and hating," of a truth.

Death is hard to bear when its angel breathes upon the face we love, and extinguishes therein the fiery spark of life; but what is death compared to such dissolution as treachery brings? If Eleanor Wyse had died when I loved her and trusted her, I should have gone mourning softly all my days, but not in pain; to find her untrue admitted no remedy, no palliation. Truth was the ruling passion of my mind; that, and nothing else, contented me. Its absence or its loss were the loss and absence of all in those whom I loved; and it was only within a brief time, as years go, that I had grown into the discovery that men are liars in spite of education or policy; what was it, then, to know this of my ideal—of Eleanor?

But let those helpless, miserable weeks go by. If I detail so much as I have, it is to show the reason of my righteous indignation—of my tenacious memory. After a time I supposed that I forgave Eleanor. I thought myself good, most Pharisaically good, to have forgiven such an injury. I made some little comedy of friendship for visible use; I visited her, though not as often as I had done before. I saw her try to supply, with the love of others, the lavish devotion and service I had given her; I saw her fail and suffer in the consciousness of want and dissatisfaction, and, self-righteously, I forgave again! Senseless that I was!—as if forgiveness rankled and grew bitter in one's heart—as if pardon, full and pure, rejoiced in the retributions of this life—fed itself with salt recollections of the past, and evil foreshadowings of the future; as if it could exist without love, without forgetfulness; as if good deeds were its pledge, or good words its seal!

No! I never forgave her. I never forgot one pang she inflicted on me, one untruth she uttered; I never trusted her word or her smile again. I gathered up every circumstance of the past, and hunted it to its source; I discovered that she had not simply deceived but deluded me, and laughed at me in the process.

How my blood boiled over these revelations! how my flesh failed with my heart! Slow, persistent fever gnawed me; my nights were without sleep or rest; my days laggard and delirious. Why I did not go crazy is yet unexplained to myself. I think I did, only that there was a method in my madness that won for it the milder name of nervousness. I was ill—I tottered on the very tempting brink of death, without awe or regret; I made no effort to live, nor any to die, except to pray that I might—the only prayer that ever passed my seared lips. I was sent away from home again; and while I was gone Eleanor married a certain Mr. Mason, of Bangor, and they removed to Illinois—in time, still further West. I was no better for this absence; and, impatient of strangers and intrusive acquaintance, I came home, and, strange as it may seem, I missed Eleanor! Habit is the anchor of half the love in this world, and my habit of loving her survived the love—or held it, perhaps—for I missed her sorrowfully.

I found Herman Van Alstyne at my uncle's when I came, and I was glad—glad of any thing to break the desperate monotony of sorrow. He knew nothing more than every one knew of this affair, except that he knew me, and from that gathered intuitively a part of the truth; and, by long patience, unwearied and delicate care—watching, waiting, forbearing, and enduring—he brought me nearer a certain degree of calm than I had believed possible, when a sudden summons called him away from Bangor; and it was during his absence that *It* began to come; as I said in the beginning, more than two years after I had lost Eleanor.

I lay still in my bed on that day of which I had spoken; the long stress of misery that I had undergone in the past years resulted in so much physical exhaustion as to have brought on the exquisite tortures of neuralgia, and it was a sudden access of this chronic rack that to-day held me prisoner. The draught I had taken was an anodyne, and under its influence I fell asleep. I must have slept an hour, when I woke abruptly with a renewed sense of something in the dusk beside me, at my pillow. I screamed as I woke into this terror, and instantly Aunt Mary came in. A cold sigh crossed my cheek; I shivered with a horror strange and unearthly. Aunt Mary asked if I had been asleep? I said yes. If I had been dreaming painfully? I did not answer that. I asked for some water, and getting it she forgot her question; but I could not bear to be alone. I begged her to sit beside me and to sleep with me, for I could not endure solitude; perpetual apprehension made me cringe in every nerve and fibre. I started at the slightest stir of leaf or insect upon the pane, and the repining autumn wind seemed to come over mile on mile of graves, bringing thence no mealy scent of white daisies—

no infant-breathing violet odors—no frutescent perfume of sweet-briar, nor funereal smells of cypress, and plaintive whispers of fir and pine; but wave after wave of cries from half-free souls; sobbing with dull pain, and moans of deprecating anguish; a cry that neither heaven nor earth answered, but which crept—a live desolation—into the ear attent, and the brain morbidly excited.

Yet gradually this left me. I kept by some kindly human presence all day, and feared night no more till—

Let me say that all this time I was imperceptibly growing better than I had been. Hope, the very ministrant of Heaven, was by tiny crevice and unguarded postern stealing into my heart, though I knew it not, and softening all my hard thoughts of Eleanor, for I am moved to the outer world rather by my own moods than theirs; sorrow and pain make me selfish and unkind; peace, joy, even unconscious hope, expand my love for all mankind. I am better, more tender, more benevolent to others, when I receive some light and life within.

One night I was all alone; the low, unearthly glimmer of a waning moon lit the naked earth, a few leaves rustled on the fitful wind that lulled, and rose, and lulled again, with almost articulate meaning. I lay listening; a long pause came, of most significant quiet—a faint sigh crossed my brow. *It* was there beside me!—unseen, unheard, but felt in the secretest recesses of life and consciousness; a spirit, whereat my marrow curdled, my heart was constricted, my blood refused to run, my breath failed—fluttered—was it death? I sprung from my pillow; the presence drew farther away. I could see nothing, but I felt that something yearning, restless, pained, and sad regarded me. I began to gather courage. I began to pity a soul that had cast off life yet could not die to life; and now it drew nearer, as if some magnetism, born of my kindlier sympathies, melted the barrier between us, close—closer—till something rustled like a light touch the cover of my bed, stirred at my ear! Good Heaven! could I bear that? I could not shriek or cry, I fell forward upon my face. It went, and the wind began its wail; now reproachful sobs filled it: the moon sank, rain gathered overhead, and dripped with sullen persistence all night upon the roof, for all night I heard it.

It is tedious to recount each instance of this visitation. For weeks it stayed beside me. I felt it on my bed at night; I felt it by my chair in the day; it swept past me in the garden paths, a cold waft of air; it watched me through the window-blinds; it hung over me sleeping; yet never was I wonted to the presence; every day thrilled me with fresh surprise, and daily it grew, for daily it became more perceivable.

At first I felt only a sense of alien life in a room otherwise solitary; then a breath of air, air from some other sphere than this, penetrative, dark, chilling; then a sound, not of voice, or pulse, but of motion in some inanimate thing, the motion of contact; then came a touch, the gentlest, faintest approach of lips or fingers, I knew not which, to my brow; and last, a growing, gathering, flickering into sight. I saw nothing at first, directly; from the oblique glance that fear impelled I drew an impression of quivering air beside me; then of a shadow, frail and variant; then a shapeless shape of mist, a cloud, dark and portentous and significant; and next those sidelong glances revealed to me an expression; no face, no feature, but, believe it who can, an expression, earnest, melancholy, beseeching; a look that pierced me, that pleaded with my soul's depth, that entreated shelter, succor, consolation, which even in my terror I longed to give.

I might perhaps have suffered physically more than I did from this visiting, but the winged hope of which I spoke before upheld me still, daily, with stronger hands.

Herman had returned to Bangor after a brief absence, and was there still. I could not see him so constantly as I did and refuse my admiration to those traits that ever rule and satisfy me. Mr. Van Alstyne passed with some people for a philosopher, with some for a reformer: there were those who called him singular and self-opinionated; there were others who revered him for his devout nature and stainless life. He was more than any of these, he was a true man: and even in his plain exterior the eye that knew him found a charm peculiar and salient; the deep-sunken, clear, earnest eyes, kindled with a spark of profound depth and meaning; the thin, sharply cut, aquiline outline; the flexible, pure, refined mouth; the bronzed coloring; the overhanging brow—all these wore beauty indefinable, fired by the sweet and vivid smile of the irradiate soul within. In his presence, calm, restful, and strengthening, no subterfuge or evasion could live. He was just, direct, and tenderly strong; it was to him, to him it is, that I owed and owe a new and higher life than I had known before; he saw my sinking and lonely soul, but he saw its self-recuperative power, and with the most delicate and careful tenderness beguiled that motive force into action. He did far more than that; he recalled to me the higher motives that anguish had well-nigh scourged out from my horizon; he taught me as a father teaches his little child a newer trust in the Father of us all. I returned to those divine consolations that he laid before me with a pierced and penitent heart; and in knowing that I was prayed and cared for on earth, I learned anew that God is more tender and more patient than his creatures, and the logic of strong emotion made the truth living and potent. In all this was I drawn toward Herman by the strongest tie that can bind one heart to another—a tie that overarches and outlasts all the fleeting passions of time, for it is the adamantine link of eternity; and had I lost him then, I should have felt for all my life that there was a relation between us, undying and sure, to be renewed and acknowledged at length where such relations respire their native air, where there is neither marrying nor giving in marriage.

But it pleased God that I should live to receive my heart's desire; what began in gratitude ended in love. I might have shrunk from admitting so potent a guest again into my soul, had any other soul sent the messenger thither; but I trusted him when I disbelieved every other creature, and with this trust had crept back to me my faith in God, in good, in life and its ends. Truly, so far as man can do it, he saved my soul alive!

Now it was the early part of December. It was still haunting me. I could see more—eyes, deep and pleading, the outline of a head, pure lineaments, seemed hovering beside me, but if I turned for a direct look they were gone. I did not fear it; my happy faith and Herman shielded me.

The year drew on. The day before Christmas came, still, crisp, but yet warm for its season; no snow shrouded the earth; the far-off sun beamed out benign and pale; the few dry leaves lay quiet as they fell; the firs upon the lawn with curved boughs waited for their ermine, stately and dark. Herman asked me to walk with him. I cloaked and hooded myself, and we went away, away into the deep woods. What we said in that sweet silence of a leafless, sunny forest is known to us two: it is not for you, reader, friendly though you be; it is enough to tell you that I had promised to be his wife, that I was homesick no more.

It was well for me that this happened that day—should I not rather say God ordered it?—for as ever in this life sorrow tramples upon the foregoing footsteps of joy, so I found upon my return a household in tears. Mr. Mason, Eleanor's husband, had written, at last, two months after it happened, and another month had the letter been in coming—ah! how ever shall I say it? Eleanor was dead! her last breath had gasped out a cry for me!

If Death is the Spoiler, so is he the Restorer; who shall dare to soil the shroud with any thing but tears? I could do no more but weep; but I mourned for Eleanor again as I had never thought to do; evil, treachery, anguish, and distrust vanished—I remembered only love.

For hours I could not see or speak with Herman, the flood of misery overpowered me; and he too sorrowed, deeply, but serenely. It was late in the evening before I recovered any sort of composure. He sent to my chamber a brief penciled request, and I went down; worn out with weeping, I obeyed like a child. I ate the food he brought me; I drank the restorative draught; quiet, but languid, I laid my head upon his breast, and, held by the firm grasp of his arm, I rested, and he consoled me; a deep and vital draught of peace slaked my soul's feverish thirst. Such peace had I never known, for it was the daughter of experience and trust.

You who, full of youth and its intact passion, give a careless hour to these pages, wonder not that I could find it just to give so noble a man a heart once given and wasted! Know that it is not the flower of any tropic palm that is fit to feed and sustain man, but the ripened clusters of its fruitage—the result of time, and sun, and storm. The first blush, the earliest kiss, the tender and timid glance are sweet indeed; but the true household fire, deep and abiding, is oftenest kindled in the heart matured by passion and by pain, tested in the stress of life, deepened and strengthened by manifold experience; and such a heart receives no unworthy guest, lights its altar-fire for no idol of wood or clay. I felt that I rendered Herman Van Alstyne far nobler and higher homage, that I did him purer justice in loving him now than it had ever been in my power to do before.

First love is a honeyed and dewy romance, fit for novels and school-girls; but of the myriad women who have lived to curse their marriage-day nine-tenths have been those who married in their ignorant girlhood, and married boys.

I have digressed to honor Herman, to vindicate myself. That Christmas-eve I lay sheltered and at rest on his arm, till the toll of midnight rang clear upon my ear. I could forever sing the angels' song now, that for years had been a blank repetition to my wretched and ungodly soul.

"Peace on earth!" was no more a chimera; I knew it at heart. "Good will to men!" that was spontaneous; I loved all in and for one. "Glory to God in the highest!" What did that ask to utter it but a full thankfulness that bore me upward like the flood-tide of a summer sea?

Blessed as I was, my common sense reminded me that it was far into the night, that I ought to sleep; so I said good-night to Herman, and crept with weak steps to my room. I fell asleep to dream of him, of Eleanor, of peace, and I woke into the deep silence that always preceded—*It.*

I woke knowing what stood beside me. Keen starlight pierced the pane, and shed a dim, obscure perception of place and outline over my room. A long, restful, sobbing sigh parted my lips; I perceived *It* was at hand; fear fled; terror died out; I turned my eyes —oh God! it was Eleanor!

Wan—frail—a flowing outline of shadow, but the face in every faultless line and vivid expression; now an expression of intense longing, of wistful prayer, of pleading that would never be denied.

I lifted my heavy arms toward the vision; it swayed and bent above me: the white lips parted; no murmur nor sound clave them, yet they spoke—"Forgive! forgive!"

"Eleanor! Yes love, darling! yes, forever, as I hope to be forgiven!" I cried out aloud. A gleam of rapture and rest relaxed the brow, the sad eyes; love ineffable glowed along each lineament, and transfused to splendor the frigid moulding of snow.

I closed my eyes to crush inward the painful tears, and a touch of lips sealed them with sacred and unearthly repose. I looked again; *It* had gone forever. The Christmas bells pealed loud and clear for dawn, and my thoughts rung their own joy bells beside the steeple chimes. Herman and Eleanor both loved me—I had forgiven; I was forgiven.

Yet must day and space echo that word once more. Hear me, Eleanor! hear me, from that mystic country where thou hast fled before!

I repeat that forgiveness again. So may Heaven pardon me in the hour of need; so may God look upon me with strong affection in the parting of soul and body, even as I pardon and love thee, Eleanor, with a truth and faith eternal! Thee, forever loved, but, ah! not now forever lost?

ELIZABETH STUART PHELPS

A good short story is a work of art which daunts us in proportion to its brevity. It would not be easy for one who has not "served his time out" at this form of creation, to understand the laws of construction involved in it, and the rigidity of obedience demanded by them. . . .

It has always taken me at least from a month to six weeks to finish a magazine story. I confess that I "toil terribly" over them. It makes little difference whether the motif *comes in a blinding flash, or in a slow, insulated, electric current:—the construction and execution remain inexorable ideals frowning above attention, patience, vitality, energy, until the work is done. One who honors this vehicle of thought is often ill with the strain, before a magazine tale of forty pages of manuscript can be apparently completed. The work upon such a story is never done. Revision calls the vision to account in that iron exaction from one's self which is so much more remorseless than the exaction that any critic can make upon one.*

I look upon a short story, properly fitted for the higher magazines of our day, as one of the very finest

*forms of expression. No inspiration is too noble for it; no
amount of hard work is too severe for it.* *

The subtlety, depth, and implications of the short fiction of Elizabeth Stuart Phelps are only recently beginning to engage the attention of contemporary readers and literary critics. The fame of her best-selling novels—*The Gates Ajar* (1868), *Beyond the Gates* (1883), and *The Gates Between* (1887)—keep her name alive so that contemporary feminists found this interesting writer easily enough when the task of rediscovering women's literary history was taken up in the early 1970s. But it has not been these novels, in which Phelps presents a kinder and gentler God than the God of the Calvinists and a utopian vision of heaven designed to comfort the many bereaved and anguished women who lost babies to early childhood diseases and fathers, sons, fiancés, and husbands in the Civil War, that have generated the most interest in Phelps during the contemporary resurgence of feminism. Rather, it has been her more feminist writings, such as the novel about a painter whose career is devastated by marriage and motherhood, *The Story of Avis* (1877), and *Doctor Zay* (1882), about a woman doctor.

Elizabeth Stuart Phelps (August 31, 1844–January 28, 1911) was the daughter of the writer Elizabeth Stuart Phelps (who died when her daughter was only eight years old) and the Andover Theological Seminary professor Reverend Austin Phelps. Both of her grandfathers were ministers as well, and she grew up surrounded by conversation and debate about theological questions. What was heaven like? Who went to heaven? Were lovers reunited in heaven?

Phelps had a long literary career, from her first published story in 1864 till her death in 1911. She published fifty-seven books, including twenty novels and five collections of short stories. Several of her stories present erotic or romantic relationships between women but those relationships are secondary to the central plot and have often gone unnoticed. For instance, in "Since I Died" the focus of

* *Chapters from a Life*, "Stories and Books" by Elizabeth Stuart Phelps, Houghton Mifflin, 1896, pp. 266–268.

the story is on the experience of a woman recently dead attempting to understand her transformed condition and struggling to communicate with the beloved whom she has left behind. The fact that her beloved is a woman almost, but not quite, escapes notice in the reader's fascination with the mystery of this voice from beyond. It is interesting to compare Phelps' description of the consciousness of a newly dead person with the descriptions collected by Dr. Elizabeth Kübler Ross of those who have had "near-death" or "out-of-body" experiences. There are remarkable similarities.

The poetic lyricism of this story—with its repeated paragraph endings ("I was restless and I ran"), the bitter but humorous dismissal of the doctor's ministrations as not worth the bother of having to hear his big boots on the stairs, and the tension between the narrator's desire to experience "the immensity" that opens before her once she leaves her body and the pull of her beloved's eyes—all combine to make a story that is difficult to put down. One reads it straight through and forgets to breathe.

Much of Phelps' early writing dealt with the constraints, unhappiness, and injustice of marriage; as pessimistic as she was about married life, she was equally optimistic about the possibilities for independent single women to live fulfilling and interesting lives. Her later writing was less optimistic about the lives of all women and seemed to posit marriage as an inescapable fate. She lived most of her literary life as a member of a strongly supportive community of women writers and shared working quarters with a beloved friend, Dr. Mary Briggs Harris. In 1888, shortly after Dr. Harris' death, Phelps married a man twenty-seven years her junior, but she found no happiness in her new conjugal state. Her heart condition deteriorated, she could no longer travel, her husband lived elsewhere, and she died alone.

"Since I Died" was first published in *Scribner's Monthly Magazine* in February 1873, and later collected in her fifth and last volume of short stories, *Sealed Orders*, in 1879. The founding editor of *Scribner's*, Josiah Gilbert Holland, was described by Edward Eggleston as ". . . the most popular and effective preacher of social and domestic moralities of his [sic] age. . . ." He refused to publish Walt Whitman whom he found threatening to the "religious and upright moral tone" of his magazine. It is interesting that he found nothing immoral or irreligious in a story about a recently dead woman torn between her earthly love for another woman and the beckoning deity.

Since I Died

How very still you sit!

If the shadow of an eyelash stirred upon your cheek; if that gray line about your mouth should snap its tension at this quivering end; if the pallor of your profile warmed a little; if that tiny muscle on your forehead, just at the left eyebrow's curve, should start and twitch; if you would but grow a trifle restless, sitting there beneath my steady gaze; if you moved a finger of your folded hands; if you should turn and look behind your chair, or lift your face, half lingering and half longing, half loving and half loth, to ponder on the annoyed and thwarted cry which the wind is making, where I stand between it and yourself, against the half-closed window.—Ah, there! You sigh and stir, I think. You lift your head. The little muscle is a captive still; the line about your mouth is tense and hard; the deepening hollow in your cheek has no warmer tint, I see, than the great Doric column which the moonlight builds against the wall. I lean against it; I hold out my arms.

You lift your head and look me in the eye.

If a shudder crept across your figure; if your arms, laid out upon the table, leaped but once above your head; if you named my name; if you held your breath with terror, or sobbed aloud for love, or sprang, or cried—.

But you only lift your head and look me in the eye.

If I dared step near, or nearer; if it were permitted that I should cross the current of your living breath; if it were willed that I should feel the leap of human blood within your veins; if I should touch your hands, your cheeks, your lips; if I dropped an arm as lightly as a snowflake round your shoulder—

The fear which no heart has fathomed, the fate which no fancy has faced, the riddle which no soul has read, steps between your substance and my soul.

I drop my arms. I sink into the heart of the pillared light upon the wall. I will not wonder what would happen if my outlines defined upon it to your view. I will not think of that which could be, would be, if I struck across your still-set vision, face to face.

Ah me, how still she sits! With what a fixed, incurious stare she looks me in the eye!

The wind, now that I stand no longer between it and yourself, comes enviously in. It lifts the curtain, and whirls about the room. It bruises the surface of the great pearled pillar where I lean. I am caught within it. Speech and language struggle over me. Mute articulations fill the air. Tears and laughter, and the sounding of soft lips, and the falling of low cries, possess me. Will she listen? Will she bend her head? Will her lips part in recognition? Is there an alphabet between us? Or have the winds of night a vocabulary to lift before her holden eyes?

We sat many times together, and talked of this. Do you remember, dear? You held my hand. Tears that I could not see fell on it; we sat by the great hall-window upstairs, where the maple shadow goes to sleep, face down, across the floor upon a lighted night; the old green curtain waved its hands upon us like a mesmerist, I thought; like a priest, you said.

"When we are parted, you shall go," you said; and when I shook my head you smiled—you always smiled when you said that, but you said it always quite the same.

I think I hardly understood you then. Now that I hold your eyes in mine, and you see me not; now when I stretch my hand and you touch me not; now that I cry your name, and you hear it not,—I comprehend you, tender one! A wisdom not of earth was in your words. "To live, is dying; I will die. To die is life, and you shall live."

Now when the fever turned, I thought of this.

That must have been—ah! how long ago? I miss the conception of that for which *how long* stands index.

Yet I perfectly remember that I perfectly understood it to be at three o'clock on a rainy Sunday morning that I died. Your little watch stood in its case of olive-wood upon the table, and drops were on the window. I noticed both, though you did not know it. I see the watch now, in your pocket; I cannot tell if the hands move, or only pulsate like a heart-throb, to and fro; they stand

and point, mute golden fingers, paralyzed and pleading, forever at the hour of three. At this I wonder.

When first you said I "was sinking fast," the words sounded as old and familiar as a nursery tale. I heard you in the hall. The doctor had just left, and you went to mother and took her face in your two arms, and laid your hand across her mouth, as if it were she who had spoken. She cried out and threw up her thin old hands; but you stood as still as Eternity. Then I thought again: "It is she who dies; I shall live."

So often and so anxiously we have talked of this thing called death, that now that it is all over between us, I cannot understand why we found in it such a source of distress. It bewilders me. I am often bewildered here. Things and the fancies of things possess a relation which as yet is new and strange to me. Here is a mystery.

Now, in truth, it seems a simple matter for me to tell you how it has been been with me since your lips last touched me, and your arms held me to the vanishing air.

Oh, drawn, pale lips! Nerveless, dropping arms! I told you I would come. Did ever promise fail I spoke to you? "Come and show me Death," you said. I have come to show you Death. I could show you the fairest sight and sweetest that ever blessed your eyes. Why, look! Is it not fair? Am I terrible? Do you shrink or shiver? Would you turn from me, or hide your strained, expectant face?

Would she? Does she? Will she? . . .

Ah, how the room widened! I could tell you that. It grew great and luminous day by day. At night the walls throbbed; lights of rose ran round them, and blue fire, and a tracery as of the shadows of little leaves. As the walls expanded, the air fled. But I tried to tell you how little pain I knew or feared. Your haggard face bent over me. I could not speak; when I would I struggled, and you said "She suffers!" Dear, it was so very little!

Listen, till I tell you how that night came on. The sun fell and the dew slid down. It seemed to me that it slid into my heart, but still I felt no pain. Where the walls pulsed and receded, the hills came in. Where the old bureau stood, above the glass, I saw a single mountain with a face of fire, and purple hair. I tried to tell you this, but you said: "She wanders." I laughed in my heart at that, for it was such a blessed wandering! As the night locked the sun below the mountain's solemn watching face, the Gates of Space were lifted up before me; the everlasting doors of Matter swung for me upon their rusty hinges, and the King of Glories entered in and out. All the kingdoms of the earth, and the power of them, beckoned to me, across the mist my failing senses made,—ruins and roses, and the brows of Jura and the singing of the Rhine; a shaft of red light on the Sphinx's smile, and caravans in sandstorms, and an icy wind at sea, and gold adream in mines that no man knew, and mothers sitting at their doors in valleys singing babes to sleep, and women in dank cellars selling souls for bread, and the whir of wheels in giant factories, and a single prayer somewhere in a den of death,—I could not find it, though I searched, —and the smoke of battle, and broken music, and a sense of lilies alone beside a stream at the rising of the sun—and, at last, your face, dear, all alone.

I discovered then, that the walls and roof of the room had vanished quite. The night-wind blew in. The maple in the yard almost brushed my cheek. Stars were about me, and I thought the rain had stopped, yet seemed to hear it, up on the seeming of a window which I could not find.

One thing only hung between me and immensity. It was your single, awful, haggard face. I looked my last into your eyes. Stronger than death, they held and claimed my soul. I feebly raised my hand to find your own. More cruel than the grave, your wild grasp chained me. Then I struggled, and you cried out, and your face slipped, and I stood free.

I stood upon the floor, beside the bed. That which had been I lay there at rest, but terrible, before me. You hid your face, and I saw you slide upon your knees. I laid my hand upon your head; you did not stir; I spoke to you: "Dear, look around a minute!" but you knelt quite still. I walked to and fro about the room, and meeting my mother, touched her on the elbow; she only said, "She's gone!" and sobbed aloud. "I have not *gone*!" I cried; but she sat sobbing on.

The walls of the room had settled now, and the ceiling stood in its solid place. The window was shut, but the door stood open. Suddenly I was restless, and I ran.

I brushed you in hurrying by, and hit the little light-stand where the tumblers stood; I looked to see if it would fall, but it only shivered as if a breath of wind had struck it once.

But I was restless, and I ran. In the hall I met the Doctor. This amused me, and I stopped to think it over. "Ah, Doctor," said I, "you need not trouble yourself to go up. I'm quite well to-night, you see." But he made me no answer; he gave me no glance; he hung up his hat, and laid his hand upon the banister against which I leaned, and went ponderously up.

It was not until he had nearly reached the landing that it occurred to me, still leaning on the banisters, that his heavy arm must have swept against and *through* me, where I stood against the oaken mouldings which he grasped.

I saw his feet fall on the stairs above me; but they made no sound which reached my ear. "You'll not disturb me *now* with your big boots, sir," said I, nodding; "never fear!"

But he disappeared from sight above me, and still I heard no sound.

Now the Doctor had left the front door unlatched.

As I touched it, it blew open wide, and solemnly. I passed out and down the steps. I could see that it was chilly, yet I felt no chill. Frost was on the grass, and in the east a pallid streak, like the cheek of one who had watched all night. The flowers in the little square plots hung their heads and drew their shoulders up; there was a lonely, late lily which I broke and gathered to my heart, where I breathed upon it, and it warmed and looked me kindly in the eye. This, I remember, gave me pleasure. I wandered in and out about the garden in the scattering rain; my feet left no trace upon the dripping grass, and I saw with interest that the garment which I wore gathered no moisture and no cold. I sat musing for a while upon the piazza, in the garden-chair, not caring to go in. It was so many months since I had felt able to sit upon the piazza in the open air. "By and by," I thought, I would go in and upstairs to see you once again. The curtains were drawn from the parlor windows and I passed and repassed, looking in.

All this while the cheek of the east was waning, and the air gathering faint heats and lights about me. I remembered, presently, the old arbor at the garden-foot, where, before I was sick, we sat so much together; and thinking, "She will be surprised to know that I have been down alone," I was restless, and I ran again.

I meant to come back and see you, dear, once more. I saw the lights in the room where I had lain sick, overhead; and your shadow on the curtain; and I blessed it, with all the love of life and death, as I bounded by.

The air was thick with sweetness from the dying flowers. The birds woke, and the zenith lighted, and the leap of health was in my limbs. The old arbor held out its soft arms to me—but I was restless, and I ran.

The field opened before me, and meadows with broad bosoms, and a river flashed before me like a scimitar, and woods interlocked their hands to stay me—but being restless, on I ran.

The house dwindled behind me; and the light in my sick-room, and your shadow on the curtain. But yet I was restless, and I ran.

In the twinkling of an eye I fell into a solitary place. Sand and rocks were in it, and a falling wind. I paused, and knelt upon the sand, and mused a little in this place. I mused of you, and life and death, and love and agony;—but these had departed from me, as dim and distant as the fainting wind. A sense of solemn expectation filled the air. A tremor and a trouble wrapped my soul.

"I must be dead!" I said aloud. I had no sooner spoken than I learned that I was not alone.

The sun had risen, and on a ledge of ancient rock, weather-stained and red, there had fallen over against me the outline of a Presence lifted up against the sky, and turning suddenly, I saw . . .

Lawful to utter, but utterance has fled! Lawful to utter, but a greater than Law restrains me! Am I blotted from your desolate fixed eyes? Lips that my mortal lips have pressed, can you not quiver when I cry? Soul that my eternal soul has loved, can you stand enveloped in my presence, and not spring like a fountain to me? Would you not know how it has been with me since your perishable eyes beheld my perished face? What my eyes have seen or my ears have heard, or my heart conceived without you? If I have missed or mourned for you? If I have watched or longed for you? Marked your solitary days and sleepless nights, and tearless eyes, and monotonous slow echo of my unanswering name? Would you not know?

Alas! would she? Would she not? My soul misgives me with a matchless, solitary fear. I am called, and I slip from her. I am beckoned, and I lose her.

Her face dims, and her folded, lonely hands fade from my sight.

Time to tell her a guarded thing! Time to whisper a treasured word! A moment to tell her that *Death is dumb, for Life is deaf!* A moment to tell her.—

CONSTANCE FENIMORE WOOLSON

The truth is, Belle, whatever one does must be done with one's might and I would rather be strong than beautiful, or even good, provided the "good" must be dull. *

Constance Fenimore Woolson (March 5, 1840–January 24, 1894) was the sixth child born to Hannah Cooper Pomeroy and Charles Jarvis Woolson in Claremont, New Hampshire. Shortly after her birth, three of her older sisters died in a scarlet fever epidemic. Soon after this tragedy, her family moved to the frontier, The Western Reserve, whose urban center was a very young Cleveland. Three more children were born there, the last one the only son. Constance, her sister Clara, and their young brother were the only Woolson children to survive to adulthood.

Her businessman father prospered and the children enjoyed good educations, travel, and a comfortable home. After her father's death in 1869, she traveled with her mother in the Eastern and

---

* Constance Fenimore Woolson to friend, Mrs. Washburn, in 1875. Quoted by Raymond S. Moore in *Constance Fenimore Woolson*, Twayne United States Authors Series, 1963.

Southern United States, staying for extended periods in St. Augustine, Florida. They were often joined by Constance's widowed sister Clara Benedict and her daughter Clare.

Woolson began publishing in the year following her father's death. Discovering that her father had left barely enough money to keep his wife fed and housed, Woolson was delighted to be able to earn with her pen the difference between subsistence and comfort for her mother and herself. After her mother's death in 1879, Woolson went abroad and spent the last fourteen years of her life in Europe; in her letters she talked often about coming back to the United States, intending to make her permanent home in St. Augustine. In January of 1894, in Venice, struggling with a second bout of influenza in six months, perhaps complicated by typhoid fever, Constance Fenimore Woolson died after a fall from a second-floor window. The debate about whether she fell by accident or intent continues.

Woolson was doubly disabled. She suffered from periodically disabling bouts of inherited biochemical depression. And she became increasingly deaf. The sense of alienation experienced by people who lose their hearing and live in a primarily hearing world is legendary. In this experience, she and the writer Ellen Glasgow have painful similarities. Her survival of the epidemic that left her with grieving parents during her earliest years and her disabilities might explain her sense of separateness from any of the worlds in which she might have moved with pleasure and ease.

"In the 1880s five of her novels. . . . dominated the American fiction of the decade. Henry James in a significant essay republished in his volume *Partial Portraits,* classed Miss Woolson with George Eliot, Turgenev, Daudet. Two of her novels, *Anne* (serialized in *Harper's* and published in book form in 1882) and *East Angels* (also serialized before book publication in 1886), have permanence unquestionably." So said Fred Lewis Pattee in "Constance Fenimore Woolson and the South" in his Address delivered at the Dedicatory Exercises of the Constance Fenimore Woolson House, May 31, 1938. John Hervey writing in the *Saturday Review of Literature* (October 12, 1929) judged Woolson "one of the finest novelists that America thus far has produced." But most of the attention accorded to Woolson during the twentieth century has revolved around her friendship with the novelist and short story writer Henry James. Common conservative assumptions about the nature of sex roles and the power-based relationships between men and women dominated interpretations of the relationship between the two writers and friends, and the understanding of her life. As time has passed, ideas about how authors influence each other have become more sophisticated. Ideas about sex roles, the suppression of the voices of marginalized "others," and the nature of literary merit have been modified by the insights of feminists, and Woolson has begun to receive scholarly attention based on her own accomplishments and character. What probably most reveals the change in attitude toward Woolson, in addition to the increasing number of scholarly publications about her and reprints of work by her, is the restoration and refunding of her archives at Rollins College in Winter Park, Florida. However, she still remains a mysterious and controversial figure.

Woolson has long been considered a regional writer and is associated in the United States both with Mackinac Island on Lake Michigan and as Florida's first regional writer. Toward the end of her life, living in Italy, and frequently visiting in Switzerland and Germany, she continued to set most of her fiction in the United States, although her last two collections of stories were *The Front Yard, and Other Italian Stories* (1895) and *Dorothy, and Other Italian Stories* (1896).

A sense of alienation, of "otherness," characterizes many of Woolson's characters including those central to her two stories in this collection. Both Felipa and Miss Moncrief seem to belong nowhere, to be as homeless as babies left behind by space travelers, to be neither a part of the world into which they were born nor eligible for inclusion in the worlds to which they aspire. Both stories have overtones of "The Little Mermaid," a myth that recurs in many forms in the writing of nineteenth-century women. Marginalized? Decentered? Displaced?

"Felipa" was first published in *Lippincott's Magazine*, June 1876. It has been considered as one of Woolson's early Florida fictions until recently. In recent years, it has come to be characterized as a "baby dyke" story, perhaps an early precursor of another southern "baby dyke" story: *Rubyfruit Jungle*.

Just what kind of character *is* Felipa, the eleven-year-old Minorcan girl? And who in this story is in love with whom? Is Catherine, the poor artist, in love with her wealthy friend, Christine? Is Christine in love with Edward? Is Christine in love with anyone? Everyone seems agreed that Edward is in love with Christine; there seems to be no ambiguity about the object of his affections. Is Felipa in love with Christine? With Edward? With both of them? What's going on here?

Is it that Woolson is a sloppy storyteller and she just didn't tell it intelligibly? Or doesn't *she* know what's happening either? Is she not telling, but *re*telling a story; that is, is she writing a story that she heard as fact but isn't sure enough about *exactly* what happened to tell it in a way that makes sense?

Or is she really a very good writer? One who insists that her readers think about what really happened, what really was the meaning, not in symbolic, but in actual terms, of "what happened"? Because if we are not given an unambiguous "story line," then our natural desire to understand what really happened makes us consider possibilities that aren't supposed to be possible, aren't supposed to be able to happen. In the sense that we don't really know who felt what and what really happened and why, this is another riddle story.

Felipa

Christine and I found her there. She was a small, dark-skinned, yellow-eyed child, the offspring of the ocean and the heats, tawny, lithe and wild, shy yet fearless—not unlike one of the little brown deer that bounded through the open reaches of the pine-barren behind the house. She did not come to us—we came to her; we loomed into her life like genii from another world, and she was partly afraid and partly proud of us. For were we not her guests? proud thought! and, better still, were we not women? "I have only seen three women in all my life," said Felipa, inspecting us gravely, "and I like women, I am a woman too, although these clothes of the son of Pedro make me appear as a boy; I wear them on account of the boat and the hauling in of the fish. The son of Pedro being dead at a convenient age, and his clothes fitting me, what would you have? It was a chance not to be despised. But when I am grown I shall wear robes long and beautiful like the señora's." The little creature was dressed in a boy's suit of dark-blue linen, much the worse for wear, and torn.

"If you are a girl, why do you not mend your clothes?" I said.

"Do you mend, señora?"

"Certainly: all women sew and mend."

"The other lady?"

Christine laughed as she lay at ease upon the brown carpet of pine-needles, warm and aromatic after the tropic day's sunshine. "The child has divined me already, Catherine," she said.

Christine was a tall, lissome maid, with an unusually long stretch of arm, long sloping shoulders, and a long fair throat; her straight hair fell to her knees when unbound, and its clear flaxen hue had not one shade of gold, as her clear gray eyes had not one shade of blue. Her small, straight, rose-leaf lips parted over small, dazzlingly white teeth, and the outline of her face in profile reminded you of an etching in its distinctness, although it was by no means perfect according to the rules of art. Still, what a comfort it was, after the blurred outlines and smudged profiles many of us possess—seen to best advantage, I think, in church on Sundays, crowned with flower-decked bonnets, listening calmly serene to favorite ministers, unconscious of noses! When Christine had finished her laugh—and she never hurried anything—she stretched out her arm carelessly and patted Felipa's curly head. The child caught the descending hand and kissed the long white fingers.

It was a wild place where we were, yet not new or crude— the coast of Florida, that old-new land, with its deserted plantations, its skies of Paradise, and its broad wastes open to the changeless sunshine. The old house stood on the edge of the dry land, where the pine-barren ended and the salt-marsh began; in front curved the tide-water river that seemed ever trying to come up close to the barren and make its acquaintance, but could not quite succeed, since it must always turn and flee at a fixed hour, like Cinderella at the ball, leaving not a silver slipper behind, but purple driftwood and bright seaweeds, brought in from the Gulf Stream outside. A planked platform ran out into the marsh from the edge of the barren, and at its end the boats were moored; for, although at high tide the river was at our feet, at low tide it was far away out in the green waste somewhere, and if we wanted it we must go and seek it. We did not want it, however; we let it glide up to us twice a day with its fresh salt odors and flotsam of the ocean, and the rest of the time we wandered over the barrens or lay under the trees looking up into the wonderful blue above, listening to the winds as they rushed across from sea to sea. I was an artist, poor and painstaking. Christine was my kind friend. She had brought me South because my cough was troublesome, and here because Edward Bowne recommended the place. He and three fellow sportsmen were down at the Madre Lagoon, farther south; I thought it probable we should see him, without his three fellow sportsmen, before very long.

"Who were the three women you have seen, Felipa?" said Christine.

"The grandmother, an Indian woman of the Seminoles who comes sometimes with baskets, and the wife of Miguel of the island. But they are all old, and their skins are curled: I like better the silver skin of the señora."

Poor little Felipa lived on the edge of the great salt-marsh alone with her grandparents, for her mother was dead. The yellow old couple were slow-witted Minorcans, part pagan, part Catholic, and wholly ignorant; their minds rarely rose above the level of their orange-trees and their fish-nets. Felipa's father was a Spanish sailor, and, as he had died only the year before, the child's Spanish was fairly correct, and we could converse with her readily, although we were slow to comprehend the patois of the old people, which seemed to borrow as much from the Italian tongue and the Greek as from its mother Spanish. "I know a great deal," Felipa remarked confidently, "for my father taught me. He had sailed on the ocean out of sight of land, and he knew many things. These he taught to me. Do the gracious ladies think there is anything else to know?"

One of the gracious ladies thought not, decidedly. In answer to my remonstrance, expressed in English, she said, "Teach a child like that, and you ruin her."

"Ruin her?"

"Ruin her happiness—the same thing."

Felipa had a dog, a second self—a great gaunt yellow creature of unknown breed, with crooked legs, big feet, and the name

Drollo. What Drollo meant, or whether it was an abbreviation, we never knew; but there was a certain satisfaction in it, for the dog was droll: the fact that the Minorcan title, whatever it was, meant nothing of that sort, made it all the better. We never saw Felipa without Drollo. "They look a good deal alike," observed Christine—"the same coloring."

"For shame!" I said.

But it was true. The child's bronzed yellow skin and soft eyes were not unlike the dog's, but her head was crowned with a mass of short black curls, while Drollo had only his two great flapping ears and his low smooth head. Give him an inch or two more of skull, and what a creature a dog would be! For love and faithfulness even now what man can match him? But, although ugly, Felipa was a picturesque little object always, whether attired in boy's clothes or in her own forlorn bodice and skirt. Olive-hued and meager-faced, lithe and thin, she flew over the pine-barrens like a creature of air, laughing to feel her short curls toss and her thin childish arms buoyed up on the breeze as she ran, with Drollo barking behind. For she loved the winds, and always knew when they were coming—whether down from the north, in from the ocean, or across from the Gulf of Mexico: she watched for them, sitting in the doorway, where she could feel their first breath, and she taught us the signs of the clouds. She was a queer little thing: we used to find her sometimes dancing alone out on the barren in a circle she had marked out with pine-cones, and once she confided to us that she talked to the trees. "They hear," she said in a whisper; "you should see how knowing they look, and how their leaves listen."

Once we came upon her most secret lair in a dense thicket of thorn-myrtle and wild smilax—a little bower she had made, where was hidden a horrible-looking image formed of the rough pieces of saw-palmetto grubbed up by old Bartolo from his garden. She must have dragged these fragments thither one by one, and with infinite pains bound them together with her rude withes of strong marsh-grass, until at last she had formed a rough trunk with crooked arms and a sort of a head, the red hairy surface of the palmetto looking not unlike the skin of some beast, and making the creature all the more grotesque. This fetich was kept crowned with flowers, and after this we often saw the child stealing away with Drollo to carry to it portions of her meals or a new-found treasure—a sea-shell, a broken saucer, or a fragment of ribbon. The food always mysteriously disappeared, and my suspicion is that Drollo used to go back secretly in the night and devour it, asking no questions and telling no lies: it fitted in nicely, however, Drollo merely performing the ancient part of the priests of Jupiter, men who have been much admired. "What a little pagan she is!" I said.

"Oh, no, it is only her doll," replied Christine.

I tried several times to paint Felipa during these first weeks, but those eyes of hers always evaded me. They were, as I have said before, yellow—that is, they were brown with yellow lights—and they stared at you with the most inflexible openness. The child had the full-curved, half-open mouth of the tropics, and a low Greek forehead. "Why isn't she pretty?" I said.

"She is hideous," replied Christine; "look at her elbows."

Now Felipa's arms *were* unpleasant: they were brown and lean, scratched and stained, and they terminated in a pair of determined little paws that could hold on like grim Death. I shall never forget coming upon a tableau one day out on the barren—a little Florida cow and Felipa, she holding on by the horns, and the beast with its small fore feet stubbornly set in the sand; girl pulling one way, cow the other; both silent and determined. It was a hard contest, but the girl won.

"And if you pass over her elbows, there are her feet," continued Christine languidly. For she was a sybaritic lover of the fine linens of life, that friend of mine—a pre-Raphaelite lady with clinging draperies and a mediæval clasp on her belt. Her whole being rebelled against ugliness, and the mere sight of a sharp-nosed, light-eyed woman on a cold day made her uncomfortable.

"Have we not feet too?" I replied sharply.

But I knew what she meant. Bare feet are not pleasant to the eye nowadays, whatever they may have been in the days of the ancient Greeks; and Felipa's little brown insteps were half the time torn or bruised by the thorns of the chaparral. Besides, there was always the disagreeable idea that she might step upon something cold and squirming when she prowled through the thickets knee-deep in the matted grasses. Snakes abounded, although we never saw them; but Felipa went up to their very doors, as it were, and rang the bell defiantly.

One day old Grandfather Bartolo took the child with him down to the coast: she was always wild to go to the beach, where she could gather shells and sea-beans, and chase the little ocean-birds that ran along close to the waves with that swift gliding motion of theirs, and where she could listen to the roar of the breakers. We were several miles up the salt-marsh, and to go down to the ocean was quite a voyage to Felipa. She bade us good-by joyously; then ran back to hug Christine a second time, then to the boat again; then back.

"I thought you wanted to go, child?" I said, a little impatiently; for I was reading aloud, and these small irruptions were disturbing.

"Yes," said Felipa, "I want to go; and still— Perhaps if the gracious señora would kiss me again—"

Christine only patted her cheek and told her to run away: she obeyed, but there was a wistful look in her eyes, and, even after the boat had started, her face, watching us from the stern, haunted me.

"Now that the little monkey has gone, I may be able at last to catch and fix a likeness of her," I said; "in this case a recollection is better than the changing quicksilver reality."

"You take it as a study of ugliness?"

"Do not be hard upon the child, Christine."

"Hard? Why, she adores me," said my friend, going off to her hammock under the tree.

Several days passed, and the boat returned not. I accomplished a fine amount of work, and Christine a fine amount of swinging in the hammock and dreaming. At length one afternoon I gave my final touch, and carried my sketch over to the pre-Raphaelite lady for criticism. "What do you see?" I said.

"I see a wild-looking child with yellow eyes, a mat of curly black hair, a lank little bodice, her two thin brown arms embracing a gaunt old dog with crooked legs, big feet, and turned-in toes."

"Is that all?"

"All."

"You do not see latent beauty, courage, and a possible great gulf of love in that poor wild little face?"

"Nothing of the kind," replied Christine decidedly. "I see an ugly little girl; that is all."

The next day the boat returned, and brought back five persons, the old grandfather, Felipa, Drollo, Miguel of the island, and—Edward Bowne.

"Already?" I said.

"Tired of the Madre, Kitty; thought I would come up here and see you for a while. I knew you must be pining for me."

"Certainly," I replied; "do you not see how I have wasted away?"

He drew my arm through his and raced me down the plankwalk toward the shore, where I arrived laughing and out of breath.

"Where is Christine?" he asked.

I came back into the traces at once. "Over there in the hammock. You wish to go to the house first, I suppose?"

"Of course not."

"But she did not come to meet you, Edward, although she knew you had landed."

"Of course not, also."

"I do not understand you two."

"And of course not, a third time," said Edward, looking down at me with a smile. "What do peaceful little artists know about war?"

"Is it war?"

"Something very like it, Kitty. What is that you are carrying?"

"Oh! my new sketch. What do you think of it?"

"Good, very good. Some little girl about here, I suppose?"

"Why, it is Felipa!"

"And who is Felipa? Seems to me I have seen that old dog, though."

"Of course you have; he was in the boat with you, and so was Felipa; but she was dressed in boy's clothes, and that gives her a different look."

"Oh! that boy? I remember him. His name is Philip. He is a funny little fellow," said Edward calmly.

"Her name is Felipa, and she is not a boy or a funny little fellow at all," I replied.

"Isn't she? I thought she was both," replied Ned carelessly;

and then he went off toward the hammock. I turned away, after noting Christine's cool greeting, and went back to the boat.

Felipa came bounding to meet me. "What is his name?" she demanded.

"Bowne."

"Buon—Buona; I can not say it."

"Bowne, child—Edward Bowne."

"Oh! Eduardo; I know that. Eduardo—Eduardo—a name of honey."

She flew off singing the name, followed by Drollo carrying his mistress's palmetto basket in his big patient mouth; but when I passed the house a few moments afterward she was singing, or rather talking volubly of, another name—"Miguel," and "the wife of Miguel," who were apparently important personages on the canvas of her life. As it happened, I never really saw that wife of Miguel, who seemingly had no name of her own; but I imagined her. She lived on a sand-bar in the ocean not far from the mouth of our salt-marsh; she drove pelicans like ducks with a long switch, and she had a tame eagle; she had an old horse also, who dragged the driftwood across the sand on a sledge, and this old horse seemed like a giant horse always, outlined as he was against the flat bar and the sky. She went out at dawn, and she went out at sunset, but during the middle of the burning day she sat at home and polished sea-beans, for which she obtained untold sums; she was very tall, she was very yellow, and she had but one eye. These items, one by one, had been dropped by Felipa at various times, and it was with curiosity that I gazed upon the original Miguel, the possessor of this remarkable spouse. He was a grave-eyed, yellow man, who said little and thought less, applying *cui bono?* to mental much as the city man applies it to bodily exertion, and therefore achieving, I think, a finer degree of inanition. The tame eagle, the pelicans, were nothing to him; and, when I saw his lethargic, gentle countenance, my own curiosity about them seemed to die away in haze, as though I had breathed in an invisible opiate. He came, he went, and that was all; exit Miguel.

Felipa was constantly with us now. She and Drollo followed the three of us wherever we went—followed the two also whenever I stayed behind to sketch, as I often stayed, for in those days I was trying to catch the secret of the salt-marsh; a hopeless effort—I know it now. "Stay with me, Felipa," I said; for it was natural to suppose that the lovers might like to be alone. (I call them lovers for want of a better name, but they were more like haters; however, in such cases it is nearly the same thing.) And then Christine, hearing this, would immediately call "Felipa!" and the child would dart after them, happy as a bird. She wore her boy's suit now all the time, because the señora had said she "looked well in it." What the señora really said was, that in boy's clothes she looked less like a grasshopper. But this had been translated as above by Edward Bowne when Felipa suddenly descended upon him one day and demanded to be instantly told what the gracious lady was saying about her; for she seemed to know by intuition when we spoke of her, although we talked in English and mentioned no names. When told, her small face beamed, and she kissed Christine's hand joyfully and bounded away. Christine took out her handkerchief and wiped the spot.

"Christine," I said, "do you remember the fate of the proud girl who walked upon bread?"

"You think that I may starve for kisses some time?" said my friend, going on with the wiping.

"Not while I am alive," called out Edward from behind. His style of courtship *was* of the sledge-hammer sort sometimes. But he did not get much for it on that day; only lofty tolerance, which seemed to amuse him greatly.

Edward played with Felipa very much as if she was a rubber toy or a little trapeze performer. He held her out at arm's length in mid-air, he poised her on his shoulder, he tossed her up into the low myrtle-trees, and dangled her by her little belt over the claret-colored pools on the barren; but he could not frighten her; she only laughed and grew wilder and wilder, like a squirrel. "She has muscles and nerves of steel," he said admiringly.

"Do put her down; she is too excitable for such games," I said in French, for Felipa seemed to divine our English now. "See the color she has."

For there was a trail of dark red over the child's thin oval cheeks which made her look unlike herself. As she caught our eyes fixed upon her, she suddenly stopped her climbing and came and sat at Christine's feet. "Some day I shall wear robes like the señora's," she said, passing her hand over the soft fabric; "and I think," she added after some slow consideration, "that my face will be like the señora's too."

Edward burst out laughing. The little creature stopped abruptly and scanned his face.

"Do not tease her," I said.

Quick as a flash she veered around upon me. "He does not tease me," she said angrily in Spanish; "and, besides, what if he does? I like it." She looked at me with gleaming eyes and stamped her foot.

"What a little tempest!" said Christine.

Then Edward, man-like, began to explain. "You could not look much like this lady, Felipa," he said, "because you are so dark, you know."

"Am I dark?"

"Very dark; but many people are dark, of course; and for my part I always liked dark eyes," said this mendacious person.

"Do you like my eyes?" asked Felipa anxiously.

"Indeed I do: they are like the eyes of a dear little calf I once owned when I was a boy."

The child was satisfied, and went back to her place beside Christine. "Yes, I shall wear robes like this," she said dreamily, drawing the flowing drapery over her knees clad in the little linen trousers, and scanning the effect; "they would trail behind me— so." Her bare feet peeped out below the hem, and again we all laughed, the little brown toes looked so comical coming out from the silk and the snowy embroideries. She came down to reality again, looked at us, looked at herself, and for the first time seemed to comprehend the difference. Then suddenly she threw herself down on the ground like a little animal, and buried her head in her arms. She would not speak, she would not look up: she only relaxed one arm a little to take in Drollo, and then lay motionless. Drollo looked at us out of one eye solemnly from his uncomfortable position, as much as to say: "No use; leave her to me." So after a while we went away and left them there.

That evening I heard a low knock at my door. "Come in," I said, and Felipa entered. I hardly knew her. She was dressed in a flowered muslin gown which had probably belonged to her mother, and she wore her grandmother's stockings and large baggy slippers; on her mat of curly hair was perched a high-crowned, stiff white cap adorned with a ribbon streamer; and her lank little neck, coming out of the big gown, was decked with a chain of large sea-beans, like exaggerated lockets. She carried a Cuban fan in her hand which was as large as a parasol, and Drollo, walking behind, fairly clanked with the chain of sea-shells which she had wound around him from head to tail. The droll tableau and the supreme pride on Felipa's countenance overcame me, and I laughed aloud. A sudden cloud of rage and disappointment came over the poor child's face: she threw her cap on the floor and stamped on it; she tore off her necklace and writhed herself out of her big flowered gown, and, running to Drollo, nearly strangled him in her fierce efforts to drag off his shell chains. Then, a half-dressed, wild little phantom, she seized me by the skirts and dragged me toward the looking-glass. "You are not pretty either," she cried. "Look at yourself! look at yourself!"

"I did not mean to laugh at you, Felipa," I said gently; "I would not laugh at any one; and it is true I am not pretty, as you say. I can never be pretty, child; but, if you will try to be more gentle, I could teach you how to dress yourself so that no one would laugh at you again. I could make you a little bright-barred skirt and a scarlet bodice: you could help, and that would teach you to sew. But a little girl who wants all this done for her must be quiet and good."

"I am good," said Felipa; "as good as everything."

The tears still stood in her eyes, but her anger was forgotten: she improvised a sort of dance around my room, followed by Drollo dragging his twisted chain, stepping on it with his big feet, and finally winding himself up into a knot around the chair-legs.

"Couldn't we make Drollo something too? dear old Drollo!" said Felipa, going to him and squeezing him in an enthusiastic embrace. I used to wonder how his poor ribs stood it: Felipa used him as a safety-valve for her impetuous feelings.

She kissed me good night, and then asked for "the other lady."

"Go to bed, child," I said; "I will give her your good night."

"But I want to kiss her too," said Felipa.

She lingered at the door and would not go; she played with the latch, and made me nervous with its clicking; at last I ordered her out. But on opening my door half an hour afterward there she was sitting on the floor outside in the darkness, she and Drollo, patiently waiting. Annoyed, but unable to reprove her, I wrapped the child in my shawl and carried her out into the moonlight, where Christine and Edward were strolling to and fro under the pines. "She will not go to bed, Christine, without kissing you," I explained.

"Funny little monkey!" said my friend, passively allowing the embrace.

"Me too," said Edward, bending down. Then I carried my bundle back satisfied.

The next day Felipa and I in secret began our labors: hers consisted in worrying me out of my life and spoiling material—mine in keeping my temper and trying to sew. The result, however, was satisfactory, never mind how we got there. I led Christine out one afternoon: Edward followed. "Do you like tableaux?" I said. "There is one I have arranged for you."

Felipa sat on the edge of the low, square-curbed Spanish well, and Drollo stood behind her, his great yellow body and solemn head serving as a background. She wore a brown petticoat barred with bright colors, and a little scarlet bodice fitting her slender waist closely; a chemisette of soft cream-color with loose sleeves covered her neck and arms, and set off the dark hues of her cheeks and eyes; and around her curly hair a red scarf was twisted, its fringed edges forming a drapery at the back of the head, which, more than anything else, seemed to bring out the latent character of her face. Brown moccasins, red stockings, and a quantity of bright beads completed her costume.

"By Jove!" cried Edward, "the little thing is almost pretty."

Felipa understood this, and a great light came into her face: forgetting her pose, she bounded forward to Christine's side. "I am pretty, then?" she said with exultation; "I *am* pretty, then, after all? For now you yourself have said it—have said it."

"No, Felipa," I interposed, "the gentleman said it." For the child had a curious habit of confounding the two identities which puzzled me then as now. But this afternoon, this happy afternoon, she was content, for she was allowed to sit at Christine's feet and look up into her fair face unmolested. I was forgotten, as usual.

"It is always so," I said to myself. But cynicism, as Mr. Aldrich says, is a small brass field-piece that eventually bursts and kills the artilleryman. I knew this, having been blown up myself more than once; so I went back to my painting and forgot the world. Our world down there on the edge of the salt-marsh, however, was a small one: when two persons went out of it there was a vacuum.

One morning Felipa came sadly to my side. "They have gone away," she said.

"Yes, child."

"Down to the beach to spend all the day."

"Yes, I know it."

"And without me!"

This was the climax. I looked up. Her eyes were dry, but there was a hollow look of disappointment in her face that made her seem old; it was as though for an instant you caught what her old-woman face would be half a century on.

"Why did they not take me?" she said. "I am pretty now: she herself said it."

"They can not always take you, Felipa," I replied, giving up the point as to who had said it.

"Why not? I am pretty now: she herself said it," persisted the child. "In these clothes, you know: she herself said it. The clothes of the son of Pedro you will never see more: they are burned."

"Burned?"

"Yes, burned," replied Felipa composedly. "I carried them out on the barren and burned them. Drollo singed his paw. They burned quite nicely. But they are gone, and I am pretty now, and yet they did not take me! What shall I do?"

"Take these colors and make me a picture," I suggested. Generally, this was a prized privilege, but to-day it did not attract; she turned away, and a few moments after I saw her going down to the end of the plank-walk, where she stood gazing wistfully toward the ocean. There she stayed all day, going into camp with Drollo, and refusing to come to dinner in spite of old Dominga's calls and beckonings. At last the patient old grandmother went down herself to the end of the long walk where they were, with some bread and venison on a plate. Felipa ate but little, but Drollo, after waiting politely until she had finished, devoured everything that was left in his calmly hungry way, and then sat back on his haunches with one paw on the plate, as though for the sake of memory, Drollo's hunger was of the chronic kind; it seemed impossible either to assuage it or to fill him. There was a gaunt leanness about him which I am satisfied no amount of food could ever fatten. I think he knew it too, and that accounted for his resignation. At length, just before sunset, the boat returned, floating up the marsh with the tide, old Bartolo steering and managing the brown sails. Felipa sprang up joyfully; I thought she would spring into the boat in her eagerness. What did she receive for her long vigil? A short word or two; that was all. Christine and Edward had quarreled.

How do lovers quarrel ordinarily? But I should not ask that, for these were no ordinary lovers: they were extraordinary.

"You should not submit to her caprices so readily," I said the next day while strolling on the barren with Edward. (He was not so much cast down, however, as he might have been.)

"I adore the very ground her foot touches, Kitty."

"I know it. But how will it end?"

"I will tell you: some of these days I shall win her, and then —she will adore me."

Here Felipa came running after us, and Edward immediately challenged her to a race: a game of romps began. If Christine had been looking from her window she might have thought he was not especially disconsolate over her absence; but she was not looking. She was never looking out of anything or for anybody. She was always serenely content where she was. Edward and Felipa strayed off among the pine-trees, and gradually I lost sight of them. But as I sat sketching an hour afterward Edward came into view, carrying the child in his arms. I hurried to meet them.

"I shall never forgive myself," he said; "the little thing has fallen and injured her foot badly, I fear."

"I do not care at all," said Felipa; "I like to have it hurt. It is *my* foot, isn't it?"

These remarks she threw at me defiantly, as though I had laid claim to the member in question. I could not help laughing.

"The other lady will not laugh," said the child proudly. And in truth Christine, most unexpectedly, took up the *rôle* of nurse. She carried Felipa to her own room—for we each had a little cell opening out of the main apartment—and as white-robed Charity she shone with new radiance, "Shone" is the proper word; for through the open door of the dim cell, with the dark little face of Felipa on her shoulder, her white robe and skin seemed fairly to shine, as white lilies shine on a dark night. The old grandmother left the child in our care and watched our proceedings wistfully, very much as a dog watches the human hands that extract the thorn from the swollen foot of her puppy. She was grateful and asked no questions; in fact, thought was not one of her mental processes. She did not think much; she felt. As for Felipa, the child lived in rapture during those days in spite of her suffering. She scarcely slept at all—she was too happy: I heard her voice rippling on through the night, and Christine's low replies. She adored her beautiful nurse.

The fourth day came: Edward Bowne walked into the cell. "Go out and breathe the fresh air for an hour or two," he said in the tone more of a command than a request.

"The child will never consent," replied Christine sweetly.

"Oh, yes, she will; I will stay with her," said the young man, lifting the feverish little head on his arm and passing his hand softly over the bright eyes.

"Felipa, do you not want me?" said Christine, bending down.

"He stays; it is all the same," murmured the child.

"So it is.—Go, Christine," said Edward with a little smile of triumph.

Without a word Christine left the cell. But she did not go to walk; she came to my room, and, throwing herself on my bed, fell in a moment into a deep sleep, the reaction after her three nights of wakefulness. When she awoke it was long after dark, and I had relieved Edward in his watch.

"You will have to give it up," he said as our lily came forth at last with sleep-flushed cheeks and starry eyes shielded from the light. "The spell is broken; we have all been taking care of Felipa, and she likes one as well as the other."

Which was not true, in my case at least, since Felipa had openly derided my small strength when I lifted her, and beat off the sponge with which I attempted to bathe her hot face. "They" used no sponges, she said, only their nice cool hands; and she wished "they" would come and take care of her again. But Christine had resigned *in toto*. If Felipa did not prefer her to all others, then Felipa should not have her; she was not a common nurse. And indeed she was not. Her fair face, ideal grace, cooing voice, and the strength of her long arms and flexible hands, were like magic to the sick, and—distraction to the well; the well in this case being Edward Bowne looking in at the door.

"You love them very much, do you not, Felipa?" I said one day when the child was sitting up for the first time in a cushioned chair.

"Ah, yes; it is so strong when they carry me," she replied. But it was Edward who carried her.

"He is very strong," I said.

"Yes; and their long soft hair, with the smell of roses in it too," said Felipa dreamily. But the hair was Christine's.

"I shall love them for ever, and they will love me for ever," continued the child. "Drollo too." She patted the dog's head as she spoke, and then concluded to kiss him on his little inch of forehead; next she offered him all her medicines and lotions in turn, and he smelled at them grimly. "He likes to know what I am taking," she explained.

I went on: "You love them, Felipa, and they are fond of you. They will always remember you, no doubt."

"Remember!" cried Felipa, starting up from her cushions like a Jack-in-the-box. "They are not going away? Never! never!"

"But of course they must go some time, for—"

But Felipa was gone. Before I could divine her intent she had flung herself out of her chair down on the floor, and was crawling on her hands and knees toward the outer room. I ran after her, but she reached the door before me, and, dragging her bandaged foot behind her, drew herself toward Christine. "You are *not* going away! You are not! you are not!" she sobbed, clinging to her skirts.

Christine was reading tranquilly; Edward stood at the outer door mending his fishing-tackle. The coolness between them remained, unwarmed by so much as a breath. "Run away, child; you disturb me," said Christine, turning over a leaf. She did not even look at the pathetic little bundle at her feet. Pathetic little bundles must be taught some time what ingratitude deserves.

"How can she run, lame as she is?" said Edward from the doorway.

"You are not going away, are you? Tell me you are not," sobbed Felipa in a passion of tears, beating on the floor with one hand, and with the other clinging to Christine.

"I am not going," said Edward. "Do not sob so, you poor little thing!"

She crawled to him, and he took her up in his arms and soothed her into stillness again; then he carried her out on the barren for a breath of fresh air.

"It is a most extraordinary thing how that child confounds you two," I said. "It is a case of color-blindness, as it were— supposing you two were colors."

"Which we are not," replied Christine carelessly. "Do not stray off into mysticism, Catherine."

"It is not mysticism; it is a study of character—"

"Where there is no character," replied my friend.

I gave it up, but I said to myself: "Fate, in the next world make me one of those long, lithe, light-haired women, will you? I want to see how it feels."

Felipa's foot was well again, and spring had come. Soon we must leave our lodge on the edge of the pine-barren, our outlook over the salt-marsh, with the river sweeping up twice a day, bringing in the briny odors of the ocean; soon we should see no more the eagles far above us or hear the night-cry of the great owls, and we must go without the little fairy flowers of the barren, so small that a hundred of them scarcely made a tangible bouquet, yet what beauty! what sweetness! In my portfolio were sketches and studies of the salt-marsh, and in my heart were hopes. Somebody says somewhere: "Hope is more than a blessing; it is a duty and a virtue." But I fail to appreciate preserved hope—hope put up in cans and served out in seasons of depression. I like it fresh from the tree. And so when I hope it *is* hope, and not that well-dried, monotonous cheerfulness which makes one long to throw the persistent smilers out of the window. Felipa danced no more on the barrens; her illness had toned her down; she seemed content to sit at our feet while we talked, looking up dreamily into our faces, but no longer eagerly endeavoring to comprehend. We were there; that was enough.

"She is growing like a reed," I said; "her illness has left her weak."

"–Minded," suggested Christine.

At this moment Felipa stroked the lady's white hand tenderly and laid her brown cheek against it.

"Do you not feel reproached?" I said.

"Why? Must we give our love to whoever loves us? A fine parcel of paupers we should all be, wasting our inheritance in pitiful small change! Shall I give a thousand beggars a half hour's happiness, or shall I make one soul rich his whole life long?"

"The latter," remarked Edward, who had come up unobserved.

They gazed at each other unflinchingly. They had come to open battle during those last days, and I knew that the end was near. Their words had been cold as ice, cutting as steel, and I said to myself, "At any moment." There would be a deadly struggle, and then Christine would yield. Even I comprehended something of what that yielding would be.

"Why do they hate each other so?" Felipa said to me sadly.

"Do they hate each other?"

"Yes, for I feel it here," she answered, touching her breast with a dramatic little gesture.

"Nonsense! Go and play with your doll, child." For I had made her a respectable, orderly doll to take the place of the ungainly fetich out on the barren.

Felipa gave me a look and walked away. A moment afterward she brought the doll out of the house before my very eyes, and, going down to the end of the dock, deliberately threw it into the water; the tide was flowing out, and away went my toy-woman out of sight, out to sea.

"Well!" I said to myself. "What next?"

I had not told Felipa we were going; I thought it best to let it take her by surprise. I had various small articles of finery ready as farewell gifts, which should act as sponges to absorb her tears. But Fate took the whole matter out of my hands. This is how it happened: One evening in the jasmine arbor, in the fragrant darkness of the warm spring night, the end came; Christine was won. She glided in like a wraith, and I, divining at once what had happened, followed her into her little room, where I found her lying on her bed, her hands clasped on her breast, her eyes open and veiled in soft shadows, her white robe drenched with dew. I kissed her fondly—I never could help loving her then or now—and next I went out to find Edward. He had been kind to me all my poor gray life; should I not go to him now? He was still in the arbor, and I sat down by his side quietly; I knew that the words would come in time. They came; what a flood! English was not enough for him. He poured forth his love in the rich-voweled Spanish tongue also; it has sounded doubly sweet to me ever since.

> "Have you felt the wool of the beaver?
>   Or swan's down ever?
>   Or have smelt the bud o' the brier?
>   Or the nard in the fire?
>   Or ha' tasted the bag o' the bee?
>   Oh so white, oh so soft, oh so sweet is she!"

said the young lover; and I, listening there in the dark fragrant night, with the dew heavy upon me, felt glad that the old simple-hearted love was not entirely gone from our tired metallic world.

It was late when we returned to the house. After reaching my room I found that I had left my cloak in the arbor. It was a strong fabric; the dew could not hurt it, but it could hurt my sketching materials and various trifles in the wide inside pockets—*objets de luxe* to me, souvenirs of happy times, little artistic properties that I hang on the walls of my poor studio when in the city. I went softly out into the darkness again and sought the arbor; groping on the ground I found, not the cloak, but—Felipa! She was crouched under the foliage, face downward; she would not move or answer.

"What is the matter, child?" I said, but she would not speak. I tried to draw her from her lair, but she tangled herself stubbornly still farther among the thorny vines, and I could not move her. I touched her neck; it was cold. Frightened, I ran back to the house for a candle.

"Go away," she said in a low hoarse voice when I flashed the light over her. "I know all, and I am going to die. I have eaten the poison things in your box, and just now a snake came on my neck and I let him. He has bitten me, and I am glad. Go away; I am going to die."

I looked around; there was my color-case rifled and empty, and the other articles were scattered on the ground. "Good Heavens, child!" I cried, "what have you eaten?"

"Enough," replied Felipa gloomily. "I knew they were poisons; you told me so. And I let the snake stay."

By this time the household, aroused by my hurried exit with the candle, came toward the arbor. The moment Edward appeared Felipa rolled herself up like a hedgehog again and refused to speak. But the old grandmother knelt down and drew the little crouching figure into her arms with gentle tenderness, smoothing its hair and murmuring loving words in her soft dialect.

"What is it?" said Edward; but even then his eyes were devouring Christine, who stood in the dark vine-wreathed doorway like a picture in a frame. I explained.

Christine smiled. "Jealousy," she said in a low voice. "I am not surprised."

But at the first sound of her voice Felipa had started up, and, wrenching herself free from old Dominga's arms, threw herself at Christine's feet. "Look at *me* so," she cried—"*me* too; do not look at him. He has forgotten poor Felipa; he does not love her any more. But *you* do not forget, señora; *you* love me—*you* love me. Say you do, or I shall die!"

We were all shocked by the pallor and the wild, hungry look of her uplifted face. Edward bent down and tried to lift her in his arms; but when she saw him a sudden fierceness came into her eyes; they shot out yellow light and seemed to narrow to a point of flame. Before we knew it she had turned, seized something, and plunged it into his encircling arm. It was my little Venetian dagger.

We sprang forward; our dresses were spotted with the fast-flowing blood; but Edward did not relax his hold on the writhing, wild little body he held until it lay exhausted in his arms. "I am glad I did it," said the child, looking up into his face with her inflexible eyes. "Put me down—put me down, I say, by the gracious señora, that I may die with the trailing of her white robe over me." And the old grandmother with trembling hands received her and laid her down mutely at Christine's feet.

Ah, well! Felipa did not die. The poisons racked but did not kill her, and the snake must have spared the little thin brown neck so despairingly offered to him. We went away; there was nothing for us to do but to go away as quickly as possible and leave her to her kind. To the silent old grandfather I said: "It will pass; she is but a child."

"She is nearly twelve, señora. Her mother was married at thirteen."

"But she loved them both alike, Bartolo. It is nothing; she does not know."

"You are right, lady; she does not know," replied the old man slowly; "but *I* know. It was two loves, and the stronger thrust the knife."

ALICE FRENCH
(OCTAVE THANET)

In her old age Alice recounted for an interviewer . . . the matter of Jane Crawford's departure: "When . . . Jennie went to Europe, Alice wept bitter tears over her going and wrote voluminous and daily letters. . . . Jennie wrote calmly in reply, while Alice wept, this time with delight, over each precious missive from her "Dear.""

In 1890, when she was forty years old, Alice French (1850–1934), publishing under the name "Octave Thanet," had nineteen years of increasingly popular and financial success as an essayist and short story writer behind her. She was working on her first novel, *We All*, which would be published the following year, and would write six more in the new century. Her pseudonym combined the first name of her beloved Octavia Putnam, with whom she had shared a twelve-by-twelve room and a double bed during their year at Andover Academy, with a word she had seen painted on the side of a freight train car. George L. McMichael, her only biog-

* *Journey to Obscurity: The Life of Octave Thanet* by George McMichael, University of Nebraska Press, Lincoln, 1965.

rapher so far, writes that she adopted the androgynous pen name "to avoid the bias of anti-feminist magazine editors. . . ."

By 1890, she had been settled in her comfortable lifelong partnership with Jane Allen Crawford for close to a decade, dividing the seasons between their home in Davenport, Iowa, and their plantation in Arkansas where Alice gave free rein to her imaginative and extravagant penchant for gourmet entertainments. The two women shared their adult lives, except for Jane's four-year marriage (the ending of which is somewhat mysterious) and Jane's departure to tour Europe.

French was born in Andover, Massachusetts, but moved with her family in 1856 to Davenport, Iowa, where her mother continued as a staunch advocate of Elizabeth Cady Stanton and her father became a wealthy manufacturer. She was the oldest of six children, from a financially and academically privileged background. As an adult she professed profoundly conservative political views. She was anti-labor union, a xenophobic who portrayed foreigners as sinister figures, and a racist caricaturist; she opposed Prohibition and helped to organize against the suffragists, whom she saw as in league with all those whom she opposed.

However, in her fortieth year, French published an edition of *The Best Letters of Lady Mary Wortley Montague (1689–1762)*, which McMichael refers to as "a quite credible scholarly work." Scholar Nancy Lyman Huse says that the book was a commissioned undertaking, work done only for money. But it is difficult to believe that French wasn't involved with her subject at a deeper level. The tie that Alice French shared with Mary Wortley was love for a woman central to the life of each of them.

In *Women of Ideas (And What Men Have Done to Them)*, Dale Spender characterizes Lady Mary Wortley Montague as "a staunch advocate of feminism." Montague and her husband lived separately, the wife appearing to have been "exiled," and for many years her only contact with her daughter and granddaughter was through letters. In these letters she set forth many of the analyses of the patriarchy with which contemporary feminists are once again acquainted. She impatiently discounts the notion of male superiority, promotes the value of education for women, and advises against marriage:

. . . (the) virgin state. . . . is undoubtedly safer than any marriage. In a lottery where there are (at the lowest computation) ten thousand blanks to a prize, it is the most prudent choice not to venture.

In *Surpassing the Love of Men,* Lillian Faderman suggests that Lady Mary Wortley Montague's major emotional involvement, begun while she was still Mary Pierrepont, was with a woman. Mary's passionate letters to her beloved Anne Wortley ended only when Anne died. Several years later, Mary married Anne's brother, Edward. When Lady Montague's friendship with Alexander Pope ended in a quarrel he thereafter referred to her in his poetry as "Sappho."

Faderman, the first to locate and identify "My Lorelei" as a story about a romantic friendship between two women, writes about Alice French:

Octave seemed to view humanity as having three sexes— men, women, and Octave Thanet. . . . Thanet saw only the model of heterosexuality around her and never questioned its morality.

"My Lorelei" was published in *The Western* in January 1880. It was French's eighth professional publication. She didn't include it in any of her eight volumes of short stories, the first of which, *Knitters in the Sun,* was published in 1887. It was not, however, the only piece of her early work that she excluded from later reprint. And she did include in her final collection, *Stories That End Well* (1911), "Max—Or His Picture" (originally published in 1899), another story in which a romantic friendship between two women is a central "fact" of the survivor's emotional history. The inclusion of "My Lorelei" in this volume is its first reprinting in more than one hundred years.

According to Huse, the story, set in Heidelberg, "is clear, vivid, and accurate in description of [the] place which Alice and her father had visited in 1874. . . . The humorous, somewhat cynical narrator has a tone reminiscent of Alice in her diaries; the beloved young woman is similar to Jennie Crawford in temperament, appearance, and even in her impending marriage to a less than admirable young man."

More needs to be done on French to develop a unified vision of this woman who wrote under an androgynous pen name, this daughter of a feminist who organized anti-suffrage meetings, this religious skeptic who learned to read from the theology books of her uncle, the Episcopal bishop of Iowa, this woman who violated the woman's sphere in almost every aspect of her life but opposed political enfranchisement for women.

French's readers would have recognized that a Lorelei was the German version of the legendary Greek siren, a half-woman who lured sailors to their deaths with her enchanting song. French/ Thanet quotes the German poet, Heinrich Heine, who had made the Lorelei famous in his poetry. Undine, with her "mysterious smile" and "delicate and elusive loveliness," whose name echoes that of the water nymph Undine whose story was told in 1811 by La Motte-Fouque. To gain a soul through marriage Undine has assumed human shape. Both Undines are unable to hold the love of the man to whom she has promised herself. But Mrs. Lynde, Constance, first tells her diary that Undine reminds her of the German Lorelei who "attract[s] a passion which [she] cannot return." She writes, ". . . I kissed her. . . . It is possible she was pleased at something; it is possible she was hurt at something. I half believe she is as puzzled over the pleasure or the pain, as I am puzzled over that curious look in her eyes." Who experiences a passion for whom? And who cannot not return the passions she attracts? Certainly it isn't Ted Tresham, Constance's good-for-nothing cousin, whose passion is unrequited. He lacks passion—at least for Undine. Although Constance begins and ends her diary with declarations of love for her husband, she tells us that since Undine's death she has "never made another friend." Is it Constance who has been lured by the siren's song?

My Lorelei

A HEIDELBERG ROMANCE

FROM THE DIARY OF MRS. LOUIS DANTON LYNDE

Heidelberg, *July* 9, 1874.—Louis is still at Frankfort. There are inconveniences in being in love with one's husband, when he has to spend half his time in Frankfort "on business." However, I will not grumble, since but for this same "business" we could not have afforded Europe for years.

We have been here two weeks; we expect to be here two months. The town is a queer, quaint, many-gabled, abominably paved place, with the famous Heidelberger Schloss shouldering its red walls through the trees of the western hills, like the Middle Ages looking down on us. When the sun sets, its rugged towers are outlined against a golden background, such as Fra Angelico gives his Madonnas. Our hotel fronts the Anlage, a charming street, of which only one side is bordered with cream-colored brick, while the other rolls back in wooded hills, where the White Caps hold their Kneipen, and the band plays on summer nights. Louis's Prussian friend, Count Von Reibnitz, recommended the hotel; indeed, he honors it with his own long-descended presence. He is a tall young man, of a florid complexion and a frank expression. He has regular features, and a great, sun-burned, white mustache, which he waxes at the ends. I cannot believe that his shoulders are so square and his waist so slender without some assistance from art. His regiment is stationed in Schwetzingen, but for some occult reason he seems to spend a great deal of his time here.

Ted Tresham is here also,—my good-natured, good-looking, and, I fear, slightly good-for-nothing cousin, whom I haven't seen for two years. His engagement does not seem to have sobered him particularly. Probably, it is merely a family affair; Miss Tresham is so rich, and his second cousin, besides. She is staying here with her aunt, Mrs. Guernsey, waiting for Uncle Tresham. When he comes, they are going home, and the young people are to be married in December. I have always had a curiosity to see Undine

Tresham, and now that I have opportunities, I improve them. She is worth seeing: when I look at her I am reminded of a German Lorelei, and I don't think it is the name altogether which suggests the comparison. No: for there are the deep, calm eyes (quite indescribable eyes); the waving, soft, brown hair, the mysterious smile,—all that delicate and elusive loveliness which the poets give to those strange creatures who attract a passion which they cannot return. She has two marked dimples and a blue vein on her cheek. Her white teeth make her smile dazzling. And she has the very sweetest voice I ever heard. Yet, I doubt my cousin may have made a great mistake. This, too, though Miss Tresham is undeniably clever, and her manners are as charming as her face. Will Coombs was in love with her once. He never asked her to marry him; she was "too jolly heartless," he said. Will has a keen streak running through his nonsense, and I fancy he was right about Undine Tresham. Graceful and cordial and winning as she is, there is an intangible mist of coldness about her, a curious remoteness, a persistent light-heartedness, that seems to spring, not from ignorance or hardness, but from sheer incapacity to feel. For instance, I cannot for my life imagine those beautiful eyes of hers filled with tears! All this from two weeks' acquaintance and Will's wild talk; decidedly, I am not timid in inference.

July 10.—I know a countess. She is the first countess of my acquaintance, therefore valued. Her name is Dunin Slepshks Wall —something! Mamma has it all neatly written out on a slip of paper, which she carries about with her, that she may be able to address the gnädige frau properly. *I* shall call her "countess." It is short, but at the same time imposing, and I have observed that they always address people so in novels. She is an amiable old woman, who rouges, and smokes cigarettes after dinner. Once she was a celebrated beauty, and she is still a brilliant talker—when she does not speak English. Unhappily, her politeness leads her to always converse with me in my own tongue. I can't tell her I don't understand English; so I sit at *table-d'hote* in a desperate state of mind, listening to her unintelligible fluency, and making frantic guesses at her meaning. Mamma can't understand her at all, and she thinks the poor woman is deaf; and when mamma looks helpless and unhappy, and murmurs, "I beg your pardon?" she yells the remark over again. Her seat at *table-d'hote* is next mine, and opposite we have two Americans. The elder is a middle-aged woman; the younger, a girl of perhaps twenty-three. They are interesting, after a fashion,—that is, the girl is; for the woman looks like nothing so much as a weak water-color, she is so faded, indistinct, and neutral-tinted. But the girl is a beauty! How Titian would rave over her crispy, red-gold hair, and topaz-brown long-lashed eyes, and creamy-white skin, with the pink glowing under the white on her oval cheeks! To me she seems like one of his gorgeous Venetian dames come to life again, with his own luxuriant grace of contour in her figure, and his own alluring splendor of coloring in her face. I suppose nine persons out of ten would call Miss Grace Wilmott (that is her name, and the water-color's title is Mrs. Moore) a magnificently handsome woman, but I don't like her; to be frank, I don't like Titian. Somehow it is an oppressive kind of beauty; there is a trifle too much of her, and then— her ribbons are never quite fresh! "Such things are women," Louis would say, and he would add that I was prejudiced because she flirts with Ted Tresham. Yesterday she blushed when he came into the room. He took the vacant seat beside her (it is not his seat at all), and one of her dimpled white hands stole under the table. I know from the sheepish look in the corner of Theodore's eye that he squeezed it! Undine and Mrs. Guernsey were not present. I wonder if he cares for his future wife; she, I fancy, is not likely to break her heart for any one. Still, it is impossible not to like her, she is so amusing, and her manners are perfect; with her aunt, for example, nothing could be better. Mrs. Guernsey is odd and fussy, and what must seem even more inexplicable to Undine, fervently enthusiastic; yet she never loses her temper, is always willing to come home before the dew falls, carries as many extra shawls as her aunt suggests, and listens with never-failing patience to the moral reflections. Far be it from me, however, to speak one slighting word of the excellent Mrs. Guernsey; she is a boon! Like mamma, she is a hungerer and a thirster for information. *I* am not. It is consequently an immense relief to have flung in our power, as it were, a comrade for mamma who is continually and indefatigably improving the time. They go off together on little instructive sprees.

July 15.—What a fascination there is about this quiet little town! Nothing is new, no one is excited; even the corps students get drunk decorously. I seem to have stepped out of the bustle and hurry and struggle of modern life. It is bliss, after Chicago. Yesterday we spent the day at the castle; there I saw a young man and a young woman sitting under the lindens. They sat there all day; half a dozen times we came back to them; always in the same attitudes,—she knitting some blue woollen article, he sitting on the grass at her feet. Occasionally he would take her hand and hold it for a few moments, smiling. He had providently spread a gay handkerchief on the grass, for his clothes were new, beyond a doubt; and he looked tranquilly and unreservedly happy. They said little; but several times the *restauration* waiters brought them beer, and at noon, they ate a great deal of bread and cheese and a large sausage, which they appeared to have brought with them. When night fell, and we went homeward, we overtook them walking hand in hand among the trees. They looked supremely satisfied with life; possibly a trifle stolid, but innocent as Arcadia. Undine glanced up at them as they passed. "They are happy," she said; "probably they are very lately married; but fancy two Americans spending a day in such a way!"

"I don't like American lovers," said I.

We all went up to the castle together,—Undine, Ted, mamma, and I. We rode up the hill in the most degraded manner, on diminutive donkeys, with a man walking behind to guide the beasts by the tail! I shall not tell Louis.

The road climbs the steepest of hills through old Heidelberg, which is picturesque and ruinous to the last degree.

All the inhabitants (save a few very bad children, who try to frighten tourists' donkeys) are over eighty, and wear ragged, dingy, blue garments.

At the castle gateway we dismounted and dismissed our donkeys. The gateway itself is a commonplace modern structure, with an iron ring let into the stone on one side. Ted explained that this was the celebrated "wishing ring." One must knock three times with it, wishing the same thing each time; then he must enter and make the circuit of the grounds in absolute silence, going out through the same gateway. If these directions are followed to the letter, whatever he has wished shall surely come to pass. Instantly out came mamma's Baedecker and glasses. "Has any one ever tried it?" she asked, eagerly.

"Hundreds," said Ted; "only ten have succeeded, though. One of these was a woman."

"Ach, *so*?" said Undine, with the absurd German inflection.

"Actually," said Ted. "I don't wonder you are surprised, but it really happened. She gagged herself with her handkerchief, and had her husband tie her hands, so she managed to walk all around and out safely, but the instant he took the handkerchief out, she gave a kind of gasping scream, and fell down dead!"

"What did she do that for?" said mamma, rather startled.

"Why, you see, she had so much to say that it killed her trying to say it all at once! What are you going to do, Undine?"

Undine, who had laid her hand on the ring, said she was going to wish.

"What will you wish for, liebchen?" said Ted, carelessly. "What have you left to want?"

She lifted her eyes to his; certainly they are the most beautiful eyes in the world. There was a little vibration in her sweet, slow voice, "I don't know, Ted;" she answered, "every thing has come to me before I have had time to want it; I can only wish to keep."

At that moment it occurred to me that I had made a little mistake about my Lorelei. Such a thought had no business to make me melancholy, but it did. I walked by Undine's side, almost as silent as she. For that matter, Ted was the only lively member of the party, since mamma was absorbed in comparing the realities with Baedecker's flights of fancy,—naturally a serious occupation,—and Undine never opened her lips. Finally, she walked out of the gate, and came back smiling. "It *is* a strain, Ted," she confessed. "I hope I shall be immortalized in the castle traditions. I feel very much exhausted; would you mind going to the *restauration* and having a cup of coffee, Mrs. Burt?"

Ted suggested champagne, but Undine asked him solemnly if he had ever tried the *restauration* champagne, and when he admitted his ignorance, she said, "The coffee is the worst of its kind, but the champagne is simply beyond words."

I am bound to say (after taking both) I think she told the truth. The *restauration* is a wooden building, glaringly modern and out of place so near the grand old ruin. Ugly wooden tables are scattered among the trees, and depressed-looking men, in shabby dress-coats, bear trays in the usual precarious manner, to the people who are seated around the tables. We soon left this scene of festivity and repaired to the museum. There mamma was in her glory. She put me to open shame, standing before some wooden-looking portraits, her bonnet perched disreputably on one side of her head, and audibly reading Baedecker's descriptions. We lost her three times in twenty minutes, and each time we found her thus. The weapons, also, seemed to exert an unaccountable fascination over her. She would take the daggers down from the wall, and run her fingers along the edge,—positively, it looked as though she meant to steal the things!

"Why, my dear," she said, to my remonstrances, "we are all alone in the room, and nobody seems to take the least care of any thing here."

Nobody did seem to take any care, but, nevertheless, I was relieved when we got her safely out of the museum. I hope we did our duty by Heidelberg Castle. Ted took us everywhere. We saw the rent tower, and the tuns, and the great chapel, and a darksome hole which Ted called the monk's chapel; but I think the monks had more sense. Finally, we came out on the terrace.

The sun had sunk below the horizon; only a few crimson streaks, like the careless strokes of an emptied brush, stained the yellow glow in the west. Far below us was spread the town, a huddle of pointed roofs and church spires; directly beneath, the Neckar ran noiselessly over its rocks; to the right and to the left stretched the hills. The near hills were green, and checkered with corn-fields and vineyards; but in the distance the dark purple outlines looked darker against the yellow sea of light. The shadows of the ruined towers lay long and heavy on the grass. Away to the right, a solitary nightingale was singing; and as we stood listening for a moment, vaguely awed by the beauty and the melancholy of the scene, some students, out of sight, began Heine's song:—

> Du hast Diamanten und Perlen,
>   Hast Alles was Menchenbegehr,
> Und hast die schönsten Augen,—
>   Mein Liebchen, was willst du mehr?

In the friendly dimness I saw Ted's arm steal around his cousin's waist. He hummed the refrain,—

Und hast die schönsten Augen,—
Mein Liebchen, was willst du mehr?

"What I wished at the gate, Ted," said Undine.

"And what was that?" said Ted, lowering his voice. "A heart, by chance?"

"No," said Undine, quietly; "I have more than I need now. But, Ted, we really ought to go. Aunt Eliza will be worried. She has a wild notion that donkeys run away. She says there is viciousness in their eyes!"

We rode home gaily enough; but that evening, passing Undine's door, it opened and she came out; by the lamp-light her face looked pale. For the first time, she seemed to me not the beautiful, cold lorelei about whom I was weaving a fanciful romance, but a girl who had no mother, and who was too rich to have many friends. Almost involuntarily, I drew her to me and kissed her. The faintest flush tinged her cheek. I can't describe how oddly she looked at me, saying, "Then, I don't chill you, Constance."

"Not to mention," said I, laughing. Then I kissed her again. It is possible she was pleased at something; it is possible she was hurt at something. I half believe she is as puzzled over the pleasure or the pain, as I am puzzled over that curious look in her eyes.

July 18.—Louis has returned.

July 21.—Yesterday Louis said, "Con, Ted will get himself into a row if he doesn't mind his pace better. I caught him walking on the Anlage with that Miss Wilmott, this evening. It doesn't look well in an engaged man." Decidedly, it does not. Lately Ted's devotion to that girl has been scandalous, even judged by American ideas. Where foreigners must place Miss Wilmott, I don't venture to imagine.

July 26.—Yesterday I was reading *Undine* to Louis, and Von Reibnitz. Undine's namesake, and the countess came in together during the reading, and would not allow me to stop. The countess, who had never read De la Motte Fouqué's charming tale, quite flattered one by her excitement over its ending. "Ah, bah!" she exclaimed, "but then Undine was a eediot! Thou art but small like her, my friend."

"She should haf some oder man to take her away from dat

villain fool," muttered Von Reibnitz. He looked at Undine as he spoke.

I believe I know now why he spends so much time in Heidelberg. Poor young man! Yesterday, after some imperious drill had torn him from us, the countess burst into a kind of Greek chorus of praise; she grew so enthusiastic that she even abandoned her cherished English, and recounted his virtues in French. Not the least of these seemed to be that his mother was the countess's twelfth cousin. For a brief period this brave, this noble young man, this best of sons, had slightly,—but the most slightly, view you,—admired "Mlle. Grase;" but who could care for her long? "Dear friends, behold the true Bertulda, so weak, so selfish—bah, so pretty!"

She made such a crowning offence of the last adjective that I laughed outright. Nevertheless, the countess is a shrewd old woman.

July 30.—For my sins, Bertulda has taken a fancy to me. She does not improve on acquaintance.

August 2.—Undine bewilders me. Does she care for Ted? If she does, how can she watch Grace Wilmott's audacious flirtation with that odd air of amusement? She has a curious smile, appearing on singularly incongruous occasions; it is almost as if she were smiling at herself. Once I asked her about her name. "My father gave it to me," she said. "It is after an aunt of mine who had a family reputation for fortitude, and my father called me after her because I never cried. You know my mother died when I was born, and there was only he to decide. He died when I was three; I don't even remember how he looked, but I have an idea I should have liked him."

"Didn't you cry often when you were a child?"

"No, somehow I never *wanted* to cry. I really don't remember crying hard but once. That was because I had no little sister. It was amusing."

"It doesn't strike me as amusing."

"You don't know the circumstances. I wasn't more than eight years old. There was a horrid little girl who lived near us,—a dreadfully disagreeable little girl,—who was always chewing gum, and when she tired of that, used to flatten the gum on my hair. It was her crude sense of humor, I suppose; but youth is not tolerant, and it was no end of trouble getting the gum out of my hair! Well, she, this unpleasant little girl, Malie Hungerford, had the sweetest little baby sister in the world. I thought it a great shame that Malie should have three sisters, while I had not even a brother. I was very fond of little Lulu, so I stole her."

"Stole her!"

"Yes, stole her out of the cradle while the nurse was talking to her friend, the ice-man, and Malie was chewing gum somewhere else; stole her, and carried her to an old woman who was to take care of her for me for a dollar a week, my Roman sash, and my new wax doll. You can fancy the conclusion of the story, of course. The old woman was a cunning old woman. She carried the baby home, running all the way. An indignant delegation of Hungerfords waited on my aunt. Poor Aunt Eliza! She began to cry, while I simply stared. 'Oh, Undine! how *could* you act so?' she said, the Hungerfords all the time glaring at me solemnly. 'I wanted a little sister,' said I. 'But, my dear,' said Mrs. Hungerford,—she was a very large woman, Constance very tall and very stout, and she always grew red in the face when she became moral and instructive,—'my dear,' said she, 'God gives little brothers and sisters—' 'Then won't He please give me one,' I interrupted, not meaning to be rude, but only awfully in earnest. 'No, He won't,' screamed Malie; 'and you can't have any, *never*!' But I didn't look at her. '*Can't I*?' I said to Mrs. Hungerford. 'Why, no, my dear,' she said, 'you can't. But you may have dear little friends, who will love you very much.' Then I cried."

"Did you always want a sister?"

"Not so much when I saw more of sisters, but I have times of wanting her still."

"Undine," said I, "suppose you try *me*; I never had a sister either, and I love you."

"Do you?" she said, looking at me with her lovely, unfathomable eyes. "I am glad. You will make a nice sister."

At least, dear, though I did not say it to you, I shall make a faithful one.

August 6.—Louis again away, Constance a martyr to Bertulda. Hardly a day passes that she does not come into my room, clad in an untidy blue cashmere wrapper, fling herself upon my lounge, and *confide*. The other day she told me how hard it was to earn her living as a companion (Mrs. Moore never denies her any thing), how sad and lonely she felt, and how much she longed for sympathy. She wept a few tears on a torn handkerchief, which she deluged with my cologne; then she took the cologne off with her to bathe her head. Of course, it has not returned. Farewell, a long farewell to all my sweetness, for she borrowed my other perfumery Thursday. Sometimes her feelings overcome her, and she cries on my handkerchiefs; that is why my stock is getting low. Grief always makes her hair come down, and she puts it up with my hair-pins. Whenever she needs a pin, she carefully selects a black pin from the cushion. There are chords—! and black pins in a foreign country touch one of mine.

August 10.—Ted has taken Mrs. Guernsey to Baden for a few days.

August 15.—Yesterday we had a most disagreeable adventure. We were to drive to Neckar Steinoch, and take dinner at a quaint little inn lauded by Von Reibnitz. Mamma, the countess, and I were to go in a carriage; Von Reibnitz and Undine were to ride. It was a lovely plan, but Bertulda spoiled it all! At the last moment, she wheedled an invitation out of mamma's soft heart. "Poor motherless child!" said mamma. "And you know, Connie, there is a vacant seat in the carriage." So she came. She looked as handsome as a snake, in a blue Chambery gauze, and a Paris hat trimmed with roses. We took dinner in the garden of the inn. The garden slopes down into the river, and from where we sat we could see trimly checkered hills and vineyards, and, peeping through the trees, a ruined tower, from which once a robber baron descended on peaceful travellers, but which now holds nothing more warlike than flocks of swallows. On the steepest of the hills, a few wretched houses were clustered about a slender church-spire, and a foot-path crawled up to them through stunted vineyards. Von Reibnitz told us that a colony of *cretins* dwelt there. They support themselves chiefly by begging, and I should judge that the whole colony had turned out in our honor. Horrible-looking beings they were,— dwarfed, maimed, deformed in strange and hideous fashions, scarred with loathsome diseases,—living hints of the appalling possibilities of our race. One bolder than the others followed us to the carriage, and clung to the door. He was a repulsively ugly man, who limped, and had somehow lost two fingers of his left hand.

Bertulda was nearest to him; she shuddered, and called out in her bad German, *"Gahen snell! ich haben nix!"* The creature only grinned, and clutched her arm. She wrenched it away, screaming to the coachman to strike the man with his whip. The coachman gave a half-reckless stroke behind him, and the *cretin* at that instant swaying forward with the motion of the carriage, the lash cut him full in his face. It was an ugly thing to see! Uglier, perhaps, though, to see his arms tossed up and his body curve backward as the sudden lurch of the carriage tumbled him into the road! The frightened horses broke into a gallop, while mamma shrieked, the countess, I fear, swore, and Bertulda gazed piteously—at her own arm! I looked back. The *cretin* was standing in the centre of the road, covered with dust. There was a wet, red line across his cheek; he wiped it with his ragged sleeve. Undine had thrown him a gold piece, but it glittered unnoticed at his feet. Not so much as glancing down, he looked from his stained sleeve to us, muttering to himself. Then a cloud of dust made a dingy ghost of him, and Undine and Von Reibnitz clattered up to the droschky. They were assailed by a little storm of questions. "Was the poor fellow hurt?" cried mamma. "Vat did he saying?" said the countess. "Did he pick up his money?" I asked.

"Oh, no, Mrs. Burt, he wasn't hurt badly," said Undine; "he was saying he would murder Miss Wilmott, madam. No, Connie, he didn't—what is the matter, Miss Wilmott?"

Bertulda was looking desperately frightened; her nerves were so shaken, in fact, that we had to stop and avert the hysterics with champagne. She had taken as much champagne as was good for her already, and the consequent spectacle was not edifying. I wish Ted had seen her.

August 16.—Yesterday Undine gave me an elegant dressing-case. I told her she gave me too many presents. She opened her eyes, "Are you not my sister?" she said. I am out of all patience with Ted. How can a man, fortunate enough to have won such an exquisite being as Undine, descend to Grace Wilmott's *beauté de diable*? Because he is a *man*, I suppose. Yesterday night they went to the cemetery,—"to hear the nightingales sing." Nice, cheerful place for a romantic stroll! As the countess says, *"Blague!"*

September 12.—Ted has a duel on his hands. Walk with Miss Wilmott—rude student—Grace frightened—student knocked down—challenge! The student says he knew Grace before,—had walked with her himself; Grace says it is a wicked lie. Maybe it is, and maybe it isn't. All this, with many unnecessary comments, was confided to me last night. It goes without saying that Undine is not to know.

September 13.—An awkward thing has just happened. Undine and I, going into the reading-room, came suddenly upon Grace Wilmott, sobbing on Ted Tresham's shoulder. "The devil!" said he. Upon my word, I don't blame him. Bertulda sank into a chair, and made a great fuss with her handkerchief. Undine, quite silent, stood in the doorway, looking from one to the other. She was dressed for dinner; the sunlight burnished the dull olive tints of her dress, there was a lace scarf flung about her shoulders, and the opals at her white throat flickered like flame. She had never looked more beautiful. I wonder if Ted didn't think so, too; anyhow, he stared at her with all his eyes. Before he could speak, she stepped between him and Grace. "Excuse me," she said, and there was not a quiver in her sweet voice, "I did not know any one was here. Before I go, let me return something that belongs to Mr. Tresham." She slipped a ring from her finger, laid it on the table near Ted, and turning, passed out of the room. There didn't seem any thing for me to do save go; so, I went—in another direction.

As for my cousin Theodore Tresham, * * * He has just been to see me. I am happy to say he looked infinitely uncomfortable. He burst out at once; he knew he had been a cursed fool, but it wasn't as bad as I thought; he swore he didn't know Miss Wilmott was in the room when he came into it; she had heard of the duel, and she felt sorry, and so—and so—"By Jove, I don't know how it *did* happen!" groaned Ted.

I said I thought I *did*; that was a nice girl to lose Undine for!

"Leave her out, can't you?" he said, gloomily. "You women are always so infernally hard on each other."

"Is Undine hard on her?"

Ted stood up; he looked more of a man than I had ever seen him. "Constance," he said, "I love Undine. And she knows it. Whatever follies and idiotic fancies for other women I may have, I always come back to her. I *have* to! She knows that, too. Tell her I am ashamed of myself, and it is the last time she shall need to forgive me. Tell her I'll do any thing she wants, if she will only let me speak to her one single time."

Well, I promised; for who dares decide what will make a woman happy? Ted as a husband I should not fancy myself, but Undine may.

Later.—I went down stairs to Undine, and conscientiously began Ted's apologies. She stopped the first of them with, "Do you think, Connie, you can invent more excuses for Ted than I?"

She had been so composed, so free from any show of either anger or grief, that I had begun to hope (yes, to *hope*, though Ted is my cousin) that she did not really care for him. In my disappointment, I said the silliest thing possible,—I told her she was far too good for him. She laughed, then she sighed; I had never heard her sigh before, and the soft little sound affected me strangely.

"I don't know about that," she said; "and besides, Constance, we don't love people because they are good, but because we can't help it."

Nothing appropriate occurring to me to say, I said nothing; but I felt, with rush of thankfulness so intense that it was pain, how much I respected Louis. Just at this point in the conversation, it was ordained that Mrs. Guernsey should come in and tell me most of the history of Heidelberg Castle. I have just escaped.

To-morrow the countess and her son are going to take mamma and me to Schwetzinger. The son is a mild-mannered young man, who is the best swordsman in Heidelberg. A wretched old German, with a villainous voice, promenades beneath my window, singing over and over again the first two lines of the Lorelei:—

> "Ich weiss nicht was solt es bedenten,
> Das ich so traurig bin!"

I am tired; I am out of spirits; I wish I could sleep a long, long time.

* * * * * *

Heidelberg, *September* 25, 1879.—How still the life stands in an old German town. I look from my window on the same shady streets, corps students, yellow-brown dogs sniffing at their masters' heels, English tourists in astonishing plaids and grays, American tourists in sombre black, honest *haus fraus* knitting in the shade, all the same. I might have left them yesterday,—and it is yesterday five years. Five years ago, I put this old journal in the pocket of my trunk, thinking then that I never should write in it again. I did not take it out again until yesterday. The trunk was too large for ordinary use, and it stood unmolested in the garret. At first I shrank from seeing the book, and yet, at the same time, shrank from destroying it; after awhile, I believe I forgot about it; but when I took the old trunk out for this journey, I remembered, and yesterday I read the journal through. Every thing comes back so freshly here, where I knew Undine, and I am glad at last that it should come. Perhaps some day I shall be glad that I have told the end of the story which I began in so unconscious and light-hearted a fashion five years ago. I might, for example, give this journal to Theodore Tresham. I have been trying to renew the old time in every way I know. This morning I climbed up to the castle; I wandered through the bare rooms and ruined arches, and I stood for a moment beneath the gateway where Undine wished "to keep." Nothing there has changed: the waiters at the *restauration* seem to wear the self-same shabby dress-coats; the very coffee was cold—as it used to be.

One thing I have not done: I have not gone to Schwetzingen, although a very pleasant party went to-day, and urged us to accompany them. But I did not go; I do not think I shall ever see Schwetzingen again. Yet it was a pleasant enough day which we spent there five years ago. I forget what we did; I only remember now the look of Louis's face as he walked into the little dining-room of the Golden Stag, where we all were, and the sound of his voice, saying, "Con, you were always brave; there has been a bad accident to Miss Tresham, and she wants you." At least I was brave enough not to make any trouble. While they were putting the horses into the lightest carriage they could find,—Von Reibnitz's dog-cart,—for there was no railroad then from Schwetzingen, Louis told me all he knew; afterwards I heard the rest. It seems Undine and Mrs. Guernsey had gone up to the castle, and were out on the terrace, when they heard wild screams, and almost instantly Grace Wilmott darted up to them, pursued by a horrible-looking man brandishing a dagger. Louis did not know then, but

it was the *cretin* of Neckar Steinoch; for weeks he had been track-
ing Grace, with the strange cunning of his distorted wits, and he
had found her alone among the ruins. The dagger belonged to
the museum, and I suppose he stole it. Grace had fled the instant
she saw him; she rushed to Undine, stumbled, and fell at her feet.
The fall probably saved her, for the *cretin* had caught her dress
and struck one furious blow; before he could strike again, Undine
had flung her arms about him. Slender as they were, they clung
like steel: though he shifted his dagger to his left hand and stabbed
her, they never loosened their grasp. "Run!" she cried to the helpless, shrieking creature by her side; "run, I can't hold him long!"
Bertulda,—well, she *was* Bertulda,—she saved herself. Mrs.
Guernsey's screams brought a dozen people to the spot, Louis
among them. He had returned unexpectedly from Frankfort, and
still wore his travelling revolver; drawing it, he pushed it under
Undine's arm, within an inch of the man's breast, and fired. The
cretin rolled over on the stones, and was dead in five minutes. But
his rusty dagger had done its work. They carried my poor girl to
the hotel, and Louis went for me. It was Von Reibnitz who brought
him the horse.

Our drive home is like a nightmare to me. When we reached
the hotel, a man ran out of the shadow of the blue and white
awnings and held out his hand to help me from the carriage.
"Yes," he said, answering the question I had not courage to ask;
"they think she may live until morning, but there is no—no hope!"
Then I saw it was Ted,—for at first the sun had shone in his face,
and I was half dazed; now I could see how white and haggard his
gay, careless face was, with red circles about the eyes, as if he had
been crying. "O Constance," he cried, wringing my hand hard,
"for God's sake, get me a chance to see her; Mrs. Guernsey is
angry, and won't let me in!"

I suppose I must have promised; somehow I got away, and
hurrying down the dark hall, almost ran into Grace Wilmott. Her
eyes were red and swollen,—it was always such an easy thing for
her to cry! She sobbed out an entreaty for me to stop.

"O Mrs. Lynde, is she really going to die? Indeed, it wasn't
my fault! And every body blames me! Oh, please stop! Oh, what
shall I do?"

I did stop. It was dark in the hall, but there was some light, and I hope she saw my face. I pointed over my shoulder. "Mr. Tresham is *there*," I said, and I left her; it was our last conversation. Mrs. Guernsey was waiting. She led me into the room. There was a table, covered with papers, drawn up to the bed, and beside it stood a tall man in black. Through the triangle made by his bent arm, I caught a glimpse of soft, brown hair; he moved, and I saw Undine's face. I went up to her,—what does it matter how I felt? I think it was then Mrs. Guernsey and the doctor went softly out of the room. Undine feebly put her hand on mine. "I knew you would come, Connie," she said; "my dear love, how hard you must have driven!"

I tried to speak,—to tell her it would hurt her to talk. She smiled and said, "Nothing will hurt me now. Connie, I wanted to speak to you alone, on business. I have left half my property to Ted; then I have left something to Aunt Eliza,—all she would take, you know she is rich; and I have left some fifty thousand in legacies to some poor people I have known; the rest I have given to you. You are my sister, Constance; you will take my money, won't you? It makes me happy to think of your having it."

"Oh, why did you save that girl?" I cried. "Oh, how can I bear it?"

Undine smiled again,—the curious smile which used to puzzle me. "Why?" she repeated. "I'm sure I don't know, myself. Yet, I suppose I would do it over again, were it to do. It seems absurd, rather, doesn't it?"

I could not speak. "How still it is!" said Undine. "Is it really so still, or is it—Connie, do you mind going to the window to see?"

I went to the window. There was straw scattered over the street, and Von Reibnitz stood like a sentinel at the corner. When I told Undine, she sighed. "How good he is!" she murmured, "I wish—" She did not finish the sentence, but a moment later she asked me to thank Von Reibnitz, and to give him a chain she had worn, which he had once admired. "Some day, I hope," she said, "he will give it to some pretty German girl, who will love him as the countess says 'the best of sons' deserves." It was a little while after this, she asked me if I had seen Ted. I told her what he had said. "Did he think I could die without seeing him?" she said. "My poor boy! But, for all that, he will marry Grace Wilmott."

"He can never look at her again!" I cried. Heaven knows, I believed it at the time!

She leaned her head half wearily on my shoulder. "I believe I could have kept him had I lived," she said; "but a memory is so weak. Constance."

"Yes, dear."

"Do you believe spirits can see those they used to love?"

"Oh, God knows, my darling, I cannot tell you. You will be happy, however it is!"

"Do you think so?" she answered, dreamily. "I have always been a kind of pagan, and I don't—feel—quite—certain."

What could I say to her? I sat silent, with a heavy heart, while one by one the street lights sprang out of the darkness, and by their gleam I took my last look of my darling's face.

They were singing over among the hills the same little love-song of Heine's, which I heard, for the first time, the day we visited the castle:—

> "Du hast Diamanten und Perlen,
> Hast Alles was Menchenbegehr,
> Und hast die schönsten Augen—
> Mein Liebchen, was willst du mehr?"

She turned those "loveliest eyes" wistfully up to mine. "*You* will always love me Con, won't you? Now call Ted. Kiss me first." Even as I kissed her, I felt her lips stir with a smile. "Connie, do you remember the day at the castle, when I wished? Well, the ring is a true fairy, for I wished Ted might love me as long as I lived, —and he will."

I laid her gently back on the pillows, but I could not see her face through my tears. I did not need to call Ted: he was watching at the door. I could hear him rush past me and fling himself on his knees before Undine, begging her, in a broken voice, to forgive him,—only to forgive him. "I never loved Grace; I never loved any one but you! You said I always came back— O my God! Constance! Constance, come here!"

Yes, he might kiss her hands and her hair, show his useless remorse in any frantic way he would,—it did not matter what he did any more, for Undine lay there with her last smile forever fixed on her beautiful mouth; as if dead she smiled at his pain, as living she smiled at her own.

All this is five years away. We left Undine in the pretty little cemetery where Ted and Grace Wilmott went to hear the nightingales sing. Last night I heard them singing by her grave.

Poor Von Reibnitz was killed in the Franco-Prussian war. He left me a little pet dog, which, as I am not fond of dogs, has been something of a trial to me.

The countess is on her Polish estates with her son. She writes me occasionally, and often alludes to her Heidelberg experience. I have no doubt she makes a capital tragic tale of it: she was always a fine talker in every language but English.

Ted Tresham married Grace Wilmott within six months after his cousin's death. I hear queer stories of his wife's extravagance and flirtations, and I take a grim satisfaction in the hearing. Our own intercourse with Ted naturally ceased with his marriage, but business matters have made a few interviews necessary. He seems subdued and changed, and looks ten years older. He has never mentioned Undine's name.

As for me, Undine's legacy has prospered with us. I am more in love with my husband than ever. My dear mother is still with us. On the whole, I am a very happy woman,—but I have never made another friend.

CONSTANCE FENIMORE WOOLSON

*"Lesbian consciousness" is really a point of view, a view
from the boundary. And in a sense every time a woman
draws a circle around her psyche, saying "this is a room
of my own" and then writes from within that "room,"
she's inhabiting "lesbian consciousness."* *

Hasn't each of us, at one time or another, wondered, "Am I the
only one in the world?" What courage and determination a person
needs to live with the belief that she is singular, isolated, and alone
forever! All kinds of characteristics render people unusual in their
"native" environments. Some are visible; others are not. A physical
difference from those among whom you live—such as a hairy face
on a woman, a sensory difference—such as deafness in a com-

---

* Harriet Desmoines in *Sinister Wisdom: Special Issue on Lesbian Literature and
Publishing,* ed. Beth Hodges, Fall 1976; quoted by Bonnie Zimmerman in " 'What
Has Never Been': Directions in Lesbian Feminist Literary Criticism" paper presented at the National Women's Studies Association Conference, June, 1979; revised version published in *Feminist Studies,* Fall, 1981, pp. 451–475; quoted in *A
Feminist Dictionary,* Cheris Kramarae and Paula A. Treichler, Pandora, 1985,
p. 228.

munity of the hearing, an intellectual difference—such as genius, a learning style difference—some form of dyslexia, a sexual orientation difference—such as homosexuality, a body type difference—such as shortness: any one of these so-called differences, each in itself meaningless in moral terms, can be the basis both for loneliness and discrimination, and for creating community with others who share the characteristic. When people who are isolated by a difference from others in their communities of birth find each other, they create whole cultures not only in celebration of having found each other, but because it is the nature of human beings to construct culture. So, for instance, deaf people create language, mount theatrical companies, craft legislation, and found schools.

But differences, when they belong to people who cannot, for whatever reasons, find others like themselves, can be the cause of terrible isolation. That isolation and the struggle for survival that accompanies it, can stimulate a variety of accommodations. Some people spend their lives trying to hide their difference and to "pass" as "normal," i.e., as "like" those among whom they find themselves. Others, who cannot pass, are often subjected by those among whom they live and who love them, or are supposed to love them, to attempts to "heal" them: psychological "therapies" designed to change them, medical and surgical interventions designed to cure them, religious rituals designed to save them, etc. Some turn to comforts that can kill them: alcohol, drugs. Some, victimized and demeaned by those among whom they find themselves, turn to crime—both to ensure their own survival and to exact retribution from those who have mistreated them. Others despair and kill themselves. And finally, out of the pain and loneliness consequent to their "difference," some create art.

Sometimes the art is coded so that only those who share the difference will understand what is really being communicated. The coded art may be filled with transformations so that those without the difference will think it is about "their" kind of people and be able to share the emotional dynamics. Sometimes the art is nonrepresentational so that audiences can appreciate it without associating it with specific images or realities of any kind.

There have been people throughout history who never found others like themselves. We have learned from recently published coming out stories that many women who found themselves attracted to other women reasoned to themselves that they *couldn't* be the only woman in the world to feel like that. But to have rejected that idea was to have wrestled with it. Not all lesbian stories are about women loving each other. There are also stories about women who didn't know they weren't the only one in the world, stories that focus on living with isolating difference, stories that tell about struggling to express through art the experience of difference. It is only recently that we are learning how to read the most coded of these stories.

"Miss Grief" is a coded story. It is about a woman who might not have known that she wasn't the only one. Perhaps if she had known she was one of many, she wouldn't have cared so much for the male narrator's opinion. The approval of representatives of conventional society is important to those with differences only when they don't know about and bond with others like themselves. Patriarchal approval is only important to lesbians who don't know about other women like themselves, who haven't experienced the sense of community and the kind of approval that women-identified women can give to each other.

"Miss Grief" is a radical story in what it has to say about the imagination of an outsider, whether the outsiderness consists of sexuality, race, class, region, disability, appearance, or some other factor that isolates a person from the majority, or puts someone outside the circle of "regular" folks. Constance Fenimore Woolson experienced the outsiderness of physical disability—she was increasingly deaf; she experienced the outsiderness of mental illness—she had inherited her father and grandfather's congenital depression. She seems to have had no interest in conventional heterosexual interactions. The reader cannot fail to wonder what the "fatal flaw" is that the Henry James–like narrator found in Miss Moncrief's writing. The "fault" that makes most sense to me is that she wrote with a lesbian imagination. The story is a time bomb, waiting to find its audience, readers who will understand the real tragedy of "Miss Grief." And because the story is a great work of art, once you read it, you cannot fail to wonder about it. Woolson pulls her reader in with the mystery of what the "flaw" in Miss Moncrief's writing might be. To arrive at the conclusion that her "flaw" is a lesbian imagination, the reader must either develop one or acknowledge that she already has one. "Miss Grief" is one of the great riddle stories of all time.

"Miss Grief" was published in *Lippincott's* in May, 1880 and never collected in one of Woolson's volumes of short stories. It was, however, reprinted in *Stories by American Authors*, Vol. IV, New York, 1884.

Miss Grief

"A conceited fool" is a not uncommon expression. Now, I know that I am not a fool, but I also know that I am conceited. But, candidly, can it be helped if one happens to be young, well and strong, passably good-looking, with some money that one has inherited and more that one has earned—in all, enough to make life comfortable—and if upon this foundation rests also the pleasant super-structure of a literary success? The success is deserved, I think: certainly it was not lightly gained. Yet even with this I fully appreciate its rarity. Thus, I find myself very well entertained in life: I have all I wish in the way of society, and a deep, although of course carefully concealed, satisfaction in my own little fame; which fame I foster by a gentle system of non-interference. I know that I am spoken of as "that quiet young fellow who writes those delightful little studies of society, you know"; and I live up to that definition.

A year ago I was in Rome, and enjoying life particularly. There was a large number of my acquaintances there, both American and English, and no day passed without its invitation. Of course I understood it: it is seldom that you find a literary man who is good-tempered, well-dressed, sufficiently provided with money, and amiably obedient to all the rules and requirements of "society." "When found, make a note of it"; and the note was generally an invitation.

One evening, upon returning to my lodgings, my man Simpson informed me that a person had called in the afternoon, and upon learning that I was absent had left not a card, but her name—

"Miss Grief." The title lingered—Miss Grief! "Grief has not so far visited me here," I said to myself, dismissing Simpson and seeking my little balcony for a final smoke, "and she shall not now. I shall take care to be 'not at home' to her if she continues to call." And then I fell to thinking of Ethelind Abercrombie, in whose society I had spent that and many evenings: they were golden thoughts.

The next day there was an excursion: it was late when I reached my rooms, and again Simpson informed me that Miss Grief had called.

"Is she coming continuously?" I said half to myself.

"Yes, sir: she mentioned that she should call again."

"How does she look?"

"Well, sir, a lady, but not so prosperous as she was, I should say," answered Simpson discreetly.

"Young?"

"No, sir."

"Alone?"

"A maid with her, sir."

But once outside in my little high-up balcony with my cigar, I again forgot Miss Grief and whatever she might represent. Who would not forget in that moonlight, with Ethelind Abercrombie's face to remember?

The stranger came a third time, and I was absent: then she let two days pass and began again. It grew to be a regular dialogue between Simpson and myself when I came in at night: "Grief to-day?"

"Yes, sir."

"What time?"

"Four, sir."

"Happy the man," I thought, "who can keep her confined to a particular hour!"

But I should not have treated my visitor so cavalierly if I had not felt sure that she was eccentric and unconventional—qualities extremely tiresome in a woman no longer young or attractive, and without money to gild them over. If she were not eccentric she would not have persisted in coming to my door day after day in this silent way, without stating her errand, leaving a note or presenting her credentials in any shape. I made up my mind that she had something to sell—a bit of carving or some intaglio supposed to be antique. It was known that I had a fancy for oddities. I said to myself, "She has read or heard of my 'Old Gold' story or else 'The Buried God,' and she thinks me an idealizing ignoramus upon whom she can impose. Her sepulchral name is at least not Italian: probably she is a sharp country-woman of mine, turning by means of pathetic lies an honest penny when she can."

She had called seven times during a period of two weeks without seeing me, when one day I happened to be at home in the afternoon, owing to a pouring rain and a fit of doubt concerning Miss Abercrombie. For I had constructed a careful theory of that young lady's characteristics in my own mind, and she had lived up to it delightfully until the previous evening, when with one word she had blown it to atoms and taken flight, leaving me standing, as it were, on a desolate shore, with nothing but a handful of mistaken inductions wherewith to console myself. I do not know a more exasperating frame of mind, at least for a constructor of theories. I could not write, and so I took up a French novel (I model myself a little on Balzac). I had been turning over its pages but a few moments when Simpson knocked, and, entering softly, said, with just a shadow of a smile on his well-trained face, "Miss Grief." I briefly consigned Miss Grief to all the Furies, and then, as he still lingered—perhaps not knowing where they resided—I asked where the visitor was.

"Outside, sir—in the hall. I told her I would see if you were at home."

"She must be unpleasantly wet if she had no carriage."

"No carriage, sir: they always come on foot. I think she *is* a little damp, sir."

"Well, let her in, but I don't want the maid. I may as well see her now, I suppose, and end the affair."

"Yes, sir."

I did not put down my book. My visitor should have a hearing, but not much more: she had sacrificed her womanly claims by her persistent attacks upon my door. Presently Simpson ushered her in. "Miss Grief," he said, and then went out, closing the curtain behind him.

A woman—yes, a lady—but shabby, unattractive and more than middle-aged.

I rose, bowed slightly, and then dropped into my chair again, still keeping the book in my hand. "Miss Grief?" I said interrogatively as I indicated a seat with my eyebrows.

"Not Grief," she answered—"Crief: my name is Crief."

She sat down, and I saw that she held a small flat box.

"Not carving, then," I thought—"probably old lace, something that belonged to Tullia or Lucrezia Borgia." But as she did not speak I found myself obliged to begin: "You have been here, I think, once or twice before?"

"Seven times: this is the eighth."

A silence.

"I am often out: indeed, I may say that I am never in," I remarked carelessly.

"Yes: you have many friends."

"Who will perhaps buy old lace," I mentally added. But this time I too remained silent: why should I trouble myself to draw her out? She had sought me: let her advance her idea, whatever it was, now that entrance was gained.

But Miss Grief (I preferred to call her so) did not look as though she could advance anything: her black gown, damp with rain, seemed to retreat fearfully to her thin self, while her thin self retreated as far as possible from me, from the chair, from everything. Her eyes were cast down: an old-fashioned lace veil with a heavy border shaded her face. She looked at the floor, and I looked at her.

I grew a little impatient, but I made up my mind that I would continue silent and see how long a time she would consider necessary to give due effect to her little pantomime. Comedy? Or was it tragedy? I suppose full five minutes passed thus in our double silence; and that is a long time when two persons are sitting opposite each other alone in a small still room.

At last my visitor, without raising her eyes, said slowly, "You are very happy, are you not, with youth, health, friends, riches, fame?"

It was a singular beginning. Her voice was clear, low and very sweet as she thus enumerated my advantages one by one in a list. I was attracted by it, but repelled by her words, which seemed to me flattery both dull and bold.

"Thanks," I said, "for your kindness, but I fear it is undeserved. I seldom discuss myself even when with my friends."

"I am your friend," replied Miss Grief. Then, after a moment, she added slowly, "I have read every word you have written."

I curled the edges of my book indifferently: I am not a fop, I hope, but—others have said the same.

"What is more, I know much of it by heart," continued my visitor. "Wait: I will show you;" and then, without pause, she began to repeat something of mine word for word, just as I had written it. On she went, and I—listened. I intended interrupting her after a moment, but I did not, because she was reciting so well, and also because I felt a desire gaining upon me to see what she would make of a certain conversation which I knew was coming —a conversation between two of my characters which was, to say the least, sphinx-like, and somewhat incandescent also. What won me a little, too, was the fact that the scene she was reciting (it was hardly more than that, although called a story) was secretly my favorite among all the sketches from my pen with which a gracious public had been favored. I never said so, but it was; and I had always felt a wondering annoyance that the aforesaid public, while kindly praising beyond their worth other attempts of mine, had never noticed the higher purpose of this little shaft, aimed not at the balconies and lighted windows of society, but straight up toward the distant stars. So she went on, and presently reached the conversation: my two people began to talk. She had raised her eyes now, and was looking at me soberly as she gave the words of the woman, quiet, gentle, cold, and the replies of the man, bitter, hot and scathing. Her very voice changed, and took, although always sweetly, the different tones required, while no point of meaning, however small, no breath of delicate emphasis which I had meant, but which the dull types could not give, escaped appreciative and full, almost overfull, recognition which startled me. For she had understood me—understood me almost better than I had understood myself. It seemed to me that while I had labored to interpret partially a psychological riddle, she, coming after, had comprehended its bearings better than I had, although confining herself strictly to my own words and emphasis. The scene ended (and it ended rather suddenly), she dropped her eyes, and moved her hand nervously to and fro over the box she held: her gloves were old and shabby, her hands small.

I was secretly much surprised by what I had heard, but my ill-humor was deep-seated that day, and I still felt sure, besides, that the box contained something that I was expected to buy.

"You recite remarkably well," I said carelessly, "and I am much flattered also by your appreciation of my efforts. But it is not, I presume, to that alone that I owe the pleasure of this visit?"

"Yes," she answered, still looking down, "it is, for if you had not written that scene I should not have sought you. Your other sketches are interiors—exquisitely painted and delicately finished, but of small scope. *This* is a sketch in a few bold, masterly lines —work of entirely different spirit and purpose."

I was nettled by her insight. "You have bestowed so much of your kind attention upon me that I feel your debtor," I said, conventionally. "It may be that there is something I can do for you— connected, possibly, with that box?"

It was a little impertinent, but it was true, for she answered, "Yes."

I smiled, but her eyes were cast down and she did not see the smile.

"What I have to show you is a manuscript," she said after a pause which I did not break: "it is a drama. I thought that perhaps you would read it."

"An authoress! This is worse than old lace," I said to myself in dismay.—Then, aloud, "My opinion would be worth nothing, Miss Crief."

"Not in a business way, I know. But it might be—an assistance personally." Her voice had sunk to a whisper: outside, the rain was pouring steadily down. She was a very depressing object to me as she sat there with her box.

"I hardly think I have the time at present—" I began.

She had raised her eyes and was looking at me: then, when I paused, she rose and came suddenly toward my chair. "Yes, you will read it," she said with her hand on my arm—"you will read it. Look at this room; look at yourself; look at all you have. Then look at me, and have pity."

I had risen, for she held my arm and her damp skirt was brushing my knees.

Her large dark eyes looked intently into mine as she went on: "I have no shame in asking. Why should I have? It is my last endeavor, but a calm and well-considered one. If you refuse I shall go away, knowing that Fate has willed it so. And I shall be content."

"She is mad," I thought. But she did not look so, and she had spoken quietly, even gently.—"Sit down," I said, moving away from her. I felt as if I had been magnetized, but it was only the nearness of her eyes to mine, and their intensity. I drew forward a chair, but she remained standing.

"I cannot," she said in the same sweet, gentle tone, "unless you promise."

"Very well, I promise; only sit down."

As I took her arm to lead her to the chair I perceived that she was trembling, but her face continued unmoved.

"You do not, of course, wish me to look at your manuscript now?" I said, temporizing: "it would be much better to leave it. Give me your address, and I will return it to you with my written opinion; although, I repeat, the latter will be of no use to you. It is the opinion of an editor or publisher that you want."

"It shall be as you please. And I will go in a moment," said Miss Grief, pressing her palms together, as if trying to control the tremor that had seized her slight frame.

She looked so pallid that I thought of offering her a glass of wine: then I remembered that if I did it might be a bait to bring her there again, and this I was desirous to prevent. She rose while the thought was passing through my mind. Her pasteboard box lay on the chair she had first occupied: she took it, wrote an address on the cover, laid it down, and then, bowing with a little air of formality, drew her black shawl around her shoulders and turned toward the door.

I followed, after touching the bell. "You will hear from me by letter," I said.

Simpson opened the door, and I caught a glimpse of the maid, who was waiting in the anteroom. She was an old woman, shorter than her mistress, equally thin, and dressed like her in rusty black. As the door opened she turned toward it a pair of small, dim blue eyes with a look of furtive suspense. Simpson dropped the curtain, shutting me into the inner room: he had no intention of allowing me to accompany my visitor farther. But I had the curiosity to go to a bay-window in an angle from whence I could command the street-door, and presently I saw them issue forth in the rain and walk away side by side, the mistress, being the taller, holding the umbrella: probably there was not much difference in rank between persons so poor and forlorn as these.

It grew dark. I was invited out for the evening, and I knew that if I went I should meet Miss Abercrombie. I said to myself that I would not go. I got out my paper for writing, I made my preparations for a quiet evening at home with myself; but it was of no use. It all ended slavishly in my going. At the last allowable moment I presented myself, and—as a punishment for my vacillation, I suppose—I never passed a more disagreeable evening. I drove homeward in a vixenish temper: it was foggy without, and very foggy within. What Ethelind really was, now that she had broken through my elaborately-built theories, I was not able to decide. There was, to tell the truth, a certain young Englishman— But that is apart from this story.

I reached home, went up to my rooms and had a supper. It was to console myself: I am obliged to console myself scientifically once in a while. I was walking up and down afterward, smoking and feeling somewhat better, when my eye fell upon the pasteboard box. I took it up: on the cover was written an address which showed that my visitor must have walked a long distance in order to see me: "A. Crief."—"A Grief," I thought; "and so she is. I positively believe she has brought all this trouble upon me: she has the evil eye." I took out the manuscript and looked at it. It was in the form of a little volume, and clearly written: on the cover was the word "Armor" in German text, and underneath a pen-and-ink sketch of a helmet, breastplate and shield.

"Grief certainly needs armor," I said to myself, sitting down by the table and turning over the pages. "I may as well look over the thing now: I could not be in a worse mood." And then I began to read.

Early the next morning Simpson took a note from me to the given address, returning with the following reply: "No; I prefer to come to you; at four; A. CRIEF." These words, with their three semicolons, were written in pencil upon a piece of coarse printing-paper, but the handwriting was as clear and delicate as that of the manuscript in ink.

"What sort of a place was it, Simpson?"

"Very poor, sir, but I did not go all the way up. The elder

person came down, sir, took the note, and requested me to wait
where I was."

"You had no chance, then, to make inquiries?" I said, knowing full well that he had emptied the entire neighborhood of any
information it might possess concerning these two lodgers.

"Well, sir, you know how these foreigners will talk, whether
one wants to hear or not. But it seems that these two persons have
been there but a few weeks: they live alone, and are uncommonly
silent and reserved. The people around there call them something
that signifies 'the Madames American, thin and dumb.' "

At four the "Madames American" arrived: it was raining
again, and they came on foot under their old umbrella. The maid
waited in the anteroom, and Miss Grief was ushered into my bachelor's parlor, which was library and dining-room in one. I had
thought that I should meet her with great deference, but she looked
so forlorn that my deference changed to pity. It was the woman
that impressed me then, more than the writer—the fragile, nerveless body more than the inspired mind. For it was inspired: I had
sat up half the night over her drama, and had felt thrilled through
and through more than once by its earnestness, passion and power.

No one could have been more surprised than I was to find
myself thus enthusiastic. I thought I had outgrown that sort of
thing. And one would have supposed, too (I myself should have
supposed so the day before), that the faults of the drama, which
were many and prominent, would have chilled any liking I might
have felt, I being a writer myself, and therefore critical; for writers
are as apt to make much of the "how," rather than the "what,"
as painters, who, it is well known, prefer an exquisitely rendered
representation of a commonplace theme to an imperfectly executed
picture of even the most striking subject. But in this case, on the
contrary, the scattered rays of splendor in Miss Grief's drama had
made me forget the dark spots, which were numerous and disfig-
uring; or, rather, the splendor had made me anxious to have the
spots removed. And this also was a philanthropic state very unusual for me. Regarding unsuccessful writers my motto had been
"Væ victis!"

My visitor took a seat and folded her hands: I could see, in
spite of her quiet manner, that she was in breathless suspense. It
seemed so pitiful that she should be trembling there before me—a

woman so much older than I was, a woman who possessed the divine spark of genius, which I was by no means sure, in spite of my success, had been granted to me—that I felt as if I ought to go down on my knees before her and entreat her to take her proper place of supremacy at once. But there! one does not go down on one's knees combustively, as it were, before a woman over fifty, plain in feature, thin, dejected and ill-dressed. I contented myself with taking her hands (in their miserable old gloves) in mine, while I said cordially, "Miss Crief, your drama seems to me full of original power. It has roused my enthusiasm: I sat up half the night reading it."

The hands I held shook, but something (perhaps a shame for having evaded the knees business) made me tighten my hold and bestow upon her also a reassuring smile. She looked at me for a moment, and then, suddenly and noiselessly, tears rose and rolled down her cheeks. I dropped her hands and retreated. I had not thought her tearful: on the contrary, her voice and face had seemed rigidly controlled. But now here she was bending herself over the side of the chair with her head resting on her arms, not sobbing aloud, but her whole frame shaken by the strength of her emotion. I rushed for a glass of wine: I pressed her to take it. I did not quite know what to do, but, putting myself in her place, I decided to praise the drama; and praise it I did. I do not know when I have used so many adjectives. She raised her head and began to wipe her eyes.

"Do take the wine," I said, interrupting myself in my cataract of language.

"I dare not," she answered: then added humbly, "that is, unless you have a biscuit here or a bit of bread."

I found some biscuit: she ate two, and then slowly drank the wine while I resumed my verbal Niagara. Under its influence—and that of the wine too, perhaps—she began to show new life. It was not that she looked radiant—she could not—but simply that she looked warm. I now perceived what had been the principal discomfort of her appearance heretofore: it was that she had looked all the time as if suffering from cold.

At last I could think of nothing more to say, and stopped. I really admired the drama, but I thought I had exerted myself sufficiently as an anti-hysteric, and that adjectives enough, for the present at least, had been administered. She had put down her empty wine-glass, and was resting her hands on the broad cushioned arms of her chair with a sort of expanded content.

"You must pardon my tears," she said, smiling: "it was the revulsion of feeling. My life was at a low ebb: if your sentence had been against me it would have been my end."

"Your end?"

"Yes, the end of my life: I should have destroyed myself."

"Then you would have been a weak as well as wicked woman," I said in a tone of disgust: I do hate sensationalism.

"Oh no, you know nothing about it. I should have destroyed only this poor worn tenement of clay. But I can well understand how *you* would look upon it. Regarding the desirableness of life the prince and the beggar may have different opinions.—We will say no more of it, but talk of the drama instead." As she spoke the word "drama" a triumphant brightness came into her eyes.

I took the manuscript from a drawer and sat down beside her. "I suppose you know that there are faults," I said, expecting ready acquiescence.

"I was not aware that there were any," was her gentle reply.

Here was a beginning! After all my interest in her—and, I may say under the circumstances, my kindness—she received me in this way! However, my belief in her genius was too sincere to be altered by her whimsies; so I persevered. "Let us go over it together," I said. "Shall I read it to you, or will you read it to me?"

"I will not read it, but recite it."

"That will never do: you will recite it so well that we shall see only the good points, and what we have to concern ourselves with now is the bad ones."

"I will recite it," she repeated.

"Look here, Miss Crief," I said bluntly, "for what purpose did you come to me? Certainly not merely to recite: I am no stage-manager. In plain English, was it not your idea that I might help you in obtaining a publisher?"

"Yes, yes," she answered, looking at me apprehensively, all her old manner returning.

I followed up my advantage, opened the little paper volume and began. I first took the drama line by line, and spoke of the faults of expression and structure: then I turned back and touched upon two or three glaring impossibilities in the plot. "Your absorbed interest in the motive of the whole no doubt made you forget these blemishes," I said apologetically.

But, to my surprise, I found that she did not see the blemishes—that she appreciated nothing I had said, comprehended nothing. Such unaccountable obtuseness puzzled me. I began again, going over the whole with even greater minuteness and care. I worked hard: the perspiration stood in beads upon my forehead as I struggled with her—what shall I call it—obstinacy? But it was not exactly obstinacy. She simply could not see the faults of her own work, any more than a blind man can see the smoke that dims a patch of blue sky. When I had finished my task the second time she still remained as gently impassive as before. I leaned back in my chair exhausted and looked at her.

Even then she did not seem to comprehend (whether she agreed with it or not) what I must be thinking. "It is such a heaven to me that you like it!" she murmured dreamily, breaking the silence. Then, with more animation, "And *now* you will let me recite it?"

I was too weary to oppose her: she threw aside her shawl and bonnet, and, standing in the centre of the room, began.

And she carried me along with her: all the strong passages were doubly strong when spoken, and the faults, which seemed nothing to her, were made by her earnestness to seem nothing to me, at least for that moment. When it was ended she stood looking at me with a triumphant smile.

"Yes," I said, "I like it, and you see that I do. But I like it because my taste is peculiar. To me originality and force are everything—perhaps because I have them not to any marked degree myself—but the world at large will not overlook as I do your absolutely barbarous shortcomings on account of them. Will you trust me to go over the drama and correct it at my pleasure?" This was a vast deal for me to offer: I was surprised at myself.

"No," she answered softly, still smiling. "There shall not be so much as a comma altered." Then she sat down and fell into a reverie as though she were alone.

"Have you written anything else?" I said after a while, when I had become tired of the silence.

"Yes."

"Can I see it? Or is it *them*?"

"It is *them*. Yes, you can see all."

"I will call upon you for the purpose."

"No, you must not," she said, coming back to the present nervously: "I prefer to come to you."

At this moment Simpson entered to light the room, and busied himself rather longer than was necessary over the task. When he finally went out I saw that my visitor's manner had sunk into its former depression: the presence of the servant seemed to have chilled her.

"When did you say I might come?" I repeated, ignoring her refusal.

"I did not say it. It would be impossible."

"Well, then, when will you come here?" There was, I fear, a trace of fatigue in my tone.

"At your good pleasure, sir," she answered humbly.

My chivalry was touched by this: after all, she was a woman. "Come to-morrow," I said. "By the way, come and dine with me then: why not?" I was curious to see what she would reply.

"Why not, indeed? Yes, I will come. I am forty-three: I might have been your mother."

This was not quite true, as I am over thirty; but I look young, while she— Well, I had thought her over fifty. "I can hardly call you 'mother,' but then we might compromise upon 'aunt,' " I said, laughing. "Aunt what?"

"My name is Aaronna," she gravely answered. "My father was much disappointed that I was not a boy, and gave me as nearly as possible the name he had prepared—Aaron."

"Then come and dine with me tomorrow, and bring with you the other manuscripts, Aaronna," I said, amused at the quaint sound of the name. On the whole, I did not like "aunt."

"I will come," she answered.

It was twilight and still raining, but she refused all offers of escort or carriage, departing with her maid, as she had come, under the brown umbrella.

The next day we had the dinner. Simpson was astonished—and more than astonished, grieved—when I told him that he was to dine with the maid; but he could not complain in words, since my own guest, the mistress, was hardly more attractive. When our preparations were complete I could not help laughing: the two prim little tables, one in the parlor and one in the anteroom, and Simpson disapprovingly going back and forth between them, were irresistible.

I greeted my guest hilariously when she arrived, and, fortunately, her manner was not quite so depressed as usual: I could never have accorded myself with a tearful mood. I had thought that perhaps she would make, for the occasion, some change in her attire: I have never known a woman who had not some scrap of finery, however small, in reserve for that unexpected occasion of which she is ever dreaming. But no: Miss Grief wore the same black gown, unadorned and unaltered. I was glad that there was no rain that day, so that the skirt did not at least look so damp and rheumatic.

She ate quietly, almost furtively, yet with a good appetite, and she did not refuse the wine. Then, when the meal was over and Simpson had removed the dishes, I asked for the new manuscripts. She gave me an old green copybook filled with short poems, and a prose sketch by itself: I lit a cigar and sat down at my desk to look them over.

"Perhaps you will try a cigarette?" I suggested, more for amusement than anything else, for there was not a shade of Bohemianism about her: her whole appearance was puritanical.

"I have not yet succeeded in learning to smoke."

"You have tried?" I said, turning round.

"Yes: Serena and I tried, but we did not succeed."

"Serena is your maid?"

"She lives with me."

I was seized with inward laughter, and began hastily to look over her manuscripts with my back toward her, so that she might not see it. A vision had risen before me of those two forlorn women, alone in their room with locked doors, patiently trying to acquire the smoker's art.

But my attention was soon absorbed by the papers before me. Such a fantastic collection of words, lines and epithets I had never before seen, or even in dreams imagined. In truth, they were like the work of dreams: they were *Kubla Khan*, only more so. Here and there was radiance like the flash of a diamond, but each poem, almost each verse and line, was marred by some fault or lack which seemed wilful perversity, like the work of an evil sprite. It was like a case of jeweller's wares set before you, with each ring unfinished, each bracelet too large or too small for its purpose, each breast-pin without its fastening, each necklace purposely broken. I turned the pages, marvelling. When about half an hour had passed, and I was leaning back for a moment to light another cigar, I glanced toward my visitor. She was behind me, in an easy-chair before my small fire, and she was—fast asleep! In the relaxation of her un-consciousness I was struck anew by the poverty her appearance expressed: her feet were visible, and I saw the miserable worn old shoes which hitherto she had kept concealed.

After looking at her for a moment I returned to my task and took up the prose story: in prose she must be more reasonable. She was less fantastic perhaps, but hardly more reasonable. The story was that of a profligate and commonplace man forced by two of his friends, in order not to break the heart of a dying girl who loves him, to live up to a high imaginary ideal of himself which her pure but mistaken mind has formed. He has a handsome face and sweet voice, and repeats what they tell him. Her long, slow decline and happy death, and his own inward ennui and profound weariness of the rôle he has to play, made the vivid points of the story. So far, well enough, but here was the trouble: through the whole narrative moved another character, a physician of tender heart and exquisite mercy, who practised murder as a fine art, and was regarded (by the author) as a second Messiah! This was mon-strous. I read it through twice, and threw it down: then, fatigued, I turned round and leaned back, waiting for her to wake. I could see her profile against the dark hue of the easy-chair.

Presently she seemed to feel my gaze, for she stirred, then opened her eyes. "I have been asleep," she said, rising hurriedly.

"No harm in that, Aaronna."

But she was deeply embarrassed and troubled, much more so than the occasion required; so much so, indeed, that I turned the conversation back upon the manuscripts as a diversion. "I cannot stand that doctor of yours," I said, indicating the prose story: "no one would. You must cut him out."

Her self-possession returned as if by magic. "Certainly not," she answered haughtily.

"Oh, if you do not care— I had labored under the impression that you were anxious these things should find a purchaser."

"I am, I am," she said, her manner changing to deep humility with wonderful rapidity. With such alternations of feeling as this sweeping over her like great waves, no wonder she was old before her time.

"Then you must take out that doctor."

"I am willing, but do not know how," she answered, pressing her hands together helplessly. "In my mind he belongs to the story so closely that he cannot be separated from it."

Here Simpson entered, bringing a note for me: it was a line from Mrs. Abercrombie inviting me for that evening—an unexpected gathering, and therefore likely to be all the more agreeable. My heart bounded in spite of me: I forgot Miss Grief and her manuscripts for the moment as completely as though they had never existed. But, bodily, being still in the same room with her, her speech brought me back to the present.

"You have had good news?" she said.

"Oh no, nothing especial—merely an invitation."

"But good news also," she repeated. "And now, as for me, I must go."

Not supposing that she would stay much later in any case, I had that morning ordered a carriage to come for her at about that hour. I told her this. She made no reply beyond putting on her bonnet and shawl.

"You will hear from me soon," I said: "I shall do all I can for you."

She had reached the door, but before opening it she stopped, turned and extended her hand. "You are good," she said: "I give you thanks. Do not think me ungrateful or envious. It is only that you are young, and I am so—so old." Then she opened the door and passed through the anteroom without pause, her maid accompanying her and Simpson with gladness lighting the way. They were gone. I dressed hastily and went out—to continue my studies in psychology.

Time passed: I was busy, amused and perhaps a little excited (sometimes psychology is delightful). But, although much occupied with my own affairs, I did not altogether neglect my self-imposed task regarding Miss Grief. I began by sending her prose story to a friend, the editor of a monthly magazine, with a letter making a strong plea for its admittance. It should have a chance first on its own merits. Then I forwarded the drama to a publisher, also an acquaintance, a man with a taste for phantasms and a soul above mere common popularity, as his own coffers knew to their cost. This done, I waited with conscience clear.

Four weeks passed. During this waiting period I heard nothing from Miss Grief. At last one morning came a letter from my editor. "The story has force, but I cannot stand that doctor," he wrote. "Let her cut him out, and I might print it." Just what I myself had said. The package lay there on my table, travel-worn and grimed: a returned manuscript is, I think, the most melancholy object on earth. I decided to wait, before writing to Aaronna, until the second letter was received. A week later it came. "Armor" was declined. The publisher had been "impressed" by the power displayed in certain passages, but the "impossibilities of the plot" rendered it "unavailable for publication"—in fact, would "bury it in ridicule" if brought before the public, a public "lamentably" fond of amusement, "seeking it, undaunted, even in the cannon's mouth." I doubt if he knew himself what he meant. But one thing, at any rate, was clear: "Armor" was declined.

Now, I am, as I have remarked before, a little obstinate. I was determined that Miss Grief's work should be received. I would alter and improve it myself, without letting her know: the end justified the means. Surely the sieve of my own good taste, whose mesh had been pronounced so fine and delicate, would serve for two. I began, and utterly failed.

I set to work first upon "Armor." I amended, altered, left out, put in, pieced, condensed, lengthened: I did my best, and all to no avail. I could not succeed in completing anything that satisfied me, or that approached, in truth, Miss Grief's own work just as it stood. I suppose I went over that manuscript twenty times: I covered sheets of paper with my copies. But the obstinate drama refused to be corrected: as it was it must stand or fall.

Wearied and annoyed, I threw it aside and took up the prose story: that would be easier. But, to my surprise, I found that that apparently gentle "doctor" would not out: he was so closely interwoven with every part of the tale that to take him out was like taking out one especial figure in a carpet: that is impossible unless you unravel the whole. At last I did unravel the whole, and then the story was no longer good, or Aaronna's: it was weak, and mine. All this took time, for of course I had much to do in connection with my own life and tasks. But, although slowly and at my leisure, I really did try my best as regarded Miss Grief, and without success. I was forced at last to make up my mind that either my own powers were not equal to the task, or else that her perversities were as essential a part of her work as her inspirations, and not to be separated from it. Once during this period I showed two of the short poems to Ethelind, withholding of course the writer's name. "They were written by a woman," I explained.

"Her mind must have been disordered, poor thing!" Ethelind said in her gentle way when she returned them—"at least, judging by these. They are hopelessly mixed and vague."

Now, they were not vague so much as vast. But I knew that I could not make Ethelind comprehend it, and (so complex a creature is man) I do not know that I wanted her to comprehend it. These were the only ones in the whole collection that I would have shown her, and I was rather glad that she did not like even these. Not that poor Aaronna's poems were evil: they were simply unrestrained, large, vast, like the skies or the wind. Ethelind was bounded on all sides, like a violet in a garden-bed. And I liked her so.

One afternoon, about the time when I was beginning to see that I could not "improve" Miss Grief, I came upon the maid. I was driving, and she had stopped on the crossing to let the carriage pass. I recognized her at a glance (by her general forlornness), and called to the driver to stop. "How is Miss Crief?" I said. "I have been intending to write to her for some time."

"And your note, when it comes," answered the old woman on the crosswalk fiercely, "she shall not see."

"What?"

"I say she shall not see it. Your patronizing face shows that you have no good news, and you shall not rack and stab her any more on *this* earth, please God, while I have authority."

"Who has racked or stabbed her, Serena?"

"Serena, indeed! Rubbish! I'm no Serena: I'm her aunt. And as to who has racked and stabbed her, I say you, *you*—YOU literary men!" She had put her old head inside my carriage, and flung out these words at me in a shrill, menacing tone. "But she shall die in peace in spite of you," she continued. "Vampires! you take her ideas and fatten on them, and leave her to starve. You know you do—*you* who have had her poor manuscripts these months and months!"

"Is she ill?" I asked in real concern, gathering that much at least from the incoherent tirade.

"She is dying," answered the desolate old creature, her voice softening and her dim eyes filling with tears.

"Oh, I trust not. Perhaps something can be done. Can I help you in any way?"

"In all ways if you would," she said, breaking down and beginning to sob weakly, with her head resting on the sill of the carriage-window. "Oh, what have we not been through together, we two! Piece by piece I have sold all."

I am good-hearted enough, but I do not like to have old women weeping across my carriage-door. I suggested, therefore, that she should come inside and let me take her home. Her shabby old skirt was soon beside me, and, following her directions, the driver turned toward one of the most wretched quarters of the city, the abode of poverty, crowded and unclean. Here, in a large bare chamber up many flights of stairs, I found Miss Grief.

As I entered I was startled: I thought she was dead. There seemed no life present until she opened her eyes, and even then they rested upon us vaguely, as though she did not know who we were. But as I approached a sudden light came into them: she recognized me, and this sudden animation, this return of the soul to the windows of the almost deserted body, was the most wonderful thing I ever saw. "You have good news of the drama?" she whispered as I bent over her: "tell me. I *know* you have good news."

What was I to answer? Pray, what would you have answered, puritan?

"Yes, I have good news, Aaronna," I said. "The drama will appear." (And who knows? Perhaps it will in some other world.)

She smiled, and her now brilliant eyes did not leave my face.

"He knows I'm your aunt: I told him," said the old woman, coming to the bedside.

"Did you?" whispered Miss Grief, still gazing at me with a

smile. "Then please, dear Aunt Martha, give me something to eat."

Aunt Martha hurried across the room, and I followed her. "It's the first time she's asked for food in weeks," she said in a husky tone.

She opened a cupboard-door vaguely, but I could see nothing within. "What have you for her?" I asked with some impatience, although in a low voice.

"Please God, nothing!" answered the poor old woman, hiding her reply and her tears behind the broad cupboard-door. "I was going out to get a little something when I met you."

"Good Heavens! is it money you need? Here, take this and send; or go yourself in the carriage waiting below."

She hurried out breathless, and I went back to the bedside, much disturbed by what I had seen and heard. But Miss Grief's eyes were full of life, and as I sat down beside her she whispered earnestly, "Tell me."

And I did tell her—a romance invented for the occasion. I venture to say that none of my published sketches could compare with it. As for the lie involved, it will stand among my few good deeds, I know, at the judgment-bar.

And she was satisfied. "I have never known what it was," she whispered, "to be fully happy until now." She closed her eyes, and when the lids fell I again thought that she had passed away. But no, there was still pulsation in her small, thin wrist. As she perceived my touch she smiled. "Yes, I am happy," she said again, although without audible sound.

The old aunt returned: food was prepared, and she took some. I myself went out after wine that should be rich and pure. She rallied a little, but I did not leave her: her eyes dwelt upon me and compelled me to stay, or rather my conscience compelled me. It was a damp night, and I had a little fire made. The wine, fruit, flowers and candles I had ordered made the bare place for the time being bright and fragrant. Aunt Martha dozed in her chair from sheer fatigue—she had watched many nights—but Miss Grief was awake, and I sat beside her.

"I make you my executor," she murmured, "as to the drama. But my other manuscripts place, when I am gone, under my head, and let them be buried with me. They are not many—those you have and these. See!"

I followed her gesture, and saw under her pillows the edges of two more copybooks like the one I had. "Do not look at them—my poor dead children!" she said tenderly. "Let them depart with me—unread, as I have been."

Later she whispered, "Did you wonder why I came to you? It was the contrast. You were young—strong—rich—praised—loved—successful: all that I was not. I wanted to look at you—and imagine how it would feel. You had success—but I had the greater power. Tell me: did I not have it?"

"Yes, Aaronna."

"It is all in the past now. But I am satisfied."

After another pause she said with a faint smile, "Do you remember when I fell asleep in your parlor? It was the good and rich food. It was so long since I had had food like that!"

I took her hand and held it, conscience-stricken, but now she hardly seemed to perceive my touch. "And the smoking?" she whispered. "Do you remember how you laughed? I saw it. But I had heard that smoking soothed—that one was no longer tired and hungry—with a cigar."

In little whispers of this sort, separated by long rests and pauses, the night passed. Once she asked if her aunt was asleep, and when I answered in the affirmative she said, "Help her to return home—to America: the drama will pay for it. I ought never to have brought her away."

I promised, and she resumed her bright-eyed silence.

I think she did not speak again. Toward morning the change came, and soon after sunrise, with her old aunt kneeling by her side, she passed away.

All was arranged as she had wished. Her manuscripts, covered with violets, formed her pillow. No one followed her to the grave save her aunt and myself: I thought she would prefer it so. Her name was not "Crief," after all, but "Moncrief:" I saw it written out by Aunt Martha for the coffin-plate, as follows: "Aaronna Moncrief, aged forty-three years two months and eight days."

I never knew more of her history than is written here. If there was more that I might have learned, it remained unlearned, for I did not ask.

And the drama? I keep it here in this locked case. I could have had it published at my own expense, but I think that now she knows its faults herself, and would not like it.

I keep it, and once in a while I read it over—not as a *memento mori* exactly, but rather as a memento of my own good-fortune, for which I should continually give thanks. The want of one grain made all her work void, and that one grain was given to me. She, with the greater power, failed—I, with the less, succeeded. But no praise is due to me for that. When I die "Armor" is to be destroyed unread: not even Ethelind is to see it. For women will misunderstand each other; and, dear and precious to me as my sweet wife is, I could not bear that she or any one should cast so much as a thought of scorn upon the memory of the writer, upon my poor dead, "unavailable," unaccepted "Miss Grief."

MARY ELEANOR
WILKINS FREEMAN

*A young writer should follow the safe course of writing
only about those subjects she knows thoroughly, and concerning which she trusts her own convictions.* *

Mary Wales (d. 1916) had been rescuing Mary Eleanor Wilkins
(1852–1930) from threatening and uncomfortable situations ever
since their shared childhood in Randolph, Massachusetts. When
Wilkins' family life ended unhappily with her father's business failure and the successive deaths of her younger sister Nan in 1876,
her mother in 1880, and her father in 1883, she was left with no
income, a personal history of indifference to conventional social
activities, a passion for literature, no professional training, no important social connections, and no prospects for or recorded interest in marriage. Mary Wales rescued Mary Wilkins one last time,
inviting her to move in with the Wales family. Wilkins returned to
Randolph from Brattleboro, Vermont, the scene of her family's

* Mary Wilkins Freeman, "Good Wits, Pen and Paper" in *What Women Can Earn*,
ed. G.H. Dodge et al., New York, 1899, p. 26.

final painful years, to live with the family of her lifelong friend and to serve her literary apprenticeship.

A portion of the Wales home became her private residence and work space, but she took her meals with the family. Mr. Wales died and the son was sent to eat in the barn with the hired help, while Mrs. Wales and the two Marys continued to share their lives. Mary Wilkins stayed with them through her years of struggle and the years of her greatest literary success.

"Mary Wilkins Freeman had in Mary Wales what many male writers have but few female ones: a kind, loving and supportive person who takes care of the practical difficulties of life, while encouraging, laughing with, and inspiring the author. Mary Wales fulfilled that role for eighteen years. Essentially, she was Mary Wilkins' 'wife.'

"Despite the outward serenity of her life, Mary [Wilkins] had terrible nightmares. She would awaken screaming, sobbing, and Mary Wales would comfort her, soothing her until the fears went away. Mary Wales was mother and sister to her, perhaps even a lover, although we cannot know that. Contemporaries called Mary Wales 'her special school friend' and her 'most constant companion.' "[1]

Her biographers make a good story out of the fact that in 1873, while still living with her family in Brattleboro, she met a young naval officer, Hanson Tyler, and is said to have fallen in love with him. During that one summer, they were together for many long hours, and then he left. Some of her biographers have implied that she waited in vain for his return, that their relationship meant more to her than to him, and that he had been cavalier while she had been vulnerable. The assumption of not only her biographers, but evidently of many of her relatives and friends, is that Wilkins loved Hanson Tyler, hoped and waited for him, and was disappointed in her hopes. He is portrayed as the great love of her life, the man who got away. The underlying assumption is that she must have loved some man and since there was no man in her life for so many years, it must be that the man she loved either didn't reciprocate or wasn't available. This assumption fails to take into account the increasing number of women during this period and in her environment who never married and never regretted not marrying, who served as models not only for the professional life

Mary Eleanor Wilkins wished for herself, but as models of satisfying personal lives that did not include marriage or heterosexual romantic love.

Freeman lived most of her life in a world of women. She was part of the great network of literary women whose hub was Annie Adams Fields, the wife of James Fields, publisher and editor of the *Atlantic Monthly,* who, after her husband's death, was a partner in a "Boston Marriage" with Sarah Orne Jewett. Jewett had been the young Mary E. Wilkins' great literary inspiration and model. Alice Brown was another member of the group gathered around the Fields.

"Two Friends," which was first published in *Harper's Bazar* June 25, 1887, was her twenty-fifth story in that periodical. Twenty of those stories were included in *A Humble Romance,* her first collection of stories, two were in her second, *A New England Nun,* and three were uncollected. "Two Friends" is one of those stories heretofore uncollected.

Harper's Bazar was a women's magazine, similar to many women's magazines published today. It included recipes, patterns for sewing, crocheting, and other types of handiwork, articles about life in the "women's sphere," cartoons, poems, and short stories. The lead article on page one of the June 25, 1887, issue advised readers on proper etiquette for engaged couples and railed against the emotional damage caused by irresponsible journalists who announced engagements without awaiting proper notification. The first page featured a large center picture of ladies' and girls' country hats and the caption promised detailed descriptions of these new seasonal hats in the accompanying four-page supplement.

Page two continued with the third installment of "Housekeeping Made Easy" and another essay in the continuing series entitled "Women and Men." This week's installation called for purity and delicacy in literature, castigating Zola and Swinburne for undermining the purification of literature achieved since the ribald and indecent days of Aphra Behn.

Page three reported on New York fashions and carried two columns of gossip about famous people. Pages four and five featured a two-page spread of the newest in infants' clothing.

Page six began with an article on Creole desserts on the top

left-hand column. In mid-column "Two Friends" began. The conclusion of this lesbian story is followed by directions for knitting
and crocheting various of the infant clothes. The final column answers letters to the editor asking for solutions to personal problems
of grooming, etiquette, and social life.

The issue ends with a page of racist cartoons, misogynist
jokes, witticisms, and a couple of pages advertising such items
as skin cleansers, an electric corset, baby formula, and sanitary
napkins.

Both Edward Foster, Wilkins' first biographer[2] and Brent Kendrick[3] have drawn connections between her life and many of the
characters and events in her novels and short stories.[4] These characters and events are always transformed—but often the connections remain clear between her work and her life. Knowing of her
proclivity to make these imaginative transformations from life in
her work, we must wonder about what it is that is being transformed in "Two Friends."

It is possible that she wrote this story as a gift to Mary Wales,
to calm any fears Wales might have had about a potential loss of
Wilkins to Tyler, and to relieve her of any sense of having been
Wilkins' "second choice." Then again, Wales may have had no
need to be calmed, reassured, or relieved. It may just have been
Wilkins' statement to a world that saw her as a woman who had
loved and lost that her situation in life was freely chosen.

ENDNOTES

1. "Mary E. Wilkins Freeman," by Emily Toth, unpublished manuscript, pp. 41–
42.

2. *Mary E. Wilkins Freeman*, by Edward Foster. New York: Hendricks House,
1956.

3. see *The Infant Sphinx: Collected Letters of Mary E. Wilkins Freeman Edited
with Biographical/Critical Introductions and Annotations*, by Brent L. Kendrick
(New Jersey, 1985).

4. ". . . Freeman chose for her subject matter the things she knew best. She once
wrote to Sarah Orne Jewett: 'I suppose it seems to you as it does to me that everything you have heard, seen, or done, since you opened your eyes on the world,
is coming back to you sooner or later, to go into stories, and things' (Letter 50).
Thus, despite her later claim that the incidents in most of her fiction were 'fictitious'

(Letter 207), it is clear that they are frequently grounded in fact. Edward Foster has suggested that her personal experiences and those of her family and friends serves as copy for much of her work. . . ." Kendrick, pp. 26–27.

Two Friends

"I wish you'd jest look down the road again, Mis' Dunbar, an' see if you see anything of Abby comin'."

"I don't see a sign of her. It's a real trial for you to be so short-sighted, ain't it, Sarah?"

"I guess it is. Why, you wouldn't believe it, but I can't see anybody out in the road to tell who 'tis. I can see somethin' movin', an' that's all, unless there's somethin' peculiar about 'em that I can tell 'em by. I can always tell old Mr. Whitcomb—he's got a kind of a hitch when he walks, you know; an' Mis' Addison White always carries a parasol, an' I can tell her. I can see somethin' bobbin' overhead, an' I know who 'tis."

"Queer, ain't it, how she always carries that parasol? Why, I've seen her with it in the dead of winter, when the sun was shinin', an' 'twas freezin' cold; no more need of a parasol—"

"She has to carry it to keep off the sun an' wind, 'cause her eyes are weak, I s'pose."

"Why, I never knew that."

"Abby said she told her so. Abby giggled right in her face one day when she met her with it."

"She didn't!"

"She did—laughed right out. She said she couldn't help it no-how: you know Abby laughs terrible easy. There was Mis' White sailin' along with her parasol h'isted, she said, as fine as a fiddle. You know Mis' White always walks kind of nippin' anyhow, an' she's pretty dressy. An' then it was an awful cold, cloudy day, Abby said. The sun didn't shine, an' it didn't storm, an' there wa'n't no earthly use for a parasol anyway, that she could see. So she kind of snickered. I s'pose it struck her funny all of a sudden. Mis' White took it jest as quick, Abby said, an' told her kind of short that her eyes were terrible weak, an' she had to keep 'em shaded all the time she was outdoors; the doctor had give her orders to. Abby felt pretty streaked about it. You don't see her comin' yet, do you?"

"No, I don't. I thought I see somebody then, but it ain't her. It's the Patch boy, I guess. Yes, 'tis him. What do you think of Abby, Sarah?"

"Think of Abby! What do you mean, Mis' Dunbar?"

"Why, I mean, how do you think she is? Do you think her cough is as bad as 'twas?"

Sarah Arnold, who was a little light woman of fifty, thin-necked and round-backed, with blue protruding eyes in her tiny pale face, pursed up her mouth and went on with her work. She was sewing some red roses on to a black lace bonnet.

"I never thought her cough was very bad anyhow, as far as I was concerned," said she, finally.

"Why, you didn't? I thought it sounded pretty bad. I've been feelin' kind of worried about her."

" 'Tain't nothin' in the world but a throat cough. Her mother before her used to cough jest the same way. It sounds kind of hard, but 'tain't the kind of cough that kills folks. Why, I cough myself half the time."

Sarah hacked a little as she spoke.

"Old Mis' Vane died of consumption, didn't she?"

"Consumption! Jest about as much consumption as I've got. Mis' Vane died of liver complaint. I guess I know. I was livin' right in the house."

"Well, of course you'd be likely to know. I was thinkin' that was what I'd heard, that was all."

"Some folks did call it consumption, but it wa'n't. See anything of Abby?"

"No, I don't. You ain't worried about her, are you?"

"Worried?—no. I ain't got no reason to be worried that I know of. She's old enough to take care of herself. All is, the supper table's been settin' an hour, an' I don't see where she is. She jest went down to the store to git some coffee."

"It's kind of damp to-night."

" 'Taint damp enough to hurt her, I guess, well as she is."

"Mebbe not. That's a pretty bonnet you're makin'."

"Well, I think it's goin' to look pretty well. I didn't know as 'twould. I didn't have much to do with."

"I s'pose it's Abby's."

"Course it's Abby's. I guess you wouldn't see me comin' out in no such bonnet as this."

"Why, you ain't any older than Abby, Sarah."

"I'm different-lookin'," said Sarah, with a look which might have meant pride.

The two women were sitting on a little piazza at the side of the story-and-a-half white house.

Before the house was a small green yard with two cherry-trees in it. Then came the road, then some flat green meadow-lands where the frogs were singing. The grass on these meadows was a wet green, and there were some clumps of blue lilies which showed a long way off in it. Beyond the meadows was the southwest sky, which looked low and red and clear, and had birds in it. It was seven o'clock of a summer evening.

Mrs. Dunbar, tall and straight, with a dark, leathery face whose features were gracefully cut, sat primly in a wooden chair, which was higher than Sarah's little rocker.

"I know Abby looks well in 'most everything," said she.

"I never saw her try on anything that she didn't look well in. There's good-lookin' women, but there ain't many like Abby. Most folks are a little dependent on their bonnets, but she wa'n't, never. Sky blue or grass green, 'twas jest made for her. See anything of her comin'?"

"I can see her," said Sarah, joyfully, in a minute.

"Abby Vane, where have you been?" she called out.

The approaching woman looked up and laughed. "Did you think you'd lost me?" she said, as she came up the piazza step. "I went into Mis' Parson's, an' I stayed longer'n I meant to. Agnes was there—she'd jest got home—an'—" She began to cough violently.

"You hadn't ought to give way to that ticklin' in your throat, Abby," said Sarah, sharply.

"She'd better go into the house out of this damp air," said Mrs. Dunbar.

"Land! the air won't hurt her none. But mebbe you had better come in, Abby. I want to try on this bonnet. I wish you'd come too, Mis' Dunbar. I want you to see if you think it's deep enough in the back."

"There!" said Sarah, after the three women had entered, and she had tied the bonnet on to Abby's head, picking the bows out daintily.

"It's real handsome on her," said Mrs. Dunbar.

"Red roses on a woman of my age!" laughed Abby. "Sarah's bound to rig me up like a young girl.

Abby stood in the little sitting room before the glass. The blinds were wide open to let the evening light in. Abby was a large, well-formed woman. She held her bonneted head up, and drew her chin back with an air of arch pride. The red roses bloomed meetly enough above her candid, womanly forehead.

"If you can't wear red roses, I don't know who can," said Sarah, looking up at her with pride and resentment. "You could wear a white dress to meetin' an' look as well as any of 'em."

"Look here, where did you git the lace for this bonnet?" asked Abby, suddenly. She had taken it off and was examining it closely.

"Oh, 'twas some I had."

"See here, you tell the truth now, Sarah Arnold. Didn't you take this off your black silk dress?"

"It don't make no odds where I took it from."

"You did. What made you do it?"

" 'Taint worth talkin' 'bout. I always despised it on the dress."

"Why, Sarah Arnold! That's jest the way she does," said Abby to Mrs. Dunbar. "If I didn't watch her, she wouldn't leave herself a thing to put on."

After Mrs. Dunbar had gone, Abby sat down in a large covered rocking chair and leaned her head back. Her lips were parted a little, and her teeth showed. She looked ghastly all at once.

"What ails you?" said Sarah.

"Nothin'. I'm a little tired, that's all."

"What are you holdin' on to your side for?"

"Oh, nothin'. It ached a little, that's all."

"Mine's been achin' all the afternoon. I should think you'd better come out an' have somethin' to eat; the table's been settin' an hour an' a half."

Abby rose meekly and followed Sarah into the kitchen with a

sort of weak stateliness. She had always had a queenly way of walking. If Abby Vane should fall a victim to consumption some day, no one could say that she had brought it upon herself by non-observance of hygienic rules. Long miles of country road had she traversed with her fine swinging step, her shoulders thrown well back, her head erect, in her day. She had had the whole care of their vegetable garden, she had weeded and hoed and dug, she had chopped wood and raked hay, and picked apples and cherries.

There had always been a settled and amicable division of labor between the two women. Abby did the rough work, the man's work of the establishment, and Sarah, with her little, slim, nervous frame, the woman's work. All the dress-making and millinery was Sarah's department, all the cooking, all the tidying and furbishing of the house. Abby rose first in the morning and made the fire, and she pumped the water and brought the tubs for the washing. Abby carried the purse, too. The two had literally one between them— one worn black leather wallet. When they went to the village store, if Sarah made the purchase, Abby drew forth the money to pay the bill.

The house belonged to Abby; she had inherited it from her mother. Sarah had some shares in the village bank, which kept them in food and clothes.

Nearly all the new clothes bought would be for Abby, though Sarah had to employ many a subterfuge to bring it about. She alone could have unravelled the subtlety of that diplomacy by which the new cashmere was made for Abby instead of herself, by which the new mantle was fitted to Abby's full, shapely shoulders instead of her own lean, stooping ones.

If Abby had been a barbarous empress, who exacted her cook's head as a penalty for a failure, she could have found no more faithful and anxious artist than Sarah. All the homely New England recipes which Abby loved shone out to Sarah as if written in letters of gold. That nicety of adjustment through which the appetite should neither be cloyed by frequency nor tantalized by desire was a constant study with her. "I've found out just how many times a week Abby likes mince pie," she told Mrs. Dunbar, triumphantly, once. "I've been studyin' it out. She likes mince pie jest about twice to really relish it. She eats it other times, but she don't really hanker after it. I've been keepin' count about six weeks now, an' I can tell pretty well."

Sarah had not eaten her own supper tonight, so she sat down with Abby at the little square table against the kitchen wall. Abby could not eat much, though she tried. Sarah watched her, scarcely taking a mouthful herself. She had a trick of swallowing convulsively every time Abby did, whether she was eating herself or not.

"Ain't goin' to have any custard pie?" said Sarah. "Why not? I went to work an' made it on purpose."

Abby began to laugh. "Well, I'll tell you what 'tis, Sarah," said she, "near's I can put it: I've got jest about as much feelin' about takin' vittles as a pillow-tick has about bein' stuffed with feathers."

"Ain't you been eatin' nothin' this afternoon?"

"Nothin' but them few cherries before I went out."

"That was jest enough to take your appetite off. I never can taste a thing between meals without feelin' it."

"Well, I dare say that was it. Any of them cherries in the house now?"

"Yes; there's some in the cupboard. Want some?"

"I'll git 'em."

Sarah jumped up and got a plate of beautiful red cherries and set them on the table.

"Let me see, these came off the Sarah-tree," said Abby, meditatively. "There wa'n't any on the Abby one this year."

"No," said Sarah, shortly.

"Kind of queer, wa'n't it? It's always bore, ever since I can remember."

"I don't see nothin' very queer about it. It was frost-bit that cold spell last spring; that's all that ails it."

"Why, the other one wa'n't."

"This one's more exposed."

The two round, symmetrical cherry-trees in the front yard had been called Abby and Sarah ever since the two women could remember. The fancy had originated somehow far back in their childhood, and ever since it had been the "Abby-tree" and the Sarah-tree." Both had borne plentifully until this season, when the Abby-tree displayed only her fine green leaves in fruit-time, and the Sarah-tree alone was rosy with cherries. Sarah had picked some that evening standing primly on a chair under the branches, a little basket on her arm, poking her pale inquisitive face into the perennial beauties of her woody namesake. Abby had been used to picking cherries after a more vigorous fashion, with a ladder, but she had not offered to this season.

"I couldn't git many—couldn't reach nothin' but the lowest branches," said Sarah to-night, watching Abby eat the cherries. "I guess you'd better take the ladder out there to-morrow. They're dead ripe, an' the birds are gittin' 'em. I scared off a whole flock to-day."

"Well, I will if I can," said Abby.

"Will if you can! Why, there ain't no reason why you can't, is there?"

"No, not that I know of."

The next morning Abby painfully dragged the long ladder around the house to the tree, and did her appointed task. Sarah came to the door to watch her once, and Abby was coughing distressingly up amongst the green boughs.

"Don't give up to that ticklin' in your throat, for pity's sake, Abby," she called out.

Abby's laugh floated back in answer, like a brave song, from the tree.

Presently Mrs. Dunbar came up the path; she lived alone herself, and was a constant visitor. She stood under the tree, tall and lank and vigorous in her straight-skirted brown cotton gown.

"For the land sake, Abby! you don't mean to say you're pickin' cherries?" she called out. "Are you crazy?"

"Hush!" whispered Abby, between the leaves.

"I don't see why she's crazy," spoke up Sarah; "she always picks 'em."

"You don't catch me givin' up pickin' cherries till I'm a hundred," said Abby, loudly. "I'm a regular cherry bird."

Sarah went into the house soon, and directly Abby crawled down the ladder. She was dripping with perspiration, and trembling.

"Abby Vane, I'm all out of patience," said Mrs. Dunbar. "There ain't no sense in your doin' so."

"Well, I've picked enough for a while, I guess."

"Give me that other basket," said Mrs. Dunbar, harshly, "an' I'll go up an' pick."

"You can pick some for yourself," coughed Abby.

"I don't like 'em," said Mrs. Dunbar, jerking herself up the ladder. "Git up off the ground, an' go in."

Abby obeyed without further words. She sat down in the sitting-room rocker, and leaned her head back. Sarah was stepping about in the kitchen, and did not come in, and she was glad.

In the course of a few months this old-fashioned chair, with its green cushion, held Abby from morning till night. She did not go out any more. She had kept about as long as she could. Every summer Sunday she had sat smartly beside Sarah in church, with those brave red roses on her head. But when the cold weather came her enemy's arrows were too sharp even for her strong mail of love and resolution.

Sarah's behavior seemed inexplicable. Even now that Abby was undeniably helpless, she was constantly goading her to her old tasks. She refused to admit that she was ill. She rebelled when the doctor was called. "No more need of a doctor than nothin' at all," she said.

Affairs went on so till the middle of the winter. Abby grew weaker and weaker, but Sarah seemed to ignore it. One day she went over to Mrs. Dunbar's. One of the other neighbors was sitting with Abby. Sarah walked in suddenly. The outer door opened directly in Mrs. Dunbar's living-room, and a whiff of icy air came in with her.

"How's Abby?" asked Mrs. Dunbar.

" 'Bout the same." Sarah stood upright, staring. She had a blue plaid shawl over her head, and she clutched it together with her red bony fingers. "I've got something on my mind," said she, "an' I've got to tell somebody. I'm goin' crazy."

"What do you mean?"

"Abby's goin' to die, an' I've got something on my mind. I 'ain't treated her right."

"Sarah Arnold, do, for pity's sake, sit down, an' keep calm!"

"I'm calm enough. Oh, what shall I do?"

Mrs. Dunbar forced Sarah into a chair, and took her shawl. "You mustn't feel so," said she. "You've been just devoted to Abby all your life, an' everybody knows it. I know when folks die we're very apt to feel as if we hadn't done right by 'em, but there ain't no sense in your feelin' so."

"I know what I'm talkin' about. I've got something awful on my mind. I've got to tell somebody."

"Sarah Arnold, what do you mean?"

"I've got to tell."

There was a puzzled look on the other woman's thin, strong face. "Well, if you've got anything you want to tell, you can tell it, but I can't think what you're drivin' at."

Sarah fixed her eyes on the wall at the right of Mrs. Dunbar. "It begins 'way back when we was girls. You know I went to live with Abby an' her mother after my folks died. Abby an' me had always been together. You remember that John Marshall that used to keep store where Simmons is, about thirty year ago. When Abby was about twenty, he begun waitin' on her. He was a good-lookin' fellar, an' I guess he was smart, though I never took a fancy to him.

"He was crazy after Abby; but her mother didn't like him. She talked again' him from the very first of it, and wouldn't take no notice of him. She declared she shouldn't have him. Abby didn't say much. She'd laugh an' tell her mother not to fret, but she'd treat him pretty well when he came.

"I s'pose she liked him. I used to watch her, an' think she did. An' he kep' comin' an' comin'. All the fellars were crazy 'bout her anyhow. She was the handsomest girl that was ever seen, about. She'd laugh an' talk with all of 'em, but I s'pose Marshall was the one.

"Well, finally Mis' Vane made such a fuss that he stopped comin'. 'Twas along about a year before she died. I never knew, but I s'pose Abby told him. He went right off to Mexico. Abby didn't say a word, but I knew she felt bad. She didn't seem to care much about goin' into company, an' didn't act jest like herself.

"Well, old Mis' Vane died sudden, you know. She'd had the consumption for years, coughed ever since I could remember, but she went real quick at last, an' Abby was away. She'd gone over to her Aunt Abby's in Colebrook to stay a couple of days. Her aunt wa'n't well neither, an' wanted to see her, an' her mother seemed comfortable so she thought she could go. We sent for her jest as soon as Mis' Vane was took worse, but she couldn't git home in time.

"So I was with Mis' Vane when she died. She had her senses, and she left word for Abby. She said to tell her she'd give her consent to her marryin' John Marshall."

Sarah stopped. Mrs. Dunbar waited, staring.

"I 'ain't told her from that day to this."

"What!"

"I 'ain't never told what her mother said."

"Why, Sarah Arnold, why not?"

"Oh, I couldn't have it nohow—I couldn't—I couldn't, Mis' Dunbar. Seemed as if it would kill me to think of it. I couldn't have her likin' anybody else, an' gittin' married. You don't know what I'd been through. All my own folks had died before I was sixteen years old, an' Mis' Vane was gone, an' she'd been jest like a mother to me. I didn't have nobody in the world but Abby. I couldn't have it so—I couldn't—I couldn't."

"Sarah Arnold, you've been livin' with her all these years, an' been such friends, an' had this shut up in your mind. What are you made of?"

"Oh, I've done everything I could for Abby—everything."

"You couldn't make it up to her in such a way as that."

"I know it. Oh, Mis' Dunbar, have I got to tell her? Have I?"

Mrs. Dunbar, with her intent, ascetic face, confronted Sarah like an embodied conscience.

"Tell her? Sarah Arnold, don't you let another sun go down over your head before you tell her."

"Oh, it don't seem as if I could."

"Don't you wait another minute. You go right home now an' tell her, if you ever want any more peace in this world."

Sarah stood gazing at her a minute, trembling. Then she pulled her shawl up over her head and turned toward the door.

"Well, I'll see," said she.

"Don't you wait a minute!" Mrs. Dunbar called after her again. Then she stood watching the lean, pitiful figure slink down the street. She wondered a good many times afterward if Sarah had told; she suspected that she had not.

Sarah avoided her, and never alluded to the matter again. She fell back on her old philosophy. " 'Tain't nothin' but Abby's goin' to git over," she told people. " 'Tain't on her lungs. She'll git up as soon as it comes warmer weather."

She treated Abby now with the greatest tenderness. She toiled for her day and night. Every delicacy which the sick woman had ever fancied stood waiting on the pantry shelves. Sarah went without shoes and flannels to purchase them, though the chance that they would be tasted was small.

Every spare moment which she could get she sewed for Abby, and folded and hung away new garments which would never be worn. If Abby ventured to remonstrate, Sarah was indignant, and sewed the more; sitting up through long winter nights, she stitched and hemmed with fierce zeal. She ransacked her own wardrobe for material, and hardly left herself a whole article to wear.

Toward spring, when her little dividends came in, she bought stuff for a new dress for Abby—soft cashmere of a beautiful blue. She got patterns, and cut and fitted and pleated with the best of her poor country skill.

"There," said she, when it was completed, "you've got a decent dress to put on, Abby, when you get out again."

"It's real handsome, Sarah," said Abby, smiling.

Abby did not die till the last of May. She sat in her chair by the window, and watched feebly the young grass springing up and the green film spreading over the tree boughs. Way over across in a neighbor's garden was a little peach-tree. Abby could just see it.

"Jest see that peach-tree over there," she whispered to Sarah one evening. It was all rosy with bloom. "It's the first tree I've seen blowed out this year. S'pose the Abby-tree's goin' to blossom?"

"I guess so," said Sarah; "it's leavin' out."

Abby seemed to dwell on the blossoming of the Abby-tree. She kept talking about it. One morning she saw some cherry-trees in the next yard had blossomed, and she called Sarah eagerly.

"Sarah, have you looked to see if the Abby-tree's blossomed?"

"Of course it has. What's to hender?"

Abby's face was radiant. "Oh, Sarah, I want to see it."

"Well, you wait till afternoon," said Sarah, with a tremble in her voice. "I'll draw you round to the front-room door after dinner, an' you can look through at it."

People passing that morning stared to see Sarah Arnold doing

some curious work in the front yard. Not one blossom was there
on the Abby-tree, but the Sarah-tree was white. Its delicate gar-
landed boughs stirred softly, and gave out a sweet smell. Bees
murmured through them. Sarah had a ladder plunged into the
roadward side of all this bloom and sweetness, and she was sawing
and hacking at the white boughs. Then she would stagger across
to the other tree with her arms full of them. They trailed on the
green turf, they lay over her shoulders like white bayonets. All the
air around her was full of flying petals. She looked like some
homely Spring Angel. Then she bound these fair branches and
twigs into the houseward side of the Abby-tree. She worked hard
and fast. That afternoon one looking at the tree from the house
would have been misled. That side of the Abby-tree was brave with
bloom.

Sarah drew Abby in her chair a little way into the front room.
"There!" said she.

"Oh! ain't it beautiful?" cried Abby.

The white branches waved before the window. Abby sat looking at it with a peaceful smile on her face.

When she was back in her old place in the sitting-room, she
gave a bright look up at Sarah.

"It ain't any use to worry," said she, "the Abby-tree is bound
to blossom."

Sarah cried out suddenly, "Oh, Abby! Abby! Abby! what shall
I do! oh, what shall I do!" She flung herself down by Abby's chair,
and put her face on her thin knees. "Oh, Abby! Abby!"

"I ain't gon' to," said Sarah, in a minute. She stood up, and
wiped her eyes. "I know you're better, Abby, an' you'll be out
pretty soon. All is, you've been sick pretty long, an' it's kind of
wore on me, an' it come over me all of a sudden."

"Sarah," said Abby, solemnly, "what's got to come has got
to. You've got to look at things reasonable. There's two of us, an'
one would have to go before the other one; we've always known
it. It ain't goin' to be so bad as you think. Mis' Dunbar is comin'
here to live with you. I've got it all fixed with her. She's real strong,
an' she can make up the fires, an' git the water an' the tubs. You're
fifty years old, an' you're goin' to have some more years to live.
But it's just goin' to be gittin' up one day after another an' goin'
to bed at night, an' they'll be gone. It can be got through with.

There's roads trod out through everything, an' there's folks ahead with lanterns, as it were. You—"

"Oh, Abby! Abby! stop!" Sarah broke in. "If you knew all there was to it. You don't know—you don't know! I 'ain't treated you right, Abby, I 'ain't. I've been keepin' something from you."

"What have you been keepin', Sarah?"

Then Abby listened. Sarah told. There had always been an arch curve to Abby's handsome mouth—a look of sweet amusement at life. It showed forth plainly toward the close of Sarah's tale. Then it deepened suddenly. The poor sick woman laughed out, with a charming, gleeful ring.

A look of joyful wonder flashed over Sarah's despairing face. She stood staring.

"Sarah," said Abby, "I wouldn't have had John Marshall if he'd come on his knees after me all the way from Mexico!"

The Long Arm

I may say, never write unless you feel that you must. But I really wonder if those rules do apply so generally that the world might not lose much good work were they strictly observed. . . . The feeling that one "must write" is . . . a . . . doubtful proposition. . . . In reality a man may write something which will live for the sake of something rather ignoble, and a woman may write something for money with which to buy a French hat. *

"The Long Arm," published in 1895, presents a story similar in many ways to "Two Friends": a life shared by two women is threatened by a suitor of one of them from long ago, but this story ends very differently. "The Long Arm," which includes a classical locked-room murder, a ratiocinating detective, false clues, misplaced suspicion that endangers the romance between a hero and an ingenue, ends with a lesbian couple's shared life destroyed. Per-

* from "The Girl Who Wants to Write" by Mary E. Wilkins Freeman, *Harper's Bazar*, June 1913, p. 272.

haps there is a transformation of realities from Wilkins' life here, too.

According to Brent Kendrick, in the years 1892–93 when Hanson Tyler finally married a woman in California, Wilkins met Dr. Charles Freeman, a New Jersey physician who had abandoned medicine for the family coal business, at a social event at the home of their mutual friend, Henry Mills Alden, editor of *Harper's Weekly* (1864–1869) and *Harper's Monthly* (1869–1919). Charles Freeman was described by the few people in her life who knew both men as someone much like Tyler.

Mary E. Wilkins married on January 1, 1902, after having broken off her engagement several times. She was forty-nine years old, a successful author, and financially independent. The marriage, reported at first to have been happy, was soon disrupted by Freeman's increasingly serious alcoholism and its associated disorders. After a number of years living separately (he with a younger man variously referred to as his valet, his groom, and his companion), she divorced him—a rare action for a woman to take in those days, regardless of provocation.

"The Long Arm" was written during the period in which Wilkins was considering the dissolution of her shared life with Mary Wales in favor of marriage. It was written after she met Freeman, who might have appeared to be a Tyler-like threat to Mary Wales. It is not a story of reassurance that the bonds between women have holding power, as is "Two Friends." It is a story about jealousy and the casual assumption of patriarchal privilege.

"The Long Arm," recovered by Kathleen L. Maio who first wrote about it in the feminist periodical *Chrysalis*[1], and discussed by Lillian Faderman in *Surpassing the Love of Men,* has been variously interpreted in recent times. In *New England Local Color Literature,* Josephine Donovan treats the story as a mother/daughter story, citing as evidence Phoebe Dole's defense of her murder of Fairbanks, the suitor of Maria, her life partner: "She's lived with me in that house for over forty years. There are other ties as strong as the marriage one, that are just as sacred. What right had he to take her away from me and break up my home?"[2] Faderman sees the same words as evidence of intense romantic friendship.

Faderman suggests that "The Long Arm" relies on public knowledge of a real lesbian murder case: ". . . in 1892 Alice Mitchell, a young Tennessee woman, who had a history of insanity, murdered Freda Ward, her female beloved, in order to 'make sure that no one else could get her. . . .' "[3]

But "The Long Arm" is above all else another version of "Two Friends." It tells the story of two women who have spent a lifetime together with the ghost of a man between them. When he tries to intrude on their life, he gets his just desserts—or does he?

This story lacks the strong sense of mutual commitment between the two women. The women in this story are not the moral equivalents of Sarah and Abby in "Two Friends." We see the same two female figures—a "managing" and devoted woman and a "feminine," delicate, and emotionally volatile woman. But each is her worst rather than her best self.

Fairbanks is as likely a murder victim for his bad behavior in business relationships as for his mistreatment of Sarah and Henry. As in an episode of "Murder, She Wrote," there are any number of likely suspects because the victim has been a victimizer. His interference in the lives of Phoebe and Maria is clearly characteristic behavior. Nothing and no one matters to him; he is the only one who counts.

However, despite the tendency to look for biographical roots to her stories, Mary E. Wilkins Freeman may just have been wishing for a new French hat. "The Long Arm" was written in 1895 as an entry in a competition. Kendrick writes:

> According to (J.E. Chamberlain's) account, Freeman noticed the prize offer and suggested that they enter the competition. He agreed. . . . For the most part, the plot of the story was Freeman's own invention, and in three days she wrote her version, titled "The Story of Sarah Tompkins." Chamberlain did the "technical work of fitting it for the Bacheller Syndicate requirement," and the story was retitled, "The Long Arm."[4]

Eighteen ninety-five was the middle of what many economic historians still view as the worst depression in the history of the United States. Not only was $1.00 of 1895 money worth about $16.00 of 1991 money, but there was no income tax, such a tax (of 2%, to be levied on only those whose income was over $4000 annually) having been declared unconstitutional by the Supreme Court on May 20, 1895. "The Long Arm" won the first prize: $2000. Freeman insisted on splitting the prize money with Chamberlain, but even $1000 would have bought a lot of French hats.

ENDNOTES

1. " 'A Strange and Fierce Delight': The Early Days of Women's Mystery Fiction," *Chrysalis*, no. 10 (n.d.), pp. 93–105.

2. *New England Local Color Literature: A Women's Tradition* by Josephine Donovan, Frederick Ungar Publishing Co., New York, 1983, pp. 129–130.

3. Quoted in *Surpassing the Love of Men*, "Lesbian Evil," p. 291; from Jonathan Katz, *Gay American History: Lesbians and Gay Men in the U.S.A.* (New York, 1976), pp. 53–58; from F. L. Sim, "Forensic Psychiatry: Alice Mitchell Adjudged Insane," *Memphis Medical Monthly*, August, 1892.

4. Kendrick, p. 122.

CHAPTER I

THE TRAGEDY

(From notes written by Miss Sarah Fairbanks immediately after the report of the Grand Jury.)

As I take my pen to write this, I have a feeling that I am in the witness-box—for, or against myself, which? The place of the criminal in the dock I will not voluntarily take. I will affirm neither my innocence nor my guilt. I will present the facts of the case as impartially and as coolly as if I had nothing at stake. I will let all who read this judge me as they will.

This I am bound to do, since I am condemned to something infinitely worse than the life-cell or the gallows. I will try my own self in lieu of judge and jury; my guilt or my innocence I will prove to you all, if it be in mortal power. In my despair I am tempted to say, I care not which it may be, so something be proved. Open condemnation could not overwhelm me like universal suspicion.

Now, first, as I have heard is the custom in the courts of law, I will present the case. I am Sarah Fairbanks, a country school teacher, twenty-nine years of age. My mother died when I was twenty-three. Since then, while I have been teaching at Digby, a cousin of my father's, Rufus Bennett, and his wife have lived with my father. During the long summer vacation they returned to their little farm in Vermont, and I kept house for my father.

For five years I have been engaged to be married to Henry Ellis, a young man whom I met in Digby. My father was very much opposed to the match, and has told me repeatedly that if I insisted upon marrying him in his lifetime he would disinherit me. On this account Henry never visited me at my own home; while I could not bring myself to break off my engagement. Finally, I wished to avoid an open rupture with my father. He was quite an old man, and I was the only one he had left of a large family.

I believe that parents should honour their children, as well as children their parents; but I had arrived at this conclusion: in nine-tenths of the cases wherein children marry against their parents' wishes, even when the parents have no just grounds for opposition, the marriages are unhappy.

I sometimes felt that I was unjust to Henry, and resolved that, if ever I suspected that his fancy turned toward any other girl, I would not hinder it, especially as I was getting older and, I thought, losing my good looks.

A little while ago, a young and pretty girl came to Digby to teach the school in the south district. She boarded in the same house with Henry. I heard that he was somewhat attentive to her, and I made up my mind I would not interfere. At the same time it seemed to me that my heart was breaking. I heard her people had money, too, and she was an only child. I had always felt that Henry ought to marry a wife with money, because he had nothing himself, and was not very strong.

School closed five weeks ago, and I came home for the summer vacation. The night before I left, Henry came to see me, and urged me to marry him. I refused again; but I never before had felt that my father was so hard and cruel as I did that night. Henry said that he should certainly see me during the vacation, and when I replied that he must not come, he was angry, and said—but such foolish things are not worth repeating. Henry has really a very sweet temper, and would not hurt a fly.

The very night of my return home Rufus Bennett and my father had words about some maple sugar which Rufus made on his Vermont farm and sold to father, who made a good trade for it to some people in Boston. That was father's business. He had once kept a store, but had given it up, and sold a few articles that he could make a large profit on here and there at wholesale. He used to send to New Hampshire and Vermont for butter, eggs, and cheese. Cousin Rufus thought father did not allow him enough profit on the maple sugar, and in the dispute father lost his temper, and said that Rufus had given him under weight. At that, Rufus swore an oath, and seized father by the throat. Rufus's wife screamed, "Oh, don't! don't! oh, he'll kill him!"

I went up to Rufus and took hold of his arm.

"Rufus Bennett," said I, "you let go my father!"

But Rufus's eyes glared like a madman's, and he would not let go. Then I went to the desk-drawer where father had kept a pistol since some houses in the village were broken into; I got out the pistol, laid hold of Rufus again, and held the muzzle against his forehead.

"You let go of my father," said I, "or I'll fire!"

Then Rufus let go, and father dropped like a log. He was purple in the face. Rufus's wife and I worked a long time over him to bring him to.

"Rufus Bennett," said I, "go to the well and get a pitcher of water." He went, but when father had revived and got up, Rufus gave him a look that showed he was not over his rage.

"I'll get even with you yet, Martin Fairbanks, old man as you are!" he shouted out, and went into the outer room.

We got father to bed soon. He slept in the bedroom downstairs, out of the sitting-room. Rufus and his wife had the north chamber, and I had the south one. I left my door open that night, and did not sleep. I listened; no one stirred in the night. Rufus and his wife were up very early in the morning, and before nine o'clock left for Vermont. They had a day's journey, and would reach home about nine in the evening. Rufus's wife bade father good-bye, crying, while Rufus was getting their trunk downstairs, but Rufus did not go near father nor me. He ate no breakfast; his very back looked ugly when he went out of the yard.

That very day about seven in the evening, after tea, I had just washed the dishes and put them away, and went out on the north doorstep, where father was sitting, and sat down on the lowest step. There was a cool breeze there; it had been a very hot day.

"I want to know if that Ellis fellow has been to see you any lately?" said father all at once.

"Not a great deal," I answered.

"Did he come to see you the last night you were there?" said father.

"Yes, sir," said I, "he did come."

"If you ever have another word to say to that fellow while I live, I'll kick you out of the house like a dog, daughter of mine though you be," said he. Then he swore a great oath and called God to witness. "Speak to that fellow again, if you dare, while I live!" said he.

I did not say a word; I just looked up at him as I sat there. Father turned pale and shrank back, and put his hand to his throat, where Rufus had clutched him. There were some purple finger-marks there.

"I suppose you would have been glad if he had killed me," father cried out.

"I saved your life," said I.

"What did you do with that pistol?" he asked.

"I put it back in the desk-drawer."

I got up and went around and sat on the west doorstep, which is the front one. As I sat there, the bell rang for the Tuesday evening meeting, and Phœbe Dole and Maria Woods, two old maiden ladies, dressmakers, our next-door neighbours, went past on their way to the meeting. Phœbe stopped and asked if Rufus and his wife were gone. Maria went around the house. Very soon they went on, and several other people passed. When they had all gone, it was as still as death.

I sat alone a long time, until I could see by the shadows that the full moon had risen. Then I went to my room and went to bed.

I lay awake a long time, crying. It seemed to me that all hope of marriage between Henry and me was over. I could not expect him to wait for me. I thought of that other girl; I could see her pretty face wherever I looked. But at last I cried myself to sleep.

At about five o'clock I awoke and got up. Father always wanted his breakfast at six o'clock, and I had to prepare it now.

When father and I were alone, he always built the fire in the kitchen stove, but that morning I did not hear him stirring as usual, and I fancied that he must be so out of temper with me, that he would not build the fire.

I went to my closet for a dark blue calico dress which I wore to do housework in. It had hung there during all the school term.

As I took it off the hook, my attention was caught by something strange about the dress I had worn the night before. This dress was made of thin summer silk; it was green in colour, sprinkled over with white rings. It had been my best dress for two summers, but now I was wearing it on hot afternoons at home, for it was the coolest dress I had. The night before, too, I had thought of the possibility of Henry's driving over from Digby and passing the house. He had done this sometimes during the last summer vacation, and I wished to look my best if he did.

As I took down the calico dress I saw what seemed to be a stain on the green silk. I threw on the calico hastily, and then took the green silk and carried it over to the window. It was covered with spots—horrible great splashes and streaks down the front. The right sleeve, too, was stained, and all the stains were wet.

"What have I got on my dress?" said I.

It looked like blood. Then I smelled of it, and it was sickening in my nostrils, but I was not sure what the smell of blood was like. I thought I must have got the stains by some accident the night before.

"If that is blood on my dress," I said, "I must do something to get it off at once, or the dress will be ruined."

It came to my mind that I had been told that blood-stains had been removed from cloth by an application of flour paste on the wrong side. I took my green silk, and ran down the back stairs, which led—having a door at the foot—directly into the kitchen.

There was no fire in the kitchen stove, as I had thought. Everything was very solitary and still, except for the ticking of the clock on the shelf. When I crossed the kitchen to the pantry, however, the cat mewed to be let in from the shed. She had a little door of her own by which she could enter or leave the shed at will, an aperture just large enough for her Maltese body to pass at ease beside the shed door. It had a little lid, too, hung upon a leathern hinge. On my way I let the cat in; then I went into the pantry and got a bowl of flour. This I mixed with water into a stiff paste, and applied to the under surface of the stains on my dress. I then hung the dress up to dry in the dark end of a closet leading out of the kitchen, which contained some old clothes of father's.

Then I made up the fire in the kitchen stove. I made coffee, baked biscuits, and poached some eggs for breakfast.

Then I opened the door into the sitting-room and called, "Father, breakfast is ready." Suddenly I started. There was a red stain on the inside of the sitting-room door. My heart began to beat in my ears. "Father!" I called out—"father!"

There was no answer.

"Father!" I called again, as loud as I could scream. "Why don't you speak? What is the matter?"

The door of his bedroom stood open. I had a feeling that I saw a red reflection in there. I gathered myself together and went across the sitting-room to father's bedroom door. His little looking-glass hung over his bureau opposite his bed, which was reflected in it.

That was the first thing I saw, when I reached the door. I could see father in the looking-glass and the bed. Father was dead there; he had been murdered in the night.

CHAPTER II

THE KNOT OF RIBBON

I think I must have fainted away, for presently I found myself on the floor, and for a minute I could not remember what had happened. Then I remembered, and an awful, unreasoning terror seized me. "I must lock all the doors quick," I thought; "quick, or the murderer will come back."

I tried to get up, but I could not stand. I sank down again. I had to crawl out of the room on my hands and knees.

I went first to the front door; it was locked with a key and a bolt. I went next to the north door, and that was locked with a key and bolt. I went to the north shed door, and that was bolted. Then I went to the little-used east door in the shed, beside which the cat had her little passage-way, and that was fastened with an iron hook. It has no latch.

The whole house was fastened on the inside. The thought struck me like an icy hand, "The murderer is in this house!" I rose to my feet then; I unhooked that door, and ran out of the house, and out of the yard, as for my life.

I took the road to the village. The first house, where Phœbe Dole and Maria Woods live, is across a wide field from ours. I did not intend to stop there, for they were only women, and could do nothing; but seeing Phœbe looking out of the window, I ran into the yard.

She opened the window.

"What is it?" said she. "What is the matter, Sarah Fairbanks?"

Maria Woods came and leaned over her shoulder. Her face looked almost as white as her hair, and her blue eyes were dilated. My face must have frightened her.

"Father—father is murdered in his bed!" I said.

There was a scream, and Maria Woods's face disappeared from over Phœbe Dole's shoulder—she had fainted. I do not know whether Phœbe looked paler—she is always very pale—but I saw in her black eyes a look which I shall never forget. I think she began to suspect me at that moment.

Phœbe glanced back at Maria, but she asked me another question.

"Has he had words with anybody?" said she.

"Only with Rufus," I said; "but Rufus is gone."

Phœbe turned away from the window to attend to Maria, and I ran on to the village.

A hundred people can testify what I did next—can tell how I called for the doctor and the deputy-sheriff; how I went back to my own home with the horror-stricken crowd; how they flocked in and looked at poor father; but only the doctor touched him, very carefully, to see if he were quite dead; how the coroner came, and all the rest.

The pistol was in the bed beside father, but it had not been fired; the charge was still in the barrel. It was blood-stained, and there was one bruise on father's head which might have been inflicted by the pistol, used as a club. But the wound which caused his death was in his breast, and made evidently by some cutting instrument, though the cut was not a clean one; the weapon must have been dull.

They searched the house, lest the murderer should be hidden away. I heard Rufus Bennett's name whispered by one and another. Everybody seemed to know that he and father had had words the night before; I could not understand how, because I had told nobody except Phœbe Dole, who had had no time to spread the news, and I was sure that no one else had spoken of it.

They looked in the closet where my green silk dress hung, and pushed it aside to be sure nobody was concealed behind it, but they did not notice anything wrong about it. It was dark in the closet, and besides, they did not look for anything like that until later.

All these people—the deputy-sheriff, and afterwards the high sheriff, and other out-of-town officers, for whom they had telegraphed, and the neighbours—all hunted their own suspicion, and that was Rufus Bennett. All believed he had come back, and killed my father. They fitted all the facts to that belief. They made him do the deed with a long, slender screw-driver, which he had recently borrowed from one of the neighbours and had not returned. They made his finger-marks, which were still on my father's throat, fit the red prints of the sitting-room door. They made sure that he had returned and stolen into the house by the east door shed, while father and I sat on the doorsteps the evening before; that he had hidden himself away, perhaps in that very closet where my dress hung, and afterwards stolen out and killed my father, and then escaped.

They were not shaken when I told them that every door was bolted and barred that morning. They themselves found all the windows fastened down, except a few which were open on account of the heat, and even these last were raised only the width of the sash, and fastened with sticks, so that they could be raised no higher. Father was very cautious about fastening the house, for he sometimes had considerable sums of money by him. The officers saw all these difficulties in the way, but they fitted them somehow to their theory, and two deputy-sheriffs were at once sent to apprehend Rufus.

They had not begun to suspect me then, and not the slightest watch was kept on my movements. The neighbours were very kind, and did everything to help me, relieving me altogether of all those last offices—in this case so much sadder than usual.

An inquest was held, and I told freely all I knew, except about the blood-stains on my dress. I hardly knew why I kept that back. I had no feeling then that I might have done the deed myself, and I could not bear to convict myself, if I was innocent.

Two of the neighbours, Mrs. Holmes and Mrs. Adams, remained with me all that day. Towards evening, when there were very few in the house, they went into the parlour to put it in order for the funeral, and I sat down alone in the kitchen. As I sat there by the window I thought of my green silk dress, and wondered if the stains were out. I went to the closet and brought the dress out to the light. The spots and streaks had almost disappeared. I took the dress out into the shed, and scraped off the flour paste, which was quite dry; I swept up the paste, burned it in the stove, took the dress upstairs to my own closet, and hung it in its old place. Neighbours remained with me all night.

At three o'clock in the afternoon of the next day, which was Thursday, I went over to Phœbe Dole's to see about a black dress to wear at the funeral. The neighbours had urged me to have my black silk dress altered a little, and trimmed with crape.

I found only Maria Woods at home. When she saw me she gave a little scream, and began to cry. She looked as if she had already been weeping for hours. Her blue eyes were bloodshot.

"Phœbe's gone over to—Mrs. Whitney's to—try on her dress," she sobbed.

"I want to get my black silk dress fixed a little," said I.

"She'll be home—pretty soon," said Maria.

I laid my dress on the sofa and sat down. Nobody ever consults Maria about a dress. She sews well, but Phœbe does all the planning.

Maria Woods continued to sob like a child, holding her little soaked handkerchief over her face. Her shoulders heaved. As for me, I felt like a stone; I could not weep.

"Oh," she gasped out finally, "I knew—I knew! I told Phœbe—I knew just how it would be, I—knew!"

I roused myself at that.

"What do you mean?" said I.

"When Phœbe came home Tuesday night and said she heard your father and Rufus Bennett having words, I knew how it would be," she choked out. "I knew he had a dreadful temper."

"Did Phœbe Dole know Tuesday night that father and Rufus Bennett had words?" said I.

"Yes," said Maria Woods.

"How did she know?"

"She was going through your yard, the short cut to Mrs. Ormsby's, to carry her brown alpaca dress home. She came right home and told me; and she overheard them."

"Have you spoken of it to anybody but me?" said I.

Maria said she didn't know; she might have done so. Then she remembered hearing Phœbe herself speak of it to Harriet Sargent when she came in to try on her dress. It was easy to see how people knew about it.

I did not say any more, but I thought it was strange that Phœbe Dole had asked me if father had had words with anybody when she knew it all the time.

Phœbe came in before long. I tried on my dress, and she made her plan about the alterations, and the trimming. I made no suggestions. I did not care how it was done, but if I had cared it would have made no difference. Phœbe always does things her own way. All the women in the village are in a manner under Phœbe Dole's thumb. The garments are visible proofs of her force of will.

While she was taking up my black silk on the shoulder seams, Phœbe Dole said—

"Let me see—you had a green silk made at Digby three summers ago, didn't you?"

"Yes," I said.

"Well," said she, "why don't you have it dyed black? those thin silks dye quite nice. It would make you a good dress."

I scarcely replied, and then she offered to dye it for me herself. She had a recipe which she used with great success. I thought it was very kind of her, but did not say whether I would accept her offer or not. I could not fix my mind upon anything but the awful trouble I was in.

"I'll come over and get it to-morrow morning," said Phœbe.

I thanked her. I thought of the stains, and then my mind seemed to wander again to the one subject. All the time Maria Woods sat weeping. Finally Phœbe turned to her with impatience.

"If you can't keep calmer, you'd better go upstairs, Maria," said she. "You'll make Sarah sick. Look at her! she doesn't give way—and think of the reason she's got."

"I've got reason, too," Maria broke out; then, with a piteous shriek, "Oh, I've got reason."

"Maria Woods, go out of the room!" said Phœbe. Her sharpness made me jump, half dazed as I was.

Maria got up without a word, and went out of the room, bending almost double with convulsive sobs.

"She's been dreadfully worked up over your father's death," said Phœbe calmly, going on with the fitting. "She's terribly nervous. Sometimes I have to be real sharp with her, for her own good."

I nodded. Maria Woods has always been considered a sweet, weakly, dependent woman, and Phœbe Dole is undoubtedly very fond of her. She has seemed to shield her, and take care of her nearly all her life. The two have lived together since they were young girls.

Phœbe is tall, and very pale and thin; but she never had a day's illness. She is plain, yet there is a kind of severe goodness and faithfulness about her colourless face, with the smooth bands of white hair over her ears.

I went home as soon as my dress was fitted. That evening Henry Ellis came over to see me. I do not need to go into details concerning that visit. It seemed enough to say that he tendered the fullest sympathy and protection, and I accepted them. I cried a little, for the first time, and he soothed and comforted me.

Henry had driven over from Digby and tied his horse in the yard. At ten o'clock he bade me good night on the doorstep, and was just turning his buggy around, when Mrs. Adams came running to the door.

"Is this yours?" said she, and she held out a knot of yellow ribbon.

"Why, that's the ribbon you have around your whip, Henry," said I.

He looked at it.

"So it is," he said. "I must have dropped it." He put it into his pocket and drove away.

"He didn't drop that ribbon to-night!" said Mrs. Adams. "I found it Wednesday morning out in the yard. I thought I remembered seeing him have a yellow ribbon on his whip."

CHAPTER III

SUSPICION IS NOT PROOF

When Mrs. Adams told me she had picked up Henry's whip-ribbon Wednesday morning, I said nothing, but thought that Henry must have driven over Tuesday evening after all, and even come up into the yard, although the house was shut up, and I in bed, to get a little nearer to me. I felt conscience-stricken, because I could not help a thrill of happiness, when my father lay dead in the house.

My father was buried as privately and as quietly as we could bring it about. But it was a terrible ordeal. Meantime word came from Vermont that Rufus Bennett had been arrested on his farm. He was perfectly willing to come back with the officers, and indeed, had not the slightest trouble in proving that he was at his home in Vermont when the murder took place. He proved by several witnesses that he was out of the State long before my father and I sat on the steps together that evening, and that he proceeded directly to his home as fast as the train and stage-coach could carry him.

The screw-driver with which the deed was supposed to have been committed was found, by the neighbour from whom it had been borrowed, in his wife's bureau drawer. It had been returned, and she had used it to put a picture-hook in her chamber. Bennett was discharged and returned to Vermont.

Then Mrs. Adams told of the finding of the yellow ribbon from Henry Ellis's whip, and he was arrested, since he was held to have a motive for putting my father out of the world. Father's opposition to our marriage was well known, and Henry was suspected also of having had an eye to his money. It was found, indeed, that my father had more money than I had known myself.

Henry owned to having driven into the yard that night, and to having missed the ribbon from his whip on his return; but one of the hostlers in the livery stables in Digby, where he kept his horse and buggy, came forward and testified to finding the yellow ribbon in the carriage-room that Tuesday night before Henry returned from his drive. There were two yellow ribbons in evidence, therefore, and the one produced by the hostler seemed to fit Henry's whip-stock the more exactly.

Moreover, nearly the exact minute of the murder was claimed to be proved by the post-mortem examination; and by the testimony of the stable man as to the hour of Henry's return and the speed of his horse, he was further cleared of suspicion; for, if the opinion of the medical experts was correct, Henry must have returned to the livery stable too soon to have committed the murder.

He was discharged, at any rate, although suspicion still clung to him. Many people believe now in his guilt—those who do not, believe in mine; and some believe we were accomplices.

After Henry's discharge, I was arrested. There was no one else left to accuse. There must be a motive for the murder; I was the only person left with a motive. Unlike the others, who were discharged after preliminary examination, I was held to the grand jury and taken to Dedham, where I spent four weeks in jail, awaiting the meeting of the grand jury.

Neither at the preliminary examination, nor before the grand jury, was I allowed to make the full and frank statement that I am making here. I was told simply to answer the questions that were put to me, and to volunteer nothing, and I obeyed.

I know nothing about law. I wished to do the best I could— to act in the wisest manner, for Henry's sake and my own. I said nothing about the green silk dress. They searched the house for all manner of things, at the time of my arrest, but the dress was not there—it was in Phœbe Dole's dye-kettle. She had come over after it one day when I was picking beans in the garden, and had taken it out of the closet. She brought it back herself, and told me this, after I had returned from Dedham.

"I thought I'd get it and surprise you," said she. "It's taken a beautiful black."

She gave me a strange look—half as if she would see into my very soul, in spite of me, half as if she were in terror of what she would see there, as she spoke. I do not know just what Phœbe Dole's look meant. There may have been a stain left on that dress after all, and she may have seen it.

I suppose if it had not been for that flour-paste which I had learned to make, I should have hung for the murder of my father. As it was, the grand jury found no bill against me because there was absolutely no evidence to convict me; and I came home a free woman. And if people were condemned for their motives, would there be enough hangmen in the world?

They found no weapon with which I could have done the deed. They found no blood-stains on my clothes. The one thing which told against me, aside from my ever-present motive, was the fact that on the morning after the murder the doors and windows were fastened. My volunteering this information had of course weakened its force as against myself.

Then, too, some held that I might have been mistaken in my terror and excitement, and there was a theory, advanced by a few, that the murderer had meditated making me also a victim, and had locked the doors that he might not be frustrated in his designs, but had lost heart at the last, and had allowed me to escape, and then fled himself. Some held that he had intended to force me to reveal the whereabouts of father's money, but his courage had failed him.

Father had quite a sum in a hiding-place which only he and I knew. But no search for money had been made, as far as any one could see—not a bureau drawer had been disturbed, and father's gold watch was ticking peacefully under his pillow; even his wallet in his vest pocket had not been opened. There was a small roll of bank-notes in it, and some change; father never carried much money. I suppose if father's wallet and watch had been taken, I should not have been suspected at all.

I was discharged, as I have said, from lack of evidence, and have returned to my home—free, indeed, but with this awful burden of suspicion on my shoulders. That brings me up to the present day. I returned yesterday evening. This evening Henry Ellis has been over to see me; he will not come again, for I have forbidden him to do so. This is what I said to him—

"I know you are innocent, you know I am innocent. To all

the world beside we are under suspicion—I more than you, but we are both under suspicion. If we are known to be together that suspicion is increased for both of us. I do not care for myself, but I do care for you. Separated from me the stigma attached to you will soon fade away, especially if you should marry elsewhere."

Then Henry interrupted me.

"I will never marry elsewhere," said he.

I could not help being glad that he said it, but I was firm.

"If you should see some good woman whom you could love, it will be better for you to marry elsewhere," said I.

"I never will!" he said again. He put his arms around me, but I had strength to push him away.

"You never need, if I succeed in what I undertake before you meet the other," said I. I began to think he had not cared for that pretty girl who boarded in the same house after all.

"What is that?" he said. "What are you going to undertake?"

"To find my father's murderer," said I.

Henry gave me a strange look; then, before I could stop him, he took me fast in his arms and kissed my forehead.

"As God is my witness, Sarah, I believe in your innocence," he said; and from that minute I have felt sustained and fully confident of my power to do what I had undertaken.

My father's murderer I will find. To-morrow I begin my search. I shall first make an exhaustive examination of the house, such as no officer in the case has yet made, in the hope of finding a clue. Every room I propose to divide into square yards, by line and measure, and every one of these square yards I will study as if it were a problem in algebra.

I have a theory that it is impossible for any human being to enter any house, and commit in it a deed of this kind, and not leave behind traces which are the known quantities in an algebraic equation to those who can use them.

There is a chance that I shall not be quite unaided. Henry has promised not to come again until I bid him, but he is to send a detective here from Boston—one whom he knows. In fact, the man is a cousin of his, or else there would be small hope of our securing him, even if I were to offer him a large price.

The man has been remarkably successful in several cases, but his health is not good; the work is a severe strain upon his nerves, and he is not driven to it from any lack of money. The physicians have forbidden him to undertake any new case, for a year at least, but Henry is confident that we may rely upon him for this.

I will now lay aside this and go to bed. To-morrow is Wednesday; my father will have been dead seven weeks. To-morrow morning I will commence the work, in which, if it be in human power, aided by a higher wisdom, I shall succeed.

CHAPTER IV

THE BOX OF CLUES

(The pages which follow are from Miss Fairbanks's journal begun after the conclusion of the notes already given to the reader.)

Wednesday night.—I have resolved to record carefully each day the progress I make in my examination of the house. I began to-day at the bottom—that is, with the room least likely to contain any clue, the parlour. I took a chalk-line and a yard-stick, and divided the floor into square yards, and every one of these squares I examined on my hands and knees. I found in this way literally nothing on the carpet but dust, lint, two common white pins, and three inches of blue sewing-silk.

At last I got the dustpan and brush, and yard by yard swept the floor. I took the sweepings in a white pasteboard box out into the yard in the strong sunlight, and examined them. There was nothing but dust and lint and five inches of brown woollen thread—evidently a ravelling of some dress material. The blue silk and the brown thread are the only possible clues which I found to-day, and they are hardly possible. Rufus's wife can probably account for them.

Nobody has come to the house all day. I went down to the store this afternoon to get some necessary provisions, and people stopped talking when I came in. The clerk took my money as if it were poison.

Thursday night.—To-day I have searched the sitting-room, out of which my father's bedroom opens. I found two bloody footprints on the carpet which no one had noticed before—perhaps because the carpet itself is red and white. I used a microscope which I had in my school work. The footprints, which are close to the bedroom door, pointing out into the sitting-room, are both from the right foot; one is brighter than the other, but both are faint. The foot was evidently either bare or clad only in a stocking—the prints are so widely spread. They are wider than my father's shoes. I tried one in the brightest print.

I found nothing else new in the sitting-room. The blood-stains on the doors which have been already noted are still there. They had not been washed away, first by order of the sheriff, and next by mine. These stains are of two kinds; one looks as if made by a bloody garment brushing against it; the other, I should say, was made in the first place by the grasp of a bloody hand, and then brushed over with a cloth. There are none of these marks upon the door leading to the bedroom—they are on the doors leading into the front entry and the china closet. The china closet is really a pantry, although I use it only for my best dishes and preserves.

Friday night.—To-day I searched the closet. One of the shelves, which is about as high as my shoulders, was blood-stained. It looked to me as if the murderer might have caught hold of it to steady himself. Did he turn faint after his dreadful deed? Some tumblers of jelly were ranged on that shelf and they had not been disturbed. There was only that bloody clutch on the edge.

I found on this closet floor, under the shelves, as if it had been rolled there by a careless foot, a button, evidently from a man's clothing. It is an ordinary black enamelled metal trousers-button; it had evidently been worn off and clumsily sewn on again, for a quantity of stout white thread is still clinging to it. This button must have belonged either to a single man or to one with an idle wife.

If one black button had been sewn on with white thread, another is likely to be. I may be wrong, but I regard this button as a clue.

The pantry was thoroughly swept—cleaned, indeed, by Rufus's wife, the day before she left. Neither my father nor Rufus could have dropped it there, and they never had occasion to go to that closet. The murderer dropped the button.

I have a white pasteboard box which I have marked "clues." In it I have put the button.

This afternoon Phœbe Dole came in. She is very kind. She had re-cut the dyed silk, and she fitted it to me. Her great shears clicking in my ears made me nervous. I did not feel like stopping to think about clothes. I hope I did not appear ungrateful, for she is the only soul beside Henry who has treated me as she did before this happened.

Phœbe asked me what I found to busy myself about, and I replied, "I am searching for my father's murderer." She asked me if I thought I should find a clue, and I replied, "I think so." I had found the button then, but I did not speak of it. She said Maria was not very well.

I saw her eyeing the stains on the doors, and I said I had not washed them off, for I thought they might yet serve a purpose in detecting the murderer. She looked closely at those on the entry-door—the brightest ones—and said she did not see how they could help, for there were no plain finger-marks there, and she should think they would make me nervous.

"I'm beyond being nervous," I replied.

Saturday.—To-day I have found something which I cannot understand. I have been at work in the room where my father came to his dreadful end. Of course some of the most startling evidences have been removed. The bed is clean, and the carpet washed, but the worst horror of it all clings to that room. The spirit of murder seemed to haunt it. It seemed to me at first that I could not enter that room, but in it I made a strange discovery.

My father, while he carried little money about his person, was in the habit of keeping considerable sums in the house; there is no bank within ten miles. However he was wary; he had a hiding-place which he had revealed to no one but myself. He had a small stand in his room near the end of his bed. Under this stand, or rather under the top of it, he had tacked a large leather wallet. In this he kept all his spare money. I remember how his eyes twinkled when he showed it to me.

"The average mind thinks things have either got to be in or on," said my father. "They don't consider there's ways of getting around gravitation and calculation."

In searching my father's room I called to mind that saying of his, and his peculiar system of concealment, and then I made my discovery. I have argued that in a search of this kind I ought not only to search for hidden traces of the criminal, but for everything which had been for any reason concealed. Something which my father himself had hidden, something from his past history, may furnish a motive for some one else.

The money in the wallet under the table, some five hundred dollars, had been removed and deposited in the bank. Nothing more was to be found there. I examined the bottom of the bureau, and the undersides of the chair seats. There are two chairs in the room, besides the cushioned rocker—green-painted wooden chairs, with flag seats. I found nothing under the seats.

Then I turned each of the green chairs completely over, and examined the bottoms of the legs. My heart leaped when I found a bit of leather tacked over one. I got the tack-hammer and drew the tacks. The chair-leg had been hollowed out, and for an inch the hole was packed tight with cotton. I began picking out the cotton, and soon I felt something hard. It proved to be an old-fashioned gold band, quite wide and heavy, like a wedding-ring.

I took it over to the window and found this inscription on the inside: "Let love abide for ever." There were two dates—one in August, forty years ago, and the other in August of the present year.

I think the ring had never been worn; while the first part of the inscription is perfectly clear, it looks old, and the last is evidently freshly cut.

This could not have been my mother's ring. She had only her wedding-ring, and that was buried with her. I think my father must have treasured up this ring for years; but why? What does it mean? This can hardly be a clue; this can hardly lead to the discovery of a motive, but I will put it in the box with the rest.

Sunday night.—To-day, of course, I did not pursue my search. I did not go to church. I could not face old friends that could not face me. Sometimes I think that everybody in my native village believes in my guilt. What must I have been in my general appearance and demeanour all my life? I have studied myself in the glass, and tried to discover the possibilities of evil that they must see in my face.

This afternoon about three o'clock, the hour when people here have just finished their Sunday dinner, there was a knock on the north door. I answered it, and a strange young man stood there with a large book under his arm. He was thin and cleanly shaved, with a clerical air.

"I have a work here to which I would like to call your attention," he began; and I stared at him in astonishment, for why should a book agent be peddling his wares upon the Sabbath?

His mouth twitched a little.

"It's a Biblical Cyclopædia," said he.

"I don't think I care to take it," said I.

"You are Miss Sarah Fairbanks, I believe?"

"That is my name," I replied stiffly.

"Mr. Henry Ellis, of Digby, sent me here," he said next. "My name is Dix—Francis Dix."

Then I knew it was Henry's first cousin from Boston—the detective who had come to help me. I felt the tears coming to my eyes.

"You are very kind to come," I managed to say.

"I am selfish, not kind," he returned, "but you had better let me come in, or any chance of success in my book agency is lost, if the neighbours see me trying to sell it on a Sunday. And, Miss Fairbanks, this is a *bonâ fide* agency. I shall canvass the town."

He came in. I showed him all that I have written, and he read it carefully. When he had finished he sat still for a long time, with his face screwed up in a peculiar meditative fashion.

"We'll ferret this out in three days at the most," said he finally, with a sudden clearing of his face and a flash of his eyes at me.

"I had planned for three years, perhaps," said I.

"I tell you, we'll do it in three days," he repeated. "Where can I get board while I canvass for this remarkable and interesting book under my arm? I can't stay here, of course, and there is no hotel. Do you think the two dressmakers next door, Phœbe Dole and the other one, would take me in?"

I said they had never taken boarders.

"Well, I'll go over and inquire," said Mr. Dix; and he had gone, with his book under his arm, almost before I knew it.

Never have I seen any one act with the strange noiseless soft speed that this man does. Can he prove me innocent in three days? He must have succeeded in getting board at Phœbe Dole's, for I saw him go past to meeting with her this evening. I feel sure he will be over very early to-morrow morning.

CHAPTER V

THE EVIDENCE POINTS TO ONE

Monday night.—The detective came as I expected. I was up as soon as it was light, and he came across the dewy fields, with his cyclopædia under his arm. He had stolen out from Phœbe Dole's back door.

He had me bring my father's pistol; then he bade me come with him out into the back yard.

"Now, fire it," he said, thrusting the pistol into my hands. As I have said before, the charge was still in the barrel.

"I shall arouse the neighbourhood," I said.

"Fire it," he ordered.

I tried; I pulled the trigger as hard as I could.

"I can't do it," I said.

"And you are a reasonably strong woman, too, aren't you?"

I said I had been considered so. Oh, how much I heard about the strength of my poor woman's arms, and their ability to strike that murderous weapon home!

Mr. Dix took the pistol himself, and drew a little at the trigger.

"I could do it," he said, "but I won't. It would arouse the neighbourhood."

"This is more evidence against me," I said despairingly. "The murderer had tried to fire the pistol and failed."

"It is more evidence against the murderer," said Mr. Dix.

We went into the house, where he examined my box of clues long and carefully. Looking at the ring, he asked whether there was a jeweller in this village, and I said there was not. I told him that my father oftener went on business to Acton, ten miles away, than elsewhere.

He examined very carefully the button which I had found in the closet, and then asked to see my father's wardrobe. That was soon done. Beside the suit in which father was laid away there was one other complete one in the closet in his room. Besides that, there were in this closet two overcoats, an old black frock coat, a pair of pepper-and-salt trousers, and two black vests. Mr. Dix examined all the buttons; not one was missing.

There was still another old suit in the closet off the kitchen. This was examined, and no button found wanting.

"What did your father do for work the day before he died?" he then asked.

I reflected and said that he had unpacked some stores which had come down from Vermont, and done some work out in the garden.

"What did he wear?"

"I think he wore the pepper-and-salt trousers and the black vest. He wore no coat, while at work."

Mr. Dix went quietly back to father's room and his closet, I following. He took out the grey trousers and the black vest, and examined them closely.

"What did he wear to protect these?" he asked.

"Why, he wore overalls!" I said at once. As I spoke I remembered seeing father go around the path to the yard, with those blue overalls drawn up high under his arms.

"Where are they?"

"Weren't they in the kitchen closet?"

"No."

We looked again, however, in the kitchen closet; we searched the shed thoroughly. The cat came in through her little door, as we stood there, and brushed around our feet. Mr. Dix stooped and stroked her. Then he went quickly to the door, beside which her little entrance was arranged, unhooked it, and stepped out. I was following him, but he motioned me back.

"None of my boarding mistress's windows command us," he said, "but she might come to the back door."

I watched him. He passed slowly around the little winding footpath, which skirted the rear of our house and extended faintly through the grassy fields to the rear of Phœbe Dole's. He stopped, searched a clump of sweetbriar, went on to an old well, and stopped there. The well had been dry many a year, and was choked up with stones and rubbish. Some boards are laid over it, and a big stone or two, to keep them in place.

Mr. Dix, glancing across at Phœbe Dole's back door, went

down on his knees, rolled the stones away, then removed the boards and peered down the well. He stretched far over the brink, and reached down. He made many efforts; then he got up and came to me, and asked me to get for him an umbrella with a crooked handle, or something that he could hook into clothing.

I brought my own umbrella, the silver handle of which formed an exact hook. He went back to the well, knelt again, thrust in the umbrella and drew up, easily enough, what he had been fishing for. Then he came bringing it to me.

"Don't faint," he said, and took hold of my arm. I gasped when I saw what he had—my father's blue overalls, all stained and splotched with blood!

I looked at them, then at him.

"Don't faint," he said again. "We're on the right track. This is where the button came from—see, see!" He pointed to one of the straps of the overalls, and the button was gone. Some white thread clung to it. Another black metal button was sewed on roughly with the same white thread that I found on the button in my box of clues.

"What does it mean?" I gasped out. My brain reeled.

"You shall know soon," he said. He looked at his watch. Then he laid down the ghastly bundle he carried. "It has puzzled you to know how the murderer went in and out and yet kept the doors locked, has it not?" he said.

"Yes."

"Well, I am going out now. Hook that door after me."

He went out, still carrying my umbrella. I hooked the door. Presently I saw the lid of the cat's door lifted, and his hand and arm thrust through. He curved his arm up towards the hook, but it came short by half a foot. Then he withdrew his arm, and thrust in my silver-handled umbrella. He reached the door-hook easily enough with that.

Then he hooked it again. That was not so easy. He had to work a long time. Finally he accomplished it, unhooked the door again, and came in.

"That was how!" I said.

"No, it was not," he returned. "No human being, fresh from such a deed, could have used such patience as that to fasten the door after him. Please hang your arm down by your side."

I obeyed. He looked at my arm, then at his own.

"Have you a tape measure?" he asked.

I brought one out of my work-basket. He measured his arm, then mine, and then the distance from the cat-door to the hook.

"I have two tasks for you to-day and to-morrow," he said. "I shall come here very little. Find all your father's old letters, and read them. Find a man or woman in this town whose arm is six inches longer than yours. Now I must go home, or my boarding-mistress will get curious."

He went through the house to the front door, looked all ways to be sure no eyes were upon him, made three strides down the yard, and was pacing soberly up the street, with his cyclopædia under his arm.

I made myself a cup of coffee, then I went about obeying his instructions. I read old letters all the forenoon; I found packages in trunks in the garret; there were quantities in father's desk. I have selected several to submit to Mr. Dix. One of them treats of an old episode in father's youth, which must have years since ceased to interest him. It was concealed after his favourite fashion—tacked under the bottom of his desk. It was written forty years ago, by Maria Woods, two years before my father's marriage—and it was a refusal of an offer of his hand. It was written in the stilted fashion of that day; it might have been copied from a "Complete Letter-writer."

My father must have loved Maria Woods as dearly as I love Henry, to keep that letter so carefully all these years. I thought he cared for my mother. He seemed as fond of her as other men of their wives, although I did use to wonder if Henry and I would ever get to be quite so much accustomed to each other.

Maria Woods must have been as beautiful as an angel when she was a girl. Mother was not pretty; she was stout, too, and awkward, and I suppose people would have called her rather slow and dull. But she was a good woman, and tried to do her duty.

Tuesday night.—This evening was my first opportunity to obey the second of Mr. Dix's orders. It seemed to me the best way to compare the average length of arms was to go to the prayer-meeting. I could not go about the town with my tape measure, and demand of people that they should hold out their arms. Nobody knows how I dreaded to go to the meeting, but I went, and I looked not at my neighbours' cold altered faces, but at their arms.

I discovered what Mr. Dix wished me to, but the discovery can avail nothing, and it is one he could have made himself. Phœbe Dole's arm is fully seven inches longer than mine. I never noticed it before, but she has an almost abnormally long arm. But why should Phœbe Dole have unhooked that door?

She made a prayer—a beautiful prayer. It comforted even me a little. She spoke of the tenderness of God in all the troubles of life, and how it never failed us.

When we were all going out I heard several persons speak of Mr. Dix and his Biblical Cyclopædia. They decided that he was a theological student, book-canvassing to defray the expenses of his education.

Maria Woods was not at the meeting. Several asked Phœbe how she was, and she replied, "Not very well."

It is very late. I thought Mr. Dix might be over to-night, but he has not been here.

Wednesday.—I can scarcely believe what I am about to write. Our investigations seem to point all to one person, and that person—— It is incredible! I will not believe it.

Mr. Dix came as before, at dawn. He reported, and I reported. I showed Maria Woods's letter. He said he had driven to Acton, and found that the jeweller there had engraved the last date in the ring about six weeks ago.

"I don't want to seem rough, but your father was going to get married again," said Mr. Dix.

"I never knew him to go near any woman since mother died," I protested.

"Nevertheless, he had made arrangements to be married," persisted Mr. Dix.

"Who was the woman?"

He pointed at the letter in my hand.

"Maria Woods!"

He nodded.

I stood looking at him—dazed. Such a possibility had never entered my head.

He produced an envelope from his pocket, and took out a little card with blue and brown threads neatly wound upon it.

"Let me see those threads you found," he said.

I got the box and we compared them. He had a number of pieces of blue sewing-silk and brown woollen ravellings, and they matched mine exactly.

"Where did you find them?" I asked.

"In my boarding-mistress's piece-bag."

I stared at him.

"What does it mean?" I gasped out.

"What do you think?"

"It is impossible!"

CHAPTER VI

THE REVELATION

Wednesday, continued.—When Mr. Dix thus suggested to me the absurd possibility that Phœbe Dole had committed the murder, he and I were sitting in the kitchen. He was near the table; he laid a sheet of paper upon it, and began to write. The paper is before me.

"First," said Mr. Dix, and he wrote rapidly as he talked, "whose arm is of such length that it might unlock a certain door of this house from the outside?—Phœbe Dole's.

"Second, who had in her piece-bag bits of the same threads and ravellings found upon your parlour floor, where she had not by your knowledge entered?—Phœbe Dole.

"Third, who interested herself most strangely in your blood-stained green silk dress, even to dyeing it?—Phœbe Dole.

"Fourth, who was caught in a lie, while trying to force the guilt of the murder upon an innocent man?—Phœbe Dole."

Mr. Dix looked at me. I had gathered myself together.

"That proves nothing," I said. "There is no motive in her case."

"There is a motive."

"What is it?"

"Maria Woods shall tell you this afternoon."

He then wrote—

"Fifth, who was seen to throw a bundle down the old well,

in the rear of Martin Fairbanks's house, at one o'clock in the morning?—Phœbe Dole."

"Was she—seen?" I gasped.

Mr. Dix nodded. Then he wrote.

"Sixth, who had a strong motive, which had been in existence many years ago?—Phœbe Dole."

Mr. Dix laid down his pen, and looked at me again.

"Well, what have you to say?" he asked.

"It is impossible!"

"Why?"

"She is a woman."

"A man could have fired that pistol, as she tried to do."

"It would have taken a man's strength to kill with the kind of weapon that was used," I said.

"No, it would not. No great strength is required for such a blow."

"But she is a woman!"

"Crime has no sex."

"But she is a good woman—a church member. I heard her pray yesterday afternoon. It is not in character."

"It is not for you, nor for me, nor for any mortal intelligence, to know what is or is not in character," said Mr. Dix.

He arose and went away. I could only stare at him in a half-dazed manner.

Maria Woods came this afternoon, taking advantage of Phœbe's absence on a dress-making errand. Maria has aged ten years in the last few weeks. Her hair is white, her cheeks are fallen in, her pretty colour is gone.

"May I have the ring he gave me forty years ago?" she faltered.

I gave it to her; she kissed it and sobbed like a child.

"Phœbe took it away from me before," she said; "but she shan't this time."

Maria related with piteous sobs the story of her long subordination to Phœbe Dole. This sweet child-like woman had always been completely under the sway of the other's stronger nature. The subordination went back beyond my father's original proposal to her; she had, before he made love to her as a girl, promised Phœbe she would not marry; and it was Phœbe who, by representing to her that she was bound by this solemn promise, had led her to write a letter to my father declining his offer, and sending back the ring.

"And after all, we were going to get married, if he had not died," she said. "He was going to give me this ring again, and he had had the other date put in. I should have been so happy!"

She stopped and stared at me with horror-stricken inquiry.

"What was Phœbe Dole doing in your backyard at one o'clock that night?" she cried.

"What do you mean?" I returned.

"I saw Phœbe come out of your back shed door at one o'clock that very night. She had a bundle in her arms. She went along the path about as far as the old well, then she stooped down, and seemed to be working at something. When she got up she didn't have the bundle. I was watching at our back door. I thought I heard her go out a little while before, and went downstairs, and found that door unlocked. I went in quick, and up to my chamber, and into my bed, when she started home across the fields. Pretty soon I heard her come in, then I heard the pump going. She slept downstairs; she went on to her bedroom. What was she doing in your backyard that night?"

"You must ask her," said I. I felt my blood running cold.

"I've been afraid to," moaned Maria Woods. "She's been dreadful strange lately. I wish that book agent was going to stay at our house."

Maria Woods went home in about an hour. I got a ribbon for her, and she has my poor father's ring concealed in her withered bosom. Again I cannot believe this.

Thursday.—It is all over, Phœbe Dole has confessed! I do not know now in exactly what way Mr. Dix brought it about—how he accused her of her crime. After breakfast I saw them coming across the fields; Phœbe came first, advancing with rapid strides like a man, Mr. Dix followed, and my father's poor old sweetheart tottered behind, with her handkerchief at her eyes. Just as I noticed them the front door bell rang; I found several people there, headed by the high sheriff. They crowded into the sitting-room just as Phœbe Dole came rushing in, with Mr. Dix and Maria Woods.

"I did it!" Phœbe cried out to me. "I am found out, and I have made up my mind to confess. She was going to marry your father—I found it out. I stopped it once before. This time I knew I couldn't unless I killed him. She's lived with me in that house for over forty years. There are other ties as strong as the marriage one, that are just as sacred. What right had he to take her away from me and break up my home?

"I overheard your father and Rufus Bennett having words. I thought folks would think he did it. I reasoned it all out. I had watched your cat go in that little door, I knew the shed door hooked, I knew how long my arm was; I thought I could undo it. I stole over here a little after midnight. I went all around the house to be sure nobody was awake. Out in the front yard I happened to think my shears were tied on my belt with a ribbon, and I untied them. I thought I put the ribbon in my pocket—it was a piece of yellow ribbon—but I suppose I didn't, because they found it afterwards, and thought it came off your young man's whip.

"I went round to the shed door, unhooked it, and went in. The moon was light enough. I got out your father's overalls from the kitchen closet; I knew where they were. I went through the sitting-room to the parlour.

"In there I slipped off my dress and skirts and put on the overalls. I put a handkerchief over my face, leaving only my eyes exposed. I crept out then into the sitting-room; there I pulled off my shoes and went into the bedroom.

"Your father was fast asleep; it was such a hot night, the clothes were thrown back and his chest was bare. The first thing I saw was that pistol on the stand beside his bed. I suppose he had had some fear of Rufus Bennett coming back, after all. Suddenly I thought I'd better shoot him. It would be surer and quicker; and if you were aroused I knew that I could get away, and everybody would suppose that he had shot himself.

"I took up the pistol and held it close to his head. I had never fired a pistol, but I knew how it was done. I pulled, but it would not go off. Your father stirred a little—I was mad with horror—I struck at his head with the pistol. He opened his eyes and cried out; then I dropped the pistol, and took these"—Phœbe Dole pointed to the great shining shears hanging at her waist—"for I am strong in my wrists. I only struck twice, over his heart.

"Then I went back into the sitting-room. I thought I heard a noise in the kitchen—I was full of terror then—and slipped into the sitting-room closet. I felt as if I were fainting, and clutched the shelf to keep from falling.

"I felt that I must go upstairs to see if you were asleep, to be sure you had not waked up when your father cried out. I thought if you had I should have to do the same by you. I crept upstairs to your chamber. You seemed sound asleep, but, as I watched, you stirred a little; but instead of striking at you I slipped into your closet. I heard nothing more from you. I felt myself wet with blood. I caught something hanging in your closet, and wiped myself over with it. I knew by the feeling it was your green silk. You kept quiet, and I saw you were asleep, so crept out of the closet, and down the stairs, got my clothes and shoes, and, out in the shed, took off the overalls and dressed myself. I rolled up the overalls, and took a board away from the old well and threw them in as I went home. I thought if they were found it would be no clue to me. The handkerchief, which was not much stained, I put to soak that night, and washed it out next morning, before Maria was up. I washed my hands and arms carefully that night, and also my shears.

"I expected Rufus Bennett would be accused of the murder, and, maybe, hung. I was prepared for that, but I did not like to think I had thrown suspicion upon you by staining your dress. I had nothing against you. I made up my mind I'd get hold of that dress—before anybody suspected you—and dye it black. I came in and got it, as you know. I was astonished not to see any more stains on it. I only found two or three little streaks that scarcely anybody would have noticed. I didn't know what to think. I suspected, of course, that you had found the stains and got them off, thinking they might bring suspicion upon you.

"I did not see how you could possibly suspect me in any case. I was glad when your young man was cleared. I had nothing against him. That is all I have to say."

I think I must have fainted away then. I cannot describe the dreadful calmness with which that woman told this—that woman with the good face, whom I had last heard praying like a saint in meeting. I believe in demoniacal possession after this.

When I came to, the neighbours were around me, putting camphor on my head, and saying soothing things to me, and the old friendly faces had returned. But I wish I could forget!

They have taken Phœbe Dole away—I only know that. I cannot bear to talk any more about it when I think there must be a trial, and I must go!

Henry has been over this evening. I suppose we shall be happy after all, when I have had a little time to get over this. He says I have nothing more to worry about. Mr. Dix has gone home. I hope Henry and I may be able to repay his kindness some day.

A month later. I have just heard that Phœbe Dole has died in prison. This is my last entry. May God help all other innocent women in hard straits as He has helped me!

KATE CHOPIN

*Human impulses do not change and can not so long as
men and women continue to stand in the relation to one
another which they have occupied since our knowledge
of their existence began.* [*]

Kate O'Flaherty Chopin (1850–1904) was born and lived all but
fourteen years of her life in St. Louis, where she was educated at
the Sacred Heart Academy. Her closest friend and schoolmate,
Kitty Garesche, abruptly became a nun the same year (1870) that
Kate married Oscar Chopin, six years her senior.

For the twelve years of her marriage, during which six children
(five sons, one daughter) were born, Kate lived with her cotton
merchant husband in Louisiana—first in New Orleans and later in
Cloutierville, Natchitoches Parish, northwest Louisiana. After Oscar's death, Kate ran his business for a year, had a notorious romance with a married man, and then suddenly returned to her

---

[*] Kate Chopin, in a review of Hamlin Garland's *Crumbling Idols* (Chicago, 1894),
in *The Complete Works of Kate Chopin*, ed. Per Seyersted, Baton Rouge, 1969, p.
79.

mother's home in St. Louis, where she was surrounded by the largely female world of her growing-up years: relatives, friends, and schoolmates.

Not long after her mother's death, Chopin embarked on a professional writing career. Although her first publications were a polka and a poem (1888–89), Chopin early recognized that "local color" was the most popular kind of fiction being written, the work for which the readiest market existed. Hence, she rarely wrote about St. Louis and its citizens: those stories did not find an enthusiastic audience. Chopin rapidly developed into a professional writer—which means that she had to take markets and audience preferences into consideration when she took up her pen. It is all the more to her credit that she was able to meet the public with her personal message on grounds that satisfied both her own artistic goals and her readers' appetites.

By 1895 she had published more than forty stories and had broken into the most esteemed literary magazines, such as the *Century* and *Vogue*. Chopin's two books of short stories, *Bayou Folk* (1894) and *A Night in Acadie* (1897), were widely praised as examples of local color; most of the stories dealt with the Creoles, Cajuns, and African-Americans of Louisiana.

Chopin used her Louisiana Creole, Cajun, and black characters as disguises for general cultural critiques. She was able to say things about women's lives in general in the guise of describing the lives of women who were part of a very small, self-contained, and "ethnic" population. Moreover, as her biographer Emily Toth has pointed out, Chopin often drew on real people, including the lover she left behind in Louisiana, for some of the most vibrant characters in her fiction.

Much of Chopin's work deals with women struggling with their desires to define and control their lives, especially intellectually and sexually. In St. Louis she maintained a salon and her son Felix later described her close friends as "pink-red liberals"; the "radical" nature of her work that espoused women's need to have meaningful work must have met with a certain encouragement and approbation among her liberal entourage. However, few were as willing to accept with the same liberal éclat a woman's sexual freedom.

Unlike the New England local colorists, Chopin had a dual

cultural heritage. She had a French background: she was bilingual and read many of the realistic and naturalistic French writers, such as her model Guy de Maupassant, in the original language. In Cloutierville, she lived in a village where French was virtually the only spoken language. However she was also an American, a Midwesterner who had lived through the Civil War in a slave state, and whose parents had owned slaves. In many ways, she was an outsider wherever she lived.

Although set in Louisiana and drawing most directly on her passionate experiences there, Chopin's first novel, *At Fault* (1890), was not successful. But her second, *The Awakening* (1899), is now considered one of the major works of the nineteenth century. It represents a synthesis of the work accomplished by writers throughout the century who were attempting to portray women as individuals defined by their own needs, perceptions, and abilities rather than by their relationships with men or children.

However, in its time, *The Awakening* received very hostile criticism from powerful reviewers and editors. Although women readers celebrated the book and invited Chopin to present her work at their clubs, the men who were the gatekeepers for her literary future refused to accept her strongest statement on women's roles and possibilities. Losing heart, and ailing at the turn of the century, Chopin wrote only about a dozen more stories before her death.

A Vocation and a Voice, her third short story collection, had been scheduled for publication in 1900, but the publisher canceled it after the furor over *The Awakening.* That collection was to include "The Falling in Love of Fedora" and other very unusual stories of passion, decadence, sensuality, and illicit drugs. It finally appeared, edited by Emily Toth, in 1991.

Chopin wrote "The Falling in Love of Fedora" in 1895 but did not publish it until February 20, 1897, in the *St. Louis Criterion,* an avant-garde periodical. Like many of her more experimental or unusual stories, it had been difficult to place: it was rejected by the *Atlantic Monthly,* for instance, because the magazine's editor felt it had "scarcely any story at all."

Perhaps because its central character somewhat resembles

Florence Hayward, a St. Louis journalist, it was published under a pen name, "La Tour." (Chopin published one other story under the same pseudonym: "Miss McEnders," a scathing personal attack on St. Louis capitalists.)

There has been very little comment about "The Falling in Love of Fedora" from Chopin scholars, although there has been the claim that it is really "about" displaced heterosexuality. Perhaps it is "about" a woman who has been torn between her love of independence and self-possession and her desire for intimacy and sensual pleasure. Fedora realizes that to have pleasure with a man is to lose power over her own life. However, having discovered that women are also available for sensual pleasure she realizes that she doesn't necessarily have to choose between intimacy and autonomy. Or is the story about something else?

The Falling in Love of Fedora: A Sketch

Fedora had determined upon driving over to the station herself for Miss Malthers.

Though one or two of them looked disappointed—notably her brother—no one opposed her. She said the brute was restive, and shouldn't be trusted to the handling of the young people.

To be sure Fedora was old enough, from the standpoint of her sister Camilla and the rest of them. Yet no one would ever have thought of it but for her own persistent affectation and idiotic assumption of superior years and wisdom. She was thirty.

Fedora had too early in life formed an ideal and treasured it. By this ideal she had measured such male beings as had hitherto challenged her attention, and needless to say she had found them wanting. The young people—her brothers' and sisters' guests, who were constantly coming and going that summer—occupied her to a great extent, but failed to interest her. She concerned herself with their comforts—in the absence of her mother—looked after their health and well-being; contrived for their amusements, in which she never joined. And, as Fedora was tall and slim, and carried her head loftily, and wore eye-glasses and a severe expression, some of them—the silliest—felt as if she were a hundred years old. Young Malthers thought she was about forty.

One day when he stopped before her out in the gravel walk to ask her some question pertaining to the afternoon's sport, Fedora, who was tall, had to look up into his face to answer him. She had known him eight years, since he was a lad of fifteen, and to her he had never been other than the lad of fifteen.

But that afternoon, looking up into his face, the sudden realization came home to her that he was a man—in voice, in attitude, in bearing, in every sense—a man.

In an absorbing glance, and with unaccountable intention, she gathered in every detail of his countenance as though it were a strange, new thing to her, presenting itself to her vision for the first time. The eyes were blue, earnest, and at the moment a little troubled over some trivial affair that he was relating to her. The face was brown from the sun, smooth, with no suggestion of ruddiness, except in the lips, that were strong, firm and clean. She kept thinking of his face, and every trick of it after he passed on.

From that moment he began to exist for her. She looked at him when he was near by, she listened for his voice, and took notice and account of what he said. She sought him out; she selected him when occasion permitted. She wanted him by her, though his nearness troubled her. There was uneasiness, restlessness, expectation when he was not there within sight or sound. There was redoubled uneasiness when he was by—there was inward revolt, astonishment, rapture, self-contumely; a swift, fierce encounter betwixt thought and feeling.

Fedora could hardly explain to her own satisfaction why she wanted to go herself to the station for young Malthers' sister. She felt a desire to see the girl, to be near her; as unaccountable, when she tried to analyze it, as the impulse which drove her, and to which she often yielded, to touch his hat, hanging with others upon the hall pegs, when she passed it by. Once a coat which he had discarded hung there too. She handled it under pretense of putting it in order. There was no one near, and, obeying a sudden impulse, she buried her face for an instant in the rough folds of the coat.

Fedora reached the station a little before train time. It was in a pretty nook, green and fragrant, set down at the foot of a wooded hill. Off in a clearing there was a field of yellow grain, upon which the sinking sunlight fell in slanting, broken beams. Far down the track there were some men at work, and the even ring of their hammers was the only sound that broke upon the stillness. Fedora loved it all—sky and woods and sunlight; sounds and smells. But her bearing—elegant, composed, reserved—betrayed nothing emotional as she tramped the narrow platform, whip in hand, and occasionally offered a condescending word to the mail man or the sleepy agent.

Malthers' sister was the only soul to disembark from the train. Fedora had never seen her before; but if there had been a hundred, she would have known the girl. She was a small thing; but aside from that, there was the coloring; there were the blue, earnest eyes; there, above all, was the firm, full curve of the lips; the same setting of the white, even teeth. There was the subtle play of feature, the elusive trick of expression, which she had thought peculiar and individual in the one, presenting themselves as family traits.

The suggestive resemblance of the girl to her brother was vivid, poignant even to Fedora, realizing, as she did with a pang, that familiarity and custom would soon blur the image.

Miss Malthers was a quiet, reserved creature, with little to say. She had been to college with Camilla, and spoke somewhat of their friendship and former intimacy. She sat lower in the cart than Fedora, who drove, handling whip and rein with accomplished skill.

"You know, dear child," said Fedora, in her usual elderly fashion, "I want you to feel completely at home with us." They were driving through a long, quiet, leafy road, into which the twilight was just beginning to creep. "Come to me freely and without reserve—with all your wants; with any complaints. I feel that I shall be quite fond of you."

She had gathered the reins into one hand, and with the other free arm she encircled Miss Malthers' shoulders.

180 of KATE CHOPIN

When the girl looked up into her face, with murmured thanks, Fedora bent down and pressed a long, penetrating kiss upon her mouth.

Malthers' sister appeared astonished, and not too well pleased. Fedora, with seemingly unruffled composure, gathered the reins, and for the rest of the way stared steadily ahead of her between the horses' ears.

ALICE BROWN

In every period of intense moral or intellectual life, there
are scores of men [sic] of whom not even the scholar takes
cognizance. The moment of England's great dramatic
blossoming is, to the million, Shakespeare's day and that
only. They agree to recognize him alone, as if he had
sprung, in isolated magnificence, from a soil nourishing
no undergrowth; they leave untouched by a glance the
stems that flourished about him only to be obscured.
. . . But let it be remembered that, as the great are but
the embodied spirit of their age, so the great who do not
absolutely "arrive" (according to that many-headed monster, the crowd) are exponents of that spirit also.*

Alice Brown (1856–1948), a New Englander who was one of the
most acclaimed short story writers in the U.S. during the peak years
of her literary career, has been lost to readers for many decades.
Although her brilliant stories were identified as among the best of
those labeled "local color," she wrote during the years of declining

---

* Alice Brown, *Mercy Warren*, Charles Scribner's Sons, New York, 1896, p. 32.

interest in literary regionalism. Despite inclusion in a few collections of local color fiction, she has presented difficulties for the literary historian. Although the best were written in the early twentieth century, her stories seem to belong to the nineteenth because of their style and focus. She often wrote about middle-aged and older women who had lived the first half of their lives in rural settings during the nineteenth century. Because their communities valued older women and maintained a place and a role for them, their lives were not significantly different from women of earlier generations. Lives begun in the middle of the old century ended close to the middle of the new, but their flavor remained unchanged.

Many of Brown's stories focus on women in community and in communication with each other, very often across the generations. She depicts young women as willing disciples to their mothers, grandmothers, or other chosen mentors in those generations. It is a spiritual discipleship in peace, grace, and joy. The greatest love in the lives of these women, the most significant "other," is often a woman of an older generation. And, of course, the model couple in this scheme is that of mother and daughter.

Alice Brown wrote about a world in which women were free to love each other, uninhibited by the new Freudian theories that had begun to reach the consciousness of the educated and artistic. Brown was familiar with these ideas; however, her female couples, whether mother and daughter or friends, live with, delight in, and love each other despite them.

Brown left little information about her family and her girlhood in New Hampshire. The younger of two children, she was born in Hampton Falls, New Hampshire, and grew up on her parents' farm. At the age of fourteen, she finished with the local school and began her years at the Robinson Seminary, a "ladies" academy, to and from which she trekked four miles each way daily till she graduated in 1876. After several years of teaching in various small towns—a job she grew to hate more and more—she left behind all the certainties she had ever known to move to Boston. She was determined to make her way in the world of letters, and she did.

She spent her professional literary life as a respected member of a community of creative women nurtured by Annie Adams

Fields (1834–1915), founder of a great and influential literary salon in Boston, wife and advisor of James Fields (one of the most prominent publishers in the United States and founding editor of the *Atlantic Monthly*), and, after her husband's death, partner in a "Boston Marriage" with Sarah Orne Jewett. Among the members of the group of writers whose center was Annie Adams Fields' salon were Sarah Orne Jewett, Mary E. Wilkins Freeman, Elizabeth Stuart Phelps, Harriet Prescott Spofford, Helen Hunt Jackson, and Louise Imogen Guiney.

Louise Imogen Guiney was a central figure in Alice Brown's life. The Irish Catholic poet was born in Boston but, unable to make an adequate living in the United States, moved to England permanently in 1900. She died there in 1920. After a first trip together to England in 1886, the two women founded the Women's Rest Tour Association "to encourage other women to take their vacations as they had, with pack and stick, in foreign lands." It was Guiney's influence that led Brown in her later years to enter into serious study of Catholicism, although she never converted.

Brown published seventeen novels, four volumes of plays, three of poetry, and four miscellaneous volumes of criticism, personal essays, and works for children during her career, which began in the early 1890s and continued for close to half a century. But it is the one hundred fifteen stories collected in eight volumes that merit the claims of literary greatness. She is the inheritor of the literary tradition of Catharine Maria Sedgwick, Lydia Maria Child, Harriet Beecher Stowe, and the great "regionalists" who befriended her as a young writer and welcomed her to their sisterhood as their youngest colleague.

Although Brown may never have been affiliated with any segment of the women's movement, her commitment to personal integrity in her own life and in the lives of her fictional characters led to frequent depictions of women who grow from complacent acceptance of the rule of generally well-intentioned males to active control of their own lives. In her personal life, the steady development and guardianship of all her own resources—intellectual, physical, economic, and spiritual—define her as a determined opponent of the ages-old patriarchal theft of women's resources.

Brown's work contains frequent celebrations of the natural world and of the life of the spirit.

"There and Here," first published in *Harper's Magazine* in October 1897, affirms a connection between this world and the next world. The story was collected in her 1904 volume, *High Noon* (Houghton Mifflin and Co.).

All eight volumes of Brown's short stories have been reprinted in recent years. They are: *Meadow-Grass: Tales of New England Life* (1895), *Tiverton Tales* (1899), *High Noon* (1904), *The County Road* (1906), *Country Neighbors* (1910), *Vanishing Points* (1913), *The Flying Teuton* (1918), and *Homespun and Gold* (1920).

There and Here

Perhaps Ruth Hollis was no more conscious at one time than another of her loneliness and heart-hunger for Rosamond Ware, the friend of her childhood, and, indeed, her entire life. It was an ever-present pain—not poignant now, but grown into that emptiness of loss which attends a broken kinship. Ruth had lived for her thirty-one years in the standstill, colonial-flavored town of Devonport. Rosamond, on the death of her father, mother, and two brothers in the space of a week, had gone to Italy to be with an older brother, a man with a jangled body and a tempered artist soul. That had not been altogether desirable, for the very fineness of his nature imposed its limitations, and he exacted much, even while he gave. She had been there eight years, from month to month prophesying her return, but never being quite able to effect it. Her unwilling feet would not drag themselves back to America. She longed for it, she brooded over shivered associations with a passionate regret, but when the moment came for clasping the lax link again, cowardice shot up in her and cried off. Her grief was poignant enough already; when she thought of voluntarily sharpening its edge, the apprehensive nerves rebelled. The house at Devonport had been given her by will, and now it was standing exactly as the family tragedy left it. The unworn garments in the closets could hardly fall more absolute prey to mice and moth; they were in ruins already. But daily the dust and mildew of time wrote a sadder record on the blurring page, and the inexorable master of all spurred himself to show what havoc he could compass, left to his own cruel will. Again and again Ruth wrote her friend, begging her to have the house opened, aired, and cleaned; not for the sake of thrift only, she urged, but because the place was dear to both of them. There they had played together at mimic living, and loved and dreamed after living began. It was her home too, according to spiritual tenure, and she had a right to speak. But Rosamond always answered, "Not yet!" Time had rent her web of life, and she was still too selfish to enlarge the rift made in the nature of things.

One late twilight, in an ice-bound spring, Ruth was wandering about the rooms of her own home, setting them in order by an observant touch here and there, and making ready to close the house for the night. The rest of the family had gone, on sudden summons, to spend a day or two with an uncle twenty miles away, whose prodigal son had come home, and who thus bade all his accessible kin to the rejoicing. Ruth, for no tangible reason, had been disinclined to go; as the day drew nearer, her unwillingness increased, and at the very last she refused entirely, promising to spend the night and the next day with Aunt Barnard, a mile's distance out of the town. The two maids, having been given sudden holiday, had already fastened their domain and departed. Ruth meant every minute to follow them, but the house so wooed her in its simmering afternoon warmth that she still lingered and dallied with her purpose. The fires were dying safely down, but there was a red glow in every room. The scented geraniums were sweet from the windows, and the stillness seemed benignant. At length, unable to conjure up more excuses for idling, she did get on her hat and cloak, and stood fastening the last button before the front window, where the snow lay dead white, and the great chestnut-tree stretched gaunt arms against the darkening blue. She stopped, with an arrested motion, in putting on her gloves. Some one was coming. It was a woman, walking very fast, yet very lightly, with a buoyant motion Ruth seemed to know. She wore a flowing cloak, and a great hat with a long feather. Ruth watched her with a tightening at her throat and a straining of the eyes. She came nearer, stopped, and waved her hand. It was growing dark so fast that a tangible veil seemed falling between them, but Ruth was sure she smiled.

"Rose!" she called wildly from the window. "Rosamond! Rosamond!"

The woman nodded. Ruth tore out of the front door, dropping her gloves behind her, and ran down the path. Now the new-comer was laughing, and Ruth felt a sudden passionate relief at the sweet familiarity of the sound. She began to see, in that instant, what her loneliness had been. She sobbed a little.

"I don't believe it," she whispered. "You are not really *you*!"

"That's your impudence," said Rosamond. "As if I'd take the trouble to be anybody else!"

They were walking into the house together, side by side and hand in hand. Ruth never knew whether they had kissed or not. It was quite likely they had not, for Rosamond was an elusive creature, who held that there are few moments when the soul is the better for the body's sacrament. Inside, the dark had fallen thick.

"Let me get a lamp," said Ruth, again with a little sob of joy completed. "I want to see you."

"No, Grandmother Wolf, not to-night. You're going over to the house with me."

Ruth turned back from the table and let her match burn out.

"Not to-night, dear," she entreated. "It's cold. It's—awful! You would break your heart."

"Ah, say yes!" coaxed Rosamond, in her old spoiled fashion. "Just to step inside and see whether we want to stay. Just to peep in. Why, Ruth, it's *home*!"

But while she spoke she was at the door, and Ruth was following her, saying, martyrwise:

"You'll have your way, of course. It's to be expected; but I do wish you wouldn't. Wait till morning, Rose. Only till the fires are built."

Rosamond laughed lightly and happily.

"Not an hour. Not a minute. Come, shut that door, and race me to the old stump. No letters in it now."

The door banged behind them, and they ran together down the frozen drive. Rose was mad with glee. She sped like a stream of darkness, softly, glidingly. She was first at the stump, and she stayed there till Ruth came up, panting.

"Over the crust now," she laughed, in a bright exhilaration.

"Come! come!" But though she ran in little dashes, and waited between, Ruth, making what shift she could to follow, crashed through and gave it up.

"Come back!" she called. "You're a fay. I'm a good twenty pounds heavier. That's according to precedent. Don't you see, it won't bear?"

But Rosamond skimmed back like a leaf, and then they went on soberly, side by side again. Ruth kept turning to look at her.

"You certainly are changed," said she; "but, oh, you're so pretty! You've got a radiance! You seem to shine! Are you my old chum?"

"Your old chum, your pal in vulgar moments, your Rose to keep."

"Then don't you wither!"

Rosamond laughed again, with that thrilling undercurrent more significant than mirth.

"I may be transplanted," said she, "but wither, no! See the little twigs pricking through the crust! Hear the tips of the pine-trees talking! Oh, what a world! what a world!"

"How you enjoy! Exactly like your old apostrophes, 'hot and hot'! You're the most universal lover I know. You're the moon that looks on many brooks. Berries? How ever do you manage to see them in this light? But then, you always were owl-eyed and cat-footed."

It was only a short stretch of road to the Ware homestead, and then a long driveway wound up through the grounds. There the thick evergreens, untrimmed for many years, so encroached upon the way that they half sheltered it from snow, and made it still accessible. Rosamond kept darting into the fir woods, to return laden with news.

"Do you remember how we used to gather cones and burn them on the Anvil Rock? The pines are full. And the hollow locust where we found the squirrel's nest? Nobody has touched it since that day, and his greatest-great-grandson lives there now. Do you remember how we used to do up nuts in our hair, and sit under the tree to let him pull them out? The hepaticas on the bank are in such a temper—you can't think! They're waked up and ready to sprout, and there's no encouragement."

"That's according to the light of the spirit. Even you can't see

under the snow, Sharp Eyes!" Ruth spoke from the dreamy acquiescence born of full content. She knew quite well that they
ought not to be going by night into a deserted house, but Rosamond's assurance had lulled her will to sleep. She was penetrated
by the wonder of seeing this dearest creature in the world, whom
she had pictured broken and desolate, so lightsome and free of
care; she had not thought beyond the happy relief.

The last sweep of the driveway brought them out in front of
the old house, spacious and still imposing, though so evidently the
subject of a lingering death. Ruth paused an instant, not daring to
look into her friend's face, and only guessing what grief must be
painted there. But Rosamond dropped her arm and ran up the
steps alone.

"Welcome home!" she called, blithely. "Welcome! Why do
you wait?"

Ruth had stopped now in a detaining after-thought. "We're
simpletons," said she. "The key is at the Daytons', where you left
it. That's a sign we're not to go in. Come back, dear, and wait till
morning."

But Rosamond held her place. "Come up here, doubter," cried
she. "When was anything lost by trying? The oracle appears because you have previously besieged the shrine. Come on! There,
now. Shall I lift the latch? Shall I?"

It yielded with the old familiar click, and the great door swung
open. Ruth gave a joyous little cry.

"You witch, you've got the key already!" She put a hand on
Rosamond's cloak, in gentle suasion. "Let me go in first. Please! I
can't bear to have you feel how cold it is, with no one to welcome
you. Why, it's light!" An airy intangibility of warmth and fragrance poured out upon them like a river delayed and eager. The
odors were familiar and sweet—a mystic alembic made of the
breath of flowers, but so fused that you could never say which was
heliotrope and which the spice of pinks. They made up a sweetness
bewildering to the sense. "Oh!" she cried again; "enchantress!
Merlin and Ariel in one!"

Rosamond shut the door behind them. The spirit of a delicate
witchery was playing on her face while she led the way into the
front room on one side of the hall; this had been the family
meeting-place and talking-place in days gone by. It lay there smil-

ing, in happy renewal of the past. A fire flickered on the hearth
with the bourgeoning of new flame above old embers. The tall
clock ticked in measureless content. The firelight seemed to fill the
room. Ruth drew a long breath of rapturous recognition.

"How like you!" she murmured. "You came days ago, weeks
ago! You put it all in order—for me. But the intention isn't all.
Somebody else might have thought of it, but nobody could have
done it."

"So you like it? Then I'm glad."

Two chairs were ready before the blaze. They threw off their
wraps, and sank into the accustomed places. They sat for a time
in silence, while the clock ticked.

"Do you remember—" began Ruth.

"Yes; that was the last time we were here together. I was
telling you, over and over again, that the lonesome house would
kill me. I behaved like a child—an ignorant, untrained child."

"I won't hear you blamed. You were beside yourself."

"I was a child," repeated Rosamond, conclusively. "I can't
imagine any one so ignorant, so pathetic in ignorance. I told you
death denied the laws of life. I could only think of my mother in
her coffin. I was a savage."

Ruth turned and looked at her in the firelight. Her face lay
soft and lovely under a very happy seriousness. She seemed absolutely serene, with the well-being of out-door things, the pine-trees,
and the snow.

"Rosamond," said her friend, impulsively, "have you got
religion?"

Rosamond laughed out. "You are so droll!" she answered at
once. "I might as well ask, have you got air in your lungs? Have
you?"

"But you're so changed, and for the better. You've grown."

"I had to grow," said Rosamond, whimsically. "Part of it at
a jump! But let's not talk about finalities. There's one thing I meant
to write you about. I made my will, two months ago, and left this
house for a home for tired women. It's to be called the Margaret
Home—for my own mother, you know. It's to be for middle-aged,
tired women: their very own, so that they can come here from the
cities and rest. I have named you executor, but I wanted to speak
about it, too. There's nothing in particular to say, for you would

always know how I should like things; still, I thought it would be well to mention it."

Ruth drew nearer, in sudden fear; but the firelight, still playing over Rosamond's face, only brought out the wholesome tints of ruddy cheek and clear gray eye.

"You're not going to die?" She spoke with that poignant, foolish alarm ever "hid in the heart of love." Rosamond smiled straight into her eyes, and her strength and beauty seemed to diffuse a certain power like beams of light. Her voice thrilled through the ear to the heart:

"I'm not going to die. I am safe, contented, happy."

"I've often thought," began Ruth, hesitatingly—"I have hoped you would marry. I never expected you to be serene, a lone stick like me. You have such an appetite for joy! How could you be contented with that one glory left out?"

Rosamond did not answer at once, but the peace of her presence still made itself felt, and Ruth was sure she had not proved her too far.

"That is one of the things I meant to tell you to-night," she began, slowly, as if she had some difficulty in making her phrases fit. "It was not left out. Three years ago I met some one in Italy. He died, and so if I— In any case, I should never have married." Her voice was still musical and unmoved, and Ruth looked at her in amazement. There seemed to be nothing to say. Rosamond went on, broodingly: "You will be glad to know how perfect it was. We understood each other from the first. Whatever it may mean to say, 'I am yours—you are mine,' was true for us. It was when that feeling came that I began to understand life a little better. It was my alphabet. I never spoke about it to you because he died so soon after we found each other. And I didn't take it well. Then I was a child too." For the first time some remote sadness crept into her voice—a tinge of regret for a beauty missed. Ruth could not answer; she was beginning not to understand. Her friend seemed to speak from the state of one charged with a knowledge not to be shared.

"However," continued Rosamond, rousing herself and calling back her former lightness, "it's absurd to wish we had been better and braver and sweeter. What's done is done, and now—'the winter is past, the rain is over and gone.' "

Ruth dared probe her no further; she felt invisible barriers.

"Is this another of your witch ways?" she asked, with a grop-ing return to the tangible. "Flowers everywhere? I've been speerin' through the dark and naming them. That's golden-rod in the big jar at my feet; asters, too. Those are columbines on the mantel, and you've put mignonette and heliotrope on the table, just where they used to stand. Do you carry the magic lamp? In my day florists never brought the seasons quite together like righteousness and peace."

Rosamond put on a merry disdain.

"Magic lamp!" quoth she—"a kitchen cupboard full. You might as well learn now that lamps seem magical only when they're out of place. Come, old lady, isn't it your bedtime? Do you still go when it's dark under the table?"

"Yes, but not to-night! Still, I suppose we ought to be getting home. I hate to leave this fire. At least, let's take some of the flow-ers with us."

"With us, forsooth! We're going to stay here."

"No, child; not in mildewed beds! I draw my line at that."

Rosamond took both her hands and drew her up from the chair.

"Come and see!" she said. "The ocular proof! I scorn to ar-gue." She led the way out into the hall, and up the broad worn stairs. Ruth followed, like a child.

"I'm a coward, and you know it," said she. "But to-night I'm not afraid. I wouldn't have believed I could be induced to stay till this hour in a deserted house with only sweet you to protect me. But here I am, and here 'I means to stick,' if you say so."

The spacious hall above was peopled with playing lights and moving shadows. The clock on the landing ticked with ancient peace. The firelight came smiling and beckoning from the two op-posite rooms at the head of the stairs. Ruth, speechless, stepped into one chamber and then the other. The fires blazed opulently; the beds were ready, turned down in the V shape both girls had learned from their mothers; it seemed to belong to their childhood together.

"Are we going to stay here?" Ruth cried. "Here together? Why, it's like Christmas! It's like heaven!"

"Into bed with you! I'm going down, but I'll come back again presently and tuck you up. And—if you lie still, like a good little lady, I'll tell you a story."

Ruth began throwing off her clothes in haste.

"Rosamond," she called blithely after her, "cover up the sitting-room fire. We forgot the fender."

So much of life is a barren gleaning after the true harvest! Little broken impressions, scintillæ of feeling, stay floating about in the memory, and happy is he who can fit them into some sort of a patch-work when days are bare again. Ruth was never so happy, so well content, she remembered afterwards, as when, with an absorbing delight in physical well-being, and a charming sense of the new and absolutely desirable, she made ready for bed, stopping here and there as she moved about the room to greet some ancient treasure with a murmur of delight. There was the red cow with one horn; they had milked her daily in other times. There were the wax flowers they had tried to imitate; but, alas! poor little handmaids, because they worked surreptitiously, with the curious secretiveness of childhood, they had no instruction, and no material save the beeswax in their mothers' work-baskets, chewed into wads by their patient teeth. There, oh joy! was Miranda, the oldest doll of all, with her abbreviated skirt and long pantalettes, sitting woodenly in a corner, quite unmoved by this strange, bright resurrection. Ruth gave her a kiss in passing—a passionate kiss for the sake of former days. She took a handful of sweet-pease from the bunch on the mantel and dropped them in Miranda's lap. Joy was cheap enough to share. Then she slipped into bed and waited. Rosamond came. She placed a chair by the bedside, and seating herself, drew Ruth's hand into hers.

"Once upon a time—" she began.

"Did you cover up the fire?"

"It's all right. Once upon a time there was a little Child, and he was always crying because he didn't know the difference between Here and There. He was always hating to be Here, and longing to be There. So one day a Strong One came and said to him, 'Come, you Silly Thing, you may go There if you want to.' And he set him on a feather of one of his wings and took him There. And There was a place you couldn't imagine if I should describe it to you. The best I can do is to say it was all flowers, and living odors, and pine-trees, and clear sunlight, and sweet winds. It's a place where everybody can be tucked up at night—"

"What makes you have any night?" asked Ruth, from her doze. "Have it all day!"

"Leave out the stars, the night dews, the counsel of the leaves! No; we must have night There. But There black is just as lovely as white; so it's all one. And the Child was happy at once, but the Strong One smiled, and said to him: 'It is always so. They are all happy at once, and they might have been before, if they had had eyes to see that Here is There and There is Here.' And the Child said—" But Ruth was soft asleep and breathing peacefully, and Rosamond smiled with great tenderness. Ruth remembered afterwards that Rosamond bent over her once to kiss her on the eyelids, but only to check herself and to draw back among the shadows.

The late moon was regnant in the chamber when she came broad awake. Rosamond was standing over her, one hand on hers.

"Oh, what made you wake me? what made you?" she cried, quite querulous in her loss. "I was dreaming such a dream! I was in a place I never saw—I can't describe it—I'm forgetting it now. But they were telling me something; the one thing, you know, that explains everything." She sat up in bed, and tried to grasp at the fleeting memory. "It's gone!" She was near crying as she said it. "I almost had the words, but they won't stay."

Rosamond paid no attention.

"Hurry!" she whispered. "Get up and dress. We are going over to your house now. Come!"

Ruth sprang out of bed, and mechanically laid hands on her clothing. She hesitated for a moment to study Rosamond's face.

"You're not frightened?" she asked. "What is it?"

"I've let you sleep too long, that's all. Don't question, my dear one. Come!"

She did, indeed, look pale, but something so sweet and comforting still hung about her and the smiling room that Ruth was not afraid. It did not come to her till afterwards that somebody—an alien somebody or something—might be in the house. Rosamond gave a quick little movement of relief when the last hook was fastened. She had Ruth's hat and cloak on her arm, and she pressed them upon her in eager haste. Then she threw her own cloak about her, and drew Ruth down the stairs. Ruth forgot to step cautiously lest they be heard; she remembered afterwards how her boots clicked, and the rustling of her dress. The fire still flick-ered in the sitting-room, and the air of the house exhaled a summer sweetness. Rosamond threw open the front door to an icy breath; she parted her lips and caught at it in sobbing relief.

"Ah," she sighed, "that's good!"

The door closed behind them, and they hurried away down the path. Rosamond swept on like a shadow, her cloak billowing behind her in the wind. A picture flashed before Ruth's vision of their coming, when they had hurried in play; now their haste was tragic.

"Rosamond!" she called, with all the breath left in her, "you've forgotten your hat. You'll get your death."

"Come! come!" called Rosamond, over her shoulder. "Hurry! hurry!"

"Then give me your hand. I can't keep up with you."

"Not now!"—her voice came back like a dying sound on the wind. "Hurry!"

They ran like fleeting clouds. Ruth was capable of more than she could have believed; but, fast as she sped, Rosamond was ever before her, a shapeless dusk in the moonlight.

"There, you mad thing—" Ruth began, as they reached her own door, but the urgency of haste clung to her, and she could not finish. She fitted the key to the lock and stood aside.

"Go in," breathed Rosamond, faintly. "Go in, dear one, dear one!"

Ruth stepped over the sill, and the door closed behind her. She turned and tugged at it with a sudden sense of loss. It would not yield. She put forth all her strength. "Rosamond," she called, "push! I can't move it!"

When the door opened, Ruth looked out on the sterile dusk of the early morning. The moon had gone down, and the earth seemed mourning her. And no one was there. She bent forward into the darkness. "Rosamond," she said. "Rosamond!"

There was no answer. A rustle came from the one oak-tree in the yard. Then there was silence, for the wind had died. In the midst of her gathering alarm a strange peace, a sense of the sweet-ness and naturalness of the world, fell upon her like a charm, and she smiled out into the darkness as if it had become a friendly face. Then, in serenity of soul, she thought it all out. Rosamond was ever a sprite; now she was playing her a trick. She had gone into the shrubbery to hide. Call, and she would not answer; leave her unnoticed, and a moment would bring her tapping at the window. She shut the door and went in. The rooms were still warm, though the hearth fires had died; and she took a fur cloak from the hall in passing, threw it about her, and sat down by the window to wait. And as she waited, the same lovely content of the evening stole over her again. She closed her eyes, and to a purring sense of spiritual warmth the dream began where it left off, and she learned the secret which explains everything. But she never could remember that dream.

She started awake with the sense of some one in the room. The fire was blazing up over new kindling; the sun lay warm on her shoulder. Her mother stood there, and the maid was bringing in wood. Ruth rubbed her eyes and worked her way out of her wraps.

"What a sleep!" she yawned. "Oh, I remember. But what made you come home?"

Her mother was looking at her very sadly. She took Ruth's hand. "I had to come," said she. "We've had bad news, and I didn't want you to hear it from any one else. Ruth, you must be brave. Rosamond died yesterday. They wired her aunt Amy from Italy."

Ruth regarded her with straining eyes. Then she began to laugh.

"My poor child," said her mother, beginning to rub the hand she held. Ruth drew it away.

"You mustn't, mummy, you mustn't," said she. "Don't be sorry for me. It isn't sad. It's lovely, only you don't know it. There's been a queer mistake. No, I won't tell you. Just come with me and I'll give you a surprise. Here's your shawl. Put it on." She threw it about her, found some gloves and pressed them upon her. Life seemed very dramatic since last night's prologue. She drew her mother along in merry haste; but at the door Mrs. Hollis left her for a moment to step back into the kitchen and whisper a word to Nora:

"Watch the way we go, and tell Mr. Hollis to follow us. Tell him I can't explain, but he must come."

Then she went out where Ruth was waiting, tapping her foot

impatiently, and scanning the path, the shrubbery, the road, lest she be caught herself by her own surprise. She ran an arm through her mother's, and hurried her down the walk. When they passed the stump post-office she laughed again; but her mother's quick look of pain recalled her.

"Poor mother!" she said, in a demure coaxing. "Wait a bit, and you'll laugh too. So Rosamond is dead?"

The tears came fast down her mother's cheeks.

"Yes, dead," she said. "You don't realize it."

Ruth tried hard to be serious.

"Not yet," she assented. "Just now you're realizing for two." They were rounding the curve of the drive. "But I don't see any smoke! The thriftless thing! she's let the fires go down." They mounted the steps together, and Ruth, in happy assurance, laid her hand upon the latch. It did not yield. Her mother stood looking wildly down the drive, and praying for her husband to come. Ruth, her self-possession inexplicably overthrown, was beating at the door.

"Rosamond!" she was calling. "Oh, Rosamond, let me in! Don't be cruel! Let me in!"

"Dear, come home," said her mother, crying bitterly. "Come home."

Ruth knelt and tried to look through the key-hole. She sprang to her feet.

"I'm going in," she said. "I will go in."

She ran round to the side piazza, on a level with the long windows, opened a blind, and broke a pane with her hand. The blood dripped down on the glass. She turned the fastening, threw up the window, and stepped in, and her mother followed. The room was dark, save for the light from that one window, for all the other blinds were closed. She ran up to the clock and looked it in the face. It was dead and still, the impassive hands pointing stolidly to a lying hour. She laid her hands upon it, as if to shake it into life. The dust lay thick over table and chairs. She threw herself upon her knees before the fireplace and thrust her hand into the ashes. They were cold.

"Mother!" she cried out, piteously. "Mother!"

"Come home, dear, come home!"

Ruth rose to her feet, sick with wonder, yet reanimated by one last hope.

"Just a minute!" she implored, and ran up the dusty stairs. The door of her own sleeping-room was closed, but she flung it open and walked shudderingly into the darkness within. The bed was unmade, with only a mildewed cover over the mattress. A mouse fled silently across the floor, a swift brown shadow. Where was the china cow? Where was Miranda? With a throb of premonitory knowledge she threw up the cover of the trunk near the bed. There lay the doll, on orderly rows of playthings packed away for doomsday; they looked as if they might have been there years.

Her mother had followed her, and Ruth turned about, trying to smile.

"I begin to understand it now," she said. "I'll go home. You mustn't think I'm crazy. I'm not." They descended the stairs together and crossed the deserted sitting-room. At the window, Mrs. Hollis paused before stepping out.

"I can't understand it," she said, musingly. "The house isn't in the least musty. It's as sweet as a garden. Sweeter!"

Ruth stopped short, arrested by the truth. The odors of the night were all about her, and as she stood there accepting them, great peace and the sense of security fell upon her like a mantle. She began to smile.

"And they might all be happy," she said to herself, "if they could only remember that There is just the same as Here!"

SARAH ORNE JEWETT

It is impossible to say how your letter has heartened me. I send you love and thanks.—it is one more unbreakable bond that holds fast between me and you. You bring something to the reading of a story that the story would go very lame without; but it is those unwritable things that the story holds in its heart, if it has any, that make the true soul of it, and these must be understood, and yet how many a story goes lame for lack of that understanding. In France there is such a code, such recognitions, such richness of allusions; but here we confuse our scaffoldings with our buildings, and so! . . . I thought that most of us had begun to grow in just such a way as she did, and so could read joyfully between the lines. . . .*

* from a letter by Jewett to her friend Sarah Whitman, written after Whitman had read "Martha's Lady." Quoted by Glenda Hobbs in "Pure and Passionate: Female Friendship in Sarah Orne Jewett's 'Martha's Lady' " in *Studies in Short Fiction*, vol. 17, no. 1, winter 1980, p. 26. Hobbs is quoting from the undated letter "Dear Friend" in *Letters of Sarah Orne Jewett*, ed. Annie Fields (Boston: Houghton Mifflin and Co., 1911), pp. 112–113.

Sarah Orne Jewett was one of the most admired and beloved writers of the nineteenth century. The survival of Jewett's writing, even in the trivializing category "local color" to which her work has been consigned, has made her rediscovery easy. Jewett is noted for two phenomena generally thought of today as lesbian: she shared a twenty-seven-year "Boston Marriage" with the widowed Annie Adams Fields and she wrote a letter (part of which is quoted in the introduction) to her admirer Willa Cather, after reading Cather's story "On the Gull's Road," urging her to forgo "cross-dressing," or the creation of male-characters-as-lovers of the women in her fiction. She said that *women* could fill the roles of lovers just as well, more authentically, in fact, than men.

Sarah Orne Jewett was born on September 3, 1849, in South Berwick, Maine, a town "within scent of the sea but not within sight of it." She was the second daughter of three born to Caroline Frances Perry and Theodore Herman Jewett. Because she was a sickly child, she was often kept home from school. Consequently, her education came while riding with her physician father as he went on his rounds in the "country of the pointed firs." On their buggy trips, he told her stories of the local people and places; she shared her impressions with him, retelling the stories that became the foundation of her written work. They discussed the books in his well-stocked library—to which she had unlimited access. In the dedication of *Country By-Ways* (1881), her fourth book, Jewett called her father her best friend, "the best and wisest man" she ever knew. Although Jewett left little in writing about her mother and their relationship, Sarah Way Sherman, author of *Sarah Orne Jewett: An American Persephone,* has been able to reconstruct some of the most important elements of that relationship, confirming what seems obvious from Jewett's stories: the daughter was emotionally tied to her mother in profound, satisfying, and nurturing ways, and achieved a sense of independent adulthood only after her mother's death—when Jewett was forty-one.

As her literary career flourished she went to Boston and met, through the sponsorship of her editor and publisher at *Atlantic Monthly,* James T. Fields and his wife, advisor, and hostess, Annie Adams Fields, the leading literary figures of her time. During these years a friendship grew between Jewett and (Mrs.) Fields that was to become the emotional center of each of their lives.

Dr. Jewett died in 1878; James T. Fields died in 1881. The following year, Sarah Orne Jewett and the widowed Annie Adams Fields took their first trip together to Europe. They were apparently thereafter accepted as a couple, and the issue or question of any sexual expression of their love for each other pales next to the greater—and nineteenth-century—understanding of the dignity, integrity, and civility women brought to friendship. After Jewett's mother's death in 1891, the couple took their second trip to Europe.

Some say that we don't or can't really *know* that Jewett was a lesbian. She did not, so far as we know now, use the word "lesbian" when she talked about who she was; in fact, we don't yet know that she used any of the terms available in the late nineteenth century to describe a woman who preferred the company and the love of other women, a woman who spent almost thirty years in a "Boston Marriage." However, when she speaks above of the "unwritable things" perhaps it is to this reality that she refers. Many scholars take for granted that she was a lesbian. Others who write about Jewett go to great lengths to deny that she was a lesbian. They "explain away" her intense romantic friendships with other women, the passionate letters she exchanged with them, the complete absence of any evidence of any interest ever in a man as a *male*. I believe she was a lesbian and knew she was, that the majority of women with whom she shared a social world were lesbians who knew that they were, and that many of Jewett's stories allude to lesbian loves, passions, and social life in language as clear as she believed she could get away with and remain "publishable." To whom was she referring in the above letter when she wrote about "most of us"?

"Martha's Lady" can be read in a great variety of ways. Martha answers Helena's plea to "Martha! I wish you would think of me sometimes after I go away. Won't you promise?" with her promise that "I shall think of you every day." Thus she commits herself to forty years in service to someone else without any apparent reciprocity or material reward.

Martha's love and service remind me of the code of chivalric love and service of the middle ages. Men committed themselves similarly to lifelong devotion to an unattainable woman of a class "above" their own. Such fealty interfered with the development of, or at least undermined, class solidarity, channeled the sexual energies of these men into protecting their noble ladies and, not coincidentally, the property interests of the men who "owned" those women, i.e., the "lords" who were their husbands.

In "Martha's Lady" Helena is the beloved of a lower class *woman* instead of a man; Martha pledges lifelong fealty to her Lady, and spends her life serving, preserving, and enhancing the life and property of Helena's relative, Harriet. The name "Harriet," a variation of "Henrietta," is the female version of Henry which means "ruler of the home."

Chivalric love is similar to the religious love characterized by a person who dedicates her or his life to adoration of the holy as it is embodied in a god, a goddess, or a saint. Both have about them the quality of a "calling" or a vocation.

Christianity has a long history of celebrating service-oriented love of religious figures, from Jesus to the many saints in whose honor men and women pledge themselves to a lifetime of celibacy, obedience, poverty, and service. We can see Martha as a nun, devoted to the worship of Helena, and the service of the "abbess" (the female form of "abbott," which comes from "father" or ruler of an abbey), Harriet. The name "Helena" refers to "Hellenic," or Greek, invoking not only a non-Christian culture, but one in which Sappho was a reigning figure. Martha's quasi-religious rituals, cherished relics, and forms of service might be those of a "religious."

Neither chivalric love nor religious devotion require the literal presence of the beloved; rather, they thrive on separation-as-presence, on ritual practices, contemplation of the beloved, and other forms of religious behavior. The most frequently modeled forms of this kind of love, both religious and chivalric, are pseudo-heterosexual; i.e., the absent or non-literal beloved is imagined as a member of the sex opposite that of the worshipper. Nuns are called "brides" of a male Christ figure; Judaism draws an analogy between heterosexual marriage and the relationship between the masculine God and the female Sabbath Bride. "Martha's Lady" also recalls the story of Martha in the Christian Bible (Luke 10:38–41 and John 11:1–12:2), the older sister of Lazarus and Mary, the one who served instead of listened.

There are all the same kinds of lesbian love and abuses of love as there are kinds and abuses of heterosexual love. "Martha's Lady" is about one kind of lesbian love, one more way that women love and have loved women, another way women have of making the love of/for a woman/women the emotional or spiritual center of their lives. Jewett's Martha experiences a love that purifies, uplifts, ennobles the lover. Her life has a transcendent purpose, a focus, a model. Such devoted love has been called transformative, elevating, raising what might have been "merely" carnal or earthly, to the spiritual.

Whether the love that Martha is encouraged to feel and is capable of sustaining for Helena is self-abusive, self-denying, limiting love or transcendent, ennobling, uplifting love can and will be debated for a long time.

"Martha's Lady" was first published in the October 1897 issue of the *Atlantic Monthly;* it was later collected in Jewett's eleventh and last collection of short stories: *The Queen's Twin and Other Stories* in 1899. Willa Cather's 1925 two-volume collection called *The Best Stories of Sarah Orne Jewett* includes "Martha's Lady."

Martha's Lady

I

One day, many years ago, the old Judge Pyne house wore an unwonted look of gayety and youthfulness. The high-fenced green garden beyond was bright with June flowers. In the large shady front yard under the elms you might see some chairs placed near together, as they often used to be when the family were all at home and life was going on gayly with eager talk and pleasure-making; when the elder judge, the grandfather, used to quote his favorite Dr. Johnson and say to his girls, "Be brisk, be splendid, and be public."

One of the chairs had a crimson silk shawl thrown carelessly over its straight back, and a passer-by who looked in through the latticed gate between the tall gate-posts, with their white urns, might think that this piece of shining East Indian color was a huge red lily that had suddenly bloomed against the syringa bush. There were certain windows thrown wide open that were usually shut, and their curtains were blowing free in the light wind of a summer afternoon; it looked as if a large household had returned to the old house to fill the prim best rooms and find them pleasant.

It was evident to every one in town that Miss Harriet Pyne, to use the village phrase, had company. She was the last of her family, and was by no means old; but being the last, and wonted to live with people much older than herself, she had formed all the habits of a serious elderly person. Ladies of her age, a little past thirty, often wore discreet caps in those days, especially if they were married, but being single, Miss Harriet clung to youth in this respect, making the one concession of keeping her waving chestnut hair as smooth and stiffly arranged as possible. She had been the dutiful companion of her father and mother in their latest years, all her elder brothers and sisters having married and gone, or died and gone, out of the old house. Now that she was left alone it seemed quite the best thing frankly to accept the fact of age at once, and to turn more resolutely than ever to the companionship of duty and serious books. She was more serious and given to routine than her elders themselves, as sometimes happened when the daughters of New England gentlefolks were brought up wholly in the society of their elders. At thirty she had more reluctance than her mother to face an unforeseen occasion, certainly more than her grandmother, who had preserved some cheerful inheritance of gayety and worldliness from colonial times.

There was something about the look of the crimson silk shawl in the front yard to make one suspect that the sober customs of the best house in a quiet New England village were all being set at defiance, and once when the mistress of the house came to stand in her own doorway she wore the pleased but somewhat apprehensive look of a guest. In these days New England life held the necessity of much dignity and discretion of behavior; there was the truest hospitality and good cheer in all occasional festivities, but it was sometimes a self-conscious hospitality, followed by an inexorable return to asceticism both of diet and of behavior. Miss Harriet Pyne belonged to the very dullest days of New England, those which perhaps held the most priggishness for the learned professions, the most limited interpretation of the word "evangelical," and the pettiest indifference to large things. The outbreak of a desire for larger religious freedom caused at first a most determined reaction toward formalism and even stagnation of thought and behavior, especially in small and quiet villages like Ashford, intently busy with their own concerns. It was high time for a little leaven to begin its work, in this moment when the great impulses of the war for liberty had died away and those of the coming war for patriotism and a new freedom had hardly yet begun, except as a growl of thunder or a flash of lightning draws one's eyes to the gathering clouds through the lifeless air of a summer day.

The dull interior, the changed life of the old house whose former activities seemed to have fallen sound asleep, really typified these larger conditions, and the little leaven had made its easily recognized appearance in the shape of a light-hearted girl. She was Miss Harriet's young Boston cousin, Helena Vernon, who, half-amused and half-impatient at the unnecessary sober-mindedness of her hostess and of Ashford in general, had set herself to the difficult task of gayety. Cousin Harriet looked on at a succession of ingenious and, on the whole, innocent attempts at pleasure, as she might have looked on at the frolics of a kitten who easily substitutes a ball of yarn for the uncertainties of a bird or a wind-blown leaf, and who may at any moment ravel the fringe of a sacred curtain-tassel in preference to either.

Helena, with her mischievous appealing eyes, with her enchanting old songs and her guitar, seemed the more delightful and even reasonable because she was so kind to everybody, and because she was a beauty. She had the gift of most charming manners. There was all the unconscious lovely ease and grace that had come with the good breeding of her city home, where many pleasant persons came and went; she had no fear, one had almost said no respect, of the individual, and she did not need to think of herself. Cousin Harriet turned cold with apprehension when she saw the minister coming in at the front gate, and wondered in agony if Martha were properly attired to go to the door, and would by any chance hear the knocker; it was Helena who, delighted to have anything happen, ran to the door to welcome the Reverend Mr. Crofton as if he were a congenial friend of her own age. She could behave with more or less propriety during the stately first visit, and even contrive to lighten it with modest mirth, and to extort the confession that the guest had a tenor voice though sadly out of practice, but when the minister departed a little flattered, and hoping that he had not expressed himself too strongly for a pastor upon the poems of Emerson, and feeling the unusual stir of gallantry in his proper heart, it was Helena who caught the honored hat of the late Judge Pyne from its last resting-place in the hall, and holding it securely in both hands, mimicked the minister's self-conscious entrance. She copied his pompous and anxious expression in the dim parlor in such delicious fashion, that Miss Harriet, who could not always extinguish a ready spark of the original sin of humor, laughed aloud.

"My dear!" she exclaimed severely the next moment. "I am ashamed of your being so disrespectful!" and then laughed again, and took the affecting old hat and carried it back to its place.

"I would not have had any one else see you for the world," she said sorrowfully as she returned, feeling quite self-possessed again, to the parlor doorway; but Helena still sat in the minister's chair, with her small feet placed as his stiff boots had been, and a copy of his solemn expression before they came to speaking of Emerson and of the guitar. "I wish I had asked him if he would be so kind as to climb the cherry-tree," said Helena, unbending a little at the discovery that her cousin would consent to laugh no more. "There are all those ripe cherries on the top branches. I can climb as high as he, but I can't reach far enough from the last branch that will bear anybody. The minister is so long and thin"—

"I don't know what Mr. Crofton would have thought of you; he is a very serious young man," said cousin Harriet, still ashamed of her laughter. "Martha will get the cherries for you, or one of the men. I should not like to have Mr. Crofton think you were frivolous, a young lady of your opportunities"—but Helena had escaped through the hall and out at the garden door at the mention of Martha's name. Miss Harriet Pyne sighed anxiously, and then smiled, in spite of her deep convictions, as she shut the blinds and tried to make the house look solemn again.

The front door might be shut, but the garden door at the other end of the broad hall was wide open into the large sunshiny garden, where the last of the red and white peonies and the golden lilies, and the first of the tall blue larkspurs lent their colors in generous fashion. The straight box borders were all in fresh and shining green of their new leaves, and there was a fragrance of the old garden's inmost life and soul blowing from the honeysuckle blossoms on a long trellis. Now it was late in the afternoon, and the sun was low behind great apple-trees at the garden's end, which threw their shadows over the short turf of the bleaching-green. The cherry-trees stood at one side in full sunshine still, and Miss Harriet, who presently came to the garden steps to watch like a hen at the water's edge, saw her cousin's pretty figure in its white dress of India muslin hurrying across the grass. She was accompanied by the tall, ungainly shape of Martha the new maid, who, dull and indifferent to every one else, showed a surprising willingness and allegiance to the young guest.

"Martha ought to be in the dining-room already, slow as she is; it wants but half an hour of tea-time," said Miss Harriet, as she turned and went into the shaded house. It was Martha's duty to wait at table, and there had been many trying scenes and defeated efforts toward her education. Martha was certainly very clumsy, and she seemed the clumsier because she had replaced her aunt, a most skillful person, who had but lately married a thriving farm and its prosperous owner. It must be confessed that Miss Harriet was a most bewildering instructor, and that her pupil's brain was easily confused and prone to blunders. The coming of Helena had been somewhat dreaded by reason of this incompetent service, but the guest took no notice of frowns or futile gestures at the first tea-table, except to establish friendly relations with Martha on her own account by a reassuring smile. They were about the same age, and next morning, before cousin Harriet came down, Helena showed by a word and a quick touch the right way to do something that had gone wrong and been impossible to understand the night before. A moment later the anxious mistress came in without suspicion, but Martha's eyes were as affectionate as a dog's, and there was a new look of hopefulness on her face; this dreaded guest was a friend after all, and not a foe come from proud Boston to confound her ignorance and patient efforts.

The two young creatures, mistress and maid, were hurrying across the bleaching-green.

"I can't reach the ripest cherries," explained Helena politely, "and I think that Miss Pyne ought to send some to the minister. He has just made us a call. Why Martha, you haven't been crying again!"

"Yes, 'm," said Martha sadly. "Miss Pyne always loves to send something to the minister," she acknowledged with interest, as if she did not wish to be asked to explain these latest tears.

"We'll arrange some of the best cherries in a pretty dish. I'll show you how, and you shall carry them over to the parsonage after tea," said Helena cheerfully, and Martha accepted the embassy with pleasure. Life was beginning to hold moments of something like delight in the last few days.

"You'll spoil your pretty dress, Miss Helena," Martha gave shy warning, and Miss Helena stood back and held up her skirts with unusual care while the country girl, in her heavy blue checked gingham, began to climb the cherry-tree like a boy.

Down came the scarlet fruit like bright rain into the green grass.

"Break some nice twigs with the cherries and leaves together; oh, you're a duck, Martha!" and Martha, flushed with delight, and looking far more like a thin and solemn blue heron, came rustling down to earth again, and gathered the spoils into her clean apron.

That night at tea, during her handmaiden's temporary absence, Miss Harriet announced, as if by way of apology, that she thought Martha was beginning to understand something about her work. "Her aunt was a treasure, she never had to be told anything twice; but Martha has been as clumsy as a calf," said the precise mistress of the house. "I have been afraid sometimes that I never could teach her anything. I was quite ashamed to have you come just now, and find me so unprepared to entertain a visitor."

"Oh, Martha will learn fast enough because she cares so much," said the visitor eagerly. "I think she is a dear good girl. I do hope that she will never go away. I think she does things better every day, cousin Harriet," added Helena pleadingly, with all her kind young heart. The china-closet door was open a little way, and Martha heard every word. From that moment, she not only knew what love was like, but she knew love's dear ambitions. To have come from a stony hill-farm and a bare small wooden house was like a cave-dweller's coming to make a permanent home in an art museum; such had seemed the elaborateness and elegance of Miss Pyne's fashion of life, and Martha's simple brain was slow enough in its processes and recognitions. But with this sympathetic ally and defender, this exquisite Miss Helena who believed in her, all difficulties appeared to vanish.

Later that evening, no longer homesick or hopeless, Martha returned from her polite errand to the minister, and stood with a sort of triumph before the two ladies who were sitting in the front doorway, as if they were waiting for visitors, Helena still in her white muslin and red ribbons, and Miss Harriet in a thin black silk. Being happily self-forgetful in the greatness of the moment, Martha's manners were perfect, and she looked for once almost pretty and quite as young as she was.

"The minister came to the door himself, and sent his thanks. He said that cherries were always his favorite fruit, and he was much obliged to both Miss Pyne and Miss Vernon. He kept me waiting a few minutes, while he got this book ready to send to you, Miss Helena."

"What are you saying, Martha? I have sent him nothing!" exclaimed Miss Pyne, much astonished. "What does she mean, Helena?"

"Only a few of your cherries," explained Helena. "I thought Mr. Crofton would like them after his afternoon of parish calls. Martha and I arranged them before tea, and I sent them with our compliments."

"Oh, I am very glad you did," said Miss Harriet, wondering, but much relieved. "I was afraid"—

"No, it was none of my mischief," answered Helena daringly. "I did not think that Martha would be ready to go so soon. I should have shown you how pretty they looked among their green leaves. We put them in one of your best white dishes with the openwork edge. Martha shall show you to-morrow; mamma always likes to have them so." Helena's fingers were busy with the hard knot of a parcel.

"See this, cousin Harriet!" she announced proudly, as Martha disappeared round the corner of the house, beaming with the pleasures of adventure and success. "Look! the minister has sent me a book: Sermons on *what*? Sermons—it is so dark that I can't quite see."

"It must be his Sermons on the Seriousness of Life; they are the only ones he has printed, I believe," said Miss Harriet, with much pleasure. "They are considered very fine; remarkably able discourses. He pays you a great compliment, my dear. I feared that he noticed your girlish levity."

"I behaved beautifully while he stayed," insisted Helena. "Ministers are only men," but she blushed with pleasure. It was certainly something to receive a book from its author, and such a tribute made her of more value to the whole reverent household. The minister was not only a man, but a bachelor, and Helena was at the age that best loves conquest; it was at any rate comfortable to be reinstated in cousin Harriet's good graces.

"Do ask the kind gentleman to tea! He needs a little cheering up," begged the siren in India muslin, as she laid the shiny black volume of sermons on the stone doorstep with an air of approval, but as if they had quite finished their mission.

"Perhaps I shall, if Martha improves as much as she has within the last day or two," Miss Harriet promised hopefully. "It is something I always dread a little when I am all alone, but I think Mr. Crofton likes to come. He converses so elegantly."

II

These were the days of long visits, before affectionate friends thought it quite worth while to take a hundred miles' journey merely to dine or to pass a night in one another's houses. Helena lingered through the pleasant weeks of early summer, and departed unwillingly at last to join her family at the White Hills, where they had gone like other households of high social station, to pass the month of August out of town. The happy-hearted young guest left many lamenting friends behind her, and promised each that she would come back again next year. She left the minister a rejected lover, as well as the preceptor of the academy, but with their pride unwounded, and it may have been with wider outlooks upon the world and a less narrow sympathy both for their own work in life and for their neighbors' work and hindrances. Even Miss Harriet Pyne herself had lost some of the unnecessary provincialism and prejudice which had begun to harden a naturally good and open mind and affectionate heart. She was conscious of feeling younger and more free, and not so lonely. Nobody had ever been so gay, so fascinating, or so kind as Helena, so full of social resource, so simple and undemanding in her friendliness. The light of her young life cast no shadow on either young or old companions, her pretty clothes never seemed to make other girls look dull or out of fashion. When she went away up the street in Miss Harriet's carriage to take the slow train toward Boston and the gayeties of the new Profile House, where her mother waited impatiently with a group of Southern friends, it seemed as if there would never be any more picnics or parties in Ashford, and as if society had nothing left to do but to grow old and get ready for winter.

Martha came into Miss Helena's bedroom that last morning, and it was easy to see that she had been crying; she looked just as she did in that first sad week of homesickness and despair. All for love's sake she had been learning to do many things, and to do them exactly right; her eyes had grown quick to see the smallest chance for personal service. Nobody could be more humble and devoted; she looked years older than Helena, and wore already a touching air of caretaking.

"You spoil me, you dear Martha!" said Helena from the bed. "I don't know what they will say at home, I am so spoiled."

Martha went on opening the blinds to let in the brightness of the summer morning, but she did not speak.

"You are getting on splendidly, aren't you?" continued the little mistress. "You have tried so hard that you make me ashamed of myself. At first you crammed all the flowers together, and now you make them look beautiful. Last night cousin Harriet was so pleased when the table was so charming, and I told her that you did everything yourself, every bit. Won't you keep the flowers fresh and pretty in the house until I come back? It's so much pleasanter for Miss Pyne, and you'll feed my little sparrows, won't you? They're growing so tame."

"Oh yes, Miss Helena!" and Martha looked almost angry for a moment, then she burst into tears and covered her face with her apron. "I couldn't understand a single thing when I first came. I never had been anywhere to see anything, and Miss Pyne frightened me when she talked. It was you made me think I could ever learn. I wanted to keep the place, 'count of mother and the little boys; we're dreadful hard pushed at home. Hepsy has been good in the kitchen; she said she ought to have patience with me, for she was awkward herself when she first came."

Helena laughed; she looked so pretty under the tasseled white curtains.

"I daresay Hepsy tells the truth," she said. "I wish you had told me about your mother. When I come again, some day we'll drive up country, as you call it, to see her. Martha! I wish you would think of me sometimes after I go away. Won't you promise?" and the bright young face suddenly grew grave. "I have hard times myself; I don't always learn things that I ought to learn, I don't always put things straight. I wish you wouldn't forget me ever, and would just believe in me. I think it does help more than anything."

"I won't forget," said Martha slowly. "I shall think of you every day." She spoke almost with indifference, as if she had been asked to dust a room, but she turned aside quickly and pulled the little mat under the hot water jug quite out of its former straightness; then she hastened away down the long white entry, weeping as she went.

III

To lose out of sight the friend whom one has loved and lived to please is to lose joy out of life. But if love is true, there comes presently a higher joy of pleasing the ideal, that is to say, the perfect friend. The same old happiness is lifted to a higher level. As for Martha, the girl who stayed behind in Ashford, nobody's life could seem duller to those who could not understand; she was slow of step, and her eyes were almost always downcast as if intent upon incessant toil; but they startled you when she looked up, with their shining light. She was capable of the happiness of holding fast to a great sentiment, the ineffable satisfaction of trying to please one whom she truly loved. She never thought of trying to make other people pleased with herself; all she lived for was to do the best she could for others, and to conform to an ideal, which grew at last to be like a saint's vision, a heavenly figure painted upon the sky.

On Sunday afternoons in summer, Martha sat by the window of her chamber, a low-storied little room, which looked into the side yard and the great branches of an elm-tree. She never sat in the old wooden rocking-chair except on Sundays like this; it belonged to the day of rest and to happy meditation. She wore her plain black dress and a clean white apron, and held in her lap a little wooden box, with a brass hinge on top for a handle. She was past sixty years of age and looked even older, but there was the same look on her face that it had sometimes worn in girlhood. She was the same Martha; her hands were old-looking and work-worn, but her face still shone. It seemed like yesterday that Helena Vernon had gone away, and it was more than forty years.

War and peace had brought their changes and great anxieties, the face of the earth was furrowed by floods and fire, the faces of mistress and maid were furrowed by smiles and tears, and in the sky the stars shone on as if nothing had happened. The village of Ashford added a few pages to its unexciting history, the minister preached, the people listened; now and then a funeral crept along the street, and now and then the bright face of a little child rose above the horizon of a family pew. Miss Harriet Pyne lived on in the large white house, which gained more and more distinction because it suffered no changes, save successive repaintings and a new railing about its stately roof. Miss Harriet herself had moved far beyond the uncertainties of an anxious youth. She had long ago made all her decisions, and settled all necessary questions; her scheme of life was as faultless as the miniature landscape of a Japanese garden, and as easily kept in order. The only important change she would ever be capable of making was the final change to another and a better world; and for that nature itself would gently provide, and her own innocent life.

Hardly any great social event had ruffled the easy current of life since Helena Vernon's marriage. To this Miss Pyne had gone, stately in appearance and carrying gifts of some old family silver which bore the Vernon crest, but not without some protest in her heart against the uncertainties of married life. Helena was so equal to a happy independence and even to the assistance of other lives grown strangely dependent upon her quick sympathies and instinctive decisions, that it was hard to let her sink her personality in the affairs of another. Yet a brilliant English match was not without its attractions to an old-fashioned gentlewoman like Miss Pyne, and Helena herself was amazingly happy; one day there had come a letter to Ashford, in which her very heart seemed to beat with love and self-forgetfulness, to tell cousin Harriet of such new happiness and high hope. "Tell Martha all that I say about my dear Jack," wrote the eager girl; "please show my letter to Martha, and tell her that I shall come home next summer and bring the handsomest and best man in the world to Ashford. I have told him all about the dear house and the dear garden; there never was such a lad to reach for cherries with his six foot two." Miss Pyne, wondering a little, gave the letter to Martha, who took it deliberately and as if she wondered too, and went away to read it slowly by herself. Martha cried over it, and felt a strange sense of loss and pain; it hurt her heart a little to read about the cherry-picking. Her idol seemed to be less her own since she had become the idol of a stranger. She never had taken such a letter in her hands before, but love at last prevailed, since Miss Helena was happy, and she kissed the last page where her name was written, feeling overbold, and laid the envelope on Miss Pyne's secretary without a word.

The most generous love cannot but long for reassurance, and Martha had the joy of being remembered. She was not forgotten when the day of the wedding drew near, but she never knew that Miss Helena had asked if cousin Harriet would not bring Martha to town; she should like to have Martha there to see her married. "She would help about the flowers," wrote the happy girl; "I know she will like to come, and I'll ask mamma to plan to have some one take her all about Boston and make her have a pleasant time after the hurry of the great day is over."

Cousin Harriet thought it was very kind and exactly like Helena, but Martha would be out of her element; it was most imprudent and girlish to have thought of such a thing. Helena's mother would be far from wishing for any unnecessary guest just then in the busiest part of her household, and it was best not to speak of the invitation. Some day Martha should go to Boston if she did well, but not now. Helena did not forget to ask if Martha had come, and was astonished by the indifference of the answer. It was the first thing which reminded her that she was not a fairy princess having everything her own way in that last day before the wedding. She knew that Martha would have loved to be near, for she could not help understanding in that moment of her own happiness the love that was hidden in another heart. Next day this happy young princess, the bride, cut a piece of the great cake and put it into a pretty box that had held one of her wedding presents. With eager voices calling her, and all her friends about her, and her mother's face growing more and more wistful at the thought of parting, she still lingered and ran to take one or two trifles from her dressing-table, a little mirror and some tiny scissors that Martha would remember, and one of the pretty handkerchiefs marked with her maiden name. These she put in the box too; it was half a girlish freak and fancy, but she could not help trying to share her happiness, and Martha's life was so plain and dull. She whispered a message, and put the little package into cousin Harriet's hand for Martha as she said good-by. She was very fond of cousin Harriet. She smiled with a gleam of her old fun; Martha's puzzled look and tall awkward figure seemed to stand suddenly before her eyes, as she promised to come again to Ashford. Impatient voices called to Helena, her lover was at the door, and she hurried away leaving her old home and her girlhood gladly. If she had only known it, as she kissed cousin Harriet good-by, they were never going to see each other again until they were old women. The first step that she took out of her father's house that day, married, and full of hope and joy, was a step that led her away from the green elms of Boston Common and away from her own country and those she loved best, to a brilliant much-varied foreign life, and to nearly all the sorrows and nearly all the joys that the heart of one woman could hold or know.

On Sunday afternoons Martha used to sit by the window in Ashford and hold the wooden box which a favorite young brother, who afterward died at sea, had made for her, and she used to take out of it the pretty little box with a gilded cover that had held the piece of wedding-cake, and the small scissors, and the blurred bit of a mirror in its silver case; as for the handkerchief with the narrow lace edge, once in two or three years she sprinkled it as if it were a flower, and spread it out in the sun on the old bleaching-green, and sat near by in the shrubbery to watch lest some bold robin or cherry-bird should seize it and fly away.

IV

Miss Harriet Pyne was often congratulated upon the good fortune of having such a helper and friend as Martha. As time went on this tall gaunt woman, always thin, always slow, gained a dignity of behavior and simple affectionateness of look which suited the charm and dignity of the ancient house. She was unconsciously beautiful like a saint, like the picturesqueness of a lonely tree which lives to shelter unnumbered lives and to stand quietly in its place. There was such rustic homeliness and constancy belonging to her, such beautiful powers of apprehension, such reticence, such gentleness for those who were troubled or sick; all these gifts and graces Martha hid in her heart. She never joined the church because she thought she was not good enough, but life was such a passion and happiness of service that it was impossible not to be devout, and she was always in her humble place on Sundays, in the back pew next the door. She had been educated by a remembrance; Helena's young eyes forever looked at her reassuringly from a gay girlish face. Helena's sweet patience in teaching her own awkwardness could never be forgotten.

"I owe everything to Miss Helena," said Martha half aloud as she sat alone by the window; she had said it to herself a thousand times. When she looked in the little keepsake mirror she always hoped to see some faint reflection of Helena Vernon, but there was only her own brown old New England face to look back at her wonderingly.

Miss Pyne went less and less often to pay visits to her friends in Boston; there were very few friends left to come to Ashford and make long visits in the summer, and life grew more and more monotonous. Now and then there came news from across the sea and messages of remembrance, letters that were closely written on thin sheets of paper, and that spoke of lords and ladies, of great journeys, of the death of little children and the proud successes of boys at school, of the wedding of Mrs. Dysart's only daughter; but even that had happened years ago. These things seemed far away and vague, as if they belonged to a story and not to life itself; the true links with the past were quite different. There was the unvarying flock of ground-sparrows that Helena had begun to feed; every morning Martha scattered crumbs for them from the side doorsteps while Miss Pyne watched from the dining-room window, and they were counted and cherished year by year.

Miss Pyne herself had many fixed habits, but little ideality or imagination, and so at last it was Martha who took thought for her mistress, and gave freedom to her own good taste. After a while, without any one's observing the change, the everyday ways of doing things in the house came to be the stately ways that had once belonged only to the entertainment of guests. Happily both mistress and maid seized all possible chances for hospitality, yet Miss Harriet nearly always sat alone at her exquisitely served table with its fresh flowers, and the beautiful old china which Martha handled so lovingly that there was no good excuse for keeping it hidden on closet shelves. Every year when the old cherry-trees were in fruit, Martha carried the round white Limoges dish with a fretwork edge, full of pointed green leaves and scarlet cherries, to the minister, and his wife never quite understood why every year he blushed and looked so conscious of the pleasure, and thanked Martha as if he had received a very particular attention. There was no pretty suggestion toward the pursuit of the fine art of housekeeping in Martha's limited acquaintance with newspapers that she did not adopt; there was no refined old custom of the Pyne housekeeping that she consented to let go. And every day, as she had promised, she thought of Miss Helena,—oh, many times in every day: whether this thing would please her, or that be likely to fall in with her fancy or ideas of fitness. As far as was possible the rare news that reached Ashford through an occasional letter or the talk of guests was made part of Martha's own life, the history of her own heart. A worn old geography often stood open at the map of Europe on the light-stand in her room, and a little old-fashioned gilt button, set with a piece of glass like a ruby, that had broken and fallen from the trimming of one of Helena's dresses, was used to mark the city of her dwelling-place. In the changes of a diplomatic life Martha followed her lady all about the map. Sometimes the button was at Paris, and sometimes at Madrid; once, to her great anxiety, it remained long at St. Petersburg. For such a slow scholar Martha was not unlearned at last, since everything about life in these foreign towns was of interest to her faithful heart. She satisfied her own mind as she threw crumbs to the tame sparrows; it was all part of the same thing and for the same affectionate reasons.

V

One Sunday afternoon in early summer Miss Harriet Pyne came hurrying along the entry that led to Martha's room and called two or three times before its inhabitant could reach the door. Miss Harriet looked unusually cheerful and excited, and she held something in her hand. "Where are you, Martha?" she called again. "Come quick, I have something to tell you!"

"Here I am, Miss Pyne," said Martha, who had only stopped to put her precious box in the drawer, and to shut the geography.

"Who do you think is coming this very night at half past six? We must have everything as nice as we can; I must see Hannah at once. Do you remember my cousin Helena who has lived abroad so long? Miss Helena Vernon, the Honorable Mrs. Dysart, she is now."

"Yes, I remember her," answered Martha, turning a little pale.

"I knew that she was in this country, and I had written to ask her to come for a long visit," continued Miss Harriet, who did not often explain things, even to Martha, though she was always conscientious about the kind messages that were sent back by grateful guests. "She telegraphs that she means to anticipate her visit by a few days and come to me at once. The heat is beginning in town, I suppose. I daresay, having been a foreigner so long, she does not mind traveling on Sunday. Do you think Hannah will be prepared? We must have tea a little later."

"Yes, Miss Harriet," said Martha. She wondered that she could speak as usual, there was such a ringing in her ears. "I shall have time to pick some fresh strawberries; Miss Helena is so fond of our strawberries."

"Why, I had forgotten," said Miss Pyne, a little puzzled by

something quite unusual in Martha's face. "We must expect to find Mrs. Dysart a good deal changed, Martha; it is a great many years since she was here; I have not seen her since her wedding, and she has had a great deal of trouble, poor girl. You had better open the parlor chamber, and make it ready before you go down."

"It is all ready, I think," said Martha. "I can bring some of those little sweetbrier roses upstairs before she comes."

"Yes, you are always thoughtful," said Miss Pyne, with unwonted feeling.

Martha did not answer. She glanced at the telegram wistfully. She had never really suspected before that Miss Pyne knew nothing of the love that had been in her heart all these years; it was half a pain and half a golden joy to keep such a secret; she could hardly bear this moment of surprise.

Presently the news gave wings to her willing feet. When Hannah the cook, who never had known Miss Helena, went to the parlor an hour later on some errand to her old mistress, she discovered that this stranger guest must be a very important person. She had never seen the tea-table look exactly as it did that night, and in the parlor itself there were fresh blossoming boughs in the old East Indian jars, and lilies in the paneled hall, and flowers everywhere, as if there were some high festivity.

Miss Pyne sat by the window watching, in her best dress, looking stately and calm; she seldom went out now, and it was almost time for the carriage. Martha was just coming in from the garden with the strawberries, and with more flowers in her apron. It was a bright cool evening in June, the golden robins sang in the elms, and the sun was going down behind the apple-trees at the foot of the garden. The beautiful old house stood wide open to the long expected guest.

"I think that I shall go down to the gate," said Miss Pyne, looking at Martha for approval, and Martha nodded and they went together slowly down the broad front walk.

There was a sound of horses and wheels on the roadside turf: Martha could not see at first; she stood back inside the gate behind the white lilacs as the carriage came. Miss Pyne was there; she was holding out both arms and taking a tired, bent little figure in black to her heart. "Oh, my Miss Helena is an old woman like me!" and

Martha gave a pitiful sob; she had never dreamed it would be like this; this was the one thing she could not bear.

"Where are you, Martha?" called Miss Pyne. "Martha will bring these in; you have not forgotten my good Martha, Helena?" Then Helena looked up and smiled just as she used to smile in the old days. The young eyes were there still in the changed face, and Miss Helena had come.

That night Martha waited in her lady's room just as she used, humble and silent, and went through with the old unforgotten loving services. The long years seemed like days. At last she lingered a moment trying to think of something else that might be done, then she was going silently away, but Helena called her back.

"You have always remembered, haven't you, Martha dear?" she said. "Won't you please kiss me good-night?"*

* A later version of the final two paragraphs reads as follows:

That night Martha waited in her lady's room just as she used, humble and silent, and went through with the old unforgotten loving services. The long years seemed like days. At last she lingered a moment trying to think of something else that might be done, then she was going silently away, but Helena called her back. She suddenly knew the whole story and could hardly speak.

"Oh, my dear Martha!" she cried, "won't you kiss me goodnight? Oh, Martha, have you remembered like this, all these long years!"

See p. 242 for further explanation.

ALICE FRENCH
(OCTAVE THANET)

Adrienne Rich has written of the compulsory orientation of women toward heterosexuality. Within the Gay population itself is another, related phenomenon: the compulsory illusion of heterosexuality. . . . When society insists that everyone pretend to be heterosexual and punishes anyone who does not give that appearance, Gay people live solidly in the closet. . . . *

What does Max—or his picture—contribute to the life of never-married Margaret Wing, principal of a school for young ladies? "Certainly, because of it, Miss Wing had greater power over her scholars." Is he as good, or even better, for her well-being, her image, dead rather than alive, in a picture frame over her desk rather than there in the flesh? ". . . its influence was the more potent that it asked for nothing." What does a man who acts as a "beard" or a "cover" or a "front" for a lesbian provide to her? "Without her mysterious sorrow . . . they would have been chilled

---

* "The Original Underground," *Another Mother Tongue: Gay Words, Gay Worlds* by Judy Grahn (Beacon Press, Boston, 1984), p. 24.

by her virtues; but as it was, their perception that she had lived deeply . . . that she had been loved . . . opened their hearts." What is the value of heterosexual success, the illusion that she had a man? "They would have admired her, now they adored her." A woman who is not otherwise oppressed on account of her race or her class, a woman who has been claimed by one man, who wears his ring, is safe to live her life as she chooses: ". . . she had refused divers offers of marriage from citizens of good repute and substance."

A woman can most practically live an autonomous, self-determined life, free from catering to male needs, when she has an absentee owner: when she is a widow. A widow has done her duty to "society" and, as long as she can take care of herself economically, she doesn't owe herself to the service of another man. Her widowhood gives her protection from further use by men, and from the harsh judgment of having been useless to men. Just imagine how many young women are freed by wars to live life on their own, lives of their own choosing! They can spend a lifetime in respectable weeds (". . . she had assumed [mourning] as her permanent garb") without ever spending a single night under some man's roof.

That is what actually happened in the lives of both Elizabeth Stuart Phelps and Constance Fenimore Woolson: each lost a sweetheart during the Civil War and both were able to live singular lives without ever suffering the emotional battering of being considered Old Maids, women never chosen by a man.

That is the kind of experience that Thanet writes about in this story: the story of a woman freed from pressure to marry by the presumption of a sort of widowhood.

"Max—Or His Picture," the most recently written and published story in this collection, is its most "coded" story. The ring with the sapphire set between two diamonds, the single rose before the picture are heavily weighted symbols from a time when books and articles about the secret language of flowers and gemstones were as popular as books about astrology are today. The ring she wears was the most common setting for a betrothal ring; the fact that it included a cashmere sapphire meant that it was a *very* expensive ring.

The story was written by one of the women most "out of

the closet" in her time, a time of great intellectual ferment and theory-making about homosexuality. Germany, the country in which French places significant parts of both this story and "My Lorelei," was the western country where the most enlightened activity relating to the subject of what we today refer to as "Gay Rights" was happening. Faderman's suggestion that Alice French . . . "seemed to view humanity as having three sexes— men, women, and Octave Thanet . . ." is not so peculiar in light of the "science" of the late nineteenth century. The creators of the new science of the psyche, in attempting to understand homo- sexuality, postulated an "intersex" or "third sex." The re- formist homosexual rights activists and "scientists" of the period agreed that "homosexual women thought like men because they were born with men's minds." Anna Rueling, writing in 1904 for the annual conference of the Scientific Humanitarian Committee, the German homosexual rights organization, believed that "The homosexual woman possessed many qualities, inclinations and capacities which we consider masculine. She particularly deviates from the feminine norm in her emotional life. While emotion is almost always—exceptions prove the rule—the predominant and deciding trait in the heterosexual woman, clear reason rules the Uranian woman."[1] As is clear from the many articles French wrote on economic, social, and political questions in her day, she was a woman ruled by what seemed to her to be "clear reason."

"Max—Or His Picture" was written as love relationships be- tween women were being pathologized, when relationships that had been seen as morally pure and socially acceptable were sud- denly being labeled perverse. Contemporary historians point out that this attack on intimacy between women accompanied the in- creasing opportunities for women to achieve economic indepen- dence. In other words, now that women were no longer bound to heterosexuality as a "career," as their only way of earning a living, other means of binding them to the service of the heteropatriarchy had to be "invented." Homosexuality as perversion, homosocial bonding as disease, was the invention that led to a whole new era and means of controlling women. As historian Blanche Wiesen Cook reminds us, "The advent of the homosexual 'closet' at the end of the 19th century was not accidental. Oscar Wilde had, after all, been released from prison on 19 May 1897. In addition to the criminal stigma now attached to homosexuality, a sudden explosion of 'scientific' publications on 'sexual disorders' and 'perversions' appeared. . . ."[2]

This collection's final story echoes the first. "My Visitation" is a story in which a woman insists that she loves a woman so passionately that she "never" can love . . . "any man as I did her," who has "but the lesser part of a heart to give any man," who "loved a woman too well to love or to marry"; nevertheless she ends up about to marry a man. She begs for understanding from her reader, presumably her young *woman* reader, who might be tempted to judge her unfaithful to her love for Eleanor, unfaithful to her own self because she is, after all her protests, marrying and claiming, finally, to love Herman Van Alstyne, a cousin of Eleanor's, come to them from Germany. She has not only agreed to marry him, but declared that her "mature" love is for him. Nevertheless, the last line in the story is a final protestation of eternal love for Eleanor, with whom she had fallen passionately in love, who had betrayed her, and died.

Just so does "Max—Or His Picture" end, with Margaret Wing proclaiming the long dead Max her "husband" and finally consenting to love him—in retrospect. But she doesn't take off the ring that everyone assumes *he* gave her, that sapphire set between diamonds, symbolizing fidelity, constancy, and love. It is the ring that *Elly* had given her, Elly, her partner in "a passionate friendship which death had ended."

French/Thanet included "Max—Or His Picture" in her collection *Stories That End Well* in 1911. It was first published in *Scribner's Magazine* in December 1899.

ENDNOTES

1. *Lesbian-Feminism in Turn-of-the-Century Germany*, edited and translated by Lillian Faderman and Brigitte Eriksson, the Naiad Press, 1980, p. vii.

2. "Female Support Networks and Political Activism: Lillian Wald, Crystal East-man, Emma Goldman" by Blanche Wiesen Cook in *A Heritage of Her Own: Toward a New Social History of American Women*, edited, with an introduction by Nancy F. Cott and Elizabeth H. Pleck, Simon and Schuster, 1979, pp. 419–420.

Max—Or His Picture

A knock sounded on the principal's door. "That's Florence," she thought; and she sighed in the same breath. The principal had secretly liked Florence Raimund the best of her two hundred girls, for three years; and, sometimes, she suspected that Florence knew it. Miss Wing sat at her desk. It was a large desk of oak, always kept in blameless order. No one could recall seeing more than one letter at a time lying on the blotter. Any others, yet unread, lay in the wicker tray to the left; the letters read but not answered were in the wicker tray to the right; the answered letters were in appropriate pigeon-holes or in ashes, Miss Wing being a firm believer in fire as a confidential agent. Above the desk hung the most interesting object in the room, to the school-girls; in fact it would be hard to gauge justly the influence this one, mute and motionless, had over their young imaginations; or how far it was responsible for the rose-tinted halo that, beyond doubt, glorified the principal for them. The object was a picture, the picture of a young man in the uniform of captain in the German cuirassiers. His thick, light hair was brushed back from a fine and candid forehead. A smile creased his cheeks under the warlike curl of his mustachios. It was a smile so happy and so friendly in its happiness, that it won the beholder. The eyes were not large, but even in the black and white of a photograph (the portrait was an ordinary cabinet *carte*) they seemed to sparkle. The young fellow's figure was superb, and held with a military precision and jauntiness. One said, looking at the whole presence, "This man is a good fellow." Viewing him more closely, one might add, "And he is in love." The picture was framed handsomely in a gilded frame. On the desk, below, an exquisite vase of Venice lifted a single, perfect rose. For fifteen years a flower had always bloomed thus. Miss Wing had hung the picture, herself, fifteen years ago. Then, she was the new principal,

and the school was but half its size; and the village people exclaimed at trusting "such a girl" with so much responsibility. During those fifteen years the new building had been built, the school
had grown and flourished; and the gray had crept into Margaret
Wing's bright hair. She had so often put on mourning for her near
kindred that she had assumed it as her permanent garb. To the
certain (and ecstatic) knowledge of the school, she had refused
divers offers of marriage from citizens of good repute and substance. But during all the changing years, the picture had kept its
place and the fresh flowers had bloomed below. No girl could remember the desk without the picture; and when the old girls visited
the school, their eyes would instinctively seek it in its old place;
always with a little moving of the heart. Yet no one ever alluded
to it to the principal; and no one, not her most trusted teacher,
nor her best loved pupil, had ever heard the principal speak of it.
The name of the pictured soldier, his story, his relation to Miss
Wing; Miss Wing's nearest kindred and friends knew as much
about all these as the school—and that was nothing. Nevertheless,
the school tradition reported part of a name on the authority of a
single incident. Years ago an accident had happened to the picture.
It was the principal's custom to carry it with her on her journeys,
however brief; always taking it down and putting it back in its
place herself. On this occasion the floor had been newly polished,
and in hanging the picture her chair on which she stood slipped
and she fell, while the picture dropped out of her grasp. One of
the girls, who was passing, ran to her aid; but she had crawled
toward the picture and would have it in her hands before she allowed the girl to aid her rise—a circumstance you may be sure not
likely to escape the sharp young eyes. Neither did these same eyes
miss the further circumstance that the jar had shifted the *carte* in
the frame and a line of writing, hitherto hidden, was staring out
at the world. The hand was the sharp, minute German hand, but
the words were English; the girl took them in at an eyeblink, as
she handed the picture to Miss Wing: "*Thine forever, Max.*" Miss
Wing made no comment, perhaps she supposed that the girl had
not seen, perhaps—in any case she was silent.

Of course, the new light flooded the school gossip, immediately. But there never came any more; every new girl was free to
work her own will on Miss Wing's romance. Was "Max" dead?

Had they parted because of any act on the woman's part? Surely he could not have been false, to receive that daily oblation of flowers. It was more likely that she thus expressed an imperishable regret. Youth, ever fanciful, played with all manner of dainty and plaintive variations on the theme. Its very mystery was its poignant charm; since each tender, young soul created a new romance and a new appeal. Elusive and pathetic, it hovered on the edge of these young lives, like the perfume of a flower. And its influence was the more potent that it asked for nothing. It is not too much to say that the spectacle of that gentle and reticent faithfulness was the strongest element in the school atmosphere. Certainly, because of it, Miss Wing had greater power over her scholars. She was a woman of ability and gentle force; by nature a little aloof, a little precise, able to feel deeply, but not able to express her sympathies or her pain. Without her mysterious sorrow, she would have seemed to young girls a thought too admirable; they would have been chilled by her virtues; but as it was, their perception that she had lived deeply, that she had suffered, that she had been loved and had loved eternally, opened their hearts. They would have admired her, now they adored her. By degrees, and insensibly to herself, she became the confessor of her little world. After they left school her girls brought her their perplexities of the heart. Wives came to her with cruel dilemmas that they shrank from revealing to their own mothers—perhaps because the mothers could not be trusted to plead for the erring husband so well; for a woman who loves, complains, not to be justified herself, but to hear her lover's misconduct excused and his love proved against her doubts. Before they left school, the girls confessed their faults and failings and strivings of conscience with the same eagerness with which they asked counsel in their innocent romances of friendship or the sorrows of trigonometry, and they accepted any penance directed, not only with patience, but a kind of exaltation natural to youth, which finds a secret joy in any exercise of its own fortitude.

To-day, however, Miss Wing sat before the picture which so many young eyes had studied with such vague yet ardent sympathy, and pondered over a confidence that had not come. The lack of its coming hurt her; and the tap on her door was welcome, for she thought, "It is she—coming to tell me. Oh, I hope he is the right man."

At her response, the door swung open with a jerk, and the dark-eyed girl who entered was catching her breath, although she tried to make the quick intakes noiseless. There was a look of pale resolution on her features.

"Have you come to let me congratulate you, my dear?" said the principal, rising. The girl colored scarlet. "I've come because I had to, because I couldn't deceive you," she blurted. "Miss Wing, it isn't so. I let Miss Parker think so; but I'm not engaged to him."

"Sit down, dear," said Miss Wing. The soft cadence of her voice did not roughen. She sat down when her guest sat, and leaned back in her desk-chair, folding her white, slim hands. There were flashing rings on the hands; and the girls used to wonder which ring "Max" had given her. They favored the sapphire, set between two diamonds, because of its beauty ("a real Cashmere, you know"), and because, whether she wore other rings or not, this always kept its place.

"Now, tell me," said Miss Wing.

"I had a letter from him this morning; it was just a note in one of Helen Grier's"—the girl's lithe form was erect in the chair, every muscle tense; she looked past Miss Wing to the wall and spoke in a toneless voice; one could see that she was driving straight on to her purpose, over her own writhing nerves—"all he said was that he had been called back to Germany——"

"Is he a German? Miss Parker said his name was Cutler."

"It is Butler," said the girl, flinging her head back, while a spark crept into her liquid, troubled, dark eyes, "but he *is* a German. Don't you know the Butler in 'Wallenstein?' You know he was a real man; and he founded a family. He—my—my friend is the Count von Butler." Miss Wing's chair, like other desk-chairs, was set on a pivot; she turned very slightly and slowly, at the same time resting her elbow on the desk. The girl ventured a timid glance at her, and thought that she looked sterner, wherefore her heart sank; but she only continued the faster: "He isn't in America just to travel; he was sent by his government to watch the Cuban war. He's very brave; and he isn't a bit like a foreigner and hasn't any nasty supercilious notions about women. Mr. Grier says he has a *future*. And really, Miss Wing, he is just like a—a—a kind of knight."

"Where did you meet him?"

"At Helen's, last summer. And he was going out to Minneapolis to see papa, I—I think. But he got a cable of his uncle's death. And his two little cousins died last year; so now he is the head of the family; and he must go to Germany, at once. For his father is dead, you know. So he wrote (in Helen's letter, because he is so—so awfully proper!) asking to let him come here and take me to drive—in the American fashion. I know who put him up to that scheme; it was Helen. I had to ask Miss Parker, because you were out; and she said if he wasn't a relation or the man I was going to marry I couldn't go. 'Of course if he were the man you expect to marry,' she said, and—and I—I said, 'But he is!' Just like that. I can't fancy how I came to say such a thing, but when it was said I didn't know how to explain; and I was so awfully ashamed; and, besides"—she lifted her eyes in the frank and direct gaze that Miss Wing always liked—"besides, I do want to see him."

"And do you expect him to ask you to marry him?" said Miss Wing, with a deepening of the color on her cheek, which went out suddenly like the flame of a lamp in the wind.

Florence Raimund blushed again, but this time she laughed: "I don't know. He is so awfully proper," said she, "and he hasn't had a chance to ask papa; but—I think he wants to."

"In that case, isn't he the man whom you expect to marry?" asked Miss Wing, dryly. "But it was deceiving her just the same. I am glad you came, Florence."

Here the girl looked up; and something in Miss Wing's eyes made her dash across the room to fling herself on her knees before the lady with an inarticulate gasp between a sob and a laugh, and the sentences came in a rush: "I *had* to come! I couldn't deceive you if I never saw him again. And besides, I hoped you'd think of some way!"

"And you escape quite unpunished?" said Miss Wing, gently.

At which the black head sank lower, while a smothered voice mumbled: "Do you think I—*liked* it, coming to tell?"

Miss Wing smoothed her hair. "It would have pained me very much if you had not come. Tell me; whether he sees you or not will he not write to your father? Do you think his feeling is so slight that a disappointment will turn it?"

The black head threw itself up and the fearless young eyes met Miss Wing's pensive, brown ones. "No, Miss Wing; I know it will make no difference."

Miss Wing stifled a sigh; it may be that she was not so sure of the firm purpose of a lover; she spoke more gently: "It is only the disappointment, then, if you can't see him?"

The girl's face quivered a little.

"Perhaps I am foolish," said Miss Wing, "but I think it *would* be a disappointment very hard to bear. Still, you must admit that parents do not send their children to school expecting them to become engaged to be married; on the contrary, there is a tacit pledge that we shall protect our wards from any entanglement. But this did not happen at school; the only question is, ought I to prevent it going any farther? My dear, do you have confidence in me?"

"Yes, Miss Wing," said the girl.

"Of course, I do not think that I ought to consent to your driving alone, together."

The girl drew a long sigh. "I suppose not," she breathed, in dismal resignation.

"But I should like him to come here, to see me; and then, if I find him to be what your father would approve, you may see him here; and we shall all have to explain things together, I fancy, to your father."

The girl drew another, a very different, sigh; and impulsively kissed Miss Wing's hand. She tried to speak; and could only murmur, "Oh, I do love you!"

"And so, if you will tell Graf von Butler—what is his Christian name, Florence?"

"Max," said the girl, very low, for she felt the presence of the picture, on which she had not once turned her eyes. Before she spoke, under a pretense of a pull at her skirt, she slipped her hand out of the hand with the sapphire ring. Yet her excited young nerves vibrated at the slight cough which came as the principal changed her position, before she said, in her usual tone: "It is a fine name. Well, Florence, will you tell Count Max von Butler that I shall hope to see him. And—will you trust me?"

The girl told her that she would trust her utterly, and she knew that it would be right; and oh, she was so happy. And she came back to say, with the tears in her eyes, "I shall be grateful to you as long as I live."

Miss Wing stood in the centre of the room, smiling, until the door closed. But then in a second she was at the door, almost fiercely but noiselessly, twisting the key in the lock. From the door she passed to the windows and dropped the shades. At last, safe from every chance of espial, she sat down again in her chair before the desk, leaned her elbows on the desk, and looked desperately, miserably, into the joyous face of the picture. She did not speak, but her thoughts took on words and sank like hot lead into her heart. "Max Butler! Max Butler! The little nephew he told about. And *he* has been alive all these years; and happy; with little sons, while I—I have lied to these trusting girls. It was wicked and shameless. I deceived myself; then I deceived them. I wonder why. I knew what they were thinking. How dared I look that honest child in the face! I suppose she wonders like the rest why I have not told anyone of my romance. And it is simply that there was nothing to tell. Nothing." She looked into the soldier's happy eyes while her lips curled and she murmured, drearily and bitterly, "I haven't even the right to be angry with you, poor lad. What did you do? *You* are not my Max; I only made him up out of my heart—like children playing a game!" Her mind drifted dizzily through shapeless and inconsequent visions of the past. She was seeing again the grim pile of the ruined castle, the masses of broken shadow, the intricate carving on arch and architrave and plinth, the wavering mass of limbs and tree-trunks on the green sward; and she, with her twisted ankle, was kneeling, trying to peer through the shrubbery for her lost companions. Did he come by chance? She had seen the handsome, young officer, daily, for a week. His great-aunt was Margaret's right-hand neighbor at the pension table d'hôte, a withered relic of Polish nobility with fine, black eyes in a face like a hickory nut; who wore shabby gowns and magnificent jewels, frankly smoked cigarettes, and seemed to have a venomous tale ready to fit any name mentioned in conversation—with one exception, her nephew's. According to her, Max's father was a swine and his mother a fool and his brother a popinjay; and his sister had no respect for her betters; but Max had a heart. It was understood at the pension that she was arranging a great match for him. In spite of the general disapproval of his aunt, he was a favorite, he was so simple, amiable, and polite. Even the American Professor admitted that for a man "who had won the Iron Cross in such a spectacular fashion, he was very modest and really more like an American than a German officer," thus paying the unconsciously arrogant compliment kept by every race for engaging aliens. Margaret's first sight of him was not under the shelter of the conventionalities. It happened that the Countess's ferocious pet (and the terror of the pension), a Great Dane, was trying to eat up a little girl, but fortunately had begun with her petticoats. The court of the house was the scene of the fray; and a large, timid cook, the only witness, was waving a copper kettle full of the meringue that she was beating in one hand and the great wire whip in the other, while she shrieked impartially on Heaven and the police. Margaret heard the din. She ran to the spot. Being a New England woman, she didn't scream; one swift glance went from the child's writhing body and the dog's horrible head to the wailing cook. In two strides she caught the kettle out of a fat and agitated German hand and hurled the whole sticky, white mass full at the dog's eyes; then, as the blinded and astounded beast flung his head back to howl, and spattered the world with meringue, she snatched up the child and sent her flying into the door and the cook. The dog was smeared with meringue, she was smeared, the child was smeared, the cook was smeared; and now a beautiful white and gold officer, who bounded over a wall and fell upon the dog with his sabre and two heels, was smeared the most lavishly of all! No wonder Frau Müller (visible, aloft, in an artless German toilet of ease and without her teeth), the countess (who was a gazing stock, for the same reason), and Augustine, her maid, the three Russians on the second floor, and the three Americans on the third, filled the windows with polyglot consternation! The consequence of it all was that when the Count von Butler was formally presented to Miss Wing, that evening, she blushed. She was too pale and listless to be pretty; but when she blushed she was enchanting. Remembering the meringue, she smiled and ventured an upward glance; and, for the first time in her life, met the admiration in the eyes of a man. At this time Margaret was thirty years old and had never been asked in marriage. She had spent most of the thirty years in a boarding school, as pupil or as teacher; and she had brought from her cloistered life a single vivid feeling, a passionate friendship which death had ended. The sapphire ring was her poor friend's last token.

To be thirty and never to have been sought like other girls, leaves a chill in the heart. It may be lonely never to have loved, but it is bleak never to have been loved. Margaret remembered her delicate, girlish dreams with a recoil of humiliation; they seemed to her almost immodest. She thought that she was too old to wear hats, and wondered whether she ought not to discard the pinks and light blues which poor Elly had liked on her, for more sedate colors. But she wore pink after she met Max Butler. Yet he never saw her save in the presence of others; he was full of little, graceful attentions, but he showed the same attention to the portly clergy-man's widow and the meritorious but cross-eyed teacher of fifty, who formed Miss Wing's "party"; it was only his eyes, his eyes always following her approving, delighting, admiring, pleading, speaking to her as they spoke to no other woman. She told herself that it was just the pleasant, foreign way; and she wrote to her friends in America, "The German officers have very agreeable, def-erential manners; I think they are much more gentle and polite and have a higher respect for women than the French or Italians." And he said no word, even of friendship, until that afternoon at the Heidelberger Schloss.

He came upon her almost immediately, scrambling up the bank at a rate which had worked woe to his uniform. He was torn, he was scratched, he was stained with mud and grass; and he was beaming with delight. "I have seen you from below," he exclaimed, in his careful English, "so I came up. Will you excuse?" Then his mood changed, perceiving her plight, and he insisted on tearing his handkerchief into strips to bind her ankle. It seemed absurd to refuse his aid, which he offered quite simply; but his hands trem-bled a little over the knots. "It will be most easy, I think," said he, "that you should let me assist you a small way, to the *restauracion*; so I can get the carriage, and you can have some ice-cream. Again, to-day, is it burned——"

She had laughed and said that she never had heard of burned ice-cream. He laughed too, and explained that it was burned as a custard, and somehow under cover of this she let him put her hand on his shoulder and his arm about her waist. She was grateful to him for the matter-of-fact manner in which he did it all, saying, "You will have to be my comrade that has been wounded, and I will help him off the field; so I did, once, with my colonel; it is better than to wait until I could bring help." In this fashion they walked for some twenty minutes. They were minutes not entirely disfigured by her physical pain, for it was a comfort to be helped by so strong and kind a friend. The comfort brightened almost into pleasure, as they drove homeward in a shabby *droschky*, with all the circuit of the horizon flooded with softest rose and gold, reflecting the cloudless glory of the West. Borne along through that unreal and lovely radiance, past the hills checkered with vineyards and ripening grain, which the sunlight blazoned in green and gold like the initials of an old missal; they talked as one friend would talk to another. At least that was her phrase, and she admitted to herself that she had not been so nearly happy since Elly died. "I didn't know a man could be so—so kind," she said.

He told her of his country and his home; and how he loved the hills that his fathers had always owned, and the rugged, simple, faithful people; he told her of the plans of his father and himself for them; he told her of his father, who had the best heart in the world, but was credited with a fierce temper simply because his voice was loud; and his mother, who was so gentle that everyone loved her; and his handsome sister, and his brother, who was a diplomat and far cleverer than he; and his little brother who died and would have no one carry him in his pain but Max ("Ah, he was the most clever and the most beautiful of us all!"), and Max, his little nephew, who looked like the dead boy. "I hope you will see my home and them all," he said; "to-morrow I shall see them, then, the same day, I shall be back here—with you."

And then, by degrees, she won him to talk of his profession, of his hopes, his ambitions, his ideals, of all those intimate and cherished things which lie at the bottom of the soul and only rise for a friend's eyes. It seemed to her that she could read his character in the hints given by his words, as one would fill an outline sketch with perspective and details. There was certainly a fascination in this revelation; candor, after all, was a virtue as well as reticence. Perhaps her new friend was a little mediæval, but he was as refined as if he had been all modern.

By now they were rattling through the modern town of Heidelberg, the plain walls of which looked bare after the lawless pomp of carving and form on the old castle; they had not even the bizarre, affected grace of the architecture then decking American countrysides. But Margaret thought how homelike and honest the houses looked; stanch and trusty, like the German. Butler, just then, was praising American buggies, from which he made a genial transition to the customs of society. "In America, is it not," says he, "the young ladies drive alone with young men?"

"Yes, very often. But not with you?"

"Oh, no, mein fraulein; this is the first time I am alone with a young lady!"

She had called herself old for so long, that there was a distinct pleasure in being "a young lady" to him, and she had not time to remember it partook of the nature of deceit, because he sent a wave of confusion over her by continuing: "In America, also, one would propose marriage to a lady, herself, before to her father?"

"It is our custom," agreed Margaret, "but"—with her prim, teacher's air—"your custom is far more decorous."

His face fell, then promptly brightened, "Perhaps it would be best to speak to both, so near the same time one can. But this is another thing you must explain me. How is it most preferable to the lady, that one shall write or shall come——"

"Oh, write," said Margaret, quickly. How silly of her to suddenly feel so frightened; she wished that she were in a room and not in a carriage with him; involuntarily she shrank back into her own corner, and she found that she was playing with the soiled and frayed edges of a tear in the cloth of the side curtain and watching her pearl-colored fingers. Those gloves she had put on new, that day. How reckless! But she had not the resolution to desist. His voice dragged a little, "Ah, yes, if she would refuse, but if—*not?*"

"In any case," said she.

"Look!" he exclaimed, "at the sunset. Ah, is it not lovely?"

Of a sudden, they were looking, not at the sunset, but into each other's eyes; and all about them was that wonderful, transfiguring glow, and it seemed as if there were nothing in the whole world that he had not said.

"Is it to the right, Herr Captain?" asked the driver, turning on his seat to divide a benign and semi-intoxicated smile between them.

Then it was hardly a moment until the yellow stucco of the pension jumped at their eyes, around a corner; and there were the clergyman's widow and the teacher at the door. They fell upon the carriage in a clamor of explanation and sympathy; they were at her side when he bowed over her hand and kissed it, saying, "Aufwiedersehen."

That was all. There was never any more. He did not come again. Or if he came, she was not there; since, the next day they were on their way to Bremen, summoned by cable to her sister's deathbed. She never heard from him or of him again. Yet she had left her American address with his aunt for any letters that might need to be forwarded, and a stiff little note of thanks and farewell—a perfectly neutral note such as any friend might give or receive. There followed weeks crowded with sorrow and business (the sister was a widow without children, and she shared her estate with her other sister); and Margaret imputed her deep depression to these natural and sufficient causes. She rated herself for vanity in reading her own meanings into a courteous young man's looks and his intelligent interest in national difference of manners. She fostered her shame with the New Englander's zest for self-torture. But, one afternoon, without warning, there fell upon her a deep and hopeless peace. It was as if some invisible power controlled and changed all the currents of her thought. She *knew* that her friend was not faithless or careless; he was dead. She began to weep, gently, thinking pitifully of his old father with the loud voice, and his fragile mother and the sister and brother and the little nephew. "Poor people," she murmured, wishing, for the first time in her life, to make some sign of her sorrow for them to them, she who always paid her toll of sympathy, but dreaded it and knew that she was clumsy. She remembered the day at the castle; and went over again, each word, each look. A sensation that she could not understand, full of awe and sweetness, possessed her. It was indescribable, unthinkable, but it was also irresistible. Under its impulse she went to a trunk in another room, from which she had not yet removed all the contents, and took out her Heidelberg photographs. She said to herself that she would look at the scenes of that day. In her search she came upon a package of her own pictures which had come the morning of the day that she had gone. She could not remember any details of receiving them, except that she had been at the photographer's the day before, and paid for them. When they came she was in too great agitation (they were just packing) to more than fling them into a tray. She could not tell why she took the *cartes* out of the envelope and ran them listlessly through her fingers; but at the last of the package she uttered a cry. The last *carte* was the picture of Max, with the inscription in his own hand, "Thine forever." It is not exact to say that with the finding of the picture her doubt of his affection for her vanished; for in truth, she had no doubts, the possession was too absolute. But the sight came upon her as the presence of a mortal being, alive and visible, comes on one, when he enters a room. And there is no question that it was a comfort; if she had really loved Max, at this time, the knowledge of his death would have been her cruelest shock; for then she could have no hope to meet him again in the world—no hope of some explanation and the happiness of life together. But she was not in love with the young German, she was touched by his admiration, she admired him tenderly, she felt the moving of a subtle attraction which she called friendship and which might pass into a keener feeling; but she did not love him. Not then. Therefore, she felt a sweetness in her pain; she could respect herself once more; she had a new and mystical joy; for was she not beloved above women? Had not her lover come to her, through what strange paths who may know, to comfort her? This is the story of the picture. She could not tell it. Nor did she; but she hung Max's portrait on the walls of her little parlor; and she hung opposite a picture of the castle; and from that day, never a day passed that it did not influence her. She used to think her thoughts before it. She came to it with her grief for the loss of kindred and friends, with her loneliness, with her anxieties, with her aspirations, her plans, her cares for others, her slowly dawning interests and affections. She was a reticent woman, who might never have allowed her heart to expand to her husband himself, beyond a certain limit; but she hid nothing from Max. In time, she fell into the habit of talking to the picture. She called him Max. The first time she spoke his name she blushed. She made her toilets for him more than for the world; but whether Max could admire them or not, it is certain that the girls knew every change in her pretty gowns. Her sense of having been loved had its effect on her manner, and a deeper effect on her heart. At thirty she was a New England nun; at forty she was the woman who understands. The love which the shrinking and critical girl repelled at its first step toward her, without knowing, the woman who pitied and who understood, attracted, quite as unconsciously.

"It is very queer, Max," she said, "that in my old age men should want to marry me. But I like you best."

Only the day before she had said that; and she had said, "I am happy, Max. Isn't it strange! But I am." Only yesterday—and now there was nothing. The Max that she had grown to love, with the gradual, imperceptible advance of affection, sweet to her shy nature—that Max had never been. No doubt all the while, over in Germany, a stout and phlegmatic German landlord had been caring for his vineyards and playing the war lord in the landwehr and living very comfortably with the doughy-looking German girl whose hair was lighter than her complexion; whom the countess wanted him to marry; a man as unlike the high-souled knight of her fancy as—as she, herself, was unlike the girl's image! Worst of all was her own weak, false behavior. "No," she cried, in an access of bitterness, "the worst is that I can't feel *that* the worst; I can only feel I have lost him, forever! I don't seem to mind that I have lost myself!"

Now she began to pace the room, trying to think clearly. Was it her duty to tell Florence the story and let her tell the girls? The red-hot agony of the idea seemed to her excited conscience an intimation that it *was* her duty from which she shrank because she was a selfish, hysterical, dishonorable coward. Horrible as such abasement would be, if it were her duty, she could do it; what she could not, what she *would* not do, was to tear the veil from that pure and mystical passion which had been the flower of her heart. "Not if it cost me my soul," she said, with the frozen quiet of despair; "it is awful, but I can't do it!" One thing did remain; she could remove the picture. That false witness of what had never been should go. No eyes should ever fall on it again. It should never deceive more. She walked toward it firmly. She lifted her hand—and it fell. "I can't!" she moaned. "I'll do it to-morrow." She could not remember, in years, so weak a compromise offered her conscience.

But she felt a sense of respite, almost relief, once having decided; and she recovered her composure enough to go to her chamber and bathe her eyes. While she was thus engaged she heard a knock. "It is he," she said, quietly; "well, the sooner the better."

It was he; he had come earlier than he expected, he explained; he was most grateful for Miss Wing's kind message. He looked like his uncle, as the members of a family will look alike. He was not so tall; he was not so handsome. Perhaps most people would call him more graceful. And his English was faultless; he must have spoken it from his childhood. In the midst of his first sentences, before they had permitted him to take a chair, his eyes travelled past Miss Wing's face. She perceived that he saw the picture; she knew that she grew pale; but, to her amazement, a calm like the calm which had wrapped her senses on the day of her finding the picture, closed about her again. "I beg pardon?" said he.

"Yes, that is Count von Butler's portrait," said she, in a clear voice, without emotion. He was not so composed. "Then it *was* you," he said. Following her example, he took a chair and looked earnestly at the pictured face. "When Miss Raimund spoke of you so warmly, I noticed that the name was the same, and I determined to inquire; but it seemed to me unlikely. Yet it is. Miss Wing, I have a message to you, from my uncle."

She noticed that there were gold motes in the air; and his pleasant, blond face seemed to waver through them; the room was full of sunlight.

"I was with him when he died."

That was a strange thing to hear when the message of his uncle's death had come to him in another country; she hoped that her brain was not going to play her false.

"It was fifteen years ago last July, you know. I never knew how many details you received, or only the bare fact in the papers."

Fifteen years! fifteen years! What was that date he was giving? That was the day on which she sailed for America, the day after —what was that story that he was telling of a visit and a fire and a child rescued and an accident? But still she listened with the same iron composure. The next words she heard distinctly.

"It was like him to lose his life that way; and he did not grudge it. Yet it was hard that I should be the only one of his blood with him. He could speak with difficulty when he told me to take a lock of hair and his signet ring to you. He dictated the address, himself, to me. 'You must be sure and take it,' he said. 'It is to the lady that I hoped would be my betrothed; you must tell grandmamma about it, too. She has my picture and she knows—but tell her'— and then, I think his mind must have wandered a little, for he smiled brightly at me, saying: '*I'll* tell her, myself,' and then the doctors came. He said nothing more, only once, they told me, he murmured something about his betrothed. But I had the ring; he took it off his finger and kissed it and gave it to me. Child as I was, I knew that it was sacred. I wrapped it in the paper; and afterward I put the lock of hair beside it. So soon as I could I went to Heidelberg, to the pension. You had gone and there was no address, no trace——"

"I left my address with the countess——"

"My aunt is dead," said the young German, gravely. "I would not criticise her, but she had her own choice of a wife for my uncle; I do not think one could trust her with addresses."

"We all gave ours to her to give to Frau Müller."

"That is why, then, I could not find you. My grandmother, also, tried. But you were gone. I thought of the banks, long after; but I found nothing. Often it has seemed dreadful that you should learn of this only through the papers. But I could not tell whether—*anything*. When I came to America, I confess it was always in my mind. I always carried my uncle's little packet with me. I will have it sent to you."

"Excuse me," said Miss Wing, gently. "Will you please bring me the glass of water—I—am afraid—I can't walk to it."

But she would not let him pour the water on his handkerchief to bathe her head. She sipped the water, and very pale, but quite herself, brought him back to his own matters. She found that it was a cousin, miscalled an uncle, in the German manner, who had died. It did not seem to her that Max's nephew could be unworthy of any girl; yet she conscientiously questioned him regarding his worldly affairs, for Florence was an only daughter whose father had great possessions and a distrust of adventurers, and at last she sent him forth to walk in the grove with his sweetheart. "And speak to her," she said, with a look that sank into his heart; "it is the American way; don't wait to write, the American way is best."

So, at last, she was alone. Alone with her lover who had always been true; whose love many waters could not quench, and it was stronger than death. She often pondered, afterward, whether there had not been some note written to her and sent with the photographs; whether the countess might not have tampered with the package, taking the note, but not suspecting the picture. But none of these puzzles troubled her to-day. She stood in front of the picture. All the years, an obscure and virginal shyness had withheld her from ever overstepping her first attitude. She told him every thought of her heart in regard to others and herself. He was her dearest friend. She called him "Max" and "my friend." Recalling the French use of the latter term, she used it sometimes with a little flutter of the heart. But those innocent endearments that a woman keeps for her lover's portrait—to make amends for not proffering them of free will to the poor fellow himself—these it would have shocked her to imagine. She never touched the picture, save reverently, to dust it, to take it down when she went away, to replace it in its station when she returned. But now, trembling, yet not blushing, she took the picture into her hands. She looked long into its eyes; she kissed it with a light and timid kiss, and swiftly hid the smiling face against her heart, pressing the frame in both hands, and touching it with her cheek bent over it, while she whispered: "You *did* tell me. You came back and told me. I love you, Max, my knight—my husband!"

A NOTE ON THE TEXT

"Two Friends" has not been published since its original appearance in a periodical except for a recent publication of this version of the story in *American Literary Realism* (Fall 1988) in anticipation of the publication of this book.

After its original appearance in a periodical, "My Visitation" was apparently not published again until Elizabeth Ammons included it in her collection of Rose Terry Cooke's stories, *"How Celia Changed Her Mind" & Selected Stories* in 1986. Hence, there was no decision to make about which version of these two stories to publish.

Although "Miss Grief" was never collected in a volume of Woolson's stories, there are two versions of the story: it was reprinted in *Stories by American Authors*, vol. IV, 1884, and reprinted in 1912. The 1912 version, which is the only one I have been able to examine, contains the version of the story reprinted recently in *Women Artists, Women Exiles: "Miss Grief" and Other Stories by Constance Fenimore Woolson* edited and with an Introduction by Joan Myers Weimer (1988).

"The Long Arm" was reprinted twice. The first was an unauthorized publication in the *Pocket Magazine* 1 (December 1895) which Chamberlain and Wilkins fought but were unable to prevent, and which Bacheller insisted on his right to, in order to recoup some of his extravagant payment for the story. The second, also apparently unauthorized, was by Carolyn Wells, in her 1927 anthology *American Detective Stories*. It has been out of print since.

In the case of the other seven stories, two versions of each exist: the original periodical version and the slightly different one collected later in a single author volume. Except for two significant differences between the versions of "Martha's Lady," all the differences between the versions of the stories are what might be called aesthetic or cosmetic rather than cogent. They are the kind of changes one might make in a perfectly complimentary costume just because there is one more chance to look in a mirror, to rearrange a curl, to shake out a pleat, to fluff a ruffle. Almost all writers will fiddle with their work endlessly, unless someone takes it away and says, "Now you are done." In all cases, I prefer and have reprinted the original version. However, for those interested in the differences, the later versions are all available in recent scholarly reprints.

There are the usual cosmetic differences in the two versions of "Martha's Lady" that are in the others, but there are also two significant differences. Two telling sentences were added to the last paragraph of the later version. This textual variant is included on p. 219 at the bottom of the page. I have reprinted the periodical version of this story, too. The only important difference in "Miss Grief" is the name "Ethelind" which was changed to "Isobel" in the later version.

There's an epidemic with 27 million victims. And no visible symptoms.

It's an epidemic of people who can't read.

Believe it *or* not, 27 million Americans are functionally illiterate, about one adult in five.

The solution to this problem is you... when you join the fight against illiteracy. So call the Coalition for Literacy at toll-free **1-800-228-8813** and volunteer.

Volunteer Against Illiteracy. The only degree you need is a degree of caring.

KARL MARX
FREDERICK ENGELS

Volume
17

MARX AND ENGELS: 1859-60

INTERNATIONAL PUBLISHERS

NEW YORK

This volume has been prepared jointly by Lawrence &
Wishart Ltd., London, International Publishers Co.
Inc., New York, and Progress Publishers, Moscow, in
collaboration with the Institute of Marxism-Leninism,
Moscow.

Editorial commissions:
GREAT BRITAIN: Jack Cohen, Maurice Cornforth,
E. J. Hobsbawm, Nicholas Jacobs, Martin Milligan,
Ernst Wangermann.
USA: James S. Allen, Louis Diskin, Philip S. Foner,
Dirk J. Struik, William W. Weinstone.
USSR: for Progress Publishers—N. P. Karmanova,
V. I. Neznanov, V. N. Sedikh, M. K. Shcheglova;
for the Institute of Marxism-Leninism—
P. N. Fedoseyev, L. I. Golman, A. I. Malysh,
M. P. Mchedlov, A. G. Yegorov.

Copyright © Progress Publishers, Moscow, 1981

Library of Congress Cataloging in Publication Data

Marx, Karl, 1818-1883

Karl Marx, Frederick Engels: collected works.

1. Socialism—Collected works. 2. Economics—
Collected works. I. Engels, Friedrich, 1820-1895.
Works. English. 1975. II. Title.
HX39.5. A 16 1975   335.4   73-84671
ISBN 0-7178-05 17-4 (v. 17)

Printed in the Union of Soviet Socialist Republics

Contents

FROM THE PREPARATORY MATERIALS

NOTES AND INDEXES

ILLUSTRATIONS

Translated by

RODNEY LIVINGSTONE

Preface

Volume 17 of the *Collected Works* of Marx and Engels comprises works written between October 1859 and December 1860. The first half of the volume is devoted to Marx's long polemic *Herr Vogt* and the letters and statements connected with the so-called Vogt Case that he sent to the editors of various newspapers. The second half consists of articles written by Marx and Engels for the American progressive newspaper *New-York Daily Tribune* between January and December 1860. All these works are linked in subject-matter with those published in volumes 16, 18 and 19 of the present edition.

As Marx and Engels had foreseen, the first world economic crisis of 1857-58 was followed by a fresh upswing of the democratic, proletarian and national liberation movements. An ever widening struggle was being waged over the tasks the bourgeois revolutions of 1848-49 had left unsolved, one of which was the now urgent necessity for the unification of Germany, and also of Italy. In this period the international situation, as the Italian war of 1859 (France and Piedmont against Austria) had shown, was charged with the danger of armed conflict.

In the complex conditions of the time the activity of the masses, particularly that of the proletariat, grew rapidly, and Marx and Engels devoted themselves to preparing the working class for the forthcoming battles. Besides elaborating revolutionary theory and crucial questions of the tactics of proletarian struggle, they concentrated more and more of their practical activity on rallying the revolutionary forces and setting up an independent political party of the working class. Their task now was not only to preserve the cadres of experienced proletarian revolutionaries, but also to

establish closer ties with the broad masses, to give the movement
its own newspaper (the attempts to turn the London German émigré
paper *Das Volk* into such an organ are described in Volume 16) and
to win more supporters.

Increasingly Marx and Engels devoted their journalistic writings
on home and foreign policy to substantiating the position of the
emerging party of the proletariat. Defending its political and
moral authority, Marx vigorously rebuffed the ideological enemies
of the working class, who were trying to slander and discredit the
active members of the Communist League. A rebuttal of these
slanderous fabrications was particularly necessary at this crucial
moment in the development of the working-class movement, when
the proletarians of many countries had begun to awaken to
political activity and showed a tendency to set up their own
political organisations and establish international connections,
when new forces were entering the working-class movement and
there was thus a real opportunity for creating a mass proletarian
party. Its nucleus was to be, as Marx and Engels envisaged, a united and well-tested group of proletarian revolutionaries. "The moment is approaching," Marx wrote to Lassalle in
September 1860, "when our 'small' and yet, in a certain sense,
powerful party' (insofar as the other parties do not know what
they want or do not want what they know) must draft a plan of its
campaign" (see present edition, Vol. 41).

Marx's long polemical work— *Herr Vogt*—reflects the struggle
waged by Marx and Engels against attempts by the ideologists and
agents of the bourgeoisie to denigrate the proletarian party. Their
exposure had become an important task and in the circumstances
of the time was not only a means of self-defence, but also a form
of active upholding and propagation of communist principles.

In his letter to Freiligrath of February 29, 1860 Marx wrote that
he and his associates were being attacked with utter ruthlessness
by the bourgeois circles of many countries, by the whole official
world "who in order to ruin us are not just occasionally infringing
the penal code but have ranged widely over its length and
breadth..." (see present edition, Vol. 41). One of the spokesmen of
this "official world" was the German scientist and politician Karl
Vogt, who had formerly sided with the petty-bourgeois democrats.
In December 1859 Vogt published a pamphlet entitled *Mein Prozess
gegen die Allgemeine Zeitung,* which was full of slanderous statements
about Marx and his associates.

In this pamphlet Vogt deliberately falsified facts and invented
charges against Marx and his associates, distorting the true picture

of the activities of the Communist League. Armed with police forgeries used in the Cologne communist trial in 1852, Vogt even went so far as to accuse Marx and his associates of mercenary, if not criminal aims. In principle there was nothing new in these insinuations. They were merely a rehash of the fabricated charges brought against members of the Communist League by Prussian police agents. The same lies had often been used by groups of petty-bourgeois émigrés hostile to the proletarian revolutionaries. "...At all times and in all places," Marx wrote, "the sycophants of the ruling class have always resorted to these despicable slanders to denigrate the literary and political champions of the oppressed classes" (see this volume, p. 69). However, Vogt's slanderous fabrications were on this occasion immediately taken up by the bourgeois press of Germany, England, Switzerland and other European countries and also found their way into the émigré press in the United States. The dissemination of anti-communist inventions assumed a massive scale. "Naturally the jubilation of the bourgeois press knows no bounds," Marx wrote to Engels on January 31, 1860 about the reaction of the bourgeois press to the publication of the Vogt pamphlet (see present edition, Vol. 41).

Marx rightly saw this as an attempt by the bourgeoisie to discredit the proletarian revolutionaries, to strike a blow at the emerging party of the proletariat and undermine its positions morally and politically in the eyes of the public. "His [Vogt's] attack on me...", Marx wrote to Engels on February 3, 1860, "is intended as a *grand coup* by vulgar bourgeois democracy ... against the whole party. It must therefore be answered by a *grand coup*. The *defensive* is not for us" (see present edition, Vol. 41). Marx's exposé *Herr Vogt* was the answer to this anti-communist campaign. The unmasking of Vogt was particularly important for Germany, where the proletarian revolutionaries were faced with the task of building up their influence among the masses in the struggle for the country's democratic unification.

Marx pursued a dual aim in his writings against Vogt. He exposed him both as an individual spreading slander and as "an individual who stands for a whole trend" (this volume, p. 26) of ideologists whom the bourgeoisie was using to discredit proletarian revolutionaries and disorganise the working-class movement. Marx was not merely answering the attacks on himself personally, was not only defending the proletarian revolutionaries' past activities, he was also fighting for the future of the proletarian party. The exposure of Vogt was "of decisive importance for the *historical*

vindication of the party and for its future position in Germany",
Marx wrote to Freiligrath on February 23, 1860 (see present
edition, Vol. 41). The importance Marx attached to defending the
party, which was still only in the process of formation, from
slander by its enemies is shown by the fact that he put aside his
work on *Capital* for nearly a year in order to write the pamphlet.

Herr Vogt is a complex, highly satirical work. The wealth of
information it contains, the importance of the problems raised, the
vast quantity of thoroughly researched and skilfully presented
material, make it one of the finest examples of Marx's polemical
writings and one of the most important of his historical works. He
succeeded in creating a broad canvas portraying the period, the
prevailing political systems, the home and foreign policies of the
ruling classes, the bourgeois court, the police and the venal press.
At the same time, he levelled revealing criticism at the anti-
proletarian trends of bourgeois liberalism and bourgeois and
petty-bourgeois democracy.

In dealing with the formation and development of the
international communist movement, Marx refuted Vogt's allegations that the Communist League was a narrow conspiratorial
organisation pursuing aims that were not revolutionary at all. In
Chapter IV of the work ("Techow's Letter") he gave a brief but
succinct description of the emergence and activities of this first
international communist organisation of the proletariat. In this
and other chapters (Chapter III, "Police Matters", and Chapter
VI, "Vogt and the *Neue Rheinische Zeitung*") he portrayed the
historical setting in which the League operated, its connections
with working-class circles and its role in the propagation of
communist ideas, and also the struggle waged by the proletarian
trend against sectarian elements. Discussing the reasons for the
split in the Communist League, Marx pointed out the harm done
by the adventurist and conspiratorial tactics of the Willich-
Schapper sectarian group, their incompatibility with the true aims
of the proletarian party, and particularly stressed the demoralising
and disorganising consequences of the voluntarist and conspiratorial trends for the working-class movement.

Herr Vogt is the first work in Marxist literature to pinpoint the
basic elements of the initial phase in the process of combining
scientific communism with the working-class movement. It
pioneers the idea of the continuity of the various stages of this
process, the various steps in the struggle for a proletarian party.
Along with Marx's *Revelations Concerning the Communist Trial in
Cologne* and *The Knight of the Noble Consciousness*, and Marx and

Engels' *The Great Men of the Exile* (see present edition, Vols. 11, 12), *Herr Vogt* marks the beginning of the Marxist historiography of the communist movement.

The portrait of the main character in the pamphlet is generalised. Marx used Vogt as an example to show that the anti-revolutionary, anti-proletarian prejudices of the unstable elements among the bourgeois intellectuals brought them into the camp of reaction and allowed the ruling classes, particularly those of such a corrupt state as Bonapartist France, to exploit them for counter-revolutionary purposes. Marx exposed Vogt as a petty politician and ridiculed him as one of the cowardly leaders of the leftist petty-bourgeois group in the Frankfurt National Assembly and a member of the imperial regency, set up by the rump of the Frankfurt Parliament at the closing stage of the 1848-49 revolution. Marx showed that Vogt's whole political activity was in fact counter-revolutionary. According to the *Neue Rheinische Zeitung*, he was "the 'faithful warner' against revolution" (this volume, p. 55). This exposure of Vogt had a great impact because he had been widely regarded as a democratic and even radical politician.

Marx considered Vogt mainly as a political figure, but some of his sharply satirical observations illuminated the nature of Vogt's philosophical views as a spokesman of German vulgar materialism.

The pamphlet's focal point is the exposure of Vogt as a paid agent of Napoleon III (Chapter VIII, "Dâ-Dâ Vogt and His Studies"; IX, "Agency"; and X, "Patrons and Accomplices"), as "one of the countless mouthpieces through whom the grotesque ventriloquist in the Tuileries spoke in foreign tongues" (this volume, p. 159). As Marx proved, Vogt performed the function of moulding European public opinion in the Bonapartist spirit and recruiting members of the liberal and democratic opposition to Bonapartism by admitting them to the "French feeding-trough". Vogt's *Studien zur gegenwärtigen Lage Europas* (Studies on the Present Situation in Europe), published a month before the outbreak of the Italian war, left Marx "in no doubt about his connection with Bonapartist propaganda" (this volume, p. 116) since it was a rehash of the official propaganda hand-outs of the Second Empire and was designed to assist the latter in its foreign-policy adventures. Subsequently, in 1870, after the fall of the Second Empire, when details of the expenditure of secret funds in 1859 were released, Vogt's name was found to be on the list of recipients. This was incontrovertible documentary proof of the charges Marx had brought against him ten years before.

Marx exposed not only Vogt but also his "patrons and

accomplices", the whole circle of paid agents, hack writers and journalists, and unprincipled politicians acting in the interests of the Second Empire. The pages describing the typical ways in which the bourgeois press serves the ruling circles ideologically in their struggle against the revolutionary working-class movement, and purveys bourgeois influence among proletarians and democrats are brilliant political satire. Marx lashed out at the venality of the Bonapartist press, whose scribes "one and all take their inspiration from one and the same illustrious— money-box" (this volume, p. 211), and had some equally hard things to say about the bourgeois press of Germany and England. He treated the action of the then liberal *Daily Telegraph,* which had reprinted Vogt's slander and refused to publish Marx's denial, as a striking example of how the press and journalism as a whole in bourgeois society become a field for private money-making, spreading lies and misinformation, derogatory rumours and scandalous gossip to satisfy the tastes of the philistine. Marx compares the newspaper to a "great central paper *cloaca*" receiving all the "social refuse" (this volume, p. 243).

The social and national demagoguery of Bonapartism, Louis Bonaparte's "leftist" gestures in social and national policy, designed to present the police state of the Second Empire as a champion of the workers' interests and a defender of oppressed nations, were particularly dangerous, Marx wrote. He drew attention to the attempts of the Bonapartist Vogt to persuade the Swiss artisans that Napoleon III was a "workers' dictator" (this volume, p. 191) deeply concerned for the welfare of the working people and their protection from exploitation by the bourgeoisie. Marx demonstrated the demoralising effect on the working class of this brand of social demagoguery, which was later to spread in other countries in the form of "police socialism". Taking Vogt's role as an accessory to the Bonapartist monarchy as an example, Marx pointed to the danger of the democratic and proletarian movements being penetrated by all kinds of hostile agents, and to the need for their timely identification and exposure.

Marx's revelations of Vogt's connections with Bonapartist circles grew into a general unmasking of the Bonapartist regime. Marx and Engels regarded the Second Empire as one of the bastions of reaction in Europe and the fight against Bonapartism as one of the international proletariat's key tasks. In *Herr Vogt* (Chapters VIII, IX and X) Marx developed and deepened the analysis of Bonapartism that he had made in his *The Eighteenth Brumaire of Louis Bonaparte* (see present edition, Vol. 11) and quotes from this work.

Dealing with Vogt's and other mercenary writers' efforts to embellish the foreign policy of the Second Empire, Marx showed the reactionary aims and methods of this policy, revealing the demagogic essence of the Bonapartist "principle of nationality", and the false concept of "natural frontiers", which were used to cover up the plans of the ruling circles to exploit the national movements in order to establish French hegemony and redraw the map of Europe in favour of the Bonapartist camarilla. Marx noted that the Bonapartist clique was trying to consolidate the dictatorial regime in France by means of "local wars" and combat the revolutionary-democratic struggle in Italy and other countries by armed force. He showed that the rulers of the Second Empire were enemies of all national liberation movements and hypocritically masked their true position by a pretence of sympathy for the Poles, Hungarians, Italians and other oppressed nations. In Marx's view the tendency of some of the national leaders to succumb to Bonapartist demagoguery, their readiness to make a deal with Bonapartism, presented a grave danger to the revolutionary development of these movements. Marx revealed the true nature of the policies pursued by the ruling circles of England, and also of Tsarist Russia, who were giving Napoleon III diplomatic support and thus contributing to the outbreak of the Italian war.

In *Herr Vogt* Marx analysed various aspects of international relations from the eighteenth century up to the 1850s and highlighted the key points of contradiction and conflict between the European powers. His interest in these problems is also documented by the excerpts, published here in the section "From the Preparatory Materials", from the book by the Hungarian historian and participant in the 1848-49 revolution Imre Szabó, *The State Policy of Modern Europe, from the Beginning of the Sixteenth Century to the Present Time*, which was a source used for several passages of *Herr Vogt*.

The writings of Marx and Engels against Bonapartism were closely linked with their struggle for the unification of Germany, and also of Italy, by revolutionary-democratic means. They saw Bonapartist France as one of the main obstacles to German and Italian unity (see present edition, Vol. 16). In *Herr Vogt* Marx exposed Vogt's pro-Bonaparte stance on this issue as well.

Marx's pamphlet against Vogt and his associates was also a kind of answer to Lassalle, whose view on the ways and means of unifying Germany, and also Italy, was expounded in his pamphlet *Der italienische Krieg und die Aufgabe Preussens* (The Italian War and the Tasks of Prussia). Lassalle justified the policy of Napoleon

III in Italy and supported the dynastic way of uniting Germany under Prussian auspices that was being canvassed by the Prussophile bourgeoisie. "Lassalle's pamphlet is an enormous blunder," Marx wrote to Engels on May 18, 1859, and in a letter of November 26 of the same year he declared even more emphatically that Lassalle "in point of fact was piping the same tune as Vogt" (see present edition, Vol. 40). Not for nothing did Lassalle try to dissuade Marx from openly opposing this Bonapartist agent. In *Herr Vogt* Marx indirectly, without naming Lassalle, was actually criticising the ideas of Lassalle's pamphlet along with the views expressed by other vulgar democrats who shared Vogt's opinion. In contrast to the nationalistic ideas of Lassalle, who did not believe in the revolutionary-democratic forces of Italy and Germany, in contrast to his attempts to justify the policy of Bonapartism and the Prussian ruling circles, Marx proposed a plan for the revolutionary-democratic unification of each of the two countries from below, through the revolutionary action of the masses. "Lassalle deviated towards a national-liberal labour policy, whereas Marx encouraged and developed an independent, consistently democratic policy hostile to national-liberal cowardice" (V. I. Lenin, *Collected Works*, Vol. 21, p. 141).

The pamphlet *Herr Vogt*, and Engels' pamphlet *Savoy, Nice and the Rhine* written a short time before (see present edition, Vol. 16), were the first works in which the founders of Marxism actually opposed in print the tactics advocated by Lassalle.

An important problem raised by Marx in *Herr Vogt* was that of how to fight the influence of bourgeois and petty-bourgeois ideology on the proletariat, an ideology emanating from circles that Marx classified as vulgar democrats (see his letters to Engels, January 28 and February 3, 1860, present edition, Vol. 41). In his Preface to the pamphlet, referring to German bourgeois and petty-bourgeois democracy, he wrote that one of the reasons that had prompted him to come out publicly against Vogt was the opportunity this offered of exposing the whole trend to which Vogt belonged. This was important as a means of securing the independence of the emerging proletarian party's ideological and tactical principles. The German petty-bourgeois democrats had evolved to the right since the revolution of 1848-49 and were steadily deteriorating into an appendage of bourgeois liberalism. Some of them, like Vogt, had taken up pro-Bonapartist positions. Marx and Engels had criticised the leaders of the petty bourgeoisie in their work *The Great Men of the Exile* (see present edition, Vol. 11). In Chapters IV and XII of *Herr Vogt* ("Techow's Letter" and

"Appendices") Marx returns to this subject and ridicules the
narrowness and political instability of the vulgar democrats, their
contempt for the true interests of the toiling masses, and the petty
quarrels between the various groups.

Brilliant both in its content and form, *Herr Vogt* is outstanding
among the best examples of political satire and journalism and
leaves one in no doubt as to Marx's extensive knowledge of
literature. Its sparkling aphorisms and literary references add to
the acerbity of its style. "This is, of course, the best polemical work
you have ever written," was Engels' comment in a letter to Marx
of December 19, 1860 (see present edition, Vol. 41), as soon as he
had read the pamphlet. Franz Mehring, who thought highly of the
pamphlet's artistic merits, although he did not fully appreciate
its significance in upholding the principles of the proletarian
party, wrote that it would afford great pleasure to the literary
connoisseur.

Marx's pamphlet is written in a spirit of militant partisanship. It
has retained its scientific and political significance both as a source
for studying the history of the international working-class movement and the struggle waged by Marx and Engels to create a
proletarian party, and as an example of their opposition to
Bonapartism and other reactionary forces. It remains a model of
the impassioned defence of the interests of the working class and is a
classic rebuttal of the opponents of communism.

The second half of the volume consists of articles by Marx and
Engels on crucial problems of the social and political development
of Europe in 1860. With the revolutionary movement again on the
upswing their writings were of especial significance as a way of
working out and popularising the tactical principles that should be
adopted by the working-class and democratic movement. In 1860
the *New-York Daily Tribune* was the only newspaper for which
Marx and Engels wrote on political subjects (the articles on
military questions that Engels contributed in 1860 to *The New
American Cyclopaedia, The Volunteer Journal, for Lancashire and
Cheshire,* and the *Allgemeine Militär-Zeitung,* are published in
Volume 18 of the present edition, as part of the cycle of works on
this subject written by Marx and Engels in those years). Though
he did not share Marx's beliefs, the editor of the paper realised
the importance of his articles (see this volume, p. 323-24).

The journalistic activities of Marx and Engels in this period show
that they were continuing their studies of the economic contours and
dynamics of the social and political development of various

countries, and the crucial points of international contradictions and
conflicts. As always they took a particular interest in the unfolding of
revolutionary events.

One of the main themes in the journalism of Marx and Engels in
1860 was the events in Italy. Their articles continue the cycle of
their works on this subject written during the Italian war (see
present edition, Vol. 16). The war resulted neither in the unification of Italy nor in its complete liberation from Austrian domination. Austria kept its grip on Venice. In return for the
cession of Lombardy to Piedmont France had been given Savoy
and Nice. With its national and social problems still unsolved, Italy
remained one of the main centres of revolutionary ferment in
Europe. In April 1860 the popular uprising in Palermo (Sicily)
against the regime of the Neapolitan Bourbons launched a new
stage in the struggle for the country's unification that took the
form of a bourgeois-democratic revolution. Marx responded to
these events with the article "Sicily and the Sicilians", drawing a
graphic picture of the hardships suffered by the people of the
island, where all land was owned by a few large landowners, where
the medieval system of land tenure was still intact, and the tenant
farmers led an impoverished existence under a crushing burden of
taxes and exorbitant rent. Marx taunted Europe's official circles for
their indifference over the brutal reprisals that the Neapolitan
authorities had taken against the insurgents. But, as Marx noted, the
people's spirit was not broken. The Sicilians "have battled, and still
battle, for their freedom" (this volume, p. 370).

Garibaldi's landing with his famous "thousand" volunteers
helped to unite the scattered guerrilla bands and develop the
revolutionary war in Sicily. Marx and Engels followed with great
sympathy the actions of Garibaldi, around whom all Italy's
patriotic forces had rallied. "If the insurrection develops much
vital power, Garibaldi's army will be swelled to more formidable
dimensions," wrote Marx in his article "Garibaldi in Sicily.—
Affairs in Prussia" (this volume, p. 382). A high evaluation of the
actions of Garibaldi's insurrectionist forces is to be found in the
articles "Garibaldi in Sicily", "Garibaldi's Movements", "Garibaldi's Progress" and "Garibaldi in Calabria", which Engels wrote at
Marx's request. Engels spoke of Garibaldi as "the man who has
borne high the flag of Italian revolution in the face of French,
Neapolitan, and Austrian battalions" (this volume, p. 386). And in
another place he said, "The Sicilian insurrection has found a
first-rate military chief" (pp. 389-90). After Garibaldi's landing in
Calabria Engels wrote that he had "shown himself to be not only a

brave leader and clever strategist, but also a scientific general" (this volume, p. 476).

Marx and Engels held that the broad scope of the popular movement in Italy offered the opportunity of achieving the unification of Italy in a democratic way. They assessed Garibaldi's successes as evidence of the superiority of Italy's revolutionary-democratic forces over the aristocratic and bourgeois monarchist camp that had assembled round Piedmont. Marx and Engels also considered Garibaldi's victories in the light of their positive international repercussions, and the revolutionary response that they had evoked among the masses in the European countries. The operations of Garibaldi's revolutionary army not only disrupted the plans of the Italian liberal-monarchist circles and the Savoyan dynasty; they also struck at the hopes nurtured by France's Bonapartist rulers of bringing Italy under its control. In the article "Interesting from Sicily.—Garibaldi's Quarrel with La Farina.—A Letter from Garibaldi", Marx joyfully reported the expulsion of Piedmont's agent La Farina from a Sicily liberated by Garibaldi's forces. Marx believed that if the movement retained "its pure popular character", and Garibaldi prevented Piedmont's ruling circles from intervening, it might lead to "rescuing Italy, not only from its old tyrants and divisions, but also from the clutches of the new French protectorate" (this volume, p. 422).

At the same time Marx and Engels were quite sober in assessing the complexity of the situation and the development of events. The liberal-monarchist circles of Piedmont were preparing, in the event of Garibaldi's campaign proving successful, to snatch the fruits of his victory and bring about the unification of Italy by dynastic means. Despite the hopes cherished by Marx and Engels, this was what happened, in the shape of the creation of the Italian monarchy headed by Victor Emmanuel II, the King of Piedmont.

A number of articles published in this volume are devoted to Germany, and more specifically to Prussia, one of the leading states of the German Confederation. In considering the principal task confronting Germany—the country's national unification— Marx and Engels developed ideas that they had already voiced in their articles of the Italian war period. The need for the unification of Germany sprang from the country's whole internal development and answered the demands of economic and social progress. In upholding the revolutionary-democratic way of solving this problem, Marx and Engels believed that only a movement involving the whole people could paralyse the opposition of the Prussian and Austrian counter-revolutionary elements. The elimination of the relics of the feudal-absolutist system, they concluded, would create favourable conditions for developing the productive forces, for social progress and rallying and organising the proletariat. "To withstand encroachments from without," Marx wrote, "or realise unity and liberty at home, she [Germany] must clear her own house of its dynastic landlords" (this volume, p. 487). Marx exposed the Prussian ruling circles' schemes for uniting the country under their aegis without any changes in its internal system by introducing and employing Prussian police and bureaucratic practices throughout the country. Opposing these plans for the Prussianisation of Germany, Marx wrote that "after the blow dealt to Austria [in the Italian war, 1859], Germany stands in need of a similar blow being dealt to Prussia, in order to get rid of 'both the houses'" (this volume, p. 378). In the article "Public Feeling in Berlin" and in other articles Marx dealt with the internal situation in Prussia. He ridiculed the sham liberalism of the Prince Regent (the future king William), the first years of whose reign—from 1858—had been proclaimed by the liberals as the beginning of a "new era", and regarded the government's manoeuvres as only a nominal rejection of "the old reactionary system of mingled feudalism and bureaucratism". In reality, he pointed out, the Prussian ruling circles had no intention of removing "the bureaucratic and police shackles" (this volume, p. 367, 368).

The articles published in this volume throw light on the beginnings of the constitutional conflict in Prussia between the liberal majority of the lower Chamber and the government, a conflict over the government plan for reorganising the army. The Bill was rejected by the Chamber, although it sanctioned the allocations "for putting the army into a state fit to encounter the dangers apprehended from without". The government launched the reform without the consent of the Provincial Diet. Marx and Engels saw the far-reaching consequences of this policy of the Prussian ruling circles, who were intent on militarising the country and creating an army "trained to passive obedience, drilled into a mere instrument of the dynasty which owns it as its property and uses it according to its caprice" (this volume, pp. 495, 496).

Marx and Engels denounced the conciliatory tactics of the German liberal bourgeoisie and also the bourgeois and petty-bourgeois democrats. They pointed to the timidity and inconsistency of their opposition to the government, their readiness to make concessions, and their actual orientation towards the unification of Germany round monarchical Prussia. In his article

"Preparations for War in Prussia" Engels pointed out ironically that the only retort from these "mock representatives" of the people to the government's military reform launched without the sanction of the Provincial Diet would be "some low grumbling, pickled with fervent assertions of dynastic loyalty, and unbounded confidence in the Cabinet" (this volume, p. 495).

Some of the articles included in this volume fill in the details of the picture of the Second Empire presented in *Herr Vogt*. They focus on the counter-revolutionary essence of the Bonapartist regime, the internal situation in France, and the mainsprings of the adventurist foreign policy pursued by its rulers. In his articles "Affairs in France", "Events in Syria.—Session of the British Parliament.—The State of British Commerce", and others, Marx showed that behind the growth of foreign trade and the spread of the railways, there were signs of the rapid economic collapse of the Second Empire—the fifty per cent increase in the national debt, the threat of financial bankruptcy, the decline of agriculture and the ruination of the peasantry. "The Empire itself," he wrote, "is the great incubus whose burden grows in a greater ratio than the productive powers of the French nation" (this volume, p. 333). The instability of the Bonapartist regime was becoming increasingly apparent and "the rebellious spirit of Gaul is rekindling from its cinders". The rulers of the Second Empire, as always, saw the way out of the crisis in foreign-policy adventures. This was what gave rise to the plan for "some fresh and thrilling crusade, to plunge his Empire again into the Lethe of war-hallucinations". This was the purpose of Napoleon III's colonial expedition to Syria (this volume, pp. 431, 430).

Marx exposed the annexationist plans of the Bonapartist circles with regard to the left bank of the Rhine, and also the demagoguery of their promises to assist in furthering the unification of the North German states around Prussia in return for the cession of the Rhineland to France (see "Preparations for Napoleon's Coming War on the Rhine", "The Emperor Napoleon III and Prussia", "Interesting from Prussia", and others).

Economic problems and also the internal development of Britain, Austria and Russia, and the situation in the colonial world, figure among the themes of the journalistic writings included in this volume, and the ideas expressed on these questions in previous years are developed in many of them.

In some of his articles Marx analysed the state of the British economy and against this background considered the general economic condition of the bourgeois world. In two surveys entitled

"British Commerce" Marx noted that one of the peculiar features of the capitalist economy was the involvement of distant regions of the globe in world trade and the interdependence of the economic processes going on in the world. These problems are also treated in Marx's articles on the Anglo-French trade agreement of 1860.

In his reviews on "The State of British Manufacturing Industry" Marx used official data—the reports of the factory inspectors—to analyse the mechanism of the industrial system and the various forms of the exploitation of the working class. Specifically, he pointed out that child labour was being widely used in British factories although Britain was at the time an advanced industrial country. In breach of laws already passed to restrict the use of child labour, the so-called apprentice system had been revived. Agreements were being made between manufacturers and boards of guardians for the employment of destitute children who had no other means of subsistence. In some industries (at the calico-printing, dyeing and bleaching factories), Marx observed, the working day of women and children of tender age was virtually unlimited and they toiled 14-15 hours a day while their real wages tended to decrease. The industrial accident rate was appalling and safety regulations were applied at by no means all factories (this volume, pp. 416-18).

Marx and Engels were by this time paying more and more attention to the situation in Russia. They attached tremendous importance to the Russian peasant movement for the abolition of serfdom and regarded this movement as a massive reserve for the European revolution (see Marx's letter to Engels of January 11, 1860, present edition, Vol. 41). In his article "Russia Using Austria.—The Meeting at Warsaw" Marx delves into the position of the various classes of Russian society on the eve of the imminent abolition of serfdom and stresses the likelihood of a deal between the Tsarist Government and the nobility in the interests of the big landowners and at the expense of the broad masses of the peasantry. He wrote that "an understanding ... has been arrived at between the existing powers at the cost of the oppressed class" (this volume, p. 486).

The above-mentioned article by Marx, Engels' articles "The Sick Man of Austria", "Austria—Progress of the Revolution", and others examine the process of the decay of the Austrian Empire, torn by internal contradictions and intensification of the national liberation struggle of the peoples within its borders. Marx associates the final disintegration of the Austrian Empire with the German revolution, which, he believed, would have "one of its centers at Vienna and the other at Berlin" (this volume, p. 487).

A number of works by Engels on military subjects have been included in the volume. Engels continued his profound study of the problems of military theory, specifically analysing the character of revolutionary wars, the influence of the advance of military technology on tactics and on the methods of warfare, and studying the history of the making and perfection of various weapons. In his articles on the Italian events Engels analysed the campaigns of Garibaldi's volunteers in Sicily and Calabria from the military point of view. In a series of articles "On Rifled Cannon" Engels considered the development of artillery. His articles "Military Reform in Germany", "British Defenses" and "Could the French Sack London?" deal with military problems in connection with international relations and the mounting military conflicts. The article "The British Volunteer Force" discusses the class composition of volunteer troops.

* * *

The volume comprises 45 works by Marx and Engels, including Marx's *Herr Vogt*, 35 articles written for the *New-York Daily Tribune* (some of them were reprinted in its special issues, the *New-York Semi-Weekly Tribune* and the *New-York Weekly Tribune*) and 9 letters and statements that Marx sent to the editors of various newspapers. There are 8 works that appear in English for the first time—*Herr Vogt* and 7 letters and statements sent by Marx to the newspapers. The other works originally written in English had not been reprinted since their publication in 1860. One of Marx's statements (written in English) was never published in his lifetime.

In the section "From the Preparatory Materials" there appear for the first time in English the passages that Marx copied from Szabó's book *The State Policy of Modern Europe, from the Beginning of the Sixteenth Century to the Present Time*.

In preparing the present volume for the press the sources used by Marx were checked and the necessary corrections made. In quoting the works of other authors Marx sometimes ran paragraphs together, omitted authors' italics and introduced his own. He also abridged some passages and gave only a general summing up of their content. The present volume retains Marx's form of quotation. The most substantial changes are indicated in footnotes and passages left out of quotations are indicated by omission marks in square brackets. For the convenience of the readers some additional paragraphing has been introduced; obvious misprints have been silently corrected.

In studying the historical material quoted in Marx's and Engels' articles, it must be borne in mind that they made use of newspaper information which in a number of cases proved to be inaccurate.

In cases where an article has no title, the editors have provided one which is given in square brackets.

The volume was compiled and the text prepared by Tatyana Yeremeyeva, who also wrote the preface and notes. Chapter XII of the pamphlet *Herr Vogt* and the section "From the Preparatory Materials" were prepared by Marina Vaninskaya, who also compiled the name index and the indexes of quoted and mentioned literature and of periodicals. The subject index was compiled by Marlen Arzumanov. The editor of the volume was Lev Churbanov (Institute of Marxism-Leninism of the CC CPSU).

The publishers express their gratitude to the editors of Marx/Engels, *Gesamtausgabe*—MEGA, Bd. 18, erste Abteilung (Institute of Marxism-Leninism of the CC, Socialist Unity Party of Germany), for the loan of materials used in preparing the volume.

The translations were made by Rodney Livingstone and edited by Nicholas Jacobs (Lawrence & Wishart), Salo Ryazanskaya, Yelena Chistyakova, Victor Schnittke (Progress Publishers) and Vladimir Mosolov, scientific editor (Institute of Marxism-Leninism of the CC CPSU).

The volume was prepared for the press by the editor Lyudgarda Zubrilova and the assistant editor Natalya Belskaya (Progress Publishers).

KARL MARX
and
FREDERICK ENGELS

WORKS

October 1859-December 1860

Karl Marx

[LETTER TO THE EDITOR OF THE *ALLGEMEINE ZEITUNG*] [1]

October 19, 1859, 9 Grafton Terrace,
Maitland Park,
Haverstock Hill, London [a]

Sir,

As long as I had a hand in the German press I attacked the *Allgemeine Zeitung* and the *Allgemeine Zeitung* attacked me. However, this does not of course prevent me from assisting the *Allgemeine Zeitung*, as far as it lies in my power, in a case in which it has in my view fulfilled the *primary* duty of the press: that of the denunciation of humbug. [b] The enclosed document would be a *legal* document here in London. [c] I do not know whether it is the same in *Augsburg*. I have procured the said document because Blind refused to stand by the statement which he had made to me and others, which I passed on to Liebknecht, and which allowed the latter no doubts about the denunciation contained in the anonymous pamphlet. [d]

Yours very sincerely,

Dr. K. Marx [e]

Published in the *Allgemeine Zeitung*, No. 300, October 27, 1859

Printed according to the newspaper

Published in English for the first time

---

[a] The *Allgemeine Zeitung* of October 27, 1859, in which this letter was published, gives the address inaccurately: "I. Grafton Terrace, Quai, Haydpark, Haverstock Hill, London." In the issue of November 21, which carried Marx's "Declaration" (see this volume, pp. 8-9), the address is given correctly.— *Ed.*

[b] Marx uses the English word.— *Ed.*

[c] This refers to the statement by the compositor Vögele to the effect that the pamphlet *Zur Warnung* was written in Blind's hand (see this volume, pp. 123-25.).— *Ed.*

[d] See this volume, pp. 122-24.— *Ed.*

[e] ."Editor of the former *Rheinische Zeitung*" (footnote added by the editors of the *Allgemeine Zeitung*).— *Ed.*

4

Karl Marx

[STATEMENT TO THE EDITORS OF *DIE REFORM*, THE *VOLKS-ZEITUNG* AND THE *ALLGEMEINE ZEITUNG*][2]

London, November 7, 1859

I see from a copy of *Der Freischütz*, No. 132, which a friend has sent me from Hamburg, that Eduard Meyen has felt obliged to place his unequivocally decisive weight into the scales of the Vogt affair.[a] The horse-power, or should I say, the donkey-power[b] of his logic is concentrated in the great thesis: that because he was a friend of Blind, and because Blind failed to send him a copy of the anonymous pamphlet, the original document I had sent to the Augsburg *Allgemeine Zeitung* must of necessity be a falsehood. In his sly little way he takes good care, of course, not to say this directly; he says it indirectly.

Incidentally, I wish that Herr Eduard Meyen would provide evidence to prove that my time is valueless enough to be squandered in attacks on the German vulgar democrats.

At the end of 1850 I broke off all relations with the German emigration in London, which really did collapse once I had pulled from under it the one thing that had held it together: its antagonism towards me. The process of dissolution was hastened, above all, by the industry of such agents as Meyen who, for example, publicly agitated against the Ruge faction on behalf of the Kinkel faction. In the nine years that have meanwhile elapsed, I have been a constant contributor to the *New-York Tribune*, a paper with 200,000 subscribers and hence a reading public roughly approximate to that of *Der Freischütz*. Have I ever even so much as mentioned the name of a single one of the German

---

[a] This refers to the item marked **, "Der Process Carl Vogt's gegen die Augsburger Allg. Ztg.", *Der Freischütz*, No. 132, November 3, 1859.— *Ed.*

[b] Marx uses the English expressions "horse-power" and "donkey-power".— *Ed.*

vulgar democrats, or spent even so much as a single word on any of the despicable attacks that these men of honour have heaped upon my head in the German and especially the German-American press over the past five years?

During this time I did indeed attack, although I did not slander, "great democrats" of the sort that were dutifully admired by Herr Eduard Meyen. Such as the great democrat Lord Palmerston.[a] My offence was all the more unforgivable because my "slanders" were reprinted not merely by English papers of the most diverse political tendencies—from the Chartist *People's Paper* to *The Free Press* of Mr. Urquhart—but also as a pamphlet at least 15,000 copies of which were produced in London, Sheffield and Glasgow without any prompting by me. During that same period, moreover, I denounced the great democrat Louis Bonaparte, first in a work in German (*Der achtzehnte Brumaire des Louis Bonaparte*),[b] which was confiscated at all the German frontiers, but which circulated in considerable numbers in the United States and which appeared in extract in the then London organ of Chartism.[3] I have continued this "slander" of the "great democrat" Bonaparte in the *Tribune* to this day in the form of analyses of his financial system, his diplomacy, his warfare and his *idées napoléoniennes*.[4] Louis Bonaparte has sent the *New-York Times* a public statement in gratitude[c] for its opposition to these "slanders". Seven years ago I even denounced the "great democrat" Stieber in the *Revelations Concerning the Communist Trial*,[d] which was pulped at the frontier of Baden and Switzerland. Herr Meyen will surely give me credit for that. Such slander is democratic nowadays since it takes place "with the permission of the high authorities". But my frequent errors in timing are revealed not only by the organ of Herr Eduard Meyen, but also by that of Herr Joseph Dumont in Cologne.[e] When in 1848 and 1849 I took the liberty of coming out for the cause of the Hungarian, Italian and Polish nationalities in the *Neue Rheinische Zeitung*, who raged and foamed at the mouth more than the organ of Herr Joseph Dumont in Cologne? But at that time, of course, no Louis Napoleon Bonaparte had given his "liberal" blessing to the cause of these nationalities. That the

---

[a] The reference is to Marx's pamphlet *Lord Palmerston* (see present edition, Vol. 12).— *Ed.*

[b] *The Eighteenth Brumaire of Louis Bonaparte* (see present edition, Vol. 11).— *Ed.*

[c] Instead of *Dankschreiben* (message of gratitude) *Die Reform* has *Denkschreiben* (memorandum), presumably a misprint.— *Ed.*

[d] See present edition, Vol. 11.— *Ed.*

[e] *Kölnische Zeitung*.— *Ed.*

former editors of the *Neue Rheinische Zeitung* have remained true
to their opinions is known even to the erstwhile Herr Joseph
Dumont, now Giuseppe Delmonte, from Frederick Engels' pamphlet *Po and Rhine*,[a] which appeared at the start of the war. But as
for Eduard Meyen's democracy "in its narrower sense", I have
ignored it for nine years and have only on two occasions, quite
recently, broken my silence. The first time was to attack Kossuth
and the second was in criticism of Herr Gottfried Kinkel. I did in
fact make a number of marginal comments of a purely grammati-
cal nature on Kinkel's aesthetic effusions in the *Hermann,* and I
published them in *Das Volk.* This was the only thing which I did write
for *Das Volk,* apart from an article on the Peace of Villafranca under
the title "Quid pro quo".[b] But in the eyes of Eduard Meyen, a "good
democrat" is doubtless just as justified in violating the "despotic"
rules of syntax as in deserting from the republican camp to that of
the royalists.[c]

I now find myself at the end of this epistle in the opposite
difficulty to Hegel's at the beginning of his *Logic.*[d] He wanted to
advance from Being to Nothing, whereas I wish to move from
Nothing to Being, namely from Eduard Meyen to a real case, the
case of Vogt. To make it brief I ask Karl Blind the following
questions:

1. Did Blind impart to me information about Vogt on May 9 on
the platform of the Urquhart meeting, information whose
substance tallies precisely with that contained in the pamphlet *Zur
Warnung?*

2. Did Blind publish an anonymous article in the London *Free
Press* of May 27, bearing the title "The Grand Duke Constantine
to be King of Hungary",[e] an article which, apart from the omission
of the name of Vogt, repeats the substance of the pamphlet *Zur
Warnung?*

3. Did Blind cause the above-mentioned pamphlet to be printed
at his expense in London in the print-shop of Herr F. Hollinger,
Litchfield Street, Soho?[f]

---

   a See present edition, Vol. 16.— *Ed.*

   b The reference is to Marx's articles "Kossuth and Louis Napoleon",
"Gatherings from the Press" and "Quid pro quo" (see present edition, Vol.
16).— *Ed.*

   c An allusion to Gottfried Kinkel's speech before the court martial in Rastatt on
August 4, 1849.— *Ed.*

   d G. W. F. Hegel, *Die Wissenschaft der Logik,* Band I, Abteilung 2, Berlin,
1833.— *Ed.*

   e See this volume, pp. 122-23.— *Ed.*

   f See this volume, pp. 116, 122, 123-24.— *Ed.*

Despite all the efforts of Meyen's democracy to misrepresent matters, and despite even that Great Unknown, the "outstanding lawyer" of Herr Joseph Dumont, everything still turns on the question: Who arranged for the pamphlet *Zur Warnung* to be printed? The only reason why the Augsburg *Allgemeine Zeitung* is being sued is the fact that this pamphlet was reprinted there. The only accusations of which Vogt feels compelled to clear his name in the eyes of the world are those contained in this pamphlet. The publisher of the pamphlet has, as Robert Peel would have said, three courses open to himself.[a] Either he has knowingly lied. I do not believe this of Karl Blind. Or else he subsequently became convinced that the information which justified his printing the pamphlet was false. In that case he is under an even greater obligation to supply an explanation. Or, finally, he holds the proof in his hand, but wishes for private reasons of his own to hush the whole business up and endures with magnanimous resignation the rotten eggs that are hurled not at himself, but at me. But must not all private considerations lapse in such a vital matter as the need to throw light on the relations between the German Imperial Regent *in partibus*[b] and the Emperor of the French *de facto*?

Karl Marx

Published in the supplement to *Die Reform*, No. 139, November 19, 1859

Printed according to the newspaper

Published in English for the first time

---

[a] This phrase is in English in the original.— *Ed.*

[b] *In partibus infidelium*—literally: in parts inhabited by infidels. The words are added to the title of Roman Catholic bishops holding purely nominal dioceses in non-Christian countries. Here the expression means "only in word".— *Ed.*

Karl Marx

DECLARATION[5]

Vogt, who knows the people he has to deal with, executed a very cunning manoeuvre when he shifted the source of the denunciation of himself from the so-called democratic camp into the socialist one. But I for my part have no interest in aiding and abetting this quid pro quo, and can therefore not permit Blind's declaration[a] in No. 313 of the *Allgemeine Zeitung* to go unanswered.

1. On May 9, on the platform of the Urquhart meeting, Blind communicated to me all the accusations against Vogt contained in the pamphlet *Zur Warnung*. He gave the same details to others, to Freiligrath, for instance. Given the complete identity of both style and substance between his verbal statement and the printed pamphlet, he was naturally regarded as its author *de prime abord*.[b]

2. In the London *Free Press* of May 27, an anonymous article of Blind's appeared with the title "The Grand Duke Constantine to be King of Hungary",[c] which in all essentials anticipated the pamphlet *Zur Warnung*. In that article Blind declared that he knew of liberals in Germany and democrats in London who had been offered "large bribes"[d] on behalf of Bonapartist propaganda. While Vogt's lawsuit was pending, I received a visit from Mr. D. Collet, the responsible editor of *The Free Press*, who asked me at *Blind's request* to make *no use* of my knowledge concerning the

---

a See this volume, pp. 125-26.— *Ed.*
b From the very outset.— *Ed.*
c See this volume, pp. 122-23.— *Ed.*
d Marx uses the English expression.— *Ed.*

authorship of the article in question. I replied to Mr. Collet—who found it quite appropriate—that I would not commit myself to anything but that my discretion in the matter would rather depend on Blind's conduct.

3. Fidelio Hollinger's declaration is simply ridiculous.[a] Fidelio Hollinger is aware that he has formally infringed English law by publishing the pamphlet *without declaring the place of publication*. He himself therefore issues a testimonial stating that he did not commit the peccadillo in question. It so happened that the reprint in *Das Volk*[b] was made from the type still standing in Hollinger's print-shop. Thus even without the need to call witnesses, a simple comparison of the pamphlet and the reprint of it in *Das Volk* would be sufficient to prove to a court that the former "came from F. Hollinger's print-shop". The transfer of the trial from Augsburg to London would, in general, resolve the entire Blind-Vogt *mystère*.

Karl Marx

November 15, 1859
9 Grafton Terrace, Maitland Park,
Haverstock Hill, London

Published in the supplement to the *Allgemeine Zeitung*, No. 325, November 21, 1859

Printed according to the newspaper

Published in English for the first time

---

[a] See Carl Vogt, *Mein Prozess gegen die Allgemeine Zeitung*, Genf, 1859, Dokumente, S. 38, and also this volume, p. 126.— *Ed.*

[b] *Das Volk*, No. 7, June 18, 1859. See also this volume, p. 119.— *Ed.*

Karl Marx

PROSECUTION OF THE AUGSBURG GAZETTE[6]

TO THE EDITOR OF *THE FREE PRESS*

9 Grafton Terrace, Maitland Park,
Haverstock Hill,
London, 4th February, 1860

Sir,

You will remember that *The Free Press* of May 27th, 1859, published an article headed: *"The Grand Duke Constantine to be King of Hungary."* In that article Mr. *Vogt,* of Geneva, although not named, was pointed at, in a manner intelligible to the German refugees, as a Bonapartist agent, who, on the outset of the Italian war, had offered *"large bribes"* to Liberals in Germany, and German Democrats in London. The writer gave vent to his intense delight at the indignant repulse those attempts at bribery had met with. *Mr. Charles Blind* I assert to be the author of that notice. You can correct me if I am in error. Some time later, there circulated in London an anonymous *German* pamphlet, entitled *Zur Warnung* (a warning), which, in point of fact, may be considered a reproduction of the article of *The Free Press,* only that it gave fuller details and Vogt's name. Having been reprinted in a German London paper, entitled *Das Volk*[a] (The People); thence the anonymous pamphlet found its way to the columns of the *Augsburger Allgemeine Zeitung*[b] (The Augsburg Gazette), which, consequently, was sued by Mr. Vogt for libel. Meanwhile I had obtained from Mr. Vögele, a compositor then employed by Mr. Hollinger, the publisher of *Das Volk,* a written declaration[c] to the effect, that the pamphlet was printed in Hollinger's office, and drawn up by *Mr. Charles Blind.* This declaration, as I told you at the time, was sent over to the *Augsburg Gazette.* The Augsburg

---

a *Das Volk,* No. 7, June 18, 1859.— *Ed.*
b "K. Vogt und die deutsche Emigration in London", *Allgemeine Zeitung,* No. 173 (supplement), June 22, 1859.— *Ed.*
c See this volume, pp. 3, 123-25.— *Ed.*

tribunal having declined to decide the case, *Mr. Blind* at last came out in the *Augsburg Gazette*.[a] Not content with a point-blank denial of his authorship of the anonymous pamphlet, he, in terms most positive, *declared the pamphlet not to have issued from Hollinger's printing office.* In proof of this latter statement, he laid before the public a declaration[b] signed by Hollinger himself, and one Wiehe, a compositor, who, as he said, had for eleven months been continuously employed by Hollinger. To this joint declaration of Blind, Hollinger and Wiehe I replied in the *Augsburg Gazette*[c]; but *Blind,* in his turn, repeated his denial, and again referred to the testimony of Hollinger and Wiehe.[d] *Vogt,* who, from the beginning, and for purposes of his own, had designed *me* as the secret author of the pamphlet, then published a *brochure*[e] full of the most infamous calumnies against myself.

Now, before taking any further step, I want to show up the fellows who evidently have played into the hands of Vogt. I, therefore, publicly declare that the statement of Blind, Wiehe and Hollinger, according to which the anonymous pamphlet was *not* printed in Hollinger's office, 3, Litchfield Street, Soho, is a *deliberate lie.* First, Mr. Vögele, one of the compositors, formerly employed by Hollinger, will declare upon oath that the said pamphlet *was* printed in Hollinger's office, was written in the hand-writing of *Mr. Blind,* and partly composed by Hollinger himself. Secondly, it can be judicially proved that the pamphlet and the article in *Das Volk,* have been taken off the same types. Thirdly, it will be shown that Wiehe was *not* employed by Hollinger for eleven consecutive months, and, especially, was *not* employed by him at the time of the pamphlet's publication. Lastly, witnesses may be summoned in whose presence Wiehe himself confessed having been persuaded by Hollinger to sign the *wilfully false declaration in the Augsburg Gazette.* Consequently, I again declare the above said *Charles Blind* to be a *deliberate liar.*

If I am wrong, he may easily confound me by appealing to an English Court of Law.

Karl Marx

Published as a pamphlet on February 4, 1860   Reproduced from the pamphlet

---

[a] This refers to Karl Blind's declaration dated "London, November 3" in the *Allgemeine Zeitung,* No. 313, November 9, 1859.— *Ed.*

[b] ibid. See also this volume, p. 126.— *Ed.*

[c] See this volume, pp. 8-9.— *Ed.*

[d] The *Allgemeine Zeitung,* No. 345, December 11, 1859.— *Ed.*

[e] Carl Vogt, *Mein Prozess....*— *Ed.*

Karl Marx

TO THE EDITORS OF THE *VOLKS-ZEITUNG*

DECLARATION [7]

I hereby make it known that I have taken steps preparatory to instituting legal proceedings for libel against the Berlin *National-Zeitung* in connection with the leading articles in Nos. 37 and 41 [a] regarding Vogt's pamphlet *Mein Prozess gegen die Allgemeine Zeitung.* I reserve the right to answer Vogt in writing at a later date since this requires putting a number of questions to people not at present in Europe.

For the moment then I shall say only this:

1. To judge by the anthology in the *National-Zeitung*—strangely the book itself has up to now been unobtainable in London either from booksellers or the acquaintances to whom Herr Vogt had earlier sent his so-called *Studien* [b] — Vogt's concoction is merely the elaboration of a sketch that he published nine months ago in his private *Moniteur,* the Biel *Handels-Courier.* [c] At the time I had his lampoon published in London without comment. Such a simple procedure was sufficient here, where the situations and personalities are well known, to provide a judgment on the Herr Professor.

2. The *pretext* which led Herr Vogt to launch his campaign against me, like the pretext for the Italian campaign, was an "idea". I was alleged to be the author of the anonymous pamphlet *Zur Warnung.* From the enclosed circular [d] in English, which I have had published here, you will see that I have taken steps to compel

---

[a] "Karl Vogt und die Allgemeine Zeitung" and "Wie man radikale Flugblätter macht", *National-Zeitung,* Nos. 37 and 41, January 22 and 25, 1860.— *Ed.*

[b] Carl Vogt, *Studien zur gegenwärtigen Lage Europas,* Genf und Bern, 1859.— *Ed.*

[c] An allusion to Vogt's article "Zur Warnung" in the *Schweizer Handels-Courier,* No. 150 (special supplement), June 2, 1859.— *Ed.*

[d] See this volume, pp. 10-11.— *Ed.*

Herr Blind and consorts either to concede the falseness of that pretext by their silence, or to be convicted of it by an English court.

Karl Marx

February 6, 1860
9 Grafton Terrace, Maitland Park,
Haverstock Hill, London

Published in the *Volks-Zeitung*, No. 35, February 10, 1860; in the supplement to the *Kölnische Zeitung*, No. 41, February 10, 1860; in *Die Reform*, No. 18, February 11, 1860; in the supplement to the *Allgemeine Zeitung*, No. 48, February 17, 1860 (with alterations)[a] and in other German papers

Printed according to the *Volks-Zeitung* checked with the manuscript

Published in English for the first time

---

[a] The manuscript of this declaration in the *Allgemeine Zeitung* written in Jenny Marx's hand and a covering note in Marx's handwriting have been preserved.— *Ed.*

Karl Marx

TO THE EDITOR OF THE *DAILY TELEGRAPH*[8]

In your to-day's impression you publish, under the title: "*The Journalistic Auxiliaries of Austria*", a letter full of libellous and scandalous imputations against my person. That letter, purporting to be written at Frankfort on the Main, but probably indited at Berlin, is, in point of fact, but a clumsy amplification of two articles contained in the Berlin *National-Zeitung* d.d. January 22 and January 25,[a] which paper will have to give account of its[b] calumnies before a Prussian Court of Law. The *false pretext*, upon which Vogt launched his libel against me,[c] is the assertion that I am the author of the anonymous *German* pamphlet: *Zur Warnung* (a warning), first circulated at London, and afterwards reprinted in the Augsburg *Allgemeine Zeitung*.[d] From the inclosed print[e] you will see that I have provoked my adversaries to bring this point to a judicial issue before an English Court of Law.

In conclusion, if you do not prefer being sued for libel, I request you to make in your next number an *amende honorable*[f] for the recklessness with which you dare vilifying a man of whose

---

_a See this volume, p. 12.— *Ed.*
_b Marx has "his".— *Ed.*
_c Carl Vogt, *Mein Prozess....— Ed.*
_d "K. Vogt und die deutsche Emigration in London", *Allgemeine Zeitung*, No. 173 (supplement), June 22, 1859.— *Ed.*
_e See this volume, pp. 12-13.— *Ed.*
_f Apology.— *Ed.*

personal character, political past, literary productions, and social standing, you cannot but confess to be utterly ignorant.

Your obedient servant,

Dr. Karl Marx

February 6, 1860
9 Grafton Terrace, Maitland Park,
Haverstock Hill, London

First published in Russian in: K. Marx and F. Engels, *Works*, Vol. XXV, Moscow, 1934

Printed according to the rough copy of the English original

Karl Marx

TO THE EDITORS
OF THE AUGSBURG *ALLGEMEINE ZEITUNG*

February 21, 1860
6 Thorncliffe Grove,
Oxford Road, Manchester

Personal

In one of the two letters dated October 16, 1859 which I have received from the editors of the Augsburg *Allgemeine Zeitung*, it says literally:

"You may rest assured of our *particular gratitude* whenever the occasion should present itself for us, highly esteemed Sir, to express to you our *thanks*."

That I neither desired nor expected either "thanks" or "particular gratitude" from the Augsburg *Allgemeine Zeitung* is made perfectly plain in my reply of October 19.[a] What I did expect, however, in this *particular matter*, was at least the common fairness[b] which no English paper, regardless of its shade of opinion, ever ventures to refuse.

The "particular gratitude" and the "thanks" are actually expressed in the following manner:

1. My first declaration[c] was *not* printed at all. There appeared instead Blind's impertinent statement[d] together with two false pieces of evidence obtained by conspiracy.[e] *Die Reform* in Hamburg published my declaration without delay.

2. In the case of my reply to Blind I had to resort to *douce violence*[f] to secure its insertion.[g] And even then it did not appear,

---

a See this volume, p. 3.— *Ed.*
b Marx uses the English phrase.— *Ed.*
c See this volume, pp. 4-7.— *Ed.*
d The *Allgemeine Zeitung*, No. 313, November 9, 1859.— *Ed.*
e Marx uses the English word.— *Ed.*
f Gentle pressure.— *Ed.*
g See this volume, pp. 8-9.— *Ed.*

as I had demanded in all fairness, in the same place as Blind's attack, namely in the main portion of the paper.

3. The Augsburg *Allgemeine Zeitung* then printed a second declaration by Blind [a] in which he had the effrontery to speak of barefaced lies and to appeal yet again to the criminally liable testimony of Wiehe and Hollinger. The paper then declared the correspondence closed and so denied me the right to reply.

4. On February 6 I sent my final declaration together with the English circular [b] to the Augsburg *Allgemeine Zeitung*. The highly esteemed editorial board pushed it to one side and instead published Blind's declaration [c] *which had only come into being as the consequence of my circular*. They naturally took good care not to publish the *billet doux* this great diplomat had enclosed. They also published Biscamp's declaration, [d] dated three days later than mine (viz., London, February 9). Finally, having convinced themselves of the fact that my declaration had long since been printed by the *Kölnische Zeitung*, the *Volks-Zeitung*, etc., they resolve on publication, [e] but—they also take upon themselves the endearing liberty of *censoring* me and making arbitrary alterations. In Cologne in 1842-43 I suffered from the twofold Royal Prussian censorship, [9] but never imagined that in the year 1860 I would in addition fall victim to the censorship of Herr Dr. Kolb & Co.

I consider that more specific characterisation of these methods is utterly pointless.

K. Marx

First published in Russian in: K. Marx and F. Engels, *Works*, Vol. XXV, Moscow, 1934

Printed according to the original

Published in English for the first time

---

[a] The *Allgemeine Zeitung*, No. 345 (supplement), December 11, 1859.— *Ed.*

[b] See this volume, pp. 10-13.— *Ed.*

[c] Karl Blind, "Gegen Karl Vogt", *Allgemeine Zeitung*, No. 44 (supplement), February 13, 1860.— *Ed.*

[d] Elard Biscamp, "Erklärung", *Allgemeine Zeitung*, No. 46 (supplement), February 15, 1860.— *Ed.*

[e] See this volume, pp. 12-13.— *Ed.*

Karl Marx

[TO THE EDITORS OF *DIE REFORM*] [10]

For Information

With regard to the effusions of Herr *Eduard Meyen* in *Der Freischütz*, Nos. 17 to 21,[a] I would say only this:

The libel action I am conducting against the Berlin *National-Zeitung* will achieve all that is necessary to provide a *legal* clarification of Vogt's pamphlet.[b] His associate Eduard Meyen cannot lay claim to a like honour. The only thing I can do for Eduard Meyen is to assign to him a niche appropriate to his dimensions in the pamphlet which is due to appear after the conclusion of the court proceedings.

Karl Marx

Manchester, February 28, 1860

Published in *Die Reform*, No. 29, March 7, 1860

Printed according to the newspaper

Published in English for the first time

---

[a] The reference is to Eduard Meyen's article "Carl Vogts Kampf gegen die Augsburger Allgem. Zeitung und die Marxianer", *Der Freischütz*, Nos. 17-21, February 9, 11, 14, 16 and 18, 1860.— *Ed.*

[b] Carl Vogt, *Mein Prozess....*— *Ed.*

Karl Marx

DECLARATION [11]

At the beginning of February 1860 the editorial board of the *Allgemeine Zeitung* were kind enough to publish a declaration by myself which began with these words:

"I hereby make it known that I have taken steps preparatory to instituting legal proceedings for libel against the Berlin *National-Zeitung* in connection with the leading articles in Nos. 37 and 41 regarding Vogt's pamphlet *Mein Prozess gegen die Allgemeine Zeitung.* I reserve the right to answer Vogt in writing at a later date." [a]

In the course of February 1860 I brought a libel suit in Berlin against F. Zabel, the responsible editor of the *National-Zeitung.* My lawyer, Legal Counsellor Weber, resolved at first on an *official investigation.* With a ruling of April 18, 1860 the Public Prosecutor refused to "take action" against F. Zabel, on the grounds that there was no *public interest* involved. On April 26, 1860 his refusal was confirmed by the Chief Public Prosecutor.

My lawyer then began *civil proceedings.* The Royal *Municipal Court* in a ruling of June 8, 1860 *prohibited* me from proceeding with my *lawsuit* on the grounds that the genuinely defamatory "utterances and statements" of F. Zabel's were *merely quotations* from other persons, and that the "intention to insult" was not present. The Royal *Court of Appeal* for its part declared in a ruling of July 11, 1860 that the alleged use of quotation did not affect the culpability of the articles, but that the defamatory passages contained in them did *not* refer to my "person". Furthermore, "in the present case" the intention to insult "could not be assumed".

---

[a] See this volume, p. 12.— *Ed.*

Thus the Royal Court of Appeal confirmed the negative ruling of
the Municipal Court. In a ruling of October 5, 1860, which I
received on October 23 of this year, the Royal *Supreme Tribunal*
found that "in the present case" no "legal error" on the part of the
Royal Court of Appeal "could be discerned". The *prohibition on suing
F. Zabel* was thus sustained and my claim did not reach the stage
of being accorded a *public hearing*.

My *reply to Vogt* will appear in a few days.

                                                              Karl Marx

London, November 24, 1860

Published in the supplement to the *Allgemeine Zeitung*, No. 336, December 1,
1860

Printed according to the newspaper

Published in English for the first
time

Karl Marx

HERR VOGT [12]

Written between February and November 1860

Published as a book in London in 1860

Signed: *Karl Marx*

Printed according to the book

Published in English for the first time

Herr Vogt.

Von

Karl Marx.

London,
A. Petsch & Co, deutsche Buchhandlung,
78, FENCHURCH STREET, E.C.

—

1·8·6·0.

Title-page of the first edition of *Herr Vogt* by Karl Marx

PREFACE

Under the date "*London*, February 6, 1860", I published a declaration[a] in the Berlin *Volks-Zeitung,* the Hamburg *Reform* and a number of other German papers, which began with these words:

"I hereby make it known that I have taken steps preparatory to instituting legal proceedings for libel against the Berlin *National-Zeitung* in connection with the leading articles in Nos. 37 and 41 regarding *Vogt*'s pamphlet, *Mein Prozess gegen die Allgemeine Zeitung.* I reserve the right to answer *Vogt* in writing at a later date."

The present publication will make it clear why I chose to answer *Karl Vogt* in writing, while challenging the *National-Zeitung* through the courts.

During February 1860 I went ahead with the libel action against the *National-Zeitung.*[b] On October 23 of this year, after the case had gone through four preliminary stages, I received a ruling from the Royal Prussian Supreme Tribunal definitively refusing me permission to put my case and so dismissing my action before it could be heard in open court. Had the latter come to pass, as I had a right to expect, I would have been spared the necessity of writing the first third of the present pamphlet. A straightforward reproduction of the verbatim report of the court proceedings would have been quite sufficient and I would have been spared the hateful task of having to answer accusations directed at my

---

[a] See this volume, pp. 12-13.— *Ed.*

[b] See Marx's letters to Legal Counsellor Weber dated February 13, 21 and 24, 1860 (present edition, Vol. 41), and this volume, pp. 19-20.— *Ed.*

own person and therefore of having to speak about myself. I have
always taken such pains to avoid this that Vogt could well expect
his cock-and-bull stories to have some success. However, *sunt certi
denique fines*.[a] Vogt's concoction, summarised by the *National-
Zeitung* in its own fashion, accused me of a series of dishonourable
actions which require a literary refutation now that the road to a
public rebuttal in the courts has been definitively barred. But even
apart from this consideration, which left me no alternative, I had
other reasons, since in any case I had to deal with Vogt's tall
stories about me and my party comrades, for examining them in
greater detail. On the one hand, there was the almost unanimous
jubilation with which the so-called liberal German press greeted
his alleged revelations. On the other hand, the analysis of his
concoction presented me with the opportunity to dissect an
individual who stands for a whole trend.

My reply to Vogt has forced me in a number of places to expose
a *partie honteuse*[b] in the history of the emigration. In doing so I
am only making use of the right to "self-defence". Moreover,
except for a few persons, the emigration can be reproached with
nothing worse than indulging illusions that were more or less
justified by the circumstances of the period, or perpetrating follies
which arose necessarily from the extraordinary situation in which
it unexpectedly found itself. I am speaking here, of course, only
of the early years of the emigration. A comparative history, say
from 1849 to 1859, of governments and of bourgeois society on
the one hand and the emigration on the other, would constitute
the most outstanding apologia of the latter that could possibly be
written.

I know in advance that the same astute men who shook their
heads sagely at the importance of Vogt's "revelations", when his
concoction first appeared, will now be unable to comprehend why
I am wasting my time refuting his childish allegations; while the
"liberal" pen-pushers who gloatingly took up Vogt's common-
places and worthless lies and hastened to hawk them around the
German, Swiss, French and American press will now find my
mode of dealing with themselves and their hero outrageously
offensive. But never mind![c]

The political and legal aspects of the present work require no
prefatory comment. I would only make one point to avoid possible

---

[a] There are certain limits after all (Horace, *Satires,* Book I, Satire 1).— *Ed.*
[b] A disgraceful affair.— *Ed.*
[c] Marx uses the English phrase.— *Ed.*

misunderstandings: men who even before 1848 agreed that the independence of Poland, Hungary and Italy has to be upheld not only as the *right* of the nations concerned, but also in the *interests* of Germany and Europe, came to advance wholly opposed ideas about the tactics to be adopted by Germany *vis-à-vis* Louis Bonaparte in connection with the Italian war of 1859.[13] This clash of opinions sprang from conflicting assessments of the *facts of the underlying situation* which it will be the prerogative of a later age to resolve. For my part, I am concerned here only with the opinions of *Vogt* and his clique. Even the views he *claimed* to uphold, and in the *fantasy* of an uncritical rabble did uphold, actually fall outside the scope of my criticism. I deal only with the views he *really* upheld.

In conclusion I wish to express my sincere gratitude for the ready assistance I have received while writing this pamphlet, not only from long-standing friends in the party, but also from many members of the emigration in Switzerland, France and England with whom I had earlier not been at all close and some of whom I still do not personally know.

London, November 17, 1860

Karl Marx

I

THE BRIMSTONE GANG [14]

Clarin: Malas pastillas gasta; ....
.... hase untado
Con ungüento de azufre.
(*Calderón*) [a]

The "*well-rounded character*", [b] as the barrister *Hermann* so delicately described his spherical client, the hereditary Vogt of Noughtborough, [15] to the District Court in Augsburg, the "well-rounded character" begins his enormous travesty of history [c] as follows:

"Among the refugees of 1849 the term **Brimstone Gang**, *or else* the no less characteristic name of the **Bristlers**, [d] referred to a number of people who after being scattered throughout Switzerland, France and England gradually congregated in London, and there they revered Herr *Marx* as their visible leader. The political principle of these fellows was the dictatorship of the proletariat, etc." (*Mein Prozess gegen die Allgemeine Zeitung* by Karl Vogt, Geneva, December 1859, p. 136).

The "Magnum Opus" [16] into which this momentous piece of information had found its way appeared in December 1859. Eight months earlier, however, in May 1859, our "well-rounded character" had published an article in the Biel *Handels-Courier* which must be regarded as an *outline* of the more extensive travesty of history. Let us consider the *original text*:

"Ever since the failure of the revolution of 1849," so brags our *Commis voyageur* from Biel, "a clique of refugees has gradually congregated in London, whose

---

[a] He's free with empty phrases; ... he has smeared himself with sulphur ointment (*El Mágico prodigioso*, Act 2).— *Ed.*

[b] Here and below Marx puns on the phrase *abgerundete Natur* which can mean both "a well-rounded character" (in the physical sense) and "an intellectually mature character". In his speech of October 24, 1859 the barrister Hermann used the phrase in the latter sense (see Carl Vogt, *Mein Prozess ...*, S. 17).— *Ed.*

[c] Cf. Johann Fischart, *Affentheurliche, Naupengeheurliche Geschichtklitterung....*— *Ed.*

[d] See this volume, pp. 38-40.— *Ed.*

members were in those days (!) known among *the Swiss emigration* as the '*Bristlers*' or the '*Brimstone Gang*'. Their leader is *Marx*, the former editor of the *Rheinische Zeitung* in Cologne—their slogan, 'Social Republic, Workers' Dictatorship'—their business, establishing contacts and hatching plots." [a] (Reprinted in the "Magnum Opus", Section 3, Documents, No. 7, pp. 31, 32.)

In the course of eight months the clique of refugees known as the "Brimstone Gang" "among the Swiss emigration" has been transformed for the benefit of a larger public into a mass "scattered throughout Switzerland, France and England" and known as the "*Brimstone Gang*" "among the refugees" in general. It is the old story of the men in buckram of Kendal green, told so merrily by Karl Vogt's prototype, the immortal Sir John Falstaff,[b] whose zoological reincarnation has forfeited nothing as to *substance*. The original text of our *Commis voyageur* from Biel makes it quite obvious that both the "*Brimstone Gang*" and the "*Bristlers*" were local *Swiss* flora. Let us try and trace their natural history.

In February 1860, having learnt from friends that a refugee association by the name of "Brimstone Gang" had indeed flourished in Geneva in the years 1849-50 and that Herr *S. L. Borkheim,* a well-situated merchant in the City of London, could provide more exact information about the origins, growth and decline of that ingenious association, I wrote to that gentleman, who was not known to me at the time, and after a personal meeting I received from him the following sketch which I print without making any alterations.

"*London,* February 12, 1860
18 Union Grove, Wandsworth Road

"Dear Sir,

"Although, until three days ago, we had not met personally, despite having lived for nine years in the same country, and for the most part in the same town, you have rightly presumed that I, as a fellow-exile, would not refuse you the information you require.

"Very well then, here is what I know about the '*Brimstone Gang*'.

"In 1849, soon after we rebels had been forced out of Baden,[17] a number of young men who as students, soldiers or businessmen had been on friendly terms in Germany before 1848, or who had become so during the revolution, gathered together in *Geneva* either of their own free will or else because they had been directed there by the Swiss authorities.

"The refugees were not in a very rosy mood. The so-called political leaders blamed each other for the failure; the military leaders criticised each other's

---

[a] Karl Vogt, "Zur Warnung", dated May 23, published in the *Schweizer Handels-Courier*, No. 150 (special supplement), June 2, 1859. Sometimes Marx ironically refers to this newspaper as the Biel *Commis voyageur.—Ed.*

[b] Shakespeare, *Henry IV*, Part I, Act II, Scene 4.— *Ed.*

retrograde attacking movements, flanking manoeuvres and offensive withdrawals; people began to call each other names such as bourgeois republicans, socialists and communists; there was a flood of pamphlets, which did nothing to restore peace; spies were thought to be everywhere and, in addition to all this, the clothes of the majority gradually turned to rags and the signs of hunger could be seen on many faces. In the midst of this misery the young people referred to above held together in friendship. They were:

"*Eduard Rosenblum,* born in Odessa of German parents; he had studied medicine in Leipzig, Berlin and Paris.

"*Max Cohnheim* from Fraustadt; he had been an office-boy, and on the outbreak of the revolution, he was doing a year as a volunteer in the artillery guards.

"*Korn,* a chemist and pharmacist from Berlin.

"*Becker,* an engineer from the Rhineland.

"And *myself,* who, after matriculating from the Werder school in Berlin in 1844, had studied in Breslau,[a] Greifswald and Berlin and was serving as a gunner in my home town of Glogau when the 1848 revolution began.

"I think none of us was more than 24 years old. We lived close together, for a time indeed in the Grand Pré, all in the same house. Finding ourselves in a small country that presented so little opportunity for earning a living, our chief occupation was to keep ourselves from being too much depressed and demoralised by the general misery of refugee life and political dejection. The climate and the surrounding country were glorious—we did not belie our Brandenburg origins and accents and found the place 'luv'ly' [fanden die *Jegend jottvoll*[b]]. What belonged to one of us, the others had too, and if none of us had anything we could always find good-natured innkeepers and other friendly souls who took pleasure in lending us money on the strength of our young, vivacious faces. We really must have looked an honest set of madcaps! I must make specific thankful mention here of Bertin, the owner of the Café de l'Europe who was truly *indefatigable* in supplying us on tick, and not only us but also many other German and French refugees. In 1856, after six years' absence, I visited Geneva on my way back from the Crimea in order, with the piety of a well-intentioned tourist, to repay my debts. Our good old fat Bertin was amazed and assured me that I was the first person to give him this pleasure, but that he did not regret the 10,000-20,000 francs still owing to him from the refugees who were by now long since scattered to the four corners of the globe. Never mentioning the money they owed him, he asked with special affection about the fate of those I had been closest to. Unfortunately there was little I could tell him.

"I return from this digression to the year 1849.

"In those days we drank merrily and sang joyfully. I remember seeing refugees of every political shade and colour at our table, including Frenchmen and Italians. Convivial evenings spent in such *dulci jubilo*[18] seemed to everyone like veritable oases amidst the otherwise barren wastes of refugee life. Even those of our friends who sat on the Grand Council of Geneva, or were later to do so, would occasionally join our revels for the sake of a little relaxation.

"Liebknecht, who is now here and whom I have only seen three or four times in last nine years, having met him each time by chance in the street, was a frequent member of the company. Students, doctors, former friends from school and university, touring on holiday, would often drink their way through many

---

[a] The Polish name is Wrocław.— *Ed.*
[b] Berlin dialect.— *Ed.*

glasses of beer and many a bottle of that good, cheap Mâcon. Sometimes we would spend days and even weeks on the Lake of Geneva without once going on shore; we sang old love-songs and, guitar in hand, paid court beneath the windows of the villas on both the Savoy and Swiss sides.

"I shall not conceal the fact that our wild behaviour occasionally brought us into collison with the police. On such occasions that dear man, the late *Albert Galeer,* who was a by no means insignificant opponent of Fazy's among the Genevan citizenry, would read us a sermon, though in the kindest manner possible. 'You are wild lads,' he would say, 'but it is true that to have such a sense of humour amid the miseries. of exile shows that you are no weaklings, either in mind or body—a certain flexibility is indispensable.' The good-natured man found it hard to rebuke us more severely than that. He was a Grand Councillor of the Canton of Geneva.

"To the best of my knowledge only one duel took place at the time, and that was fought with pistols by a Herr R...n and myself. But the quarrel was not political. My second was a Genevan in the artillery who spoke nothing but French, and *Oskar Galeer* acted as adjudicator. He was the Grand Councillor's brother, a young man who unfortunately later died prematurely of a nervous disease while still a student in Munich. A second duel, also unpolitical in origin, was to have taken place between Rosenblum and a refugee lieutenant von F...g from Baden, who returned home soon after and, I believe, rejoined the resuscitated Baden army. On the morning fixed for the battle the quarrel was settled amicably before a blow was struck thanks to the intervention of Herr Engels [19]—presumably the same man who is now said to be in Manchester and whom I have not seen again since those days. This Herr Engels was *passing* through Geneva and we drank many bottles of wine in his entertaining company. The acquaintance with him was very welcome to us, if I recollect rightly, especially because we could allow his purse to take charge of the proceedings.

"We were associated neither with the so-called blue or red [20] republicans, nor with the socialist or communist party leaders. We reserved the right to form our own opinions freely and independently (I will not say always correctly) about the political activities of Imperial Regents, members of the Frankfurt Parliament [21] and other speech-making bodies, about generals of the revolution no less than the corporals and Dalai Lamas of communism. For this reason as well as for other reasons which diverted us we even founded a weekly paper entitled

RUMMELTIPUFF

Organ of Rapscallionocracy*

"The paper only survived two issues. Later, when I was arrested in France prior to being deported to this country, the French police confiscated my papers and diaries and I can no longer remember clearly whether it was official ban or lack of funds that brought about the paper's demise.

"To the 'philistines'—and they were to be found in the ranks of the so-called bourgeois republicans as well as among the so-called communist workers[a]—we were known as the *'Brimstone Gang'.* I sometimes imagine that we must have given

* "If my memory serves me right, this epithet had been applied to all the liberal parties in the Parliament of one of the German petty principalities, or in the Frankfurt Parliament. We wished to immortalise it." (*Borkheim*)

---

[a] This presumably refers to the advocates of utopian workers' communism.—*Ed.*

the name to ourselves. At any rate it was only attached to us in its cosy German sense. I am on the friendliest terms with fellow-exiles, who are friends of Herr Vogt, and with others who were, and probably still are, friends of yours. But I rejoice to say that I have never found the members of what I have called the 'Brimstone Gang' referred to by anyone in a disrespectful tone in connection with either political or private matters.

"This 'Brimstone Gang' is the only one known to me. It existed in Geneva from 1849 to 1850. The few members who constituted this dangerous band were compelled, with the exception of *Korn,* to leave Switzerland in the middle of 1850, as they belonged to the category of undesirable aliens. Our departure meant the end of the 'Brimstone Gang'. I know nothing of other 'Brimstone Gangs', or whether other groups went by the name anywhere else, nor what goals they might have been pursuing.

"*Korn* remained, I believe, in Switzerland and is said to have settled down as a pharmacist. *Cohnheim* and *Rosenblum* went to Holstein before the battle of Idstedt[22] in which, I believe, both took part. Later, in 1851, they sailed to America. Rosenblum returned to England at the end of the same year and left again in 1852 for Australia and I have heard nothing more of him since 1855. *Cohnheim* is said to have been for some time now editor of the *New-Yorker Humorist. Becker* likewise emigrated to America in 1850. Unfortunately I have no definite subsequent news of him.

"I myself stayed in Paris and Strasbourg during the winter of 1850-51 and, as I mentioned earlier, in February 1851 the French police sent me to England by brute force—for three months I was dragged from one prison to the other, 25 in all, and for the most part in heavy iron chains while *en route.* I now live here where, having devoted the first year to learning the language, I am engaged in business. My interest in the course of political events in my native land is as persistent and lively as ever, but I have held aloof from all the activities of the political cliques among the refugees. I am doing tolerably well or, as the English would say: Very well, sir, thank you.—You have only yourself to blame if I have made you wade through this long and at all events not very important story.

"I remain, Sir, your humble servant,

Sigismund L. Borkheim"

Thus far Herr *Borkheim's* letter. In anticipation of its historical significance the "Brimstone Gang" took the precaution of carving its own civic register into the Book of History. For the first issue of the *Rummeltipuff* is adorned by woodcut portraits of its founders.

The prodigies of the "Brimstone Gang" had taken part in Struve's republican putsch of September 1848. They then sat in Bruchsal Gaol until May 1849[23] and finally fought as combatants in the campaign for the Imperial Constitution, and as a result were pushed across the Swiss frontier. At some point in 1850 two of their matadors, Cohnheim and Rosenblum, arrived in London where they "congregated" around Herr *Gustav Struve.* I did not have the honour of a personal acquaintance with them. But they established contact with me politically by attempting to form a counter-committee[24] under Struve's leadership in opposition to the London Refugee Committee[25] which was directed at the time by Engels, Willich, myself and others. Their manifesto, hostile to us, appeared in the Berlin *Abend-Post* and elsewhere over the signatures of Struve, Rosenblum, Cohnheim, Bobzin, Grunich and Oswald.

In the heyday of the Holy Alliance the *Charcoal Gang* (or Carbonari[26]) was a mine richly productive of police activities and aristocratic fantasies. Was it the intention of our Imperial Gorgellantua[a] to exploit the "Brimstone Gang" in the same way as the Charcoal Gang had been exploited for the benefit of ye olde Teutonic burghers? If there were a *Saltpeter Gang,* it would round off the policemen's Trinity. Possibly, also, *Karl Vogt* is averse to brimstone because he cannot take the smell of gunpowder. Or is it that, like other patients, he cannot endure a medicine specific to his disease? It is well known that the magic Dr. *Rademacher* classifies diseases according to their antidotes.[27] The category of sulphur diseases would include what Hermann, the barrister in the District Court in Augsburg, referred to as his client's *"well-rounded character"*,[b] what Rademacher calls a "drum-like distension of the peritoneum", and what the even greater Dr. Fischart describes as "the great vaulted belly from France".[c] Thus all Falstaffian natures suffered from the sulphur disease in more than one sense. Or can it be that *Vogt's* zoological conscience has reminded him that sulphur is fatal to scab-mites, and that it is therefore utterly repugnant to scab-mites that have several times changed skin? For, as recent research has shown, only the mite that has shed its skin is capable of procreation and has therefore achieved self-awareness. What a charming contrast: *sulphur* on the one hand, the *self-aware scab-mite* on the other! But in any case, Vogt was obliged to prove to his "Emperor"[d] and to the liberal Teutonic burghers that all disasters "since the failure of the revolution of 1849" stem from the *Brimstone Gang* in Geneva, rather than from the *December Gang* in Paris.[28] To punish me for my many outrages, committed over a period of years, against the head and members of the "Gang of December 10", Vogt

---

[a] An allusion to Vogt. Gorgellantua or Gurgelgrosslinger=Gargantua. Gorgellantua occurs in Johann Fischart's adaptation of Rabelais' *Gargantua et Pantagruel.*—*Ed.*

[b] See this volume, p. 28.—*Ed.*

[c] Johann Fischart, *Affentheurliche, Naupengeheurliche Geschichtklitterung...,* S. 130.—*Ed.*

[d] Napoleon III.—*Ed.*

appointed me the leader of the Brimstone Gang which he has so reviled and which I had not heard of before the appearance of his "Magnum Opus". To render comprehensible the just indignation of this "agreeable companion"[a] I may cite here some of the passages referring to the "December Gang" from my book *Der achtzehnte Brumaire des Louis Bonaparte,* New York, 1852. (Cf. loc. cit., pp. 31, 32 and 61, 62.[b])

"This gang[29] dates from the year 1849. On the pretext of founding a benevolent society, the lumpenproletariat of Paris had been organised into secret sections, each section being led by Bonapartist agents, with a Bonapartist general[c] at the head of the whole. Alongside decayed aristocratic *roués* with dubious means of subsistence and of dubious origin, alongside ruined and adventurous offshoots of the bourgeoisie, were vagabonds, discharged soldiers, discharged jailbirds, escaped galley slaves, rogues, mountebanks, *lazzaroni,*[30] pickpockets, tricksters, gamblers, *maquereaux,*[d] brothel-keepers, porters, casual labourers, organ-grinders, ragpickers, knife-grinders, tinkers, beggars—in short, the whole indefinite, disintegrated mass, thrown hither and thither, which the French term *la bohème*; from this kindred element Bonaparte formed the core of the Gang of December 10. A 'benevolent society'—in so far as, like Bonaparte, all its members felt the need of benefiting themselves at the expense of the labouring nation.

"This Bonaparte, who constitutes himself chief of the lumpenproletariat, who here alone rediscovers in mass form the interests which he personally pursues, who recognises in this scum, offal, refuse of all classes the only class upon which he can base himself unconditionally, is the real Bonaparte, the Bonaparte *sans phrase,* unmistakable even when, later on, having become all-powerful, he pays his debt to a number of his former fellow-conspirators by decreeing their transportation to Cayenne along with the revolutionaries. An old crafty *roué,* he conceives the historical life of the nations and their performances of state [*Haupt- und Staatsaktionen*] as comedy in the most vulgar sense, as a masquerade where the grand costumes, words and postures merely serve to

---

[a] Marx applies to Vogt the expression *angenehmer Gesellschafter* which the latter used in reference to Jérôme Napoleon (see Carl Vogt, *Mein Prozess...,* Dokumente, S. 24).— *Ed.*

[b] *The Eighteenth Brumaire of Louis Bonaparte* (see present edition, Vol. 11, pp. 148-49, 150, 195-97). In the extracts quoted here Marx leaves out a number of passages and slightly alters others.— *Ed.*

[c] Jean Pierre Piat.— *Ed.*

[d] Pimps.— *Ed.*

mask the pettiest knavery. Thus on his expedition to Strasbourg, where a trained Swiss vulture had played the part of the Napoleonic eagle. For his irruption into Boulogne he puts some London lackeys into French uniforms. They represent the army.[31] In his Gang of December 10, he assembles 10,000 rogues who are to play the part of the people, as Nick Bottom that of the lion [a]....

"What the national *ateliers* were for the socialist workers, what the *Gardes mobiles*[32] were for the bourgeois republicans, the Gang of December 10, the party fighting force characteristic of Bonaparte, was for him. On his journeys the detachments of this gang packing the railways had to improvise a public for him, stage public enthusiasm, roar *vive l'Empereur,* insult and beat up republicans, of course under the protection of the police. On his return journeys to Paris they had to form the advance guard, forestall counter-demonstrations or disperse them. The Gang of December 10 belonged to him, it was *his* work, his very own idea. Whatever else he appropriates is put into his hands by the force of circumstances; whatever else he does, the circumstances do for him or he is content to copy from the deeds of others. But *he* with official phrases about order, religion, family and property in public, before the citizens, and with the secret society of the Schufterles and Spiegelbergs, the society of disorder, prostitution and theft, behind him—that is Bonaparte himself as original author, and the history of the Gang of December 10 is his own history....

"Bonaparte would like to appear as the patriarchal benefactor of all classes. But he cannot give to one class without taking from another. Just as at the time of the Fronde it was said of the Duke of Guise that he was the most *obligeant* man in France because he had turned all his estates into his partisans' obligations to him, so Bonaparte would fain be the most *obligeant* man in France and turn all the property, all the labour of France into a personal obligation to himself. He would like to *steal* the whole of France in order to be able to *make a present* of her to France, or, rather, in order to be able to *buy France anew* with French money, for as the chief of the Gang of December 10 he must needs buy what ought to belong to him. And all the state institutions, the Senate, the Council of State, the legislative body, the courts, the Legion of Honour, the soldiers' medals, the wash-houses, the public works,

---

[a] The reference is to Shakespeare's *A Midsummer Night's Dream,* Act I, Scene 2.— *Ed.*

the railways, the *état-major*[a] of the National Guard excluding privates, and the confiscated estates of the House of Orleans—all become parts of the institution of purchase. Every place in the army and in the government machine becomes a means of purchase.

"But the most important feature of this process, whereby France is taken in order to be given back, is the percentages that find their way into the pockets of the head and the members of the Gang of December 10 during the transaction. The witticism with which Countess L.,[b] the mistress of M. de Morny, characterised the confiscation of the Orleans estates: '*C'est le premier vol* de l'aigle*',[c] is applicable to every flight of this *eagle,* which is more like a *raven.* He himself and his adherents call out to one another daily like that Italian Carthusian admonishing the miser who, with boastful display, counted up the goods on which he could yet live for years to come: '*Tu fai conto sopra i beni, bisogna prima far il conto sopra gli anni.*'** Lest they make a mistake in the years, they count the minutes.

"A gang of shady characters push their way forward to the court, into the ministries, to the head of the administration and the army, a crowd of the best of whom it must be said that no one knows whence he comes, a noisy, disreputable, rapacious *bohème* that crawls into braided coats with the same grotesque dignity as the high dignitaries of Soulouque. One can visualise clearly this upper stratum of the Gang of December 10, if one reflects that Véron-Crevel*** is its preacher of morals and Granier de Cassagnac its thinker. When Guizot, at the time of his ministry, utilised this Granier on a hole-and-corner newspaper against the dynastic opposition, he used to boast of him with the quip: '*C'est le roi des drôles*', 'he is the king of the buffoons.'[d] One would do wrong to recall the Regency[34] or Louis XV in connection with

---

* *Vol* means flight and theft. [Note by Marx to *The Eighteenth Brumaire of Louis Bonaparte.*]

** "Thou countest thy goods, thou shouldst first count thy years." [Note by Marx to *The Eighteenth Brumaire of Louis Bonaparte.*]

*** In his novel *Cousine Bette,* Balzac delineates the thoroughly dissolute Parisian philistine in Crevel, a character based on Dr. Véron, owner of the *Constitutionnel.* [Note by Marx to *The Eighteenth Brumaire of Louis Bonaparte.*]

---

a General Staff.— *Ed.*

b Lehon.— *Ed.*

c "It is the first flight (theft) of the eagle."[33]— *Ed.*

d Quoted in the article by Emile Dupont, "Chronique de l'intérieur", *La Voix du Proscrit,* No. 8, December 15, 1850, p. 118.— *Ed.*

Louis Bonaparte's court and clique. For 'often already, France has experienced a government of mistresses; but never before a government of *hommes entretenus*.'...*[a]

"Driven by the contradictory demands of his situation and being at the same time, like a conjurer, under the necessity of keeping the public gaze fixed on himself, as Napoleon's substitute, by springing constant surprises, that is to say, under the necessity of executing a coup d'état *en miniature* every day, Bonaparte throws the entire bourgeois economy into confusion, violates everything that seemed inviolable to the Revolution of 1848, makes some tolerant of revolution, others desirous of revolution, and produces actual anarchy in the name of order, while at the same time stripping its halo from the entire state machine, profanes it and makes it at once loathsome and ridiculous. The cult of the Holy Coat of Trier[35] he duplicates in Paris with the cult of the Napoleonic imperial mantle. But when the imperial mantle finally falls on the shoulders of Louis Bonaparte, the bronze statue of Napoleon will crash from the top of the Vendôme Column."[36]

---

* The words quoted are those of Madame Girardin. [Note by Marx to *The Eighteenth Brumaire of Louis Bonaparte*.]

[a] *Hommes entretenus*: kept men.—*Ed.*

II

THE BRISTLERS

> "But, sirrah, there's no room for faith, truth, nor honesty in this bosom of thine; it is all filled up with guts and midriff."
>
> *(Shakespeare)* [a]

"Bristlers" **or** *"Brimstone Gang"* is what it says in the original Biel gospel ("Magnum Opus", Documents, p. 31). *"Brimstone Gang"* **or else** *"Bristlers"* is what we find in the "Magnum Opus" (p. 136). [b]

According to both versions the "Brimstone Gang" and the "Bristlers" are one and the same gang. The "Brimstone Gang" was, as we have seen, dead and buried by the middle of 1850. Therefore the "Bristlers" too? Our "well-rounded character" is the civilising agent attached to the December Gang, and civilisation, according to Fourier, is distinguished from barbarism by the fact that in it lies simple are replaced by lies composite. [c]

Our "composite" Imperial Falstaff informs us ("Magnum Opus", p. 198) that a certain *Abt* is the "lowest of the low". What admirable self-effacement: Vogt puts himself in the positive, but his Abt in the superlative, appointing him, as it were, his Field Marshal Ney. When Vogt's original gospel appeared in the Biel *Commis voyageur*, [d] I requested the editors of *Das Volk* [37] to reprint the original rigmarole without further comment. Despite this they followed the reprint with this note:

"The above rigmarole stems from the pen of a dissolute creature called *Abt*, who, eight years ago in Geneva, was unanimously found guilty of a variety of

---

[a] *Henry IV*, Part I, Act III, Scene 3. Marx quotes in English.— *Ed.*

[b] Carl Vogt, *Mein Prozess...*, S. 31, 136.— *Ed.*

[c] Charles Fourier, *Théorie de l'unité universelle. Oeuvres complètes*, Vol. 2, Paris, 1843, pp. 78-79, and Vol. 5, Paris, 1841, pp. 213-14.— *Ed.*

[d] Marx means Karl Vogt's article "Zur Warnung" in the *Schweizer Handels-Courier*, No. 150 (special supplement), June 2, 1859 (see this volume, p. 29).— *Ed.*

dishonourable actions by a court of honour of German refugees" (*Das Volk*, No. 6, June 11, 1859).

The editors of *Das Volk* took Abt for the author of Vogt's original rigmarole; they forgot that Switzerland had two Richmonds in the field,[38] a *Vogt, as well as an Abt.*

In the spring of 1851, then, the "lowest of the low" invented the *"Bristlers"*, whom Vogt pilfered from his Field Marshal in the autumn of 1859. The sweet habit of plagiarism acquired in making books on natural history instinctively clings to him in those dealing with his police activities. For a time the President of the Workers' Association in Geneva had been a brushmaker [*Bürstenmacher*] called *Sauernheimer*. Abt bisected Sauernheimer's profession and name, took the beginning of the former and the end of the latter and from the two halves thus obtained he ingeniously formed the whole: "*Bürstenheimer*" [Bristler]. This title he originally bestowed on *Sauernheimer*, as well as on his closest friends: *Kamm* from Bonn, a brushmaker by trade, and also **Ranickel**, a bookbinder's apprentice from Bingen. He appointed Sauernheimer general and Ranickel adjutant of the Bristlers, while Kamm became a Bristler *sans phrase*. Later, when two refugees belonging to the Workers' Association in Geneva, *Imandt* (who is at present professor at the college in Dundee) and *Schily* (a lawyer, formerly of Trier, now in Paris), brought about Abt's expulsion at the hands of a court of honour of the Association, Abt published an abusive pamphlet [39] in which he elevated the whole Workers' Association in Geneva to the rank of "*Bristlers*". It is clear, then, that there were Bristlers in general and Bristlers in particular. "*Bristlers*" in general included the Genevan Workers' Association, the same association which Vogt tricked into giving him a *testimonium paupertatis* which was published in the *Allgemeine Zeitung*[a] at a time when he had been driven into a corner, the same association on which he fawned during the celebrations in memory of Schiller and Robert Blum (1859). "Bristlers" in particular were, as I have mentioned, Sauernheimer, who is totally unknown to me and who has never been to London; Kamm who, having been turned out of Geneva, went to the United States via London, where he looked up Kinkel and not me; and finally *Ranickel,* or **the Ranickel,**[b] who remained as the adjutant of the

---

[a] This refers to the declaration of the German Workers' Educational Association in West Switzerland printed in the *Allgemeine Zeitung*, No. 235, August 23, 1859.— *Ed.*

[b] The name suggests *Ranunkel*=ranunculus and also, by metathesis, *Karnickel*=(1) rabbit and (2) a fool or Simple Simon. Marx puns below on *Ran-Igel*=hedgehog.— *Ed.*

Bristlers in Geneva where he "congregated" around our "well-rounded character". And indeed, in his own person he represents the proletariat in Vogt's eyes. As I shall have more to say about *the Ranickel* later on, here are a few preliminary facts about the beast. *Ranickel* took part in Hecker's ill-starred campaign and after its defeat he joined the detachment of refugees under Willich in Besançon.[40] Still under Willich he went through the campaign for the Imperial Constitution after which he fled with him to Switzerland. Willich was in his eyes the communist Mohammed who would bring about the millennium with fire and sword. A vain, long-winded, foppish melodramatic actor, *the Ranickel* was more tyrannical than the tyrant. In Geneva he raged in a red fury against the "parliamentarians" in general and, like a second Tell, against the "Land-Vogt" in particular, whom he threatened to "strangle". But when he was introduced to Vogt by Wallot, a refugee from the thirties and a boyhood friend of Vogt's, *Ranickel*'s thirst for blood dissolved in the milk of human kindness.[a] "*That* fellow was *the Vogt's*," as Schiller says.[b]

The adjutant of the Bristlers became the adjutant of General Vogt, who has only failed to achieve military renown because Plon-Plon thought the Neapolitan captain *Ulloa* (another general by courtesy[c]) bad enough for the task his "*corps de touristes*" had to perform in the Italian campaign, and so held his Parolles in reserve for the great adventure with "the lost drum" that will unfold on the Rhine.[41] In 1859 Vogt promoted his *Ranickel* from the proletariat to the middle classes, obtained a business for him (*objets d'art*, bookbinding and stationery) and in addition procured for him the custom of the Geneva Government. The adjutant of the Bristlers now became Vogt's "maid of all work",[d] his Cicisbeo, intimate friend, Leporello, confidant, correspondent, gossip-bearer and scandal-monger, but above all, after the Fall of our Fat Jack,[e] he acted as his spy and as recruiting officer for Bonaparte among the workers. A Swiss paper recently reported the discovery of a third species of hedgehog, viz., the Ran or Rhine hedgehog [*Ran- oder Rhein-Igel*] which combines the qualities of both the canine and porcine varieties in itself and which has been found in

---

[a] Marx uses the English phrase "the milk of human kindness" which comes from *Macbeth*, Act I, Scene 5.— *Ed.*

[b] *Wilhelm Tell*, Act I, Scene 4.— *Ed.*

[c] Marx uses the English phrase. For more about Ulloa see Engels' letter written to Marx approximately July 23, 1860, present edition, Vol. 41.— *Ed.*

[d] Marx uses the English phrase.— *Ed.*

[e] Sir John Falstaff was addressed as Jack by his drinking mates.— *Ed.*

a hole on the River Arve, the country-seat of Humboldt-Vogt. Was this *Ran-Igel* aimed at our *Ranickel*?

N.B. The only refugee in Geneva with whom I had any contact was *Dr. Ernst Dronke,* a former co-editor of the *Neue Rheinische Zeitung*[42] and at present a businessman in Liverpool. He was opposed to the activities of the "Bristlers".

The following letters from *Imandt* and *Schily* I would only preface with the remark that, on the outbreak of the revolution, Imandt left university in order to take part as a volunteer in the war in Schleswig-Holstein. In 1849 Schily and Imandt led the storming of the arsenal in Prüm[43] and from there they forced a passage to the Palatinate with their troops and the weapons they had seized. There they joined the ranks of the army of the Imperial Constitution. Having been expelled from Switzerland in the early summer of 1852 they made their way to London.

                                              "Dundee, February 5, 1860
"Dear Marx,

"I am at a loss to understand how Vogt can attempt to connect you with affairs in Geneva. It was common knowledge among the refugees there that of all of us *only Dronke* was in communication with you. The *Brimstone Gang* was before my time and the only name I can recall in connection with it is *Borkheim.*

"The *Bristlers* were the Genevan Workers' Association. The name originated with *Abt.* At the time the Association served as nursery for Willich's secret league of which I was chairman. When, at my instigation, Abt was found by the Workers' Association, to which many refugees belonged, to be a scoundrel and unworthy to associate with refugees and workers, he published a lampoon shortly afterwards in which he accused Schily and myself of the absurdest crimes. Whereupon we revived the whole affair in a different place and before a completely different audience. He rejected our demand that he should come forward with proofs to back up his libellous allegations, and without its being necessary for Schily or myself to say a word in our own defence, *Dentzel* proposed a motion that Abt be declared an infamous slanderer. The motion was approved unanimously for a second time, on this occasion by a meeting of refugees consisting almost entirely of parliamentarians. I am sorry that my tale is so very meagre, but it is the first time in eight years that I have had cause to think back to all *that* trash. I would not like to be condemned to write about it and *I shall be most astonished if you can bring yourself to immerse your hand in such a brew.*

                                              "Adieu,

                                                    Your *Imandt"*

A well-known Russian writer[a] who had been on very friendly terms with Herr Vogt during his stay in Geneva, wrote to me very much along the lines of the concluding words of the above letter:

_____
[a] Nikolai Ivanovich Sazonov.— *Ed.*

42 Karl Marx

"Paris, 10 Mai 1860

"Mon cher Marx!

"J'ai appris avec la plus vive indignation les calomnies qui ont été répandues sur votre compte et dont j'ai eu connaissance par un article de la *Revue contemporaine,* signé *Édouard Simon.*[a] Ce qui m'a particulièrement étonné c'est que Vogt, que je ne croyais ni bête, ni méchant, aît pu tomber dans l'abaissement moral que sa brochure révèle. Je n'avais besoin d'aucun témoignage pour être assuré, que vous étiez incapable de basses et sales intrigues, et il m'a été d'autant plus pénible de lire ces diffamations que dans le moment même où on les imprimait, vous donniez au monde savant la première partie du beau travail[b] qui doit renouveler la science économique et la fonder sur des nouvelles et plus solides bases... Mon cher Marx, ne vous occupez plus de toutes ces misères; tous les hommes sérieux, tous les hommes consciencieux sont pour vous, mais ils attendent de vous autre chose que des polémiques stériles; ils voudraient pouvoir étudier le plus tôt possible la continuation de votre belle œuvre.—Votre succès est immense parmi les hommes pensants et s'il vous peut être agréable d'apprendre le retentissement que vos doctrines trouvent en Russie, je vous dirai qu'au commencement de cette année le professeur—[c] a fait à Moscovie un cours public d'économie politique dont la première leçon n'a pas été autre chose que la paraphrase de votre récente publication.[44] Je vous adresse un numéro de *La Gazette du Nord,* où vous verrez combien votre nom est estimé dans mon pays. Adieu, mon cher Marx, conservez-vous en bonne santé et travaillez comme par le passé, à éclairer le monde, sans vous préoccuper des petites bêtises et des petites lâchetés. Croyez à l'amitié de votre dévoué..."[d]

---

a "Un tableau de moeurs politiques en Allemagne. Le procès de M. Vogt avec la gazette d'Augsbourg", *Revue contemporaine,* February 15, 1860. For Marx's analysis of this article see this volume, pp. 93-94, 112-13.— *Ed.*

b The reference is to Marx's work *A Contribution to the Critique of Political Economy* (see present edition, Vol. 30).— *Ed.*

c Ivan Kondratyevich Babst.— *Ed.*

d "My dear Marx, I have learnt with the greatest indignation of the slanders that have been circulated about you and of which I was apprised by an article in the *Revue contemporaine* signed by *Édouard Simon.* What has astonished me most of all is that Vogt whom I thought to be neither stupid nor malicious should have morally sunk so low as his pamphlet reveals. I need no evidence to persuade me that you are incapable of base and sordid intrigues and it was all the more painful to read these slanders when, at the very moment they were being printed, you were presenting to the learned world the first part of the admirable work which will give new life to the science of economics and provide it with new and more solid foundations.... My dear Marx, you must ignore all this wretched pettiness; all serious men, all scrupulous men are on your side, but they expect something other than sterile polemics from you; they would like to study the continuation of your admirable work as soon as possible.—Among thinking men your success is enormous, and if it gives you pleasure to hear of the echo your works have found in Russia, I can tell you that at the beginning of this year Professor— gave a course of public lectures on political economy in Moscow, the first hour of which was nothing but a paraphrase of your recent publication. I am sending you an issue of *La Gazette du Nord* from which you will be able to see how high your reputation stands in my

Szemere, the former Hungarian Minister, also wrote to me in similar vein:

"Vaut-il la peine que *vous* vous occupiez de toutes ces bavardises?" [a]

I have briefly indicated in the Preface my reasons for immersing my hand in Vogt's brew (to use Imandt's forceful expression) despite these and similar attempts at dissuasion. To return to our *Bristlers.* The following letter from *Schily* is printed here verbatim, not even omitting the parts that do not refer to "*nos moutons*". I have however shortened the description of the Brimstone Gang since it would merely repeat what we already know from Borkheim's account, and certain other passages have been saved for *later* as I must to some extent treat "my agreeable subject" artistically and not blurt all my secrets out at once.

"Paris, February 8, 1860
46 Rue Lafayette

"Dear Marx,

"It was very agreeable to have a direct sign of life from you in the shape of your letter of January 31 [b] and you will find me all the more ready to give you the information you require about these episodes in Geneva as I intended to write to you about them *proprio motu.*[c] The first thing that struck me, and not only me but also all my Geneva acquaintances here with whom I had occasion to discuss the matter, was that Vogt, as you write, lumps you together with people who are quite unknown to you. And so, in the interests of the truth, I had taken upon myself the task of conveying to you the relevant information about the 'Bristlers', the 'Brimstone Gang', etc. So you can see that both your questions: '(1) Who were the Bristlers and what were their activities? and (2) What was the Brimstone Gang, who belonged to it, what did they do?' came at a very opportune moment. I must begin by pointing out, however, that you are guilty of an error in chronology, for priority belongs by rights to the *Brimstone Gang.* If it was Vogt's wish 'to have a bit of fun' and terrify the German philistines by conjuring up the devil or even by calling down fire and brimstone on their heads, he should have found rather more diabolical figures for his models than those harmless and jolly ale-house geniuses to whom we, the senior members of the Geneva emigration, used to refer jokingly and without any unfriendly ulterior motive as the Brimstone Gang, a title which they too accepted in good part. They were the merry sons of the Muses who had taken their *examina* and done their *exercitia practica* in the various South German putsches, finishing up in the campaign for the Imperial Constitution. After the failure they were gathering strength in Geneva in the company of their examiners and instructors in revolution for the time when business would be resumed.... It is

country. Adieu, my dear Marx, keep in good health and labour as in the past for the enlightenment of the world without concerning yourself with petty stupidities and petty acts of cowardly malice. I remain your devoted friend...." — *Ed.*

[a] "Is it really worth *your* while to bother your head with all this tittle-tattle?" (From Szemere's letter of February 5, 1860.) — *Ed.*

[b] Marx's letter to Schily dated January 31 is not available. — *Ed.*

[c] Of my own accord. — *Ed.*

obvious that anyone who either was never in Geneva or arrived there after the dissolution of the Gang could not have belonged to it. It was a purely local and ephemeral flora (a brimstone flora would be the right name for this corrosive substance), though probably because of the *Rummeltipuff* with its whiffs of revolution, it proved to have too strong a scent for Federal Swiss nerves. For Druey blew and the flower was scattered to the winds. It was not until a considerable period had elapsed that *Abt* came to Geneva, followed a few years later by *Cherval*, and while both of them smelled, 'each in his own way', it was not, as Vogt alleges, in that forgotten bouquet which had long since wilted and been torn apart.

"The activities of the Gang may be more or less summed up in the words: *toiling in the vineyard of the Lord.*[a] In addition they edited the *Rummeltipuff* with its motto: 'Dwell in the land and thrive on *red wine!*'[b] In it they exercised their wit and humour on everything under the sun: they denounced false prophets, flayed the parliamentarians (*inde irae*[c]), and spared neither themselves nor us, their audience, but caricatured everyone whether friend or foe with an admirable conscientiousness and impartiality.

"I do not need to tell you that they had no connection with you and never wore your *Bundschuh.*[45] Nor can I conceal from you the fact that that footwear would have been little to their taste. These soldiers of the revolution were for the time being lounging around in the slippers of the armistice until the revolution itself would reanimate them and re-equip them with its own buskin (the seven-league boots of resolute progress).[46] And anyone who had been so bold as to disturb their siesta with Marxist political economy, workers' dictatorship, etc., would have been given a very cool reception indeed. For Heaven knows, the work *they* did required nothing further than a Master of Ceremonies and their economic researches were confined almost entirely to the 'jug' and its *reddish* contents. One of their members, Backfisch, an honest farrier from the Odenwald, once expressed the opinion that 'the right to work was all very well, but the duty to work was one he would prefer to be spared....'

"Let us then replace the sacrilegiously abused tombstone of the Brimstone Gang. To prevent any further desecration of their grave a Hafiz should be employed to sing the *requiescat in pace.*[d] But, failing that, may they herewith accept this obituary *pro viatico et epitaphio*[e]: 'They knew the smell of powder.' Whereas their sacrilegious historiographer has merely managed to smell out brimstone.

"The *Bristlers* first emerged at a time when the Brimstone Gang only lived on verbally in legend, in the records of Genevan philistines and the hearts of Genevan beauties. The brushmakers and bookbinders, Sauernheimer, Kamm, Ranickel, etc., came into conflict with Abt. When Imandt, myself and others resolutely took their side we too became the targets of his hostility. Abt was then summoned to appear before a general assembly of refugees and members of the Workers' Association, combined to form a *cour des pairs*[f] or a *haute cour de justice*.[g] Abt did in fact appear

---

[a] Matthew 20:4.— *Ed.*
[b] A pun on Psalm 37:3. Proverbia (in German): "Dwell in the land and verily thou shalt be fed" (lit. "feed thyself honestly" in Luther's version). Schily replaced *redlich* (honestly) with *rötlich,* literally "reddishly".— *Ed.*
[c] Hence the outcry (Juvenal, *Satires,* Book I, Satire 1).— *Ed.*
[d] Rest in peace. Psalms 4:9.— *Ed.*
[e] For their extreme unction and epitaph.— *Ed.*
[f] Court of peers.— *Ed.*
[g] High court.— *Ed.*

and not only failed to provide proof of the accusations he had hurled at various people, but even declared quite openly that he had made them up quite arbitrarily, as reprisals for just as arbitrary accusations that his enemies had levelled at him: *'Tit for tat, reprisals make the world go round!'*—was his view of the matter. Having made a valiant plea for his system of tit for tat, thoroughly convincing the noble peers of the great practical advantages to be derived from it, and after proofs of the accusations against him had been brought, he was declared to have confessed his malicious slanders, was found guilty of the other misdeeds imputed to him and was formally outlawed. In revenge he christened the noble peers, originally only the above-named guild-members, the *'Bürstenheimers'* [Bristlers], which, as you see, is a happy combination of the trade and name of the first-named. You should revere him, therefore, as the progenitor of the family of Bürstenheim, without however your being in a position to claim to be one of or related to the clan, whether the term is applied to the guild or the peerage. For you ought to know that those of them that did busy themselves with 'organising the revolution' did so not as your supporters but as your opponents. They revered Willich as God the Father or as their Pope and anathematised you as the Antichrist or antipope, so that Dronke, who was regarded as your only supporter and *legatus a latere*[a] in the diocese of Geneva, was excluded from all councils of the Church except the oenological ones, where he was *primus inter pares*. But the Bristlers, like the Brimstone Gang, were the merest Ephemeridae, and Druey had only to give one mighty puff and they scattered in all directions.

"The fact that a pupil of Agassiz[b] should have got involved in these fossils of the Geneva emigration and have unearthed such fantastic tales as those served up in his pamphlet is the more astonishing since as regards the species of Bristleriana he actually possesses a perfect specimen in his own zoological cabinet in the shape of a mastodon of the order of ruminants: **Ranickel**, the very prototype of the Bristler. So the rumination seems to have been imperfectly performed, or else not properly studied by the above-mentioned pupil.

"There you have all you asked for *et au delà.*[c] But now I too should like to ask you something, namely your opinion about the wisdom of introducing an inheritance tax *pro patria, vulgo*: for the state. It would form the state's principal source of income, eliminate the taxes which at present burden the poorer classes and of course would only apply in cases of sizeable estates.... Besides this inheritance tax I am interested in two German institutions: 'the consolidation of landed property' and 'mortgage insurance', institutions which I wish were better appreciated in this country. At the present time they are not at all understood, for the French in general, with but few exceptions, when they gaze across the Rhine see nothing but nebulosities and sauerkraut. An exception was provided recently by *L'Univers*[d] which, after lamenting immoderately about the fragmentation of landed property, added quite correctly: 'Il serait désirable qu'on appliquât immédiatement les remèdes énergiques, dont une partie de l'Allemagne s'est servie avec avantage: le remaniement obligatoire des propriétés partout où les $^7/_{10}$ des propriétaires d'une commune réclament cette mesure. La nouvelle répartition facilitera le

---

[a] Cardinal, emissary. Dronke was sent to Switzerland as an emissary of the Communist League in the summer of 1850.— *Ed.*

[b] Vogt had been an assistant to the Swiss naturalist Agassiz.— *Ed.*

[c] And more besides.— *Ed.*

[d] The full title of the newspaper is *L'Univers réligieux, philosophique, politique, scientifique et littéraire.*— *Ed.*

drainage, l'irrigation, la culture rationelle et la voirie des propriétés.'ᵃ On top of this comes *Le Siècle* which is in general somewhat myopic, but which is completely blind when it comes to consider German affairs, thanks to a chauvinism which it displays as proudly as Diogenes showed off his threadbare cloak—it serves up this stuff, disguised as patriotism, daily to its subscribers. This chauvinist, then, having fired off the obligatory salvo at *L'Univers*, its *bête noire*, went on to say: 'Propriétaires ruraux, suivez ce conseil! Empressez-vous de réclamer le remaniement obligatoire des propriétés; *dépouillez les petits au profit des grands.* O fortunatos nimium agricolas—trop heureux habitants des campagnes—sua si bona—s'ils connaissaient l'avantage à remanier obligatoirement la propriété.'ᵇ As if the large landowners could out-vote the smallholders where *each man* had a vote.

"For the rest I let God's water flow freely over His land, give unto Caesar the things that are Caesar's, and unto God the things that are God's,ᶜ and even 'the Devil's share',ᵈ and remain your old affectionate friend,

Schily"

It follows from the foregoing that as there existed a "Brimstone Gang" in Geneva in 1849-50, and an association called the "Bristlers" in 1851-52, two societies connected neither with each other nor with myself, the revelations of our parliamentary clown about the existence of the *"Brimstone Gang* or *Bristlers"* are flesh of his flesh, a *lie* to the fourth power, "like the father that begets it: gross as a mountain, open, palpable".ᵉ Just imagine a historian shameless enough to report: At the time of the first French Revolution there was a group of people known by the name of the *"Cercle social"*[47] **or else** by the no less characteristic title of *"Jacobins"*.

As regards the life and deeds of the "Brimstone Gang *or* Bristlers" that he concocted, our merry joker was careful to keep the costs of their production down to a minimum. I shall give but a single instance of this:

"One of the chief occupations of the Brimstone Gang," the well-rounded one informs his astounded audience of philistines, "was to compromise people at home in Germany in such a way that they were forced to pay money and no longer resist the attempts to blackmail them" (a fine how-do-you-do[48]; "they *were forced to no longer*

ᵃ "It would be desirable that energetic remedies be introduced immediately, such as those that have proved so successful in part of Germany: the compulsory reorganisation of land holdings wherever it is demanded by ⁷/₁₀ of the owners in a community. The new distribution of land would facilitate drainage, irrigation, the rational exploitation of the land and the planning of roads."—*Ed.*

ᵇ "Rural landowners, follow this advice! Hasten to demand the compulsory reorganisation of land holdings; *rob the small owners to enrich the large ones.* O *fortunatos nimium agricolas*—too happy country-dwellers—*sua si bona*—if they only knew the advantages of the compulsory reorganisation of land holdings." (The Latin expression quoted here is a paraphrase from Virgil's poem *Georgics*.)—*Ed.*

ᶜ Matthew 22:21.—*Ed.*

ᵈ Shakespeare, *Henry IV*, Part I, Act I, Scene 2.—*Ed.*

ᵉ ibid., Act II, Scene 4.—*Ed.*

resist the attempts to blackmail them"), "in exchange for which the gang should preserve the secret of their having been compromised. Not just *one* letter, but *hundreds* were written to Germany by these men" (namely Vogt's homunculi) "and all of them contained the naked threat that the person in question would be denounced for complicity in this or that act of revolution unless a certain sum of money had been received at a specified address by a given date" ("Magnum Opus", p. 139).

Why did Vogt fail to print even *"one"* of these letters? Because the "Brimstone Gang" wrote *"hundreds"* of them. If threatening letters were as plentiful as blackberries[a] Vogt would swear that we should have no threatening letter. If he were summoned to appear tomorrow before a court of honour of the Grütli Association[49] to give an account of the "hundreds" of "threatening letters", he would instead of producing a single letter pull a bottle of wine from his jerkin, smack his lips, cock a snook and with a great belly-laugh worthy of Silenus, he would exclaim like his Abt: "Tit for tat, reprisals make the world go round."

---

[a] Adaptation of Falstaff's "if reasons were as plentiful as blackberries" (Shakespeare, *Henry IV*, Part I, Act II, Scene 4).— *Ed.*

III

POLICE MATTERS

"Welch' Neues Unerhörtes hat der Vogt
Sich ausgesonnen!"

(*Schiller*)[a]

"I say quite bluntly," says Vogt, striking the gravest pose of which such a buffoon is capable, "I say quite bluntly: Everyone who engages in political machinations with Marx and his associates will sooner or later fall into the hands of the police. For these machinations are no sooner under way than they are made known and betrayed to the secret police and hatched out by them as soon as the time appears to be ripe" (these machinations are eggs, it would seem, and the police are the broody hens that hatch them out). "The instigators, Marx & Co., are of course sitting in London out of reach" (while the police are sitting on the eggs). "*I would not be at a loss to provide proofs of this assertion*" ("Magnum Opus", pp. 166, 167).[b]

Vogt is not "*at a loss*" [*verlegen*], Falstaff was never "*at a loss*" either. As "*mendacious*" [*verlogen*] as you please, but "*at a loss*"? Come, your "proofs" [*Belege*], Jack, your "proofs".[c]

1. CONFESSION

"*Marx* himself says on p. 77 of his pamphlet *Revelations Concerning the Communist Trial in Cologne*,[d] published in 1853: '*After* 1849 just as before 1848, only *one* path was open to the proletarian party—that of *secret association*. Consequently after 1849 a whole series of clandestine proletarian societies sprang up on the Continent, were *discovered by the police,* condemned by the courts, broken up by the gaols and *continually resuscitated* by the force of circumstances.' *Marx,*" Vogt declares, "here euphemistically describes himself as 'circumstance'" ("Magnum Opus", p. 167).

Marx says, then, that "the police have discovered a whole series of secret societies since 1849" that were restored to life by the

---

a "What new, unheard-of plan has Vogt invented now?" (*Wilhelm Tell*, Act I, Scene 3.)— *Ed.*

b Carl Vogt, *Mein Prozess....* The italics are Marx's.— *Ed.*

c Shakespeare, *Henry IV*, Part I, Act II, Scene 4.— *Ed.*

d See present edition, Vol. 11, p. 446.— *Ed.*

force of circumstances. Vogt says it was *Marx* and not the "circumstances" that "resuscitated the secret societies". Thus Vogt has furnished proof that whenever Badinguet's police discovered Marianne,[50] Marx in collusion with Pietri set it up again.

"*Marx himself* says." I shall now quote what Marx himself says in its proper context:

"With the defeat of the revolution of 1848-49 the party of the proletariat on the Continent lost use of the *press, freedom of speech and the right to associate,* i.e. the *legal instruments* of party organisation, which it had enjoyed for once during that short interval. The social status of the classes they represented enabled both the bourgeois-liberal and the petty-bourgeois democratic parties to remain united in one form or another and to assert their common interests more or less effectively despite the reaction. After 1849 just as before 1848, only *one* path was open to *the proletarian party*—that of *secret association. Consequently* after 1849 a whole series of clandestine proletarian societies sprang up on the Continent, were discovered by the police, condemned by the courts, broken up by the gaols and continually resuscitated by the force of circumstances. Some of these secret societies aimed directly at the overthrow of the existing state. This was fully justified in *France....* Other secret societies aimed at organising the proletariat into a party, without concerning themselves with the existing governments. This was necessary in countries like *Germany....* There is no doubt that here too the members of the proletarian party would take part once again in a revolution against the *status quo, but it was no part of* **their** *task to prepare this revolution, to agitate, conspire or to plot for it.... The Communist League,*[51] *therefore, was no conspiratorial society...*" (*Revelations, etc.,*[52] *Boston* edition, pp. 62, 63).[a]

But our merciless Land-Vogt regards even "propaganda" as a crime, except of course for the propaganda organised by Pietri and Laity. Our Land-Vogt will even condone "agitation, conspiracy and plotting", but only when its central office is in the Palais Royal[53] with Hearty Harry, Heliogabalus Plon-Plon. But "propaganda" among proletarians! Fie!

After the above-quoted passage, so significantly mutilated by our Examining Magistrate Vogt, I continue in the *Revelations* as follows:

---

[a] See present edition, Vol. 11, pp. 445-46. Marx introduces additional italics and also bold type in quoting.—*Ed.*

"It is self-evident that a secret society of this kind" (like the *Communist League*) "[...] could have had but few attractions for individuals who on the one hand concealed their personal insignificance by strutting around in the theatrical cloak of the conspirator, and on the other wished to satisfy their narrow-minded ambition on the day of the next revolution, and who wished above all to seem important at the moment, to snatch their share of the proceeds of demagogy and to find a welcome among the quacks and charlatans of democracy. Thus a group broke off from the *Communist League,* or if you like it was broken off, a group that demanded, if not real conspiracies, at any rate the *appearance* of conspiracies, and accordingly called for a direct alliance with the democratic heroes of the hour; this was the Willich-Schapper group. It was typical of them that Willich was, together with *Kinkel,* one of the *entrepreneurs* in the business of the German-American Revolutionary Loan" [54] (pp. 63, 64). [a]

And how does Vogt translate this passage into his "euphemistic" police mumbo-jumbo? Listen:

"As long as *both*" (parties) "cooperated, they worked, *as Marx himself says,* to create secret societies and to **compromise societies and individuals** *on the Continent*" (p. 171).

Our fat rascal forgets only to quote the page in the *Revelations* where Marx "*of course says this himself*".

"Egli è bugiardo e padre di menzogna." [b]

2. THE REVOLUTIONARY CONGRESS IN MURTEN

"Charles the Bold", our "bold Charles", *vulgo* Karl Vogt, now delivers his account of the defeat of Murten. [55]

"Large numbers of workers and refugees were cajoled and bullied"—namely by *Liebknecht*—"until finally [...] it was agreed that there should be *a revolutionary congress* in Murten. The delegates of the branch societies were to assemble there *in secret* in order to confer about the *final organisation of the League* and the *exact moment for the armed uprising.* All preparations were made in *absolute secrecy,* the summonses were conveyed *only* by Liebknecht's trusted friends and correspondents. The delegates converged on Murten from *all* sides, *on foot, by boat and by carriage,* and were immediately welcomed by gendarmes, who knew in advance about the whats, the whys and the *hows.* The whole company that had been arrested *in this manner* was detained for a while in the Augustinian monastery in Fribourg and then transported to England and America. Herr Liebknecht was treated with quite *exceptional* consideration" ("Magnum Opus", p. 168).

---

[a] See present edition, Vol. 11, p. 449.— *Ed.*

[b] "'Twas said he was a liar and the father of lies" (Dante, *The Divine Comedy,* Inferno, Canto XXIII).— *Ed.*

"Herr Liebknecht" had taken part in Struve's putsch in September 1848, then was kept in Baden gaols until the middle of May 1849, was freed as a result of the military insurrection in Baden, served as a common soldier in the Baden People's Artillery, was incarcerated once more as a rebel in the casemates in Rastatt by Vogt's friend Brentano; having been freed again during the campaign for the Imperial Constitution he joined the division commanded by Johann Philipp Becker and finally crossed the French border with Struve, Cohnheim, Korn and Rosenblum from where they made their way to Switzerland.

At the time I knew even less about "Herr Liebknecht" and his Swiss "revolutionary congresses" than about the drinking-meetings with mine host Benz in Kessler Street in Berne where the assembled parliamentarians regaled each other with the speeches they had made in St. Paul's Church,[56] counted and distributed future posts of the Empire among themselves, and helped to while away the hard night of exile by listening to the lies, farces, ribaldry and rodomontades of Charles the Bold who, not without a touch of humour, awarded himself the letters patent of *"Imperial Wine Bibber"* in honour of an old German lay.

The "lay" begins with these words:

"Swaz ich trinken's hân gesëhen,
   daz ist gar von kinden geschëhen:
   ich hân einen swëlch gesëhen,
   dem wil ich meisterschefte jëhen.
"Den dûhten becher gar entwiht,
   ër wolde näpf noch kophe niht.
   ër tranc ûz grôzen kannen.
   ër ist vor allen mannen
   ein vorlauf allen swëlhen
"von ûren und von ëlhen
   wart solcher slünd nie niht getân."[a]

---

[a] "The drink and drinking I have seen
   Are fit alone for callow youth,
   But one great tippler has there been
   Fit to wear the crown in truth.
"Normal cups he had forsworn,
   Pots and jugs he'd laugh to scorn,
   He would guzzle tankards tall,
   The staunchest drinkers he would balk,
   He was the greatest of them all.
"Neither bison nor the elk
   Could quaff their drink in such a gulp."
(From the thirteenth-century comic poem "Weinschwelg". Marx quotes in Middle High German.)—*Ed.*

But to return to the "revolutionary congress" in Murten. "Revolutionary congress"! *"Final* organisation of the League"! "Moment for the armed uprising"! *"Absolutely secret* preparations"! "Very *secret* meeting converging from all sides on foot, by boat and by carriage"! "Charles the Bold" evidently did not study my analysis of Stieber's methods in the *Revelations* without profit.

The facts of the matter are simply these: Liebknecht was—early in 1850—the President of the Geneva Workers' Association. He proposed a union of all the hitherto unconnected German workers' associations in Switzerland. The proposal was accepted. Whereupon it was decided to send a circular to twenty-four different workers' associations, inviting them to Murten to discuss the problems of the intended organisation and of establishing a joint newspaper. The debates in the Geneva Workers' Association, the circular, the discussions of the latter in the other twenty-four workers' associations—all this was done *in public* and the congress at Murten was likewise arranged *in full view of the public.* Had the Swiss authorities desired to ban it they could have done so four weeks before it was due to be held. But the liberal Herr *Druey,* who was on the look-out for a victim he could devour and thus placate the sabre-rattling Holy Alliance, preferred to have his police stage a *coup de théâtre.* Liebknecht, who as President of the Workers' Association had signed the document proclaiming the congress, was accorded the honour of being regarded as one of the chief ringleaders. He was separated from the other delegates, was granted free lodging in the uppermost turret of the tower in Fribourg, from where he enjoyed a fine view of the surrounding country, and he even had the privilege of walking for an hour each day upon the battlements. The only special feature of the way he was treated was the fact of solitary confinement. His repeated request to be allowed to join the other prisoners was repeatedly rejected. Vogt, however, knows full well that the police do not put their *"moutons"*[a] in solitary confinement, but place them as "agreeable companions" among the mass.

Two months later Liebknecht, together with a certain Gebert, was transported by the Fribourg Chief of Police to Besançon, where both he and his companion received a compulsory French passport to London, with the warning that if they deviated from the prescribed route they would be deported to Algiers. As a result of this unexpected journey Liebknecht lost most of the

---

[a] Spies.— *Ed.*

personal effects he had in Geneva. Apart from this, however, Messrs. Castella, Schaller and the other members of the then Fribourg Government are to be commended for their humane treatment of Liebknecht and the other prisoners of Murten. These gentlemen were mindful of the fact that they themselves had been captive or on the run but a few years before and they openly expressed the disgust they felt at being obliged to execute the orders of the Grand Cophta Druey.[57] The captive refugees were not given the *kind* of treatment that the refugee "parliamentarians" had expected. A certain Herr H., an associate of the parliamentarians who is still in Switzerland, felt it incumbent on himself to publish a pamphlet in which he denounced the prisoners in general and Liebknecht in particular for upholding "revolutionary" ideas that exceeded the limits of parliamentary reason. And it seems that "Charles the Bold" is still inconsolable about the "quite exceptional consideration" accorded to Liebknecht.

Plagiarism is a general characteristic of all the concoctions of our "bold hero", and this one is no exception. For the Swiss liberals invariably "liberalised" their acts of expulsion by accusing their victims of spying. After *Fazy* had expelled *Struve* he denounced him publicly as a "Russian spy". Likewise *Druey,* who accused *Boichot* of being a French *mouchard. Tourte* slandered *Schily* in a similar manner after he had suddenly had him arrested in the street in Geneva and sent to the *tour des prisons* in Berne. *"Le commissaire maire fédéral Monsieur Kern exige votre expulsion"*[a] was the reply of the high and mighty *Tourte* when Schily asked the reason for the brutal treatment meted out to him. *Schily: "Alors mettez-moi en présence de Monsieur Kern."*[b] *Tourte: "Non, nous ne voulons pas que M. le commissaire fédéral fasse la police à Genève."*[c] The logic of this reply was altogether worthy of the letter this same *Tourte,* who was then Swiss Ambassador in Turin, wrote to the President of the Confederation[d] informing him that Cavour was working with might and main to prevent the cession of Savoy and Nice at a time when this cession was already a *fait accompli.* But it is possible that certain diplomatic railway

---

a "The Federal Commissioner, Mayor Kern, demands your expulsion."—*Ed.*
b "Very well, then, take me to M. Kern."—*Ed.*
c "No, no, we won't have the Federal Commissioner playing policeman in Geneva."—*Ed.*
d See *Correspondence Respecting the Proposed Annexation of Savoy and Nice to France...,* No. 34, p. 34, Hudson to Russell, received February 16, 1860.—*Ed.*

connections were responsible for the failure of Tourte's normal discernment at the time. Scarcely was Schily locked up in the severest solitary confinement in Berne when Tourte began to "liberalise" his police brutality by whispering in the ears of German refugees (Dr. Fink, for example) that "Schily had secretly been in contact with Kern and had sent him information about refugees in Geneva, etc." The Geneva paper *Indépendant* itself included among the notorious sins of the Geneva Government of the day "the systematic calumniation of the refugees, which has been raised to the level of a principle of state". (See Appendix 1.)

At the very first representations of the German police, Swiss liberalism violated the right of asylum by driving out the so-called "leaders"—and this right of asylum had just been granted on condition that the remnant of the revolutionary army would refrain from fighting a last battle on Baden soil. But later, after the "leaders", it was the turn of the "misguided led". Thousands of Baden soldiers were given passports for home on false pretences and when they arrived there they were immediately welcomed by gendarmes, who knew in advance about "the whats, the whys and the hows". Then came the threats of the Holy Alliance and with them the police farce in *Murten*. But even the "liberal" Federal Council [58] did not venture to go as far as the "bold Charles". Nothing at all about "revolutionary congress", "final organisation of the League", "exact moment for the armed uprising". The investigation which for propriety's sake had to be started, vanished into thin air.

"Threats of war" from abroad and "political-propagandistic tendencies", that was all the "embarrassed" Federal Council could stutter by way of excuse in its official report. (See Appendix 2.) The grand police actions of "Swiss liberalism" did not cease with the "revolutionary congress in Murten". On January 25, 1851 my friend Wilhelm Wolff ("Parliamentary Wolf" as he was known among the "Parliamentary Sheep") wrote to me from Zurich:

"The recent measures taken by the Federal Council have reduced the number of refugees from 11,000 to 500, and the Council will not rest until the remnant has been harried out of the country too, leaving only those who possess either a considerable fortune or powerful connections."

The refugees who had fought for the revolution stood in the most natural opposition to the heroes of St. Paul's Church who had talked it into the grave. The latter did not scruple to deliver their opponents into the hands of the Swiss police.

Vogt's loyal follower, the *Ranickel* monstrosity, himself wrote to *Schily* after the latter's arrival in London:

"Try to keep a few columns open in one of the Belgian newspapers for explanations, and do not fail to make the life of those *rascally German dogs* (the parliamentarians) in America miserable for having **sold** *themselves to that goitrous diplomat* (*Druey*)."

It is now apparent what "Charles the Bold" meant when he said:

"I was labouring *with all my strength* to set limits to all these revolutionary antics and to provide the refugees with *shelter*, either on the Continent or *overseas*." ᵃ

The following description was to be found, long ago, in No. 257 of the *Neue Rheinische Zeitung* dated

"Heidelberg, March 23, 1849: Our friend *Vogt*, 'champion' of the Left, imperial jester of the moment, imperial Barrot of the future, the 'faithful warner' against revolution—he has joined forces with—some like-minded people? By no means! But with a few reactionaries of the deepest dye ... and for what purpose? In order to convey or to *deport* to America all those 'characters' living in Strasbourg, Besançon and elsewhere on the German frontier.... What Cavaignac's iron rule imposes as a punishment these gentlemen would like to mete out in the name of Christian charity.... Amnesty is dead, long live *deportation*! And of course this was accompanied by the *pia fraus*ᵇ that the refugees had themselves expressed the desire to emigrate, etc. But now the *Seeblätter* receives word from Strasbourg that these intentions to deport them have unleashed an angry storm of protest among *all* the refugees, etc. [...] In fact they all hope to return to Germany soon, even at the risk (as Herr Vogt touchingly remarks) of having to join some 'mad escapade'."ᶜ

But enough of "Charles the Bold's" revolutionary congress in Murten.

3. CHERVAL

"The virtue of this jest will be the incomprehensible lies that this same fat rogue will tell us." ᵈ

In my *Revelations Concerning the Communist Trial in Cologne* an entire chapter is devoted to the *Cherval plot*.[59] In it I show that Stieber with Cherval (a pseudonym for Crämer) as his instrument, and Carlier, Greif and Fleury as midwives, brought the so-called

---

ᵃ Carl Vogt, *Mein Prozess...*, S. 165.— *Ed.*

ᵇ Pious deception.— *Ed.*

ᶜ Marx quotes the *Neue Rheinische Zeitung* from his notebook. There are some alterations in the use of italics as compared with the original.— *Ed.*

ᵈ Shakespeare, *Henry IV*, Part I, Act I, Scene 2. Marx quotes in English and gives the German translation.— *Ed.*

Franco-German September plot in Paris into the world,* with the
intention of providing the prosecution with just that *"factual
evidence of an indictable offence"* against the Cologne prisoners
the lack of which the "Indictment Board of Cologne" had criticised.

So decisive were the proofs I delivered to the defence during
the Cologne trial,[60] so convincing the demonstration of a total lack
of connection between Cherval, on the one hand, and the accused
at Cologne and myself, on the other, that Stieber, who had sworn
by Cherval on October 18 (1852), forswore him again on October
23, 1852 (*Revelations,* p. 29[a]). Driven into a corner he abandoned
the attempt to link Cherval and his plot with us. Stieber was Stieber,
but even Stieber was a far cry from Vogt.

I think it is quite unnecessary for me to repeat here the
information I gave in the *Revelations* about the so-called September plot. At the beginning of May 1852 Cherval returned to
London, from where he had moved to Paris on business in the
early summer of 1850. The Paris police let him escape from them
a few months after he was sentenced in February 1852. In London
he was greeted at first as a political martyr and welcomed into the
German Workers' Educational Society, from which my friends and
I had resigned as early as *mid-September 1850.*[61] But this delusion
was short-lived. The truth about his deeds of heroism in Paris
soon became known and during that same month, May 1852, he
was publicly expelled from the Society for his infamous conduct.
The accused in Cologne, who had been imprisoned early in May
1851, were still in detention awaiting trial. I realised from a notice
sent from Paris by the spy *Beckmann* to his paper, the *Kölnische
Zeitung,* that the Prussian police were attempting retrospectively to
forge a link between Cherval, his plot and the accused in Cologne.
I accordingly kept on the look-out for reports about Cherval. It so
happened that in July 1852 the latter offered his services as an
Orleanist agent to M. de R.,[b] a former Minister during Louis
Philippe's reign and a well-known eclectic philosopher. The
connections which M. de R. retained in the Paris Prefecture of
Police enabled him to obtain extracts from their dossier on

---

* I did not learn until after the *Revelations* were in print that de la Hodde
(under the name Duprez) as well as the Prussian police agents *Beckmann* (then
correspondent of the "Kölnische Zeitung") and *Sommer* were also involved.

ª See present edition, Vol. 11, p. 420.— *Ed.*
ᵇ Charles François Marie de Rémusat (see Marx's letter to Engels, July 13, 1852,
present edition, Vol. 39).— *Ed.*

Cherval. In the French police report Cherval was referred to as *Cherval nommé Frank, dont le véritable nom est Crämer.*[a] For a long time he had worked as an agent for Prince Hatzfeldt, the Prussian Ambassador in Paris; he was the betrayer of the *complot franco-allemand* and was now simultaneously a spy for the French, etc. In the course of the Cologne trial I gave these reports to one of the counsel for the defence, Herr *Schneider II*, and empowered him to name my source if need arose. When Stieber said under oath during the session of October 18 that the Irishman Cherval, who on Stieber's own testimony had served a gaol sentence in Aachen in 1845 for forging bills of exchange, was at that moment still under arrest in Paris, I informed Schneider II by return of post that, under the pseudonym of Cherval, the Rhenish Prussian Crämer was "still!" in London, was in daily communication with Greif, the Prussian lieutenant of police, and that, as he was a condemned Prussian criminal, the English would extradite him as soon as they received an application from the Prussian Government. To have brought him to Cologne as a witness would have overthrown the entire Stieber system.

Under pressure from Schneider II Stieber finally remembered on October 23 having heard that Cherval had fled from Paris, but he swore high and low that he had no knowledge of the present whereabouts of the Irishman or of his alliance with the Prussian police. In fact at that time Cherval was attached to Greif in London by a fixed weekly salary. The debates about the "Cherval mystery" at the Cologne Assizes, that had been provoked by my reports, drove Cherval from London. I heard that he had gone on a police mission to Jersey. I had long lost sight of him when by chance I came across a report from the Geneva correspondent of the *Republik der Arbeiter,*[b] which appears in New York, stating that Cherval had turned up in Geneva in March 1853 under the name of *Nugent,* and that he had vanished from there once more in the summer of 1854. He visited Vogt in Geneva, then, a few weeks after my *Revelations* with the compromising statements about him had been published in Basle by Schabelitz.

Let us now return to the Falstaffian travesty of history. According to Vogt, Cherval arrived in Geneva *immediately* after his fictitious escape from Paris and before that he was allegedly "sent" by the secret Communist League from London to Paris "a

---

[a] Cherval, called Frank, whose real name is Crämer.— *Ed.*

[b] "Korrespondenzen. Genf, den 16. April 1854", *Republik der Arbeiter*, No. 22, May 27, 1854.— *Ed.*

few months" prior to the discovery of the September plot (loc. cit.,
p. 172). Hence while the interval between May 1852 and March
1853 thus disappears altogether, the interval between June 1850
and September 1851 shrinks to "a few months". What wouldn't
Stieber have given for a Vogt who could have testified on oath
before the Assizes at Cologne that the "secret Communist League
in London" had sent Cherval to Paris in June 1850, and what
wouldn't I have given to see Vogt sweating on the witness stand
next to his Stieber! What a fine company they make: the swearing
Stieber with his bird, the Greif [griffin], his Wermuth [vermouth],
his Goldheimchen [golden cricket] and his *Bettelvogt* [beadle].
Vogt's Cherval brought with him to Geneva "*recommendations
to all friends of Marx & Co., from whom Mr. Nugent soon became
inseparable*" (p. 173). He "took up his quarters with the family of a
correspondent of the *Allgemeine Zeitung*" and gained access to
Vogt probably as the result of my recommendations (in the
Revelations). Vogt employed him as a lithographer (loc. cit., pp.
173[-74]) and entered with him so to speak into a "scientific
intercourse" as he had done earlier with Archduke John and
was to do later with Plon-Plon. One day, while he was working in
the "office" of the Imperial Regent,[62] "Nugent" was recognised by
an "acquaintance" as Cherval and accused of being an "*agent
provocateur*". In fact Nugent was not only working for Vogt in
Geneva but was also busily engaged in "founding a clandestine
society".

   "Cherval-Nugent presided, *kept the minutes and corresponded with London*" (loc.
cit., p. 175). He had "*taken a few not very discerning* but otherwise worthy workers
into his confidence" (ibid.), however "among the members *there was also an associate
of the Marx clique* known to everyone as a suspect minion of the German police"
(loc. cit.).

   "*All* the friends" of Marx, from whom Cherval-Nugent
"became inseparable", are now suddenly transformed into "*one*
associate", and this *one* associate promptly dissolves again into "*the
associates of Marx* who had remained behind *in Geneva*" (p. 176),
with whom Nugent later "continues to correspond from Paris"
and whom he magnetically "attracts to himself" in Paris (loc. cit.).
   Yet another instance, then, of his favourite "transformation" of
the buckram "cloth" of Kendal green!
   What Cherval-Nugent purposed with his society was the

   "mass production of forged banknotes and treasury bills which when put into
circulation were expected to undermine the credit of the despots and ruin their
finances" (loc. cit., p. 175).

Cherval, it seems, was trying to emulate the celebrated Pitt who, as is well known, set up a factory not far from London during the war against the Jacobins to produce false French assignats.

"Various stone and copper plates had *already* been engraved for this purpose by Nugent himself; the gullible members of the secret league had *already* been selected to go to France, Switzerland and Germany with packets of these"—stone and copper plates?—no—"*these counterfeit banknotes*" (the banknotes were, of course, put into packets before they were printed) (p. 175),

but Cicero-Vogt was *already* standing behind Cherval-Catiline with his sword drawn. A peculiar characteristic of all Falstaffs is that as well as big bellies they also have big mouths. Just look at our Gurgelgrosslinger who has already set limits to "revolutionary antics" in Switzerland and arranged for whole shiploads of refugees to find *a livelihood overseas,* look how he postures, how melodramatically he acts, how he magnifies Stieber's Paris skirmish with Cherval (see *Revelations*[a])! Here he lay, and thus he bore his point![b]

"The plan of the whole *conspiracy*" (loc. cit., p. 176) "*had been monstrously conceived.*" "All the workers' associations were to have Cherval's project laid at their door." There had *already* been "some confidential inquiries from foreign embassies", they were *already* on the point of "compromising Switzerland, especially the Canton of Geneva".

But the Land-Vogt was vigilant. He carried out his first rescue of Switzerland, an experiment he later repeated several times with steadily increasing success.

"*I* cannot deny," the weighty man exclaims, "*I* cannot deny that I contributed **a substantial part** in frustrating these *devilish plans*; *I* cannot deny that I made use of the police of the Geneva Republic for this purpose; *I* regret to this day" (disconsolate Cicero) "that the zeal of some deluded enthusiasts served to warn the wily ringleader and enabled him to evade arrest" [p. 177].

But at all events, Cicero-Vogt had "frustrated" the Catiline conspiracy, rescued Switzerland, and "contributed" **his substantial part** (wherever he carries that). According to him Cherval reappeared in Paris a few weeks later and there "he made no attempt to hide himself, but showed himself *in public* like other *citizens*" (loc. cit., p. 176). And we all know how *public* is the *life* of the citizens of Paris in the counterfeit Empire.

---

[a] See present edition, Vol. 11.— *Ed.*

[b] Falstaff's words (slightly paraphrased) from Shakespeare's *Henry IV*, Part I, Act II, Scene 4.— *Ed.*

While Cherval thus gads about in Paris "in public", poor[a] Vogt always has to hide in the Palais Royal under Plon-Plon's table when he visits Paris!

I rather regret that after Vogt's powerful Zachariad[63] I must now give the following letter from *Johann Philipp Becker.* A veteran of the German emigration, active as a revolutionary from the Hambach Festival[64] to the campaign for the Imperial Constitution, in which he fought as commander of the 5th Army Division (the Berlin *Militär-Wochenschrift,* a voice that is by no means partial, testified to his military achievement), Johann Philipp Becker is too well known to require any recommendation from me. I need only say, therefore, that his letter was written to R.,[b] a German businessman in London with whom I am on friendly terms, that I do not know Becker personally and that he has never been connected with me politically. Finally, I should note that I have omitted the opening section of his letter which deals with business matters as well as most of the passages referring to the "Brimstone Gang" and the "Bristlers" since we are already familiar with the material they contain. (The original of the letter is in Berlin along with other documents connected with my suit.)

"*Paris,* March 20, 1860

"...I recently saw Vogt's pamphlet against Marx.[c] I found its contents very distressing, all the more so since, as I was living in Geneva at the time, I am perfectly familiar with the history of the so-called Brimstone Gang and the notorious Cherval. It is evident that the events have been totally distorted and with an utter disregard for justice have been falsely connected with the political activities of the economist Marx. I do not know Herr Marx personally, nor have I ever had any association with him whatever, but I have known Herr Vogt and his family for upwards of twenty years and am bound to him by much closer bonds of affection. I must bitterly deplore and unreservedly repudiate the frivolous and unscrupulous manner in which Vogt has entered the lists on this occasion. It is unworthy of a man to include distorted and even imaginary facts as weapons in his armoury. It is really very painful to see that Vogt unthinkingly, and apparently suicidally, destroys his congenial field of activity, compromises his position and stains his own reputation; and this would be the case even if he could be wholly acquitted of the charge of being in the pay of Napoleon. On the other hand, how gladly would I have seen him use every honest means to clear his name of such grave accusations. As it is, his behaviour hitherto in this unedifying business impels me to give you a description of the so-called Brimstone Gang and the worthy Herr Cherval so that you may judge for yourself the extent to which Marx may be held responsible for their existence and their activities.

"A word, then, about the rise and fall of the Brimstone Gang, for scarcely

---

[a] Marx uses the English word.— *Ed.*

[b] Georg Friedrich Rheinländer.— *Ed.*

[c] Carl Vogt, *Mein Prozess...*.— *Ed.*

anyone is in a better position than I am to give you this information. During my stay in Geneva at that time I had an opportunity to observe the activities of the emigrants not only thanks to my position; but in addition, as an older man and always mindful of the general cause, I had a particular interest in closely following their every move so as to be able whenever possible to forestall and prevent the occasional foolish ventures which were so forgivable in people whom misfortune had so harassed and even reduced to despair. My 30 years' experience had taught 'me only too well how richly every emigration is endowed with illusions."

(What follows has been largely anticipated in the letters of Borkheim and Schily.)[a]

"...This company, essentially a company of idlers, was referred to jestingly and mockingly as the Brimstone Gang. It was a club which consisted, as it were, of a motley crowd brought together by chance; it had neither president nor programme, neither statute nor dogma. There is no question of its having been a secret society, or of its having had any political or other goal to pursue systematically; they merely wanted to show off and that with an openness and frankness that knew no bounds. Nor did they have any connection with Marx, who for his part could certainly have known nothing of their existence and whose socio-political views moreover diverged widely from theirs. And in addition these fellows evinced a strong urge to be independent that verged on self-conceit and it is extremely unlikely that they would have been willing to subordinate themselves to any authority either in theory or in practice. They would have laughed Vogt's paternalistic admonitions out of court, no less than they would have ridiculed Marx's policy instructions. I was in a position to obtain very precise information about everything that went on in those circles since my eldest son [b] used to meet the Big White Chiefs every day.... In all, the whole farce of this gang, devoid of any ties,[c] scarcely outlasted the winter of 1849-50; the force of circumstances scattered our heroes to the winds.

"Who would have thought that after ten years' slumber the long-forgotten Brimstone Gang would be set alight once more by Professor Vogt in order to ward off imagined aggressors by spreading a foul stench which was then transmitted by obliging journalists with great enthusiasm acting as it were as electromagnetic-sympathetic conductors. Even Herr von Vincke, that liberal *par excellence*, mentioned the Brimstone Gang in connection with the Italian question and used it as an illustration in the modest Prussian Chamber. And the otherwise blameless citizens of Breslau in their *sancta simplicitas* have in honour of the Brimstone Gang prepared a carnival jest and fumigated the whole city with sulphur fires as the symbol of their loyalty.

"Poor innocent Brimstone Gang! After your blessed end you had willy-nilly to turn into a veritable volcano, to become the bogy that frightens timid subjects into a wholesome respect for the police, to vulcanise all the fat-heads of the world and blacken every overheated brain down to its roots—just as Vogt, in my opinion, has burnt his fingers for ever.

"Now then, *as for Crämer, vulgo Cherval*. This socio-political and common scoundrel came to Geneva in 1853, pretending to be an Englishman by the name

---

[a] See this volume, pp. 29-32, 43-46.—*Ed.*

[b] Gottfried Becker.—*Ed.*

[c] A pun in the original: *bandlose Bande. Bandlose* means "without ties", *Bande* means "band", "gang".—*Ed.*

of Nugent. This was in fact the surname of the woman who accompanied him, ostensibly as his wife, and who really was English. He spoke both French and English fluently and for a long time carefully avoided speaking German for he seemed to be doing everything in his power to pass for a native Englishman. Being competent in both lithography and chromolithography, he boasted of having introduced this latter art into Geneva. In society he was very adept, he knew how to make his presence felt and to show himself to advantage. He soon obtained a sufficient amount of work, drawing objects from nature and antiquity for professors of the Academy. At first he lived a retired life and later, when he did seek company it was exclusively in the circle of French and Italian refugees. At that time I founded an *office de renseignements*[a] and a daily paper *Le Messager du Léman* and I had an assistant called *Stecher*,[b] a refugee from Baden who had formerly been headmaster in a secondary school. He was a talented draughtsman and strove to improve his standing by studying chromolithography. He found a teacher in the Englishman Nugent. Stecher was now full of stories about this skilful, kindly and generous Englishman and about the pleasant and graceful Englishwoman. Stecher also taught singing in the Workers' Educational Association and he occasionally brought his teacher Nugent with him. It was there that I first had the pleasure of meeting him and that he condescended to speak German; he spoke it so fluently and with such a command of the Lower Rhenish dialect that I said to him: 'But you can't possibly be an Englishman!' He persisted in his assertion, however, explaining that his parents had placed him in a school in Bonn when he was very young and that he had remained there until his eighteenth year, during which time he had got used to the local dialect. Stecher, who remained enchanted by the 'nice' man almost to the last, helped to make the belief that he was an Englishman more credible. But this incident made me rather distrustful of the would-be son of Albion and I urged caution on my fellow-members in the Association. Some time later I met the Englishman in the company of some French refugees and approached just as he was boasting of his heroism during the Paris uprisings. This was the first occasion on which I learned that he was also interested in politics. This made him all the more suspect so I made fun of the 'leonine bravery' he claimed to have displayed, to give him the chance to exhibit it against me in the presence of the Frenchmen. But as he answered my biting mockery by cringing like a cur I judged him contemptible from that moment on.

"From then on he avoided me whenever he could. In the meantime, with Stecher's aid, he organised evening dances in the bosom of the German Workers' Association, enlisting additional musical talent free of charge in the shape of an Italian, a Swiss and a Frenchman. At these balls I again met the Englishman, this time as a veritable *maître de plaisir*[c] and completely in his element; uproarious merriment and pleasing the ladies suited him much better than his leonine bravery. However, he was not politically active in the Workers' Association, where he did nothing but hop, skip and jump, drink and sing. In the meantime however I heard from Fritz, a goldsmith from Württemberg, that our 'intrepid revolutionary Englishman' had founded a League consisting of him (Fritz), another German, a few Italians and Frenchmen, making seven members in all. I implored Fritz to have nothing to do with this political tightrope-walker, at any rate as far as serious matters were concerned, and begged him both to resign from the League at once and induce his associates to do likewise. Some time later my bookseller sent me a

---

[a] Information bureau.— *Ed.*
[b] See Appendix 3 (p. 304 of this volume).— *Ed.*
[c] Master of ceremonies.— *Ed.*

pamphlet by *Marx* dealing with the communist trial in Cologne[a] and in this Cherval was unmasked as Crämer and sharply attacked as a scoundrel and a traitor. At once I began to suspect that Nugent might be Cherval, above all because, according to the pamphlet, he came from the Rhineland and this corresponded to his accent. Also he was alleged to be living with an Englishwoman, which was the case here too. I at once told Stecher, Fritz and others of my suspicions and circulated the pamphlet to this end. Mistrust of Nugent spread quickly; *Marx's pamphlet had its effect.* Soon Fritz came to me explaining that he had resigned from the 'League' and that the others would follow his example. He also revealed to me the League's secret aim. The 'Englishman' intended to destroy the credit of the nations by manufacturing government securities and using the profits that would be gained in this manner to start a European revolution, etc. At about this time a French refugee called Laya, who had formerly been a lawyer in Paris, was giving lectures on socialism. Nugent attended them and Laya, who had defended him at his trial in Paris, identified him as Cherval, and told him so. Nugent implored Laya not to betray him. I learned of it from a French emigrant friendly with Laya and I spread the news at once. Nugent had the effrontery to appear once again in the Workers' Association whereupon he was exposed as the German Crämer and the Frenchman Cherval and was expelled. Ranickel from Bingen is said to have been his most violent assailant on this occasion. To crown it all the Genevan police began to show an interest in him because of the League, but the manufacturer of government securities had disappeared without a trace.

"In Paris he engaged in decorating porcelain and since I was in the same line of trade I met him in the course of business. But I found him the same irresponsible and incorrigible windbag as before.

"But how Vogt could have dared to connect the Genevan activities of this rogue with those of *Marx* and to describe him as one of his confederates or tools is utterly beyond my comprehension, especially as this was supposed to have been at the very time that he was the object of such a violent attack by *Marx* in the pamphlet referred to above. *It was after all Marx who unmasked him and who drove him from Geneva where, according to Vogt, he was actively engaged on Marx's behalf.*

"When I reflect how it was possible for a scientist like Vogt thus to go astray my mind reels. Is it not lamentable to find the praiseworthy reputation brought about by a happy coincidence of events so recklessly destroyed in such a wasteful and sterile fashion! Would it be surprising if after witnessing such deeds the whole world were to receive Vogt's scientific researches with scepticism, suspecting all the while that he might have arrived at his scientific conclusions with the same recklessness and the same lack of scruple, basing them on erroneous notions rather than on positive facts, painstakingly studied?

"If to become a statesman and a scientist nothing but ambition were required even *Crämer* might become both. *Unfortunately, with his Brimstone Gang and his Cherval, Vogt has degenerated into a sort of Cherval himself. And indeed there are intrinsic similarities between the two, brought about by their hankering for material comfort, for the safety of their own persons, for the joys of conviviality and for frivolous trifling with serious matters....* In anticipation of friendly news from you I send you my warmest greetings.

"Yours,

J. Ph. Becker

---

[a] *Revelations Concerning the Communist Trial in Cologne* (see present edition, Vol. 11).— *Ed.*

"P. S. Glancing once more at Vogt's pamphlet I observe to my further surprise that the 'Bristlers' too have been duly honoured. So I am adding a few words to outline their story....

"Furthermore, I also saw in the pamphlet that he claims that Nugent-Cherval-Crämer *came to Geneva on a mission for Marx*.[a] I must add therefore that he did not drop the pretence of being an Englishman up to the very last moment in Geneva and that he *never gave the slightest indication that he had ever had any contact whatever with any German emigrant,* which would in any case have scarcely been reconcilable with his wish to preserve his incognito. Even here and now, when the matter must have lost its former significance for him, he is reluctant to admit his German origin and steadfastly denies all earlier acquaintance with Germans.

"Hitherto I still believed that Vogt had light-mindedly allowed himself to be mystified by others, but now his actions increasingly seem to be motivated by malicious perfidy. I am less sorry for him than before and my sympathy is reserved now for his worthy and good old father[b] who will suffer many a bitter moment because of this business.

"I will not only permit you, I actually request you to make known this information among your circle of acquaintances in the interest of truth and of the good cause.

"With warm greetings,

Yours,

J. Philipp B." (See Appendix 3.)

4. THE COMMUNIST TRIAL IN COLOGNE

From the "office" of the Regent of the Empire in Geneva to the Royal Prussian Court of Assizes in Cologne.

"In the Cologne trial *Marx* played an outstanding part." Undoubtedly.

"In Cologne *his confederates* were on trial."[c] Granted.

The Cologne accused were held in detention for $1^1/_2$ years pending the trial.

The Prussian police and the Embassy, Hinckeldey with his entire clan, postal and municipal authorities, the Ministries of the Interior and of Justice—all made the most strenuous efforts during these $1^1/_2$ years to give birth to a *corpus delicti.*

Here then, in his research into my "activities", Vogt has at his disposal, as it were, the assistance of the Prussian state and he even had authentic material contained in my *Revelations Concerning the Communist Trial in Cologne,* Basle, 1853, a copy of which he discovered in the Geneva Workers' Association and which he borrowed and "studied". This time, then, young Karl really will

---

[a] Carl Vogt, *Mein Prozess...,* S. 176.—*Ed.*

[b] Philipp Friedrich Wilhelm Vogt.—*Ed.*

[c] Carl Vogt, *Mein Prozess...,* S. 169-70.—*Ed.*

settle my hash. But no! For once Vogt is "at a loss", he just sets off a few of his home-made smoke-bombs and stink-bombs* before beating a hasty retreat, stammering:

> "*The Cologne trial is of no particular significance for us*"[a] ("Magnum Opus", p. 172).

In the *Revelations* I was compelled to attack Herr *August Willich* among other people. Willich commenced his defence in the *New-Yorker Criminal-Zeitung* of October 28, 1853** by describing my work as "*a masterly critique of the savage procedures adopted by the central police of the German Confederation*".[b] *Jacob Schabelitz fils,* the publisher of the pamphlet, wrote to me from *Basle* on December 11, 1852 after receiving the manuscript:

> "Your exposure of the perfidy of the police is unsurpassable. You have erected a permanent monument to the present regime in Prussia."[c]

He added that his judgment was shared by experts, chief among these "experts" being a man who is at present a Genevan friend of Herr Karl Vogt.

Seven years after the publication of the *Revelations* Herr Eichhoff of Berlin, whom I do not know at all, made the following statement in court (it is well known that Eichhoff was on trial,[65] accused of having slandered Stieber):

> "He had made a detailed study of the Cologne communist trial and not only adhered to his original opinion that Stieber had committed perjury but had to extend it to assert that everything Stieber said during the trial was false.... The verdict passed on the accused in Cologne was due entirely to Stieber's testimony.... Stieber's whole testimony was perjury from start to finish" (first supplement to the Berlin *Vossische Zeitung,* May 9, 1860).[d]

---

* "*Smoke-bombs* or *stink-bombs* are used chiefly in mine warfare. One works with an ordinary flare-charge which must however contain rather more *sulphur* than usual and as much feathers, horn, hair and other rubbish as the charge will take. This is put in a container and the shell fired with a fuse" (F. C. Plümicke, *Handbuch für die Königlich Preussischen Artillerie-Offiziere,* Erster Teil, Berlin, 1820).

** I replied with a pamphlet called *The Knight of the Noble Consciousness,* New York, 1853. [See present edition, Vol. 12.]

---

a Italics by Marx.— *Ed.*

b This refers to August Willich's slanderous article "Doctor Karl Marx und seine Enthüllungen", published in the *Belletristisches Journal und New-Yorker Criminal-Zeitung,* October 28 and November 4, 1853.— *Ed.*

c See present edition, Vol. 39. Marx gives a summary rather than the exact words of the quoted passage.— *Ed.*

d Karl Wilhelm Eichhoff [,Erklärung vor dem Criminalgericht 8.-15. Mai 1860], *Königlich privilegirte Berlinische Zeitung von Staats- und gelehrten Sachen,* No. 108 (supplement), May 9, 1860.— *Ed.*

Vogt himself admits:

"He" (Marx) "did *everything in his power* to provide the defence with the materials and instructions necessary for the conduct of their case...."

It is a known fact that "false documents, manufactured by the agents themselves", i. e. Stieber, Fleury, etc., "were presented to the court" (in Cologne) "as 'evidence' and that in general an abyss of perfidy was *exposed* among this police rabble that makes one shudder to contemplate" ("Magnum Opus", pp. 169, 170).

If Vogt can show his hatred of the coup d'état by making propaganda for Bonapartism, why should not I reveal "my collusion" with the secret police by *exposing* their abysmal perfidy? If the police had genuine proofs, why manufacture false ones?

But, lectures Professor Vogt,

"nevertheless the blow *only* fell on the members of the Marxian League in Cologne, only on the Marx party".

Indeed, Polonius! Had not the blow fallen on another party earlier on in Paris; did it not also strike another party later on in Berlin (the Ladendorf trial), and yet another in Bremen (League of the Dead),[66] etc., etc.?

As to the *verdict* passed on the Cologne accused I shall quote a relevant passage from my *Revelations*:

"The miracles performed by the police were originally necessary to conceal the completely *political nature* of the trial. 'The revelations you are about to witness, Gentlemen of the Jury,' said Saedt when opening for the prosecution, 'will prove to you that this trial is not a political trial.' But now" (at the conclusion of the case) "he emphasises its political character so that the police revelations should be forgotten. After the 1 1/2-year preliminary investigation the jury needed objective evidence in order to justify itself before public opinion.

"After the five-week-long police comedy they needed 'politics *pure and simple*' to extricate themselves from the sheer mess. Saedt therefore did not only confine himself to the material that had led the Indictment Board to the conclusion that 'there was no factual evidence of an indictable offence'. He went even further. He attempted to prove that the law against conspiracy does not require any indictable action, but is simply a law with a political purpose, and the category of conspiracy is therefore merely a pretext for burning political heretics in a legal way. The success of his attempt promised to be all the greater because of the decision to apply the new [Prussian] Penal Code that had been promulgated after the accused had been arrested. On the pretext that this code contained extenuating provisions the servile court was able to permit its retroactive application. But if it was simply a political trial why a preliminary investigation lasting $1\,^1/_2$ years? For political reasons" (loc. cit., pp. 71, 72).

"With the unmasking of the minute-book" forged and planted by the Prussian police themselves "the case had advanced to a new stage. The jury was no longer free merely to find the defendants guilty or not guilty; they must either find the defendants guilty—or the government.

"To acquit the accused would mean condemning the government" (loc. cit., p. 70).[a]

That the Prussian Government of the day put a similar construction on the situation is plain from a communication that Hinckeldey sent to the Prussian Embassy in London while the Cologne trial was still in progress. In this he said that *"the whole existence of the political police depended on the outcome of the trial".* He accordingly asked for a person who could appear in court in the guise of the witness H.[b] (who had disappeared), for which performance he would receive 1,000 talers reward. This person had actually been found when Hinckeldey's next letter arrived:

"The State Prosecutor hopes that *thanks to the happy constitution of the jury* it will be possible to get a verdict of guilty even without further extraordinary measures, and he" (Hinckeldey) "therefore asks you not to trouble yourselves further." (See Appendix 4.)

It was in fact the *happy constitution of the jury in Cologne* which inaugurated the Hinckeldey-Stieber regime in Prussia. "A blow will be struck in Berlin if the Cologne accused are condemned" was the view of the police rabble attached to the Prussian Embassy in London, as early as October 1852, even though the police mine (the Ladendorf conspiracy) did not explode in Berlin until the end of March 1853. (See Appendix 4.)

The liberal outcry that follows an age of reaction is all the louder the greater the cowardice displayed by liberals in putting up with the reaction for years on end without protest. Thus at the time of the Cologne trial, all my efforts to expose Stieber's system of deception in the liberal Prussian press were unavailing. The motto of the press, printed on its banner in block letters, ran: Reliability is the first duty of the citizen, and in this sign shalt thou—live.[67]

---

a See *Revelations Concerning the Communist Trial in Cologne* (present edition, Vol. 11, pp. 454-55, 453). Except for the words "pure and simple", the italics were introduced by Marx in *Herr Vogt.—Ed.*

b Hermann Wilhelm Haupt.— *Ed.*

5. JOINT FESTIVAL OF THE GERMAN WORKERS'
EDUCATIONAL ASSOCIATIONS IN LAUSANNE
(JUNE 26 AND 27, 1859)

Our hero takes to his heels and with undiminished pleasure he
retreats to—Arcadia. We meet him again in a "secluded corner of
Switzerland", in Lausanne, at a "Joint Festival" of a number of
German workers' educational associations which took place
towards the end of June. Here Karl Vogt saved Switzerland for
the second time. While Catiline was sitting in London, our Cicero
with the gay-coloured jacket thundered in Lausanne:

"Jam, jam intelligis me acrius vigilare ad salutem, quam te ad perniciem
reipublicae." [a]

By happy chance there exists an authentic report on the
above-mentioned "Joint Festival" and on the deed of valour
performed during it by our "well-rounded character". Written by
Herr G. Lommel with the collaboration of Vogt, it is entitled *Das
Centralfest der Deutschen Arbeiterbildungsvereine in der Westschweiz
(Lausanne 1859)*, Geneva, 1859, Markus Vaney, rue de la Croix
d'or. Let us compare the authentic report with the "Magnum
Opus", which appeared five months later. The report contains
Cicero-Vogt's speech *"delivered by himself"* and in it he begins by
explaining the mystery of his presence at this gathering. He
appears among the workers, he harangues them, because

"grave accusations have latterly been made against him, accusations which, if
they were true, were bound utterly to destroy the confidence placed in him and
completely undermine all his political activities". "I have come," he goes on, "I have
specifically come here to protest publicly against the" (above-mentioned) "malicious
underhand dealings" *(Report,* pp. 6-7).

He has been accused of Bonapartist intrigues, he has to rescue
his political activities and as is his wont he defends his skin with
his tongue. After indulging in empty talk for an hour and a half,
he recollects Demosthenes' admonition that "action, action and
once again action is the soul of eloquence". [b]

But what is action? In America there is a small animal called a
skunk which has only *one* method of defending itself at moments
of extreme danger: its offensive smell. When attacked it releases a
substance from certain parts of its body which, if it touches your
clothes, will ensure that they have to be burnt and, if it touches

---

[a] "You will already be aware that I attend with greater zeal to the salvation of
the state than you to its destruction" (Cicero, *Speeches against Catiline,* I, 4).— *Ed.*

[b] Demosthenes, *The Olynthiac,* Second Speech, Chapter Four.— *Ed.*

your skin, will banish you for a period from all human society. The smell is so horribly offensive that when hunters see that their dogs have accidentally started a skunk they will hurriedly take to their heels in greater panic than if they had found that a wolf or a tiger was pursuing them. For powder and lead is an adequate defence against wolves and tigers, but no antidote has been found to the *a posteriori* of a skunk.

That is what action is, says our orator, a naturalised citizen of the "Kingdom of Animals",[a] and bespatters his supposed persecutors with the following skunk-like effluent:

"But I would like to warn you of one thing above all else, and that is of the machinations of a small group of depraved men whose aims and efforts are all directed towards seducing the worker away from his job, implicating him in conspiracies and communist intrigues, and finally, after living from the sweat of his brow, driving him cold-bloodedly" (i. e. after he has finished sweating) "to his destruction. Now *once again* this small group is using every possible method" (just keep it as general as possible!) "to ensnare the workers' associations in its toils. Whatever they may say" (about Vogt's Bonapartist intrigues) "you may rest assured that their true aim is to exploit the worker for their own selfish ends and finally to abandon him to his fate" (*Report,* p. 18. See Appendix).

The shameless impertinence with which this "skunk" accuses me and my friends of *"living from the sweat of the workers' brow",* when we have always sacrificed our private interests in order to defend those of the working class, and have done this *gratis,* is not even original. The *mouchards* of the December Gang hurled similar slanders at Louis Blanc, Blanqui, Raspail, etc. And not only that, for at all times and in all places the sycophants of the ruling class have always resorted to these despicable slanders to denigrate the literary and political champions of the oppressed classes. (See Appendix 5.)

After this action our "well-rounded character" is incidentally no longer able to keep a straight face. The buffoon goes on to compare his "persecutors" who are walking about freely, with the "Russians *taken prisoner* at Zorndorf".[b][68] And he compares himself with—who would have guessed it!—*Frederick the Great.* Falstaff-Vogt remembers that Frederick the Great ran away from the first battle at which he was present. How much greater then is *he* who ran away without even waiting for the battle.*

* Kobes I[69] relates in *Jacob Venedey's* pamphlet *Pro domo und pro patria gegen Karl Vogt,* Hanover, 1860: "He was a witness to the fact that the Imperial Regent,

---

[a] An allusion to the title of Karl Vogt's book, *Untersuchungen über Thierstaaten,* in which the author treats his subject as a vulgar materialist.— *Ed.*

[b] Georg Lommel, op. cit., S. 19.— *Ed.*

Thus far the adventures of the Joint Festival at Lausanne according to the authentic report. And "now just look" (as Fischart puts it) "at our clammy-handed, parasitically stout, slovenly cook and pot holder"[a] and see what a fine police *purée à la* Eulenspiegel he serves up five months later for the benefit of the German philistines.

"*They* wanted at *all costs to create complications in Switzerland*; some sort of blow was to be aimed ... at the policy of neutrality. *I was informed* that the Joint Festival of the Workers' Educational Associations was to be used to induce the workers to follow a route which they had firmly rejected. It was hoped that the lovely Festival would provide an opportunity for forming a *secret committee* to enter into communication with like-minded people in Germany and take God knows what *steps*" (Vogt does not know, *even though he was informed*). "There were all sorts of dark rumours and mysterious talk about the active intervention of the workers in German political affairs. *I at once resolved to oppose these intrigues* and to exhort the workers anew to turn a deaf ear to *all proposals of this sort.* At the conclusion of the speech referred to above I gave a solemn warning, etc." ("Magnum Opus", pp. 180 [-81]).

Cicero-Vogt has already forgotten that at the start of his speech he let slip what had brought him to the Joint Festival—not the neutrality of Switzerland but the need to save his own skin. His speech does not contain a single word about the intended plot against Switzerland, the conspiratorial intentions at the Joint Festival, the secret committee, the active intervention of the workers in German politics or proposals of "*this*" or any other "sort". Not a word about all these Stieberiads. His final warning was nothing but the warning of the honest Sikes in the Old Bailey who warned the jurymen not to listen to the "infamous" detectives who had caught him stealing.

"The events which immediately followed," Falstaff-Vogt declares ("Magnum Opus", p. 181), "confirmed my *forebodings.*"

Karl Vogt, was not present when we and the four other Imperial Regents forced the Government of Württemberg to bring the Parliament to an honourable end with sword and bayonet. It is an amusing story. The other four Imperial Regents had already entered the carriage to go to the Assembly Room, as agreed, and there together with the Rump Parliament [...] to put on a bold front" (it is well known that the Rump Parliament had no head). [Venedey says here: *die Brust bieten* (literally, to present the breast). The phrase is an adaptation of the German idiomatic expression *die Stirn bieten* (to present the forehead) which means "to put on a bold front". Marx puns on Venedey's substitution of *Brust* (breast) for *Stirn* (forehead) to stress that the Rump Parliament had no head.] "Karl Vogt slammed the carriage-door shut and called to the coachman: 'You go on ahead, the carriage is full up, I shall follow on!' But Karl Vogt only appeared [...] after all possible danger was over" (loc. cit., pp. 23, 24).

---

[a] Johann Fischart, *Affentheurliche, Naupengeheurliche Geschichtklitterung...*, S. 73.— *Ed.*

What does he mean, *forebodings*! But Falstaff has already forgotten that a few lines before he did not have "forebodings", but that he had been "informed", *informed* of the plans of the conspirators, and *informed in detail*! And what, you vengeful angel,[a] were the *events* which immediately followed?

"An article in the *Allgemeine Zeitung* imputed tendencies to the Festival and to the life of the workers which these" (i. e. the Festival and the life) "did not in the least have in mind." (Just as Vogt had imputed tendencies to the Murten Congress and the workers' organisations in general.) "This article and a *reprint* of it in the *Frankfurter Journal* led to a confidential inquiry from the Ambassador of a South German state in which the Festival was given the importance"—"*imputed*" to it by the article in the *Allgemeine Zeitung* and the reprint in the *Frankfurter Journal*?—by no means!—"which it **ought to have had** if the *intentions of the Brimstone Gang had not been frustrated.*" [b]

Ought to have had! Yes indeed!

Although the most superficial comparison of the "Magnum Opus" and the authentic report on the Joint Festival is enough to clear up the mystery of Cicero-Vogt's second rescue of Switzerland, I nevertheless wished to ascertain whether there was any factual basis, however slender, that might have given him the "matter" which provided him with his "energy".[70] I wrote, therefore, to the editor of the authentic report, Herr *G. Lommel* in Geneva.[c] Herr Lommel must have been on friendly terms with Vogt since he not only collaborated with him on the report on the Joint Festival in Lausanne but also, in a subsequent pamphlet about the Schiller and Robert Blum memorial celebrations in Geneva,[d] he covered up the fiasco that Vogt had brought upon himself there. In his reply of April 13, 1860, Herr Lommel, who is personally unknown to me, wrote:

"*Vogt's* story that he had frustrated a dangerous conspiracy in Lausanne is *the sheerest fairy-tale* or **lie**; he only went to Lausanne because it was an opportunity to make a speech which he could afterwards print. In the speech, which lasted $1\frac{1}{2}$ hours, he defended himself against allegations that he was in the pay of Bonaparte. I still have the manuscript in safe keeping."

---

[a] An allusion to Goethe's *Faust*, Erster Teil, Marthens Garten. But instead of Goethe's *du ahnungsvoller* (foreboding) *Engel* Marx has *du ahndungsvoller* (vengeful) *Engel.—Ed.*

[b] Carl Vogt, *Mein Prozess...*, S. 181, 182. In the last sentence the italics are Vogt's. He is referring to the article in the *Allgemeine Zeitung*, No. 215 (supplement), August 3, 1859.— *Ed.*

[c] Marx to Lommel, April 9, 1860 (present edition, Vol. 41).— *Ed.*

[d] Georg Lommel, *Das Centralfest der Deutschen Arbeiterbildungsvereine in der Westschweiz*, Genf, 1859.— *Ed.*

A Frenchman living in Geneva, when asked about the same Vogtian conspiracy, replied bluntly:

"Il faut connaître cet individu" (namely Vogt), "surtout **le faiseur**, *l'homme important*, toujours hors de la nature et de la vérité." [a]

Vogt himself declares on p. 99 of his so-called *Studien*[b] that he "had never laid claim to *prophetic* gifts". But we know from the Old Testament that the ass could see what the prophet had missed.[c] And so we can understand how Vogt managed to *see* the conspiracy which in November 1859 he had forebodings of having "frustrated" in June 1859.

6. MISCELLANY

"If my memory does not deceive me," our Parliamentary Clown writes, "the circular" (i. e. an alleged address to the proletarians dated London 1850) "was indeed written by a follower of Marx's known as Parliamentary Wolf, and it was allowed to fall into the hands of the Hanover police. Here too we find *this same channel turning up* in the history of the circular 'of the patriots to the men of Gotha'" ("Magnum Opus", p. 144).

A channel turns up! A prolapsus ani,[d] perhaps, you zoological jester?

As to "Parliamentary Wolf"—and we shall see later on why, like a bad dream, Parliamentary Wolf weighs so heavily on the memory of our Parliamentary Clown—he published the following statement in the Berlin *Volks-Zeitung*, the *Allgemeine Zeitung* and the Hamburg *Reform*:

"*Statement*. Manchester, February 6, 1860: I see from the letter of a friend that the *National-Zeitung* (No. 41 of this year) has brought the following passage to the attention of the public in a leading article based on Vogt's pamphlet:

"'In 1850 another *circular* was dispatched from London to *the proletarians* in Germany, written, as Vogt believes he remembers, by Parliamentary Wolf, alias Casemate Wolf. The circular was allowed simultaneously to fall into the hands of the Hanover police.' I have seen neither the relevant issue of the *National-Zeitung* nor the Vogt pamphlet and would like therefore to direct my answer solely to the passage just cited:

"1. In 1850 I was living not in London but *in Zurich*, and I did not move to London until the summer of 1851.

"2. I have never in the whole of my life written a circular addressed either to 'proletarians' or to anyone else.

---

[a] "One must know this fellow who is above all a **charlatan,** a *self-important*, unnatural, untruthful man."—*Ed.*

[b] Carl Vogt, *Studien zur gegenwärtigen Lage Europas*, Genf und Bern, 1859, S. 99. Marx's italics.—*Ed.*

[c] Numbers 22:21-33.—*Ed.*

[d] Prolapse of the rectum.—*Ed.*

"3. As to the insinuation about the Hanover police *I hereby return this shamelessly invented accusation to its author with contempt.* If the remainder of Vogt's pamphlet is as full of impudent lies as the part that refers to me it is a worthy fellow to the *fabrications of Chenu, de la Hodde* & Co.

W. Wolff" [a]

There you are: just as *Cuvier* could construct the whole skeleton of an animal from a single bone, *Wolff* has correctly constructed Vogt's whole fabrication from a single fragmentary quotation. *Karl Vogt* can indeed stand beside *Chenu* and *de la Hodde* as *primus inter pares.*

The last "proof" adduced by Vogt, who is still "by no means at a loss", to demonstrate my *entente cordiale* with the secret police in general and "my relations with the *Kreuz-Zeitung* party in particular", consists in the argument that my wife is the sister of the retired Prussian Minister Herr von Westphalen ("Magnum Opus", p. 194). Now how to parry the cowardly stratagem of our fat Falstaff? Perhaps the Clown will forgive my wife the cognate Prussian Minister [b] when he learns of the agnate Scotsman [c] who was beheaded in the market-place in Edinburgh as a rebel in the war of liberation against James II. It is well known that it is only by accident that Vogt still carries his own head around. For at the Robert Blum celebrations of the German Workers' Educational Association in Geneva (November 13, 1859) he reported

"how the Left of the Frankfurt Parliament was for a long time undecided who to send to Vienna, Blum or him. Finally, the matter was decided by lot, by drawing a piece of straw, which fell upon Blum, or rather against him" (*Die Schillerfeier zu Genf usw.*, Geneva, 1859, pp. 28, 29).

On October 13 Robert Blum set out from Frankfurt for Vienna. On October 23 or 24 a deputation of the extreme Left in Frankfurt arrived in Cologne on the way to the Democratic Congress in Berlin.[71] I met these gentlemen, among whom were several Members of Parliament who had close bonds with the *Neue Rheinische Zeitung.* These parliamentarians, of whom one was summarily shot during the campaign for the Imperial Constitution, a second died in exile, while the third still lives, whispered all sorts of strange and sinister stories in my ear about Vogt's intrigues in connection with Robert' Blum's mission to Vienna.

---

[a] Wilhelm Wolff, "Erklärung", *Allgemeine Zeitung,* No. 44 (supplement), February 13, 1860. Also published in the Hamburg *Reform* on February 11, 1860 and in the Berlin *Volks-Zeitung* on February 24, 1860.— *Ed.*

[b] Ferdinand von Westphalen.— *Ed.*

[c] Archibald Campbell Argyll.— *Ed.*

However,

> Bid me not speak, bid me be silent,
> To keep the secret I am bound.[a]

The Robert Blum celebrations of November 1859 in Geneva to which we have already referred treated our "well-rounded character" most unkindly. On entering the premises, waddling like an obsequious Silenus at the heels of his patron, James Fazy, a worker was heard to say: There's Harry with Falstaff after him. When he told a delightful anecdote designed to present himself as the *alter ego* of Robert Blum, it was only with difficulty that some infuriated workers were prevented from storming the podium. And when, finally, forgetting how he had frustrated the revolution in June, he himself "called yet again for the barricades"[b] (*Schillerfeier*, p. 29) a mocking echo repeated: "Barricades—shmarricades!" Abroad, however, people know so well just what value they are to place on Vogt's revolutionary mouthings that the "confidential inquiry from a South German Ambassador",[c] usually unavoidable, was unforthcoming on this occasion and *no* article appeared in the *Allgemeine Zeitung*.

Vogt's entire Stieberiad from the "Brimstone Gang" to the "retired Minister" reveals the sort of Mastersinger of whom Dante says:

> Ed egli avea fatto del cul trombetta.*

---

* And he made a trumpet of his rear. (*Kannegiesser*) [Dante, *The Divine Comedy*, Inferno, Canto XXI. Kannegiesser is the name of the German translator.]

---

[a] Mignon's song in Goethe's novel *Wilhelm Meisters Lehrjahre*, Fünftes Buch, Kapitel 16.— *Ed.*

[b] The closing line of the poem about Robert Blum which Vogt quoted concluding his speech at the Blum celebrations (see Georg Lommel, *Die Schiller-Feier in Genf. Nebst einem Nachtrag enthaltend die diesjährige Todtenfeier für Robert Blum*, Genf, 1859, S. 29).— *Ed.*

[c] Carl Vogt, *Mein Prozess...*, S. 181-82.— *Ed.*

IV

TECHOW'S LETTER

What else does our *"well-rounded character"* pull out of that

"tristo sacco
Che merda fa di quel, che si trangugia."

(*Dante*)*

A letter from Techow dated London, August 26, 1850:

"I cannot characterise these activities better" (i. e. of the "Brimstone Gang") "than by imparting to you the contents of a letter from a man whom all who have ever known him will acknowledge as a man of honour, a letter which I may permit myself to publish because *it*"[a] (the man of honour or the letter?) "was expressly intended *for communication*" (to whom?) "and the considerations" (whose?) "which earlier militated against *publication* no longer obtain" ("Magnum Opus", p. 141).

Techow arrived in London from Switzerland at the end of August 1850. His letter is addressed to *Schimmelpfennig*, formerly a lieutenant in the Prussian army, who lived in Berne at the time. Schimmelpfennig was supposed to "communicate the letter to our friends", i. e. the members of the *Centralisation*,[72] a secret society now extinct for nearly a decade, set up by German refugees in Switzerland with a rather mixed membership and a strong leavening of parliamentarians. Techow was a member of the society, but Vogt and his friends were not. How then did Vogt come into possession of Techow's letter and who authorised him to publish it?

* "The sordid sack
  That turns to dung the food it swallows." [*The Divine Comedy*, Inferno, Canto XXVIII.]

---

[a] The German *er* used here can refer either to the man of honour or the letter.— *Ed.*

Techow himself wrote to me on the subject from Australia on April 17, 1860:

"At any rate, *I* have *never* had occasion to give Herr *Karl Vogt any authorisation* in connection with this matter."

Of the "friends" of Techow to whom the letter was to be communicated only two are still living in Switzerland. Both may speak for themselves:

E.[a] *to Schily, April 29, 1860, Upper Engadine, Grisons Canton*:
"When Vogt's pamphlet *Mein Prozess gegen die Allgemeine Zeitung* appeared, containing a letter from Techow to his friends in Switzerland dated August 26, 1850,[b] we, the friends of Techow still living in Switzerland, resolved to write to Vogt to express our disapproval of his *unauthorised* publication of the letter. Techow's letter had been addressed to Schimmelpfennig in Berne and the intention was to distribute copies of it among friends.... I am glad that we were not mistaken in our belief that none of Techow's friends, none of those who had a right to see the letter of August 26, had used it after the manner of the man who has by accident come into possession of it. On January 22 a letter was dispatched to Vogt protesting against the *unauthorised* publication of Techow's letter, forbidding *any further misuse* of it and demanding the return of the letter. On January 27 Vogt replied: 'Techow's letter was intended to be shown to his friends; the friend who had it in his possession had handed it over with the express wish that it should be published ... and he would only return the letter to the man from whom *he* had received it.'"

B.[c] *to Schily, Zurich, May 1, 1860*[73]:
"The letter to Vogt was written by me after I had discussed the matter with E.... R.[d] was not among the 'friends' for whom Techow's letter was intended. From the contents of the letter, however, it was *perfectly clear to Vogt* that it had been addressed to me among others, but he took good care not to ask me for permission to publish it."

The solution to the riddle is contained in a passage from *Schily's* letter quoted earlier[e] and which I have saved up for this moment. He writes:

"I must say something here about **Ranickel** because it is *through him that Techow's letter must have fallen into Vogt's hands*, a point in your letter which I had almost overlooked. This letter was written by Techow to friends he had lived with in Zurich: Schimmelpfennig, B. and E. As their friend and Techow's, I was also able to read it later on. When I was brutally and summarily expelled from Switzerland (without any previous order of expulsion having been made I was simply arrested in the street in Geneva and immediately transported from there), I was not permitted to go back to my lodgings to arrange my affairs. From the prison in Berne I wrote to a reliable man in Geneva, a master shoemaker called

---

a Karl Emmermann.— *Ed.*
b See Carl Vogt, *Mein Prozess...*, S. 142-61.— *Ed.*
c Friedrich von Beust.— *Ed.*
d Ranickel.— *Ed.*
e See this volume, pp. 43-46.— *Ed.*

Thum, asking him to find one or other of my friends who might be still in Geneva (for I did not know whether the same fate had not befallen any of them), who could pack up my belongings and send the most valuable of them to me in Berne, putting the remainder *into safe keeping* for the time being. I wanted that person to sort out my papers taking particular care to ensure that nothing should be forwarded to me which could not survive the transit through France. Thum did as I asked him and Techow's letter remained behind. My belongings included a number of papers relating to a rebellion of the parliamentarians against the Geneva local committee for the distribution of money for the refugees (the committee consisted of three Geneva citizens, among them Thum, and two refugees, Becker and myself). *Ranickel* was familiar with these as he had taken the side of the committee against the parliamentarians. For this reason I had asked Thum as the treasurer and archivist of the committee to take out those papers with *Ranickel's* help. It may now be the case that, having a legitimate reason for being present while my papers were being sorted, Ranickel somehow got his hands on Techow's letter. Perhaps it was given him by one of the sorters. I do not by any means dispute the *transfer of the letter into his possession,* as distinct from the transfer of *property rights* from me to him. On the contrary, I claim the latter quite explicitly. *I soon wrote to Ranickel from London asking him to send me the letter. However, he did not do so* and his *culpa manifesta*[a] dates from that time. At the beginning it was probably only *levis*[b] but it then mounted, depending on the extent of his complicity in the unauthorised publication of the letter, to *magna* or *maxima culpa*[c] or even to *dolus.*[d] I do not doubt for a single moment that his publication of the letter was *unauthorised* and that none of the addressees had given their permission, but I shall nevertheless write to E. for confirmation of this. Nor can it be doubted that *Ranickel* assisted in the publication, given his notorious intimacy with Vogt. And even though I do not wish in the least to criticise that intimacy, I cannot refrain from pointing out the contrast with their earlier relationship. For **Ranickel** had not only been one of the greatest enemies of the parliamentarians in general; he had also uttered the most blood-curdling threats in regard to the Imperial Regent in particular. 'I'll strangle the fellow,' he would shout, 'even if I have to go to Berne to do it', and we had to forcibly restrain him from carrying out his regicidal intention. But now that the scales seem to have fallen from his eyes, and Saul has turned into Paul,[e] I am very curious to see how he will worm his way out of another obligation: that of becoming the *avenger of Europe.* I have fought a hard struggle, he would say in the days when he was hesitating between Europe and America, but now it is at an end. I shall remain and—*avenge myself!!* Let Byzantium tremble."[f]

Thus far *Schily's* letter.

Ranickel, then, unearthed[g] Techow's letter among the papers left behind by Schily. Notwithstanding Schily's request for it from

---

[a] Manifest guilt.—*Ed.*

[b] Slight.—*Ed.*

[c] Great or maximum guilt.—*Ed.*

[d] Evil intent.—*Ed.*

[e] The Acts of the Apostles 9 : 15-17.—*Ed.*

[f] "Trema, Bisanzio!"—quoted from Gaetano Donizetti's opera *Belisario,* Act II, Scene 3 (libretto by Salvatore Cammarano).—*Ed.*

[g] Marx uses the verb *aufstiebern*—an adaptation of the verb *aufstöbern* (ferret out, unearth)—formed by analogy with *Stieber,* the name of a German police agent.—*Ed.*

London, he retained it. The letter *misappropriated* in this way was handed by "friend" *Ranickel* to "friend" Vogt, and "friend" Vogt, with his characteristic delicacy of conscience, declared himself authorised to publish the letter since Vogt and *Ranickel* are "friends". Anyone, therefore, who writes a letter to be "communicated" to "friends", necessarily writes for the benefit of "friends" *Vogt* and *Ranickel—arcades ambo.*[a]

I must apologise if this peculiar sort of jurisprudence leads me back to long-past and half-forgotten events. But Ranickel has started it and I must follow.

The *"Communist League"* was founded in Paris in 1836, originally under another name.[b] The organisation that gradually evolved was as follows: a certain number of members formed a "community", the different communities in the same town constituted a "district" [*Kreis*] and a varying number of districts were joined together into "leading districts" [*leitende Kreise*]. At the head of the whole stood the "Central Authority" which was elected at a congress consisting of deputies from all the districts, but which had the right to add to its own numbers and, in emergencies, to nominate its successor on a provisional basis. The Central Authority was based first in Paris, and then, from 1840 to the beginning of 1848, in London. The chairmen of the communities and districts and the Central Authority itself were elected. This democratic constitution, utterly unsuitable for conspiratorial secret societies, was not incompatible, to say the least, with the tasks facing a propaganda association. The activities of the "League" consisted first of all in founding public German workers' educational associations, and the majority of the associations of this sort, which still exist in Switzerland, England, Belgium and the United States, were founded either directly by the "League" or else by people who had at one time belonged to it. The constitution of these workers' associations is accordingly the same everywhere. One day per week was devoted to discussion, another to social activities (singing, recitations, etc.). Libraries were set up everywhere, and where possible classes in elementary education were started for the instruction of the workers. The "League" standing behind the public educational associations, and guiding them, found them both the most convenient forum for

---

[a] Literally "Arcadians both", i.e. each deserves the other—an expression used by Virgil in *Bucolics* (Eclogues), 7, 4, and later by Byron, who wrote: "'Arcades ambo' id est—blackguards both" (*Don Juan*, IV, 93).—*Ed.*

[b] The League of the Just.—*Ed.*

public propaganda and also a reservoir whose most useful members could replenish and swell its own ranks. In view of the itinerant life of German artisans it was only on rare occasions that the Central Authority had to send special emissaries.

As far as the secret doctrine of the "League" is concerned, it underwent all the transformations of French and English socialism and communism, as well as their German versions (e. g. ·Weitling's fantasies). After 1839, as is made clear in the Bluntschli report,[a] the religious question came to play the most important role alongside the social problem. The various phases undergone by German philosophy from 1839 to 1846 were followed with the most lively interest in these workers' societies. The secret form of the society goes back to its Paris origins. The chief purpose of the League—propaganda among workers in Germany—dictated the retention of this form in later years. During my first stay in Paris[b] I established personal contact with the leaders of the "League" living there as well as with the leaders of the majority of the secret French workers' associations, without however becoming a member of any of them. In Brussels, where Guizot's expulsion order had sent me, I, together with Engels, W. Wolff and others, founded the German Workers' Educational Society,[74] which is still in existence. At the same time we published a series of pamphlets,[c] partly printed, partly lithographed, in which we mercilessly criticised the hotchpotch of Franco-English socialism or communism and German philosophy, which formed the secret doctrine of the "League" at that time. In its place we proposed the scientific study of the economic structure of bourgeois society as the only tenable theoretical foundation. Furthermore, we argued in popular form that it was not a matter of putting some utopian system into effect, but of conscious participation in the historical process revolutionising society before our very eyes. In consequence of these activities the London Central Authority entered into correspondence with us and at the end of 1846 they sent one of their members, a watchmaker called *Joseph Moll*, who later fell as a soldier of the revolution on the field of battle in Baden,[d] to Brussels to invite us to join the "League". Moll allayed

---

[a] Johann Caspar Bluntschli, *Die Kommunisten in der Schweiz nach den bei Weitling vorgefundenen Papieren...*, Zürich, 1843.—*Ed.*

[b] From late October 1843 to February 3, 1845.—*Ed.*

[c] The only one extant is *Circular Against Kriege* (see present edition, Vol. 6).—*Ed.*

[d] See Frederick Engels, *The Campaign for the German Imperial Constitution* (present edition, Vol. 10, pp. 225-26).—*Ed.*

our doubts and objections by revealing that the Central Authority intended to convoke a Congress of the League in London where the critical views we had expressed would be laid down in an open manifesto as the doctrine of the League. He argued, however, that if backward and refractory elements were to be overcome, our participation in person was indispensable, but that this could only be arranged if we became members of the "League". Accordingly, we joined it. The Congress, at which members from Switzerland, France, Belgium, Germany and England were represented, took place,[a] and after heated debate over several weeks it adopted the *Manifesto of the Communist Party*[b] written by Engels and myself, which appeared in print at the beginning of 1848 and was later translated into English, French, Danish and Italian. On the outbreak of the February revolution the London Central Authority entrusted me with the leadership of the "League". During the revolutionary period in Germany, its activities died down of themselves, since more effective avenues existed now for the realisation of its ends. When, in the late summer of 1849, I arrived in London after being expelled from France for a second time, I found that the Central Authority had been reconstructed from the ruins and that the links with the reconstituted districts of the League in Germany had been re-established. *Willich* arrived in London a few months later and was admitted to the Central Authority at my suggestion. He had been recommended to me by *Engels,* who acted as his adjutant in the campaign for the Imperial Constitution. To round off the history of the League I would only remark that there was a split in the Central Authority on September 15, 1850.[c] Its majority, including Engels and myself, transferred the seat of the Central Authority to *Cologne,* which had long been the "leading district" for Central and Southern Germany and which, after London, was the most important centre of intellectual activity.

We resigned from the London *Workers' Educational Society* at the same time. The minority on the Central Authority, however, including Willich and Schapper, set up a separate League[75] which maintained relations with the Workers' Educational Society and also resumed contact with Switzerland and France, which had been interrupted since 1848. On November 12, 1852 the accused in the Cologne communist trial were condemned. A few days later, at my

---

    [a] The Second Congress of the Communist League was held in London between November 29 and December 8, 1847.— *Ed.*

    [b] See present edition, Vol. 6.— *Ed.*

    [c] See present edition, Vol. 10, pp. 625-30.— *Ed.*

suggestion, the League was declared dissolved.[a] I included a document, relating to the dissolution, dated November 1852, in the dossier on my action against the *National-Zeitung*. The reason given there for the dissolution of the League is that with the arrests in Germany, i.e. from as early as the spring of 1851, *all* contact with the Continent had in any case ceased to exist and that moreover circumstances were no longer favourable for a propaganda society of this sort. A few months later, at the beginning of 1853, the Willich-Schapper separate League also died a natural death.

The issues of principle which underlay the split mentioned above are set out in my *Revelations Concerning the Communist Trial*,[b] which contains an extract from the minutes of the meeting of the Central Authority of September 15, 1850. The immediate practical cause of the split was *Willich*'s efforts to involve the "League" in the revolutionary escapades of the German democratic emigration. The disagreement was exacerbated by wholly opposed interpretations of the political situation. I shall cite only *one* example. Willich had conceived the idea that the quarrel between Prussia and Austria on the question of the Electorate of Hesse and the German Confederation [76] would lead to serious conflicts and create an opportunity for the practical intervention of the revolutionary party. On November 10, 1850, shortly after the split in the "League", he published a proclamation along these lines entitled *Aux démocrates de toutes les nations*[c] over the signatures of the Central Authority of the "separate League" as well as those of French, Hungarian and Polish refugees. Engels and I, on the other hand, as can be seen in the *Neue Rheinische Zeitung. Revue* (double issue, May to October 1850, Hamburg, pp. 174, 175), maintained on the contrary that "*None of this noise will lead to anything.... Without a drop of blood having been shed, the parties to the dispute*", i. e. Austria and Prussia, "will come together on the benches of the Federal Diet" [77] in Frankfurt "without there being the slightest diminution in their petty mutual jealousies, or in their dissensions with their subjects, or in their irritation at *Russian* supremacy".[d]

---

[a] See Marx's letter to Engels dated November 19, 1852 (present edition, Vol. 39). A copy of the letter is to be found in Marx's notebook for 1860.— *Ed.*

[b] See present edition, Vol. 11.— *Ed.*

[c] *Le Constitutionnel*, November 18, 1850. The text of this proclamation is quoted by Marx in his letter to Engels dated December 2, 1850 (see present edition, Vol. 38).— *Ed.*

[d] See "Review, May to October [1850]" (present edition, Vol. 10, p. 528). The italics were introduced by Marx in *Herr Vogt.—Ed.*

Now it may be judged from the following document whether *Willich's* individuality (whose worth incidentally we do not intend to dispute) and the then (1850) still fresh memories of his experiences in Besançon enabled him "impartially" to consider conflicts which contradictory views had rendered inevitable and had constantly renewed:

    "*The German Brigade in Nancy*
          to
    Citizen Joh. Philipp Becker in Biel,
    President of the German military
    association 'Self-Help' [78]

"*Citizen,*

"We are writing to inform you, as the elected representative of all German republican refugees, that in Nancy a brigade of German refugees has been formed which bears the name: 'German Brigade in Nancy.'

"The refugees who make up the present Brigade are composed partly of former members of the Vesle Brigade and partly of units of the Besançon Brigade. Factors of a purely democratic nature are responsible for the removal of the latter from Besançon.

"The fact is that in everything that he did, Willich very rarely consulted the Brigade. Hence the principles governing the Besançon Brigade were not generally discussed and decided by all members, but were decreed *a priori* by Willich and put into effect without the approval of the Brigade.

"Furthermore, Willich also provided evidence of his despotic nature *a posteriori* in the form of a number of orders worthy of a Jellachich or a Windischgrätz, but not a republican.

"Willich ordered a man called Schön, who wished to resign from the Brigade, to take off his new shoes which had been purchased from the savings of the Brigade, disregarding the fact that Schön too had contributed his share to these savings, which consisted chiefly of the daily 10 sous per capita which the French paid by way of subsidy.... Schön wanted to take his shoes with him, but Willich forced him to leave them behind.

"Several valuable members of the Brigade were for trivial offences such as absence from roll-call, drill, lateness (in the evening), petty quarrels, etc., ordered by Willich, who *did not consult* the Brigade, to leave Besançon. They could go to Africa, he remarked, for they had no right to remain in France, and if they did not go to Africa he would see to it that they were extradited to Germany. He claimed that the French Government had given him authority to do this, but upon subsequent inquiry the Prefecture in Besançon declared this to be untrue. Almost every day at roll-call, Willich announced: Whoever does not like it here can go, if he wishes, the sooner the better; he can go to Africa, etc. On one occasion he also uttered the general threat that anyone who refused to obey his orders could either go to Africa or he, Willich, would have him extradited to Germany. This led to our making the above-mentioned inquiry at the Prefecture. As a result of these daily threats many people were fed up with life in Besançon where, as they said, one was constantly provoked into chucking up the whole paltry business. If we wish to be slaves, they said, we can go to Russia and we need not have started the fight in Germany in the first place. In short, they declared that they could no longer endure it in Besançon at any price without coming into serious conflict with Willich. They therefore left Besançon, but as at that time there was no other brigade which they could join, and as they could not live on the 10 sous on their own, they had no other choice but to sign on for Africa, and this they did. In this way Willich reduced thirty worthy citizens to despair and he is to blame for their loss to the national cause.

"Furthermore, Willich was unwise enough always to praise his old colleagues at roll-call while denigrating the new ones, and this led to constant friction. On one occasion Willich even declared at roll-call that the Prussians were far superior to the South Germans in head, heart and body, or as he put it, in physical, moral and intellectual abilities. The South Germans, in contrast, were easy-going, or rather, stupid was what he wanted to say, but he did not quite dare. In this way Willich managed to infuriate the South Germans, who were in a great majority. We have left the worst to the end:

"Two weeks ago the 7th Company allowed a man called Baroggio whom Willich had arbitrarily expelled from the barracks to spend an extra night in their room. Despite Willich's refusal to permit this they kept him in their room and defended it against Willich's supporters, fanatical tailors. Willich then ordered ropes to be brought and the rebels to be bound. The ropes really were brought, but although Willich had the will to have his order carried through, he did not have the power.... It is for these reasons that they have left the Brigade.

"We have not written this letter in order to accuse Willich. For Willich's character and intentions are good, and many of us respect him. But we did not like the manner in which he attempts to achieve his ends nor all the means he uses. Willich means well. But he believes to be wisdom itself and the *ultima ratio* and thinks that everyone who opposes him, even on petty issues, is either a fool or a traitor. In short, Willich acknowledges no opinion other than his own. He is a spiritual aristocrat and despot; when he has resolved on a thing, he does not easily shrink from using the means necessary to put it into practice. But enough: we know Willich now. We know his strengths and his weaknesses; this is why we are no longer in Besançon. Incidentally, when we left Besançon we all declared that we were leaving Willich, but that we did not wish to resign from the German military association 'Self-Help'.

"This applies to the members of the Vesle Brigade also....

"Assuring you of our enduring respect, we conclude with fraternal greetings from the Brigade in Nancy.

"Approved in general assembly, November 13, 1848.

"Nancy, November 14, 1848

"In the name and on the instructions of the Brigade,
                                                    B..., Secretary"

Let us now return to *Techow*'s letter. As with other reptiles, its poison is in the tail, namely in the postscript of September 3 (1850). It refers to a duel between Herr *Willich* and my friend, *Konrad Schramm,* who died a premature death. In the duel, which took place in Antwerp in the beginning of September 1850, *Techow* and *Barthélemy,* a Frenchman, acted as Willich's seconds. *Techow* wrote to Schimmelpfennig "for communication to our friends":

"They" (i.e. Marx and his followers) "have let their champion *Schramm* loose against Willich who had attacked him" (Techow means: whom he had attacked) "with invective of the most vulgar sort and finally challenged him to a duel." ("Magnum Opus", pp. 156, 157.)

My refutation of this stupid piece of gossip was published seven years ago in the pamphlet, cited earlier, *The Knight of the Noble Consciousness*, New York, 1853.

At the time Schramm was still alive. Like Willich he was living in the United States.

Willich's second, Barthélemy, had not yet been hanged; Schramm's second, the worthy Polish officer Miskowsky, had not yet been burnt to death,[79] and Herr Techow could not yet have forgotten the letter he had written for "communication to our friends".

In the above-mentioned pamphlet there is a letter from my friend *Frederick Engels*, dated *Manchester, November 23, 1853*, at the end of which he writes:

"*In the meeting of the Central Authority, when it came to a challenge to a duel between Schramm and Willich*,[80] I*" (Engels) "am supposed" (according to Willich) "to have committed the crime of having 'left the room' together with Schramm shortly before the scene took place, *and, therefore, of having prepared the whole scene in advance.* Previously" (according to Willich) "it was *Marx* who was alleged to have 'egged on' Schramm, now for a change *I* am supposed to have done so. A duel between a Prussian lieutenant, an old hand at pistol shooting, and a *commerçant*, who perhaps had never had a pistol in his hand, was truly a remarkable means to 'get rid' of the lieutenant. Yet friend Willich maintained everywhere, orally and in writing, that we had wanted to get him shot.... Simply, Schramm was furious at Willich's shameless behaviour, and to the great astonishment of us all he challenged him to a duel. A few minutes before, Schramm himself had no inkling that it would come to this. Never was an action more spontaneous.... Schramm departed" (from the room) "only after being personally addressed by Marx, who wanted to avoid any further scandal.

                                        Fr. Engels" (*The Knight, etc.*, p. 7.)ᵃ

How far I was from foreseeing that *Techow* would allow himself to become a vehicle for this stupid piece of gossip can be seen from the following passage of the same pamphlet:

"Originally, *as Techow himself told Engels and me after his return to London*, Willich was firmly convinced that through Schramm I aimed at his removal from this world, and he put this idea in writing everywhere. On closer reflection, however, he found it impossible that a diabolical tactician like myself could hit on the

---

ᵃ See present edition, Vol. 12, pp. 492, 493. The italics were introduced by Marx in *Herr Vogt.—Ed.*

idea of getting rid of him by means of a duel with Schramm" (loc. cit., p. 9).[a]

The gossip that Techow imparted to Herr Schimmelpfennig for "communication to our friends" was hearsay which he simply repeated. *Karl Schapper*, who took Willich's side when later the split in the League occurred and who witnessed the challenge, has written this letter to me about it:

> "5 Percy Street, Bedford Square,
> September 27, 1860
>
> "Dear Marx,
>
> "Concerning the row between Schramm and Willich:
>
> "It broke out during a meeting of the Central Authority as the result of a fierce argument between the two which arose *by chance* in the course of the discussion. I can still remember very well that you did *everything* possible to restore calm and to settle the affair and that you appeared to be as much taken by surprise by this sudden explosion as I myself and everyone else present.
>
> "Salute,
> Your *Karl Schapper*"

Finally, it is worth mentioning that a few weeks *after* the duel, in a letter dated *December 31, 1850*, Schramm himself accused me of *being partial to Willich*. The disapproval which Engels and I had openly expressed, both before the duel and after it, had momentarily annoyed him. His letter and other papers of his and Miskowsky's concerning the duel, which have come into my hands, are available for perusal by his relatives. They should not be exposed to the gaze of the public.

When Konrad Schramm next visited me in London in mid-July 1857 after his return from the United States, his impetuous, tall, youthful frame had already collapsed under the impact of galloping consumption, which however had merely heightened the effect of his strikingly handsome features. With the sense of humour peculiar to him and which never left him for a moment, the first thing he showed me, laughing as he did so, was the notice of his death which an indiscreet friend had already published in a German paper in New York on the basis of a rumour.[b] On medical advice Schramm went to St. Hélier in Jersey, where Engels and I saw him for the last time. Schramm died on January 16, 1858. At his burial, which was attended by the entire liberal population of St. Hélier and the whole of the emigration resident

---

[a] ibid., p. 496. The italics were introduced by Marx in *Herr Vogt.—Ed.*

[b] See Marx's letter to Engels dated April 9, 1857 (present edition, Vol. 40). The paper referred to is *Neue Zeit.—Ed.*

there, the funeral oration was given by one of the best English popular orators, G. *Julian Harney*, who was known earlier as one of the Chartist leaders and who had been friendly with Schramm during his stay in London. Schramm's ardent, fiery and enterprising nature, which could never be curbed by mundane concerns, was combined with critical understanding, original intelligence, ironic humour and naive geniality. He was the Percy Hotspur of our party.

To return to Herr *Techow*'s letter. A few days after his arrival in London, he had a long meeting with us late one evening[a] in a tavern where Engels, Schramm and myself acted as hosts. He describes the meeting in his letter of August 26, 1850 to Schimmelpfennig, "for communication to our friends".[b] I had never met him before and only saw him once or twice afterwards, and then only briefly. Nevertheless, he at once made a penetrating analysis of me and my friends, closely examining our minds, hearts and entrails, and hastened to send a letter containing a psychological description behind our backs to Switzerland, carefully advising his "friends" that it should be secrètly reproduced and distributed.

Techow is much concerned with the state of my "heart". I will generously refrain from following him into this territory. *"Ne parlons pas morale"*,[c] as the Parisian grisette says when her friend starts to talk politics.

Let us dwell a while on the recipient of the letter of August 26, the former Prussian lieutenant *Schimmelpfennig*. I do not know the gentleman personally and have never seen him. I shall quote from two letters to convey his character. The first, which I give only in extract, was addressed to me by my friend *W. Steffen*, a former Prussian lieutenant and teacher in the Divisional School. It is dated *Chester, November 23, 1853*[81] and he writes:

"Willich once sent an adjutant called *Schimmelpfennig* over" (to Cologne). "He paid me the compliment of summoning me to him and he was firmly convinced that he could assess the whole situation right from the start better than anyone who was involved in it from day to day. He therefore formed a very low opinion of me when I told him that the officers of the Prussian army would be far from considering themselves fortunate to be able to fight under his banner and Willich's and that they were certainly not inclined to proclaim Willich's republic at once. He became even angrier when no one showed himself foolish enough to offer to duplicate the proclamation which he had brought with him in readiness and which exhorted the officers to declare themselves in favour of what he called democracy.

---

[a] On August 21, 1850.— *Ed.*
[b] See Carl Vogt, *Mein Prozess...*, S. 142-61.— *Ed.*
[c] "Don't let's talk morality."— *Ed.*

"In a fury, he departed from what he described to me as '*a Cologne enslaved by Marx*'. He arranged for the duplication of his nonsense elsewhere and dispatched it to a large number of officers with the result that the chaste mystery of his cunning plan to convert Prussian officers to the republican cause was prostituted by the 'Spectator' of the *Kreuz-Zeitung*."

At the time of this adventure, Steffen, who only came to England in 1853, was completely unknown to me. Even more revealing is *Schimmelpfennig's* self-characterisation in the following letter to the same *Hörfel* who was later exposed as a French police agent. He was the heart and soul of the Revolutionary Committee founded in Paris at the end of 1850 by Schimmelpfennig, Schurz, Häfner and other friends of *Kinkel* in those days and he was on terms of intimacy with those two matadors Schurz and Schimmelpfennig.

Schimmelpfennig to Hörfel (in Paris, 1851):

"Here" (in London) "the following events have taken place.... We have written to all our friends with any influence" (in America) "asking them to prepare the way for the loan" (the Kinkel Loan) "first of all *by talking for some time about the power of conspiracy, both personally and in the press,* and by emphasising that people worth their salt will *never* leave the field of battle— *neither* the Germans, the French nor the Italians." (History does *not* have *no* date?[a]) "... *Our work is now off to a good start.* If you drop people who are too obstinate, they will soon think better of it and come to accept the conditions imposed. Since the *work* is now firm and secure, I shall tomorrow establish contact with Ruge and Haug.... *My own social position, like yours, is very oppressive.* **It is vital that our affairs should get moving soon.**" (Namely the business of Kinkel's Revolutionary Loan.)

"Your *Schimmelpfennig*"

This letter of Schimmelpfennig's is to be found in the *Enthüllungen* which A. *Ruge* published in the *Herold des Westens*, Louisville, September 11, 1853. Schimmelpfennig, who was already living in the United States when they appeared, never impugned the authenticity of the letter. Ruge's *Enthüllungen* are reprinted from a document entitled "*Aus den Akten des Berliner Polizeipräsidiums*". It consists of marginal notes by Hinckeldey and of papers which were either found by the French police in the possession of Schimmelpfennig and Hörfel in Paris, or were unearthed at Pastor Dulon's in Bremen, or, lastly, were entrusted to the German-American press during the Frogs-and-Mice War between Ruge's Agitation Union and Kinkel's Émigré Society,[82] by the feuding brothers themselves. Typical is the irony with which

---

[a] Marx ridicules Schimmelpfennig's ungrammatical sentence by alluding to an equally ungrammatical statement made by Prince Lichnowski, a reactionary deputy of the Frankfurt National Assembly, who said at one of the sessions: "Für das historische Recht gibt es *kein* Datum *nicht*" ("With regard to historical right there does *not* exist *no* date") (cf. present edition, Vol. 7, p. 369).— *Ed.*

Hinckeldey remarks that Schimmelpfennig abruptly cut short his journey through Prussia as missionary on behalf of Kinkel's Revolutionary Loan because "he *imagined* that he was being pursued by the police"! The same *Enthüllungen* contain a letter from *Karl Schurz*, "the representative of the Paris Committee" (i.e. that of Hörfel, Häfner, Schimmelpfennig, etc.) "in London", in which we find:

> "It was decided yesterday that of the members of the emigration here Bucher, Dr. Frank, Redz from Vienna and *Techow*, who will soon be here, should be asked to join the discussions. N.B. *Techow should not be informed of this decision for the time being, either verbally or in writing*, before his arrival." (*Karl Schurz* to his "dear men" in Paris, *London, April 16, 1851*.)

It was to one of these "dear men", Herr *Schimmelpfennig*, that *Techow* addresses his letter of August 26, 1850 for "communication to our friends". He begins by informing the "dear man" of theories which I had been trying to keep a strict secret, but which he at once detected at our single encounter by means of the proverb "*in vino veritas*".

> "I," Herr Techow recounts to Herr Schimmelpfennig, "for communication to our friends", "I ... declared finally that I had *always* **imagined** them" (i.e. Marx, Engels, etc.) "*to be above all the nonsense about a communist paradisiacal barn à la Cabet*, etc." ("Magnum Opus", p. 150.)[a]

Imagined! So Techow did not even *know* the elementary facts about our views, but was nevertheless magnanimous and condescending enough to *imagine* that they were not exactly "nonsense".

Leaving scientific works to one side, even if he had read the *Manifesto of the Communist Party*, which he later calls my "Proletarian Catechism",[b] he would have found in it a detailed chapter with the title "Socialist and Communist Literature", and at the end of this chapter a section entitled "Critical-Utopian Socialism and Communism", in which it says:

"The Socialist and Communist systems properly so called, those of Saint-Simon, Fourier, Owen and others, spring into existence in the early undeveloped period, described above, of the struggle between proletariat and bourgeoisie.... The founders of these systems saw, indeed, the class antagonisms, as well as the action of the decomposing elements in the prevailing form of society. But the proletariat offered to them the spectacle of a class without any historical initiative or any independent political movement. Since the development of class antagonism keeps even pace with the

---

[a] Carl Vogt, *Mein Prozess...*, S. 150. Marx's italics and bold type.—*Ed.*
[b] ibid., S. 152.—*Ed.*

development of industry, the economic situation, as they find it, does not as yet offer to them the material conditions for the emancipation of the proletariat. They therefore search after a social science, after social laws, *that are to create these conditions.* Social action is to yield to their personal inventive action, *historically* created conditions of emancipation to *fantastic* ones, and the gradual class organisation of the proletariat to an *organisation of society specially contrived by these inventors.* Future history resolves itself, in their eyes, into the *propaganda and the practical* carrying out of their social plans.... The significance of Critical-Utopian Socialism and Communism bears an inverse relation to historical development.... Therefore, although the originators of these systems were, in many respects, revolutionary, their disciples have, in every case, formed mere reactionary sects [...] and [...] still *dream* of experimental realisation of their social Utopias, of founding isolated 'phalanstères', of establishing 'Home Colonies', of *setting up a 'Little Icaria'*—duodecimo editions of the New Jerusalem...*" (*Manifesto of the Communist Party,* 1848, pp. 21, 22).[a]

In the concluding words *Cabet*'s Icaria, or "paradisiacal barn", to use Techow's expression, is explicitly referred to as a "duodecimo edition of the New Jerusalem".

Techow's self-confessed total ignorance of the ideas that Engels and I had published in print years before our encounter with him is the factor that completely accounts for his misunderstanding. A few quotations will serve adequately to characterise *him*:

"He" (Marx) "laughs at the fools who blindly repeat his Proletarian Catechism after him, just as he laughs at communists like Willich and at the bourgeoisie. The only men he respects are *aristocrats,* those who are pure aristocrats, and are conscious of being so. *To oust them from power* he requires a force which he can find only in the proletariat. *This is why his system is tailored to fit that force*" ("Magnum Opus", p. 152).

---

* *Phalanstères* were Socialist colonies on the plan of Charles Fourier; *Icaria* was the name given by Cabet to his Utopia and, later on, to his American Communist colony. [*Note by Engels to the English edition of 1888.*]

"Home Colonies" were what Owen called his Communist model societies. *Phalanstères* was the name of the public palaces planned by Fourier. *Icaria* was the name given to the Utopian land of fancy, whose Communist institutions Cabet portrayed. [*Note by Engels to the German edition of 1890.*]

---

[a] Here and below Marx quotes from the first German edition of the *Manifesto of the Communist Party,* published in London in 1848 (see present edition, Vol. 6, pp. 514-15, 516). The italics were introduced by Marx in *Herr Vogt.—Ed.*

Techow thus "imagines" that I have written a "Proletarian Catechism". He means the *Manifesto* which criticises and, if he likes, "ridicules" socialist and critical utopianism of every kind. Only, this "ridiculing" was not such a simple matter as Techow "imagines", but required a fair amount of work, as he could see from my book against Proudhon, *Misère de la philosophie* (1847).[a] Techow further "imagines" that I have "tailored" a "*system*", whereas, on the contrary, even in the *Manifesto* which was intended directly for workers, I rejected systems of *every* kind and in their place I insisted on "a critical insight into the conditions, the line of march and the ultimate general results of the real movement of society".[b] Such an "insight" cannot be blindly repeated, nor can it be "tailored" like a cartridge pouch. Of rare naivety is the view of the relations between aristocracy, bourgeoisie and proletariat, as Techow "imagines" them and *imputes* them to me.

I "respect" the aristocracy, "laugh" at the bourgeoisie, and I "tailor a system" to fit the proletariat, using them to "oust the aristocracy from power". In the first section of the *Manifesto,* entitled "Bourgeois and Proletarians" (see *Manifesto,* p. 11),[c] it is argued in detail that the economic and, hence too, in one form or another, the political *sway of the bourgeoisie* is the essential precondition both of the existence of the modern proletariat and of the creation of the "material conditions for its emancipation". "The development of the modern proletariat" (see *Neue Rheinische Zeitung. Revue,* January 1850, p. 15) "is, in general, conditioned by the development of the industrial bourgeoisie. Only *under its rule* does the proletariat gain that extensive national existence which can raise its revolution to a national one, and does it itself create the modern means of production, which become just so many means of its revolutionary emancipation. Only *its rule* tears up the material roots of feudal society and levels the ground *on which alone a proletarian revolution is possible.*"[d] I declared accordingly in the same "Review" that any revolution in which England did not take part was no more than a "storm in a teacup".[83] Engels had already advanced the same opinion in 1845 in *The Condition of the Working-Class in England.*[e] Hence in countries where an aristocracy

---

[a] See present edition, Vol. 6.— *Ed.*

[b] ibid., p. 497.— *Ed.*

[c] ibid., pp. 495-96.— *Ed.*

[d] Karl Marx, *The Class Struggles in France, 1848 to 1850* (see present edition, Vol. 10, p. 56). The italics were introduced by Marx in *Herr Vogt.—Ed.*

[e] See present edition, Vol. 4.— *Ed.*

in the Continental sense of the term—and this is what Techow meant by "aristocracy"—has still to be "ousted from power", the very first prerequisite of a proletarian revolution is in my opinion missing, namely the existence of an *industrial proletariat* on a national scale.

Techow could have found my view of the attitude to the bourgeois movement adopted by the German workers in particular expressed very clearly in the *Manifesto.*

"In Germany they [the Communists] fight with the bourgeoisie whenever it acts in a revolutionary way, against the absolute monarchy, the feudal landowners and philistinism [*Kleinbürgerei*]. But they never cease, for a single instant, to instil into the working class the clearest possible recognition of the hostile antagonism between bourgeoisie and proletariat, etc." (*Manifesto,* p. 23.) [a]

When I stood before a bourgeois jury in Cologne charged with "rebellion", I argued along the same lines: "Modern bourgeois society still has *classes,* but no longer *social estates.* Its development lies in the struggle between these classes, but the latter stand united against the estates and their monarchy by the grace of God." ("*Zwei politische Prozesse,* verhandelt vor den Februar-Assisen zu Köln 1849", p. 59.) [84]

What else did the liberal bourgeoisie do in its appeals to the proletariat between 1688 and 1848 but "tailor systems and phrases" in order to use the *proletariat's* strength to oust the aristocracy from power? So Herr Techow discovers that the core of the matter [b] hidden in my secret theory is *bourgeois liberalism of the crudest sort! Tant de bruit pour une omelette!* [c] Since, on the other hand, Techow knew perfectly well that "Marx" was no bourgeois liberal, he was left finally with no choice but "to go away with the impression that *his* personal supremacy was the goal of all his actions". "All my actions", what a temperate description of my single interview with Herr Techow!

Techow further confides to his Schimmelpfennig, "for communication to our friends", that I had expressed the following monstrous opinion:

---

[a] Karl Marx and Frederick Engels, *Manifesto of the Communist Party* (see present edition, Vol. 6, p. 519). Marx quotes the German edition of 1848.— *Ed.*

[b] Marx uses the idiomatic expression *des Pudels Kern* from Goethe's *Faust,* Erster Teil, Studierzimmer.— *Ed.*

[c] Much ado about an omelette!—an exclamation which Jacques Vallée, Sieur des Barreaux, is supposed to have made when a thunderstorm occurred while he was eating an omelette on a fast-day.— *Ed.*

"In the end it is a matter of complete indifference whether this miserable Europe were to be destroyed, a thing which must happen **within a short space of time** without a social revolution, and whether afterwards America would exploit the old system at Europe's expense." ("Magnum Opus", p. 148.)[a]

My conversation with Techow took place at the end of August 1850. In the February 1850 issue of the *Neue Rheinische Zeitung. Revue,* i.e. eight months *before* Techow culled this secret from my lips, I revealed the following views to the German public:

"Now we come *to America.* The most important thing to have occurred here, more important than the February revolution, is the discovery of the Californian gold-mines. Already now, after barely eighteen months, one may predict that this discovery will have much more impressive consequences than the discovery of America itself.... For the second time world trade is taking a new direction ... the Pacific Ocean will have the same role as the Atlantic has now and the Mediterranean had in antiquity and in the Middle Ages—that of the great water highway of world commerce; and the Atlantic will decline to the status of an inland sea, like the Mediterranean nowadays. The only chance the civilised nations of Europe will *then* have, not to fall into the same industrial, commercial and political dependence to which Italy, Spain and Portugal are now reduced, lies in a social revolution." (*Revue,* No. 2, February 1850, pp. [76,] 77.)[b]

But the idea that old Europe will be "destroyed *within a short space of time*" and America will accede to the throne the following morning, belongs to Herr Techow. The clarity of my own view of America's immediate prospects at that time can be seen from another passage in the same "Review": "*Over-speculation* will develop very soon, and even if British capital becomes involved on a large scale [...] nevertheless this time *New York* will remain the centre of the whole swindle and, as in 1836, will be the first to suffer when it collapses." (*Revue,* double issue, May to October 1850, p. 149.)[c] This prognosis for America, which I made in 1850, was fully borne out by the great trade crisis of 1857. As to "old Europe", on the other hand, having given an account of the revival of its economy, I go on to say: "With this general prosperity, in which the productive forces of bourgeois society

----

[a] In this passage Marx left out Vogt's italics and introduced bold type.—*Ed.*

[b] See present edition, Vol. 10, pp. 265-66. The word "*then*" in the last sentence was introduced by Marx in *Herr Vogt.*—*Ed.*

[c] Here and immediately below Marx quotes, with minor alterations, from "Review, May to October [1850]" (see present edition, Vol. 10, pp. 506 and 510). The italics were introduced by Marx in *Herr Vogt.*—*Ed.*

develop so luxuriantly ... there can be no talk of a real revolution.... The various quarrels in which the representatives of the individual factions of the Continental party of Order now indulge and mutually compromise themselves, far from providing the occasion for revolution, are, on the contrary, possible only because the basis of the relationships is *momentarily* so secure and, what the reaction does not know, *so bourgeois.* All reactionary attempts to hold up bourgeois development will rebound off it just as certainly as *all moral indignation and all enthusiastic proclamations of the democrats.* A new revolution is possible only in consequence of a crisis" (loc. cit., p. 153).

And in fact European history has only re-entered an acute and, if one wishes, revolutionary phase since the crisis of 1857-58. In fact it was precisely during the reactionary period from 1849 to 1859 that industry and trade on the Continent, and along with them the material foundations for the political domination of the bourgeoisie, developed to an extent unheard of previously. In fact during this period "all moral indignation and all enthusiastic proclamations of the democrats" rebounded off the realities of economic conditions.

If *Techow* took the serious side of our discussions so humorously, he made up for it by the seriousness with which he responded to their humorous side. With a woebegone face he reports to his *Schimmelpfennig* "for communication to our friends":

"Furthermore, *Marx* stated: In revolutions officers are always the greatest threat; [...] from La Fayette to Napoleon, a series of traitors and treacheries. *One ought always to have dagger and poison in readiness for them.*" ("Magnum Opus", p. 153.)[a]

Even Techow will not wish to claim that the platitude about the treasonable activities of "the military" is an original opinion of mine. My originality is supposed rather to consist in the "dagger and poison" always to be held in readiness. Did Techow not know even then that really revolutionary governments, such as the *Comité du salut public,*[85] kept antidotes in readiness for "the military" that were very drastic though less melodramatic? The dagger and poison really belong to the stock-in-trade of a Venetian oligarchy. If Techow were to scrutinise his letter once again, he would perhaps notice the irony in the "dagger and poison". *Vogt's* fellow-scoundrel, **Edouard Simon,** the notorious Bonapartist **spy**, translated the last part of Techow's letter in the

---

[a] In this passage the italics are Vogt's.— *Ed.*

Revue contemporaine (XIII, Paris, 1860, p. 528, in his "Le procès de M. Vogt, etc.") adding his own gloss:

"*Marx* n'aime pas beaucoup voir des officiers dans *sa bande.* Les officiers sont trop dangereux dans les révolutions.

"*Il faut toujours tenir prêts pour eux le poignard et le poison!*

"Techow, qui est officier, se le tient pour dit; il se rembarque et retourne en Suisse." [a]

According to *Edouard Simon,* poor Techow was in such a panic at the thought of the "dagger and poison" I was holding in readiness, that he immediately took to his heels, boarded ship and returned to Switzerland. The Imperial Vogt prints the passage about "dagger and poison" in bold type, to send a shiver down the spine of the German philistines. However, the same merry gentleman wrote in his so-called *Studien*:

"*Today the knife and the poison of the Spaniard are shining in even greater glory*—for it was the independence of the nation that was at stake" (loc. cit., p. 79).[b]

Quite by the way: the Spanish and English historical sources dealing with the period 1807-14 have long since disproved the tales about poison invented by the French. But for the tub-thumping politicians, of course, they survive unscathed.

I now come, lastly, to the "tittle-tattle" in Techow's letter and shall provide a few illustrations of his historical impartiality:

"The talk centred at first on the question of competition between them and us, Switzerland and London. [...] *They had to maintain the rights of the old League,* which because of its own specific party policy of course could not tolerate another league operating in the *same* area" (the proletariat) ("Magnum Opus", p. 143).[c]

The rival organisation in Switzerland to which Techow refers here and as whose representative he, as it were, approached us, was the already-mentioned "*Revolutionary Centralisation*". Its Central Committee was located in Zurich and its President was a lawyer, a former Vice-President of one of the pocket parliaments of 1848 and a member of one of the provisional governments in Germany in 1849.[d] In *July 1850 Dronke* went to Zurich [86] where, as a

---

[a] "*Marx* does not much care to see officers in *his gang.* Officers are too dangerous in revolutions.

"*One ought always to have dagger and poison in readiness for them!*

"Techow, who is an officer, did not need to be told twice; he re-embarked and returned to Switzerland" (Edouard Simon, "Un tableau de moeurs politiques en Allemagne. Le procès de M. Vogt avec la gazette d'Augsbourg", *Revue contemporaine*, t. 13, Paris, February 15, 1860). The italics are Simon's.— *Ed.*

[b] Carl Vogt, *Studien zur gegenwärtigen Lage Europas,* S. 79. Marx's italics.— *Ed.*

[c] Carl Vogt, *Mein Prozess...*, S. 143.— *Ed.*

[d] Samuel Erdmann Tzschirner.— *Ed.*

member of the London "League", he was given a sort of legal
contract by that lawyer "for communication" to me. I quote from
it verbatim:

"Considering the necessity for a union of all truly revolutionary elements, and
since all members of the Revolutionary Central Committee have acknowledged the
proletarian character of the next revolution, even though not all were able
unreservedly to accept the programme adopted in London (the Manifesto of 1848),
the Communist organisation and the Revolutionary Centralisation have agreed on the
following points:

"1. Both parties agree to continue working side by side—the Revolutionary
Centralisation will strive to prepare for the next revolution by attempting to unite
all revolutionary elements, the London association will try to prepare for the rule
of the proletariat by concentrating *primarily* on the organisation of *proletarian
elements*;

"2. The Revolutionary Centralisation will instruct its agents and emissaries that,
when forming branches in Germany, members who seem to be qualified to join the
Communist organisation should have their attention drawn to the existence of an
organisation devoted primarily towards the furtherance of proletarian interests;

"3. and 4. That the leadership in the 'Revolutionary Central Committee' for
Switzerland will only be entrusted to *genuine supporters* of the London Manifesto,
and that there should be a general exchange of information."

It is evident from this document, which is still in my possession,
that there was no question of two secret societies "operating in the
same area" (the proletariat), but of an alliance between two
societies with *different aims* operating in *different areas.* It is equally
evident that the "Revolutionary Centralisation" declared itself
willing to act as a sort of branch organisation of the "Communist
League", in addition to pursuing its own ends.

The proposal was rejected because it was incompatible with the
principles of the "League".

"Then it was *Kinkel*'s turn.... To this they replied.... They had never striven for
cheap popularity, on the contrary! [...] As far as Kinkel was concerned they would
not have begrudged him his cheap popularity in the least, had he kept quiet. But
once he had published that Rastatt speech in the Berlin *Abend-Post*,[a] peace was no
longer possible. They had known perfectly well that there would be a general
outcry; they had clearly foreseen that the existence of their present paper"
(*Rheinische Zeitung. Revue*) "was at stake. Moreover, their fears had been realised.
They had been ruined by the whole affair, they had lost all their subscribers in the
Rhine Province and had to close the paper down. But it would do them no harm"
(loc. cit., pp. 146-48).[b]

First a factual correction. It is not true that the *Revue* was closed
down at this point, since one more, double issue came out three

---

[a] Gottfried Kinkel's speech before the court martial in Rastatt on August 4,
1849, *Abend-Post*, Nos. 78 and 79, April 5 and 6, 1850.—*Ed.*

[b] Carl Vogt, *Mein Prozess...*, S. 146-48.—*Ed.*

months afterwards.[a] Nor had we lost *a single subscriber* in the Rhine Province, as my old friend *J. Weydemeyer,* a former Prussian lieutenant of artillery and, at that time, editor of the *Neue Deutsche Zeitung* in Frankfurt, can testify since it was he who was kind enough to collect the subscriptions for us. For the rest, Techow, who had only a hearsay acquaintance with the writings of Engels and myself, nevertheless must at least have read our critique— which he himself criticises—of Kinkel's speech. Why then send this confidential information to his "dear men" in Switzerland? Why "reveal" to them what we had ourselves revealed to the public five months previously? We wrote in the critique referred to:

"We know in advance that we shall provoke the general wrath of the sentimental swindlers and democratic spouters by denouncing this speech of the 'captured' Kinkel to our party. To this we are completely indifferent. Our task is that of ruthless criticism ... and in maintaining this our position *we gladly forego cheap democratic popularity.* Our attack will by no means worsen Herr Kinkel's position; *we denounce his amnesty* by confirming his confession that he is not the man people allege to hold him for, and by declaring that he is worthy, not only of being amnestied, but even of entering the service of the Prussian state! Moreover, his speech has been published" (*Neue Rheinische Zeitung. Revue,* April 1850, pp. 70, 71).[87]

Techow asserts that we "compromised" the *petits grands hommes*[b] of the revolution. However, he does not use the word "compromise" in the *police* sense of Herr Vogt. On the contrary, he means the operation by means of which we stripped off the offensive covering of those sheep who had dressed up in revolutionary wolf's clothing, thus preserving them from the fate of the celebrated Provençal troubadour[c] who was torn to pieces by the dogs because they took the wolf's pelt seriously which he wore to go hunting.

As an instance of our offensive attacks Techow singles out the incidental gloss on General *Sigel* to be found in Engels' account of the "campaign for the Imperial Constitution" (see *Revue,* March 1850, pp. 70-78).[d]

---

[a] The issue in question— *Neue Rheinische Zeitung. Politisch-ökonomische Revue,* No. 5-6—appeared in late November 1850.— *Ed.*

[b] Little great men.— *Ed.*

[c] Vidal Peire.— *Ed.*

[d] See present edition, Vol. 10, pp. 174-79.— *Ed.*

Now Engels' critique, which is based on documentary evidence, should be compared with the following malicious and trite twaddle about that same General *Sigel,* published about a year after our meeting with Techow by the London "Emigration Association" run by Techow, Kinkel, Willich, Schimmelpfennig, Schurz, H. B. Oppenheim, Eduard Meyen, etc. Moreover, this was published solely because Sigel belonged to Ruge's "Agitation Union", instead of Kinkel's "Emigration Association".

On December 3, 1851 the *Baltimore Correspondent,*[a] which was at the time a sort of Kinkel *Moniteur,* published the following description of *Sigel* beneath the title *"The Agitation Union in London"*:

"Let us take another look at these worthy men who regard everyone else as an *'immature politician'. Sigel, the supreme commander.* If anyone ever asks the muse of history how such an insipid nonentity was given the supreme command she will be even more at a loss for an explanation than in the case of that mooncalf Napoleon. The latter is at least 'his uncle's nephew'; Sigel, however, is only 'his brother's brother'. His brother[b] became a popular officer as a result of his critical remarks about the government, remarks which had been provoked by his frequent arrests for *disorderly behaviour.* The young Sigel thought this *reason enough* in the early confusion prevailing at the outbreak of the revolution to proclaim himself supreme commander and Minister of War. The Baden artillery, which had often proved its worth, had plenty of older and more experienced officers who should have taken precedence over this *young Lieutenant Sigel,* and they were more than a little indignant when they had to obey a *young, insignificant* man whose *inexperience was only matched by his incompetence.* But there was Brentano, who was so mindless and treacherous as to permit anything that might ruin the revolution. It is a ridiculous fact, but a fact nevertheless, *that Sigel promoted himself to the rank of commander-in-chief* and that Brentano approved his nomination in retrospect.... It is certainly noteworthy that Sigel left the bravest soldiers of the republican army in the lurch at the desperate and hopeless battles in Rastatt and the Black Forest without the reinforcements he had promised while he himself drove around Zurich with the epaulettes and in the carriage of Prince von Fürstenberg and paraded as an interesting unfortunate supreme commander. This is the well-known magnitude of this mature politician who, 'understandably proud' of his earlier heroic deeds, imposed himself as supreme commander for a second time, on this occasion in the Agitation Union. This is the great *well-known man,*[c] the *'brother of his brother'.*"[d]

Impartiality requires us to lend an ear also to Ruge's "Agitation Union" in the person of its spokesman *Tausenau.* In an open letter addressed "To Citizen Seidensticker", London, *November 14, 1851,*

---

[a] *Der Deutsche Correspondent* (Baltimore).— *Ed.*

[b] Albert Sigel.— *Ed.*

[c] Presumably an analogy with The Great Unknown, i.e. Sir Walter Scott, who was called so because until 1827 his novels appeared anonymously.— *Ed.*

[d] This passage is also quoted in the pamphlet *The Great Men of the Exile* by Marx and Engels (see present edition, Vol. 11, p. 324).— *Ed.*

Tausenau writes with reference to the "Emigration Association" led by Kinkel, Techow, etc.:

"...They affirm their conviction that the union of all in the interest of the revolution is an urgent patriotic duty. The German Agitation Union shares this conviction, and its members have proved this by their sustained efforts to achieve unity with Kinkel and his supporters. But as soon as a basis for political co-operation seemed to be established it vanished once again, and new disappointments followed the old ones. High-handed actions in violation of previous agreements, separate interests in the guise of conciliation, the systematic 'fixing' of majorities, the emergence of unknown quantities as party leaders, attempts to impose a secret finance committee are but a few of the devious tricks and chess moves that immature politicians always resort to in exile in the belief that they are guiding the fortunes of their country, while in reality the very first glow of the revolution will dissipate all such vanities and scatter them to the winds.... We were denounced officially and in public by Kinkel's supporters; the **reactionary German press, which was barred to us,** is packed with reports favourable to Kinkel and hostile to us. Finally Kinkel made the journey to the United States in order to use his project of the so-called German Loan as a means of imposing a union on us, or rather a status of subordination and dependence which is the *goal of everyone who proposes a financial merger between two parties.* Kinkel's departure was kept so secret that we did not learn of it until we read in the American press about his arrival in New York.... All this, and other considerations of the same sort, were compelling motives to persuade serious revolutionaries who did not overestimate themselves, but who in the *knowledge of their previous achievements* could with self-confidence assert that at any rate *clearly defined sections of the people stood behind them,* to enter an association which seeks in its own way to further the interests of the revolution." [a]

Further it is held against Kinkel that the funds he had collected were to be used for the benefit of "a clique", as "his entire behaviour here" (in London) "and in America makes plain", as do also "the majority of the guarantors nominated by Kinkel himself".

Tausenau concludes by saying:

"We *promise* our friends neither interest on their money nor the repayment of their patriotic donations; but we know that we shall vindicate their confidence in us through our positive achievements" (fair services?) "and scrupulous accounting and *that one day, when we come to publish their names, the gratitude of the nation will await them*" (*Baltimore Wecker* of November 29, 1851).

This was the sort of "literary activity" maintained in the columns of the German-American press for three years by the democratic heroes of the "Agitation Union" and the "Emigration Association" who were later joined by the "Revolutionary League of Two Worlds" [88] founded by Goegg. (See Appendix 6.)

The refugee row in the American press, incidentally, was inaugurated by a paper battle [89] between the parliamentarians Zitz and Roesler of Oels.

---

[a] This passage is contained in Marx's notebook for 1860.— *Ed.*

One more fact by way of characterising Techow's "dear men". Schimmelpfennig, to whom Techow's letter "for communication to our friends" was addressed, had set up a so-called Revolutionary Committee in Paris at the end of 1850 (as we have already mentioned) together with Hörfel, Häfner, Goegg and others (K. Schurz joined in at a later date).

A few years ago a document written by a former member of the Committee to a political refugee here[90] was handed to me to use as I pleased. The document is still in my possession.

It says, among other things:

"Schurz and Schimmelpfennig were in effect the whole Committee. They also acquired some sort of associates but they were merely for show. These two gentlemen firmly believed at that time that they could soon put their Kinkel, whom they had virtually made their property, at the head of affairs in Germany. They particularly detested Ruge's sarcasms and the criticism and demonic activity of Marx. At a meeting of these gentlemen with their associates they gave us a really very interesting description of Marx and conveyed to us an exaggerated impression of the pandemonic dangers he represented.... Schurz-Schimmelpfennig proposed a motion to *destroy* Marx. The means they *recommended* were *insinuations and intrigues,* and **the most shameless slanders.** A vote in favour and a resolution, if one can use these words to describe their childish antics, then took place. The next step was the character sketch of Marx published in the *literary section* of the *Hamburger Anzeiger*[a] at the beginning of 1851. It was written by *L. Häfner* on the basis of the above-mentioned description by Schurz and Schimmelpfennig."

In any event there is the most striking affinity between Häfner's essay and Techow's letter, although neither the one nor the other can equal *Vogt*'s *Lousiad.* It is important not to confuse the *Lousiad* with the *Lusiads* of Camoens. The original *Lousiad* was rather a mock heroic epic by *Peter Pindar.*[91]

---

[a] Leopold Häfner's article was published in the *Hamburger Nachrichten* on February 28, 1851.— *Ed.*

V

IMPERIAL REGENT AND COUNT PALATINE

> Vidi un col capo sì dì merda lordo,
> Che non parea, s'era laico, o cherco,
> Quei mi sgridò: perchè se' tu sì 'ngordo
> Di riguardar più me che gli altri brutti.
>
> (*Dante*)*

Vogt, repulsed by the Bristlers, experiences a powerful need to show why the "Brimstone Gang" had singled him out as the *bête noire*. For this reason *Cherval* and the "frustrated conspiracy" at the Joint Festival in Lausanne are supplemented by the adventure of the "fugitive Imperial Regent", an adventure which had no less reality than they. *Vogt*, we must not forget, was at one time Governor of the parliamentary island of Barataria.[92] His story goes like this:

"Early in 1850 the *Deutsche Monatsschrift* of Kolatschek made its appearance. [...] Immediately after the publication of the first number, *the Brimstone Gang, acting through one of its comrades who left for America without delay, issued* a pamphlet with the title *Der flüchtige Reichsregent Vogt mit seinem Anhange und die Deutsche Monatsschrift von Adolf Kolatschek,* a work which was also mentioned by the *Allgemeine Zeitung....* The Brimstone Gang's whole system is revealed yet again in this pamphlet" (loc. cit., pp. [162-]163).[a]

He goes on to explain at tedious length how, in the pamphlet referred to, an anonymous article on *Gagern* which had been written by Professor *Hagen* was "attributed" to the fugitive Imperial Regent, Vogt, because

---

* I there made out a smeared
   Head—whether clerk or lay was hard to tell,
   It was so thickly plastered with the merd.
   "Why stand there gloating?" he began to yell,
   "Why stare at me more than the other scum?" (*Kannegiesser*) [*The Divine Comedy*, Inferno, Canto XVIII. Kannegiesser is the name of the German translator.]

---

a Here and below Marx quotes from Vogt's *Mein Prozess...*, S. 162-63. The italics are Marx's.— *Ed.*

"the Brimstone Gang knew" that Hagen "was living in Germany at the time, that he had been harassed by the Baden police and that he could not be named without exposing him to molestation of the most unpleasant sort" (p. 163).

In his letter of February 6,[a] *Schily* wrote to me from Paris:

"That *Greiner* who, to the best of my knowledge, has never been to Geneva, has been linked with the Brimstone Gang, is the result of his obituary notice to the 'fugitive Imperial Regent' for which *d'Ester* was held responsible and outlawed in parliamentary circles until I set matters right in a letter to one of Vogt's friends and colleagues." [b]

Greiner was a member of the Provisional Government of the Palatinate. Greiner's rule was an "unrelieved horror" (see *Vogt's Studien,* p. 28), that is for my friend *Engels,* whom he had arrested on a trumped-up charge in Kirchheim. Engels has himself given a detailed account of the whole tragicomedy in the *Neue Rheinische Zeitung. Revue* (February 1850, pp. 53-55).[c] And that is all I know about Herr *Greiner.* The fact that the fugitive Imperial Regent has managed to implicate me in his quarrel with "Count Palatine" reveals "yet again" the "whole system" by means of which our ingenious raconteur has composed the story of the life and deeds of "the Brimstone Gang".

What endears him to me, however, is the true Falstaffian humour he displayed in causing the Count Palatine to depart for America "without delay". The Count Palatine, having let fly his pamphlet at the "fugitive Imperial Regent" like a Parthian shot, was suddenly overwhelmed with horror. Which caused Greiner to flee from Switzerland to France, from France to England. Even the Channel did not seem to offer sufficient protection and so he fled headlong to a Cunard steamer[d] in Liverpool where he breathlessly cried out to the Captain: "Away, across the Atlantic!" And the "stern mariner"[e] replied:

"I'll save you from the hands of the *Vogt*
But from the might of the storm another must lend his aid."[f]

---

[a] Marx quotes from Schily's letter of February 8, 1860.— *Ed.*
[b] Ludwig Simon.— *Ed.*
[c] See *The Campaign for the German Imperial Constitution* (present edition, Vol. 10, pp. 200-02).— *Ed.*
[d] Marx uses the English word.— *Ed.*
[e] Marx uses the English phrase.— *Ed.*
[f] Schiller, *Wilhelm Tell,* Act I, Scene 1.— *Ed.*

VI

VOGT AND THE *NEUE RHEINISCHE ZEITUNG*

"Sîn kumber was manecvalt."[a]

Vogt himself claims that his "purpose" in writing his "Magnum Opus" (p. 162) is to clarify "the *development of his personal attitude to this clique*" (Marx and Co.). Curiously enough, he only describes conflicts that he has never experienced and only experiences conflicts that he has never described. So it is necessary to confront his tall stories with a piece of real history. Anyone who leafs through the *Neue Rheinische Zeitung* (June 1, 1848-May 19, 1849) will discover that in 1848 Vogt's name does not occur, apart from a single exception,[b] either in its leading articles or in its correspondence columns. It will be found only in the daily reports of the parliamentary debates and to Vogt's immense satisfaction the Frankfurt reporter[c] never failed to record conscientiously the "applause" accorded to him for "the speeches delivered by himself". We saw that whereas the Right wing in Frankfurt had at their disposal the united forces of a harlequin like *Lichnowski* and a *clown* like *von Vincke,* the Left was forced to rely entirely on the sporadic outbreaks of farce from its one and only *Vogt.* We realised that he stood in need of encouragement,

> "that *important fellow,*
> the children's wonder — *Signor Punchinello*",[d]

---

[a] "His griefs were manifold"—an adapted line from *Der Edel Stein,* a collection of fables by Ulrich Bonerius.— *Ed.*

[b] This refers to the article "Ein Aktenstück des Märzvereins" in the *Neue Rheinische Zeitung,* No. 181, December 29, 1848.— *Ed.*

[c] Gustav Adolph Schlöffel.— *Ed.*

[d] Marx gives these lines in English.— *Ed.*

and so let the Frankfurt reporter have his head. After the middle of September 1848 his reports underwent a change of tone.

In the debates on the Truce of Malmö, Vogt tried to stir up a rebellion with his revolutionary rantings.[a] At the decisive moment he did his utmost to prevent the acceptance of the resolutions which had been passed by the popular assembly on the Pfingstweide and approved by a section of the extreme Left.[94] After the barricade fighting had been crushed, with Frankfurt openly transformed into an army camp and a state of siege proclaimed, this same Vogt declared on September 19 that he was in favour of *urgently* discussing Zachariä's resolution endorsing the measures already taken by the Imperial Ministry and expressing gratitude to the Imperial troops.[b] Before *Vogt* rose to speak even *Venedey*[c] had protested against the *"urgency"* of these resolutions, declaring that such a discussion at such a time was unworthy of the Assembly. But Vogt was *inferior* to Venedey. By way of punishment I inserted the word "windbag" into the parliamentary report[d] after the word "Vogt", as a hint to the Frankfurt reporter.

In the following October Vogt not only neglected his duty of waving his harlequin's wooden sword above the heads of the then boisterous and fiercely reactionary majority. He did not even dare to sign the protest tabled by *Zimmermann* of Spandau[e] on October 10 in the name of some 40 deputies, opposing the law for the protection of the National Assembly.[95] The law, as Zimmermann correctly pointed out, signalled the most shameless interference with the popular rights that had been gained in the March revolution—right of assembly, freedom of speech and of the press. Even *Eisenmann*[f] handed in a similar protest. But *Vogt* was *inferior* to *Eisenmann.* When he did venture forth again at the founding of the "Central March Association"[96] his name finally made its appearance in an article in the *Neue Rheinische Zeitung*

---

[a] Vogt's speech in the Frankfurt National Assembly on September 15, 1848, *Stenographischer Bericht über die Verhandlungen der deutschen constituirenden Nationalversammlung zu Frankfurt am Main*,[93] Bd. 3, S. 2091-94.— *Ed.*

[b] The speeches by Vogt and Zachariä in the Frankfurt National Assembly on September 19, 1848, ibid., S. 2188.— *Ed.*

[c] Venedey's speech in the Frankfurt National Assembly on September 19, 1848, ibid., S. 2187.— *Ed.*

[d] Report on the sitting of the Frankfurt National Assembly on September 20, 1848, *Neue Rheinische Zeitung*, No. 110, September 23, 1848.— *Ed.*

[e] Zimmermann's speech in the Frankfurt National Assembly on October 10, 1848, *Stenographischer Bericht...*, Bd. 4, S. 2531.— *Ed.*

[f] Eisenmann's speech in the Frankfurt National Assembly, ibid., pp. 2531 et seq.— *Ed.*

(December 29, 1848), in which the "March Association" was designated the "unconscious tool of the counter-revolution", its programme was critically torn to shreds and *Vogt* was represented as one half of the two-headed figure whose other half was *Vincke.* More than a decade later both "Ministers of the Future" acknowledged their affinity and chose the *partition of Germany* as the motto of their unity.

That our assessment of the "March Association" was correct was not only confirmed by its later "development". The Heidelberg "People's League", the Breslau "Democratic Association", the Jena "Democratic Association", etc., all rejected its importunate offers of love with scorn, and those members of the extreme Left who had joined it confirmed our criticism of December 29, 1848, by announcing their resignation on April 20, 1849. Vogt, however, in the quiet grandeur of his soul, heaped coals of fire on our heads as can be seen from the following quotation:

"*Neue Rheinische Zeitung, No. 243,* Cologne, March 10, 1849. 'The Frankfurt so-called March Association' of the so-called 'Imperial Assembly' has had the insolence to send *us* the following lithographed letter:

"'The March Association has decided to compile a list of *all newspapers* which *have given us space in their columns* and to distribute it to all associations with which we are connected in order that with the assistance of this association the newspapers indicated will be given preference in being supplied with any relevant *announcements.* In informing you herewith of this list, *we believe it is unnecessary to draw your attention to the importance of the paid announcements of a newspaper* as the chief source of income for the whole enterprise. [...] Frankfurt, end of February 1849.

The Managing Committee
of the Central March Association'

"In the enclosed *list* of newspapers which have given space in their columns to the March Association and to which the supporters of the March Association should give preference in supplying 'relevant announcements', one finds also the *Neue Rheinische Zeitung,* which, *in addition, is given the honour of an asterisk.* We hereby announce [...] that our newspaper has never given space in its columns to the so-called March Association.... If, therefore, the March Association in its lithographed report to those newspapers which have really given it space in their columns designates our newspaper as one of its organs, this is simply calumny against the *Neue Rheinische Zeitung* and absurd boasting on the part of the March Association....

"To the dirty remark of the profit-greedy competition-goaded patriots about the importance of the paid announcements of a newspaper as a *source of income for the whole enterprise,* we, of course, do not reply. The *Neue Rheinische Zeitung* has always differed from the patriots not only generally but also in that it has never regarded political movement as a territory for swindlers or a source of income." [a]

Shortly after this brusque rejection of the source of income proffered by Vogt and Co. the *Neue Rheinische Zeitung* was tearfully held up as a model of "true German disunity" at a meeting of the Central Commercial Association. [b] At the conclusion of our reply to this Jeremiad (*Neue Rheinische Zeitung*, No. 248) Vogt is described as a "provincial academic beer-blusterer and an *unsuccessful Imperial Barrot*". [c] True, at that time (March 15), he had not yet compromised himself on the question of the Emperor. But we had made our minds up once and for all about Herr Vogt and could therefore regard his future treason as a foregone conclusion, even before it was clear to Vogt himself.

From then on, incidentally, we abandoned Vogt and Co. to the attentions of the young *Schlöffel,* who was both brave and intelligent. He had arrived in Frankfurt from Hungary early in March after which he kept us informed of all the storms in the Imperial frog-pond.

Vogt, meanwhile, had sunk so low—he himself had of course done more to bring this about than the *Neue Rheinische Zeitung*— that even *Bassermann* could venture to brand him an *"apostate and renegade"* in the session of April 25, 1849. [d]

F. Engels, one of the editors of the *Neue Rheinische Zeitung,* was forced to flee because of the part he played in the Elberfeld uprising, [97] and I myself was driven out of Prussia shortly afterwards, after repeated efforts to silence me through legal proceedings had failed thanks to the jury, and after the *Neue Preussische Zeitung,* the organ of the coup d'état Ministry, [98] had repeatedly denounced the "Chimborazo insolence [e] of the *Neue Rheinische Zeitung,* compared to which the *Moniteur* of 1793

---

[a] Karl Marx, "The March Association" (see present edition, Vol. 9, pp. 36-37).— *Ed.*

[b] Marx puns on *März* (March) and *Kommerz* (commerce).— *Ed.*

[c] Karl Marx, "The Frankfurt March Association and the *Neue Rheinische Zeitung*" (see present edition, Vol. 9, p. 85). The italics were introduced by Marx in *Herr Vogt.—Ed.*

[d] *Stenographischer Bericht...,* Bd. 8, S. 6303.— *Ed.*

[e] The Chimborazo is a peak of the Andes. "Chimborazo insolence" means "monumental insolence".— *Ed.*

seemed rather pale" (see the *Neue Rheinische Zeitung,* No. 299).[a] Such "Chimborazo insolence" was highly appropriate in a Prussian fortress-town and at a time when the victorious counter-revolution sought to intimidate people by means of unashamed brutality.

On May 19, 1849 the last number of the *Neue Rheinische Zeitung* (the Red Number) appeared. As long as the *Neue Rheinische Zeitung* existed, Vogt had endured in silence. If a parliamentarian did lodge a complaint, he did so in all modesty. For example:

"Sir, the *sharp criticism* in your newspaper is valued by me no less because *it observes all parties and all persons with equal strictness*" (see No. 219 [supplement], February 11, 1849, *Wesendonck's* complaint).[b]

A week after the demise of the *Neue Rheinische Zeitung,* Vogt, operating under the mantle of parliamentary immunity, finally thought he could seize his long-awaited opportunity to convert the "matter" he had accumulated deep in his heart into "energy".[99] The position was that one of the editors of the *Neue Rheinische Zeitung, Wilhelm Wolff,* had replaced a retired Silesian deputy[c] in the Frankfurt Assembly, which was "in the process of dissolution" at the time.[100]

In order to understand the following scene in the parliamentary session of May 26, 1849, it must be borne in mind that the uprising in Dresden and the local movements in the Rhine Province had already been crushed. The Empire was about to intervene in Baden and the Palatinate, the main Russian army was marching on Hungary and, finally, the Imperial Ministry had simply quashed resolutions approved by the Assembly. On the agenda were two "Proclamations to the German Nation", the first edited by Uhland and emanating from the majority, the other stemming from the Committee of Thirty,[101] whose members belonged to the Centre. Presiding over the Assembly was *Reh* from Darmstadt who later turned into a rabbit[d] and "detached" himself from the Assembly, which was "in complete disarray". I quote from the official stenographic report, Nos. 229, 228. Session in St. Paul's Church.[e]

Wolff from Breslau: "Gentlemen, I have registered my opposition to the Proclamation to the Nation, the proclamation that was composed by the majority

---

[a] Karl Marx, "The *Kreuz-Zeitung*" (see present edition, Vol. 9, p. 437).— *Ed.*
[b] Hugo Wesendonck, "Erklärung. Düsseldorf, 8. Februar 1849".— *Ed.*
[c] Gustav Adolf Stenzel.— *Ed.*
[d] Marx plays on the surname *Reh,* a homonym of *Reh* (roe deer).— *Ed.*
[e] *Stenographischer Bericht...,* Bd. 9, S. 6749.— *Ed.*

and that has been read aloud here, because I think it utterly inadequate to the needs of the present time. I find it altogether too feeble. It is good enough to appear as an article in the newspapers which represent the party that has devised it, but it is not good enough for a Proclamation to the German Nation. Since a second Proclamation has now been read out I may remark in passing that I would be even more strongly opposed to it than to the first one, for reasons that I do not need to enter into here." (A voice from the Centre: "Why not?") "I am speaking solely of the majority Proclamation. It is true that it is couched in such moderate terms that even Herr Buss had little to say against it, and that is without doubt the worst recommendation for any proclamation. No, gentlemen, if you wish to have any influence on the people at all you should not address it in the manner adopted in this Proclamation. You must not speak about legality, the legal basis, etc., but of illegality just like the governments, like the *Russians*—and by Russians I understand the Prussians, Austrians, Bavarians and Hanoverians." (Commotion and laughter.) "All these have been subsumed under the name *Russians*." (Loud laughter.) "Yes, gentlemen, the *Russians* are represented in this Chamber too. You must tell them: 'In the same way as you adopt the legal standpoint, so do we.' This is the standpoint of force, and in parenthesis you ought to explain legality by saying that you will oppose the Russian cannon with force, with well-organised storming-parties. *If any* proclamation is to be issued, issue one which begins by *outlawing the first traitor to the people, the Imperial Regent*." [a] (Interruption: "Order!"—Lively applause from the gallery.) *"All the Ministers likewise."* (Renewed commotion.) "Oh, I shall not let myself be intimidated: *he is the first traitor to the people.*"

President: "I think that Herr Wolff has ignored and offended against every propriety. He cannot describe the *Archducal Imperial Regent* as a *traitor to the people in this House* and I must therefore call him to order. I must also request the galleries for the last time not to intervene further in the debate."

Wolff: "For my part, I accept the call to order and declare that it was my *intention* to transgress the bounds of order and to state *that he and his Ministers are traitors*." (From all sides of the House: "Order. This is scandalous.")

President: "I must ask you to be seated."

Wolff: "Very well, *I protest*. I wanted to speak here in the *name of the people* and to say what the *people is thinking*. I protest against every proclamation framed in these terms." (Great tumult.)

President: "Gentlemen, will you please allow me to speak for a moment. Gentlemen, the *incident* that has just taken place is, I may say, the *first* there has been *since Parliament has been in session here*." (It was indeed the first and *the only incident* to take place in that Debating Society.) "No speaker has ever before declared that it was his intention to disrupt the *order*, the very *foundations* of this House." (*Schlöffel* had replied to a similar call to order, in the session of April 25: "I accept the call to order, all the more as I hope that *the time will soon come when this Assembly will be called to order in a very different way.*") [b]

"Gentlemen, I deeply regret that Herr Wolff, who has only just become a member of this House, should have made his *début* in this manner" (Reh looks at the matter from a theatrical point of view). "Gentlemen, I have called him to order because he has permitted himself *greatly to affront the respect and consideration that we owe to the person of the Imperial Regent.*"

----

[a] Archduke John.— *Ed.*
[b] *Stenographischer Bericht...*, Bd. 8, S. 6751.— *Ed.*

The debate then proceeded. Hagen and Zachariä made long speeches, the one for and the other against the proclamation of the majority. Finally,

Vogt from Giessen rose from his seat: "Gentlemen, allow me a few words, I shall not weary you. It is perfectly true that this Parliament *is no longer what it was* when it *assembled* last year, gentlemen, and we *thank Heaven*" (our Vogt of "blind faith" [a] thanks Heaven) "that *it is become so*" (*is become*, indeed! [b]) "and that those who lost faith in the people and who betrayed the cause of the people at the decisive moment, have now left this Assembly! Gentlemen, I *have asked permission to speak*" (so the thanksgiving we have just heard was just humbug), "in order to defend the *crystal-clear stream*" (defence of a stream) "that flowed from the poet's soul" (Vogt is becoming soulful) "into this proclamation against the *unworthy filth* that has been thrown into it *or* hurled at it" (but the stream had already been absorbed by the proclamation), "to defend these *words*" (as with everything that Vogt touches, the stream has been changed into *words*) "against the *muck* that has been heaped up in this latest movement and which threatens to engulf and besmirch everything. Yes, gentlemen! That" (namely the muck) "is muck *and* filth" (the muck is filth!) "which is being thrown in *this way*" (in what way?) "*at everything pure that can be imagined*, and I wish to express my *deep indignation*" (Vogt in deep indignation, *quel tableau!* [c]) "at the fact that *this sort of thing*" (what sort of thing?) "could have happened." [d]

And his very speech is—muck. [e]

Wolff had not said a single word about *Uhland's editing* of the proclamation. As the President repeatedly declared, he had been called to order, he had conjured up the whole storm, because *he* had declared that the *Imperial Regent and all his Ministers were traitors to the people* and had called on Parliament to do likewise. But for Vogt the "Archducal Imperial Regent", the "worn-out Habsburg" (*Vogt's Studien*, p. 28) and *"all his Ministers"* represent *"everything pure that can be imagined"*. With Walther von der Vogelweide he sang:

> "des fürsten milte ûz ôsterrîche
> fröit dem süezen rëgen gelîche
> beidiu liute und ouch daz lant." [f]

---

[a] Vogt of "blind faith" (*der "Köhlergläubige" Vogt*)—an ironical allusion to Vogt's book *Köhlerglaube und Wissenschaft...*, Giessen, 1855.— *Ed.*

[b] Marx ridicules the ungrammatical verb form used by Vogt: *geworden wird.— Ed.*

[c] What a sight!— *Ed.*

[d] *Stenographischer Bericht...*, Bd. 9, S. 6751.— *Ed.*

[e] Variation on a verse from Ludwig Uhland's "Des Sängers Fluch": "Und was er spricht, ist Geissel" ("His very speech is a whiplash").— *Ed.*

[f] "The Prince of Austria's generosity,
Like gentle rain, bestows felicity
Both on the people and on the land."— *Ed.*

Did Vogt already, even at that time, enjoy the "scientific relationship" with Archduke John that he later confessed to? (See Documents in the "Magnum Opus", p. 25.)

Ten years later the same Vogt declared in the *Studien* (pp. 27[-28]):

"So much at least is certain: the National Assembly in France and its leaders at the time underestimated the abilities of Louis Napoleon just as the leaders of the Frankfurt National Assembly underestimated *those of Archduke John*, and both the old foxes *made their respective detractors pay dearly for their mistake.* We are far from wanting to equate the two men. The terrible ruthlessness, etc., etc." (of Louis Bonaparte).— "All this makes him cut a far superior figure to the old and worn-out Habsburg." [a]

During the very same session *Wolff* challenged *Vogt* to a duel with pistols—a challenge which was transmitted by deputy Würth from Sigmaringen—and when the aforesaid Vogt preferred to preserve his skin intact for the Empire,* he threatened to thrash him. On leaving St. Paul's Church, however, *Wolff* discovered Charles the Bold flanked by two ladies, and bursting into laughter he left him to his fate. Although he is a wolf, with a wolf's heart and teeth, Wolff is a lamb when he sees the fair sex. His only, really quite innocuous, revenge was an article in the *Neue Rheinische Zeitung. Revue* (April issue, 1850, p. 73) entitled "*Nachträgliches aus dem Reich*" in which he wrote about the Ex-Imperial Regent as follows:

"In these critical days the Central March people have been extremely industrious. Before withdrawing from Frankfurt they had published an address to the various March associations and to the German people: 'Fellow-citizens! The eleventh hour has struck!' In order to assemble a people's army they issued a new proclamation 'to the German nation' from Stuttgart, and lo and behold! the hand on the Central March clock had stood still, or like the clock on Freiburg Minster, had lost the number XII. However that might be, this proclamation too began with the words: 'Fellow-citizens! The eleventh hour has struck!' Oh if only it had struck earlier, and had pierced your heads, at least at the time when *Karl Vogt*, the Central March hero, was pacifying the Franconian revolution [102] in Nuremberg to his own satisfaction and to the satisfaction of the wailers who were fêting him **....

---

* In the pamphlet by Jacobus Venedey already referred to, Kobes I tells the following story: "In the same session in which Gagern embraced Gabriel Riesser after the latter's speech on the Emperor, ... Karl Vogt embraced Zimmermann in St. Paul's Church with mock pathos and noisy exclamations, and so I called out to him: 'Stop these roguish pranks.' Vogt thought it expedient to reply in provocative and abusive terms and when I challenged him personally, he had the courage, after a friend had made a number of journeys between the two of us, to withdraw his insult" (loc. cit., pp. 21, 22).

** Vogt later justified his valiant deeds in Nuremberg with the words: "He had been given no guarantees for his own personal safety."

---

[a] Carl Vogt, *Studien zur gegenwärtigen Lage Europas*, S. 27-28. Marx's italics.— *Ed.*

The Regency set up its offices in the government building in Freiburg. The Regent *Karl Vogt*, who was also Foreign Minister and the incumbent of many other Ministries, once more took the well-being of the German people[a] very much to heart. Having studied their problems in long days and nights he came up with a very timely invention, that of '*Imperial Regency passports*'. These passports were simple, beautifully lithographed and could be obtained gratis by anyone whose heart desired one. They only had the one small defect of being recognised as valid only in Vogt's Chancellery. It is possible that later on one or other of them will find its way into an Englishman's collection of curios."[b]

Wolff did not follow Greiner's example. Instead of "departing at once for America" as soon as the *Revue* "had appeared", he remained for a year in Switzerland, awaiting the revenge of the Land-Vogt.

---

[a] Wolff has: "of the German Empire".— *Ed.*
[b] *Neue Rheinische Zeitung. Politisch-ökonomische Revue,* IV. Heft, April 1850, S. 75, 76.— *Ed.*

VII

THE AUGSBURG CAMPAIGN

Shortly after the citizen of the Canton of Thurgau [103] had concluded his Italian war, the citizen of the Canton of Berne[a] launched his Augsburg campaign.

"There" (in London) "it was *the Marx clique* that had *always* supplied the greater part of the reports" (of the *Allgemeine Zeitung*), "and *ever since 1849 its relations with the 'Allgemeine Zeitung' had been continuous*" ("Magnum Opus", p. 194).[b]

Although Marx has only been living in London since the end of 1849,[c] i.e. since he was expelled from France for the second time, the "Marx clique" appears to have lived in London *always*, and although the Marx clique has "*always* supplied **the greater part of the reports** of the *Allgemeine Zeitung*", "its relations" with the *Allgemeine Zeitung* have only been "*continuous* ever since 1849". At all events, Vogt's chronology is divided—and this is not to be wondered at since before 1848 the man "had not yet contemplated any political activity" (loc. cit., p. 225)—into two great periods, viz., the period "*always*" up to 1849, and the period from 1849 up to "this" year.

Between 1842 and 1843 I edited the old *Rheinische Zeitung*, which waged a life-and-death war with the *Allgemeine Zeitung*. From 1848 to 1849 the *Neue Rheinische Zeitung* revived the polemic. What remains, then, of the period "*always up to 1849*"

---

[a] i.e. Vogt. See his *Studien zur gegenwärtigen Lage Europas*, S. 6.— *Ed.*

[b] Carl Vogt, *Mein Prozess...*, S. 194. The words "the Marx clique" were italicised by Vogt, the rest of the italics are Marx's.— *Ed.*

[c] Marx arrived in London about August 26, 1849.— *Ed.*

apart from the fact that Marx had fought against the *Allgemeine Zeitung "always"*, while Vogt had been its "constant collaborator" from 1844 to 1847? (See "Magnum Opus", p. 225.)

Now for the second period of world history *à la* Vogt.

The reason why I maintained "continuous relations with the *Allgemeine Zeitung*" from London, "*continuous ever since* **1849**", is that "*from* **1852**" a certain *Ohly* had been chief London correspondent of the *Allgemeine Zeitung*. It is true that Ohly had *no* relations whatever with me, either before or after 1852. I have *never* seen him in my life. Inasmuch as he played any part among the London refugees it was as a member of Kinkel's *Emigration Association*. But this has no bearing on the case, for,

"The former oracle of Altenhöfer, that old Bavarian who had learnt English, was my" (Vogt's) "*fellow-countryman, the blond Ohly,* who having started out as a communist, *strove to attain a loftier poetic standpoint in politics and literature.* At first in Zurich, but from 1852 in London, he was the chief correspondent of the *Allgemeine Zeitung* until he ended his days in a madhouse." ("Magnum Opus", p. 195.)

Edouard Simon, the police spy, has Frenchified this Vogtiad as follows:

"En voici d'abord un qui de son point de départ communiste, avait cherché à s'élever aux plus hautes conceptions de la politique." ("Loftier poetic standpoint in *politics*" was beyond the genius even of an Edouard Simon.) "A en croire M. Vogt, cet adepte fut l'oracle de la Gazette d'Augsbourg jusqu'en 1852, époque où il mourut dans une maison de fous"[a] (*Revue contemporaine*, Vol. XIII, Paris, 1860, p. 529).

"*Operam et oleum perdidi,*"[b] Vogt may well say of his "Magnum Opus" and his *Ohly*. Whereas he makes his "fellow-countryman" the London correspondent of the *Allgemeine Zeitung from 1852*, until he "ends his days in a madhouse", Edouard Simon says that "if we may believe Vogt, Ohly had been the oracle of the *Allgemeine Zeitung up to 1852* when he" (who, it will be noted, is still alive) "*died* in a madhouse". But Edouard Simon knows his Karl Vogt. Edouard knows that once one has resolved to "believe" Karl, it is quite irrelevant *what* one believes, whether it is what he says, or the opposite of what he says.

"*Herr Liebknecht,*" says Karl Vogt, "replaced him" (namely *Ohly*) "as correspondent of the *Allgemeine Zeitung.*" "Only after Liebknecht had been openly *proclaimed*

---

[a] "This is a man who, having started out as a communist, strove to raise himself to the loftier conceptions of politics. If we may believe Herr Vogt, this adept was the oracle of the Augsburg Gazette up to 1852 when he died in a madhouse."— *Ed.*

[b] "I have wasted oil and labour", Plautus, *Poenulus,* Act I, Scene 2, where it is spoken by a whore whose efforts to repair the ravages of time have proved vain. *Oleum* is a pun on Ohly.— *Ed.*

a member of the *Marx party*,[a] was he accepted as a correspondent by the *Allgemeine Zeitung*" (loc. cit., p. 169).

That proclamation was made during the Cologne communist trial, i.e. at the *end* of 1852.

In fact in the spring of 1851 Liebknecht became a contributor to the *Morgenblatt* where he reported on the Great Exhibition in London.[104] Through the mediation of the *Morgenblatt* he was made correspondent of the *Allgemeine Zeitung* in *September 1855*.

"His" (Marx's) "comrades do not write a single line of which Marx *has not been previously informed*" (loc. cit., p. 194).

The proof is simple: "He" (Marx) "has absolute control over his people" (p. 195) whereas Vogt is absolutely obedient to his Fazy and Co. We are confronted here by a peculiarity of Vogt's myth-making. The pygmy standards of Giessen or Geneva, the small-town framework and the fug of Swiss taverns are everywhere. Naively translating the leisurely provincial cliquism of Geneva to one of the great cities of the world, London, he will not allow Liebknecht to write "a single line" in the West End of which I "have not been previously informed" four miles away in Hampstead. And I perform the identical services of a La Guéronnière[b] every day for a whole host of "comrades" scattered all over London and writing their reports to the four corners of the globe. A delightful profession—and a profitable one!

With the unmistakable delicacy of the artist, Vogt's mentor, Edouard Simon, who does not know London, but is at least familiar with conditions in Paris, provides the account of his uncouth "friend from the country" with the veneer of the big city:

"Marx, comme chef de la société, ne tient pas lui-même la plume, mais ses fidèles n'écrivent pas une ligne sans l'avoir consulté: *La Gazette d'Augsbourg* sera d'autant mieux servie" (loc. cit., p. 529). That is to say, "Marx as head of the society *does not write himself*, but his trusted associates do not write a single line without first consulting him. In this way the *Augsburger Zeitung* is the better served."

Does Vogt appreciate all the subtlety of this correction?

I had as much to do with Liebknecht's reports to the *Allgemeine Zeitung* from London as I had with Vogt's reports to the *Allgemeine Zeitung* from Paris. Moreover, Liebknecht's reports were praiseworthy in every respect—a critical presentation of *English* politics, which he described in exactly the same way in the

---

[a] Vogt has: "of Marx's society".— *Ed.*

[b] La Guéronnière was Chief Censor during the Second Empire in France.— *Ed.*

Allgemeine Zeitung as in his reports for the radical German-American newspapers written at the same time. Vogt himself, who has anxiously searched through whole years of the *Allgemeine Zeitung* in the hope of discovering something detrimental in Liebknecht's letters, confines his critique of their contents to stating that the symbol used by Liebknecht to indicate his authorship consisted of *"two thin slanting lines"* ("Magnum Opus", p. 196).

The fact that the lines were on a slant showed of course that the reports themselves were not quite straight. But even worse, they were *"thin"*! If only Liebknecht had chosen instead of two "thin lines", two round blobs of grease for his reports! But even if there is nothing reprehensible about his reports apart from these "two thin slanting lines", there is still the objection that they were printed at all in the *Allgemeine Zeitung*. And why should they not? It is a known fact that the *Allgemeine Zeitung* allows the most widely divergent views to be expressed in its columns, at least on such neutral topics as that of English politics, and in addition it is the only German paper with a more than local significance in the eyes of the world. Liebknecht could without hesitation dispatch his London letters to the very newspaper for which *Heine* wrote his "Paris Letters" and *Fallmerayer* his "Oriental Letters".[105] Vogt reports that lewd persons also wrote for the *Allgemeine Zeitung*. It is well known that he himself was a contributor from 1844 to 1847.

As far as *Frederick Engels* and myself are concerned—I mention Engels because we work to a common plan and after prior agreement—it is true that in 1859 we did enter into a "relationship" of a sort with the *Allgemeine Zeitung*. That is to say during January, February and March 1859 I published a series of leading articles in the *New-York Tribune* in which *inter alia* the theory advanced by the *Allgemeine Zeitung* about a "Central European great power" and that paper's claim that it was in the *Germans' interest* to maintain Austria's rule in Italy were subjected to searching criticism. Shortly before the outbreak of war, and with my agreement, *Engels* published *Po and Rhine*, Berlin, 1859,[a] a pamphlet directed specifically against the *Allgemeine Zeitung*. To quote Engels' own words (from his pamphlet *Savoy, Nice and the Rhine*, Berlin, 1860, p. 4) it provided scientific military proof that "Germany does not need any part of Italy for its defence and that

---

[a] Karl Marx, "The War Prospect in Prussia", and Frederick Engels, *Po and Rhine* (see present edition, Vol. 16).—*Ed.*

France, if only military considerations counted, would certainly have much stronger claims to the Rhine than Germany to the Mincio".[a] This polemic against the *Allgemeine Zeitung* and its theory of the necessity of Austrian despotic rule in Italy went hand in hand with a polemic directed against *Bonapartist* propaganda. For instance, I argued in detail in the *Tribune* (see e.g. February 1859) that the financial and internal political problems of the *"bas empire"* [106] had reached a critical point and that only a foreign war could prolong the rule of the coup d'état in France and hence the counter-revolution in Europe.[b] I demonstrated that the *Bonapartist* liberation of Italy was a mere pretext to keep France in subjection, to subject Italy to the rule of the coup d'état, to shift France's "natural frontiers" to Germany, to transform Austria into a tool of Russia and to force the nations into a war waged by the legitimate counter-revolution against the illegitimate counter-revolution. All this took place before the ex-Regent of the Empire, Karl Vogt, issued his clarion call from Geneva.

Ever since Wolff's article in the *Neue Rheinische Zeitung. Revue* (1850),[c] I had completely forgotten the "well-rounded character". I was reminded of the merry fellow once more in the spring of 1859, on an evening in April, when Freiligrath gave me a letter of Vogt's to read together with an accompanying political *"Programme"*.[107] This was no act of indiscretion since Vogt's circular was intended "for communication" to the friends not of Vogt, but of the addressee.

Asked what I found in the "Programme", I replied: "Political hot air." I could see at once that the old joker had not changed, from his request to Freiligrath to persuade Herr *Bucher* to become political correspondent for the propaganda sheet to be published in Geneva.[d] Vogt's letter was dated April 1, 1859. It was well known that in the reports he sent from London to the Berlin *National-Zeitung* since January 1859, Bucher advocated views directly antithetical to those in Vogt's Programme. But all cats are grey to the man of "critical immediacy".

After this incident which I did not think of sufficient importance to mention to anyone, I received a copy of Vogt's *Studien*

---

[a] See present edition, Vol. 16, p. 572.— *Ed.*

[b] See "The Money Panic in Europe", *New-York Daily Tribune*, No. 5548, February 1, 1859 (present edition, Vol. 16).— *Ed.*

[c] Wilhelm Wolff, "Nachträgliches aus dem Reich...", *Neue Rheinische Zeitung. Politisch-ökonomische Revue*, Heft 4, April 1850.— *Ed.*

[d] Presumably *Die Neue Schweiz.— Ed.*

zur gegenwärtigen Lage Europas, a woeful document which left
me in no doubt about his connection with Bonapartist propaganda.

On the evening of May 9, 1859 I found myself on the platform
at a public meeting arranged by David Urquhart because of the
Italian war. Before the meeting had got under way I saw a solemn
figure approaching me portentously. From the Hamlet-like
expression on his countenance I realised at once that "something
was rotten in the state of Denmark".[a] It was the *homme d'état, Karl
Blind.* After a few preliminaries he began to talk about Vogt's
"intrigues" and he assured me with much shaking of the head
that Vogt was in receipt of Bonapartist subsidies for his
propaganda, that a South German writer, whose name he could
"unfortunately" not reveal, had been offered 30,000 guilders as a
bribe by Vogt—I was in some doubt as to which South German
writer could possibly be worth 30,000 guilders—that there had
been attempts at bribery in London, that as early as 1858 there
had been a meeting between Plon-Plon, Fazy & Co. in Geneva
where the Italian war had been discussed and the Grand Duke
Constantine of Russia had been named as the future King of
Hungary, that Vogt had also tried to enlist him (Blind) for his
propaganda, and that he had *proofs* of Vogt's treasonable intrigues
against his country. Blind then withdrew to his seat at the other
corner of the platform next to his friend J. Fröbel; the meeting
began and in a detailed report[b] D. Urquhart tried to present the
Italian war as the fruit of Franco-Russian intrigue.*

---

* Vogt naturally connects the attacks on *Lord Palmerston* by the Marx clique with
my hostility to this self-important personage and his "friends" ("Magnum Opus",
p. 212). It would appear, then, that this is a suitable place to comment briefly on
my relations with D. Urquhart and his party. Urquhart's writings on Russia and
against Palmerston had interested but not convinced me. In order to arrive at a
firm view I undertook the laborious analysis of *Hansard's Parliamentary Debates* and
the diplomatic Blue Books from 1807 to 1850. The first fruits of these studies were
a series of leading articles in the *New-York Tribune* (end of 1853) in which I
demonstrated Palmerston's involvement with the St. Petersburg Cabinet on the
basis of his transactions with Poland, Turkey, Circassia, etc. Shortly afterwards I
had these articles reprinted in *The People's Paper,* the organ of the Chartists edited
by Ernest Jones, together with additional passages about Palmerston's activities.[108]
In the meantime, *The Glasgow Sentinel* had also reprinted one of the articles
("*Palmerston and Poland*"),   which attracted the attention of Mr. D. Urquhart.
After a meeting with me he persuaded Mr. Tucker in London to bring out some of

---

   [a] Shakespeare, *Hamlet,* Act I, Scene 4.— *Ed.*
   [b] David Urquhart's report was discussed in the article "Mr. Urquhart's Address
on Neutrality" in *The Free Press,* No. 5, May 27, 1859.— *Ed.*

Towards the end of the meeting *Dr. Faucher*, foreign-news editor of *The Morning Star* (the organ of the Manchester School[111]), came up to me to tell me that a new London German weekly, *Das Volk*, had just appeared. *Die Neue Zeit*, a workers' paper published by Herr *A. Scherzer* and edited by *Edgar Bauer*, had just folded up as the result of an intrigue by *Kinkel*, the publisher of the *Hermann*. Hearing this news, *Biscamp*, who had been a reporter for *Die Neue Zeit* up to that time, gave up his teaching post in the South of England in order to go to London and set up *Das Volk* in opposition to the *Hermann*. The German Workers' Educational Society and other London societies supported the newspaper, which like all such workers' newspapers was naturally edited and written gratis. Although as a free-trader[b] he, Faucher, did not agree with the general policy of *Das Volk*, he was opposed to there being a monopoly in the German press in London and therefore, together with some London acquaintances, he had set up a Finance Committee in support of the paper. Biscamp had already written to Liebknecht, whom he had not yet met, with a request for literary contributions, etc. Finally, Faucher asked me to join in the venture.

Although Biscamp had been living in England since 1852, we had not yet made each other's acquaintance. The day after the Urquhart meeting Liebknecht brought him to my home. From lack of time I could not accept the invitation to write for *Das Volk* for the moment, but I promised to ask my German friends in

the articles in pamphlet form. These Palmerston pamphlets were later sold in various editions in numbers ranging from 15,000 to 20,000. Following my analysis of the Blue Book on the fall of Kars—it was published in the London organ of the Chartists in April 1856[a]—I received a letter of thanks from the Sheffield Foreign Affairs Committee.[109] (See Appendix 7.) While looking through the diplomatic manuscripts in the possession of the British Museum I came across a series of English documents, going back from the end of the eighteenth century to the time of Peter the Great, which reveal the continuous secret collaboration between the Cabinets of London and St. Petersburg, and seem to indicate that this relationship arose at the time of Peter the Great. Up to now, all I have published of a detailed investigation into the subject has been an introduction with the title *Revelations of the Diplomatic History of the 18th Century*. This appeared first in the Sheffield and subsequently in the London *Free Press*,[110] both published by Urquhart. The last-named has received occasional contributions from me since its foundation. My interest in Palmerston and British-Russian diplomatic relations in general arose, as one can see, without my having had the slightest suspicion that the figure of Herr Karl Vogt was standing behind that of Lord Palmerston.

---

[a] "The Fall of Kars", *The People's Paper*, Nos. 205-08, April 5, 12, 19 and 26 (see present edition, Vol. 14).— *Ed.*

[b] Marx uses the English term.— *Ed.*

England for subscriptions, financial donations and literary contributions. In the course of the conversation we came to speak of the Urquhart meeting and this led on to Vogt, whose *Studien* Biscamp had already read and correctly evaluated. I told him and Liebknecht of the contents of Vogt's "Programme" and also of Blind's revelations, adding, however, with respect to the latter, that South Germans were inclined to paint in rather exaggerated colours. To my surprise, No. 2 of *Das Volk* (May 14) printed an article with the title "Der Reichsregent als Reichsverräther" [The Imperial Regent as Imperial Traitor][a] (see "Magnum Opus", Documents, pp. 17, 18) in which Biscamp mentioned two of the facts reported by Blind—the 30,000 guilders, which, however, he reduced to 4,000, and the Bonapartist sources of Vogt's funds. For the rest his article consisted of witticisms in the manner of *Die Hornisse*, which he had edited in Cassel with *Heise* in 1848-49. In the meantime, as I learned long after the appearance of the "Magnum Opus" (see Appendix 8), the London Workers' Educational Society had commissioned Herr Scherzer, one of its leaders, to invite the workers' educational associations in Switzerland, Belgium and the United States to support *Das Volk* and to combat Bonapartist propaganda. Biscamp himself sent a copy of the above-mentioned article published in *Das Volk* on May 14, 1859 to Vogt, who simultaneously received Herr A. Scherzer's circular from his own Ranickel.

With his familiar "critical immediacy" Vogt at once cast me in the role of the demiurge behind these attempts to ensnare him. Without hesitation he at once published an *outline* of his later travesty of history[b] in the oft-quoted "*special supplement to No. 150 of the 'Schweizer Handels-Courier'*". This original gospel which first revealed the mysteries of the Brimstone Gang, the Bristlers, Cherval, etc., beneath the date Berne, May 23, 1859 (and hence more recently than the gospel according to the Mormons[112]), bore the title **Zur Warnung**[c] and its content corresponds to that of a piece translated from a pamphlet[113] by the notorious E. About.*

---

* A word about the Biel *Commis voyageur*, the local *Moniteur* of the "fugitive Imperial Regent". The publisher and editor of the Biel *Handels-Courier* is a

[a] This refers to the anonymous article "Der Reichsregent". One of the paragraphs in it begins with the words "Der Reichsregent als Reichsverräther!"—*Ed.*

[b] See Johann Fischart, *Affentheurliche, Naupengeheurliche Geschichtklitterung....*—*Ed.*

[c] Carl Vogt, "Zur Warnung", *Schweizer Handels-Courier*, No. 150 (special supplement), June 2, 1859; see also *Mein Prozess...*, Dokumente, S. 31-33.—*Ed.*

Vogt's anonymous original gospel *Zur Warnung* was reprinted, as I have already remarked, in *Das Volk*[a] at my request.

In the beginning of June I left London to visit Engels in Manchester, where a subscription of about £25 was collected for *Das Volk*. This contribution, whose "nature" induced the "curious" Vogt to cast his "eyes across the Channel" towards Augsburg and Vienna ("Magnum Opus", p. 212), came from Frederick Engels, Wilhelm Wolff, myself and finally three German physicians[b] resident in Manchester, whose names are recorded in one of the legal documents I sent to Berlin. As to the money collected in London by the original Finance Committee, Vogt should consult Dr. Faucher.

Vogt informs us on p. 225 of the "Magnum Opus":

> "But it has always been a *device* of the *reactionaries* to require the democrats to do everything *for nothing* while *they*" (that is the reactionaries, not the democrats) "*claim* the right to demand payment and to be paid."

What a *reactionary* device on the part of *Das Volk*, which is not only edited and written for nothing but *even induces* those who work on it to *pay*! If that is not proof of the connection between *Das Volk* and the reaction, then Karl Vogt is at his wit's end.

During my stay in Manchester an event of decisive importance took place in London. Liebknecht discovered in the compositor's room of Hollinger (*who printed "Das Volk"*) the proof-sheet of the anonymous pamphlet against Vogt entitled *Zur Warnung*. He read it through cursorily, immediately recognised Blind's revelations and to crown it all learnt from *A. Vögele*, the compositor, that *Blind* had given the manuscript, which was in his handwriting, to Hollinger for printing. The corrections on the proof-sheet were also in *Blind*'s handwriting. Two days later Hollinger sent Liebknecht the proof-sheet, which he in turn sent to the *Allgemeine Zeitung*. The type for the pamphlet survived and was used later for a reprint in *Das Volk*, No. 7 (June 18, 1859).[c]

With the publication of the "*warning*" by the *Allgemeine Zeitung*[d]

---

certain Ernst Schüler, a political refugee of 1838, a postmaster, wine merchant, bankrupt and at present solvent once more thanks to the fact that his newspaper, which was subsidised by British, French and Swiss advertisements during the Crimean war, now numbers 1,200 subscribers.

[a] No. 6, June 11, 1859.— *Ed.*

[b] Louis Borchardt, Eduard Gumpert and Martin Heckscher.— *Ed.*

[c] In the article "Warnung zur gefälligen Verbreitung".— *Ed.*

[d] "K. Vogt und die deutsche Emigration in London", *Allgemeine Zeitung*, No. 173, June 22, 1859.— *Ed.*

begins the Augsburg campaign of the ex-Vogt of the Empire. He sued the *Allgemeine Zeitung* for reprinting the pamphlet.

In the "Magnum Opus" (pp. 227-28) Vogt travesties Müllner's "'Tis me, 'tis me; I am the robber Jaromir".[114] He merely translates "to be" into "to have".

> "*I have sued* because I knew all along that the shallowness, futility and baseness of the editorial board which parades as the 'representative of High German culture', would be forced into the open. *I have sued* because I knew all along that the connection of its esteemed editors and the Austrian policies they have been exalting to the heavens with the Brimstone Gang and the dregs of the revolution, could not remain hidden from the public."

And so on through another four "*I have sued*'s". The suing Vogt becomes quite sublime,[a] or Longinus is right when he says that there is nothing in the world that is drier than a man with dropsy.[b]

> "Personal considerations," the "well-rounded character" declares, "were the least of my motives when I went for the law."

In reality matters stood quite differently. No calf could show greater reluctance to go to the slaughter than Karl Vogt to go to court. While his "close" friends, the Ranickel, Reinach (formerly a peripatetic *chronique scandaleuse* about Vogt) and the garrulous Mayer from Esslingen, a member of the Rump Parliament, confirmed him in his terror of the court, he was bombarded with urgent requests from Zurich to proceed with his "suit". At the Workers' Festival in Lausanne the fur-dealer Roos told him in front of witnesses that he could no longer have any respect for him if he did not take legal proceedings. Nevertheless, Vogt resisted: He did not give a rap for the Augsburg and London Brimstone Gang and would remain silent. Suddenly, however, he spoke. Various newspapers announced the forthcoming trial and the Ranickel declared:

> "*The Stuttgart people would not leave him*" (*Vogt*) "*any peace*. He" (Ranickel) "had not given his approval."

We may note in passing that since the "well-rounded one" found himself in a tight corner, an action against the *Allgemeine Zeitung* was undoubtedly the most promising stratagem. Vogt's self-apologia in response to an attack on him by J. Venedey, who had accused him of Bonapartist intrigues,[115] saw the light in the

---

[a] A pun in the original: *der geklagt habende* (who has sued) and *wird erhaben* (becomes sublime).— *Ed.*

[b] Cassius Longinus, *On the Sublime.*— *Ed.*

Biel "Handels-Courier" of June 16, 1859,[a] and hence arrived in London *after* the appearance of the anonymous pamphlet, which concluded with the threat:

"If, however, *Vogt* attempts to deny these accusations, a thing he will hardly dare, this revelation will be followed by No. 2."[b]

Vogt had now issued a denial and revelation No. 2 did not follow. Secure on this front, mischief could only come from his dear friends, whom he knew well enough to rely on their cowardice. The more he exposed himself in public by resorting to legal action, the more surely he could bank on their discretion, for in the person of the "fugitive Imperial Regent" it was in a way the entire Rump Parliament that was standing in the pillory.

Parliamentarian *Jacob Venedey tells tales* out of school in his *Pro domo und pro patria gegen Karl Vogt,* Hanover, 1860, *pp. 27-28*:

"Apart from the letters produced by Vogt in his own account of his lawsuit, I have read a further letter of Vogt's which reveals, much more clearly than the letter to Dr. Loening,[c] Vogt's position as the accomplice of those who were making strenuous efforts to localise the war in Italy. I have copied out a few passages from this letter for my own information, but unfortunately I cannot publish them because the man to whom the letter was addressed only showed them to me on condition that I would not publish them. *Attempts have been made from personal and party considerations to cover up Vogt's part in this affair which in my view cannot be justified either from a party point of view or in terms of a man's duty to his country. This restraint on the part of many people* explains why Vogt can still have the temerity to present himself as a German party leader. *It appears to me, however, that the party to which Vogt belonged has by this means become in part responsible for his activities."* *

If then his action against the *Allgemeine Zeitung* was not risking all that much, an offensive in that direction provided General Vogt with the most favourable base of operations. It was Austria that was denigrating the Imperial Vogt through the *Allgemeine Zeitung,* and moreover, Austria in league with the communists! Thus the Imperial Vogt appeared as the interesting victim of a

---

* See also p. 4 of the same pamphlet where it is stated: "This practice of 'making allowances' from party considerations, the want of moral principle implied in admitting among themselves that Vogt has been playing a disgraceful game with his own country [...] and then permitting Vogt to sue people for slander when they have only asserted what all know and think and of which they know and even possess the proofs—all this I find quite nauseating, etc."

---

[a] Carl Vogt, "Erklärung", *Schweizer Handels-Courier,* No. 162 (special supplement). Vogt's statement was dated Geneva, June 10, 1859. He also included it in his *Mein Prozess...,* Dokumente, S. 20-25.—*Ed.*

[b] "Warnung zur gefälligen Verbreitung", *Das Volk,* No. 7, June 18, 1859.—*Ed.*

[c] Carl Vogt, *Mein Prozess...,* Dokumente, S. 36.—*Ed.*

monstrous coalition of the enemies of bourgeois liberalism. And the "Little Germany" press, which was already prejudiced in the Imperial Vogt's favour, as a diminisher of the Empire,[116] would jubilantly bear him aloft on its shield!

In the beginning of July 1859, shortly after my return from Manchester, Blind paid me a visit in consequence of an incident of no importance in this context. He was accompanied by Fidelio Hollinger and Liebknecht. During this meeting I gave it as my opinion that Blind was the author of the pamphlet *Zur Warnung.* He protested the opposite. I repeated what he had told me on May 9[a] point by point, for in fact his assertions then constituted the entire contents of the pamphlet. He admitted all that but nevertheless insisted that he was not the author of the pamphlet.

About a month later, in August 1859, Liebknecht showed me a letter he had received from the editors of the *Allgemeine Zeitung* who urgently asked him for proof of the allegations made in the pamphlet *Zur Warnung.* At his request I agreed to go with him to Blind's home in St. John's Wood, for even if Blind was not the *author,* he at any rate had known as early as the beginning of May what the pamphlet did not reveal to the world until the beginning of June, and he could, moreover, *"prove"* what he knew. Blind was not there. He had gone to a seaside resort. Liebknecht, therefore, wrote to him explaining the purpose of our visit. No answer. Liebknecht wrote to him a second time.[117] Finally, the following statesman-like document arrived:

"Dear Herr Liebknecht,

"Your two letters, which had been wrongly addressed, arrived almost simultaneously. As you will understand I have absolutely no wish to meddle in the affairs of a newspaper with which I am quite unconnected. All the less in the given case, since, *as I have already stated, I had* **nothing whatever to do** *with the problem in question.* As to *the remarks* you cite *that were made in the course of a private conversation,* it is *obvious that these were completely misinterpreted.* There is evidently a misunderstanding here which I shall discuss with you in due course. I am sorry that your visit to me with Marx was in vain and

"I remain, respectfully yours,

K. Blind

"St. Leonard's, September 8"

This cool diplomatic note according to which *Blind* had **"nothing whatever to do"** with the denunciation of Vogt, reminded me of an article which had appeared anonymously in

---

[a] See this volume, p. 116.— *Ed.*

The Free Press in London on May 27, 1859 and which went as follows[a]:

> "*The Grand Duke Constantine to be King of Hungary*
>
> "A Correspondent, who encloses his card, writes as follows:—
>
> "Sir,—Having been present at the last meeting* in the Music Hall, I heard the statement made concerning the Grand Duke Constantine. I am able to give you another fact: So far back as last summer, Prince Jérôme-Napoléon detailed to some of his confidants at Geneva a plan of attack against Austria, and prospective rearrangement of the map of Europe. I know the name of a Swiss senator to whom he broached the subject. Prince Jérôme, at that time, declared that, according to the plan made, Grand Duke Constantine was to become King of Hungary.
>
> "I know further of *attempts* made, in the beginning of the present year, to *win over* to the Russo-Napoleonic scheme *some of the exiled German Democrats, as well as some influential Liberals in Germany. Large pecuniary advantages were held out to them as a bribe.*[b] I am glad to say that these offers were rejected with indignation." (See Appendix 9.)

This article—though it does not name Vogt but, as far as the German emigration in London was concerned, unmistakably points to him—does in effect contain the *core* of the pamphlet *Zur Warnung* that appeared later on. The author of the *"future King of Hungary"*, whom patriotic zeal drove to make an anonymous denunciation of Vogt, had of course to grasp the golden opportunity that the Augsburg trial had thrown into his lap, the opportunity to reveal the treachery in a court of law in full view of the whole of Europe. And who was the author of the "future King of Hungary"? *Citizen Karl Blind.* The form and content of the article had already made that obvious to me in May and this was now *officially confirmed* by Mr. Collet, the editor of *The Free Press*, after I had explained to him the importance of the dispute that was pending and after I had shown him Blind's diplomatic note.

On September 17, 1859, Herr *A. Vögele*, the compositor, gave me a written declaration (printed in the "Magnum Opus", Documents, Nos. 30, 31), in which he testifies not that *Blind* was the *author* of the pamphlet *Zur Warnung*, but that he (A. Vögele) and his employer, *Fidelio Hollinger, had set the type for it in the Hollinger print-shop*, that *the manuscript was in Blind's hand* and that *Blind had occasionally been mentioned by Hollinger as the author of the pamphlet.*

---

* This was the meeting held by D. Urquhart on May 9, mentioned above.

---

[a] In the German original the letter is given in Marx's translation. In the present edition the original English text is given, which Marx supplies in Appendix 9.— *Ed.*

[b] Marx quotes this sentence in English in brackets after the German translation. The italics in this paragraph are Marx's.— *Ed.*

Armed with Vögele's declaration and the "future King of Hungary", *Liebknecht* again wrote to *Blind* asking for "proofs" of the denunciations made by that statesman in *The Free Press,* pointing out at the same time that he had now a piece of evidence about *his* involvement in the publication of *Zur Warnung.* Instead of answering *Liebknecht, Blind* sent Mr. Collet to me. Mr. Collet was supposed to ask me in *Blind's name* to make no public use of my knowledge of the authorship of the said article in *The Free Press.* I replied that I could give no such assurance. *My* discretion would keep pace with *Blind's* courage.

In the meantime, the date set down for the hearing of the case in Augsburg was drawing nearer. *Blind* remained silent. *Vogt* had attempted in various public announcements to make *me* as the secret source of it all responsible both for the pamphlet and the *proof* of the facts given in it. To ward off this manoeuvre, to vindicate Liebknecht and to defend the *Allgemeine Zeitung,* which in my view had performed a good deed in denouncing Vogt, I informed the editors of the *Allgemeine Zeitung* via Liebknecht that I was prepared to let them have a document regarding the origin of the pamphlet *Zur Warnung,* if I received a written request from them. That is how the *"lively correspondence came about which is at present carried on by Marx and Herr Kolb"* as Herr Vogt states on p.194 of the "Magnum Opus".* My *"lively correspondence with Herr Kolb"* consisted in two letters from Herr *Orges* to me, both of the same date, in which he asked me for the document I had promised, which I then sent him together with *a few lines* from myself.**

The two letters from Herr *Orges,* which were in reality just a double edition of the same letter, arrived in London on October 18, 1859, while the court proceedings were due to begin in Augsburg on the 24th. I therefore wrote at once to Herr Vögele to arrange a meeting next day in the office at the Marlborough Street Police Court, where he should give his declaration about the pamphlet *Zur Warnung* the legal form of an *affidavit.**** My letter

* It is true that in No. 319 of the *Allgemeine Zeitung,* Herr *Kolb* mentions "a very detailed *letter* from Herr *Marx which he has not printed".* But this "detailed letter" has been *printed* in the Hamburg *Reform,* No. 139, *supplement of November 19, 1859.* The "detailed letter" was a declaration from me intended for *publication,* and I sent it also to the Berlin *Volks-Zeitung.* [See this volume, pp. 4-7.]

** My covering note [see this volume, p. 3] and Vögele's declaration can be found in the "*Magnum Opus*", *Documents,* pp. 30, 31. Herr Orges' letters to me are contained in Appendix 10.

*** An *affidavit* is a statutory declaration given before a court, which, if false, is liable to all the penalties incurred by perjury.

did not reach him in time. Hence, on October 19,* against my original intention, I was compelled to send the above-mentioned written declaration of September 17 instead of the affidavit.**

The court proceedings in Augsburg, as is well known, turned into a true comedy of errors. The *corpus delicti* was the pamphlet *Zur Warnung* sent by W. *Liebknecht* to the *Allgemeine Zeitung* and reprinted by it. The publisher and the author of the pamphlet, however, were involved in a game of blind-man's buff. *Liebknecht* could not compel his witnesses, who were in London, to appear before the court in Augsburg; the editors of the *Allgemeine Zeitung*, embarrassed by this legal impasse, spouted a lot of political gibberish; Dr. Hermann regaled the court with the tall stories of our "well-rounded character" about the Brimstone Gang, the Lausanne Festival, etc.; and the court finally dismissed *Vogt's* suit because the plaintiff had brought the case to the *wrong* court. The confusion reached its climax when the case in Augsburg had been concluded and the report on the proceedings[a] reached London with the *Allgemeine Zeitung. Blind,* who had unswervingly preserved his statesman-like silence up to that moment, suddenly leaped into the public arena scared by the testimony of *Vögele,* the compositor, which had been produced by me. Vögele had *not* declared that Blind *was the author* of the pamphlet, but only that he had been referred to as such by Fidelio Hollinger. However, Vögele did declare categorically that the *manuscript of the pamphlet had been written in Blind's hand, with which he was familiar, and that it had been set and printed in Hollinger's print-shop. Blind* could be the *author* of the pamphlet even if it had neither been written down in Blind's handwriting, nor set up and printed in Hollinger's print-shop. Conversely, the pamphlet could have been *written down* by *Blind* and printed by Hollinger, even though Blind was *not* the author.

In No. 313 of the *Allgemeine Zeitung,* beneath the date London,

---

* Since I write illegibly my letter of October 19 was regarded by the Augsburg Court as dated October 29. Vogt's lawyer, Dr. Hermann, Vogt himself, the dignified *Berlin "National-Zeitung" et hoc genus omne* [and that whole tribe] of "*critical immediacy*" did not doubt at all that a letter written in London on October 29 could arrive in Augsburg by October 24.

** That this quid pro quo was the result of pure chance—namely the belated arrival of my letter to Vögele—can be seen from his subsequent affidavit of February 11, 1860.

---

[a] The report in question, "Prozess Vogt gegen die Redaction der Allgemeinen Zeitung", was published in the *Allgemeine Zeitung,* Nos. 300 and 301, October 27 and 28, 1859.— *Ed.*

November 3 (see "Magnum Opus", Documents, pp. 37, 38), the
citizen and statesman Blind declared that he was *not the author* of
the pamphlet, and as *proof* he was "publishing" the "**following
document**":

"a) I hereby declare that the assertion of the compositor Vögele printed in the
Allgemeine Zeitung, No. 300, to the effect that the pamphlet *Zur Warnung*
mentioned there was *printed in my print-shop* or that Herr *Karl Blind* was its author,
is a *malicious fabrication.*

"3 Litchfield Street, Soho,
London, November 2, 1859

Fidelio Hollinger"

"b) The undersigned, who *has lived and worked* in No. 3 Litchfield Street for the
past eleven months, for his part *testifies to the correctness of Herr Hollinger's statement.*

"London, November 2, 1859

J. F. Wiehe, Compositor"

Vögele had nowhere *asserted* that *Blind* was the *author* of the
pamphlet. Fidelio Hollinger therefore invents Vögele's assertion so
as to be able to dismiss it as a *"malicious fabrication".* On the other
hand, *if* the pamphlet was *not* printed in Hollinger's print-shop,
how can the same Fidelio Hollinger be certain that *Karl Blind* was
not its author?

And how can the circumstance that the *compositor Wiehe "has
lived and worked for eleven months"* (up to November 2, 1859) with
Hollinger enable him to testify to the *"correctness of Fidelio
Hollinger's statement"*?

My reply[a] to *Blind*'s declaration (in No. 325 of the *Allgemeine
Zeitung,* see "Magnum Opus", Documents, pp. 39, 40) concluded
with the words: *"The transfer of the trial from Augsburg to London
would resolve the entire Blind-Vogt mystère."*

Blind, with all the moral indignation of a beautiful soul cut to
the quick, returned to the attack in the *"supplement to the
'Allgemeine Zeitung' of December 11, 1859"*:

"Having **repeatedly**" (we must take note of this) "**based my testimony** *on the*
documents signed *by Herr Hollinger, the printer, and Herr Wiehe, compositor,* I
declare here for the last time that the *allegation* (which is latterly put forward
merely as an insinuation) that *I am the author* of the pamphlet frequently referred
to is a *downright untruth.* The other statements about me contain *distortions of the
crudest sort."*

In a postscript to this declaration the editors of the *Allgemeine
Zeitung* remarked that "this discussion is of no further interest to
the general public" and they therefore request "the gentlemen

---

[a] See this volume, pp. 8-9.— *Ed.*

concerned to abstain from further replies", a request which our "well-rounded character" interpreted as follows at the end of the "Magnum Opus":

"In other words, the editors of the *Allgemeine Zeitung* request Messrs. *Marx, Biscamp** and *Liebknecht,* who stand revealed as barefaced liars, not to compromise themselves and the *Allgemeine Zeitung* any further."

Thus, for the time being, the Augsburg campaign came to an end.

Reverting to the tone of his *Lousiad,* Vogt made "Vögele the compositor" bear *"false witness"* to me and *Liebknecht* ("Magnum Opus", p. 195). He explained the origins of the pamphlet by suggesting that *Blind*

"may well have conceived various suspicions and have spread them abroad. *The Brimstone Gang then used them to fabricate a pamphlet and other articles which they then attributed to Blind who found himself driven into a corner"* (loc. cit., p. 218).

And if the Imperial Vogt failed to resume his indecisive campaign in London, as he had been challenged to do, this was partly because London was *"a backwater"* ("Magnum Opus", p. 229), but partly because the disputants "were accusing each other of lying" (loc. cit.).

The man's "critical immediacy" can only approve of the intervention of the courts if the parties are *not disputing* about the truth.

I now pass over three months and resume the thread of my story in the beginning of February 1860. Vogt's "Magnum Opus" had not yet reached London, but we had received the *anthology* of the Berlin *National-Zeitung,* which contained the following statement:

"It was very easy for the *Marx party* to lay the authorship of the pamphlet at *Blind*'s door, just because the latter had previously uttered similar views in

---

* In a letter dated October 20 from London, Biscamp had written to the editors of the *Allgemeine Zeitung* in connection with the Vogt affair, ending up by offering his services as news correspondent.[a] I knew nothing of this letter until I saw it in the *Allgemeine Zeitung.* Vogt has invented a moral doctrine according to which my support of a newspaper which has since folded up makes me responsible for the subsequent private letters written by its editor. How much more responsible would this make Vogt for Kolatschek's *Stimmen der Zeit* since he was a paid contributor to Kolatschek's *Monatsschrift.* When Biscamp was editing *Das Volk,* he made the greatest sacrifices. He gave up a job he had had for many years in order to take on the editorship; he edited the paper *gratis* in very trying circumstances and finally he jeopardised his position as news correspondent for German papers, such as the *Kölnische Zeitung,* so that he could work in accordance with his convictions. Everything else did not and does not concern me.

[a] The *Allgemeine Zeitung,* No. 300 (supplement), October 27, 1859.— *Ed.*

conversation with *Marx* and in the article in *The Free Press*. By using Blind's statements and turns of phrase the pamphlet could be *fabricated* so that it looked like *his* work."

Blind, like Falstaff who thought discretion the better part of valour,[a] esteemed silence as the whole art of diplomacy, and so he began to be silent once again. To loosen his tongue I published a circular in English over my signature and dated London, February 4, 1860. (See Appendix 11.)

The circular, addressed to the editor of *The Free Press*, stated *inter alia*:

"Now, before taking any further step, I want to show up the fellows who evidently have played into the hands of Vogt. I, therefore, publicly declare that the statement of Blind, Wiehe and Hollinger, according to which the anonymous pamphlet was *not* printed in Hollinger's office, 3, Litchfield Street, Soho, *is an infamous lie*." *

Having presented the evidence in my possession I end with the words:

"Consequently, I again declare the above said *Charles Blind* to be an *infamous liar* (deliberate liar). If I am wrong, he may easily confound me by appealing to an English Court of Law."[b]

On February 6, 1860 a London daily (the **Daily Telegraph**)— to which I shall return in due course—reproduced the anthology of the *National-Zeitung,* under the title *"The Journalistic Auxiliaries of Austria".*[c] However, I initiated an action for libel against the *National-Zeitung,* gave the *Daily Telegraph* notice of similar proceedings[d] and set about assembling the necessary legal material.

On February 11, 1860 the compositor Vögele swore an affidavit before the Police Court in Bow Street. He repeated the essential contents of his declaration of September 17, 1859, namely that the manuscript of the pamphlet was in **Blind's handwriting** and that

---

* In the English original I said "a deliberate lie". The *Kölnische Zeitung* translated this as "*infame Lüge*" (infamous lie). I accept this translation, even though "*durchtriebene Lüge*" would be closer to the original.

---

a Shakespeare, *Henry IV*, Part I, Act V, Scene 4.— *Ed.*

b Marx's circular (letter to the editor of *The Free Press* dated February 4, 1860, see this volume, p. 11) was written in English. The original text is reproduced here and in Appendix 11. The last sentence does not occur in the latter.— *Ed.*

c Marx gives the title in English and supplies the German translation in brackets.— *Ed.*

d See this volume, pp. 14-15.— *Ed.*

it had been composed **in Hollinger's print-shop,** partly by him (Vögele) and partly by *F. Hollinger.* (See Appendix 12.)

Incomparably more important was the affidavit taken out by the compositor *Wiehe,* whose testimony Blind had **repeatedly,** and with growing self-confidence, quoted in the *Allgemeine Zeitung.*

Apart from the original (see Appendix 13) I am therefore giving here a word-for-word translation [a]:

"One of the first days of November last—I do not recollect the exact date—in the evening between nine and ten o'clock I was taken out of bed by Mr. *F. Hollinger,* in whose house I then lived, and by whom I was employed as compositor. He presented to me a paper to the effect, that, during the preceding eleven months I had been *continuously* employed by him, and that during all that time a certain German flysheet '*Zur Warnung*' (A Warning) had *not* been composed and printed in Mr. Hollinger's Office, 3, Litchfield Street, Soho. In my perplexed state, and not aware of the importance of the transaction, I complied with his wish, and copied, and signed the document. Mr. *Hollinger* promised me *money,* but I never received anything. *During that transaction Mr. Charles Blind,* as my wife informed me at the time, *was waiting in Mr. Hollinger's room.* A few days later, Mrs. Hollinger called me down from dinner and led me into her husband's room, *where I found Mr. Blind alone. He presented me the same paper* which Mr. Hollinger had presented me before, and *entreated me*[b] *to write, and sign a second copy, as he wanted two, the one for himself, and the other for publication in the Press. He added that he would show himself grateful to me.* I copied and signed again the paper.

"I herewith declare the truth of the above statements and that:

"1) During the eleven months mentioned in the document I was for six weeks **not** employed by Mr. Hollinger, but by a Mr. Ermani.

"2) I did **not** work in Mr. Hollinger's Office just at that time when the flysheet '*Zur Warnung*' was published.

"3) I heard at the time from Mr. Vögele, who then worked for Mr. Hollinger, that he, Vögele, had, **together with Mr. Hollinger** himself, *composed* the flysheet in question, and that the manuscript was in *Blind's handwriting.*

"4) The types of the pamphlet were still standing when I returned to Mr. Hollinger's service. *I myself broke them into columns* for the reprint of the flysheet (or pamphlet) 'Zur Warnung' in the German paper *Das Volk* published by Mr. Hollinger, 3, Litchfield Street, Soho. The flysheet appeared in No. 7, d.d. 18th June 1859, of *Das Volk.*

"5) I saw Mr. Hollinger give to Mr. William Liebknecht of 14, Church Street, Soho, the proofsheet of the pamphlet 'Zur Warnung', on which proofsheet Mr. *Charles Blind with his own hand had corrected four or five mistakes.* Mr. Hollinger hesitated at first giving the proofsheet to Mr. Liebknecht, and when Mr. *Liebknecht* had withdrawn, he, Hollinger, expressed to me and my fellow workman Vögele his regret for having given the proofsheet out of his hands.

Johann Friedrich Wiehe

---

[a] The original English text is given in Appendix 13. The various types of emphasis were introduced by Marx.— *Ed.*

[b] In his translation Marx gives the English words "entreated me" in brackets after the German equivalent.— *Ed.*

"Declared and signed by the said Friedrich Wiehe at the Police Court, Bow Street, this 8th day of February, 1860, before me,

Th. Henry, Magistrate of the said court" (Police Court)

(Bow Street)

The two *affidavits* of the compositors *Vögele* and *Wiehe* proved that the *manuscript of the pamphlet had been written in Blind's hand, composed in Hollinger's print-shop and that Blind himself had corrected the proofs.*

And the *homme d'état* wrote to Julius Fröbel from London on July 4, 1859:

"A violent attack on Vogt has *appeared* here, accusing him of corruption. *I do not know who is responsible for it.* It contains a number of allegations *of which we had not previously heard.*"[a]

And the same *homme d'état* wrote to Liebknecht on September 8, 1859, saying that

"he had nothing whatever to do with the problem in question".

Not content with these achievements citizen and statesman *Blind had fabricated a false declaration* and contrived to *induce the compositor Wiehe to sign it* by promises of money from *Fidelio Hollinger* and proofs of his own gratitude in the future.

This, his own fabrication with a signature obtained by false pretences and together with Fidelio Hollinger's false testimony, he not only sent to the *Allgemeine Zeitung,* but in his second declaration he even *"refers" "repeatedly"* to these *"documents",* and hurls the reproach of "downright untruth" at my head with every sign of moral indignation.

I had copies made of the two affidavits of Vögele and Wiehe and circulated them in different circles, whereupon a meeting took place at Blind's house attended by *Blind, Fidelio Hollinger,* and Blind's house-friend Herr *Karl Schaible,* M.D., a quiet decent fellow who plays the role of tame elephant in Blind's political operations.

In the *Daily Telegraph* of February 15, 1860 there appeared an item that was later reprinted in German newspapers and which went as follows:

"The Vogt-Pamphlet
"To the Editor of *The Daily Telegraph*
"Sir,
"In consequence of erroneous statements which have been current, I feel I owe it to Mr. Blind, as well as to Mr. Marx, formally to declare that neither of them is

[a] Marx probably quotes this letter from the *National-Zeitung*, No. 41, July 4, 1859.— *Ed.*

the *author* of the pamphlet directed some time ago against Professor Vogt, at Geneva. That pamphlet originates from me; and on me the responsibility rests. I am sorry both with regard to Mr. Marx and Mr. Blind, that circumstances beyond my control should have prevented me from making this declaration earlier.

"London, 14 February, 1860

Charles Schaible, M.D."

Herr *Schaible* sent me this declaration.[a] I reciprocated his politeness by return of post by sending the affidavits of the compositors Vögele and Wiehe and wrote that his (Schaible's) declaration made no difference either to the false statements that *Blind* had sent to the *Allgemeine Zeitung*, or to *Blind's conspiracy*[b] *with Hollinger* to obtain Wiehe's signature for the *false document he had fabricated*.

Blind perceived that he was no longer on the firm territory of the *Allgemeine Zeitung*, but under the perilous jurisdiction of England. If he wanted to invalidate the *affidavits* and the "grave insults" of my circular based on them, he and Hollinger would have to swear *counter-affidavits*; but felony is no joke.

Eisele-Blind[118] is not the author of the pamphlet, because Beisele-Schaibele publicly declares himself its author. Blind has only *written* the manuscript of the pamphlet; he has only *had it printed* by Hollinger, corrected the proofs in his own hand, *fabricated false statements* together with Hollinger in order to refute these facts and sent them to the *Allgemeine Zeitung*. But he is nevertheless a wronged innocent, because he was not the *author* or *originator* of the pamphlet. He acted only as *Beisele-Schaibele's secretary*. It is just for this reason that on July 4, 1859 he did not know *"who"* had brought the pamphlet into the world and on September 8, 1859 he had *"nothing whatever to do with the problem in question"*. It may therefore reassure him that *Beisele-Schaible* is the *author* of the pamphlet in the literary sense of the word, but *Eisele-Blind* is its *author* in the technical sense of the English law, and the *responsible publisher* in the sense of all civilised legislation. *Habeat sibi!*[c]

A final word of farewell to Herr Beisele-Schaible.

The lampoon published by *Vogt* against me in the Biel *Handels-Courier*, dated *Berne, May 23, 1859*, bore the title *Zur Warnung*. The pamphlet composed by *Schaible* and written out

---

[a] On this see Marx's letters to Engels of February 15, 1860 and to Legal Counsellor Weber of February 24, 1860 (present edition, Vol. 41).— *Ed.*

[b] Marx uses the English word.— *Ed.*

[c] So be it! Genesis 38:23.— *Ed.*

and published by his secretary *Blind* in the beginning of June
1859, in which Vogt was arraigned as an agent of Louis
Bonaparte, and accused in some detail of both *"giving"* and
"taking bribes", also bears the title *Zur Warnung*. Furthermore, it
is signed X. Although in algebra X represents an unknown
quantity, it also happens to be the last letter of my name. Were the
title and the signature on the pamphlet an attempt to make
Schaible's "warning" look like *my* reply to Vogt's "warning"?
Schaible had promised a Revelation No. 2 as soon as Vogt
ventured to deny Revelation No. 1. Vogt not only issued a denial;
he instituted an action for libel in reply to Schaible's "warning".
And Herr Schaible's Revelation No. 2 has not appeared to this
day. At the head of his pamphlet Schaible had printed the words:
"For distribution!" And when Liebknecht was obliging enough to
"distribute" it through the *Allgemeine Zeitung*, "circumstances
beyond his control" sealed Herr Schaible's lips from June 1859 to
February 1860, when they were unsealed again by the affidavits
taken out in the Police Court in Bow Street.

However that may be, Schaible, the original denouncer of Vogt,
has now publicly accepted responsibility for the information given
in the pamphlet. Hence the Augsburg campaign ends not with the
victory of the defendant Vogt, but with the appearance on the
battlefield at long last of the accuser Schaible.

VIII

DÂ-DÂ VOGT AND HIS STUDIES

"SINE STUDIO" [119]

About a month before the outbreak of the Italian war, Vogt published his so-called *Studien zur gegenwärtigen Lage Europas,* Geneva, 1859. *Cui bono?*[a]

Vogt knew that

"in the approaching war *England* would remain *neutral*" (**Studien**, p. 4).

He knew that *Russia,*

"in agreement with France, would do *everything in its power* to injure Austria, short of actual hostilities" (*Studien,* p. 13).[b]

He knew that *Prussia*—but let him say for himself what he knows about Prussia.

"Even the most short-sighted will have realised by now *that there is an understanding between the Prussian Government and the Imperial Government of France*; that Prussia will not take up arms to defend Austria's non-German provinces; that it will give its approval to all measures necessitated by the defence of the territory of the Confederation; but apart from this *it will prevent any attempt by the Confederation or any of its members to intervene in support of Austria,* and in the subsequent peace negotiations it will expect *to be rewarded in the northern plains of Germany for* **these** *pains*" (loc. cit., pp. [18-]19).

To sum up: In Bonaparte's imminent crusade against Austria, England will *remain neutral,* Russia will adopt a *hostile stance* towards Austria, Prussia will restrain the bellicose members of the Confederation, and Europe will localise the war. As with the Russian war earlier on, Louis Bonaparte will now conduct the Italian war with the permission of the supreme authorities, he will

---

[a] Who benefits?— *Ed.*

[b] The quotation actually begins with the words "would do everything".— *Ed.*

act, as it were, as the secret general of a European coalition. What then is the purpose of Vogt's pamphlet? Since Vogt knows that England, Russia and Prussia are acting against Austria, what compels him to write *for Bonaparte*? But it appears that, quite apart from the old Francophobes with "the now childish Father Arndt and the ghost of the wretched Jahn at their head" (loc. cit., p. 121), a sort of national movement was convulsing "the German people" and was echoed in all kinds of "Chambers and newspapers" "while the governments only joined the dominant current hesitatingly and with reluctance" (loc. cit., p. 114). It appears that the "belief in an imminent threat" moved the German "people" to issue a "call for common measures" (loc. cit.). The French **Moniteur** (see *inter alia* the issue of March 15, 1859) looked on at this German movement with "astonishment and regret".[a]

"A sort of crusade against France," it declares, "is preached in the Chambers and in the press of some of the states of the German Confederation. They accuse France of entertaining ambitious plans, which it has disavowed, and of preparing for conquests of which it does not stand in need", etc.

In rebuttal of these "slanders" the *Moniteur* argues that "the Emperor's" attitude towards the Italian question should "rather inspire the greatest sense of security in Germany", that German unity and nationhood are, so to speak, the hobby-horses of Decembrist France, etc. The *Moniteur* concedes, however (see April 10, 1859), that certain German anxieties may appear to have been "provoked" by certain Parisian pamphlets—pamphlets in which Louis Bonaparte urgently exhorts himself to provide his people with the "long-desired opportunity" *"pour s'étendre majestueusement des Alpes au Rhin"* (to extend its frontiers majestically from the Alps to the Rhine).

"But," the *Moniteur* asserts, "Germany forgets that France stands under the protection of a legislation which does not authorise any preventive control on the part of the government."[b]

This and similar declarations by the *Moniteur* produced the very opposite effect to the one intended, or so it was reported to the Earl of Malmesbury (see the Blue Book *On the Affairs of Italy. January to May 1859*[c]). But where the *Moniteur* failed, *Karl Vogt* might perhaps succeed. His *Studien* are nothing but a *compilation*

[a] "Partie non officielle. Paris, le 14 mars", *Le Moniteur universel*, No. 74, March 15, 1859.—*Ed.*

[b] *Le Moniteur universel*, No. 100, April 10, 1859.—*Ed.*

[c] Cowley to Malmesbury, April 10, 1859 (extract). Here and below Marx uses the English title of the Blue Book.—*Ed.*

in German of *Moniteur* articles, *Dentu* pamphlets[120] and Decembrist maps of the future.

———————

Vogt's tub-thumping about *England* has only one point of interest—as an illustration of the general style of his *Studien*. Following his French sources he transforms the English Admiral, *Sir Charles Napier,* into *"Lord" Napier (Studien,* p. 4). The literary Zouaves attached to the Decembrists have learnt from the theatre of Porte St. Martin[121] that every distinguished Englishman is a Lord at the very least.

"England has never been able," *Vogt* declares, "to harmonise with Austria for long. Even though a *momentary* community of interests may have united *them for a while,* political necessity always separated them again *immediately.* On the other hand, England constantly formed close alliances with Prussia", etc. (loc. cit., p. 2.)[a]

Indeed! The common struggle of England and Austria against Louis XIV lasted with brief interruptions from 1689 to 1713, i.e. almost a quarter of a century. In the war of the Austrian Succession England fought for about six years together with Austria against Prussia and France. It was not until the Seven Years' War[122] that England became the ally of Prussia against Austria and France, but as early as 1762 Lord Bute left Frederick the Great in the lurch and put forward proposals for the "partition of Prussia" first to the Russian minister Golitsin and then to the Austrian minister Kaunitz. In 1790 England concluded a treaty with Prussia against Russia and Austria, but it faded away before the year was out. During the Anti-Jacobin War Prussia withdrew from the European Coalition with the Treaty of Basle,[123] despite Pitt's subsidies. Austria, on the other hand, urged on by England, fought on with brief interruptions from 1793 to 1809. As soon as Napoleon was eliminated and even before the conclusion of the Congress of Vienna, England concluded a secret treaty (of January 3, 1815) with Austria and France against Russia and Prussia.[124] In 1821, in Hanover, Metternich and Castlereagh made a new agreement against Russia.[125] Thus whereas the British themselves, both historians and parliamentarians, mostly refer to Austria as their "*ancient ally*",[b] *Vogt* has discovered from his original source, French pamphlets published by *Dentu,* that Austria and England were always at loggerheads apart from cases of a

———————

[a] In this passage the italics are Marx's. The punctuation is slightly altered.— *Ed.*
[b] Marx uses the English phrase and gives the German translation in brackets.— *Ed.*

"momentary community of interests", while England and Prussia were constant allies, which probably explains why Lord *Lyndhurst* warned the House of Lords during the Russian war with Prussia in mind: "*Quem tu, Romane, caveto!*" [a] Protestant England has antipathies towards Catholic Austria, liberal England towards conservative Austria, free-trade England towards protectionist Austria, solvent England towards bankrupt Austria. But emotional factors have always been alien to English history. It is true that Lord *Palmerston,* during his thirty years' rule of England, occasionally glossed over his vassalage to Russia by parading his Austrian antipathies. From "antipathy" to Austria, for example, he rejected in 1848 Austria's proposal, approved by Piedmont and France, for England to mediate in Italy, a proposal according to which Austria would have withdrawn to Verona and the line of the Adige, Lombardy would have become part of Piedmont, if it so decided, Parma and Modena would have fallen to Lombardy, while Venice would have formed an independent Italian state under an Austrian Archduke and given itself a constitution. (See *Blue Book on the Affairs of Italy,* Part II, July 1849, Nos. 377, 478.) These conditions were at any rate better than those of the Treaty of Villafranca.[126] After Radetzky had defeated the Italians at all points, Palmerston put forward the same terms that he himself had earlier rejected. As soon as Russia's interests required the opposite approach, however, such as during the *Hungarian* war of independence, he refused the assistance for which the Hungarians asked on the basis of the treaty of 1711 [127]—despite his "antipathy" to Austria—and even refused to make any protest against Russian intervention on the grounds that

"the political independence and liberties of Europe are bound up with the maintenance and integrity of Austria as a great European Power" (sitting of the House of Commons, July 21, 1849).[b]

Vogt's story continues:

"The interests of the United Kingdom ... are *everywhere in opposition* to them" (to the interests of Austria) (loc. cit., p. 2).

"Everywhere" is at once transformed into the Mediterranean.

"England wishes at all costs to preserve its influence in the Mediterranean and the countries along its coastline. Naples and Sicily, Malta and the Ionian Islands, Syria and Egypt are points of support of its policy oriented towards the *East Indies.* At *all* these points, Austria has set up the *greatest* obstacles to it" (loc. cit.).

------

[a] "Be on your guard against him, Romans!" (Horace, *Satires,* Book I, Satire 4, paraphrased.)—*Ed.*

[b] *The Times,* No. 20235, July 23, 1849.—*Ed.*

It is amazing to see how much *Vogt* takes on trust from the original Decembrist pamphlets published by Dentu in Paris! The English had imagined hitherto that they had been fighting the Russians and the French in turn for Malta and the Ionian Islands, but never the Austrians. They imagined that France, not Austria, had earlier sent an expedition to Egypt and was establishing itself at this very moment in the isthmus of Suez; that France, not Austria, had made conquests on the North coast of Africa and, allied with Spain, had striven to snatch Gibraltar from Britain; that England had concluded the treaty of July 1840 referring to Egypt and Syria against France and with Austria[128]; that in "*the policy oriented towards the East Indies*" England had everywhere encountered the "greatest obstacles" set up by Russia, not Austria. They imagined that in the only serious dispute between England and Naples—the sulphur question of 1840—it was a *French,* not an Austrian, company whose monopoly of the Sicilian sulphur trade triggered off the conflict.[129] And lastly, that on the other side of the Channel, there was occasional talk of transforming the Mediterranean into a "*lac français*", but never into a "*lac autrichien*". However, an important particular has to be considered in this context.

In the course of 1858 a map of Europe appeared in London entitled *L'Europe en 1860* (Europe in 1860).[a] This map, which was put out by the French Embassy and for 1858 contained several prophetic hints—Lombardy-Venice, for example, were annexed by Piedmont, and Morocco by Spain—redrew the political geography of the whole of Europe with one exception, that of France, which apparently remained within its old frontiers. The territories designed for it were, with sly irony, donated to impossible owners. Thus *Egypt* fell to *Austria* and the note in the margin of the map read: "*François Joseph I, l'Empereur d'Autriche et d'Egypte*" (Francis Joseph I, Emperor of Austria and Egypt).

Vogt had the map of *L'Europe en 1860* before him as a sort of Decembrist compass. Hence his dispute between England and Austria on account of *Egypt* and *Syria.* Vogt prophesies that this conflict would "end in the destruction of one of the disputants", *if,* as he remembers just in time, "*if* Austria *possessed a navy*" (loc. cit., p. 2). However, the historical scholarship peculiar to the *Studien* reaches its climax in the following passage:

---

[a] A description of the map was published in *The Times,* Nos. 23228 and 23229, February 12 and 14, 1859.— *Ed.*

"When Napoleon I *once* attempted to break *the English Bank*, the latter *one day*[a] resorted to counting the sums, instead of weighing them out, as it had always done previously; the Austrian Treasury finds itself in the same position, or even in a much worse one, for 365 days every year" (loc. cit., p. 43).

It is well known that the Bank of England ("the English Bank" is another figment of Vogt's imagination) suspended payments in cash from February 1797 until 1821,[130] during which 24 years English banknotes could not be exchanged for metal at all, whether weighed or counted. When the suspension first began there was as yet no Napoleon I in France (although a General Bonaparte was engaged on his first Italian campaign), and when cash payments were resumed in Threadneedle Street, Napoleon I had ceased to exist in Europe. Such "studies" even surpass La Guéronnière's account of the conquest of Tyrol by the "Emperor" of Austria.

Frau von Krüdener, the mother of the Holy Alliance, used to distinguish between the good principle, the *"white angel of the North"* (Alexander I), and the evil principle, the *"black angel of the South"* (Napoleon I).[b] Vogt, the adoptive father of the new Holy Alliance, transforms both, Tsar and Caesar, Alexander II and Napoleon III, into *"white angels"*. Both are the predestined liberators of Europe.

Piedmont, Vogt claims, *"has **even** gained the respect of Russia"* (loc. cit., p. 71).[c]

What more can be said of a state *than that it has even gained the respect of Russia*. Especially after Piedmont had ceded the naval port of Villafranca to Russia, and as the selfsame *Vogt* points out in regard to the purchase of the Jade Bay by Prussia[131]:

"A naval port on alien territory, without organic connections to the land to which it belongs, is such ridiculous nonsense that its existence can only acquire meaning if it is, as it were, regarded as a target of future aspirations, as a raised pennant on which to train one's sights" (*Studien*, p. 15).

It is common knowledge that Catherine II had already striven to obtain naval ports on the Mediterranean for Russia.

Tender consideration towards the "white angel" of the North leads *Vogt* into crude exaggerations which violate "the modesty of

---

The italics are Marx's except for the words "one day"; the punctuation is slightly altered.— *Ed.*

[b] See J. Turquan, *Une illuminée au XIX*e *siècle* (*la baronne de Krüdener*),*1766-1824*, Paris, p. 194.— *Ed.*

[c] Marx's italics and bold type.— *Ed.*

nature", insofar as this was still respected by his original source in
Dentu. In *La vraie question. France-Italie-Autriche,* Paris, 1859
(published by Dentu) he read on p. 20:

> "And besides, with what right could the Austrian Government invoke the
> inviolability of the treaties of 1815, when it has itself broken them with the
> *confiscation of Cracow* whose independence the treaties guaranteed?" *

He translates his French original in this way:

> "It is strange to hear such language from the mouth of the *only government*[a]
> which up to *now has insolently violated the treaties* [...] by raising its sacrilegious hand,
> without cause, in the midst of peace, against the *Republic of Cracow,* which had been
> guaranteed by the treaties, and incorporating it *without more ado* into the Empire"
> (loc. cit., p. 58).

It was of course out of "respect" for the treaties of 1815 that
Nicholas destroyed the Constitution and autonomy of the Kingdom of Poland, which were guaranteed by the treaties of 1815.
Russia had no less respect for the integrity of *Cracow* when it
occupied the free city with Muscovite troops in 1831. In 1836
Cracow was again occupied by the Russians, Austrians and
Prussians; it was treated like a conquered nation in every respect
and as late as 1840 it vainly appealed to England and France,
invoking the treaties of 1815. Finally, on February 22, 1846,
Russians, Austrians and Prussians again occupied Cracow, to
incorporate it into Austria.[132] Thus all *three Northern powers*
violated the treaties and the Austrian confiscation of 1846 was
only the sequel to the Russian invasion of 1831. Out of courtesy
towards the "white angel of the North" Vogt forgets the
confiscation of Poland and falsifies the history of the confiscation
of Cracow.**

The circumstance that *Russia* is "consistently hostile to Austria
and sympathetic to France", leaves Vogt in no doubt about Louis
Bonaparte's inclination to liberate all nations, just as the fact that
"his" (Louis Bonaparte's) "policies·are *today* in the *closest* agreement with those of Russia" (p. 30) raises no doubts in his mind
about Alexander II's inclination to liberate all nations.

---

* "De quel droit, d'ailleurs, le gouvernement autrichien viendrait-il invoquer
l'inviolabilité de ceux (traités) de 1815, lui qui les a violés en confisquant Cracovie,
dont ces traités garantissaient l'indépendance?"

** Palmerston, who fooled Europe with his ridiculous protest, had worked
unceasingly in the intrigue against Cracow ever since 1831. (See my pamphlet
Palmerston and Poland, London, 1853.) [See present edition, Vol. 12.]

---

[a] The words "only government" were italicised by Vogt. The other italics in this
passage are Marx's.— *Ed.*

Hence in the East Holy Russia must be regarded as the "friend of aspirations to freedom" and of "popular and national development", just like Decembrist France in the West. This slogan was given out for all the agents of December 2.

"Russia," Vogt found in *La foi des traités, les puissances signataires et l'empereur Napoléon III*, Paris, 1859, a work published by Dentu, "Russia belongs to the family of the Slavs, a chosen race.... Astonishment has been expressed at the chivalrous concord that has suddenly sprung up between France and Russia. Nothing could be more natural: *agreement on principles, unanimity of purpose,* submission to *the law of the holy alliance of the governments and peoples,* not to set traps and constrain others, but to guide and support the divine movements of the nations. From this perfect concord" (between Louis Philippe and England there was only an *entente cordiale,* but between Louis Bonaparte and Russia there is *la cordialité la plus parfaite*) "the most happy things have resulted: railways, *emancipation of the serfs,* trading posts in the Mediterranean, etc." *

Vogt immediately latches on to the "emancipation of the serfs" and suggests that

"the present impulse ... may well make Russia the ally of aspirations to freedom, rather than their enemy" (loc. cit., p. 10).

Like his Dentu original, he attributes the impulse for the so-called emancipation of the serfs in Russia to Louis Bonaparte and for this purpose he transforms the Anglo-Turkish-French-Russian war, which provided the impulse, into a *"French war"* (loc. cit., p. 9).

It is well known that the call to emancipate the serfs first rang out, loud and persistently, under Alexander I. Tsar Nicholas was occupied with emancipation of the serfs throughout his life; in 1838 he created a Ministry of Domains for this very purpose; in 1843 he instructed this Ministry to make the necessary preparations and in 1847 he even issued decrees favourable to the peasantry about the disposal of land belonging to the nobility[133] which he only reversed in 1848 from fear of the revolution. Hence, if the emancipation of the serfs has assumed more substantial dimensions under the "benevolent Tsar", as *Vogt* genially calls Alexander II, this would appear to be the result of economic developments which even a Tsar cannot subdue. Besides, the emancipation of the serfs as the *Russian Government sees it,* would

---

* "La Russie est de la famille des Slaves, race d'élite... On s'est étonné de l'accord chevaleresque survenu soudainement entre la France et la Russie. Rien de plus naturel: accord des principes, unanimité du but ... *soumission à la loi de l'alliance sainte des gouvernements et des peuples,* non pour leurrer et contraindre, mais pour guider et aider la marche divine des nations. De la cordialité la plus parfaite sont sortis les plus heureux effets: chemins de fer, *affranchissement des serfs,* stations commerciales dans la Méditerranée, etc." *La foi des traités, etc.,* Paris, 1859, p. 33.

increase the aggressive power of Russia a hundredfold. It is simply intended to perfect autocratic rule by tearing down the barriers which the big autocrat has hitherto encountered in the shape of the many lesser autocrats of the Russian nobility, whose might is based on serfdom, as well as in the shape of the self-administrating peasant communes, whose material foundation, common ownership of land, is to be destroyed by the so-called emancipation.

The Russian serfs happen to interpret the emancipation differently from the government, and the Russian nobility understands it in yet a third sense. Hence the "benevolent Tsar" discovered that a genuine emancipation of the serfs is incompatible with his own autocratic rule, just as the benevolent Pope Pius IX discovered in his day that the emancipation of Italy was incompatible with the existence of the Papacy. The "benevolent Tsar", therefore, regards wars of conquest and the traditional foreign policy of Russia, which, as the Russian historian Karamzin remarks, is "immutable",[a] as the only way to postpone the revolution within. In his work *La vérité sur la Russie,* 1860, Prince *Dolgorukov* has subjected to devastating criticism the tissue of lies about the millennium that is supposed to have dawned under Alexander II, myths zealously disseminated throughout Europe since 1856 by writers in the pay of Russia, loudly proclaimed in 1859 by the Decembrists and blindly repeated by Vogt in his *Studien.*

According to *Vogt,* even before the outbreak of the Italian war the alliance forged between the "white Tsar" and the "Man of December" for the express purpose of liberating the subject nationalities, had shown its worth in the Danubian principalities, where the unity and independence of the Romanian nation were confirmed by the election of Colonel Cuza as ruler of Moldavia and Wallachia.[134]

"Austria protested with might and main, *France and Russia applauded*" (loc. cit., p. 65).

In a memorandum [135] (printed in the *Preussisches Wochenblatt,* 1855) drawn up in 1837 for the Tsar of the time[b] by the Russian Cabinet, we can read:

"Russia prefers not to annex *immediately* states with alien elements.... In any event it seems more fitting to allow countries whose acquisition has been *resolved*

---

[a] Н. М. Карамзинъ, *Исторія Государства Россійскаго,* Т. XI, Спб., 1824, стр. 23 (N. M. Karamzin, *The History of the Russian State,* Vol. XI, St. Petersburg, 1824, p. 23).— *Ed.*

[b] Nicholas I.— *Ed.*

upon to exist for a time under separate, but entirely dependent leaders, as we have done in Moldavia and Wallachia, etc." [a]

Before Russia annexed the Crimea it proclaimed its *independence*. In a Russian proclamation of December 11, 1814, it is stated *inter alia*:

"The Emperor Alexander, your protector, appeals to you, Poles: Arm yourselves for the defence of your country and the maintenance of your *political independence*." [b]

And above all the Danubian principalities! Ever since Peter the Great's invasion of the Danubian principalities, Russia has laboured in the cause of their *"independence"*. At the Congress of Niemirov (1737) the Empress Anne demanded that the Sultan should concede the independence of the Danubian principalities under Russian protection. At the Congress of Focşani (1772) Catherine II insisted on the independence of the principalities under *European protection*.[136] Alexander I continued these efforts and put the seal on them by transforming Bessarabia into a Russian province (by the Peace of Bucharest, 1812[137]). Nicholas even gladdened the hearts of the Romanians through Kiselev by bestowing on them the *Règlement organique,* which established the most hideous form of serfdom while the whole of Europe applauded him for this code of liberty, which is still in force.[138] By his quasi-unification of the Danubian principalities under Cuza, Alexander II only went one step further in the century-and-a-half's policy of his forbears. *Vogt* now discovers that this unification under a Russian vassal means that "the principalities will constitute a dam blocking the advance of Russia towards the South" (loc. cit., p. 64).

Since Russia has been applauding the election of Cuza (loc. cit., p. 65) it is as clear as daylight that the benevolent Tsar must be doing all he can to block his own "path to the South" even though "Constantinople remains an eternal goal of Russian policy" (loc. cit., p. 9).

There is nothing new in proclaiming Russia the protector of liberalism and of national aspirations. Catherine II was celebrated as the standard-bearer of progress by a whole host of French and

---

[a] "Zur Signatur der russischen Politik", *Preussisches Wochenblatt*, No. 23, June 9, 1855. Marx gives a summary rather than the exact words of the passage in question.— *Ed.*

[b] The source used by Marx has not been established. The text of the proclamation can be found in D'Angeberg's *Recueil des traités, conventions et actes diplomatiques concernant la Pologne.—Ed.*

German Enlighteners. The "noble" Alexander I (*Le Grec du Bas Empire*[a] as Napoleon meanly described him) in his day played the hero of liberalism throughout Europe. Did he not make Finland happy by bestowing on it the blessings of Russian civilisation? Did he not in his magnanimity give France not only a Constitution, but even a *Russian* Prime Minister, the Duc de Richelieu? Was he not the secret head of the "Hetairia",[139] while simultaneously at the Congress of Verona, he urged Louis XVIII through his hired agent Chateaubriand to campaign against the Spanish rebels? [140] Did he not use Ferdinand VII's confessor to incite Ferdinand to send an expedition to quell the rebellious Spanish-American colonies, while at the same time he promised the President of the United States of North America[b] his assistance against the intervention of any European power on the American continent? Did he not send Ypsilanti to Wallachia as the "leader of the Holy Hellenic Host", and use the same Ypsilanti to betray the host and arrange for the assassination of Vladimirescu, the Wallachian rebel leader? Before 1830 Nicholas, too, was eulogised in every language, in verse and in prose, as the hero who would liberate the subject nationalities. In 1828-29, when he undertook a war against Mahmood II, for the liberation of the *Greeks*, after Mahmood had refused to allow a Russian army to move in to suppress the Greek uprising, Palmerston speaking in the British Parliament declared that the enemies of Russia, the liberator, were necessarily the "friends" of the greatest monsters in the world: Dom Miguel, Austria and the Sultan. Did not Nicholas in paternal solicitude give the Greeks a president, namely Count Capo d'Istria, a Russian general? But the Greeks were not Frenchmen and they murdered the noble Capo d'Istria. And although Nicholas had mainly appeared in his role as guardian of legitimacy ever since the July 1830 revolution, he did not cease for a moment to work for the "liberation of the subject nationalities". A few illustrations will suffice. The constitutional revolution in *Greece* in September 1843 was led by Katakasi, the Russian minister in Athens and formerly the responsible supervisor over Admiral Heiden at the time of the disaster at Navarino.[141] The centre of the *Bulgarian* rebellion in 1842 was the Russian consulate in Bucharest. There in the spring of 1842, the Russian general Duhamel received a Bulgarian

---

a Greek of the Byzantine Empire; figuratively, confidence-trickster. See Emmanuel Las Cases, *Mémorial de Sainte-Hélène...*, t. 2, Paris, 1824, p. 407, and François René Chateaubriand, *Congrès de Vérone*, Vol. I, Paris, 1838, pp. 186-87.— *Ed.*

b James Monroe.— *Ed.*

deputation whom he presented with a plan for a general insurrection. Serbia was to act as reserve for the revolt and the Russian general Kiselev was to become Hospodar of Wallachia. During the *Serbian* uprising (1843) Russia used its Embassy in Constantinople to drive the Turks to resort to violence against the Serbs, and then made use of this pretext to appeal to the sympathy and fanaticism of Europe against the Turks. *Italy,* too, was by no means excluded from the liberation plans of Tsar Nicholas. *La Jeune Italie,* which was for a time the Paris organ of the Mazzini party, recounts in an issue in November 1843:

"The recent disturbances in the Romagna and the movements in Greece were more or less connected with each other.... The Italian movement failed because the real democratic party refused to join it. The *Republicans* would *not aid* in a movement instigated by *Russia.* Everything was prepared for a general insurrection in Italy. The movement was to commence in Naples, where it was expected that a section of the army would take the lead or make common cause with the patriots. After the outbreak of the revolution, Lombardy, Piedmont and the Romagna would rise and an *Italian Empire* was to be established under the Duke of Leuchtenberg, the son of Eugène Beauharnais and the son-in-law of the Tsar. 'Young Italy'[142] *frustrated this plan.*"[a]

The Times of November 20, 1843 commented as follows on this information from *La Jeune Italie:*

"If that great end—the establishment of a new Italian Empire the head of which would be a Russian Prince—could be attained, so much the better; but there was another—an immediate, though perhaps not quite so important advantage to be gained by any outbreak in Italy—the causing of alarm to Austria and the withdrawal of her attention from the fearful[b] projects of Russia *on the Danube.*"

After Nicholas had made an unsuccessful approach to "Young Italy" in 1843, he sent Mr. von Butenev to Rome in March 1844. Butenev proposed to the Pope[c] in the name of the Tsar that Russian Poland should be ceded to Austria in exchange for Lombardy, which was to become a North Italian kingdom under Leuchtenberg. *The Tablet* of April 1844, which was at that time the English organ of the Roman Curia, commented as follows:

"The bait for the Roman Curia contained in this beautiful plan lay in the fact that Poland would fall into Catholic hands, while Lombardy would remain in the possession of a Catholic dynasty as before. But the diplomatic veterans of Rome perceived that while Austria can barely maintain its hold on its own possessions and in all human probability will be forced sooner or later to relinquish its Slav

---

[a] Here and below Marx probably drew on the item "Express from Paris", *The Times*, No. 18458, November 20, 1843. The italics are Marx's.— *Ed.*

[b] In the original Marx gives the word "fearful" in brackets after its German equivalent.— *Ed.*

[c] Gregory XVI.— *Ed.*

provinces, the cession of Poland to Austria, even if this part of the proposal were seriously intended, would be nothing more than a loan to be repaid at a later date. Whereas North Italy with the Duke of Leuchtenberg would in fact fall under Russian protection and before long would infallibly come beneath the Russian sceptre. The warmly recommended plan was consequently put aside for the present." [a]

Thus far *The Tablet* of 1844.

The only factor that has served as a justification for the existence of Austria as a political entity since the middle of the eighteenth century has been its resistance to the advance of Russia in Eastern Europe, a resistance conducted in a helpless, inconsistent and cowardly, but obstinate manner. This resistance leads *Vogt* to the discovery that "Austria is the source of all discord in the East" (loc. cit., p. 56). With "a certain childlike innocence" so becoming to his tubbiness, he explains the alliance of Russia and France against Austria as the result of the latter's *ingratitude* for the services rendered it by Nicholas during the Hungarian revolution, to say nothing of the liberating predilections of the "benevolent Tsar".

"In the Crimean war Austria went to the very edge of hostile, armed neutrality. It is self-evident that such an attitude, which moreover bore all the marks of *falsity and scheming*, was bound to be bitterly resented by the Russian Government and impel it to draw closer to France" (loc. cit., pp. 10, 11).

According to *Vogt*, Russia pursues a sentimental policy. The *gratitude* Austria expressed to the Tsar at Germany's expense during the Warsaw Congress in 1850 and in the march on Schleswig-Holstein [143] does not satisfy the grateful *Vogt*.

The Russian diplomat *Pozzo di Borgo* in his celebrated dispatch from Paris in October 1825,[144] having listed Austria's intrigues to frustrate Russia's plans for intervention in the East, goes on to say:

"Our policy obliges us, therefore, to present our most terrifying face towards this state" (Austria) "to convince it by our preparations that if it ventures any movement against us we shall unleash upon it the greatest storm it has ever experienced."

He goes on to threaten war from without and revolution from within, and having hinted at a possible peaceful solution in the suggestion that Austria should annex any Turkish "provinces that appealed to it" and having described Prussia as a subordinate ally of Russia, he continues:

---

[a] "The Papacy and the Great Powers", *The Tablet*, No. 205, April 13, 1844. Marx gives a summary rather than the exact words of the passage in question. He may have used some other source too.— *Ed.*

"*If the Viennese court had yielded to our good purposes and intentions,* the plan of the Imperial Cabinet would long since have achieved fulfilment—a plan which embraces not only the annexation of the Danubian principalities and Constantinople, but even provides for the expulsion of the Turks from Europe."

It is well known that in 1830 a secret treaty was concluded between Nicholas and Charles X. Its terms laid down that France would permit Russia to take possession of Constantinople and would receive the Rhine provinces and Belgium in return. Prussia would be given Hanover and Saxony, and Austria would receive a part of the Turkish provinces on the Danube. Under Louis Philippe, at Russia's suggestion, this plan was again laid before the Russian Cabinet by Molé. A little while after, Brunnow went to London with the document where it was shown to the English Government as proof of France's treachery and helped to set up the anti-French coalition of 1840.

Let us now see how, according to the ideas of *Vogt,* who obtained his inspirations from his original Paris sources, Russia was *supposed* to exploit the Italian war in agreement with France. It might be thought that the "national" composition of Russia and especially the *"Polish nationality"* might well create certain difficulties for a man for whom "the principle of nationality was the Lodestar".[a] However:

"The principle of nationality stands high in our estimation, but the principle of free self-determination stands even higher" (loc. cit., p. 121).

When Russia annexed by far the largest portion of *Poland* proper by virtue of the treaties of 1815, it gained a position which extended so far westward, and drove as it were a wedge not only between Austria and Prussia, but also between East Prussia and Silesia, that even at the time Prussian officers (such as Gneisenau) pointed out that such frontiers could not be tolerated in relation to so powerful a neighbour. However, it was not until 1831, when the defeat of Poland put the whole territory at the mercy of Russia, that the true significance of the wedge became clear. The subjugation of Poland was no more than a pretext for constructing the grandiose chain of fortresses at Warsaw, Modlin and Ivangorod. Its real purpose was complete strategic control of the basin of the Vistula, and the establishment of a base from which to launch attacks to the North, South and West. Even Haxthausen, who enthused about the orthodox Tsar and all things Russian, regards this as a very definite danger and a threat to Germany.

---

[a] Carl Vogt, *Studien...*, Einleitung, S. ix.— *Ed.*

The Russian fortifications on the Vistula pose a greater threat to Germany than all the French fortresses put together, especially if and when Polish national resistance were to cease completely and Russia were able to use Poland's war potential as its own force of aggression. Hence *Vogt* comforts Germany with the thought that *Poland* has become *Russian* from an act of free self-determination.

"There can be no doubt," he says, "that thanks to the great efforts of the Russian people's party, *the gulf that yawned between Poland and Russia has been narrowed significantly* and it perhaps requires only a *small impulse to close it completely*" (loc. cit., p. 12).

This small impulse was to be provided by the Italian war. (However, in the course of this war Alexander II became convinced that Poland had not yet reached such Vogtian heights.) The idea was that owing to the law of gravity *Poland,* which had been absorbed into Russia by an act of "free self-determination", would as a central body attract the detached limbs of the former Kingdom of Poland, which were now wasting away under foreign rule. To facilitate this process of attraction *Vogt* counsels Prussia to seize the opportunity and rid itself of its "Slav appendage" (loc. cit., p. 17), that is *Posen* (loc. cit., p. 97) and probably also *West Prussia* since only East Prussia is recognised to be a "genuine German land". The limbs detached from Prussia would, of course, at once revert to the central body absorbed by Russia and the "genuine German land" of East Prussia would be transformed into a Russian enclave. On the other hand, as far as *Galicia* is concerned, which is also shown as a part of Russia on the map of *L'Europe en 1860,* its separation from Austria lay directly in line with the war to free Germany from the non-German possessions of Austria. *Vogt* recollects that

"before 1848 the picture of the Russian Tsar could be seen more frequently in [...] Galicia than that of the Austrian Emperor" (loc. cit., p. 12) and "in view of the uncommon skill displayed by Russia in weaving its intrigues, Austria would have serious cause for anxiety here" (loc. cit.).

It is perfectly self-evident, however, that in order to rid itself of the "internal enemy" Germany should simply allow the Russians "to advance troops to the frontier" (p. 13) to lend their support to these intrigues. While Prussia is detaching itself from its Polish provinces, Russia using the Italian war should separate Galicia from Austria, just as in 1809 Alexander I had received a piece of Galicia in payment for his purely theatrical support of Napoleon I. It is well known that Russia successfully reclaimed parts of Poland

148 Karl Marx

that had originally gone to Austria and Prussia, partly from Napoleon I and partly from the Congress of Vienna. According to Vogt, in 1859 the time had come for the *whole* of Poland to be united with Russia. *Vogt demands not the emancipation of the Polish nationality* from Russians, Austrians and Prussians, but the *absorption by Russia and the annihilation of the entire former Kingdom of Poland. Finis Poloniae!*[145] This "Russian" conception of the "reconstruction of Poland", which was rife throughout Europe immediately after the death of Tsar Nicholas, was denounced as early as March 1855 by *David Urquhart* in his pamphlet *The New Hope of Poland.*[a]

But *Vogt* had not yet done enough for Russia.

"The extraordinary civility," says our *agreeable companion*, "indeed the almost brotherly feelings with which the Russians treated the *Hungarian* revolutionaries formed too great a contrast with the behaviour of the Austrians for it not to have had repercussions. Russia did indeed crush the party" (N.B.: according to *Vogt* the Russians crushed not *Hungary* but the *party*), "but treated it with forbearance and courteousness, and thereby laid the foundations for an attitude which may be characterised by saying that when faced with two evils one must choose the lesser of the two, and *that in the present case, Russia is not the greater*" (loc. cit., pp. 12, 13).

With what "extraordinary civility, forbearance, courteousness", and indeed almost "brotherly feelings" does Plon-Plon's Falstaff conduct the Russians to Hungary, making himself into the "channel" for the illusion which destroyed the Hungarian revolution of 1849. It was *Görgey*'s party which disseminated the belief in a Russian prince as the future King of Hungary, a belief which broke the will of the Hungarian revolution to resist.*

Without having particular support in any one race the Habsburgs naturally based their dominion over Hungary *before* 1848 on the dominant nationality—the *Magyars*. We may remark in passing that Metternich was the great protector of the nationalities. He misused them by playing them off against each other, but he needed them in order to misuse them. He therefore

---

* According to the Polish Colonel Lapinski, who fought against the Russians in the Hungarian revolutionary army up to the fall of Komorn,[b] and later in Circassia, "it was the Hungarians' misfortune that they did not know the Russians" (Theophil Lapinski, *Feldzug der Ungarischen Hauptarmee im Jahre 1849*, Hamburg, 1850, p. 216). "The Viennese Cabinet was completely in the hands of the Russians ... it was on their advice that the leaders were murdered ... while the Russians did everything to gain the sympathies of all, *Austria was ordered by them* to make itself even more hated than ever in the past" (loc. cit., pp. 188, 189).

---

a Marx gives the English title and supplies the German translation in brackets.— *Ed.*

b Komárom.— *Ed.*

preserved them. We may compare the situation in Posen and Galicia. After the revolution of 1848-49 the Habsburg dynasty, having used the Slavs to subdue the Germans and Magyars, tried to follow in the footsteps of Joseph II and to impose the rule of the German element in Hungary by force. The fear of Russia prevented the Habsburgs from embracing their rescuers, the Slavs. Their overall reactionary policy in Hungary was aimed more against their saviours, the Slavs, than against their defeated enemies, the Magyars. Hence, as *Szemere* has shown in his pamphlet *Hungary, 1848-1860*, London, 1860, fighting against its own saviours, the Austrian reaction therefore drove the Slavs back under the wing of the Magyars. Austrian rule *over* Hungary and the rule of the Magyars *in* Hungary coincided, therefore, both *before* and *after* 1848. Russia is in a quite different position, whether it rules Hungary directly or indirectly. Taking the racial and religious affinities together, Russia would immediately have the *non-Magyar majority* of the population at its disposal. The Magyar race would instantly succumb to the union of the Slavs, who are akin to the Russians ethnically, and the Wallachians, who are akin to them religiously. Russian domination in Hungary, therefore, is synonymous with the *destruction of Hungarian nationality*, i.e. of a Hungary historically bound up with Magyar rule.*

Vogt, who proposes that the *Poles* by an act of "free self-determination" should be absorbed by *Russia*, also wants to drown the *Hungarians* in a *sea of Slavs* by subjecting them to Russian rule.**

But *Vogt* has still not done enough for Russia.

---

* General *Moritz Perczel*, famous for his part in the Hungarian revolutionary war, withdrew from the group of Hungarian officers around Kossuth in Turin while the Italian campaign was still in progress. In a public declaration he explained the reasons for his resignation—on the one hand, there was Kossuth, who merely acted as a Bonapartist bogyman, on the other hand, there was the prospect of a *Russian* future for Hungary. In his reply (from St. Hélier, April 19, 1860) to a letter from me in which I inquired for further information about his declaration, he said *inter alia*: "I shall never consent to act as a tool to rescue Hungary from the claws of the Double Eagle merely to force it into the **deadly embrace** of the Northern Bear."

** Mr. *Kossuth* was never in any doubt about the correctness of the views set forth in the present work. He knew that *Austria* can maltreat Hungary, but not annihilate it. "The Emperor Joseph II," he writes to the Grand Vizier Reshid Pasha from Kütahya, February 15, 1851, "the only man of genius produced by the Habsburg family, exhausted the extraordinary resources of his rare intellect and of the then still common notions of the power of his House, in the attempt to Germanise Hungary, and integrate it within the state as a whole. But Hungary

Among the "non-German provinces" of Austria on behalf of
whom the German Confederation should *not* "take up its sword"
against France and Russia, which "stands whole-heartedly on the
side of France", are not only Galicia, Hungary and Italy, but in
particular *Bohemia and Moravia,* as well.

"Russia," Vogt says, "provides the firm centre around which the Slav
nationalities increasingly strive to congregate" (loc. cit., pp. 9-10).

Bohemia and Moravia belong to the "Slav nationalities". As
Muscovy developed into Russia, so must Russia develop into Pan-
Slavonia. "With the *Czechs* ... at our side we shall *succumb to every
enemy*" (loc. cit., p. 134). We, i.e. Germany, must attempt to rid
ourselves of the Czechs, i.e. of Bohemia and Moravia. "No
guarantee for non-German possessions of the rulers" (loc. cit.,
p. 133). "*No non-German provinces in the Confederation any longer*"
(loc. cit.) but only German provinces in France! Hence we must not
only "*give* the present French Empire *a free hand* [...] as long as it
does **not** *violate the territory* of the German *Confederation*" (Preface,
p. 9), but we must also allow **Russia** "a free hand" as long as it
only violates *"non-German provinces in the Confederation".* Russia will
help Germany develop its "unity" and "nationhood" by advancing
troops to the "Slav appendages" of Austria exposed to Russia's
"intrigues". While Austria is kept busy in Italy by Louis Bonaparte
and Prussia forces the sword of the German Confederation back
into its sheath, the "benevolent Tsar" will "be able secretly to
support" revolutions in *Bohemia and Moravia* "with money, arms
and munitions" (loc. cit., p. 13).

And "with the Czechs at our side we must succumb to every
enemy"!

emerged from the struggle with renewed vigour.... In the last revolution Austria
only raised itself from the dust in order to collapse once again at the feet of the
Tsar, its master, who never *gives* his aid but only *sells* it. And Austria had to pay
for this aid dearly" (*Correspondence of Kossuth,* p. 33). On the other hand, he
maintains in the same letter that only Hungary and Turkey together can frustrate
the *Pan-Slavist intrigues* of Russia. He writes to *David Urquhart* from Kütahya,
January 17, 1851: "*We must crush Russia,* my dear Sir! and, headed by you, we will! I
have not only the resolution of will, but also that of hope! and this is no vain word,
my dear Sir! no sanguine fascination; it is the word of a man, who is wont duly to
calculate every chance: of a man though very weak in faculties, not to be shaken in
perseverance and resolution, etc." (loc. cit., p. 39.)[a]

---

[a] The letter was quoted in the article "Data by Which to Judge of Kossuth",
The Free Press, No. 5, May 27, 1859. Marx quotes the original English text and
gives the German translation in brackets.— *Ed.*

How magnanimous of the "benevolent Tsar", then, to relieve us of Bohemia and Moravia with all their Czechs which as "Slav nationalities must" naturally "congregate around Russia".

Let us examine how our Vogt of the Empire protects the Eastern German frontier by incorporating Bohemia and Moravia in Russia. Bohemia Russian! But Bohemia lies in the middle of Germany, separated from Russian Poland by Silesia, and from the Galicia and Hungary Russified by *Vogt*, by a Moravia also Russified by Vogt. Thus Russia acquires an expanse of German federal territory 50 German miles long and 25-35 miles broad.[a] Its Western frontier will advance westwards by a full 65 German miles. Since the distance between Eger[b] and Lauterburg in Alsace is no more than 45 German miles as the crow flies, North Germany will be totally separated from South Germany by the French wedge in the West and even more by the Russian wedge in the East, and the *partition of Germany would be complete!* The direct route from Vienna to Berlin would pass *through Russia*, and the same would apply even to the direct route from Munich to Berlin. Dresden, Nuremberg, Regensburg and Linz would be our frontier towns bordering on Russia; our position *vis-à-vis* the Slavs would, at least in the South, be the same as it was *before* Charlemagne (while in the West Vogt does not allow us to go back as far as Louis XV), and we could simply erase 1,000 years of our history.

What could be accomplished with the aid of Poland, could be accomplished even better with the aid of Bohemia. If Prague were transformed into a fortified encampment, with secondary fortresses at the confluence of the Moldau and the Eger[c] with the Elbe, the Russian army in Bohemia could calmly stand and wait for the German army which, divided from the outset, would approach from Bavaria, Austria and Brandenburg. Falling upon the smaller German units it would be able to destroy them while allowing the larger ones to run up against the fortresses.

Let us look at a linguistic map of Central Europe, taking, for example, a Slav authority, the *"slovanský zeměvid"* of Šafařík.[146] According to this the Slav-language frontier runs from the Pomeranian coast near Stolp via Zastrow south of Chodziehen[d] on the Netze, and advances westwards to Meseritz. However, from there it suddenly curves south-east. Here the massive German

---

[a] A German mile is equal to 7,420 metres.— *Ed.*
[b] Modern name: Cheb.— *Ed.*
[c] Now the Vltava and the Ohře.— *Ed.*
[d] Modern names: Stölpchen (Stölpgen), Jastrow and Colmar.— *Ed.*

territory of Silesia drives a deep wedge between Poland and Bohemia. In Moravia and Bohemia the Slavonic language again protrudes far to the west, although it is greatly eroded by the advance of German from all directions and the whole area is interspersed with German towns and linguistic islands, just as in the north, the whole Lower Vistula and the best part of East and West Prussia are German and push forward uncomfortably towards Poland. Between the most westerly point of the Polish tongue and the most northerly point of Bohemian, the Lusatian or Wendish linguistic enclave lies in the middle of German-speaking territory, but in such a way that it almost cuts off Silesia.

For the Russian Pan-Slavist *Vogt,* who has Bohemia to play with, there is no doubt where the natural frontier of the Slav Empire lies. It goes from Meseritz directly to Lieberose and Lübben, then south of where the Elbe passes through the mountains on the Bohemian frontier, after which it follows the Western and Southern frontier of Bohemia and Moravia. Everything to the east of this is Slav: the few German enclaves and other interlopers on Slav soil can no longer withstand the development of the great Slav nation. And anyway they have no right to be where they are. Once this "Pan-Slavist state of affairs" has been brought about, a similar rectification of the frontiers will become inevitable in the south. Here too a German wedge has of its own accord thrust itself between the North and South Slavs and occupied the valley of the Danube and the Styrian Alps. *Vogt* cannot tolerate this wedge and, being consistent, he therefore has Russia annex Austria, Salzburg, Styria and the German parts of Carinthia. In this construction of the Slav-Russian Empire, Vogt has already demonstrated, Austria notwithstanding, that according to the well-tested axioms of the "principle of nationality" small numbers of Magyars and Romanians as well as various groups of Turks must fall to Russia (for the "benevolent Tsar" also contributes to the "principle of nationality" by his subjugation of Circassia and the extermination of the Crimean Tartars!)—as a punishment for being wedged between the North and South Slavs.

In this operation, we Germans lose—nothing more than East and West Prussia, Silesia, parts of Brandenburg and Saxony, the whole of Bohemia, Moravia and the rest of Austria apart from Tyrol (part of which falls to the Italian "principle of nationality")—and our national existence to boot!

But let us just consider the first stage, according to which Galicia, Bohemia and Moravia become *Russian!*

In such circumstances German Austria, Southwest Germany and North Germany can never act in concert, except—and this would inevitably come about— *under Russian leadership.*

Vogt makes us Germans sing what his Parisians sang in 1815:

> "Vive *Alexandre,*
> Vive *le roi des rois,*
> Sans rien *prétendre,*
> Il nous donne *des lois.*" [a]

Vogt's "principle of nationality", which he desired to realise in 1859 through the alliance between the "white angel of the North" and the "white angel of the South", should according to *his* views prove its worth by the absorption of Polish nationality, the disappearance of Magyar nationality and vanishing of German nationality in— *Russia.*

I have not mentioned his original source in *Dentu's* pamphlets on this occasion because I was reserving a *single* conclusive quotation as proof that everything that he either hints at or blurts out stems from slogans issued by the Tuileries. In the *Pensiero ed Azione's* issue of May 2-16, 1859, in which *Mazzini* forecasts events that later took place, he remarks *inter alia* that the first condition of the alliance agreed between Alexander II and Louis Bonaparte was: *"abbandono assoluto della Polonia"* (absolute abandonment of Poland by France, which *Vogt* translates as "completely closing the gulf yawning between Poland and Russia").

"Che la guerra si prolunghi e assuma ... proporzioni europee, l'insurrezione delle provincie oggi turche preparata di lunga mano e quelle dell' *Ungheria,* daranno campo all'Allianza di rivelarsi... Principi russi governerebbo le provincie che surgerebbo *sulle rovine* dell'Impero Turco e dell' *Austria... Constantino di Russia* è già proposto ai malcontenti ungheresi." (See *Pensiero ed Azione,* May 2-16, 1859.) ("If the war be prolonged so as to assume ... European proportions, the insurrection of the Turkish provinces, prepared a long time since, and that of Hungary, would enable the alliance to assume palpable forms.... Russian princes would govern the states established on the ruins of the Turkish Empire and Austria.... Constantine of Russia is already proposed to the Hungarian malcontents.") [b]

---

[a] "Long live *Alexander,*
Long live *the king of kings;*
He gives us *laws* and *never*
Asks for the least of things."
(*Le Peuple de 1850,* No. 26, September 27).— *Ed.*

[b] From Mazzini's manifesto entitled "La Guerra". Marx translated it into English and published it with a brief introduction in the *New-York Daily Tribune* (see present edition, Vol. 16, p. 357).— *Ed.*

But *Vogt's Russophile posture* is only secondary. He is merely repeating one of the catch-phrases issued by the Tuileries and his aim is merely to prepare Germany for manoeuvres agreed between Louis Bonaparte and Alexander II if certain contingencies of the war against Austria should eventuate. In fact, he merely echoes slavishly the Pan-Slavist phraseology of his original Paris pamphlets. His true task is to sing the *Lay of Ludwig*[147]:

> "Einan kùning wèiz ih, hèizit hêr Hlùdowîg
> ther gêrno Gôde" (i.e. the nationalities) "dionôt." [a]

We saw earlier how *Vogt* praised Sardinia by pointing out that *"it had even gained the respect of Russia"*. We now have the parallel assertion.

"There is no mention of Austria," he says, "in" (Prussia's) "declarations ... in the event of an imminent war between North America and Cochin China the wording would be the same. But the German mission of Prussia, its German obligations, the old Prussia—that is where the emphasis is put for preference. *France*" (in accordance with his statement on p. 27 that "France is now summed up [...] exclusively in the person of its ruler") "*therefore bestows praise through the 'Moniteur' and the rest of the press.*—Austria fumes" (*Studien*, p. 18).

"The fact that Prussia correctly interprets its *'German mission'* follows from the *praise bestowed on it* by Louis Bonaparte in the *Moniteur* and the rest of the Decembrist press." What brazen impudence! We remember how from a feeling of tenderness towards the "white angel of the North" Vogt made Austria the *sole* offender against the treaties of 1815 and the sole state to confiscate Cracow. He now performs the same labour of love for the benefit of the "white angel of the South".

"This ecclesiastical state against whose republic" (republic of an ecclesiastical state!) "*Cavaignac*, the representative of the doctrinaire republican party [...] and the military counterpart of Gagern" (a fine parallel!),"perpetrated the abominable *act of massacre*" (to commit massacre against the republic of a state!), "a crime which, however, did not help him to reach the presidential chair" (loc. cit., p. 69).

So it was *Cavaignac* and not *Louis Bonaparte* who perpetrated "the *abominable act of massacre*" against the *Roman Republic*! Cavaignac did indeed send a navy to Civitavecchia in November 1848 for the personal protection of the Pope. But it was only in the following year, on *February 9, 1849*, several months after Cavaignac had failed to get the presidential chair, that the temporal rule of the Pope was abolished and *the republic proclaimed in Rome*. So Cavaignac could not possibly murder a republic that

---

[a] "I know of a king, he is called Lord Ludwig
who gladly serves God" (i.e. nationalities).—*Ed.*

did not yet exist while he was in power. On April 22, 1849 Louis Bonaparte sent General Oudinot with 14,000 men to Civitavecchia after he had tricked the National Assembly into giving him the funds necessary for the expedition against Rome by solemnly declaring several times over that his intention was merely to resist an invasion of the Roman states planned by Austria. It is well known that the Paris catastrophe of June 13, 1849[148] arose from the resolution moved by Ledru-Rollin and the Montagne to exact vengeance for the "abominable act of massacre against the Roman Republic" which was also an "abominable breach of the French Constitution" and an "abominable violation of the resolution of the National Assembly", from *Louis Bonaparte,* who was responsible for all these abominations, *by instituting proceedings for impeachment against him.* We see how "abominably" the base sycophant of the coup d'état, how brazenly *Karl Vogt falsifies* history in order to elevate the mission of Lord "Hlùdowîg" to liberate the subject nationalities in general and Italy in particular beyond all doubt.

Vogt remembers from the *Neue Rheinische Zeitung* that alongside the class of the lumpenproletariat it is the class of peasant smallholders that in France constitutes the sole social basis of the *bas empire.* He now adjusts this as follows:

"The present Empire has no party among the educated, no party [...] in the French bourgeoisie—only two masses *belong* to it, the army and the rural proletariat,[a] *which cannot read or write.* But this constitutes $9/10$ of the population and embraces the mighty organised instrument with whose aid resistance can be smashed, and the *herd of mortgage helots* who own nothing but their *vote*" (p. 25).

The non-urban population of France, including the army, amounts to scarcely $2/3$ of the total population. *Vogt* transforms less than $2/3$ into $9/10$. Moreover, he transforms the whole non-urban population of France, of which around $1/5$ consists of well-to-do landowners and another $1/5$ of people with neither land nor other possessions, lock, stock and barrel into smallholders, "mortgage helots". Finally, he abolishes all reading and writing in France outside the cities. Just as he earlier distorted history, so now he falsifies statistics in order to enlarge the pedestal of his hero. Having done this he installs his hero on this pedestal.

"Thus France is now indeed summed up exclusively in the person of its ruler, of whom Masson" (also an authority) "said 'he possesses great qualities as a statesman and a sovereign, an unshakable will, sure sense of tact, vigorous resolution, a stout heart, a bold, noble spirit and utter ruthlessness'" (loc. cit., p. 27).

---

[a] Vogt in his *Studien* has *Landvolk* (rural people).— *Ed.*

"wie saeleclîche stât im an
allez daz, daz êr begât!
wie gâr sîn lîp ze wunsche stât!
wie gênt îm so gelîche inein
die fînen keiserlîchen bein."

(*Tristan*)[a]

Vogt snatches the censer from Masson's hands in order to swing it himself. To Masson's catalogue of virtues he adds "cold calculation", "bold planning", "serpentine cunning", "tenacious patience" (p. 28) and then, as the Tacitus of the antechamber, he stammers: "The *origins* of this reign are *monstrous*", which is certainly—nonsense. Above all he has to melodramatise the grotesque figure of his hero into a great man and so "*Napoléon le Petit*"[149] becomes a "*man of destiny*" (loc. cit., p. 36).

"Even if *present circumstances*," Vogt exclaims, "lead to a *change*" (what a modest word: a *change*!) "in the government" (of this man of destiny), "we shall not be behindhand with our *warmest congratulations,* even though we can see *no prospect* of this for the time being!" (loc. cit., p. 29.)

How serious the warm fellow is with his congratulations *in petto*[b] can be seen from the following:

"Hence with a **lasting peace** the *internal situation* becomes **more and more untenable day by day,** because the French army is much more closely involved with the parties of the educated than is the case, for example, in the German states, in Prussia and Austria; because these parties find an echo, above all among the officers, so that one fine day the *only active pillar* of the power that the Emperor holds in his hands might slip away" (loc. cit., pp. [26-]27).[c]

So the "*internal situation*" became "*more and more untenable day by day*" with a "**lasting peace**". This is why *Vogt* had to assist Louis Bonaparte to *violate the peace.* The army, the "only active pillar" of his "power", threatened to "slip away". This is why Vogt had to prove that it was Europe's task to bind the French "army" to Louis Bonaparte once again by means of a "localised" war in Italy. And indeed at the end of 1858 it looked as though things were going to end dreadfully[150] with Badinguet, as the Parisians unrespectfully call the "nephew of his uncle". The general trade crisis of 1857-58 had paralysed French industry.* The government

---

* It is in fact the industrial prosperity that has sustained the regime of Louis Bonaparte for so long. As the result of the discoveries in Australia and California

---

[a] "Everything he does, how divinely it becomes him! What a perfect body he has! How evenly those royal legs move together!" (Gottfried von Strassburg, *Tristan und Isolde.*) Marx quotes according to an entry he made in his notebook entitled *Vogtiana* (1860).— *Ed.*

[b] Up his sleeve.— *Ed.*

[c] The italics and bold type are Marx's.— *Ed.*

manoeuvres to prevent the crisis from becoming acute made the
malady chronic, so that the stagnation in French trade dragged on
until the outbreak of the Italian war. On the other hand, grain
prices fell so low between 1857 and 1859 that a loud cry went up
at various *congrès agricoles* to the effect that French agriculture was
being ruined by low prices and the heavy burdens imposed on it.
Louis Bonaparte's absurd attempt to raise grain prices artificially
by a fiat designed to force the bakers throughout France to set up
granaries only reveals the helpless confusion of his government.

The foreign policy of the coup d'état exhibited nothing but a
series of unsuccessful attempts to play Napoleon—mere trials,
invariably crowned by official withdrawals. For example, his
intrigue against the United States of America, his manoeuvres to
revive the slave trade,[151] the melodramatic threats directed against
England. The insolence with which Louis Bonaparte at that time
ventured to treat Switzerland, Sardinia, Portugal and Belgium—
even though in Belgium he could not even prevent the fortification of Antwerp—only throws the fiasco of his policy *vis-à-vis* the
great powers into even starker relief. In the British Parliament
"Napoléon le Petit" became a standard expression and *The Times*
heaped ridicule on the "Man of Iron" in its articles at the end of
1858, by describing him as the "Man of Gutta-Percha". In the
meantime, Orsini's hand-grenades [152] had burst like a thunderbolt,
illuminating the internal situation in France. It turned out that
Louis Bonaparte's regime was just as insecure as it had been in the
first days after the coup d'état. The *Lois de sûreté publique*[153]
revealed his total isolation. He had to abdicate to his own generals.
In an unprecedented development, France was divided into 5
General Captaincies, in the Spanish manner. With the introduction
of the Regency Pélissier was in fact recognised as the highest
authority in France.[154] Moreover, the renewed *terreur* intimidated
no one. Instead of presenting a terrible appearance, the Dutch
nephew of the battle of Austerlitz only looked grotesque.[155]
Montalembert was able to play Hampden in Paris, Berryer and
Dufaure to disclose the hopes of the bourgeoisie in their
summings-up and in Brussels Proudhon to proclaim Louis-
Philippism with an *acte additionnel,*[156] while Louis Bonaparte himself
disclosed the growing power of Marianne to the whole of Europe.

and their effects on the world market, French export trade had more than
doubled, a hitherto unprecedented advance. And in general the failure of the
February revolution may be attributed in the last analysis to California and
Australia.

In the course of the uprising in Chalon [157] the officers, on hearing that a republic had been proclaimed in Paris, cautiously inquired at the Prefecture whether a republic had actually been proclaimed, instead of just falling upon the insurgents, an event which demonstrated in a striking manner that even the army regarded the restored Empire as a pantomime, whose closing scene was drawing near. Scandalous duels of the arrogant officers in Paris coincided with scandalous deals on the Stock Exchange in which the top leaders of the Gang of December 10 were involved. The Palmerston Government in England fell because of its alliance with Louis Bonaparte! [158] And lastly, a treasury that could only be replenished by resorting to exceptional subterfuges! Such was the situation of the *bas empire* at the end of 1858. The Brummagem[a] Empire would collapse, or else the absurd farce of a Napoleonic empire *within* the frontiers of the treaties of 1815 would have to cease. But for this a *localised war* was essential. The mere prospect of a war with Europe would then have sufficed to produce an explosion in France. A child could understand what *Horsman* said in the British Parliament:

"We know that France will support the Emperor as long as our vacillation allows him success in his foreign policy, but we have grounds to believe that it will abandon him as soon as we show resolute opposition."

All depended on *localising* the war, i.e. on conducting it with the supreme sanction of Europe. To begin with, France itself had to be prepared gradually for the war with the aid of a series of hypocritical peace negotiations and their repeated failure. Louis Bonaparte came to grief even here. Lord Cowley, the English Ambassador in Paris, had gone to Vienna with proposals drawn up by Louis Bonaparte and approved by the (Derby) Cabinet in London. In Vienna (see the Blue Book quoted above[b]), under English pressure, the proposals were unexpectedly accepted. Cowley had just returned to London with the tidings of a "peaceful solution" when suddenly the news came that Louis Bonaparte had abandoned his own proposals and had supported the convocation of a congress suggested by Russia to discipline Austria. The war became possible only through the intervention of Russia. If Russia had no longer needed Louis Bonaparte in order to carry out its own plans—either *to enforce them with French assistance* or *to use the French to beat Austria and Prussia into passive instruments of Russia*—Louis Bonaparte would have fallen

---

a Marx uses the English word.— *Ed.*

b This refers to *Correspondence Respecting the Affairs of Italy* (see this volume, p. 134).— *Ed.*

then. But despite Russia's covert support, despite the promises of Palmerston, who had given his blessing at Compiègne to the conspiracy of Plombières,[159] everything depended on the attitude of Germany, since on the one hand the Tory Cabinet was still at the helm in England, and on the other hand the silent rebellion of France against the Bonapartist regime would have been driven out into the open by the prospect of a European war.

Vogt himself lets slip that he sang his *Lay of Ludwig* neither from a lively sympathy for Italy, nor from fear of the timid, conservative despotism of Austria, which was as clumsy as it was brutal. On the contrary, he believed that if Austria, which, it should be noted, was *forced* to start the war, should gain the advantage in Italy at first,

"the revolution would certainly be unleashed in France, the Empire would be overthrown and the future would be different" (loc. cit., p. 131). He believed that "the Austrian armies would in the last resort be unable to withstand the liberated forces of the French people" (loc. cit.) and that "the victorious armies of Austria, by provoking revolutions in France, Italy and Hungary, would themselves create the enemy who would crush them".[a]

But the issue for him was not the liberation of Italy from Austria, but the enslavement of France by Louis Bonaparte.

What further proof is required that *Vogt* was merely one of the countless mouthpieces through whom the grotesque ventriloquist in the Tuileries spoke in foreign tongues?

It will be remembered that at the time when Louis Bonaparte first discovered his mission to liberate the subject nationalities in general and Italy in particular, France presented a spectacle unprecedented in its history. The whole of Europe marvelled at the stubborn obstinacy with which it rejected the *"idées napoléoniennes"*.[b] People still remember very well the enthusiasm with which even the *"chiens savants"* [c] of the *Corps législatif* welcomed Morny's assurances of peace [d]; the irritated tone in which the *Moniteur* lectured the nation, now for its immersion in material interests, now for its lack of patriotic vigour and its doubts about Badinguet's talents as a general and his wisdom as a politician [e];

---

a Marx's italics.— *Ed.*

b An allusion to N.-L. Bonaparte's book *Des idées napoléoniennes*, Paris, 1839. — *Ed.*

c "Trained dogs".— *Ed.*

d This refers to Morny's speech at the opening of the Legislative Assembly on February 8, 1859, *Le Moniteur universel*, No. 40, February 9, 1859.— *Ed.*

e "Partie non officielle. Paris, le 4 mars", *Le Moniteur universel*, No. 64, March 5, 1859.— *Ed.*

the soothing official messages to all the chambers of commerce throughout France and the imperial assurance that "*étudier une question n'est pas la créer*".[a] At the time, the English press, astonished at the extraordinary spectacle, was crammed full of well-meaning nonsense about the transformation of the French into a peace-loving people, the Stock Exchange treated the issue of "war" or "not war" as a "duel" between Louis Bonaparte, who wanted war, and the nation, which did not, and bets were placed as to who would prevail, the nation or "his uncle's nephew". To give an idea of the situation as it was at the time I shall simply quote a few passages from the London *Economist*, which, as the organ of the City, as the spokesman of the Italian war and as the property of Wilson (the recently deceased Secretary of the Treasury for India and a tool of Palmerston), was highly influential:

"Alarmed at the colossal uproar which has been created, the French Government is now trying the soothing system" (*The Economist, January 15, 1859*).

In its issue of *January 22, 1859*, in an article entitled "*The Practical Limits of the Imperial Power in France*", *The Economist* says:

"Whether the Emperor's designs for a war in Italy are or are not carried out to their completion, *one* fact at least has become conspicuous enough,—that his plans have received a very severe and probably unexpected check in the chilling attitude assumed by popular feeling in France and the complete absence of any sympathy with the Emperor's scheme.... He proposes a war [...] and the French people show nothing but alarm and discontent;—the Government securities are depreciated, the fear of the tax-gatherer subdues every gleam of political or martial enthusiasm, the commercial portion of the nation is simply panic-struck, the rural districts are dumb and dissatisfied, fearing fresh conscriptions and fresh imposts;—the political circles which have supported the Imperial régime most strongly, as a *pis aller* against anarchy,[b] discourage war for exactly the same reason for which they support that régime [...] it is certain that Louis Napoleon has found an extent and depth of opposition throughout all classes in France to a war, even in Italy, which he did not anticipate." *

* Lord Chelsea, who deputised for Lord Cowley in Paris during the latter's absence, writes: "The official disavowal" (in the *Moniteur* of March 5, 1859) "of all warlike intentions on the part of the Emperor, this Imperial message of peace,[c] has been received *by all classes of Paris* with feelings of what may be called exultation" (No. 88 of the Blue Book *On the Affairs of Italy. January to May 1859*). [Marx quotes in English and gives the German translation in brackets.]

---

[a] "To study a question is not to create it."— *Ed.*

[b] *Pis aller* means "last resort". *The Economist* has "as against the alternative of anarchy".— *Ed.*

[c] "Partie non officielle. Paris, le 4 mars", *Le Moniteur universel*, No. 64, March 5, 1859.— *Ed.*

Faced with this mood of the French people *that* section of the original Dentu pamphlets was launched which "in the name of the people" peremptorily called on the "Emperor" "at last to assist France in the majestic extension of its frontiers from the Alps to the Rhine" and no longer to resist the "nation's pugnacious spirit and desire to bring about the liberation of the subject nationalities". *Vogt* plays the same tune as the prostitutes of December. At the very moment when Europe stood amazed at France's obstinate longing for peace, *Vogt* made the discovery that "*today,* the fickle nation" (the French)*"appears to be filled with a warlike passion"* (loc. cit., pp. 29, 30), and Lord Hlùdowîg was only following the "dominant trend of the age" which was intent on the "independence of the nationalities" (loc. cit., p. 31). Naturally, he did not believe a *single* syllable of what he was writing. In the *Programme* in which he called upon democrats to co-operate in his Bonapartist propaganda he makes it crystal clear that the Italian war was *unpopular* in France.

"*I cannot foresee any immediate threat to the Rhine*; *but* one could *arise in the future.* A war *there* or against England would make Louis Napoleon almost popular; *the Italian war does not possess this popular aspect*" ("Magnum Opus", Documents, p. 34).*

If now one portion of the original Dentu pamphlets sought to rouse the French nation from its "peace lethargy" with the aid of the traditional visions of conquest and to put the private wishes of Louis Bonaparte into the mouth of the nation, the other portion, with the *Moniteur* in the vanguard, had the task of convincing Germany in particular of the Emperor's repugnance to foreign conquests and of his ideal mission as the Messiah who would bring freedom to the subject nationalities. The proofs of the disinterestedness of his policy on the one hand and of his desire to free the subject nationalities on the other are easy to remember because they are constantly repeated and revolve round only two axes. Proof of the disinterestedness of Decembrist policies— *the Crimean war.* Proof of his desire to free the subject nationalities— *Colonel Cuza and the Romanian nationality.* The tone was set by the

* *N. B.* In his *Studien* he echoes the *Moniteur* and the original Dentu pamphlets to the effect that "it is a peculiar whim of fate which compels this man" (Louis Bonaparte) "to place himself in the forefront as the *liberator of the subject nationalities*" (p. 35), that one "must agree to *assist* this policy as long as it keeps within the framework of the liberation of subject nationalities" and *must wait "until this liberation has been brought about by this man of destiny"* (p. 36). In his *Programme* for the democrats, on the other hand, he says: "We can and *must warn against such a helper*" ("Magnum Opus", Documents, p. 34).

Moniteur. See the *Moniteur* of March 15, 1859 on *the Crimean war.* The *Moniteur* of April 10, 1859 writes about the *Romanian nationality:*

"In Germany as in Italy it" (France) "desires that the nationalities recognised by the treaties should continue to exist and become even stronger. In the *Danubian principalities* he" (the Emperor) "has endeavoured to help the legitimate wishes of these provinces to triumph so that an order based on national interests might be established in this part of Europe too."

See also the pamphlet published by *Dentu* at the beginning of 1859 with the title *Napoléon III et la question roumaine.* With regard to *the Crimean war:*

"Lastly, what compensation has France requested for the blood it has shed and the millions it has expended in the East in the service of an exclusively European cause?" (*La vraie question,* Dentu, Paris, 1859, p. 13.)

This theme, played with endless variations in Paris, was translated so well into German by *Vogt* that *E. About,* that gossipy magpie of Bonapartism, appears to have translated *Vogt's* German translation back into French. See *La Prusse en 1860.* Here too we are again pursued by the *Crimean war* and *Romanian nationality under Colonel Cuza.*

"But this much at least is clear," *Vogt* announces, echoing the *Moniteur* and Dentu's original pamphlets, "that France did not conquer a single square foot of land" (in the Crimea) "and that after such a *victorious campaign* the *uncle* would not have rested content with the meagre gain of having proved his superiority in the art of warfare" (*Studien,* p. 33). "Here we can see an *essential* difference between the present and the old Napoleonic policies" * (loc. cit.).

---

* Incidentally, "*Napoléon le Petit*" also copied the catchword "liberation of subject nationalities" from the real Napoleon. In *May 1809,* for example, Napoleon issued a proclamation from Schönbrunn to the *Hungarians,* in which he says *inter alia:* "Hungarians! The moment is come to recover your *independence....* I ask *nothing* of you. I only desire to see you a *free and independent nation.* Your union with Austria has been your bane, etc." [a] On May 16, 1797 Bonaparte concluded a treaty with the Republic of Venice whose first article states: "In future peace and understanding shall govern relations between France and the Venetian Republic." He revealed his intentions in concluding this peace three days later in a secret dispatch to the French Directory which opens with these words: "You receive herewith the treaty that I have concluded with the Republic of Venice and under the terms of which General Baraguay d'Hilliers has occupied the city with 5,000-6,000 men. In making this peace I had a number of aims in mind." As the final aim he mentions: "To silence all the talk in Europe since it will now seem as if our occupation of Venice is merely a temporary operation which *the Venetians themselves* urgently requested." Two days later, on May 26, Bonaparte wrote to the Venice municipality: "The treaty concluded

---

[a] "Proclamation Addressed to the Hungarians by Napoleon I. From Schoenbrunn, in May, 1809" (see Bartholomäus Szemere, *Hungary, from 1848 to 1860,* London, 1860).— *Ed.*

As if Vogt had to prove to us that *"Napoléon le Petit"* is not the real Napoleon! With just as much justification *Vogt* could have prophesied in 1851 that the nephew, who had nothing to set against the first Italian campaign and the expedition to Egypt but the Strasbourg adventure, the expedition to Boulogne and the sausage review of Satory,[160] could never emulate the 18 Brumaire, to say nothing of acquiring the Imperial Crown. There was after all "an essential difference between the present and the old Napoleonic policies". Yet another difference was between waging a war against a European coalition and waging one with the permission of a European coalition.

The "glorious campaign in the Crimea" in which England, France, Turkey and Sardinia in concert "captured" half a Russian fortress after two years, and in exchange lost a whole Turkish fortress (Kars) to the Russians, and at the conclusion of peace were forced humbly to "request" the enemy at the Paris Congress [161] for "permission" to evacuate their troops without interference and ship them home—that was indeed anything but "Napoleonic". It

in Milan can be signed by the municipality in the meantime—the secret articles by three of its members. I shall always do everything in my power to provide you with proofs of my desire to consolidate *your liberties* and to see *this unfortunate Italy* at last occupy the place it deserves on the world stage, *free and independent of all alien rule."* A few days later he wrote to General Baraguay d'Hilliers[a]: "On receipt of this letter present yourself to the Provisional Government of Venice and point out to them that in accordance with the principles which now unite the Republics of France and Venice, and with the immediate protection granted to Venice by the French Republic, it is essential to place its sea power on a footing that will inspire respect. *On this pretext* you will take possession of everything, while at the same time you will do all in your power to remain on good terms with the Venetians and to recruit all the sailors of the Republic to our service—while *constantly speaking in the name of Venice.* In brief, you must manage matters so that you can transport the entire stock of ships and naval supplies in the harbour of Venice to Toulon. By virtue of a secret article in the treaty, the Venetians are obliged to provide the French Republic with naval supplies to the value of 3 million for the Toulon navy, but *it is my intention* to take possession on behalf of the French Republic of *all* the Venetian ships and *all* their naval supplies for the benefit of Toulon" (see *Correspondance secrète et confidentielle de Napoléon,* 7 vols., Paris, 1817). These commands were carried out to the letter; and as soon as Venice had been plundered of *all* its naval and war supplies, Napoleon, without the slightest hesitation, handed over his new ally, *the liberated Republic of Venice,* whom he had solemnly sworn to defend at whatever the risk, to *the despotic yoke of Austria.*

---

[a] Napoléon Bonaparte, "Au chef de division commandant la marine française dans le golfe Adriatique. Montebello, le 25 prairial, an 5 (13 juin 1797)", *Correspondance inédite...,* v. 5, livre 1, pp. 304-05. Baraguay d'Hilliers is named by mistake here.— *Ed.*

was glorious only in *Bazancourt*'s novel.[a] But the Crimean war proved all sorts of things. Louis Bonaparte *betrayed* his ostensible allies (the Turks) in order to gain the alliance of the ostensible enemy. The first success of the Paris peace was the sacrifice of the "Circassian nationality" and the extermination of the Crimean Tartars by the Russians, and likewise the destruction of the national hopes that the Poles and Swedes had pinned to a West European crusade against Russia. A further moral of the Crimean war was: Louis Bonaparte could *not* afford a *second Crimean war*, could not afford to lose an old army and gain new national debts in exchange for the knowledge that France was rich enough "*de payer sa propre gloire*",[b] that the name of Louis Napoleon figured in a European treaty, that "the conservative and dynastic press of Europe" unanimously acknowledged "the ruling virtues, the wisdom and the moderation of the Emperor"—a fact which *Vogt* counts to Louis Bonaparte's credit (loc. cit., p. 32)—and that at the time the whole of Europe paid him all the honour due to a genuine Napoleon, on the express condition that Louis Bonaparte, following the example of Louis Philippe, should quietly stay within "the limits of practical reason", i.e. of the treaties of 1815, and not forget for a single moment the fine line that distinguishes a buffoon[c] from the hero he represents. The political combinations, the ruling powers and the social conditions that provided the leader of the December Gang with the opportunity to play at being Napoleon, first in France and then even beyond French territory, do in fact belong to *his* epoch, and not to the annals of the Great French Revolution.

"This fact at any rate is established, that present French policy in the East has fulfilled the aspirations of one nationality" (the *Romanian*) "for unification" (*Studien,* pp. 34-35).

Cuza, as we have mentioned, is keeping the place open for either a Russian governor or a Russian vassal. On the map of *L'Europe en 1860* a Grand Duke of Mecklenburg figures as that vassal. Russia naturally allowed Louis Bonaparte all the *honour* for *this* Romanian emancipation, reserving all its advantages for itself. Austria stood in the way of further benevolent intentions. Hence the Italian war had the function of *remodelling* Austria, *changing it from an obstacle into an instrument*.

---

a *L'Expédition de Crimée jusqu'à la prise de Sébastopol,* t. I-II, Paris, 1857.— *Ed.*
b "To pay for its own fame".— *Ed.*
c Marx uses the word *Pickelhäring,* the name for the buffoon in Old German comedies.— *Ed.*

The ventriloquist in the Tuileries was already playing the tune of "Romanian nationality" on his innumerable mouthpieces as early as 1858. One of *Vogt's* authorities, *Mr. Kossuth,* was thus in a position to give an answer as early as November 20, 1858 in a lecture in Glasgow[a]:

"Wallachia and Moldavia receive a Constitution, hatched in the caverns of secret diplomacy.... It is in reality no more nor less than a charter granted to Russia for the purpose of disposing of the Principalities."[b]

Thus the "principle of nationality" was abused by Louis Bonaparte in the Danubian principalities so as to mask the fact that they were being handed over to Russia, just as in 1848-49 the *Austrian Government* had abused the "principle of nationality" to strangle the Magyar and German revolution with the aid of the Serbs, Slovenes, Croats, Wallachians, etc.

Good care is taken both by the Russian consul in Bucharest and by the rabble of Moldavian and Wallachian Boyars, most of whom are not even Romanian but a motley mosaic of adventurers from God-knows-where—a sort of oriental December Gang—that the *Romanian people* should still groan beneath the burdens of a villeinage so monstrous that it could *only* have been set up by *Russians* with their *règlement organique* and could only be sustained by an oriental *demi-monde.*

Vogt, in the attempt to deck out the wisdom quarried from his original Dentu sources with his own eloquence, says:

"Austria already had enough on her hands with one Piedmont in the South; it had no need of another in the East" (loc. cit., p. 64).

Piedmont annexes *Italian* lands. So are the Danubian principalities, the least warlike of the Turkish lands, to annex Romanian territory, that is, conquer Bessarabia from Russia, and Transylvania, the Banat of Temesvár and the Bukovina from Austria? *Vogt* not only forgets the "benevolent Tsar", he also forgets that in 1848-49 *Hungary* did not seem in the least inclined to part with these more or less Romanian provinces, that it answered their "cry of distress" with a drawn sword, and that on the contrary it was *Austria* which used "propaganda about the principle of nationality" as a weapon *against Hungary.*

But the historical scholarship of his *Studien* shows itself in its full splendour when *Vogt,* relying on half-remembered bits from

---

[a] Kossuth actually gave the lecture on November 19 (Kossuth, *L'Europe, l'Autriche et la Hongrie,* Bruxelles, 1859, pp. 54-55).— *Ed.*

[b] Marx gives this sentence in English in brackets after its German equivalent.— *Ed.*

an ephemeral pamphlet, which he had skimmed through, with perfect calm

"*deduces* the wretched condition of the principalities ... from the destructive poison of the *Greeks* **and** *Fanariots*" (loc. cit., p. 63).

He had no idea that the *Fanariots* (so called after a district in Constantinople) are these very same *Greeks* who have lorded it in the Danubian principalities under Russian protection since the beginning of the eighteenth century. They are, in part, the descendants of the *limondji* (lemonade-sellers) of Constantinople that are now once again playing at "Romanian nationality" by order of the Russians.

———————

While the white angel of the North advances from the East, destroying the various nationalities for the benefit of the Slav race, the white angel of the South advances from the opposite direction as the standard-bearer of the principle of nationality, and

"we must *wait until* the liberation of the subject nationalities has been brought about by this man of destiny" (*Studien,* p. 36).

Now while these combined operations of the two angels and the "two greatest external enemies of Germany's unity" (*Studien,* 2nd edition, Afterword, p. 154) are being conducted "in close concert"—what role is assigned to *Germany* by our Imperial Vogt, who is, however, no "Augmentor of the Realm" [a]?

"The most short-sighted persons," Vogt remarks, "*must* have realised by now that there is an understanding between the Government of Prussia and the Imperial Government of France, that Prussia will not unsheath its sword to defend the non-German provinces of Austria" (including Bohemia and Moravia, of course), "that it will give its approval to all measures affecting the defence of the territory of the Confederation" (excluding its "non-German" provinces), "but will otherwise prevent any intervention of the Confederation or its individual members on Austria's behalf, so that in the subsequent peace negotiations *it will receive its reward for these efforts in the North German plains*" (*Studien,* 1st edition, pp. 18-19).

By proclaiming from the housetops, even before the outbreak of the war against Austria, the secret entrusted to him by the Tuileries that Prussia was acting in "secret *understanding*" with the "external enemy of Germany", who would reward it with territory "in the North German plains", Vogt was of course giving Prussia the best possible assistance in achieving its alleged ends. He roused

———————

[a] Medieval title bestowed on the German Emperor.— *Ed.*

the suspicions of the other German governments both towards Prussia's initial attempts to neutralise them and towards its military preparations and its claim to the supreme command during the war.

"Whatever path Germany has to choose in the present crisis," Vogt says, "one thing is certain: that as a whole it must pursue one definite path with energy, whereas as things are the unhappy Federal Diet, etc." (loc. cit., p. 96).

By spreading the view that Prussia goes arm in arm with "the external enemy" and that this will lead to its devouring the Northern plains, Vogt presumably intends to restore the unity in the Federal Diet which is so badly lacking. *Saxony*, in particular, is reminded explicitly that Prussia has already once occasioned "the loss of some of its finest provinces" (loc. cit., p. 93). The "purchase of the Jade Bay" is denounced (loc. cit., p. 15).

"*Holstein* was to have been the reward for Prussia's participation" (in the Turkish War) "when the notorious theft of the dispatch gave the negotiations a different turn" (loc. cit., p. 15). "Mecklenburg, Hanover, Oldenburg, Holstein and other miscellaneous appendages ... these fraternal German states are the bait at which Prussia greedily snatches"—and does so moreover "at every possible opportunity" (loc. cit., pp. 14, 15).

And as Vogt reveals, on this occasion it has been firmly hooked by Louis Bonaparte. On the one side, as the result of its secret "understanding" with Louis Bonaparte Prussia must and will "reach the coasts of the North Sea and the Baltic at the expense of its German brothers" (loc. cit., p. 14). On the other side,

"Prussia will have obtained a *natural frontier* only when the *watershed* of the Erzgebirge and the Fichtelgebirge is extended *through* the white Main and *along* the Main up to Mainz" (loc. cit., p. 93).

Natural frontiers in the depth of Germany! Formed, moreover, by a *watershed* which *passes through a river*! It is this sort of discovery in the realm of physical geography—to which we may add the channel that rose to the surface (see "Magnum Opus")—that puts "the well-rounded character" on a par with Alexander von Humboldt. At the same time as he was preaching to the German Confederation on the confidence it must have in the leadership of Prussia, Vogt, not satisfied with the "ancient rivalry between Prussia and Austria on German, etc., territory", invented another rivalry between these two states which "has so frequently broken out on *non-European* soil" (loc. cit., p. 20). This *non-European* soil is probably on the moon.

In fact Vogt simply translates into words the map of *L'Europe en 1860* published by the *French* Government in 1858. The map shows Hanover, Mecklenburg, Brunswick, Holstein, the Electorate of Hesse together with sundry territories such as Waldeck, Anhalt, Lippe, etc., as having been annexed to Prussia, while "*l'Empereur des Français conserve ses* (!) *limites actuelles*", the Emperor of the French preserves his (!) existing frontiers. "Prussia down to the Main" is also a slogan of Russian diplomacy. (See, for example, the memorandum of 1837 mentioned above.[a]) A Prussian North Germany would counterbalance an Austrian South Germany, separated by natural frontiers, tradition, denomination, dialect and tribal differences. The *division* of Germany *into two parts* would be completed by simplifying the contradictions within it and the Thirty Years' War [162] would be declared in permanence.

According to the first edition of the *Studien*, Prussia was supposed to receive such a *"reward"* for its "efforts" in forcing the sword of the German Confederation back into its sheath during the war. In Vogt's *Studien,* as on the French map *L'Europe en 1860,* it is *not Louis Bonaparte, but Prussia* that seeks and achieves the enlargement of its territory and attains natural frontiers as a result of the *French* war against Austria.

Vogt only reveals Prussia's true task in the Afterword to the second edition of his *Studien,*[b] which appeared while the Franco-Austrian war was still in progress. Prussia was to initiate a "**civil war**" (see the 2nd edition, p. 152) so as to establish a "unified central power" (loc. cit., p. 153), to incorporate Germany in the Prussian monarchy. While Russia advances from the East and Austria is held down by Louis Bonaparte in Italy, Prussia is to embark on a *dynastic "civil war"* in Germany. Vogt guarantees the Prince Regent[c] that

"the war that has broken out" in Italy "will last out the year 1859 at the very least, whereas the unification of Germany, if prosecuted resolutely, will not take *as many weeks* as the Italian campaign months" (loc. cit., p. 155).

The civil war in Germany will only be a matter of weeks! Apart from the Austrian troops which would immediately march on Prussia, Italian war or no Italian war, Prussia would meet resistance, as *Vogt* himself explains, from "*Bavaria*[d] ... which is entirely under Austrian influence" (*Studien*, 1st edition, p. 90), from *Saxony,* which would be the first to be threatened and which

---

[a] See this volume, p. 141.— *Ed.*

[b] The Preface to the first edition of the *Studien* was dated "March 31, 1859", and the Afterword to the second edition, "June 6, 1859".— *Ed.*

[c] William, Prince of Prussia.— *Ed.*

[d] Vogt's italics.— *Ed.*

would no longer have any reason to do violence to its "sympathies for Austria" (loc. cit., p. 93), from "Württemberg, Hesse-Darmstadt and Hanover" (loc. cit., p. 94), in short from *"nine-tenths"* (loc. cit., p. 16) of the *"German governments"*. And these governments, as *Vogt* further demonstrates, would not lack support in the event of such a *dynastic* "civil war", especially if initiated by Prussia at a time when Germany was threatened by its "two greatest external enemies".

"The court" (in Baden), says Vogt, "goes along with Prussia, but the people, and there is no doubt about that, certainly does not share the predilections of the ruling family. The Breisgau, no less than Upper Swabia, is bound much more closely to the Emperor and the Imperial state by ties of sympathy, religious confession and old memories of the Austrian Forelands, to which it formerly belonged, than one would have supposed after such a long separation" (loc. cit., pp. 93-94). "With the exception of Mecklenburg" and "perhaps" the Electorate of Hesse, "in *North Germany* the attitude to the theory of incorporation is one of mistrust and Prussia's policy is accepted only with reluctance. The instinctive *feeling of dislike, indeed of hatred,* aroused by Prussia in *South Germany* ... has not been eliminated or talked out of existence by the full-throated cry of the Imperial party.[a] It lives on in the people, and no government, not even that of Baden, can resist it for long. *Thus Prussia has no real support either among the German people, or in the governments of the German Confederation"* (loc. cit., p. 21).

Thus speaks Vogt. And for that very reason, according to that same *Vogt*, a *dynastic "civil war"* initiated by Prussia in "secret understanding" with the "two greatest external enemies of Germany", would only be a matter of *"weeks"*. But there is more to come.

"The Old Prussian provinces go along with the government—the *Rhineland and Westphalia* with Catholic Austria. If the popular movement there does not succeed in pushing the government over to Austria's side, *the immediate consequence would be to reopen the gulf between the two parts of the monarchy"* (loc. cit., p. 20).

Thus, according to *Vogt,* if the simple non-intervention of Prussia on Austria's behalf was enough to reopen the gulf between Rhineland-Westphalia and the Old Prussian provinces, then clearly, in the eyes of the same *Vogt,* a "civil war", undertaken by Prussia with the aim of expelling Austria from Germany, was bound to wrench Rhineland-Westphalia from Prussia for good and all. But "what does Germany matter to these papists?" (loc. cit., p. 119), or as he really thinks, what do these papists matter to Germany? The *Rhineland and Westphalia* are ultramontane *"Roman-Catholic"* and not *"true German"* provinces. Hence they must be expelled from the territory of the Confedera-

---

[a] i.e. the supporters of Austria.—*Ed.*

tion just like Bohemia and Moravia. And this process of expulsion is to be accelerated by the *dynastic "civil war"* recommended to Prussia by *Vogt*. And in fact in its map published in 1858 of *L'Europe en 1860*, which served *Vogt* as a compass throughout his *Studien*, the *French* Government, which had annexed Egypt to Austria, also showed the Rhine provinces as countries of *"Catholic nationality"* and annexed by *Belgium*—an ironic formula for the annexation of Belgium and the Rhine provinces by France. The fact that *Vogt* goes even further than the map of the French Government and throws in Catholic Westphalia as an extra, can be explained by the "scientific relations" between the fugitive Regent of the Empire and Plon-Plon, the son of the ex-King of Westphalia.[a]

To sum up: On the one hand, Louis Bonaparte will give Russia leave to extend its rule from Posen to Bohemia and from Hungary right down to Turkey. On the other hand, he himself will establish a united and independent Italy on France's frontier by force of arms, and all that—*pour le roi de Prusse*[b]; all that to give Prussia an opportunity to bring Germany under its wing by means of a civil war and to "secure" the "Rhine provinces for ever" against France (loc. cit., p. 121).

"But, it will be said, the territory of the Confederation is in danger, the hereditary foe threatens, his real goal is the Rhine. Then, defend the Rhine and defend the territory of the Confederation" (loc. cit., p. 105),

and in fact defend the territory of the Confederation by ceding Bohemia and Moravia to Russia, and defend the Rhine by starting a German "civil war" with the aim, among others, of tearing Rhineland and Westphalia from Prussia.

"But, it will be said, Louis Napoleon ... desires to satisfy his Napoleonic thirst for conquest by some means or other! We do not think so, we have the example of the Crimean campaign before our eyes!" (loc. cit., p. 129.)

Apart from his scepticism about the Napoleonic thirst for conquest and his faith in the Crimean campaign, *Vogt* has yet another argument *in petto*. The Austrians and the French will follow the example of the Kilkenny cats[163] and keep on biting each other in Italy until there is nothing left of them but their tails.

"It will be a terribly bloody, stubborn and perhaps indecisive war" (loc. cit., pp. 127, 128). "Only by exerting its strength to the very utmost will France, together with Piedmont, be able to triumph, and it will not recover from these efforts for decades" (loc. cit., p. 129).

---

[a] Jérôme Bonaparte.— *Ed.*
[b] For the King of Prussia, i.e. for nothing.— *Ed.*

This prospect of a *long-lasting* Italian war silences his critics. And the method by which *Vogt* manages to prolong Austria's resistance to French arms in Italy and to cripple France's aggressive power, is indeed original enough. On the one hand, the French are given *carte blanche* in Italy; on the other hand, the "benevolent Tsar" is given leave by manoeuvres in Galicia, Hungary, Moravia and Bohemia and by revolutionary machinations within the country and military demonstrations on its frontiers

"to hold down a significant part of the Austrian forces in those parts of the monarchy which are exposed to Russian attack or vulnerable to Russian intrigue" (loc. cit., p. 11).

And lastly, by means of a dynastic "civil war" simultaneously unleashed in Germany by Prussia, Austria will be compelled to withdraw its main forces from Italy to protect its German possessions. It is obvious that in such circumstances Francis Joseph and Louis Bonaparte will not conclude a Treaty of Campoformio[164] but "will both bleed to death in Italy".

Austria will not make any concessions to the "benevolent Tsar" in the East and accept the long-standing offer of indemnification in Serbia and Bosnia. Nor will it guarantee the Rhine provinces to France and fall on Prussia in league with Russia and France. Not on your life! It will insist on "bleeding to death in Italy". In any event, however, Vogt's "man of destiny" would indignantly reject such a compensation on the Rhine. Vogt knows that

"the foreign policy of the present Empire has only one principle, that of self-preservation" (loc. cit., p. 31).

He knows that Louis Bonaparte

"is intent on pursuing a single idea [...] that of preserving his power" (over France) (loc. cit., p. 29).

He knows that the "Italian war does not increase his popularity in France" whereas the acquisition of the Rhine provinces would make him and his dynasty "popular". He says:

"The Rhine provinces are indeed a pet ambition of the French chauvinist and perhaps, if one were to go into it, one would discover only a very small minority of the nation which did not bear this wish deep in its heart" (loc. cit., p. 121).

On the other hand, "perceptive Frenchmen", and therefore presumably also Vogt's "man of destiny who is as wise as a serpent", know that

"they can only hope to see this realised" (namely France's acquisition of the natural frontier of the Rhine) "as long as Germany possesses 34 different governments. [...] Let a real Germany come into existence, with unified interests and a firm organisation—and the Rhine frontier will be secure for all time" (loc. cit., p. 121).

For this very reason, Louis Bonaparte, who at Villafranca offered the Emperor of Austria Lombardy in exchange for a guarantee of the Rhine provinces (see the statement by Kinglake in the House of Commons, July 12, 1860[a]), would have indignantly rejected Austria's offer of the Rhine provinces in exchange for French aid against Prussia.

Vogt's original *Dentu* sources likewise not only indulged in lyrical effusions on the subject of German unity under the aegis of Prussia*: they also spurned every suggestion of ambitions in the Rhine provinces with virtuous indignation.

"The Rhine!... What is the Rhine?—A frontier. Frontiers will soon be anachronisms" (*La foi des traités, etc.*, Paris, 1859, p. 36).**

In the millennium that is to be established by Badinguet on the foundations of the principle of nationality, who will be concerned about the Rhine frontier, or indeed any frontiers at all!

"Does France insist on compensation for the sacrifices it is prepared to make in the cause of equity, of legitimate influence and in the interest of European equilibrium? Does it demand the left bank of the Rhine? Does it so much as lay claim to Savoy and the County of Nice?" (*La vraie question, etc.*, Paris, 1859, p. 13.)***

* "La Prusse est l'espoir de l'Allemagne ... l'esprit allemand a son centre à Berlin ... l'esprit allemand cherche *l'unité* de son corps, la vérité de la Confédération. C'est par cet entraînement que s'élève la Prusse... D'où vient-il que, lorsque l'Italie réclame l'intégrité, l'unité nationale, ce que l'Allemagne désire, celle-ci favorise l'Autriche, négation vivante de toute nationalité?... C'est que la Prusse n'est pas encore la tête; c'est que la tête est l'Autriche qui, pesant avec ces forces hétérogènes sur l'Allemagne politique, l'entraîne à des contradictions avec l'Allemagne véritable" (*La foi des traités, etc.*, p. 34). ["Prussia is the hope of Germany ... the German spirit has its centre in Berlin ... the German spirit seeks the *unity* of its body, a real Confederation. It is this desire that induces Prussia to rise.... How does it come about that while Italy demands national integrity and unity, which Germany too longs for, the latter can still favour Austria, the living negation of all nationality?... The reason is that Prussia is not yet in command; the reason is that Austria is still in command and weighing with its heterogeneous forces on the political entity called Germany, and brings it into contradiction with the real Germany."]

** "Le Rhin!... Qu'est-ce que le Rhin? Une frontière. Les frontières seront bientôt des anachronismes" (loc. cit., p. 36).

*** "La France stipule-t-elle des dédommagements pour les sacrifices qu'elle est prête à faire dans un but d'équité, de juste influence, et dans l'intérêt de l'équilibre

---

[a] *The Times*, No. 23671, July 13, 1860.—*Ed.*

France's renunciation of Savoy and Nice as proof of France's renunciation of the Rhine! Vogt did not translate that into German.

Before the start of the war it was of crucial importance for Louis Bonaparte, if he was unable to lure Prussia into an understanding, at least to make the German Confederation believe that he had done so. Vogt attempts to disseminate this belief in the first edition of his *Studien*. During the war it became even more important for Louis Bonaparte to induce Prussia to take steps that would provide Austria with proof or apparent proof of such an understanding. In the second edition of the *Studien*, which appeared while the war was in progress, Vogt therefore calls on Prussia in an Afterword to conquer Germany and initiate a dynastic "civil war" which, as the text of his book makes clear, would be "bloody, stubborn and perhaps indecisive" and would cost Prussia Rhineland and Westphalia at the very least. And in the Afterword to the same book he solemnly assures his readers that it will "only cost a matter of weeks". Vogt's voice is in truth not that of the siren. Hence Louis Bonaparte, seconded in his knavish plot by bottle-holder[a] *Palmerston*, was forced to present *Prussian proposals he himself had drawn up* to Francis Joseph in Villafranca; Austria had to use Prussia's modest claims to the military leadership of Germany as an excuse for concluding a peace* which Louis Bonaparte had to excuse in France by saying that the Italian war was threatening to become a general war which

"would bring about German unity and thus accomplish a work which ever since Francis I it had been the object of French policy to prevent".**

européen? Demande-t-elle la rive gauche du Rhin? Élève-t-elle même des prétentions sur la Savoie et sur le Comté de Nice?" (*La vraie question, etc.*, p. 13.)

* A few days after the conclusion of peace in Villafranca the *Prager Zeitung* printed the following official declaration: "This insistence" (Prussia's insistence on taking over the supreme command of the federal army *under federal control*) "provides clear proof that *Prussia is striving for hegemony in Germany and thus for the expulsion of Austria from Germany.* Since faithless Lombardy is infinitely less valuable than *the maintenance of our position in Germany*, we sacrificed it so as to achieve peace which had become an urgent necessity for us *in view of Prussia's attitude*."[b]

** *Galignani's Messenger* of Paris, which only carries leading articles by way of exception and then in response to special official request, states in its issue of July 22, 1859 [Marx quotes in English]: "To give another province to the King of Piedmont, it would not only have been necessary to support a war against

---

[a] Marx uses the English expression.— *Ed.*

[b] "Politische Übersicht, Wien, 13. Juli", *Prager Zeitung*, No. 165, July 15, 1859.— *Ed.*

After France had acquired Savoy and Nice as a result of the Italian war, and with them a position worth more than an army in the event of a war on the Rhine, "German unity under Prussian hegemony" and "cession of the left bank of the Rhine to France" became interchangeable factors in the probability calculations of the 2nd December. The map of *L'Europe en 1860* published in 1858 was interpreted by the map *L'Europe pacifiée* (Europe pacified?) which appeared in 1860. According to this map Egypt was no longer given to Austria and the Rhine provinces together with Belgium were annexed by France in return for the "*Northern plains*" that were now assigned to Prussia.*

Finally, *Persigny* made an official pronouncement in Etienne that, if only in the "interest of European equilibrium", any further centralisation on the part of Germany would entail the advance of France to the Rhine.** But neither before nor after the Italian war had the grotesque ventriloquist of the Tuileries expressed himself with such insolence as through the mouthpiece of the fugitive Imperial Regent.

---

two-thirds of Europe, but *German unity would have been realised,* and a work thus accomplished, which ever since the time of Francis I it has been the object of French policy to prevent." ["Latest Intelligence", *Galignani's Messenger,* No. 13876, July 22, 1859.]

* Plon-Plon's special organ, *L'Opinion nationale,* said in an article of July 5, 1860: "The day of demanding the return of territories by force is past. The Emperor has too much tact and too accurate a feeling for the trend of public opinion for that.... But is *Prussia* obliged by oath never to think of *German unity*? Can it guarantee never to cast a covetous eye on Hanover, Saxony, Brunswick, Hesse, Oldenburg and Mecklenburg? Today the rulers embrace each other and their sincerity is certainly genuine. But who knows what the people will demand of them in a few years' time? And if, under the pressure of public opinion, Germany is *unified* would it be fair, would it be reasonable not to allow *France to expand its territory at the expense of its neighbours?*... If the Germans were to think it right and proper to alter their hitherto existing political constitution and to put a strong centralised government in the place of the impotent Confederation, then we cannot guarantee *that France would not think it right and proper to demand compensation and assurances from Germany.*"

** The Imperial Pecksniff excels himself in the Dentu pamphlet *La politique anglaise,* Paris, 1860. According to this a few million Germans and Belgians have to be purloined in order to improve the moral constitution of France, whose southerly element requires a greater admixture of northern solidity. Having argued that for political and military reasons France *requires the frontiers given it by nature itself,* it continues: "A second factor makes such an annexation" (of the Rhine provinces and Belgium) "necessary. France desires and demands a rational freedom (*une sage liberté*) and the southerly element plays an important role in its public institutions. This southerly element has many wonderful qualities ... but it lacks stamina and

Vogt "the New Swiss, citizen of the Canton of Berne and member of the Council of States [165] for Geneva" (loc. cit., Preface), opens the *Swiss* section of his *Studien* with a prologue (loc. cit., pp. 37-39) in which he calls upon Switzerland to utter a *paean of joy* at the replacement of Louis Philippe by Louis Bonaparte. It is true that Louis Bonaparte was demanding that the Federal Council should "put controls on the press", but "the Napoleonides seem in this respect to have extremely sensitive skins" (loc. cit., p. 36). A mere skin disease, so engrained in the family that it is transmitted not only in the family blood, but even — *teste* Louis Bonaparte—by the mere family name. However,

"The persecution of innocent men in Geneva which has been carried out by the Federal Council on *instructions from the Emperor* against poor devils whose only crime was that they were Italians; the establishment of consulates; the harassment of the press; the senseless police regulations of every conceivable kind and, finally, the negotiations about the cession of the Vallée des Dappes,[166] have all played an essential part in obliterating in the minds of the Swiss the memories of those *services* which *the Emperor really rendered* in the *Neuchâtel affair*,[167] and in particular for the very party which has now turned most violently against him" (loc. cit., pp. 37, 38).

Magnanimous Emperor, ungrateful party! The Emperor's aim in the Neuchâtel affair was by no means the creation of a precedent for the violation of the treaties of 1815, the humiliation of Prussia and the establishment of a protectorate over Switzerland. What he was really concerned with was "*to render*" Switzerland "*a real service*", in his capacity as "New Swiss, citizen of the Canton of Thurgau and artillery captain of Oberstrass". The accusation of ingratitude levelled by *Vogt* against the anti-Bonapartist party in Switzerland in March 1859, was extended to the whole of Switzerland in June 1860 by another servant of the Emperor, M. de *Thouvenel. The Times* of June 30, 1860 writes that

"A few days ago a meeting took place between Dr. Kern and M. de Thouvenel in the Foreign Ministry in Paris in the presence of Lord Cowley. Thouvenel informed the honourable representative of Switzerland that the doubts and protestations of the Federal Government were insulting inasmuch as they seemed to imply a want of faith in the government of His Imperial Majesty. Such treatment was base ingratitude in view of the *services* which the Emperor Napoleon had *rendered*[a] the Confederation on many occasions, and in particular in the

firmness. It stands in need of patient steadfastness, the cold, unbending resolution of our northern brothers. The frontiers destined for us by providence, therefore, are as essential to our freedom as to our independence."

---

[a] Marx gives the English words "services" and "rendered" in brackets after their German equivalents.— *Ed.*

Neuchâtel affair. However that may be, since Switzerland had been so *blind* as to mistrust her benefactor, she must herself bear the consequences."

Nevertheless *Vogt* tried to open the eyes of the *blind* anti-Bonapartist party in Switzerland as early as March 1859. On the one hand, he points to "the real services" which "the Emperor has rendered". On the other hand, "the Imperial harassments shrink to vanishing point" beside the royal harassments under Louis Philippe (loc. cit., p. 39). For example, in 1858 the Federal Council "on instructions from the Emperor" expelled some "poor devils whose only crime was that they were Italians" [a] (p. 37); in 1838, notwithstanding Louis Philippe's threats, it refused to expel Louis Bonaparte, whose only crime was to have used Switzerland as a base from which to conspire against Louis Philippe.• In 1846, despite Louis Philippe's "warlike gestures", Switzerland ventured upon the Sonderbund war,[168] for it refused to let itself be bullied by the peaceful King; in 1858 it was hardly prudish in its reaction to Louis Bonaparte's groping in the Vallée des Dappes.

"Louis Philippe," Vogt says himself, "had dragged out a miserable existence in Europe, snubbed by everybody, even by the lesser legitimate rulers, because he had not dared to conduct a strong foreign policy" (loc. cit., p. 31). However, "*Imperial policy vis-à-vis Switzerland* is without any doubt that of a powerful neighbour *who knows that in the end he can enforce whatever he likes*" (loc. cit., p. 37).

Therefore, Vogt concludes, with a logic worthy of *Grandguillot*, "*from a purely Swiss point of view one can only rejoice heartily*" (p. 39) because instead of "Louis Philippe who was snubbed by everybody" Switzerland has received a "powerful neighbour who knows that *with respect to Switzerland he can do whatever he likes*".

This prologue, which establishes the necessary mood, is followed by a German translation of the note of the Federal Council of March 14, 1859,[b] and curiously enough Vogt is full of praise for this note in which the Federal Council referred to the treaties of 1815,[169] though the same Vogt declares that it is "hypocrisy" to refer to these treaties. "Get along with your hypocrisy!" (loc. cit., p. 112.) *

* In reality it was not the "treaties" which had protected Swiss neutrality, but the fact that the interests of the various neighbouring powers cancelled each other out. "The Swiss feel," wrote Captain Harris, the English chargé d'affaires in Berne, in a letter to Lord John Russell after an interview with Frey-Hérosé, the Federal President, "that ... recent events have fundamentally altered the balance of power

[a] In early 1858 Napoleon III demanded that the Swiss Government should extradite the political refugees accused of being implicated in the Orsini conspiracy.— *Ed.*

[b] Carl Vogt, *Studien...*, S. 80-83.— *Ed.*

Vogt now goes on to consider "from which side *the first attack on Swiss neutrality will come*" (loc. cit., p. 84) and proves, quite unnecessarily, that the French army, which had no need to conquer Piedmont this time, would march through neither the Simplon nor the Great St. Bernard. At the same time he discovers a non-existent land route "over the Mont Cenis, via Fénestrelle and through the Stura valley" (loc. cit., p. 84). He means the Dora valley. From *France*, then, there is no threat to Switzerland.

"But respect for Swiss neutrality *on the part of Austria* cannot be looked for with similar confidence, and various factors even suggest that in certain eventualities Austria is indeed prepared to violate it" (loc. cit., p. 85). "Of significance in this respect is *the concentration of a military force in Bregenz and Feldkirch*" (loc. cit., p. 86).

Here the thread which runs through the *Studien* and leads straight from Geneva to Paris becomes visible.

The Blue Book on *The Affairs of Italy. January to May 1859* published by the Derby Cabinet says that "the concentration of an Austrian military force near Bregenz and Feldkirch" was a rumour assiduously cultivated by Bonapartist agents in Switzerland without a jot of factual evidence to support it (No. 174 of the Blue Book in question: letter from Captain Harris to Lord Malmesbury, Berne, March 24, 1859). In this connection Humboldt-Vogt also made the discovery that in Bregenz and Feldkirch

"one is in the immediate vicinity of the valley of the Rhine, which is the starting-point for *three* great Alpine passes with viable roads, viz., the Via Mala, the Splügen and the Saint Bernard, the latter leading to the Ticino, the first two to Lake Como" (loc. cit., p. 86).

In reality the Via Mala leads firstly over the Splügen, secondly over the Saint Bernard and thirdly nowhere else.

After all this Polonius chatter designed to direct the apprehensions of the Swiss from the Western to the Eastern frontier, "the well-rounded character" at last rolled on to its real task.

"Switzerland," Vogt announces, "is utterly *in the right* when it *firmly rejects* the obligation not to permit troop movements on this railway" (from Culoz to Aix and Chambéry) "and will confine itself, should the case arise, to make use of the neutralised territory only insofar as it is necessary for the defence of its own territory" (loc. cit., p. 89).

among Switzerland's neighbours, as ever since the Neuchâtel affair, Prussia has been indifferent, Austria paralysed, and France incomparably more powerful than before."[a]

---

[a] Harris to Russell, received January 25, *Correspondence Respecting the Proposed Annexation of Savoy and Nice to France...*, London, 1860, p. 12.— *Ed.*

And he assures the Federal Council that "the whole of Switzerland will support the *policy indicated in its note of March 14* to a man".

Vogt published his *Studien* at the end of March. It was not until April 24 that Louis Bonaparte used the above-mentioned railway for troop movements and he did not declare war until even later. Thus Vogt, who was privy to the details of the Bonapartist plan of war, knew very well *"from which side the first attack on Swiss neutrality would come"*. His mission was explicitly to decoy Switzerland into condoning an initial violation of its neutrality, which would lead logically to the annexation of the neutralised territory of Savoy by the December Empire. Patting the Federal Council on the back, he attributes to the note of March 14 the meaning that it *ought to have* from the point of view of the Bonapartists. The Federal Council stated in its note that Switzerland would fulfil its "mission" of neutrality as stipulated in the treaties, "faithfully and with complete impartiality". It goes on to quote an article of the treaties according to which *"no troops belonging to any other power may pass through* or be stationed there" (in the neutralised territory of Savoy). It does not mention *at all* that it would permit the French to use the railway which passes through the neutralised territory. Conditionally, as a "measure designed to secure and defend the territory of the Confederation", it reserves the right of the Confederation to a "military occupation" of the neutralised territory. The fact that *Vogt* deliberately and on instructions from above *distorts* the note of the Federal Council is not only evident from its own wording; it is corroborated also by the statement made in the House of Lords on April 23, 1860 by Lord *Malmesbury*, then British Foreign Secretary:

"When the French troops were about to march through Savoy into Sardinia" (more than a month *after* the Federal Council's note of March 14), "the Swiss Government, true to the neutrality upon which depends its independence, [...] at first objected that these troops had no right to pass through the neutralised territory." [a]

And by what means did Louis Bonaparte and the Swiss party allied with him manage to allay the doubts of the Federal Council? Vogt, who was aware at the end of March 1859 that French troop trains would violate the neutralised territory at the end of April 1859, was naturally able to foresee by the end of March the euphemism which Louis Bonaparte would use at the end of April to palliate his act of violence. He casts doubt on whether the

---

[a] Marx gives the quoted passage in English in a footnote.— *Ed.*

"head of the line from Culoz to Aix and Chambéry comes within the neutral territory" (loc. cit., p. 89) and shows that "the demarcation of neutral territory was not carried out with the purpose of cutting off communications between France and Chambéry", so that morally the railway in question does not come within the neutral territory.*

Let us, on the other hand, listen to what Lord *Malmesbury* says about it:

"Subsequently, there being some question as to whether the line of railway did not avoid the neutralised portion of Savoy, the Swiss Government withdrew their objection, and allowed the troops of France to pass. I think that they were wrong in doing so.[a] We thought the maintenance of the neutrality of such European consequence ... that we protested at the French Court against the passage of those troops to Sardinia on 28 April 1859."

This protest led to Palmerston accusing Malmesbury of "pro-Austrian" sympathies, as he "had uselessly offended the French Government",[b] just as *Vogt* in his "Magnum Opus" (p. 183) accuses *Das Volk* of

"doing everything in its power to embarrass Switzerland", on behalf of Austria, of course.... "Read the articles which *Das Volk* published about the question of neutrality and the passage of the French troops through Savoy if you wish to have tangible evidence of these views, which are fully shared by the *Allgemeine Zeitung*".**

* The fact that the railway *does* come within the neutralised territory was explicitly conceded in a note addressed to Captain Harris on November 18, 1859 by Stämpfli, the President of the Confederation, and Schiess, the Chancellor. It says there: "Il pourrait être aussi question d'un autre point qui concerne la neutralité de la Savoie ... nous voulons parler du chemin de fer dernièrement construit de Culoz à Chambéry, à l'égard duquel on peut se demander s'il devait *continuer à faire partie du territoire neutralisé*." ["A further question could arise concerning the neutrality of Savoy ... we refer to the railway recently constructed between Culoz and Chambéry, regarding which it may be questionable whether it can *continue to form part of the neutralised territory*."]

** Vogt accuses *Das Volk* in particular of having attempted "to bring about a conflict between the Swiss Confederation and its more powerful neighbours". When the annexation of Savoy actually took place, the *Eidgenössische Zeitung,* a Bonapartist paper, criticised the official journal, *Der Bund,* because "its views on Savoy and France were a feeble echo of the policy which had aimed at involving Switzerland in the conflicts of Europe ever since 1848" (see *Der Bund*, Berne, No. 71, March 12, 1860). It is evident that the Bonapartist scribes receive the phrases ready-made.

---

[a] Marx gives this sentence in English in brackets after its German equivalent.— *Ed.*

[b] Marx gives this phrase in English in brackets after its German equivalent.— *Ed.*

The reader will now have "tangible evidence" that the entire
section of Vogt's *Studien* that deals with Switzerland had no other
purpose than to prepare the ground for the *first violation of Swiss
neutrality* by his "man of destiny". It was the first step towards the
annexation of Savoy and hence of French Switzerland. The fate of
Switzerland depended on the vigour with which it opposed this
first step, maintained its rights by availing itself of them at the
decisive moment and raised the matter at European level at a time
when the support of the English Government was assured and
Louis Bonaparte, who was just launching into his localised war,
would not venture to throw down the gauntlet. Once the English
Government had become officially committed, it could not back
out.* *Hence* the mighty efforts of our "New Swiss, citizen of the
Canton of Berne and member of the Council of States for
Geneva" to distract attention by representing it as a **right** to be
asserted by Switzerland and as a courageous gesture of defiance
towards Austria to *grant permission* to the French troops to march
through the neutralised territory. After all, he had saved
Switzerland from Catiline-Cherval!

At the same time as Vogt reiterates and amplifies the denial put
out in his original *Dentu* pamphlets with regard to ambitions on
the Rhine frontier, he avoids making *any* reference, even the most
tentative, to the renunciation of Savoy and Nice contained *in the
same pamphlets*. Even the names of Savoy and Nice do not appear
at all in his *Studien*. Now, as early as February 1859, Savoyard
delegates in Turin had protested against the Italian war on the
grounds that the annexation of Savoy by the December Empire
would be the price of purchasing the French alliance. This protest
had never reached Vogt's ears. Nor had the terms of the
agreement reached at Plombières by Louis Bonaparte and Cavour
in *August 1858* (published in one of the first issues of *Das Volk*[a])
even though they were well known in émigré circles. In the issue
of *Pensiero ed Azione* already cited (May 2-16, 1859), *Mazzini* had
predicted, literally:

"But if Austria were to be defeated right at the start of the war and if it were to
revive the proposals which it had put to the English Government for some time in
1848, namely the surrender of Lombardy on condition that it could keep Venice,
then peace would be accepted. The only conditions to be implemented would be

---

* "Had those provinces (Chablais and Faucigny) been occupied by the Federal
troops ... there can be little doubt they would have remained in them up to this
moment" (L. Oliphant, *Universal Suffrage and Napoleon III*, London, 1860, p. 20).

---

a "Mazzini und Monsieur Bonaparte", *Das Volk*, No. 5, June 4, 1859.— *Ed.*

the enlargement of the Sardinian monarchy and the *cession of Savoy and Nice to France.*" *

Mazzini published his prediction in the middle of May 1859 and the second edition of Vogt's *Studien* appeared in the middle of June 1859, but it did not contain a single word about Savoy and Nice. Even before Mazzini and the Savoyard delegates, as early as *October 1858,* a month and a half after the conspiracy at Plombières, the President of the Swiss Confederation informed the English Ministry in a dispatch that

"he had reason to believe that a conditional agreement about the cession of Savoy had been reached between Louis Bonaparte and Cavour".**

In the beginning of June 1859 the President of the Confederation again informed the English chargé d'affaires in Berne of his fears about the imminent annexation of Savoy and Nice.*** *Vogt,* the professional saviour of Switzerland, never received the least intimation either of the protest of the Savoyard delegates or of Mazzini's revelations, or of the anxieties of the Swiss Federal Government which persisted from October 1858 to June 1859. Indeed, as we shall see later, *even in March 1860,* when the secret of Plombières was circulating in all the streets of Europe, it took care to keep out of Vogt's way. "Silence is the virtue of slaves",[a] the motto of the *Studien,* refers presumably to their failure to mention the threatened annexation. They do, however, contain *one* oblique reference to it:

"But even assuming," Vogt says, "even assuming that the *improbable* were to take place and that territory in Italy, whether to the south or the north, were to be the prize for victory.... *Undoubtedly, from an extremely narrow German point of view ... one might fervently wish* that the French wolf will get his teeth into *an Italian bone*" (loc. cit., pp. 129, 130).

---

* "Ma dove l'Austria, disfatta in sulle prime, affacciasse proposte eguali, a quelle ch'essa affacciò per breve tempo nel 1848 al Governo Inglese, abbandono della Lombardia a patto di serbare il Veneto, la pace ... sarebbe accettata: le sole condizioni dell'ingrandimento della Monarchia Sarda e della cessione della Savoia e di Nizza alla Francia, riceverebbero esecuzione."

** In the speech mentioned above, Lord *Malmesbury* said: "There is a despatch now in the Foreign Office, dated as long back as October 1858 ... from the President of the Swiss Republic, stating that he had reason to believe that some conditional agreement had been come to between the Emperor of the French and Count Cavour with respect to Savoy."

*** See No. I of the first Blue Book *On the Proposed Annexation of Savoy, etc.*

---

a Paraphrased dictum from Heinrich Heine's *Reisebilder,* Zweiter Teil, Italien. III. Die Stadt Lucca, Kap. XVII.— *Ed.*

Italian territory to the north of course meant Nice and Savoy.
After the New Swiss, citizen of the Canton of Berne and member
of the Council of States for Geneva has called on Switzerland
"from a purely Swiss point of view" (loc. cit., p. 39) to *"rejoice with all
its heart"* at having Louis Bonaparte for a neighbour, it suddenly
occurs to the fugitive Regent of the Empire that "undoubtedly,
from an extremely narrow German point of view" he would "fervently
wish" that the French wolf "will get his teeth into the bone" of
Nice and Savoy, and *hence, of French Switzerland.**

Some time ago a pamphlet appeared in Paris with the title
Napoléon III, not *Napoléon III et l'Italie*, or *Napoléon III et la
question Roumaine*, or *Napoléon III et la Prusse*,[a] but quite simply
Napoléon III, Napoleon III without any qualification. Couched
entirely in hyperboles, it is a panegyric on Napoleon III written by
Napoleon III. The pamphlet was translated by an *Arab* called
Dâ-Dâ into his native tongue.[b] In the Afterword the intoxicated
Dâ-Dâ is unable to contain his enthusiasm any longer and
overflows into radiant verse. In the Foreword, however, he is still
sober enough to confess that his pamphlet had been published at
the behest of the local authorities in Algiers and was destined for
distribution among the indigenous Arab tribes beyond the
Algerian frontiers so that "the idea of unity and nationhood
under a common leader might take hold of their imagination".

---

* The wish which, "from an extremely narrow German point of view", Vogt
has to force Italian "bones" between the jaws of the "French wolf" to give the wolf
indigestion, will undoubtedly be fulfilled in increasing measure. The semi-official
Revue contemporaine—Vogt's special patron, incidentally—on October 15, 1860
carries a report from Turin of October 8 which states *inter alia: "Genoa and
Sardinia* would be the legitimate prize for a new (French) war on behalf of Italian
unity. I may add that the possession of Genoa would be the necessary instrument
of our influence on the peninsula and the only effective means of preventing the
sea power whose establishment we had aided from defecting from an alliance with
us at a later date in order to enter into league with someone else. *Only with our knee
on Italy's throat can we be sure of its loyalty. Austria, a good judge on this point, knows this
very well. We shall apply pressure less crudely, but more effectively than Austria,—that is the
only difference."* [Quoted from "La situation de l'Italie, Turin, le 8 octobre 1860".]

[a] Marx refers to the following pamphlets: Arthur La Guéronnière, *Napoléon III,
portrait politique,* Paris, 1853 and *L'empereur Napoléon III et l'Italie,* Paris, 1859;
A. Lévy, *L'empereur Napoléon III et les principautés roumaines,* Paris, 1858; and
Edmond About, *La Prusse en 1860,* Paris, 1860.— *Ed.*

[b] La Guéronnière, *Portrait politique de l'empereur Napoléon III,* trad. en arabe par
M. Rochaid Dahdah, Paris, 1860.— *Ed.*

This common leader who would lay the foundations for "the unity of the Arab nation" is, as Dâ-Dâ makes clear, none other than "the sun of beneficence, the glory of the firmament,—the Emperor Napoleon III". Vogt, although his writing is unrhymed,[a] is none other than *the German Dâ-Dâ*.

That *Dâ-Dâ Vogt* should employ the word "*studies*" to describe his German paraphrase of the "*Moniteur*" *articles, Dentu pamphlets and revised maps of Europe* inspired by the sun of beneficence and the glory of the firmament, is the best joke that has ever occurred to him in the course of his hilarious career. It even surpasses his Regency of the Empire, the Imperial Wine-Bibbing and his invention of the Imperial passports. The fact that the "educated" German citizen was able to accept in good faith "studies" in which Austria fought against Britain for the possession of *Egypt*, Austria and Prussia were waging their struggle on *non-European* terrain, Napoleon I compelled the Bank of England to weigh its gold instead of counting it, Greeks and Fanariots were racially distinct, a land route went from Mont Cenis through Fenestrelle via the Stura valley, etc.,—all this bears witness to the high pressure which a ten-year-long reaction had exerted on his liberal skull.

Curiously enough, the same liberal German sluggard who had applauded the crude exaggerations of *Vogt's German version of the original Decembrist pamphlets,* leaped up in fury from his sleep when *Edmond About* produced a prudently restrained French *retranslation* of Dâ-Dâ's compilation with the title *La Prusse en 1860* (originally *Napoléon III et la Prusse*). This chattering magpie of Bonapartism, incidentally, has a dash of waggishness. As evidence of Bonapartist sympathies for Germany, *About* points out, e.g., that the December Empire no more distinguishes between *Dâ-Dâ Vogt* and *Humboldt* than it does between *Lazarillo Hackländer* and *Goethe*.[b] At any rate his bracketing of *Vogt* with *Hackländer* suggests a more profound study on the part of About than is to be found anywhere in the *Studien* of our German Dâ-Dâ.

---

[a] Marx puns on the word *ungereimt,* which means "unrhymed" and also "without rhyme or reason".— *Ed.*

[b] Edmond About. *La Prusse en 1860,* Paris, 1860, p. 6.— *Ed.*

IX

AGENCY

"So muosens alle strîten.
in vîl angestlîchen zîten
wart gescheiden doch her dan
... der *Vogt* da von Bërne." [a]

(*Klage*) *

In a Programme which Dâ-Dâ Vogt in a fit of great hilarity has dated *April 1*, namely April 1, 1859,[c] he called upon democrats of every shade of opinion to collaborate in a paper which was to appear in Geneva and propagate the Decembrist-Russian views of his *Studien*. Circumspect as the Programme naturally had to be, the cloven hoof can occasionally be glimpsed beneath the blotting-paper in which it is wrapped. But we shall not dwell on this aspect of it.

At the conclusion of his Programme Vogt asks his readers to give him the names of "like-minded comrades" who "would be

---

* In *Iwein*, on the other hand, *Hartmann* makes the *Vogt* say, evidently alluding to his dispute with the bears of Berne[b]:

"von Bêrn mac wol heizen ich,
wand ich dâ nîht ze schaffen hân."
["Von Bern I may be called
Though no business have I there."]

This *Hartmann* is not to be confused with Vogt's friend, the lyrical parliamentary mollusc of the same name.

---

[a] "Thus, all to war must go
In times of grief and woe.
He had to take leave of that place
...the *Vogt* of Berne." [170] — *Ed.*
[b] i.e. the people of Berne.— *Ed.*
[c] Carl Vogt, *Mein Prozess...*, Dokumente, S. 33-37.— *Ed.*

prepared to support similar aims in newspapers and journals to which they had access". At the Joint Festival in Lausanne he declared he had formulated a Programme with an invitation to

"*those people who* were in agreement with it and were prepared to work for it, in exchange for an appropriate remuneration, in organs of the press at their disposal" (*Centralfest, etc.,* p. 17).[a]

Lastly, in a letter to *Dr. Loening* he writes:

"Can you put me in touch with *people* who could influence newspapers and journals in this sense from Frankfurt? I am in a position to offer respectable remuneration for the contributions offprints of which I am sent" ("Magnum Opus", Documents, p. 36).

The *"like-minded comrades"* of the Programme become *"those people who"* at the Joint Festival of Lausanne, and they in turn are transformed into *"people",* people *sans phrase,* in the letter to Dr. Loening. Vogt the Treasurer in Chief and Inspector General of the German press has had "funds placed at his disposal" (loc. cit., p. 36) with which to commission not only articles "in newspapers and journals", but even "pamphlets" (loc. cit.). It is easy to see that an agency on this scale stands in need of quite substantial "funds".

> "—er sante nach allen den hêrren
> die in diusken rîchen wâren;
> er klagete in allen sîn nôt,
> unde bôt in ouch sîn golt rôt."
>
> (*Kaiserchronik*)[b]

But to what purpose were newspapers, journals and pamphlets to be "influenced" and "sent to" Vogt by *those people who* would then receive "respectable" remuneration from him? "It is Italy that is at stake", that is all; for in order to ward off the danger threatening on the Rhine it "appears advantageous" to Herr Vogt "to bleed Louis Bonaparte in Italy" (*Programme*, loc. cit., p. 34). No, "it is not Italy that is at stake" (letter to Dr. Loening, loc. cit., p. 36). "Hungary is at stake" (letter to Herr H. in N., loc. cit.). No, Hungary is not at stake. "What is at stake ... is something that I cannot disclose" (loc. cit., Documents, p. 36).

---

[a] Georg Lommel, *Das Centralfest der Deutschen Arbeiterbildungsvereine in der Westschweiz*, Genf, 1859, S. 17.— *Ed.*

[b] "For all the noble lords sent he
   That dwelt in the lands of Germany.
   All them of his great need he told,
   And offered them his bright red gold." [171]— *Ed.*

As controversial as the question of what is at stake is the problem of the source from which these respectable "funds" flow. It lies in "a remote corner of French Switzerland" ("Magnum Opus", p. 210). No, "it is Hungarian ladies from the West" (letter to Karl Blind, supplement to No. 44 of the *Allgemeine Zeitung* of February 13, 1860).[a] On the contrary, it is some *masculini* "within the reach of the German and especially the Austrian police" (*Centralfest,* p. 17). The size of his funds is no less chameleon-like than their purpose and source. They amount to "a few francs" ("Magnum Opus", p. 210). "The funds are small" (*Centralfest,* p. 17). The funds are adequate to provide respectable remuneration for all those able to exert a Vogtian influence in the German press and in pamphlets. To cap it all there are even two accounts of the formation of the funds. Vogt has "*scraped them together* slowly and painfully" ("Magnum Opus", p. 210). No, they "have been placed at his disposal" (loc. cit., Documents, p. 36).

"If I am not mistaken," says the "well-rounded character", "to *bribe* means to offer someone money or other advantages to perform actions or make utterances contrary to his own convictions" (loc. cit., p. 217).

Hence anyone whose convictions bid him to allow himself to be *bought* cannot be *bribed,* likewise anyone whose convictions run counter to this cannot be bribed. For example, if the department of the Paris Ministry responsible for the foreign press offers Swiss newspapers copies of the Paris *Lithographierte Correspondenz* which appears daily and costs 250 francs, at half or a quarter of the price, or even for nothing, and if it intimates to "editors who are well disposed" that they can expect a cash bonus of 50, 100 or 150 francs each month "depending on their success", this cannot be called bribery by any stretch of the imagination. The editors whose convictions run counter to the daily *Correspondenz* and the monthly bonus are not compelled to accept the one or the other. And has Granier de Cassagnac been "bribed", or La Guéronnière, or About, or Grandguillot, or Bullier, or Jourdan of *Le Siècle,* or Martin or Boniface of *Le Constitutionnel,* or Rochaid Dâ-Dâ Albert? Has a remunerative action or utterance ever come into conflict with the convictions of any of these gentlemen? Or again, did Vogt bribe the agent of a certain Swiss newspaper formerly hostile to him when he placed several hundred copies of his *Studien* at his disposal free of charge? In any event it is a strange

---

[a] In Karl Blind's article "Gegen Karl Vogt". — *Ed.*

invitation, Vogt's invitation to journalists to work in the spirit of their own convictions in organs at their disposal and to be rewarded for their efforts by the organ of Herr Karl Vogt in Geneva. The fact that Vogt makes no distinction between the fee paid by a particular newspaper to its own contributors and the secret subsidies which a third party draws from an anonymous source and offers to the correspondents of newspapers quite unconnected with him and even to the press of a whole nation—this quid pro quo shows the extent to which the German Dâ-Dâ "familiarised" himself with the morality of December 2.

"At the source there sat a youth."[a] But at which source?

Instead of the weekly *Die Neue Schweiz* intended by Vogt, there appeared somewhat later in Geneva the *Neue Schweizer Zeitung*, founded by Herr *A. Brass*, Dâ-Dâ's friend of many years' standing. One cool morning in November Herr Brass declared to the astonishment of the whole of Geneva that he had

"written to Vogt spurning the *French feeding-trough* that Vogt had tried to set before him".

At the same time he declared his willingness to stand by his denunciation before a court (*Neue Schweizer Zeitung, November 12, 1859*). And the cock or rather the capon that had crowed so merrily until that moment suddenly fell silent as soon as he was attacked on his own dung-heap. The "New Swiss, citizen of the Canton of Berne and member of the Council of States for Geneva" now stood publicly accused in the middle of Geneva by one of his "notorious" friends of having *attempted to bribe him* with *French* money. And the Genevan Councillor fell silent.

It should not be imagined that Vogt could simply ignore the *Neue Schweizer Zeitung* with an air of superiority. The denunciation of his actions had appeared, as we have said, in the issue of November 12, 1859. Shortly after this the same paper published a piquant description of Plon-Plon and the *Revue de Genève*, the organ of *James Fazy,* the dictator of Geneva, immediately retorted in a four-column leading article (*Revue de Genève,* December 6, 1859). It protested "*au nom du radicalisme genèvois*", in the name of Genevan radicalism. Such was the importance attached to the *Neue Schweizer Zeitung* by James Fazy himself. The four-column leading article of the *Revue de Genève* shows the unmistakable signs of Vogt's helping hand. Brass himself is half-excused. He had not contrived the attack on Plon-Plon, but

---

[a] From Schiller's poem "Der Jüngling am Bache".—*Ed.*

had merely been led astray. In the authentic Vogtian style the *corpus delicti* is placed at the doorstep of the same L. Häfner whom Vogt suspected, in the "Magnum Opus" too (p. 188), of spreading "unsavoury pieces of personal gossip about the Emperor and Prince Napoleon". There is also Vogt's inevitable allusion to "the notorious former Baden lieutenant Clossmann" as the Berne correspondent of the *Allgemeine Zeitung* (cf. "Magnum Opus", p. 198). Let us dwell for a moment on the protest which master and servant, *James Fazy* and *Karl Vogt,* published on December 6, 1859 in the *Revue de Genève* "in the name of Genevan radicalism" and in vindication of Plon-Plon.

Brass is accused of attempting "to validate his German opinion of France by insulting a Prince of the House of Bonaparte". As had long been common knowledge in Geneva, *Plon-Plon* was a liberal of the purest water who during his exile had magnanimously refused "to play a part of any sort at the court of Stuttgart or even Petersburg". Nothing would be more ridiculous than to impute to him, as does the libellous article in the *Neue Schweizer Zeitung,* the idea of forming a small sovereign realm here and there, an Etruscan kingdom, for instance.

"Prince Napoleon, who is acutely aware of his own **genius** and his own *talents,* has too lofty an opinion of himself to stoop to such petty thrones."

Rather does he prefer "as citizen-prince" *(prince-citoyen)* to play the part of Marquis Posa at the court of his exalted cousin in France, "the centre of high civilisation and the fount of general inspiration". "His cousin loves and respects him, whatever people may say of this." The Prince is not only Bonaparte's Marquis Posa. He is "the disinterested friend" of Italy, of Switzerland, in short, of the subject nationalities.

"Prince Napoleon, like the Emperor, is a great economist.... Undoubtedly, if the sound principles of political economy ever triumph in France, this will be due in no small measure to the influence of Prince Napoleon."

He was and is "the advocate of the most far-reaching freedom of the press", the enemy of all preventive measures on the part of the police, the adherent of "ideas of freedom in the broadest sense of the word, both in theory and practice". If this Egeria finds that the Emperor's malicious entourage has made him deaf to his voice, he makes a dignified withdrawal, but "without sulking". It is simply "*his merits* that have exposed him to the slanders of Europe". The

"enemies of France fear him because he relies on the revolutionary support of the peoples of Europe to restore to them their nationhood and their liberty".

Hence he is a misunderstood genius, Marquis Posa, Egeria, an economist, the protector of the subject nationalities, a democrat of the purest water and—can it be possible?—Plon-Plon is *"habile comme général et brave comme tout officier fançais"* ("a skilful general and valiant like every French officer").

"He proved this in the Eastern campaign, during and following the battle on the Alma." And in the Italian campaign "he ably organised his army corps of 50,000 men" (the celebrated *corps de touristes*; I was almost tempted to write *corps de ballet*) "and within a short space of time he made a hard march through mountainous country without his men wanting for anything".

The French troops in the Crimea are known to have said of anyone who got into a funk that he was suffering from *la maladie Plon-Plonienne,* and it is likely that Plon-Plon only withdrew from the peninsula because of the increasing shortage of provisions.[172]

"We," the *Revue de Genève* concludes triumphantly, "we have portrayed him", namely Plon-Plon, "as he really is".

Three cheers for General Plon-Plon!

No wonder therefore that *Vogt* can announce that he received his war chest from "democratic hands". Plon-Plon, the *Prince Rouge,*[a] is the ideal of both Vogt and Fazy; he is, as it were, the enchanted prince of European democracy. *Vogt* could not receive his money from purer democratic hands than those of Plon-Plon. Even if some of the monies made over directly to Mr. Kossuth by Plon-Plon's exalted cousin had been transmitted to Vogt through Hungarian hands, their "origins would still be *monstrous*".[b] But from the hands of Plon-Plon...! And even if the monies that *Vogt* obtained from Klapka's friend, Countess K.,[c] at the time of the Neuchâtel affair might come from more delicate hands, they could not possibly come from purer or more democratic ones. A well-known French writer has said that *"Plon-Plon est voluptueux comme Héliogabale, lâche comme Ivan III et faux comme un vrai Bonaparte"*.[d] Plon-Plon's most disastrous achievement is that he has turned his cousin into *un homme sérieux*. Victor Hugo could still say of Louis Bonaparte *"n'est pas monstre qui veut"*.[e] But ever since Louis Bonaparte invented Plon-Plon, the business side

---

[a] Red Prince.— *Ed.*

[b] Carl Vogt, *Studien...,* S. 28.— *Ed.*

[c] Countess Károlyi.— *Ed.*

[d] "Plon-Plon is as dissolute as Heliogabalus, as cowardly as Ivan III and as false as a real Bonaparte" (Victor Hugo, *Napoléon le Petit,* paraphrased).— *Ed.*

[e] "One is not a monster because one wishes to be one" (ibid.).— *Ed.*

of the Imperial Janus has been concentrated in the hands of the man in the Tuileries, and the grotesque side in the man residing in the Palais Royal. The false Bonaparte, who is his uncle's nephew without being his father's son,[173] appeared authentic when compared with this authentic Bonaparte. So that the French still say: "*l'autre est plus sûr*".[a] Plon-Plon is both the Don Quixote and the Hudibras of the *bas empire*. Hamlet thought it disquieting that the dust of Alexander might have been used to stop a bung-hole.[b] What would Hamlet have said if he had seen the disintegrated head of Napoleon on the shoulders of Plon-Plon?*

Although *Vogt* obtained the main supplies of money for his war chest *"from the French feeding-trough"*, it is of course possible that to conceal this he also organised ostentatious collections of "a few francs" from more or less democratically inclined friends. The contradictions about the source, quantity and formation of his funds are thus quite easily resolved.

Vogt's agency did not confine itself to the *Studien,* the *Programm* and the setting up of a recruitment office. At the *"Joint Festival" in Lausanne* he informed the German workers in Switzerland of Louis Bonaparte's mission to liberate the subject nationalities, and he did so of course in more radical terms than he had used in the *Studien,* which had been intended for the liberal German philistines. In the latter case his penetrating study of the relation between "matter and energy"[174] had led him to the conclusion that there could be no question of "undermining and destroying the existing governments in Germany" (*Studien,* Preface, p. VII), and he appealed to the "German bourgeois" in particular (loc. cit., p. 128) "to take to heart" the consideration that the Bonapartist "liberation" of Italy would help to ward off "revolution" in Germany. He informed the German workers, on the other hand, that "Austria is the *only pillar* shoring up their" (i.e. the German rulers') "existence" (*Centralfest, etc.,* p. 11).[c]

---

* Vogt recounts that as early as 1852 he was supposed to embark on a voyage of discovery (Bacchic procession?) with Plon-Plon, to whom he had been enthusiastically recommended by a "Proudhonist" because of his "astounding studies in natural history" "*mais do que promettia a força humana*" ["which showed promise of superhuman strength", Camoëns, *Lusiads,* First Canto] ("Magnum Opus", Documents, p. 24).

---

[a] "The other one is safer."— *Ed.*

[b] Shakespeare, *Hamlet,* Act V, Scene 1.— *Ed.*

[c] Here and below Marx quotes Vogt's speech at the Joint Festival of the German Workers' Educational Associations in Lausanne (Georg Lommel, *Das Centralfest der Deutschen Arbeiterbildungsvereine in der Westschweiz*).— *Ed.*

"As I have just pointed out," he said, "Germany does not exist as far as the outside world is concerned, it has still to be created, and I am convinced that it can only be created *in the form of a federation of republics* similar to the Swiss Confederation" (loc. cit., p. 10).

He said this on June 26 (1859), while on June 6, in the Afterword to the second edition of the *Studien* he entreated the Prince Regent of Prussia[a] to bring Germany beneath the sway of the House of Hohenzollern by force of arms and a dynastic civil war. Monarchic centralisation by force of arms is, of course, the shortest way to a federal republic "similar to the Swiss Confederation". He further developed the theory of the *"external enemy"*, France, with which Germany should ally itself in opposition to the *"internal enemy"*, Austria.

"If I am presented with the choice," he exclaimed, "between the Devil (Habsburg) and his grandmother (Louis Bonaparte), *I will choose the latter,* since she is an old woman and must die."

This direct appeal to Germany to throw itself into the arms of Decembrist France on the pretext of hatred for Austria seemed to him too compromising to be put into print, so in the *published* speech we find this emended version:

"And if we are obliged to take up sides in the dispute between the Devil and his grandmother we think it would be best *if the two were to kill and devour each other,* thus saving us the trouble" (*Centralfest, etc.,* p. 13).

Finally, whereas in the *Studien* he raises the standard of Louis Bonaparte as the Emperor of the peasants and soldiers, when faced with an audience of workers he declares that

"it is *especially the great majority of workers in Paris* who have been won over to Louis Bonaparte".

In the view of the French workers

"Louis Bonaparte is doing everything the Republic should have done *since he is giving work to the proletariat and ruining the bourgeoisie, etc.*" (*Centralfest, etc.,* p. 9).

Thus Louis Bonaparte is a *workers' dictator* and eulogised as such before the German workers in Switzerland by the very same *Vogt* who in the "Magnum Opus" flared up in bourgeois indignation at the mere mention of the words "workers' dictatorship"![b]

The Paris programme which laid down the line to be followed by the Decembrist agents in Switzerland on the question of the

---

[a] William.— *Ed.*
[b] Carl Vogt, *Mein Prozess...*, S. 136-40. Vogt has "dictatorship of the proletariat".— *Ed.*

annexation of Savoy consisted of three points: (1) For as long as
possible rumours of the imminent danger were to be
completely ignored and if necessary they were to be dismissed as
an Austrian invention. (2) At a more advanced stage it should be
put about that Louis Bonaparte wished to incorporate the
neutralised territory into Switzerland. (3) And finally, once the
annexation had been carried out it should be used as a
justification for a *Swiss alliance with France,* i.e. for Switzerland's
voluntary submission to a Bonapartist protectorate. We shall now
see how faithfully master and servant, *James Fazy* and *Karl Vogt,*
the dictator of Geneva and the member of the Council of States
for Geneva created by him, adhered to the terms of this
programme.

We have already seen in the *Studien* that Vogt assiduously
avoided all mention of the idea on behalf of which his man of
destiny was embarking on war. The same silence prevails at the
Joint Festival in Lausanne, in the National Council,[175] at the
celebrations in memory of Schiller and Robert Blum, in the Biel
Commis voyageur and, lastly, in the "Magnum Opus". And yet the
"idea" was even older than the conspiracy of *Plombières.*[176] As early
as *December 1851,* a few days after the coup d'état, one could read
in *Le Patriote savoisien.*

"The official positions in Savoy are already being shared out in the
antechambers of the Elysée. Its newspapers find the subject a great source of
amusement." *

On December 6, 1851 M. Fazy considered Geneva as good as
lost to the December Empire.**

On July 1, 1859 *Stämpfli,* who was President of the Confederation at the time, had an interview with Captain Harris, the British
chargé d'affaires in Berne. He repeated his fears that in the event
of the expansion of Sardinian rule in Italy, the annexation of
Savoy by France was a settled matter, and he emphasised that the
annexation of North Savoy in particular would completely *expose*
one flank of Switzerland and this would entail the loss of Geneva
in the near future (see the first Blue Book *On the Proposed*

---

* "On se partage déjà les places ... de la Savoie dans les antichambres de
l'Elysée. Ses journaux plaisantent même assez agréablement là-dessus."
** "Peut-être le citoyen Thurgovien que nous avons si bien défendu contre
les menaces de Louis-Philippe, nous fera-t-il la grâce de vouloir bien se constituer
comme médiateur, *et reprendre de nous Genève*" ["Perhaps the citizen of Thurgau
whom we defended so well against the threats of Louis Philippe will do us the
favour of offering himself as mediator and *recover Geneva from us*"] (*Revue de
Genève,* December 6, 1851).

Annexation of Savoy and Nice, No. I). Harris reported to Malmesbury, who for his part instructed Lord Cowley in Paris to ask Walewski to explain the nature of the Emperor's intentions. Walewski in no way denied that

"France and Sardinia had more than once discussed the problem of annexation and that the Emperor entertained the idea that if Sardinia was to be enlarged and become an Italian Kingdom, it was not unreasonable to expect that she should, on the other hand, make territorial concessions to France" (loc. cit., No. IV).[a]

Walewski's reply was written on July 4, 1859 and hence pre-dated the peace of Villafranca. In August 1859 Petétin's pamphlet[b] appeared in Paris, preparing Europe for the annexation of Savoy. *That same August,* after the summer session of the Swiss National Assembly, Herr Vogt slunk into Paris to receive his instructions from Plon-Plon. To put people off the scent he arranged for his fellow-scoundrels, Ranickel and Co., to spread the rumour in Geneva that he had gone for a cure on the Lake of Lucerne.

> "ze Pârîs lëbt er mangen tac,
> vil kleiner wîsheit er enpflac,
> sîn zerung was unmâzen grôz;...
> ist ër ein esel und ein gouch,
> daz sëlb ist ër zuo Pârîs ouch."[c]

In September 1859 the Swiss Federal Council saw the threat of annexation looming nearer (loc. cit., No. VI) and on November 12 it resolved to address a memorandum to this effect to the great powers. On November 18 President Stämpfli and Chancellor Schiess handed an official note to the English chargé d'affaires in Berne (loc. cit., No. IX). *James Fazy,* who had returned in October from his abortive journey to Tuscany where he had vainly striven to advance the cause of Plon-Plon's Etruscan kingdom, now tried to stem the rumours of annexation in his usual loud and cantankerous manner and with an affectation of rage: no one has ever dreamt of annexation, either in France or in Sardinia. As the danger drew nearer, the confidence of the *Revue de Genève* increased accordingly and in November and December 1859 its

---

a Cowley to Russell, received July 5, 1860.— *Ed.*
b Anselme Petétin, *De l'annexion de la Savoie.*— *Ed.*
c "In Paris many a day he dwelt,
    For learning no great love he felt;
    He ate and drank more than his fill....
    Since he is ass and fool together,
    He doesn't change in Paris either."
(Ulrich Bonerius, *Der Edel Stein,* Berlin, 1816.)— *Ed.*

Corybantic cult[177] of the Napoleonides surpassed all bounds (see, for example, the article on Plon-Plon quoted above[a]).

With the year 1860 we enter the second phase of the annexation affair.

Issuing denials or just turning a deaf ear was no longer in the interest of the Decembrists. The problem now rather was to make Switzerland more amenable to the idea of annexation and manoeuvre it into a false position. The second point of the Tuileries programme had to be put into action, i.e. the alleged intention of donating the neutral territory to Switzerland had to be publicised as loudly as possible. These efforts of the Swiss Decembrists were of course supported by simultaneous manoeuvres in Paris. Thus *Baroche,* the Minister of the Interior, told the Swiss Ambassador, *Dr. Kern,* at the beginning of January 1860, that

"should any change in the ownership of Savoy occur hereafter it should only be made with due regard to those provisions of the Treaties of 1815 which stipulated that a portion of it sufficient to ensure a good line of defence should be at the same time ceded to Switzerland" (see the Blue Book, op. cit., No. XIII).[b]

And even on February 2, 1860, on the same day that *Thouvenel* told the British Ambassador, Lord Cowley, that the annexation of Savoy and Nice was a "possibility", he informed him at the same time that

"indeed, in the opinion of the French Government, it would be well if in these circumstances the districts of Chablais and Faucigny should be united *permanently* to Switzerland" (loc. cit., No. XXVII).[c]

The dissemination of this illusion was designed not only to make the Swiss more amenable to the idea of the annexation of Savoy by the December Empire, but also to blunt their subsequent protest, and to compromise them in the eyes of Europe by making them the accomplices, albeit the cheated accomplices, of the Decembrists. *Frey-Hérosé,* President of the Confederation since 1860, avoided the pitfall and even informed Captain Harris of his misgivings about the supposed advantages of incorporating the neutralised territory into Switzerland. For his part, *Harris* warned the Federal Government about the Bonapartist intrigue, so that

---

[a] The leading article in the *Revue de Genève,* December 6, 1859 (see this volume, p. 187).—*Ed.*

[b] Grey to Russell, received January 10, *Correspondence Respecting the Proposed Annexation of Savoy and Nice to France...,* p. 9.—*Ed.*

[c] Cowley to Russell, received February 8, ibid., p. 28.—*Ed.*

"Switzerland should not appear as a Power eager for annexation or extension of territory" (loc. cit., No. XV).[a]

On the other hand, *Sir James Hudson,* the British Ambassador in Turin, wrote to Lord John Russell after a lengthy interview with *Cavour:*

"I have good ground for believing that Switzerland also is anxious to annex to herself a portion of Savoy. Consequently, it ought to be clearly understood, that when France is blamed for seeking this cession, Switzerland is no less to blame.... This question therefore, becoming more complicated by this double attack, renders the position of Sardinia more defensible" (loc. cit., No. XXXIV).[b]

Finally, as soon as Louis Bonaparte threw away the mask, Thouvenel quite unceremoniously revealed the mystery behind the slogan of the Swiss annexation of the neutral territory. In a dispatch to the French chargé d'affaires in Berne he openly derided the Swiss protest against the French annexation of Savoy, and how? By using the "plan for the *partition* of Savoy" foisted on Switzerland by Paris (see Thouvenel's dispatch of March 17, 1860).[c]

And what did the Swiss agents of December meanwhile contribute to the web of delusion? In January 1860, in the course of discussion with the British chargé d'affaires in Berne, *James Fazy* was the first to represent the annexation of Chablais and Faucigny to Switzerland not as something promised by Louis Bonaparte, but as the desire of Switzerland and of the inhabitants of the neutralised districts (loc. cit., No. XXIII). *Vogt,* who until that moment had never dreamt of the possibility of a French annexation of Savoy, was suddenly inspired by the spirit of prophecy, and *The Times,* which had never mentioned the name Vogt since its inception, suddenly announced in a correspondence dated January 30:

"The Swiss Professor Vogt pretends to know that France will procure for Switzerland Faucigny, Chablais, and the Genevese, the neutral provinces of Savoy, if the Grand Council of the Republic will let her have the free use of the Simplon" (*The Times,* February 3, 1860).[d]

Even more! At the end of January 1860 James Fazy assured the British chargé d'affaires in Berne that *Cavour,* with whom he had had a long interview in Geneva hardly two months previously, was foaming with rage at the idea of making any concession to France

---

[a] Harris to Russell, received January 25, ibid., p. 12.— *Ed.*
[b] Hudson to Russell, received February 16, ibid.— *Ed.*
[c] *Le Moniteur universel,* No. 82, March 22, 1860.— *Ed.*
[d] "Austria", *The Times,* No. 23533, February 3, 1860.— *Ed.*

(see the Blue Book,[a] op. cit., No. XXXIII). Thus while Fazy plays guarantor for Cavour to England, Cavour exculpates himself in English eyes by revealing the territorial ambitions of the same Fazy (loc. cit., No. XXXIII). And finally, *Tourte,* the Swiss Ambassador in Turin, hastens to the British Ambassador, Hudson, as late as February 9, 1860 to assure him that

"no engagement subsists between Sardinia and France for the cession of Savoy to France, and that Sardinia is not in the least disposed to cede or exchange Savoy to France" (loc. cit.).[b]

The decisive moment was drawing nearer. The Paris *Patrie* of January 25, 1860 began to prepare the way for the annexation of Savoy in an article entitled "*Les voeux de la Savoie*". In another article, on January 27, "*Le comté de Nice*", it foreshadowed in its Decembrist style the annexation of Nice. On February 2, 1860 Thouvenel announced to the British Ambassador, Cowley, that even before the war France and Sardinia had agreed that the annexation of Savoy and Nice was a "possibility". However, an official note on France's *actual* decision to absorb Savoy and Nice was not given to Lord Cowley until February 5 (see Lord Cowley's speech in the House of Lords on April 23, 1860)[c] and Dr. Kern was not told until February 6. And both the British and Swiss Ambassadors were explicitly informed that the neutralised territory was to be absorbed into Switzerland. *Prior* to these official announcements, *James Fazy* was instructed from the Tuileries that Sardinia had *already* ceded Savoy and Nice to France in a secret treaty and that the treaty contained *no clause in favour of Switzerland. Prior* to Thouvenel's official announcements to Lord Cowley and Dr. Kern, *Fazy* was to sugar the Imperial pill and present it to his Genevan subjects. On *February 3,* therefore, he arranged for his blindly devoted tool, *John Perrier,* to organise a popular meeting on the premises of the *Club populaire* of Geneva, a meeting which he attended apparently by chance, on the pretext that

"he had just heard (*je viens d'entendre*) that the treaties were being discussed which may have been concluded between France and Sardinia for the cession of Savoy. Unfortunately, such a treaty was signed on *January 27* by the Sardinian Government; but from this *positive fact* we cannot yet deduce that our security is really threatened.... It is true that there is no written reservation made in the treaty

---

[a] Harris to Russell, received February 6, *Correspondence Respecting the Proposed Annexation of Savoy and Nice to France...*, p. 24.— *Ed.*

[b] Hudson to Russell, received February 16, ibid.— *Ed.*

[c] *The Times,* No. 23602, April 24, 1860.— *Ed.*

in favour of our rights over the Sardinian neutralised territory; but we do not know whether in the intention of the contracting parties there may not exist some reservation in this sense.... It may have been taken into consideration, and, so to speak, understood as taken for granted (*sous-entendu comme allant de soi*)....We should beware of introducing any spirit of premature distrust.... We should rely on the sympathy" (for the coup d'état monarchy) "...and abstain from any hostile word."

(See Fazy's "confidential" speech, in its own way a masterpiece of demagogy, in the *Revue de Genève* of February 3, 1860.) The British chargé d'affaires in Berne found Fazy's prophetic knowledge remarkable enough for him to send a special dispatch to Lord John Russell about it.[a]

The *official* treaty relating to the cession of Savoy and Nice to France was due to be concluded on March 24, 1860. So there was no time to be lost. The Swiss patriotism of the Genevan Decembrists had to be officially established before the official proclamation of the annexation of Savoy. Signor *Vogt* therefore journeyed to Paris early in March, accompanied by General *Klapka,* who might well be acting *de bonne foi,*[b] with the intention of bringing *his* influence to bear on Plon-Plon, the Egeria of the Palais Royal, the misunderstood genius, and, in full view of the whole of Switzerland, of throwing *his personal weight* into the scales in favour of the incorporation of the neutralised territory into Switzerland. From the Lucullan table of Plon-Plon—in the art of gastronomy, as is well known, Plon-Plon rivals both Lucullus and Cambacérès, so that if Brillat-Savarin were to rise from the grave, even he would marvel at Plon-Plon's *genius, economics, liberal ideas, military talent* and *personal valour* in this field—from the Lucullan table of Plon-Plon, where as an "agreeable companion" he tucked in heartily, Falstaff-Vogt called on the Swiss to show their valour (see his long letter from Paris in the supplement to the Biel *Commis voyageur* of *March 8, 1860*). Switzerland should prove that

"its militia was not there *just* to parade and play at being soldiers". The "cession of the neutralised territory to Switzerland" was an illusion. "The abandonment of Chablais and Faucigny to France was a *first* step, to be followed by others." "*Mounted on the two stilts: nationality and natural frontiers,* one can advance from the Lake of Geneva to the Aar and right up to Lake Constance and the Rhine—if one's legs are strong enough."

But—and this is the point—Falstaff-Vogt *still does not give credence* to what the French Minister Thouvenel himself had

---

[a] Harris to Russell, received February 9, *Correspondence Respecting the Proposed Annexation of Savoy and Nice to France....—Ed.*

[b] In good faith.—*Ed.*

officially revealed a month before and what all Europe knew by now—that the cession of Savoy and Nice had been agreed on · *as long ago as August 1858 in Plombières,* as the price of French intervention against Austria. His "man of destiny" had only just been driven against his will into the arms of chauvinism by the priests and coerced into confiscating the neutralised territory.

"Evidently," our embarrassed apologist stammers, "evidently the leading circles have been **looking** for a counterweight to the *steady growth of the clerical movement* and hope that this might be found in so-called chauvinism—in that most narrow-minded sense of nationality that knows of nothing beyond the acquisition of *a* **bit** (!) of territory."

After Vogt, intoxicated by the smells issuing from Plon-Plon's kitchen, had laid about him so heartily in the Biel *Commis voyageur,* he romanced wildly in the same mouthpiece on his return from Paris about the absolute love of the French to be found among the inhabitants of Nice. He thus came into a disagreeable conflict with *Vegezzi-Ruscalla,* one of the chief leaders of the Italian National Association and the author of the pamphlet *La nazionalità di Nizza.* And when the same hero who had played Winkelried from the safety of Plon-Plon's table came to speak in the National Council in Berne, the warlike clarion call turned into a diplomatic piping on the flute, which recommended calmly to carry on the negotiations with *the Emperor who had always been amicably disposed towards the Swiss* and which warned emphatically against any *alliance with the East.* The President of the Confederation, *Frey-Hérosé,* made some strange insinuations regarding *Vogt,* who on the other hand had the satisfaction of seeing his speech praised by the *Nouvelliste Vaudois.*[a] The *Nouvelliste Vaudois* is the organ of Messrs. Blanchenay, Delarageaz and other Vaudois magnates, in short of the Swiss Western railway, just as the *Neue Zürcher-Zeitung* is the organ of Zurich Bonapartism and the Northeastern railway. To characterise the patrons of the *Nouvelliste Vaudois* it is enough to point out that on the occasion of the well-known dispute about the Oron railway five Vaudois government councillors were repeatedly and with impunity accused by the opposition press of having each received a present of 20 shares to the value of 10,000 francs from the Paris *Crédit Mobilier,*[178] the chief shareholder of the Swiss Western railway.

A few days after *Vogt* had set off in the company of Klapka to visit the Egeria of the Palais Royal, *James Fazy,* accompanied by

---

[a] Marx is drawing on data from a letter by Georg Lommel of April 19, 1860. There is an entry to this effect in Marx's notebook.— *Ed.*

John Perrier, embarked on a journey to the sphinx in the Tuileries.[a] It is known that Louis Bonaparte relishes the role of sphinx and maintains his Oedipuses just as former kings of France maintained their own court jesters. In the Tuileries, *Fazy* interposed himself between Switzerland and the sphinx. As we have said, *John Perrier* was his companion. This John is the very shadow of his James, he does everything the latter desires, nothing which he does not desire, lives through him and for him, became a member of the Grand Council of Geneva through him, prepares all festivals and toasts for him and acts, in short, as his Leporello and his Fialin. Both returned to Geneva having achieved nothing as far as the threat to Switzerland was concerned, and with astonishing success, as far as the threat to Fazy's own position was concerned. Fazy thundered in public, saying that the scales had now fallen from his eyes and that in future he would hate Louis Bonaparte as passionately as he had loved him hitherto. A strange love, this nine-year-long passion of the republican Fazy for the murderer of two republics! Fazy acted the disillusioned patriot with such virtuosity that the whole of Geneva wallowed in Fazy-enthusiasm and the demise of Fazy's illusions was felt almost more keenly than the loss of the neutralised provinces. Even Théodore de Saussure, the head of the aristocratic opposition and his enemy of many years' standing, confessed that it was no longer possible to doubt the sincerity of James Fazy's Swiss patriotism.

Having been the recipient of such well-merited popular ovations, the tyrant of Geneva hastened to the National Council in Berne. Shortly after his departure, his loyal squire, his Paris travelling companion, in short, his own *John Perrier,* embarked on a voyage of the Argonauts of a very special sort. A band of Swiss drunkards (at least this is how they were described in the columns of the London *Times*), chosen from the company of *"fruitiers"*, Fazy's democratic bodyguard, set sail unarmed under *Perrier's* leadership for *Thonon* at which spot of the neutralised territory they intended to stage an *anti-French* demonstration. To this day no one can say in what this demonstration consisted or was supposed to consist, whether the Argonauts intended to search for the Golden Pelt[b] or to sell their own skins. For no Orpheus accompanied Perrier's Argonauts and no Apollonius has sung of

---

[a] An allusion to Karl Grün's pamphlet *Louis Bonaparte, die Sphinx auf dem französischen Kaiserthron,* Hamburg, 1860.— *Ed.*

[b] Marx ironically writes *goldenes Fell* (Golden Pelt) instead of *goldenes Vlies* (Golden Fleece).— *Ed.*

their deeds. It seems to have involved a sort of symbolic occupation of the neutralised territory by a Switzerland represented by *John Perrier* and his band. The real Switzerland now found its hands so full with diplomatic excuses and declarations of loyalty and indignant repudiations of *John Perrier*'s symbolic occupation of Thonon as to make Louis Bonaparte appear the soul of magnanimity when he contented himself with the actual occupation of Thonon and the rest of the neutralised territory.

John Perrier was arrested in Geneva with several thousand francs in his pockets. On the basis of Perrier's testimony M. *Ducommun,* the Vice-Chancellor of the state and editor of the *Revue de Genève,* a young man without private means, and dependent for his incumbency of these two posts on *James Fazy,* President of the State Council and owner of the *Revue de Genève,* was likewise arrested. He confessed to having given Perrier the money which had been taken from a fund set up to establish a volunteer corps—a fund whose existence had been quite unknown to the Geneva radicals up to that moment. The judicial investigation ended with the dismissal firstly of Ducommun and then of Perrier.

On March 24 Nice and Savoy, together with the neutralised territory, were officially ceded to Bonaparte by Victor Emmanuel. On March 29-30 *John Perrier,* who had returned from Paris to Geneva with *Fazy,* embarked on his Argonaut adventure, a burlesque demonstration which just at the crucial moment made any real demonstration impossible. In Berne, *James Fazy* insisted that "he had no knowledge of the incident".* In the former neutral territory *Laity* boasted that if the Swiss had actually launched an attack there his Emperor would have at once ordered three divisions to march into Geneva. *Vogt,* finally, was quite in

---

* The realisation that with the annexation of North Savoy Geneva had become an enclave of France and, in no less measure, the impact of the French fortification of the harbour of Thonon, have recently, as everybody knows, greatly roused the anti-Decembrist feeling of the ancient Republic. However, the authentic outbreaks of popular indignation are accompanied by false ones, inspired from Paris and set in motion in part by French police personnel. Thus, for example, we can read in the *Saturday Review* of September 22, 1860: "A party of self-styled Swiss were giving vent to gross insults against the Empire at Thonon, when a blundering gendarme, in an excess of official zeal, seized them, and insisted on looking at their passports. They turned out to be Frenchmen, with papers perfectly *en règle....* The gravest fact relating to these artificial collisions is, that in one of the earliest and the worst of them, *a close adherent of Mr. Fazy*" (friend Perrier) *"was prominently implicated."*[a]

---

[a] Marx gives the last sentence in brackets in English after its German equivalent.— *Ed.*

the dark about the secret of the journey of the Argonauts, *for* a few days before it took place he made a prophylactic *denunciation to the Genevan police* warning them of a conflict due to be engineered from Geneva on the Savoy frontier—but in so doing he was laying a false trail. I have in my possession a letter from a refugee living in Geneva, a former friend of Vogt's, to a refugee living in London. It says *inter alia*:

"*Vogt* was putting it about that I was continuously dashing backwards and forwards between West Switzerland and Savoy organising a revolution to the detriment of Switzerland and the advantage of powers hostile to it. This was only a few days before *Perrier's* adventure about which Vogt was undoubtedly in the know, but of which I was as ignorant as yourself. Evidently he attempted to cast suspicion on me and to ruin me. Fortunately, *he also denounced me to Duy, the Director of Police* who summoned me and was not a little surprised when I burst into laughter at his opening question and said: 'Aha! that well-known intrigue of Vogt's!' He then asked for details about my relations with *Vogt*. My statement was also confirmed by a government secretary, a member of the Helvetia,[179] who went to the Central Assembly in Berne on the following day where he met Vogt's brother and criticised Karl's behaviour to him, whereupon Gustav replied laconically that he had long since gathered from Karl's letters how things stood with his politics."[a]

If, to begin with, silence, denials and sermons of confidence in Louis Bonaparte were supposed to blind the Swiss to the impending danger, if later on the clamour about the intended incorporation of Faucigny, Chablais and the Genevese into Switzerland was designed to make the annexation of Savoy by France acceptable for the people, and if, finally, the burlesque at Thonon was intended to break any serious resistance, then, in accordance with the Paris programme, the annexation which had actually taken place and the danger that could no longer be denied were now to be put forward to induce the Swiss to surrender voluntarily, *i.e. to enter an alliance with the December Empire.*

This task was of such an extreme delicacy that its accomplishment could only be entrusted to *James Fazy* himself. His servant *Vogt* was allowed to warn against an *alliance with the East,* but only Fazy himself could advocate an *alliance with the West.* He first hinted at the necessity of this in the *Revue de Genève.* On *April 18, 1860* an excerpt from a London letter was circulating in Geneva which said, among other things:

"Our influential fellow-citizens should be warned to be on their guard against the advice of *J. Fazy,* who may well recommend that Switzerland should *abandon its neutrality.* It is highly likely that this advice emanates from the *French Government*

---

[a] Marx is quoting Georg Lommel's letter of April 19, 1856.—*Ed.*

itself, whom *James Fazy* has served zealously down to this very day.... He now
assumes the posture of a good Swiss who is striving to thwart the designs of the
French. However, I am told by someone who has always shown himself to be well
informed that this is all just a snare. As soon as Switzerland has declared that it
neither can nor will continue to remain *neutral,* the French Government will take
notice of this and force it into an alliance as in the days of the First Empire."

Whereupon *Fazy* caused this reply to appear in the *Revue de
Genève*:

"The day that Savoy is united with France the neutrality of Switzerland will
cease of itself, so that any advice to that effect from Fazy would be superfluous."

Three months later, on *July 10, James Fazy* made a speech in the
Swiss National Council in which

"fuming and raging and shaking his clenched fist at the Bonapartist financiers
and the barons of the Confederation—he denounced them as *le gouvernement
souterrain*[a]—he marched straight into the Bonapartist camp".

The official French party of Zurich and the Vaud, seemingly the
chief victim of his attack, therefore allowed him to continue
blustering.

"Europe, and *Germany in particular,* has left Switzerland in the lurch. *Neutrality
has thereby become impossible*; *Switzerland must look around for* **alliances**, but where?"

The old demagogue then muttered something to the effect that

"France, which was so near and closely related, would one day recognise and
make good the wrong it had done. It might even become a republic, etc. But the
financiers and barons of the Confederation who had outlived their day should not
be allowed to initiate *the new policy.* Helvetia, the people must do that: Just wait and
see, the next elections will teach you a lesson. The troops of the Confederation are
most welcome in Geneva. However, if their presence raises the slightest doubts
about the existing government of Geneva, then away with them. Geneva is able to
look after itself and to defend itself."

On *July 10,* then, *James Fazy* elaborated in the National Council
upon what he had hinted at in the *Revue de Genève* of *April
18*—*"the new policy", the alliance between Switzerland and France,* i.e.
the annexation of Switzerland by the Decembrists. Well-informed
Swiss thought that it was premature for Fazy to drop the
anti-Bonapartist mask he had been wearing since his return from
the Tuileries. However, it is precisely Fazy who displays a virtuosity
in the art of calculated indiscretion that to some extent is reminiscent
of that of Palmerston.

It is well known that the most disreputable members of the
"gouvernement souterrain" moved a vote of censure on *Stämpfli* in

---

[a] The underground government.— *Ed.*

the National Council, because as Federal President he had grasped the situation and at one point had made the correct decision to use Federal troops to defend the neutralised territory against French violations. The motion of censure was defeated by an enormous majority, but *Vogt's* vote was not among them.

"Very typical," I was told in a letter from Switzerland at the time, "of *Karl Vogt* was his absence during the discussions in the Swiss Council of States on the motion of censure on *Stämpfli*, the President of the Confederation. As representative of the Canton of Geneva under threat from Bonaparte Vogt had perforce to vote for Stämpfli, the most energetic defender of this Canton. He is, moreover, both a personal friend of Stämpfli's and also greatly indebted to him. Vogt's father and two of his brothers earn their bread as employees of the Canton of Berne; a third brother was recently given a lucrative post as a senior Federal statistician, thanks to Stämpfli's mediation. Consequently it was hardly possible for Vogt to vote against his friend, benefactor and man of the people in an open ballot. On the other hand, it was even less possible for a Plon-Plonist to approve publicly a policy which was fighting Bonapartist aggression to the death. Hence his running away and sticking his head in the sand, but this left his broad backside clearly visible and exposed to a beating—the usual stratagem and the mundane destiny of the modern Falstaff."

The slogan of *"Austrianism"*, which had emanated from the Tuileries, and had then been echoed so loudly by *James Fazy* in the *Revue de Genève* and by his servant *Vogt* in the Biel *Commis voyageur,* in the *Studien* and in the "Magnum Opus", etc., now finally rebounded on Switzerland. Around the middle of April a poster appeared everywhere on the walls of Milan entitled: *"Conflict between Napoleon and Switzerland."* In it we read:

"Savoy appeared to Switzerland as an appetising tit-bit and, *egged on by Austria,* Switzerland hastened to obstruct the plans of Napoleon III on a matter that is exclusively the concern of Italy and France.... England and the other great powers of the north, *except Austria,* are not in the least opposed to the incorporation of Savoy. *Switzerland alone, spurred on by Austria,* which attempts to stir up trouble and rebellion in all the states allied to Sardinia, put in its veto.... *Switzerland* is an *abnormal state* which cannot resist the *tide of the great principle of nationality* for a long time. Germans, Frenchmen and Italians are not capable of submitting to the same laws. If Switzerland knows this it should reflect that in the Canton of Ticino it is the language of Foscolo and Giusti that is spoken, it should not forget that a large part of its population belongs to the great and magnanimous nation that calls itself *French.*"

In short, it appears that Switzerland is an *Austrian* invention. While *Vogt* was at such pains to rescue *Switzerland* from the clutches of *Austria,* he charged one of his most trusted accomplices with the task of rescuing *Germany.* This was the garrulous Swabian, *Karl Mayer of Esslingen,* Rump parliamentarian, a would-be great man and at present owner of a bijouterie factory. At the ceremony to dedicate the banner of the Neuchâtel German

Workers' Association, held at The Crown in St. Blaise, the official speaker, Rump parliamentarian and jeweller, *Karl Mayer of Esslingen,* called upon Germany

"just *to allow* the French across the Rhine because otherwise things would never improve in Germany".

Two representatives of the Workers' Association of Geneva who returned in the new year (1860) after attending the ceremony, reported the incident. When their account was confirmed by the representatives of a number of other West Swiss associations, the Genevan headquarters released a circular containing a general warning about Bonapartist intrigues among German workers in Switzerland. I quote from a report of the circular lying before me:

"According to a reminiscence of the First Empire when a few Germans also tried to uphold Napoleon's dominion of the world truly believing that the colossus would not survive the demise of its hero and that then a unified Germany would at any rate be one of the provinces into which the Frankish Empire would disintegrate, and such a Germany would find it easier to win freedom—it was dismissed as political quackery to believe that one could drain a living body of blood and trust to the fantastic miracle that fresh blood would be produced to replace it. Moreover, the attempt was denounced to deny a great people the strength to help itself and the right to determine its own destiny. Finally, it was noted that Germany's hoped-for Messiah had just demonstrated in Italy precisely what *he* understood by the liberation of subject nationalities, etc., etc. The circular was addressed, as it stated, only to those Germans who were choosing the wrong means to achieve a good end, but it refused to become involved with **venal journalists** and **ambitious ci-devants.**"

Simultaneously, the *Aargauer Nachrichten, organ of the Helvetia,* castigated

"the logic that the hedgehog should be allowed to enter the mole's burrow so that one could better catch hold of it and throw it out again, according to which fine logic the Ephialtes of this world should be given a free hand so that Leonidases might arise. **A certain professor** was behaving like Duke Ulrich of Württemberg in reverse; for the Duke attempted to return home from exile by making use of the Bundschuh,[180] after the Riding Boot did not want to have anything to do with him, while **the above-mentioned professor** had ruined his relations with the Shoe and so was trying to patch things up with the Boot, etc."

This denunciation of *Professor Vogt* was significant because it appeared in an organ of the Helvetia. By way of compensation, as it were, he was given a favourable reception in *L'Espérance,* a paper founded in 1859 in Geneva by the French Treasury and which .appeared in large format and with no expense spared. It was the task of *L'Espérance* to preach in favour of the annexation of Savoy and the Rhineland in particular and of Louis Bonaparte's Messianic destiny to liberate the subject nationalities in general. It is common knowledge in *Geneva* that *Vogt* was an *habitué* of the editorial office of *L'Espérance* and one of its most active contributors. I myself have been informed of details which put this fact *beyond all doubt.* What *Vogt* hints at in his *Studien*, what he had his accomplice *Karl Mayer*, the garrulous Swabian, Rump parliamentarian and jeweller *from Esslingen*, proclaim so loudly at Neuchâtel, is developed further in *L'Espérance*. For example, it says in its issue of *March 25, 1860*:

"If war with France is the only hope of the German patriots, what reason can they have for wishing to weaken the government of that country and to prevent it from attaining its *natural frontiers?* Could it be that the German people is far from sharing this hatred of France? However that may be, *there are some very sincere German patriots, in particular* among the most progressive German democrats" (namely the Vogt of the Empire, the Ranickel, Karl Mayer from Esslingen and *tutti quanti*), "*who do not regard the loss of the left bank of the Rhine as a great misfortune, but who on the contrary are convinced that* only after that loss *political life will begin in Germany*, a revived Germany founded on the alliance and merging with the civilisation of the European West." *

Having been so precisely informed by *Vogt* of the views of the most progressive elements among the German democrats, *L'Espérance* declared in a leading article on May 30 that

"a plebiscite on the left bank of the Rhine would soon show that everyone there was in favour of the French".[c]

Der Postheiri, a humorous Swiss magazine, then overwhelmed *L'Espérance* with bad jokes, referring to it as the "miserable jade" which in addition to the light laurels of Bacchus Plon-Plon now had also to endure the "weighty paunch" of his Silenus on its back.

The precision with which the Decembrist press manoeuvres were orchestrated can be seen in the following example. On *May*

---

* "Si la seule espérance des patriotes allemands est fondée sur une guerre avec la France, quelle raison peuvent-ils avoir de chercher à affaiblir le gouvernement de ce pays et l'empêcher de former ses[a] frontières naturelles? Serait-il que le peuple en Allemagne est loin de partager cette haine de la France? Quoi qu'il en soit, il y a des patriotes allemands très sincères, et notamment parmi les démocrates les plus avancés, qui ne voient pas un grand malheur dans la perte de la rive gauche du Rhin, qui sont, au contraire, convaincus que c'est après cette perte seulement que commencera la vie politique d'une Allemagne régénérée, appuyée sur l'alliance et se confondant avec la civilisation de l'Occident européen" (*L'Espérance*, March 25, 1860).[b]

---

[a] In *L'Espérance*: "et l'empêcher de reclamer les" ("and to prevent it from claiming the").— *Ed.*

[b] Marx quotes from the article "Allemagne. Correspondance particulière de l'Espérance". The italics and bold type are Marx's.— *Ed.*

[c] "Le Rhin", *L'Espérance*, No. 149, May 30, 1860.— *Ed.*

30 L'Espérance in Geneva spoke of the cession of the left bank of the Rhine to the Decembrists by plebiscite; on *May 31* Louis Jourdan in *Le Siècle* in Paris started to dig the trenches for the annexation of the Rhine,[a] and in the *beginning of June Le Propagateur du Nord et du Pas-de-Calais* opened up with crude artillery fire against Belgium. Shortly before the statements of the Genevan mouthpiece, *Edmond About* declared in *L'Opinion nationale* that Sardinia's aggrandizement had compelled the Emperor "de prendre la Savoie ... c.-à-d. *nous fermons notre porte*",[b] and, he continued, if Germany's desire for unification led to a similar enlargement of Prussia, "alors nous aurions à veiller à notre sûreté, *à prendre la rive gauche du Rhin*, c.-à-d. *nous fermerions notre porte*".[c] This frivolous door-keeper was immediately followed by A. A.,[d] that ponderous blockhead, the correspondent of *L'Indépendance belge*, a sort of Joseph Prudhomme and Sybil Extraordinary of the "providence" dwelling in the Tuileries.[e] Meanwhile the enthusiasm for *German unity* peculiar to *L'Espérance* and the same paper's indignant denunciation of German anti-Decembrists who had fallen into the clutches of *Austria*, had reached such giddy heights that *James Fazy*, who was forced to observe certain diplomatic proprieties and who was moreover on the point of converting his *Revue de Genève* into *La Nation suisse*, magnanimously condescended to declare in the *Revue* that it was possible to oppose Bonapartism without being an Austrian.

Karl Vogt, German Dâ-Dâ, owner of a Decembrist recruitment office for the German press, Fazy's sub-agent, "agreeable companion" in the Palais Royal, Plon-Plon's Falstaff, Ranickel's "friend", prompter to the Biel *Commis voyageur*, contributor to *L'Espérance*, protégé of Edmond About, bard of the *Lousiad—Karl Vogt* had still to plumb the ultimate depths of depravity. In Paris he was to appear before the eyes of the world in the *Revue contemporaine*, arm in arm with **Monsieur Edouard Simon.** Let us consider for a moment what the *Revue contemporaine* is and who *Monsieur Edouard Simon*.

The *Revue contemporaine* was originally the official Decembrist publication in sharp contrast to the *Revue des deux Mondes*, which

---

a Louis Jourdan's article "Les frontières naturelles".— *Ed.*

b "To take Savoy ... in other words, *we are closing our door*".— *Ed.*

c "Then we should have to look to our security, *occupy the left bank of the Rhine*, in other words, *we should close our door*".— *Ed.*

d An allusion to the item "Autre correspondance. Paris, 27 avril" signed A. A., which appeared in *L'Indépendance belge*, No. 120, April 29, 1860.— *Ed.*

e i.e. of Napoleon III.— *Ed.*

received contributions from the elegant writers, the men of the *Journal des Débats*, Orleanists, Fusionists, and above all professors of the *Collège de France* and members of the *Institut*.[181] Since the latter could not be directly assigned to the *Revue contemporaine*, the attempt was made to detach them from the *Revue des deux Mondes* and so indirectly to force them to join the Decembrist *Revue*. However, the coup did not have much success. The proprietors of the *Revue contemporaine* even found it inexpedient to do business with the editorial committee foisted onto them by M. *La Guéronnière*. But since the ventriloquist of the Tuileries stood in need of mouthpieces tuned in various keys, the *Revue contemporaine* was then transformed into a *semi-official* magazine while the *Revue européenne* with the editorial committee imposed by *La Guéronnière* was installed as *official* review.

Now to **Monsieur Edouard Simon**, by nature a Rhine-Prussian Jew called *Eduard Simon*, who however cuts the most comical capers to pass himself off as an authentic Frenchman, while his style constantly betrays the fact that he is a Rhine-Prussian Jew translated into French.

Shortly after the Schiller festivities (November 1859) in the home of a London acquaintance I met a highly respectable businessman who had lived many years in Paris. He gave me a detailed account of the Parisian Schiller festivities, Schiller societies, etc. I interrupted him with a question about how German societies and meetings in Paris had managed to accommodate themselves to the Decembrist police. He replied with a humorous grin:

"Naturally, there is no meeting without a *mouchard*,[a] nor any society without its *mouchard*. To avoid all complications we decided once and for all to adopt the simple tactic—*probatum est*[b]—of attracting a *known spy* and voting him on to the committee from the start. And we always have **Edouard Simon** at our disposal, a man who might have been made for the job. You are aware that *La Guéronnière*, who was formerly Lamartine's lackey and the manufacturer of long rigmaroles for Émile de Girardin, is now the Emperor's favourite, his privy stylist and at the same time the supreme censor of the French press. Well, *Edouard Simon* is *La Guéronnière's* lap-dog, and," he added screwing up his nose, "he is a cur with a very unpleasant smell at that. *Edouard Simon* was unwilling to work *pour le roi de Prusse*,[c] as I am sure you will find understandable, but decided that he would perform an incalculable service for civilisation and himself if he were to make common cause with the Decembrist system. He is a fellow with a small mind and a nasty character, but in the sphere of petty intrigue he is not without a certain ability. La Guéronnière installed his *Edouard Simon* in *La Patrie* to write some of the leading articles. This well illustrated the tact of the privy stylist. For the

---

[a] Spy.— *Ed.*

[b] It has been shown to work.— *Ed.*

[c] For the King of Prussia, i.e. for nothing.— *Ed.*

proprietor of *La Patrie,* a banker called *Delamarre,* is an arrogant, headstrong, surly parvenu who cannot endure anyone around him who is not an utterly servile and pliable creature. So *Edouard Simon* was the right man for the position, since despite his poisonous malice, he can be as smooth as an angora cat. Under the republic *La Patrie* was, as you know, one of the most brazen mouthpieces of the *rue de Poitiers.*[182] Since the December coup it has quarrelled with *Le Pays* and *Le Constitutionnel* for the honour of being recognised as the semi-official organ of the Tuileries and ever since the signal was given it has gone in for the annexation-fever in a big way. You know of those beggars who pretend to have epileptic attacks on the street so as to swindle passers-by of a few coppers. It was indeed an honour to *La Patrie* that it was allowed to be the first to announce the imminent annexation of Savoy and Nice. Scarcely had the annexation taken place when it enlarged its format, for, as M. Delamarre naively declared: 'La Savoie et le Comté de Nice ayant été annexés à la France, la conséquence naturelle est *l'agrandissement de la Patrie.'* [a] Who is not put in mind of the witticism of a Parisian cynic who when asked *'Qu'est-ce que la patrie?'* replied *'Journal du soir'.*[b] If moreover the Rhine provinces were annexed, what an increase there would be then in *La Patrie* and its format and in the *salaire* of *Edouard Simon*! As far as economic policy is concerned *La Patrie* believes that the salvation of France is to be achieved by abolishing the *tourniquet de la Bourse,*[c] as a result of which business on the Exchange and hence throughout the land would again soar to the desired level. *Edouard Simon* is equally enthusiastic about the abolition of the *tourniquet de la Bourse.* However, our *Edouard Simon* is not only a writer of leading articles for *La Patrie* and La Guéronnière's lap-dog. He is the most sincere friend and informer of the new *Jerusalem,* alias the Prefecture of Police, and of M. *Palestrina* in particular. In short, gentlemen," the narrator concluded, "a committee with M. **Edouard Simon** in its bosom is by that very fact in the very best *police odour."*

And Herr ... gave a curiously shrill laugh as if there were a further ineffably secret connection between Monsieur *Edouard Simon* and the *odeur de mauvais lieu.*[d]

Mr. *Kinglake* has drawn the attention of the House of Commons to the pleasant confusion of foreign policy, the police and the press, so characteristic of the Decembrist agents (session of the House of Commons, July 12, 1860).[e] Of course, **Monsieur Edouard Simon**—Vogt's infamous[f] *Eduard* is not to be confused with Vogt's gentle *Kunigunde,* alias *Ludwig Simon of Trier**— **Monsieur Edouard Simon,** La Guéronnière's lap-dog, Delamarre's

---

* Thanks to the intervention of the gentle Kunigunde some of Vogt's attacks against me were inserted in a local sheet in my home town of Trier. They included

---

[a] "Savoy and the county of Nice having been annexed by France, the natural consequence is *the enlargement of the Patrie"* (*Patrie* can mean both "motherland" and the title of the newspaper).— *Ed.*

[b] "What is the motherland?" "An evening paper."— *Ed.*

[c] Whirligig of the Stock Exchange.— *Ed.*

[d] The smell of a place of ill-repute.— *Ed.*

[e] Mr. Kinglake's speech was reported in *The Times,* No. 23671, July 13, 1860.— *Ed.*

[f] Marx puns on the word *ruchbar* (notorious, infamous) which in this context can also mean "ill-smelling".— *Ed.*

poodle, Palestrina's spy [a] and general dogsbody, clearly belongs if not to the cream at least to the Limburg cheese of the 10th December, to the Second Circle where

"s'annida
Ipocrisia, lusinghe, e chi affatura,
Falsità, ladroneccio, e *simonia,*
Ruffian, baratti, e simile lordura".[b]

Many weeks before the publication of the "Magnum Opus" *Karl Vogt* had commissioned his *Edouard Simon* to review it in the French press. *Edouard Simon* opted for *double emploi.* First, he privately translated the "Magnum Opus" for M. *La Guéronnière* and in this connection his patron then assigned him to the *Revue contemporaine.* It was in vain that the editorial board of the *Revue contemporaine* humbly pleaded that if *Edouard Simon* were to appear in their columns it should at least be anonymously. La Guéronnière was inexorable. *Edouard Simon* made his debut in the *Revue contemporaine* of February 15, 1860 with an advertisement for his friend *Vogt* under the title: "*Un tableau de mœurs politiques de l'Allemagne. Le procès de M. Vogt avec la Gazette d'Augsbourg*" (Political Portrait of Germany. Herr Vogt's Action against the Augsburg Gazette), signed—**Edouard Simon**.

The "Romanic" *Edouard Simon* does not believe that "he needs to hurl invective at the noble German race in order to prove himself a good Frenchman" (*Revue contemporaine,* loc. cit., p. 531), but as a "good Frenchman" and a "Romanic by birth" he must at least exhibit his innate ignorance of German affairs. Thus among other statements he asserts of his *Karl Vogt*: "He was one of the *three Regents*[c] of the short-lived Empire." * *Monsieur Edouard Simon*

---

references to my "carnal miscegenation" with the *Allgemeine.* What an association of ideas for the chaste Kunigunde! Very shocking indeed! [Marx wrote the last sentence in English. The reference is to an item published in the Trier *Volksblatt* on November 7, 1859. Marx mentions it also in a letter to Engels of November 19, 1859 (see present edition, Vol. 40).]

* "Il fut un des trois régents de l'empire éphémère" (loc. cit., p. 518).

<a> Marx uses the word *Spitzel* which means "spy" but in this context also suggests "spitz".— *Ed.*

<b> "Hypocrites, flatterers, dealers in sorcery.
Panders and cheats, and all such filthy stuff,
With theft, and *simony* and barratry
All have their nest."
(Dante, *The Divine Comedy,* Inferno, Canto XI, adapted.)— *Ed.*

<c> Marx's italics.— *Ed.*

does not know of course that the Empire *in partibus*[a] groaned under the rule of a *pentarchy*,[b] and "as a Frenchman" he imagines that if only for the sake of symmetry there were three parliamentary Regents of the Empire in Stuttgart corresponding to the three wise kings of Cologne.[183] "Friend" *Vogt*'s jokes in the "Magnum Opus" "frequently go beyond the limits of French taste".* Edouard the Frenchman will remedy this and will "strive to make a judicious selection".** "Friend" *Vogt* has a natural liking for "garish colours" and "is not exactly subtle in his use of language".*** Naturally! For "friend" Vogt is only a German who has been annexed, just as Dâ-Dâ is only an Arab who has been annexed, whereas *Edouard Simon* is a "good Frenchman" by birth and belongs to the "Romanic" race. Did Herr Orges and Herr Dietzel ever go so far in their slander of the "Romanic race"?

Monsieur Edouard Simon amuses his superiors by exhibiting one of the "three" wise German Rump-Kings to the Paris public, with the agreement, moreover, and on the instructions of that Holy German Rump-King, and parading him as a voluntary prisoner in the wake of the triumphal carriage of the Imperial Quasimodo. It is obvious, says *Edouard Simon*, after quoting from *Vogt*'s "Magnum Opus",

"it is obvious that it did not matter to Herr *Vogt* from where help might come in favour of German unity, provided only that it did come; *he even regarded the French Empire as particularly well fitted to hasten the realisation of the solution he favoured. Perhaps Herr Vogt abandoned his old antecedents* **too cheaply** (?!), *and his former colleagues who had sat with him on the extreme Left of the Frankfurt Parliament must have been astonished to see this intransigent opponent of every unified power, this passionate zealot of anarchy, **display such lively sympathies for the sovereign who has subdued anarchy in France**".****

* "Il dépasserait le but au goût des Français" (loc. cit., p. 519).
** "Nous nous efforcerons de choisir" (loc. cit.).
*** "M. Vogt aime beaucoup les couleurs tranchantes, et il n'est pas précisément un gourmet en matière de langage" (loc. cit., p. 530).
**** "On le voit, M. Vogt se souciait peu d'où vînt le secours en faveur de l'unité allemande, pourvu qu'il vînt; l'empire français lui semblait même singulièrement propre à hâter le dénoûment qu'il désire. Peut-être en cela M. Vogt faisait-il bon marché de ses antécédents, et il dut paraître étrange, à ses anciens collègues qui siégeaient avec lui à l'extrême gauche dans le Parlement de Francfort, de voir ce fougueux antagoniste de tout pouvoir unique, ce fervent zélateur de l'anarchie manifester de si vives sympathies envers le souverain qui l'a vaincue en France" (loc. cit., p. 518).

---

a The words *in partibus infidelium* (in lands inhabited by infidels) were added to the title of Catholic bishops appointed to purely nominal dioceses in non-Catholic countries. Here *in partibus* means non-existent.— *Ed.*
b Marx means the five Imperial Regents (Franz Raveaux, Karl Vogt, Heinrich Simon, Friedrich Schüler and August Becher).— *Ed.*

Edouard transfers the "fugitive Regent of the Empire" from the un-"committed" Left to the extreme Left of the Frankfurt Parliament. The man who voted in favour of "the hereditary German Emperor" [184] is transformed into an "intransigent opponent of every unified power", and the member of the Central March Association who preached "order" at any price to the motley parties inhabiting the taverns of Frankfurt becomes a "passionate zealot of anarchy". And all this to put the achievement of the 10th December in capturing the "fugitive Regent of the Empire" into its proper perspective. All the more precious are the *"lively sympathies"* which Herr *Vogt* "cherishes for the man who had subdued anarchy in France", all the more valuable his present recognition *"that the French Empire is particularly well fitted to bring about the unity of Germany"*, and all the more comprehensible is "friend" *Simon's* broad hint that "friend" *Vogt* "perhaps abandoned his antecedents *too cheaply* (*de bon marché*)", i.e. the December man at any rate did not have to pay *"too dearly"*. And in order to remove every doubt that might have remained in higher places that "friend" *Vogt* might not be as utterly reliable as "friend" *Simon,* Monsieur Edouard Simon explains with a grin and a wink, rubbing his hands the while, that *Vogt* in his passion for order, *"if he has understood him rightly, has even notified the Genevan authorities of revolutionary intrigues"** that have come to his attention,* just as Monsieur Edouard Simon "notified" Messrs. Palestrina and La Guéronnière.

It is common knowledge that About and Jourdan and Granier de Cassagnac and Boniface and Dr. Hoffmann, that the monks of *L'Espérance,* the knights of *Les Nationalités,* the bellows of *L'Opinion nationale,* the penny-a-liners[a] of *L'Indépendance, The Morning Chronicle,* the *Nouvelliste Vaudois,* etc., that the La Guéronnières and the Simons, the stylists, civilisationists, Decembrists, Plon-Plonists, Dentuists and dentists one and all take their inspiration from one and the same illustrious—**money-box.** So we see that Dâ-Dâ *Vogt* is no solitary partisan fighting a lonely battle, but is subsidised, indoctrinated, enlisted, enrolled along with the *canaille,* bound up with Edouard Simon, annexed by Plon-Plon, and sticking to them through thick and thin. The remaining question is whether *Karl Vogt* has been *paid* for his agency?

---

* "Si nous l'avons bien compris, il a *même* appelé l'attention des *autorités* de Genève sur ces menées" (loc. cit., p. 529).

---

[a] Marx uses the English expression.— *Ed.*

"If I am not mistaken, to bribe means to offer someone money or other advantages to perform actions or make utterances contrary to his own *convictions*" ("Magnum Opus", p. 217).

And Plon-Plonism is the sum of *Vogt's* convictions. So that even if he was *paid* in cash, he was by no means *bribed*. But the modes of payment are at least as various as the different forms of coinage.

Who knows whether Plon-Plon did not promise his Falstaff the post of governor of the Mouse Tower near the Binger Loch? [185] Or nomination as corresponding member of the *Institut*, now that About in his *La Prusse en 1860* has made French naturalists quarrel over the honour of corresponding *simultaneously* with the living *Vogt* and the dead *Dieffenbach*? Or perhaps he held out prospects of a restoration of his Regency of the Empire?

I know of course that current reports provide a more prosaic explanation. Thus it is said that "with the change of circumstances since 1859" there has been a change in the circumstances of our "agreeable companion"[a] (who had shortly before been one of the managers of a joint-stock company which had run aground and became the subject of a criminal investigation[186]). His anxious friends tried to explain away these developments by claiming that an Italian mining company had presented Vogt with a large number of shares in recognition of his contributions to "mineralogy", a gift which he had turned into cash during his first stay in Paris. People conversant with the situation but who do not know each other, have written to me almost simultaneously from Switzerland and France informing me that the "agreeable companion" had assumed the fairly profitable superintendence of an estate called "La Bergerie" near Nyon (in the Vaud). The estate is the widow's seat which Plon-Plon purchased for the Iphigenia of Turin.[b] I have even seen a letter written by a "New Swiss" who was still on terms of intimacy with *Vogt* long after "the change in circumstances of 1859" to a "Mr. P. B. B. of 78 Fenchurch Street, London" early in 1860 in which he *mentions a very considerable sum of money* which his ex-friend had received from the treasury in Paris, not as a *bribe*, but as *payment in advance*.

Such items of news and worse have made their way to London,

---

[a] Carl Vogt, "Zur Warnung", *Schweizer Handels-Courier*, No. 150 (special supplement), June 2, 1859.— *Ed.*

[b] Princess Clothilde of Savoy, daughter of the Sardinian King Victor Emmanuel.— *Ed.*

but for my part I would not give a brass farthing for them. I rather believe *Vogt* implicitly, when he says that

"it is no one's business where I" (*Vogt*) "get my money from. *I shall continue to try to obtain whatever resources are needed to achieve my political ends*, and conscious *that I am working for a good cause I shall continue to obtain them* **from wherever I can**" ("Magnum Opus", p. 226) —

hence also from the Paris treasury.

Political ends!

> "Nugaris, cum tibi, Calve,
> Pinguis aqualiculus propenso sesquipede extet." [a]

Good cause! This is apparently the German idealistic expression for what the Englishman with his coarse materialism calls "the good things of this world".[b]

Whatever *Dr. Schaible* may think of it, why should we not believe *Vogt* implicitly, since in the same "Magnum Opus" he declares with equal seriousness at the end of his *tall stories* about the Brimstone Gang, etc.:

"That concludes this phase of **contemporary history**. *What I have described are no mere day-dreams*; **they are pure facts!**" ("Magnum Opus", p. 182.)

Why shouldn't his *agency* be just *as pure* as the **facts** recounted in the "Magnum Opus"?

For my part, I am firmly convinced that, in contrast to all the other writing, agitating, politicising, conspiring, propagandising, boasting, Plon-Plonising, plotting and self-compromising members of the *December Gang*, it is solely and exclusively the unique Vogt who regards his Emperor as "*l'homme qu'on aime pour lui-même*".[c]

"*Swerz niht geloubt, der sündet*", as Wolfram von Eschenbach says,[d] or "He errs who does not believe it", as a contemporary song says.

---

[a] "You're drivelling, Calvus, with your
    Fat little paunch protruding in front of you eighteen inches."
(Persius, *Satires*, Book I, First Satire.)— *Ed.*

[b] Marx uses the English phrase.— *Ed.*

[c] "A man whom one loves for his own sake."— *Ed.*

[d] "He sins who does not believe it" (Wolfram von Eschenbach, *Parzival*, IX. Buch).— *Ed.*

X

PATRONS AND ACCOMPLICES

Principibus placuisse viris non ultima laus est.[a]

As guarantors of his "good behaviour"[b] the ex-Vogt of the Empire proposes

"Kossuth" and "the two other men — *Fazy*, the regenerator of Geneva, and *Klapka*, the defender of Komorn"[187] — whom he "proudly calls his friends" ("Magnum Opus", p. 213).

I call them his *patrons.*

After the battle of Komorn (July 2, 1849) *Görgey* usurped the supreme command of the Hungarian army in defiance of the orders of the Hungarian Government, which had dismissed him.

"If an energetic man had stood at the head of the government," writes Colonel *Lapinski*, who was still a supporter of *Kossuth* when he wrote his book, "a stop could have been put to all of Görgey's intrigues even at that time. *Kossuth* needed only to come into the camp and say a few words to the army and all of Görgey's popularity would not have saved him from defeat.... But *Kossuth* did not come; he was not forceful enough to oppose Görgey in public and so *while he intrigued against the general in secret, he attempted to justify the latter's misdemeanours in the eyes of the world.*" (Th. Lapinski, *Feldzug der Ungarischen Hauptarmee, etc.,* pp. 125, 126).

On his own admission, Kossuth was officially informed of Görgey's intended betrayal some time later by General *Guyon* (see David Urquhart, *Visit to the Hungarian Exiles at Kutayah*[c]).

"It is true that Kossuth did say in the course of a fine speech in Szeged that if he knew that anyone was a traitor he would murder him with his own hands. He may have had Görgey in mind as he spoke. However, not only did he not carry out this somewhat theatrical threat, he did not even tell all his Ministers just whom he

---

[a] To have pleased great men is not the greatest glory (Horace, *Epistles*, I, 17).— *Ed.*

[b] Marx uses the English phrase.— *Ed.*

[c] Kütahya.— *Ed.*

had under suspicion; while he *was busy forging miserable plans against Görgey* with some of them, [...] *he always spoke of him with the greatest respect and even wrote letters to him couched in the most amicable terms.* Others may understand him but I cannot understand how it was possible for him to realise that the salvation of the nation wholly depended on the fall of a dangerous man and yet to make no more than a tentative gesture to bring him down, while at the same time supporting him, winning new adherents and admirers to his cause by expressing his confidence in him, and thus placing all the power into his hands. While Kossuth vacillated *in this pusillanimous way,* working now for Görgey and now against him ... *Görgey,* who was more consistent and resolute than Kossuth, put his evil plan into practice" (Th. Lapinski, loc. cit., pp. 163, 164).

On August 11, 1849, on Görgey's *orders,* Kossuth issued a manifesto, ostensibly from the fortress of Arad, announcing his abdication and conferring on Görgey "supreme government authority in both military and civilian affairs". He went on to say:

"After the unfortunate outcome of the battles which *God* has *visited* upon the nation in recent days, *there is no longer any hope that we can continue our defensive struggle against the combined forces of the two great powers* [...] *with any prospect of success.*" [a]

Having thus stated at the beginning of the manifesto that Hungary's cause was *irrevocably* lost, and moreover as a result of *Divine visitation, Kossuth* goes on to make Görgey "responsible *before God* for deploying the power" placed by Kossuth at his disposal "*for the salvation*" of Hungary. He trusted Görgey enough to deliver Hungary up to him, but too little to deliver up his own person to him. His personal distrust of Görgey was so intense that he contrived it so that the arrival of his deed of abdication in Görgey's hands coincided with his own arrival on Turkish soil. This is why he concludes his manifesto with the words:

"If my death can be of any use to my country, I shall sacrifice my own life with joy."

What he had sacrificed on the altar of his country, handing it over to Görgey, was the *government,* the *title* to which however he at once usurped again under Turkish protection.

In Kütahya His Excellency, the Governor *in partibus,* received a copy of the first Blue Book on the Hungarian catastrophe laid before Parliament by Palmerston.[b] As he wrote to David Urquhart, the study of these diplomatic documents convinced him that "*Russia had a spy, nay an agent even, in every Cabinet*" and that *in the*

---

[a] Lajos Kossuth, "An die Nation! Festung Arad am 11. August 1849". Quoted in Theophil Lapinski's *Feldzug der Ungarischen Hauptarmee...,* Hamburg, 1850, S. 175.— *Ed.*

[b] *Correspondence relative to the Affairs of Hungary, 1847-1849. Presented to both Houses of Parliament by Command of Her Majesty.* August 15, 1850, London.— *Ed.*

Russian interest Palmerston had betrayed dear Hungary.[a]* And the
first words that fell from his lips when he stepped onto English
soil in Southampton were: "Palmerston, the dear friend of my
bosom!"[b]

After he was freed from internment in Turkey Kossuth sailed to
England. Off the coast of Marseilles, where he was forbidden to
land, he issued a manifesto whose tenor and phraseology were
those of French social democracy.[c] Having set foot on English soil
he at once *repudiated*

> "that *novel doctrine,* social democracy, which rightly or wrongly is held to be
> incompatible with social order and the security of property. Hungary neither has
> nor wishes to have anything to do with these doctrines, if only for the extremely simple
> reason that in Hungary there is no opportunity nor even the slightest inducement for
> them to be introduced."[d] (Cf. the letter from Marseilles.)

During the first two weeks of his stay in England he changed his
confession of faith as frequently as his audience—he was all things
to all men. Count *Kasimir Batthyány* gave this explanation of his
public breach with Kossuth which took place at this time:

> "It is not just the *bévues*[e] that Kossuth has committed in the first two weeks since
> his release that have induced me to take this step, but all my experience of him,
> everything I have seen, suffered, allowed, endured, and, as you will recall,
> disguised and concealed, at first in Hungary and then in exile,—in short it is a
> matter of the opinion I have formed about the man.... Permit me to remark that
> whatever Mr. Kossuth has said or may say in Southampton, Wisbech or London, in
> England, in short, cannot undo what he said in Marseilles. In the land of the
> 'young giant'" (America) "he will again sing a different tune, for just as he is
> unscrupulous[f] in other matters and bends like a reed beneath any gust of wind, so
> too does he gainsay his own words *sans gêne,*[g] and does not hesitate to hide behind

---

* Kossuth did not understand then how Palmerston's feigned hostility to Russia
"could" deceive anyone of ordinary intelligence. "*How could a man of any intellect*
for a single moment believe that the Minister who allowed Russia's intervention in
Hungary, would give the word of attack against her?" (Letter dated Kutayah,
December 17, 1850. *Correspondence of Kossuth.*)

---

[a] Marx uses the English phrase "dear Hungary".— *Ed.*

[b] Marx quotes this sentence in English and gives its German equivalent in
brackets.— *Ed.*

[c] Lajos Kossuth, "An die Marseiller Democratie" [Bord des Mississippi, 29.
September 1851], quoted in Gustav von Alvensleben's *L. Kossuth nach der Capitulation
von Vilagos,* Weimar, 1852, S. 65-66.— *Ed.*

[d] From Kossuth's speech at a workers' meeting at Copenhagen House. Quoted
in *Authentic Life of His Excellency Louis Kossuth...,* London, 1851, p. 76.— *Ed.*

[e] Blunders.— *Ed.*

[f] Marx gives the English words "unscrupulous" and, further on in the text, "a
most undeserving heart" in brackets after their German equivalents.— *Ed.*

[g] Without the slightest embarrassment.— *Ed.*

the great names of men now dead whom he has ruined, such as my poor cousin, Louis Batthyány.... I do not hesitate to declare that before Kossuth leaves England you will have good reason to regret the honours you have squandered on a most undeserving heart" (*Correspondence of Kossuth*, letter of Count Batthyány to Mr. Urquhart, Paris, October 29, 1851).

Kossuth's performance in the United States, where he spoke *against* slavery in the North and *for* slavery in the South, left behind nothing but a great sense of disappointment and 300 dead speeches. Bringing the curtain down hastily on this peculiar episode, I would only remark that he strongly recommended the *Germans* in the *United States*, and in particular the *German emigration*, to conclude an alliance between Germany, Hungary and Italy, to the *exclusion of France* (and not just the coup d'état government, but France itself, and even the French emigration together with the parties in France represented by it). No sooner had he returned to London than he attempted *to establish relations with Louis Bonaparte* through the agency of Count Szirmay, a dubious character, and through Colonel Kiss in Paris (see my letter in the *New-York Tribune* of *September 28, 1852* and my public declaration in the same paper on November 16, 1852[a]).

During the Mazzini rising in Milan in 1853[188] a proclamation appeared on the walls of the town addressed to the Hungarian troops stationed there and calling on them to join the Italian insurgents.[b] It bore the signature: *Louis Kossuth.* Scarcely had the news of the defeat of the insurgents reached London when Kossuth hastened to publish a statement in *The Times*[c] and other English papers, declaring the proclamation to be a *forgery* and thereby publicly contradicting his friend Mazzini. The proclamation was nevertheless *authentic.* Mazzini had obtained it from Kossuth, he owned the original manuscript in Kossuth's handwriting and he had acted in concert with Kossuth. Convinced that Austrian despotism in Italy could only be overthrown by the united action of Italy and Hungary, Mazzini then first tried to replace Kossuth with a more reliable Hungarian leader, but after this attempt had failed because of the divisions within the Hungarian emigration, he forgave his unreliable ally and mag-

---

a Karl Marx, "Movements of Mazzini and Kossuth.—League with Louis Napoleon.—Palmerston" and "Kossuth, Mazzini, and Louis Napoleon. To the Editor of *The N. Y. Tribune*, London, November 16, 1852" (see present edition, Vol. 11).— *Ed.*

b L. Kossuth, "In the Name of the Hungarian Nation. To the Soldiers Quartered in Italy, February 1853", *The Times*, No. 21348, February 10, 1853.— *Ed.*

c "Italy. The 'Voce della Verita!'", *The Times*, No. 21366, March 3, 1853.— *Ed.*

nanimously abstained from an exposure which was bound to destroy Kossuth's reputation in England.

The same year, 1853, it will be remembered, saw the beginning of the Russo-Turkish war. On December 17, 1850 Kossuth had written to David Urquhart from Kütahya:

"Take away the Turkish supremacy from Turkey and it will cease to be. And after all, as matters stand, *Turkey is indispensably necessary to the freedom of the world.*" [a]

His enthusiasm for the Turks was even greater in a letter he wrote to the Grand Vizier *Reshid Pasha* on February 15, 1851. In extravagant phrases he offered his services to the Turkish Government. On January 22, 1852, during his tour of the *United States,* he wrote to *David Urquhart*:

"Would you feel inclined, knowing how much the interests of Hungary and Turkey were identical, to plead my cause at Constantinople? The Porte did not know who I am when I was there. My reception in England and America, and the position in which the chances of fortune, and I may say Providence, have placed me, could show the Porte that I am a true friend, and perhaps a not uninfluential one, of Turkey and her future."

On November 5, 1853 he wrote to Mr. *Crawshay* (an Urquhartist), offering to go to Constantinople as an ally of Turkey, but "not with empty hands",[b] and therefore asked Mr. Crawshay to raise funds

"by private applications addressed confidentially to such liberal men as might well afford the assistance he required".

In this letter he says: "I hate and despise the artifice of making revolutions." At the same time as he was penning letters to the Urquhartists that overflowed with hatred of revolutions and love for the Turks, he issued manifestos together with Mazzini which proclaimed the expulsion of the Turks from Europe and the transformation of Turkey into an "oriental Switzerland", and also signed the exhortations to revolution in general put out by the so-called Central Committee of European Democracy.[189]

Since as early as the end of 1853 Kossuth had aimlessly squandered the money he had collected in America in 1852 by his speechifying in the name of Hungary, and since moreover his plea to Mr. Crawshay fell on deaf ears, the Governor abandoned his intended chivalrous journey to Constantinople, but instead he sent

---

[a] Here and below Marx quotes from the article "Data by Which to Judge of Kossuth", *The Free Press*, No. 5, May 27, 1859. The italics are in the article.— *Ed.*

[b] Marx gives the English words "not with empty hands" and, below, "I hate and despise the artifice of making revolutions" in brackets after their German equivalents.— *Ed.*

his agent, Colonel *Johann Bangya,* supplying him with the best possible recommendations.*

* I myself had made the acquaintance of *Bangya* in London in 1850, together with his friend at the time, the present *General Türr.* His underhand dealings with parties of every complexion, Orleanists, Bonapartists, etc., and his association with policemen of every "nationality" made me suspect him, but he dispelled my suspicions quite simply by showing me a document in *Kossuth's* own hand in which he (who had formerly been provisional chief commissioner of the police in Komorn[a] under Klapka) was appointed chief commissioner of the police *in partibus.* As a secret chief of police in the service of the revolution he naturally had to keep in "touch" with police in the service of the governments. In the course of the summer of 1852 I discovered that he had appropriated a manuscript[b] I had asked him to convey to a bookseller in Berlin and steered it into the hands of a German government. After I had written to a Hungarian in Paris[c] describing this incident and a number of other striking peculiarities of the man's, and after the Bangya mystery had been completely cleared up thanks to the intervention of a third person well informed in the matter,[d] I sent an open denunciation, signed by myself, to the *New-Yorker Criminal-Zeitung* early in 1853.[e] In a letter, still in my possession, in which he attempted to justify his actions, Bangya emphasised that I had less reason than anyone to regard him as a spy, since he had always (and this was perfectly true) avoided discussing with me the affairs of my own party. Although Kossuth and his supporters did not drop Bangya at the time, my revelations in the *Criminal-Zeitung* made it nevertheless difficult for him to continue operating in London and so he was all the more ready to grasp the opportunity provided by the troubles in the Orient of employing his talents in another setting. Soon after the conclusion of the Peace of Paris in 1856 I saw from the English newspapers that a certain *Mehemed Bey,* a colonel in the Turkish service, formerly a Christian known under the name of Johann Bangya, had sailed from Constantinople to Circassia, in the company of some Polish refugees, and that once there he figured as Sepher Pasha's Chief of the General Staff, and as what might be termed the "Simon Bolívar" of the Circassians. In the columns of the London *Free Press,* of which many copies are sent to Constantinople, I drew attention to the liberator's past.[f] On January 20, 1858 Bangya was, as is mentioned in the text, sentenced to death in Aderbi by a military tribunal of the Polish Legion under the command of Colonel Th. Lapinski for plotting treason against Circassia. As Bangya was a Turkish colonel, Sepher Pasha decided that execution of the sentence was incompatible with the respect due to the Sublime Porte and therefore shipped the condemned man to Trebizond from where he soon returned to Constantinople, a free man. In the meantime the Hungarian emigration in Constantinople had enthusiastically taken up his cause against the Poles. Shielded from the Divan (which, since he was a "colonel", had moreover to feed both him and his harem) by the protection of the Russian Embassy, and from the Poles by

---

[a] Komárom.— *Ed.*

[b] The pamphlet *The Great Men of the Exile* by Marx and Engels (see present edition, Vol. 11).— *Ed.*

[c] Gustav Zerfy (see Marx's letter to him of December 28, 1852, present edition, Vol. 39).— *Ed.*

[d] Bartholomäus Szemere.— *Ed.*

[e] See Karl Marx, "Hirsch's Confession" (present edition, Vol. 12).— *Ed.*

[f] Karl Marx, "A Traitor in Circassia", *The Free Press,* No. 34, April 1, 1857.— *Ed.*

A military tribunal held in Aderbi in Circassia on *January 20, 1858* unanimously passed a sentence of death on "*Mehemed Bey,* formerly *Johann Bangya d'Illosfalva,* who on his own admission and on the evidence of witnesses had been found guilty of high treason and conducting a secret correspondence with the enemy" (the Russian general Philipson).[d] However, this did not prevent him from living peacefully in Constantinople to this very day. In a handwritten confession submitted to the tribunal, *Bangya* said *inter alia.*

"My political action was entirely dictated by the chief of my country, *Louis Kossuth....* Provided with letters of introduction from my political chief, I came to Constantinople on the 22nd December, 1853."[e]

He goes on to describe how he became a Moslem and entered the Turkish service with the rank of colonel.

"My instructions" (from Kossuth) "insisted that I should get attached in some way or other to troops which were to take part in operations on the Circassian coast."

His task there was to prevent the Circassians from taking any part in the war against Russia. He carried out his mission successfully and towards the close of the war he sent "Kossuth a detailed account of the situation in Circassia" from Constantinople. Before his second expedition to Circassia, which he undertook together with the Poles, he received an order from Kossuth to collaborate with certain Hungarians, among whom was General Stein (Ferhad Pasha).

the prejudices of his fellow-countrymen, Bangya coolly proceeded to publish a self-apologia in the *Journal de Constantinople.* However, a Circassian deputation arrived presently and this put an end to his games. The Hungarian emigration officially dropped their favourite, though *de très mauvaise grâce.*[a] All the papers relating to the military tribunal in Aderbi, including Bangya's own confession of guilt, and all the documents produced later in Constantinople were sent on to London by the Polish emigration, and once there they were published in extracts in *The Free Press* (May 1858).[b] The documents were also published more extensively by me in the *New-York [Daily] Tribune* on June 16, 1858.[c]

---

a With great reluctance.— *Ed.*

b "Extract from the Minutes of the Council of War, held at Aderbi...", *The Free Press*, No. 16, May 12, 1858.— *Ed.*

c See "A Curious Piece of History", *New-York Daily Tribune*, No. 5352.— *Ed.*

d "Sentence. January 20, 1858", *The Free Press*, No. 16, May 12, 1858.— *Ed.*

e Here and below Marx quotes from "Confession of Bangya before the Council of War", *ibid.— Ed.*

"Captain Franchini," he says, *"military secretary to the Russian Ambassador,*[a] was present at several of our conferences. The object was to win over Circassia to Russian interests in a peaceable, slow, but sure manner. [...] Before the expedition set out from Constantinople" (mid-February 1857), "I received letters and instructions from Kossuth approving my plan of operations."

Bangya's treachery came to light in Circassia when a letter to Philipson, the Russian general, was intercepted.

"In conformity with my instructions," Bangya says, "I was to get in touch with the Russian general. For a long time I could not make up my mind to do this, but at last I received *orders so precise* that it was impossible for me to hesitate any longer."

The proceedings of the military tribunal in Aderbi and especially *Bangya's confession* made a great sensation in Constantinople, London and New York. Kossuth was repeatedly and urgently pressed, even from the Hungarian side, to make a public statement, but to no avail. To this day he has maintained timorous silence on Bangya's mission in Circassia.

In the autumn of 1858 Kossuth was busy hawking around England and Scotland moderately priced lectures in which he denounced the Austrian concordat[190] and Louis Bonaparte. The passionate fanaticism with which he warned the English to beware of the treacherous designs of Louis Bonaparte, whom he described as the secret ally of Russia, can be seen, e.g., from *The Glasgow Sentinel* of November 20, 1858.[b] When Louis Bonaparte revealed his Italian plans early in 1859, Kossuth denounced him in *Mazzini's Pensiero ed Azione* and warned "all true republicans", Italians, Hungarians and even Germans, to beware of allowing themselves to be used as a cat's-paw by the Imperial Quasimodo. In February 1859 Kossuth ascertained that Colonel Kiss, Count Teleki and General Klapka, all of whom had long since belonged to the red camarilla of the Palais Royal, were hatching a conspiracy with Plon-Plon to provoke an uprising in Hungary. Kossuth now threatened a public polemic in the English press unless he too were admitted to the "secret league". Plon-Plon was more than willing to open the doors of the conclave to him. Travelling under the name of Mr. Brown and furnished with an English passport, Kossuth went to Paris in the beginning of May. He hastened to the Palais Royal and expounded his plans for a Hungarian uprising to Plon-Plon at great length.[191] On the evening of May 3 the Prince Rouge accompanied the ex-Governor to the Tuileries in his own carriage, to present him there to the saviour of society. Throughout the meeting with Louis

---

[a] Apollinary Petrovich Butenev.— *Ed.*

[b] This refers to the article "Louis Kossuth and Panslavism".— *Ed.*

Bonaparte, words failed the normally so eloquent speaker, so that Plon-Plon had to act as spokesman and present Kossuth's programme to his cousin. Kossuth later praised the almost literal accuracy of Plon-Plon's rendering. Having listened attentively to his cousin's exposition, Louis Bonaparte declared that there was only one obstacle preventing him from adopting Kossuth's proposals, and this was Kossuth's republican convictions and republican connections. Thereupon the ex-Governor solemnly abjured his republican faith, protesting that he neither was a republican now, nor had he ever been one, but that political necessity alone and a strange concatenation of circumstances had forced him into an alliance with the republican party of the European emigration. As proof of his anti-republicanism he offered Plon-Plon the Hungarian crown in the name of his country. At that time, this crown had not yet been abolished. Moreover, Kossuth was not officially authorised to auction it, but everyone who has followed his appearances abroad with any attention will have observed that he had long been accustomed to speak of his "dear Hungary"[a] much as a backwoods squire will speak of his estate.*

I take his repudiation of republicanism to be sincere. A civil list of 300,000 florins, claimed in Pest to maintain the dignity of the executive; the transfer of the patronage of the hospitals from an Austrian Archduchess[b] to his sister[c]; the attempt to christen a number of regiments with the name of Kossuth; his efforts to form a camarilla; the stubbornness with which he clung to the title of governor when abroad, a title which he had renounced in the moment of danger; his entire subsequent behaviour, much more that of a pretender than a refugee—all that points to tendencies alien to republicanism.

After his formal cleaning of the suspicion of republicanism, an agreement was reached placing 3 million francs at Mr. Kossuth's disposal. There was nothing objectionable about this clause in itself since money was needed to finance the military organisation of the Hungarian refugees, and why should the Governor be denied the same right to receive subsidies from his new ally as had

---

* That such matters come to light appears less strange if it is borne in mind that at least two loquacious parties were involved here. Incidentally, English papers reported these facts during Kossuth's stay in London (in the late summer of 1859).

---

^a Marx uses the English expression.— *Ed.*
^b Maria Theresa.— *Ed.*
^c Zsuzsánna Meszlenyi.— *Ed.*

been enjoyed by all the despotic powers of Europe who had been subsidised by England throughout the anti-Jacobin war? Kossuth was given 50,000 francs[a] on the spot as an advance on his personal expenses and he secured certain other pecuniary advantages, a sort of insurance premium, in the event of the premature end to the war. Financial flair and melodramatic emotions are by no means mutually exclusive. After all, as his ex-Finance Minister, Dušek, must be aware, even during the Hungarian revolution Kossuth had taken the precaution of receiving his salary not in Kossuth-notes but in silver or in Austrian banknotes.

Before Kossuth left the Tuileries it was agreed that he should undertake to neutralise the alleged "Austrian tendencies" of the Derby Ministry by launching a neutrality campaign in England. It is known how the voluntary support of the Whigs and the Manchester School enabled him to carry out this initial part of the agreement with the greatest success. A lecturing tour from the Mansion House in London to the Free Trade Hall in Manchester formed an antithesis to the Anglo-Scottish tour of autumn 1858 when he hawked his hatred of Bonaparte and Cherbourg, "the standing menace to England",[b] at a shilling per head.

The larger part of the Hungarian emigration in Europe had withdrawn its support for Kossuth since the end of 1852. The prospect of an invasion of the Adriatic coast with French assistance brought the majority back to his flag. His negotiations with the military sector of his new-found supporters were not without a certain Decembrist flavour. In order to be in a position to assign a larger amount of French money to them he advanced them to higher military rank, lieutenants, for instance, were promoted to major. To begin with each man received travelling expenses to Turin, then a lavish sum for a uniform (the cost of a major's outfit amounted to £150), and finally six months' advance of salary with the promise of one year's retirement pay after the conclusion of peace. The salaries themselves were not unduly high: 10,000 francs[c] for the supreme general (Klapka), 6,000 francs for the generals, 5,000 for the brigadiers, 4,000 for the lieutenant-colonels, 3,000 for the majors, and so on. The Hungarian forces assembled in Turin consisted almost entirely of officers without

---

[a] *The Free Press* of September 28, 1859 ("Particulars of Kossuth's Transaction with Louis Napoleon"), and the *New-York Daily Tribune* of September 24, 1859 ("Kossuth and Louis Napoleon") have: "75,000 francs".— *Ed.*

[b] Marx uses the English phrases "lecturing tour" and "the standing menace to England".— *Ed.*

[c] *The Free Press* of September 28, 1859 has: "12,000 francs".— *Ed.*

the rank and file, and I have heard many bitter words about this from the "lesser" Hungarian emigration.

General Moritz Perczel, as has already been mentioned, resigned publicly as soon as he had seen through the diplomatic game. Despite Louis Bonaparte's order to the contrary, *Klapka* insisted on a landing near Fiume, but *Kossuth* made sure that the Hungarian refugee corps stayed within the theatrical limits laid down by the director of the troupe.

The rumours of the peace signed at Villafranca had hardly arrived in Turin when Kossuth, terrified of being handed over to the Austrians, took to his heels and escaped to Geneva, secretly, behind the back of the military forces at his disposal. At the time neither the name of Francis Joseph, nor that of Louis Bonaparte, stood in such bad odour in the Hungarian camp in Turin as that of Louis Kossuth, but for the fact that the comic side of his latest escapade somewhat overshadowed all criticism. On his return Kossuth published in London a letter to his tame elephant, a certain McAdam in Glasgow,[a] declaring himself to be disillusioned, but not cheated and closing with the emotional statement that he had nowhere to lay his head and that therefore all letters for him should be sent to his friend F. Pulszky who had offered shelter to the refugee. The more than Anglo-Saxon gruffness with which the London press intimated to Kossuth that he should use the Bonapartist subsidies to rent himself a house in London convinced him that for the time being his role in London was at an end.

Apart from his talent as an orator Kossuth also possesses the great gift of silence as soon as the audience shows definite signs of displeasure or he finds himself at a loss for words by which to justify himself. Like the sun he knows all about eclipses. That he was capable of consistency at least once in his life was demonstrated by his recent letter to Garibaldi in which he warned him not to make an attack on Rome lest he offend the Emperor of the French, "the only support of the oppressed nationalities".[b]

Just as, in the first half of the eighteenth century, Alberoni was known as the colossal cardinal, so we may think of Kossuth as a colossal *Langenschwarz.* He is essentially an improviser who is

---

[a] Passages from the letter were quoted in a leading article in *The Times,* No. 23428, October 4, 1859. A statement by McAdam to the effect that Kossuth's letter was a private one was published in *The Times,* No. 23431, October 7. Marx mentioned the fact in a letter to Bartholomäus Szemere on October 8 (see present edition, Vol. 40).— *Ed.*

[b] Cf. Kossuth's letter to Garibaldi, Turin, September 14, in L. Kossuth, *Meine Schriften aus der Emigration,* Bd. III, S. 24.— *Ed.*

moulded by the impressions he receives from the audience facing him at a given moment, not an author who stamps his original ideas on the world. Like Blondin on his rope, Kossuth dances on his tongue. Cut off from the mood of his people he was bound to lapse into mere virtuosity and the vices of the virtuoso. The insubstantiality of thought characteristic of the improviser is inevitably reflected in the ambivalence of his actions. If Kossuth was once the Aeolian harp through which the hurricane of the people reverberated, he is now merely the Dionysian ear which echoes in a murmur the whisperings in the mysterious apartments of the Palais Royal and the Tuileries.

It would be quite unjust to place *General Klapka,* Vogt's second patron, on the same level as Kossuth. Klapka was one of the best Hungarian revolutionary generals. Like the majority of officers who gathered in Turin in 1859 he regards Louis Bonaparte much as Franz Rákóczy regarded Louis XIV. In their eyes Louis Bonaparte represents France's military power, a power which might serve Hungary but which, if only on geographical grounds, could never endanger it.* But why does Vogt appeal to the authority of Klapka? Klapka has never made a secret of the fact that he belongs to Plon-Plon's red camarilla. So that "friend" Klapka can vouch for "friend" Vogt? Klapka has shown no great talent in the selection of his friends. One of his closest friends in Komorn was Colonel *Assermann.* Let us hear about this Colonel Assermann from Colonel *Lapinski,* who served under Klapka up to the surrender of Komorn and who subsequently distinguished himself in Circassia fighting against the Russians.

---

* Although I can understand how Klapka can entertain such views, it is astonishing to find similar ones in the above-quoted work of Szemere's[a] and I have frankly told him what I think of it in this respect.[b] I find it even harder to understand his latest statement about the Austrian concession.[192] I am aware that Szemere does not allow private considerations to influence his decisions on public affairs and that he had very important reasons for declaring that with the concessions granted by Vienna, the Hungarians could take all they wanted in Pest; that any Hungarian insurrection from abroad, especially with the aid of the French, would necessarily provoke Russian intervention in Hungary, whether for or against Austria; and finally, that the autonomy granted to Transylvania, Slavonia and Croatia, as well as to the Voivodina, would at this particular moment ensure that the Vienna Cabinet had the loyalty of these "nationalities" against the Magyars just as it did in 1848-49. All that is true enough, but could have been said without appearing to recognise the Hungarian Constitution "in usum delphini"[193] in the mutilated Viennese edition.

---

[a] This refers to Bartholomäus Szemere's pamphlet *Hungary, from 1848 to 1860,* London, 1860.— *Ed.*

[b] Marx to Szemere, June 2, 1860 (see present edition, Vol. 41).— *Ed.*

"The betrayal at Világos," [194] Lapinski says, "threw the numerous and idle staff officers in Komorn into a state of great terror.... The scented gentlemen with golden collars, many of whom were able neither to hold a rifle nor to command three men, were full of fear running about in confusion and devising plans to save their own skins at any price. These men, who had managed on one pretext or another to leave the main army and withdraw to the cosy safety of the impregnable fortress, without having to perform any labour over and above putting their signature to a receipt once a month acknowledging that their salaries were correct and in order, were terrified by the thought that they were now faced with a life-and-death struggle.... It was these wretches who conjured up dreadful visions of internal unrest, mutiny, etc., in order to make the general surrender the fortress as quickly as possible [...] if they could only save themselves and their property. The latter was of special concern to many of them, for all their endeavours throughout the revolution had been concentrated on enriching themselves, and a number had succeeded. Some individuals managed to enrich themselves quite easily for often half a year would pass before it was necessary to give an account of the funds they had received. Since this was a situation which favoured treachery and fraud many people may have dipped their hands more deeply into the cash-box than they could have justified.... The armistice had been concluded: how was it used? From the supplies in the fortress, which would have lasted *a year,* unnecessarily large rations were distributed among the villages, while no provisions were brought in from the surrounding area; even the hay and oats which the peasants in the nearby villages wanted to sell was left lying there so that a few weeks later the Cossacks' horses devoured the property of the peasants while we in the fortress complained about the lack of supplies. The cattle in the fortress were for the most part sold off outside the town on the pretext that there was a shortage of fodder. *Colonel Assermann* presumably did not know that meat can be pickled. A large part of the grain was also sold off on the grounds that it was going mouldy; this was done openly, and even more such things were done secretly. With such a man as *Assermann* at his side and with a number of similar individuals in his entourage *Klapka* had of course quickly to abandon every good idea that came into his head; those gentlemen took good care of that..." (Lapinski, loc. cit., pp. 202-06).[a]

The memoirs of both Görgey and Klapka[b] provide no less eloquent testimony to Klapka's lack of character and political understanding. All the errors he committed during the defence of Komorn stem from this defect.

"If Klapka with his knowledge and patriotism *also had a firm will of his own,* and if he had acted in accordance with opinions he had formed himself, rather than with those *suggested* to him by fools and cowards, the defence of Komorn would sparkle in the annals of history like a meteor" (loc. cit., p. 209).

On August 3, Klapka had gained a brilliant victory over the besieging Austrian corps at Komorn, he had scattered it and put it out of action for some time. He followed this up by taking Raab[c]

---

[a] Theophil Lapinski, *Feldzug der Ungarischen Hauptarmee im Jahre 1849.*—*Ed.*

[b] Arthur Görgey's *Mein Leben und Wirken in Ungarn in den Jahren 1848 und 1849,* Bd. 1-2, Leipzig, 1852, and *Memoiren von Georg Klapka. April bis October 1849,* Leipzig, 1850.—*Ed.*

[c] Now Györ.—*Ed.*

and could easily take Vienna as well, but for eight days remained irresolute and inactive at Raab and then returned to Komorn where he was met by the news of Görgey's surrender and found a letter from the latter awaiting him. The enemy requested an armistice so that the scattered besieging corps of the Austrians and the Russians advancing from Rima Szombat[a] could be concentrated near Komorn and invest the fortress at their leisure. Instead of attacking and defeating the enemy formations piecemeal before they could join up, Klapka again vacillated irresolutely, but rejected the request of the Austrian and Russian spokesmen for an armistice. At that moment, says Lapinski,

"an adjutant of the Emperor Nicholas arrived in Komorn on August 22.... But, said the Russian Mephisto in honeyed tones, *surely you will grant us a two weeks' armistice, General. It is His Majesty, my gracious Emperor, who is asking you!* This worked like a quick poison. Where the efforts of the Austrian spokesmen and the arguments of the Russian negotiators had failed, this cunning Russian emissary succeeded with a few brief words. *Klapka* could not resist the subtle compliment and signed an armistice for 14 days. The fall of Komorn dates from this act".[b]

Klapka allowed the armistice to be used by *Colonel Assermann,* as we have already mentioned, to disperse *in two weeks* the *provisions* of the fortress, *which would have lasted a whole year.* At the end of the armistice Grabbe invested Komorn from the Vag, while the Austrians, whose forces had gradually grown to 40,000 men, camped on the right bank of the Danube. The inactive life behind the walls and fortifications demoralised the troops inside Komorn. Klapka did not launch a single attack on the Russian besieging corps, which had seen no action yet and was only 19,000 strong. The enemy's preparations for the siege were not disturbed for an instant. In fact, from the moment he had signed the armistice, Klapka prepared everything not for defence but for capitulation. The only energy he showed was of an inquisitorial nature and was directed at the upright officers who were opposed to capitulation.

"In the end," *Lapinski* says, "it became dangerous to say anything about the Austrians if one wished to avoid arrest."

Finally, on September 27, the capitulation was signed.

"In view of the power, of the desperate situation of the nation, which had put its last hopes in Komorn," Lapinski says, "in view of the situation in Europe and the impotence of Austria, which would have made the greatest sacrifices for the sake of Komorn, *the surrender conditions were as wretched as could be imagined.*"[c]

---

[a] Rimavska Sobota.— *Ed.*
[b] Theophil Lapinski, op. cit., S. 201-02.— *Ed.*
[c] Ibid., S. 230.— *Ed.*

They "were just sufficient to enable us to escape quickly from Komorn over the frontier", but they did not contain the slightest guarantee either for Hungary or even for the revolutionary generals in the hands of the Austrians. Moreover, they were drawn up in great haste and were so imprecise and ambiguous that it was easy for Haynau to violate them later on.

So much for *Klapka*. If Vogt is lacking in "character", Klapka is the last man to make good the deficiency.

Vogt's third patron is "*Jaimes Fazy, the regenerator of Geneva*",[a] as he is described by Vogt, his court jester. The following letters, written by *Johann Philipp Becker*[b] to the addressee of his letter reproduced earlier,[c] contain a portrait of Fazy which is so apt that any additional comment will only spoil it. I would make only one preliminary remark. The most nauseating feature of Vogt's so-called *Studien* is the hypocritical show of Lutheran and even Calvinist horror of the "*ultramontane party*".[195] Thus, for example, he confronts Germany with the absurd alternative of either giving Louis Bonaparte a free hand or submitting to the domination of the Austrian concordat, and "verily we should rather prefer to undergo a second period of national humiliation" (*Studien,* p. 52). In the nasal tones of the puritan he fumes about

"the ultramontane party, the sworn enemy of humanity, this monster that is attacking its very core" (loc. cit., p. 120).[d]

He has of course never heard of the fact which even Dupin Aîné revealed in the Decembrist Senate, that

"under Louis Bonaparte's régime the congregations, associations and foundations of all kinds directly subject to the Order of Jesuits have become more numerous than they were under the *ancien régime,* and that all the state regulations which restricted the ultramontane organs of propaganda even before 1789 have been systematically dismantled by Decembrist legislation and administration".

But Vogt must at any rate know that the rule of his local Bonaparte, M. *James Fazy,* is based on a long-standing coalition between the so-called radical party and the ultramontane party. When the Vienna Congress incorporated Geneva, the traditional home of Calvinism, into the Swiss Confederation, it added to its

---

a Carl Vogt, *Mein Prozess...,* S. 213.— *Ed.*

b Becker wrote them at Marx's request (see Marx's letter to him of April 9, 1860, present edition, Vol. 41). For tactical reasons Becker addressed them to Georg Friedrich Rheinländer.— *Ed.*

c See this volume, pp. 60-64.— *Ed.*

d The words in quotation marks are Marx's summary of several passages from the *Studien.—Ed.*

territory, along with certain Savoyard districts, a rural Catholic population and the *crème* of the ultramontane priesthood. It is the alliance with this "sworn enemy of humanity, this monster" which has made *Fazy* the *dictator* of Geneva and *Vogt Fazy's member of the Council of States.* So much by way of introduction.

"*Paris*, July 2, 1860

"Dear R...,

"At long last I really must comply with your wish and give you my opinion of M. James Fazy....

"Just as the political sciences are of no avail unless one knows how to apply them in real life, so too statesmanship is sterile unless it is based on science and philosophical thought. A so-called statesman who has nothing but theory will not fool anyone and he will soon reveal his incapacity. On the other hand, a man who has a one-track talent for statesmanship can more easily conceal his lack of knowledge and intellectual prowess, he may pass for a practical statesman and gain the support of the great market of mediocrity. Whether or not the rule of such a man can advance the culture of a nation and can create conditions ensuring its undisturbed progress, lies beyond the powers of judgment of the blindly adulating crowd. If there is only the appearance that things are going well and are improving and if only everything is done in the name of freedom and civilisation!

"M. *James Fazy* is an outstanding specimen of the breed of political virtuosos. This astute man is distinguished not only for his statecraft but largely for his political craftiness. He resorts to all sorts of artifices and produces *tours de force* as often as the 'public interest' requires it, but with his usual cunning avoids every *salto mortale*. Full of guile in his manipulation of roles behind the scenes, a skilful director and prompter, he is the *ne plus ultra* of a French actor. His 'strength of character', which recoils from nothing if only it will serve his purposes, would be much to be admired, were it not for the fact that it is so intimately bound up with the disreputable nature of those purposes. Once one is familiar with the man's lack of principles and moral character, one will be less inclined to admire his ingenuity in devising means and his adroitness in employing them. This political virtuoso contrives by a sleight of hand boldly to appropriate everything good that occurs in the life of the people he governs; he then presents it to the great mass of the people in his own name so that they believe and are prepared to swear that it has all been brought about by or through the agency of 'Papa Fazy'. With equal skill he manages to shrug off the responsibility for everything that is bad or unpopular and to blame it on others. In his government he will not endure any independent personality, his colleagues must submit to being arbitrarily repudiated or forced to act as godfather for his abortive undertakings. Submitting to his despotic brutality *à discrétion*,[a] they have always to be prepared to act as the scapegoats and whipping-boys for the sake of the people and the glory of their President. Just as a crowned monarch will always ask himself whether a political measure will damage his dynasty, however much it may be to the advantage of the people, before he 'is pleased' to approve it, so too Papa Fazy asks himself, whenever he plans to take action: 'Will it not topple my presidential chair?' Hence our hero always adapts his policies to circumstances and lives from hand to mouth: on one day he will act out an uproarious comedy in the government, the next day he will perform a conjuring trick in the Grand Council and the day after that he will produce a sensational

---

[a] Unconditionally.— *Ed.*

coup at a popular assembly, and the great mass, skilfully cosseted by him, only too happy to believe in a visible and audible God whom it can worship and pray to, becomes credulous and believes in pennies from heaven when it is only a heavy shower beating down on the roofs. I do not wish to suggest that the people of Geneva are immature and lacking in intelligence; on the contrary, I am convinced that hardly anywhere can one find a more active public life, a more vigorous and conscious endeavour to evolve a free civil society than here on the banks of the Lake of Geneva. I shall return later to the subject and attempt to explain why M. Fazy has nevertheless been able on so many occasions to secure a majority of votes.

"All that has been achieved in Geneva in fifteen years by an energetic generation he has chalked up to the credit of his rule, or he has caused his lackeys and worshippers to do so. The demolition of the fortifications, the impressive extension and improvement of the capital of the Canton, for instance, pass for his achievement. But every administration, including that of M. Fazy, would have been ruthlessly pushed aside if it had attempted to resist the mighty pressure from the populace to tear down fortifications that had become useless and to expand a town in which health conditions were increasingly deteriorating because of the terrible overcrowding. This question thus also became a question of Fazy's own survival and he energetically took it in hand—honour to whom honour is due—and has helped to carry out many improvements to the general satisfaction of the public. But without arrogant insolence no individual can set himself up as the originator or creator of what has been achieved by the strenuous and joint efforts of a whole generation to satisfy a great need of the age. It is only society as a whole that creates, and then only in a relative sense, an integral whole, to which the members according to their strength and position contribute a larger or smaller share. Blind faith in the authorities is a superstition like any other and is detrimental to any healthy development.

"I am well aware that our M. Fazy is like everyone else in that he only does those things which he cannot refrain from doing, and he only refrains from doing things that he cannot do, and that like every living being, in his desire to develop his own individuality completely, he pursues his own needs. It is just as impossible to expect him to act otherwise as to demand that a cat should go into the water of its own accord or a horse climb trees. If he acted differently he would not be James Fazy, and if he were not James Fazy he might perhaps be Louis Bonaparte or something of the sort. If greatness in a man who possesses power is to keep a people in leading-strings, to dazzle them with conjuring tricks, without impressing the stamp of intensive progress on their moral and intellectual culture, but instead branding society with the marks of corruption, then Fazy would surely be great and worthy of being envied by tyrants more powerful than he.

"He is as capable as anyone of sustaining contradictory policies and from them he produces the magic formula with which, as with a compass, he steers his little ship of state. At one moment radicalism will supply the crew and ultramontanism the cargo, at another, it will be the other way about—just as it suits the book and the latest tactics of the helmsman. So the machine of state is constantly in motion, heaving from one side to the other, like the balance wheel of a watch. And with what a happy effect! The radicals swear that things are moving forwards, the ultramontanists are convinced that they are going backwards. Both views are correct; both sides are happy in their faith and the Lord God Fazy remains at the helm.

"Now, my dear friend, let these lines be enough for the moment.

"Warmest greetings from

Your *Joh. Philipp Becker*"

"Paris, July 20, 1860

"Dear R...,

"So you think that my portrait of Fazy is perhaps somewhat exaggerated. By no means, my dear friend! Moreover, one cannot just think and judge things and people according to one's whims, but only in accordance with the logic of one's understanding and inner experience. Anyone whose words differ from his thoughts in such matters, and whose acts differ from his words, is untrue to himself and a scoundrel.

"Fazy, who received his earliest education in a Herrnhut school [196] in Neuwied and speaks good German, still gives the appearance, at the age of 65, of judging Germany and its people according to the impressions gained at that model institution. Nothing German, and even Swiss German, is to his taste, and only in rare cases does he make an exception of this. As a native of Geneva and as a man who has spent a long time in the United States of North America, he is intimately familiar with republican institutions, with the methods of agitation and, owing to his natural disposition, especially with the various stratagems of intrigue. He is more of a demagogue than a democrat and his chief political slogan, his badge: *laissez aller et laissez faire*,[197] would not be so bad, if only he could refrain from having a finger in every pie in which people attempt to do something without the blessing of the state. His interventions are designed either to achieve something that adds to his own glory, or where this proves to be impossible, to frustrate the enterprise, as he did in the project of Herr Mayer and others to establish the Banque de Crédit et d'Échange and to set up a Chamber of Commerce. During the Genevan revolution of 1846 [198] M. James acted in accordance with the precept: away from the danger zone makes for a long life, and he thought more of how to escape than of how to win. He was just on the point of leaving Geneva in secret when Albert Galeer, the heart and soul of the entire movement, made a last mighty effort to resolve the struggle which had long raged indecisively, and gained a total victory. Galeer, who was single-mindedly devoted to the cause and cared nothing for fame, firmly believed, at least at that time, that Fazy was motivated by a sincere love of the people. He was not at all put out when that hero, who had been saved from a precipitate flight in the nick of time, posed as the conqueror at a popular assembly immediately after the victory. Galeer himself could not contemplate a government post for himself immediately after the revolution, especially as he was not a Genevan, but a citizen of the Canton of Berne and so could neither vote nor be elected according to the confederate laws in force at the time. It is true that citizenship was soon conferred on him and after that he was elected into the Grand Council and was also given a post as translator of state papers. As the focus of the most energetic among the young people of Geneva he became a firm pillar of radical rule. Thanks to him Fazy's position as the hero of the great mass was strengthened still further. Using the phraseology of French radicalism which he had acquired when working on *Le National* in Paris in the day of Louis Philippe, James Fazy agitated in the press and on the podium, disguising his true thoughts and desires to his heart's content. Nevertheless, despite all his demagoguery a year had scarcely passed before he began to be seriously accused in various circles of entertaining secret relations with the leaders of the ultramontane party, and soon after of being a Francophile. In German Switzerland, where people look at these things more coolly and their judgments are more detached, they seem to have seen through his game even earlier. Towards the end of 1847, immediately after the conclusion of the Sonderbund War,[199] M. James Fazy went to the offices of the War Department to pay a call on General Ochsenbein; I was the only person there, as Ochsenbein was with the rest of the officers visiting the wounded in the hospitals. When Ochsenbein returned I told him that M. Fazy had called, to which he responded contemptuously: 'Oh, that perfidious hypocrite!' General Ochsenbein, the former President of the Swiss Confederation and head of the Berne Government, who for years has been living on an Imperial French pension in Switzerland, may now perhaps think more charitably of an old colleague who is certainly his equal. However, it is a noteworthy fact that M. Fazy was never elected into the Federal Council by the Swiss National Assembly, despite all the efforts of his friends and himself, and despite the tendency, so dominant in this Assembly as almost to have become an inflexible dogma, to ensure that the important cantons should be guaranteed a turn in the Central Government. He always was a recalcitrant in relation to, and when possible tried to put a spoke in the wheel of, the federal authority which provided him with no opportunity to exercise power, and instead limited the cantonal sovereignty so convenient for him.

"When, early in 1849, the Federal police deemed it politically expedient to persecute me for organising a Sicilian legion,[200] I went to Geneva where Fazy told me that I could organise to my heart's content and had no need to concern myself about the Federal Council. I am well aware that M. Fazy will instantly sacrifice anyone as soon as things take a bad turn for the person concerned, even if the law is on that person's side, and I have later experienced this myself in an incident which is too complicated to explain in a letter but to the facts of which the Federal Commissars Dr. Kern and Trog can testify.

"As far as the refugees were concerned, he used the watchword of humanity to resist the measures of the Federal Council and with callous arbitrariness persecuted refugees who were in his bad books. Above all, outstanding people close to Galeer, in whom he suspected a future rival, were subjected to ruthless persecution. Mazzini had good cause to fear him more than the Federal police. The tall Heinzen was abhorrent to him and had to leave the Canton almost at once. 'He thumps around as if the ground belonged to him', was the only explanation Fazy naively offered. Struve was arrested while out walking with his wife, even though there had been no instructions from the Federal Council, and was pushed over the frontier to the Canton of Vaud on the grounds that he was a *Russian* spy. Galeer managed to get to Fazy in time and tried to rectify this error. The two became embroiled in loud discussions since Fazy believes he is more convincing the more he shouts and the more indignant he pretends to be. Struve had to remain a Russian spy. If I remember rightly this scene took place in the Hôtel des Bergues in the presence of Mr. Herzen, the Russian refugee with whom the head of the Geneva Government liked to dine. However, this gentleman certainly had no part in the sordid accusations brought against Struve. Fazy is undoubtedly a greater Russophile than Struve, for I once heard him say in a speech at some celebration: 'The works of Jean Jacques Rousseau are more read and better understood in Russia than in Germany.' It is true that his principal intention here was to snipe at Galeer's German friends and the Germans in general.

"Galeer, who up till then had gone along with Fazy through thick and thin on political matters and whom I spoke to just after he had crossed swords with Fazy on Struve's account, told me sadly: 'I am through with Fazy now. As a matter of honour I can no longer associate with him. The man is a veritable monster politically, a mere animal in his desires. If I were to remain in league with him this would mean helping to destroy the cause of the people from within. Only if he is confronted by a truly liberal party, will he be compelled to uphold the banner of radicalism to save his position. As long as he is opposed only by the old aristocracy things will only get worse, since he has long been flirting with the ultramontane party and can really do what he likes. Moreover, he is no true Swiss in his attitudes and looks more to Paris than to Berne. I have for a long time now had reason enough to turn my back on him but I was prevented by the fact that I had been accustomed to look on him as a worthy man for so long. Only repeated internal struggles and the external clash today have finally prevailed on me to settle accounts with him.'

"All the people with independent minds and especially the members of the young school of political economy gathered round Galeer, and the committed radical and socialist elements thus 'united' soon became known as the democratic party. Henceforth radicalism, with few exceptions, consisted solely in conscious or unconscious servility towards Fazy, who had now found, in the Catholic districts of Savoy united with Geneva after 1815, a lever by which to control the majority. The ultramontane priests, all-powerful in that region, now entered into an alliance with 'radicalism', which was the upshot of Fazy's activity. Galeer was subjected to the basest sort of calumny, persecuted and was finally removed from his post. The young democratic party now found itself caught between the party of the aristocrats on the one hand and the party of the united old radicals and the ultramontanists on the other, and was as yet unable to put up its own independent list at the approaching elections. And although M. James Fazy refused to include the names of some of the democrats in his own list, Galeer and his friends, scorning the offers of the aristocratic party, resolved to give their votes this time to Fazy, looking for victory to the future. So if Fazy had been sincere in what he said about progress and a radically bourgeois development he would have had no need to attach himself to the filthy wing of the eternally backward-looking ultramontanists. In order to prosecute the malicious attacks and accusations against Galeer with greater effect the satellites of His Excellency, the 'radical' President, founded a special abusive paper to relieve that astute lord and master of the necessity of befouling his own *Moniteur,* the *Revue de Genève,* with his invective, more and more of which now appeared in the paper of his whipping-boys, whom he could disown at will. Galeer, whose health was weak, succumbed to this dastardly campaign and died in the course of the same year (1851) when he was still no more than thirty-five years of age. How often did I not hear it said in Geneva: '*Our good, noble Galeer was the victim of the inexorable revenge of our jesuitical tyrant.*' In the following elections Galeer's friends entered into the alliance offered by the aristocratic party, and they did so all the more willingly since the latter declared themselves content with the fall of Fazy and with a very modest share in the government. Galeer, who always remained true to his principles, would probably have rejected this alliance even now, but, as the members of his party said, to what end has M. Fazy given us the fine example of his alliance with the ultramontane party, why should we be ashamed of joining up with the decent wing of the aristocratic party when Fazy does not blush to be associated with the indecent wing of the ultramontanists? Can we not progress at least as far with the cultured aristocracy as M. Fazy claims to with the ignorant ultramontanists?

"When it came to the elections, then (I believe they took place in November 1853) many radicals and even a number of Fazy's ministerial colleagues went over to the democrats, so that the hero of 1846 was unseated from his presidential chair by a great majority. The ex-President, who had run up lots of debts, now found himself in an extremely embarrassing situation. In this context I must digress to reveal a number of characteristic facts about his life.

"Even before entering the government M. James Fazy had run through a substantial inheritance in fine style. Up to his ears in debts and mercilessly pursued by his creditors, he sought as soon as he had arrived at the presidential chair quickly to abolish the practice of arresting debtors. Of course, he was acting 'in the interests of personal liberty'. In 1856 I was told by a Genevan citizen plagued by debts: 'It is a good thing that we had a spendthrift as head of the government. Though he could not abolish debts, at least he abolished the debtors' prison.'

"In the beginning of the fifties, however, M. Fazy found himself in sore straits materially, so that a 'grateful people' had to come to his rescue and make him a present of a large building site that had become available with the razing of the fortifications. And why not indeed? Since he had been instrumental in cleaning this area of the fortifications, why should he not 'annex' a portion of it, especially as greater potentates than he do not disdain to do things of that sort. M. Fazy was now able to sell many large building sites and build a big beautiful house for himself. Unfortunately, he soon incurred new debts and could not pay the wages of his builders. Early in 1855 he was forced to endure being shouted at on the street by a master carpenter to whom he owed a few thousand francs: 'Pay me, you rogue, so that I can buy bread for my children.' It was in these circumstances that the hard-pressed man became an ex-President, and, to crown it all, he found himself in an even more painfully embarrassing situation. What happened was that the Caisse d'Escompte, a radical bank, was forced to suspend payments. Fazy's friends in the bank, themselves overburdened with debts, had advanced credit to him and to each other far beyond what was permitted in the statutes and was actually at the disposal of the bank. The director, who is in jail to this day, had been even less restrained—bad examples ruin good habits—in advancing credit to himself. Thus the Caisse d'Escompte found itself on the brink of a grave emergency: bankruptcy. The savings of a hundred thrifty workers' families were in jeopardy. Good counsel and, even more urgently, action were needed, cost what it might, otherwise Fazism would have been swept away by the deficit like chaff in the wind. Naturally enough in the circumstances, there could be no question of raising money for the Caisse d'Escompte directly. However, at that time there was another bank in Geneva labouring to establish itself, the Banque Générale Suisse. A considerable amount of capital had to be procured for this bank so that in return it would rescue the Caisse d'Escompte from its financial ebb and M. Fazy from the flood of debts. Fazy had to act as rescuer in order to be rescued himself. In case of success he was guaranteed a substantial commission expressed in so and so many per cent and the Caisse d'Escompte the badly needed additional capital. So on behalf of the Banque Générale Suisse and also *pro domo*,[a] M. Fazy went to *Paris* where, after a sojourn lasting several weeks and, as rumour would have it, *thanks to the gracious assistance of 'His Majesty'*,[b] he succeeded in persuading the Crédit Mobilier[201] to provide millions of francs towards the rescue operation. At around the same time (November 1855) the preparations for the new elections were being made and the *sauveur*[c] therefore sent letters home to Geneva in advance, announcing that he would presently arrive bearing in person his cargo of millions. This was a healing plaster for the stricken hearts of the shareholders of the Caisse d'Escompte, and a magic wand for the ultramontane-radical voters. At that time a good likeness of him appeared in a caricature showing him as a gigantic swan entering the harbour of Geneva weighed down with sacks of gold. A joker told me at the time that according to the story he had heard over a beer Fazy had brought back 50 million, over a glass of wine the sum rose to 100 million and when the absinthe was reached it had become 200 million. In the eyes of his children, the reputation of Papa Fazy's miraculous powers was fully restored. The democrats,

---

[a] For his own benefit.— *Ed.*

[b] Napoleon III.— *Ed.*

[c] Saviour.— *Ed.*

fondly imagining that their victory at the hustings was assured, did not exert themselves very much. A society of muscular young men that had been formed some time before—*les fruitiers*—now established themselves as Fazy's bodyguard. They terrorised the electorate in the most brutal manner possible and their idol ascended the presidential throne once more.

"This time, however, it soon became perfectly clear that the ultramontane faction had not lent their massive support for nothing, but that they were determined to have their share of the rewards of victory. M. Marilley, the Bishop of Fribourg, an eternal agitator and trouble-maker who had been driven out of Switzerland as a result of the Sonderbund War, left France and reappeared in Geneva one fine day with the official permission of M. Fazy. Once in Geneva he began to celebrate 'Holy' Mass once again. The entire city reverberated with anger, and popular fury soon echoed throughout Switzerland. It was too much even for the blindest radicals, the most subservient *fruitiers*. A popular assembly was convened without delay and the head of the government was presented with a vote of no-confidence. His colleague, Councillor Tourte, although himself merely a disciple and pupil of Fazy, suddenly displayed a very dubious desire for independence and he thundered away at his lord and master without any scruples whatever. However, M. Fazy had taken good care to absent himself from the country before the arrival of the Lord Bishop, just as he always did leaving his colleagues to drink what he had brewed. M. de Marilley, of course, had to leave the city and the country without more ado. Papa Fazy however wrote from Berne giving his unruly children a dressing down and asserting that he had been the victim of a misunderstanding, the government had not handled the affair correctly, he had merely acted in the 'interest of freedom of religion' and had simply permitted the Bishop to make a visit. After the storm had abated a much wronged Papa Fazy returned to Geneva. It was now all the simpler to re-establish his injured authority and restore faith in his pure love of freedom and of his country, by the simple device of uttering a few oracular statements which ring very true and fit any situation, because his colleagues were decent enough to shoulder the main responsibility. But Fazy had thus achieved the satisfactory end of demonstrating to his friends of the ultramontane faction *that he was always prepared to do for them—whatever lay in his power*. For a number of years now M. James Fazy has been a very wealthy man. Not only is the Banque Générale Suisse said to have guaranteed him a certain percentage for the duration of his life, but he has also, as head of the government, revealed great understanding of his own interests in such matters as the development of railways in his own Canton, etc. In his large and beautiful mansion (the Hôtel Fazy on the Quai du Mont Blanc) the beau monde moves among the *cercle des étrangers*.[a] And ever since Piedmont found the 'gambling dens' of the Savoy spas incompatible with its political morality, the compassionate President of the Republic of Geneva has touchingly offered such a den asylum in his roomy dwelling. Long live freedom! *Laissez aller et laissez faire! Allez chez moi et faites votre jeu!*[b]

"Darling, what more can you desire?[c]

Your *Johann Philipp Becker*"

---

[a] Circle of foreigners.— *Ed.*

[b] Let people do as they think best. Come to my place and make your stake.— *Ed.*

[c] From Heinrich Heine's cycle of poems, "Die Heimkehr", No. 64, *Buch der Lieder,* Erster Teil.— *Ed.*

Leaving *Vogt's* patrons, I descend now to his *accomplices.*

> Peace and goodwill to this fair meeting,
> I come not with hostility, but greeting.[a]

At the head of the procession, from which I intend only to single out a few of the more striking figures, we encounter the Berlin *National-Zeitung,* under the command of Herr **F. Zabel.** A comparison between the review of the "Magnum Opus" which appeared at Vogt's prompting in the *Revue contemporaine* from the pen of M. Edouard Simon[b] and the corresponding articles in the *National-Zeitung, Breslauer Zeitung,* etc., almost leads one to the conclusion that the "well-rounded character" issued two programmes, one dealing with the Italian campaign, the other with the Augsburg campaign. What on earth could have induced Herr *F. Zabel,* that fat and tedious bore of the *National-Zeitung,* who is usually so cautious, to kick over the traces and translate Vogt's street-songs into leading articles?

The first detailed reference to the *National-Zeitung* appeared in No. 205 of the *Neue Rheinische Zeitung* on January 26, 1849, in a leading article beginning with the words *"Signpost to Schilda".*[202] However, the arms of this signpost are too long to reprint them here. In a leading article of the *Neue Rheinische Zeitung,* No. 224 of February 17, 1849, it is stated:

"The Berlin *National-Zeitung* represents *triviality portentously expressed.* Some recent samples. They are taken from its discussion of the Prussian circular note.... Althoughs and buts! Can and may and seem! Consider and wish that the Prussian Government may wish! Like the inmate of a bagnio each phrase has a hundredweight tied to it, and is therefore weighty. Each 'if', each 'although', each 'but' is a real *Dr. utriusque juris.*[c] And if you take all that Christian-Germanic padding, all those cotton rags in which the *National-Zeitung* has solicitously enveloped its wisdom and unwrap them just as carefully, what remains? ... *Political hot air,* in black and white, Berlin leading articles *en grande tenue*[d].... The *National-Zeitung* is obviously written for the *thinking reader,* just like Rotteck's *Weltgeschichte*[203].... The French have an apt formula for thought of this kind which is active purely at a linguistic level. *'Je n'aime pas les épinards et j'en suis bien aise; car si je les aimais, j'en mangerais beaucoup, et je ne peux pas les souffrir.'* 'I do not like spinach and that is a good thing; *for if* I liked it I would not be able to eat enough of it and I can't stand it.' ... The *National-Zeitung* has Prussia's happiness at heart and so it wants—another Ministry. What it wants in any case is—a *Ministry.* And this is the only thing which the patrons of the *National-Zeitung* are definite and self-confident about."

---

[a] Marx quotes the verses in English and gives the German translation in a footnote.— *Ed.*

[b] Edouard Simon, "Un tableau de moeurs politiques en Allemagne...", *Revue contemporaine,* t. 13, Paris, 1860.— *Ed.*

[c] Doctor of both laws (civil and canon).— *Ed.*

[d] In full dress.— *Ed.*

In the *Neue Rheinische Zeitung,* No. 296,[a] the following can be found:

"*Berlin, May 9, 1849....* It is interesting to observe the attitude of the Berlin press towards the Saxon revolution. *The 'National-Zeitung' knows only one emotion: the fear of being banned.*"

But fear is an elixir of life, as the *National-Zeitung* has demonstrated throughout the decade of Manteuffel's rule.

The *National-Zeitung* has proved the truth of Pope's dictum:

> Still her old empire to restore she tries,
> For, born a goddess, Dullness never dies.*[204]

The only thing that distinguishes Pope's realm of *Dullness* from that of the *National-Zeitung* is that in the former "now[b] Dunce the second reigns like Dunce the first", whereas in the latter, the old dunce, *Dunce the first,*[c] still holds sway.

The *Breslauer Zeitung,* which follows hard on the heels of the *National-Zeitung,* is now in raptures about the Hohenzollern Ministry as it had been about the Manteuffel Ministry before it. Early in 1860 I received the following letter[d]:

"Breslau, February 27, 1860

"Dear Marx,

"I saw in the *Volks-Zeitung* your address and your declaration against the *National-Zeitung.*[e] An article similar to that in the *National-Zeitung* appeared also in the *Breslauer Zeitung* from the pen of its *daily* contributor, **Dr. Stein.** This is the same Dr. Stein who used to sit with D'Ester on the extreme left of the Berlin National Assembly and who proposed the famous motion against the officers of the Prussian army. This great Stein with the diminutive body was suspended from his post as teacher. When the new Ministry was installed he set himself the task of agitating on its behalf, not just in the past year, in preparation for the elections, but even now, to bring about a merger of the Silesian democrats and the constitutionalists. Despite this his application to the present Ministry for permission to give private lessons has been refused, not just once but over and over again. The previous Ministry had tacitly allowed him to teach, while the present one prohibits him from doing so on the grounds that it is unlawful. He has now gone to Berlin to obtain permission there but without success, as you can see elsewhere in the

---

* It is impossible to find a German equivalent for Dullness. It is more than boredom, it is ennui elevated into a principle, soporific lifelessness, blunted stupor. As a quality of style Dullness is what the *Neue Rheinische Zeitung* called "triviality portentously expressed". [Marx quotes the two lines from Alexander Pope in English and gives the German translation at the beginning of this footnote.]

---

a Of May 12, 1849.— *Ed.*

b Pope has "still".— *Ed.*

c Marx uses the English phrase "Dunce the first".— *Ed.*

d An entry in Marx's notebook says the letter was written by Peter Nothjung.— *Ed.*

e See this volume, pp. 12-13.— *Ed.*

same issue of the *Volks-Zeitung* which printed your declaration. *Dr. Stein* has now made the Brimstone Gang play their part in the procession of fools in the *Breslauer Ressourcen-Gesellschaft*. Nevertheless, *Dr. Stein, Schlehan, Semrau* and their cronies have to put up with one humiliation after the other at the hands of the constitutionalists; but men of their stamp will not let themselves be deflected from their patriotic purposes. What do you say to this fine company?"

What should I say about my colleague Stein, for in fact, Stein was my colleague, since I was for a full six months, in 1855, a correspondent of the *Neue Oder-Zeitung*[205] and this was the only German paper for which I wrote while I was abroad. Clearly, Stein is a man with a stony [*steinern*] heart and even the refusal to allow him to give private lessons could not soften him. The *Neue Rheinische Zeitung* hammered away at Stein a great deal in order to knock him into shape. Thus in No. 225, for example:

"Cologne, February 16, 1849.... As for Herr Stein himself, we recall the time when he attacked the republicans on fanatically constitutional grounds, when in the *Schlesische Zeitung* he *roundly* **denounced** *the representatives of the working class* and *had them denounced* by a schoolteacher whose ideas were akin to his own and who is now a member of the 'Association for Law and Order'. Just as pitiful as the Agreers Assembly itself was the so-called democratic group of this Assembly. It could be foreseen that these gentlemen, in order to be *re-elected,* would now recognise the *imposed Constitution.* It is even more characteristic of the standpoint of these gentlemen that *after* the elections they are disavowing in the democratic clubs what *before* the elections they assented to at meetings of the electors. This petty, crafty liberal slyness was never the diplomacy of revolutionaries." [206]

The [*Neue*] *Rheinische Zeitung* had not sculptured this stone [*Stein*] in vain, as he demonstrated as soon as Manteuffel had dictated the dictated Chamber out of existence once again, for Dr. Julius Stein then proclaimed in the "chief democratic club in Breslau":

"We" (the extreme Berlin Left) "have regarded the German question as a lost cause from the outset.... People must *now* realise that *no united Germany is possible as there are still German Princes*" (*Neue Rheinische Zeitung*, No. 290).

It is indeed a heart-rending sight, it is enough to melt a stone, to see how Schwerin time and time again rejects this same Stein, even though he is no longer a stumbling-block [*Stein des Anstosses*], and refuses to use him—as a building stone [*Baustein*].[a]

I do not know if my readers have ever themselves seen a copy

---

[a] Cf. Psalms 118:22, Matthew 21:42 and Luke 20:17.—*Ed.*

of *Punch,* the London equivalent of the *Kladderadatsch.* The title-page shows a picture of Punch sitting down and behind him stands his dog Toby with a grumpy expression on his face and a pen behind his ear, both of which point to his being a born penny-a-liner.[a] If it is fair to compare small things with large[b] then one could perhaps compare Vogt with Punch, especially since the latter has lost his wit, a misfortune that struck him in 1846 with the abolition of the Corn Laws.[207] His companion, however, Toby the dog, can only be compared to himself or to—**Eduard Meyen.** And in fact if Eduard Meyen were ever really to die he would not stand in need of any Pythagorean migration of the soul. Toby has already taken care of that during his lifetime. I would not go as far as to claim that Eduard Meyen sat for the artist who designed the title vignette, but in any case I have never in my life seen a greater similarity between a man and a dog. But there is nothing surprising about this, since Eduard Meyen is a penny-a-liner by nature, and the penny-a-liner is by nature—Toby. E. Meyen has always inclined to devote his obtrusively versatile pen to ready-made party-organisation-literary-enterprise institutions. An imposed programme saves one the trouble of thinking for oneself, the feeling of togetherness with a more or less organised mass of people stifles the sense of one's own inadequacy, and the realisation that a war-chest is available can overcome, momentarily at least, even Toby's professional peevishness. Thus we find Eduard Meyen attached to the unfortunate Central Democratic Committee, that empty nut which grew out of the German Democratic Assembly in Frankfurt am Main in 1848.[208] As an exile in London he was engaged as the most indefatigable producer of the lithographed flysheets on which a portion of the money Kinkel had raised by loan to manufacture a revolution was frittered away, a circumstance which did not of course prevent the selfsame Eduard Meyen from rushing with bag and baggage into the camp of the Prince Regent[c] to beg for an amnesty and in fact to obtain permission to go to Wandsbek and pester the Hamburg *Freischütz* with articles on foreign policy. Vogt, who was busy enlisting the services of "people who" would "follow his Programme" and were prepared to bring him articles, and who was dangling the tempting sight of a well-filled war-chest before their eyes, came as a godsend to Eduard Meyen, who was running around without a

---

[a] Here and below Marx uses the English term.— *Ed.*

[b] Cf. Virgil, *Georgics,* Book IV, 176.— *Ed.*

[c] William, Prince of Prussia.— *Ed.*

master just then, for no one was willing to pay the dog tax during those hard times. And you can just imagine the howls of rage when Toby heard a rumour that I was about to cheat Vogt's party literary-enterprise institution of its credit and its pen-pushing pugs of their fees! *Quelle horreur!* Vogt's instructions to his Eduard Meyen about the obligatory treatment of the "Magnum Opus" were just as detailed as those given to Edouard Simon, and in fact Eduard Meyen did adorn 5 numbers of *Der Freischütz* (Nos. 17-21, 1860) with pieces from the "Magnum Opus".[a] But what a difference! Whereas Edouard Simon corrected the original, Eduard Meyen bowdlerised it. The simplest evidence of the objective understanding of a given topic is surely the ability to *copy* printed matter, but our Eduard Meyen is utterly incapable of copying even a single line correctly. Toby's mind lacks even the strength requisite for correct copying. Just listen:

Der Freischütz, No. 17:

"The paper" (*Allgemeine Zeitung*) "... has now been found guilty ... also ... of having made use of the assistance of a revolutionary party which Vogt has stigmatised as the *Brimstone Gang of the German republicans.*"

When and where has Vogt prated about the Brimstone Gang of the German republicans?

Der Freischütz, No. 18:

"It is Liebknecht who has launched an attack on Vogt in the *Allgemeine Zeitung*,[b] by repeating there the accusations made by Biscamp in the London *Volk*. However, the accusations did not develop their full force until Marx sent to the offices of the *Allgemeine Zeitung* a pamphlet that had appeared in London and which he attributed to Blind."

Vogt was able to tell many lies but even his lawyer, Hermann, forbade him the lie that the article by Biscamp, which had *not* been reprinted in the *Allgemeine Zeitung*, was "repeated" there by Liebknecht. Nor has Vogt ever thought of maintaining that it was I who sent the pamphlet *Zur Warnung* to the *Allgemeine Zeitung*. On the contrary, he says quite explicitly: "It was Herr Liebknecht ... who sent the libellous pamphlet to the *Allgemeine Zeitung*" ("Magnum Opus" p. 167).

Der Freischütz, No. 19:

"Blind positively denied that he was the pamphlet's author, and the printer certified that it was not *given* to him to print by Blind. What is however certain is that

---

[a] This refers to Eduard Meyen's article "Carl Vogts Kampf gegen die Augsburger Allgem. Zeitung und die Marxianer" published in *Der Freischütz* in February 1860.— *Ed.*

[b] Wilhelm Liebknecht [An die Redaction der *Allgemeinen Zeitung*, Augsburg], *Allgemeine Zeitung*, No. 300, October 27, 1859.— *Ed.*

the lampoon was immediately taken over in the same type-setting in *Das Volk*, and that Marx caused it to be published in the *Allgemeine Zeitung,* etc."

In his "Magnum Opus" Vogt on the one hand prints Fidelio Hollinger's declaration asserting that the pamphlet *had not been set* in his print-shop,[a] and, on the other, my counter-declaration that the original type of the lampoon was *still* standing at Hollinger's when it was reprinted in *Das Volk.*[b] What chaos did our unfortunate Toby make out of this!

Der Freischütz, No. 19:

"As far as the people themselves are concerned" (Engels and I are supposed to say in Techow's letter) "they are pure rationalists who have no patience with nationality."

No *sentimentality,* my dear Toby; no sentimentality, writes Techow, according to Vogt.

Der Freischütz, No. 20:

"Marx ... did not prevent the duellists from going to *Ostend* to fight a pistol duel. Techow acted as Willich's second, etc. After this incident [...] Techow broke off relations with Marx and his League."

Eduard Meyen is not content to substitute *Ostend* for *Antwerp.* He had probably heard about the Frenchman in the West End of London complaining that the English write "London" and pronounce it "Constantinople". Techow, who had only met me once in his life at the time of his correspondence and who moreover writes explicitly that he had at first intended to *join* me and my League, is made by Eduard Meyen to *break off* relations with me and my League, of which he was never a member.

Der Freischütz, No. 21:

"This incident" (the Joint Workers' Festival in Lausanne) "explains the violent attack on Vogt which was made in *Das Volk* in London."

In the "Magnum Opus" Vogt himself gives the date of the "violent attack" on him in *Das Volk*—*May 14, 1859.*[c] (The pamphlet appeared in *Das Volk* on June 18, 1859.) However, the Lausanne Joint Festival took place on *June 26 and 27, 1859,* i.e. long *after* the "violent attack" which according to Meyen it provoked.

But we have quoted enough of Toby's reading. It is not surprising that Toby having managed to read all sorts of things in

---

[a] Carl Vogt, *Mein Prozess...,* Dokumente, S. 38.—*Ed.*
[b] ibid., S. 39-40. See also this volume, pp. 8-9.—*Ed.*
[c] ibid., S. 17.—*Ed.*

Vogt that were not there should also have made this discovery:

"Vogt's book will take its rightful place among the boldest, wittiest and most useful polemics in our literature" (*Der Freischütz*, No. 17).

Just think of this wretched Toby, incapable as he is of even copying out two lines of a printed book correctly, just think of him condemned to sit in Wandsbek, having to decipher the book of world history[209] every day, straining to read a record of events barely hinted at in the obscurest of scripts, copying away by the hour and having to produce life-size photographs of the dissolving views[a] of the present in the columns of *Der Freischütz*! Unhappy Wandsbek Messenger![b] Happy Hamburg reader of *Der Freischütz*!

A few days ago the London *Times* published a strange news item which went through the entire English press and bore the title: "A Man Shot by a Dog." It seems therefore that Toby knows how to use a gun and thus it is not surprising to find Eduard Meyen sing in *Der Freischütz*: "A marksman am I in the pay of the Regent."[c]

The *Kölnische Zeitung* confined itself to a few malicious little paragraphs and insinuations in favour of Vogt. A week after the "Magnum Opus" had appeared it spread the fairy-tale in its columns that it was already out-of-print, probably so as not to have to lay violent hands upon it. But what an irony of history!

If only I had been able to foresee in 1848-49, at the time of the *Neue Rheinische Zeitung*, when we had daily to cross swords with our Cologne neighbour for the Poles, Hungarians and Italians, that this very same *Kölnische Zeitung* would in 1859 become the chivalrous protagonist of the principle of nationality, and that the simple Herr **Jusepp Dumont** would emerge from his chrysalis as Signor Giuseppe Del Monte! But of course at that time no Louis Bonaparte had as yet given the nationalities the superior blessing of morality and liberalism, and the *Kölnische Zeitung* will always remember that Louis Bonaparte has saved society. The red fury with which it attacked *Austria* at the time can be seen from the *Neue Rheinische Zeitung*, No. 144[d]:

"Cologne, November 15 (1848). At a moment when the whole of Germany cries out in indignation because the blood-stained minion of the Austrian bandit, because a Windischgrätz could dare to have the deputy **Robert Blum** shot down

---

[a] Marx uses the English phrase "dissolving views".— *Ed.*

[b] Marx here puns on *Wandsbeker Bote*—Wandsbek Messenger, a celebrated paper published by the poet Matthias Claudius from 1770 to 1775.— *Ed.*

[c] See B. von Braunthal, *Dàs Nachtlager in Granada.*— *Ed.*

[d] This refers to the item "Köln, 15. November" in the *Neue Rheinische Zeitung* of November 16, 1848. Marx quotes from his notebook.— *Ed.*

like a dog—at such a moment it is fitting to take note of two German papers of which one has attempted with almost unheard-of perfidy to vilify the last few days of the dead man's life, while the other pursues him to the grave with its insipid cretinism. We are referring to the *Kölnische Zeitung* and the *Rheinische Volks-Halle* (*vulgo* Narrhalla[a]).... In No. 292 the *Kölnische Zeitung* reported: 'On the 22nd of this month' (October) 'the *enthusiastic leaders* of the democratic party ... left Vienna; so did ... **Robert Blum.**' The *Kölnische Zeitung* made this statement without any qualification, but set its denunciation of Blum in Garamond type to print it more firmly on the reader's memory. The *Kölnische Zeitung* reached the heights of perfection in its subsequent issues. It was not ashamed to find space in its columns even for the articles of the most black and yellow paper of the camarilla, news items from the journal of the Archduchess Sophie [...], the most infamous of all Austrian papers [...] " (there then follows a quotation including this passage): "'Robert Blum earned no laurels in Vienna.... For he spoke in the great hall of the internal enemies—timorousness, lack of courage and of stamina; but if there were to arise *other enemies* in addition to these internal ones—he hoped this would not be the case—but if there were still people in the city who preferred the victory of the military to the victory of freedom, then the life-and-death battle waged before the walls of the city must be just as ruthlessly waged against them too.... In Herr Blum's speech there lay the madness of a Septembrist[210].... If Herr Blum really spoke those words then we must say quite frankly that he has **dishonoured himself.**' So much for the *Kölnische Zeitung.*"

By means of an ingenious system of concealed plumbing, all the lavatories of London empty their physical refuse into the Thames. In the same way every day the capital of the world spews out all its social refuse through a system of goose quills, and it pours out into a great central paper *cloaca*—the *Daily Telegraph.* Liebig rightly criticises the senseless wastefulness which robs the Thames of its purity and the English soil of its manure.[b] L e v y, however, the proprietor of this central paper cloaca, is an expert not only in chemistry, but even in alchemy. Having transformed the social refuse of London into newspaper articles, he transforms the newspaper articles into copper, and finally the copper into gold. At the entrance which leads to the central paper cloaca, the following words are written *di colore oscuro*: "*hic ... quisquam faxit oletum!*"[c] or as *Byron* translated it so poetically "*Wanderer, stop and—piss!*"[d]

Levy, like Habakkuk, *est capable de tout.*[e] He is capable of printing a leading article three columns long on a single case of rape. Earlier this year he treated his numerous public of gourmets to an

---

[a] Roughly=fool's paradise, a pun on Valhalla.— *Ed.*

[b] Justus von Liebig, *Die Chemie in ihrer Anwendung auf Agricultur und Physiologie,* Braunschweig, 1840, S. 216.— *Ed.*

[c] In sombre colours: "Here ... it is permitted to make bad odours!" The Latin words are a paraphrased line from Persius, *Satires,* Book I, First Satire.— *Ed.*

[d] Byron, "Epitaph".— *Ed.*

[e] Is capable of everything.— *Ed.*

asafoetida stew that had been ingeniously brewed from ingredients of a certain court case that were so nauseating that the judge ordered the court to be cleared of women and children. Unfortunately Levy had spiced the stew with the name of an innocent person. The resulting libel action brought against Levy ended with his conviction and the public condemnation of his newspaper by the English judiciary. As everyone knows, libel actions, like all other actions, are shamelessly expensive in England; they are in a sense the privilege of the *coffre fort*.ᵃ However, a number of unemployed lawyers in the City now discovered that Levy was fair game; they joined forces and offered their services gratis as a speculation to anyone who wished to take action against Levy for libel. Levy himself thereupon complained loudly in his paper that a new kind of blackmail had become fashionable: libel actions against Levy. Since then it has become precarious to sue Levy. One lays oneself open to ambiguous talk, for just as you can read on walls in London the notice: Commit no Nuisance, so too you can find written on the entrances to the English courts: *Commit Levy*.ᵇ

Politicians refer to the *Daily Telegraph* as "Palmerston's mobpaper", but Levy's refuse barge only carries politics as ballast. The *Saturday Review* aptly described his penny-rag as "cheap and nasty".

"It is a fatal symptom," it says *inter alia,* "that it should have given such a definite preference for dirt to cleanliness. In every case it will exclude the most important report in order to leave space for a disreputable article."

Nevertheless, Levy also has a prudery of his own. He criticises immorality in the theatre, for instance, and like a second Cato the Censor, he pursues the dress of the ballet dancers, which according to him starts too late and ends too soon. Such fits of virtue only take Levy out of the frying-pan into the fire. O Logic! a London theatrical journal, *The Players,* exclaims, O Logic! where is thy blush? How the rogueᶜ must have laughed in his sleeve!... The *Telegraph* as guardian of the decency of female costume on the stage! Holy Jupiter, what will happen next? Earthquakes and fiery comets are the least that can be expected now. Decency! "I thank thee, Jew, for teaching me that word."ᵈ And as Hamlet

---

ᵃ Of the strong-box, i.e. of the rich.— *Ed.*

ᵇ Here and below Marx uses English: "Commit no Nuisance", "Commit Levy", "mobpaper", "cheap and nasty".— *Ed.*

ᶜ Marx gives the English word in brackets after its German equivalent.— *Ed.*

ᵈ Shakespeare, *The Merchant of Venice,* Act IV, Scene 1. In Marx's original the English sentence is followed by its German equivalent in brackets.— *Ed.*

advises Ophelia, the "Player" advises Levy to clear off to a nunnery: "Get thee to a nunnery,[a] Levy!" Levy in a nunnery! And perhaps "nunnery" is just a printing error for a nonaria[b] so that we should really read it "Get thee to a nonaria, Levy!" and in that case, everyone will be

"multum gaudere paratus,
Si Cynico" (the cynic Levy) "barbam petulans nonaria vellat".[c]

The *Weekly Mail* maintains that although Levy really fools no one,[d] he has changed "i" into "y", and it is true that among the 22,000 Levites[211] whom Moses counted in the journey through the wilderness, there was not a single Levi who spelled his name with a "y". Just as Edouard Simon spares no effort to be regarded as belonging to the Romance people, so Levy is determined to be an Anglo-Saxon. Therefore, at least once a month he attacks the un-English policies of Mr. Disraeli, for Disraeli, "the Asiatic mystery",[e] is, unlike the *Telegraph*, not an Anglo-Saxon by descent. But what does it profit Levy to attack Mr. D'Israeli and to change "i" into "y", when Mother Nature has inscribed his origins in the clearest possible way right in the middle of his face. The nose of the mysterious stranger of Slawkenbergius (see *Tristram Shandy*) who had got the finest nose from the promontory of noses[f] was just a nine days' wonder in Strasbourg,[g] whereas Levy's nose provides conversation throughout the year in the City of London. A Greek epigrammatist describes the nose of a certain Castor which could be used for all sorts of things: as a shovel, a trumpet, a sickle, an anchor, etc. He concludes his description with the words:

"Οὕτως εὐχρήστου σκεύους Κάστωρ τετύχηκε,
Ῥῖνα φέρων πάσης ἄρμενον ἐργασίας"*

* Thus was Castor equipped with a tool that was truly amazing,
Owning a nose that served almost every conceivable purpose."
[Anonymous epigram from *Anthologia Graeca*, XI, 203, Verses 7 and 8.]

---

^a Shakespeare, *Hamlet,* Act III, Scene 1.— *Ed.*
^b Harlot.— *Ed.*
^c "...always ready to be delighted,
Should the harlot playfully tug at the beard of the Cynic" (Persius, *Satires,* Book I, First Satire).— *Ed.*
^d Marx puns on the idiom "ein X für ein U vormachen" (to put an X in place of a U) which means to try to fool someone.— *Ed.*
^e Marx gives the English phrase in brackets after its German equivalent.— *Ed.*
^f Marx uses English: "finest nose" and "promontory of noses".— *Ed.*
^g Cf. Laurence Sterne, *The Life and Opinions of Tristram Shandy, Gentleman,* Vol. IV, Slawkenbergius.— *Ed.*

But even Castor could not have guessed the purpose to which
Levy puts his nose. The English poet comes nearer to it in the
lines:

> "And 'tis a miracle we may suppose,
> No nastiness offends his skilful nose."[a]

Indeed the great skill of Levy's nose consists in its ability to
titillate with a rotten smell, to sniff it out a hundred miles away
and to attract it. Thus Levy's nose serves the *Daily Telegraph* as
elephant's trunk, antenna, lighthouse and telegraph. It is therefore
no exaggeration to say that Levy writes his paper with his nose.

The clean-minded *Daily Telegraph* was of course the *only*
English paper in which Vogt's *Lousiad,* not only could, but had to
be printed. In Levy's organ an article two-and-a-half columns long
appeared on February 6, 1860, with the title: "The Journalistic
Auxiliaries of Austria",[b] which was in fact a mere translation into
malodorous English of the two leading articles from the Berlin
National-Zeitung. To lead the reader astray, the article bore the
superscription: "From an occasional correspondent, Frankfort on
the Main, February 2."[c] I knew of course that the only
correspondent of the *Telegraph* was based in Berlin where Levy's
nose had sniffed him out with its customary virtuosity. I therefore
wrote at once to a friend in Berlin asking him to see if he could
discover the name of Levy's correspondent.[212] My friend, a man
whose learning has been acknowledged even by Alexander von
Humboldt, was obdurate enough to insist that there was no *Daily
Telegraph* in London and consequently no correspondent belonging to it in Berlin. I therefore turned to another acquaintance in
the City on the Spree. Reply: the Berlin correspondent of the
Daily Telegraph exists and is called—**Abel**. I thought this might
well conceal a gross mystification. Abel was obviously just an
abbreviation of Zabel. Nor was I led astray by the fact that Zabel
cannot write English. If Abel can edit the *National-Zeitung* as Zabel
without knowing any German, why should not Zabel be able to
contribute to the *Telegraph* as Abel without knowing any English.
So Zabel, Abel, Abel, Zabel? How to find a way out of this Babel?
I examined the Berlin organ of wisdom once again, comparing it
with Levy's, and this time I discovered the following passage in
No. 41 of the *National-Zeitung:*

---

[a] Marx quotes in English and gives the German translation in a footnote.— *Ed.*
[b] Marx gives the title in English and supplies the German translation in
brackets.— *Ed.*
[c] Marx gives the words of the superscription in English and supplies the
German translation in brackets.— *Ed.*

"Liebknecht strangely enough adds: 'We asked the *magistrate* (?) to authenticate our signatures.'"

This passage about the magistrate and Zabel's astonished question mark after the word "magistrate" puts one in mind of the Swabian who "as soon as he got off the ship in Asia asked: 'Isn't there some good fellow from Bebbingen here?'" Levy's paper omits not only the entire passage, but even the question mark, which proves conclusively that Levy's correspondent does not share F. Zabel's belief that London police-court judges or magistrates[a] are the same thing as the Berlin *Magistrat*.[213] Hence Zabel was not Abel and Abel was not Zabel. In the meantime, however, other acquaintances in Berlin had heard of my difficulties. One of them wrote: "Among the 22,000 Levites in *Numbers* there is an Abel, but it is spelt Abigail." Another wrote: "On this occasion it is Abel who killed Cain, not Cain who killed Abel." In this way I went deeper and deeper into the maze until, finally, the editor of a London newspaper assured me with the dry earnestness of the English that Abel was not a joke, but a Jewish-born man of letters in Berlin whose full name was **Dr. Karl Abel**. This noble youth had served for a considerable time under Stahl and Gerlach as a zealous drudge for the *Kreuz-Zeitung*, but with the change of Ministry he had changed, if not his skin, at least his colours. The over-eager zeal of the renegade would indeed explain why Levy's Berlin correspondent imagines that the freedom of the press in England has been specially designed to allow him to peddle his compulsive admiration of the Hohenzollern Ministry. Hypothetically, then, we may assume that there is an Abel in Berlin as well as a Levy in London—*par nobile fratrum*.[b]

Abel supplies his Levy simultaneously from everywhere under the sun: from Berlin, Vienna, Frankfurt am Main, Stockholm, Petersburg, Hong Kong, etc.,—a much greater achievement than De Maistre's *Voyage autour de ma chambre*. But whatever address Abel chooses when he writes to his Levy, his dominant sign of the Zodiac remains constant: Cancer. In contrast to the procession in Echternach where those taking part move two steps forward and one step back,[214] Abel's articles take one step forward and two steps back.

"No crab more active in the dirty dance,
    Downward to climb, and backward to advance." (*Pope*)[c]

---

[a] Marx gives the English term in brackets after its German equivalent.— *Ed.*

[b] A noble pair of brothers (Horace, *Satires*, Book II, Satire 3).— *Ed.*

[c] Alexander Pope, *The Dunciad*, Book II. Marx quotes in English and gives the German translation in a footnote.— *Ed.*

Abel has an undeniable talent for providing his Levy with the state secrets of the Continent. For example, if the *Kölnische Zeitung* publishes a leading article it has borrowed from the *Baltische Monatsschrift* on the state of the Russian finances, Abel will let a month go by and will suddenly send the *Kölnische Zeitung*'s article to London from Petersburg, not omitting to hint of course that he acquired the statistical secrets *entre deux cigares,* not indeed from the Tsar himself, or even from the Russian Minister of Finance, but assuredly from one of the directors of the State Bank. And he will declare triumphantly: "I am in a position to state, etc." [a] Or the official *Preussische Zeitung* puts out a ministerial feeler, for instance indicating Herr von Schleinitz's unauthoritative ideas about the problem of the Electorate of Hesse. This time Abel wastes no time. The very same day he writes to his Levy openly from Berlin about the problem of the Electorate of Hesse. A week later he reports: The *Preussische Zeitung,* the organ of the Ministry, has printed the following article on the problem of the Electorate of Hesse and "I owe it to myself" to point out that a week ago I myself, etc. Or he translates an article from the *Allgemeine Zeitung,* and gives it a date-line perhaps from Stockholm. This is inevitably followed by the phrase, "I must warn your readers" to beware—not of the article he has copied, but of some other article in the *Allgemeine Zeitung* that he has not copied. Yet, whenever he happens to mention the *Kreuz-Zeitung* he makes the sign of the cross so as to disguise his true identity.

As to Abel's style, we can give the reader an idea of what it is like by saying that it is a poor imitation of the styles of Stern Gescheidt, Isidor Berlinerblau and Jacob Wiesenriesler.

With Abel's permission we shall make a digression at this point. The original Stern Gescheidt is another accomplice of Vogt. He is a certain **L. Bamberger** who in 1848 was the editor of a provincial rag in Mainz [b] and is at present a *loup-garou* [c] married "on full pay" in Paris and a *Decembrist democrat* "in the *simplest* meaning of the word". To grasp the significance of this "simple" meaning, it is necessary to be acquainted with the jargon of the Paris Stock Exchange synagogue. Stern Gescheidt's "simple" democracy is identical with what Isaac Péreire calls *"la démocratisation du crédit",*

---

[a] This phrase and, below, the expressions "I owe it to myself" and "I must warn your readers" are in English in the original. The German equivalents are given in brackets.— *Ed.*

[b] The *Mainzer Zeitung.—Ed.*

[c] Werewolf.— *Ed.*

the democratisation of credit. This consists in transforming the entire nation, and not just certain strata in it, into a gambling den so that the people can be swindled *en masse.*[215] Under Louis Philippe the oligarchic Stock Exchange wolf had been so strait-laced that he confined his depredations to the national wealth accumulated by the upper bourgeoisie; under the aegis of Louis Bonaparte, however, all is fair game[a] for the democratic Stock Exchange wolf, who like the Roman Emperor exclaims: *non olet,*[b] adding with Stern Gescheidt Bamberger: *"It's the quantity that does it."* This is Stern Gescheidt's democracy in its extreme "simplicity". More recently, Stern Gescheidt Bamberger has come to be known under the name of *"Hurrah, on to Italy!"*[c] In contrast to that, during the campaign for the Imperial Constitution he answered to the name of *"Ouch, away from Kirchheimboland!"* I have in my possession a priceless manuscript describing the heroic deeds of Stern Gescheidt Bamberger, who absconded from Kirchheimboland and led the volunteer corps of the Rhine-Palatinate by the nose. He was much too smart[d] not to have sensed that the bloated, blood-streaked soil of December was gold-bearing for smart treasure-seekers. So he went to Paris where, as his friend Isidor Berlinerblau alias *H. B. Oppenheim* puts it so aptly, "one feels freer than one knows". Stern Gescheidt, whose "circulation was coming to a standstill" in 1858 (see the declaration of the Banque de France on circulation in 1858-59[e]), was overjoyed when he suddenly saw the dirty soil of December glistening with the bright colours of high-faluting ideas. Stern Gescheidt, as smart as he is brightly democratic, realised that if Paris had a flood which were to wash over the soil of December, it would sweep away the *Credit* in his ledger, while leaving the *Debit* behind. It is common knowledge that Stern Gescheidt Bamberger has added a tenth, Hebrew, muse to the nine Greek ones: it is "the muse of time", as he calls the Stock Exchange list.

But to return to Abel. Abel's style is saturated with the *odor specificus* inseparable from the *Daily Telegraph,* the paper cloaca of

---

[a] Marx writes "fish" in the original.— *Ed.*

[b] It doesn't smell (these words are usually attributed to Emperor Vespasian who introduced a tax on public lavatories).— *Ed.*

[c] An allusion to Ludwig Bamberger's book *Juchhe nach Italia!* published anonymously in Berne and Geneva in 1859.— *Ed.*

[d] Marx uses the word *gescheit,* punning on the name Gescheidt. On Bamberger's part in the events of 1849 see Engels' *The Campaign for the German Imperial Constitution* (present edition, Vol. 10, pp. 196 and 224).— *Ed.*

[e] "The Bank of France", *The Times,* No. 23203, January 14, 1859.— *Ed.*

the capital of the world. When Levy finds himself genuinely moved by the scent of Abel's news reports, Abel's learning and the energy and zeal with which Abel writes from 20 different latitudes at the same time—at such moments of the greatest exaltation Levy has a very special term of endearment for Abel: he calls him his "industrious bug".[a]

Poetic justice demands that at the end of the comedy the "well-rounded character" should not get stuck together with Abel in the London muck, but who is to pull him out of it? Who is to be his saviour? A mudlark is to be his saviour, namely *Baron* **von Vincke,**[b] a squire of the red earth,[c] a knight of the joyful countenance, *chevalier sans peur et sans reproche.*[216]

As already mentioned, the *Neue Rheinische Zeitung* as early as 1848 revealed the identity of the opposites Vogt and Vincke,[d] and Vogt himself had a presentiment of this identity as early as 1859 when he wrote in his *Studien:*

"Herr von Vincke as the apostle of a new political freedom ... really verges *on the realm of the ridiculous*" (loc. cit., p. 21),

i.e. Vogt's own realm. However, on March 1, 1860 Vincke publicly extended the hand of friendship in a speech in which, as Johann Philipp Becker expressed it, he "used the *Brimstone Gang* as an illustration of the modest Prussian Chamber". Hardly a year had passed since he had recommended to that same house the pamphlet *Po and Rhine*[e] whose sulphurous origins he had of course been unable to detect, since he lacked Levy's nose. When moreover Vincke began to play the Italian just like Vogt, when Vincke, like Vogt, insulted the Poles and when Vincke, like Vogt, proclaimed the partition of Germany, the feuding brothers fell into each other's arms for ever.

It is well known that like poles are bound to repel each other. So for a long time Vogt and Vincke repelled each other. Both men drivel too much so that each imagined that the other wished to prevent him from speaking.

Vogt is a great zoologist, as Ranickel testifies, and so is Vincke, as is demonstrated by his pig-farm at Ickern.

---

[a] Alexander Pope, *The Dunciad,* Book I. Marx uses the English phrase and gives the German translation and the author's name in a footnote.— *Ed.*

[b] Marx puns on the name Vincke and the word *Mistfinke* (mudlark, filthy fellow).— *Ed.*

[c] Westphalia.— *Ed.*

[d] This refers to an item in the column "Deutschland" in the *Neue Rheinische Zeitung,* No. 181, December 29, 1848.— *Ed.*

[e] See present edition, Vol. 16.— *Ed.*

In Spanish drama there are always two clowns per hero. Calderón equips even St. Cyprian, the Spanish Faust, with a Moscon and a Clarin.[a] In the same way, in the Frankfurt Parliament, the reactionary General von Radowitz had two comic adjutants, his harlequin Lichnowski and his clown Vincke. Vogt, however, the liberal counter-clown, had to do everything on his own, for Jacobus Venedey only knew how to act the sentimental role of Pantalone, and so inevitably, he came to resent Vincke. Vincke liked occasionally to take off the fool's cap and bells. On June 21, 1848, for example, he declared in Parliament:

"He sometimes imagined that he was in a theatre rather than in such an assembly."[b]

And at a party of the Tories of the Frankfurt Parliament he made an appearance as the *Prince of Fools,* sat on a barrel and sang[217]:

"The Prince of Fools am I,
I'll booze until I die."

This too offended his counterpart. Furthermore, Vogt and Vincke could not intimidate each other so they both imagined that their best course was for each to set upon the other. Falstaff Vogt knew what to think of the knight without fear or reproach, and vice versa. The Westphalian Bayard had in his time studied law at German universities, not so much the Roman *corpus juris*[218] for, as he said, his ancestors of the red earth had not defeated Varus for nothing. To make up for it he threw himself on Teutonic law, i.e. the *students' code of behaviour,* whose basis he thoroughly explored in every direction and subsequently made notorious as the *legal basis.*[c] As a result of this profound and casuistical research into the students' code of behaviour he later on, whenever faced with a duel, always found some Duns-Scotian hair which at the decisive moment interposed itself as hair-splittingly sharply between our knight and the shedding of blood as the naked sword in the bridal bed which separated the princess from the *locum tenens.*[d] From the adventure with the Supreme Court advocate Benda at the time of the United Diet of 1847[219] to the no less notorious adventure with the

---

[a] Calderón, *El Mágico prodigioso.—Ed.*

[b] The *Neue Rheinische Zeitung,* No. 25, June 25, 1848.—*Ed.*

[c] A reference to Georg Vincke's speech in the Frankfurt National Assembly on June 21, 1848, in which he said "my standpoint is that of the undermined legal basis" (ibid.).—*Ed.*

[d] Substitute.—*Ed.*

Prussian Minister of War[a] in the Chamber of Deputies in 1860, this hair-splitting always intervened with the regularity of a recurrent fever. We can see how unfair was the reproach, recently levelled at the squire, that he had lost his legal basis. It is not his fault if his legal basis consists entirely of trapdoors. Moreover, since the students' code of behaviour is really only applicable in the higher reaches of legal debate, the ingenious squire replaces it at the ordinary parliamentary level by the *code of the cudgels*.

In the frog-pond of Frankfurt Vincke once bitterly referred to his counterpart Vogt as the *"Minister of the Future"*.[b] But it really struck home when he heard in Ickern that Vogt, mindful of the maxim

> "Once a position of power you've found,
> You're lord and master the whole year round",[c]

had not only become Imperial Regent, but even Minister of Foreign Affairs *in partibus,* and he grumbled irritably that the rights of seniority had been ignored. For as early as the United Diet of 1847 Vincke as a frondeur had been against the Ministry and as a representative of the nobility against the bourgeois opposition. Hence on the outbreak of the March revolution he thought that he above all others was predestined to save the crown. But his rivals became Ministers of the Present, whereas he was appointed *"Minister of the Future"*, a post that he has filled with unbroken success to this day.

In revenge he shook the dust of Berlin from his feet and went to St. Paul's Church in Frankfurt, where he joined the extreme Right wing, acting as a clown, claqueur and bully for General Radowitz.

Our finch[d] was a fanatical and zealous Austrian as long as this had the approval of the authorities. He thundered frantically against the *nationalities.*

"On the left they are infatuated with every conceivable nationality in turn—Italians, Poles, and now even Magyars" (session of October 23, 1848).[220]

The three knights Vincke, Lichnowski and Arnim played a musical trio:

---

[a] Albrecht Roon.— *Ed.*

[b] Report on the session of the Frankfurt National Assembly of September 16, 1848 in the *Neue Rheinische Zeitung,* No. 106, September 19, 1848 in the column "Deutschland".— *Ed.*

[c] Johann Fischart, *Affentheurliche, Naupengeheurliche Geschichtklitterung...,* S. 76.— *Ed.*

[d] Marx puns on *Fink* (finch) and Vincke.— *Ed.*

"To ox's bellow and cow's fart
The ass provides the underpart."

They performed this with such virtuosity in opposition to those who spoke in support of Poland (session of June 5, 1848)[a] that even the President's bell ran out of breath, and when Radowitz went so far as to put forward military and "natural" arguments in favour of incorporating the Mincio into the German Empire (session of August 12, 1848),[b] Vincke stood on his head and signalled his applause with his legs, to the delight of the whole gallery and the secret admiration of Vogt. As the chief claqueur for the resolutions by means of which the Frankfurt frog-pond stamped the dynastic subjugation of Poland, Hungary and Italy with the approval of the German people, the squire of the red earth shouted even more excitedly when the claims of the German nation had to be sacrificed because of the humiliating armistice of Malmö. To secure a majority for the ratification of the cease-fire, diplomatic and other observers sneaked down from the gallery and joined the Right-wing benches. The fraud was discovered and Raveaux pressed for a new vote. The finch protested that it was not a matter of who voted but of what was voted for (session of September 16, 1848).[c] During the September rising in Frankfurt that had been provoked by the resolution approving the Malmö armistice the Westphalian Bayard vanished without a trace, but reappeared after the state of siege had been proclaimed and avenged himself in a series of reactionary somersaults for the fright which no one could ever make up to him.

Not content with his verbal fulminations against Poles, Italians and Hungarians, he proposed that the Archduke John of Austria should be made president of the provisional central authority (session of June 21, 1848),[d] but he obsequiously added the rider that the Habsburg executive of the German Parliament should neither implement nor proclaim, nor in any way concern itself with the Parliament's plebeian resolutions. He even fell into a rage when, just to make a change, his colleagues in the majority voted that the Imperial Administrator should at least graciously deign to secure the previous agreement of the Parliament on matters of war and peace or the conclusion of treaties with foreign powers (session of June 27, 1848). And the extreme heat which the finch

[a] The *Neue Rheinische Zeitung*, No. 10, June 10, 1848.— *Ed.*
[b] ibid., No. 76, August 15, 1848.— *Ed.*
[c] ibid., No. 106, September 19, 1848.— *Ed.*
[d] ibid., No. 25, June 25, 1848.— *Ed.*

generated in his noisy efforts to extort from the German
Parliament a vote of confidence for the Imperial Minister
Schmerling and his associates by way of reward for their and the
Imperial Administrator's complicity in the bloody and infamous
betrayal of Vienna[221] (session of October 23, 1848), triumphantly
refuted Fischart's slanderous words:

> "Oh, what cold mouths
> Are Westphalian mouths!"[a]

Thus Vincke was amiably pro-Habsburg until the Fata Morgana
of Little Germany[222] suddenly came into view, looming above the
parliamentary Sahara, and the squire perceived a life-size ministerial portfolio with a finch under its arm. Since the walls of St. Paul's
Church had unusually long ears, he might well flatter himself that
the noise he had made in Frankfurt with his outbursts about
loyalty to the Hohenzollern dynasty had produced an agreeable
effect in Berlin. Had he not declared before a crowded St. Paul's
Church on June 21, 1848:

> "I have been sent here by the electorate to defend the rights not only of the
> people, but also of the princes. I always comfort myself with the saying of the
> Great Elector[b] who once described the inhabitants of the Mark[c] as his most loyal
> and obedient subjects. And we in the Mark are proud of it."[d]

And our Bayard from the Mark proceeded from phrases to
fisticuffs in the celebrated parliamentary battle in which he won
his spurs (sessions of August 7 and 8, 1848). What happened was
that when Brentano, in the course of the debate on the proposed
amnesty for Friedrich Hecker, let fall an ambiguous reference to
one of the Hohenzollern princes from the rostrum, the finch had
a veritable attack of loyalty rabies and rushing from his seat he
hurled himself upon Herr Brentano and tried to drag him from
the rostrum, shouting "Come down, you dirty dog!" Brentano was
not to be dislodged. Later on the squire assaulted him a second
time and threw down the gauntlet of knighthood, though
naturally he reserved the right to later and more mature
reflections on scruples arising from the legal basis. Brentano
accepted his challenge with the words:

> "Outside the church you may say whatever you wish to me; but if you do not let
> go of me here I shall hit you in the face."

---

[a] Johann Fischart, *Affentheurliche, Naupengeheurliche Geschichtklitterung...*, S. 68.— *Ed.*

[b] Frederick William.— *Ed.*

[c] A county in Westphalia.— *Ed.*

[d] In this passage Marx summarises Vincke's speech, which was reported in the *Neue Rheinische Zeitung*, No. 25, June 25, 1848.— *Ed.*

The squire then reached into his quiver of invective and showered the Left with a series of dirty dogs until Reichardt shouted at him: "Von Vincke, you are a skunk" (session of August 7, 1848).[a] The finch tried to cut short the debate on the disagreement between the Brandenburg Ministry and the Berlin Agreers Assembly by simply proposing that the Assembly should proceed to the next item on the agenda.

"Ever since Wrangel's triumphant entry into Berlin," he said, "order had reigned, stocks have risen on the Exchange.... The Berlin Assembly has no right to issue proclamations to the people, etc."[b]

The members of the Agreers Assembly had hardly been dispersed before our knight without fear or reproach fell upon them with even greater fury.

"We lack the political experience," he lamented in the session of December 12, 1848, "needed for a republic. This has been proved to us by the members of the former Berlin Assembly who approved resolutions dictated by base personal ambitions."[c]

He sought to appease the storm this provoked by declaring that

"he was ready to defend his words against anyone, in a *chivalrous manner*", but, the cautious knight added, "he was not referring to any member of this Assembly, only the members of the dispersed Berlin Assembly".[223]

This was the defiant challenge that our Bayard of the Mark hurled at the entire army of dispersed Agreers. One of them heard his call, pulled himself together and succeeded in bringing about an unheard-of event: he managed to induce our squire of the red earth to venture bodily onto the battlefield at Eisenach. Bloodshed seemed inevitable when, at the decisive moment, our Bayard smelled a Duns-Scotian rat. His opponent bore the name of Georg Jung and while the laws of honour enjoined the knight without fear or reproach to do battle with dragons, they would not allow him under any circumstances to take up the cudgels with a namesake of the dragon killer.[d] The finch simply could not be made to give up this *idée fixe*. He swore by all that is holy that he would rather slit his stomach like a Japanese *daimio*[224] than touch

---

[a] Joseph Reichardt made this remark on August 8. It was included in the report on the session published in the *Neue Rheinische Zeitung*, No. 72, August 11, 1848.— *Ed.*

[b] Georg Vincke's speech of November 14, 1848, ibid., No. 145, November 17, 1848.— *Ed.*

[c] Georg Vincke's speech of December 12, 1848, ibid., No. 169, December 15, 1848.— *Ed.*

[d] St. George.— *Ed.*

a hair of the head belonging to a man with the name of Georg,
especially if he was below duelling age.[a] The knight invulnerable
to duels showed all the less restraint in his onslaughts in St. Paul's
Church against Temme and other persons unpalatable to the
government who were safely under lock and key in the gaol at
Münster (session of January 9, 1849).[b] While he scorned no detail
that might ingratiate him in high places his zeal to prove his
loyalty surpassed itself in his titanic efforts to bring about the
creation of a lesser Germany and a greater crown for Prussia.
Warwick the King-Maker was a child compared to Vincke the
Emperor-Maker.

Our Bayard from the Mark now imagined that he had heaped
enough burning coals on the heads of the ingrates of March 1848.
When the Ministry of Action[225] fell, Vincke vanished for a time
from St. Paul's Church and held himself in readiness. He did
likewise on the fall of the von Pfuel Ministry. But as the mountain
still failed to come to Mahomet, Mahomet resolved to go to the
mountain. Having been elected in the first available rotten
borough,[c] the knight of the red earth suddenly reappeared in
Berlin as a deputy in the imposed Chamber,[d] fully expectant that
the reward for his deeds in Frankfurt would now be forthcoming.
Moreover, the knight felt entirely at home in the state of siege
which would not deny him any unparliamentary freedom. He
lapped up the hisses and jeers with which the people of Berlin
greeted him as he stood with the other "imposed" deputies in
front of the palace, waiting to be admitted to the White Hall, all
the more eagerly as Manteuffel had dropped a delicate hint to the
effect that they were inclined in the very highest places to accept
the gift of the lesser German crown from the hands of the
Emperor-Makers of Frankfurt if only to find a vacant ministerial
portfolio in payment for a certain service. Full of such sweet
dreams the finch sought to make himself useful for the time being
by acting as the dirty boy of the Cabinet. He drew up a draft
address to the Crown on lines laid down by the *Kreuz-Zeitung*,[e]

---

a Marx puns on the name Jung and the adjective *jung* (young).— *Ed.*

b The *Neue Rheinische Zeitung*, No. 196, January 16, 1849.— *Ed.*

c Marx uses English: "rotten borough" and, below, "dirty boy".— *Ed.*

d i.e. the Chamber set up under the Constitution imposed by Frederick William IV
in December 1848. It was dissolved in February 1849.— *Ed.*

e This refers to a motion Georg Vincke tabled in the Second Chamber of the
Prussian National Assembly on March 31, 1849 (see the *Neue Rheinische Zeitung*,
No. 262, April 3, 1849).— *Ed.*

inveighed against amnesty,[a] and was only willing to accept the imposed Constitution on the express condition that it would be revised and revoked[b] by a "strong state power". He insulted the Left-wing deputies suffering from the rigours of the state of siege, etc., and patiently awaited the hour of his triumph.

The catastrophe drew nearer, the Frankfurt deputation bringing the offer of the Imperial Crown had arrived in Berlin and on April 2 (1849) Vincke put forward the most loyal amendment to the proposals about the Emperor,[c] an amendment for which Manteuffel voted in all innocence. As soon as the session was over Vincke rushed into a neighbouring second-hand shop where he personally purchased a portfolio, a portfolio of black cardboard, with a red velvet cover edged in gold. The following day our knight of the joyous countenance sat contentedly in his seat in the middle of the Chamber, grinning like a triumphant faun—but the words he heard from Manteuffel's mocking lips were "never, never, never" [226]; and the fearless squire, the colour drained from his cheeks, and quivering like an electric eel with emotion, gasped to his friends: "Hold me back, or I shall do something terrible." The *Kreuz-Zeitung*, whose prescriptions Vincke had been anxiously following for months and to whose proposed address of the Chamber he had stood godfather, the *Kreuz-Zeitung*, to hold him back, published an article on the following day with the headline "The Nation in Danger" in which it declared *inter alia*:

"*The Ministry remains* and the King's[d] answer to Herr von Vincke and his associates is that they should not involve themselves in matters which do not concern them." [e]

Finding himself cheated our knight *sans peur et sans reproche* left Berlin for Ickern with a nose longer than Levy had ever had, a nose, moreover, which simply could not have been fobbed off onto anyone except a—*Minister of the Future!*

Having spent many a long anxious year vegetating in the pursuit of practical zoology in Ickern, our Cincinnatus of the red earth awoke one fine day in Berlin to find himself the official

---

[a] Georg Vincke's speech of March 22, 1849, *Neue Rheinische Zeitung*, No. 255, March 22, 1849.—*Ed.*

[b] A pun in the original: *ausgemerzt* (eradicated) puts the reader in mind of *März* (March) and the March revolution in Germany.—*Ed.*

[c] See the *Neue Rheinische Zeitung*, No. 263, April 4, 1849.—*Ed.*

[d] Frederick William IV.—*Ed.*

[e] "Das Vaterland ist in Gefahr!", *Neue Preussische Zeitung*, April 3, 1849. The *Neue Rheinische Zeitung* commented on this article in its issue No. 260, April 7, 1849.—*Ed.*

leader of the opposition in the Prussian Chamber of Deputies. Having had such ill luck with his rightist speeches in Frankfurt he now embarked on left-handed speeches in Berlin. It was not possible to discover whether he represented the opposition of confidence or the confidence of the opposition. But however that may be, he once again overplayed his hand. He soon became so indispensable to the Cabinet on the opposition benches that he was forbidden ever to take his leave of them. The squire of the red earth thus remained—a *Minister of the Future.*

In the circumstances the finch became tired of the whole business and so he concluded his famous Treaty of Ickern. *Vogt* gave it him in black and white: as soon as Plon-Plon had conquered the first parliamentarian island of Barataria[a] on the German continent, and as soon as he had peopled it with Sch-Oppenheimers[b] and had installed his Falstaff as its Regent, Vogt would appoint the Westphalian Bayard to be his Prime Minister and confer on him the right to adjudicate in all matters concerning duelling. Furthermore, he would make him Real and Privy General Masterbuilder in charge of all the roads,* and would moreover raise him to a princely rank giving him the title of a Prince of Fools. Lastly, he would have a coin struck in the *metal*[c] that passes for money in the insular realm of Vogt and this coin would have engraved on it a pair of Siamese twins, with Vogt on the right as Plon-Plon's Regent, Vincke on the left as Vogt's Minister, and a vine-adorned inscription wound round the voluminous double-figure, stating

> "Cheek by jowl with you
> I throw down this challenge to the age."[d]

---

* See the pamphlet *Auch eine Charakteristik des liberalen Abgeordneten von Vincke und erbauliche Geschichte des Sprochhövel-Elberfelder Wegbaues,* Hagen, 1849.

---

[a] The island of which Sancho Panza became Governor in *Don Quixote,* Book II, Chap. 44.— *Ed.*

[b] A pun on the name Oppenheim and Schoppen (pint pot). *Sch-Oppenheimers* suggests "boozers".— *Ed.*

[c] A pun on *Blech,* which means both "sheet metal" and, in a figurative sense, "nonsense".— *Ed.*

[d] Adaptation of the lines: "Arm in arm with you I throw down this challenge to the age." From Schiller's *Don Carlos,* Act I, Scene 9.— *Ed.*

XI

A LAWSUIT

At the end of January 1860 two numbers of the Berlin *National-Zeitung* arrived in London containing two leading articles, the first bearing the title *"Karl Vogt und die 'Allgemeine Zeitung'"* (*National-Zeitung*, No. 37), and the second, *"Wie man radikale Flugblätter macht"* (*National-Zeitung*, No. 41). Under these headings **F. Zabel** presented a version of Vogt's *"Magnum Opus"*[a] prepared *in usum delphini*.[227] The "Magnum Opus" itself did not reach London until much later. I decided at once to start proceedings for libel against this **F. Zabel** in Berlin.

In the previous ten years a vast number of vilifications of myself had appeared in the German and German-American press, but they only rarely drew any literary response from me, and then only if a real party interest seemed to be at stake, as with the Cologne communist trial. In my view the press has *the right to insult* writers, politicians, actors and other public figures. If I regarded an attack to be worth answering my motto in such cases was: *à corsaire, corsaire et demi.*[b]

Here the position was different. *Zabel* accused me of a series of *criminal* and *infamous* actions and he did so for the benefit of a public whose political prejudices inclined it to credit the greatest atrocities and who, moreover, in view of my eleven-year absence from Germany, had nothing to enable it to form a judgment of me. Quite apart from any political considerations, I therefore owed it to my family, my wife and children, to have Zabel's *defamatory* accusations tested in a court of law.

---

[a] Carl Vogt, *Mein Prozess gegen die Allgemeine Zeitung.—Ed.*
[b] Pay rogues in their own coin.— *Ed.*

The method of procedure I selected excluded from the outset any legal comedy of errors along the lines of Vogt's action against the *Allgemeine Zeitung*. Even if I had indulged in the fantastic idea of appealing against Vogt before the same Fazyesque court which had already quashed one criminal action in Vogt's interests,[a] there were a number of important and even decisive points that could *only* be settled in Prussia and not in Geneva. Conversely, the only one of Zabel's statements for which he might have sought proof from Vogt was based on alleged documents which Zabel could produce just as easily in Berlin as his friend Vogt in Geneva. My "complaint" against Zabel contained the following points:

1. In No. 37 of the *National-Zeitung* dated January 22, 1860, in an article entitled "Karl Vogt und die 'Allgemeine Zeitung'" Zabel writes:

"*Vogt* reports on p. 136 et seq.: Among the refugees of 1849 the term *Brimstone Gang,* or the name of the *Bristlers,* referred to a number of people who, originally scattered throughout Switzerland, France and England, gradually congregated in London, *where they revered Herr Marx as their visible leader.* The political principle of *these fellows* was the 'dictatorship of the proletariat' and with the aid of this illusion they succeeded in deceiving for a while not only some of the best among the refugees but also the workers from Willich's volunteer corps. *They continued the work of the 'Rheinische Zeitung'*[b] among the refugees. In 1849 this paper had counselled against any participation in the movement and had also constantly attacked all the members of Parliament because the Imperial Constitution was the only aim of the movement. *The Brimstone Gang maintained a frightfully strict discipline among its supporters.* Any of them who sought in any way to make a decent living in the bourgeois world was branded a traitor to the revolution merely for attempting to become independent. It was expected that the revolution would break out again at any moment and it was vital to keep its soldiers mobile and ready to be sent into battle. With the aid of rumours, letters, etc., dissension, brawling and duels were artificially fomented in this carefully nurtured class of loafers. Each one suspected the other of being a spy and a reactionary; distrust was universal. *One of the chief occupations of the Brimstone Gang was to compromise people at home in Germany in such a way that they were forced to pay money so that the gang should preserve their secret without compromising them. Not just one, but hundreds of letters were written to people in Germany, threatening to denounce them for complicity in this or that act of revolution unless a certain sum of money had been received at a specified address by a given date.* Following the principle that 'whoever is not unconditionally for us, is against us', the reputation of anyone who opposed these intrigues was 'ruined', not just among the refugees, but also by means of the press. *The 'proletarians' filled the columns of the reactionary press in Germany with their denunciations of those democrats who did not subscribe to their views; they became the confederates of the secret police in France and Germany.* To *fill* in the picture Vogt publishes among other documents a long letter by Techow, a former lieutenant, dated

---

[a] The action against the joint-stock company La Cimentaire. See Appendix 16 and also Marx's letter to Engels of November 16, 1860 (present edition, Vol. 41).— *Ed.*

[b] The *Neue Rheinische Zeitung.*— *Ed.*

August 26, 1850, in which the principles, the intrigues, the feuds and the various hostile secret unions of the 'proletarians' are described, and in which we see how Marx, puffed up with Napoleonic pride in his intellectual superiority, *rules the members of the Brimstone Gang with a rod of iron."*

We should note at once, so as better to understand what follows, that *Zabel,* who was ostensibly allowing *Vogt* to "speak for himself" in the passage quoted above, now goes on in his own name to throw further light on the Brimstone Gang, by mentioning one after the other the Cherval trial in Paris, the communist trial in Cologne, the pamphlet I wrote about the last,[a] Liebknecht's revolutionary congress in Murten and his relations with the *Allgemeine Zeitung* in which I acted as mediator, Ohly, who is "likewise a channel of the Brimstone Gang", and lastly, Biscamp's letter of October 20, 1859 to the *Allgemeine Zeitung.*[b] He concludes with the statement:

"A week after Biscamp *Marx,* too, wrote to the *Allgemeine Zeitung,* offering it a 'legal document' as evidence against Vogt about which we shall perhaps speak at a later date. *These then are the correspondents of the 'Allgemeine Zeitung'."*

Of the whole of this leading article No. 1, I made use only of the section printed under 1. in my submission, and in that passage I was concerned only with the following sentences:

"One of the chief occupations of the Brimstone Gang" (commanded by *Marx*) "was to compromise people at home in Germany in such a way that they were forced to pay money so that the gang should preserve their secret without compromising them. Not just one, but hundreds of letters were written to people in Germany, threatening to denounce them for complicity in this or that act of revolution unless a certain sum of money had been received at a specified address by a given date."

Here, of course, what I required from Zabel was *proof that his claims were true.* In my first advice to my lawyer, Legal Counsellor *Weber* in Berlin, I wrote that I did not require Zabel to produce "hundreds of threatening letters",[c] or even one, but just a single line showing that any one of my notorious party associates had been guilty of the infamous deeds imputed to them. Zabel, after all, only needed to turn to Vogt, who could have sent him dozens of "threatening letters" by return. And if by any chance Vogt were unable to produce even a single line from the hundreds of threatening letters, he would in any case still be able to give the names of the several hundred "people in Germany" who had been

---

[a] Karl Marx, *Revelations Concerning the Communist Trial in Cologne* (present edition, Vol. 11).— *Ed.*

[b] See this volume, p. 127.— *Ed.*

[c] See Marx's letter to Weber of February 13, 1860 (present edition, Vol. 41).— *Ed.*

plundered in the manner described. Since these people are to be found in "Germany" they would undoubtedly be more accessible to a court in Berlin than to one in Geneva.

Thus my ground of complaint against Zabel's leading article No. 1 confined itself to a single point: *political compromising of people in Germany for the purpose of extorting money from them.* In order at the same time to refute the other statements made in his leading article No. 1, I produced a series of facts. Here I did not require Zabel to *prove that his claims were true*; I showed that *they were false*.

As to the *Brimstone Gang or Bristlers, Johann Philipp Becker*'s letter[a] has thrown sufficient light on them. As far as the *character of the Communist League* was concerned, and my involvement with it, *H. Bürgers* of Cologne, one of the condemned in the Cologne communist trial, belonged to those people who could have been subpoenaed as witnesses to Berlin and made to testify under oath during the proceedings. Furthermore, *Frederick Engels* had discovered amongst his papers a letter dated November 1852[b] and *authenticated* by its postmarks in London and Manchester, in which I informed him of the dissolution of the League at my suggestion together with the reasons for that dissolution as they were set forth in the resolution: viz. that since the arrest of the accused in Cologne all contacts with the Continent had been broken off and that a propaganda society of this kind was no longer opportune. As for Zabel's shameless allegations about my contacts "with the secret police in Germany and France", these were supposed to have been verified partly by the Cologne communist trial and partly by the Cherval trial in Paris. I shall have more to say about the latter in due course. With reference to the former I sent my defence counsel a copy of my *Revelations Concerning the Communist Trial in Cologne,* which had appeared in 1853, and pointed out that the lawyer Schneider II could be subpoenaed from Cologne to Berlin where he could testify under oath to my part in uncovering the nefarious activities of the police.[c] Zabel's claim that my party associates and myself had "filled the columns of the reactionary press in Germany with denunciations of those democrats who did not subscribe to our views"—this claim was to be confronted with the fact that I *never* either directly or indirectly wrote for German newspapers from abroad, with the single

---

[a] See this volume, pp. 60-64.— *Ed.*

[b] Marx to Engels, November 19, 1852 (see present edition, Vol. 39). An extract from this letter is contained in Marx's notebook.— *Ed.*

[c] See Marx's letters to Weber of February 24 and March 3, 1860 (present edition, Vol. 41).— *Ed.*

exception of the *Neue Oder-Zeitung.* My printed contributions to that paper and, if need be, the testimony of one of its editors, Dr. Elsner, would prove that I *never* thought it worth the trouble to mention even one "democrat" by *name.* As for *Liebknecht's* reports to the *Allgemeine Zeitung,* they began in the spring of 1855, three years after the "League" was dissolved, and moreover they appeared *without my knowledge,* and as a scrutiny of the back numbers will reveal they contain accounts of English politics written from his political standpoint, but not a word about "democrats". When, during my absence from London, Liebknecht sent a pamphlet printed in London and attacking the "democrat" Vogt[a] to the *Allgemeine Zeitung,* he was perfectly entitled to do so for he knew that the pamphlet had been published by a "democrat" whom the "democrat" Vogt had himself invited to collaborate on his "democratic" propaganda, i.e. whom Vogt had recognised as a "democrat" of equal standing with himself. Zabel's comic tale making me a "correspondent of the *Allgemeine Zeitung*" was utterly refuted by a letter written to me by *Herr Orges* a few days before the opening of the Augsburg trial (see Appendix 10), in which he, *inter alia,* sought to correct my presumed "liberal" prejudices against the *Allgemeine Zeitung.* Lastly, Zabel's lie that "a week *after* Biscamp Marx, too, wrote to the *Allgemeine Zeitung*" collapsed of its own accord since Biscamp's letter was dated October 20, 1859 and the brief note I sent to Herr Orges along with the "document" he had asked for, was already in the hands of the Augsburg Court on October 24, 1859 and so could not possibly have been written in London on October 29, 1859.

For the benefit of the court it seemed appropriate to supplement the evidence already mentioned with a few documents which would serve to reflect back on "democrat" Zabel the grotesquely defaming light in which he had sought to place my situation within the emigration and my "intrigues" abroad.

I first lived in Paris from the end of 1843 until early in 1845, when I was expelled by Guizot. To indicate my position within the French revolutionary party during my stay in Paris I sent my counsel a letter from *Flocon* which in the name of the Provisional Government of 1848 revoked Guizot's decree of expulsion and invited me to return to France from Belgium (Appendix 14). I lived in Brussels from the beginning of 1845 until the end of February 1848, when Rogier had me expelled from Belgium. Subsequently the Brussels Municipal Council dismissed the police

---

[a] *Zur Warnung* by Karl Blind.—*Ed.*

commissar who had arrested my wife and myself on the occasion of my expulsion. In Brussels there was an international democratic association [228] in which the aged General *Mellinet* who had saved Antwerp from the Dutch held the office of Honorary President. The lawyer *Jottrand,* a former member of the Belgian Provisional Government, was President; the Vice-President for the Poles was *Lelewel,* a former member of the Polish Provisional Government; the Vice-President for the French was *Imbert,* who had been Governor of the Tuileries after the February revolution of 1848, and I held the post of Vice-President for the Germans, having been elected at a public meeting consisting of the members of the German Workers' Association and the entire German emigration in Brussels. A letter from Jottrand to me at the time of the establishment of the *Neue Rheinische Zeitung* (Jottrand belongs to what is known as the American school of republicanism, i.e. a trend alien to me), and a few otherwise insignificant lines from my friend Lelewel provide a sufficient indication of my position in the democratic party in Brussels. I added them therefore to the material in my defence (Appendix 14).

After I had been driven out of Prussia in the spring of 1849 and out of France in the late summer of the same year, I went to London, where following the dissolution of the League (1852) and the departure of most of my friends from London, I have been living without joining *any* associations whether public or secret, and indeed without society of any sort. I do, however, from time to time, with the permission of "democrat" Zabel, give free lectures on political economy to a select group of workers. *The German Workers' Educational Society in London,* from which I resigned on September 15, 1850, celebrated its twentieth anniversary on February 6, 1860. It invited me to attend the celebrations, at which it passed a unanimous resolution *"to brand as slander"* Vogt's allegation that I had "exploited" the German workers in general and the London workers in particular. Herr Müller, who was at that time the President of the Workers' Society, had this resolution authenticated on March 1, 1860 at the Police Court in Bow Street. Together with this document I sent my lawyer a letter from the English lawyer and leader of the Chartist Party, Ernest Jones (Appendix 14), in which he expresses his indignation about the "infamous articles" [a] of the *National-Zeitung* and draws

---

[a] Marx uses the English phrase and gives the German translation in brackets.— *Ed.*

attention *inter alia* to my unpaid collaboration over a period of years on the London organs of the Chartist Party. (It should be noted, incidentally, that Ernest Jones, who was born and brought up in Berlin, knows more German than Zabel.) I may also mention here that when the English Labour Parliament assembled in Manchester at the end of 1853,[229] Louis Blanc and I were the only members of the London emigration to be invited to attend as honorary members.

Finally, since our honorary Vogt has represented me as "living from the sweat of the workers", from whom I have never either asked or received a penny, and since "democrat" Zabel has suggested that I have "compromised people in Germany" politically "in such a way that they were forced to pay money so that the gang should preserve their secret without compromising them", I requested Mr. *Charles A. Dana,* the managing editor[a] of the *New-York Tribune,* the first Anglo-American paper which has 200,000 subscribers and is thus almost as widely known as the Biel *Commis voyageur* and Zabel's "organ of democracy",[b] to give me a statement in writing about my ten-year-long paid collaboration on the *Tribune,* the *Cyclopaedia Americana,* etc. His letter, extremely flattering for me (see Appendix 14), was the last document I thought it necessary to forward to my lawyer to defend myself against the stink-ball No. 1 of Vogt and Zabel.

2. In Zabel's leading article No. 2, "Wie man radikale Flugblätter macht" (*National-Zeitung,* No. 41, January 25, 1860), it is stated:

"*Where* the *money* for this generously distributed paper" (i.e. *Das Volk*) "*came from,* is known to the gods; men, however, are well aware that *Marx* and Biscamp have no money to spare."

Looked at in isolation this passage might appear to be no more than a frank expression of astonishment, as if I were to say: "How a certain stout party whom I knew in my student days in Berlin as a dunce bereft of all intellectual and material charms—he was the owner of a day nursery and his literary accomplishments prior to the revolution of 1848 were confined to a few furtive contributions to a literary local rag—how the above-mentioned stout dunce managed to become editor-in-chief of the *National-Zeitung,* a shareholder in it and 'a democrat in possession of spare money'—that is known to the gods. Men, however, who have read

---

[a] Marx uses English: "managing editor".—*Ed.*

[b] The *Schweizer Handels-Courier* and the *National-Zeitung.*—*Ed.*

a certain novel by Balzac[a] and who have made a study of the Manteuffel era, may be able to hazard a guess."

Zabel's remark acquires quite a different, and far more malicious inflection from the circumstance that it follows his allegations about my connections with the secret police of France and Germany and my conspiratorial and police efforts to extort money with the aid of threatening letters, and leads on directly to the "manufacture of counterfeit paper money on a massive scale" to be treated under 3. Obviously he intends to imply that I obtained financial contributions for *Das Volk* in a disreputable manner.

In order to refute Zabel in court I obtained an affidavit from Manchester dated March 3, 1860 according to which all the money I gave to *Das Volk* (with the exception of a specified amount out of my own pocket) came, not, as Vogt opined, from "the other side of the Channel", but from the pockets of my friends in Manchester (see "The Augsburg Campaign").[b]

3. "To throw light on" the "tactics" of the "*'proletarian' party* **under Marx**", F. Zabel narrates the following story (leading article No. 2 *inter alia*):

"In this way a conspiracy of the most infamous sort was devised in 1852, which aimed at damaging the Swiss workers' associations by **manufacturing counterfeit paper money on a massive scale**. *See Vogt for further details*, etc."

This is how Zabel interprets Vogt's assertions about the *Cherval affair* and makes me the moral source and criminal accomplice in the "manufacture of counterfeit paper money on a massive scale". The evidence I assembled in refutation of these allegations by "democrat" Zabel extended over the whole period from Cherval's admission to the "Communist League" to his flight from Geneva in 1854. An affidavit taken out by *Karl Schapper* at the Police Court at Bow Street on March 1, 1860[c] proved that Cherval had been admitted to the League in London *before* I myself joined it. It showed further that when he was in Paris, where he lived from the summer of 1850 until the spring of 1852, he entered into relations not with myself, but with the rival League of Willich and Schapper which was hostile to me. Finally, it proved that after his feigned escape from the prison of St. Pélagie and his return to

---

[a] Presumably *Illusions perdues*.— *Ed.*

[b] See this volume, pp. 118, 119.— *Ed.*

[c] On this see Marx's letter to Karl Schapper of February 27, 1860 (present edition, Vol. 41). Extracts from the letter and from the affidavit are contained in Marx's notebook.— *Ed.*

London (spring 1852), he joined the public *German Workers' Educational Society* there to which I had ceased to belong in September 1850. Here he was finally exposed, condemned and expelled. Moreover, the lawyer Schneider II in Cologne could be made to testify under oath that the revelations about Cherval made *while* the Cologne communist trial was in progress, the account of his relations with the Prussian police in London, etc., all came from me. My *Revelations,* which were published in 1853, proved that I had publicly denounced him *after* the conclusion of the trial. Finally, Johann Philipp Becker's letter[a] provided information about Cherval's Geneva period.

4. Having with genuinely dunce-like logic babbled about the pamphlet *Zur Warnung,* which had been aimed at Vogt, and having done his best to discredit Vögele's testimony[b] about the *origins* of the pamphlet, which testimony I had forwarded to the *Allgemeine Zeitung,* "democrat" F. Zabel concludes his peroration in leading article No. 2 as follows:

> "He" (Blind) "is obviously not a member of the *Marx party in the narrower sense.* It appears to us that the *latter* did not find it too difficult to turn him into a scapegoat, and if the charges levelled at Vogt were to carry any weight, they had to be attributed to a definite person who would have to be responsible for them. The *Marx party* could very easily saddle Blind with the authorship of the pamphlet because and after he had expressed similar views to those contained in it in *conversation with Marx* and in an article in *The Free Press. By making use of Blind's assertions and turns of phrase the pamphlet could be* **fabricated** *and made to look as if* **he** *had concocted it....* Anybody is at liberty to regard either *Marx* or Blind as its author", etc.

Zabel here accuses me of having **fabricated** a document, viz. the pamphlet *Zur Warnung,* in **Blind's name** and of having subsequently, in a false testimony sent by me to the *Allgemeine Zeitung,* represented Blind as the author of the *pamphlet fabricated* by myself. The legal refutation of "democrat" Zabel's allegations was as decisive as it was simple. It consisted of Blind's letter to Liebknecht, cited earlier on, of Blind's article in *The Free Press,*[c] the two affidavits of Wiehe and Vögele (Appendices 12 and 13) and the printed declaration of M. D. Schaible.[d]

Vogt, who is known to have jeered at the Bavarian Government in his *Studien,*[e] launched an action against the *Allgemeine Zeitung* at

---

[a] See this volume, pp. 60-64.—*Ed.*

[b] ibid., Appendix 12.—*Ed.*

[c] ibid., pp. 122, 122-23.—*Ed.*

[d] ibid., pp. 130-31.—*Ed.*

[e] Carl Vogt, *Studien zur gegenwärtigen Lage Europas,* S. 91.—*Ed.*

the end of August 1859. As early as September the *Allgemeine Zeitung* had to request a postponement of the hearing and although the postponement had been granted the trial actually took place on *October 24, 1859.* If this was possible in the *obscurantist state of Bavaria,* what might not be expected from the *enlightened state of* **Prussia,** quite apart from the proverbial truth that "in Berlin there are judges".

My lawyer, *Counsellor Weber,* formulated my case thus:

"The editor of the *National-Zeitung,* Dr. Zabel, has repeatedly and publicly libelled me in leading articles in Nos. 37 and 41 of that paper of this year. In particular he has accused me (1) of acquiring and having acquired money in a dishonourable and criminal manner; (2) of having fabricated the anonymous pamphlet *Zur Warnung* and of having not only represented a certain Blind as its author to the *Allgemeine Zeitung* against my better knowledge, but also of having sought to prove this assertion with the aid of a document of whose inaccurate contents I must have been convinced."

Counsellor Weber elected to proceed first by means of an *official investigation,* i.e. he denounced Zabel's libels to the Public Prosecutor with the idea that proceedings against Zabel should then be initiated by the Public Prosecutor's Office. This resulted in the following *"ruling"* which was handed down on *April 18, 1860*:

"The original documents are returned to Dr. Karl Marx c/o Counsellor Weber, together with the notification that *no issue of public importance* is raised by this matter which could make it desirable for me to take any action (Article XVI of the Prolegomena to the Penal Code of April 14, 1851).[a] Berlin, April 18.

"Public Prosecutor at the Royal Municipal Court,

(signed) **Lippe**"

My counsel appealed to the Chief Public Prosecutor and on *April 26, 1860* he received a second *"ruling"* worded thus:

"To the Royal Counsellor Weber, acting on behalf of Dr. Karl Marx of London. I hereby return to you the documents accompanying the complaint of April 20 of this year concerning the denunciation against Dr. Zabel. The only criterion by which the Public Prosecutor may act in considering what discretion he is allowed by Article XVI of the Prolegomena to the Penal Code is, of course, the question whether prosecution is required by any discernible public interest. Concurring with the judgment of the Royal Public Prosecutor I must answer this question negatively in the present instance, and I accordingly reject your complaint. Berlin, April 26, 1860.

"Chief Public Prosecutor at the Royal High Court,

(signed) **Schwarck**"

---

[a] "Gesetz über die Einführung des Strafgesetzbuchs für die Preussischen Staaten. Vom 14. April 1851", *Gesetz-Sammlung für die Königlichen Preussischen Staaten 1851.—Ed.*

I found these two refusals on the part of Public Prosecutor *Lippe* and Chief Public Prosecutor *Schwarck* entirely justified. In every state throughout the world, and hence presumably in the state of Prussia also, the public interest is interpreted as the *interest of the government.* As far as the Prussian Government was concerned there neither was nor could there be *"any discernible public interest"* in the *prosecution* of "democrat" Zabel for libels against my person. If anything, the interest lay in the opposite direction. Moreover, the Public Prosecutor does not have the judicial authority to pass judgment; he has to follow blindly the regulations laid down by his superior, the *Minister of Justice* in the final instance, and he must do this regardless of his own views or convictions.

In actual fact, then, I am quite in agreement with the decisions of Messrs. Lippe and Schwarck, although I have legal reservations about Lippe's reference to Article XVI of the Prolegomena to the Penal Code of April 14, 1851. There is no paragraph in the Prussian Code which obliges the Public Prosecutor's Office to give a reason for its *refusal* to intervene. Nor is there any single syllable about this in the Article XVI referred to by Lippe. So why quote it?

My lawyer now proceeded to launch a *civil action,* and I breathed a sigh of relief. Though the Prussian Government had no public interest in prosecuting F. Zabel, I had the strongest private interest to defend myself. And I could now act in my own name. The *verdict* was a matter of indifference to me, if only I could compel F. Zabel to appear at the bar of a public court. But just imagine my astonishment! I was told that it was not yet a matter of instituting legal proceedings, but of a court hearing to settle the question whether I had a *right to bring an action* against F. Zabel.

I was disconcerted to discover that, according to the Prussian judicial regulations, before the judge can hear the action and proceed to judgment, every plaintiff must plead his case to the same judge to enable the latter to see whether the plaintiff has the *right to sue.* In the course of this preliminary investigation the judge may call for additional evidence, or he may suppress part of the old evidence, or he may find that the plaintiff has no **right** *to sue.* If he sees fit to allow the right to sue, the judge arranges the hearing; the case is heard and is settled by a verdict. If the judge refuses the right to sue, he simply stops the action by a decree, by a *ruling.* This procedure applies not only to actions for libel, but to all civil cases. Thus an action for libel, like any other civil action, can be dismissed in all instances by such an official *ruling* and therefore will never be settled.

It will be granted that a code of law which does not recognise the *right* of the private individual *to sue* in his own private interests, ignores the simplest and most basic laws of civil society. The right to sue, a self-evident right of the independent private individual, is turned into a privilege granted by the state through the agency of its judiciary. In every legal conflict the state intervenes placing itself between the private individual and the gateway to the court, which is its *private property* and which it opens or closes as it thinks fit. First the judge *gives a ruling* in his capacity as an official; later on he *gives his verdict,* in his capacity as a judge. The same judge who, without hearing the accused, without hearing the pros and cons of the case, *prejudges* the issue of whether there are grounds for an action, and who, let us say, places himself on the side of the plaintiff, who thus decides to a certain degree *in favour of* the legitimacy of the complaint, who decides therefore to a certain degree against the defendant, this very same judge is supposed subsequently, in the actual trial, to *decide impartially* between the plaintiff and defendant, i.e. to pass a verdict on his own prejudgment. B. boxes A.'s ears. A. cannot sue the attacker until he has civilly acquired a licence to do so from the court official. A. withholds from B. a piece of land that belongs to him. B. requires a preliminary licence enabling him to assert his property rights before the court. He may receive it or he may not. B. libels A. publicly in the press, and an official of the judiciary, sitting in camera, may "rule" that A. may not sue B. It is easy to see what monstrous injustices may be perpetrated because of this procedure even in civil cases in the strict sense of the word. Still more so in case of libels made in the press against political parties. In all countries, and even in Prussia, judges are known to be human beings like everyone else. Even one of the Vice-Presidents of the Royal Prussian Supreme Tribunal, *Dr. Götze,* has declared in the Prussian Upper House that Prussian law was embarrassed by the disturbances of the years 1848, 1849 and 1850, and needed some time to orientate itself. Who can guarantee that Dr. Götze has not miscalculated the time required for orientation? The fact that in Prussia the right to take action against a slanderer, for example, depends on the *interim "ruling"* of an official whom the government, moreover, may punish for so-called "derelictions of duty while in office", with censure, fines, forced transfer and even dishonourable dismissal from the judiciary (see the interim ordinance of July 10, 1849 and the Law concerning discipline of May 7, 1851[a])—how shall I even begin to make this credible, if not clear, to English readers?

For it is my intention to publish an English pamphlet about my case against F. Zabel.[230] And when Edmond About wrote his *La Prusse en 1860* what would he not have given for the information that in the entire realm of the Prussian monarchy the *right to sue* does not exist anywhere but in the Rhine Province, which has been "blessed" with the possession of the *Code Napoléon*[231]! Men must *suffer* everywhere under the courts, but only in a very few countries are they forbidden to *sue*.

In the circumstances it is understandable that *my action* against *Zabel* in the *Prussian courts* had to change into *my dispute with the Prussian courts* about *Zabel*. Leaving the theoretical beauties of the law to one side, let us now cast a glance at the charms of applying it in practice.

On June 8, 1860 the Royal *Municipal Court* in Berlin issued the following *"ruling"*:

"*Ruling regarding the suit for libel brought on June 5, 1860*
"*Marx contra Zabel*. M. 38 de 1860
"1. The suit is dismissed for *lack of an indictable offence,* because the two incriminating leading articles of the local 'National-Zeitung' *merely make the political views of the Augsburg 'Allgemeine Zeitung'* and the *history of the anonymous pamphlet* 'Zur Warnung' the object of discussion. *The statements and assertions contained therein, insofar as they are those of the author himself* and **are not merely quotations from other persons,** *do not exceed the bounds of legitimate criticism.* In accordance with § 154 of the Penal Code, therefore, since *the intention to insult* is evident neither *from the form* of these utterances, nor *from the circumstances* in which they were made, they cannot be held to be punishable.

Berlin, June 8, 1860

"Royal Municipal Court, Criminal Division
"Commission I for Libel Cases (L.S.[b])"

Thus the *Municipal Court* forbids me to *sue F. Zabel* and absolves *Zabel* of the irksome necessity of having to answer for his public libels! And why? *"For lack of an indictable offence."* The Public Prosecutor's Office refused to take action against Zabel on my behalf because *no discernible public interest was involved.* The *Municipal Court* forbids me to proceed against Zabel on my own behalf because there is *no indictable offence.* And why is there no indictable offence?

---

[a] "Verordnung, betreffend die Dienstvergehen der Richter ... vom 10. Juli 1849" and "Gesetz, betreffend die Dienstvergehen der Richter ... vom 7. Mai 1851".— *Ed.*
[b] *Locus sigilli*: the place of the seal.— *Ed.*

First: "Because the two leading articles of the *'National-Zeitung'* *merely relate to the political views of the 'Allgemeine Zeitung'*."

Because Zabel has for the time being deceitfully transformed me into a *"correspondent of the 'Allgemeine Zeitung'"* he has the right to make me the whipping-boy in his feud with that paper, and I do not even have the right to complain about this "ruling" of the mighty Zabel! Brimstone Gang, Bristlers, *complot franco-allemand,* revolutionary congress in Murten, Cologne communist trial, fabrication of counterfeit paper money in Geneva, *"work of the 'Rheinische Zeitung'"*, etc., etc.— all this "**merely** *relates to the political views of the 'Allgemeine Zeitung'*".

Second: F. Zabel had *"no intention to insult"*. Of course not! The good fellow only had the intention of killing me off politically and morally with his lies.

When "democrat" F. Zabel asserts in the *National-Zeitung* that I have counterfeited money on a massive scale, fabricated documents in the name of third persons, politically compromised people in Germany so as to extort money from them by threatening to denounce them, etc., it is evident that according to legal terminology he can have had only one of two things in mind: either to libel me or to denounce me. If the first, then he is legally punishable; if the second, then he must prove the truth of his assertions in a court of law. What do I care for any other private intentions of "democrat" F. Zabel?

Zabel libels me, but without "the intention to insult". He injures my reputation like the Turk who cut off the head of a Greek, but without intending to injure him.

If one speaks of "insulting" and "the intention to insult", if one speaks of the kind of infamous actions which "democrat" F. Zabel imputes to me, then the specific *"intention"* to *"insult"*, the *utterly malicious intention* of the *good* Zabel—why it breathes from every pore of his leading articles Nos. 1 and 2.

Vogt's "Magnum Opus", appendices included, has no fewer than 278 pages. And F. Zabel, who is accustomed "to draw out the thread of his verbosity finer than the staple of his argument",[a] our conceited F. Zabel, Dunce Zabel has succeeded in compressing these 278 pages into approximately five small newspaper columns without forgoing a *single one* of Vogt's libels against me and my party. F. Zabel provides an anthology of the most scurrilous parts and a table of contents for the less drastic portions. F. Zabel, accustomed to expanding two molecules of ideas into 278 pages,

---

[a] Shakespeare, *Love's Labour's Lost,* Act V, Scene 1.— *Ed.*

now condenses 278 pages into two leading articles without losing a single atom of dirt in the process. *Ira facit poetam.*[a] How potent a malice it must have been to transform the hydrocephalic Zabel into a hydraulic press of such force!

On the other hand, his malice blinds him to such an extent that he ascribes miraculous powers to me, actual miraculous powers, only to enable him to make one more slanderous insinuation at my expense.

Having begun in the first leading article with a description of the Brimstone Gang under my command, and having happily turned me and my associates into the *"confederates of the secret police in France and Germany"*, having recounted, *inter alia,* that "these people" hated Vogt because he was continuously rescuing Switzerland from their clutches, he goes on:

"Now when last year Vogt had brought an action against the *Allgemeine Zeitung,* the *latter* received a *communication* from *another* London *accomplice, Biscamp....* In the most shameless manner the writer offered ... his services as a second correspondent along with Herr Liebknecht. [...] *A week after Biscamp Marx,* too, *wrote to the 'Allgemeine Zeitung', offering it a 'legal document'* as evidence against Vogt about *which"* [b] (the document, the evidence or Vogt?) *"we shall perhaps speak at a later date."*

Zabel gave this promise on January 22 and carried it out as early as January 25 in the *National-Zeitung,* No. 41, where we can read:

"So Blind denies being the author of the pamphlet; he is ... referred to as such for the first time in *Biscamp's letter to the 'Allgemeine Zeitung' of October 20.... To strengthen the case* for Blind's authorship *Marx wrote to the 'Allgemeine Zeitung' on October 29.*"

So F. Zabel credits me, not once, but twice, first on January 22 and then again on January 25, having had three days to think it over, with the magic power of writing a letter in London on *October 29, 1859* which had been in the possession of the Augsburg District Court on *October 24, 1859.* And both times he credits me with this magic power in order to establish a link between the "document" I forwarded to the *Allgemeine Zeitung,* and the objectionable letter sent to it by Biscamp,[c] i.e. to make my letter look like the *pedisequus*[d] to Biscamp's. So was it not malice, pigheaded malice which made F. Zabel stupid to the point of

---

[a] Anger makes the poet (Virgil, *The Aeneid,* Book VII, 507, paraphrased).— *Ed.*

[b] In German: *von dem,* but *dem* can refer either to the document, the evidence or Vogt.— *Ed.*

[c] See this volume, p. 127.— *Ed.*

[d] Sequel.— *Ed.*

beginning to believe in magic, far beyond the average degree of duncedom?

But, the *Municipal Court* "argues further", Zabel's leading article No. 2 *"merely makes the history of the anonymous* pamphlet *Zur Warnung"* the "object of discussion". The *object?* Read *pretext.*

Eisele-Beisele, concealed this time under the name of *"German Patriots",* had, it appears, sent an "open letter" in November 1859 to the "National Association" which was printed in the reactionary *Neue Hannoversche Zeitung.*[232] This "open letter" offended against the "democracy" of Zabel, a democracy in which the heroic courage to attack the Habsburg dynasty was neatly balanced by the servility shown to the Hohenzollern dynasty. The *Neue Preussische Zeitung* took the opportunity provided by the "open letter" to make the not very original discovery that once democracy has got under way it need not necessarily end up in— **F. Zabel** and his "organ of democracy". Zabel flew into a rage and wrote leading article No. 2, *"Wie man radikale Flugblätter macht"* [*"How Radical Pamphlets Are Made"*].

"By inviting the *Kreuz-Zeitung,"* Zabel begins portentously, "to go through the history of the pamphlet (*Zur Warnung*) *with the help* of the documents and *explanations* provided *by Vogt,* we express the hope that it will finally admit that we were in the right when we said two months ago that the open letter to the National Association was something for it, not for us, that it had been designed *for its columns,* not for ours."

So "democrat" Zabel, who has been so radically initiated by Vogt into the mysteries of radicalism, wishes for his part to read the *Kreuz-Zeitung* a lecture on the mystery of "how radical pamphlets are made", or as the Municipal Court expresses it: "he **merely** *wishes to make the history of the pamphlet 'Zur Warnung' the object of discussion".* And how does F. Zabel set about his task?

He starts with the "tactics" of the "'proletarian' party *under Marx"*. First, he recounts how, *in the name* of a Workers' Association but behind its back, the "proletarians *under Marx"* send letters from London for foreign workers' associations "which *are to be compromised"*, hatch "intrigues", set up a secret league, etc.; and how they, finally, compose "documents" which "inevitably attract the protests of the police" to those associations "which are to be compromised". Thus in order to teach the *Kreuz-Zeitung* "how radical pamphlets are made", Zabel begins by explaining that "the 'proletarian' party *under Marx"* manufactures police "reports" and "documents", which are not "pamphlets" at all. In order to explain "how radical pamphlets are made" he goes on to recount that the "proletarians *under Marx*" manufactured *"counterfeit paper money on a massive scale"* in Geneva in 1852, which are likewise not "radical pamphlets". In order to demonstrate "how radical pamphlets are made", he reports that the "proletarians *under Marx*" carried out *"manoeuvres"* hostile to the Swiss and compromising for the associations during the Lausanne Joint Festival in 1859—and these too are not "radical pamphlets". He explains that "Biscamp and *Marx*" with the aid of funds whose source was known only "to the gods" produced *Das Volk,* which was not a "radical pamphlet" either but a weekly journal. And after all this he puts in a good word for the immaculate purity of Vogt's recruiting agency, which once again was no "radical pamphlet". In this way he fills 2 of the $3\frac{1}{4}$ columns of the article entitled *"How Radical Pamphlets Are Made".* Thus for these $\frac{2}{3}$ of the article the *history* of the anonymous pamphlet serves merely as a *pretext* for reproducing those of Vogt's slanders which *F. Zabel,* his "friend" and accomplice, has not dealt with under the heading *"Political Views of the 'Allgemeine Zeitung'".* Lastly at the very end Dunce I comes to the art of "making radical pamphlets", namely to "the history" of the pamphlet *Zur Warnung.*

"Blind denies being the author of the pamphlet; he is impudently referred to as such for the first time in Biscamp's letter to the *Allgemeine Zeitung* of October 20.... *To strengthen the case* for Blind's authorship *Marx* wrote to the *Allgemeine Zeitung* on October 29: 'I have obtained the *accompanying document* because Blind refused to stand by statements which he made to me and to other persons.'"

Now Zabel suspects this document in particular because Liebknecht ... "strangely enough" adds: "We requested the magistrate (?)" (this question mark stands in Zabel's text) "to authenticate our signatures" and Zabel has resolved once and for all not to recognise any magistrate but the Berlin magistrate. Zabel goes on to report the contents of Vögele's declaration which had caused Blind to send the statements of Hollinger and Wiehe to the *Allgemeine Zeitung* to prove *that the pamphlet had not been printed on Hollinger's press* and was therefore not *composed* by Blind. He continues:

"*Marx, always ready with an answer,* replied in the *Allgemeine Zeitung* on November 15."

Zabel lists the various points in my reply. Marx says this ... Marx says that..., "**in addition**, *Marx* refers". So since I do not say anything *"in addition"*, surely Zabel has informed his readers of *all* the points I make in my reply? But we know our Zabel! He conceals, leaves out, *suppresses* the decisive point of my reply.[a] In my declaration of November 15[b] I make a number of points, all of which are numbered. Thus "1. ... 2. ... and finally, 3. ...": "It so happened that the reprint" (of the pamphlet) "in *Das Volk* was made from the type still standing in Hollinger's print-shop. Thus *without the need to call witnesses,* a simple comparison of the pamphlet and the reprint of it in *Das Volk* would be sufficient *to prove to a court that the former came from F. Hollinger's print-shop.*" That's the conclusive piece of evidence, Zabel said to himself. My readers must not hear of this. So he spirits away the strongest point of my reply and instead burdens my conscience with a suspect gift of repartee.[c] Thus Zabel's account of "the history of the pamphlet" contains two intentional falsehoods. He falsifies first the chronology and then the contents of my declaration of November 15. His *twofold falsification* prepares the way for his conclusion *that I "fabricated" the pamphlet,* and that I did so in such a way that it "looked like Blind's fabrication" and hence that in sending Vögele's testimony to the *Allgemeine Zeitung* I likewise sent a false testimony, and did so *knowingly.* The accusation of fabricating documents with the intention of saddling a third person with responsibility for them does not, in the view of the Berlin *Municipal Court,* "exceed the bounds of legitimate criticism" and even less does it imply "an intention to insult".

At the end of his recipe describing "how radical pamphlets are made" it suddenly occurs to Zabel that there is *one* shameless invention of Vogt's that he has omitted to make use of, and so right at the end of his leading article No. 2 he hastily adds the following note:

"In 1850 another circular" (as Vogt recollects) "written by Parliamentary Wolf, *alias Casemate Wolf,* was sent to the 'proletarians' in Germany, and *simultaneously* allowed to fall into the hands of the Hanover police."[d]

With this pretty police anecdote about one of the former editors of the *Neue Rheinische Zeitung,* our stout party, democrat Zabel, grins and takes his leave of his readers. The words "alias

---

[a] Marx puns on the words *unterschlagen* (suppress) and *schlagend* (decisive).— *Ed.*

[b] See this volume, pp. 8-9. The italics were introduced by Marx in *Herr Vogt.—Ed.*

[c] Marx puns on the words *Schlagkraft* (forcefulness, striking power, here— strongest point) and *Schlagfertigkeit* (gift of repartee).— *Ed.*

[d] From the article "Wie man radikale Flugblätter macht", *National-Zeitung,* No. 41, January 25, 1860.— *Ed.*

Casemate Wolf" belong not to Vogt but to F. Zabel. His Silesian readers were to be clearly informed that he is talking about their countryman *W. Wolff,* the former co-editor of the *Neue Rheinische Zeitung.* How assiduously our good Zabel toils to ensure that the connection between the *Neue Rheinische Zeitung* and the police in France and Germany is established down to the last detail! His Silesians might imagine otherwise that it was Zabel's own *B. Wolff* that was under discussion, Zabel's natural superior[a] who, as is well known, rearranges world history with the aid of telegrams and in "secret league" with such well-known manufacturers of false reports as *Reuter* in London and *Havas* in Paris. *Sigmund Engländer,* the notorious secret police agent, is the heart and soul of the Reuter bureau and hence the presiding genius of the trinity *B. Wolff-Reuter-Havas.*

Despite all this and despite democrat Zabel's intention not to insult, the Berlin *Municipal Court* declares that Zabel's two leading articles do indeed "contain statements and assertions" which "exceed the bounds of legitimate criticism" and are therefore "punishable", or at least *actionable.* So produce this Zabel! Hand him over and let him wriggle in court! Not so fast! the *Municipal Court* exclaims. The "statements and assertions" contained in the two leading articles, the Municipal Court says, do not, "*insofar as they are those of the author*" (Zabel) "himself **and are not merely quotations from other persons**", exceed "the bounds of legitimate criticism" and are not "punishable". Hence Zabel is not only not punishable, he is not even actionable and "the costs are therefore to be borne by the plaintiff". So the libellous part of Zabel's "statements and assertions" is "**mere quotation**". *Voyons!*

It will be remembered from the opening part of this chapter that my action for libel was based on four passages in Zabel's two leading articles. In the passage dealing with *Das Volk*'s financial resources (*sub* 2 of the points listed above), *Zabel himself does not claim* to quote nor does he quote in fact, for:

Zabel (National-Zeitung, No. 41)	Vogt ("Magnum Opus", p. 212)
"Where the money for this generously distributed paper" (*Das Volk*) "came from, is known to the gods; men, however, are well aware that Marx and Biscamp have no money to spare."	"The regular correspondent of the *Allgemeine Zeitung* is a collaborator on this paper" (*Das Volk*) "which was established with the aid of unknown funds, for neither Biscamp nor Marx have the requisite means *for it*" (i.e. to establish a paper on the basis of *unknown funds?*).

---

[a] Marx gives the English phrase in brackets after its German equivalent.— *Ed.*

In the second incriminating passage (see above *sub* 4), in which I am accused of fabricating a document in Blind's name, Zabel even states *explicitly* that **he** is speaking in *his own* name, as Zabel, and not in Vogt's.

"It appears to **us**", as monarch in the Kingdom of Dullness[a] Zabel naturally makes use of the *pluralis majestatis*,[b] "it *appears* to **us** that the latter" (the Marx party) "did not find it too difficult to turn him" (Blind) "into a scapegoat.... By making use of Blind's assertions and turns of phrase the pamphlet could be *fabricated* and made to *look* as if *he*" (Blind) "had concocted it" (*National-Zeitung*, No. 41).

The third of the incriminating passages (see above *sub* 3) must be "quoted" again in full:

"In this way a conspiracy of the most infamous sort was devised in 1852, which aimed at damaging the Swiss workers' associations by manufacturing counterfeit paper money on a massive scale. (*See Vogt for further details.*) This conspiracy would have caused the greatest difficulties for the Swiss authorities if it had not been uncovered in time."

Is this "**merely a quotation**", as the *Municipal Court* maintains, is it in fact a quotation of any kind? It is indeed partly plagiarised from Vogt, but it is *not a quotation in any sense of the word.*

In the first place *Zabel himself* does not claim that he is quoting, but implies that he is speaking in his own right when he remarks in a parenthesis: "See Vogt for further details." And now look at the passage itself! In Geneva it was known that *Cherval* did not arrive in Geneva before *spring 1853* and that his "conspiracy" and flight took place in *spring 1854*. So Vogt, writing in Geneva, does not venture to assert that the "conspiracy ... was devised in **1852**". This lie he leaves to our good Zabel in Berlin. Furthermore, Vogt says:

"Various stone and copper plates had already been *engraved* for this purpose" (the manufacture of counterfeit banknotes, etc.) "by Nugent" (Cherval) "himself" ("Magnum Opus", p. 175).

Hence various stone and copper plates had . *already* been engraved for the forgery, but the banknotes and treasury bills had *not yet* been manufactured. According to *Zabel,* however, "the manufacture of counterfeit paper money" had already taken place, and *"on a massive scale",* moreover. Vogt states that the statutory "purpose" of Cherval's conspiracy was

"to attack despotism with its own weapons, by manufacturing counterfeit banknotes and treasury bills on a massive scale" (loc. cit.).

---

[a] Marx uses the English word.— *Ed.*
[b] The royal plural.— *Ed.*

Zabel deletes the attack on despotism and holds fast to the "manufacture of counterfeit paper money on a massive scale". In Zabel, then, what we have is an ordinary criminal act which is not even palliated for the benefit of the members of the "secret league" by the pretence of a political purpose. And *this* is how Zabel "**quotes**" from the "Magnum Opus" throughout. *Vogt* felt it necessary to turn his tall stories into a "book". So he fills it with details, spins it out, scrawls, splutters, colours, daubs, arranges, develops, complicates, explains, fantasises, *fa del cul trombetta*[a] with the result that at every point his Falstaffian soul shines through the purported facts, which are once more dissolved by his own narrative, though he is not aware of this, into the void from which they had emerged. Zabel, by contrast, who had to compress the book into two leading articles and did not wish to omit a single slander, suppresses[b] everything but the *caput mortuum*[b] of every purported "fact", he strings the dry bones of these slanders together and then counts his rosary with the zeal of a Pharisee.

Take the following case. Starting with the fact revealed first by myself, that Cherval was a secret police agent and *agent provocateur* in the pay of various embassies, Vogt's imagination takes wing. He says *inter alia*:

"Various stone and copper plates had *already* been engraved for this purpose" (forgery) "by Nugent" (Cherval) "himself; the gullible members of the secret league had *already* been selected to go to France, Switzerland and Germany with packets of these" (as yet unmanufactured) "counterfeit banknotes. But *denunciations had already been made to the police* and scandalously enough these also incriminated the workers' associations, etc." ("Magnum Opus", p. 175.)

Vogt thus makes Cherval *denounce* his own operations to the police even though he has done *no more* than engrave the stone and copper plates for the intended forgery, even before the purpose of his conspiracy has been achieved, before a *corpus delicti* has appeared and anyone apart from himself has been compromised. But the Vogtian Cherval is eager to "scandalously" incriminate "the workers' associations" in his "conspiracy". The *foreign embassies* that make use of Cherval are as stupid as he is and are equally precipitate

"in indicating to the Swiss police in confidence that political intrigues were being devised in the workers' associations, etc."[c]

---

a Makes a bugle of his rear (Dante, *The Divine Comedy*, Inferno, Canto XXI).— *Ed.*

b Literally: dead head; a term used in chemistry for the residuum left after distillation; here: remainder, residue.— *Ed.*

c op. cit., S. 176.— *Ed.*

Simultaneously, these ambassadorial numskulls, who are too impatient to allow the conspiracy hatched by Cherval on their orders to come to fruition and who, in their childish impatience, reveal the identity of their own agent to no purpose, have police lying in wait at "the frontiers" to receive Cherval's emissaries, "if matters had developed to such a pitch" as they had prevented them from developing, "to receive them with counterfeit bank-notes" whose manufacture they had thwarted,

"and turn the whole affair into an occasion for a general witch-hunt in which masses of innocent people would have had to pay for the misdeeds of a few wicked men". [a]

When *Vogt goes on* to say that "the plan of the whole conspiracy had been *monstrously conceived*", everyone will agree that its conception was *monstrously stupid,* and when he concludes with the boast

"I cannot deny that I contributed **a substantial part** in frustrating these *devilish plans*", [b]

everyone will get the point and collapse with laughter at the whimsical devil. But compare this with the ascetic account given in Zabel's annals!

"In this way a conspiracy of the most infamous sort was devised in 1852, which aimed at damaging the Swiss associations by manufacturing counterfeit paper money on a massive scale. (See Vogt for further details.) This conspiracy would have caused the greatest difficulties for the Swiss authorities if it had not been uncovered in time."

Here, condensed into a single brief sentence, we find a whole bundle of facts, as dry as they are scandalous. "A conspiracy of the most infamous sort" dated 1852. "Manufacture of counterfeit paper money on a massive scale", i.e. an ordinary criminal act. The intentional compromising of the "Swiss workers' associations", i.e. betrayal of one's own party. The "greatest difficulties" which might have arisen for the "Swiss authorities", i.e. *agent provocateur* against the Swiss Republic in the interests of Continental despots. Lastly, "timely discovery of the conspiracy". Here criticism is deprived of all the vital clues provided by Vogt's account, they have been simply conjured away. One has to believe or disbelieve. And this is how Zabel treats the entire "Magnum Opus" insofar as it deals with my party associates and myself. As *Heine* so rightly says, no human being is as dangerous as an addle-brained ass.

---

[a] ibid., S. 177.— *Ed.*
[b] ibid.— *Ed.*

Lastly, the fourth incriminating passage (see above *sub* 1) with which leading article No. 1 opens its revelations about the "Brimstone Gang". It is true that *Zabel* begins with the words: *"Vogt reports on p. 136 et seq."* But Zabel does not make it clear whether he is summarising or quoting. He takes care not to use quotation marks. In fact, *he does not quote.* There could be no doubt about it from the outset since he condenses pp. 136, 137, 138, 139, 140 and 141 of the "Magnum Opus" into 51 lines of about 48 letters each, does not indicate omissions, but packs the sentences as tightly as Dutch herrings, and lastly even has space in these 51 lines for reflections of his own. Wherever he comes upon a particularly vile sentence, he incorporates it more or less as it stands. For the rest, he mixes up his excerpts so that they do not follow the pagination of the "Magnum Opus" but are brought in as and when they suit his purpose. He equips the head of one Vogtian sentence with the tail of another Vogtian sentence. Or again, he composes a *single* sentence from the keywords of a dozen of Vogt's sentences. Should it occur that in Vogt's original the stylistic rubble prevents the light from falling right on the slander, Zabel clears away the rubble. For example, *Vogt* talks of

"compromising people at home in Germany in such a way that *they could no longer resist the attempts to blackmail them* and were forced to pay money".

According to *Zabel,* however, this reads:

"compromising people in such a way that they were forced to pay money".

Elsewhere Zabel *alters* anything that appears to him to be *ambiguous* in Vogt's unstylish mess. Thus *Vogt:*

"they were forced to pay money so that the gang should preserve the secret of *their* having been compromised".

Whereas in *Zabel:*

"so that the gang should preserve their secret *without* compromising [them]".

Finally, *Zabel* interpolates entire sentences of his *own* invention, such as:

"The Brimstone Gang maintained a frightfully strict discipline among its supporters" and "they"—namely *"the fellows who continued the work of the 'Rheinische Zeitung' among the refugees"*—"**they became the confederates of the secret police in France and Germany**."

Thus of the four passages regarded by me as libellous three stem *from Zabel on Zabel's own admission,* while the fourth alleged "quotation", although containing quotations, is *not a quotation,* and even less is it *"merely a quotation",* as the *Municipal Court* maintains, and least of all is it a quotation *"from other persons"* in the plural, as the same *Municipal Court* contends. Conversely, among all Zabel's *"statements and assertions"* about me there is not *a single line* of "criticism and appraisal" ("legitimate" or "illegitimate").

But even supposing that *the actual assumption of the Municipal Court* is as true as it is false; even supposing that *Zabel's* libellous statements about me were merely *quotations*, would the *Municipal Court* because of this circumstance be *legally justified* in *forbidding* me to bring an *action* against *F. Zabel?* On the contrary, in a "ruling" handed down by the **Royal Prussian High Court** which we shall give *in extenso*, we find that

> "It would **not** *affect* the situation as laid down in §156 of the Penal Code if the facts set out in the aforementioned articles turned out to be *the author's own assertions* or **quotations** from the assertions of third persons."

So whether he quotes or not, "democrat" Zabel remains responsible for his "assertions". The *Municipal Court* has already *declared* that Zabel published assertions about me which are in themselves "punishable"; *but* these assertions are **quotations** and **hence** unassailable. Away with this pretext, which is *legally untenable*, cries the **High Court**. So finally I shall be able to lay hands on Zabel; the doors of the law will open, *Italiam, Italiam!*[a]

My lawyer appealed from the *Municipal Court* to the *High Court* and on *July 11, 1860* he received the following *"ruling"*:

> "In the leading articles published in Nos. 37 and 41 of the *National-Zeitung* on January 22 and 25 of this year under the titles 'Karl Vogt and the *Allgemeine Zeitung*' and 'How Radical Pamphlets Are Made', a libel on the plaintiff Dr. Karl Marx of London cannot be found. Even though it would not affect the situation as laid down in §156 of the Penal Code if the facts set out in the aforementioned articles turned out to be the author's own assertions or the assertions of third persons, it would be wrong to restrict the right of the press to subject the activities of the parties and the published expression of their disagreements to analysis and criticism, insofar as the form of the polemic does not indicate an *intention to insult.* In the present case this intention *cannot be presumed to exist.*
>
> "In the aforementioned articles light is thrown above all on the conflict that prevailed between the views of Dr. Karl Vogt, on the one hand, and the Augsburg *Allgemeine Zeitung*, on the other, concerning the support expressed for the interests of the Italians and for the interests of Austria on the occasion of the recent war; in this context the intervention of the so-called *German emigration* in London on the side of the Augsburg *Allgemeine Zeitung* and against Vogt, as well as some of the *factional quarrels* and the machinations of these refugees among themselves, are also discussed!

---

[a] Virgil, *The Aeneid,* Book III.— *Ed.*

"If in the course of these discussions the relations of *the plaintiff* to these parties and his partial involvement in their aspirations and in particular his efforts to assist the Augsburg '*Allgemeine Zeitung*' *in its polemic* against Vogt by supplying it with evidence are drawn into the debate, the relevant allegations concerning this involvement which are contained in the two articles are *not so much refuted as the plaintiff intended, but rather confirmed* by the facts *which he himself includes in his complaint.* If on the other hand he goes on to assert that he is *identified, in a defamatory manner,* with those political activities, on which the articles in question admittedly pass severe strictures, referring to them as *eccentric,* and even unprincipled and *dishonourable,* this assertion cannot be regarded as substantiated. *For* when the first article *quotes* from Vogt's account: 'that the refugees of 1849 gradually congregated in London, where they revered the above mentioned Marx as their visible leader'; and refers to a letter by Techow: 'in which we see how Marx, puffed up with Napoleonic pride in his intellectual superiority, rules the members of the Brimstone Gang with a rod of iron'—what we have here is in essence only a description of what Vogt calls the 'Brimstone Gang', and not an invective against Marx, who is portrayed rather as a restraining influence and intellectually superior. Least of all is his person associated with those people who are accused of blackmail and denunciation. Likewise, in the second article, it is nowhere stated that the plaintiff ascribed the authorship of the pamphlet *Zur Warnung* to the abovementioned Blind *against his better knowledge,* and that he *knowingly* sent false testimonies of third persons to that effect to the Augsburg *Allgemeine Zeitung.* However, the fact that the testimony of the compositor Vögele was disputed is conceded by the plaintiff himself in his complaint when he cites the conflicting statements by Hollinger, the printer, and Wiehe, the compositor. Furthermore, on his own admission a certain Schaible later disclosed that he was the author of the pamphlet, and he did this moreover only *after* the two articles in the *National-Zeitung* had appeared.

"The appeal of the 21st of last month against the negative ruling of the Royal Municipal Court of the 8th of the same month is adjudged to be without foundation and is therefore dismissed. Twenty-five silver groschen in costs for assessing the unfounded appeal are to be paid to the Treasury of the local Municipal Court without delay on pain of distraint.

"Berlin, July 11, 1860

Criminal Senate of the Royal High Court
Second Division
Guthschmidt Schultze

"To D. Phil. Karl Marx c/o Legal
Counsellor Weber"

When I first received this "*ruling*" from my lawyer, I did not notice the address and conclusion on the first reading and, unfamiliar as I am with Prussian law, I imagined that I had been sent a copy of the *defence* handed in to the High Court by "democrat" F. Zabel. I said to myself that what Zabel had to say about "the views" (see Appendix 15) "of Dr. Karl Vogt and the Augsburg *Allgemeine Zeitung*", and about "the interests of the Italians and the interests of the Austrians", all this must have accidentally strayed into his petition from a leading article intended for the *National-Zeitung*.

In any event, "democrat" F. Zabel does not mention in so much
as a *single syllable* either these views or those interests in the four
columns that concern *me* in his two leading articles (which
themselves amount to hardly six columns). In his petition Zabel
says that I

"assisted the Augsburg *Allgemeine Zeitung* in its *polemic* against Vogt by
supplying it with evidence".

He refers to *Vogt's legal action against the "Allgemeine Zeitung"*
as the *polemic of the "Allgemeine Zeitung" against Vogt*. If legal action and polemic were identical things why should I require the
permission of the Public Prosecutor, the Municipal Court, the
High Court, etc., for my "polemic" against Zabel? And Zabel even
asserts that the "relevant allegations" in his two leading articles
concerning my relations with the *Allgemeine Zeitung* were "*not so
much* refuted as I had intended, *but rather confirmed* by the facts I
had myself included". Not so much—but rather! In *jus*[a] it must be
either-or. And what "relevant allegations" were made by Zabel?

The "relevant allegations" in Zabel's leading article No. 1
concerning my relations with the *Allgemeine Zeitung* were as
follows:

1. Liebknecht became correspondent for the *Allgemeine Zeitung*
on the strength of a reference which I had given him officially. I
declared, in my complaint, that Zabel was lying, but thought it
unnecessary to advance any further "facts" on such an absurdity.
2. According to Zabel I sent a "legal document" to the *Allgemeine
Zeitung* from London on October 29, which in fact had been in
the possession of the Augsburg District Court on October 24, and
he found this "allegation" confirmed by the "facts" produced by
me! From the facts I had advanced in my complaint, Zabel could
indeed see that, quite apart from any political motives, it had
become necessary for me to send in a document relating to *the
origins* of the pamphlet *Zur Warnung,* because Vogt had *publicly*
attempted to saddle me with the authorship of it even before the
institution of legal proceedings. 3. Zabel's "allegation" that I was
one of the correspondents of the *Allgemeine Zeitung* was refuted
by me with the aid of authentic documents. Zabel's *leading article
No. 2,* "How Radical Pamphlets Are Made", contained, as shown
earlier on, no "allegations" concerning my relations with the
Allgemeine Zeitung, other than the "allegation" that I myself had
fabricated the pamphlet, that I had then laid it at Blind's door and

---

a Law.— *Ed.*

tried to prove that it was his work by means of Vögele's false testimony. Were all these "relevant allegations not so much refuted as I had intended, but rather confirmed by the facts included 'in my complaint'"? Zabel himself admits the opposite.

Could Zabel have known that Schaible had written the pamphlet *Zur Warnung*? Did Zabel have to believe that compositor Vögele's testimony, which on my own admission was "disputed", was in fact correct? But where in the world have I laid down that Zabel must have this knowledge or that belief? My complaint refers "rather" to Zabel's "relevant allegation" that I "*fabricated* the pamphlet and made it *look* as if *he*" (Blind) "had concocted it" and that I later used Vögele's testimony to try and prove that it was Blind's work.

Finally, I came across an argument in Zabel's defence which at least looked interesting.

"If on the other hand he" (the plaintiff Marx) "goes on to assert that he is *identified,* in a *defamatory* manner, with those political activities" (of the Brimstone Gang), "on which the articles in question" (Zabel's leading articles) "admittedly pass severe strictures, referring to them as *eccentric,* and even *unprincipled* and *dishonourable,* this assertion cannot be regarded as substantiated... *Least of all is his person associated with those people who are accused of blackmail and denunciation.*" [a]

Zabel is manifestly not one of those Romans of whom it is said: "*memoriam quoque cum voce perdidissimus.*" [b] He has lost his memory, but not his tongue. He transforms not just brimstone but the Brimstone Gang from its crystalline state into a liquid and from a liquid into a gas, and he uses the red gas to throw dust in my eyes.[c] The Brimstone Gang, he claims, is a "party" with whose "activities" he has never "*identified*" me, and with whose "blackmail and denunciations" he never even associated people "associated" with me. It is essential to convert this sulphurous gas back into the original flowers of sulphur.

In *leading article No. 1 (National-Zeitung, No. 37, 1860)* Zabel opens his "relevant allegations" about the *Brimstone Gang* by describing "*Marx*" as its "visible leader". The second member of the Brimstone Gang whom he alludes to "to fill in the picture", but does not name, is Frederick Engels. He refers in particular to the letter in which Techow reports on his meeting with Fr. Engels, K. Schramm and myself. Zabel draws attention to the two last as illustrations of the "Brimstone Gang". Immediately after he mentions *Cherval* as a London emissary. Then it is Liebknecht's turn.

---

[a] See this volume, p. 283.— *Ed.*

[b] "We lost our memories along with our vices" (Tacitus, *Vita Julii Agricolae*).— *Ed.*

[c] Marx puns on *roter Dampf* (red gas) and *blauen Dunst vormachen* (literally: to produce blue smoke; figuratively: to throw dust in someone's eyes).— *Ed.*

"This Liebknecht, *in nomine omen*,[a] one of the most servile supporters of *Marx*....
Immediately after his arrival Liebknecht took up service with *Marx*, and his labours
were to the complete satisfaction of his master."

"*Ohly*", who marches directly behind Liebknecht, is "**likewise** a
channel of the Brimstone Gang". Finally, "another London
accomplice, Biscamp". All these details follow in quick succession in
leading article No. 1, but at the end of leading article No. 2 yet
another member of the Brimstone Gang is named, *W. Wolff*—
"Parliamentary Wolf, alias Casemate Wolf"—who had been
entrusted with the vital mission of "sending out circulars".
According to Zabel's "relevant allegations", then, the *Brimstone
Gang* consists of: Marx, leader of the Brimstone Gang; F. Engels,
illustration of the Brimstone Gang; Cherval, London emissary of
the Brimstone gang; Liebknecht, "one of the most servile
supporters of Marx"; Ohly, "**likewise** a channel of the Brimstone
Gang"; Biscamp, "*another*" London "accomplice"; lastly, Wolff,
the Brimstone Gang's writer of circulars.

In his first 51 lines Zabel makes this miscellaneously constituted
Brimstone Gang figure variously under the *names*: "Brimstone
Gang or Bristlers", "fellows who continued the *work of the*
Rheinische Zeitung among the refugees", the "*proletarians*" or, as
we find in leading article No. 2, "the 'proletarian' party under
Marx".

So much for the personnel and the names of the Brimstone
Gang. In his "relevant allegations" Zabel gives a brief and
impressive account of its *organisation.* "*Marx*" is the "*leader*". The
"*Brimstone Gang*" itself comprises the circle of his "*close*"
supporters or, as Zabel says in his second leading article, "*the Marx
party in the narrower sense*". Zabel even provides a touchstone for
defining "*the Marx party in the narrower sense*". A member of the
Marx party in the narrower sense must have seen Biscamp at least
once in his life.

"He" (Blind), Zabel writes in leading article No. 2, "he declares that he has
never seen Biscamp in the whole of his life. He is *obviously not a member of* **the
Marx party in the narrower sense**."

The "Marx party in the narrower sense", or the Brimstone
Gang proper, is therefore the aristocracy of the gang, not to be
confused with the third category, the mass of "*supporters*" or "this
carefully nurtured *class of loafers*". So first comes leader Marx,
then the "Brimstone Gang" proper, or "the Marx party in the

---

[a] The name says everything. *Lieb-knecht*—dear servant.— *Ed.*

narrower sense", and lastly, the mass of "supporters" or the "class of loafers". The Brimstone Gang, subdivided into these three categories, enjoys a truly Spartan discipline. "The *Brimstone Gang*," says Zabel, "maintained a frightfully strict discipline among its *supporters*." While at the same time "*Marx* ... rules the members of the *Brimstone Gang* with a rod of iron". It is obvious that in such a well-organised "gang" as this, its characteristic "activities", its "chief occupations", the deeds the gang carries out qua gang, all take place on the orders of its leader and they are explicitly presented by Zabel as the actions of this leader with his rod of iron. And what was, if we may use the term, the official occupation of the gang?

"One of the chief occupations of the Brimstone Gang was to compromise people at home in Germany in such a way that they were forced to pay money so that the gang should preserve their secret without compromising them. Not just one, but hundreds of letters were written to people in Germany, threatening to denounce them for complicity in this or that act of revolution unless a certain sum of money had been received at a specified address by a given date.... The reputation of anyone who opposed **these** intrigues was ruined, not just among the refugees, but also by means of the press. The 'proletarians' filled the columns of the reactionary press in Germany with *their denunciations* of those democrats who did not subscribe to their views; they became the *confederates* of the secret police in France and Germany, etc." (*National-Zeitung*, No. 37.)[a]

After beginning the "relevant allegations" about the Brimstone Gang with the observation that I was its "visible leader", and after listing its "chief occupations", namely blackmail, denunciation, etc., Zabel concludes his general description of the Brimstone Gang with the words:

"...*They became the confederates of the secret police in France and Germany.* To *fill in* the picture Vogt publishes a letter by Techow, a former lieutenant, dated August 26, 1850 ... in which we see how *Marx, puffed up with Napoleonic pride in his intellectual superiority, rules the members of the Brimstone Gang with a rod of iron.*"

Having caused me to be "revered" as the "visible leader" of the Brimstone Gang in his introductory remarks, Zabel fears that the reader might imagine that behind the visible leader there was an invisible one, or that, like the Dalai Lama, I was content to be "revered". So at the end of his description he transforms me (in *his* words, not *Vogt*'s) from the merely "visible" leader into the leader who wields a rod of iron, from the Dalai Lama into the Napoleon of the "Brimstone Gang". And it is precisely this remark that he cites in his petition as *proof* that he does *not* "*identify*" me with the "political activities" of the Brimstone Gang,

---

[a] Here and below cf. this volume, pp. 260-61.— *Ed.*

on which "severe strictures are passed" and which are "referred to as *eccentric*, and even *unprincipled* and *dishonourable*". Of course he doesn't! Or not entirely! He does "*identify*" me with them, but *not* "in a *defamatory manner*". "Rather" he has done me the *honour* of appointing me the Napoleon of blackmailers, threatening-letter writers, *mouchards, agents provocateurs*, forgers, etc. Zabel clearly takes his conception of honour from the vocabulary of the *December Gang*. Hence the epithet "Napoleonic". But I am taking him to court because of this very *honour* he has shown me! With the "facts" adduced in my complaint I have **proved**, and proved so decisively that Zabel absolutely refuses to follow me to any public court, **proved** that all his "relevant allegations" about the Brimstone Gang are Vogtian inventions and lies, and that Zabel only "quotes" them in order to be able to "*honour*" me as the Napoleon of this Brimstone Gang. But am I not depicted by him as "a restraining influence and intellectually superior"? Does he not describe me as maintaining *discipline* in the gang? He himself explains what this restraint, this superiority and this *discipline* consisted in.

"The Brimstone Gang maintained a *frightfully strict discipline* among its supporters. Anyone who sought in any way to secure a decent living in the bourgeois world was branded a traitor to the revolution merely for attempting to become independent.... With the aid of rumours, letters, etc., dissension, brawling and duels were fomented in this carefully nurtured class of loafers, etc."

But Zabel is not content with this *general description* of the "political activities" of the Brimstone Gang with which he has honourably "identified" me.

Liebknecht, a "notorious member of the Marx party", "one of the most servile supporters of Marx, whose labours were to the complete satisfaction of his master", intentionally compromises the workers in Switzerland with the "revolutionary congress in Murten" and joyfully "leads" them "into the arms" of the waiting "gendarmes". "In the Cologne trial the authorship of the forged minute-book was attributed to this Liebknecht." (Zabel omits to add, of course, that this lie of Stieber's was publicly *shown* to be a lie of Stieber's during the actual proceedings.) *Wolff*, the former co-editor of the *Neue Rheinische Zeitung*, is accused of sending "a circular to the proletarians" from London and at the same time "allowing it to fall into the hands of the Hanover police".

While Zabel thus presents people who are "notoriously" connected with me as agents of the secret police, on the one hand, he also connects me with a "notorious" secret police agent, *agent provocateur* and forger, namely Cherval, on the other. Immediately following his general description of the Brimstone Gang he makes "a number of people" including *Cherval* travel from London to Paris "in the double role of revolutionary seducers of workers and confederates of the secret police" and bring about the "so-called communist trial", etc. In leading article No. 2 he takes up the story:

"In this way a conspiracy of the most infamous sort was devised in 1852 which involved the manufacture of counterfeit paper money on a massive scale (**see Vogt for further details**), etc."

Now if the reader of the *National-Zeitung* carries out Zabel's peremptory instructions and *sees for further details in Vogt*, what does he find? He finds that Cherval was sent by me to Geneva where under my direct orders he set in motion "the most infamous conspiracy involving counterfeit paper money", etc. The reader, referred by Zabel to Vogt, will further find this:

"However, the personal involvement of Marx is quite irrelevant in this context, for, as we have already remarked, *it is a matter of complete indifference whether Marx does something himself or has it done by a member of his gang; his control over his people is absolute.*"

But Zabel could not rest content even with this. At the end of his two leading articles he felt impelled to whisper a final word into the ear of his readers. He says:

"He" (Blind) "declares at the same time that he has never seen Biscamp in the whole of his life. He is obviously not a member of the *Marx party in the narrower sense. It appears to us* that the latter" (i.e. the Marx party in the narrower sense) "did not find it too difficult to turn him" (Blind) "into a scapegoat.... The *Marx party* could very easily saddle Blind with the authorship of the pamphlet because ... he had expressed similar views to those contained in it in conversation with *Marx* and in an article in *The Free Press*. By making use of Blind's assertions and turns of phrase *the pamphlet could be fabricated* and made to look as if *he*" (Blind) "had concocted it."

Hence *"the Marx party"* or *"the Marx party in the narrower sense"* alias the Brimstone Gang "fabricated" the pamphlet so that it looked as if Blind had concocted it? Having unfolded this hypothesis Zabel summarised its implications in the following laconic words: "*Anybody is now at liberty* **to regard** *either* **Marx** or *Blind* **as its author**."

Thus it is not the Marx party or Blind, and not even Blind or the Marx party in the narrower sense, *vulgo* Brimstone Gang, but Blind or Marx, *Marx sans phrase*. Hence the Marx party, the Marx party in the narrower sense, the Brimstone Gang, etc., were merely pantheistic names for *Marx,* the person Marx. Zabel not only *"identifies"* Marx with the "party" of the Brimstone Gang, he *personifies* the Brimstone Gang in Marx. And the *selfsame* Zabel has the effrontery to assert before a court that, in his leading articles, he did not *"identify* the plaintiff" Marx with the "activities" of the Brimstone Gang in a "defamatory manner". With his hand on his heart he swears that *"least of all"* has he "associated" my "person with those people" whom he "accuses of blackmail and denunciation"! What a figure Zabel will cut in the public session of the court, I thought to myself. What a figure indeed! With this consoling exclamation, I turned once more to the document I had received from my lawyer and read it through again, vaguely noticing that it was signed by some such names as Müller and Schultze.[a] But I soon discovered my error. What I had in my hands was not Zabel's proposed petition, but—a *"ruling"* handed down by the *High Court* over the signatures of *Guthschmidt and Schultze,* a ruling that refused me the *right to proceed with my action* against Zabel, and, to cap it all, by way of punishing me for my "complaint" it ordered me to pay 25 silver groschen to the Treasury of the Berlin Municipal Court without delay, on pain of distraint. I was indeed *attonitus.*[b] However, on carefully reading the *"ruling"* once more my astonishment faded away.

Example I

Zabel prints in the leading article of the *"National-Zeitung"*, No. 37, 1860:	Messrs. Guthschmidt and Schultze read in the leading article of the *"National-Zeitung"*, No. 37, 1860:

Zabel prints in the leading article of the *"National-Zeitung"*, No. 37, 1860:

"Vogt reports on p. 136 et seq.: Among the refugees of 1849 the term Brimstone Gang, or the name Bristlers, referred to a number of people who, originally scattered throughout Switzerland, France and England, gradually congregated in London, where they revered Herr Marx as their visible leader."

Messrs. Guthschmidt and Schultze read in the leading article of the *"National-Zeitung"*, No. 37, 1860:

"For when the first article *quotes* from Vogt's account: 'that the *refugees of 1849* gradually congregated in London, where they revered the above mentioned Marx as their visible leader'".

Zabel says: Among the refugees of 1849 *the term Brimstone Gang, or the name Bristlers,* referred to *a number of people, etc.,* who gradually congregated in London, where they revered myself as their visible leader. Messrs. *Guthschmidt* and *Schultze,* however, make Zabel say: *The refugees of 1849 gradually congregated in London* (which is not even true since a large proportion of the refugees congregated in Paris, New York, Jersey, etc.) where they revered me as their visible leader, an honour which I have not

---

[a] The names of two philistines, the characters of many skits and jokes in the satirical journal *Kladderadatsch.—Ed.*

[b] Thunderstruck.—*Ed.*

received, nor is it imputed to me by either Zabel or Vogt. Now Messrs. *Guthschmidt and Schultze* are by no means giving a summary, they *quote in inverted commas* a sentence *nowhere* printed by Zabel as if it were *quoted* by Zabel in his first article "from Vogt's account". Messrs. *Guthschmidt and Schultze* evidently had before them a *secret edition* of No. 37 of the *National-Zeitung,* known neither to me nor the public. This must be the explanation of all these misunderstandings.

This *secret edition* of No. 37 of the *National-Zeitung* differs from the vulgar edition of the same issue not just by a *different formulation* of particular sentences. The *entire context* of the first leading article in the *vulgar edition* has nothing but a few words in common with its context in the *secret edition.*

Example II

Having appointed me the leader of the Brimstone Gang, Zabel goes on to say in No. 37 of the "National-Zeitung":
"These fellows" (the Brimstone Gang) "...continued the work of the *Rheinische Zeitung* among the refugees.... One of the chief occupations of the Brimstone Gang was to compromise people at home in Germany in such a way that they were forced to pay money.... The 'proletarians' filled the columns of the reactionary press in Germany with their denunciations ... they became the confederates of the secret police in France and Germany. To *fill in* the picture" (of the "Brimstone Gang" or "proletarians") "Vogt publishes a letter by Techow ... in which the principles, the *activities,* etc., of the 'proletarians' are described, and in which we see how Marx, puffed up with Napoleonic pride in his intellectual superiority, rules the members of the Brimstone Gang with a rod of iron."

After Zabel has appointed me the leader of the refugees of 1849, Messrs. Guthschmidt and Schultze read in No. 37 of the "National-Zeitung":
"and when it" (the first article in the *National-Zeitung*) "*goes on* to refer to a letter by Techow, 'in which we see how Marx, puffed up with Napoleonic pride in his intellectual superiority, rules the members of the Brimstone Gang with a rod of iron'".

Given that judges have the legal authority to grant or refuse private individuals the right to bring an action, it is clear that Messrs. *Guthschmidt and Schultze* were not only justified in refusing me the right to sue Zabel, they were obliged to do so. For the context of the leading article in No. 37 of the *secret edition* of the *National-Zeitung,* which they reproduce *in nuce,*[a] flatly precludes

---

[a] In brief.—*Ed.*

any *corpus delicti.* For what in fact does Zabel say in this *secret edition*? In the first place he confers on me the undeserved honour of causing me to be "revered" as the "visible leader" by the entire community of refugees living in London in 1849. And why should I wish to *"bring an action"* against him for that? And secondly, he does me the no less undeserved honour of making me "rule with a rod of iron" over a *Brimstone Gang* without connecting me with that gang in any other way whatever, more or less as I had ruled over Zabel and his companions in 1848-49. And what is there in that to make me *"bring an action"* against Zabel?

It is obvious what confusions can arise when the law permits officials of the judiciary to *"give a ruling"* and *"rule"* in secret on the question of whether or not someone has the right to bring an action against another person, e.g. for libel in the *National-Zeitung.* The plaintiff *sues* on the basis of a vulgar edition of No. 37 of the *National-Zeitung* of which perhaps 10,000 copies are available to the public, and the judge bases his *ruling* on a secret edition of the same issue produced *for him alone.* So little care is taken in this procedure to preserve the identity even of the *corpus delicti.*

By making the right of private individuals to bring an action dependent on a judicial permit in each particular case, Prussian law proceeds from the assumption that the state is a paternal authority which must regulate and act as guardian over the civil existence of its children. But even from the standpoint of Prussian law the "ruling" of the *High Court* seems strange. The intention of Prussian law is evidently to prevent the bringing of frivolous actions and therefore, if I understand its spirit correctly, and if I am right in assuming that its aim is not the systematic refusal of justice, it gives the judge the right to refuse permission for a case to proceed, but only if the *complaint* is *prima facie*[a] *unfounded,* if the suit appears frivolous on the face of it. Is that the case in the present instance? The *Municipal Court* concedes that Zabel's leading articles *in fact* contain "defamatory" and hence "punishable" statements about me. It only places *F. Zabel* beyond the reach of my legal vengeance because *F. Zabel* has *"merely quoted"* his libels. The *High Court* declares: defamatory statements are equally punishable by law whether they are quoted or not quoted, but it goes on to *deny* for its part that Zabel's leading articles contain any defamatory statements about myself whether quoted or unquoted. Thus the *Municipal Court* and the *High Court* have not merely *divergent,* but directly *conflicting* views of the *facts of the case.* The

---

a At first view.— *Ed.*

one finds defamatory statements about me where the other fails to do so. The *contradictory* judicial findings about the *facts of the case* demonstrate clearly that *prima facie* there are *grounds* for complaint. If Papinian and Ulpian say: This printed statement is defamatory; and if Mucius Scaevola and Manilius Brutus assert the opposite: This printed statement is not defamatory, what will the nation of quirites [233] think? Why should the people not believe with Ulpian and Papinian that Zabel had in fact published defamatory statements about me in Nos. 37 and 41 of the *National-Zeitung*? And if I assure the nation of the quirites that Mucius Scaevola and Manilius Brutus have given me a secret certificate stating that Zabel's *"defamatory"* statements and assertions in no way referred to my person, the nation of the quirites will undoubtedly shrug their shoulders and say: *à d'autres.*[a]

Since the *High Court* is the final court of appeal as far as the *facts of a case* are concerned, in this case therefore it was the court of last instance that had to decide whether Zabel's two leading articles *in fact* contained defamatory statements about me and whether the intention to insult was present; and since the *High Court* denies that the *facts of the case* provided sufficient grounds for action, a further appeal to the **Supreme Tribunal** could only relate to the question whether the *substantive findings* of the High Court were not based on an *error in law*. In its *"ruling"* the *High Court* had **established** that Zabel had accused the *Brimstone Gang* of "unprincipled and dishonourable activities", "denunciations and blackmail", the same Brimstone Gang that in the same leading article the same Zabel had expressly described as *"the Marx party"*, or *"the Marx party in the narrower sense"*, with "Marx" as its visible "leader", ruling it with a rod of iron. Was the High Court within its *legal* rights in not regarding this as an insult to me? My lawyer, Counsellor *Weber,* comments on the question as follows in his submission to the *Supreme Tribunal*:

"It is true that it is nowhere stated in so many words" (by Zabel) "that Marx had extorted or forged money, or denounced anybody. But is anything more explicit required than the statement: Marx was the leader of a party which was engaged in the above-mentioned criminal and immoral activities? No sensible and unprejudiced person can deny that the leader of an association whose purpose and chief activities consist in the execution of crimes, not only condones these activities, but initiates and organises them and enjoys their fruits. And this leader is, unquestionably, doubly responsible, both as participant and as the intellectual inspiration, even if it cannot be proved in any particular instance that he was actually implicated in a specific act of crime. *The view expressed in the disputed ruling"* (of the High Court) *"would imply that a man's good name was utterly at the*

---

[a] Tell us another one.— *Ed.*

mercy of anyone who wished to discredit him. Instead of fraudulently asserting that A. had committed murder, a would-be slanderer would need only to say that somewhere or other a gang was engaged in committing murder and that A. was the leader of the gang. The view expressed by the High Court grants this slanderer complete impunity. According to the correct view, however, the same punishment for slander should be imposed on the slanderer irrespective of whether he falsely accuses a man of being a robber or a robber-chief."

From the standpoint of ordinary *common sense* a libel has undoubtedly been committed. Does it also exist in the *view of Prussian law*? The High Court says no, my lawyer says yes. If the High Court has ruled, contrary to the Municipal Court, that the *form of a quotation* should not grant *immunity* to a libeller, why should not the Supreme Tribunal rule, contrary to the High Court, that the libeller is *not protected* by the *"tapeworm"* form? My lawyer appealed to the **Supreme Tribunal**, hence so to speak to the *Areopagus* itself, on this *legal point,* on the argument that there had been an *error in law* on the part of the High Court in its appraisal of the facts of the case. The *Supreme Tribunal "ruled"*:

"I. Your appeal of August 23 of this year against the ruling on July 11 of this year of the Criminal Senate of the Royal High Court in the action for libel brought by Dr. K. Marx against Dr. Zabel, editor of the *National-Zeitung,* is hereby dismissed as without foundation after consideration of the relevant documents. II. For the Royal High Court did not find an objective defamation of the plaintiff in the two leading articles of the *National-Zeitung* in question, nor did it find that there was an intention to insult the plaintiff. It was right, therefore, to refuse permission to proceed with the proposed action for libel. The question whether there is an objective act of defamation, or an intention to insult, essentially pertains to matters of fact and the conclusions regarding them can only be disputed by appeal to the Royal Supreme Tribunal if the decision of the Appeal judge is based on an error in law. III. However, such an error is not evident in the present instance. IV. The costs of this ruling are to be borne by you and for this purpose 25 silver groschen should be deposited with the Treasury of the local Royal Municipal Court within a week.

"*Berlin,* October 5, 1860

Royal Supreme Tribunal, *von Schlickmann*

"To Legal Counsellor *Weber* in Berlin"

For the sake of clarity I have numbered the various sections of the *"ruling"* of the *Supreme Tribunal.*

Sub I. Herr *von Schlickmann* states that the appeal against the High Court has been *"dismissed".* *Sub* II. Herr *von Schlickmann* informs us of the respective spheres of competence of the High Court and the Supreme Tribunal—evidently a didactic digression irrelevant to the matter in hand. *Sub* IV. Herr Weber is ordered to pay the sum of 25 silver groschen into the Treasury of the Berlin

Municipal Court within a week. This is a *consequence* of the "ruling", but certainly not its *reason*.

Where then is the "dismissal" of the appeal *substantiated*? Where is the answer to the very detailed case set out by my lawyer? It is:

Sub III. "However, such an error is **not** *evident* in the present instance."

If we strike out the little word *not* from this sentence *sub* III, the explanation reads: "However, such an error is *evident* in the present instance." And this of course would overturn the ruling of the High Court. Thus this ruling is sustained only by the word *"not"* with which Herr *von Schlickmann* "dismisses" in the name of the Supreme Tribunal the appeal put forward by Counsellor Weber.

Αὐτότατος ἔφη.[a] *Not!* Herr *von Schlickmann* does *not* refute the legal objections raised by my lawyer; he does *not* discuss them; he does *not* even *mention* them. Of course, Herr *von Schlickmann* had reasons enough for his "ruling", but he fails to state them. *Not!* The demonstrative force of this little word lies entirely in the authority of the man who utters it, in the position he holds in the hierarchy. In itself "not" proves nothing. *Not!* Αὐτότατος ἔφη.

Thus the *Supreme Tribunal* too **forbade** me to **bring an action** against "democrat" **F. Zabel.**

Thus ended *my lawsuit with the Prussian courts.*

---

[a] He himself hath spoken (the words are attributed to the disciples of Pythagoras).— *Ed.*

XII

APPENDICES

1. SCHILY'S EXPULSION FROM SWITZERLAND

A letter from Schily about his expulsion from Switzerland which exemplifies the treatment meted out to non-parliamentary refugees[234] can unfortunately only be printed in extract, owing to lack of space. The letter begins by recounting how two German refugees, B. and I.,[a] both friends of Schily, left Geneva, were arrested during their journey through Switzerland and, having been liberated by Druey, returned again to *Geneva*.

"At their request," Schily continues, "I went to Fazy to find out whether anyone was looking for them and he reassured me by saying that there was no reason at Cantonal level to disturb their incognito and that no inquiries about them had reached him at Federal level either. I would do well, however, to have an interview with the *chef du département de justice et de police*, M. Girard, mentioning his name and what he had told me. This I did, with more or less the same success and leaving my address behind in case there were any Federal inquiries. A few weeks later I was visited by a police officer who requested me to give him the address of B. and I. I refused, hurried around to the aforementioned Girard and upon being threatened by him with expulsion unless I gave him the address, I explained to him that according to our previous agreement I could be appealed to as an *intermédiaire*, but not as a *dénonciateur*. To which he replied: 'Vous avez l'air de vouloir vous interposer comme ambassadeur entre moi et ces réfugiés, pour traiter de puissance à puissance.'[b] I replied: 'Je n'ai pas l'ambition d'être accrédité ambassadeur près de vous.'[c] And in fact I was then dismissed without any of the ceremony to which ambassadors are entitled. On my way home I learnt that B. and I. had just been discovered, and that they had been arrested and led off, so that I could regard Girard's threat as superseded by events. But I had reckoned without April 1, for on this ominous day in 1852 I was requested by a police officer, in the middle of the street, to accompany him to the Hôtel de Ville, where some questions

---

a Elard Biscamp and Peter Imandt.— *Ed.*

b "It looks as if you would like to act the ambassador between me and these refugees, to mediate as between equal powers."— *Ed.*

c "I have no ambition to become an ambassador accredited to you."— *Ed.*

were to be put to me. Once arrived there it was explained to me by State Councillor Tourte, the Genevan Commissar for the expulsion of refugees and *ad latus*[a] to Trog, his counterpart at Federal level, who happened to be in Geneva at the time, that I was expelled and that he must send me to Berne without delay; all of this to his greatest regret, since there was no complaint against me at Cantonal level, but the Federal Commissar insisted on my expulsion. To my request to be allowed to see the latter he replied: 'Non, nous ne voulons pas que le commissaire fédéral fasse la police ici.'[b] This statement, of course, contradicted his earlier one and in general he now abandoned his role of Genevan State Councillor, which consisted in resisting Federal demands for expulsion with liberal prudery, in yielding only to force, sometimes also yielding, with pleasure or resignation, to the application of gentle pressure.[c] Another feature of this role was to noise it abroad that the person expelled was a spy and that it had been necessary to remove him in the interests of the 'good cause'.... Thus Tourte told the refugees afterwards that he had had to get rid of me because I was in league with the Federal Commissar, together with whom I had sought to frustrate *his* (Tourte's) measures to protect the refugees, i.e. that I was in league with the same Commissar who, much to *his* regret, had given orders to expel me. *Quelles tartines!*[d] What lies and contradictions! And all for a little *aura popularis!*[e] Of course, wind is what that gentleman uses to keep his balloon airborne. Grand Councillor and State Councillor of Geneva, member of the Swiss Council of States or National Council, a born Counsellor of Confusion, he needs only to become a member of the Federal Council[235] to ensure that Switzerland will enjoy peaceful days in accordance with the saying: *Providentia Dei et confusione hominum Helvetia salva fuit.*"[f]

On arriving in London Schily sent a letter of protest about Tourte's slander to the Genevan *Indépendant,* which was under the influence of *Raisin,* whom we shall mention later, and which had shortly before printed a scathing attack on the assinine slanderous fabrications with which "the liberal *faiseurs*[g] were driving the refugees out of Switzerland". His letter was *not* published.

"From the Hôtel de Ville in Geneva," Schily continues, "I was transferred to gaol, and on the following day I was sent by mail coach to Berne with a police guard. There M. Druey held me in close confinement for two weeks in the so-called Old Tower...."

In his correspondence with the imprisoned Schily, which we shall refer to in due course, *Druey* placed all the guilt on the Canton of Geneva, while for his part Tourte had asserted that the entire responsibility lay with the Federal authorities, since *there was*

---

[a] Assistant.— *Ed.*

[b] "No, we don't want the Federal Commissar playing the policeman here."— *Ed.*

[c] Marx uses English: "gentle pressure".— *Ed.*

[d] What follies!— *Ed.*

[e] Whiff of popularity (a phrase from Cicero's *De haruspicum responso,* 20, 43).— *Ed.*

[f] The providence of God and the confusion of man have been the salvation of Switzerland.— *Ed.*

[g] Busybodies.— *Ed.*

no complaint against him on the part of the Canton of Geneva. He had received a similar assurance shortly before from *Raisin,* the Genevan examining magistrate. Schily has this to say, among other things, about the latter gentleman:

"On the occasion of the Federal Shooting Competition which was held in Geneva in the summer of 1851, *Raisin* had taken over the editorship of the *Journal du tir fédéral,* which appeared in French and German. He engaged me to work on the paper, promising me a fee of 300 francs in exchange for which I was supposed *inter alia* to record *flagrante delicto*[a] the opening and closing speeches in German of the President of the Committee Tourte. I owe a debt of gratitude to Tourte for having made my task much easier by his habit of addressing more or less the same enthusiastic words to the various deputations of marksmen, varying his phrases slightly according to whether he was eulogising the Bear of Berne, the Bull of Uri,[b] or other members of the Confederation. In particular, when he would come to the refrain 'But if the moment of danger ever arrives, then we shall, etc.', I would calmly lay down my pen and when *Raisin* asked *why,* I could answer: *c'est le refrain du danger, je le sais par coeur.*[c] Instead of my hard-earned fee of 300 francs, I managed only to extract 100 from *Raisin,* and only with the greatest difficulty although he did open up the prospect of collaborating on a political review he intended to establish in Geneva in order to be independent of all the existing parties and be able to oppose any side and especially the then 'liberal' government of Fazy and Tourte, even though he belonged to it himself. He was the very man for such an enterprise—able, as he used to boast, 'd'arracher la peau à qui que ce soit'....[d] Accordingly, he commissioned me to establish contacts for this journal in the course of a journey through Switzerland which I undertook after my Federal Shooting labours. I did so and on my return I drew up a written report on the results achieved. In the meantime, however, the wind had begun to blow from another direction and he found himself returning full sail from his expedition of piracy into the peaceful harbour of the existing government. *J'en étais donc pour mes frais et honoraires,*[e] for which I vainly pestered him and continue to do so to this day, and have still received nothing even though he is now a wealthy man.... Shortly before my arrest he asserted categorically that there was no question of my being expelled, his friend Tourte had himself assured him that it was not necessary for me to take any preventive measures with regard to Girard's threats, etc. ... In reply to a letter which I sent him *de profundis,*[f] from my old prison tower, asking him for a small instalment of the money he owed me and for an explanation of the incident (my arrest, etc.), he preserved a stubborn silence, even though he assured the person who brought him the message that he would comply with all my requests....

"A few months later I received a letter from K.,[g] a reliable, unprejudiced man, informing me that my expulsion had been the work of the refugee *parliamen-*

---

[a] In the very act of committing an offence.— *Ed.*

[b] An allusion to the arms of the Cantons of Berne and Uri.— *Ed.*

[c] "It is the refrain about danger, I know it by heart."— *Ed.*

[d] "To skin a man alive."— *Ed.*

[e] That was the last I heard of my expenses and fees.— *Ed.*

[f] Literally: out of the depths. Figuratively: from a state of extreme suffering (Psalms 130:1).— *Ed.*

[g] Presumably a letter from Friedrich Kamm written in 1852.— *Ed.*

tarians, and this was confirmed *mordicus*[a] by a few lines written by *Ranickel,* which he enclosed. This view was also confirmed by many experienced observers with whom I later had an opportunity to discuss the matter.... Yet I did not hate the parliamentarians like that hyena *Reinach,* who used to drag the late-lamented Imperial Regent *Vogt,* day after day, from the Imperial tomb to the dinner table in Berne where Vogt sat like the reincarnation of the 'chained Prometheus', and then, *entre poire et fromage,*[b] would savagely devour both his mummy and the reincarnated form to the horror of those present. It is true that I was no admirer of the parliamentarians' deeds, quite the reverse! But is it likely that these gentlemen intended to punish me for this by an Imperial ban—regarding Switzerland as part of the Empire because both the Imperial Constitution[236] and the most recent resolution of the Imperial Diet lie buried there? I think it more likely that the presumption of their persecution of myself is connected with the parliamentary rebellion mentioned in my previous letter[c] against the Geneva Refugee Committee formed by myself, Becker and a number of Genevan citizens.... Why these gentlemen wished to usurp the right to distribute the refugee funds was a matter about which even they differed among themselves. Some of them, among them Dentzel from the little Chamber of Baden, *preferred,* contrary to *our* practice of giving aid above all to penniless workers, to wipe away the tears of professional sufferers, heroes of the revolution, patriotic sons of the nation, who had seen better days.... *Is fecit cui prodest,*[d] as the saying goes in the trade, and since my activities were, it is true, inconvenient to these gentlemen, the suspicion arose that they had made use of their influence in important places to bring about my removal. It was known that they had the *aurem principis*[e] or, at any rate, they were close enough to it to whisper something or other about my *restiveness,* and that *princeps* Tourte especially had frequently gathered them around himself...."

Having described how he was moved from the Old Tower in Berne to Basle and then over the French frontier, Schily continues:

"As far as the expense entailed in expelling refugees is concerned, I cherish the hope that the costs were defrayed not by the Federal Treasury, but by that of the Holy Alliance. For one day a considerable time after our entry into Switzerland, *Princess* **Olga** was sitting at luncheon in a Berne restaurant with the *Russian* chargé d'affaires there.[f] *Entre poire et fromage (sans comparaison* to the terrible *Reinach)* Her Highness remarked to her table companion: 'Eh bien, Monsieur le baron, avez-vous encore beaucoup de réfugiés ici?' 'Pas mal, Princesse,' he replied, 'bien que nous en ayons déjà beaucoup renvoyé. M. Druey fait de son mieux à cet égard, *et si de nouveaux fonds nous arrivent,* nous en renverrons bien encore.'[g] This was overheard and passed on to me by the waiter on duty, a quondam volunteer in the Imperial campaign where he served under my august command."

---

[a] Convincingly.— *Ed.*

[b] Over the dessert.— *Ed.*

[c] Schily's letter of February 8, 1860 (see this volume, pp. 43-46).— *Ed.*

[d] He did it who benefits by it (Seneca, *Medea,* III, 500-01).— *Ed.*

[e] Ear of the authorities.— *Ed.*

[f] Pavel Alexeyevich Krüdener.— *Ed.*

[g] "Well, Baron, are there still many refugees here?" "Quite a few, Your Highness, although we have already sent many of them back. M. Druey does his best in this respect, *and if we receive new funds* we shall be able to send back even more."— *Ed.*

During Schily's removal his travel-effects vanished mysteriously and irretrievably.

"It has remained a mystery to this very day how my effects could have vanished in Le Havre from the chaos of bundles accompanying a German émigré train (into which we had been incorporated in Basle by *Klenk,* the emigration agent, whom the Federal authorities had hired to transport us to Le Havre, with the result that all the luggage belonging to the refugees and emigrants had become hopelessly confused), *unless* it had been achieved *with the aid of a list of the refugees and their baggage.* Perhaps the Swiss Consul in Le Havre, the merchant *Wanner,* to whom we were sent for further transportation, knows more about it. He promised that we would be fully compensated. Druey later confirmed this promise in a letter which I sent to *Advocate Vogt in Berne* to enable him to pursue the matter in the Federal Council. However, I have not been able to get it back from him up to now, *nor have I ever received a reply to any of the letters I wrote to him.* On the other hand, in the summer of 1856 my complaint was rejected by the Federal Council and I was warned to keep the peace, without being given any reasons for this decision....

"All this and all the expulsions involving so many gendarmes, handcuffs, etc., are mere trivia, however, compared to the peculiarly cosy good-neighbourly arrangement of sending home the so-called less serious offenders of the Baden campaign, providing them with special travel passes and directing them to report on their arrival to the local authorities where, instead of being allowed to resume their occupations, as they had been led to expect, they were subjected to all sorts of unexpected penances. The silent sufferings of all those extradited in this way (for extradition is the correct word) are still waiting for their chronicler and avenger.

"The Swiss Tacitus speaking of Switzerland says that it does a man credit 'if his faults may be mentioned without detracting from his greatness'. There is no lack of materials for praise of this kind; to praise Switzerland in this manner does not spoil its figure ... *qui aime bien châtie bien.*[a] And in fact I for my part have an irrepressible love for Switzerland by and large. I like both the country and the people. Keeping a gun as part of his household equipment, always ready and skilful in using it to protect historical traditions of good repute and modern achievements of good quality, the Swiss in my eyes definitely deserves respect. He is entitled to the sympathies of others because he himself feels sympathy for others who struggle to improve their situation. 'I would rather that God had lost his best pair of angels,' a Swiss farmer said in his annoyance at the failure of the South German uprising. He might not have been prepared to risk a team of *his* horses for it, but he would have been more likely to risk his skin and his gun. In his heart of hearts the Swiss is not *neutral,* even if he practises neutrality because of, and in order to preserve, his inherited possessions. Incidentally the old crust of neutrality which cloaks his better nature will probably soon burst asunder with all these foreign feet trampling on it—for that is after all the essence of neutrality—and there will be a big bang and that will clear the air."

Thus far Schily's letter. In the Prison Tower in Berne he was not able to arrange a personal meeting with Druey, but he did manage to exchange letters with that gentleman. In reply to a letter from Schily inquiring into the reasons for his arrest and asking permission to consult his lawyer, Herr Wyss in Berne, Druey wrote on *April 9, 1852:*

---

a He who loves well chastises well.—*Ed.*

"... L'autorité genèvoise a ordonné votre renvoi du Canton, vous a fait arrêter et conduire à Berne à la disposition[a] de mon département, parce que vous vous êtes montré un des réfugiés les plus remuants et que vous avez cherché à cacher I. et B., que vous vous étiez engagé à représenter à l'autorité. Pour ce motif et parce que votre séjour ultérieur en Suisse nuirait *aux relations internationales de la Confédération,* le Conseil fédéral a ordonné votre renvoi du territoire suisse, etc. ... Comme votre arrestation n'a pas pour but un procès criminel ou correctionnel, mais *une mesure de haute politique*[b] ... il n'est pas nécessaire que vous consultiez l'avocat. *D'ailleurs, avant de ... autoriser l'entrevue que vous me demandez avec M. l'avocat Wyss, je désire savoir le but de cette entrevue."* [c]

The letters which Schily was permitted, after numerous complaints, to write to his friends in Geneva had all to be submitted beforehand to M. Druey to inspect. In one of these letters Schily used the expression *"Vae victis".*[237] Druey wrote to him about it in a letter dated *April 19, 1852:*

"Dans le billet que vous avez adressé à M. J.,[d] se trouvent les mots: *vae victis...* Cela veut-il dire que les autorités fédérales vous traitent en vaincu? S'il en était ainsi, ce serait *une accusation mensongère,* contre laquelle je devrais protester." [e]

Schily replied to the mighty Druey in a letter dated *April 21, 1852:*

"Je ne pense pas, M. le conseiller fédéral, que cette manière de caractériser les mesures prises à mon égard puisse me valoir le reproche d'une *accusation mensongère;* du moins un pareil reproche ne serait pas de nature à me faire revenir de l'idée que je suis traité avec dureté; au contraire, adressé à un *prisonnier, par celui qui le tient en prison,* une telle réponse me paraîtrait une dureté de plus." [f]

---

[a] Marx has: "déposition".— *Ed.*

[b] Marx has: "police".— *Ed.*

[c] "...The Genevan authorities have ordered your expulsion from the Canton; they have had you arrested and conducted to Berne and put at the disposition of my department, because you have shown yourself to be one of the most restive of the refugees and have tried to conceal the whereabouts of I. and B., of which you were obliged to inform the authorities. For this reason and because your further residence in Switzerland would have harmed the *international relations of the Confederation,* the Federal Council has resolved on expelling you from Swiss territory, etc. ... Since the purpose of your arrest was not the institution of any criminal or civil action against you, but is *a measure necessitated by considerations of high politics* ... there is no need for you to consult a lawyer. *In any event before ... authorising the interview you request with M. Wyss, your lawyer, I should have to know for what purpose you want to consult him."*— *Ed.*

[d] Abraham Jacoby.— *Ed.*

[e] "The note you have written to M. J. contains the words: *vae victis....* Is that supposed to mean that the Federal authorities treat you as one treats a defeated opponent? If this is the implication, it is *a lying accusation* against which I should feel bound to protest."— *Ed.*

[f] "I do not believe, Federal Councillor, that the way in which I have described the measures taken in my regard can be thought to merit the reproach of making *lying accusations;* at the very least such a reproach is hardly likely to persuade me that I am not being treated harshly; on the contrary, for me *as a prisoner to receive an answer like this from the person who keeps me in prison* seems to be another harsh act."— *Ed.*

Towards the close of *March 1852,* shortly before Schily's arrest
and the deportation of other *unparliamentary* refugees, the
reactionary *Journal de Genève* published all sorts of wild gossip
about communist plots among the German refugees in Geneva:
Herr Trog was said to be busy cleaning out a nest of German
communists with a brood of 84 communist dragons inside it, etc.
Alongside this reactionary Genevan paper a scribbler in Berne
who belonged to the parliamentary gang—it must be assumed that
it was **Karl Vogt** since he repeatedly claims in the "Magnum
Opus" that it was he who had rescued Switzerland from the
clutches of the communist refugees—was busy spreading similar
news in the *Frankfurter Journal* over the initials "ss". For example,
he wrote that the Genevan Committee to aid German refugees, a
committee consisting of communists, had been overthrown because
of its inequitable distribution of the available funds, and that it
had been replaced by upright men (namely parliamentarians) who
would soon put an end to these evil practices. He wrote further
that the dictator of Geneva seemed at last to be prepared to
comply with the ordinances of the Federal Commissars, since two
German refugees belonging to the communist faction had shortly
before been put under arrest and brought from Geneva to Berne,
etc.[238] The *Schweizerische National-Zeitung,* which appears in
Basle, published an answer from Geneva in its issue No. 72, of
March 25, 1852, in which it said *inter alia:*

"Every unbiassed person knows that just as Switzerland is concerned only with
the consolidation and constitutional development of its political achievements, so
too the feeble remnants of the German emigration in this country are occupied
entirely with earning their daily bread and other perfectly harmless pursuits, and
that the fairy-tales about communism are the product of hallucinations on the part
of philistines or else are concocted by politically or personally interested *informers.*"

After the Berne parliamentary correspondent of the *Frankfurter
Journal* had been described as one of these *informers*—the article
concludes:

"The refugees here are of the opinion that in their ranks there are a number of
so-called 'decent men' on the pattern of the former 'Biedermen and Bassermen of
the Empire'[a] who, driven by nostalgia for the flesh-pots of home,[239] seek to pave
the way for their own pardon at the hands of their native rulers by reactionary
expectorations of this kind. We should like to send them our best wishes for a

---

[a] A pun on the names of Friedrich Karl Biedermann and Friedrich Daniel
Bassermann, *Biedermann* means "honest man" and, in an ironical sense, "philistine".
Bassermansch means "homeless tramp" or "beggar".— *Ed.*

speedy departure as they will then cease to compromise the refugees and the government that gives them asylum."

Schily was known to the refugee *parliamentarians* as the author of this article. It appeared in the Basle *National-Zeitung* on *March 25,* and on *April 1* Schily's wholly unmotivated arrest took place. "Tantaene animis caelestibus irae?"[a]

2. THE REVOLUTIONARY CONGRESS IN MURTEN

After the Murten scandal[b] the German refugees in Geneva, with the exception of the refugee *parliamentarians,* issued a protest addressed "To the Supreme Department of Justice and the Police of the Confederation", from which I print the following passage[240]:

"... The monarchs did not rest content with their previous diplomatic gains. They rattled their sabres all around Switzerland and threatened military occupation so as to make a clean sweep of the refugees. The Federal Council at any rate has expressed its concern about this danger in an official document. And lo and behold! There were further deportations, justified this time by the notorious assembly in Murten and the claim that traces of political and propagandistic activities had been uncovered by the investigation following it. As far as the facts are concerned this claim must be categorically rejected.... From the legal point of view, however, it is important to bear in mind that wherever the rule of law obtains, *actions proscribed by the law can only be punished by penalties laid down by the law,* and this holds good for deportation too, if it is not to appear as the arbitrary action of the police. Or was perhaps here too the intention to play off *diplomacy* against us and to say: we have been forced to act thus out of *consideration for foreign powers,* in the interests of international relations? Very well, then, if this is the position, the *cross of the Confederation*[c] should hide its head in shame before the *Turkish crescent,* which, when the myrmidons searching for refugees knock on the Porte,[d] shows its horns and does not eat humble pie.[e] If this is the position, then give us our passports so that we can go to *Turkey* and when the door has closed behind us, hand over the keys to the Swiss bastion of liberty to the *Holy Alliance* as a *feudum oblatum,*[f] and hold them in future as the insignia of chamberlains of the Holy Alliance, with the motto: *Finis Helvetiae!"* [g]

---

[a] "Can heavenly spirits cherish resentment so dire?" Virgil, *Aeneid,* I, 11.— *Ed.*

[b] See this volume, pp. 50-55.— *Ed.*

[c] Switzerland's national flag.— *Ed.*

[d] A pun in the original: *an der Pforte klopft* (literally, "knocks on the door". *Pforte* in German means both "door" and "the Porte", i.e. the Turkish Government).— *Ed.*

[e] In the original: *nicht zu Kreuze kriecht*—"does not crawl to the cross".— *Ed.*

[f] Feudal fief.— *Ed.*

[g] End to Switzerland! (by analogy with *Finis Poloniae!*—End to Poland! See p. 148 of this volume).— *Ed.*

3. CHERVAL

I realised from Joh. Ph. Becker's letter[a] that the "associate of Marx" or the "associates" of Cherval mentioned by the Vogt of the Empire[b] could only be Herr *Stecher,* now resident in London. Up to that time I had not had the honour of making his personal acquaintance, although I had heard many complimentary descriptions of his great and many-sided artistic talents. In consequence of Becker's letter we met for the first time. The following is a letter from my "associate" to me.[c]

"17 Sussex St., London W. C.
October 14, 1860

"Dear Herr Marx,

"I am glad to be able to give you some information about *Nugent* (Cherval-Crämer) who was mentioned in Vogt's pamphlet of which you were kind enough to send me an extract. In March 1853 I came to Geneva after a trip to Italy. Nugent arrived in Geneva at around the same time and I made his acquaintance in a lithography workshop. I had myself just taken up lithography and since Nugent had a thorough knowledge of it, and since he was extremely agreeable, energetic and industrious by nature, I accepted his proposal to share an atelier with him. What Vogt says about Nugent's activities in Geneva is roughly the same as what I heard for myself at the time, if you discount the usual exaggerations to be expected from journalists or pamphleteers. There was very little success. I knew only one of the group, a good-natured and hard-working, but otherwise imprudent and light-minded young man. And since he was one of the leaders it must be presumed that N. was everything in the group and the others nothing but curious listeners. I am convinced that neither stone nor copper plates were ever engraved, although I heard N. talk of such matters. My own acquaintances were mainly Genevans and Italians. I was aware that later on I was thought to be a spy by Vogt and other German refugees, whom I did not know. But I took no notice of it—the truth will always out. I was not even offended; it was so easy to arouse suspicion as there were spies aplenty and to discover who they were was not always a simple matter. I am almost certain that Nugent did not correspond with anyone in Geneva after he had been expelled from there. I later received two letters from him inviting me to join him in Paris to help him with a project on medieval architecture, which I did. In Paris I found Nugent to be utterly remote from politics and correspondence. All this of course suggests that I myself could be '*the associates of Marx*' since I neither saw nor heard of *anyone else whom Nugent had induced to come to Paris.* Of course Herr Vogt could not know that I had never had any contact with you, either direct or indirect, and that I probably never would have had, if I had not moved to London where by chance I have had the pleasure of meeting you and your esteemed family.

"With best wishes to you and your ladies,

H. Cal. Stecher"

---

[a] See this volume, pp. 60-64.— *Ed.*
[b] See Carl Vogt, *Mein Prozess...,* S. 175.— *Ed.*
[c] This letter has not been found.— *Ed.*

4. THE COMMUNIST TRIAL IN COLOGNE

In this section I wish to make public information concerning the Prussian Embassy in London and its correspondence with Prussian authorities on the Continent during the Cologne trial. This information is based on the confessions of Hirsch which were published by *A. Willich* in April 1853 in the *New-Yorker Criminal-Zeitung* under the title "Die Opfer der Moucharderie, Rechtfertigungsschrift von Wilhelm Hirsch".[a] Hirsch, who is at present in a Hamburg gaol, was the principal tool of Police Lieutenant Greif and his agent Fleury. It was on instructions from them and under their direction that he forged the *false* Minute-Book submitted as evidence by Stieber in the course of the communist trial. I give here a number of excerpts from Hirsch's memoirs.

(During the Great Exhibition) "the German associations were kept under surveillance by a police triumvirate: Police Superintendent Stieber for Prussia, a Herr Kubesch for Austria and Police Commissioner Huntel of Bremen".

Having volunteered to act as an informer, Hirsch had an interview in London with *Alberts* who was Secretary at the Prussian Embassy. He gives this account of their first meeting:

"The meetings of the Prussian Embassy in London with its secret agents take place at a public house well fitted for the purpose. The Cock, in Fleet St., Temple Bar, is so unobtrusive that but for a golden cock pointing to the entrance the casual passer-by would hardly notice it. I went through a narrow passage leading to the interior of this old English tavern and asked for Mr. Charles, whereupon a corpulent personage introduced himself to me with such an amiable smile that anyone seeing us would have taken us to be old friends. The Embassy agent (for this is what he was) seemed to be in very high spirits and his mood was still further improved by brandy and water. He enjoyed it so much that for a long time he seemed to have completely forgotten the purpose of our meeting. Mr. Charles at once revealed that his true name was *Alberts* and that he was the *Embassy Secretary*. To begin with, he informed me that in fact he had nothing to do with the police but that he would act as an intermediary in this case... A second meeting took place at his home in 39 Brewer St., Golden Square, and it was here that I made the acquaintance of Police Lieutenant *Greif*. Greif looked the true policeman: medium height, dark hair and a beard of the same colour cut in the regulation style, with the moustache meeting the side-whiskers and the chin left shaven. His eyes looked anything but intelligent and they protruded fiercely in a permanent glare, apparently the result of frequent association with thieves and rogues.... Like Herr Alberts, Herr Greif introduced himself to me by the pseudonym of Mr. Charles. The latest Mr. Charles was at least in a more serious mood and he even felt it was necessary to test me.... Our first meeting ended with his instructing me to give him an accurate report on all the activities of the revolutionary émigrés.... On the next

---

[a] This article was published in instalments in the *Belletristisches Journal und New-Yorker Criminal-Zeitung* on April 1, 8, 15 and 22, 1853. Excerpts from it are contained in Marx's notebook. For his assessment of it see his article "Hirsch's Confessions" (present edition, Vol. 12).— *Ed.*

occasion Herr Greif introduced me to what he called 'his right hand', namely 'one of his agents', he added. This turned out to be a tall elegantly dressed young man who also gave his name as Mr. Charles. The whole political police seems to have adopted this pseudonym and I now had three Charleses to deal with. The latest specimen seemed to be the most remarkable. He said that 'he too had been a revolutionary but that all things were possible and I had only to go along with him'."

Greif left London for some time and parted from Hirsch

"expressly commending me to the latest Mr. Charles who, he said, acted always on his instructions. I should not hesitate to confide in him. Moreover, even if certain things should appear strange to me I should not be surprised. To make this clearer he added: 'The Ministry sometimes requires various things, *chiefly documents; if these are unobtainable we should find some way out!*'"

Hirsch states further that the latest Charles was *Fleury*.

"He had earlier been employed in the office of the *Dresdner Zeitung*, which was edited by L. Wittig. When he was in Baden, he was, as a result of recommendations he had brought from Saxony, sent by the provisional government to the Palatinate to take in hand the organisation of the Landsturm, etc. When the Prussians occupied Karlsruhe he was taken prisoner, etc. He suddenly reappeared in London towards the end of 1850 or early in 1851; from the outset he went here by the name of de Fleury and was known by this name in refugee circles. He was hard up, at least he seemed to be, stayed in the refugee barracks set up by the Refugee Committee and drew subsidies. Early in the summer of 1851 his position suddenly improved; he moved into a respectable apartment and at the end of the year he married the daughter of an English engineer. He turned up later in Paris as a police agent.... His real name is *Krause* and he is the son of Krause the cobbler who was executed some 15 or 18 years ago in Dresden together with Backhof and Beseler for the murder of Countess Schönberg and her maid.... Fleury-Krause told me many times that he had been working for different governments since he was 14."

It is this same *Fleury-Krause* whom Stieber admitted in open court in Cologne to be a secret Prussian police agent working directly under Greif. In my *Revelations Concerning the Communist Trial in Cologne* I wrote of Fleury:

"Fleury is not indeed the Fleur de Marie of the police prostitutes, but he is a flower[a] and he will bear blossom, albeit only fleurs-de-lys." *

This prophecy has in a sense been fulfilled; some months after the communist trial Fleury was sentenced in England to several years in the hulks[b] for forgery.

---

* *Fleurs-de-lys* [lilies] is the French colloquial name of the letters T. F. (*travaux forcés*, forced labour), the brand-mark of criminals. [Note by Engels to the 1885 edition of the *Revelations*. See present edition, Vol. 11, p. 442.]

---

[a] A pun: Fleur de Marie—the heroine in Eugène Sue's novel *Les mystères de Paris*, fleur—a flower.— *Ed.*

[b] Marx uses the English word.— *Ed.*

"As the right-hand man of Police Lieutenant Greif," Hirsch writes, "Fleury dealt directly with the Prussian Embassy during Greif's absence."

Fleury was in contact with Max Reuter who stole the letters from Oswald Dietz, at that time archivist of the Schapper-Willich League.[241]

"Stieber," says Hirsch, "had learned from the agent of the Prussian Ambassador in Paris Hatzfeldt, the notorious *Cherval*, of the letters written by the latter to London. Stieber got Reuter to find out where they were, whereupon Fleury stole them on Stieber's orders and with Reuter's aid. These are the stolen letters which Herr Stieber was not ashamed to exhibit 'as such' to the jury in Cologne.... In autumn 1851 Fleury had been in Paris with Greif and Stieber after the latter had, through the mediation of Count Hatzfeldt, made contact with *Cherval*, or more correctly, *Joseph Crämer* with whose assistance he hoped to engineer a plot. With this end in view consultations were held in Paris between Messrs. Stieber, Greif, Fleury, two other police agents, Beckmann[*] and Sommer, and the famous French spy *Lucien de la Hodde* (who went by the name of Duprez) and they gave Cherval directions according to which he was to tailor his correspondence. Fleury often laughed in my presence over the scuffle he had provoked between Stieber and Cherval. And the man called Schmidt who in the guise of secretary of a revolutionary league in Strasbourg and Cologne had gained admission to the society founded at *the behest of the police* by Cherval, was none other than M. de Fleury.... Fleury was undoubtedly the sole agent of the Prussian secret police in London and all proposals and offers that the Embassy received went through his hands.... Messrs. Greif and Stieber were accustomed to relying on his judgment."

Fleury informed Hirsch:

"Herr Greif has told you what has to be done.... At Police Headquarters in Frankfurt they are themselves of the opinion that our primary aim must be to make *the position of the political police secure*; the means we use to achieve this are immaterial; the September plot in Paris is already *one step in this direction.*"[a]

Greif returned to London and expressed satisfaction with Hirsch's work but demanded more. In particular he wanted reports on *"the secret meetings of the Marx party"*.

"At all costs," the Police Lieutenant concluded, "we must draw up reports on the League meetings. Do it any way you wish as long as you don't overstep the limits of credibility. I am too *occupied* to attend to it myself. M. de Fleury will work with you as my representative."

Greif's occupation at that time consisted, as Hirsch states, in a correspondence via de la Hodde-Duprez with Maupas concerning

---

* The same man[b] who figures in the Arnim Trial. [Note by Marx in the 1875 edition of the *Revelations,* to which Appendix 4 to *Herr Vogt* was supplemented.] He was already then Paris correspondent for the *Kölnische Zeitung* and was to remain so for many years. [Engels' addition to Marx's note in the 1885 edition of the *Revelations.*]

---

a Beckmann.— *Ed.*
b See this volume, pp. 55-56.— *Ed.*

the arrangements for the mock escape of Cherval and Gipperich from the St. Pélagie gaol. On being assured by Hirsch that

> "Marx had not founded any new central organisation of the League in London ... Greif agreed with Fleury that in the circumstances we should for the time being prepare reports on meetings of the League ourselves. He, Greif, would vouch for their authenticity, and in any case his submissions would be accepted".

So Hirsch and Fleury set to work. "The content" of their reports on the secret meetings of the League I held

> "was provided", Hirsch states, "by reports of discussions that took place from time to time; the admission of new members, the founding of new sections in obscure corners of Germany, or a new organisation; speculation to the effect that in Cologne Marx's imprisoned friends did or did not have any prospects of being released; letters that had come from this person or that, and so on. On this last point Fleury usually took care to mention people in Germany who had become suspect as a result of political investigations or who had been involved in some political activity or other. Very often, however, we had to have recourse to our imagination and then we would report on the activities of a non-existent member of the League. But Herr Greif said that the reports were excellent and that anyway we had to have them at all costs. Some of the writing was done by Fleury alone but mostly I had to help him as he was unable to describe the smallest detail without errors of style. In this way the reports came into being and without a moment's hesitation Herr Greif declared his willingness to vouch for their authenticity".

Hirsch then describes how Fleury and he visited Arnold Ruge in Brighton, and Eduard Meyen (of Tobian memory[a]) and stole letters and lithographed material from them. Not content with this, Greif-Fleury rented a lithographic press from Stanbury Press, Fetter Lane, and together with Hirsch began to produce "radical pamphlets". That "democrat", F. Zabel, could learn a lesson or two here. Let him take note of this:

> "The first pamphlet I" (Hirsch) "wrote was entitled An das Landproletariat at Fleury's suggestion; and we managed to make a few good copies of it. Herr Greif sent these copies as documents emanating from the Marx party. To make it seem more plausible we included in the reports of the so-called League meetings, which came into being in the manner described above, a few words about the dispatch of such a pamphlet. One other product of this kind was fabricated; its title was An die Kinder des Volkes and I do not know under whose auspices Herr Greif sent this one in. We later abandoned this trick chiefly because it was so costly."

At this point Cherval arrived in London after his mock escape from Paris and was attached to Greif at a weekly salary of £1 10s.,

> "in return for which he was required to make reports on the contacts between the German and French émigrés".

Publicly exposed and expelled from the Workers' Society as a spy,[242]

---

[a] See this volume, p. 239.— Ed.

"Cherval very understandably described the German émigrés and their organs as being as insignificant as could be—since he found it quite impossible to get hold of any information on the subject which he could pass on. By way of compensation he compiled a report for Greif on the non-German revolutionary party which put Munchausen's tall stories in the shade".

Hirsch now returns to the Cologne trial.

"Herr Greif had already been questioned a number of times about the contents of the League reports prepared at his instance by Fleury in so far as they had any bearing on the Cologne trial.... There were also particular commissions in connection with the trial. On one occasion Marx was alleged to be corresponding with *Lassalle* via an 'ale-house' and the Public Prosecutor required further information.... Rather more naïve was the Public Prosecutor's request asking for precise information about the financial assistance that Lassalle in Düsseldorf was allegedly sending to the defendant Röser in Cologne ... it was believed that the true source of the money was in London."

I have already recounted in Section III, 4 how Fleury, acting on instructions from Hinckeldey, was to find someone in London who would be willing to appear before the jury in Cologne in the guise of H.,[a] the witness who had disappeared, etc. After a detailed account of this incident Hirsch goes on:

"Herr Stieber had meanwhile urgently requested Greif to supply him, if at all possible, with the original minutes of the League meetings that he had been reporting on. Fleury was of the opinion that he could produce an original minute-book if only the requisite people were available. Above all, however, he would need *specimens of the handwriting of some of Marx's friends*. I made use of this last remark in order to extricate myself from the whole undertaking; Fleury alluded to the topic only once again and after that he said nothing more. Around this time Stieber suddenly appeared in Cologne with a Minute-Book of the League's central organisation in London.... I was even more astonished when I found that the minutes as reported in extract in the papers were absolutely identical with the reports concocted by Fleury at Greif's behest. It was evident that Herr Greif or Herr Stieber himself had had a *copy* made somehow or other, *for the minutes in this allegedly original document bore signatures while those submitted by Fleury had none.* From Fleury himself I learned about this miracle only that 'Stieber can contrive anything, it will be a sensation!'"

As soon as Fleury heard that "Marx" had had the handwriting of the ostensible signatories of the minutes (Liebknecht, Rings, Ulmer, etc.) witnessed in a London Police Court[b] he wrote the following letter:

"*To the Royal Police Presidium in Berlin;* dated from London.
"It is the intention of Marx and his friends here to discredit the signatures on the League Minutes by having handwriting specimens legally authenticated. These specimens are to be produced in the Court of Assizes as the really authentic ones. Everyone familiar with the English laws knows that on this point they can be

---

a Haupt (see this volume, p. 67).— *Ed.*
b Marx uses English: Police Court.— *Ed.*

manipulated and that a person who vouches for the authenticity of a thing does not actually give any true guarantee. The person who gives you this information does not recoil from giving you his name in a matter like this where the truth is at stake. *Becker,* 4, Litchfield St." "Fleury knew the address of Becker, a German refugee living in the same house as *Willich.* It might very easily happen later on that the suspicion of authorship would fall on the latter who was an opponent of Marx.... Fleury looked forward eagerly to the scandal that would result. The letter would be read out in court, but of course too late, he thought, for any doubts about its authenticity to arise before the trial was over.... The letter, signed by Becker, was addressed to the *Police Presidium in Berlin,* however it went not to Berlin but to 'Police Officer Goldheim, Frankfurter Hof in Cologne', and an *envelope for this letter* arrived at the Police Presidium in Berlin with a note stating that *'Herr Stieber in Cologne would give a complete explanation as to its use....'* Stieber made no use of this letter; he was unable to do so because he was forced to drop the whole *Minute-Book.*"

With regard to the Minute-Book Hirsch says that

"Herr Stieber declared" (in court) "that he had had the Minute-Book in his hands for two weeks but had scrupled to produce it; he declared further that it had come to him by a courier called Greif.... Hence Greif had personally delivered his own work. How can this be reconciled with a letter of Herr *Goldheim's* in which he informed the Embassy that 'the Minute-Book was produced so late only in order to avoid scrutiny as to its authenticity....'"

On Friday, October 29, Herr Goldheim arrived in London.

"As Herr Stieber had to face the fact that it was not possible to uphold the authenticity of the Minute-Book he sent a deputy to negotiate with Fleury about it on the spot. At issue was the question whether a proof could not be obtained after all. His discussions were fruitless and he returned without any decision having been reached. Fleury was left in a state of despair for Stieber was now resolved to expose him rather than compromise the police chiefs. But I did not realise that this was the cause of Fleury's disquiet until Herr Stieber made his declaration soon afterwards. In panic, M. Fleury now resorted to his last expedient. He brought me a specimen of handwriting for me to use to copy out a declaration, sign it 'Liebknecht' and take an oath before the Lord Mayor of London that I was Liebknecht.... Fleury told me that the handwriting was that of the person who had written the Minute-Book and that *Herr Goldheim had brought it with him*" (*from Cologne*). "But if Herr Stieber had received the Minute-Book per Greif, the courier from London, how was it possible for Herr Goldheim to bring a specimen of the handwriting of the alleged Minute-Book writer from Cologne at the very moment when Greif had just arrived back in London?.... What Fleury gave me consisted of a few phrases and a signature...." Hirsch "copied the handwriting as closely as he could and wrote that the undersigned, i.e. Liebknecht, declared that the signature of Liebknecht legally witnessed by Marx and Co. was false and that this, his signature was the only genuine one. When I had finished and had the handwriting in my hands" (i.e. the specimen given him by Fleury to copy), "which fortunately I still possess, I told Fleury, who was not a little taken aback, that I had had second thoughts and would not go through with it. Inconsolable at first, he then announced that he would swear to it himself....For safety's sake he would *have the writing countersigned by the Prussian Consul*; and he went to the Consulate at once. I waited for him in a tavern; when he got back he had the countersignature and he next went to the Lord Mayor to swear the oath. But the plan fell through as the Lord Mayor wanted further guarantees and Fleury could not give them—so the oath remained unsworn.... Late in the evening I saw M. de Fleury again, and for the last time. That very day he had been unpleasantly surprised to read Herr Stieber's declaration concerning him in the *Kölnische Zeitung.* 'But I know that Stieber could not have acted differently, otherwise he would have had to compromise himself,' M. de Fleury said very truly by way of consoling himself.... '*There will be a great explosion in Berlin if the Cologne prisoners are convicted,*' M. de Fleury said to me at one of our last meetings".

Fleury's last meetings with Hirsch took place at the *end of October 1852.* Hirsch's confessions are dated the *end of November 1852*; and at the *end of March 1853* came the *"explosion in Berlin"* (the Ladendorf conspiracy).* [243]

* The reader will be interested to see the testimonials that Stieber himself gave his two accomplices Fleury-Krause and Hirsch. He writes of the first in the *Black Book,*[244] II, p. 69:

"No. 345. *Krause,* Carl Friedrich August, from Dresden. He is the son of Friedrich August Krause, a farmer executed for his part in the murder of Countess Schönberg in Dresden in 1834, and afterwards" (after his execution?) "a corn-dealer, and of his widow Johanna Rosine née Göllnitz, who is still living. Carl Friedrich was born on January 9, 1824, in the vineyard houses at Coswig near Dresden. From October 1, 1832, he went to the charity school in Dresden; in 1836 he was admitted to the orphanage in Antonstadt, Dresden, and in 1840 he was confirmed. He was then apprenticed to Herr Gruhle, a Dresden merchant, but in the following year he was arrested and detained by the Dresden Municipal Court for *repeated theft.* However, the period of detention was counted towards his sentence and he was released. After this he lived with his mother without taking a job, but in March 1842 he was arrested again for *breaking and entering* and this time he was sentenced to *four years' imprisonment.* On October 23, 1846, he came out of gaol and returned to Dresden and began to *associate with the most notorious thieves.* Then, the Rehabilitation Society took him up and found him a job in a cigar factory and he remained in this job without interruption or any further misdemeanour until March 1848. But after that date he gave in to his idleness again and began to frequent political societies" (as a government spy; see above his admission to Hirsch in London). "Early in 1849 he became a salesman of the *Dresdner Zeitung* edited by the republican literateur E. L. Wittig who is now in America but who at that time was in Dresden. In May 1849 he took part in the Dresden uprising and became commandant of the barricade in the Sophienstrasse. He fled to Baden after the uprising was quelled and there he was empowered by the provisional government of Baden (the decrees of June 10 and 23, 1849) to raise a Landsturm and requisition supplies for the insurgents. He was taken prisoner by Prussian soldiers but on October 8, 1849, he escaped from Rastatt." (Just as, later on, Cherval "escaped" from Paris. But now comes the part of the bouquet which has the authentic police aroma—it should be borne in mind that this was printed two years after the Cologne Trial.) "According to a report in the Berlin *Publizist,* No. 39 of May 15, 1853, taken from a book printed in New York with the title *Die Opfer der Spionage*[a] by Wilhelm Hirsch, a Hamburg shop-assistant" (O Stieber, you foreboding angel![b]), "Krause

---

a *Die Opfer der Moucharderie, Rechtfertigungsschrift von Wilhelm Hirsch.—Ed.*
b See this volume, p. 71.—*Ed.*

5. SLANDERS

When the communist trial in Cologne was over, Vogt-like calumnies about my "exploitation" of the workers were busily disseminated, especially in the German-American press. Some of my friends living in America—Messrs. J. Weydemeyer, Dr. A. Jacoby (a practising doctor in New York and one of the defendants in the Cologne communist trial) and A. Cluss (an official in the U.S. Navy Yard in Washington)—published a detailed refutation of these absurdities dated New York, November 7, 1853. Their article contained the comment that I was in the right to preserve *silence* about my private affairs insofar as it was a matter of gaining the *approval* of the philistines. "But when faced by the *hostility* of the mob, the philistines and the

turned up in London late in 1850 or early in 1851 as a political émigré bearing the name of *Charles de Fleury*. At first he lived in somewhat straitened circumstances but later, in 1851, his position improved. For after he was admitted to the Communist League" (another Stieber lie), "he worked as an agent for a number of governments in the course of which, however, he became involved in a number of swindles."

So much for Stieber's gratitude to his friend Fleury who, moreover (as we noted above), was sentenced to several years' imprisonment in London for forgery just a few months after the Cologne trial.

Concerning the worthy Hirsch we can read (op. cit., p. 58):

"No. 265. Hirsch, Wilhelm, shop-assistant from Hamburg. It appears that he went to London not as a refugee but of his own accord." (Why this wholly superfluous lie? After all, Goldheim tried to arrest him in Hamburg!) "But once there he associated with refugees and especially with the communist party. He played a double game. On the one hand, he was active on behalf of the revolutionary party, while, on the other, he offered to spy on political criminals and forgers for a number of continental governments. But he himself became implicated in the *worst possible frauds* and swindles. In particular, he was guilty of *forgery*, so that everyone should be on their guard *against him*. Together with various other individuals he even *manufactured false paper money* merely in order to extract high rewards from the police for uncovering forgeries. He was eventually unmasked by both sides" (namely, both by police forgers and non-police ones?) "and he has now returned from London to Hamburg where he lives in poor circumstances."

Thus far Stieber on his London accomplices to whose "truthfulness and reliability" he is never tired of testifying. It is interesting to see how utterly impossible it is for this model Prussian to speak the simple truth. He cannot even restrain himself from smuggling[a] quite purposeless lies into the—true and false—facts taken from the documents. On the testimony of such professional liars—and they are more numerous now than ever—hundreds of people are sent to prison and in this lies what is nowadays called salvation of the state. [This note to Appendix 4 was added by Engels in the 3rd (1885) edition of the *Revelations Concerning the Communist Trial in Cologne*.]

---

[a] A pun on the name *Stieber* and the verb *hineinstiebern* (to smuggle in, insert).— *Ed.*

degenerate idlers, it does harm to the cause in our view and so *we* break that silence."[a]

6. THE WAR BETWEEN FROGS AND MICE[b]

In my pamphlet *The Knight, etc.,* from which I quoted above, I wrote on p. 5:

"...On July 20, 1851 the 'Agitation Union' was founded, and on July 27, 1851 the German 'Émigré Club'. From that day ... dates the struggle on both sides of the ocean between the 'Émigrés' and the 'Agitators', the great war between frogs and mice.

> Now who will give me words and who the tongue,
> To sing of such brave deeds in sonorous sounds!
> For ne'er was strife upon this earth begun
> More proudly fought on bloodier battle grounds;
> Compared to this all other wars are roses.
> To tell of it my lyric art confounds
> For on this earth there ne'er was seen such glory
> Or noble valour bright as in this story.

> (After Boiardo, *Orlando innamorato,*
> Canto 27.)"[c]

Now it is by no means my intention to go into the details of "the story" of this strife or into the agreement entitled, *verbotenus,*[d] "The Preliminary Agreement about the *Treaty on the Alliance*" (under which name it was publicised throughout the entire German-American press), which was reached between *Gottfried Kinkel* in the name of the Émigré Club, and *A. Goegg* on behalf of the "Revolutionary League of the Two Worlds", on August 13, 1852. I would only remark that with a few exceptions the entire *parliamentary* emigration joined in the farce on one side or the other. (Of course, names like *K. Vogt* were at that time avoided by every party if only for propriety's sake.)

At the end of his revolutionary pleasure and fund-raising tour of the United States, Gottfried Kinkel, the passion flower of German philistinism, wrote a *"Denkschrift über das deutsche Nationalanlehn zur Förderung der Revolution",* dated Elmira, N. Y., February 22, 1852, in which he gave vent to views which at least

---

[a] J. Weydemeyer, A. Cluss, A. Jacoby, "An die Redaktion der *New-Yorker Criminal-Zeitung,* November 7, 1853", *New-Yorker Criminal Zeitung,* No. 37, November 25, 1853.— *Ed.*

[b] See this volume, p. 87.— *Ed.*

[c] See present edition, Vol. 12, p. 488.— *Ed.*

[d] Literally.— *Ed.*

possess the merit of great simplicity. Gottfried believes that
engineering a revolution is much like making a railway. Once the
money is there, the railway, or the revolution will follow in due
course. Whereas the nation should cherish a longing for revolution
in its heart, the makers of revolution should have cash in their
pockets, and everything therefore depends on "a small well-
equipped band of men with a **plentiful** supply of money". It is
remarkable into what bizarre byways of thought even melodramatic
minds are driven by England's commercial wind. Since everything
here, even public opinion,[a] is organised with the aid of shares, why
not float a joint-stock company "for the promotion of the
revolution"?

In a public meeting with *Kossuth,* who was also engaged at that
time on a revolutionary fund-raising campaign in the United
States, *Gottfried* expressed himself in highly aesthetic terms:

"Even from your clean hands, Governor, the gift of freedom would be a bitter
pill, and I would moisten it *with the tears of* **my shame.**"[b]

Hence *Gottfried,* having looked the gift-horse so sharply in the
mouth, assured the governor that if the latter should present to
him "the revolution in the east" with his right hand, he, Gottfried,
would present to him "the revolution in the west" in return. Seven
years later, in the *Hermann,* a paper he had founded himself, the
very same Gottfried assured his readers that he was a man of rare
consistency,[c] and that having proclaimed the Prince Regent[d] as
Emperor of Germany before the military court in Rastatt,[245] he had
always kept this as his motto.

Count Oskar Reichenbach, one of the three original regents and
the Treasurer of the Revolutionary Loan, published the accounts
in *London* on *October 8, 1852,* together with a statement in which
he dissociated himself from the enterprise. At the same time he
declared that "in any event I neither can nor will hand the money
over to citizens Kinkel, etc." Instead he invited the shareholders to
hand in their provisional loan certificates in exchange for the
money in his hands. His own resignation as treasurer, etc., he said,

"was motivated by political and legal considerations.... The assumptions on
which the idea of the loan was based have not been realised. The sum of 20,000

---

[a] Marx uses the English phrase: "public opinion".— *Ed.*

[b] G. Kinkel, "Denkschrift über das deutsche Nationalanlehn zur Förderung der
Revolution", *New-Yorker Staats-Zeitung,* March 2, 1852.— *Ed.*

[c] G. Kinkel, "Brief des Herausgebers an einen Freund in Amerika", *Hermann,*
March 26, 1859.— *Ed.*

[d] William.— *Ed.*

dollars which had to be raised before the loan could be proceeded with, has therefore not been acquired.... The proposal to found a periodical and to promote agitation found no echo. Only political charlatans or revolutionary monomaniacs could deem the loan to be practicable at present and imagine that an equitable, and hence impersonal, actively revolutionary use of the money by all party groups is possible at this moment."

But Gottfried's faith in revolution could not be shaken so easily and so he procured a "resolution" that allowed him to carry on the business under another name.

Reichenbach's statement of the accounts contains some interesting data.

"The Trustees," he says, "cannot be held responsible for contributions which may have been made later by the committees *to persons other than myself*, and I would ask the committees to take note of this when calling in the certificates and settling accounts."

According to his computations £1,587 6s. 4d. was *received*, of which London had contributed £2 5s., and *"Germany"* £9. The *expenditure* amounted to £584 18s. 5d. and was broken down as follows: *Kinkel*'s and *Hillgärtner*'s *travel expenses*: £220; *other travel expenses*: £54; lithographic press: £11; cost of provisional certificates: £14; *lithographed correspondence, stamps, etc.*: £106 1s. 6d. *On Kinkel*'s *instructions, etc.*: £100.

The Revolutionary Loan ended up with £1,000, which Gottfried Kinkel keeps in the Westminster Bank as earnest money for the first German provisional government. And despite all this, there is still no provisional government. Perhaps Germany believes that 36 actual governments are quite sufficient.

Certain American loan funds which were not incorporated into the central London Treasury were at least employed here and there for patriotic purposes. Such was the case with the £100 which Gottfried Kinkel gave to Karl Blind early in 1858 to transform into "radical pamphlets", etc.

7. PALMERSTON-POLEMIC

"Council Hall, Sheffield, May 6th, 1856

"Doctor,

"The Sheffield Foreign Affairs Committee instruct me to convey to you an expression of their warm thanks for the great public service you have rendered by your admirable *exposé* of the Kars-Papers[a] published in the *People's Paper*.

"I have the honour, &c.

"Dr. Karl Marx"[b]   Wm. Cyples, *Secretary*

---

[a] Marx's series of articles "The Fall of Kars" (see present edition, Vol. 14).— *Ed.*
[b] Marx quotes the letter in English.— *Ed.*

8. STATEMENT BY HERR A. SCHERZER

Herr *A. Scherzer,* a man who has played a praiseworthy role in the workers' movement since the 1830s, wrote to me from London on April 22, 1860:

"Dear Citizen,

"I cannot let the occasion pass without protesting about a passage in the monstrous tissue of lies and the infamous calumnies of Vogt's pamphlet which concerns me personally. I am referring to the statement in Document No. 7, printed in the supplement to the *Schweizer Handels-Courier,* No. 150, of June 2, where it says: 'We know that at this very time fresh efforts are being made from London. Letters signed by A. Sch... are being sent from there to both associations and individuals, etc.' These 'letters' appear to be the reason why Herr K. Vogt wrote elsewhere in his book: 'At the beginning of this year (1859) a new arena for political agitation seemed to be opening up. The opportunity was seized in a moment so as to regain some influence if possible. The tactics have not altered in this respect for years. A committee about which "no-one knows nothing", as it says in the old song, circulates letters through an equally unknown president or secretary, etc., etc. Having reconnoitred the terrain in this manner, a number of "travelling brethren" turn up in the country and at once start to organise a secret league. The association which is to be compromised learns nothing of these goings-on which remain the work of a number of sectarian individuals. For the most part even the correspondence conducted in the name of the association remains quite unknown to it, but the letters refer always to "our association", etc., and the inquiries of the police, which follow inexorably, and are based on documents that have fallen into their hands, always affect the association as a whole, etc.'

"Why did Herr K. Vogt not *print the whole letter* which he alludes to in Document No. 7? Why not 'reconnoitre' the source he has relied on for his information? It would have been easy for him to discover that the public *Workers' Educational Society in London* chose its correspondence committee, to which I had the honour to be elected, in *open* session. When Herr Vogt speaks of unknown secretaries and the like, I am very pleased to be unknown to him, but am happy to be able to say that I am known to thousands of German workers, who have all derived benefit from the erudition of the men whom he vilifies now. Times have changed. The period of secret societies is past. It is ridiculous to talk of secret leagues or sects, when problems are dealt with openly in a workers' society, where strangers attend as visitors at every meeting. The letters signed by me were so formulated that it was impossible for anyone to come to harm in consequence. We German workers in London had only one interest at heart and that was to learn about the mood of the workers' associations on the Continent, and to found a newspaper which would represent the interests of the working class and which would do battle with writers in the pay of the enemy. It naturally did not occur to a single German worker to act in the interests of a Bonaparte, a thing of which only a Vogt or people of his kind are capable. We undoubtedly hate the despotism of Austria with a far deeper loathing than Herr Vogt, but we do not seek its defeat in the victory of another despot. Every people must liberate itself. Is it not striking that Herr Vogt arrogates for himself the very means which he accuses us of having used against his own activities? Herr Vogt asserts that he is not in the pay of Bonaparte, and that he only received money to set up a newspaper from democratic sources. In saying this he hopes to exonerate himself, but how can he be so obtuse, with all his learning, to cast suspicion on workers, and hurl accusations at them for concerning themselves with the well-being of their country and for making propaganda about the need to establish a newspaper?

"With my most sincere respects,

A. Scherzer"

9. BLIND'S ARTICLE IN *THE FREE PRESS* OF MAY 27, 1859[a]

"*The Grand Duke Constantine to be King of Hungary*

"A Correspondent, who encloses his card, writes as follows:—

"Sir,—Having been present at the last meeting in the Music Hall, I heard the statement made concerning the Grand Duke Constantine. I am able to give you another fact:—

"So far back as last summer, Prince Jérôme-Napoléon detailed to some of his confidants at Geneva a plan of attack against Austria, and prospective rearrangement of the map of Europe. I know the name of a Swiss senator to whom he broached the subject. Prince Jérôme, at that time, declared that, according to the plan made, *Grand Duke* Constantine *was to become King of Hungary*.

"I know further of attempts made, in the beginning of the present year, to win over to the Russo-Napoleonic scheme some of the exiled German Democrats, as well as some influential Liberals in Germany. Large pecuniary advantages were held out to them as a bribe. I am glad to say that these offers were rejected with indignation."[b]

10. HERR ORGES' LETTERS

"Dear Sir,

"I heard today from Herr Liebknecht that you would be kind enough to put a legal document at our disposal, *relating to the origins* of the pamphlet against Vogt.[c] May I ask you urgently to send it to us as quickly as possible, so that we can produce it in court. Please, send the document against a receipt and charge us for any expenses you may have incurred. Incidentally, my dear Sir, the liberal party sometimes misjudges the *Allgemeine Zeitung*. We (the editors) have gone through fire and water and have passed all the tests of political commitment. If you do not consider the separate piece of work, the individual article, but our whole activity you will probably come to realise that no German newspaper strives as we do, without haste, but without rest, for unity and freedom, power and culture, for spiritual and material progress, for greater patriotic awareness and higher moral standards of the German nation, and that no paper achieves more than ours. You should judge our deeds by their effects. Asking you once more most urgently to grant my request, and assuring you of my greatest respect,

"Yours sincerely,

Hermann Orges

"*Augsburg*, 16/10"

---

[a] See this volume, pp. 122-24.— *Ed.*
[b] Marx quotes this report in English.— *Ed.*
[c] See this volume, pp. 119-24.— *Ed.*

The second letter, dated the *same* day, was only an *extract* of the first, and was posted, as Herr Orges states, "only for safety's sake". In it he likewise requests "the most urgent dispatch of the document *about the origins* of the well-known pamphlet against Vogt, a document which, as Herr Liebknecht writes, you have been so kind as to put at our disposal".

11. CIRCULAR AGAINST K. BLIND

I include here only the concluding section of my circular against Blind of February 4, 1860, which was written in English[a]:

"Now, before taking any further step, I want to show up the fellows who evidently have played into the hands of Vogt. I, therefore, publicly declare that the statement of Blind, Wiehe and Hollinger, according to which the anonymous pamphlet was *not* printed in Hollinger's office, 3, Litchfield Street, Soho, is a *deliberate lie*. First, Mr. Vögele, one of the compositors, formerly employed by Hollinger, will declare upon oath that the said pamphlet *was* printed in Hollinger's office, was written in the hand-writing of *Mr. Blind,* and partly composed by Hollinger himself. Secondly, it can be judicially proved that the pamphlet and the article in *Das Volk* have been taken off the same types. Thirdly, it will be shown that Wiehe was *not* employed by Hollinger for eleven consecutive months, and, especially, was *not* employed by him at the time of the pamphlet's publication. Lastly, witnesses may be summoned in whose presence Wiehe himself confessed having been persuaded by Hollinger to sign the *wilfully false declaration in the Augsburg Gazette.*[b] Consequently, I again declare the above said *Charles Blind* to be a *deliberate liar.*

Karl Marx"

From the London "Times", February 3rd.

"Vienna, January 30th.—The Swiss Professor Vogt pretends to know that France will procure for Switzerland Faucigny, Chablais, and the Genevese,[c] the neutral provinces of Savoy, if the Grand Council of the Republic will let her have the free use of the Simplon."[d]

---

[a] Marx quotes this excerpt from the circular in English (see this volume, pp. 10-11).— *Ed.*

[b] The Augsburg *Allgemeine Zeitung.*— *Ed.*

[c] Genevois.— *Ed.*

[d] Marx quotes this report in English (see also this volume, p. 195).— *Ed.*

12. VÖGELE'S AFFIDAVIT

"I declare herewith:

that the German flysheet *Zur Warnung* (A Warning) which was afterwards reprinted in No. 7 (d.d. 18th June 1859) of *Das Volk* (a German paper which was then published in London) and which was again reprinted in the *Allgemeine Zeitung* of Augsburg (the Augsburg Gazette)—that this flysheet was composed partly by Mr. Fidelio Hollinger of 3, Litchfield Street, Soho, London, partly by myself, who was then employed by Mr. Fidelio Hollinger, and that the flysheet was published in Mr. F. Hollinger's Printing office, 3, Litchfield Street, Soho, London; that the manuscript of the said flysheet was in the handwriting of Mr. Charles Blind; that I saw Mr. F. Hollinger give to Mr. William Liebknecht of 14, Church Street, Soho, London, the proofsheet of the flysheet *Zur Warnung*; that Mr. F. Hollinger hesitated at first giving the proofsheet to Mr. W. Liebknecht, and, that, when Mr. W. Liebknecht had withdrawn, he, Mr. F. Hollinger, expressed to me, and to my fellow workman J. F. Wiehe, his regret for having given the proofsheet out of his hands.

"Declared at the Police Court, Bow Street, in the County of Middlesex, the eleventh day of February 1860, before me, *Th. Henry*, one of the Police Magistrates of the Metropolis.

"L.S.   A. Vögele"[a]

13. WIEHE'S AFFIDAVIT

"One of the first days of November last—I do not recollect the exact date—in the evening between nine and ten o'clock I was taken out of bed by Mr. F. Hollinger, in whose house I then lived, and by whom I was employed as compositor. He presented to me a paper to the effect, that, during the preceding eleven months I had been continuously employed by him, and that during all that time a certain German flysheet *Zur Warnung* (A Warning) had not been composed and printed in Mr. Hollinger's Office, 3, Litchfield Street, Soho. In my perplexed state, and not aware of the importance of the transaction, I complied with his wish, and copied, and signed the document. Mr. Hollinger promised me money, but I never received anything. During that transaction Mr. Charles Blind, as my wife informed me at the time, was waiting in Mr. Hollinger's room. A few days later, Mrs. Hollinger called me down from dinner and led me into her husband's room, where I found Mr. Charles Blind alone. He presented me the same paper which Mr. Hollinger had presented me before, and entreated me to write, and sign a second copy, as he wanted two, the one for himself, and the other for publication in the Press. He added that he would show himself grateful to me. I copied and signed again the paper.

"I herewith declare the truth of the above statements and that:

"1) During the 11 months mentioned in the document I was for *six weeks not* employed by Mr. Hollinger, but by a Mr. Ermani. 2) I did not work in Mr. Hollinger's Office just at that time when the flysheet *Zur Warnung* (A Warning) was published. 3) I heard at the time from Mr. Vögele, who then worked for Mr. Hollinger, that he, Vögele, had, together with Mr. Hollinger himself, composed the flysheet in question, and that the manuscript was in Mr. Blind's handwriting. 4) The types of the pamphlet were still standing when I returned to Mr. Hollinger's service. I myself broke them into columns for the reprint of the

---

[a] Marx gives this document in English (see also this volume, p. 128).—*Ed.*

flysheet (or pamphlet) *Zur Warnung* (A Warning) in the German paper *Das Volk* published at London, by Mr. Fidelio Hollinger, 3, Litchfield Street, Soho. The flysheet appeared in No. 7, d. d. 18th June 1859, of *Das Volk* (The People). 5) I saw Mr. Hollinger give to Mr. William Liebknecht of 14, Church Street, Soho, London, the proofsheet of the pamphlet *Zur Warnung*, on which proofsheet Mr. Charles Blind with his own hand had corrected four or five mistakes. Mr. Hollinger hesitated at first giving the proofsheet to Mr. Liebknecht, and when Mr. Liebknecht had withdrawn, he, F. Hollinger, expressed to me and my fellow workman Vögele his regret for having given the proofsheet out of his hands.

"Declared and signed by the said Johann Friedrich Wiehe at the Police Court, Bow Street, this 8th day of February, 1860, before me *Th. Henry*, Magistrate of the said court.

"L.S.   *Johann Friedrich Wiehe*" [a]

14. FROM THE TRIAL PAPERS

"*Gouvernement Provisoire*
République Française. Liberté, Egalité, Fraternité.

Au nom du Peuple Français

"Paris, 1 Mars 1848

"Brave et loyal Marx,

"Le sol de la république française est un champ d'asile pour tous les amis de la liberté. La tyrannie vous a banni, la France libre vous rouvre ses portes, à vous et à tous ceux qui combattent pour la cause sainte, la cause fraternelle de tous les peuples. Tout agent du gouvernement français doit interpréter sa mission dans ce sens. Salut et fraternité.

Ferdinand Flocon, Membre du gouvernement provisoire" [b]

"Bruxelles, le 19 Mai 1848

"Mon cher Monsieur Marx,
"J'entends avec un grand plaisir par notre ami Weerth que vous allez faire paraître à Cologne une *Nouvelle Gazette Rhénane* dont il m'a remis le prospectus. Il

---

[a] Marx gives this document in English (see also this volume, pp. 129-30).— *Ed.*
[b] "*Provisional Government*
French Republic. Liberty, Equality, Fraternity.
In the name of the French People

"Paris, March 1, 1848

"Honest, worthy Marx,

"The soil of the French Republic is a place of asylum for all the friends of freedom. Tyranny has expelled you, a free France opens its doors to you once more, to you and to all those who fight for the sacred cause, the fraternal cause of all the peoples. Every official of the French Government should interpret his task in this sense. With fraternal greetings.

Ferdinand Flocon, Member of the Provisional Government."— *Ed.*

est bien nécessaire que cette feuille nous tienne au courant en Belgique des affaires de la démocratie allemande, car il est impossible d'en rien savoir de certain ici par la *Gazette de Cologne,* la *Gazette Universelle* d'Augsbourg et les autres gazettes aristocratiques de l'Allemagne que nous recevons à Bruxelles, non plus que par notre *Indépendance Belge* dont toutes les correspondances particulières sont conçues au point de vue des intérêts de notre aristocratie bourgeoise. M. Weerth me dit qu'il va vous joindre à Cologne pour contribuer à l'entreprise de la *Nouvelle Gazette Rhénane*: et il me promet en votre nom l'envoi de cette feuille en échange du *Débat social* que je vous enverrai de mon côté. Je ne demande pas mieux aussi que d'entretenir avec vous une correspondance sur les affaires communes à nos deux pays. Il est indispensable que les Belges et les Allemands ne restent pas trop étrangers les uns aux autres, dans l'intérêt commun des deux pays: car il se prépare en France des événements qui ne tarderont pas à mettre en jeu des questions qui toucheront les deux pays ensemble. Je reviens de Paris où j'ai passé une dizaine de jours que j'ai employés de mon mieux à me rendre compte de la situation de cette grande capitale. Je me suis trouvé, à la fin de mon séjour, juste au milieu des affaires du 15 mai.[246] J'assistais même à la séance où s'est passé le fait de l'irruption du peuple dans l'assemblée nationale.... Tout ce que j'ai compris, à voir l'attitude du peuple parisien et à entendre parler les principaux personnages qui sont en ce moment dans les affaires de la république française, c'est qu'on s'attend à une forte réaction de l'esprit bourgeois contre les événements de février dernier; les affaires du 15 mai précipiteront sans doute cette réaction. Or, celle-ci amènera indubitablement dans peu de temps un nouveau soulèvement du peuple... La France devra bientôt recourir à la guerre. C'est pour ce cas-là que nous aurons à aviser, ici et chez vous, sur ce que nous aurons à faire ensemble. Si la guerre se porte d'abord vers l'Italie nous aurons du répit... Mais si elle se porte sur-le-champ vers ce pays-ci je ne sais pas trop encore ce que nous aurons à faire, et alors nous aurons besoin du conseil des Allemands... En attendant j'annoncerai dans le *Débat social* de dimanche la publication prochaine de votre nouvelle feuille... Je compte aller à Londres vers la fin du mois de juin prochain. Si vous avez occasion d'écrire à Londres à quelques amis, veuillez les prier de m'y faire accueil. Tout à vous cordialement,

L. Jottrand, Avt." ᵃ

ᵃ "My dear Mr. Marx, I hear with great pleasure from our friend Weerth that you intend to publish a *Neue Rheinische Zeitung* in Cologne of which he has sent me the prospectus. It is extremely necessary for this paper to keep us in Belgium informed about the affairs of German democracy, since it is not possible to learn anything definite about this from the *Kölnische Zeitung*, the Augsburg *Allgemeine Zeitung* and the other aristocratic German papers which we receive here in Brussels, any more than from our *Indépendance Belge,* all of whose special reports are written from the standpoint of the interests of our bourgeois aristocracy. Herr Weerth has told me that he is going to join you in Cologne to collaborate on the *Neue Rheinische Zeitung* and he has promised me in your name to send me copies of it in exchange for the *Débat social* which I shall forward to you. I can ask nothing better than to correspond with you about the affairs common to our two nations. It is in the interest of both our countries that Belgians and Germans should become better acquainted with each other, for in France events are about to take place which in a short time will pose problems affecting both our countries. I have just come back

"Bruxelles, 10 Février, 1860

"Mon cher Marx,
"N'ayant pas de vos nouvelles, depuis très longtemps, j'ai reçu votre dernière[a] avec la plus vive satisfaction. Vous vous plaignez du retard des choses, et du peu d'empressement de ma part de vous répondre à la question que vous m'aviez faite. Que faire: l'âge ralentit la plume; j'espère cependant que vous trouverez mes avis et mon sentiment toujours les mêmes. Je vois que votre .dernière est tracée à la dictée par la main de votre secrétaire intime, de votre adorable moitié: or Madame Marx ne cesse de se rappeler du vieux hermite de Bruxelles. Qu'elle daigne recevoir avec bonté mes salutations respectueuses.
"Conservez-moi, cher confrère, dans vos amitiés. Salut et fraternité.

Lelewel"[b]

---

from Paris after spending ten days there during which time I did my best to gain an understanding of what is happening in this great metropolis. At the end of my stay I found myself in the midst of the events of May 15. I was even present at the session of the National Assembly during which the people rushed into the Chamber.... As far as I have understood both from seeing the attitude of the people of Paris and from listening to the speeches of the leading statesmen in the French Republic at the present time, a powerful reaction is expected against the events of February last on the part of the bourgeoisie; the events of May 15 will doubtless hasten this reaction. And this will undoubtedly lead in a short time to a new uprising by the people.... France will soon have to have recourse to war. It is for this reason that we ought to consider here and in your country what common action we should take in that event. If to start with the war is directed against Italy we shall have a breathing space; ... but if it is directed against this country from the very beginning I do not yet know what we should do, and we should then be in need of the advice of the Germans.... In the meantime I shall announce the approaching publication of your new paper in the Sunday edition of the *Débat social....* I plan to go to London towards the end of June. Should you have occasion to write to any of your friends in London, I would be grateful if you could ask them to receive me kindly.

"With cordial greetings,

L. Jottrand, Lawyer"

See also this volume, pp. 263-66.—*Ed.*

---

[a] This refers to Marx's letter to Lelewel of February 3, 1860 (present edition, Vol. 41).—*Ed.*

[b] "My dear Marx, not having heard any news from you for a long time, I was very glad to receive your last communication. You complain about the delay and the lack of urgency on my part in answering the question you put to me. But what can one do: age slows down the pen. Nevertheless, I hope that you will find my opinions and my feelings the same as ever. I see that your last letter was written at your dictation by the hand of your private secretary, your charming wife. So Madame Marx still remembers the old hermit in Brussels. Please, convey to her my respectful greetings.
"Continue to include me, dear colleague, among your friends. With fraternal greetings.

Lelewel".—*Ed.*

"5, Cambridge Place,
Kensington, London,
February 11th, 1860

"My dear Marx,

"I have read a series of infamous articles against you in the *National-Zeitung* and am utterly astonished at the falsehood and malignity of the writer. I really feel it a duty that every one who is acquainted with you, should, however unnecessary such a testimony must be, pay a tribute to the worth, honour and disinterestedness of your character. It becomes doubly incumbent in me to do so, when I recollect how many articles you contributed to my little magazine, the *Notes to the People,* and subsequently to the *People's Paper,* for a series of years, utterly gratuitously; articles which were of such high value to the people's cause, and of such great benefit to the paper. Permit me to hope that you will severely punish your dastardly and unmanly libeller.

"Believe me, my dear Marx, most sincerely, yours,

Ernest Jones

"Dr. Karl Marx" [a]

"Tribune Office,
New York,
March 8th, 1860

"My dear Sir,

"In reply to your request I am very happy to state the facts of your connection with various publications in the United States concerning which I have had a personal knowledge. Nearly nine years ago I engaged you to write for the *New York Tribune,* and the engagement has been continued ever since. You have written for us constantly, without a single week's interruption, that I can remember; and you are not only one of the most highly valued, but one of the best paid contributors attached to the journal. The only fault I have had to find with you has been that you have occasionally exhibited too German a tone of feeling for an American newspaper. This has been the case with reference both to Russia and France. In questions relating to both, Czarism and Bonapartism, I have sometimes thought that you manifested too much interest and too great anxiety for the unity and independence of Germany. This was more striking perhaps in connection with the late Italian war than on any other occasion. In that I agreed perfectly with you: *sympathy with the Italian people.* I had as little confidence as you in the sincerity of the French Emperor, and believed as little as you that *Italian liberty* was to be expected from him; but I did not think that Germany had any such ground for alarm as you, in common with other patriotic Germans, thought she had.

"I must add that in all your writings which have passed through my hands, you have always manifested the most cordial interest in the welfare and progress of the labouring classes; and that you have written much with direct reference to that end.

"I have also at various times within the past five or six years been the medium through which contributions of yours have been furnished to *Putnam's Monthly,*[247] a literary magazine of high character; and also to the *New American Cyclopaedia,* of which I am also an editor, and for which you have furnished some very important articles.

---

[a] Marx gives the letter in English.— *Ed.*

"If any other explanations are needed I shall be happy to furnish them. Meanwhile I remain, yours very faithfully,

> *Charles A. Dana,* Managing Editor of the *N. Y. Tribune*

"Dr. Charles Marx" [a]

15. DENTU PAMPHLETS

I have shown that the Dentu pamphlets are the source from which the German Dâ-Dâ derives his wisdom about world history in general and "*Napoleon's salutary policy*" in particular. The "*salutary policy of Napoleon*" is a phrase from a recent leading article by "democrat" *F. Zabel.* What the *French themselves* think and know about these pamphlets can be seen from the following extract from the Paris weekly, the *Courrier du Dimanche, No. 42,* of *October 14, 1860.*

"Pour ce qui regarde le moment actuel, prenez dix brochures au hasard, et vous reconnaîtrez que neuf au moins ont été pensées, élaborées, écrites ... par qui? par des romanciers de profession, par des chansonniers, par des vaudevillistes, par des sacristains!

"Parle-t-on dans les gazettes de mystérieuses entrevues entre les puissances du Nord, de la Sainte-Alliance qui ressuscite? Vite voilà un faiseur agréable de couplets assez littéraires, et même (jadis) passablement libéraux, qui court chez l'inévitable *M. Dentu* et lui apporte sous ce titre ronflant: La coalition, une longue et fade paraphrase des articles de M. Grandguillot. L'alliance anglaise semble déplaire parfois à M. Limayrac? Vite, un M. Châtelet, chevalier de l'ordre de Grégoire le Grand,[248] et qui doit être sacristain quelque part, si j'en crois son style, publie ou republie un long et ridicule factum: *Crimes et délits de l'Angleterre contre la France.* Déjà l'auteur du *Compère Guillery* (Edmond About) avait jugé à propos de nous édifier sur les arcanes politiques de la monarchie prussienne, et avait donné du haut de ses chutes théâtrales, des conseils de prudence aux chambres de Berlin. On annonce que M. Clairville va prochainement élucider la question de l'isthme de Panama, si fort embrouillée par M. Belly; et sans doute quelques jours après la conférence royale du 21 Octobre,[249] on verra paraître à toutes les vitrines de nos libraires une splendide brochure rose qui portera ce titre: *Mémoire sur l'entrevue de Varsovie par le corps de ballet de l'Opéra.*

"Cette invasion, en apparence inexplicable, des questions politiques par les *dii minores* de la littérature, se rattache à bien des causes. Nous en citerons ici une seule, mais qui est la plus immédiate et la plus incontestable.

"Dans le marasme presque universel d'esprit et de coeur, ces messieurs, qui font le triste métier d'amuseurs publics, ne savent plus par quel moyen secouer et réveiller leurs lecteurs. Les vieilles gaîtés de leurs refrains et de leurs anecdotes leur reviennent sans cesse. Eux-mêmes se sentent aussi mornes, aussi tristes, aussi ennuyés que ceux qu'ils entreprennent de dérider. Voilà pourquoi à bout de ressources, ils se sont mis, en désespoir de cause, à écrire les uns des mémoires de courtisanes, les autres des brochures diplomatiques.

"Puis, un beau matin, un aventurier de la plume, qui n'a jamais fait à la politique le sacrifice d'une heure sérieuse d'étude, qui n'a pas même au coeur le

---

[a] Marx gives the letter in English.— *Ed.*

semblant d'une conviction, quelle qu'elle soit, se lève et se dit: 'J'ai besoin de frapper un grand coup! Voyons! que ferai-je pour attirer sur moi l'attention générale qui me fuit d'instinct? Écrirai-je un opuscule sur la question Léotard ou sur la question d'Orient? Révélerai-je au monde surpris le secret de boudoirs où je n'entrai jamais, ou celui de la politique russe qui m'est plus étrange encore? Dois-je m'attendrir en prose voltairienne sur *les femmes éclaboussées* ou en prose évangélique sur les malheureuses populations maronites[250] traquées, dépouillées, massacrées par le fanatisme mahométan? Lancerai-je une apologie de mademoiselle Rigol-boche ou un plaidoyer en faveur du pouvoir temporel? Décidément, j'opte pour la politique. J'amuserai encore mieux mon public avec les rois et les empereurs, qu'avec les lorettes.' Cela dit, notre surnuméraire de la littérature bohème compulse le *Moniteur,* hante quelques jours les colonnades de la Bourse, rend visite à quelques fonctionnaires et sait enfin de quel côté souffle le vent de la curiosité à la ville, ou celui de la faveur à la cour; il choisit alors un titre que ce vent puisse enfler d'une façon suffisante et se repose content sur ses lauriers. Aussi bien son oeuvre est faite désormais; car aujourd'hui, en matière de brochure, il n'y a que deux choses qui comptent, le titre et les relations que l'on suppose entre l'écrivain et 'de hauts personnages'.

"Est-il nécessaire de dire, après cela, ce que valent les brochures qui nous inondent? Ramassez un jour tout ce que vous avez de courage, tâchez de les lire jusqu'au bout et vous serez effrayés de l'ignorance inouïe, de la légèreté intolérable, voire même de l'amoindrissement de sens moral qu'elles décèlent dans leurs auteurs. Et je ne parle pas ici des plus mauvaises... Et chaque année nous courbe plus bas, chaque année voit apparaître un nouveau signe de décadence intellectuelle, chaque année ajoute une honte littéraire nouvelle à celles dont il nous faut déjà rougir. De telle sorte que les plus optimistes se prennent quelquefois à douter de demain, et se demandent avec angoisse: Sortirons-nous de là?"[a]

---

[a] "As to the present state of affairs, pick any ten pamphlets at random and you will find that at least nine of them have been devised, worked out and written ... by whom? By professional novelists, song-writers, vaudeville-writers or sextons.

"If the newspapers mention mysterious meetings between the northern powers or a project to resurrect the Holy Alliance, immediately some amiable person manufacturing fairly literary songs, and even (formerly) passably liberal songs, will run off to the inevitable *M. Dentu* and supply him, under the resounding title: 'La Coalition', with a lengthy and insipid paraphrase of the articles of M. Grandguillot. If the alliance with England seems sometimes to displease M. Limayrac, a M. Châtelet, knight of the Order of Gregory the Great, and a man who must be a sexton somewhere or other, to judge him by his style, quickly publishes or republishes a long, ridiculous account: *Crimes et délits de l'Angleterre contre la France.* The author of *Compère Guillery* (Edmond About) has already deemed it expedient to edify us with stories about the political secrets of the Prussian monarchy and from the heights of his theatrical fiascos he has honoured the Chambers of Berlin with his prudent advice. It has been announced that M. Clairville will soon elucidate the problem of the Isthmus of Panama which has been so thoroughly obscured by M. Belly; and no doubt a few days after the royal conference of October 21 we shall see in the windows of all our bookshops a splendid pink pamphlet bearing the title: *Mémoire sur l'entrevue de Varsovie par le corps de ballet de l'Opéra.*

"This apparently inexplicable invasion of the political arena by the *lesser gods* of literature has many causes. We shall only mention one here, but that one is the most palpable and the most indisputable of all.

The phrase "*the salutary policy of Napoleon*" quoted above was taken from the *National-Zeitung*. Strangely enough the Paris correspondent of the *Manchester Guardian* which is regarded throughout England as a paper publishing mostly reliable news—has reported the following curiosity:

"Paris, November 8.... Louis-Napoleon spends his gold in vain in supporting such newspapers as the *National-Zeitung*." (*Manchester Guardian* of November 12, 1860.) [a]

"Amidst the almost universal decline of intellect and heart, the gentlemen who have the dreary task of amusing the public are at a loss for the means to astonish and rouse their readers. They continually reproduce the old jokes of their refrains and their anecdotes. They are themselves as depressed, as melancholy and as bored as those whom they undertake to cheer up. This is why out of sheer despair, when they have come to their wits' end, some of them begin to write the memoirs of courtesans, and others diplomatic pamphlets.

"Then, one fine morning, an adventurer of the pen who has never sacrificed a single hour of serious study to politics, who does not even have the ghost of a genuine conviction of any sort in his heart, gets out of bed and says to himself: 'I must strike a great blow! Let's see, what shall I do to attract the notice of the general public which instinctively ignores me? Shall I write an article on the Leotard affair or on the Eastern Question? Shall I reveal to an astonished world the secrets of boudoirs which I have never entered, or the mysteries of Russian politics of which I know even less? Shall I melt with emotion in the Voltairean manner about the fate of *fallen women*, or bewail in Biblical prose the wretched Maronite population persecuted, plundered and slaughtered by Moslem fanaticism? Shall I sing the praises of Mademoiselle Rigolboche or pen an apologia of temporal power? I have it: I shall settle for politics. I shall entertain my public better with kings and emperors than with loose women.' Having said which, our supernumerary of the literary *Bohème* wades through the *Moniteur*, hangs around the colonnades of the Stock Exchange for several days, visits a few officials and in the end he knows which way the wind of the town's curiosity is blowing, or the direction of the favour of the Court. He then selects a title capable of capturing a sufficient portion of this wind, whereupon he rests on his laurels. He has now done everything necessary; for these days only two things are needed to make a pamphlet: the title and the relations that may be supposed to exist between the author and 'people in high places'.

"Is it still necessary, after all this, to speak of the value of the pamphlets which are flooding the market? If one day you pluck up all your courage and try to read them right through to the end you will be appalled by the extraordinary ignorance, the unbearable frivolousness and especially the utter debasement of moral principles that they reveal in their authors. And I am not speaking of the worst of them.... And every year sees the standard sink still lower, every year brings new evidence of intellectual decadence, every year brings a new literary dishonour to add to those which already make us blush. Things have come to such a pass that even the greatest optimists sometimes wonder what the morrow will bring and anxiously ask themselves: Shall we ever be able to escape from all this?"—*Ed.*

[a] Marx quotes the passage from *The Manchester Guardian* in English and gives the German translation in brackets.—*Ed.*

However, I think that the normally so well-informed correspondent of the *Manchester Guardian* is mistaken this time. For F. Zabel is said to have gone over to the Bonapartist camp to prove that he is *not in the pay of Austria*. At any rate, this information reached me from Berlin and it fits well into the— *Dunciad*.

16. POSTSCRIPT

a) K. VOGT AND *LA CIMENTAIRE*

While the last of these pages were being printed, I accidentally came across the *October issue* (1860) of the *Stimmen der Zeit*. A. Kolatschek, the former publisher of the *Deutsche Monatsschrift*, the organ of the refugee parliamentarians, and hence, in a manner of speaking, the literary superior of the "fugitive Regent of the Empire", tells the following story about his *friend Karl Vogt* on p. 37:

> "The Geneva joint-stock company, *La Cimentaire*, which numbered none other than Herr *Karl Vogt* himself among its *directors*, was founded in 1857. By 1858 the shareholders were down to their last farthing and the public prosecutor immediately put one of the directors in gaol on charges of fraud. At the time of the arrest Herr Vogt happened to be away in Berne; he returned in haste, the man who had been arrested was set at liberty, the charges were suppressed 'for fear of causing a scandal', but the shareholders lost everything. But after such an example as this it cannot really be maintained that property is very well protected in Geneva and the error of Herr *Karl Vogt* in this respect is all the stranger since he was, as we have mentioned, *one of the directors of the company concerned*. And even in France in similar cases it is customary to search for the culprits among the directors, to put them into gaol and to use their property to satisfy the civil claims of the shareholders."

This should be compared with the account given by Joh. Ph. Becker in his letter (in Chapter X) about the bank incident which drove M. *James Fazy* into the arms of the Decembrists.[a] Such details as this are a great help in solving the riddle of how *"Napoléon le Petit"* became the greatest man of his age. As is well known *"Napoléon le Petit"* himself had to choose between a coup d'état and—Clichy.[251]

b) KOSSUTH

The following excerpt from a memorandum of a conversation with *Kossuth* proves incontrovertibly that Kossuth knows perfectly well that it is *Russia* that constitutes the greatest threat to

---

[a] See this volume, pp. 230-35.— *Ed.*

Hungary. The memorandum[252] comes from one of the most celebrated radical members[a] of the present House of Commons.[b]

"*Memorandum of a conversation with M. Kossuth on the evening of May 30th, 1854,* at....

"... A return to strict legality in Hungary (said he, viz. *Kossuth*) might renew the union of Hungary and Austria, and *would prevent Russia from finding any partisan in Hungary*. He (Kossuth) would not offer any opposition to a return to legality. He would advise his countrymen to accept with good faith such a restoration, if it could be obtained, and would pledge himself not in any way to be an obstacle to such an arrangement. He would not himself return to Hungary. He would not himself put forward such a course for Austria as he had no belief in Austria's return to legality, except under pressure of dire necessity. He gave me authority to say, such were his sentiments, and if appealed to, he would avow them, though he could not commit himself to any proposal, as he could not expect Austria to abandon her traditional scheme of centralisation till forced to do so.... He would have consented in 1848 to Hungarian troops being sent to resist attacks of the Piedmontese" (M. Kossuth went much further in 1848 since he ensured that Hungarian troops would be sent against the Italian "rebels" by delivering a violent speech in the Imperial Diet in Pest), "but would not employ them to coerce Austrian Italy, as he would not consent to foreign troops in Hungary."[253]

The mythopoeic power of popular fantasy has always shown itself in the creation of "great men". *Simon Bolivar* is undeniably the most convincing illustration of this. As for *Kossuth,* he is, for example, celebrated as the man who abolished feudalism in Hungary. Nevertheless he is in no way connected with the three great measures: universal taxation, the abolition of the feudal burden of the peasantry and the abolition without compensation of the tithes paid to the Church. The motion for *universal taxation* (the nobility having previously been exempt) was put by *Szemere*; the motion to do away with corvée, etc., by *Bonis,* the deputy for Szabolcz, and the clergy itself, acting through Jekelfalussy, a deputy and a canon, voluntarily relinquished its rights to raise tithes.[254]

c) EDMOND ABOUT'S LA PRUSSE EN 1860

At the end of Chapter VIII I expressed the opinion that E. *About*'s pamphlet *La Prusse en 1860*, or as it was originally called, *Napoléon III et la Prusse,* was a retranslation into French of an excerpt of Dâ-Dâ Vogt's German compilation of the Dentu pamphlets.[c] The only objection to this view was the total ignorance

---

[a] William Sandford.— *Ed.*

[b] Marx uses the English term and gives the text of the memorandum, which follows, in English too.— *Ed.*

[c] See this volume, pp. 182-83.— *Ed.*

of the German language on the part of that unsuccessful comedy writer, E. About. But was it out of the question for the *compère Guillery* to have discovered a *commère allemande*[a] somewhere or other in Paris? Who this *commère* was remained a matter of conjecture. *La Prusse en 1860* was known to have been published as a vademecum for Louis Bonaparte's trip to Baden-Baden[255]; it was designed to foreshadow his request to the Prince Regent and to make it clear to Prussia that in the December 2 Empire Prussia possessed, in the concluding words of the pamphlet, an "allié très utile qui est peut-être appelé à lui" (Prussia) "rendre de grands services, *pourvu qu'elle s'y prête un peu*".[b] E. About had already revealed in French (see Chapter IX, "Agency"[c]) in *L'Opinion Nationale* as early as the spring of 1860 that "*pourvu qu'elle s'y prête un peu*" translated into German means: "on the condition that Prussia sells the Rhine Province to France". In view of these aggravating circumstances I could not name anyone as the German prompter of E. About, the unsuccessful comedy writer and Dentu pamphletist, simply on the basis of a conjecture. But I am now justified in declaring that the German *commère* of the *compère* Guillery is none other than Vogt's gentle Kunigunde— *Herr Ludwig Simon of Trier.* This was hardly suspected by the German refugee in London[d] who penned the well-known answer to About's pamphlet.[e]

---

[a] *Compère*—godfather, *commère allemande*—German godmother.— *Ed.*

[b] "A very useful ally, who is still ready to render her" (Prussia) "great service, *provided that she will help herself.*"— *Ed.*

[c] See this volume, pp. 211-12.— *Ed.*

[d] S. L. Borkheim.— *Ed.*

[e] *Napoléon III und Preussen. Antwort eines deutschen Flüchtlings auf die Broschüre "Preussen in 1860" von Edmond About,* London, 1860.— *Ed.*

New-York Tribune.

VOL. XIX.....No. 5,862.   NEW-YORK, TUESDAY, FEBRUARY 7, 1860.   PRICE TWO CENTS.

Karl Marx

AFFAIRS IN FRANCE [256]

Paris, Jan. 17, 1860

Louis Napoleon has been converted to Free-trade, and is about to inaugurate a new era of peace. He can hardly fail to be enrolled as a member of the Society of Friends,[257] and the year 1860 will, in the annals of Europe, be recorded as the year 1 of the Millennium. This extraordinary news going the round of the London Press dates its origin from a letter of Louis Bonaparte published in the *Moniteur*, dated Jan. 15, 1860, and addressed to Mr. Fould, Minister of State.[a] The first effect of the letter was to send the Funds down at Paris and to send them up at London.

Now, before all things, it seems necessary to scrutinize somewhat closely the *corpus delicti*—that is, the Imperial letter—upon which the whole superstructure of the new era is about to be reared. Louis Bonaparte informs Mr. Fould that

"the moment has arrived for applying ourselves to the means of giving a greater development to the different branches of national wealth."

The almost identical announcement[b] appeared in the *Moniteur* of January, 1852, when the *Coup d'état* inaugurated the era of the *Crédit Mobilier*, the *Crédit Foncier*, and other *Crédits ambulants*.[258] And this is not all. Since that eventful epoch, every yearly financial bulletin issued under the auspices of the French autocrat has laid all its stress upon and proved by an awful array of official figures the circumstance that the Empire had been as good as its word,

---

[a] Here and below see *Le Moniteur universel*, No. 15, January 15, 1860. Further on Marx calls this letter a "manifesto".— *Ed.*

[b] "Au nom du peuple français", *Le Moniteur universel*, No. 15, January 15, 1852.— *Ed.*

and that, under its fostering sway, all the branches of national industry *had* taken an immense development.

Thus one finds himself in a fix. Either the proclamations of the *Coup d'état* were untimely, and the financial bulletins issued after the *Coup d'état* were spurious, or the present proclamation is a mere hoax.

At all events, this much appears incontrovertible, on the own showing of the new Imperial manifesto, that the economical benefits which French society was to derive from the resurrection of Bonapartism belong not to the past, but to the future tense. Let us, then, see by what new contrivance the happy economical change is to be brought about.

In the first instance, Louis Bonaparte tells Mr. Fould, who must have been somewhat startled at the profound discovery of his master, that "our foreign commerce must be developed by the exchange of products," a stupendous truism, indeed. Foreign commerce consisting in the exchange of national products for foreign products, it cannot be denied that, to develop French foreign commerce, the exchange of French products must be developed. The principal result which Louis Bonaparte expects from the new development of French foreign commerce he is about to start, is "to spread prosperity among the working classes," the which, as implicitly confessed by the man of the *Coup d'État*, and as shown by recent French writers (see, for instance, the works of the late Mr. Colins[a]), have visibly decayed within the last ten years. Unhappily, one great fact strikes the most superficial observer. French foreign commerce *has* made immense strides from 1848 to 1860. Amounting in 1848 to about 875 millions francs, it has risen to more than double that sum in 1859. An increase of commerce by more than 100 per cent in the short space of ten years, is a thing almost unprecedented. The causes that have brought about that increase are to be found in California, Australia, the United States, and so forth, but certainly not in the archives of the Tuileries.[259] It appears, then, that despite the immense increase of French foreign commerce within the last ten years—an increase to be traced to revolutions in the markets of the world quite beyond the petty control of the French police—the situation of the mass of the French nation has not improved. Consequently, there must have been at work some

---

[a] Marx refers to Jean Guillaume Colins' works *L'économie politique. Sources des révolutions et des utopies prétendues socialistes,* Vols. I-III, Paris, 1856-1857, and *Science sociale,* Paris, 1857.— *Ed.*

agency powerful enough to frustrate the natural results of commercial progress. If the development of French foreign commerce accounts for the apparent ease with which the second Empire has been allowed to indulge its expensive vagaries, the prostration of the nation, despite its doubled exports, betrays the cost at which that Imperial ease is purchased. If the Empire could not have subsisted *without* that development of French foreign commerce, that commercial progress has failed *with* the Empire to bear its legitimate fruits.

The Austrian Emperor, having banished the deficit from his States by dint of a ukase, why should Louis Bonaparte, by dint of another ukase, not command the increase of French foreign commerce? Still he apprehends some hitch in his way.

"We must first," he says, "improve our agriculture, and free our industry from all interior impediments which place it in a position of inferiority."

That French agriculture is badly in want of improvement, is the standing topic of French economists; but how is Louis Bonaparte to do the thing? In the first place, he will grant loans to agriculture at a moderate "interest." French agriculture is notoriously the concern of more than two-thirds of the French nation. Will Louis Bonaparte impose taxes upon the remaining third, in order to grant loans "at a moderate rate" to the majority of the nation? The idea is in fact too preposterous to be insisted upon. On the other hand, it was the confessed aim of his *Crédits Fonciers* to direct loanable capital to the land. The only thing they have proved efficient in is not in ameliorating agriculture, but in ruining small freeholds and accelerating the concentration of landed estates. After all, we have here again the old worn-out panacea—institutions of credit. Nobody will deny that the second Empire marks an epoch in the development of French credit, but that it has overshot the mark, and that, with its own credit, its credit-fostering influence has gone to the wall. The only novelty seems to be that the semi-official credit machinery having been stretched and worked to its utmost, Louis Bonaparte now dreams of converting the Government itself into a direct loan-shop. While any such attempt must be fraught with immense dangers, it would as necessarily collapse as did his grain granaries, intended to screw up the prices of corn.[260] Draining, irrigating, and cleaning the ground, are all very good things in their different lines, but their only possible effect is to multiply agricultural products. They cannot raise, and they are not intended to raise, the prices of those products. Now then, even if Louis Bonaparte should find by

some miraculous methods the ways and means required for those
ameliorations on a national scale, how are they to mend the
depreciation of agricultural produce which the French peasant has
labored under for these five years? But then, Louis Napoleon will
set about a consecutive amelioration of the means of communication. The coolness with which this proposition is made, beats even
Bonapartist impudence. Look only to the development of French
railways since 1850. The annual expense for these "means of
communication" amounted, from 1845 to '47, to about
175,000,000 of francs; from 1848 to '51, to about 125,000,000;
from 1852 to '54, to nearly 250,000,000 (double the expenditure
of 1848-'51); from 1854[a] to '56, to nearly 550,000,000; from 1857
to '59, to about 500,000,000. In 1857, when the general crisis
broke in upon the commercial world, the French Government
stood aghast at the immense sums still required for the railways in
progress or already conceded. It prohibited the railway companies
from raising, by means of securities, debentures, &c., more than
212,500,000 francs annually, interdicted the getting up of new
companies, and circumscribed within fixed limits the work to be
annually undertaken. And, after all this, Louis Bonaparte speaks
as if railways, canals, and so forth, were now first to be invented!
A forcible reduction of the canal dues, which he hints at, is, of
course, an operation involving the breach of public contracts,
frightening the capital embarked in those enterprises, and
certainly not calculated to allure new capital into the same
channels. Lastly, to find a market for agricultural products,
manufacturing industry is to be stimulated. Yet, as we have
already stated, manufacturing industry has made immense strides
during the second Empire, but with all that, with the unprecedented increase of exports, with the immense development of
railways and other means of communication, with the exaggeration of a credit system formerly unknown in France, French
agriculture languishes, and the French peasantry decays. How
shall we account for the strange phenomenon? The fact that
255,000,000 of francs are added yearly to the funded debt, not to
speak of the impost of blood for the army and the navy, offers a
sufficient answer. The Empire itself is the great incubus whose
burden grows in a greater ratio than the productive powers of the
French nation.

Louis Bonaparte's prescriptions for French industry, if we
deduct all that is mere phraseology, or is still looming in the

---

[a] Thus in the original.— Ed.

future, are simply these: Suppression of the duties on wool and cotton, and successive reductions on sugar and coffee. Now, this is all very well, but all the gullibility of English free-traders is required to call such measures free trade. Whoever is acquainted with political economy, knows full well that the abolition of duties on agricultural raw material forms a main item in the doctrine of the mercantile school of the eighteenth century. These "interior impediments" which weigh upon French production, are as nothing if compared with the *octrois*,[261] dividing France into as many independent countries as there are towns, paralyzing the internal exchange, and barring the creation of wealth by crippling its consumption. Those *octrois*, however, have increased under the Imperial régime, and will continue to increase. The diminution of duties on wool and cotton is to be made up by suppressing the sinking fund, so that the last restraint upon the growth of the public debts, although merely nominal, will be done away with.

On the other hand, the woods are to be cleared, the hills to be leveled, and the moors to be drained, by applying to those purposes the 160,000,000 of francs said to form the remnant disposable from the last war loans, in three yearly installments, which will make less than 54,000,000 of francs on an annual average. Why, the embankment of the Loire alone, so pompously announced by the Imperial Cagliostro some five years ago, and then no longer thought of, would absorb the whole sum in less than three months. What then remains of the manifesto! "The inauguration of an era of peace," as if that era had not long since been proclaimed at Bordeaux. "*L'Empire c'est la paix.*"[a]

Written on January 17, 1860

First published in the *New-York Daily Tribune*, No. 5862, February 7, 1860

Reproduced from the newspaper

---

[a] The words quoted are taken from Napoleon III's speech in Bordeaux on October 9, 1852, shortly before the plebiscite and the proclamation of the second Empire. They were a demagogic attempt to win the sympathy of the people.— *Ed.*

Karl Marx

ENGLISH POLITICS

London, Jan. 27, 1860

The most interesting topics touched upon in the parliamentary address[a] debates were the third Chinese war, the commercial treaty with France, and the Italian complication.[262] The Chinese question, it ought to be understood, involves not only an international question, but also a constitutional question of vital import. The second Chinese war,[263] undertaken on the arbitrary behest of Lord Palmerston, having led first to a vote of censure against his Cabinet, and then to a forcible dissolution of the House of Commons—the new House, although elected under his own auspices, was never called upon to cashier the sentence passed by its predecessor. To this very moment Lord Palmerston's second Chinese war stands condemned by a parliamentary verdict. But this is not all.

On the 16th of September, 1859, the account of the repulse on the Peiho was received in England. Instead of summoning Parliament, Lord Palmerston addressed himself to Louis Bonaparte, and conversed with the autocrat on a new Anglo-French expedition against China.

"During three months," as Lord Grey says, "the British ports and arsenals resounded with the din of preparation, and measures were taken for dispatching artillery, stores, and gun-boats to China, and for sending land forces of not less than 10,000 men, in addition to the naval forces."[b]

---

[a] Victoria, "The Queen's Speech. The Address, January 24, 1860," *The Times*, No. 23525, January 25, 1860.— *Ed.*

[b] Here and below Marx quotes Lord Grey's speech in the House of Lords on January 24, 1860 during the parliamentary address debates. See *The Times*, No. 23525, January 25, 1860.— *Ed.*

The country having thus been fairly embarked in a new war, on the one hand by a treaty with France, on the other by a vast expenditure incurred without any previous communication to Parliament, the latter, on its meeting, is coolly asked "to thank her Majesty for having informed them of what had occurred, and the preparations that were making for the expedition to China." In what different style could Louis Napoleon himself have addressed his own *corps législatif,* or the Emperor Alexander his senate?

In the debate on the address in the House of Commons in 1857, Mr. Gladstone, the present Chancellor of the Exchequer, with reference to the Persian war,[264] had indignantly exclaimed:

"I will say, without fear of contradiction, that the practice of commencing wars, without first referring to Parliament, is utterly at variance with the *established practice* of the country, *dangerous to the Constitution, and absolutely requiring the intervention of this House,* in order to render the repetition *of so dangerous a proceeding* utterly impossible." [a]

Lord Palmerston has not only repeated the proceeding, "so dangerous to the Constitution"; he has not only repeated it this time with the concurrence of the sanctimonious Mr. Gladstone, but as if to try the strength of ministerial irresponsibility, wielding the rights of Parliament against the Crown, the prerogatives of the Crown against Parliament and the privileges of both against the people—he had the boldness to repeat the dangerous proceeding within the same sphere of action. His one Chinese war being censured by the Parliament, he undertakes another Chinese war in spite of Parliament. Still, in both Houses, only one man mustered courage enough to make a stand against this ministerial usurpation; and, curiously to say, that one man belonging not to the popular, but to the aristocratic branch of the Legislature. The man is Lord Grey. He proposed an amendment to the address in answer to the Queen's speech to the purport that the expedition ought not to have been entered upon before the sense of both Houses of Parliament was taken.

The manner in which Lord Grey's amendment was met, both by the spokesman of the ministerial party and the leader of her Majesty's opposition, is highly characteristic of the political crisis which the representative institutions of England are rapidly approaching. Lord Grey conceded that, in a formal sense, the Crown enjoyed the prerogative of entering upon wars, but since Ministers were interdicted from spending one single farthing on

---

[a] Marx quotes Gladstone from Lord Grey's speech.— *Ed.*

any enterprise without the previous sanction of Parliament, it was the constitutional law and practice that the responsible representatives of the Crown should never enter upon warlike expeditions before notice having been given to Parliament, and the latter been called upon to make provision for defraying the expenditure which might be thus incurred. Thus, if the council of the nation thought fit, it might check, in the beginning, any unjust or impolitic war contemplated by ministers. His Lordship quoted then some examples in order to show how strictly these rules were formerly adhered to. In 1790, when some British vessels were seized by the Spaniards on the north-west coast of America, Pitt brought down to both Houses a message from the Crown[a] calling for a vote of credit to meet the probable expenses. Again in December 1826, when the daughter of Dom Pedro[b] applied to England for assistance against Ferdinand VII of Spain, who intended an invasion of Portugal to the benefit of Dom Miguel, Canning brought down a similar message[c] notifying to Parliament the nature of the case and the amount of expenditure likely to be incurred. In conclusion Lord Grey broadly intimated that the ministry had dared to raise taxes upon the country without the concurrence of Parliament, since the large expenditure already incurred must have been defrayed one way or other; and could not have been defrayed without encroaching upon money-grants provided for entirely different demands.

Now which sort of reply did Lord Grey elicit on the part of the Cabinet? The Duke of Newcastle, who had been foremost in protesting against the lawfulness of Palmerston's second Chinese war, answered in the first instance that "the very wholesome practice had arisen of late years of never moving an amendment to the address, unless some great *party object* was to be attained."[d] Consequently, Lord Grey being not prompted by factious motives, and pretending not to aspire to put Ministers out in order to put himself in, what, for the life of the Duke of Newcastle, could he mean by infringing upon that "very wholesome practice of late years"? Was he crotchety enough to fancy that they were to break

---

[a] George III, "Message respecting Vessels captured by Spain at Nootka Sound. 1790, 5 May", *The Parliamentary History of England from the Earliest Period to the Year 1803*, London, 1816, Vol. 28, pp. 764-66.— *Ed.*

[b] Maria II da Gloria.— *Ed.*

[c] George IV [Message respecting Portugal, December 11, 1826], *Hansard's Parliamentary Debates*, London, 1826, Vol. 16, pp. 334-36.— *Ed.*

[d] Here and below Marx quotes the Duke of Newcastle's speech in the House of Lords on January 24, 1860. See *The Times*, No. 23525, January 25, 1860.— *Ed.*

lances except for great party objects? In the second instance, was it not notorious that the constitutional practice, so anxiously adhered to by Pitt and Canning, had been over and over again departed from by Lord Palmerston? Had that noble Viscount not carried on a war of his own in Portugal in 1831, in Greece in 1850, and, as the Duke of Newcastle might have added, in Persia, in Afghanistan[265] and in many other countries? Why, if Parliament had allowed Lord Palmerston to usurp to himself the right of war and peace and taxation during the course of thirty years, why, then, should they all at once try to break from their long servile tradition? Constitutional law might be on the side of Lord Grey, but prescription was undoubtedly on the side of Lord Palmerston. Why call the noble Viscount to account at this time of the day, since never before had he been punished for similar "wholesome" innovations? In fact, the Duke of Newcastle seemed rather indulgent in not accusing Lord Grey of rebellion for his attempt at breaking through Lord Palmerston's prescriptive privilege of doing with his own—the forces and the money of England—as he liked.

Equally original was the manner in which the Duke of Newcastle endeavored to prove the legality of the Peiho expedition. There exists an Anglo-Chinese treaty of 1843, by dint of which England enjoys all the rights conceded by the Celestials to the most favored nations.[266] Now Russia, in her recent treaty with China, has stipulated for the right of sailing up the Peiho.[267] Consequently, under the treaty of 1843, the English had a right to such passage. This, the Duke of Newcastle said, he might insist upon "without any great special pleading." Might he, indeed! On the one side there is the ugly circumstance that the Russian treaty was only ratified, and, consequently, dates its actual existence only from an epoch posterior to the Peiho catastrophe. This, of course, is but a slight *husteron proteron*.[a] On the other hand, it is generally known that a state of war suspends all existing treaties. If the English were at war with the Chinese at the time of the Peiho expedition, they, of course, could appeal neither to the treaty of 1843, nor to any other treaty whatever. If they were not at war, Palmerston's Cabinet has taken upon itself to commence a new war without the sanction of Parliament? To escape the latter part of the dilemma, poor Newcastle asserts that since the Canton bombardment,[268] for the last two years, "England had *never* been *at peace*

---

[a] The latter (put as) the former—a figure of speech in which what should come last is put first; inversion of the natural order.— *Ed.*

with China." Consequently the Ministry had pushed on hostilities, not recommenced them, and consequently he might, without special pleading, appeal to the treaties effective only during a time of peace. And to highten the beauty of this queer sort of dialectics, Lord Palmerston, the chief of the Cabinet, asserts at the same time, in the House of Commons, that England all this time over, "*had never been at war with China.*" [a] They were not so now. There were, of course, Canton bombardments, Peiho catastrophes, and Anglo-French expeditions, but there was no war, since war had never been *declared,* and since, to this moment, the Emperor of China [b] had allowed transactions at Shanghai to proceed in their usual course. The very fact of his having broken, in regard to the Chinese, through all the legitimate international forms of war, Palmerston pleads as a reason for dispensing also with the constitutional forms in regard to the British Parliament, while his spokesman in the House of Lords, Earl Granville, "with regard to China," disdainfully declares "*the consultation of Parliament by Government*" to be "*a purely technical point.*" [c] The consultation of Parliament by Government a purely technical point! What difference, then, does still remain between a British Parliament and a French *Corps Législatif?* In France, it is, at least, the presumed heir of a national hero [d] who dares to place himself in the place of the nation, and who at the same time openly confronts all the dangers of such usurpation. But, in England, it is some subaltern spokesman, some worn-out place-hunter, some anonymous nonentity of a so-called Cabinet, that, relying on the donkey power of the parliamentary mind and the bewildering evaporations of an anonymous press, without making any noise, without incurring any danger, quietly creep their way to irresponsible power. Take on the one hand the commotions raised by a Sulla [269]; take on the other the fraudulent businesslike maneuvers of the manager of a joint stock bank, the secretary of a benevolent society, or the clerk of a vestry, and you will understand the difference between imperialist usurpation in France and ministerial usurpation in England! Lord Derby, fully aware of the equal interest both factions have in securing ministerial impotence and irresponsibility, could, of course, "not concur with the noble Earl

---

[a] Lord Palmerston's speech in the House of Commons on January 25, 1860, *The Times,* No. 23526, January 26, 1860.— *Ed.*

[b] Hsien Fêng.— *Ed.*

[c] The Earl of Granville's speech in the House of Lords on January 24, 1860, *The Times,* No. 23525, January 25, 1860.— *Ed.*

[d] The reference is to Napoleon III and Napoleon I.— *Ed.*

[Grey] in the strong views which he takes of the *laches* of Government."[a] He could not quite concur in Lord Grey's complaint that "the Government ought to have called Parliament together, to have consulted them on the Chinese question," but he "certainly would not support him by his vote, should he press the amendment to a division."

Consequently, the amendment was not pressed to a division, and the whole debate, in both Houses, on the Chinese war, evaporated in grotesque compliments showered by both factions on the head of Admiral Hope for having so gloriously buried the English forces in the mud.

Written on January 27, 1860   Reproduced from the newspaper

First published in the *New-York Daily Tribune*, No. 5868, February 14, 1860

---

[a] Lord Derby's speech in the House of Lords on January 24, 1860, *The Times*, No. 23525, January 25, 1860.— *Ed.*

Karl Marx

THE NEW TREATY BETWEEN FRANCE
AND ENGLAND

London, Jan. 28, 1860

The commercial treaty with France[270] will not be communicated to the House of Commons before the 6th of February. Still, with what was broached during the address debates—with what is insinuated by the French papers, and with what is gossiped at London and Paris, one may, Mr. Gladstone's solemn warnings[a] notwithstanding, already venture upon some general appreciation of this "sweet changeling."[271] It was on Monday, the 23d of January, that the treaty was duly signed at Paris, Rouher, Minister of Commerce, and Baroche, ad interim Minister of Foreign Affairs, acting as its French godfathers, while, on the part of England, the same function was performed by Lord Cowley and Mr. Cobden. That Mr. Michel Chevalier—the ex-St. Simonian— had his hand in the pie, and that general regret is felt throughout the whole realm of France that Louis Napoleon had not the tact of allowing this distinguished personage (viz.: Mr. Chevalier) to inscribe his name to the treaty by the side of his "English confrère,"[b] is a piece of news which that "distinguished personage" himself was so condescending as to send over to London and have inserted in the various free-trade organs. But, what is not known by the journals, is that *Père Enfantin*, the ex-high-priest of St. Simonism, was the principal actor on the French side. Is it not truly wonderful how those St. Simonians, from *Père Enfantin* down to Isaac Péreire and Michel Chevalier, have been turned into the main economical pillars of the second Empire. But to return to

---

[a] Gladstone's speech in the House of Commons on January 25, 1860, *The Times*, No. 23526, January 26, 1860.— *Ed.*

[b] Colleague.— *Ed.*

Mr. Chevalier's "English *confrère*," the Lancashire ex-manufac-
turer, who, of course, felt not a little elated at the honor of putting his own sign-manual to an international treaty. If one should
consider the circumstance that reciprocity treaties, and commercial treaties generally, save the treaties with barbarians, have
always been loudly denounced by the English free-traders, led
by Mr. Cobden, as the worst and most perfidious form of pro-
tectionism; if it be further considered that the present treaty,
even judged from the reciprocity stand-point, seems a rather
ludicrous arrangement; and, lastly, if the political aims and
purposes the treaty is destined to screen be duly weighed, people
might feel inclined to pity Mr. Richard Cobden as the innocent
victim of a Palmerstonian machination. Yet there is another side to
the medal. Mr. Cobden, as is generally known, did once receive, in
exchange for his Anti-Corn law[272] success, some £60,000 sterling
on the part of the grateful manufacturing interest. Mr. Cobden
invested the principal in American shares, and, consequent upon
the crisis of 1857, lost almost everything. The hopes he still
cherished when setting out on his voyage to the United States,
proved delusory. Mr. Cobden returned to England a ruined man.
To appeal to a national subscription some national pretext was
wanted, some transaction that might be puffed, and again exhibit
Mr. Cobden in the light of the guardian angel of the United
Kingdom, "securing plenty and comfort to millions of lowly
households." Well, the Anglo-French treaty *did* the thing, and, as
you will see, from the provincial papers, a new subscription to the
amount of £40,000, intended to compensate the great free-trade
apostle for his American losses, already goes the round very
"feelingly." There is no doubt that if Disraeli, for instance, had
introduced to the Commons such a treaty, Mr. Cobden at the head
of the free-traders would have risen to move for a vote of
non-confidence in a Cabinet attempting to carry the legislation
back to the darkest fallacies of the unenlightened past.

From the following tables[a] the number of protective duties
levied during the year 1858 by England on French articles may be
inferred:

Articles.	Duty.
Baskets	£2,061
Butter	7,159
China and Porcelain Ware	1,671
Clocks	3,928

[a] "Commercial Treaties and Free Trade", *The Economist*, No. 857, January
28, 1860, p. 85.—*Ed.*

Coffee	4,311
Eggs	19,934
Embroidery	5,572
Flowers, artificial	20,412
Fruit	7,347
Lace	1,858
Boots, Shoes, and other Leather Manufactures	8,883
Gloves	48,839
Musical Instruments	4,695
Oil, chemical	2,369
Paper-Hangings	6,713
Plaiting of Straw, for hats, &c	11,622
Silks	215,455
Brandy and other Spirits	824,960
Sugar	275,702
Tea	14,358
Tobacco	52,696
Watches	14,940
Wine	164,855

Most of the duties thus levied were protective duties, as those on baskets, clocks, lace, boots, gloves, silks, etc. Others, like the duties on brandy, etc., were higher than the English excise duty on British spirits, and so far protective. Even mere duties for revenue, such as the duty on wine, might be considered by a consequent free-trader as protective duties, because it is almost impossible to levy taxes on a foreign article without protecting some similar, if not identical, article in the home market. For instance, a revenue duty on foreign wine may be considered a protective duty for native beer, etc. By dint of the treaty just concluded all British duties on French manufactures will be abolished at once, while the duties on brandy, wine, and other articles, will be assimilated to English excise duties, or to the Custom-House duty now raised on similar products (wine for instance) if introduced from British colonies. On the other hand, the French changes of tariff will not be completely carried out before October, 1861, as will be seen from the following statement, borrowed from a French Government paper[a]:

July 1, 1860—Suppression of the import duties on cotton and wool.
July 1, 1860—Belgian tariff applied to English coal and coke.
October 1, 1860—Duty of 7 francs the 100 kilogs. substituted for the present duties on iron.
December 31, 1860—Diminution of the duties on the importation of machinery.

---

[a] "Foreign correspondence. Paris, Thursday", The Economist, No. 857, January 28, 1860.— Ed.

June 1, 1861—Removal of the prohibition on hemp threads and fabrics, and the adoption of duties not exceeding 30 per cent.

October 1, 1861—Removal of all other prohibitions, to be replaced by protective duties ad valorem for five years, and not exceeding 25 per cent afterward.

Save the reduction of the duty on English coal to the same rate now paid by Belgian coal, all the concessions apparently made by France appear of a very equivocal character. The price of a tun of pig iron No. 1 (Wales) amounts, for instance, at present, to £3 10/, but the French duty on iron will amount to nearly another £3. That the 30 per cent ad valorem duty on prohibited articles will be virtually protective is conceded by the London *Economist*. So far as the reductions, real or apparent, on English articles are put off to future periods, the English Government acts, in fact, the part of an insurance office for Louis Napoleon's tenure of power for the terms specified. The true secret, however, of the commercial treaty, viz.: that "*it is no commercial treaty at all*," but a simple hoax, intended to puzzle John Bull's commercial mind, and to cloak a deep-laid political scheme, has been masterly exposed by Mr. Disraeli during the address debates.[a] The substance of his revelation was this:

"Some years ago, the Emperor of the French made a communication similar to the letter lately addressed by him to the Minister of the Interior,[b] in which communication he proposed the entire extinction of the prohibitive system, and the adoption of measures similar to those contained in his late manifesto.[c] In 1856, a bill in this sense was introduced into the *Corps Législatif* [...], but, before being passed, was laid before the 86 Provincial Councils of France,[d] which, with the exception of 6, all adopted the proposal with an understanding that a certain period of time should elapse before the new system should be brought into play. Consequently, the Emperor agreeing with this proposition, some public document expressed his resolution to carry this system into effect, and appointed July, 1861, as the period with which it should commence." All, therefore, that France engages by the treaty to do in July, 1861, "was already provided by the course of law in France."

Written on January 28, 1860   Reproduced from the newspaper

First published in the *New-York Daily Tribune*, No. 5868, February 14, 1860

---

[a] Benjamin Disraeli's speech in the House of Commons on January 24, 1860, *The Times*, No. 23525, January 25, 1860.— *Ed.*

[b] *The Times* has "the Minister of State".— *Ed.*

[c] See this volume, p. 330.— *Ed.*

[d] *The Times* has "86 Councils General, the departmental Parliaments of France".— *Ed.*

Frederick Engels

MILITARY REFORM IN GERMANY[273]

The Italian war of 1859, even more than the Crimean war,[274] established the fact that the French military organization was the best in Europe. Of all European armies, excepting the French, the Austrian army certainly ranked highest; and yet, in the short campaign of 1859, though its soldiers covered themselves with glory, the army, as a whole, could not win a single battle. With all due allowance for bad generalship, want of unity of command, and for the incompetent meddling of the Emperor, still the unanimous impression of the Austrian regimental officers and of the men was, that part of their want of success was due to an organization less adapted for real war than that of their opponents. And if the Austrian army—thoroughly reorganized as it had been only a few years before—was found to be deficient, what was to be expected from other armies whose organization was of even a more ancient date?

That the French were superior in this particular, was a fact not to be wondered at. No nation with any military aptitude can carry on petty warfare for twenty-five years on so colossal a scale as that of Algeria,[275] without thereby developing to a high pitch the capabilities of its troops. While England and Russia had waged their wars in India and the Caucasus principally with troops set apart for this service, the greater part of the French army had passed through the Algerine school. France really had made the most of this school, which had been expensive in men and money, but very effective and fruitful in valuable military experience. After this, the Crimean war, another school on a larger scale, served to enhance the confidence of the soldier by showing him that what he had learned in his campaigns against nomadic tribes and irregulars, was quite as useful and applicable in a contest with regular troops.

That with such opportunities, a nation endowed with peculiar genius for the military profession, should have brought its warlike organization to a perfection exceeding anything attained by its neighbors—a fact proved beyond dispute at Magenta and Solferino[276]—nevertheless excited wonder, especially in Germany. The military pedants of that country had been so secure in their presumed superiority over the volatile, unsteady, undisciplined, immoral French, that the blow stunned them. On the other hand, the younger and more intelligent portions of the Austrian and other German armies, always opposed to martinetism, now at once began to speak out. The Austrian officers, fresh from Magenta, were the first to say, what is perfectly true, that the French carry no knapsacks in battle; that they have no stocks, no stiff collars, no tight coats or trousers; they are dressed in loose trousers, and a loose great coat with collar turned down, and neck and chest quite free; their head covered with a light cap, and they carry their cartridges in their trousers pockets. Where the men of the Austrians arrive fatigued, and out of breath, the French come up fresh and singing, and ready for any physical effort. Thus reported the letters of the Austrian officers fresh from the battle-field, and Prussian, Bavarian, and other officers soon chimed in. The awful fact was there. Soldiers had actually dared to face the enemy without all the cumbersome paraphernalia which compose almost all the glorious pomp and circumstance of war, and which taken together are equivalent to a strait-jacket; and in spite of the absence of this strait-jacket they had been victorious on every field. This fact was so very serious that even the German Governments could not close their eyes to it.

Thus military reform became the watchword of the day in Germany, to the great dismay of old fogies in general. The most revolutionary theories in matters military were not only pro-pounded with impunity, but even taken into consideration by governments. The first point was of course that of the equipment of the soldier, which had formed the most conspicuous difference between the two armies on the battle-field, and the discussion of this project was as interminable as the varieties of taste. An immense deal of ingenuity was expended on military tailoring. Caps, helmets, shakos, hats, coats, blouses, capotes, collars, cuffs, trousers, gaiters, and boots were discussed with vivacity and loquacity as if on such things alone had depended the fate of the day at Solferino. The Austrians were the most extravagant in their military fashions. From an almost exact copy of the French model (barring the color) they passed through all the intermediate stages, up to the blouse and slouched, wide-awake hat. Imagine the stiff, conservative, staid, Imperial Royal Austrian soldier in the coquettish dress of the French chasseur, or, still worse, in the blouse and felt hat of the revolutionary German free corps of 1848. A greater satire could not be passed on the Austrian military system than that either of these extremes should have been taken seriously into consideration. As usual, the debate has been exhausted rather than settled; military old fogyism has recovered part of the lost ground, and in Austria, at least, the alterations in the uniform will, upon the whole, be trifling; while in the other German armies scarcely any change appears probable, except that the Prussian helmet, that pet invention of the romantic Frederick William IV, seems doomed to descend to the grave even before its inventor.

Next came the great knapsack question. That the French went into battle without their knapsacks was a piece of imprudence which could be justified by nothing but their good luck, and the warmth of the season. But should it become a habitual thing with them, the first reverse in cold or rainy weather would punish them severely for it. In fact, the general adoption of this usage would imply nothing less than that in every battle the beaten army should lose not only its artillery, colors, and stores, but the whole of the individual baggage of its infantry also. In consequence, a few rainy bivouacs would completely break up the infantry, reduced as it would be to such clothing as every man might happen to be dressed in. The real question, however, would seem to be, how the individual baggage of the soldier can be reduced to a minimum, and this is a point of importance which might easily be settled in a satisfactory way, if the items composing it were considered merely as to their real utility in a campaign; but the discussion in Germany has not settled it.

Beside the clothes question and the knapsack question, the organization of the various subdivisions of the army is also a matter much disputed. How many men should make a company, how many companies a battalion, how many battalions a regiment, how many regiments a brigade, how many brigades a division, and so forth. This is another point upon which a great deal of bosh may be uttered with the most serious and important face in the world. In every army the system of elementary tactics confines to certain limits the strength and number of companies and battalions; the strength of brigades and divisions find their minimum and maximum by the strength adopted in neighboring armies, so that in case of a conflict the disproportion between the larger tactical units may not be too great. To try to solve such questions not by the actual conditions as given by the facts of the case, but by an attempted recourse to first principles, is mere fudge, worthy perhaps of German philosophers but not suited to practical men. The increase in the number of the Austrian regiments of infantry of the line from 63 to 80, with a reduced number of battalions, will no more insure them "better luck next time" than the widening of their trousers and the turning down of their collars.

But while man-millinery and abstruse speculations on the normal strength and composition of a brigade occupy attention, the great defects and evils of the German military system are unheeded. What, indeed, are we to think of officers who most furiously discuss the cut of a pair of pantaloons, or of a collar, and who submit quietly to have in the German federal[277] army some twenty different calibers of field artillery, and an almost incalculable variety of calibers for small-arms? The introduction of rifled muskets, which offered such a splendid occasion for equalizing the calibers all over Germany, has not only been shamefully neglected, but has made matters worse. It is worth while to look for a moment at this confusion of calibers. Austria, Bavaria, Württemberg, Baden, and Hesse-Darmstadt, have one caliber—0.53 of an inch. With that practical good sense which the South Germans have shown in many instances, they have carried this most important reform, which establishes unity of caliber for five corps of the federal army. Prussia has two calibers; one the so-called *Zündnadelgewehr*, or needle-gun,[a] about 0.60 of an inch, and the old smooth-bore musket, lately rifled on Minié's principle, about 0.68. The latter, however, is to be superseded by the former as soon as possible. The Ninth Army Corps has three different rifled and two or three different smooth-bore calibers; the Tenth has at least ten, and the reserved division has as many calibers almost as battalions. Now imagine this motley army in an active campaign. How is it possible that the ammunition belonging to each contingent can always be at hand when wanted, and if not, that contingent is helpless and useless? Excepting Austria, the South Germans and Prussia, no contingent can, from this circumstance alone, be of any real use in a lengthened contest. The same is true of the artillery. Instead of fixing at once upon one common caliber at least corresponding to the old six-pounder, which would

---

[a] See Frederick Engels' *The History of the Rifle*, present edition, Vol. 18.—*Ed.*

thus in time become the universal caliber of rifled field guns, the Prussians, the Austrians, the Bavarians are now casting rifled ordnance quite independently of each other, which will only serve to increase the diversity of calibers already existing. An army in which such fundamental defects exist might do better than spend its time in quarreling about collars and inexpressibles, and the normal strength of brigades and battalions.

There can be no military progress in Germany so long as the idea is cherished in high quarters that armies are made for parade and not for battle. Crushed for a while by Austerlitz, Wagram, and Jena,[278] and by the popular enthusiasm of 1813-15, this pedantry soon raised its head again, reigned supreme until 1848, and, in Prussia, at least, seems to have attained its culminating point during the last ten years. Had Prussia been involved in the Italian war, Pélissier could scarcely have helped inflicting another Jena upon her army, and the fortresses on the Rhine alone would have saved her. Such is the condition to which an army has been reduced which, in respect of its men, stands second to none in the world. In any future conflict between the French and the Germans, we may reasonably expect to see reproduced the features of Magenta and Solferino.

Written in late January and early February 1860

First published in the *New-York Daily Tribune*, No. 5873, February 20, 1860 as a leading article

Reproduced from the newspaper

Karl Marx

THE ENGLISH BUDGET

London, Feb. 11, 1860

The last was a great night, in the Parliamentary sense of the word. Mr. Gladstone, in an immense speech,[a] simultaneously divulged the mysteries of his budget and of the commercial treaty, linking both carefully together, and propping the frailty of the one by the boldness of the other. As to the treaty, now laid with all its details before the world, you will find the sketch I gave you many weeks ago[b] to have been quite correct, and, in fact, I have nothing to add to the general criticism I ventured upon at the time. Consequently, I propose considering Mr. Gladstone's budget as a simple operation of English finance, a treatment of the subject the more called for since the impending Parliamentary debates are sure to enlighten us, by the by, on the diplomatic undercurrent of Mr. Gladstone's facts and figures.

Now, whatever inconsistencies may be traced in the details of the budget; whatever political objections may be raised against the prudence of answering a deficit of more than 14 per cent on the total revenue, and a vast increase of expenditure, by one full sweep of many existing duties, part of which did hardly weigh upon the mass of the people; nevertheless, common fairness obliges me to say that Mr. Gladstone's budget is a great and bold stroke of financial ingenuity, and that the British Free-Trade doctrines once accepted—apart from some glaring incongruities necessitated by the treaty with France, as well as by the tenderness every British Chancellor of the Exchequer will always bring to

---

[a] Marx analyses the Budget for 1860-61, introduced by Gladstone, Chancellor of the Exchequer, in his speech in the House of Commons on February 10, 1860 (*The Times*, No. 23540, February 11, 1860).— *Ed.*

[b] See this volume, pp. 341-44.— *Ed.*

bear upon the rent-rolls of the 50,000 paramount landlords—it is a fair budget. The position of Mr. Gladstone was fraught with difficulties created by himself. He was the man, who in 1853, in his so-called standard budget prospectively extending over a space of seven years, had pledged himself to definitely do away with the income tax in 1860-61.[a] He again, in a supplementary budget,[b] called into life by the Russian war, had promised to abolish, at no distant date, the war duty on tea and sugar. The same man, now that his promissory bills have fallen due, comes forward with a scheme in which the latter duty is maintained, while the income tax is enhanced from 9d. to 10d. in the pound; that is to say, by 11 1-9 per cent. But, you will remember that, in my strictures on his budget of 1853, I tried to prove that, if the financial legislature of free-trade meant anything, it meant indirect taxation being displaced by direct taxation.[279] I dwelt at the time on the incompatibility of Mr. Gladstone's pledge of going on with the removal of custom and excise duties, with his simultaneous pledge of altogether expunging the income tax from the tax-gatherer's list. The income tax, only that it is partially, unjustly, and even stupidly laid on, is the best item in English financial law. That Mr. Gladstone, instead of seriously taxing landed property, maintains a war duty upon such first necessities as tea and sugar, is a cowardice due much more to the aristocratic structure of Parliament than to any narrowness of mind on his part. If he had dared lay his hands on the rent-rolls, the Cabinet, whose prospects of life are precarious enough, would have gone to the wall in no time. It is an old proverb that the belly has no ears, but it is no less true that rent-rolls have no conscience.

Before giving a succinct statement of the alterations contemplated by Mr Gladstone, I shall first call the attention of the reader to some incidental remarks dropped in the course of his speech. First, then, the Chancellor of the Exchequer admitted that the common opinion of free-trade being incarnated in the English financial system was mere slang. Secondly, he admitted that England had no commerce worth speaking of with France, while France, on the contrary, had a very extensive and expanding trade with England. Thirdly, he could not help confessing that Palmerstonian policy, embarking upon "friendly expeditions" behind the

---

[a] Gladstone's speeches in the House of Commons on April 18, 1853, *The Times*, No. 21406, April 19, 1853 and February 10, 1860, *The Times*, No. 23540, February 11, 1860.— *Ed.*

[b] Gladstone's speech in the House of Commons on May 8, 1854, *The Times*, No. 21736, May 9, 1854.— *Ed.*

back of Parliament, had turned the scale, and paralyzed the increase accruing to the Exchequer from the extension of British commerce and industry. Lastly, although gilding the bitter pill with a sweet envelope, and presenting it in as handy a shape as French apothecaries are used to present you the most abominable pharmaceutical stuff, he could not but own that the same dear ally, to whom Great Britain is just about sacrificing nearly two millions of income, is the mainspring of British military and naval expenditure being swollen, for the year 1860-61, to the stupendous amount of 30 millions. Eighteen millions, it should be recorded, was the maximum of war expenditure, which the Iron Duke,[a] twenty-four years since, entreated English rationalism to swallow.

After these preliminary remarks I come to the changes proposed by Mr. Gladstone. They are divided into two categories, the one resulting from the treaty with France, the other embracing subsidiary changes which Mr. Gladstone was compelled to introduce in order to free his budget from the reproach of being a concession extorted from a foreign despotic power, and imparting to it the more acceptable color of being a general reform of the existing tariff.

The changes introduced by the commercial treaty with France are these: There will at once be a clean sweep, absolutely and entirely, of manufactured goods off the British tariff, with the exception, for a limited period, of three articles only, viz.: cork, gloves, and another trifling article. The brandy duty will be reduced from 15s. a gallon to the level of the colonial duty of 8s. The duty on all foreign wines will be immediately diminished from nearly 5s. 10d. per gallon to 3s. a gallon. England engages further to reduce the duty from April 1, 1861, to a scale proportioned to the quantity of spirit contained in the wine. All duties upon foreign articles which are also produced in England, and there subject to an excise duty, will be reduced to the standard of the home excise. Such is the pith of the first set of changes to be introduced.

The alterations which, independently of the treaty with France, are to give the present budget the character of a general reformation of British financial legislature are these:

There are to be abolished immediately and entirely the duties on butter, tallow, cheese, oranges, and lemons, eggs, nutmegs, pepper, licorice, and various other articles, of which the total duty is about £382,000 a year. Reductions are to take place in the

---

[a] The Duke of Wellington.— *Ed.*

present duty raised on timber from 7/ and 7/6 to the colonial rate of 1/ and 1/6.[a] On currants, from 15/9 to 7/; on raisins and figs, from 10/ to 7/; on hops, from 45/ to 15/. Lastly, the excise upon paper is to be abolished.

The account of the financial year 1860[-61] stands thus[b]:

EXPENDITURE.

Funded and Unfunded Debt	£26,200,000
Consolidated Fund Charges	2,000,000
Army and Militia	15,800,000
Navy and Packet Service	13,900,000
Miscellaneous and Civil Service	7,500,000
Revenue Department	4,700,000
Total	£70,100,000

INCOME.

Customs	£22,700,000
Excise	19,170,000
Stamps	8,000,000
Other Taxes	3,250,000
Income Tax	2,400,000
Post-Office	3,400,000
Crown Lands	280,000
Miscellaneous Revenue	1,500,000
Total	£60,700,000

Now, on comparing expenditure with income, it will be found that a deficit to the amount of nearly £10,000,000 sterling is avowed, for which Mr. Gladstone, as already said, thinks to make up by the increase of the Income Tax from 9/ to 10/ and by the maintenance of the war duties on tea and sugar. The minor alterations, by which he proposes getting a penny here, and another penny there, it is not necessary to dwell upon in this general survey of the British Budget for 1860-61.

Written on February 11, 1860   Reproduced from the newspaper

First published in the *New-York Daily Tribune*, No. 5878, February 25, 1860

---

[a] Gladstone has these figures in his speech: "I propose to reduce the duty on timber from 7s. 6d. and 15s. to the colonial rate of 1s. and 2s."—*Ed.*

[b] *The Times*, No. 23540, February 11, 1860.—*Ed.*

Frederick Engels

ON RIFLED CANNON

I

[*New-York Daily Tribune*, No. 5914, April 7, 1860]

The first attempts at increasing the range and precision of ordnance by rifling the bore, and thereby giving the shot a rotation vertical to the line of propulsion, date from the 17th century. There is a small rifled gun at Munich, manufactured in Nuremberg in 1694; it has eight grooves and a bore of about two inches diameter. During the whole of the 18th century, experiments were made, both in Germany and in England, with rifled cannon, some of them breech-loading. Though the calibers were small, the results obtained were very satisfactory; the English two-pounders in 1776, at a range of 1,300 yards, gave a lateral deflection of two feet only—a degree of precision which no other gun at the time was capable of approaching. In the same year, these rifled cannon were for the first time used for projecting oblong shot.

These experiments, however, remained for a long while without any practical results. The current of military opinion at that time altogether went against rifled arms. The rifle itself was then a very clumsy instrument, its loading was a slow and tedious operation, requiring considerable skill. It was a weapon unfit for general warfare at a period when rapid firing, whether of deployed lines, of heads of columns, or of skirmishers, was one of the chief desiderata in battle. Napoleon would have no rifles in his army; in England and Germany, a few battalions only were equipped with them; in America and Switzerland alone, the rifle remained the national weapon.

The Algerian war was the occasion to bring the rifle again into credit, and to cause improvements in its construction which were but the beginning of that colossal revolution in the whole system of firearms which is even now far from its conclusion. The smooth-bore muskets of the French were no match for the long *espingardas* of the Arabs; their greater length and better material, which admitted of a heavier charge, enabled the Kabyles and Bedouins to fire on the French at distances where the regulation musket was utterly powerless. The Duke of Orleans,[a] having seen and admired the Prussian and Austrian chasseurs, organized the French chasseurs on their model, who soon, for armament, equipment, and tactics, became the first troops of their class in the world. The rifle with which they were armed was far superior to the old rifle, and it soon underwent further changes, resulting, finally, in the general introduction of rifled muskets in the whole of the infantry of Europe.

The range of infantry fire having thus been increased from 300 to 800, and even 1,000 yards, the question arose whether field artillery, which hitherto had commanded all distances from 300 up to 1,500 yards, would still be able to hold its own against the new small-arms. The fact was, that the greatest efficacy of common field guns lay just within that range which was now disputed to it by the rifle; canister was scarcely effective beyond 600 or 700 yards; round shot gave no very satisfactory results, with the six or nine-pounder, beyond 1,000 yards; and shrapnel (spherical case-shot), to be very formidable, required a coolness and a correct estimation of distances which are not always to be found on the field of battle, when the enemy is advancing; while the shell-practice of the old howitzers against troops was anything but satisfactory. The armies which had the nine-pounder gun for their smallest caliber, such as the English, were still the best off; the French eight-pounder, and, still more, the German six-pounder, became almost useless. To obviate this, the French introduced, about the beginning of the Crimean war, Louis Napoleon's so-called invention, the light twelve-pounder, *canon obusier*,[b] from which solid shot, with a charge of one-fourth instead of one-third its weight, as well as shell, was to be fired. This gun was a mere plagiarism upon the English light twelve-pounder, which had already been again abandoned by the English; the system of firing shells from long guns had been long in practice in Germany; so that there was nothing at all new in this pretended improvement. Still, the arming of the whole French artillery with 12-pounders, even of a diminished range, would have given it a decided

---

a Ferdinand.— *Ed.*
b Howitzer.— *Ed.*

superiority over the old 6 and 8-pounders; and to counteract this, the Prussian Government, in 1859, resolved upon giving heavy 12-pounders to all its foot batteries. This was the last move in the cause of the smooth-bore gun; it showed that the whole subject was exhausted, and the defenders of the smooth-bore driven *ad absurdum*. There could, indeed, not be anything more absurd than to arm the whole artillery of an army with those lumbering, stick-in-the-mud Prussian 12-pounders, and that at a time when mobility and rapidity of maneuvering is the greatest desideratum of all. The French light 12-pounder having a relative superiority only to other artillery, and none at all as regarded the new small-arms, and the Prussian heavy 12-pounder being a palpable absurdity, there remained nothing but either to drop field artillery altogether, or to adopt rifled cannon.

In the mean time, experiments with rifled cannon had continually been carried on in various countries. In Germany, the Bavarian Lieut.-Col. Reichenbach experimented with a small rifled gun and cylindro-conoidal shot, as early as 1816. The results were very satisfactory as to range and precision, but the difficulties of loading and extraneous obstacles prevented the subject from being followed up. In 1846, the Piedmontese Major Cavalli constructed a breech-loading rifled gun which attracted considerable attention. His first gun was a thirty-pounder, charged with a cylindro-conoidal hollow shot weighing 64 pounds, and 5 pounds powder; at $14\,^3/_4$ degrees elevation he obtained a range (of first gauge) of 3,050 metres or 3,400 yards. His experiments (continued up to the latest period, partly in Sweden, partly in Piedmont) had the important result of leading to the discovery of the regular lateral deflection of all shot fired from rifled ordnance, which is caused by the pitch of the grooves, and which is always in the direction to which the grooves turn; this once being ascertained, its correction by what is called a lateral or horizontal tangent-scale, was also invented by Cavalli. The results of his experiments were highly satisfactory. At Turin, in 1854, his thirty-pounder, with 8-pound charges, 64-pound shot, gave the following results:

Elevation.	Range.	Lateral irregular deflection.
10°	2,806 metres	2.81 metres
15°	3,785 metres	3.21 metres
20°	4,511 metres	3.72 metres
25°	5,103 metres	4.77 metres

giving a range, at 25 degrees, of above three miles, with a lateral deflection from the line of aim (as corrected by the horizontal tangent-scale) of less than 16 feet! The largest French field howitzer, at a range of 2,400 metres, equal to 2,650 yards, gave lateral deflections averaging 47 metres, or 155 feet; ten times as large as those of the rifled gun at twice the range.

Another system of rifled ordnance which created attention, a little after Cavalli's first experiments, was that of the Swedish Baron Wahrendorff. His gun was also breech-loading, and his shot cylindro-conoidal. The difference, however, in the shot was this: while Cavalli's shot was of hard metal, and had wings to fit in the grooves, Wahrendorff's shot was covered with a thin layer of lead, and slightly larger in diameter than the bore of the rifled portion of the gun. After being introduced into the chamber, which was large enough to receive it, the shot was propelled by the explosion into the rifled bore, and the lead being pressed into the grooves effectually, did away with all windage, and prevented the escape of any portion of the gases formed by the explosion. The results obtained with these guns in Sweden and elsewhere were quite satisfactory, and if Cavalli's guns were introduced into the armament of Genoa, those of Wahrendorff figure in the casemates of Waxholm in Sweden, Portsmouth in England, and in some Prussian fortresses. Thus, the introduction of rifled ordnance into practical use had begun, although only for fortresses. There remained only the one step to introduce them into field artillery, and this has been done in France and is now being done in all European artilleries. The various systems on which the rifling of field ordnance is now, or may be, profitably carried on, will form the subject of a second paper.

II

[*New-York Daily Tribune*, No. 5926, April 21, 1860]

The French were, as we said in our preceding paper, the first to introduce rifled cannon into practical warfare. For five or six years past, two officers, Col. Tamisier and Lieut.-Col. (now Col.) Treuille de Beaulieu, had experimentalized on the subject by order of the Government, and the results arrived at were found satisfactory enough to warrant their being made the base of a reorganization of the French artillery immediately before the outbreak of the late Italian war. Without entering upon the history of the experiments, we will at once pass to a description of the system now adopted in the French artillery.

In accordance with that desire for unity so characteristic of the French, they adopted one caliber only for field artillery (the old French four-pounder bore of 85 $^1/_2$ millimetres, or nearly 3 $^1/_2$ inches), and one for siege artillery (the old 12-pounder of 120 millimetres, or 4 $^3/_4$ inches). All other guns, except mortars, are to be done away with. The material selected is generally the common gun-metal, but also cast-steel, in some cases. The guns are muzzle-loading, as the French experiments with breech-loaders gave no satisfaction. There are six grooves in each gun, 5 millimetres deep and 16mm. broad, of a rounded form; the pitch of the rifling appears to be but low, but there are no details known respecting it. The windage on the body of the shot is about $^1/_2$ to 1 mm.; that on the *ailettes* or warts which enter the grooves rather less than 1 mm. The shot is cylindro-ogival, and hollow, weighing about 12 pounds when filled; it has six *ailettes*, one for every groove, three standing near the point, and three near the base; they are very short—about 15 mm. long. The fuse-hole passes downward from the point, and is closed by a fuse or by a piston, with a percussion-cap for shot filled with powder, and by an iron screw, when the shot is not to explode; in this latter case it is filled with a mixture of sawdust and sand, so as to give it the same weight as when filled with powder. The length of bore of the gun is 1,385 mm., or 16 times its diameter; the weight of the brass gun is but 237 kilogrammes (518 pounds). To regulate the line of aim by the deviation (lateral deflection) of the shot in the direction of the pitch of the rifling—a deviation common to all projectiles launched from rifled barrels—the right trunnion carries what is called a horizontal tangent-scale. The gun, as well as its carriage, is reported to be of very elegant workmanship, and, from its small size and neatness, to look more like a model than a real engine of war.

Armed with this gun, the French artillery entered upon the Italian campaign, where it indeed astonished the Austrians by its great range, but certainly not by its accuracy of fire. The guns very often, indeed generally, overshot the mark, and were more dangerous to reserves than to first lines—in other words, where they hit better than the common guns, they hit people at whom they were not aimed at all. This is certainly a very questionable advantage, as in nine cases out of ten it implies that the objects at which the guns were aimed were *not* hit. The Austrian artillery, with as clumsy a material as any in Europe, made a very decent appearance when opposed to them, and came up to close quarters (that is, 500 or 600 yards) with these formidable opponents, unlimbering under their most effective fire. There is no doubt that, great as the superiority of the new French guns is over their old smooth-bored ones, they did not perform anything like what was expected from them. Their extreme practicable range was 4,000 metres (4,400 yards), and undoubtedly it was but an impudent Bonapartist exaggeration when it was said that they could easily hit a single horseman at 3,300 yards.

The reasons for these unsatisfactory performances, in actual war, are very simple. The construction of these guns is utterly imperfect, and if the French adhere to it, in two or three years their artillery will possess the worst materiel in Europe. The first principle in rifled arms is that there must be *no windage*; otherwise the shot, loosely rolling about in the barrel and grooves, will not rotate round its own longitudinal axis, but rotate, in a spiral line of flight, round an imaginary line, the direction of which is determined by the accidental position of the shot when leaving the muzzle, and the spiral rounds will increase in diameter with the distance. Now, the French guns have considerable windage, and cannot do without it so long as the explosion of the charge is relied upon to light the fuse of the shell. This, then, is one circumstance which explains the want of accuracy. The second is the irregularity of the propelling force created by the greater or less escape of gas through windage during the explosion of the charge. The third is the greater elevation, with the same charge, necessitated through this windage; it stands to reason that where no gas at all can escape between shot and bore, the same charge propels further than where part of the gas escapes. Now, the French guns appear to require not only a very great charge for rifled guns (one-fifth of the weight of the shot), but also a pretty high elevation. The greater range obtained by rifled bores over smooth ones, even with smaller charges, is chiefly obtained by the absence of windage, and the certainty of having the whole explosive force of the charge applied to the expulsion of the shot. By admitting windage, the French sacrifice part of the propelling force, and have to replace it by increased charges to a limited degree, and by greater elevation beyond that. Now, there is nothing so contrary to accuracy at any distances as great elevation. So long as the line of flight of the shot does not, at its highest point, much exceed the hight of the object aimed at, so long a mistake in estimating the distance is of little importance; but at long range, the shot takes a very high flight, and comes down at an angle on an average twice as great as that under which it began its flight (this, of course, is confined to elevations up to about 15 degrees). Thus, the higher the elevation the more the line in which the shot strikes the ground approaches the vertical; and an error in estimating the distance of not more than ten or twenty yards may preclude the possibility of hitting at all. At ranges beyond even 400 or 500 yards, such errors are unavoidable, and the consequence is the astonishing difference between the capital shooting on the practice-ground, with measured distances, and the execrable practice on the battle-field, where the distances are unknown, the objects moving, and the moments for reflection very short. Thus, with the new rifles, the chance of hitting beyond three hundred yards on the battle-field is very small, while under three hundred yards, from the low flight of the ball, it is very great; in consequence of which, the charge with the bayonet becomes the most effective means of dislodging an enemy, as soon as the attacking body has come up to that distance. Suppose one army to carry rifles which at 400 yards give no higher trajectory than the rifles of their opponents give at 300 yards, the former will have the advantage of beginning an effective fire at 100 yards greater distance, and as but three or four minutes are required to charge through 400 yards, this advantage is not a mean one in the decisive moment of a battle. It is similar with cannon. Sir Howard Douglas, ten years ago, declared[a] that gun far the best which gives the greatest range with the least elevation. With rifled cannon the importance of this point is still greater, as the chance of error in estimating distance increases with the longer range, and as the ricochets of any other than spherical shot cannot be relied upon. This is one of the disadvantages of rifled guns; they must hit with the first impact, if they are to hit at all, while round-shot, if it falls short, will rebound and continue its flight in very nearly its original direction. Here, then, a low trajectory is of the very highest importance, as every degree more of elevation reduces the chance of hitting with the first impact in an increasing ratio, and therefore the high line of flight produced by the French guns is one of their most serious defects.

But the whole of the deficiencies of these guns are crowned and enhanced by one defect, which suffices to stamp the whole system. They are produced by the machinery and on the principles formerly serving for the manufacture of the old smooth-bored guns. With the very great windage of these old guns, and the varying weights and diameters of the shot, mathematical precision

---

a Howard Douglas, *A Treatise on Naval Gunnery. Dedicated by Special Permission to the Lords Commissioners of the Admiralty*, London, 1851.— *Ed.*

in the manufacture was but a secondary consideration. The manufacture of firearms, up to a very few years ago, was the most backward branch of modern industry. There was far too much hand labor and far too little machinery. For the old smooth-bore arms this might be allowable; but when arms were to be manufactured which were expected to have great precision at long distances, this system became intolerable. To insure the certainty that every musket should shoot perfectly alike at 600, 800, 1,000 yards, and every cannon at 2,000, 4,000, 6,000 yards, it became necessary that every part of every operation should be performed by the most perfect and self-acting machinery, so as to turn out one weapon the mathematical counterpart of the other. Deviations from mathematical precision, inappreciable under the old system, now became defects rendering the whole weapon useless. The French have not improved their old machinery to any noticeable extent, and hence the irregularities in their firing. How can guns be made to give the same range at the same elevation, all other circumstances being alike, when none of them is identical with the other in every particular? But irregularities in manufacture which at 800 yards produce differences of a yard, at 4,000 will produce differences of a hundred yards in range. How, then, can such guns be expected to be true at long ranges?

To recapitulate: the French rifled guns are bad, because they must have windage; because they require, comparatively, great elevations, and because their workmanship is not at all up to the requirements of rifled long-range guns. They must soon be superseded by different constructions, or they will reduce the French artillery practice to the worst in Europe.

We have purposely examined these guns a little in detail, as they gave us, thereby, an opportunity of explaining the chief principles of rifled ordnance. In a concluding article we shall consider the two systems proposed, which in England are now contesting for superiority—systems both of which are founded upon loading by the breech, absence of windage, and perfect workmanship—the Armstrong system and that of Whitworth.

III

[New-York Daily Tribune, No. 5938, May 5, 1860]

We now come to the description of the two kinds of breech-loading rifled cannon which at the present moment contend for superiority in England, and which, both invented by civilians, certainly surpass in efficiency anything hitherto produced by professional artillerists—the Armstrong gun and the Whitworth gun.

Sir William Armstrong's gun had the advantage of priority, and of being praised by the whole press[a] and official world of England. It is, undoubtedly, a highly effective machine of war, and far superior to the French rifled gun; but whether it can beat Whitworth's gun may well be doubted.

Sir Wm. Armstrong constructs his gun by wrapping, round a tube of cast steel, two layers of wrought-iron tubes in a spiral form, the upper layer laid on in the opposite direction to the lower one, in the same way as gun-barrels are made from layers of wire. This system gives a very strong and tough material, though a very expensive one. The bore is rifled with numerous narrow grooves, one close to the other, and having one turn in the length of the gun. The oblong—cylindro-ogival—shot is of cast iron, but covered with a mantle of lead, which gives it a diameter somewhat larger than the bore; this shot, along with the charge, is introduced by the breech into a chamber wide enough to receive it; the explosion propels the shot into the narrow bore, where the soft lead is pressed into the grooves, and thus does away with all windage while giving the projectile the spiral rotation indicated by the pitch of the grooves. This mode of pressing the shot into the grooves, and the coating of soft material required for it, are the characteristic features of Armstrong's system; and if the reader will refer to the principles of rifled ordnance, as developed in our preceding articles, he will agree that, in principle, Armstrong is decidedly in the right. The shot being larger in diameter than the bore, the gun is necessarily breech-loading, which, to us, also seems a necessary feature in all rifled ordnance. The breech-loading apparatus itself, however, has nothing whatever to do with the principle of any particular system of rifling, but may be transferred from one to the other; we leave it, therefore, entirely out of our consideration.

The range and precision attained with this new gun are something wonderful. The shot was thrown to some 8,500 yards, or nearly five miles, and the certainty with which the target was hit at 2,000 or 3,000 yards much exceeded what the old, smooth-bore guns could show at one-third of these distances. Still, with all the puffing of the English press, the scientifically interesting details of

---

[a] See *The Times*, Nos. 23524, 23526, 23545, 23547 and 23585, January 24 and 26, February 17 and 20, and April 4, 1860.— *Ed.*

all these experiments were studiously kept secret. It was never stated with what elevation and charge these ranges were obtained; the weight of the shot and that of the gun itself, the exact lateral and longitudinal deviations, &c., were never particularized. Now, at last, when the Whitworth gun has made its appearance, we learn some details of one set of experiments at least. Mr. Sidney Herbert, Secretary of War, has stated in Parliament[a] that a 12-pounder gun of 8 cwt., with 1 lb. 8 oz. of powder, gave a range of 2,460 yards, at 7 degrees elevation, with an extreme lateral deviation of three, and an extreme longitudinal deviation of 65 yards. At eight degrees elevation, the range was 2,797 yards; at nine, above 3,000 yards; the deviations remaining nearly the same. Now, an elevation of seven to nine degrees is a thing unknown in the practice of smooth-bore field artillery. The official tables, for instance, do not go beyond four degrees elevation, at which the 12-pounder and 9-pounder give a range of 1,400 yards. Any higher elevation in field guns would be useless, from giving too high a line of flight, and thereby immensely reducing the chance of hitting the mark. But we have some experiments (quoted in Sir Howard Douglas's *Naval Gunnery*) with heavy ship guns of smooth bore at higher elevations. The English long 32-pounder at Deal, in 1839, gave ranges, at 7 degrees, of 2,231 to 2,318; at 9 degrees, from 2,498 to 2,682 yards.[b] The French 36-pounder, in 1846 and '47, gave ranges, at 7 degrees, of 2,270; at 9 degrees, of 2,636 yards.[c] This shows that, at equal elevations, the ranges of rifled guns are not so very superior to those of smooth-bore cannon.

The Whitworth gun, in almost every respect, is the opposite of the Armstrong gun. Its bore is not circular, but hexagonal; the pitch of its rifling is very near twice as high as that of the Armstrong gun; the shot is of a very hard material, without any coating of lead; and, if it is breech-loading, it is not necessarily so, but merely as a matter of convenience and of fashion. This gun is of a recently-patented material, called "homogeneous iron," of great strength, elasticity, and toughness; the shot is a mathematically exact fit to the bore, and cannot, therefore, be introduced without the bore being lubricated. This is done by a composition of wax and grease being inserted between charge and shot, which at the same time tends to decrease whatever windage there may be

---

[a] In his speech in the House of Commons on February 17, 1860 (see *The Times*, No. 23546, February 18, 1860.— *Ed.*

[b] See Howard Douglas' *A Treatise on Naval Gunnery*, London, 1851, p. 563.— *Ed.*

[c] ibid., p. 585.— *Ed.*

left. The material of the gun is so tough that it will easily stand 3,000 rounds without any damage to the bore.

The Whitworth gun was brought before the public in February last, when a series of experiments were made with it at Southport, on the Lancashire coast. There were three guns—a 3-pounder, 12-pounder, and 80-pounder; from the long reports[a] we select the 12-pounder as an illustration. This gun was 7 feet 9 inches long, and weighed 8 cwt. The common 12-pounder, for round shot, is 6 feet 6 inches long, and weighs 18 cwt. The ranges obtained with Whitworth's gun were as follows: At 2 degrees elevation (where the old 12-pounder gives 1,000 yards), with a charge of $1\,^3/_4$ lb., the range varied from 1,208 to 1,281 yards. At 5 degrees (where the old 32-pounder gives 1,940 yards), it ranged from 2,298 to 2,342 yards. At 10 degrees (range of old 32-pounder, 2,800 yards), it averaged 4,000 yards. For higher elevations a 3-pounder gun was used, with 8 oz. charge; with 20 degrees, it ranged from 6,300 to 6,800, with 33 and 35 degrees, 9,400 to 9,700 yards. The old 56-pounder, of smooth bore, gives, at 20 degrees, a range of 4,381 yards, at 32 degrees, of 5,680 yards. The precision obtained by the Whitworth gun was very satisfactory, and at least as good as that of the Armstrong gun in lateral deflection; as to longitudinal variations, the experiments do not admit of a satisfactory conclusion.

IV[b]

[New-York Daily Tribune, No. 5950, May 19, 1860]

The Whitworth gun is constructed upon the principle of reducing windage to the utmost minimum, by a mathematical fit of the shot to the bore, and doing away with what little may remain by the effect of the lubricating composition. In this respect it is inferior to Armstrong's gun, which has no windage at all; and this we consider its principal defect. The polygonal bore, however, would be impossible without this defect, and at all events it deserves to be acknowledged that with such an originally defective system, such great results have been obtained. Whitworth has undoubtedly brought to its highest perfection the system which

---

[a] See "Experiments with Mr. Whitworth's Breech-Loading Cannon", *The Times*, No. 23547, February 20, 1860.— *Ed.*

[b] This section was discovered to have been by Engels after the publication of the German and the Russian editions of the *Collected Works,* and appears here for the first time since its publication in the newspaper.— *Ed.*

gives hard, unyielding shot and allows windage. His gun is immensely superior to the rough empiricism of the French rifled ordnance. But while Armstrong's gun, and other guns depending on soft-coated shot to be forced into the grooves by pressure, may be perfected *ad infinitum*, Whitworth's gun will have no such future; it has already attained the highest perfection compatible with its fundamental principles.

To recapitulate:

We find that at the *practicable elevation* of field-artillery, the best rifled guns known give a range but *very little* superior to the old smooth-bored gun. There is, however, some advantage, and this remains an item in their favor. But the great *advantages* of rifled ordnance for field-artillery are these:

1. The same weight of shot can be projected by a gun having a much smaller bore, and with a much smaller charge than with the old smooth-bored gun, which was only fit for spherical shot. Consequently, the weight of the gun is considerably reduced. The old 12-pounder had a bore of about $4\,^1/_2$ inches, and weighed 18 cwt.; its charge was four pounds of powder. The new 12-pounder has a bore of about $3\,^1/_2$ inches, or nearly that of the old 9-pounder; its weight, 8 cwt.; charge, from $1\,^1/_2$ to $1\,^3/_4$ pounds. The French new 12-pounders, with the old 4-pounder's bore, are still lighter. This is an immense advantage. It gives to the field-gun a mobility hitherto unknown, and renders it almost as fit to go over any ground as infantry. More than four horses to a gun will henceforth be useless.

2. At the distances hitherto practicable for field-artillery, it gives a far greater chance of hitting; it lowers the trajectory, and reduces to a minimum both lateral and longitudinal deflections. At an exchange of round shot and shells with percussion fuses, a rifled battery will always beat a smooth-bored one of equal weight of shot.

As to heavy ordnance, it will be all-powerful against stone walls, especially by shell-practice with percussion fuses. This has already been proved by experiment, both in France and Germany. It will give ships and siege batteries a chance of bombarding towns at distances from 4,000 to 9,000 yards. In every other respect it will not alter materially the hitherto existing relations of besiegers and besieged, and of ships against batteries on shore.

On the other hand, the *disadvantages* of rifled ordnance are:

1. The common case-shot becomes either impossible or ineffective from the irregular line of flight imparted to the balls by the spiral rotation.

2. Firing with shell with time-fuses (and shrapnel shot with ditto) becomes almost impracticable, as the absence or reduction of windage prevents the flame of the explosion from communicating with the fuse which necessarily must be at the point of the oblong shot.

In spite of these drawbacks, rifled ordnance has now become a matter of necessity for every army. The question now is only, how these drawbacks can be obviated. That they will be so there can be no doubt. But it is certain that the same rules obtain in rifled ordnance which regulate the construction and use of rifled small arms. The exaggerated ideas of five-mile ranges in the one are as ridiculous as the notion of hitting a man with the new rifles at 800 or 1,000 yards; and still the advantages given by rifled bores in either case, are so great that it is imperative upon every army which may ever be called upon to fight with civilized foes, to do away with all smooth-bored barrels, both in small arms and artillery.

Written in March and May 1860

First published in the *New-York Daily Tribune*, Nos. 5914 (as a leading article), 5926, 5938 and 5950, April 7 and 21, May 5 and 19, 1860; parts I and II reprinted in the *New-York Semi-Weekly Tribune*, Nos. 1556 and 1558, April 24 and May 1, 1860

Reproduced from the *New-York Daily Tribune*

Karl Marx

PUBLIC FEELING IN BERLIN

Berlin, April 10, 1860

If an intelligent foreigner who had visited Berlin but two months ago and then left it were now to return to the "metropolis of intelligence," the thorough change in the physiognomy, tone and temper *"meiner lieben Berliner"* (of my beloved Berliners)[a] could not fail to strike his mental eye. Still, some months ago small talk obtained in all the ranks of the metropolitan society. People congratulated each other, in subdued accents, on the nightmare of a decennial reaction having at last ceased to crush their brains—that the worst was over. This silly theme was sounded to all keys, and the unavoidable afterthought that the change had been brought about not by any vigorous and healthy effort on the part of the Prussian subjects, but rather by the sickly affection of the Prussian King's head; that the change was therefore the work of nature, not the deed of man. This uncomfortable afterthought falsified even the first joys of the new era[280] triumphantly announced by the dully-deadly pens of the Berlin daily press. Such was the pusillanimity prevailing that, not to frighten the Prince Regent[b] out of his new-fangled liberalism, all the candidates in the general election to the Second Chamber were put to this simple test: Did they profess confidence in the Hohenzollern Cabinet[c] installed by the Prince Regent? Were their names in no way obnoxious to the mild liberalism of the new Government? Instead of men to take up the grievances of the country, there were wanted bottle-holders with ready-cut votes for the Cabinet. That the new Cabinet actually did not touch the bureaucratic and police shackles forged by its predecessors, while its very profes-

---

[a] An allusion to Frederick William IV's address to the Berlin population on March 19, 1848 (see the *Allgemeine Preussische Zeitung*, No. 80, March 20, 1848).— *Ed.*

[b] William, Prince of Prussia.— *Ed.*

[c] The Cabinet headed by Karl Anton Hohenzollern.— *Ed.*

sions of faith were characterized by weak duplicity, shy reserve, and equivocal reticence—these facts were hoodwinked; and it was furthermore proclaimed a patriotic duty to hoodwink them. All the opposition papers, whether styling themselves Constitutional or Democratic, turned downright Ministerial.

After the peace of Villafranca, when *Herr von Schleinitz*, the Prussian Minister of Foreign Affairs, published a sort of Blue Book on the Italian war[281]—when his dispatches, true patterns of weak-minded verbosity, showed him up the worthy successor of the man[a] who, in the last century, had concluded the peace of Basle, and, in this century, had prepared the catastrophe of Jena[282]—when we saw him humbly receiving lessons of constitutionalism on the part of Little Johnny,[b] the British Jack-of-all-Trades, crouching in the dust before Prince Gorchakoff, exchanging *billets-doux* with the Man of December,[c] superciliously frowning upon his Austrian colleague,[d] to be finally kicked by all his correspondents—even then the Prussian press and our Berlin Liberals worked themselves into real fits of enthusiasm with respect to the superhuman wisdom evinced by the Prussian Government, which, not content with doing nothing itself, had contrived to preclude Germany from all action.

Soon after there took place at Breslau[e] a meeting between the Russian Czar and Gorchakoff on the one side, and the Prince Regent with his Ministerial satellites on the other.[283] A new deed of enfeoffment of Prussia to her Muscovite neighbor was duly signed—the first, but necessary result, this, of the peace of Villafranca. Even in 1844 such an event would have aroused a storm of opposition throughout the country. Now it was extolled as an earnest of far-seeing statecraft. The *nihilism* of the Prince Regent's foreign policy coupled with the continuance of the old reactionary system of mingled feudalism and bureaucratism, which was forsaken in *name* only, seemed to our friends, the Berlin Liberals, and the Prussian press of all colors, save the special organs of the old Camarilla, sufficient reasons to claim the Imperial crown of little Germany (that is to say, Germany minus German Austria) for the representative of the Prussian dynasty. It is difficult to find in the records of history a similar piece of judicial blindness, but we remember that after the battle of

---

a Karl August Hardenberg.—*Ed.*
b John Russell.—*Ed.*
c Napoleon III.—*Ed.*
d Johann Bernhard Rechberg.—*Ed.*
e Wrocław.—*Ed.*

Austerlitz,[284] Prussia also crowed for some days on her own dunghill, *quasi re bene gesta.*[a]

After the termination of the Italian war, it was a spectacle as pitiful as it was disgusting to hear the Prussian press, with the Berlin papers at its head, instead of venturing upon the faintest criticism of the stupid diplomacy of her[b] native rulers; instead of boldly challenging the "liberal" Ministry to bridge at last, in internal affairs, the broad chasm between the nominal and the real; instead of denouncing the silent but obstinate encroachments on civil liberty dared upon by the host of Manteuffel's officials, still snugly ensconced in their old strongholds; instead of all that, to hear them sing panegyrics on the splendor of renovated Prussia; to see them dart their pointless shafts at humbled Austria; to see them stretch their unnerved hands at the German Imperial crown, and, to the utter astonishment of all Europe, demean themselves like maniacs in a fool's paradise. Altogether, it seemed as if the great international drama now enacted on the European stage, did only concern our Berlin friends as spectators who, from the gallery or pit, have to applaud or hoot, but not to act.

All this has been changed now as by a magician's wand. Berlin is at this moment, with the exception perhaps of Palermo and Vienna, the most revolutionary town in Europe. The fermentation pervades all ranks, and seems more intense than in the days of March, 1848. How has this phenomenon been brought about, and so suddenly, too? By a combination of events at the top of which range Louis Bonaparte's last exploits on the one hand, and the new army reforms[c] proposed by the liberal Government on the other. Then, of course, the state of confidence and of willful self-delusion could not last forever. The incidents, furthermore, by which the Ministry has been forced to dismiss Stieber,[285] the Police Director, the low criminal, who, together with his master, the late Hinckeldey, had swayed supreme power in Prussia ever since 1852; and last, not least, the publication of Humboldt's correspondence with Varnhagen von Ense[d] have done the rest. The fool's paradise has vanished before the breath from beyond the grave.

Written on April 10, 1860   Reproduced from the newspaper

First published in the *New-York Daily Tribune,* No. 5932, April 28, 1860

---

[a] As if everything were well.— *Ed.*

[b] i.e. Prussia's.— *Ed.*

[c] See this volume, pp. 345-49.— *Ed.*

[d] *Briefe von Alexander von Humboldt an Varnhagen von Ense aus den Jahren 1827 bis 1858,* Leipzig, 1860. Humboldt's letters contain sharp criticism of the Prussian Government.— *Ed.*

Karl Marx

SICILY AND THE SICILIANS

Throughout the history of the human race no land and no people have suffered so terribly from slavery, from foreign conquests and oppressions, and none have struggled so irrepressibly for emancipation as Sicily and the Sicilians. Almost from the time when Polyphemus promenaded around Etna, or when Ceres taught the Siculi [286] the culture of grain, to our day, Sicily has been the theater of uninterrupted invasions and wars, and of unflinching resistance. The Sicilians are a mixture of almost all southern and northern races; first, of the aboriginal Sicanians, with Phoenicians, Carthaginians, Greeks, and slaves from all regions under heaven, imported into the island by traffic or war; and then of Arabs, Normans, and Italians. The Sicilians, in all these transformations and modifications, have battled, and still battle, for their freedom.

More than thirty centuries ago the aborigines of Sicily resisted as best they could the superior weapons and military skill of Carthaginian and Greek invaders. They were made tributary, but never wholly subdued by the one or the other. For a long time Sicily was the battle-field of Greeks and Carthaginians; her people were ruined and partly enslaved; her cities, inhabited by Carthaginians and Greeks, were the central points whence oppression and slavery radiated through the interior of the island. These early Sicilians, however, never missed an opportunity to strike for liberty, or at least to take as much revenge as possible on their Carthaginian masters and on Syracuse. The Romans finally subdued Carthaginians and Syracusans, selling into slavery as many of them as possible. On one occasion 30,000 inhabitants of Panormus, the modern Palermo, were thus sold. The Romans worked Sicily with numberless gangs of slaves, in order to feed with Sicilian wheat the poor proletarians of the Eternal City. For this purpose, they not only enslaved the inhabitants of the island, but imported slaves from all their other dominions. The terrible cruelties of Roman Proconsuls, Praetors, Praefects, are known to every one who is in any degree familiar with the history of Rome, or with the oratory of Cicero. Nowhere else, perhaps, did Roman cruelty hold such saturnalia. The poor freemen and yeomen, if unable to pay the crushing tribute exacted of them, were pitilessly sold into bondage, themselves or their children, by the tax-gatherers.

But both under the Syracusan Dionysius and under the Roman rule, the most terrible slave insurrections took place in Sicily, in which the native people and the imported slaves often made common cause. During the breaking up of the Roman Empire, Sicily was visited by various invaders. Then the Moors got hold of it for a time; but the Sicilians, and above all the genuine people of the interior, resisted always, more or less successfully, and step by step maintained or conquered various small franchises. The dawn had scarcely begun to spread over the medieval darkness, when the Sicilians stood forth, already armed, not only with various municipal liberties, but with rudiments of a constitutional government, such as at that time existed nowhere else. Earlier than any other European nation, the Sicilians regulated by vote the income of their Governments and Sovereigns. Thus the Sicilian soil has ever proved deadly to oppressors and invaders, and the Sicilian Vespers [287] stand immortal in history. When the House of Aragon brought the Sicilians into dependence on Spain, they knew how to preserve their political immunities more or less intact; and this they did alike under the Hapsburgs and the Bourbons. When the French Revolution and Napoleon expelled the tyrannical reigning family from Naples, the Sicilians—incited and seduced by English promises and guaranties—received the fugitives, and in their struggles against Napoleon sustained them both with their blood and their money. Every one knows the subsequent treachery of the Bourbons, and the subterfuges or impudent denials by which England has tried and still tries to varnish her own faithless abandonment of the Sicilians and of their liberties to the tender mercies of the Bourbons.

At the present day, political, administrative, and fiscal oppression crushes all classes of the people; and these grievances therefore stand in the foreground. But nearly the whole soil is still in the hands of comparatively few large landowners or barons.

372

The medieval tenures of land are still preserved in Sicily, except that the tiller is not a serf; he ceased to be such about the eleventh century, when he became a free tenant. The conditions of his tenure are, however, generally so oppressive, that the immense majority of agriculturists work exclusively for the advantage of the tax-gatherer and of the baron, producing scarcely anything beyond the taxes and rents, and themselves remaining either wretchedly, or, at least, comparatively poor. Producing the celebrated Sicilian wheat and excellent fruits, they themselves live poorly on beans the whole year through.

Sicily now bleeds again, and England looks calmly on at these new saturnalia of the infamous Bourbon, and his not less infamous minions, lay or clerical, Jesuits or Guardsmen.[288] The fussy declaimers of the British Parliament rend the air with their empty talk about Savoy and the dangers of Switzerland, but have not a word to say of the massacres in the Sicilian cities. No voice raises the cry of indignation throughout Europe. No ruler and no Parliament proclaims outlawry against the bloodthirsty idiot of Naples.[a] Louis Napoleon, alone, for this or that purpose—of course not for any love of liberty, but for the aggrandizement of his family or of French influence—may perhaps stop the butcher in his work of destruction. England will howl about perfidy, will spout fire and flames against Napoleonic treachery and ambition; but the Neapolitans and the Sicilians must eventually be gainers, even under a Murat or any other new ruler. Any change must be for the better.

Written in late April and early May 1860

First published in the *New-York Daily Tribune*, No. 5948, May 17, 1860 as a leading article; reprinted in the *New-York Semi-Weekly Tribune*, No. 1563, May 18, 1860

Reproduced from the *New-York Daily Tribune*

---

[a] Francis II.— *Ed.*

Karl Marx

PREPARATIONS FOR NAPOLEON'S COMING WAR ON THE RHINE

I

Berlin, May 1, 1860

The notion that Louis Bonaparte is about to put the German question on the tapis prevails here among all classes of society. In to-day's *National-Zeitung*, a correspondent even affirms that he knows, from sources most authentic, that Badinguet (as Louis Bonaparte is familiarly styled at Paris) has definitely resolved upon a Rhenish campaign, and that Lord John Russell had just been informed of this scheme when, some weeks ago, he rose from his seat to frighten the House of Commons by fierce invectives against the Emperor of the French, and the sudden announcement that England was now going in search for new alliances. The tone and temper of French semi-official prints are far from allaying these apprehensions. Read, for instance, the following extract from *Bullier's Correspondence*,[289] a Paris publication from which most of the provincial journalists in France derive their inspiration:

"A friend of mine, who is addicted to prophetic pleasantries, said to me the other day: 'You'll see the Emperor go to the Rhine to offer his alliance to the King of Prussia,[a] coupled with a slight rectification of frontiers.' I replied by a quotation from the pamphlet *Napoleon III et l'Italie*[b]: It is better to settle a Territorial modification in a friendly way than to have to do it the day after a victory."

Not long after the treaty of commerce with England[c] was concluded, the French Government threw out a hint to the Prussian Embassador[d] at Paris that an application for a similar treaty between France and the Zollverein[290] would be favorably received, but the Prussian Government answering that the

---

[a] Frederick William IV.— *Ed.*

[b] La Guéronnière, *L'empereur Napoléon III et l'Italie*, Paris, 1859, pp. 63-64.— *Ed.*

[c] See this volume, pp. 341-44.— *Ed.*

[d] A. Pourtalès.— *Ed.*

Zollverein was not at all desirous to make such a treaty, surprise
and displeasure were expressed in terms far from courteous.
Moreover, the Prussian Government was, at the time, fully
informed of the negotiations which the agents of Louis Bonaparte
had recently opened with the Bavarian Court, in order to induce
the latter to cede to France the fortress of Landau, which, it was
said, having been left to France by the treaty of 1814, had been
unjustly taken from her by the treaty of 1815.[291] The popular
rumors of an impending rupture with France are, consequently,
strengthened by official suspicion.

Prussia's position at present bears, in some respects, a strong
likeness to that of Austria after the conclusion of the Oriental war.
Austria seemed then to have got off best of all the Powers. She
flattered herself that she had humbled Russia, her dangerous
neighbor, without incurring any trouble beyond the mobilization
of her forces. Having played the armed mediator while the
Western Powers had to bear the brunt of war, she might, after the
proclamation of peace, fancy she had broken, by the arms of the
Western Alliance, the ascendency Russia had won over her since
the Hungarian events of 1849, and there were indeed at that time
many compliments bestowed upon the clever diplomatic tactics of
the Vienna Cabinet. In point of fact, however, the ambiguous
attitude maintained by Austria during the Oriental war, left her
without allies, and enabled Louis Bonaparte to *localize* the Italian
war. Prussia, in her turn, maintained her resources intact during
the Italian war. She shouldered her arms, but had not used them,
and contented herself with spilling, instead of blood, the patient
ink of her political wiseacres. After the peace of Villafranca,
Prussia seemed to have weakened the rival House of Hapsburg
through the instrumentality of French victories, and opened to
herself the road to paramount power in Germany. Still, the very
pretexts on which the treaty of Villafranca was proclaimed ought
to have rent the delusions she labored under. While Louis
Bonaparte declared that Prussia's armaments and threats of an
eventual intervention had blunted the sword of France, Austria
declared that her own power of resistance had split upon the
equivocal neutrality of Prussia. During the whole war, Prussia had
displayed pretensions ludicrously contradicted by her acts. Before
Austria and the minor German States she appealed to her duties
as a European Power; before England and Russia she appealed to
her obligations as the paramount German Power; and, resting her
claims on these double pretensions, she demanded from France to
be acknowledged as the armed mediator of Europe. To her claims

as the German Power, *par excellence*, she acted up by allowing Russia to intimidate, in a circular[a] of unprecedented insolence, the minor German courts, and by timidly listening, in the person of Herr von Schleinitz, to Lord John Russell's flippant lectures on the "constitutional" law of nations.

Her claims as a European Power she made good by hushing up the warlike impulses of the minor German princes, and by an attempt to turn the military defeats of Austria into as many titles for usurping the place formerly held by her rival in the councils of the German Confederation. When at last forced, by the progress of the French arms, to assume something like a warlike attitude, she met with the cold resistance of the minor German States, which hardly thought it worth while to dissimulate their distrust as to the ultimate intentions of the Prussian Court. The peace of Villafranca found Prussia completely insulated, not only in Europe, but in Germany, while the subsequent annexation of Savoy, by greatly contracting the exposed front of France, greatly improved her chances of a victorious campaign on the Rhine.

Under these circumstances, the line of policy which Prussia now affected to follow, both in her internal and external relations, appears alike faulty. Despite all the vainglorious declamations of the Prussian newspapers and Representative Chambers, nothing has been altered in her internal affairs, save the phraseology of her officials. The propositions on army reform,[b] while not at all strengthening her military force for the impending emergency, aim at a permanent enlargement of the standing army, already too large; the overburdening of the financial resources, already overstrained, and the annihilation of the only democratic institution of the country—the Landwehr.[292] All the reactionary laws on the press, the right of association, the municipal administration, the relations of landlords and peasants, the bureaucratic tutelage, the ubiquity of the police, have been carefully maintained. Even the infamous statutes relating to marriages contracted between nobles and the common stock of mankind, have not been rescinded. The very idea of restoring the Constitution, overthrown by a *coup d'état*, is hooted at as a wild dream.

I will give you one single instance of the civil liberty now enjoyed by a Prussian subject. A native of Rhenish Prussia[c] had,

---

[a] Gorchakov's "Circularschreiben an die russischen Gesendtschaften vom 15. (27.) Mai 1859", *Allgemeine Zeitung*, No. 167, June 16, 1859.— *Ed.*

[b] See this volume, pp. 345-49.— *Ed.*

[c] Peter Nothjung. See Engels' letter to Ferdinand Lassalle of March 15, 1860, present edition, Vol. 41.— *Ed.*

during the worst period of the reaction, been condemned by a packed Jury, because of what was then called a political crime, to seven years imprisonment in a Prussian fortress. The period of his punishment, not abridged by the liberal ministry, having come to an end, he repaired to Cologne, there to be driven out by order of the police. He then set out for his native town, but, strange to say, was informed by the authorities that, having absented himself for seven years from the place, he had lost his citizenship, and must look for another abode. He retorted that his absence had not been a voluntary one, but all in vain. From Berlin, where he then resorted, he was again ejected on the plea that he had no means of existence to show, except his personal resources of labor and knowledge; all his property having been consumed during his imprisonment. He at last betook himself to Breslau, where an old acquaintance of his employed him as one of his agents, but being one morning summoned to the police, he was told that his permission of residence could be prolonged only for a few weeks, if, in the mean while, he should not have procured citizenship in Breslau. On his appliance to the Breslau municipal authority, many petty difficulties were thrown in his way, which, being removed by the interference of zealous friends, his petition for citizenship was at last granted, but, together with the grant, he received a big bill, parading an array of fees, all to be paid by any happy mortal on his entrance into the ranks of Breslau citizens. If his friends had not possessed the means by clubbing, to raise the sum required, this Prussian subject would, like the Wandering Jew, have found no place in his glorious fatherland where to rest his head.

II

Berlin, May 2, 1860

After the conclusion of the peace of Villafranca, the Prussian Government, which for months had flattered itself with the idle hope of being acknowledged as the armed mediator of Europe, and of rearing, upon the ruins of the Hapsburg Empire, the edifice of Hohenzollern greatness, seemed to have awakened to a sense of the immense dangers looming in the future. Their policy, at once irresolute, vacillating, and perfidious, had left them without allies, and even von Schleinitz, whose long-winded dispatches had become a standing joke with the diplomatic world, could hardly conceal from himself the truth that, so soon as the internal state of France should again drive the Man of December beyond the French frontiers, Prussia was to be the predestined object of another localized war.

Had not Louis Napoleon, in a moment of apparent openheartedness, dropped some words to the effect that he knew what Germany stood in need of—unity, that he was the man to impart it; and that the Rhenish Provinces would be not too high a price for the purchase of so precious a commodity. Quite true to the tradition of Prussia's past, the first idea of the Prince Regent[a] and his satellites was to throw themselves upon the mercy of Russia. Had not Frederick William I acquired Pomerania by a treaty of division concluded with Peter the Great against Charles XII of Sweden?[293] Had not Frederick II carried the day in the Seven Years' War, and annexed Silesia by the withdrawal of Russia from her Austrian ally?[294] Had not the several divisions of Poland,[295] planned between the Court of Berlin and the Court of Petersburg, swelled out the diminutive dimensions of the Prussian monarchy? Had not, at the Congress of Vienna, the unbounded servility of Frederick William III, who stood by Alexander I, when, in 1814, England, Austria, and France showed some indication to opposition and resistance, been rewarded by the annexation of Saxony and the Rhenish Provinces to Prussia?[296] Prussia, in one word, had in its encroachments upon Germany, always enjoyed the patronage and the support of Russia, on the express condition, of course, of helping that latter Power to subject the countries bordering on the fatherland, and of playing the part of its humble vassal on the European stage. In October, 1859, the Prince Regent and Alexander II, surrounded by diplomatists, generals and courtiers, met each other at Breslau, there to conclude a treaty,[297] the articles of which have, till now, remained an unfathomable secret, not for Louis Bonaparte or Lord Palmerston, but for Prussian subjects, whose liberal representatives have proved themselves, of course, much too polite to interpellate Herr von Schleinitz, the Foreign Minister, on such a delicate question. This much, however, is sure, that the Bonapartist press took no fright at the Breslau conference; that ever since then the relations between Russia and France have grown more ostentatiously intimate; that that conference did not prevent Louis Bonaparte, either from seizing upon Savoy, or threatening Switzerland, and throwing out hints upon some unavoidable "rectification of the Rhenish frontiers," and, finally, that Prussia herself, despite the comfortable prospect

---

a William, Prince of Prussia.— *Ed.*

of again being allowed to form Russia's vanguard, has, in these latter times, eagerly seized upon the bait of an English alliance, only thrown out at London to amuse the British House of Commons for a week or two.

However, Lord John Russell's indiscreet betrayal in the shape of a Blue Book,[a] of Herr von Schleinitz's coquetry with the Tuileries during the last Italian war, gave the death-blow to the Anglo-Prussian alliance, which the Prussian Government considered for a moment as a scheme really entertained, but which was known at London to be nothing beyond a phrase hiding a Parliamentary trick. After all, despite the conference with Alexander II, at Breslau, and Lord John Russell's "search for new alliances," Prussia now, as after the treaty of Villafranca, finds herself completely insulated and singly exposed to the French theory of the natural frontiers.[298]

Can it be believed that under such trying circumstances the only expedient which the Prussian Government has hit upon is to renew its scheme of a little Germany with a Hohenzollern at its head, and, by the most insolent provocations, not only to drive Austria into the hostile camp, but to estrange the whole of Southern Germany? Yet, incredible as it may appear, and the more incredible since this line of policy is fervently recommended by the Bonapartist press, such is the case. The nearer the danger draws, the more anxious appears Prussia to display her hunger for a new division of Germany. By the way, it is likely enough that, after the blow dealt to Austria, Germany stands in need of a similar blow being dealt to Prussia, in order to get rid of "both the houses,"[b] but at all events nobody will suspect the Prince Regent and Herr von Schleinitz of acting upon such pessimist principles. Ever since the treaty of Villafranca the leanings of the Regent's policy have been betrayed in little press skirmishes and small occasional debates on the Italian question, but, on the 20th of April, in the Prussian Lower House, on [the] occasion of the debates on the Kurhessian question,[c] the cat was let out of the bag.

I have before explained this Kurhessian question to your readers,[d] and shall therefore now limit myself to explaining in a

---

[a] *Correspondence respecting the Affairs of Italy from the Signing of Preliminaries of Villafranca to the Postponement of the Congress,* London, 1860.— *Ed.*

[b] Cf. "a plague o'both your houses", Shakespeare, *Romeo and Juliet,* Act III, Scene 1.— *Ed.*

[c] See the *Königlich privilegirte Berlinische Zeitung,* No. 93, April 20, 1860.— *Ed.*

[d] Karl Marx, "Trouble in Germany", present edition, Vol. 16.— *Ed.*

few words the main points upon which the debates turned. The Kurhessian Constitution of 1831 having been destroyed by the Arch-Elector[a] in 1849-50, under Austrian auspices, Prussia for a moment affected a desire to draw the sword on behalf of the protesting representative Chamber, but in November, 1850, on the meeting between Prince Schwarzenberg and Baron Manteuffel at Olmütz, when Prussia altogether surrendered to Austria, acknowledged the restoration of the old German Diet,[299] betrayed Schleswig-Holstein, and recanted all her pretensions to supremacy, she also yielded her knight-errantry on behalf of the Kurhessian Constitution of 1831.

In 1852, the Arch-Elector octroyed a new constitution which was guaranteed by the German Diet, despite the protest of the Kurhessian people. After the Italian war, the question, on the secret instigation of Prussia, was again mooted. The Kurhessian Chambers again declared for the validity of the Constitution of 1831, and fresh petitions for its reestablishment went up to the Diet at Frankfort. Prussia then asserted the Constitution of 1831 to be alone valid, but, as she cautiously added, it ought to be adapted to the monarchical principles of the Diet. Austria, on the other hand, insisted that the Constitution of 1852 was legal, but ought to be amended in a liberal sense. Thus the dispute was a verbal one, a mere quibble, the gist of which was a trial of the respective power wielded by the Hohenzollern and the Hapsburg over the German Confederation. A vast majority of the Diet decided at last for the validity of the Constitution of 1852; viz., on the Austrian side, and against Prussia. The motives which swayed the votes of the minor German States were transparent. Austria they knew to be too much involved in foreign difficulties, and too unpopular, to attempt anything beyond the conservation of the general *status quo* in Germany, while they suspected Prussia of ambitious schemes of innovation. By not acknowledging the competency of the vote of the Diet of 1851, they would have put in jeopardy the competency of all the other resolutions of the Diet since 1848. Last, not least, they did not like the Prussian strategy of dictating to the minor German Princes and encroaching upon their sovereignty, by affecting to take up the grievances of the Kurhessian people against the Arch-Elector. Consequently the motion of Prussia was lost.

Now, on the 20th of April, when this matter came to be debated at Berlin in the House of Deputies, Herr von Schleinitz, in the

---

[a] Friedrich Wilhelm I.—*Ed.*

name of the Prussian Government, explicitly declared[a] that Prussia would not think herself bound by the vote of the German Diet; that, in 1850, when the Prussian Constitution was fabricated, there existed no German Diet, that body having been swept away by the earthquake of 1848, whence it followed that all resolutions of the German Diet which should run counter to the plans of the Prussian Government were void of legal force; and, lastly, that, in fact, the German Diet belonged to the dead, although the German Confederation, of course, continued to exist. Now, is it possible to imagine any step more foolish on the part of the Prussian Government? The Austrian Government declared the old Constitution of the German Empire to be defunct, after Napoleon I had really put the extinguisher upon it. The Hapsburg then proclaimed only a fact. The Hohenzollern, on the contrary, now proclaims the nullity of the Federal Constitution of Germany at a moment when Germany is threatened with a foreign war, as if to afford the Man of December legal pretexts for entering into separate alliances with the minor German States, which, till now, were precluded from such a course of action by the laws of the Diet. If Prussia had proclaimed the right of the Revolution of 1848, the nullity of all the counter-revolutionary acts committed by herself and the Diet since that time, and the restoration of the institutions and laws of the Revolutionary epoch, she would have commanded the sympathies of all Germany, Austrian Germany included.

As it is, she has only divided the German Princes without uniting the German people. She has, in fact, opened the door by which to let in the Zouaves.

Written on May 3-4, 1860   Reproduced from the newspaper

First published in the *New-York Daily Tribune*, No. 5950, May 19, 1860

---

[a] Von Schleinitz's speech in the Prussian Diet on April 20, 1860, *Stenographischer Bericht*, Bd. 2, Berlin, 1860, S. 794-95. Presumably Marx used the material from "Debates in the Prussian Chamber", *The Times*, No. 23604, April 26, 1860.— *Ed.*

Karl Marx

[GARIBALDI IN SICILY.—]
AFFAIRS IN PRUSSIA

Berlin, May 28, 1860

The prevailing topic of conversation here, as everywhere all over Europe, is, of course, Garibaldi's adventures in Sicily. Now, you are aware that never before has the telegraph been put to such impudent work as in the present instance, both on the part of Naples and Genoa or Turin. Locusts have never poured upon Europe in such multitude as do now the electric *canards*. It seems, therefore, worth while to state, in a few words, the views here entertained of Sicilian affairs in the most competent military circles. In the first instance, the insurrection, as is generally known, was kept up for a whole month before the arrival of Garibaldi; but, of paramount importance as this fact is, it may be overvalued, as shown by the Paris *Constitutionnel*. The military forces Naples disposed of in Sicily before Gen. Lanza was sent over with fresh troops could hardly amount to 20,000 men, the far greater part of whom had to be concentrated in the fortresses of Palermo and Messina, so that the flying corps left available for the pursuit of the insurgents might boast of several successful encounters, disperse the enemy on certain points, and harass him in different directions, but must prove altogether insufficient to thoroughly stifle the insurrection. At the present moment, there seem to be about 30,000 Neapolitan troops gathered at Palermo, two-thirds of them holding the fortress, while one-third encamp beyond its precincts. Fifteen thousand Neapolitans are said to hold Messina. Now Garibaldi had, according to the latest news, not pushed beyond Monreale. It is true that this place is situated on hills which command Palermo from the land side, but to improve the opportunities offered by this position, Garibaldi as yet lacks the principal requisite—siege artillery. The immediate chances of

Garibaldi, whose army musters about 12,000 men, will consequently depend upon two main circumstances—the rapid spread of the
insurrection throughout the island, and the attitude of the
Neapolitan soldiers at Palermo. If the latter waver, and get into
quarrels with the foreign mercenaries intermingled with them,
Lanza's means of defense may break up in his own hands. If the
insurrection develops much vital power, Garibaldi's army will be
swelled to more formidable dimensions. If Garibaldi should get
into Palermo, he will sweep everything before him save Messina,
where the difficult task will again begin. You remember that, in
1848-49, the Neapolitans had lost everything save Messina, serving
as a *tête-de-pont* between Sicily and Naples; but Messina then
sufficed to regain the whole island. The fall of Palermo, and the
military hold by the patriots of the whole island, except Messina,
would, however, this time prove more decisive than in 1848-49,
because of the altered political conjunctures. If Garibaldi masters
Palermo, he will be officially supported by the "King of Italy." If
he fails, his invasion will be disavowed as a private adventure.
There is something of ironical pathos in the words addressed to
Victor Emmanuel by Garibaldi, who tells the King that he will
conquer for him a new province, which he hopes the King will not
again bargain away, like Nice, Garibaldi's birthplace.[a]

Among the topics of Prussian politics, the first place in the
public mind is naturally occupied by the Prince of Prussia's private
letter to the Prince Consort of England,[300] of which the Prince de
La Tour d'Auvergne, Louis Bonaparte's Embassador at the Court
of Berlin, had not only the impudence to present a copy to Herr
von Schleinitz, the Prussian Foreign Minister, but went the length
of asking explanations on some of its passages reflecting on the
character and plans of the great Paris *saltimbanque*.[b] This incident
reminds one of a similar accident that happened shortly before the
ratification of the treaty of Unkiar-Skelessi, 1833.[301] The Grand
Vizier having at that time communicated a copy of the secret
treaty, drawn up by Count Orloff, to the British Embassy at
Constantinople, was much bewildered when a day later, to his not
agreeable surprise, Count Orloff returned him the identical copy,
with the spiteful advice, to find better confidants for the future.
At Berlin everybody feels sure that the Prince Regent's letter,
having been transmitted by post via *Ostend,* not via *Calais,* was

---

[a] Giuseppe Garibaldi's address to Victor Emmanuel, *Allgemeine Zeitung*,
No. 143, May 22, 1860.— *Ed.*
[b] Quack.— *Ed.*

tampered with at the English Post-Office, where a numerous *personnel* is notoriously employed in prying into suspected letters—a practice carried to such a degree that at the time of the Coalition-Cabinet, the Earl of Aberdeen confessed that he dared not confide to the post his own letters addressed to his metropolitan friends. Lord Palmerston, having thus got a copy of the Prince Regent's letter, is supposed, out of spite against Prince Albert and in the interest of the Anglo-French-Russian alliance, to have placed a copy of that letter into the hands of the French Embassador[a] at London. At all events the course of the intended and much talked-of Anglo-Prussian alliance runs anything but smooth.

Some months ago, when Lord John Russell one fine morning discovered that England must go in search of new alliances,[b] and when that intimation was received with much childish enthusiasm in the official circles of Berlin, out came all at once, in the form of an English Parliamentary paper, a dispatch addressed by Lord Bloomfield[c] to the Foreign Office at Downing street, narrating a private conversation he had held during the last Italian war with Herr von Schleinitz, and sadly compromising the good faith of Prussian foreign policy. Lord John at the time pleaded guilty of a most strange indiscretion, but the first blow to the new alliance was dealt. The second blow has been given by the miscarriage of the Prince Regent's letter.

You will have seen that in his speech from the throne the Prince[d] speaks very emphatically of the maintenance of treaty rights and the united front Germany is ready to show against any encroachment upon the independence and integrity of the common fatherland. The unpleasant impression produced upon the Paris stock exchange by the apparent menace has been allayed through the Russian journal *Le Nord*,[e] which, in a tone of ironically condescending *bonhommie*,[f] divests the Prince's speech of all serious meaning, calls to mind similar phrases uttered by him

---

[a] Jean Gilbert Persigny.— *Ed.*

[b] John Russell's speech in the House of Commons on March 26, 1860, *The Times*, No. 23578, March 27, 1860.— *Ed.*

[c] For Lord Bloomfield's dispatch to Lord John Russell see "Nouvelles de l'Angleterre. Berlin, 14 janvier, 1860", *L'Indépendance belge*, No. 73, March 13, 1860.— *Ed.*

[d] The Prince of Prussia's speech from the throne at the closing of the Prussian Diet on May 23, 1860, *Königlich privilegirte Berlinische Zeitung*, No. 120, May 24, 1860.— *Ed.*

[e] "Resumé politique", *Le Nord*, No. 148, May 27, 1860.— *Ed.*

[f] Good nature.— *Ed.*

during the Italian war, and, in conclusion, characterizes the whole passage as a mere compliment paid to popular feeling. As to the rest of the Prince's speech, it is, in fact, but a summary of legislative failures. The only important projects debated by the Chambers—the projected laws on marriage, municipal administration, and reform of the land tax, from which the nobility in the greater part of the monarchy still remain exempt, have all proved abortive. The Prince, moreover, complains of his pet measures relating to the army reform not having yet received legislative sanction.

Though the Government has proved unable, even with the present Chamber of Representatives—whose large majority consists of Ministerialists—to carry its proposed army reform, it has at last got an extra vote of nine millions and a half of dollars, to be laid out in military expenditures; while simultaneously, as I am informed by letters from the provinces, the intended changes in the army organization are quietly but practically introduced, so as to leave to the Chambers, when reassembling, no other alternative than that of sanctioning what will then have become a *fait accompli*. The gist of the intended army reform is pointed out in the *Baltische Monatsschrift*, a Russian-German monthly, published at Riga, and printed under the sanction of the Russian Governor-General of Livonia, Esthonia, and Courland.

"The Prussian army reform," says that paper, "which was introduced immediately after the peace of Villafranca, can hardly serve any other purpose than that of emancipating the Government from the direct appeal to the whole people—[an appeal] which, with the old military system, became unavoidable, whenever the Government thought it necessary to support its policy by warlike demonstrations. Under the present political combinations of Europe, a State like Prussia, still striving for its full acknowledgment as one of the great Powers, can neither suspend its whole pacific life on every occasion that seems to necessitate the employment of its military forces, nor can it in every case guarantee to the nation when once called to arms the ensuing of actual war. There lies hidden in the *Landwehr* system a certain democratical antagonism against the monarchic principle. The mobilizations of 1850 and 1859, following each other within a relatively short interval, and leading both times to no warlike action, but only to demobilization, seem to have impaired with the great part of the Prussian people the authority of the State, even in foreign affairs. From the very circumstances accompanying both mobilizations, the conclusion seemed to have been drawn by the popular mind that the Government was bound to obtain the consent of public opinion in every instance of a general armament. Even the official declarations made by Prussia in regard to the attitude she observed during the Italian conflict contain the confession of the mobilization of the *Landwehr* having encountered *unexpected difficulties*."[a]

---

[a] The *Baltische Monatsschrift*, 1859, Bd. I, Heft I, S. 47-48.— *Ed.*

Hence the Russian-German paper concludes that Prussia ought to get rid of the *Landwehr system*, in its present form, but, at the same time, intimates with an ironical sneer that "such an alteration of one of the most popular institutions, just at a moment when Prussia affects to stand on liberalism," is a very delicate operation. I may here remark that this *Baltische Monatsschrift*, published under Czarist auspices at Riga, forms to some degree the counterpart of the *Strassburger Correspondent*, published under Bonapartist auspices at Strassburg. Both skirmish on the German frontiers, the one from the east, the other from the west. The writers of the one may be considered as literary Cossacks, the writers of the other as literary Zouaves.[a] Both affect great tenderness for Germany, and abound in wise counsels to the land whose vernacular they still condescend to use. Both try to prepare the fatherland for great changes impending, and both smell of the *entente cordiale* just now linking the Caesarism of Paris to the Czarism of Petersburg; but here the likeness ends. The Strassburg paper, although perfumed with that peculiar scent of false melodramatic dignity characteristic of the Bohemian literature of the Second French Empire, is still written in the homely style that belongs to Southern Germany. It affects common sense, and certainly does not pretend to any literary distinction. The Riga monthly, on the contrary, struts with a didactic stateliness and a metaphysical profoundness savoring of the traditions of the Königsberg University. After all, I consider the ebullitions of patriotic rage with which the German press assails both the *Monatsschrift* and the *Correspondent*, but mainly the latter, as silly exhibitions of childish incompetency.

Written on May 28, 1860   Reproduced from the newspaper

First published in the *New-York Daily Tribune*, No. 5972, June 14, 1860

---

[a] See Marx's letter to Engels of April 24, 1860, present edition, Vol. 41.—*Ed.*

Frederick Engels

GARIBALDI IN SICILY [302]

After a variety of the most contradictory information, we receive, at last, something like trustworthy news of the details of Garibaldi's wonderful march from Marsala to Palermo. It is, indeed, one of the most astonishing military feats of the century, and it would be almost unaccountable were it not for the prestige preceding the march of a triumphant revolutionary general. The success of Garibaldi proves that the Royalist troops of Naples still hold in terror the man who has borne high the flag of Italian revolution in the face of French, Neapolitan, and Austrian battalions, and that the people of Sicily have not lost their faith in him, or in the national cause.

On the 6th of May, two steamers leave the coast of Genoa with about 1,400 armed men, organized in seven companies, each of them, evidently, destined to become the nucleus of a battalion to be recruited among the insurgents. On the 8th, they land at Talamone on the Tuscan coast, and persuade the commander of the fort there, by some sort of argument or other, to furnish them with coal, ammunition, and four field pieces. On the 10th, they enter the harbor of Marsala, at the extreme western end of Sicily, and disembark with all their material, in spite of the arrival of two Neapolitan men-of-war, who are powerless, at the right moment, to prevent them; the story about British interference in favor of the invaders has proved false, and is now abandoned even by the Neapolitans themselves. On the 12th, the small band had marched to Salemi, 18 miles distant in the interior, and on the road toward Palermo. Here the chief men of the revolutionary party appear to have met Garibaldi, to have consulted with him, and collected insurrectionary reenforcements amounting to some 4,000 men;

while these were being organized, the insurrection, repressed but not quelled a few weeks before, was kindled afresh all over the mountains of Western Sicily, and, as was proved on the 16th, not without effect. On the 15th, Garibaldi, with his 1,400 organized volunteers and 4,000 armed peasantry, advances northward across the hills upon Calatafimi, where the country road from Marsala joins the high road from Trapani to Marsala. The defiles leading to Calatafimi, across a spur of the lofty Monte Cerrara, called the Monte di Pianto Romano, were defended by three battalions of Royal troops, with cavalry and artillery, under Gen. Landi. Garibaldi at once attacked this position, which was at first obstinately defended; but although in this attack Garibaldi could not have employed against the 3,000 or 3,500 Neapolitans more than his volunteers and a very small portion of the Sicilian insurgents, the Royalists were successively driven out of five strong positions, with the loss of one mountain-gun and numerous killed and wounded. The loss of the Garibaldians is stated by themselves at 18 killed and 128 wounded. The Neapolitans profess to have conquered one of Garibaldi's flags in this engagement, but, as they found a flag left behind on board one of the abandoned steamers at Marsala, they are quite capable of having exhibited this same flag at Naples as a proof of their pretended victory. Their defeat at Calatafimi, however, did not compel them to abandon that town the same evening. They left it on the following morning only, and after that they appear not to have offered any further resistance to Garibaldi until they reached Palermo. They did reach it, but in a terrible state of dissolution and disorder. The certainty of having succumbed to mere "filibusters and armed rabble" reproduced in their minds all at once the terrible image of that Garibaldi, who, while defending Rome against the French, could yet find time to march to Velletri and send to the right-about the advanced guard of the whole Neapolitan army, and who had since conquered, on the slopes of the Alps, warriors of a far superior mettle to any that Naples produces.[303] The hurried retreat, without a show even of further resistance, must have still increased their despondency and the tendency to desertion which already existed in their ranks; and when all at once they found themselves surrounded and harassed by that insurrection which had been prepared at the meeting at Salemi, their cohesion was utterly lost; of Landi's brigade nothing but a disorderly and dispirited mob, greatly reduced in numbers, reentered Palermo in small successive bands.

Garibaldi entered Calatafimi on the day that Landi had left it—on the 16th; marched on the 17th to Alcamo (10 miles); on the 18th to Partinico (10 miles), and beyond that place toward Palermo. On the 19th, incessant torrents of rain prevented the troops from moving.

In the mean time, Garibaldi had ascertained that the Neapolitans were throwing up intrenchments around Palermo, and strengthening the old, decayed ramparts of the town on the side facing the Partinico road. They were still at least 22,000 strong, and thus far superior to any forces that he could bring against them. But they were dispirited; their discipline was loosened; many of them began to think of passing over to the insurgents; while their generals were known, both to their own soldiers and to their enemy, to be imbeciles. The only trustworthy troops among them were the two foreign battalions. As matters stood, Garibaldi could not have ventured upon a direct front attack upon the town, while the Neapolitans could not undertake anything decisive against him, even if their troops were fit for it, as they must always leave a strong garrison in the town and never move too far away from it. With a General of the common stamp in the place of Garibaldi, this state of things would have led to a series of desultory and undecisive engagements, in which he might have trained a portion of his levies to warfare, but in which also the Royal troops would very soon have recovered a good deal of their lost confidence and discipline, for they could not help being successful in some of them. But such a kind of warfare would neither suit an insurrection nor a Garibaldi. A bold offensive was the only system of tactics permitted to a revolution; a striking success, such as the deliverance of Palermo, became a necessity as soon as the insurgents had arrived in sight of the city.

But how was this to be done? Here it was that Garibaldi brilliantly proved himself a General, fit not for petty partisan warfare only, but also for more important operations.

On the 20th and succeeding days, Garibaldi attacked the Neapolitan outposts and positions in the neighborhood of Monreale and Parco, on the roads leading to Palermo from Trapani and Corleone, thus making the enemy believe that his attack would take place chiefly against the south-western face of the town, and that here his main forces were concentrated. By a skillful combination of attacks and feigned retreats, he induced the Neapolitan General to send more and more troops out of the town in this direction, until, on the 24th, some 10,000 Neapolitans appeared outside the town, toward Parco. This was what Garibaldi intended. He at once engaged them with part of his forces, slowly retreated before them so as to draw them further and further away from the town, and when he had got them as far as Piana,[a] across the main range of hills, which run across Sicily, and here divide the Conca d'Oro (the golden shell, the Valley of Palermo) from the Valley of Corleone, he at once threw the main body of his troops across another part of the same ridge, into the Valley of Misilmeri, which opens out to the sea, close to Palermo. On the 25th he took up his headquarters at Misilmeri, eight miles from the capital. What he further did with the 10,000 men entangled on a single line of bad road in the mountains, we are not informed, but we may be sure that he kept them well occupied with some fresh apparent victories, so as to make sure they would not come back too soon to Palermo. Having thus reduced the defenders of the town by nearly one-half, and transferred his line of attack from the Trapani road to the Catania road, he could proceed to the grand attack. Whether the insurrection in the town preceded Garibaldi's assault, or whether it was produced by his knocking at the gates, the conflicting dispatches leave unsettled; but certain it is, that on the morning of the 27th, all Palermo rose in arms and Garibaldi thundered at the Porta Termini, on the south-east face of the town, where no Neapolitan expected him. The remainder is known—the gradual clearing of the town, with the exception of the batteries, the citadel, and the Royal palace, from the troops; the subsequent bombardment, the armistice, the capitulation. Authentic details of all these proceedings are still wanting; but the main facts are pretty certain.

In the mean time, we must declare that Garibaldi's maneuvers preparatory to the attack on Palermo at once stamp him as a General of a very high order. Hitherto we knew him as a very skillful and very lucky guerrilla-chief only; even in the siege of Rome his mode of defending the town by constant sallies gave him scarcely an opportunity of rising above that level. But here we have him on fair strategic ground, and he comes from the trial a proven master of his art. His manner of enticing the Neapolitan commander into the blunder of sending one-half of his troops out of reach, his sudden flank-march and reappearance before Palermo, on the side where he was least expected, and his energetic attack while the garrison was weakened, are operations far more imprinted with the stamp of military genius than anything that occurred during the Italian war of 1859. The

---

[a] Piana dei Greci.— *Ed.*

Sicilian insurrection has found a first-rate military chief; let us hope that the politician Garibaldi, who will soon have to appear on the stage, may keep unsullied the glory of the General.

Written about June 7, 1860

First published in the *New-York Daily Tribune*, No. 5979, June 22, 1860 as a leading article; reprinted in the *New-York Semi-Weekly Tribune*, No. 1573, June 22, 1860

Reproduced from the *New-York Daily Tribune*

Karl Marx

THE EMPEROR NAPOLEON III AND PRUSSIA[304]

Berlin, June 12, 1860

The following are extracts from Mr. About's newest pamphlet,[a] which will be published in Paris in the course of a few days:

"Let Germany know that the friendship of France has its value. [...] Did not our soldiers rush to the Black Sea to rescue the Ottoman Empire from destruction? [...] Has not the emancipation of the Moldo-Wallachians [...] been effected solely by our influence, without bloodshed? Italy [...] has entered the paths of independence and unity under our auspices—our armies paved the way along which it now marches onward, led by Piedmont; and if Heaven shall permit this great work to be accomplished, and that a nation of 26,000,000 of souls shall be organized at our gates, France will not take umbrage, [...] for she feels that order cannot be established in Europe so long as there are oppressed nationalities and *kings who are insupportable to their subjects.*"

"Never was that noble nation" (Germany) "so great as from 1813 to 1815, for never was it so united. When a Frenchman speaks with admiration of the campaigns which were so terrible to France, his testimony is worthy of attention. The sentiment of German honor and independence, surging up against conquest, worked miracles. Germany has but one passion—one heart. It raised itself up as one man, and the defeat of our incomparable armies showed what united Germany could do."

"Well, let Germany be again united. France ardently desires it, for she loves the Germanic nation with disinterested affection. Were we devoured by that brutal ambition attributed to us by certain Princes, we should not impel Germany to unity. [...] Let Germany be united and form so compact a body as to render invasion impossible. France sees without fear an Italy of 26 millions of souls rising on her southern frontier; she would not fear to see one of 32 millions of Germans on her eastern confines."

"The Germans begin to see [...] the folly of keeping up 37 different Governments," and are resolved to become united.

Prussia will be their nucleus, because Prussia represents freedom of trade and thought, whereas Austria represents prohibition, despotism and all the horrors

---

[a] Edmond About, *La Prusse en 1860*, Paris, 1860.— Ed.

engendered by its Concordat.[305] Therefore will they rally round Prussia. But Prussia must choose between the right divine and the rights of the people. "While some Princes are clinging to a false legitimacy, really legitimate empires are being founded on the basis of universal suffrage. The King of Naples[a] affirms that his subjects belong to him, and they oppose an armed repudiation of these pretensions. The Emperor of the French[b] and the King of Sardinia[c] declare with modern philosophy that peoples belong to themselves alone, and two great nations with all but unanimity select them for their chiefs. Will the Prince of Prussia[d] declare for the right divine [...] or the rights of the people? [...] It is the more necessary [...] that he should make this declaration, as in 1849, [...] a National Assembly, the issue of universal suffrage, brought a legitimate crown to the King[e] in his palace. What did he? He declared for the right divine against the popular right; he would not accept the crown unless offered to him by Princes, and the Prussian clodhoppers applauded saying: '[...] We would not have a throne on which Democracy has spat.' [...] Saxony and Baden had dismissed their Sovereigns. Two Prussian armies marched in the name of divine right and invaded Saxony and Baden. The Saxon King[f] was replaced on his throne, as was also the Duke of Baden[g]; and after all had thus been adjusted, and the Baden Democratic Army had sought shelter in Switzerland, the Prussians shot in cold blood 26 German patriots.

"A Prussian Democrat lately wrote to the people in Württemberg, 'Why don't you join us?' They replied, 'If we were Prussians we should all be exiled, with the poet Uhland at our head.'

"Nothing is more strange nor more true than this assertion. Since 1848 all the princes of Europe, including even the Pope, have granted amnesties. The Prussian amnesty has not yet appeared. If the Regent' wishes to deserve well of his country, "let him summon back the exiles [...] and become the testamentary executor of the Parliament of 1849, as the Napoleons are testamentary executors of the French Revolution!

"Let us here correct certain erroneous notions which exist in Germany. They suppose, on the strength of certain feudal journals, that the French Empire[h] is in a state of slavery—that the Imperial rule has gagged thought, suppressed the national representation, and tossed our liberties to the dogs.

"The Prussians believe themselves to be more free and happy than we are, under their liberal and parliamentary Government. It is true that the Emperor of the French works out the grandeur and prosperity of France" with a dictatorial power: but it is essentially democratic, "as it was confided to him by the people."[i]

But is not feudalism rampant in Prussia?

"The French army is devoted to the Emperor, but it does not belong to him but to the nation. Does the Prussian army belong to the King or to the nation? 'To the

---

[a] Francis II.— *Ed.*
[b] Napoleon III.— *Ed.*
[c] Victor Emmanuel II.— *Ed.*
[d] William.— *Ed.*
[e] Frederick William IV.— *Ed.*
[f] Frederick Augustus II.— *Ed.*
[g] Leopold.— *Ed.*
[h] Edmond About has "la nation française".— *Ed.*
[i] This sentence reads as follows in the French original: "Il est vrai que l'empereur Napoléon travaille à la grandeur et à la prospérité de la France avec un pouvoir très-étendu. Mais ce pouvoir, c'est la nation qui le lui a confié."— *Ed.*

King,' said the other day the Prime Minister Hohenzollern, 'the Deputies of the nation have nothing to do with the affairs of the army.'

"It is true that with us the liberty of the press is subjected to severe restrictions, but the right to print and publish is not confiscated; it is only postponed. The nation consents to remain silent around a Prince who does great things, as the friends of a philosopher or a great writer keep silent in his cabinet. As for the right, it remains intact, and Frenchmen [...] will have the right to reclaim it, in good time and place, should the Emperor forget (!) to restore it to them. The writers of Berlin are more free, perhaps," despite their taxes, and caution-money, etc., "but who shall guarantee to them the duration of their privilege? [...] The hand which gave may take away. The difference between us and them is that we lend our liberties to the Emperor, whereas they borrow theirs from the Regent.

"The Germans fancy that we have allowed ourselves to be despoiled of our Parliamentary régime. True. Our Parliament has changed since 1848. It is no longer a coterie representing 400,000 or 500,000 persons; it is the whole nation which sends its Deputies to the Corps Législatif. This Assembly, chosen, like the Emperor himself, by universal suffrage, no longer enjoys the ridiculous privilege (!) of interrupting the march of public affairs, of replacing action by speeches, union by coalition, the public interest by private vanity, the serious progress of a great people by the flattering of some petty oratorical ambition—but it enjoys the inestimable right of voting all the taxes and all the laws of the Empire." "Have we any reason to be jealous of the Prussian Constitution? Is the principle of Ministerial responsibility applied in Prussia? Not yet. Have the Chambers the recognized right to refuse to vote the taxes? No. And what are the Prussian Chambers? That which corresponds with our Corps Législatif, or (!) the House of Commons, is united by a mechanism rather ingenious than democratic." [...] A District is given, which pays 300,000 francs direct taxation. The tax-payers are separated into three squads, the 15 or 20 large proprietors who pay 100,000 francs, are the first class of electors; the second class consists of 200 or 300 who pay another 100,000 francs, and the third, of the 2,000 or 3,000 who pay the remainder. Each of these classes elect [...] six Electors, and these eighteen Electors elect a Deputy. Therefore the middling classes can never be represented, and "this is why M. de Vincke, who sat on the Conservative side in the Frankfort Parliament, is now, without having changed his opinions, the most advanced democrat of the Prussian Chambers. Can liberal Germany do much with such a Chamber?" And even when it evinces some desire for progress, is it not cramped and pushed back by the Upper House?—"an Assembly consisting of nobles who have seats by right or by birth, and members selected by the King from candidates presented to him by the nobility, the Universities and large towns—on one side the right of birth, on the other the Sovereign's choice. It is recruited from no other sources, therefore is it opposed to all liberal measures." It lately "rejected the principle of civil marriages by a large majority. It nearly raised an insurrection against the Minister[a] who proposed that the nobles should be compelled to pay taxes like the other classes of the citizens.

"This Constitution is not perfect. They will do well to modify it if Germany should resolve to throw itself into the arms of Prussia.

"It is very desirable that Prussia should show a little more fairness toward the Governments which are based on universal suffrage. We do not reproach the Court of Berlin for the violence of the German press, nor do we expect the Prince Regent to gag his subjects even when they insult us; but we must be permitted to remark that if the *Siècle* and *Opinion nationale* express themselves in offensive terms

---

[a] Count von Roon.— *Ed.*

against a Sovereign who is not the enemy of France, the *Moniteur*, or at least the semi-official journals hasten to repair the injury by administering a severe reprimand.

"It would also be extremely desirable that the political men of Prussia should abstain from fulminating in the Prussian Parliament attacks openly directed against France. When M. de Vincke talks in the Prussian Chamber of Deputies of reconquering from us Alsace and Lorraine, the French nation is not sufficiently excited by this frivolity to take up arms; but it takes pleasure in declaring that such imprudences are never committed in France."

"Since the accession of Napoleon III, and especially since the annexation of Nice and[a] Savoy, German writers and perhaps even German Princes have somewhat loudly manifested an unjust mistrust of French policy. They persist in attributing to us the project of annexing the Rhenish Provinces, and encroaching on the soil of Germany. This groundless alarm is so loudly expressed and so obstinately persevered in *that it might inspire us with bad thoughts were we less equitable. It is certain that if you accost in the street the most gentle and inoffensive man, and you say to him: Sir, you mean to slap my face, you may swear that you have no such intention, but I know that you intend to slap my face. You need not swear to the contrary, for I won't believe you on your oath, for I know that you do mean to slap my face. But I am stronger than you. I am not afraid of you. I will crush you like a fly, and I defy you to slap my face. Would not the gentlest and most inoffensive man find good reason to do what was demanded of him, and would he not inflict the slap on the face of his provoker?*[b]

"But, no provocations will cause France to depart from the line which she has traced for herself. [...] We have too much justice to think of conquering the territory of a foreign nationality. Would to Heaven that the German Confederation was animated by the same ideas! It would not have taken the Duchy of Posen, nor attacked the north of Schleswig, nor declared Trieste to be a German town. As for us, we do not fear to affirm that Lorraine and Alsace are French, because they themselves have proved it against Germans. *We keep what belongs to us.* We demand nothing more! We believe that all the natural frontiers, all the rivers of Europe, are not worth half so much for the defense of our territory as a regiment of Zouaves or Chasseurs-à-pied with fixed bayonets.

"May we be permitted to add one piece of advice to these friendly counsels? It will prove how deeply we are interested in German unity and the future of Prussia.

"Much as the name of Prussia, its Constitution, the person of its august Regent excite the sympathies of Germany, still more so, perhaps, does its bureaucracy inspire feelings of abhorrence, not only in Germany but among honest men of all countries. On the 12th of May, 1860, a ray of light fell on the maneuvers of the Prussian police, and revealed the most singular admixture of clumsiness and immorality, zeal, and imprudence, incendiary provocation and splashing Machiavellism.

"Here are the facts as they have been narrated to the Prussian Parliament by an honorable deputy of the Grand Duchy of Posen, Mr. Niegolewscki. Three Prussian bureaucrats, M. de Puttkammer, President of the Province of Posen, M. de Baerensprung, President of the Police, and Mr. Post, Secretary-Interpreter, were in search of some means whereby they might make manifest their zeal and entitle themselves to the gratitude of the Government. M. de Puttkammer is a great personage, something more than a Prefect, something less than a Minister, M. de Baerensprung is a man of note and importance. Post is a poor devil of no note.

---

[a] The words "Nice and" were introduced by Marx.— *Ed.*

[b] Italicised by Marx.— *Ed.*

"The first thinks, the second dictates, the third writes. These three worthies, by dint of digging into their bureaucratic brains, conceive the grand idea of getting up an insurrection in Posen, that they may have the honor and glory of putting it down. The part of a provocative agent, against which even Vidocq recoiled, inspired them with no disgust. They disguise themselves as Poles discontented with Prussian rule. They establish in their bureaus a false democratic committee, and put themselves in communication with the Central Committee residing in London. 'Send us,' they write, 'send us emissaries, proclamations, arms.' On the other hand, they send money to London, the money of the Budget, the thalers wrung from unfortunate tax-payers. Here are taxes well employed. The treasurer of the enterprise was M. Stolzenberg, the Secretary of Police. The letters were to be addressed to Madame Ruch, wife of a counselor in the Supreme Tribunal.

"The London Committee did not take the bait very readily. It hesitated, was mistrustful. It seemed to scent the treason. But the bureaucratic trio implored with such humility for some letters and circulars; it spoke with such admiration of General Mazzini; with so much emotion of the prose of Félix Pyat, the very bread of life, that some revolutionary men in London, including even Mazzini himself, entered into correspondence with them. This perfidious game was played for three years, and would have been played on till now, had it not been suddenly stopped by a thunderbolt from M. Niegolewscki.[a]

"The eloquent orator of Posen laid on the table the original text of 24 letters, written by Mr. Post, dictated by M. Baerensprung and inspired by Mr. Puttkammer. The first is dated August 19, 1858; the last April, 1860. No one, not even the Minister of the Interior, M. de Schwerin, ventured to contest the authenticity of these documents. We have had them translated by a sworn interpreter. They prove that the Prussian police excited the Committee in London to send incendiary proclamations to the Grand Duchy of Posen; that it paid the expenses for printing them in London, and caused them to be distributed to suspected persons, that they might afterward be seized and the police might then manifest their zeal to the detriment of some of the King of Prussia's subjects; that Puttkammer, Baerensprung, and their accomplices, by means of entreaties and promises, induced the Committee in London to dispatch to them an emissary named Rewitt, who was furnished by them" (the Police) "with a passport; that they allowed him to circulate freely, that he might compromise as many people as possible; that they then arrested him, and had him condemned to two years' imprisonment". After this fine exploit, M. de Baerensprung, the savior of order, which he had disturbed, [...] set up as a candidate for Parliament, and was rejected. "But he still carried on his correspondence with Mazzini, and the Committee in London, swearing to them that Rewitt had been betrayed by the Polish nobility (letter of July 5, 1859), and that numbers of the nobility were in the police. (Letter of July 19, 1859.)

"These functionaries, in their letters, held up the nobility and clergy, including Prince Czartoryski, to the execration of the London Committee. They talk about seizing the estates of the nobles, and parceling them out among the people. [...] On the 27th March, 1859, they see that the Emperor of the French is about to make a generous effort in favor of Italian independence. They write to the London Committee to forestall it. They beg Mazzini to stir up the country before the arrival of the French army. [...] They beg him to hoist the red flag before Napoleon shall be able to mix himself up in Italian affairs. [...] On the 21st of May, they thank the

---

[a] Niegolewscki's speech in the Chamber of Deputies on May 12, 1860, *Allgemeine Zeitung*, No. 136, May 15, 1860.— *Ed.*

Committee in London for sending them [...] the 'receipt for making Orsini's shells.' It needs no ghost to tell us for what purpose they obtained this receipt. We know that these gentlemen belonged to the police, therefore they could not be conspirators; their intentions must have been pure. They doubtless intended to warn the Emperor against danger, and this was their reason for putting a postscript to their letter: 'How long will the French democrats delay making another attempt against Napoleon?' [...] After Villafranca, you might have supposed that every German would have been pleased that Venice was preserved to Austria; but they wrote to Mazzini: 'The revolution will break out in Italy, Hungary, Germany, Prussia, and perhaps in France, and even in Poland. The eyes of the world are opened to the treachery of Napoleon, and all oppressed nations are glad to get rid of him.' And, further on, these Prussian police agents write: 'What is going on in France? Will no second Orsini come forth? Do the Republicans mean to do nothing to overthrow the tyrant?' (Aug. 20, 1859.)

"We do not wish to fix too high the responsibility for these imprudences. The police has been more clumsy than culpable, for it has not had the tact to conceal its most secret papers from the gaze of honest men. But the Prussian Government should lead its police out of these tortuous paths; it is always wrong to counsel crime, even as a means for trying of what stuff men are made.

"Every one knows that if Orsini had succeeded in his criminal attempt he would have assassinated the future liberator of Italy, and have done more harm than good to his country. We may also add that if these Prussian police, without any evil intent, and simply out of a stupid zeal, had got up another Orsini, they would have deprived Prussia of a useful ally, who is still ready to render her good service, provided that she will help herself."[a]

Compiled on June 12, 1860

First published in the *New-York Daily Tribune*, No. 5986, June 30, 1860

Reproduced from the newspaper

---

[a] The concluding words from Edmond About's pamphlet, beginning with "a useful ally", are cited by Marx at the end of *Herr Vogt* (see this volume, p. 329).— *Ed.*

Karl Marx

INTERESTING FROM PRUSSIA

Berlin, June 13, 1860

This evening the Prince Regent[a] will leave for Baden-Baden, where a sort of conference between Louis Napoleon and a council of crowned German heads is to take place on the 16th and 17th inst.[306] The Prince Regent's suite will be formed by Gen. von Manteuffel, the chief of the Military Cabinet; Gen. von Alvensleben, Lieut.-Col. von Schimmelmann, von Loë, *chef d'escadron*, Count von Pückler, the Court Marshal, Privy Councilor von Illaire, Mr. Borkmann, the Regent's Secretary, and Prince von Hohenzollern-Sigmaringen, the chief of the Cabinet and a member of the Royal family. You will remember that on the occasion of the private letter addressed by the Prince Regent to the Prince Consort of England, intercepted at London and thence communicated to Louis Bonaparte,[b] the latter insisted upon a personal interview with the Prince Regent as the best means of clearing away the misunderstanding that seemed to have sprung up between France and Prussia. Shortly afterward, on the Prince Regent's visit to Saarbrücken and Trier, towns situated on the confines of France, Louis Napoleon again intimated his wish to improve this opportunity for meeting the Prince. This proposal was, however, declined. Meanwhile, the rumor having got abroad of the Prince Regent's intention to stay for a month at Baden-Baden, Max, the King of Bavaria,[c] took it into his head to propose to the Regent a sort of conference at the watering-place with the Princes of Southern Germany, who wanted to come to a friendly understand-

---

a William, Prince of Prussia.— *Ed.*
b See this volume, pp. 382.— *Ed.*
c Maximilian II.— *Ed.*

ing with Prussia, and by this very meeting to show a united front against France. The Prince Regent, jumping at once into this scheme, which was also embraced by the Grand Duke of Baden, the King of Württemberg, and the Grand Duke of Hessen-Darmstadt,[a] one fine morning the French Embassador at Berlin[b] officially notified Herr von Schleinitz, the Prussian Foreign Minister, that his august master, in order to dispel the distrust, whose innocent object France appeared to be, thought a friendly interview at Baden-Baden, with the actual chief of the Prussian State, a great benefit to both Germany and France. On the Prussian Minister's reply that unjust suspicions, not likely to be dispelled by such an interview, hovered also over Prussia, and that besides a confidential conference of German Princes at Baden-Baden had already been convened, the French Embassador, on further information from Paris, rejoined that Louis Napoleon would delight in finding together the greatest possible number of German Princes, and that, moreover, he had some important communication to personally impart, which would allow of no further delay. At this point the Hohenzollern power of resistance gave way.[c] A Vienna dispatch conveyed at once to Berlin the expression of Austria's displeasure at the intended rendezvous, but the other German Courts were more or less soothed by a circular note of the Prussian Foreign Minister.[d] Consequent upon this circular note, the King of Hanover[e] unexpectedly arrived at Berlin this morning, and declared spontaneously his willingness of accompanying to Baden-Baden the Prince Regent, who then, by a telegraphic dispatch, summoned also the King of Saxony[f] to the conference. It need hardly be said, that the Dukes of Coburg-Gotha and Nassau[g] will follow in the track.

Thus, a meeting of German Princes, originally purporting to mean a demonstration against France, has turned into a sort of levee, held by Louis Bonaparte, on German soil, and crowded by the Kings, Grand Dukes, and other little potentates of the German Confederation. On the part of the Prince Regent it looks like

---

[a] Friedrich I Wilhelm Ludwig, William I and Ludwig III.— Ed.

[b] La Tour d'Auvergne-Lauraguais.— Ed.

[c] For the preparation for a friendly interview at Baden-Baden see "Prusse", Le Nord, June 15, 1860.— Ed.

[d] Alexander Schleinitz, "Preussische Circulardepesche, 6. Juni, 1860", Allgemeine Zeitung, No. 261, September 17, 1860.— Ed.

[e] Ernest Augustus.— Ed.

[f] Johann Nepomuk Maria Joseph.— Ed.

[g] Ernst II and Adolf.— Ed.

contrition for the sin of having uttered his suspicions as to the French usurper's aggressive schemes, and on the part of the smaller princely fry as a precaution taken for not being sold by their huger *confrère*[a] to their common enemy. The lead in the humiliation of the crowned heads before the Quasimodo of the French Revolution was notoriously taken by Queen Victoria and the King of Sardinia.[307] The Czar's personal interview at Stuttgart with the Man of December, in 1857,[308] could surprise nobody beyond the coffee-house politicians, duped by the ostentatious coquetry of the Petersburg Court with the tenets of legitimacy. After the battle of Solferino, the Hapsburg's Villafranca meeting with his victor was a matter of business, not of courtesy. The Prince Regent, together with the minor stars clustering around him, has neither to plead an alliance, like Victoria and Victor Emmanuel, nor a conspiracy, like Alexander II, nor a defeat, like Francis Joseph; but, leaving the motives aside, he may plead the general precedent put by his betters. At all events, he has seriously impaired his factitious popularity by the acceptance of Louis Bonaparte's overture, and the more so since the latter, only a few weeks ago, had the impudence of intimating, through a dispatch of his Foreign Minister, M. de Thouvenel, to the Grand Dukes of Hessen-Darmstadt and Baden, that, for the future, they ought to sign their letters to the French Emperor with the words: "*Votre frère et serviteur.*"[b] Such was, indeed, the formula Napoleon I had invented for the German Princes, forming part of the Rhenish Confederation, of which he was the protector, and to which belonged Baden and Hessen-Darmstadt, together with Württemberg, Bavaria, and other German principalities.[309] In order to prevent Louis Bonaparte from introducing M. de Thouvenel into the presence of the highly-offended monarchs of Baden and Hessen-Darmstadt, the Prince Regent and his crowned associates have unanimously forborne to be accompanied by their respective Foreign Ministers; but, then, do these gentlemen really fancy that the affront was offered to them by the servant, instead of the servant's master?

As to the "important communication" which the Dutch savior of society is about to impart to the crowned heads of Germany, there is every reason to believe that, imitating Metternich's operations on the successive Congresses of Vienna, Aix-la-Chapelle,[c] Troppau,

---

a Colleague.— *Ed.*
b "Your brother and servant."— *Ed.*
c Aachen.— *Ed.*

Laibach and Verona,[310] Louis Napoleon will try his utmost to convince the Prince Regent of the existence of a vast conspiracy among the revolutionists, straining every nerve to bring about a collision between France and Prussia, in order to enthrone the Red Republic in Paris and a Central Republic in Germany. All the Bonapartist organs in Switzerland, Belgium, and Germany, swarm, since a fortnight, with paragraphs full of similar dark insinuations; and a confidential Bonapartist agent at Geneva—a well-known German naturalist[a]—has already triumphantly announced that the anti-Bonapartists' eruptions of the German press would very soon be stopped by the competent authorities.

While the Prince Regent and his German *dii minorum gentium*[b] are thus to be convinced of the necessity to gather round the general savior of society, the Prussian people is to be belabored in the opposite sense by M. About's new pamphlet, "The Emperor Napoleon III and Prussia."[c] Although this pamphlet has as yet been retained, some stray copies of it have already found their way to Berlin, and by another letter I have sent you the most remarkable passages from this newest Tuileries manifesto.[d] The Prussian people must choose, says the oracle from the Seine, between the feudalism of Austria and the democratic principle of the French Empire. It is only by the latter that, resolving of course to give its mighty neighbor some material guaranties, the German people can hope to realize the unity so much coveted by it. Having traced the shortcomings of the present Prussian Government in a very superficial manner, the author of the pamphlet sets out on informing the Prussians of the true nature of the "democratic principle" so characteristic of the second French Empire, and which consists, to say it shortly, in the election of its chief by what is called in modern Gaul, "general suffrage." It is true, and M. About does hardly dare deny it, that every sort of liberty has been sequestrated in France to the profit of the Dutch adventurer, but then, this sequestration was based on general suffrage. It is in this way, with the aid of France, and on the same democratic basis, that a Teutonic Empire under the auspices of a Hohenzollern ought to be reared in Germany. The operation is a very simple one. Prussia has only to cede part of her "legitimate" possessions

---

[a] Karl Vogt.— *Ed.*

[b] Literally, "lesser gods"; here, minor princes.— *Ed.*

[c] The reference is to Edmond About's *La Prusse en 1860*, Paris, 1860.— *Ed.*

[d] See this volume, pp. 391-96.— *Ed.*

to France and to simultaneously encroach, under the form of an appeal to general suffrage, on the possessions of the minor princes, and she will at once be transformed from a feudal into a democratic state. It must be owned that this new "democratic principle" discovered by Louis Bonaparte and his sycophants is no innovation, but, on the contrary, has for about two centuries been flourishing in holy Russia. The Romanoff family was seated on the throne by general suffrage. Hence democracy reigns from the Niemen to the Amoor. Perhaps it might be retorted by the prophets of the new "democratic principle" that the Romanoffs were freely elected; that no *coup d'état* preceded the appeal to the people; and that, on their accession to the throne, a general state of siege failed to keep the electoral urns within the proper limits of the democratic principle. At all events, since Louis Bonaparte cannot afford to become a "legitimate" prince, the next best thing he can do is to convert his brother sovereigns of Italy and Germany into "democratic" princes, after the pattern of the Lesser Empire. The Roman Emperors, of course, were no truly "democratic" sovereigns, because modern progress requires the principle of hereditary monarchy to be engrafted upon the principle of "general suffrage," so that, when a fellow by hook or crook has once succeeded in usurping a throne, and coloring his usurpation by the farce of general election, his dynasty must forever be supposed to remain the living incarnation of the people's general will. (*Rousseau's volonté générale.*)[a]

In another letter I propose surveying the state of the Schleswig-Holstein complications, which impart to the Baden-Baden Conference its actual importance. For the present, I shall only mention that on the 10th of June an interview took place at the castle of Kronburg between the King of Sweden and the King of Denmark.[b] A fortnight before this rendezvous the Swedish Foreign Minister[c] had sent to the Danish Foreign Minister[d] a note to the purport that it was very desirable that the King of Denmark's suite should contain no persons the encounter with whom might prove embarrassing for his Swedish Majesty. In other words, the King of Denmark was called upon to clear his company

---

[a] Marx refers to Jean-Jacques Rousseau's *Contrat social ou principes du droit politique*, London, 1782, v. 5, p. 254.— *Ed.*

[b] Charles XV and Frederick VII.— *Ed.*

[c] Kristoffer Rutger Ludvig Mandeström.— *Ed.*

[d] Carl Christian Hall.— *Ed.*

from the presence of his wife, the Countess Daner, *ci-devant*[a] Mademoiselle Ramussen. Accordingly, the King of Denmark thought fit to leave his girl behind him.

Written on June 13, 1860   Reproduced from the newspaper

First published in the *New-York Daily Tribune*, No. 5986, June 30, 1860

---

[a] Formerly.— *Ed.*

Frederick Engels

THE BRITISH VOLUNTEER FORCE

The great review of volunteers which took place in London a few weeks ago has attracted attention to the citizen soldiers of Great Britain. The volunteers must not be confounded with the militia, which is a separate arm of her Majesty's service. On the 1st of April, the militia numbered, according to Government statistics, 50,000. Of these, 23,735 were embodied, England contributing 13,580, Ireland 7,471, and Scotland 2,684. The militia represents the lower classes; the volunteers the middle class. The assertion of the London *Times*[a] that in the ranks of the troops reviewed on the 22d "all classes were represented" is merely a way of giving things a popular coloring. It is not quite three months since a deputation of respectable mechanics waited on the authorities for the purpose of being supplied with arms, to "defend their country," in case of invasion. Their application was refused. The only working men admitted into the volunteer corps are those whose outfit and expenses their employers provide, and whose services are understood to be permanently at the command of those employers.

The total strength of the British volunteer force, notwithstanding the larger figures of many recent statistical tables, is short of 90,000. It is true that Col. Macmurdo declared, at a dinner given some time since to the St. George's Rifle Corps, that there were 124,000 registered for voluntary service; but when pushed for particulars he included half the militia in his estimate. The newspapers count every regiment at the nominal strength of 800 or 1,000 men, when in reality few ever muster on parade more

---

[a] *The Times*, Nos. 23655 and 23658, June 25 and 28, 1860.— *Ed.*

than 500 or 600. Mr. Sidney Herbert, whose position at the Horse Guards entitles him to be an authority on the subject, stated in Parliament a day or two before the great turnout in London, that "on paper, the force has maintained considerable numbers, who, however, cannot be accounted for, and never answer at roll-call."[a]

The speech in which this passage occurs appears in the same number of *The Times* that chronicles "the magnificent success" of the national volunteer review. Even the Hyde Park parade itself furnishes a striking illustration of the exaggerated manner in which the London Press speak of such matters. *The Times* of the 20th anticipated that "no less than 35,000 men would appear before her Majesty."[b] Tom Taylor, writing to *The Manchester Guardian* from London on the 21st, says that there were over 46,000 in the Metropolis. Yet the whole number of soldiers who passed before the Queen, according to Col. Macmurdo, who would hardly underestimate them, was 18,300. Certainly, this is not a very extraordinary army to be over-jubilant about. In October, 1803, nearly 13,000 native Londoners were inspected in the garb of volunteers; and, by way of comparing British military valor of those days with that of the present time, we subjoin a brief statement of the volunteer force, registered in Jan., 1804:

Total of effective rank and file	341,687
Field-officers	1,246
Captains	4,472
Subalterns	9,918
Staff-officers	1,100
Sergeants	14,787
Drummers	6,733
Grand total	379,943

Even the 124,000, to which England hopes to raise her present voluntary army, would not figure creditably beside this table. One man in every ten of the present able-bodied of Great Britain's male population would amount to 500,000 men. It does not appear from these facts that Englishmen are becoming more

    [a] Sidney Herbert's speech in the House of Commons on June 26, 1860, *The Times*, No. 23657, June 27, 1860. Instead of "and never answer at roll-call", *The Times* has "and never appear on parade".— *Ed.*

    [b] "London, Friday, June 22, 1860", *The Times*, No. 23653, June 22, 1860. The figure in *The Times* is 30,000.— *Ed.*

desirous to take up arms in defense of their native land than they ever were before, the statements of London journals to the contrary notwithstanding. According to the careful statistics of a writer in *The Army and Navy Gazette*, we find the total militia and volunteer force of England to be, of militia 50,160, and of volunteers 88,400, making 138,560 in all. Of these, the writer of *The Gazette* states that at least 20,000 would, from various causes, prove unavailable in case of need, so that 118,560 men constitute the grand total of England's militia and volunteers.

Written between June 25 and 28, 1860

First published in the *New-York Daily Tribune*, No. 5994, July 11, 1860 as a leading article; reprinted in the *New-York Semi-Weekly Tribune*, No. 1579, July 13, 1860

Reproduced from the *New-York Daily Tribune*

Karl Marx

BRITISH COMMERCE

The Board of Trade Returns[a] for the five months ending May 31, 1860, which have just been issued at London, show but a trifling change in the movement of British exports, if compared with the exports during the first five months of 1859.

From £52,337,268, to which they had amounted in 1859, they rose to £52,783,535 in 1860[b]—this small surplus being altogether due to an increase in the month of May last.

The first feature that strikes us on comparing the respective exports during the first five months of 1860 and 1859, is a considerable decline in the British export trade to the British East Indies, as will be seen from the following statement:

PRINCIPAL BRITISH ARTICLES EXPORTED TO THE EAST INDIES
IN THE FIVE MONTHS ENDING MAY 31.

	Quantities.		Value.	
	1859.	1860.	1859.	1860.
Beer and ale, barrels	168,355	166,461	£507,308	£491,609
Cottons, yards	396,022,733	311,163,765	4,884,982	3,977,289
Cotton yarn, lbs.	17,411,542	15,044,812	1,002,439	903,516
Iron (bar, bolt, rod), tuns	16,851	12,194	127,678	90,954
Iron (cast), tuns	12,138	4,108	132,946	42,912
Iron (wrought), tuns	11,823	10,554	188,126	195,659
Sheets and rails [c]	31,582	79,117	169,072	437,170

---

[a] For the analysis of the British commerce Marx makes use of the table "Exports of the Principal and other Articles of British and Irish Produce and Manufactures in the Five Months ended 31st May, 1860, compared with the corresponding Months of the Year 1859", *The Economist*, No. 879, June 30, 1860, pp. 36-38.— *Ed.*

[b] ibid., p. 38.— *Ed.*

[c] *The Economist* has "nails" here and in the table on p. 409.— *Ed.*

	Quantities.		Value.	
	1859.	1860.	1859.	1860.
Earthen ware and porcelain	....	....	£34,530	£24,039
Haberdashery and millinery	....	....	83,832	42,126
Leather—saddlery and harness	....	....	16,780	15,600
Machinery—steam engines	....	....	73,087	100,846
Other kinds	....	....	165,899	196,928
Tin plates	....	....	19,127	6,441
Total			£7,405,806	£6,525,089
Decrease				£876,717

From the above table it appears that the aggregate decrease in the main exports to the East Indies amounts to about one million sterling; that it is heaviest in the leading articles (cotton and cotton yarns); and that the only exception consists of commodities immediately connected with railway building. It ought, moreover, to be kept in view that the commercial news received by the last Overland Mail is highly unfavorable, and points to an overcharged market; so that, consequently, the value of the exports as declared in England, and as estimated on a range of prices far beyond the average, will by no means be realized in India. Now, there can be no doubt that the Indian trade has been overdone. The artificial demand raised by the Government during the Indian rebellion [311]; the stimulus given to commercial activity by the subsiding of the revolutionary disturbances, and the contraction of most of the other markets of the world, consequent upon the general crisis of 1857-58—all these circumstances concurred to swell the bulk of the Indian trade beyond its natural capacities. Still, according to all past experience, the newfangled prosperity market might have borne the bombardment by cotton goods for some years longer, but for the sage interference of the British Government. Mr. Wilson, it seems, was expressly dispatched to Calcutta for the purpose of convulsing the Anglo-Indian trade, by the joint operation of clumsy fiscal measures in the interior, and of burdensome customs duties levied on imports from abroad. Has ever, in the whole history of commerce, such a spectacle been witnessed as that of the United Kingdom allowing its most important colonial market to be crippled by the spontaneous acts of its own Government, at the very same time that it cringes before the French Emperor,[a] and bears with his political encroachments, on the pretext of a factitious alleviation in the French customs duties?

The exports to the Australian market, although they show some decline in cottons, exhibit, on the whole, an increase both in quantity and value. However, to arrive at a just appreciation of the present state of the markets in the Australian Colonies, we ought to turn from the Board-of-Trade returns to the last commercial intelligence received. Advices from Adelaide to the 26th of April complain of a continuance of excessive shipments from England, and a general prevalence of speculation, swindling and overtrading. An extensive weeding out, it was said, of insolvent firms had become necessary. In Sydney, New South Wales, several failures had already taken place, including nine houses with an aggregate of liabilities of £400,000, of which amount three-fourths was expected to be ultimately deficient, the loss falling on the banks and English creditors. From a list just received of Australian insolvencies during the last 17 years, it appears that the number in 1858 was three times as great as in 1857, and in 1859 there was a further increase of 50 per cent; and this year, up to the middle of April, the rate had experienced a fresh advance of about 7 per cent. The total liabilities of failed firms from 1822 to 1859 were £5,981,026; and the assets, stated in schedules, amounted to £3,735,613; but of the latter amount, not 50 per cent was ever realized.

The considerable decline that has taken place in the value, and in most cases, also, in the quantity of the British goods exported to the United States, will be illustrated by the following extract:

PRINCIPAL ARTICLES EXPORTED TO THE UNITED STATES IN
THE FIVE MONTHS ENDING MAY 31.[b]

	Quantities.		Value.	
	1859.	1860.	1859.	1860.
Coals, tuns	68,020	106,925	£67,785	£66,196
Cotton, yards	88,441,112	84,208,598	1,562,918	1,491,721
Linens, yards	25,476,444	20,974,699	776,780	643,676
Pig Iron, tuns	37,510	21,497	106,476	62,919
Bar, bolt, rod, tuns	48,063	37,824	394,426	293,294

---

  [a] Napoleon III.— Ed.
  [b] The New-York Daily Tribune has a misprint here, "May 1" instead of "May 31".— Ed.

	Quantities.		Value.	
	1859.	1860.	1859.	1860.
Wrought, tuns	16,024	16,488	£200,576	£189,854 [a]
Sheets and rails, tuns	12,107	4,622	61,721	24,559
Seed Oil, gals.	795,808	511,602	95,154	57,230
Silk manufacture, lb.	119,719	58,836	128,133	68,866
Woolens, mix. stff., yds.	22,697,619	18,250,639	892,026	733,000
Earthenw'e & porcel'n	......	......	234,492	281,532
Haberdash'y & milli'y	......	......	719,754	637,035
Tin plates	......	......	524,615	464,630

France was, of course, the country to make up for the contraction of the markets of the East Indies, the Australian Colonies, and the United States. However, on a closer examination, the English export trade to France will be found to have lost nothing of its traditionally diminutive dimensions. As to cottons and twist, Mr. Milner Gibson, the President of the Board of Trade, seems to have been ashamed of the sorry figure he cut, and, consequently, thought fit to altogether expunge them from the returns. Ditto with linens and linen yarns, and silk manufactures. The value of the exports during the respective epochs of 1859 and 1860 shows a falling off for the current year in thrown silk from £130,260 to £88,441,[b] in silk twist and yarn from £50,520 to £29,643, in machinery from £98,551 to £64,107, and in coals from £253,008 to £206,317, while some increase has taken place in the export of iron, copper, wool, woolens, and worsted yarns.

The import of French wine has increased, but in no greater proportion than that of all other descriptions of wine. In conclusion, we may remark that the symptoms of contraction in the principal markets, if taken together with the very distressing harvest prospects, the heavy calls upon the money market by the English and other Governments, and the unsettled political state of Europe, seem to forebode anything but a prosperous season for the Autumn of 1860.

Written in late June and early July 1860

Reproduced from the newspaper

First published in the *New-York Daily Tribune*, No. 5998, July 16, 1860 as a leading article

---

[a] The figure in the *New-York Daily Tribune* is 199,859, which is a misprint.— *Ed.*

[b] *The Economist*, No. 879, June 30, 1860, pp. 37, 38, 36.— *Ed.*

Karl Marx

THE STATE OF BRITISH MANUFACTURING INDUSTRY

I

[*New-York Daily Tribune*, No. 6016, August 6, 1860]

London, July 10, 1860

The reports of the Inspectors of Factories,[a] which have just been issued, comprise three reports only; the district lately vacated by Mr. Leonard Horner having been annexed partly to Sir John Kincaid's district (Scotland), and partly to Mr. Redgrave's district, now comprising 3,075 factories and printworks; while Mr. Robert Baker's district (Ireland, and some parts of England) remains within its old boundaries. The following is a general abstract, showing the total number of accidents reported to the three Inspectors during the six months ended the 30th April, 1860:

ACCIDENTS ARISING FROM MACHINERY.[b]

	Ad'ts.		Y'g per.		Child.		Total.		
Nature of Injury	M.	F.	M.	F.	M.	F.	M.	F.	Total.
Causing death	14	3	7	2	2	2	23	7	30
Amputat'n of right hand or arm	5	6	3	1	1	—	9	7	16
Amputat'n of left hand or arm	4	1	7	3	1	—	12	4	16
Amputat'n of part of right hand	23	24	29	22	15	7	67	53	120
Amputat'n of part of left hand	16	17	21	18	8	7	45	42	87

[a] In writing this article Marx made use of the *Reports of the Inspectors of Factories to Her Majesty's Principal Secretary of State for the Home Department, for the Half Year ending 30th April 1860*, London, 1860.— *Ed.*

[b] ibid., p. 4.— *Ed.*

	Ad'ts.		Y'g per.		Child.		Total.		
Nature of Injury........	M.	F.	M.	F.	M.	F.	M.	F.	Total.
Amp. of any part of leg or foot	5	—	1	—	—	—	6	—	6
Fract. of limbs and bones of trunk	30	11	43	11	11	4	84	26	110
Fracture of hand or foot	39	43	30	37	20	15	89	95	184
Injuries to head and face	20	17	23	29	11	4	54	40	94
Lac'tns, contus'ns, and other injur's not enum. above	268	255	315	352	128	66	711	673	1,384
Total	424	377	479	465	197	105	1,100	947	2,047

ACCIDENTS NOT ARISING FROM MACHINERY.

| Total .... | 83 | 30 | 59 | 26 | 21 | 10 | 163 | 66 | 229 |

The reports are unanimous in bearing witness to the extraordinary activity of trade during the half year. Such was the demand for work that in some branches of industry the supply of labor was insufficient. This difficulty was less prevalent in the woolen manufactures, where improved machinery allowed the manufacturers to dispense with manual labor, than in cotton and worsted factories, where much machinery has been standing for want of hands, particularly of the younger. Some vicious methods have been adopted in past times to meet this transitory deficiency of labor. In the infancy of the factory system, when manufacturers were in want of labor, it was obtained directly by application to the overseers of some distant parish, who forwarded a certain number of apprentices, children of tender age, who were bound to the manufacturers for a term of years. The children being once apprenticed, the Poor-Law officers congratulated their respective parishes on their deliverance from idle mouths, while the manufacturer proceeded to make the best of his bargain by keeping them at the most economical rate, and by screwing from them all the labor of which they were capable. Hence the first of the series of Factory acts passed in 1802, 42 Geo. III, Cap. 73, has for its title, "An Act for the Preservation of the Health and Morals of Apprentices and Others Employed in Cotton and Other Mills, and Cotton and Other Factories," and was merely intended to mitigate the evils of the apprenticeship system. But as improvements were made in machinery, a different kind of labor was wanted, when trade became brisk and the population of the neighborhood failed to supply the mills with their full complement of hands. These manufacturers sent to Ireland, and brought over Irish families; but Ireland has ceased to be the market from which a supply of labor can be procured on English demand, and manufacturers have now to look to the Southern and Western counties of England and Wales for families which can be tempted by the present rate of wages in the Northern counties to commence a new career of industry. Agents have been sent throughout the country, to set forth the advantages offered to families by removing to the manufacturing districts, and they are empowered to make arrangements for the emigration to the North. Many families are said to have been forwarded by these agents. Still, the importation into a manufacturing town of a man with his wife and family has this peculiar disadvantage, that while the younger members of the family, who can soon be taught, and whose services become valuable in a comparatively short period, are most in request, there is no ready demand for the labor of the man and his wife, unskilled in factory labor. This has induced some manufacturers to return, in some measure, to the old apprenticeship system, and to enter into engagements for specific periods, with boards of guardians, for the labor of destitute pauper children. In these cases, the manufacturer lodges, clothes and feeds the children, but pays them no regular wages. With the return of this system, complaints of its abuse seem also to have revived. However, this kind of labor, it should be remembered, would only be sought after when none other could be procured, for it is a high-priced labor. The ordinary wages of a boy of 13 would be about 4 shillings per week; but to lodge, to clothe, to feed and to provide medical attendance and proper superintendence for 50 or 100 of these boys, and to set aside some remuneration for them, could not be accomplished for 4 shillings a head per week.[a]

A comparison of the rate of wages paid to factory operatives in 1839 and that paid in 1859 proves the highly interesting fact that the rate of wages has risen, at least nominally, in factories where the hours of work were restricted to 60 per week, while, with a few exceptions, a real reduction has been suffered in the printing, bleaching, and dyeing works in which the labor of children, young

---

[a] These facts and the following are taken from the "Report of A. Redgrave, Esq., Inspector of Factories, for the Half Year ending the 30th April 1860", *Reports of the Inspectors of Factories...*, pp. 26-27.— *Ed.*

persons, and women is unrestricted, and where they are at times employed fourteen and fifteen hours per day. The following statements have reference to the cotton trade in Manchester and its neighborhood:

WEEKLY WAGES.[a]

	1839.	1859.
Hours of work per week	69	60
Occupations.		
Steam-engine tender	24sh.	30sh.
Warehouse boys	7	8
Warehouse men	18	22
Carding department—Scutchers (young women and girls)	7	8
Skippers (young men)	11	14
Overlookers	25	28
Card minders (boys from 14 to 18)	6	7
Drawing-frame tenders (young women)	6 6d	8
Spinning department—Spinners on self-acting mules ...	16 to 18	20 to 22
Piecers (women and young men)	8	10
Overlookers	20	20
Doubling department—Doublers (women)	7	9
Doffers (girls)	4	5
Overlookers	24	28
Jobbers (young men)	10	13

In the reeling, gassing, and power-loom departments, there has also been a slight increase of wages. The anticipations of those who warned the factory operatives that they would seriously suffer by the diminution of their hours of work, have thus been completely disappointed. Compare, on the other hand, the movement of wages in those branches where the hours of daily labor are legally unrestricted:

CALICO-PRINTING, DYEING, BLEACHING,
SIXTY HOURS PER WEEK.[b]

	Weekly Wages.	
	1839.	1859.
Color-mixer	35	32
Machine-printer	40	38
Foreman	40	40

---

[a] op. cit., p. 31.— *Ed.*
[b] op. cit., p. 32.— *Ed.*

	[Continued] Weekly Wages.	
	1839.	1859.
Block-cutter	35	25
Block-printer	40	28
Dyer	18	16
Washer and laborer	16 and 15	16 and 15

FUSTIAN-DYEING, SIXTY-ONE HOURS PER WEEK.

Dressers	18	22
Bleachers	21	18
Dyers	21	16
Finishers	21	22

By far the most interesting portion of the Reports of Mr. Alexander Redgrave and Sir John Kincaid relates to the development and extension of cooperative societies for the erection and working of mills in Lancashire, and also to some degree in Yorkshire. These cooperative societies, which have multiplied since the passing of the Limited Liability Act, are generally composed of operatives. Each society has a capital of £10,000 and upward, divided into shares of £5 and £10, with power to borrow in certain proportions to the capital subscribed, the money borrowed being made up of small loans by operatives and persons of the like class. In Bury, for instance, upward of £300,000 will be required to put the cooperative mills there built and building into working order. In cotton-spinning mills the spinners and persons employed are frequently shareholders in the same mill, working for wages and receiving interest upon their shares. In cotton-weaving sheds, the partners frequently hire and work looms. This is attractive to operatives, because no great capital is required to start them in their undertaking. They purchase the yarn ready for the loom, weave the cloth, and the factory operation is completed; or else they receive the yarn from some manufacturer who trades with them, and return to him the woven fabric. But this cooperative system is not confined to the spinning and weaving of cotton. It has extended to the trade on a variety of articles of consumption, such as flour, groceries, draperies, etc.

The following report, drawn up by Mr. Patrick, one of Sir John Kincaid's sub-inspectors, contains some valuable information in regard to the progress of this new system of mill-ownership, which, I am afraid, will be put to a severe test by the next industrial crisis.

"May 16, 1860

"There has been a cooperative company in existence at Rochdale, under the style of the 'New Bacup and Wardle Commercial Company,' for about twelve years. They are incorporated under the Joint Stock Companies Act, and unlimited. They commenced operations at Clough House Mill, Wardle, near Rochdale, with power to raise a capital of £100,000, in shares of £12 10s., £20,000 of which was paid up. They then increased to £30,000, and about five years ago built a large factory, Far Holme Mill, near Stackstead, of 100-horse power steam, in addition to Clough House Mill; and the half year ending October last they paid a dividend at the rate of 44 per cent on the paid-up capital (Mr. Patrick reports on the 11th June, that the New Bacup and Wardle Commercial Company, 'Far Holme Mill, Bacup,' have just declared another dividend of 48 per cent on the paid-up capital), and they have now increased their capital to the sum of £60,000, and have largely increased their Far Holme Mill, near Stackstead, in this neighborhood, requiring two more engines of 40-horse power each, which they are about to put down. The large majority of shareholders are operatives who work in the factory, but receive wages as workmen, and have no more to do with the management than to give their vote to the annual election of the Committee of Management. I have been through the Far Holme Mill this morning, and can report that, so far as the Factory Act is concerned, it is as well conducted as any in my division. I think, though I did not ask them the question, that they have borrowed money at 5 per cent interest.

"There has been another in existence in the neighborhood of Bacup about six years, trading under the firm of the 'Rossendale Industrial Association.'

"They built a factory; but, I am told, were not thriving, in consequence of the want of sufficient funds. This, also, was on the cooperative system. The firm has now been changed to 'The Rossendale Industrial Company,' and are incorporated under the Limited Liabilities Act, with power to raise a capital of £200,000. £40,000 has been taken in shares of £10 each, and they have borrowed about £4,000. This £4,000 has been borrowed from small capitalists, in sums from £150 down to £10, without any mortgages being given. When this cooperative company first started, every shareholder was an operative. In addition to the Wear Mill, that referred to as having been built by the Rossendale Industrial Association, they have now bought of Messrs. R. Mum Bros., Irwell Mills, in Bacup, and are working the two.

"The prosperity and success of the New Bacup and Wardle Commercial Company seem to have given rise to the new companies that are now formed in my immediate vicinity, and preparing large factories to carry on their business. One is the 'New-Church Cotton Spinning and Weaving Company,' under the Limited Liabilities Act, with power to raise £100,000 in £10 shares, £40,000 of which is already paid, and the Company has borrowed £5,000 on mortgage at five per cent. This Company has already started, having taken an unoccupied factory of 40-horse power, Vale Mill, New-Church, and they are building the 'Victoria Works,' which will require an engine of 100-horse power. They calculate upon employing 450 people when complete, which they think will be in February next.

"Another is 'The Ravenstall Cotton Manufacturing Company,' also limited, with a nominal capital of £50,000, in £5 shares, with power to borrow to the extent of £10,000. About £20,000 is already paid up, and they are erecting at Hareholme a factory requiring an engine of 70-horse power. I am told that in both of these companies nine-tenths of the shareholders are of the operative class.

"There is another cooperative company which has sprung up within the last six months. 'The Old Clough Cotton Company,' which purchased from Messrs. R. & J. Mum, two old mills, called Irwell Springs, and are on the same principle as the others, but not having been able to go there to-day I am not able to give all particulars about it. The power, however, has been returned as 13-horse and the number of hands employed 76, and I believe all the shareholders to be of the operative class.

"There are several who take part of a factory, one or two rooms, as the case may be, and in some instances even part of a room, but then these are masters of that part, although they work with and as their own workmen, hire and pay wages as any other manufacturer, without the workpeople employed having interest in the business. There are many more of these at Bacup than there are now. Some have given it up, while others have succeeded and either built mills for themselves or rent large premises. There are more of this sort at Rochdale than any other place in my division." [a]

II

[New-York Daily Tribune, No. 6032, August 24, 1860]

London, July 14, 1860

After the *résumé* given in my last letter [b] of the Factory Reports of Sir John Kincaid and Mr. Redgrave, it still remains for me to take notice of the report of Mr. Robert Baker, [c] Inspector of Factories for Ireland and part of Cheshire, Lancashire, Gloucestershire, Yorkshire, Staffordshire, Leicestershire, Herefordshire, Shropshire, Worcestershire, and Warwickshire. The total number of accidents in Mr. Baker's district amounted to 601, of which 9 per cent only occurred to children, while 33 per cent happened to persons above 18 years of age. [d] A closer analysis of these accidents will prove, firstly, that the ratio of accidents to population is greatest in those branches of industry where the machinery employed is not subject to legal control, and, secondly, that in the textile fabrics, where the same sort of machinery is employed, the bulk of accidents falls upon the largest mills. In regard to the employment of 198,565 operatives, belonging to the district of Mr. Baker, the latter gives, for the last half year, the following statement [e]:

----

[a] "Report of Sir John Kincaid, Inspector of Factories, for the Half Year ending the 30th April 1860", *Reports of the Inspectors of Factories...*, pp. 11-12.— *Ed.*

[b] See this volume, pp. 410-16.— *Ed.*

[c] "Report of Robert Baker, Esq., Inspector of Factories, for the Half Year ending the 30th April 1860", *Reports of the Inspectors of Factories...*, pp. 49-85.— *Ed.*

[d] op. cit., pp. 52, 53.— *Ed.*

[e] loc. cit., p. 53.— *Ed.*

Persons employed.		Accidents from machinery.
In Cotton Mills, among.............	107,106	1 to every 261
In Woolen Mills	14,982	1 to every 348
In Flax Mills	33,918	1 to every 389
In Silk Mills	33,874	1 to every 2,251
In Worsted Mills	2,896	1 to every 424
In other Fabrics	5,789	nil

In all these textile fabrics, the machinery is protected—that is to say, provided with such contrivances for the security of the operatives that use it as are prescribed by the protective clauses of the Factory Act. If we now turn, for example, to Nottingham, where a large number of persons, and especially of children, are employed among machinery which is *not* protected by the law, we shall find that there were entered on the books of the General Hospital, in 1859, 1,500; and on those of the Dispensary, 794 accidents; making a total of 2,294 among a population estimated to not exceed 62,583. This gives the number of accidents within the borough of Nottingham as 1 to every 27, a proportion compared with which the accidents in the protected textile fabrics appear almost insignificant. Again, in Birmingham, which is full of employments of every kind, both with and without connection with power, where there are only two small textile factories, and where, generally, there is no compulsory protection to the machinery among which the young workers are engaged, the proportion of accidents to population was as 1 to 34. The great advantages derived from the protective clauses of the Factory Act, and from the more general enforcement of these clauses, is also shown by a comparison of all the accidents reported to all the Inspectors for the half years ending the 31st of October, 1845, and the 30th of April, 1846, with the half years ending with October and April, 1858 and 1859. In the latter period, the gross diminution of accidents was equal to 29 per cent, although there had taken place an increase of workers of 20 per cent, at the lowest estimate.

Now, as to the distribution of accidents between larger and smaller mills, I think the following facts, stated by Mr. Baker, to be decisive: During the last half year, out of the 758 cotton factories of his district, employing 107,000 persons, all the accidents which occurred happened in 167 factories, employing about 40,000 persons; so that in 591 factories, employing 67,000 persons, there were no accidents at all.[a] In like manner, out of 387

---

[a] op. cit., pp. 54-55.— *Ed.*

smaller mills all the accidents happened in 28 mills; out of 153
flax mills all the accidents happened in 45 mills, and out of 774
silk factories all the accidents happened in 14 mills, so that in a
large proportion of each branch of trade there were no accidents
whatever by machinery, and in every branch the bulk of the
accidents happened in the largest mills. The latter phenomenon
Mr. Baker tries to account for by the two causes, that in the largest
mills the transition state from old, unprotected, to new machinery
is, comparatively, most protracted and gradual; and, secondly, that
in these larger concerns the rapidity with which the hands are
collected together grows in the same ratio as the moral control
exercised over such establishments diminishes.

"These two causes," says Mr. Baker, "operate most distinctly in the production
of accidents. In the former, the remains of the old machinery which has never
been protected, and wherein gathering parts of wheels still remain, are even more
destructive from that very circumstance, since, in the safety of the new, the danger
of the remaining old is forgotten, while, in the latter, the perpetual scramble for
every minute of time, where work is going on by an unvarying power, which is
indicated at, perhaps, a thousand horses, necessarily leads to danger. In such mills,
moments are the elements of profit—the attention of everybody's every instant is
demanded. It is here, where, to borrow one of Liebig's sentiments, there may be
seen a perpetual struggle between life and inorganic forces; where the mental
energies must direct, and the animal energies must move and be kept equivalent to
the revolutions of the spindles. They must not lag, notwithstanding the strain upon
them either by excessive excitement or heat; nor be suspended for an instant by
any counter-attention to the various movements around, for in every lagging there
is loss. Thus it is that fingers are laid upon wheels supposed to be secure, either
from their position, or from the slowness of their motion when the attention is
wrongly directed elsewhere. Thus, workmen, in hastening to produce a certain
amount of pounds weight of yarn within a given time, forget to look under their
machines for their little 'piecers.' Thus many accidents arrive from what is called
self-carelessness."[a]

During the last half year, all the textile manufactures, that of
silk excepted, were highly prosperous in Ireland as well as the
English districts of Mr. Baker. The only check which seemed to
keep the different branches of industry within bounds, was the
increasing scarcity of raw material. In the cotton trade, the
erection of new mills, the formation of new systems of extension,
and the demand for hands had, at no former time, been
exceeded. Nothing was more remarkable than the new movements
in search of raw material. Thus, in imitation of the Cotton Supply
Association of Lancashire, a Flax Supply Association had been
founded at Belfast. While "for the five years ending with 1853,
the average importation of flax, with the flax crop of Ireland

---

[a] op. cit., p. 56.— Ed.

added, had amounted to 113,409 tuns per annum, it was, for the last five years, ending with 1858, only 101,672 tuns, showing a diminution of 12,000 tuns per annum, with an increased annual value of exports of £1,000,000."[a] The price of wool, already above the average, during the period over which the last Factory Reports extend, has since then been continually rising. The rapid extension of the woolen manufactories, and the increased demand for mutton both in Great Britain and in the Colonies, may be considered as the permanent causes of this rise in the wool prices. As an accidental cause menacing to shorten the usual supply of wool, must be considered the peculiar character of the season; many sheep having died during the Winter from bad or improper food, and many lambs having perished during the Spring from cold, want of food, and by a disease that proved fatal in a few hours.[b]

The only trade that was seriously checked during the last six months, consequent upon the conclusion of the Anglo-French Commercial Treaty,[c] and the fears entertained concerning the effects of foreign competition, is the silk trade. The pressure thus exercised has been gradual, so that at the moment I write this letter more than 13,000 weavers are out of employment in Coventry alone, every loom being stopped. This crisis is the more to be regretted, since, as I remarked in a letter on the Factory Reports of 1859, there had been springing up at Coventry a number of cottage silk factories, in which the workmen employed their own families, with now and then a little hired labor. These factories had, since the commencement of 1860, been considerably increased in number. They are, in fact, a recurrence to the former domestic manufacturers, only with the addition of steam-power, but wholly different to the new cooperative system of Lancashire and Yorkshire. With them the householder is the master, the weaver the renter of power, sometimes the employer of other labor, as well as that of his own family. He has either bought his two looms out and out, or upon credit, and is paying for them so much a week; or he has hired them, probably from his landlord, who is a builder and speculator. He, besides, hires the power wanted. There is said to be as much difference now between the work thus done upon the weaver's loom and that done upon the

---

[a] op. cit., p. 57. Robert Baker cites the figures given by the President of the Chamber of Commerce in his speech of December 1859.— Ed.

[b] op. cit., p. 58.— Ed.

[c] See this volume, pp. 341-44.— Ed.

master's, as there is almost between the French ribbon and the English one. Still it is apprehended, and Mr. Robert Baker, in his report, seems to share this apprehension, that this domestic labor, combined with the employment of mechanical power, will be unable to stand commercial shocks. It is probable that the English manufacturer, to cope with his French rival, will be compelled to recur to the employment of capital on a large scale, which must break up the cottage silk factories competing at his own door.

Written on July 10 and 14, 1860   Reproduced from the newspaper

First published in the *New-York Daily Tribune*, Nos. 6016 and 6032, August 6 and 24, 1860

Karl Marx

INTERESTING FROM SICILY.—
GARIBALDI'S QUARREL WITH LA FARINA.—
A LETTER FROM GARIBALDI

London, July 23, 1860

According to a telegram received to-day from Palermo, Col. Medici's impending attack on Milazzo had decided the King of Naples[a] to give orders for the complete evacuation of Sicily by the Neapolitan army, and their withdrawal to his continental dominions. Although this telegram stands in need of confirmation, it seems beyond dispute that Garibaldi's cause is working on, despite the disease his troops suffer from, and the diplomatic intrigues his Government is pestered with.

Garibaldi's open breach with the Cavour party, viz.: the expulsion from Sicily of La Farina, the notorious marplot, and of Signors Griscelli and Totti,[b] Corsicans by birth, and Bonapartist police agents by profession, has given rise to very contradictory comments on the part of the European press. A private letter of Garibaldi's to a London friend,[312] which has been communicated to me with the permission to state its principal contents in the *Tribune*, will leave no doubt as to the real bearing of the case. Garibaldi's letter is of a date anterior to his decree of the 7th inst., by which the three aforesaid plotters were summarily removed from the island, but it fully explains the points at issue between the General and the Minister—between the popular Dictator and the dynastic Grand Vizier; in one word, between Garibaldi and Cavour. The latter, in secret understanding with Louis Bonaparte, whom Garibaldi stigmatizes as "*cet homme faux*" (that false man), and with whom he foresees "the necessity of measuring his sword some fine morning"—Cavour, then, had determined upon

---

[a] Francis II.— *Ed.*

[b] "Affaires des deux Siciles", *Le Constitutionnel*, No. 198, July 16, 1860.— *Ed.*

annexing, piece-meal, such slices of Italian territory as Garibaldi's sword might cut out, or as popular risings might sever from their old allegiance. This process of piece-meal annexation to Piedmont was to be accompanied by a simultaneous process of "compensation" for the second Empire. As Savoy and Nice had to be paid for Lombardy and the Duchies, so Sardinia and Genoa were to pay for Sicily; every new act of separate annexation calling for a new separate diplomatic transaction with the protector of Piedmont. A second dismemberment to the benefit of France, quite apart from the outrage on the integrity and independence of Italy which it involved, would at once have put an extinguisher on the patriotic movements at Naples and Rome. The conviction spreading that to coalesce under Piedmontese auspices, Italy must grow less and less, would have enabled Bonaparte[a] to maintain at Naples and Rome separate governments, independent in name, but for all practical purposes, French vassalages. Hence Garibaldi thought it his principal task to cut off all pretext for French diplomatic interference, but, as he understood, this could only be done by preserving to the movement its pure popular character, and divesting it of all appearance of connection with mere schemes of dynastic aggrandizement. Sicily, Naples, and Rome once liberated, the moment would have come for merging them into the kingdom of Victor Emmanuel, if the latter would take upon himself to keep them, and defend them, not only from Austria, the enemy in front, but also from France, the enemy in the rear. Relying, perhaps, somewhat too much on the good will of the English Government, and the necessities of Louis Bonaparte's situation, Garibaldi presumes that so long as he does not annex to Piedmont any territory, and exclusively relies for the liberation of Italy upon Italian arms, Louis Bonaparte will not dare to interfere in open violation of the pretexts upon which he commenced the Italian crusade. However that may be, this much is sure—that Garibaldi's plan, whether successful or not, is the only one that, under present circumstances, holds out any chance of rescuing Italy, not only from its old tyrants and divisions, but also from the clutches of the new French protectorate. And to baffle this plan was the special errand upon which Cavour had dispatched La Farina to Sicily, supported by the two Corsican brothers.

La Farina is a native of Sicily, where, in 1848, he distinguished himself among the Revolutionists by his hatred against the

---

[a] Napoleon III.— *Ed.*

Republican party and his intrigues with the Piedmontese doctrinaires rather than by real energy or memorable exploits. After the failure of the Sicilian revolution and during his stay at Turin, he published a voluminous history of Italy,[a] in which he did his best to exalt the Savoy dynasty, and to slander Mazzini. With soul and body bound to Cavour, he imbued the "National Association for Italian unity" [313] with a Bonapartist spirit; and having become its chairman, handled it as an instrument not for furthering but for impeding all attempts at independent national action. It was quite in keeping with these antecedents that, when the first rumor got afloat of Garibaldi's intended expedition to Sicily, La Farina ridiculed and reviled the very idea of such an expedition. When, nevertheless, immediate steps were taken in preparation of the bold adventure, La Farina put in movement all the resources of the "National Association" with a view to obstruct it. When his opposition had failed in discouraging the general and his men, and when at last the expedition sailed, La Farina, with cynical sneers, indulged in forebodings of the most sinister kind, making himself bold to predict the immediate and total failure of the enterprise. So soon, however, as Garibaldi had taken Palermo and proclaimed himself Dictator, La Farina rushed to join him, being provided with a commission from Victor Emmanuel, or rather from Cavour, which gave him power to assume the command of the island in the name of the King, directly after the annexation had been voted. Being, as he himself admits, despite his ill-omened antecedents, at first most courteously received by Garibaldi, he at once began to assume the airs of the master, to intrigue against the Ministry of Crispi, conspire with the French police agents, rally around himself the aristocratic liberals eager to close the revolution by a vote of separate annexation, and propose, instead of the necessary steps for the expulsion of the Neapolitans from Sicily, plans for the expulsion from the public administration of the Mazzinians, and other men not to be relied on by his master, Cavour.

Crispi, with the undermining of whose Ministry La Farina opened his intrigues, had for a long time been an exile in London, where he was counted among Mazzini's friends, and made the deliverance of Sicily the all-absorbing subject of his exertions. In the Spring of 1859 he went under a Wallachian name and character to Sicily at great personal risk, visited every great town

---

[a] Giuseppe La Farina, *Storia d'Italia dal 1815 al 1850*, Vols. I-VI, Torino, 1851-1852.— *Ed.*

there, and planned an insurrection for the month of October. The events of the Autumn delayed the insurrection, first till November, and then till the present year. In the mean time Crispi applied to Garibaldi, who, while refusing to excite an insurrection, gave the promise to aid it after it had once broken out and so far consolidated itself as to prove what were the real feelings of the Sicilians. During the expedition Crispi, with his wife, the only woman of the expedition, accompanied Garibaldi and fought in every action, his wife superintending the attendance on the sick and wounded. It was this man whom Signor La Farina wanted first to throw overboard, with the secret hope, of course, of flinging the Dictator after him. Garibaldi, out of consideration for Victor Emmanuel, and under the high pressure of the aristocratic liberals, consented, although under protest, to form a new Ministry and dismiss Crispi, whom he, however, retained as a personal counselor and friend. But Garibaldi had hardly made this sacrifice when he became aware that the dismissal of the Crispi Ministry had only been insisted upon in order to quarter upon him a Cabinet which, in all but name, was not his, but La Farina's or Cavour's Cabinet, and which, encouraged by the presence of La Farina, and relying upon Cavour's protection, would in a very short time counteract his whole plan of liberation, and turn all their influence throughout the country against the Nizzardist intruder, as Garibaldi was already nicknamed. It was then that he saved his own cause, not less than that of Sicily and Italy, by the expulsion of La Farina with the two Corsican brothers, the acceptance of the resignation of La Farina's ministerial nominees, and the appointment of a patriotic Ministry, among whom we may name Signor Mario.

Written on July 23, 1860   Reproduced from the newspaper

First published in the *New-York Daily Tribune*, No. 6018, August 8, 1860

Frederick Engels

BRITISH DEFENSES [314]

The plan for the National Defenses of England, just laid before Parliament,[a] proposes to confine all the outlay to the fortification of the dockyards, together with some minor works, barely sufficient to protect the larger harbors of the country from insult by small hostile squadrons, and with the erection of strong and extensive forts at Dover and Portland, for the purpose of securing sheltered anchorage to fleets and detached vessels. The whole of the money is to be spent on the circumference of the country, on the coast-line accessible to an enemy's fleet; and as it is impossible to defend the whole length of coast, a few important points, especially the naval arsenals and dockyards, are selected. The interior of the country is to be left entirely to its own resources.

Now, when England once confesses that her wooden walls no longer protect her, and that she must have recourse to fortification as a means of national defense, it stands to reason that she should first shelter from attack her naval arsenals—the cradles of her fleet. That Portsmouth, Plymouth, Pembroke, Sheerness, and Woolwich (or whatever place may be selected in its stead), should be made so strong as to be able to beat off any attack by sea, and to hold out for a reasonable time against a regular siege by land, nobody will doubt. But it is perfectly ridiculous to call the providing for this danger a system of national defense. In fact, in order to elevate the scheme to this dignity, it appears to have been necessary to make it far more complicated and expensive than was required for the mere protection of the dockyards.

A country like France or Spain, which is exposed to invasion on its land frontier as much as to naval attacks and descents on its

---

[a] See *Report of the Commissioners appointed to consider the Defences of the United Kingdom; together with the Minutes of Evidence and Appendix; also Correspondence relative to a Site for an internal Arsenal. Presented to both Houses of Parliament by Command of Her Majesty*, London, 1860; on the debates see *The Times*, No. 23680, July 24, 1860.—*Ed.*

coast, is obliged to make its naval depots fortresses of the first rank. Toulon, Carthagena, Genoa, even Cherbourg, may be subjected to the combined attack which destroyed the arsenals and dockyards of Sevastopol.[315] They ought, therefore, to have a very strong land-front with detached forts to keep the dockyards out of range of a bombardment. But this does not apply to England. Supposing even that a naval defeat had for a moment placed in doubt England's maritime supremacy; even then an invading army, landed on British soil, could never depend upon the liberty of its communications, and must, therefore, act rapidly and decisively. This invading army would not be in a state to undertake a regular siege; and if it was, nobody in his senses would expect the invader to go and settle down quietly before Portsmouth and to waste his resources in a lengthened siege, instead of marching straight upon London, and at once provoking a decision on the main issue while his moral and material ascendency is at its hight. If it comes to that, that troops and material can be safely landed in England sufficient to attack London, and at the same time to besiege Portsmouth, then England is at the brink of ruin, and no land-forts around Portsmouth can save her. As with Portsmouth, so with the other naval arsenals. Let the sea-fronts be made as strong as they can; but on the land-fronts, everything is superfluous which goes beyond keeping off the enemy far enough to protect the dockyard from bombardment, and securing it against a fortnight's regular siege. But if we are to judge from the estimates, and from some plans respecting the proposed defenses of Portsmouth, which have got into the London *Times*, there is to be a great waste of brick and mortar, of ditch and parapet, of money and, in case of war, of men too. The engineering staff appear positively to revel in this luxury of planning fortifications which, to them, has so long been a forbidden joy. England is menaced with a vegetation of forts and batteries springing up as rapidly as mushrooms, and as rank as the creepers of a tropical forest. The Government seem to insist upon it that there must be something to show for the money; but that will be the principal use of all these splendid structures.

So long as the dockyards are not safe against a *coup de main*,[a] so long invasions might be undertaken, with the sole aim of destroying one of them, and then retiring. Thus they serve, so to say, as safety-valves for London. But as soon as they are secured against an attack by main force, and even against a regular attack, for fourteen days—and this is evidently necessary—there is no

---

[a] Sudden attack.— *Ed.*

other object left for an invasion except London. All minor ends are secured; local invasions are no longer to any purpose; an invasion must go in for the chance of annihilating England or suffer annihilation in its turn. Thus, the very fact of the fortification of the dockyards weakens London. It compels the invading power to concentrate all its strength on the attempt at once upon London. London, we are told by Lord Palmerston, must be defended in the field. Suppose this to be so: the stronger the army, the safer London will be. But where is that strong army to come from, if Portsmouth, Plymouth, Chatham, and Sheerness, and, perhaps, Pembroke, are converted into first-rate fortresses of the size of Cherbourg, Genoa, Coblentz, or Cologne, requiring garrisons of from 15,000 to 20,000 men to defend them? Thus, the stronger you make the dockyards, the weaker you render London and the country. And this is what you call national defenses.

In any case, one lost battle would decide the fate of London; and, considering the immense commercial centralization of the country, and the dead lock to which the occupation of London would bring all the industrial and commercial machinery of England, there can be no doubt that one battle would decide the fate of the whole kingdom. And thus, while twelve millions are proposed to be spent on the security of the dockyards, the very heart of the country is to remain unprotected, and is left to hinge on the result of one battle!

There is no good in mincing the matter. Let the dockyards, by all means, be fortified in a rational manner, which could be done for less than half the money now proposed to be squandered upon them; but if you want national defenses, set at once about fortifying London. It is no use saying, as Palmerston does, that this is impossible. It is the same talk that was heard when Paris was to be fortified. The surface inclosed in the continuous rampart round Paris is not much less than that occupied by London; the line of forts encircling Paris has an extent of 27 miles, and a circle round London six miles from Charing Cross would give a periphery of 37 miles. This circle might very well represent the average distance of the forts from the center; and ten miles more will not render the line too long, if a proper system of radial and circular railway communication facilitates the rapid movements of the reserves. Of course, London cannot be defended in the off-hand way, proposed in the *Cornhill Magazine*, where six large forts are to do all; the number of forts must be twenty at least; but, on the other hand, London need not be fortified in the pedantic style of Paris, for it will never have to stand a siege. To defend it against a *coup de main*, against the resources which an invading army can bring against it within a fortnight after landing, is all that is required. The continuous inclosure may be dispensed with; the villages and groups of houses on the outskirts may be made to serve in its stead quite effectually, if the plan of defense be properly prepared beforehand.

With London thus fortified, and the dockyards strengthened on the sea fronts and protected on the land fronts against a forcible, irregular attack, and even a slight siege, England might defy any invasion, and the whole might be done for something like fifteen millions sterling. The dockyards would not absorb, in all, more than 70,000 regulars and 15,000 volunteers; while the whole rest of the line, the militia, and the volunteers—say 80,000 line and militia, and 100,000 volunteers—would defend the intrenched camp around London, or accept battle in front of it; and while the whole country north of London would remain at full liberty to organize fresh bodies of volunteers and depots for the line and militia. The enemy would in all cases be compelled to act; he could not, even if he would, then escape the attraction of the great intrenched camp of London, and he would have only the choice either to attack it and be beaten, or to wait, and thereby increase every day the difficulties of his position.

Instead of this, the Government plan of national defenses would bring matters to this pass, that if the forces of England consisted of 90,000 line and militia and 115,000 volunteers, the garrisons would, at least, absorb 25,000 regulars and 35,000 volunteers, leaving for the field in which to defend London, 65,000 regulars and 80,000 volunteers, while 35,000 men who might be very badly wanted on the day of battle, would be sitting quietly and unmenaced behind stone walls which nobody had thought of attacking. But not only would this army be weakened by 35,000 men, it would be deprived of a fortified position out of which it could not be driven except by a regular siege; it would have to expose its 80,000 badly officered and inexperienced volunteers to a fight in the open field, and it would thus fight in circumstances very much less favorable than the army placed as above described.

Written about July 24, 1860

First published in the *New-York Daily Tribune*, No. 6020, August 10, 1860 as a leading article; reprinted in the *New-York Semi-Weekly Tribune*, No. 1588, August 14, 1860

Reproduced from the *New-York Daily Tribune*

Karl Marx

[EVENTS IN SYRIA.— SESSION OF THE BRITISH PARLIAMENT.— THE STATE OF BRITISH COMMERCE]

London, July 28, 1860

The Blue Book on the Syrian disturbances[a] having only just been issued, and Lord Stratford de Redcliffe having announced for Tuesday next his interpellation respecting the Syrian affairs,[b][316] I delay entering on this momentous subject, and would only warn your readers to not be carried away by the sentimental declamations of the Decembrist press, the feelings of horror at the atrocious outrages of wild tribes, and the natural sympathy felt for the sufferers. But there are a few points which ought steadily to be fixed upon. In the first instance, the Russian Empire, consequent upon the internal collisions that have arisen out of the serf emancipation movement and the dilapidated state of finances, finds itself in a fix out of which the present Government knows not how to get itself safe by a war on a grand scale. War appears to them the only means of shifting off the impending revolution so confidentially predicted in Prince Dolgoroukow's *La vérité sur la Russie.* Consequently, it is about three months since Prince Gorchakoff tried to reopen the Oriental question by issuing his circular[c] on the grievances of the Christians in Turkey, but his appeal, reechoed only by a solitary voice from the Tuileries, fell flat on the ears of Europe.

---

[a] *Papers, 1858-1860, respecting past or apprehended Disturbances in Syria,* in four parts, London, 1860.— *Ed.*

[b] Lord Stratford de Redcliffe's interpellation of August 3, 1860, *The Times,* No. 23690, August 4, 1860.— *Ed.*

[c] Gorchakov's circular of May 20, 1860 to Russian Embassies in foreign countries, *Russky Invalid,* No. 111, May 26, 1860, pp. 447-48.— *Ed.*

Even from that time Russian and French agents were bestirring themselves to bring about a politico-religious row—the former on the Dalmatian, the latter on the Syrian coast—both movements supporting each other, since the troubles in Montenegro and the Herzegovina compelled the Porte to withdraw almost the whole Turkish army stationed in Syria, so as to leave the arena open to the high-pitched antagonism of the barbarous clans of the Lebanon. The Emperor of the French found himself placed in the same necessity as the orthodox Czar,[a] of looking out for some fresh and thrilling crusade, to plunge his Empire again into the Lethe of war-hallucinations. The Italian movement, slipping out of his leading-strings, and taking a course contrary to the direction he wanted to impart to it, had, as was delicately hinted in the *Constitutionnel*,[b] become a *bore* in the opinion of Paris. His attempts at wheedling the Prince Regent of Prussia[c] into a violent "consolidation of Germany," to be paid by a "moral compensation" for France in the shape of the Rhenish Provinces, turned out a signal failure, and even cast some ridicule on the *entrepreneur* of the emancipation-of-nationalities dodge. The conflict Louis Napoleon found himself involved in with the Pope[317] damaged the prop on which his sway over the peasantry rests—the Catholic clergy of France.

The Imperial exchequer was reduced for some time to, and continues in a state of, exhaustion, which it was vainly tried to cure by throwing out the hint of the expediency of an *emprunt de la paix* (a peace-loan). This was too much even for Decembrist France. To eke out one loan contracted on the pretext of war by a subsequent loan contracted on the pretext of peace, was a presumption abhorrent even to the Paris stock-jobbers. Some faint voice in the emasculated Paris press dared to insinuate that the blessings of the second Empire were as great as expensive, the nation having bought them by an increase to the amount of fifty per cent of the public debt. The project of a peace loan of 500,000,000f. was consequently dropped, a retreat that only encouraged Mr. Favre to descant in the *Corps Législatif* on the impending "financial crash," and to tear to pieces the flowery gauze which the Imperial Budgetmonger had thrown over the State chest. The strictures in the *Corps Législatif* among the "*chiens savants*" (the learned dogs) of the mock representation, hazarded

---

[a] Alexander II.— *Ed.*

[b] See Ernest Dréolle's article "Paris, 10 juillet", *Le Constitutionnel*, No. 193, July 11, 1860.— *Ed.*

[c] William.— *Ed.*

by Mr. Favre and Mr. Olivier,[a] on the characteristic features of the Decembrist régime, as well as the furious onslaught on the intrigues of the "old parties,"[318] with which the official, the semi-official, and officious press of Paris teems, coincided in bearing witness to the stern fact, that the rebellious spirit of Gaul is rekindling from its cinders, and that the continuance of the usurper's rule again depends on the enactment of a grand war-spectacle, as it did two years after the *coup d'état*, and again two years after the conclusion of the Crimean episode. It is evident that the Autocrat of France and the Autocrat of Russia,[b] laboring both under the same urgent necessity of sounding the war-trumpet, act in common concert. While Bonapartist semi-official pamphlets[c] offered to the Prince Regent of Prussia[d] "German Union," backed by a "moral compensation" for France, the Emperor Alexander, as has just been publicly stated, without a denial on the part of the Berlin governmental press, in the publications of the German "National Association,"[319] openly proposed to his uncle[d] the annexation to Prussia of the whole of Northern Germany up to the main, on the condition of a cession to France of the Rhenish Provinces, and of connivance at the progress of Russia on the Danube. It is this fact simultaneously thrown out by both the Autocrats that has brought about the rendezvous at Teplitz between the Emperor of Austria and the Prince Regent.[320] The conspirators of Petersburg and Paris had, however, in case their temptations of Prussia should fail, kept in reserve the thrilling incident of the Syrian massacres, to be followed by a French intervention which, as it would not do to enter through the main gate, would open the back door of a general European war. In respect to England I will only add, that, in 1841, Lord Palmerston furnished the Druses with the arms they kept ever since, and that, in 1846, by a convention with the Czar Nicholas, he abolished, in point of fact, the Turkish sway that curbed the wild tribes of the Lebanon, and stipulated for them a quasi-independence[321] which, in the run of time, and under the

---

[a] Émile Olivier's speech in the *Corps Législatif* on June 26, 1860, *Le Moniteur universel*, No. 180, June 28, 1860.— *Ed.*

[b] Napoleon III and Alexander II.— *Ed.*

[c] Marx is referring to the following pamphlets published by Dentu in Paris in 1859 and 1860: *La vraie question, France-Italie-Autriche; Napoléon III et la question roumaine; La foi des traités, les puissances signataires et l'empereur Napoléon III;* Edmond About, *La Prusse en 1860* (concerning the last-named pamphlet, see this volume, pp. 391-96 and 400-01.).— *Ed.*

[d] William.— *Ed.*

proper management of foreign plotters, could only beget a harvest of blood.

You are aware that the present Parliamentary session stands unrivalled by a startling succession of Government failures. Apart from Mr. Gladstone's abortion of protective duties, not one single important measure has been carried. But while the Government were withdrawing bill after bill, they had contrived to smuggle through the second reading a little resolution,[a] consisting of one single little clause, which, if carried, would have brought about the greatest constitutional change witnessed in England ever since 1689.[322] That resolution simply proposed the abolition of the local English army in India, its absorption into the British army, and consequently the transfer of its supreme command from the Governor-General at Calcutta to the London Horse Guards, alias the Duke of Cambridge. Quite apart from the other serious consequences such a change must be fraught with, it would put part of the army out of the control of Parliament, and, on the grandest scale, add to the Royal patronage. It seems that some members of the Indian Council, who unanimously objected to the Government project, but, by virtue of the Indian Act of 1858,[323] can occupy no seats in the House of Commons, whispered their protests into the ears of some M.P.s, and so it came that when the Government already considered their dodge to be safe, a sudden Parliamentary émeute,[b] led by Mr. Horsman,[c] broke through their intrigue in the very nick of time. It is a truly ludicrous spectacle, this perplexity of a Cabinet unexpectedly found out, and the bewilderment of a House of Commons fretting at the snares laid to its own profound ignorance.

The declared value of the exports for last month shows the progress of the downward movement of British commerce. I have singled out in a previous letter[d] [that], compared with the exports of June, 1859, there is a falling off of nearly a million and a half sterling for June, 1860.

The returns for the month of June in the last three years are as follows[e]:

----

a Moved in the House of Commons on June 12, 1860, *Hansard's Parliamentary Debates*, Vol. 159, 1860, p. 395.— *Ed.*

b Riot.— *Ed.*

c Edward Horsman's speech in the House of Commons on July 26, 1860, *The Times*, No. 23683, July 27, 1860.— *Ed.*

d See this volume, pp. 406-09.— *Ed.*

e For these and the following data see the article "The Board of Trade Returns", *The Economist*, No. 883, July 28, 1860.— *Ed.*

1858.	1859.	1860.
£10,241,433	£10,665,891	£9,236,454

For the half year ending with the 30th June, the declared value of the exports is less by a million than in the same six months of last year:

1858.	1859.	1860.
£53,467,804	£63,003,159	£62,019,989

The falling off of the last month is distributed over the cotton, cotton yarn, linen, hardware, and cutlery, iron and worsted trade. Even in the exports of manufactured woolen goods, the trade in which has hitherto shown a steadily increasing prosperity, this month excepted, "woolen and worsted yarn" shows a decline. The export of cotton goods for the *six months* to British India has declined from £6,094,430, in the first half of 1859, to £4,738,440 in the first half of 1860, or by [about] £1,360,000 worth of goods.[a]

With regard to the imports the most striking feature is the huge bulk of the cotton arrivals. In June, 1860, 2,102,048 cwts. have been received, as against 1,655,306 cwts. in the June of last year, and 1,339,108 cwts. in June, 1858.[b] The increase for the six months is no less than three millions of hundredweights; so that the half year receipts are greater by more than 60 per cent. The cotton imported in the month of May, 1860, is worth more by £1,800,000 than the import in 1859. No less than six millions and a half sterling have been spent in raw cotton in the first five months of 1860, beyond what was so spent in the same period of the previous year.

If the rapid decrease in the export of cotton goods and yarns be compared with the still more decided increase in the cotton imports, it will be understood that some cotton crisis is approaching, the more so since the new arrivals of the raw material fall upon unusually replete cotton stores.

Written on July 28, 1860   Reproduced from the newspaper

First published in the *New-York Daily Tribune*, No. 6021, August 11, 1860

---

[a] op. cit.— *Ed.*
[b] op. cit.— *Ed.*

Frederick Engels

COULD THE FRENCH SACK LONDON?

The report of the British National Defense Commission, which was recently published in London,[a] states that if the Emperor of the French were disposed to send a hostile army to England, it would be impossible for "all the available vessels of the Royal Navy" to prevent it from landing at some point of the 2,147 miles of coast line of England and Wales, not to speak of that of Ireland. It having been also conceded, at various times before and since the publication of the famous de Joinville pamphlet,[b] that a landing of 100,000 or more Frenchmen could be effected in the British Islands, under skillful management, the only important point to be considered is, what power of resistance Great Britain has at her command to meet such an invasion.

In compliance with an order of the House of Commons, the strength of the British land forces was reported in May last. It was as follows: Total regimental establishments, 144,148; effectives of all ranks on the 1st of May, 133,962; embodied militia, 19,333. When this statement was made public, an almost universal cry from all parts of the three Kingdoms was raised, as to the manner in which the $75,000,000 appropriated for the army estimates were spent, since an analysis of the 144,148 men, given as the available material of the line, "revealed the startling fact that scarcely 30,000 infantry could be mustered for offensive or defensive purposes, at a given place."

---

[a] *Report of the Commissioners appointed to consider the Defences of the United Kingdom*, London, 1860. See this volume, pp. 425-28.— *Ed.*

[b] François Ferdinand de Joinville's *De l'État des forces navales de la France*, Francfort s/M., 1844.— *Ed.*

Mr. Sidney Herbert and his associates of the Horse Guards, immediately held a consultation, and the London *Times* endeavored to quiet the anxiety of the people. It said[a]:

"We took occasion to examine the figures by which these allegations were supported, and explained in some detail the actual position of affairs."

It tried to

"show that if by the term 'troops' it was intended to describe only infantry of the line, the state of the case had been pretty accurately given, but that in reality the force at home comprised strong divisions of other arms of the service, so that its aggregate strength was by no means so small as might have been imagined."

The result of this nervousness on the part of the public, and of the consultation at the Horse Guards, was a completely new table of statistics,[b] putting down the military forces of Great Britain, at home, at 323,259; or 179,111 men more than the statement submitted two months previously. The discrepancy is not difficult of explanation. The first was issued with the intention to show the number of men that could, under favorable circumstances, and on receiving reasonable notice, be made available for immediate duty; the last to supply the sum total of every man and boy entered on the military pay-roll, and consequently receiving a share of the $75,000,000, beside including 227,179 volunteers and militia, of whom fully 200,000 have no existence as soldiers. Then there are 33,302 men accounted for, as belonging to "depots." Lest we may be charged with prejudice in describing what these "depots" are, we will cite the London *Times* as authority[c]:

"The troops in the depots really belong, not to the home, but the foreign establishments. They are portions of the battalions serving abroad, and there is nothing strange in their being comparatively ineffective for duty at home."

In short they are merely an ineffective body, composed of recruits not over three months in the service, who are shipped off quarterly, or oftener, when enlisted, to the regiments abroad, and old invalids who have been left at home as useless,

"so that, what with those who are exhausted and those who are untaught, the corps itself is never in the condition of a regular battalion."

So much for the depots. Now as to the volunteers and militia. It is only necessary to repeat that at least 200,000 exist at present, only on paper. Mr. Maguire recently proved in Parliament that nearly every regiment of militia had from 200 to 300 men more

[a] "London, Saturday, June 23, 1860", *The Times*, No. 23654, June 23, 1860.— *Ed.*
[b] ibid.— *Ed.*
[c] "London, Monday, June 4, 1860", *The Times*, No. 23637, June 4, 1860.— *Ed.*

on the books of the Horse Guards than could ever be got together on parade. Mr. Sidney Herbert made a similar admission.[a] Of the Irish militia regiments, whose members are compelled, from hardship and poverty, to report themselves more punctually than their English neighbors, many now estimated at 800—the Waterford for instance—have only 400. The estimate giving the strength of militia and volunteers of England at 138,560 is probably as near the mark as it is possible for an impartial statistician to make it.

The force of the regular army at home, according to the recent report from the War-Office, is 68,778. The Household cavalry (1,317), Royal Engineers (2,089), the Army Hospital corps of discarded invalids, the military train, and other partially unavailable troops, are here included. To avoid trespassing on disputed grounds, we will admit that the entire 68,000 are available. This, supposing all militia and volunteers embodied, and under arms, would give a grand total of 206,560 men. We will even add the Irish police to the list, which will increase it to about 237,000. The nominal strength of the regular army and embodied militia, just now, is given at 100,000; about 16,000 in excess of the real figures; but we will take it as it stands. Conceding that 15,000 of the volunteers could be assembled at a given point, within three days of the landing of the French, England would still have at her disposal an army of 115,000. Of these, it must be borne in mind that fully 25,000 are novices in the use of arms. Now, all the navy yards, arsenals and Government strongholds, would require extra garrisons, for there are never more than 8,000 marines ashore at the naval ports. Ireland, without attaching any importance to the influence of the "national petition," in creating a friendly disposition to the soldiers of McMahon, will need an army. All volunteers or militia would not suffice to keep order in the Emerald Isle, with the prospect of a fight in view. Her Majesty's authorities should at least detail 10,000 regulars, and 25,000 irregulars for that country, beside the police. This would make about 55,000 in all, and would leave only 80,000 soldiers to England and Wales, to guard arsenals, armories, and navy yards. It is idle to suppose that less than 20,000 serviceable troops would be sufficient for this important duty, allowing even the worn-out or inexperienced men in the depots to be able to hold their own. So Napoleon's 100,000 Frenchmen, Zouaves, &c., would be opposed by 60,000 red coats, of whom little more than 45,000

---

[a] Sidney Herbert's speech in the House of Commons on June 26, 1860, *The Times*, No. 23657, June 27, 1860.—*Ed.*

would belong to the line. The probable result of a rencounter between the two forces, thus brought face to face, hardly admits of a doubt.

It will be objected that France could not equip and dispatch across the Channel 100,000 men, without its becoming known. It may be; but England would not know where the blow would fall, and would naturally tremble for the safety of her possessions bordering the Mediterranean, and try to reenforce her garrisons there lest the threatened attack on London might be intended to cover ulterior designs on Malta and Gibraltar. She would send over to those places, in a few vessels of the Channel fleet, 20,000 or 30,000 soldiers, who would not be "volunteers," thus throwing on the latter the weight of resisting the enemy at home. Some distinguished writers assert that even the sacking of London would eventually be less injurious to England, than her banishment from Malta and Gibraltar.

But it will be argued that the mere announcement of national danger would be sufficient to arouse every Briton in the land, from the Cheviot Hills to Cornwall, to hurl the intruder into the sea. This is plausible. But experience teaches us that no matter how intense the patriotism of the masses may be, the fact that they, as a general thing, have no arms, and do not know how to use them if they had, renders their disposition in an emergency of very little value. Cane-swords and pitchforks may be weapons exceedingly dangerous to human life in the Seven Dials,[a] or in the Provinces, but it is not reasonable to assume that they would be irrepressible in repelling the Zouaves. It may also be seriously doubted whether the middle classes, who almost exclusively represent the volunteer force, would be so ready to answer muster, with the French on their native island, as they are when summoned to receive the congratulations of her Majesty. At all events, it is not more absurd to admit the possibility of the invading army numbering 150,000 than to suppose the volunteers can turn out 120,000; since a cordial invitation from Buckingham Palace cannot succeed in bringing, at the end of a twelve months' recruiting, more than 18,300.

Some doubts having been expressed as to the force actually reviewed at Hyde Park, we quote a paragraph from *The Manchester Guardian*, of the second day's parade. The "private correspondent" alluded to is Mr. Tom Taylor, an intimate and confidential friend of Col. McMurdo:

---

[a] A working-class district in the centre of London.— *Ed.*

"Our private correspondent, as our readers may recollect, has stated the number at 18,300, on the official authority of Col. McMurdo, which is a little lower than the amount given by Sir. John Burgoyne's calculation. But the martial bearing of the Volunteers evidently struck Sir John more than their mere number."

In estimating the forces that could probably be concentrated to oppose invaders, we have purposely made the most liberal calculation in favor of Great Britain. Our statement of the regular army admits as efficient every man, sick and well, whose name is on the military books. The militia and volunteers have been considered as 115,000 strong, which those well informed on the matter may deem excessive. The acknowledged ability of French field officers, the excellence of French military discipline, the general superiority of French tactics; and, on the other hand, the well-established stupidity of many of the highest officers in the English army; the slovenly management of the regulars and volunteers (after five weeks' notice had been given one regiment of militia actually mustered, in May last, with 135 barefoot members); even the conceded inferiority of the *ensemble* of a British to a French fighting army—all these have not been considered, although they are most important elements in a discussion of the subject.

In view of these facts, it appears certain that if Napoleon landed to-morrow, at a judiciously selected port in England, with 150,000 or even 100,000 men, he could "sack London" and escape the "annihilation" which a London journal recently stated would be his inevitable fate "if he put a hostile foot on Saxon soil."

Written between July 26 and 28, 1860   Reproduced from the newspaper

First published in the *New-York Daily Tribune*, No. 6021, August 11, 1860 as a leading article

Karl Marx

THE RUSSO-FRENCH ALLIANCE

London, August 3, 1860

The observations made in my last letter[a] upon the secret connection between the Syrian massacres and the Russo-French alliance, have received unexpected confirmation from the other side of the Channel, in the shape of a pamphlet published at M. Dentu's on Tuesday last, entitled *La Syrie et l'Alliance Russe*, and ascribed to the penmanship of M. Edmond About. M. Dentu, as you are aware, is the French Government publisher, who has issued all the semi-official pamphlets which from time to time initiated Europe into the "studies"[b] just indulged at the Tuileries. The above-mentioned pamphlet derives a peculiar interest from the circumstance that its publication followed closely on the love-letter addressed by the Man of December to Persigny,[324] which was destined to mesmerize John Bull, and of which Lord John Russell, at the very moment he refused to lay it before the House, forwarded a copy to the London *Times*.[c] The subjoined extracts contain the substance of *La Syrie et l'Alliance Russe*:

"As at the time of the Crusades, Christian Europe is moved by the horrible crimes of which Syria has just been the scene. Seven hundred thousand Christians are delivered up to the merciless fanaticism of two millions of Mussulmans, and the Turkish Government, by its inexplicable inaction, appears to avow itself their accomplice. Assuredly, France would have forgotten all her traditions had she not immediately claimed the honor of protecting the lives and properties of those who,

---

[a] See this volume, pp. 429-32.— *Ed.*

[b] Marx is evidently alluding to Carl Vogt's work *Studien zur gegenwärtigen Lage Europas*, Geneva and Berne, 1859.— *Ed.*

[c] Issue No. 23687, August 1, 1860.— *Ed.*

in former days, were the soldiers of Peter the Hermit and Philip Augustus.... It is, therefore, high time to think of a remedy for a situation which could not last any longer without leading to a great calamity—the total extermination of the Christian subjects of the Porte. The expedition which the Turkish Government talks so much about is totally insufficient to restore order. The Powers which have co-religionists in Syria, and which are justly alarmed for their safety, must be prepared bodily to interfere. If they tarried, it would no longer be time to protect victims; their only duty would be to avenge martyrs.

"Two nations are especially interested in defending the Cross on those distant shores—France and Russia. What would be the probable consequence of the union of their arms, and the result on the ulterior organization of Europe? This is what we are about to investigate.

"At certain periods of history we find that under the impulse of certain laws of attraction and agglomeration peoples form political combinations unknown to the past. We are 'assisting' at one of these critical moments in the life of mankind. The Syrian question is but one of the knots of a very complicated situation. The whole of Europe is in a state of expectation and anxiety, waiting for a vast solution which may settle the basis of a lasting peace both in Europe and in the East. Now that object can only be attained in so far as the organization of our continent shall be in conformity with the wishes and requirements of the present questions of nationalities struggling beneath the yoke. Hostile religious tendencies, incompatibility of tempers, languages radically opposed to each other, keep up in certain European States an undercurrent of agitation, which prevents the restoration of confidence, and hinders the progress of civilization. Peace, that ultimate term of the ambition of all Governments, can only be permanently secured when the permanent causes of disturbance we have just indicated shall have disappeared. We therefore wish to arrive at a double result.

"1. Wherever such a thing is possible, to favor the formation of a homogeneous and national State, the mission of which would be to absorb and concentrate, in a mighty unity, populations having ideas or tendencies in common.

"2. To try and carry out that principle without having recourse to arms.

"At first sight, France and Russia appear to have realized the ideal of monarchies. Though 400 leagues divide them, these two Powers have arrived by the most different roads at that unity which alone is able to create durable empires, not ephemeral circumscription, the limits of which may be changed any day by the fortune of war.... The Czars, meditating for the last 135 years over the will of Peter the Great,[325] have not ceased to cast covetous glances on European Turkey....Must France continue to protest against the pretensions of the Czars to the decaying Empire of the Sultan? We think not. *If Russia lent us her cooperation for the reannexation of the Rhine frontier, it appears to us that a kingdom would not be too high a price for her alliance. Thanks to such a combination, France might resume her real limits, as traced by the geographer Strabo, 18 centuries ago.* [Then follows a quotation from Strabo, enumerating the advantages of Gaul as the seat of a powerful empire.] It can easily be understood that France should desire to reconstruct that divine work [I presume the frontiers of Gaul], thwarted for so many centuries by the fraud of man, and this is so much in the nature of things, that at a period when we were not thinking of territorial aggrandizement, Germany was nevertheless subject to periodical fits of uneasiness, and flung at us, as a pledge of defiance, Becker's patriotic song[326].... We know that we are not alone in having plans of aggrandizement. Now, if Russia regards Constantinople in the same way as we look at the Rhine, can one not turn these analogous pretensions to some account, and force upon Europe the acceptance of a combination which would allot Turkey to

Russia, to France that Rhine frontier, which Napoleon I considered in 1814 as a *sine qua non* condition of his existence as a sovereign?

"There are only two millions of Turks in Europe, whereas there are thirteen millions of Greeks, whose spiritual head is the Czar.... The Greek insurrection,[a] which lasted nine years, was but the prelude of the movement which the massacres in Syria may act upon as a signal to break out. The Greek Christians are only waiting for an order from their Chief at St. Petersburg,[b] or their Patriarch at Constantinople, to rise against the infidels; and there are but few far-sighted politicians who do not anticipate a solution of the Eastern question in a sense favorable to Russia, and that at no distant time. It is not, therefore, surprising, that at the call of their co-religionists, and encouraged by the predictions of Stalezanew, the Russians should be prepared to cross the Pruth at the first moment.

"If we cast an eye on our frontiers, the considerations which justify our tendencies appear to be quite as important as those which actuate Russia. Let us set aside all historical recollections, and all geographical motives, take one by one the provinces inclosed by the Rhine, and examine the reasons that militate in favor of their annexation.

"First we meet with Belgium. In good faith it is difficult to question the striking analogy which has induced some historians to call the Belgians the French of the North. In fact, throughout that country the educated classes use no language but French, and the Flemish dialect is only understood by the lower classes of the population in some few localities. Moreover, Belgium is throughout attached to Catholicism, and it is to France, her sister, by origin, idiom and religion, that she is indebted for her independence. We will not recall the fact that Belgium, conquered by our armies in 1795, formed nine French departments until 1814. Nevertheless, it would appear that our yoke was not so very heavy, as in 1831, Belgium, having been unable to obtain from the Great Powers the permission of being annexed to France, offered, by a vote of the two Chambers, the Belgian Crown to the Duke de Nemours, the son of the King of the French. The refusal of the latter induced them subsequently to offer it to the Duke of Saxe Coburg, now Leopold I; but the precedent we refer to appears to us highly important, and it leads to the presumption that if Belgium were consulted she would not be less generous than Savoy, and would prove once more the attraction of the prestige which the greatness of France causes her to feel. The opposition of a few members of the upper classes would be very soon stifled by popular acclamations.

"Before falling into the sea, the Rhine divides itself into three branches, two of which run in rather northerly directions—the Yssel, which flows into the Zuyderzee, and the Waal, a confluent of the Meuse. If France had once more to trace her limits, might she not take the line of the Rhine, properly so called, instead of that of the Waal or the Yssel, so as to slice off as little as possible of Southern Holland? That is what she would assuredly do. Moreover, it is not on the side of Holland that it is indispensable to rectify our frontier by taking the line of the Rhine as a basis. Belgium, with her present frontiers, would be enough to satisfy the want of extension which of late has been so loudly claimed by public opinion. The line of the Scheldt was, moreover, the frontier conceded to France by the treaty of Lunéville in 1801."

Next follows a short passage demonstrating, by similar arguments, the necessity of annexing the Grand Duchy of Luxemburg,

---

[a] The reference is to the 1821-29 national uprising in Greece.— *Ed.*
[b] A probable reference to the Russian Tsar.— *Ed.*

"which formed under the Empire the *Département des Forêts.*"[a] The pamphleteer then proceeds to show the necessity for the annexation of Rhenish Prussia:

"Belgium and Luxemburg once in our power, our task is not over.... To complete our frontiers we must not take less than two-thirds of Rhenish Prussia, the whole of Rhenish Bavaria, and about one-third of the Grand Duchy of Hesse. All these territories formed, under the Empire, the departments of Roer of the Rhine, and Moselle of the Sarre, of Mont Tonnerre,[b] and the Grand Duchy of Berg. In 1815, they were distributed among several possessors, to render their recovery by us more difficult. A remarkable fact is, that these provinces, annexed to the French Monarchy, were but a few years in direct intercourse with us, and, nevertheless, our temporary stay among them has left the most enduring marks. What sympathy is lavished on the French traveler in those parts, we willingly appeal to those who have traveled there. For the last 45 years not a single French soldier has garrisoned those towns on the banks of the Rhine, and yet it is marvelous to see the touching reception our uniform meets with there. Catholics like us—like us they are Frenchmen. *Was it not at Aix-la Chapelle[c] that our Emperor, Charlemagne, held his Court?...* Contiguous to France, the Rhenish Provinces must become the political, as they are the natural dependencies of France."

The writer then returns to Russia, and after showing that the Crimean war forms no barrier to the alliance between France and Russia, *as they had not then come to an understanding*, gives the following piece of information concerning one of the claims of France to the gratitude of Russia:

"It must be kept in mind that France did not lend herself to the plans of England in the Baltic. We do not know whether an attack on Cronstadt would have succeeded in any case; it was not attempted, thanks, we have reason to believe, to the opposition of France."

After an excursion to the Italian campaign, the writer does not doubt that in the end Prussia will join the Franco-Russian alliance:

"But to attach the Cabinet of Berlin to our policy, it must be withdrawn from the influence of England. How can this be brought about? By so contriving that Prussia shall cease to be our neighbor on the Rhine, and by promising to support her legitimate pretensions to preponderance in Germany. The exchange of these Rhenish Provinces causes Bavaria and Prussia to take their compensations from Austria. The English alliance can only secure to Prussia the *status quo*—the French alliance throws open to her a boundless horizon.

"The alliance between France, Russia, and Prussia loyally concluded, as we have reason to hope it will be, the consequences that flow from it are most natural.... We have demonstrated above what 1,800 years ago Strabo had laid down as beyond question—that the Rhine was the natural frontier of Northern France. Now, Prussia is the greatest sufferer from this extension of territory. For the last 45 years she has kept the Rhine as the dragon used to keep watch over the garden of the

---

[a] Forestry Department.— *Ed.*
[b] Ruhr-Rhine, Moselle-Saar, Donnersberg.— *Ed.*
[c] Aachen.— *Ed.*

Hesperides. Let this cause of hostility between France and Prussia disappear; let the left hand of the Rhine become French once more; in exchange for her good offices, Prussia would find a compensation in Austria—that Power would be punished for her bad faith and clumsiness. Let all be organized for a durable peace.

"Let the populations be consulted, so that no violent annexation should take place. With Russia at Constantinople, France on the Rhine, Austria diminished, and Prussia preponderating in Germany, where can any cause for disturbance or revolution be found in Europe? Would England dare to contend single-handed against Russia, Prussia, and France? We cannot admit such a thing. If, however, it did happen, if Great Britain should venture to commit such an imprudence, she might receive a severe lesson. Gibraltar, Malta, the Ionian Islands are a security for her keeping quiet; those are the weak points of her armor. But though she will be reduced to a sterile agitation in her island, and be compelled to be a passive spectator of what takes place on the continent, she will barely be permitted to offer her opinion, thanks to the five or six thousand men she will send to Syria.

"The moment has arrived when our policy must be clearly defined. It is in Syria that France must pacifically conquer the frontier of the Rhine, by cementing the alliance of Russia. But we must take care not to give Russia an unlimited extension. The provinces north of the Bosphorus must suffice for her ambition. Asia Minor must remain neutral ground. Were it, indeed, possible to look at a practical subject in a poetical and practical light, we would say our choice is made; a man has just come forward who seems the incarnation of the idea we should wish to see represented in Syria—Abd-el-Kader. He is sufficiently orthodox as a Moslem to conciliate the Mussulman population; he is sufficiently civilized to distribute justice equally to all; he is attached to France by ties of gratitude; he would protect the Christians, and reduce to obedience the turbulent tribes ever ready to disturb the repose of Asia Minor. To make of Abd-el-Kader the Syrian Emir would be a noble reward for our prisoner's services."

The critical remarks on Edmond About's pamphlet were written on August 3, 1860

Reproduced from the newspaper

First published in the *New-York Daily Tribune*, No. 6025, August 16, 1860

Karl Marx

THE PAPER TAX.—THE EMPEROR'S LETTER

London, Aug. 7, 1860

The great faction fight of the session, which came off yesterday night, in a full House of Commons, proved a failure in the scenical sense, although it was a triumph in the ministerial sense. Mr. Gladstone's resolutions[a] for reducing the customs duties on paper to the level of the excise duties—some slight charge being added to the customs duties to counterbalance the incidental inconveniences of the excise duty—were carried by a majority of 33. But the House of Commons had it all their own way. There was the arena, and there were the gladiators, with their retainers behind them, but there was no audience worth mentioning. Before the battle had commenced, its issue was known and its bulletin promulgated. Hence the indifference of the public. The coalized parties, forming the so-called "Great Liberal Party,"[327] notoriously sway a Parliamentary majority, so that a defeat of the Cabinet could only have proceeded from a split in the ranks of the majority. This point, however, had been settled in Lord Palmerston's official residence, whither he had summoned the liberal members of all shadows and shades. The resolution itself proceeded from the Manchester fraction of the Ministry, Lord Palmerston having only been able to retain the support of Messrs. Gladstone and Milner Gibson by pledging himself to raise Mr. Gladstone's resolution to the rank of a Cabinet question. He had betrayed them by his management of the Paper Duty Abolition bill. This time they had bound him over to a certain line of conduct. The regular Whigs were the only fraction of the majority

---

[a] Moved on August 6, 1860. See *The Times*, No. 23692, August 7, 1860.— *Ed.*

suspected of hatching treasonable designs; but the harsh voice of their master and the menace suspended over their heads of a new dissolution of Parliament sufficed to bring them back to the stern behests of discipline. Thus many hours before the curtain was drawn, all London had become acquainted with the exact result of the party trial, and, save the habitués of the Strangers' Gallery, nobody cared to assist the sham-fight at St. Stephen's.[328] It was indeed a rather dull affair, enlivened only by the sweeping oratory of Mr. Gladstone, and the highly finished pleading of Sir Hugh Cairns.[a] Mr. Gladstone tried to represent the opposition raised against his bill as a last desperate stand made by Protection against Free Trade. When he sat down, the cheers that drowned his concluding words, seemed to hail him as the true chief of the liberal party, of which Lord Palmerston is the by no means beloved despot. Sir Hugh Cairns, on the part of the Conservatives, proved by close argumentation, and with great analytical power, that the reduction of the customs duty on paper to the level of the excise duty was in no way stipulated for by the commercial treaty with France. His antagonist, Sir Richard Bethell, the Whig Attorney-General, had the bad taste to show ill temper at the success of his rival, to sneer at Sir Hugh's "forensic eloquence,"[b] and thus to draw upon his own devoted head a regular volley of Tory interruptions.

The great faction fight of the session being over, whole flocks of honorable members are sure to desert the House, so that Lord Palmerston, by the sheer process of exhaustion, may now succeed in passing any little bill he has set his heart upon—i.e. the monstrous Indian bill for the amalgamation of the local European army with the British army.[329] If any new striking proof were wanted of the depth of degradation Parliamentarism has reached in England, this Indian bill and the treatment it received in the House of Commons would afford it. Every man in the House, of any authority on, and any experience in, Indian affairs, had opposed the bill. The majority themselves confessed not only their complete ignorance, but they betrayed their dark suspicions as to the ulterior views of the framers of the bill. They could not but confess that the bill had been smuggled into the House under false pretenses; that the most important papers indispensable for a

---

[a] Hugh Cairns' speech in the House of Commons on August 6, 1860, *The Times*, No. 23692, August 7, 1860.— *Ed.*

[b] Richard Bethell's speech in the House of Commons on August 6, 1860, *The Times*, No. 23692, August 7, 1860.— *Ed.*

just appreciation of the case had been fraudulently withheld; that the Indian Minister[a] had introduced the bill despite the unanimous dissent of the Indian Council, a dissent which, by an open infraction of the new constitution bestowed upon India in 1858,[330] he had omitted to lay on the table of the House; and lastly, that the Cabinet had not even attempted at showing any reason for driving, toward the end of the session, and after the withdrawal of every measure of import, with such indecent haste, a bill through the House which, in point of fact, radically changed the British Constitution by an immense addition of patronage to the crown, and by the creation of an army that, in every practical respect, would become independent of the vote of supplies. Still, this bill may now be carried, the chiefs of both factions having, as it appears, come to a secret understanding with the Court.

Louis Napoleon's letter to his beloved Persigny continues to form the chief topic of conversation here and on the other side of the Channel. It seems that, in the first instance, the protest of the Porte against the Syrian expedition, as originally planned between France and Russia,[331] met with a strong support on the part of Austria and Prussia, while Lord Palmerston, having just singled out, during the fortification debates, Louis Napoleon as the great object of British suspicion, could not but throw his weight into the balance of Turkey and the German Powers. It appears, moreover, that the Man of December got somewhat frightened, not only at the dictatorial tone assumed by Russia, but still more at the sneers circulated in the saloons of the "*anciens partis*"[b] and the low murmurs audible in the Faubourgs in regard to the "*alliance Cosaque.*"[c]

To make the latter palatable to Paris, a far greater complication of things must have been arrived at. Under these distressing circumstances, and in an evidently uneasy state of mind, Louis Napoleon penned his letter, several passages of which are highly perfumed with the scent of the ludicrous.

An Englishman may indulge in a downright laugh at the phrase addressed by Louis Napoleon to Lord Palmerston: "Let us understand one another in good faith like *honest men as we are, and not like thieves* who desire to cheat each other"; but the exquisitely bad taste blended with the power of ridicule of the original French "*entendons nous loyalement comme d'honnêtes gens, que nous sommes, et*

---

[a] Sir Charles Wood.— *Ed.*
[b] Old parties.— *Ed.*
[c] Cossack alliance.— *Ed.*

non comme Des Larrons qui veulent se duper mutuellement," [a] can only be appreciated by a French ear. No Frenchman can read that passage without being reminded of a similar sentence occurring in the famous play of "*Robert Macaire.*" [332]

I subjoin some data for a comparison between French and English state expenditure. [b] According to the provisional or prospective budget, the total revenue of France for the year 1860 is estimated at 1,825 millions of francs, or £73,000,000 sterling, derived from the following sources:

I. Direct Taxes, land, house, personal patentes	£18,800,000 [c]
II. Enregistrement (stamps and domaines)	14,300,000
III. Woods, forests, and fisheries	1,500,000
IV. Customs and tax on salt	9,100,000
V. Contributions indirectes (excise, etc.)	19,500,000
VI. Post-Office	2,300,000
VII. Miscellaneous..	7,500,000

The English revenue for 1859 (the financial accounts for 1860 have not yet been issued) was as follows, in both cases round numbers only being given:

I. Taxes (including income tax)	£10,000,000
II. Stamps	8,250,000
III. Crown Lands	420,000
IV. Customs	24,380,000
V. Excise	18,500,000
VI. Post-Office	3,200,000
VII. Miscellaneous..	2,100,000

The comparative public expenditure of the two countries was as follows:

	France.	England.
Interest on the debt	£22,400,000	£28,500,000
Army and Navy...	18,600,000	22,500,000
Civil List of the Crown	1,000,000	400,000
Cost of collecting the Revenue	8,000,000	4,500,000
Other expenses	23,000,000	9,000,000
Total	£73,000,000	£65,000,000

---

[a] Napoleon III's letter to Jean Persigny of July 25, 1859, "Paris, 1 [er] août", *Le Constitutionnel*, No. 215, August 2, 1860.— *Ed.*

[b] The tables are taken from the article "Taxation in France", *The Economist*, No. 884, August 4, 1860, p. 840.— *Ed.*

[c] The *New-York Daily Tribune* gives 18,000,000—a misprint.— *Ed.*

From the last tabular statement it will be seen that the interest on the public debt is in Bonapartist France rapidly mounting to the British level; that Continental centralization keeps the Army and Navy at a cheaper cost than insular oligarchy; that one Louis Napoleon wants for his private expenses twice and a half more money than a British sovereign; and finally, that in a bureaucratic country, like France, the cost of collecting the revenue grows at a rate disproportionate to the amount of the revenue itself.

Written on August 7, 1860					Reproduced from the newspaper

First published in the *New-York Daily Tribune*, No. 6030, August 22, 1860

Frederick Engels

GARIBALDI'S MOVEMENTS

London, August 8, 1860

The crisis in Southern Italy is at hand. If we are to trust the French and Sardinian papers, 1,500 Garibaldians have landed on the coast of Calabria and Garibaldi is hourly expected.[a] But even if this news be premature, there can be no doubt that Garibaldi will have transferred the seat of war to the Italian mainland before the middle of August.

To understand the movements of the Neapolitans, it must be kept in mind that there are two opposing undercurrents at work in their army: the moderate Liberal party, officially in power, and represented by the Ministry, and the Absolutist camarilla, to which most of the chiefs of the army are attached. The orders of the Ministry are counteracted by the secret orders of the Court and by the intrigues of the generals. Hence conflicting movements and conflicting reports. To-day we hear that all royal troops are to leave Sicily, to-morrow we find them preparing a fresh base of operations at Milazzo. This state of things is inherent to all half-and-half revolutions; the year 1848 furnishes examples of it all over Europe.

While the Ministry offered to evacuate the island, Bosco, who seems to be the only resolute man among the parcel of old women bearing Neapolitan generals' epaulettes, quietly attempted to turn the north-eastern corner of the island into a stronghold from which the reconquest of the island might be attempted, and for this purpose marched to Milazzo with a picked force of the best men to be had in Messina. Here he fell in with Medici's brigade of

---

[a] See "Affaires des deux Siciles", *Le Constitutionnel,* No. 220, August 7, 1860.— *Ed.*

Garibaldians. He did not, however, venture any serious attack on them, until Garibaldi himself had been sent for and brought some reenforcements. Here the insurgent chief, in his turn, attacked the royals, and, after an obstinate fight of above twelve hours' duration, defeated them completely. The forces engaged on either side were about equal, but the position held by the Neapolitans was very strong. However, neither positions nor men could withstand the dash of the insurgents, who drove the Neapolitans right through the town into the citadel. Here nothing remained to them but to capitulate, and Garibaldi allowed them to embark, but without arms. After this victory, he marched at once to Messina, where the Neapolitan general consented to give up the outer forts of the town on condition of not being molested in the citadel. This citadel being unable to hold more than a few thousand men, will never be a serious obstacle to any offensive operations of Garibaldi, and he therefore did quite right in sparing the town of a bombardment, which would inevitably have followed any attack. As it is this series of capitulations at Palermo, Milazzo, and Messina, must do more to destroy the confidence of the royal troops in themselves and in their chiefs, than twice as many victories. It has become a matter of course that the Neapolitans always capitulate before Garibaldi.

From this moment it became possible for the Sicilian Dictator to think of landing on the continent. His steam navy does not as yet appear to be sufficiently large to warrant him in attempting a landing further north, somewhere within six or eight marches from Naples, say in the Bay of Policastro. He, therefore, seems to have decided on crossing the Straits where they are narrowest, that is, on the extreme north-eastern point of the island, north of Messina. On this point he is said to have concentrated about 1,000 vessels, very likely most of them fishing and coasting felucas, such as are common on those coasts, and if the landing of the 1,500 men under Sacchi be confirmed, they will form his advanced guard. The point is not the most favorable for a march on Naples, as it is the part of the mainland furthest away from the Capital; but if his steam navy cannot transport something like 10,000 men at once, he cannot select any other, and then he has at least this advantage, that the Calabrians will at once join him. If, however, he can cram some ten thousand men on board his steamers, and can rely on the neutrality of the Royal navy (which appears resolved not to fight against Italians), then he may still land a few men in Calabria as a feint, and himself go with the main body to the Bay of Policastro, or even to that of Salerno.

The force at present at the disposal of Garibaldi consists of five brigades of regular infantry, of four battalions each; of ten battalions of Cacciatori dell' Etna[a]; of two battalions of Cacciatori delle Alpi,[b] the élite of his army; of one foreign (now Italian) battalion under Col. Dunne, an Englishman; of one battalion of engineers; one regiment and a squadron of cavalry; and four battalions of field artillery; in all 34 battalions, four squadrons, and 32 guns, equal to some 25,000 men in all, of whom, rather more than one-half are North Italians, the rest Italians. The whole, nearly, of this force might be used for the invasion of Naples, as the new formations now being organized will soon suffice to observe the citadel of Messina, and protect Palermo and the other towns from insult. Still, this force looks very small when compared with what the Neapolitan Government disposes of on paper.

The Neapolitan army consists of three regiments of the guard, fifteen ditto of the line, four foreign regiments, each of two battalions, or together 44 battalions; of 13 battalions of chasseurs; of nine regiments of cavalry, and two of artillery—in all 57 battalions, and 45 squadrons, on the peace-footing. Inclusive of the 9,000 gens d'armes, who also are organized on a perfectly military footing, this army, on the peace-footing, counts 90,000 men. But, during the last two years, it has been raised to the full war complement; third battalions of regiments have been organized, the depot squadrons have been put to active service, the garrison troops have been completed; and this army now consists, on paper, of above 150,000 men.

But what an army is this! Externally fine to look at for a martinet, there is no life, no spirit, no patriotism, no fidelity in it. It has no national military traditions. When Neapolitans fought as such, they were always defeated. Only in the wake of Napoleon were they ever associated with victory. It is not a National army. It is a purely Royal army. It was raised and organized for the express and exclusive purpose of keeping down the people. And even for that it appears unfit; there are plenty of anti-royalist elements in it, and they now break forth everywhere. The sergeants and corporals, especially, are Liberals almost to a man. Whole regiments shout "*Viva Garibaldi!*" No army ever underwent such disgrace as this one did from Calatafimi to Palermo; and if the foreign troops and some Neapolitans fought well at

---

[a] Etna riflemen.— *Ed.*
[b] Alpine riflemen.— *Ed.*

Milazzo, it is not to be forgotten that these picked men form but a small minority of the army.

Thus it is almost certain that, if Garibaldi lands with a force sufficient to obtain a few successes on the continent, no concentration of Neapolitan masses will be able to oppose him with any chance of success; and we may next expect to hear that he is continuing his triumphal career, with 15,000 men against tenfold odds, from the Scilla to Naples.

Written about August 7, 1860

First published in the *New-York Daily Tribune*, No. 6031, August 23, 1860; reprinted in the *New-York Semi-Weekly Tribune*, No. 1592, August 28, 1860

Reproduced from the *New-York Daily Tribune*

Karl Marx

[THE NEW SARDINIAN LOAN.—THE IMPENDING FRENCH AND INDIAN LOANS]

London, Aug. 14, 1860

The new Sardinian loan of £6,000,000 has been closed, and three times the sum required is said to have been subscribed. Thus it appears that the bonds of the new Italian Kingdom are rising in the market at the very time that Austria is struggling in vain with a debt whose magnitude ought to be measured not by the resources of the country, but by the weakness of its Government, and while Russia, mighty Russia, having been driven from the European loan market, was forced to recur again to its own paper-money machinery. Still, even in regard to Sardinia, the new loan reminds us of the ugly fact that in modern times almost the first act in a people's struggle for freedom or independence seems, by some monstrous fatality, to consist in contracting a new servitude. Is every public debt not a mortgage saddled upon the industry of a whole people, and a curtailment of its freedom? Does it not give rise to a new set of invisible tyrants, known under the name of public creditors? However that may be, if the French, in less than a decade, have almost doubled their public debt in order to remain slaves, the Italians must be allowed to incur the same liabilities in order to become freemen.

Piedmont proper, exclusive of the provinces newly added,[333] was in 1847 taxed to the amount of £3,813,452, while this year it will have to pay £6,829,000.[a] It has been stated by English papers, *The Economist*, for instance, that the commerce of Piedmont, consequent upon the liberal changes introduced into its tariff, had also greatly increased, and in illustration of this progress we are treated to the following figures:

In 1854 the imports were only	£12,497,160
In 1857 they were	19,123,040

---

[a] Marx took all the data from *The Economist*, No. 885, August 11, 1860, pp. 867-68.— *Ed.*

In 1854 the exports were £8,595,280
In 1857 they increased to .... 14,050,040[a]

Now, I beg to remark that this increase is more apparent than real. The leading articles of Sardinian export consist of silk, silk manufactures, twine, spirits, and oil; but it is generally known that during the first three quarters of 1857 the prices of all those articles had assumed a most bloated aspect, and would, consequently, greatly swell the sum total of the Sardinian commercial returns. The official statistics of the Kingdom give, moreover, the values only, not the quantities of the articles exported and imported, so that the figures for the year 1857 may be altogether exceptional. No public accounts for the years 1858-60 having as yet been issued, it remains to be seen whether or not the commercial crisis in 1858 and the Italian war in 1859 have checked the industrial progress of the country. The following tabular statements, showing the official estimates of the revenue and expenditure for the current year (1860) of Sardinia proper, afford evidence that part of the new loan will be employed to cover the deficit, while another part of it is wanted for new preparations for war:

Sardinian Revenue for 1860.

Customs	£2,411,824
Land-tax, house-tax, stamps, etc	2,940,284
Railroads and telegraphs	699,400
Post-Office	242,000
Fees received at Foreign Office	12,400
Fees received at Home Office	21,136
Profits on some branches of Public Instruction	580
Mint	6,876
Miscellaneous	193,888
Extraordinary resources	301,440
Total	£6,829,828

Sardinian Expenditure for 1860.

Finance Department	£4,331,676
Public Justice	243,816
Foreign Affairs	70,028
Public Instruction	117,744
Ministry of the Interior	407,152
Public Works	854,080

---

[a] The *New-York Daily Tribune* has 19,050,040 instead of 14,050,040.— *Ed.*

Military expenditure	£2,229,464
Marine expenditure	310,360
Extraordinary expenses	1,453,268
Total	£10,017,588

Comparing the expenditure amounting to £10,017,588 to the revenue of £6,829,828, we find a deficit of £3,187,760. On the other hand the newly acquired provinces are estimated to yield an annual revenue of £3,435,552, and to cost an annual expenditure of £1,855,984, so that they would leave a clear surplus of £1,600,000.[a] According to this calculation, the deficit of the whole kingdom of Sardinia, including the newly acquired provinces, would be reduced to £1,608,282. It is only just that Lombardy and the Duchies should pay part of the expenses Piedmont has incurred in the Italian war; but, in the run of time, it might prove a highly dangerous experiment to charge taxes upon the new provinces, almost twice as large as their cost of administration requires, with a single view to relieving the exchequer of the old provinces.

People conversant with the undercurrents of the Paris money market continue to give out that another French loan is looming in a not remote future. The only thing wanted is a specious opportunity for raising the wind. The *emprunt de la paix*,[b] as you know, has proved a failure. *Partant pour la Syrie*[334] has till now been rehearsed on too small a scale to justify a fresh appeal to the enthusiasm of the *grande nation*. It is, therefore, presumed that, should nothing new turn up, and the prices of corn go on increasing, a loan will be raised on the pretext of providing against the possible disasters of dearth. In connection with French finances it may be remarked as a curious fact, that Mr. Jules Favre, who dared to predict in the midst of the *Corps Législatif* the impending crash of the Imperial Exchequer,[c] has been elected *Bâtonnier* of the Paris Bar. The French advocates, as you are aware, have from the times of the old monarchy saved some tatters of their ancient feudal constitution. They still form a sort of corporate body, called the *Barreau*, the yearly elected chief of

---

[a] This figure is cited by *The Economist*, p. 867. The exact figure is £1,579,568. Hence the figure £1,608,282 in the next sentence.— *Ed.*

[b] The peace loan—a loan whose purpose was to increase military contingents. The question was debated in the *Corps Législatif* (see *Le Moniteur universel*, No. 117, April 27, 1859).— *Ed.*

[c] Jules Favre's speech in the *Corps Législatif* on July 13, 1860, *Le Moniteur universel*, No. 195, July 15, 1860.— *Ed.*

which, viz., the *Bâtonnier*, represents the order in its relations with the tribunals and the Government, at the same time that he watches over its internal discipline. Under the restoration, and under the following regime of the citizen King,[a] the election of the Paris *Bâtonnier* was always considered a great political act, involving a demonstration for or against the Ministry of the day. Mr. Jules Favre's election must, I believe, be considered the first anti-Bonapartist demonstration ventured upon by the Paris Bar, and consequently deserves to be chronicled among the events of the day.

In yesterday's sitting of the House of Commons, before a House hardly large enough to make up a quorum, Sir Charles Wood, that true pattern of the genuine Whig place-hunter, carried a resolution[b] empowering him to contract a new loan of Three Millions Sterling on behalf of the Indian Treasury. According to his statement, the Indian deficit was in 1858-59 (the financial year always beginning with and ending in April) £14,187,000, in 1859-60 £9,981,000, and is estimated for 1860-61 at £7,400,000. Part of that deficit he promised to cover from the yield of Mr. Wilson's newly-introduced taxes—a very questionable prospect, after all—while the other part was to be provided for by the new loan of three millions. The public debt, which in 1856-57, the year before the Rebellion, amounted to £59,442,000, had now increased to £97,851,000. At a still more rapid rate the interest on the debt had grown. From £2,525,000 in 1856-57 it had risen to £4,461,000 in 1859-60. Although the revenue had been forcibly expanded by the imposition of new taxes, still it could not keep pace with the expenditure which, even according to Mr. Charles Wood's own statement, was increasing in every direction, save that of Public Works. To make up for an outlay of three millions on fortified barracks, there has been put during the present, and will be put during the following year, "almost a perfect stop to public works and public buildings of a civic character." This "perfect stop" Sir Charles seemed to consider one of the beauties of the system. Instead of 40,000, as in 1856-57, there are now kept 80,000 European soldiers in India; and, instead of a native army of hardly 200,000, one of above 300,000 men.

Written on August 14, 1860   Reproduced from the newspaper

First published in the *New-York Daily Tribune*, No. 6035, August 28, 1860

---

[a] Louis Philippe.— *Ed.*

[b] Sir Charles Wood's resolution of August 13, 1860, *The Times*, No. 23698, August 14, 1860.— *Ed.*

Frederick Engels

THE SICK MAN OF AUSTRIA

The Emperor Francis Joseph of Austria seems permitted to live only that he may prove the truth of the old Latin maxim, that he whom the gods mean to destroy they first make mad. From the beginning of the year 1859 he has done nothing but deliberately trample under foot every chance that was offered to him to save himself and the Austrian Empire. The sudden attack on Piedmont with a portion only of his forces—the superseding of Marshal Hess in the command of the army by the Emperor and his clique—the irresolution which led to the battle of Solferino—the sudden conclusion of peace at the very moment when the French had arrived before his strongest positions—the obstinate refusal of all concessions in the internal organization of the Empire until it was too late, form an unequaled series of foolish blunders to be committed by one individual in so short a time.

But, as luck would have it, Francis Joseph had still another chance. The barefaced double-dealing of Louis Napoleon rendered necessary that alliance between Prussia and Austria which the preceding humiliations of Austria, her daily increasing difficulties at home and abroad, had first rendered possible. The interviews of Baden and Teplitz [335] sealed that alliance. Prussia, for the first time acting as the representative of the rest of Germany, promised her assistance in case Austria was attacked, not only by Italy, but by France also; while Austria promised to make concessions to public opinion, and change her internal policy. Here was indeed a hope for Francis Joseph. A fight with Italy single-handed he might not fear, even in case of troubles in Hungary, for his new policy was to be the best guaranty of security in that quarter. With a separate Constitution based upon the one abolished in 1849, Hungary would have been satisfied; a liberal Constitution for the whole of the Empire would have fulfilled the present wishes of the German nucleus of the monarchy, and counteracted in a great measure the separate tendencies of the Slavonic provinces. The finances once under popular control, public credit would have recovered itself, and the same Austria, now weak, poor, prostrate, exhausted, and a prey to internal divisions, would have soon regained strength under the protection of the 700,000 bayonets which Germany held ready to defend her. To insure all this, but two things were required of Austria: to follow up a genuine liberal policy at home, sincerely and without reserve, and to remain on the defensive in Venice, abandoning the remainder of Italy to its fate.

But neither the one nor the other, it appears, can or will Francis Joseph do. He can neither throw overboard his power as an absolute monarch, which is every day being dissolved more and more into vapor, nor can he forget that position of protector of the petty Italian tyrants, which he has already lost. Insincere, weak, and obstinate at the same time, he seems to fly from his internal difficulties to an aggressive war abroad, and rather than cement his Empire by the sacrifice of a power which is slipping from his hands, he appears to have thrown himself once more into the arms of his personal cronies, and to be preparing a descent into Italy which may end in the breaking up of the Austrian monarchy.

There may or there may not be a note or other communication sent from Vienna to Turin, on the subject of Garibaldi's landing in Calabria; but it is quite probable that Francis Joseph has made up his mind to consider this landing a case for his intervention in favor of the King of Naples.[a] Whether this be true, we shall soon see. But what can be the cause of this sudden revulsion of Austrian policy? Has the recent fraternization with Prussia and Bavaria turned the head of Francis Joseph? It is not likely; for, after all, that fraternization of Teplitz was a humiliation for him, and a triumph for Prussia only. Does Francis Joseph intend to collect under his standard the armies of the Pope[b] and of the King of Naples before Garibaldi has shattered them to atoms and incorporated their Italian elements with his own followers? That would be a very insufficient motive. In any campaign whatever, these troops will want for nothing, while, in the position in which

---

a Francis II.— *Ed.*
b Pius IX.— *Ed.*

Austria will place herself by such a foolish aggression, she will want for everything. There can be no other cause for it than the state of internal Austrian politics. And here we have not to seek long. The Council of the Empire, reenforced by some of the most conservative and aristocratic elements of the different Provinces, and intrusted, *in time of peace,* with the control of the finances of the country, is about to discuss the question of popular representation and constitutions for the Empire and the single provinces composing it. The motions made to this effect by the Hungarian members have an overwhelming majority in the Committee, and will be passed in the same triumphant manner in the Council, in the face of the Government. In one word, *the second Austrian Revolution seems to have set in.* The Council of the Empire—a weak counterfeit of the French Notables—exactly as they did, declares itself incompetent, and calls for the States General.[336] The Government, in the same financial difficulties as that of Louis XVI, and weaker still by the diverging tendencies of the various nationalities composing the Empire, is not in a position to resist. Concessions wrested from the Government are sure to be followed by fees and demands. The States General soon formed themselves into the National Assembly. Francis Joseph feels the ground tremble under his feet, and to escape from the impending earthquake will perhaps fly into a war.

If Francis Joseph acts up to his menace, commencing a crusade for legitimacy in Naples and the Papal States, what will be the end of it? There is not a Power or State in Europe which has the slightest interest in the maintenance of the Bourbons, and if Francis Joseph interferes in their behalf, he will have to bear the consequences. Louis Napoleon is sure to cross the Alps in defense of non-intervention; and Austria, with the public opinion of all Europe dead against her, with ruined finances, insurrection in Hungary, and a brave but far outnumbered army, will be fearfully beaten. Perhaps she will receive her death-blow. As to Germany coming to her aid, it is perfectly out of the question. The Germans will most decidedly decline to fight either for the King of Naples or for the Pope. They will take care to have the territory of the Confederation respected (which both French and Italians will be but too glad to submit to), and if Hungary rises, they will look on quite as coolly. Nay, the German provinces of the Empire will, very likely, support the demands of the Hungarians, as they did in 1848, and demand a Constitution for themselves. The Austrian press, restricted as it is by the Government, still shows unmistakable signs of the existence, even in Austria, of a widespread sympathy with Garibaldi. The current of opinion has changed from the channel it followed last year; Venice is now considered a very bad kind of property, and the struggle of the Italians for independence, since it is carried on without French assistance, is looked on in a favorable light by the Viennese public. Francis Joseph will find it exceedingly difficult to make even his own German subjects take up the cause of the Bourbon of Naples, of the Pope, of the petty Dukes of Emilia. A people which is just entering on a revolution against absolutism, is not likely to stick up for the dynastic interests of its ruler. The Viennese have proved this before, and it is possible enough that the passage of the Po by the Austrian troops may become the signal for the use of more violent means by the movement party in Vienna as well as in Hungary.

Written on August 16, 1860

First published in the *New-York Daily Tribune*, No. 6039, September 1, 1860 as a leading article; reprinted in the *New-York Semi-Weekly Tribune*, No. 1594, September 4, and in the *New-York Weekly Tribune*, No. 991, September 8, 1860

Reproduced from the *New-York Daily Tribune*

Karl Marx

THE CROPS IN EUROPE

London, August 21, 1860

The more the season advances the gloomier become the harvest prospects and the fainter grow the hopes still founded on a possible return of fine weather. The character of the past Summer was altogether exceptional, not only throughout the United Kingdom, but over the whole of Northern Europe, Northern France, Belgium, and the Rhenish Provinces included. In regard to this country the season has been justly described in these words:

"After the cold, backward Spring, June proved so extremely wet that in many districts turnips could not be sown, mangel-wurzel hoed, nor any of the usual operations of the period performed. Then, after about ten days of fine weather, the season became so unsettled that two days together without rain have been rather a surprise. But, in addition to the excess of moisture, the present, we may say the past Summer, has been remarkable for the absence of sunshine and the very low temperature which have prevailed even when there has been no rain."[a]

The average fall of rain for the year being about 20 inches, and the fall of rain during the months of May and June having reached the figure of 11.17, it appears that these two months have given over half a year's supply of water. During the last week, at the commencement of which a favorable change seemed impending, the weather proved more unsettled and boisterous than ever, real deluges of rain being, on the 16th and 18th inst., accompanied by thunder-storms and the tempests of the south-west wind. Consequently the wheat prices at Mark Lane[337] advanced yesterday about two shillings the quarter over the rates of last Monday's[b] market.

---

[a] "The Wet Summer", *The Economist*, No. 886, August 18, 1860, p. 899.— *Ed.*

[b] August 13; see *The Times*, Nos. 23698 and 23704, August 14 and August 21, 1860.— *Ed.*

Hay-making has been already seriously interfered with and belated by the incessant wind, rain, and cold. The grass having been laid and constantly saturated with water, it is feared that much of its nutritive substance has been washed away, so that a great part of it will not do for fodder, but must be used for litter, and will thus prove a very serious loss, greatly increasing the consumption of Spring corn. Much of it is still to be gathered, and much is irretrievably lost.

"There can be little doubt," says *The Gardeners' Chronicle* of Saturday last, "that the wheat crop generally is considerably injured. Of 140 reports received from as many correspondents in England and Scotland, no fewer than 91 declare the crop to be below the average, and if the chief wheat-growing districts be selected, it will be found that the proportion of unfavorable returns is quite as large. Thus, five out of six reports from Lincolnshire, three out of five from Norfolk and Suffolk, and all from the counties of Oxford, Gloucestershire, Wilts, Hants, and Kent, are unfavorable."

A great deal of the wheat crop has rotted at the root before the grain was mature, and in many districts it has been blighted and mildewed. While wheat is thus attacked by the disease, and in many districts to a large extent, the potato disease, which commenced in 1845, continued with great virulence for the four subsequent years, and gradually abated since 1850, has reappeared in an aggravated form, not only in Ireland, but in many districts of England and the Northern Continent.

The Freeman's Journal thus resumes the general harvest prospects of Ireland:

"The oat crop is generally looked upon as all but lost. Except in a few inconsiderable districts, it has not yet ripened; but remains perfectly green, and beaten to the ground by the violence of the weather. Wheat promises to share in the calamity which generally threatens the grain crops. Little of it has been yet cut, and this crop, the condition of which inspired the most sanguine expectations only a few weeks since, is now causing farmers the deepest concern. [...] With regard to the potato crop, the general opinion is, that if the present weather continues for another month, it must be inevitably lost." [a]

According to the Wexford *Independent,*

"the potato disease is progressing, and in some places fully one-third of the produce is found affected, irrespective alike of size and description, and in proportion to the time of planting."

This much appears, therefore, certain: The general harvest will be much belated beyond its usual term, and the existing stores

---

[a] Quotations from *The Freeman's Journal* were given in the article "The Harvest" in *The Times,* No. 23703, August 20, 1860.— *Ed.*

consequently be run short. The partial failure of hay, coupled with the potato disease, will press to an unwonted extent upon the cereals; and the yield of all sorts of corn, especially wheat, will fall far below the average. Till now, the imports from abroad, instead of showing an excess over the imports during the years 1858 and 1859, exhibit, on the contrary, a marked comparative decline. On the other hand, corn prices, although, on an average, they rule now 26 per cent higher than at the same period of last year, have as yet been kept down by the news of the plentiful harvests in America and Southern Russia, by the hope of a favorable turn in the weather, and by the extreme caution the late collapse in the leather trade had imposed upon *all* monetary transactions. The conclusion to which I am led by a comparison of the present prices with those of similar seasons since 1815, is, that the average price of wheat, which may be taken now to amount to 58/@59/ the quarter, will have to rise, in England at least, to 65/@70/. The effect of such a rise in the price of breadstuffs will be considerably aggravated by its coincidence with a progressive decline in the export trade of the country. From £63,003,159, which sum they realized during the six months ending June 30, 1859, the British exports have sunk to £62,019,989 during the corresponding period of 1860,[a] and, as I have shown in a former letter,[b] the contraction was mainly due to a decline in the sale of cotton goods and yarns, consequent upon the markets of Asia and Australia having been glutted. While the exports are thus falling off, the imports have considerably risen, if compared with the corresponding period of 1859. We find, in fact, the imports for the five months ending May 31, 1859, £44,968,863; 1860, £57,097,638.

This excess of imports over exports must necessarily aggravate the drain of bullion and the consequent unsettled state of the money market which characterizes all periods of failing harvests, and extraordinary purchases of foreign corn. If, in England, the effect of the imminent monetary pressure is not likely to stretch far beyond the sphere of political economy, it is quite another thing on the Continent, where serious political disturbances are almost unavoidable whenever a monetary crisis coincides with a failing harvest and a great increase of taxation. Already the most serious apprehensions are entertained at Paris, where the magistrate is just busied with buying up whole lots of old houses, in

---

[a] The figures quoted here and at the end of the paragraph were given in *The Economist*, No. 886, August 18, 1860, p. 895.— *Ed.*

[b] See this volume, pp. 406-08.— *Ed.*

order to have them pulled down, and thus cut out work for the
"*ouvriers*." [a] The Paris prices of best wheat range at this moment as
high, if not somewhat higher than the London prices, namely at
60/6 to 61/. The last dodges by which Louis Bonaparte tried to
divert the public mind, viz.: the Syrian expedition, the advance-
ment of Spain to a "great power," [338] the transactions with Prussia,
and the attempts at interference with Garibaldi's progress, having
all turned out dead failures, he must needs meet the dangers of a
bad season, a monetary pressure and a stinted exchequer at the
very moment when his political "prestige" is evidently at a
considerable discount. If any proof for the latter assertion were
wanted, is there not his letter to "*Mon cher Persigny*"? [b] [339]

Written on August 21, 1860

First published in the *New-York Daily
Tribune*, No. 6043, September 6, 1860;
reprinted in the *New-York Semi-Weekly
Tribune*, No. 1595, September 7 and in
the *New-York Weekly Tribune*, No. 991,
September 8, 1860 without the last
paragraph

Reproduced from the *New-York
Daily Tribune*

---

[a] "Workmen".— *Ed.*
[b] "My dear Persigny."— *Ed.*

Karl Marx

[CORN PRICES.—EUROPEAN FINANCES
AND WAR PREPARATIONS.—THE ORIENTAL QUESTION]

London, Aug. 25, 1860

The state of the weather having not improved during this week, a rise of 6 shillings per sack took place in the value of town-made flour, at Mark Lane yesterday, and orders for the purchase of nearly 1,000,000 quarters of produce were at once forwarded to foreign ports. Importers share now pretty generally the opinion I advanced in a late letter[a] as to the inevitable further rise in the quotations of the grain market. The recent measures taken by France in regard to the corn trade bring that country into direct competition with the British corn merchant. You are aware that there exists in France a sliding scale, regulating the import and export duties on grain, and that this sliding scale varies for the eight different circles which the whole country is divided into with respect to the corn trade. Now, by a decree published in the *Moniteur* of the 23d inst.,[b] this sliding scale has been altogether suspended. The decree enacts that grain and flour imported by land or by sea, in French or foreign vessels, shall, wherever they may come from, only pay, up to the 30th of September, 1861, the minimum of duties fixed by the law of the 15th of April, 1832[c]; also, that vessels laden with grain and flour shall be exempt from tunnage dues; and finally, that vessels so laden leaving any foreign port at any date previous to the said 30th of September, 1861, shall only pay the said minimum, and shall be free from tunnage

---

[a] See this volume, p. 461.—*Ed.*

[b] *Le Moniteur universel*, No. 235.—*Ed.*

[c] "Loi relative à l'importation et à l'exportation des céréales [le 15 avril 1832]", *Le Moniteur universel*, No. 109, April 18, 1832.—*Ed.*

dues. The minimum referred to, is 25 cents the hectolitre (about $2^3/_4$ bushels).[a] Consequently, while France in the years 1858 and 1859 sent more wheat—2,014,923 quarters—and more flour—4,326,435 cwt. to England than any other country, it will now seriously compete with England in the purchase of grain in the foreign markets—the provisional suspension of the French sliding scale affording the wanted facilities for such competition.

The two main markets of export which both England and France find themselves limited to are the United States and Southern Russia. In regard to the latter country, the news as to the state of the harvest is of the most contradictory character. On the one hand, it is asserted that the harvest is most plentiful; on the other, that heavy rains and high floods having damaged the crops in all parts of the Empire, the roads and corn-fields of the southern provinces had been greatly devastated by locusts, a scourge which made its first appearance in Bessarabia, and whose depredations it was vainly attempted to circumscribe within a limited area by an army of 20,000 men drawing a cordon around them. The ultimate extent of the disaster cannot, of course, be estimated, but at all events it must tend to accelerate the upward movement of food prices. Some London papers fancy that the drain of bullion inseparable from large and sudden corn imports may be counterbalanced in its usual effect upon the money market by the gold supplies from Australia. No notion could be more preposterous. We witnessed, during the crisis of 1857, a lower ebb of the bullion reserves than in any similar epoch before the discovery of Australia and California. On former occasions I have shown by incontrovertible facts and figures that the extraordinary gold imports into England since 1851 have been more than counterbalanced by extraordinary gold exports. There is, moreover, the fact that the bullion reserves in the Bank of England have, since 1857, not only not exceeded the average amount, but were continually falling off. While they amounted in August, 1858, to £17,654,506, they had declined to £16,877,255 in August, 1859, and to £15,680,840 in August, 1860.[b] As the gold drain has not yet set in, this phenomenon may be accounted for by the circumstance that the prospect of a failing harvest is only beginning to operate, while, till now, the rate of interest has

---

[a] "Foreign correspondence", *The Economist*, No. 887, August 25, 1860, p. 931.—*Ed.*

[b] "Bank Returns and Money Market", *The Economist*, No. 887, August 25, 1860, p. 934.—*Ed.*

continued to be higher at London than at the other principal exchanges of the Continent, viz.: Amsterdam, Frankfort, Hamburg, and Paris.

Continental Europe exhibits at this moment a very curious spectacle. France is known to labor under heavy financial difficulties, but she is creating armaments on a scale as gigantic, with an energy as untiring, as if she owned Aladdin's lamp. Austria totters on the very brink of bankruptcy, but, somehow or other, the money is found for feeding an immense army, and crowding the fortresses of the Quadrilateral[a] with rifle cannon. And Russia, where all the monetary operations of the Government have failed, and the national bankruptcy is talked of as a probable event—where the army grumbles in consequence of arrears not paid, and even the loyalty of the Imperial Guard is put to a severe test, their pay having been withheld for the last five months—Russia, nevertheless, is pouring her troops down to the Black Sea, and holds 200 ships ready at Nicolaieff, in order to embark them for Turkey. The inability of the Russian Government to cope with the slave question, the money question, and the reviving Polish question, seems to have decided it to try war as a last resource of national soporification. The complaints arising from all parts of the Empire, and all ranks of Russian society, are consequently, by Government order, drowned in the fanatical cry of revenge for the poor, down-trodden Christians of Turkey. Day by day the Russian press teems with illustrations and demonstrations as to the necessity of an intervention in Turkey. The following extract from the *Invalid*[b] may be considered a fair sample[340].

"The Oriental question has reached a stage which is certain to keep it before the Powers for a long time to come, and, as it now engrosses the attention of all Europe, it would ill become us to leave it undiscussed in our columns. Those only who are indifferent to the interests of humanity can allow this topic to pass by unnoticed. We, however, are obliged not only to relate the details of Oriental occurrences, but also to allude to the eventualities of the future, especially as it behooves us to show the public what measures must be taken in order to do away with such an unnatural state of things, forming, as it does, the disgrace of our century and civilization.

"Considering what acts of barbarism the Turks are allowed to commit, we are, in deference to truth and justice, compelled to acknowledge that Europe must be held accountable for the origin and consequences of Mussulman fanaticism. We will not hesitate to speak out frankly. What were the motives that prompted Europe to engage in an unjust war against Russia in 1853-4? Europe herself put forward two

---

[a] Mantua, Peschiera, Verona and Legnago (on this see Engels, "Po and Rhine", present edition, Vol. 16).— *Ed.*

[b] *Russky Invalid.—Ed.*

objects as the grounds of the Crimean campaign[a]: One was, to thwart the power and ambition of Russia; the other to prevent the oppression of Christians by the Turks. Europe, consequently, acknowledged the existence of such oppression, but in order to remove it, declared her determination to maintain the integrity of Turkey as a necessary condition of the balance of power. The war being at an end, diplomacy began to busy itself with the means for the attainment of this double object. The first step was to receive Turkey into the family of European Powers, and to protect her against the overweening interference of any one of their number. This being easy enough of accomplishment, one of the two objects was consequently secured. But how is it with the other? Have any guarantees been given for the protection of Christians against murder and every description of ill usage? Alas! Europe in this respect put her faith in words, papers, and documents, without any solid security being accorded for their fulfillment. As early as the 8th of August, 1854, when the cessation of hostilities was contemplated,[b] the Porte was called upon to grant an equal share of religious rights to its Christian and Mussulman subjects.[c] The same demand was raised by the St. Petersburg Cabinet in the memorials of the 28th December, 1854[d]; and finally, the preliminary conditions of peace drawn up at Vienna on the 1st of February, 1856, and afterward embodied in the minutes of the first sitting of the Paris Congress, were made to include the following words: 'The rights of the rayahs will be protected, without prejudice, however, to the independence and sovereign dignity of the Sultan. Austria, France, Great Britain, and the Porte, are of accord respecting the maintenance of the Turkish Christians in the enjoyment of their political and religious rights; and they will request the consent of Russia to this proposition in the instrument of peace.'

"The same object occupied the Congress in various other sittings, as may be seen from the minutes of the 28th of February, and of the 24th and 25th of March. In all this, it was desirous of attaining two objects mutually destructive of each other—to preserve the sovereign rights of the Sultan, and to place those of his Christian subjects under the guardianship of Europe. The Congress altogether forgot that the same rights of the Christians, which it was so desirous of establishing, had been conceded over and over again by the Porte in its previous treaties with Europe—treaties which, moreover, had already abolished the sovereign power of that monarch, who, as Europe now said, ought to be assisted in its maintenance. To establish a little harmony between these two contradictory points, the Sultan, while induced to issue the celebrated Hatti-Humayouni, was acknowledged to have acted from his own free will and sovereign inclination. So he had to promise that he would respect and increase the rights of his Christian subjects, and this promise was received into the treaty of peace, by way of guaranty for its fulfillment as one of its constituent parts. On these conditions, the Congress, in the 9th clause of the treaty, resigned all further interference with the internal affairs of Turkey.

"But has the Congress really obtained any guaranty for the carrying out of the Hatti-Humayouni? Have any effective obligations been entered into by the Sultan?

---

[a] The words "as the grounds of the Crimean campaign" do not occur in the *Russky Invalid.—Ed.*

[b] The *Russky Invalid* has here "and the famous Four Points drawn up".— *Ed.*

[c] The *Russky Invalid* reads "the Porte was called upon to preserve the religious rights of all the Christians".— *Ed.*

[d] The *Russky Invalid* has "The same demand was raised in the memorials of the 28th December, 1854, submitted to the St. Petersburg Cabinet."— *Ed.*

Of this, nothing was provided. For, although the wisdom of the Hatti-Humayouni is much extolled in the treaty, that document, as all Europe predicted, has remained a dead letter. But, worse than this—Europe, in virtue of the new treaty, is deprived of all right of legal interference,[a] even though the Hatti-Humayouni may never have been executed, and notwithstanding the perpetration of the most horrible atrocities only four years after its issue. [...] Quite recently, Russia warned all the Cabinets of Europe that the fanaticism of the Turks[b] had diminished neither in zeal nor fierceness; that new outbreaks were soon to be expected, although, indeed, there had never been any interval of relaxation. But even then Europe was satisfied with the promises of the Porte, and indulged herself in the hope that the guilty parties would be punished, and law and order speedily restored. It needed the wholesale slaughter at the hands of these savages to effect a change in her opinions. Then at length Europe resolved to interfere,[c] though not without such delay and circumlocution as would justify the belief that she intended to let the guilty ones escape. Everything was made to depend on the letter of the treaty of the 30th March, 1856; and, just as in the case of Italy last year, the sufferings of a people weighed nothing against the text of a diplomatic document.[d]

"But our opinion on all this is very different. The treaty of Europe with Turkey, in our eyes, guarantees the principles of humanity, religion, and civilization. If Turkey violates these principles, she alone brings upon herself the interference of Europe.[e]

"Until the year 1856, the Powers of Europe, in virtue of several treaties concluded with the Porte, owned a legal right of remonstrance respecting the position of the Christian rayahs. To-day, however, it may be questioned whether or not this right has been abrogated by the treaty of the 30th March, 1856. Has Europe resigned the privileges of protecting its co-religionists? It has if it ever reckoned upon the execution of the Hatti-Humayouni, of the 18th February; if it ever believed that reforms promised are one and the same with reforms carried out; if it ever hoped that the customs, passions, and laws of the Mussulmans[f] are capable of a change. But, of course, Europe never was, never could be, of that opinion. Carried away by the belief that the integrity of the Ottoman Empire is a *sine qua non* for the balance of power, she allowed the Sultan to enter into her family of States. But this was only accorded on the condition that Turkey, dissevering herself from Mussulman traditions, should become European in her institutions; that a sword should no longer be the only law-giver between believers and unbelievers; that the Christians should no longer be the slaves of their masters and the property of the royal rayahs cease to form the common plundering-ground of Mussulmans. This, indeed, was the leading idea of Europe in 1856. With all its wrath against Russia, the natural consequence of a sanguinary and unjust war, it did not release the Porte from its previous obligations; but, on the contrary, demanded a progressive improvement in the situation of the Christians. To secure the attainment of this object was the only purpose of the common protectorate of Europe over the Porte and for this price alone Europe guaranteed the integrity of the Sultan's dominions. Without this, neither the war nor the peace would have been justifiable. Without this, Turkey would never have been received into the family of

---

[a] The *Russky Invalid* has "mediation" instead of "legal interference".— *Ed.*
[b] The *Russky Invalid* has "Mussulmans".— *Ed.*
[c] The *Russky Invalid* has "mediate".— *Ed.*
[d] The *Russky Invalid* has "against the letter of the Vienna treaties".— *Ed.*
[e] The *Russky Invalid* has "the mediation and its consequences".— *Ed.*
[f] The *Russky Invalid* has "laws of the Koran".— *Ed.*

Powers, nor protected in the integrity of her possessions. The two conditions are so intimately connected that they cannot be separated; every one can see that, who wishes to see at all.

"The form of the condition, it is true, might have been less effective than it is; if the letter of the treaty ruled supreme. Europe, in virtue of the 9th clause, has formally resigned her right of interference[a] in the internal affairs of Turkey; but even in this clause mention is made of the Hatti-Humayouni of the 18th February, in accordance with which the Christians are to be placed on an equal footing of right with the Mussulmans. It is but in harmony with the laws of sound logic to infer, that if the Hatti-Humayouni has been disregarded, the 9th clause falls to the ground.

"In vain Turkey now affects to quell the latest outbreak[b] in Syria. That outbreak was unavoidable, considering that the situation of the Christians has not been ameliorated, but on the contrary, rendered worse than before. In vain England strives to prevent the interference[a] of Europe; it is just possible she has her own policy, and is swayed by political and commercial motives, the justice and importance of which we do not care to consider; but she cannot base her objections on the 9th clause of the Paris Treaty. [...] In vain Europe seeks to conceal the fact of her interference, under the plea that it has been undertaken in consequence of a wish of the Sultan. We say that all this is in vain; and although Ilion did not believe in the prophecies of Cassandra, we have at least the satisfaction of knowing that Ilion was destroyed."

Written on August 25, 1860   Reproduced from the newspaper

First published in the *New-York Daily Tribune*, No. 6046, September 10, 1860

---

[a] The *Russky Invalid* has "mediation".— *Ed.*
[b] The *Russky Invalid* has "In vain Turkey now vigorously opposes mediation".— *Ed.*

Frederick Engels

GARIBALDI'S PROGRESS

As events develop themselves they begin to give us an insight into the plan which Garibaldi had prepared for the liberation of Southern Italy, and the more we see of it the more we admire the vastness of its proportions. Such a plan could not have been conceived, or its execution attempted in any country but Italy, where the National party is so perfectly organized, and so completely under the control of the one man who has drawn his sword with brilliant success for the cause of Italian unity and independence.

The plan was not confined to the liberation of the Kingdom of Naples only; the Papal States were to be attacked simultaneously, so as to find occupation for Lamoricière's army and the French at Rome,[341] as well as for Bombalino's[a] troops. About the 15th of August, 6,000 volunteers transferred gradually from Genoa to the Gulf of Oranges (Golfo degli Aranci), on the north-east coast of the Island of Sardinia, were to cross over to the Papal coast, while at the same time the insurrection in the various Provinces of the Neapolitan Continent was to break out, and Garibaldi was to cross the Straits of Messina into Calabria. Some reported expressions of Garibaldi's as to the cowardice of the Neapolitans, and the intelligence received by the last steamer that he had entered Naples, and been triumphantly received there, render it probable that an insurrection in the streets of that city, which the flight of the King rendered unnecessary, was a part of the plan.

The landing in the Papal States, as is already known, was prevented partly by Victor Emmanuel's representations, partly and

---

[a] Francis II.— *Ed.*

principally by Garibaldi's convincing himself that these men were not in a fit state to undertake an independent campaign. He accordingly took them to Sicily, left part at Palermo, sent the remainder round the island in two steamers to Taormina, where we shall find them again presently. In the mean time the Neapolitan movements in the provincial towns took place as agreed upon, and in a manner which showed both how well the revolutionary party was organized, and how much the country was ripe for an outbreak. On the 17th of August, the insurrection broke out at Foggia, in Apulia. The dragoons, forcing the garrison of the town, joined the people. General Flores, commanding the district, sent two companies of the 13th Regiment who, on arrival, did likewise. Then did Gen. Flores come himself, accompanied by his staff; but he could do nothing and had to leave again. This proceeding clearly shows that Flores himself did not wish to offer serious resistance to the revolutionary party. Had he been in earnest he would have sent two battalions instead of two companies, and when he came himself, would have come at the head of as strong a force as he could muster, instead of coming with a few adjutants and orderlies. In fact, the circumstance alone that the insurgents allowed him to leave the town again is sufficient to show that there was at least some tacit understanding. Another movement broke out in the Province of Basilicata. Here the insurgents collected their forces at Carletto Perticara, a village on the River Lagni (this must be the place called Corleto by the telegrams).

From this mountainous and remote district they marched to Potenza, the chief town of the Province, where they arrived, 6,000 strong, on the 17th. The only resistance they found, was offered by about 400 gendarmes, who, after a short engagement, were dispersed, and afterward came in one by one to surrender. A provincial government was formed in the name of Garibaldi, and a prodictator installed.[a] It is reported that the Royal Intendant (governor of the Province) accepts this office—another sign how hopeless the cause of the Bourbons is considered to be even by their own organs. Four companies of the Sixth Regiment of the line were sent from Salerno to put down this insurrection, but when they came to Auletta, about 23 miles from Potenza, they refused to march further, and cried *Viva Garibaldi*. These are the only movements of which any details have reached us. But we are further informed that other places have joined the insurrection;

---

[a] See "Affaires d'Italie", *Le Constitutionnel*, No. 241, August 28, 1860.— *Ed.*

for instance, Avellino, a town not 30 miles from Naples; Campobasso, in the Province of Molise (on the Adriatic), and Celenza in Apulia, for this must be the place called Cilenta in the telegrams; it is situated about half-way between Campobasso and Foggia; and now Naples itself is added to the number.

While thus the Neapolitan provincial towns at least carried out their apportioned share of the work, Garibaldi was not idle. Scarcely returned from his trip to Sardinia, he made his final arrangements for crossing over to the continent. His army now consisted of three divisions, commanded by Türr, Cosenz, and Medici. The two latter, concentrated about Messina and the Faro,[a] were marched toward the northern coast of Sicily, between Milazzo and Faro, as if they were intended to embark there and land on the Calabrian coast, north of the Straits, somewhere about Palmi or Nicotera. Of Türr's division, the brigade Éber was encamped near Messina, the brigade Bixio had been sent to the interior, to Bronte, to repress some disorders. Both were at once ordered to Taormina, where, on the evening of the 18th of August, the brigade Bixio, along with the men brought from Sardinia, embarked on the two steamers, the *Torino* and *Franklin,* and some on transports taken in tow.

About ten days previous Major Missori, with 300 men, had crossed the Straits and safely passed through the Neapolitans to the high and broken ground of Aspromonte. Here he was joined by other small bodies, thrown across the Straits from time to time, and by Calabrian insurgents, so that by this time he commanded a body of about 2,000 men. The Neapolitans had sent about 1,800 men after his little band when landed, but these 1,800 heroes managed so as never to come up with the Garibaldians.

On the 19th, at daybreak, Garibaldi's expedition (for he was on board *himself*) landed between Melito and Cape Spartivento, on the extreme southern end of Calabria.

They found no resistance. The Neapolitans had been so completely deceived by the movements threatening a landing north of the Straits, that the country south of them was completely neglected by them. Thus 9,000 men were thrown across, beside the 2,000 got together by Missori.

Having been joined by these, Garibaldi at once marched on Reggio,[b] which was occupied by four companies of the line and four of chasseurs. This garrison must, however, have received

---

[a] Faro di Messina.— *Ed.*

[b] Reggio di Calabria.— *Ed.*

some reenforcements, as some very severe fighting is reported to have taken place in or before Reggio on the 21st.[a] After the storming of some outworks of Garibaldi, the artillery in the fort of Reggio refused to fire any longer, and Gen. Viale capitulated.[b] In this engagement Col. Deflotte (the Republican member for Paris in the French Legislative Assembly of 1851) was killed.

The Neapolitan flotilla in the Straits distinguished itself by doing nothing. After Garibaldi had landed, a naval commander telegraphed to Reggio that it was impossible for the ships to offer any resistance, as he had with him eight large men-of-war and seven transports! No more did this flotilla oppose the passage by the division of Gen. Cosenz, which must have taken place on the 20th or 21st, at the narrowest place of the Straits, between Scilla and Villa San Giovanni, on the very spot where both the ships and troops of the Neapolitans were most concentrated. Cosenz's landing was marked by a signal success. The two brigades Melendez and Briganti (the Neapolitans say battalions instead of brigades), and the fort of Pezzo (not Pizzo, as some telegrams say; this place is situated far to the north, beyond Monteleone), surrendered to him, as it appears, without a blow. This is said to have taken place on the 21st, on which day also Villa San Giovanni was occupied after a short engagement.[c]

Thus in three days Garibaldi had made himself master of the whole coast of the Straits, including some of the fortified points; the few forts still occupied by Neapolitans were now useless to them.

The two following days appear to have been occupied by the passage of the remainder of the troops and of the materiel—at least we do not hear of any further engagements until the 24th, when a severe contest is reported to have taken place at a place called in the telegrams *Piale*, which we do not find on the maps. It may be the name of some mountain torrent, the ravine formed by which might have served as a defensive position to the Neapolitans. This engagement is said to have been undecided. After some time the Garibaldians offered an armistice, which the Neapolitan commander referred to his General-in-Chief at Monteleone. But before an answer could arrive, the Neapolitan soldiers appear to have come to the conclusion that they had done quite enough for their King, and dispersed, leaving the batteries unoccupied.

---

[a] *Le Constitutionnel*, No. 240, August 27, 1860.— *Ed.*

[b] *Le Constitutionnel*, No. 241, August 28, 1860.— *Ed.*

[c] ibid.— *Ed.*

The main body of the Neapolitans, under Bosco, appears during all this time to have quietly remained at Monteleone, some thirty miles from the Straits. They do not seem to have been very eager to fight the invaders, so Gen. Bosco went over to Naples to fetch six battalions of Chasseurs, which are, next to the Guards and foreign troops, the most reliable portions of the army. Whether these six battalions were themselves infected by the spirit of dejection and demoralization reigning in the Neapolitan army remains to be seen. Certain it is, that neither they nor any other troops have been able to prevent Garibaldi from marching victoriously, and probably unchecked, to Naples, to find that the Royal family had fled, and the gates of the city open to his triumphant entrance.

Written about September 1, 1860   Reproduced from the newspaper

First published in the *New-York Daily Tribune*, No. 6056, September 21, 1860 as a leading article

Frederick Engels

GARIBALDI IN CALABRIA

We are now in possession of detailed information respecting the conquest of Lower Calabria by Garibaldi, and the entire dispersion of the Neapolitan corps charged with its defense. In this part of his triumphal career, Garibaldi has shown himself to be not only a brave leader and clever strategist, but also a scientific general. The attack, by main force, of a chain of coast-forts is an undertaking which requires not only military talent, but also military science; and it is gratifying to find that our hero, who never passed a military examination in his life, and can scarcely be said ever to have belonged to a regular army, was as much at home on this kind of battle-field as on any other.

The toe of the Italian boot is formed by the mountain chain of Aspromonte, which ends in the peak of Montalto, about 4,300 feet high. From this peak, the waters flow toward the coast in a number of deep ravines, extending from Montalto as from a center, like the radii of a semicircle, the periphery of which is formed by the coast. These ravines, with the beds of their respective mountain torrents dried up in this season, are called *fiumare*, and form as many positions for a retreating army. They may indeed be turned by the Montalto, especially as there are bridle-paths and footpaths running along the crest of each spur and of the main chain of Aspromonte itself; but the complete absence of water on the high land would make it rather a difficult maneuver to do so in Summer with a large force. The spurs of the hill run down to the coast, where they descend toward the sea in steep and irregularly broken rocks. The forts guarding the straits between Reggio and Scilla are constructed partly on the beach, but more generally on low, projecting rocks close to the shore. The consequence is that they are all of them commanded and looked into by the more elevated rocks close to the rest, and although the commanding points may be inaccessible to artillery, and mostly out of the range of old Brown Bess,[342] so as to be considered of no consequence when the forts were erected, their importance has become decisive since the introduction of the modern rifle; they are mostly within its range, and thus they now do command the forts in reality. Under these circumstances, a forcible attack on these forts, despising the rules of regular sieges, was perfectly justified. What Garibaldi had to do was, evidently, to send a column along the high road which skirts the shore under the fire of the forts, for a feigned front attack on the Neapolitan troops; and to take another column over the hills as high up the *fiumare* as might be rendered necessary by the nature of the ground, or by the extent of front offered by any Neapolitan defensive position, thus turning both troops and fort, and having the advantage of the commanding position in every engagement.

Accordingly, on the 21st August, Garibaldi sent Bixio, with part of his troops, along the coast toward Reggio, whilst he himself, with a small detachment and the troops of Missori, which had rejoined him, went by the higher ground. The Neapolitans, eight companies, or about 1,200 men, occupied a *fiumare* just outside Reggio. Bixio, being the first to attack, sent one column to the extreme left on the sandy beach, while he himself advanced on the road. The Neapolitans very soon gave way; but their left wing, in the hills, held out against the few men of Garibaldi's advanced guard until Missori's men came up and drove them in. Then they retreated to the fort, which is situated in the middle of the town, and to a small battery on the beach. The latter was taken by a very gallant rush of three of Bixio's companies, who went in through an embrasure. The large fort was cannonaded by Bixio, who found two Neapolitan heavy guns, with ammunition, in this battery; but this would not have compelled it to surrender, had not Garibaldi's sharpshooters taken up the commanding hights, from which they could see and pick off the gunners in the batteries. This told; the artillerymen forsook the platforms, and ran into the casemates: the fort surrendered, the men partly joining Garibaldi, but mostly going home. While this was going on at Reggio, the attention of the Neapolitan steamers being engaged by this fight, by the destruction of the stranded steamer *Torino,* and by a sham embarcation of Medici's men in Messina, Cosenz succeeded in getting 1,500 men, in 60 boats, out of the Faro Lagore, and landing them on the north-west coast, between Scilla and Bagnara.[a]

---

[a] Bagnara Calabria.— *Ed.*

On the 23d, a small engagement took place near Salice,[a] a little beyond Reggio; fifty Garibaldians, English and French, commanded by Col. De Flotte, defeated four times their number of Neapolitans. De Flotte fell on this occasion. On the same day, Gen. Briganti, who commanded a brigade in Lower Calabria under Viale, had an interview with Garibaldi as to the conditions of his passing over into the Italian camp; this interview, however, had no other result but to show that the Neapolitans were completely demoralized. From this moment, there was no longer any question as to victory, but only as to surrender. Briganti and Melendez, the chief of the second movable brigade of Lower Calabria, had taken up a position close to the coast, between Villa San Giovanni and Scilla, extending their left toward the hills near Fiumara-di-Muro. Their united forces might be computed at some 3,600 men.

Garibaldi, placing himself in communication with Cosenz, who had landed in the rear of this body, drew a complete net round them and then quietly awaited their surrender, which took place on the 24th, toward evening. He kept their arms, and permitted the men to go home if they liked, which most of them did. The fort of Punta-di-Pezzo surrendered also, and the posts of the Alla Fiumare, Torre del Cavallo, and Scilla followed the example, discouraged as much by the rifle-shots from the commanding hights as by the general defection of the other forts and the troops in the field. Thus not only was the perfect command of both sides of the straits secured, but the whole of Lower Calabria conquered, and the troops sent to its defense taken prisoners and dismissed to their homes in less than five days.

This series of defeats broke every capability of further resistance in the Neapolitan army. The officers of the remaining battalions of Viale, at Monteleone, came to the conclusion to defend their position for an hour, to save appearances, and then to lay down their arms. The insurrection in the other provinces made rapid progress; whole regiments refused to march against the insurgents, and desertions took place in bodies, even among the troops guarding Naples. And thus the road to Naples was finally opened to the hero of Italy.

Written about September 6, 1860   Reproduced from the newspaper

First published in the *New-York Daily Tribune*, No. 6058, September 24, 1860 as a leading article

---

[a] Saliche Calabria.— *Ed.*

Karl Marx

BRITISH COMMERCE

London, Sept. 8, 1860

The *Tribune* was the first paper which called attention to the serious decline of the British export trade to the East Indies, a decline most conspicuous in the great staple articles, viz.: cotton goods and cotton yarns.[a] The reaction hence arising has begun to be felt in Lancashire and Yorkshire, at the very moment when the home market is contracting in consequence of a harvest which is full five weeks later than that of last year, and, despite the improving prospects since Thursday, the 30th of August, will, at all events, fall below an average yield. The British Chambers of Commerce have, consequently, taken the alarm, and assailed the central government with protests against the New Indian Customs' Act, by which the duty upon the staple imports from Great Britain was increased from 5 to 10 per cent.; that is to say, at a rate of 100 per cent. The English press, which, till then, had cautiously abstained from touching this point, has thus at last been compelled to break through its reserve. The London *Economist* treats us to the "Trade of India", and "The Cause of its Depression."[b] Apart from the circumstance of *The Economist* being considered the first English authority in matters of this kind, its articles on India derive peculiar interest from their connexion with the writing-desk of Mr. Wilson, the present Indian Chancellor of the Exchequer. The first part of the article, an attempt at disengaging the late Indian customs legislation from all responsibility for the present contraction of the Indian market, is best answered by the necessity

---

[a] See this volume, pp. 406-08.— *Ed.*

[b] "The Trade of India. The Cause of Its Depression", *The Economist*, No. 889, September 8, 1860, pp. 977, 978.— *Ed.*

to which the Governor-General at Calcutta has been put, of
convening, at Calcutta, a committee, to consist of representatives
of the Revenue Boards of Calcutta, Bombay, and Madras, and
their respective Chambers of Commerce, and to be charged with
the task of revising and readjusting the tariff lately introduced.
That tariff, as I stated when first introducing this subject to your
readers,[a] did not create the Indian commercial crisis, whose
outbreak it, however, accelerated by its sudden introduction at a
time when the Indian commerce was already bloated to a size
beyond its natural capacity. The glut of British commodities in the
Indian market and of Indian commodities in the English market is
avowed by *The Economist*.

"We believe," he says, "it will be admitted on all hands that the enormous
profits made in the Indian trade during a portion of last year, led to a sudden and
large increase of supplies to the market, more than was required for any
consumption, as far as this country was concerned, and to a very extensive
speculative trade by the native capitalists for the supply of the markets in the
interior from the seaports. For example, the exports of cotton piece goods to
British India amounted [...] in 1859 to the value of £12,043,000 against £9,299,000
in 1858 and £5,714,000 in 1857; and of yarns the exports were in 1859 £2,546,000
against £1,969,000 in 1858, and £1,147,000 in 1857. For a long time goods were
taken off as rapidly as they arrived, and as long as prices continued to rise, there
was no lack of speculative Mahajuns[b] to make purchases and to consign to the
markets of the interior; and there is no doubt, from the best information we can
obtain, that *large stocks of goods accumulated at all the markets in the North-West*. Upon
this point the testimony of Mirzapur, Allahabad, Lucknow, Agra, Delhi, Amritsar and
Lahore is uniform."[c]

The Economist then proceeds to detail some circumstances which
contributed to consolidate in a certain sense the glut in the Indian
markets. The main cause—the continuance of large supplies from
England—he does not even allude to. In the first instance, then,
the Autumn crops of 1859 throughout northern India, consequent
upon the drouth generally prevailing, fell much below an average,
and were affected both as to quality and quantity. Hence a high
range of the prices of provisions through the Winter and Spring,
which, later on in the season, was still more enhanced by famine
prospects. Furthermore, with scarcity and high prices, there was
raging the disease.

"Throughout the whole of the North-West, the cholera prevailed to so alarming
an extent among the densely-peopled cities, that the ordinary business of life was in
many cases suspended, and the population fled as from an invading enemy."

---

[a] See this volume, pp. 406-08.— *Ed.*

[b] Usurers.— *Ed.*

[c] *The Economist*, No. 889, September 8, 1860, p. 978; Marx's italics.— *Ed.*

But, worst of all,

"Upper India was threatened, for a month or six weeks before the departure of the last mail, with a misfortune most appalling. The rains, upon which alone the Autumn crops depend, usually fall by the middle or at latest the end of June. This year, up to the middle of July, not a drop of rain had fallen. From the north-west frontier down to Lower Bengal, from the Khyber pass to Benares, including the great Doabs of the Sutlej, the Jumna, and the Ganges, all was one arid, hard, and immovable surface of parched earth. It was only in the few exceptional places which were moistened by the rivers passing through them, or by the tributaries of the great irrigation works, the Jumna and Ganges canals, that any cultivation was possible. The prospect of a famine equal to that of 1837 and 1838 created on all hands the greatest apprehension. Prices rose still more. Cattle were dying in numbers or being drawn to the hills in place of tilling the soil, and the people are described as being on the borders of starvation."[a]

The worst apprehensions, however, have been set to rest, according to the telegraphic accounts received and published at Calcutta during the eight days previous to the departure of the last mail, which left on the 27th of July. Rains had at last fallen copiously, and in proper time to avert a famine, if not to secure a good crop.

The details given by *The Economist* go far to prove that for the next future there exists not the least prospect of a revival in the Indian trade, which had already fallen off about £2,000,000 for the first half year of 1860 as compared with the first half year of 1859. The Australian markets exhibit also all the symptoms of contraction consequent upon over-trade. The trade with France, which was all at once to assume immense proportions by virtue of the Commercial Treaty,[b] has on the contrary declined by more than £1,000,000, as will be seen by the following statement[c]:

Six months ended June 30,	1859.	1860.
Imports from France	£9,615,065	£8,523,983
Exports to France	2,358,912	2,324,665
Total	£11,973,977	£10,848,648

The heavy decline in the British import trade from France may be accounted for by the high prices of provisions in France during this year, while in 1859 corn and meal had formed a principal item in the French exports to England. Great stress is laid on the increased rate at which the United States, in return for the present

---

[a] loc. cit.— *Ed.*
[b] See this volume, pp. 341-44.— *Ed.*
[c] *The Economist*, No. 888, September 1, 1860, p. 953.— *Ed.*

large exports of provisions to the United Kingdom, are presumed to become consumers of English manufactures. But though there will always be some proportion between the exports and the imports of a country, the above conclusion seems somewhat rash, if we are to judge from the movements of the Anglo-American trade in the first half years of 1859 and 1860. There we shall find[a]:

	1859.	1860.
British Export to the United States...	£11,625,920	£9,366,647
British Imports from United States...	17,301,790	25,618,472

so that during the same epoch, in which the British imports from the United States increased by more than 8,000,000, the British exports to the United States decreased by more than 2,000,000. The only branches of international British trade which have enlarged are the Anglo-Turkish trade, the Anglo-Chinese trade, and the Anglo-German trade. Now Turkey is just being convulsed by Russian and French interference. China is convulsed by the English themselves, and Germany, while suffering in many parts from a deficient harvest, stands on the eve of grave political convulsions at home, and serious collisions abroad. As to the Anglo-Chinese trade, I still remark that some part of its increase is certainly due to the war demand; that part of the increased exports to China were only so many goods abstracted from the Indian market, and thrown, by way of experiment, on the Chinese market, and, lastly, that the import from China continues to be of much more importance than the export to China, as will be seen from the following figures[a]:

Six months ending June 30.

	1859.	1860.
Imports from China, including Hong Kong	£5,070,691	£5,526,054
Exports to China, exclusive of Hong Kong	1,001,709	1,622,525
Exports to Hong Kong	976,703	1,236,262
Total	£7,049,103	£8,384,841

Meanwhile, unexpected failures in most branches of business continue to feed a general feeling of distrust. The subjoined

---

[a] loc. cit.— Ed.

summary of the till-now-ascertained liabilities and assets of the late failures in the leather trade will show that the assets, on an average, but amount to 5s. 6d. in the pound, leaving to the holders of the bills of the fallen firms a loss of £1,471,589.

LIABILITIES. [a]

Firms.

In bankruptcy	9	£1,530,991
Winding up or compromised	15	499,806
Particulars not published	10	....
Total	34	£2,030,797

ASSETS.

		Amounts.	In the £.	Defic'y
In bankruptcy	9	£342,652	4s. 6d.	£1,188,339
Winding up or compromised	15	216,556	8s. 8d.	283,250
Particulars not published	10	....	....	....
Total	34	£559,208	5s. 6d.	£1,471,589

Written on September 8, 1860

Reproduced from the newspaper

First published in the *New-York Daily Tribune*, No. 6063, September 29, 1860

[a] *The Economist*, No. 889, September 8, 1860, p. 992.— *Ed.*

Karl Marx

RUSSIA USING AUSTRIA.—THE MEETING AT WARSAW

Berlin, 17th September, 1860

Of all the countries in Europe, Germany presents, at this moment, the most curious, the most intricate, and the most lamentable spectacle. The real state of German affairs will be best understood from a simple juxtaposition of two facts, the recent meeting of the German National Association at Coburg, and the impending meeting of the principal German princes at Warsaw. [343] While the former aspires to the unification of the fatherland, by abandoning German Austria and confiding in Prussia, the Regent of Prussia[a] himself rests his prospects of resistance against French aggression upon the restoration of the Holy Alliance under Russian auspices. Russian foreign policy, as is well known, does not care one straw for principles, in the common meaning of the term. It is neither legitimist nor revolutionary, but improves all opportunities of territorial aggrandizement with the same facility, whether they be obtained by siding with insurgent peoples or with struggling princes. In regard to Germany, it has become the invariable policy of Russia to shift sides. She first combines with France, in order to break the resistance of Austria to her Oriental schemes, and then sides with Germany in order to enfeeble France and draw a bill upon German gratitude, to be discounted on the Vistula or the Danube. In the progress of a European complication, she will always prefer a coalition with the German princes to an alliance with the French upstarts, for the simple reason that her real force consists in her diplomatic superiority, and not in her material power. A war with Germany, her immediate neighbor, springing from an alliance with France, would reveal the real

---

[a] William, Prince of Prussia.— *Ed.*

impotency of the Northern Colossus; while in a war with France, Russia must, from her geographical position, always form the reserve, forcing Germany to do the real work, and keeping in store for herself the fruits of the victory. Coalesced empires resemble in this point the different corps of an army. The vanguard and the center have to bear the decisive shock, but the reserve decides the battle and carries the day. German dreamers may flatter themselves with the delusive hope that Russia, while laboring under the high pressure of an internal social struggle, in the emancipation movement, will for once give the lie to Karamzin, the Russian historian's maxim that Russian foreign policy never changes.

It has been presumed that an immense empire, distracted by a struggle of classes, and distressed by a financial crisis, would be but too glad to let Europe alone; but then the real nature of the Russian internal movement has been misunderstood. Whatever may have been his real intentions, it is no more possible for a benevolent Czar[a] to conciliate the abolition of serfdom with the continuance of his own autocracy than it proved for a benevolent Pope,[b] in 1848, to reconcile Italian unity with the vital conditions of the Papacy. Simple as the phrase of Russian serf emancipation sounds, it implies meanings the most different and aspirations the most contradictory. The vail that, in the beginning of the movement, was thrown, by a kind of general enthusiasm, over the conflicting tendencies, must necessarily be torn asunder, so soon as steps are taken to proceed from the verbal to the real. Serf emancipation, in the sense of the Czar, amounted to the destruction of the last checks still restraining the Imperial autocracy. On the one hand the relative independence of the nobles, resting upon their uncontrolled sway over the majority of the Russian people, would have been removed; on the other hand, the self-administration of the rural serf communities, based on their common property in the enslaved soil, would have been broken up by the Government scheme which aimed at the abolition of the "communist" principle. Such was serf emancipation as understood by the Central Government. The nobles, in their turn—that is to say, that influential portion of the Russian aristocracy which despaired of maintaining the old state of things—had made up their minds to grant the emancipation of the serfs on two conditions: monetary indemnity, converting the

---

[a] Alexander II.— *Ed.*
[b] Pius IX.— *Ed.*

peasants from their serfs into their mortgagees, so that, so far as material interests go, nothing would have been changed, for two or three generations at least, save the form of servitude—its patriarchal form being supplanted by its civilized form. Beside this indemnity to be paid by the serfs, they wanted another indemnity to be paid by the State. For the local power over their serfs, which they declared themselves ready to surrender, they wanted to make up by political power to be wrested from the Central Government, investing them in substance with a constitutional share in the general management of the empire.

Lastly, the serfs themselves preferred the simplest formula of the emancipation question. What they understood by it was the old state of things, minus their old landlords. In this mutual strife, where the Government, despite menaces and cajoling, split upon the opposition of the nobles and the peasants—the aristocracy upon the opposition of the Government and of their human chattels, the peasantry upon the combined opposition of their central lord and their local lords—an understanding, as is usual in such transactions, has been arrived at between the existing powers at the cost of the oppressed class. The Government and the aristocracy have agreed together to shelve the emancipation question for the present, and to again try their hands at foreign adventures. Hence the secret understanding with Louis Bonaparte in 1859 [344], and the official congress at Warsaw with the German princes in 1860. The Italian war had sufficiently broken the self-reliance of Austria to transform her from an obstacle into a tool of the Russian schemes of foreign policy, and Prussia, which had made a fool of herself by combining, during the continuance of the war, the airs of ambitious perfidy with an utter nullity of action, cannot, threatened as she is by France on her Rhenish frontiers, but follow in the wake of Austria. It was one of the great delusions of the Gotha party [345] to fancy that the blows Austria was likely to receive on the part of France would dissolve her into her constituent parts, so that Austrian Germany, disconnected from its ties with Italy, Poland, and Hungary, might easily enter into the formation of one great German empire. A long historical experience has shown us that every war which Austria may have to wage with France or Russia would not free Germany from her weight, but only make her subservient to the schemes of France or Russia. To break her up into her constituent parts by one great blow, would be bad policy on the part of those Powers, if they were possessed of the force to strike the blow; but to enfeeble Austria, in order to turn its remaining influence to their own account, was and must always be the main object of their diplomatic and military operations. Nothing but a German revolution, with one of its centers at Vienna and the other at Berlin, could shatter to pieces the Hapsburg empire, without endangering the integrity of Germany, and without subjecting its non-German dominions to French or Russian control.

The impending Warsaw Congress would immensely strengthen Louis Bonaparte's position in France, if the prospect of a conflict in Italy between the truly national party and the French party did not spoil his opportunity. As it is, one must hope that the Warsaw Congress will at last open the eyes of Germany, and teach her that either to withstand encroachments from without or realize unity and liberty at home, she must clear her own house of its dynastic landlords.

Written on September 17, 1860   Reproduced from the newspaper

First published in the *New-York Daily Tribune*, No. 6072, October 10, 1860

Karl Marx

AFFAIRS IN PRUSSIA.
[—PRUSSIA, FRANCE AND ITALY]

Berlin, September 27, 1860

The Prince Regent[a] who, as I have already told your readers, since his accession to supreme power, is a sullen and dogged Legitimist at the core of his heart, despite the gaudy insignia of liberalism he has been decked out with by the official oracles of the Prussian fool's paradise, has just caught an occasion of publicly giving vent to his long compressed feelings. It is a strange fact, but nevertheless it is a fact, that the Prince Regent of Prussia has for the nonce shut out the Garibaldians from the fortress of Messina, and saved that important military stronghold for his beloved brother, King Bombalino[b] of Naples. The Prussian Ambassador at Naples, Count of Perponcher, a personage as notorious for his staunch Legitimism as Baron of Canitz, the Prussian Ambassador at Rome, had, like most of his colleagues, followed King Bombalino to Gaeta, where the Prussian war corvette *Loreley* was placed for the protection of German subjects. Now on the 15th of September, the citadel of Messina was on the point of capitulating. The officers had declared for Victor Emmanuel, and sent a deputation to Gaeta in order to tell the King that the place was no longer tenable. On the following day that deputation was shipped back to Messina by the war corvette *Loreley*, with a Prussian Commissary on board, who, on the arrival of the vessel, proceeded immediately to the citadel, where he had a long conversation with the Neapolitan commander. Beside his personal eloquence, the Prussian agent exhibited a bundle of dispatches on the part of the King, encouraging the General to resistance, and strongly inveigh-

---

[a] William, Prince of Prussia.— *Ed.*

[b] Francis II.— *Ed.*

ing against every proposition of giving up, even under the most favorable conditions, the forts still sufficiently provisioned for several months. During the stay of the Prussian Commissary, cries of "Evviva il Re!"[a] were heard ringing from the citadel, and when he left, the transactions entered into, with a view to stipulate the terms of the capitulation, were at once broken off. On the arrival of this news, Count Cavour hastened to lodge a complaint at Berlin because of "the abuse of the Prussian flag," and the violation of the promise to preserve perfect neutrality in the revolutionary war of Italy. Despite the justness of the complaint, Count Cavour of all men was the man least fitted to prefer it. Herr von Schleinitz, whose dispatches had, during the war of 1859,[346] obtained some notoriety for their soft-sawder style, their seesaw reasonings, and the incomparable art of drawing out the thread of their verbosity finer than the staple of their argument— Herr von Schleinitz eagerly improved the opportunity to insinuate himself with the Prince Regent, and to change for once his humble sotto voce[b] for the shrill tones of haughtiness. He administered a peremptory rebuke to Count Cavour, who was plainly told that Sicily had not yet become a Sardinian province, that the treaty obligations were daily violated by the Court of Turin, and that if Cavour wanted to protest against foreign intervention in Italy, he had better lodge his protest at the Tuileries.

The withdrawal of the French Embassador from Turin is here considered a transparent dodge, since it is perfectly known that immediately after the meeting at Chambéry between Louis Bonaparte and Messrs. Farini and Cialdini, the latter was intrusted with the command of the Piedmontese invasion of the Papal States. That invasion was planned at Chambéry with a view to taking the game out of the hands of Garibaldi and replacing it into the hands of Cavour, the French Emperor's most pliant servant. The revolutionary war in Southern Italy is known to be considered at the Tuileries not as a fortuitous avalanche of a ball once set rolling, but as the deliberate act of the independent Italian party who, ever since Louis Napoleon's ingress of the *via sacra*,[347] had proclaimed the rising of the South as the only means of taking off the nightmare of French protection. In point of fact, Mazzini in his proclamation to the Italian people, dated May 16, 1859, stated plainly:

---

[a] "Long Live the King!"—*Ed.*
[b] Undertone.—*Ed.*

"With due reserve the people of the North may rally round the banners of Victor Emmanuel, wherever the Austrian is encamped or neighboring; the insurrection of the South must take a different and more independent course. Rising, rising united, installing a Provisional Government, arming, selecting a strategical point where it may keep its ground and attract the volunteers of the North, Naples and Sicily may still save the cause of Italy, and constitute its power, represented by a national camp. Thanks to that camp and the Northern volunteers, Italy, at the end of the war, whatever be the intentions of its initiators, may still become the supreme arbiter of its own destinies.... Such a popular manifestation would exclude every new division of Italy, every importation of new dynasties, every peace of the Adige or the Mincio, every abandonment of every part of the Italian soil. And the name of Rome is inseparable from the name of Italy. There, in the sacred city, stands the palladium of our national unity. It is the duty of Rome not to swell the Sardinian army by a mob of volunteers, but to prove to Imperial France that the prop of the Papal despotism at Rome will never be acknowledged the sword-bearer of Italian independence.... If Rome forgets its duties, we must act for the Romans. Rome represents the unity of the fatherland. Sicily, Naples, and the volunteers of the North must constitute its army."

Such were the words of Mazzini in May, 1859, reechoed by Garibaldi[a] when, at the head of the popular army created in Sicily and Naples, he promised to proclaim the Unity of Italy from the top of the Quirinal.[348]

You will remember how Cavour, from the beginning, did everything in his power to beset Garibaldi's expedition with difficulties; how, after the first success won by the popular hero, he sent La Farina, in company with two Bonapartist agents, over to Palermo, in order to deprive the conqueror of his dictatorship; how, later on, every military move of Garibaldi was met, on the part of Cavour, first by diplomatic and at last by military countermoves.[b] After the fall of Palermo and the progress to Messina, Garibaldi's popularity towered so high among the people and the army of Paris, that Louis Napoleon considered it prudent to try the wheedling method. When Gen. Türr, at that time disabled from active service, had repaired to Paris, he became quite overwhelmed with Imperial flatteries. He was not only an honored guest at the Palais Royal, but was even admitted to the Tuileries,[349] initiated into the Emperor's unbounded enthusiasm for his "annexed" subject, the Nizzard hero, and laden with tokens of good will, such as rifled cannon, and so forth. At the same time Türr's mind was impressed with the Emperor's

---

[a] Giuseppe Mazzini, "La Guerra", *Pensiero ed Azione*, No. 17, May 2-16, 1859; Giuseppe Garibaldi's address to the people of Palermo on September 10, 1860, *L'Indépendance belge*, No. 261, September 17, 1860; see also *The Times*, No. 23728, September 18, 1860.— *Ed.*

[b] See this volume, pp. 421-24.— *Ed.*

conviction that Garibaldi, after he had made sure of Naples and the Neapolitan Navy, could do nothing better than to try, in unison with the Hungarian refugees, a landing at Fiume, there to plant the banner of a Hungarian revolution. But Louis Napoleon proceeded from altogether false premises when he supposed that Türr was the man, or even fancied himself to be the man, to exercise the least control over Garibaldi's course of action. Türr, whom I know personally, is a brave soldier and an intelligent officer, but beyond the sphere of military activity he is a mere zero, below the average of common mortals, lacking not only training of mind and a cultivated intellect, but that natural shrewdness and instinct which may stand in place of education, learning, and experience. He is, in one word, an easy-going jolly good fellow, gifted with an extraordinary degree of credulity, but certainly not the man to politically control anybody, not to speak of Garibaldi, who, with a fire of soul, still owns his grain of that subtle Italian genius you may trace in Dante no less than in Machiavelli. Türr, then, having proved a miscalculation, such at least he is spoken of in the entourage of the Tuileries. Kossuth was tried and dispatched to Garibaldi to bring him round to the views of the Emperor, and to bring him off his true scent, which points to Rome. Garibaldi used Kossuth as a means of stirring the revolutionary enthusiasm, and had him consequently feasted with popular ovations, but knew wisely how to distinguish between his name, representing a popular cause, and his mission, hiding a Bonapartist snare. Kossuth returned to Paris quite chopfallen; but, to give an earnest of his fidelity to the Imperialist interests, has now, as reported by the *Opinion nationale*, the Plon-Plon *Moniteur*, addressed a letter to Garibaldi, wherein he calls upon the latter to conciliate himself with Cavour, to abstain from every attempt at Rome, in order to not estrange France, the true hope of the oppressed nationalities, and even to let Hungary alone, the latter country being not yet ripe for an insurrection.

I need not tell you that here, at Berlin, the shares of ministerial liberalism have experienced a heavy fall, consequent upon the impending Warsaw Congress; where, not only the rulers by the grace of God are to shake hands, but their respective Ministers of Foreign Affairs: Prince Gorchakoff, Count Rechberg, and our own Herr von Schleinitz, are to meet in the snug corner of a gilded antechamber, there to give an orthodox turn to the coming history of mankind.

The transactions of Prussia with Austria, as to a new commercial treaty between the Zollverein and Austria, such as foreshadowed

by the treaty of February 19, 1853,[350] may now be considered to
be broken off, since the Prussian Cabinet has positively declared
that any assimilation, or even approximation of tariffs was out of
the question.

Written on September 27, 1860   Reproduced from the newspaper

First published in the *New-York Daily
Tribune*, No. 6076, October 15, 1860

Frederick Engels

PREPARATIONS FOR WAR IN PRUSSIA

Berlin, Oct. 23, 1860

The anger and the dread felt by our Liberals at the Prince Regent's[a] participation in the Warsaw Congress, find, as is usual with the grievances of genuine Prussian Liberals, their vent in bitter aspersions of Austria and its new-fangled Constitution.[351] In the first place, Francis Joseph will never be forgiven, for having bereft these gentlemen of their greatest consolation, and the standing topic of their verbose self-righteousness, viz., the contrast between "constitutional" Prussia and "absolutist" Austria. The Austrian patent, of course, is open, not only to cavils, but to serious misgivings of every kind. The circumstances under which and the hands by which the gift is bestowed, stamp it with the character of a shift, rather than a sincere concession. Once before, on the 4th of March, 1849, Francis Joseph promulgated the outlines of a constitution, only to cancel them the following year, after the fortune of war had declared on his side.[352] But, then, there exists no instance on the records of history of princes having ever curtailed their own privileges, and yielded to popular claims, except under a heavy pressure from without, and there exists no instance of their having kept faith whenever they could dare to break their oaths and their pledges with impunity. The old Hungarian Constitution[353] has not been restored in its integrity, since the two most important rights of voting the ways and means, and the levies of troops, are transferred from the Diet at Pesth to the Central Imperial Council at Vienna, which latter being intended to form the States General of the whole empire, finds itself invested with attributes likely to become permanent sources

---

[a] William, Prince of Prussia.— Ed.

of strife between itself and the different national or provincial Diets. The Constitutions of the German and Slavonic provinces being limited to the most general and vague outlines, may be made nothing or everything of. The greatest fault found with the patent on the part of the Magyars is the separation of Croatia and Servia and Transylvania from Hungary, and the grant to those provinces of different independent Diets; but if the events of 1848-49 be recalled to mind, it may be justly doubted whether the Croats, Slavonians, Serbs, and Wallachians will be inclined to share in this Magyar grievance, and back it by their support. The Vienna statesmen, in this instance, seem rather to have played a clever trick upon the principle of nationality, and turned it to their own account.

But, as for the general Diet of the whole empire, under the name of the Imperial Council, seated at Vienna and composed of the respective delegates appointed by the different Diets of Galicia, Hungary, Transylvania, Croatia, Servia, Venetia, and the German provinces, being placed beyond the pale of allegiance to the Diet of the German Confederation, will it not cut asunder the relations that have hitherto obtained between German Austria and the German Confederation? This is the great theme now harped upon by official Prussian Liberalism, which will never stand in want of arguments for its pet idea, the exclusion of Austrian Germany from the German Confederation. But all this reasoning proceeds from a false premise in clinging to the letter of Francis Joseph's patent. While the latter must be considered, on the part of the Austrian dynasty, as a clever device, it affords to the various peoples crushed under Hapsburg sway a precious handle for working out their own destinies and reopening the era of revolutions. For the present, the Austrian Constitution will have done much good in humbling the Pharisean pride of the Prussian mock Liberals, and stripping the Hohenzollern dynasty of the only advantage it could boast over its rival, that of carrying on the old concern of the bureaucrat and the soldier under the more respectable form of constitutionalism.

To give you an insight into the real state of this much-vaunted, "regenerated" Prussia, it will be necessary to recur to the changes that have lately taken place in the organization of the Prussian army. You will remember that the Prussian Chamber of Deputies, while lacking on the one side the courage to affront public opinion by an open sanction of the Government proposals for the reorganization of the army, and lacking on the other side the courage to make a decided stand against the martinet leanings of the Prince Regent, hit upon the usual expedient of weakness—a middle course, neither fish nor flesh. It refused to pass the Government plan for the reorganization of the army, but voted $9,500,000 for putting the army into a state fit to encounter the dangers apprehended from without.[a] In other words, the Prussian Deputies voted the ways and means wanted by the Government for carrying out its plan, but voted them on false pretexts. Hardly had the Prussian Parliament been adjourned when the Ministry, openly breaking through the conditions on which the grant was obtained, began, without further ado, to introduce the changes in the organization of the army willed by the Prince Regent and rejected by the so-called representatives. During the recess of the Parliament, the standing army has been *doubled*, being raised from 40 regiments to 72 regiments of the line and 9 regiments of the guard. The permanent annual expenses for the military budget have thus, by the supreme will of the Prince Regent, and in open violation, not only of the will of the people, but of the vote of its mock representatives, been raised by 100 per cent. But do not fancy the Prince of Hohenzollern or any of his colleagues risks the fate of Strafford.[354] There will be some low grumbling, pickled with fervent assertions of dynastic loyalty, and unbounded confidence in the Cabinet, and this will be all. Now, considering that even the old army organization, founded as it was upon a merely agricultural population, had become an intolerable drawback upon the resources and the productive activity of a people which in the course of time had engaged in manufactures, it will be easily understood how the army, now doubled in numbers, must grind down the best energies of the masses, and drain the springs of national wealth. The Prussian army may now boast of being the largest in Europe in proportion to population and national resources.

You know that a Hohenzollern ruler, when speaking of himself, or when spoken of by his cabinet and his officials, goes by the name of *Kriegsherr*, that is to say, "Lord of War." Now this, of course, does not mean that Prussian kings and regents lord it over the chances of war. Their great anxiety to keep peace, and their known propensity for being thrashed in the open field show better. By that title of "Lord of War," so dearly cherished by Hohenzollern rulers, it is rather understood that the true prop of their kingly power must be sought for, not in the people, but in a

---

[a] On this sitting of the Prussian Diet (February 10, 1860) see the *Stenographische Berichte über die Verhandlungen*, Bd. I, Berlin, 1860, S. 95-106.— *Ed.*

portion of the people, separated from the mass, opposed to it, distinguished by certain badges, trained to passive obedience, drilled into a mere instrument of the dynasty which owns it as its property and uses it according to its caprice. A Prussian king would, therefore, rather abdicate than allow his army to swear obedience to the Constitution. Hence a Hohenzollern ruler, being the king of his people only as far as he is the "Lord of War," in other words, the proprietor of the army, must, before all things, dote on it, fondle it, flatter it, and feed it with always increasing morsels of the national wealth. This great aim has been obtained by the new military organization. The number of officers has been doubled, and the rapid promotion to higher grades in the French, Austrian, and Russian armies, which the Prussian officers had cast longingly anxious eyes upon, has been secured to them without exposing their lives and limbs to the least hazard. Hence there is just now prevailing, not among the common soldiers, but among the officers of the Prussian army, a vast amount of enthusiasm for the Prince Regent and his "liberal" Ministers. At the same time the aristocratic fox-hunters, grumbling at the liberal phrases of the new régime, have been quite conciliated by the new occasion afforded them for fastening their younger sons on the purse of the country. There is one drawback to all this, even from the dynastic standpoint. Prussia has now concentrated all its available forces into one standing army. That army once beaten, there will be no reserve to fall back upon.

Written on October 23, 1860   Reproduced from the newspaper

First published in the *New-York Daily Tribune*, No. 6097, November 8, 1860

Karl Marx

GREAT BRITAIN—A MONEY STRINGENCY[a]

London, Nov. 10, 1860

An event long ago predicted has set in, a drain of bullion, and, consequent upon it, a rise in the rate of discount. Yesterday the Bank of England raised the rate of discount from 4 to $4^1/_2$ per cent. In the corresponding month of 1859 the bank rate did not exceed 3 per cent, despite the then enormous shipments of silver to the East, amounting to £13,234,305. The obvious object of the Bank was to put a check on the drain of bullion from its vaults, which, amounting to £16,255,951 on the 26th of September last, is now reduced to £13,897,085, not including £43,000 taken from the Bank yesterday. The drain, beginning on Sept. 26, has been constantly on the increase until it has reached this week almost £300,000. The large imports of corn were, of course, sure to lead, sooner or later, to an emigration of the precious metals, but the payments of the corn bills being not yet due, the present drain cannot be accounted for in this manner, and, moreover, it takes place concurrently with a rate of discount higher in London than in Paris, Amsterdam, Brussels and Hamburg, while simultaneously the gold export leaves no profit as an exchange operation.

Whither, then, does the gold go? To the vaults of the Bank of France. The present discount rate of the Bank of France is only 3 per cent, although that concern has lost about £4,000,000 since the end of August, while its discounts for August and September have increased by about £3,000,000. Any vulgar bank would, under such circumstances, have raised its rate of discount, but Louis Bonaparte, afraid to cause a *visible* disturbance of the

---

[a] Marx based his analysis on the article "The Rise in the Bank Rate of Discount", *The Economist* of November 10, 1860, pp. 1232 and 1242.—*Ed.*

money market, orders the Bank to purchase gold at a loss, and
will force it to continue proceeding with this certainly not
mercantile operation. On the other hand, the Bank of England
proves that it is unable to check the present drain by the rise in
the rate of interest. Yesterday, for instance, no bullion was taken
from the Issue Department of the Bank, but a considerable
quantity in sovereigns was drawn from the Banking Department.
It is one of the necessary consequences of Sir Robert Peel's blessed
bank acts of 1844 and 1845 [355] that the mercantile public are
constantly misled as to the real amount of the precious metals
exported, since the Banking Department furnishes no public
returns of the sovereigns withdrawn from its chest.

The rise in the official discount rate of the Bank of England,
especially if continuing, will, of course, impose upon the Bank of
France the necessity of following in the same direction, and thus
prevent Louis Bonaparte from any longer commanding the Bank
Directors to buy gold at a loss, in order to hide a visible
derangement of the money market. Still, the English drain of
bullion will not be stopped by that eventuality, since, in proper
time, the corn bills must fall due and be paid for in cash.

Written on November 10, 1860   Reproduced from the newspaper

First published in the *New-York Daily
Tribune*, No. 6111, November 24, 1860

Frederick Engels

AUSTRIA—PROGRESS OF THE REVOLUTION

London, Dec. 24, 1860

The revolution in Austria gets along at a racing pace. Only two months ago, Francis Joseph acknowledged by his *diploma* of the 20th October,[356] that his empire was in a state of revolution, and tried to remedy it by bribing Hungary by a promise that her ancient Constitution, in some curtailed shape or other, was to be restored. The diploma, although a concession to the revolutionary movement, was in its conception one of those master-strokes of treacherous policy which form such a prominent part in Austrian diplomacy. Hungary was to be bought by concessions apparently very great, and made to appear still greater by being placed side by side with the scanty allowance allotted to the German and Slavonic provinces, as well as with the mockery of an Imperial Parliament which the diploma proposed to establish. But in the details of the work the cloven foot of treachery was apparent enough to turn the contemplated master-stroke into a piece of egregious folly and a pledge given to the revolutionary movement of the helpless weakness of the Government. Not only was the voting of supplies and soldiers to be taken from the Hungarian Diet and to be transferred to the Central Parliament and partly even to the Emperor alone—as if a Government just compelled to eat all the political leek it had grown during the last ten years, was still strong enough to withhold such rights from its very conquerors—but the scanty and vague nature of the rights conferred on the other portions of the empire and on the central representation at once proved, by contrast, the insincerity of the whole affair. And when the provincial constitutions for Styria, Carinthia, Salzburg, and Tyrol[357] were published—constitutions giving the lion's share of representation to the nobility and clergy, and maintaining the old distinction of estates—when the old Ministry remained in office, there could be no longer any doubt as to what was intended. Hungary was to be soothed, and then to be made the cat's-paw to help absolutist Austria out of her troubles; and absolutist Austria once strong again, Hungary knew well enough from experience what her fate would be. The very fact of the unlimited and indiscriminate establishment of the Hungarian language as the only official language in Hungary, was intended for nothing else but to excite the Slavonians, Roumans, and Germans of Hungary against the Magyar race. The Hungarian old Conservatives (*vulgo*, Aristocrats), who had concluded this bargain with the Emperor, lost all standing at home by it; they had attempted to barter away the two most essential rights of the Diet. In fact, the Imperial diploma deceived nobody. While in the German provinces public opinion at once compelled the old municipal councils (appointed by the Emperor after the Revolution) to give way before new men, who are now being chosen by popular election, the Hungarians began to reestablish their old county officers and county assemblies which, before 1849, formed all the local authorities in the country.[358] In either case, it is a good sign that the opposition party at once secured local and communal power, instead of merely clamoring for an ephemeral change of Ministry and neglecting to secure the important positions left open to it in more modest spheres of action. In Hungary, the forms of the ancient local administration, as reorganized in 1848, at once placed all the civil power in the hands of the people, and left to the Vienna Government no other alternative but to cede or to have recourse at once to military force. Here, then, the movement naturally went on most rapidly. The demand for the full restoration of the Constitution, as amended in 1848, and including all the laws agreed upon in that year between the Diet and the King, arose from one end of the land to the other. Not satisfied with that, the immediate repeal of the tobacco monopoly (introduced illegally since 1848), and of all other laws imposed without the consent of the Diet, was asked for. The levying of taxes was openly declared illegal, until the Diet should have voted them; not one-third of the taxes due were paid; the young men called out to serve in the army were called upon to resist enrolment, or to abscond; and Imperial eagles were pulled down, and, worst of all, in this transition state the Government had no means to resist this agitation. Wherever the county assemblies were convoked they pronounced themselves unanimously in this sense;

and the Conference of Hungarian notables assembled at Gran,[a] under the Presidency of the Primate of Hungary,[b] in order to propose to the Government a basis for the election of a Diet, without deliberation almost, and unanimously, declared the democratic electoral law of 1848 to be still in force.

That was more than the old Conservatives had expected when they made the compromise with the Emperor. They were completely "*débordés.*"[c] The revolutionary waves threatened to drown them. The Government itself saw that something must be done. But what could the Cabinet of Vienna do?

The attempt at bribing Hungary was on the eve of signally failing. What, if the Cabinet now tried to bribe the Germans? They never enjoyed such rights as the Hungarians, perhaps less would satisfy them. The Austrian monarchy, to exist, must use the various nationalities among its subjects in turns against each other. The Slavonians could be used in the utmost extremity only; they were too much connected with Russia by Panslavist agitation; be it then for the Germans. Count Goluchowski, the hated Polish aristocrat (a renegade from the Polish cauşe to that of Austrian service), was sacrificed, and Chevalier von Schmerling was made Minister of the Interior. He had been Minister of the German ephemeral empire in 1848, and afterward of Austria; this post he quitted when the Constitution of 1849 was definitively abolished. He passed for a Constitutionalist. But there was, again, so much hesitation and indecision before he was definitively called in, that the effect was again lost. People asked what good was Schmerling if all the other Ministers remained? There was a cooling down of all hopes, even before he was definitively appointed; and instead of a frank concession, his nomination only appeared as another proof of weakness. But while in the German Provinces the opposition was satisfied with securing local power, and receiving every move of the Government with undisguised distrust, and dissatisfaction, in Hungary the movement went on. Before even Schmerling had been nominated, the old Conservative Hungarians called into office, Szécsen and Vay at their head, acknowledged the impossibility of retaining their positions; and the Ministry of the Emperor had to undergo the humiliation of inviting two Hungarian Ministers of 1848, colleagues up to Autumn of that year of Batthyány, who was shot, of Kossuth and Szemere—of

---

a Estergom.— *Ed.*

b János Scitovszky.— *Ed.*

c Overwhelmed.— *Ed.*

inviting Messrs. Déak and Eötvös, to enter the Ministry of the man who had trodden down Hungary with Russian assistance. They are not appointed yet; the system of hesitation and vacillation, of higgling and haggling about trifles, is in its full glory yet, but if they accept, they are sure to be ultimately appointed.

Thus Francis Joseph is being driven from one concession to another, and if it should come to pass that in January the two Diets should meet, one at Pesth for Hungary, and her annexes, and the other at Vienna for the remaining provinces of the empire, fresh concessions will be wrung from him. But instead of reconciling his subjects, every fresh concession will exasperate them more by the undisguised insincerity with which it is given. And what with the reminiscences of the past—with the maneuvers of the Hungarian emigration in the pay of Louis Napoleon; with the fact that a liberal Austria is impossible, because Austria's foreign policy must always be reactionary, and, therefore, at once create collisions between the Crown and the Parliament, and with Louis Napoleon speculating upon this fact—it is probable enough that 1861 may see the Austrian empire dissolve into its component parts.

Written on December 24, 1860   Reproduced from the newspaper

First published in the *New-York Daily Tribune*, No. 6152, January 12, 1861

FROM THE PREPARATORY MATERIALS

Karl Marx

[EXTRACTS FROM IMRE SZABÓ'S WORK *THE STATE POLICY OF MODERN EUROPE, FROM THE BEGINNING OF THE SIXTEENTH CENTURY TO THE PRESENT TIME.* IN TWO VOLUMES, LONDON, 1857][359]

[Volume I]

1) *1520-1559. Francis I and Charles V*

(*1523.* Dissolution of the Union of Calmar[360]; Gustavus Vasa elected king of Sweden.)

1520. Charles (V) crowned emperor at Aix-la-Chapelle[a] (master of *Burgundy, Spain, Sicily, Naples* and *Navarre* and *Austria* (since Maximilian I's death in 1519)).

Milan, claimed by Louis XII by the right of his grandmother, of the family of Visconti, conquered by Francis I in 1515 from the Sforzas; now claimed by Charles as a fief of the Empire. Francis also revived the claims of France to Naples and Burgundy. Thus commenced a 14 years' war, apparently for the sake of Milan. Henry VIII in the Austrian alliance. French (after defeat of Bicoco[b]) forced by a Spanish army to abandon the Duchy of Milan. Rome, Venice, Florence and Genoa enter the Austrian alliance. Francis I without an ally; Charles Bourbon (the Constable) goes over to Charles.

Second French campaign (in Italy) under General Bonnivet. The French routed. Charles Bourbon enters the Provence, English prepare to invade Picardy. Francis drives the invaders out of the French territory, reconquers the Duchy of Milan (after the battle of Marignano).

1525. Francis beaten before Pavia, carried away prisoner to Madrid. Coalition against Charles—the small states of Italy, new pope (Clement VII), Henry VIII, Louise of Savoy (the regent of France, Francis' mother). *1526.* Francis accepts Madrid peace to get free.

League between Francis, Pope, Venice, Milan, Florence, Henry VIII.[361]

Bourbon with the Imperialists drives Sforza[c] from Milan, sacks Rome. Francis and Henry VIII declare war to Charles.

French army makes itself master of Rome, besieges Naples. Malady in the French camp, return to France.

Charles checked by the Lutheran princes of Germany and the arms of Soliman. Ottomans occupy almost the whole of Hungary, of which Ferdinand, the brother of Charles, endeavoured to possess himself. Soliman advances to the walls of Vienna.

---

[a] Aachen.— *Ed.*

[b] Bicocca.— *Ed.*

[c] Francesco II.— *Ed.*

1529. Treaty of Cambray (traité des dames).[362] Francis again renounces his claims to Milan, Naples, and Flanders. As to Burgundy, one chief point of the quarrel, only temporary arrangement: the marriage of Francis with Eleonora of Portugal, Charles' sister, being again stipulated.

Charles turns upon the Lutherans. The *princes now [have] two lines of policy, with regard to home and foreign affairs*; Pope even seeks the alliance of the infidels.

1530. Diet of Augsburg.[363] Condemnatory decree against innovation. Protestants form the *league of Schmalkalden,*[364] seek the aid of France and England. Francis enters upon the proposal; concludes also alliance with *John Zapolya,*[a] *of Hungary,* the rival of Ferdinand of Austria, and sends Rincon to Constantinople, to secure the *Sultan's assistance.* Francis marries his son[b] to Catherine of Medici, the pontiff's niece, while Henry VIII severs England from the see of Rome.[365]

1532. Temporary peace of Nuremberg (between Charles and the Protestants). Charles' expedition against Barbarossa.[c]

1535. Francis, after 6 years of peace, recommences war (*third war*), reappears in Italy; successful; dictates at Milan and Savoy. Charles returns victor from Algiers, drives the French from Italy, penetrates into the Provence where [he is] finally repulsed.

1538. Peace at Nice for 10 years. But 2 French envoys (Rincon to the Porte, Fregosa for Venice) by orders of Charles seized in Italy, assassinated. Francis recommences war. Five armies put in motion, but in vain.

1544. Peace of Crespy: Francis renounces his claims to Naples and Artois; bind[s] himself not to meddle with Navarre. (Henry VIII had again turned on the part of Charles.)

1547. † *Francis I;* his son *Henry II.* Charles turns upon the league of Schmalkalden.

1547. Victory of the Imperialists through Maurice of Saxony of Mühlberg, dissolving the league. Charles proclaims the Interim.[366] Maurice, having secured the co-operation of Henry II, surprises the Emperor in Tyrol (Charles forced *1552* to conclude the *peace of Passau* with the Protestants) same year in which the French poured into the Duchy of Lorraine, there to seize Metz, Toul and Verdun. Charles driven back from Metz and *1556* withdraws from the public scene, divides his dominions between his brother, Ferdinand of Austria, and his son Philip II. War in Italy and the Netherlands continues between Henry II and Philip II.

1559. Treaty of Château Cambresis.[d] Each party was bound to restore all the conquests made since 1551[367]; France abandoning more than 180 strong places besides Savoy. Marriage of Elizabeth, daughter of Henry II, to Philip II. Henry II †.

This (the reign of Charles V) the period of Habsburg supremacy proper. France is the first to attack it, but supported by Lutherans in Germany, Soliman, Hungary (Zapolya) and the Pope (Clément), also by the jealousy of the small Italian states.

II) *1559-1618. The Netherlands and Philip II*

1559. Francis II in France. (Religious wars in France.) *1566.* Commencement of the troubles in the Netherlands.

[a] Janos Zápolya.— *Ed.*
[b] Henry II.— *Ed.*
[c] Hadher Barbarossa.— *Ed.*
[d] Cateau-Cambrésis.— *Ed.*

First page of Marx's manuscript with extracts from Imre Szabó's work *The State Policy of Modern Europe, from the Beginning of the Sixteenth Century to the Present Time*

1572. William of Orange proclaimed governor of Holland, Zealand, Utrecht. *1579.* Union of Utrecht.

Elizabeth in England. *1562* (after treaty of Elizabeth with Protestants in France) treaty with *Charles IX* (of France). In this treaty comprehended Ferdinand (Emperor) and Philip II.

1572. Massacre of St. Bartholomew.

Till *1585* the Netherlands left to themselves. *1585.* Alliance treaty of Elizabeth with the Netherlands.

1589. Henry III, the last of the Valois, murdered. *Henry of Navarre (Henry IV).*

1593. Alliance at the Hague between Elizabeth and Henry IV; Netherlands included in it.

1598. Peace of Vervins between Henry IV and Philip II (mutual restitution of the conquests since 1559). This peace proclaimed the wane of Spanish preponderance (in the same year *Edict of Nantes*). *Philip II* †. *Philip III. (1588.* Destruction of the Armada.) Death of Elizabeth. *James I.*

1609. Treaty between Henry and Spain for the cessation of hostilities with the *United Provinces* (form of a truce of 12 years; in fact, an acknowledgment of the independence of the Low Countries). (The Spanish branch of the Habsburgs still maintained its sway over Italy and had acquired Portugal in 1581).

Henry IV's plan for the remodelling of Europe (abasement of Austria).[368] Provisions: *Italy: Pope secular Prince* (Rome, Naples, Apulia, Calabria under him); *Venice* (Republic; united with Florence, Modena, a few other small states); *Duke of Savoy* (to become king of Lombardy).

Bohemia (elective kingdom; to be annexed to it Moravia, Silesia, Lusatia[a]). *Hungary* (annexed to it the arch-duchy of Austria, Styria, Carinthia). *Poland* also to be aggrandized. *Switzerland* (to be added to it Tyrol, Alsace, and other territories). *Netherlands* (to be republic).

The House of Austria to be reduced to Spain and a few islands off the coast of the Mediterranean.

† *Henry IV* 1610.

(This period [witnesses the] downfall of the older branch of the Habsburgs.)

III) *1618-1648. (Thirty Years War)*

1617. Treaty between Gustav Adolphus and Michael Feodorowich (first Romanoff). Sweden confirmed in the possession of Carelia, Kexholm[b] and Ingria.[c] Muscovite excluded from the Gulf of Finland and the Baltic. Adolphus rendered himself master (against Poland) of Livonia and Polish Prussia. End of the 16th century extinction of the Jagellon dynasty.

Hungary and Bohemia now under the Habsburgs: the former aided, and, at the same time, clogged by Turkey in its attempts to throw off the Habsburgs.

Under Ferdinand I, Maximilian, Rudolph II (filling the XVIth century) Austria takes no part in the wars between Spain and France; appeases the Sultans with tributes and vies for Hungary.

1606. Hungary pacified by the *treaty of Vienna (Rudolph II).* Transylvania's

---

[a] Region in the middle reaches of the Elbe, Spree and Neisse rivers, inhabited by the West Slavonic tribe of Lusatians.— *Ed.*

[b] Priozersk.— *Ed.*

[c] The Izhora land subject to Novgorod.— *Ed.*

independence acknowledged.[369] Turkey checked by Abbas, Shah of Persia; arrested her progress to Europe.

Accession of *Ferdinand II* (archduke of Styria).

1618 commencement of the troubles in Bohemia. Bohemians offer the crown to *Frederick V* (elector of the Palatinate); his ally *Bethlen*[a] (prince of Transylvania).

28 Aug. 1619. Ferdinand II elected emperor of Germany, concludes alliance with Maximilian of Bavaria, Spain, Pope,[b] and Mary de Medicis (in the minority of Louis XIII, married to Anne, daughter of Philip III). (Duke of Angoulême *1620* concludes for France treaty with Ferdinand II at Ulm.) Philip III †. Philip IV. Protestants in Germany [find an] ally in Christian IV of Denmark; Wallenstein's army. Beginning of the war.[370] Prince of Wales married with Henrietta of France.[c]

1624. Richelieu's entrance into office.

1625. Richelieu makes war on Spain by occupying the Valtelina. *Charles I* (in England).

1626. Bethlen forced to make peace with Ferdinand II.[371] Denmark (participating in the war from 1625) forced to make a separate peace with *Ferdinand II* (1629).

1629. Ferdinand II's decree of Restitution.[372] La Rochelle surrenders to Richelieu.

1629. Richelieu mediates peace between Sweden and Poland.[373] Gustavus Adolphus (with the promise of subsidies of France) lands an army in Pomerania.

1631. Treaty between France and Sweden.

(1629, after the death of Gonzaga, Duke of Mantua,[d] Charles, Duke of Nevers, and Ferdinand of Guastalla pretenders to it. Former supported by France, latter by Austria. French army forces the pass of Susa, confirms Nevers.)[374]

1632. Battle of Lützen. Gustav Adolphus †.

1634. Defeat of the Swedes at Nördlingen. Direct participation of France in the war of Germany. France takes possession of Alsace, after its fortified places were given up to the French by their Swedish allies. New league with the Netherlands set on foot by Richelieu. *Elector of Saxe*[e] goes over to the Emperor; *peace of Prague.*[375]

War simultaneously recommenced in Spain, Italy, the Netherlands, on the Rhine and the Danube. Richelieu invades Spain. (*1635*) Marshals Châtillon and Brézé entered the Netherlands; Créqui, in unison with the Duke of Savoy,[f] in Italy; Guébriant and Turenne cooperate with the Swedes on the Rhine, another body penetrates into Spain.

Austria and Spain on the one side; France, Sweden, and the Netherlands on the other the principals.

1637. Ferdinand II † Ferdinand III Emperor.

1640. Fresh war in Hungary about to commence by *George Rakoczy,*[g] *Prince of Transylvania,* in alliance with France and Sweden; the latter (France) ditto with the Catalonians, where a rise [takes place]. Revolution in Portugal; expulsion of the Spaniards. Emperor assured by a truce with the Turks, then masters of the half of Hungary. Victories of the French army in Italy, Spain, Flanders, on the Rhine.

---

a Gábor Bethlen.— *Ed.*
b Paul V.— *Ed.*
c Henrietta Maria.— *Ed.*
d Vincenzo II Gonzaga.— *Ed.*
e Johann Georg I.— *Ed.*
f Victor Amadeus I.— *Ed.*
g György I Rákóczy.— *Ed.*

4 December 1642. Richelieu †. *1643.* Louis XIII †. *Mazarin* (Anne's of Spain Regency).[376]

1645. Assembling of the Plenipotentiaries at *Münster* (chiefly there treated the affairs of Sweden and the Protestants), and *Osnabruck*[a] (the affairs of France principally).[377] (155 negotiators.) (Savoy ally of France.)

Circular of the French ambassador: "*the interests of France identical with German liberty*". Victories by French and Swedes.

"The Hollanders no more feared their hereditary enemies, the Spaniards, but the French, their ancient allies, now the object of their distrust" (Bougeant[b]). "They (the Hollanders) insensibly came to the conviction that security consisted in having the Spaniards as a barrier against France" (l.c.). *Preliminary agreement between the Spanish and Dutch ambassadors.*

1648. Victories of the Swedes. Ratification of peace between Spain and Holland.[378]

October 1648. Peace. (Spain excluded from it.)

France obtained: Upper and Lower Alsace, Brisac,[c] right of keeping a garrison in Philipsburg, the three bishoprics of Metz, Toul and Verdun. *Sweden* received Higher Pomerania, Stettin, Gortz, etc., port of Wismar; bishoprics of Verden and Bremen, with vote in the German diet. Brandenburg, Mecklenburg, Hanover, Hesse, etc., compensated chiefly by ecclesiastical property. (*Pignerol,*[d] formerly belonging to Savoy, [turned over] to France.) In Italy Austria confirmed in Milan and Tuscany. Acknowledged independence of Holland and Switzerland

(de facto since 1315).

With reference to religion all settled on the basis of the peace of Passau and Augsburg (1552 and 1556). Emperor grants general amnesty to the empire, except his own provinces.

(Bohemia forgotten.)[379]

Weakening of the younger house of Austria.

IV) *1648-1660. Gallo-Spanish War.*
Peace of the Pyrenees

Cromwell.

1654. War in Flanders between Mazarin and Spain.

1654. Peace between England and Holland.[380]

1655. Coalition between England and France. Commercial English treaty with France. *1657* Cromwell sends the French an aid of 6,000 men, acquires Dunkirk.

1657. † Ferdinand III. *1658* Leopold Emperor. Cromwell †.

1657. Coalition against Sweden of Denmark, Poland, Muscovy, Austria. (*Charles Gustavus* king of Sweden.) His only ally: Prince Rakoczy of Transylvania.

1659. Conferences between Mazarin and Don Louis de Haro, on the island of Pheasants (in the river of Bidasoa). Marriage between Louis XIV and *Maria*

---

[a] Osnaburg.— *Ed.*

[b] Guillaume Hyacinthe Bougeant, *Histoire du traité de Westphalie, ou des négociations qui se firent à Münster et à Osnabrüg, pour établir la paix entre toutes les puissances de l'Europe*, Paris, 1751.— *Ed.*

[c] Breisach.— *Ed.*

[d] Pinerolo.— *Ed.*

512 Karl Marx

Theresa, daughter of Philip IV (entire renunciation on the part of the Infanta). *Treaty of the Pyrenees.*[381] France gets in the Low Countries the county *of Arras*, several places in Flanders, Hainault and the Duchy of Luxemburg. On the Pyrenees Roussillon and Conflans.[a] Duke of Lorraine bound to allow a military passage to France.

March 1661 Mazarin †.

1654. Queen Christina resigns in favour of Charles X (son of the sister of Gustav Adolphus[b]). He is allied with the elector of Brandenburg,[c] invades Poland. Then league of Denmark with Muscovy, Holland against him. *1660* he compels the Danes to peace, gets Scania,[d] Oeland,[e] several places on the island of Rügen, exemption from the Sound Duties.[382] *1660* Charles X †; his son, *Charles XI*, succeeds. Renews treaty with Denmark, makes *peace of Oliva*[383] with Poland, which cedes to him Livonia, Esthonia, and Oesel. *1661* peace with Muscovy on the status quo ante bellum.

"Thus did Sweden confirm its preponderance in the north, at the very moment when France became all-powerful in the south and west of Europe."

V) *1660-1697. Wars of Louis XIV. Peace of Ryswick*

Restoration in England.

Dunkirk sold to Louis XIV by Charles II. War between England and Holland. England by De Ruyter and Tromp forced to *peace of Breda (1667)*. (Louis XIV acted in this war with Holland.) Louis XIV assists Portugal against Spain.

1665. Philip IV of Spain (Louis XIV's father-in-law) †. *Carlos II* (scarcely 4 years old, his son). (Philip IV's 2nd daughter[f] consort of the Emperor Leopold.) Louis XIV lays claim by the *"right of devolution"*[384] to the Spanish Netherlands.

1667. Louis XIV (Turenne) conquers greatest part of the Spanish Netherlands. *1668* (winter) subdues *Franche-Comté.*

January 23, 1668. Triple Alliance between England, Holland and Sweden. France was to relinquish its conquests in the Spanish Netherlands or Franche-Comté.

May 1668. Louis XIV at Aix-la-Chapelle peace with Spain (retains his conquests in the Netherlands, relinquishes Franche-Comté).

1670. Conspiracy of the nobles in Hungary against the Habsburg rule. Leopold treaty with Louis XIV. Hungary subdued, Leopold turned to the Dutch.

1671. Secret treaty of Louis XIV with Charles II of England.

1672. French invasion of Holland.

1673. Charles forced to abandon the French alliance. Coalition of Spain, the Emperor,[g] Brandenburg, Holland, Denmark against France. Sweden her only ally. Theatre of war from Holland transferred to the Spanish Netherlands and the German frontiers.

1675. Negotiations commence at *Nimeguen,*[h] where:

10 August 1678. Separate treaty between Louis XIV and Holland. *September 1678* Spain made peace. Abandons Franche-Comté for the restitution of some

---

[a] Albertville.— *Ed.*
[b] Catherine.— *Ed.*
[c] Frederick William.— *Ed.*
[d] Malmöhus.— *Ed.*
[e] Halland.— *Ed.*
[f] Margarita Theresa.— *Ed.*
[g] Leopold I.— *Ed.*
[h] Nijmegen.— *Ed.*

places in the Spanish Netherlands. Finally *Leopold* makes peace[385]; Louis stipulates with Denmark, Brunswick, Brandenburg for the restitution to Sweden of the conquests made upon her during the war. Louis XIV triumphs at the coast of Sicily over the united fleets of Holland and Spain. But the peace of Nimeguen did not settle Louis' right over a few towns in Alsace.

1681. Chamber of Reunion in Metz.[386]

Emperor tries to make war; but war with Hungary and Turkey; *1684* makes peace with Louis XIV at Ratisbonne.[a]

1686. League between Holland, Austria, Savoy, Brandenburg.

1688. Louis XIV sends an army to the Rhine. Accession of William III in England. Great offensive alliance against France (England, Holland, Emperor Leopold, Spain, Brandenburg, Victor Amadeus of Savoy).

1689. Declaration of war against France by Holland, England, Spain, and Austria.[b] (Separate treaty between Holland, England and the Emperor in May 1689.) (Emperor or his heirs shall be assisted in taking the eventual succession of the Spanish Monarchy. His son, Joseph, king of Hungary, shall be elected Emp. of Germany.) (France to be reduced to the terms of the treaties of Westphalia and the Pyrenees.)

August 1696. Separate peace at Turin between Louis XIV and Victor Amadeus of *Savoy.* Pignerol given up to Savoy.

1697. Peace of Ryswick.[387] First peace between France, Holland and England. Then Spain. Mutual restitution. *July 1697* peace with the Emperor. Kiel, Fribourg, Brisac, Philipsburg exchanged by Louis XIV for Strasburg. Apart from this, restitution of all places acquired during the war, beyond Alsace.

VI) *1697-1715. War of the Spanish Succession.* *Peace of Utrecht*

October 11, 1698. Partition treaty (of Spain) at the Hague between Louis XIV and William III. (Two Sicilies, Tuscany, Guipuscoa allotted to the Dauphin.[c] Milan to archduke Charles, 2nd son of the emperor. Spain and its other possessions to the Elector of Bavaria[d] and his heirs.)

February 1698. † the Elector of Bavaria.

March 11, 1700. Second Partition Scheme between William and Louis.

(Dauphin to receive, besides the dominions in the 1st treaty, Lorraine, for which Milan to the Duke of Lorraine. All the other dominions of the Spanish crown to the Archduke Charles.)

1699. Peace of Carlowitz between the Porte, Austria, Venice, and Poland.

1700. League between Czar Peter, Poland and Denmark against Sweden, defeat of the Russians at Narva by Charles XII.

October 1700. Will of *Carlos II*, appointing the Duke of Anjou,[e] 2nd son of the Dauphin, his heir. *November 1700* Carlos II †. Philip V acknowledged by Duke of Savoy, Duke of Mantua,[f] Portugal, and lastly, *King William.*

---

[a] Regensburg.— *Ed.*

[b] Marx took this from the chronological table at the end of Szabó's book, p. 384.— *Ed.*

[c] Louis.— *Ed.*

[d] Joseph Ferdinand.— *Ed.*

[e] Philip of Anjou (Philip V).— *Ed.*

[f] Ferdinando Carlo, Gonzaga di.— *Ed.*

February 1701. Louis XIV marches troops into the Spanish Netherlands which he forces the Dutch garrisons to evacuate; letter patent by which he acknowledges the right of Philip to succeed to the throne of France.[a]

September 1701. Second Great Alliance.[388] James II †. *Louis XIV* acknowledges the Pretender.[b] William †. Partial war between Austria and France in Italy.[389]

1702. Queen Anne renews the alliance. *May.* War against France declared by England, Holland, Emperor.[c] (Portugal, Hanover, Prussia accede) ([also] several of the smaller German states). (Bavaria, Brunswick, Cologne, Duke of Savoy for Louis XIV.)

1704. Gibraltar captured by the English. *1706* victory of Ramillies (Marlborough). Civil war in Hungary.[390] Austria conquers Naples.

1707. Charles XII in Saxony.

(Hungary in war against Austria since 1703.)

1709. Battle of Pultava.[d] Charles XII to Turkey.

1710. Declarations of war by the Porte to Russia.

1711. Peace of the Pruth between Turkey and Russia. Preliminaries of Peace between England and France.

April 1711. † Emperor Joseph. The Archduke Charles, his son,[e] heir to all his dominions.

In the preliminaries (*between England and France*):

Dunkirk demolished; Gibraltar and Port *Mahon,* Newfoundland and Hudson Bay for England.

January 12, 1712. General Congress opened at Utrecht. (Philip renounces his claims to France.) (Duke of Berry and Duke of Orleans renounce their claims to Spain.)

April 1713. Peace of Utrecht concluded between England, France, Spain and Holland. France ceded to England, besides the above, her possessions in the island of St. Christopher, Nova Scotia, Port Royal. In the name of Spain Louis ceded Upper Guelder to Prussia, acknowledged the king-title of Frederick I, and his sovereignty over Neufchatel. Savoy received Sicily and the right of succession [to the] throne, in default of the issue of Philip V. Frontier between France and Savoy the summits of the Alps. Holland obtains a commercial treaty and the exchange of a few places. *April 11,* 1713. Commercial treaty between France and England.

1711. Hungary pacified by the treaty of Szatmar. Czar Peter promised to assist him [f] with 30,000 men, if allowed to keep Livonia as a fief of the German empire. Short campaign, France on the Rhine superior to Austria.

Sept. 7, 1714. Peace of Baden between France and Austria. France acknowledges the right of the Emperor to Naples, Milan, Tuscany, Spanish Netherlands; restores Brisac and Fribourg. Electors of Bavaria and Cologne to be restored to their states.

1715. New league against Sweden joined by George I and Prussia.

Philip V not yet acknowledged by Austria. Not until *1715* treaty between Holland and Austria, which concedes Holland a few places in the Spanish Netherlands, in addition to the right of garrisoning several other places.

1 September 1715. Louis XIV †.

---

[a] Szabó has "formal renunciation on the part of Philip V of the throne of France" (Vol. I, p. 167).— *Ed.*

[b] James Stuart.— *Ed.*

[c] Leopold I.— *Ed.*

[d] Poltava.— *Ed.*

[e] A slip of the pen. It should read "his brother".— *Ed.*

[f] Charles VI.— *Ed.*

VII) *1715-1721*

George I [and] Duke of Orleans united in league against Spain. (Alberoni.)

1699. Peace of Carlowitz. Peter gets Azov; abandonment of all Hungary to Austria save the *Banat*; Morea rendered back to Venice; Podolia and Ukraine to Poland.

Under the treaty between England (Hanover), Prussia, Poland (Saxony) and Denmark, the Czar received the Baltic provinces; Prussia Stettin and dependencies, August of Saxony rex Poloniae Courland, Hanover Bremen-Verden, Denmark the island of Rügen with a part of Swedish Pomerania.[a] *1719.* Aaland conferences opened on April 24.[391] Agreed in Aaland isles that: Czar assists Charles XII to recover from Prussia Stettin and the part of Pomerania occupied by Prussian troops. Czar assists Sweden with 20,000 men for carrying on the war in Germany, and assists Charles to acquire Norway as indemnity for the Baltic provinces ceded to Russia. Czar assists Charles to gain back Bremen and Verden from George I, etc.

(also Restoration of Stuarts).

Death of Charles XII. Peace of the new Swedish Government with England, Denmark and Prussia.

(*Treaty of Stockholm*, November 1, 1719.)

Treaty of Nystadt (in Finland), *August 30, 1721.* (Sweden cedes Livonia, Esthonia, Ingria, part of Carelia, district of Wiborg, islands Oesel, Dago, Moen, and the other islands off the coasts of the said provinces. Czar restores Finland except a part, to be determined at the regulation of the frontiers.)[392]

(Under the peace of Stockholm Schleswig fell to Denmark. Peter marries his daughter Anne to Duke of Holstein,[b] takes up his "rights". Originally, he in alliance with Denmark against this Duke.)

"Transformation of the north of Europe, based on the dismemberment of Sweden."

VIII) *1715-1740. General Embroilment of Europe*

War between Spain and Austria in Italy. Austria supported by England. War of England and France against Spain.

Alberoni sent into exile.

January 1720. Spain accedes to the Quadruple Alliance.[393] *Sicily* made over to the Emperor,[c] Savoy receives Sardinia in exchange for it. Parma, Placentia,[d] Tuscany promised, on the death of the last Medici,[e] to Don Carlos, son of Philip V by his second wife, Elizabeth of Parma.

---

[a] Marx put this paragraph after the words "*1719.* Aaland conferences opened on April 24". The editors have transferred it to maintain the chronological order.— *Ed.*

[b] Charles I.— *Ed.*

[c] Charles VI.— *Ed.*

[d] Piacenza.— *Ed.*

[e] Cosimo III.— *Ed.*

1724. Congress of Cambray (England, France, Spain, and Austria).
1725. Secret treaties between Spain and Austria. Counter-treaty of Hanover.[394]
1728. (Opened 14 June) *Congress of Soissons.*
1729. Peace of Seville between Spain, England and France.
1731. Treaty of Vienna between Austria, England and Holland. Death of king Augustus.
September 1733. Stanislaus Leszinsky proclaimed king of Poland. Russia (ruled by Anne since 1730) with Austria (Karl VI) are for the son[a] of the deceased king, who promised the emperor the guarantee of the Pragmatic Sanction,[395] and to the Czarina not to reclaim Courland, formerly a fief of Poland. *War about the crown of Poland.* France attacks Austria.

Marshal Berwick operates on the Rhine. Another French army, under Villars, crosses the Alps, and, joined by Charles Emanuel of Sardinia, drove the Austrians from Milan. Shortly afterwards Don Carlos (of Spain) (son of Elizabeth) penetrated into Naples and Sicily, where he was proclaimed king, dispersing (with the aid of the population, exasperated at the tyranny of the Austrian rule) the whole imperial army; and there was soon nothing left in Italy in Austrian hands, save the fortress of Mantua. Only 1,500 French troops sent to Danzic.

1735. Peace of Vienna (October) between France and Austria. (August III of Saxony shall be king of Poland. Stanislaus, with the kingly title, *receives the Duchies of Lorraine and Bar, to revert after his death to France.* Don Carlos retains Naples, Sicily, and the Austrian coast of Tuscany.) The Duke of Lorraine receives in exchange for his hereditary dominions the possession of Tuscany. *Sardinia shall receive Novara, Tortona, and a few other places in the Milanese.* Parma and Piacenza to be given to the Emperor. All the other conquests made by the allied armies to be restored. *Guarantee of the Pragmatic Sanction* by France, Spain, the maritime powers and Russia. (Marie Therese, the Emperor's daughter, marries Francis of Lorraine.[b])

1736. Russo-Austrian war against the Porte. Russians invade the Crimea. Munich takes Perekop, lays waste the southern part of the peninsula.

1737. Munich takes Oczakow. Gen. Lascy (Russ) again penetrates into the Crimea. *Congress of Niemirov.* Russia demanded: 1) the abolition of all former treaties; 2) cession of the Crimea, the Kuban, and the other Tartar provinces; 3) independence of the Danubian provinces, under the protectorate of Russia; 4) Czar to be acknowledged (his title as *Emperor*); 5) free navigation in the Euxine,[c] the Bosphorus, the Hellespont, and the Mediterranean.

Austria asked large territories beyond the Danube, including Belgrade, Widdin, several portions of Moldavia and Wallachia.

1739. Peace of Belgrade: Everything restituted to the Porte except Azov. Further: The Porte remained in the possession of Belgrade, Orsova, and the disputed parts of Wallachia and Bosnia. (Never had Hungary had a better opportunity for recovering her independence. Rakoczy, ex-prince of Transylvania, in Turkey together with anti-Austrian Hungarian chiefs.)

War in India[d] between Spain and England. English declaration of war against Spain.[e]

---

[a] Augustus III.— *Ed.*
[b] Francis Stephen (Francis I).— *Ed.*
[c] The Black Sea.— *Ed.*
[d] Szabó has "in the Indies". This refers to the West Indies.— *Ed.*
[e] Marx took this sentence from the chronological table at the end of Szabó's book, p. 386.— *Ed.*

1740. † Frederick William I, of Prussia; † Emperor Charles VI; † Anna of Russia.

1713-1740. Barren unison of France with England. Pitiable state of Sweden, divided into Hat (French) and Bonnet (Russian) parties, the latter of which soon gained the ascendancy.

IX) *1740-1763. Austrian Succession War.*
Seven Years War

1740. Invasion of Silesia by Frederick II.

1741. Treaty of Nymphenburg, based on the partition of Austria (between France, Elector of Bavaria,[a] Spain, August III (of Saxony and Poland), and Prussia). Habsburg saved by Hungarian enthusiasm, and the treacherous policy and half measure of Cardinal Fleury. *1741* (spring). Fred. II marches into Moravia. Sardinia, subsequently gained over to the other side, prepares for the invasion of Milan.

1742. England declares for Austria. *June 11* peace at Breslau between Frederick and Austria (he gets Lower Silesia). War between France and Austria goes on in Germany and Italy. *Frankfort* (1742) *Charles VII* (Bavaria) crowned Emperor.

To prevent Russia from rendering aid to Maria Theresia, French bring about a Russo-Swedish war; soon ended to Russia's profit. *1743* peace of Abo; Sweden to cede different places in Finland; to designate, at the behest of the Czarina,[b] the Duke of Holstein Gottorp,[c] successor to the Swedish crown.

1745. Treaty of Warsaw between England, Saxony and Austria against Frederick.

(*1743. Treaty of Worms* between Austria, England and Sardinia.) Frederick again enters the French alliance.

(*1744. Spring.* France and England declare war against each other.)[d]

1745 (December). Peace of Dresden between Frederick and Austria: renewal of the treaty of Breslau, by which Frederick retained Silesia, promising his vote to Francis of Lorraine, consort of Maria Theresia. Emperor Charles Albert of Bavaria had died, his son[e] had made peace with Maria Theresia. (This the second separate Austro-Prussian peace.)

This peace enabled Maria Theresia to send large reinforcements to Italy where Milan, Parma and Piacenza had fallen into the hands of the Gallo-Spanish armies; scale turned.

England victorious in the Indies and the Mediterranean. Philip V of Spain †. Withdrawal of the Spanish troops from Italy. While Belleisle beaten in Italy, victories of Marshal de Saxe[f] and Lowendal in the Netherlands. Saxe in *1747* progresses through the territories of the Dutch Republic, reduction of the fortress Bergen-op Zoom. Maritime victories by the Engl. admirals Anson, Warren and Hawke. Russian army of 40,000 set in motion by Elizabeth, allured by the promise of English subsidies.

---

[a] Charles VII (Charles Albert).— *Ed.*

[b] Elizabeth (Petrovna).— *Ed.*

[c] Adolphus Frederick.— *Ed.*

[d] Marx put this after the words "*1745* (December). Peace of Dresden between Frederick and Austria". The editors have transferred it in accordance with Marx's marginal notes.— *Ed.*

[e] Maximilian III Josef.— *Ed.*

[f] Maurice von Saxe.— *Ed.*

1748. October. Peace of Aix-la-Chapelle which Maria Theresia could not but accept. Restitution of conquests by France and England. France gave up for Cape Breton the places in the Netherlands, and restored to England Madras; dispute about the frontiers in Canada left for subsequent decision. Parma, Piacenza, Gustalla[a] given to Don Philip and his male heirs. Sardinia remains in status quo, Assiento treaty for England prolonged for 4 years, guarantee of the English succession, expulsion of the Stuarts from France. Guarantee of the Pragmatic Sanction, confirmation of Lower Silesia to Frederick II. Germs of the new war the pending differences between France and England.

1751-3. Kaunitz' secret negotiations at Paris. Makes first abbé de Bernis, then Duc de Choiseul Minister.

1754. War recommences between France and England in America; dispute about the boundaries of Nova Scotia, or Acadia, ceded to England in the Utrecht treaty [396]; building of French forts along the Ohio, occupation by the French of the neutral islands of the Antilles, Tobago, St. Vincent, St. Lucia.

January 1756. Anglo-Prussian treaty of Westminster. Against it *Gallo-Austrian* defensive alliance of Versailles (*May 1756*). At the same time negotiations between Austria, Saxony, and (Elizabeth) Russia. *June 1756.* Capture of Fort Mahon by the French. Frederick defeats the Saxons at Pirna (surrender of 18,000 men) (autumn 1756).

1757 (winter). Austria, France, Russia, Sweden, and several "circles" of Germany collect force of 400,000 men against Frederick. Spring 1757 Fred. beats the Austrians at Prague; beaten by Daun at Collin,[b] forced to retreat to Saxony. Defeat of the Hanovero-Hessian troops by Richelieu.[397] (*Convention at Closter Seven*, by which Duke of Cumberland bound to disband the Han. Hess. troops.) Frederick persuades Richelieu to inaction, while he falls upon Soubise and the Germans under Prince Hildburghausen. *November 5 his victory at Rosbach*, while Richelieu remained inactive in his quarters at Halberstadt. Then to Silesia. *Victory at Lissa.*[398]

1758. Accession of Pitt (Lord Chatham) to the head of affairs.

December 1758. Second Gallo-Austrian treaty at Versailles. Louis XV engages to subsidise the Swedes, to maintain 100,000 army (French) in Germany, and to maintain also the Saxon army—Silesia and Glatz to be restituted to the empress,[c] the Rhenish provinces to be conquered from Prussia, to be ceded to Austria, the revenues, however, during the time of war, to be given to France. France forgot her maritime war,[399] to fight the battles of Austria.

1759. Defeat of Prussians at Hochkirchen.

1759-60. English victorious in the East Indies, in America (capture of Quebec by Wolfe, hence, the conquest of Canada) and in the West Indies.

Choiseul in Austria's interest.

1761. Family compact between the French and Spanish Bourbons. Chatham will anticipate Spain. Supplanted by *Lord Bute.* Invasion of Portugal by Spain.

January 1762. † Elizabeth of Russia. *Peter III* emperor. The propositions made to the Czar by *Lord Bute*, through the Russian minister, Prince Golitsin, to reduce Prussia to peace on any conditions, declined.

(Fred. II informed of these despatches by Peter III.)

Bute's secret negotiations with Austria for the dismemberment of Prussia met with no better success.

---

a Guastalla.— *Ed.*

b Kolin.— *Ed.*

c Maria Theresa.— *Ed.*

February 1763. Peace between England, France, Spain at Paris. England received Nova Scotia, Canada, Cape Breton, while France a share in the fisheries of Newfoundland. Mississippi declared the boundary between Louisiana and the British settlements. France yielded to England, in the West Indies, Grenada and the neutral islands of St. Vincent, Domingo,[a] Tobago. In Africa the English restored Gorea, retained Senegal; Menorca restored to England. France recovered her small possessions in the East Indies, but engaged to maintain no troops in Bengal. Spain gave up to England Florida, confirms her right to cut logwood in the bay of Honduras, but Spain replaced in Cuba and Havanah. Portugal in the *status quo ante bellum.*

Peace at Hubertusburg[400] between Fred. and Austria (nothing else than a confirmation of the peace at Breslau and Dresden[b]). (Fred. engages to give his vote for Archduke Joseph, son of Maria Theresa, at the pending election of the king of the Roumans.) No territorial change in Europe after the 7 years' war.

If Frederick raised Prussia to the rank formerly occupied by Sweden (since the peace of Westphalia[401]), he is prudent enough to profit by, but too weak to arrest, the *progress of Muscovite ambition....* Fred. II had no great political plan. Silesia his whole and single idea.

The distinctive character of this period the decline of France. In the first war the alliances of France with Frederick, twice thrown overboard by him, failed to wrest the German sceptre from dilapidated Austria. In the second war, France, allied with that same Austria, Saxony, Sweden and Russia, failed even to dispossess Frederick of Silesia.

X) *1763-1774. Partition of Poland.*
Peace of Kainardji

Augustus III, Saxon king of Poland, †. *June 1762. Catherine* usurps throne of Russia. Catherine and Frederick declare for Poniatowski. *Defensive alliance between them,* contains secret clause not to permit any changes in the anomalous constitution of Poland.[402]

1764. Russian troops march into Poland. *September* enthrone Poniatowski. Russian minister[c] at Warsaw real president of the assemblies of Poland. Catherine declares for the dissidents (Greeks and Protestants), also supported by England and Sweden, as the guarantees of the peace of Oliva.

Diet of 1767. Prince Repnin, the Russian ambassador, assumes the part of a dictator. *Polish Confederacy of Bar* (in Podolia). War with the Russians; the remnant of the Bar confederates driven into the dominions of the Porte, excited by France to mingle in the Russo-Polish war. At the end of 1768 or the beginning of 1769 the Sultan[d] throws the Russian Ambassador[e] in the 7 towers.

1770. Russo-Turkish war.[f]

(*Corsica* sold to France by Genoa.)[g]

---

[a] Dominica.— *Ed.*

[b] See this volume, p. 517.— *Ed.*

[c] Nikolai Vasilyevich Repnin.— *Ed.*

[d] Mustafa III.— *Ed.*

[e] Alexei Mikhailovich Obreskov.— *Ed.*

[f] Marx took this from the chronological table at the end of Szabó's book, p. 386.— *Ed.*

[g] Marx put this after the words "*1772. Partition of Poland*". The editors have transferred it in accordance with the way the material is presented in Szabó's book.— *Ed.*

1772. Partition of Poland. By the partition Prussia obtained *West Prussia* (600,000 souls; master of the Vistula, the inlets and outlets of Polish commerce); Catherine: *Lithuania* and the country between the rivers Dvina and Dnieper (1,800,000 souls); Austria: Lodomeria, Gallicia, and other parts surrounding Hungary (3,000,000 souls).

July 1774. (Peace of Kainardji.) (Independence of the Crimea.) Azov, Kinburn, Kertch, Yenikale for Russia, etc. The right of Russia to make verbal applications at Constantinople, in behalf of Moldavia and Wallachia.

Austria obtains the *Bukovina* part of Moldavia (Austria, the ally of Turkey).

XI) *1774-1783. American War of Independence.*[a]
Peace of Paris

1763. Rigorous regulations (British) to prevent smuggling; stamp duty.[403]

1773. Boston demonstration (ship-cargoes with tea thrown into the sea).

December 1776. (Franklin arrives in France.)

6 February 1778. Treaty between France and the revolted Colonies.[b]

April 1778. French fleet under Count d'Estaing with a considerable land force sets sail for America.

Joseph (of Austria) attempts to annex Lower Bavaria (after the death of the Elector Maximilian Joseph) to Austria.

Potato war.[404]

He tries also to open by force of arms the free navigation of the Scheldt.

1779. Spain joins with France in the war against England.

1780. Russia proclaims the Armed Neutrality.[c][405]

3 September 1783. Peace of Versailles between France, Spain, America, England.

May 1784. Peace between England and Holland.

XII) *1783-1790. Final annexation of the Crimea*
to the Russian Empire

Austria in alliance with Russia, ready to share in the spoil.

1790. Prusso-Turkish Alliance.... Congress of Reichenbach (entire conciliation of Prussia and Austria[406]).... Peace of Werila (on the basis of the status quo) between Sweden and Russia[407].... Discontent of the Hungarians and Belgians.... Peace of Szistova between Austria and Turkey[408].... Peace of Jassy (between Russia and Turkey).[409]

Austria, since the days of Charles V, was never able either to conquer, or to recover, a single province.

[Volume II][410]

Ia) *1790-1796*

1791, August 25. Austro-Prussian declaration of Pilnitz.

1792 (April 20). French declaration of war against Austria.

---

[a] Szabó has "The war of the British-American colonies..." (*The State Policy...,* Vol. I, p. 296).— *Ed.*

[b] Marx took this item from the chronological table at the end of Szabó's book, p. 386.— *Ed.*

[c] Item taken by Marx from Szabó's chronological table (ibid., p. 387).— *Ed.*

1792 (July 25, Coblenz). Brunswick's proclamation.
1793, 21 January. Louis Capet executed.
1793, 25 March. Convention of Pitt with Russia, followed by treaties of alliance and subsidies with Sardinia, Spain, the Bourbon Princes of Italy, Prussia, Austria, Portugal, and several petty states of Germany

(against France).

1st Coalition. (While sending his troops into the heart of France, the Prussian king[a] plotted with Catherine a second partition of Poland.)
July 1793. Second partition of Poland. Prussia: Danzic and Thorn.

(The new constitution of Poland had been proclaimed May 3, 1791.) (Throne hereditary.) (Russian campaign in Poland 1792.) (Convention between Prussia and Russia of St. Petersburg, January 23, 1793. Prussians enter Poland. Russia got nearly the half of Lithuania (the Palatinates of Podolia, Polotsk and Minsk, the half of Novogrodek,[b] Brest, Volhynia) (3 millions of inhabitants).[c]

Catherine vehemently inveighed against *France,* keeping her forces at home. *April 1794.* (Subsidiary agreement between Prussia and England.)

March 24, 1794. Kościuszko (dictator). Insurrection at Warsaw and Vilna. Austria despatches also an army. *November 9, 1794.* Suworow enters Warsaw.

3 January 1795. Separate Declaration of Petersburg between Austria and Russia (relating to the division). *October 24, 1795.* Prussia signs with Austria the convention of Petersburg. Cracow for Austria. Russia obtained the remainder of Poland and Lithuania as far as the Niemen, and the confines of Brest and Novogrodek, greater part of Samogitia, all of Courland and Semigalia. In little Poland that part of the territory of Chelm situated on the right bank of the Bug, and the remainder of Volhynia. (1,200,000.)

Austria [obtains], besides principal part of Cracow, Palatinates of Sandomir and Lublin, part of the district of Chelm, Palatinates of Brest, Podolactia[d] and Masovia (on the left bank of the Bug) (about 1 million of souls).

Prussia part of Masovia and Podolactia on the right bank of the Bug, in Lithuania part of the Palatinate of Troki and Samogitia and small district in little Poland, part of the Palatinate of Cracow (about 1 million).

---

[a] Frederick William II.— *Ed.*
[b] Novogrudok.— *Ed.*
[c] This paragraph is not based on Szabó's book, but on some other source.— *Ed.*
[d] Podlachia.— *Ed.*

III partition of Poland

Russia hitherto the greatest gainer by the French war. The first in impressing upon England, Austria, Prussia the dangers of the revolutionary principles, Catherine pursued her separate interests, without furnishing a single Cossack or a single rouble for the "common cause". Her few vessels sent to the assistance of England had the appearance of mockery.

5 April 1795. Basel Peace of France with Prussia. Definite and secret treaty in August. Prussia ceded her possessions on the left bank of the Rhine, to be indemnified by the secularisation of several German bishoprics. Spain follows. (France holds only Spanish part of St. Domingo.[411]) Tuscany [made] peace with France earlier on. Two powers of the Baltic neutral. England now only with Sardinia and Austria. Belgium incorporated into France. Parts of Holland ceded to France.[412]

IIa) *1796-1801 (peace of Luneville)*

April 1796. (3 consecutive battles—Bonaparte—decide the fate of Sardinia.) (France obtained Savoy, Nice and the right to occupy several fortresses.) Bonaparte in Lombardy. The colonies of the Batavian republic had fallen into the hands of Great Britain.

Catherine † *17 November 1796.*

18 April 1797. Peace preliminaries at Leoben signed by Austria.

Cisalpine Republic (Modena, Ferrara, Romagna, Mantua). *Ligurian republic* (Genoa, etc.)

17 October 1797. Peace of Campoformio. (Austria renounces the Netherlands, consents to the acquisition of the left bank of the Rhine by France. *Receives Venice* and the *Dalmatian part of the Venetian territory.* Albania and the Venetian or Ionian islands become French.)[413]

(*May 19, 1798.* Bonaparte leaves Toulon for Egypt.) (Malta Bonaparte conquers in June 1798.)[a] *March 15, 1798. Rastatt Congress.*[414]

December 1798. Treaty between England and Russia. (Both [form] separate alliance with Turkey and Sicily.) Swiss Republic under French Protectorate. Occupation by the French of the Papal states.

Second Coalition.

April 1799. Dissolution of the Rastatt Congress.

Austria enters *the 2ⁿᵈ coalition.* By and by Portugal, Bavaria, Elector of Mayence,[b] Duke of Württemberg[c] enter it. War in Italy and Germany. Naples overthrown. *Parthenopean Republic.*[415] Piedmont [becomes] French under false pretences (de facto. *Charles Emanuel IV* withdraws to Sardinia.)

(*9 October 1799.* Bonaparte lands in France.)

June 14, 1799. Marengo. British take Malta. *Emperor Paul: armed neutrality* with Denmark, Sweden and Prussia.

March 23, 1801. Paul †. Alexander I.

9 February 1801. Peace of Luneville. (Rhine recognised by Austria as the boundary of France. Division of Venetian territory. Cession of Belgium to France.) (Cisalpine, Ligurian, Helvetian, Batavian republics recognised.)

---

a Marx took this from the chronological table at the end of Szabó's book.— *Ed.*

b Friedrich Karl Joseph, Baron of Erthal.— *Ed.*

c Frederick I.— *Ed.*

IIIa) *1801-1805*

January 1802. Bonaparte president of the Italian republic.
27 March 1802. Peace of Amiens (France, England, Spain, Holland). (England retains Trinidad and Ceylon.) (Malta to be evacuated by the English, independent.) (France promises to evacuate Naples, Papal states; England all the ports and islands in the Mediterranean and Adriatic. Republic of the Ionian islands, integrity of Turkey guaranteed.)
May 18, 1803. England declares war to France.
May 18, 1804. Bonaparte Emperor. *2 December 1804* crowned by Pope.[a]

IVa) *1805-1807. 3ᵈ Coalition. Peace of Tilsit*

Petersburg the pivot of new combinations against France.
11 April 1805. Coalition Treaty between England and Russia. (*Sweden* already bound to England[b] by a treaty of December 1804, by which Stralsund was made the dépôt of the English.)

Declar. Petersburg of August 9, exchanged between Austria with England and Russia.

17 October 1805. Capitulation of Ulm. *2 December* Austerlitz.
26 December 1805. Separate peace of Pressburg (Austria and Bonaparte). (Napoleon recognised as king of Italy. Austria loses her Venetian part. Cedes Tyrol to Bavaria; other parts to Baden and Württemberg. Bavaria and Württemberg kingdoms, Baden Grand Duchy.)
January 23, 1806. Pitt †. Fox negotiates with France. *Russia thwarts the peace negotiations.* September 13, 1806. Fox †.

July 12, 1806 (*Paris. Confederation of the Rhine,* 16 German princes.)

6 August 1806. Austria resigns the title of German Emperor. (*Empire at an end.*)

October 14, 1806. Battle of Jena and Auerstädt.
June 14, 1807. Battle of Friedland.
July 7, 1807. Peace of Tilsit. (Warsaw and part of West Prussia given to *August III* (Saxony) and raised into a kingdom; East Prussia to the Czar. *Secret articles*: Moldavia and Wallachia to Russia, Morea and Candia[c] to France, Continental System. Deposition of Bourbons in Spain.)

Va) *1807-1814. (Peace of Paris)*

October 1808. Congress of Erfurt. Conquests of Russia in Sweden (Finland) and Turkey (Danubian Principalities).

(At the same time the Russians engaged in backstage dealings[d] with Prussia and Austria against France.)

---

[a] Pius VII.— *Ed.*
[b] Marx has "Russia", probably a slip of the pen.— *Ed.*
[c] Crete.— *Ed.*
[d] The original is illegible here.— *Ed.*

March 1809. Austrian Manifesto calls the Tyroleans to arms. Archduke John into Italy, Ferdinand marched upon Warsaw, Charles into Bavaria.

12 May 1809. Napoleon enters Vienna. *5, 6 July* Wagram. *10 Oct.* Peace at Schönbrunn. (Austria cedes Carinthia, part of Tyrol, the territory of Trieste, part of Croatia, Hungarian Adriatic Coast with Fiume. King of Saxony[a] received West Gallicia; *Russia another part of Austrian Poland,* for her tardy and reluctant manoeuvres during the campaign, as the ally of France.) (*Austria had received secret assurances of the neutrality of the Czar.*)

September 1809. Peace of Russia with Sweden. (*It obtained Finland and the Aaland isles.*)

December 1810. Ukase issued by Russia against the principles of the Continental System.

By the end of 1811, the whole of the plots between the northern courts and the court of St. James ripe for execution. Pozzo di Borgo and Prince Luberminski channels between Petersburg and London. Bernadotte already looked upon as a sure card. Prussia and Russia already favoured with arms and ammunition by England. General rising in Italy prepared by Pozzo.

1812. Peace of Bucharest under English mediation[b]; acquisition by Russia of Bessarabia and part of Moldavia.

1813, February. Prusso-Russian treaty of Kalisch.

1814, April 12. Abdication of Napoleon.

1814, May 30. Peace of Paris. (France limits of 1792. Certain augmentations on the North side.[c])

VIa) *May 1814 to November 1815*

1 November 1814. Opening of the Congress of Vienna.

9 January 1815. Secret treaty between Austria, France, and England.

1 March 1815. Bonaparte lands in France.

June 18, 1815. Waterloo. (*September 26, 1815.* Holy Alliance.)

End of June 1815. Congress of Vienna ends. ("Kingdom of Poland" to Russia; part of the Duchy of Warsaw (Posen) to Prussia. Gallicia to Austria. Prussia received half of Saxony, part of Swedish Pomerania, several provinces of Westphalia, and on the left bank of the Rhine. Belgium and Luxemburg to Holland. *Austria* obtains (in exchange for Belgium) besides its former possessions the whole of Venice, Mantua, etc. (Modena, Tuscany and Parma for other members of the Habsburg family.) Naples restored to Ferdinand.[d] Genoa to Piedmont. Denmark must give up Norway to Sweden. Austria gets president of the Frankfort diet.[416] *Switzerland*: Valois,[e] Neufchatel, Geneva added to it. Several settlements in the Indies, the Cape of Good Hope, Malta, the Ionian islands, Heligoland—spoils from France, Holland, Venice, the Knights of St. John and Denmark to England.)

26 September 1815. Holy Alliance.

20 November 1815. Second Paris Treaty. France obliged to give up several frontier fortresses on the side of the Rhine, Netherlands, Alps.

---

[a] Frederick Augustus I.— *Ed.*

[b] Marx took this sentence from the chronological table at the end of Szabó's book, p. 388.— *Ed.*

[c] Presumably this refers to Holland (see Szabó, *The State Policy...,* Vol. I, p. 92).— *Ed.*

[d] Ferdinand I.— *Ed.*

[e] Valais.— *Ed.*

VIIa) *1815-1825*

October 1817. Festival of the German students at Wartburg. Burschenschaft.[417] Abolition of the constitution (of 1812) of Sicily. Ditto of Cortes in Spain.[418]

September 1818. Congress of Aix-la-Chapelle. Evacuation of France. The war in Portugal. War between Spain and her American colonies. *Periodical meetings* proposed by Metternich, to keep down the revolutionary spirit. *November 15* protocol signed with relation to those meetings. Castlereagh had signed it. France also taken into the Holy Alliance; [Castlereagh] departs on command of his ministry. (Metternich, Hardenberg, Nesselrode the triumvirate.)

1819. Congress at Carlsbad under Austro-Prussian auspices; afterwards transferred to Vienna. Remodelled the German constitution. Police-Commission at Maynz.[419] Carbonari (formed in 1809 around the throne of Emperor Francis[a]).[420] Pope[b] thunders against Carbonarism and Freemasons.

January 1820. Ferdinand of Spain[c] forced to restore the constitution of the Cortes, ditto *Ferdinand king of Naples (6 July).* (General William Pepe, leader of the Carbonari.)

August 1820. Proclamation issued in Lombard-Venetia by Emp. Francis I against Carbonarism.

October 1820. Congress at Troppau. Armed interference against Naples proposed by Metternich. (Dissent of Castlereagh) (who, however, "will leave Austria unembarrassed in her cause"); the congress transferred to

Laybach (1821).

February 1821. Austrian army enters Naples under Baron Fremont.[d] Outbreak in Sardinia, Wallachia, Greece. Austrian armed intervention in Sardinia.

1822. September. Congress of Verona. Protest of Canning. French intervention in Spain.

28 January 1823. Crown speech of Louis XVIII. Announces the intervention in Spain. Alexander I distinctly announced his resolve to aid France if attacked by England. (Metternich began to equivocate.)

Counter-revolution in Portugal. (1822 House of Braganza had granted constitution similar to that of Spain.[421] (King John VI.) (Made counter-revolution with the aid of his son, Don Miquel and the Count Amarazda.[e]) *Canning* forbids Spanish Intervention; acknowledges the independence of the American Colonies.)

December 2, 1823. Message to the American Congress of James Monroe, the President. *1825.* Mexico acknowledged by Canning.

September 1824. Louis XVIII †. Charles X.

1 October 1825. Alexander I ("The White Angel" of Madame de Krüdener[f]) †. *Nicolaus.*

VIIIa) *1825-1834*

Mohamed II (Reformer). (Mutiny of the Janissaries, discontent of the Ulemas,[422] defection of several Pashas.) ("Hetäria".) (First established in Moscow.[423]) (Alexander's Ionian minister,[424] Capo d'Istria, chief instrument in the Greek

---

[a] Francis I.— *Ed.*

[b] Pius VII.— *Ed.*

[c] Ferdinand VII.— *Ed.*

[d] Johann Maria Philipp Frimont.— *Ed.*

[e] Dom Miguel and Count of Amarante.— *Ed.*

[f] See this volume, p. 138.— *Ed.*

movement.) (Ali Pasha, of Janina, gives in 1821 signal to the general rising of the Greeks.) (Alexander Ypsilanti in Wallachia first rising. Simultaneous risings in the Peloponnesus, the Archipelago, etc. Destruction of the Janissaries.)

February 1825. Ibrahim Pasha (son of Mehemet Ali) lands in Morea.

Quarrel of Turkey with Russia, before Alexander's death.

4 April 1826. Anglo-Russian Protocol (of Petersburg) on Greece.

Treaty of Ackerman October 1826 (between Russia and Turkey). (Stipulations with regard to the Principalities[a] and Servia.)

March 1826. King John VI of Portugal †. (His eldest son Don Pedro gives Portugal to his daughter Maria.) Metternich intrigues with and for the Sultan.[b]

6th July 1827. Treaty (on Greece) signed in London by France, England, and Russia (mediation upon the belligerents).

October 20, 1827. Navarino Disaster. (Canning meanwhile †.)

Spring 1828. Russian army crosses the Pruth. Occupies the Principalities. Pozzo, bosom friend of La Ferronnays, French Minister, privy to every secret communication proceeding from Vienna.

14 September 1829. Treaty of Adrianople; the mouth of the Danube acquired by Russia. Count Capo d'Istria President of Greece.

1830, July. Accession of Louis Philippe. September. Revolution in Belgium.

1831. Rise of the Poles. Risings in Italy. Settlement of the Belgian affairs. Settlement of the Greek affairs.[c]

October 1831. Finis Poloniae.[d]

20 January 1831. Declaration of Belgian independence.

1833, February. Treaty of Unkiar Skelessi *(10 July).*[425]

7 May 1832. Otto of Bavaria King of Greece.

(Russia which extorted, under the cover of the Greek war, the treaty of Ackerman, and then that of Adrianople, was the sole gainer among the European powers.)

1832. On Metternich's initiative reactionary measures in Germany.

IXa) *1834-1846*

1828. (Revolt of Don Miquel.) *1832.* Don Pedro lands in Terceira.

Ferdinand of Spain † 1833. *July 1, 1833.* (Sir Charles Napier destroys the Miquelite squadrons at Cape St. Vincent.)

April 1834. Quadruple Alliance (England, France, Spain, Portugal).[426]

Treaty of July 15, 1840.[427]

6 November 1846. Cracow incorporated into Austria.

XIa) *1846-1850*[e]

Pope Pius IX. Swiss Confederation wages war [against the Sonderbund[428]]. *Revolution of February 1848.*

---

[a] Moldavia and Wallachia.— *Ed.*

[b] Mahmood II.— *Ed.*

[c] Marx took this item from the chronological table at the end of Szabó's book, p. 389.— *Ed.*

[d] See this volume, p. 148.— *Ed.*

[e] Marx omitted Chapter X ("Theories of International Law") of Szabó's book.— *Ed.*

November 1846. Pope issues order for the convocation of a "Consulta di Stato".[429]

Pressburg diet of 1847.

9 August 1848. Charles Albert (Sardinia) forced to buy the *armistice at Solasco* (lasts until *mid-March* 1849).

25 November 1848. Flight of Pius.

May 1848. Frankfort Assembly.

March 23, 1849. Battle of Novara.

14 April 1849. Independence of Hungary proclaimed.

9 February 1849. Republic proclaimed at Rome.

30 June 1849. Rome falls. *13 August 1849.* Hungary surrenders.

August 22, 1849. Venice surrenders.

1848, July. Entry of the Russians into the Principalities.

Duke of Genoa[a] becomes king of Sicily.

1849.[430] *February.* The Russians in Transylvania.

    March 15. The Russians expelled from Transylvania.

    March 23. Defeat of the Sardinians at Novara.

    April 14. Dethronisation (Hungary) of the Habsburgs.

    February 9. Rome Republic.

April 1849. Treaty of Balta Liman.

    April 22. French embark for Civita Vecchia.

    June. Russians enter *Hungary.*

    June 30. Rome surrenders to the French.

    August 13. Surrender of the chief Hungarian corps to the Russians.

    August 22. Surrender of Venice.

XIIa) *1850-1853*

1850, January. Greece blockaded by the English.

    May 24. Three Kings' Treaty (Prussia, Saxony, Hanover).[b]

    October. Warsaw conferences.

    December. Austro-Russian conferences at Dresden.

1851, December 2. Coup d'Etat.

1851, Russians withdraw from the principalities.

1852, December 2. French Empire proclaimed.

    December 6. Its recognition announced in the British Parliament.

1852, May. Danish succession treaty.

XIIIa) *1853-56*[c]

Compiled in June 1860

First published in: Marx and Engels, *Works,* Second Russian Edition, Vol. 44, Moscow, 1977

Printed according to the manuscript in English and German

Published in English for the first time

---

[a] Ferdinando Maria Alberto.— *Ed.*

[b] Frederick William IV, Frederick Augustus II and Ernest Augustus.— *Ed.*

[c] Here the manuscript breaks off.— *Ed.*

NOTES
AND
INDEXES

NOTES

¹ This letter is the first document bearing on the Vogt case (see Note 12). In the spring of 1859 Karl Vogt had published his pamphlet *Studien zur gegenwärtige Lage Europas* (Genf und Bern, 1859) in which he put forward a Bonapartist conception of foreign policy. In June 1859, an anonymous pamphlet, *Zur Warnung* (*A Warning*), appeared in London. It was published in the London newspaper *Das Volk*, No. 7, June 18, 1859 under the heading *Warnung zur gefälligen Verbreitung* (*A Warning. With a Request for Circulation*—in *Herr Vogt* and his letters Marx refers to it as *Zur Warnung*) in the column "Reichsverraetherei", and it exposed Vogt's Bonapartist intrigues and his attempts to bribe some journalists to present a Bonapartist picture of developments. As Marx shows, the pamphlet was written by Karl Blind. Wilhelm Liebknecht sent a proof sheet of *Zur Warnung* to the Augsburg *Allgemeine Zeitung* (see this volume, p. 114) which published it in its No. 173 on June 22, 1859 in the article "Karl Vogt und die deutsche Emigration in London" ("Karl Vogt and the German Emigrés in London"). This induced Vogt to bring an action against the *Allgemeine Zeitung*.

Blind denied authorship of *Zur Warnung* thus making it impossible for the *Allgemeine Zeitung* to refute Vogt's complaint. This caused Marx to send its editors a statement by the compositor Vögele confirming Blind's authorship (see this volume, pp. 117-19).

The present letter by Marx was published by the *Allgemeine Zeitung*, No. 300, October 27, 1859 under the editorial heading "Prozess Vogt gegen die Redaction der *Allgemeinen Zeitung*" ("Vogt's Action against the Editors of the *Allgemeine Zeitung*") in the column "Neuste Posten" alongside the relevant statements by E. Biscamp, A. Vögele and W. Liebknecht. p. 3

² The *Volks-Zeitung* and the *Allgemeine Zeitung* did not publish this statement. The *Reform* carried it in the Supplement to its No. 139 on November 19, 1859 under the editorial heading "Zum Prozesse von Carl Vogt contra die Augsburger *Allgemeine Zeitung*" ("Concerning Carl Vogt's Lawsuit against the *Allgemeine Zeitung*"). The statement was prefaced with the following editorial note: "In view of the great interest *Carl Vogt's* lawsuit against the Augsburg *Allgemeine Zeitung* has evoked everywhere, we would not deny Herr K. Marx acceptance of the following letter which casts a new light on the grave and

utterly *unproved* accusations made by *Karl Blind* against the former member of the Frankfurt Parliament."   p. 4

3 Excerpts from *The Eighteenth Brumaire of Louis Bonaparte* first appeared in English in the Chartist *People's Paper* in "A Review of the Literature on the Coup d'état" written by Johann Georg Eccarius, a Communist League member, and published in instalments from October to December 1852 (see this edition, Vol. 11). The last part of the "Review" (*The People's Paper*, Nos. 32 and 33, December 11 and 18) contained passages from the first chapter of *The Eighteenth Brumaire*.   p. 5

4 Here and below Marx refers to the book *Des idées napoléoniennes* written by Louis Bonaparte in England and published in Paris and Brussels in 1839.
                                                                        p. 5

5 Apart from the *Allgemeine Zeitung*, No. 325, November 21, 1859 (Supplement), this "Declaration" was published in Karl Vogt's *Mein Prozess gegen die Allgemeine Zeitung*, Genf, 1859 (Dokumente, Nr. 12).   p. 8

6 This declaration, published as a leaflet in London in February 1860, was repeatedly referred to by Marx as a circular because he had sent it, together with the "Declaration" of February 6, 1860 (see this volume, pp. 12-13), to a number of German newspapers. Marx translated the closing part of the circular into German and included it in the main body of his *Herr Vogt* (see this volume, pp. 127-28). He also included this section, in English, in the Appendix (11) to this work.   p. 10

7 Besides the newspapers listed under Marx's text this "Declaration" was published in the Berlin *Publicist* (see Marx's letter to Engels of February 13, 1860, present edition, Vol. 41). Marx also sent copies of the "Declaration" to the *National-Zeitung* and the *Frankfurter Journal* (see his letter to Engels of February 7, 1860) but these papers did not publish it.
   Die Reform printed the "Declaration" with the editorial note: "The pamphlet is headed 'Prosecution of the Augsburg Gazette' and is available for inspection at the editorial office."
   The opening part of the "Declaration" was included by Marx in the Preface to *Herr Vogt* (see this volume, p. 25).   p. 12

8 This letter was not published. A copy of it, written in Marx's hand, is extant. (See Marx's letters to Engels of February 9 and 14, 1860 and to Legal Counsellor Weber of February 24, 1860, present edition, Vol. 41.)   p. 14

9 This refers to the strict twofold censorship imposed by the Prussian Government on the *Rheinische Zeitung*, which was edited by Marx.   p. 17

10 As can be seen from an entry in Marx's notebook for 1860 this declaration was also sent to the Hamburg *Freischütz* which, however, did not publish it. p. 18

11 Marx sent this "Declaration" to the *Volks-Zeitung* and *Die Reform*.   p. 19

12 Marx's exposé *Herr Vogt* was written in reply to Vogt's pamphlet *Mein Prozess gegen die Allgemeine Zeitung*, Genf, 1859, which heaped slander on Marx and his associates in the Communist League. Vogt wrote his pamphlet after the

Allgemeine Zeitung had reprinted the pamphlet *Zur Warnung,* which exposed Vogt's Bonapartist intrigues (see Note 1). Vogt had brought an action against the newspaper. His complaint was dismissed, and in December 1859 he published his pamphlet. The bourgeois press gave his slanderous accusations the broadest publicity. On January 31, 1860 Marx wrote to Engels: "The jubilation of the bourgeois press is, of course, unbounded" (see present edition, Vol. 41). The Berlin *National-Zeitung* gave a résumé of Vogt's pamphlet in two leading articles (Nos. 37 and 41, January 22 and 25, 1860). A number of European periodicals, notably the Hamburg *Freischütz* (Nos. 17-21, April 1860), the *Breslauer Zeitung,* the London *Daily Telegraph* (February 5, 1860) and the Paris *Revue contemporaine* (XIII, February 15, 1860), also gave it extensive coverage.

In the interests of the proletarian party, then in process of formation, Marx decided to answer Vogt through the press. He did so in his exposé *Herr Vogt.* He also intended to bring an action for libel against the *National-Zeitung.* In late January 1860 he began gathering the material for his book against Vogt and his action against the *National-Zeitung.* With this aim in view he wrote dozens of letters to people with whom he was connected in his political and revolutionary activity and received from them material exposing Vogt. Letters arrived from J. Ph. Becker, G. Lommel (as Marx wrote to Engels on November 13, 1860, Lommel's letter provided the basis for Chapter IX, "Agency", of *Herr Vogt*), S. Borkheim and others. C. A. Dana, C. D. Collet, L. L. Jottrand, J. Lelewel, B. Szemere, M. Perczel, N. I. Sazonov and others sent letters bearing witness to Marx's faultless political record. Marx was also supported by Ernest Jones, which led to the resumption of their old friendship. In mid-February 1860 Marx began sending evidence against Friedrich Zabel, editor of the *National-Zeitung,* to Legal Counsellor Weber, who instituted legal proceedings against Zabel. However, between April and October 1860 Marx's complaint was dismissed at every level of the Prussian judiciary.

While supplying evidence for his action, Marx continued to work on his exposé of Vogt. His preparatory materials for it, contained above all in his notebooks for 1858-60, and the numerous direct and indirect references to various sources in the book itself, testify to the vastness of the factual material Marx had gone through. He studied the political and diplomatic history of the seventeenth, eighteenth and nineteenth centuries and made copious notes on foreign policy from books and periodicals of different orientations, from Bonapartist pamphlets brought out by the Dentu publishers, from *Hansard's Parliamentary Debates,* from *Blue Books* and from other sources.

In September Marx by and large concluded his work on *Herr Vogt.* However, following the dismissal of his charge against Zabel, he wrote one more chapter, "A Lawsuit", in which he criticised the Prussian judiciary. In a letter to Engels dated October 2, 1860 Marx gave a summary of *Herr Vogt* which, with some alterations, he later incorporated in the book as its table of contents. In the letter, Section 5 of Chapter III was entitled "Central Festival of Workers in Lausanne"; in the book its title is "Central Festival of the German Workers' Educational Associations in Lausanne (June 26 and 27, 1859)"; Chapter VIII bears the title "Vogt's Studies" in the letter, and "Dâ-Dâ Vogt and His Studies" in the book. The latter change accentuates the similarity of views of the Bonapartist Vogt and the contemporary Arab journalist Dâ-Dâ, who translated Bonapartist pamphlets into Arabic on the instructions of the Algerian authorities.

Marx considered several titles for his book. Originally he intended to call it *Ex-Imperial Vogt* or *Dâ-Dâ Vogt* (see his letter to Engels of September 25, 1860). Both versions met with the objections of Engels, and it was at his suggestion that the book was entitled *Herr Vogt* (see Marx's letters to Engels of October 2 and November 13, 1860 and Engels' letters to Marx of October 1 and 5, 1860 in Vol. 41 of the present edition). Originally every chapter had a résumé at the end, but Marx omitted them because the book, as he wrote in his letter to Engels of December 6, 1860, had "grown without my noticing it".

Publication of *Herr Vogt* involved serious difficulties, both financial ones and those connected with the revelations contained in this scathing polemic (see, for instance, Marx's letters to Engels of September 15 and 25 and to Lassalle of September 15, 1860). The book was sent to the printers in September 1860 (Marx to Lassalle, September 15, 1860) and appeared on December 1, 1860. The publisher was A. Petsch (London) and the printer R. Hirschfeld. In his letter to Marx of December 5, 1860 Engels deplored the numerous misprints and spelling mistakes, and also the absence of résumés at the end of chapters. Such résumés, he wrote, would have been "extremely effective" and, at the same time, "brought out the artistry of the whole arrangement which is truly admirable".

Marx took steps to ensure the wide circulation of the book as a means of exposing Vogt and other Bonapartist agents among journalists. Advertisements of its publication were sent to more than 40 newspapers, mostly German ones, in Germany, Switzerland and America, and also to a number of British papers (Marx to Engels, December 12, 1860 and January 22, 1861). But only a few newspapers published them: the *Genfer Grenzpost*, No. 12, December 22, 1860, the Hamburg *Reform* (supplements to Nos. 150 and 152, December 15 and 19, 1860) and *Freischütz*, the Berlin *Publicist* and *Neue Preussische Zeitung*, and the *Kölnische Zeitung* (Marx to Engels, December 26, 1860 and January 8 and 22, 1861, Engels to Marx, January 7, 1861). Most papers ignored the book. In his letter to Engels of January 22, 1861 Marx wrote with bitterness: "The scoundrels ... want to consign it to oblivion." The censorship and the police authorities, in particular those of the Bonapartist Second Empire, reacted guardedly. A report from Paris in the *Allgemeine Zeitung* of April 19, 1861 said: "By way of warning to booksellers *Herr Vogt* by Karl Marx was placed on the list of proscribed books, thus frustrating the appearance of a muchabridged French version which is now printing" (Marx to Engels, May 16, 1861).

The book was duly appreciated by Marx's friends and acquaintances. On receiving it Engels wrote to Marx: "That thing is grand. Especially the chapters 'Studies' and 'Agency'; cela est écrasant." Two days later he wrote: "The more I read of the book, the better it pleases me." And still later: "It's certainly the best piece of polemical writing you have ever done" (Engels to Marx, December 3, 5 and 19, 1860). W. Wolff's comment was: "It is a masterpiece from beginning to end." Contemporaries greatly appreciated Marx's closely reasoned arguments. For instance, P. Imandt wrote in January 1861 that it had banished whatever doubts he still had about Vogt's treachery in 1849. Lassalle, who originally objected to the very idea of writing a polemic against Vogt, was forced to admit that there were solid grounds for accusing Vogt of association with Bonapartist circles. This was also granted by people whose views widely differed from Marx's. For instance, L. Bucher, as Marx wrote to Engels on December 19, 1860, admitted the validity of Marx's arguments and that the book had destroyed "any prejudice he might have had against Marx's agitational activities".

A number of bourgeois and petty-bourgeois journalists attempted to refute Marx's exposé of Vogt as a Bonapartist agent. This was the purpose of Eduard Meyen's libellous article "Die neue Dunciation Karl Vogt's durch K. Marx" ("The New Dunciation of Karl Vogt by Karl Marx") in *Der Freischütz*, Nos. 155 and 156, December 27 and 29, 1860 and No. 1, January 1, 1861 (Marx to Engels, January 3, 1861). Marx was also attacked by Bettziech (pen name of the German petty-bourgeois democrat H. Beta) in the *Magazin für die Literatur des Auslandes*, No. 2, January 9, 1861. Complimentary notices on the book were published in the *Kölnischer Anzeiger* (Marx to Engels, January 18, 1861).

No second edition of *Herr Vogt* appeared during the lifetime of Marx and Engels. Only a few short excerpts were reprinted. Thus a passage from Chapter X ("Patrons and Accomplices") appeared in the *Breslauer Zeitung*, No. 115, March 9, 1861 under the heading "Zur Charakteristik Kossuth's" ("Concerning Kossuth") and in the Leipzig *Demokratisches Wochenblatt*, Nos. 16-18, April 18 and 25 and May 2, 1868 under the heading "Der enthüllte Kossuth" ("Kossuth Exposed"). Appendix 4 ("The Communist Trial in Cologne") from Chapter XII was reprinted in the Leipzig *Volksstaat*, organ of the Social-Democratic Party, Nos. 7 and 8, January 20 and 22, 1875 under the heading "Enthüllungen über den Kölner Kommunistenprozess" ("Revelations Concerning the Communist Trial in Cologne"). The same section was reproduced in the Nachtrag (Appendix) to the authorised (second) edition of Marx's *Revelations Concerning the Communist Trial in Cologne* (Leipzig, 1875). Under the heading "Nachtrag aus der Leipziger Auflage von 1875" ("Appendix from the Leipzig Edition of 1875") Engels also included it, with a small addendum, in the third edition of the *Revelations*, which he published in 1885.

Herr Vogt appears in English for the first time in these *Collected Works*. Only Appendix 4 ("The Communist Trial in Cologne") appeared in English earlier, in the collection: Karl Marx and Frederick Engels, *The Cologne Communist Trial*, translated with an Introduction and Notes by Rodney Livingstone, Lawrence and Wishart and International Publishers, London and New York, 1971.   p. 21

13 This refers to the war between the Kingdom of Sardinia (Piedmont) and France, on the one hand, and Austria, on the other (April 29 to July 8, 1859). It was launched by Napoleon III, who, under the banner of the "liberation of Italy", strove for aggrandizement and sought to strengthen the Bonapartist regime in France with the help of a successful military campaign. The Piedmont ruling circles hoped that French support would enable them to unite Italy, without the participation of the masses, under the aegis of the Savoy dynasty ruling in Piedmont. The war caused an upsurge of the national liberation movement in Italy. The Austrian army suffered a series of defeats. However, Napoleon III, frightened by the scale of the national liberation movement in Italy, abruptly ceased hostilities. On July 11, the French and Austrian emperors concluded a separate preliminary peace in Villafranca (see Note 126).

In this passage Marx alludes to his differences with Ferdinand Lassalle on the ways of unifying Italy and Germany. In his pamphlet *Der italienische Krieg und die Aufgabe Preussens. Eine Stimme aus der Demokratie (The Italian War and the Task of Prussia. The Voice of a Democrat)* published in Berlin in 1859, Lassalle advocated the dynastic unification of Germany under the aegis of Prussia (see the preface to this volume, pp. XVII-XVIII).   p. 27

14 The *Brimstone Gang* (Schwefelbande)—the name of a students' association at Jena University in the 1770s whose members were notorious for their brawls; subsequently the expression "Brimstone Gang" became widespread.   p. 28

15 Marx often puns on the name of Karl Vogt. *Vogt* or *Landvogt* was the name of provincial governors and other administrators in the German Empire in the Middle Ages. The "hereditary Vogt of Noughtborough (Nichilburg)" is an allusion to a character in Johann Fischart's satirical novel *Affentheurliche, Naupengeheurliche Geschichtklitterung: von Thaten und Rahten der vor kurtzen langen und je weilen vollenwolbeschreyten Helden und Herrn: Grandgoschier, Gorgellantua und Pantagruel. Königen inn Utopien, Iedewelt und Nienenreich, Soldan der Neuen Kannarrien und Oudyssen Inseln: auch Grossfürsten im Nubel Nibel Nebelland, Erbvögt auff Nichilburg, und Niderherren zu Nullibingen, Nullenstein und Niergendheym Etwan von M. Franz Rabelais Französisch entworffen.* Achte Ausgabe, 1617. Fischart's work, a German adaptation of François Rabelais' novels *Gargantua* and *Pantagruel*, was published in 1757. Below Marx frequently uses phrases from it.   p. 28

16 By "Magnum Opus" Marx means, here and below, Vogt's book *Mein Prozess gegen die Allgemeine Zeitung*, as distinct from Vogt's other, shorter writings on the same subject.   p. 28

17 This refers to the closing stage of the campaign in support of the Imperial Constitution which was adopted by the Frankfurt National Assembly on March 28, 1849. Most German states refused to recognise the Constitution. The people were its sole defender. Led by petty-bourgeois democrats, they launched an armed struggle in its support in the spring of 1849. The most violent uprisings occurred in the Bavarian Palatinate and Baden. However, in July the joint Prussian, Bavarian and Württemberg troops crushed the resistance of the Palatinate and Baden insurgent army and forced the remaining units to withdraw into Switzerland. The Baden and Palatinate events marked the end of the German revolution of 1848-49. Engels described them in *The Campaign for the German Imperial Constitution* and *Revolution and Counter-Revolution in Germany* (see present edition, Vols. 10 and 11).   p. 29

18 *In dulci jubilo* (in sweet merriment)—the opening words of a fourteenth-century Christmas carol. Later the phrase occurred in various student songs.

                                                                                      p. 30

19 Engels took part in the Baden-Palatinate uprising and on July 12, 1849, after its defeat, crossed over into Switzerland together with the detachment of August Willich, whose adjutant he was. He first settled in Vevey, but later moved to Lausanne. In September he met with members of the Communist League in Berne and Geneva. In early October, after obtaining a permit to leave Switzerland (see present edition Vol. 10, p. 595) he left for London where Marx wanted him to take part in the publication of the *Neue Rheinische Zeitung. Politisch-ökonomische Revue* and in reorganising the Communist League (Marx to Engels, end of July, August 17 and 23, 1849, present edition, Vol. 38).

                                                                                      p. 31

[20] The *blue republicans*—bourgeois republicans; *red republicans*—democrats and socialists of various trends.   p. 31

[21] The *Frankfurt Parliament* or the German National Assembly, opened in Frankfurt am Main on May 18, 1848. It was convened to unify the country and draw up a Constitution. The liberal deputies, who were in the majority, turned the Assembly into a mere debating club. At the decisive moments of the revolution, the liberal majority condoned the counter-revolutionary forces. In spring 1849, the liberals left the Assembly after the Prussian and other governments had rejected the Imperial Constitution that it had drawn up. What remained of the Assembly (the Rump) moved to Stuttgart and was dispersed by the Württemberg forces on June 18.

The *Regency of the Empire* was formed in Stuttgart on June 6, 1849 by what remained of the Frankfurt National Assembly. The Regency consisted of five deputies representing the Left faction (moderate democrats), including Karl Vogt. Their attempts to ensure by parliamentary means the implementation of the Constitution drawn up by the Frankfurt Assembly and rejected by the German princes ended in total failure.   p. 31

[22] The *battle of Idstedt* (June 24-25, 1850) was the closing episode of the war waged by the duchies of Schleswig and Holstein against Denmark. Under the impact of the March 1848 revolution in Germany a national liberation uprising had flared up in the two duchies, which were subject to the King of Denmark but populated mainly by Germans. The uprising became part of the struggle for the unification of Germany. The ruling circles of Prussia, which was at war with Denmark over Schleswig and Holstein, feared a popular outbreak and an intensification of the revolution. They therefore sought an agreement with the Danish monarchy to the detriment of overall German interests, which also had a negative effect on the operations of the Prussian army. The war lasted intermittently until July 1850. The Schleswig-Holstein army was defeated at Idstedt. As a result, the two duchies remained part of the Kingdom of Denmark.   p. 32

[23] On September 21, 1848 German refugees led by Struve invaded Baden from Swiss territory. Supported by the local republicans, Struve proclaimed a German Republic in the frontier town of Lörrach and formed a provisional government. The insurgent detachments were soon dispersed by troops, and Struve, Blind and other leaders of the uprising were imprisoned in Bruchsal by decision of a court-martial. They were released during another uprising in Baden in May 1849.   p. 32

[24] This refers to attempts by Struve and other German democrats to form a refugee *Democratic Association* and a Central Bureau of the United German Emigration. The activities of the petty-bourgeois democrats were to a considerable extent directed against the Social-Democratic Refugee Committee, then led by Marx and Engels (see Note 25), and aimed at bringing the proletarian sections under their influence. A critical assessment of these activities is given in the "Address of the Central Authority to the League, June 1850", written by Marx and Engels (see present edition, Vol. 10, p. 371) and in Engels' letter to Joseph Weydemeyer of April 22, 1850 (see present edition, Vol. 38).   p. 33

[25] The London *German Refugee Committee* was set up on September 18, 1849 on Marx's initiative under the auspices of the German Workers' Educational

Society. Besides Marx and other members of the Communist League, it included a number of petty-bourgeois democrats. At a meeting of the Society on November 18, the Committee was transformed into the *Social-Democratic Refugee Committee,* the aim being to dissociate the proletarian section of the London refugees from the petty-bourgeois elements (the report on the meeting was dated December 3, 1849). The new Committee included only members of the Communist League: Karl Marx (who was elected chairman), Heinrich Bauer, August Willich, Karl Pfänder and Frederick Engels. Besides providing material assistance for the refugees, predominantly those belonging to the proletarian wing, the Committee played an important part in restoring ties between members of the Communist League, in uniting the supporters of Marx and Engels in London and in reorganising the Communist League. In mid-September 1850, following the split in the Communist League, when most members of the Educational Society, to which the Committee was accountable, came under the influence of the Willich-Schapper sectarian group, Marx and Engels, together with their followers, withdrew from the Educational Society and the Committee (for details see present edition, Vol. 10, pp. 483 and 632).

p. 33

26 *Carbonari*—members of secret political societies in Italy and France in the first half of the nineteenth century. In Italy they fought for national independence, unification of the country and liberal constitutional reforms. In France their movement was primarily directed against the rule of the restored Bourbon dynasty (1815-30).   p. 33

27 By calling J. G. Rademacher a doctor of magic, Marx alludes to the former's book *Rechtfertigung der von den Gelehrten misskannten, verstandesrechten Erfahrungsheillehre der alten scheidekünstigen Geheimärzte und treue Mittheilung des Ergebnisses einer 25-jährigen Erprobung dieser Lehre am Krankenbette,* Berlin, 1846-1847 (*Vindication of the Neglected Rational Empirical Science of Medicine of the Old Doctors of Magic, Experts in Analytical Chemistry. With a Truthful Account of the Results of a 25-Year-Long Application of this Science at the Sick-Bed*).   p. 33

28 By the *December Gang* Marx means the secret Society of December 10 founded in 1849 and so called to commemorate the election of Louis Bonaparte, the Society's patron, to the Presidency of the French Republic on December 10, 1848. Marx describes the December 10 Society further in the text. The Society played an active part in the Bonapartist coup d'état of December 2, 1851 which established the counter-revolutionary regime of the Second Empire (1852-70) headed by Napoleon III.   p. 33

29 In the passage from *The Eighteenth Brumaire of Louis Bonaparte* quoted here Marx consistently substitutes the word "gang" *(Bande)* for "society" *(Gesellschaft).*   p. 34

30 *Lazzaroni*—a contemptuous name for declassed proletarians, primarily in the Kingdom of Naples. These people were repeatedly used by reactionary governments against liberal and democratic movements.   p. 34

31 This refers to Louis Bonaparte's attempts during the July monarchy to stage a coup d'état by means of a military mutiny. On October 30, 1836 he succeeded, with the help of several Bonapartist officers, in inciting two artillery regiments of the Strasbourg garrison to mutiny, but they were disarmed within a few

hours. Louis Bonaparte was arrested and deported to America. On August 6, 1840, taking advantage of a partial revival of Bonapartist sentiments in France, he landed in Boulogne with a handful of conspirators and attempted to raise a mutiny among the troops of the local garrison. This attempt likewise proved a failure. Louis Bonaparte was sentenced to life imprisonment, but escaped to England in 1846.   p. 35

32 The *National ateliers* (workshops) were instituted by the Provisional Government immediately after the February revolution of 1848. By this means the government sought to discredit Louis Blanc's ideas on the "Organisation of Labour" in the eyes of the workers and, at the same time, to utilise those employed in the national workshops, organised on military lines, against the revolutionary proletariat. Revolutionary ideas, however, continued to gain ground in the national workshops. The government took steps to reduce the number of workers employed in them, to send a large number off to public works in the province and finally to liquidate the workshops. This precipitated a proletarian uprising in Paris in June 1848. After its suppression, the Cavaignac Government issued a decree on July 3 disbanding the national workshops.

For an assessment of the national workshops see Karl Marx, *The Class Struggles in France, 1848 to 1850* (present edition, Vol. 10, p. 63).

The *Gardes mobiles* (Mobile Guards), set up by a decree of the Provisional Government on February 25, 1848 with the secret aim of fighting the revolutionary masses, were used to crush the June uprising of the Paris workers. Later they were disbanded on the insistence of Bonapartist circles, who feared that in the event of a conflict between Louis Bonaparte and the republicans, the *Gardes mobiles* would side with the latter.   p. 35

33 This witticism by Countess Lehon and the caustic remark by Madame de Girardin on the Bonapartist regime, both of which Marx quotes at the end of the paragraph, were forwarded to him, together with many other items used in *The Eighteenth Brumaire,* by Richard Reinhardt, a German refugee in Paris and Heinrich Heine's secretary. In his letter to Ferdinand Lassalle of February 23, 1852 Marx quotes a letter to him from Reinhardt, in particular the following passage: "As for de Morny, the minister who resigned with Dupin, he was known as the *escroc* [swindler] of his mistress' (Countess Lehon's) husband, a circumstance which caused Émile de Girardin's wife to say that while it was not unprecedented for governments to be in the hands of men who were governed by their wives, none had ever been known to be in the hands of *hommes entretenus* [kept men]. Well, this same Countess Lehon holds a salon where she is one of Bonaparte's most vociferous opponents and it was she who, on the occasion of the confiscation of the Orleans' estates, let fall '*C'est le premier vol de l'aigle*'. [A pun: "It is the first flight of the eagle" and "It is the first theft of the eagle".] Thanks to this remark of his wife's, Émile de Girardin was expelled" (see present edition, Vol. 39).   p. 36

34 This refers to the Regency of Philippe of Orleans in France from 1715 to 1723 during the minority of Louis XV.   p. 36

35 The *Holy Coat of Trier*—a relic exhibited in the Catholic Cathedral at Trier, allegedly a garment of Christ of which he was stripped at his crucifixion. Generations of pilgrims came to venerate it.   p. 37

36 The *Vendôme Column* was erected in Paris between 1806 and 1810 as a tribute
    to the military victories of Napoleon I. It was made of bronze from captured
    enemy guns and crowned by a statue of Napoleon; the statue was removed
    during the Restoration but re-erected in 1833. In the spring of 1871, by order
    of the Paris Commune, the Vendôme Column was destroyed as a symbol of
    militarism.   p. 37

37 *Das Volk*—a German-language weekly published in London from May 7 to
    August 20, 1859—was founded as the official organ of the German Workers'
    Educational Society in London. The first issue appeared under the editorship
    of the German journalist Elard Biscamp, a petty-bourgeois democrat. Begin-
    ning with issue No. 2 Marx took an active part in its publication: he gave advice
    to the editors, edited articles himself and organised material support. In issue
    No. 6 of June 11, the Editorial Board officially named Karl Marx, Frederick
    Engels, Ferdinand Freiligrath, Wilhelm Wolff and Heinrich Heise as its
    contributors (see present edition, Vol. 16, p. 624). Marx's first article in the
    paper—"Spree and Mincio"—was printed on June 25 (see present edition,
    Vol. 16). Under Marx's influence *Das Volk* began to turn into a militant
    revolutionary working-class newspaper. In the beginning of July, Marx became
    its virtual editor and manager.
        Das Volk carried Marx's preface to his work *A Contribution to the Critique of
    Political Economy*, six of his articles, including the unfinished series *Quid pro
    Quo*, seven articles by Engels and his review of Marx's *Contribution to the Critique
    of Political Economy*, and reviews of the *Hermann*, the newspaper of the German
    petty-bourgeois democrats, by Marx and Biscamp (they appeared in the column
    "Gatherings from the Press"). Furthermore, many articles and political reviews
    written by different authors were edited by Marx. In all, sixteen issues
    appeared. *Das Volk* ceased publication for lack of money.
        Articles published in *Das Volk* reflected the elaboration by Marx and Engels
    of questions of revolutionary theory and the tactics of proletarian struggle,
    covered the class battles of the proletariat and implacably combated petty-
    bourgeois ideology. From a position of proletarian internationalism the
    newspaper analysed the course of the Austro-Italo-French war of 1859 and the
    issues involved in the unification of Germany and Italy, exposed the foreign
    policy of Britain, Prussia, France, Russia and other reactionary states and
    waged a consistent struggle against Bonapartism and its overt and covert
    supporters.   p. 38

38 *Two Richmonds in the field* is an expression used to denote a second, unexpected
    adversary. It originates from Shakespeare's *Richard III* (Act V, Scene 4).
                                                                            p. 39

39 This presumably refers to Abt's pamphlet *Carl Vogt und Carl Marx oder die
    Bürstenheimer*, Leipzig, Heidelberg. A notice in No. 27 (July 5, 1861) of the
    Stimmen der Zeit. Wochenschrift für Politik und Literatur, a weekly published by
    Adolph Kolatschek, said that the pamphlet would be published in the
    supplement to No. 39, and contained the following editorial note: "The
    work in question reached the editor as early as January of this year. The
    delay in publication is by no means due to any fault on the part of the
    author."
        It is possible that friends had forwarded the manuscript of the pamphlet to
    Marx.   p. 39

⁴⁰ In April 1848 a republican uprising took place in Baden. Led by the petty-bourgeois democrats Friedrich Hecker and Gustav Struve, it started with republican detachments invading Baden from Switzerland. The uprising was poorly organised and was crushed by the end of April.

Later some participants in the Baden uprising joined the unit formed by August Willich from German émigré workers and artisans in Besançon, France, in November 1848. Its members received allowances from the French Government, payment of which was, however, discontinued at the beginning of 1849. Later the unit was incorporated in Willich's volunteer detachment which took part in the Baden-Palatinate uprising in May-June 1849.   p. 40

⁴¹ The great adventure with "the lost drum" is Marx's ironic way of referring to the manoeuvres of Napoleon III and the Bonapartist circles in France aimed at capturing the left bank of the Rhine. Vogt supported these manoeuvres in the press. Marx compares them to a comic episode in Shakespeare's *All's Well That Ends Well* (Act III, Scenes 5 and 6, Act IV, Scenes 1 and 3). By Parolles Vogt is meant.   p. 40

⁴² The *Neue Rheinische Zeitung. Organ der Democratie* appeared in Cologne daily from June 1, 1848 to May 19, 1849. The editorial board included Karl Marx (Editor-in-Chief), Heinrich Bürgers, Ernst Dronke, Ferdinand Freiligrath, Georg Weerth, Wilhelm Wolff, Ferdinand Wolff and Frederick Engels.

The *Neue Rheinische Zeitung* was founded by Marx as a militant periodical intended to exert a direct influence on the masses, educate and unite them politically and ideologically and pave the way for the creation of a mass party of the German proletariat. As a rule, Marx and Engels wrote the editorials, formulating the paper's stand on the key questions of the revolution.

The consistent revolutionary tendency of the *Neue Rheinische Zeitung*, its active internationalism and its attacks on the government, aroused the displeasure of the bourgeois shareholders and led to the persecution of its editors by the authorities and a smear campaign in the feudal monarchist and liberal bourgeois press. It was particularly the paper's articles in defence of the June 1848 uprising of the Paris proletariat that frightened away the shareholders. Persecution of the *Neue Rheinische Zeitung* editors by the judicial authorities and the police became particularly severe after the counter-revolutionary coup in Prussia in November-December 1848.

In May 1849, under the conditions of the general counter-revolutionary offensive, the Prussian Government expelled Marx from Prussia on the pretext that he was not a Prussian citizen. Marx's expulsion and new repressive measures against other editors of the *Neue Rheinische Zeitung* resulted in the paper ceasing publication. The last issue, No. 301, printed in red ink, appeared on May 19, 1849. In their farewell address "To the Workers of Cologne", the editors wrote that "their last word everywhere and always will be *emancipation of the working class*".   p. 41

⁴³ The *arsenal in Prüm* was stormed by democrats and workers from Trier and neighbouring townships on May 17 and 18, 1849. Their aim was to seize the arms and extend the uprising in defence of the Imperial Constitution to the left bank of the Rhine. The insurgents succeeded in capturing the arsenal, but government troops soon arrived on the scene and the movement was suppressed.   p. 41

⁴⁴ Sazonov obviously had in mind Professor I. K. Babst, who had given a series of lectures in political economy in Moscow. An account of the first lecture was

published in the *Moskovskiye vedomosti*, No. 19, January 24, 1860. In Sazonov's opinion, this lecture reflected some of the ideas contained in the *Preface* of Marx's *A Contribution to the Critique of Political Economy*.   p. 42

45 The *Bundschuh* was a secret revolutionary peasant union active in Germany on the eve of the Peasant War of 1525. Schily uses the name to designate the Communist League, led by Marx and Engels.   p. 44

46 An allusion to the *Club of Resolute Progress*. Founded in Karlsruhe on June 5, 1848, it represented the more radical wing of the petty-bourgeois democratic republicans (Struve, Tzschirner, Heinzen and others) discontented with the conciliatory policy of the Brentano government and the increasing strength of the Rightist elements within it. The Club suggested that Brentano should extend the revolution beyond Baden and the Palatinate and introduce radicals into the government. Brentano refused, so the Club tried, on June 6, to force the government's hand by threatening an armed demonstration. The government, however, supported by the civic militia and other armed units, proved the stronger party in the conflict. The Club of Resolute Progress was disbanded.   p. 44

47 *Cercle social*—an organisation established by democratic intellectuals in Paris in the first years of the French Revolution. Its chief spokesmen, Claude Fauchet and Nicolas Bonneville, demanded the egalitarian division of the land, restrictions on large fortunes and employment for all able-bodied citizens.
                              p. 46

48 Here Marx has "auch eine schöne Gegend", i.e. "a beautiful landscape too". The phrase originated from a story about a woman who, trying to console the mother of a soldier killed at the Battle of Leipzig (1813), said: "But it was a beautiful landscape."   p. 46

49 The *Grütli Association (Grütliverein)* was a Swiss petty-bourgeois reformist organisation founded in 1838 as an educational society for artisans and workers. The name *Grütliverein* was to emphasise the Swiss national character of the association. Legend has it that in 1307 representatives of three Swiss cantons met in Grütli meadow and formed an alliance to fight against the arbitrary rule of the Austrian governors (Vogts). Hence Marx's ironic reference to Karl Vogt.   p. 47

50 *Badinguet* was the nickname of Napoleon III. He was called so because in 1846 he escaped from prison disguised in the clothes of the stonemason Badinguet.
    Marianne was the name of a secret republican society in France founded in 1850. Its aim was to fight against the Bonapartist regime of the Second Empire.
                              p. 49

51 The *Communist League* was the first German and international communist organisation of the proletariat formed under the leadership of Marx and Engels in London early in June 1847, as a result of the reorganisation of the League of the Just (a secret association of refugee workers and artisans that was set up in Paris in the 1830s and had communities in Germany, France, Switzerland and England). The programme and organisational principles of the Communist League were drawn up with the direct participation of Marx and Engels. The League's members took an active part in the bourgeois-democratic

revolution in Germany in 1848-49. Although the defeat of the revolution dealt a blow to the League, in 1849-50 it was reorganised and continued its activities. In the summer of 1850 disagreements arose in the League between the supporters of Marx and Engels and the sectarian Willich-Schapper group, which tried to impose on the League its tactics of immediately unleashing a revolution without taking into account the actual situation and the practical possibilities. The discord led to a split within the League in September 1850. Because of police persecutions and arrests of League members in May 1851, the activities of the League as an organisation practically ceased in Germany. On November 17, 1852, on a motion by Marx, the League's London District announced the dissolution of the League (see Marx's letter to Engels of November 19, 1852). On February 24, 1860 Marx sent this letter to Legal Counsellor Weber (see present edition, Vol. 41).

The Communist League played an outstanding role as the first proletarian party guided by the principles of scientific communism, as a school of proletarian revolutionaries and as the historical forerunner of the International Working Men's Association. (On the Communist League see this volume, pp. 78-82.)   p. 49

52 See Marx's *Revelations Concerning the Communist Trial in Cologne* (present edition, Vol. 11, pp. 445-49). This work was published as a pamphlet in Basle, Switzerland, in January 1853 (the edition used by Vogt). In the USA it was first published in instalments in the democratic Boston *Neu-England-Zeitung* and at the end of April 1853 it was printed in pamphlet form by the same newspaper. In *Herr Vogt* Marx quotes the *Revelations* from the Boston pamphlet. p. 49

53 The *Palais Royal* in Paris was the residence of Jerôme Bonaparte (the youngest brother of Napoleon I) and his son, Prince Joseph (nicknamed Plon-Plon).
                                                                     p. 49

54 The *German-American Revolutionary Loan* was a loan that Gottfried Kinkel and other petty-bourgeois émigré leaders tried to raise in 1851 and 1852 among German refugees and Americans of German origin with a view to immediately inciting a revolution in Germany. To win support for the loan, Kinkel toured the USA in September 1851. The project proved a total failure. In a number of their works Marx and Engels ridiculed the loan as an adventurist and harmful attempt artificially to engineer a revolution during a lull in the revolutionary movement.   p. 50

55 At the *battle of Murten* (June 22, 1476), fought in the course of the Burgundian Wars, the troops of Duke Charles the Bold of Burgundy were defeated by the Swiss.   p. 50

56 In *St. Paul's Church,* Frankfurt am Main, the Frankfurt National Assembly met in 1848 and 1849.   p. 51

57 The *Grand Cophta* was the name of the omnipotent and omniscient Egyptian priest who headed the nonexistent Masonic "Egyptian Lodge" which the famous eighteenth-century impostor "Count" Cagliostro (Giuseppe Balsamo) claimed to have founded.   p. 53

58 The *Federal Council*—the Government of the Swiss Confederation.   p. 54

59 In September 1851 arrests were made in France among members of local communities belonging to the Willich-Schapper group, which was responsible

for the split in the Communist League in September 1850. The petty-bourgeois conspiratorial tactics of the group, ignoring realities and aiming at an immediate uprising, enabled the French and Prussian police, with the help of the agent-provocateur Cherval, who headed one of the group's local communities in Paris, to fabricate the case of the so-called Franco-German plot. Cherval was both an agent of the Prussian envoy in Paris and a French spy. In February 1852 the accused were sentenced on a charge of plotting a coup d'état. With the connivance of the French and Prussian police Cherval was allowed to escape from prison. The attempts of the Prussian police to incriminate the Communist League led by Marx and Engels failed. Konrad Schramm, a League member, arrested in Paris in September 1851, was soon released owing to lack of evidence. Nevertheless, the Prussian Police Superintendent Stieber, one of the organisers of the Cologne Communist trial in 1852, repeated the false police accusations. Marx exposed Stieber's perjury in his *Revelations Concerning the Communist Trial in Cologne* (see the chapter "The Cherval Plot", present edition, Vol. 11, pp. 407-19).

On his arrival in London in May 1852 Cherval was admitted to the German Workers' Educational Society led by Schapper but was soon expelled because of his role of provocateur in the so-called Franco-German plot.   p. 55

60 The *Cologne trial* (October 4-November 12, 1852) was organised and stage-managed by the Prussian Government. The defendants were members of the Communist League arrested in the spring of 1851 on charges of "treasonable plotting". The forged documents and false evidence presented by the police authorities were not only designed to secure the conviction of the defendants but also to compromise their London comrades and the proletarian organisation as a whole. Seven of the defendants were sentenced to imprisonment in a fortress for terms ranging from three to six years. The dishonest tactics resorted to by the Prussian police state in fighting the international working-class movement were exposed by Engels in his article "The Late Trial in Cologne" and, in greater detail, by Marx in his pamphlet *Revelations Concerning the Communist Trial in Cologne* (see present edition, Vol. 11).   p. 56

61 The *German Workers' Educational Society* in London was founded in February 1840 by Karl Schapper, Joseph Moll and other members of the League of the Just (an organisation of German craftsmen and workers, and also of emigrant workers of other nationalities). After the reorganisation of the League of the Just in the summer of 1847 and the founding of the Communist League, the latter's local communities played the leading role in the Society. During various periods of its activity, the Society had branches in working-class districts in London. In 1847 and 1849-50, Marx and Engels took an active part in the Society's work, but on September 17, 1850, Marx, Engels and a number of their followers withdrew because the Willich-Schapper sectarian and adventurist faction had temporarily increased its influence in the Society, causing a split in the Communist League (see present edition, Vol. 10, pp. 483, 632). In the late 1850s, Marx and Engels resumed their work in the Educational Society, which was active up to 1918, when it was closed down by the British Government.   p. 56

62 Karl Vogt was one of the five members of the Imperial Regency (see Note 21).   p. 58

[63] An allusion to the denunciatory prophecies of Zacharias, one of the twelve minor prophets of the Old Testament.   p. 60

[64] The *Hambach Festival* was a political demonstration held by members of the liberal and radical bourgeoisie at the castle of Hambach (in the Bavarian Palatinate) on May 27, 1832 to urge the unification of Germany, constitutional reforms and the transformation of Germany into a federal republic.   p. 60

[65] The German socialist Eichhoff was Berlin correspondent of the weekly *Hermann*. In September and October 1859 he anonymously published in it a series of articles headed "Stieber" in which he exposed the part played by Wilhelm Stieber, chief of the Prussian political police, in organising the government-inspired trial of members of the Communist League in Cologne in 1852. Stieber sued Eichhoff for libel. In May 1860 a Berlin court sentenced Eichhoff to 14 months imprisonment (see Marx's letters to Engels of January 31, 1860 and to Freiligrath of February 29, 1860, present edition, Vol. 41).
                                                              p. 65

[66] The *Ladendorf trial*—the trial of Ladendorf, Gercke, Falkenthal, Levy and several other persons arrested in 1853 on the basis of a denunciation by police agent Hentze, a former member of the Communist League. The trial was held in Berlin in 1854. On trumped-up charges of plotting, the defendants were sentenced to various terms of imprisonment (from three to five years).

The *League of the Dead* was a secret conspiratorial organisation in Bremen in the 1840s and early 1850s. It was uncovered by the police in 1852.   p. 66

[67] Here Marx paraphrases two expressions: "Tranquillity is the first duty of the citizen", a dictum coined by the Prussian minister Schulenburg-Kehnert in his address to the population of Berlin of October 17, 1806, following the defeat at Jena (*Le Moniteur universel*, No. 304, October 31, 1806, "Prusse", Berlin, du 18 octobre), and "In hoc signo vinces" ("By this sign thou shalt conquer"). Legend has it that on the eve of a battle against his rival Maxentius in 312, the Roman Emperor Constantine (274-337) saw in the sky the sign of the Cross and over it the words "In hoc signo vinces". The Church associates this legend with Constantine's "conversion" from the persecution of Christianity to its protection.   p. 67

[68] At the *battle of Zorndorf*, fought in the course of the Seven Years' War on August 14 (25), 1758, the Prussian army, commanded by Frederick II, clashed with the Russian forces. Both sides suffered heavy losses. The outcome of the battle was inconclusive.   p. 69

[69] *Kobes I* was the nickname of Jacob Venedey, who was born in Cologne. In the Cologne dialect, Kobes stands for Jacob. Venedey owed the nickname to Heinrich Heine, who in a satirical poem headed "Kobes I" ridiculed him as a model philistine.   p. 69

[70] An ironic allusion to the book *Kraft und Stoff* (Energy and Matter) (1855) by the German physiologist Ludwig Büchner, a vulgar materialist like Vogt. p. 71

[71] This refers to the Second Democratic Congress of representatives of democratic and workers' organisations from various German towns which was held in Berlin from October 26 to 30, 1848.   p. 73

72 A reference to the *Revolutionary Centralisation,* a secret organisation founded at
the beginning of 1850 by German refugees in Switzerland, mostly petty-
bourgeois democrats. Its Central Committee, based in Zurich, was headed by
S. E. Tzschirner, a leader of the Dresden uprising in May 1849. Prominent
members were P. Fries, T. L. Greiner, F. Sigel, G. A. Techow and J. Ph. Becker,
all participants in the 1849 Baden-Palatinate uprising. Members of the
Communist League, K. L. J. d'Ester, K. Bruhn and W. Wolff, also belonged to
this organisation. In July and August 1850 the leaders of the Revolutionary
Centralisation approached the Central Authority of the Communist League with a
proposal to amalgamate. On behalf of the League's Central Authority Marx and
Engels rejected the proposal as detrimental to the class independence of the
proletarian party. By the end of 1850, the Revolutionary Centralisation had
disintegrated as a result of the mass expulsion of German refugees from
Switzerland.   p. 75

73 Beust's letter to Schily of May 1, 1860 was a postscript to Emmermann's letter
to Schily part of which Marx quotes immediately above. Marx commented on
Emmermann's and Beust's letters (particularly on the latter, which contained
derogatory statements about Marx) in his letter to Engels of May 7, 1860 (see
present edition, Vol. 41).   p. 76

74 The German Workers' Educational Society in Brussels (Deutscher Arbeiter-
verein) was founded by Marx and Engels at the end of August 1847 to provide
a political education for German workers living in Belgium and spread the
ideas of communism among them. With Marx, Engels and their associates at its
head, the Society became the legal centre rallying German revolutionary
proletarians in Belgium and maintaining direct contact with Flemish and
Walloon workers' clubs. Its most active members belonged to the Brussels
community of the Communist League. The Society played an important part in
founding the Brussels Democratic Association. Its activities ceased after the
February 1848 revolution in France when the Belgian police arrested and
deported its members.   p. 79

75 The reference here is to the Willich-Schapper group, which Marx and Engels
called the *Sonderbund*—perhaps an allusion to the separatist union of seven
economically backward Catholic cantons of Switzerland formed in the 1840s to
resist progressive bourgeois reforms. This sectarian adventurist group split
away from the Communist League after September 15, 1850 (see Note 51) and
formed an independent organisation with its own Central Authority. In view of
the factionalists' refusal to abide by the decision to transfer the Central
Authority to Cologne and because of their disorganising activities, the Cologne
Central Authority expelled them from the League at the proposal of the
League's London District and gave notification of this in its Address of
December 1, 1850 (see present edition, Vol. 10, pp. 625-30 and 633). By their
activities the Willich-Schapper group helped the Prussian police uncover the
League's illegal communities in Germany and fabricate a case in Cologne in
1852 against prominent members of the League (see present edition, Vol. 11,
pp. 445-52).   p. 80

76 The *German Confederation (der Deutsche Bund)* was an ephemeral union of
German states formed by decision of the Congress of Vienna in June 1815 and
originally comprising 35 absolutist feudal states and 4 free cities. The

Confederation aggravated the political and economic fragmentation of Germany and impeded its development.

After the defeat of the 1848-49 revolution, a struggle for hegemony in Germany developed between Prussia and Austria. The latter sought to restore the German Confederation, which had virtually fallen apart during the revolution. Prussia hoped to achieve supremacy by forming a union of German states under its own aegis. In the autumn of 1850 the Austro-Prussian rivalry was intensified by the clash of interests over the Electorate of Hesse-Cassel, where a constitutional conflict had developed between the local Chamber and the Elector as a result of which the Chamber was disbanded and martial law introduced. In this situation Austria and Prussia vied for the right to carry out punitive operations against the Hesse constitutional movement. In early November 1850 Prussian and Austrian troops clashed on the territory of Hesse-Cassel. However, under pressure from Nicholas I, Prussia was forced to yield to Austria and temporarily desist from its plans for establishing hegemony in Germany (see Note 143).   p. 81

77 The *Federal Diet (Bundestag)*—the central body of the German Confederation. It consisted of representatives of the member states and held its sessions in Frankfurt am Main. Having no actual power, it nevertheless served as an instrument of monarchist feudal reaction.   p. 81

78 The German military association "Self-Help" (Deutscher republikanischer Wehrbund "Hilf Dir") was set up at the initiative of J. Ph. Becker in Gross-Hüningen in October 1848. It was to unite Germans living abroad, particularly political refugees and artisans in Switzerland and France. The Association's Central Committee was in Biel, Berne Canton. Becker was the political leader, A. Willich the military. A German column was formed in Besançon with branches in Nancy, Vesul, Lyons and other towns. The idea of rallying all German unions in Switzerland failed to materialise.   p. 82

79 H. L. Miskowsky was burnt to death during a fire in a wooden barracks in Whitechapel in 1854 (see Marx's letter to Engels of May 6, 1854, present edition, Vol. 39).   p. 84

80 The meeting in question was held in late August 1850.   p. 84

81 In Marx's exposé *The Knight of the Noble Consciousness,* in which this letter is quoted in full, it is dated November 22 (see present edition, Vol. 12, pp. 504-05). The original of the letter is not extant.   p. 86

82 An allusion to *Batrachomyomachia* (The Battle of the Frogs and the Mice), an anonymous Greek poem which parodies Homer's *Iliad.*

Marx and Engels give a detailed description of A. Ruge's Agitation Union and G. Kinkel's Émigré Club (Marx calls it Émigré Society here) and also of the relations between the two émigré petty-bourgeois organisations in their exposé *The Great Men of the Exile* (see present edition, Vol. 11, pp. 310-25).   p. 87

83 This idea was formulated in the "Review, May to October 1850" in a section which Engels later included in Chapter IV of *The Class Struggles in France, 1848 to 1850,* 1895 edition (see present edition, Vol. 10, pp. 509-10 and 134-35). Marx expressed the same idea even earlier in his article "The Revolutionary Movement" (present edition, Vol. 8, p. 214).

"A storm in a teacup" is an expression used by Montesquieu about a series of riots in the republic of San Marino.   p. 90

84 Marx quotes from his speech at the trial of the Rhenish District Committee of Democrats (see present edition, Vol. 8, p. 336). The minutes of the trial were published in the *Neue Rheinische Zeitung*, Nos. 226 and 231-33, February 19, 25, 27 and 28, 1849 and as a separate pamphlet under the heading *Zwei politische Prozesse. Verhandelt vor den Februar-Assisen in Köln*, Köln, 1849. Verlag der Expedition der *Neuen Rheinischen Zeitung*. The pamphlet also included a report on the trial of the *Neue Rheinische Zeitung* of February 7, 1849.   p. 91

85 The *Comité de salut public* (Committee of Public Safety) was established by the Convention on April 6, 1793; during the Jacobin dictatorship (June 2, 1793-July 27, 1794) it was the leading body of the revolutionary government in France.   p. 93

86 Ernst Dronke was sent to Switzerland as an emissary of the Communist League in July 1850 after Marx and Engels had learnt about the activity of the Revolutionary Centralisation from a letter by Wilhelm Wolff of May 9, 1850. Dronke wrote about his work in Switzerland and Germany in his letters to the League's Central Authority of July 3, 1850 and to Engels of July 3 and 18, 1850.   p. 94

87 This quotation is from the article "Gottfried Kinkel" by Marx and Engels (see present edition, Vol. 10, p. 345).

   The article castigated the unworthy conduct of the petty-bourgeois democrat Kinkel before the court-martial in Rastatt which tried him for his part in the campaign for the Imperial Constitution. Speaking in court in his own defence on August 4, 1849 Kinkel denied his involvement in the revolutionary movement and eulogised the Hohenzollern dynasty. Marx and Engels gave a satirical portrayal of Kinkel in their exposé *The Great Men of the Exile* (see present edition, Vol. 11).   p. 96

88 Marx probably means the American Revolutionary Union for Europe (*Amerikanischer Revolutionsbund für Europa*), a German-American émigré organisation set up in Philadelphia in the summer of 1852 and consisting mostly of former members of the Agitation Union.   p. 98

89 Marx means the polemic between Gustav Adolf Roesler and Franz Heinrich Zitz, former deputies to the Frankfurt National Assembly, who attacked each other between July and September 1850 in the German-American newspapers *Deutsche Schnellpost für Europäische Zustände, öffentliches und sociales Leben Deutschlands* (New York) and *New-Yorker Democrat*.   p. 98

90 This probably refers to the manuscript "Drei Jahre in Paris" ("Three Years in Paris"), a description of the German emigration in 1849 to 1851 by the petty-bourgeois refugee Leopold Häfner. Marx was familiar with it (see his letter to Adolph Cluss of September 3, 1852, present edition, Vol. 39). p. 99

91 Marx is referring to Vogt's pamphlet *Mein Prozess gegen die Allgemeine Zeitung* as the *Lausiade* (from the German word *Laus*, i.e. *louse*) by analogy with the *Lousiad*, a satirical epic by the English poet Peter Pindar (pen name of John Wolcot).

Lusiads (*Os Lusiadas*) is an epic by Luis de Camoens (c. 1524-1580), the great poet of the Portuguese Renaissance.   p. 99

92 Marx ridicules Vogt's ephemeral power as Imperial Regent (see Note 21) by comparing his status to Sancho Panza's imaginary governorship of the island of Barataria (*barato* means "cheap" in Spanish) in Cervantes' *Don Quixote*.

                                                                                                          p. 100

93 Here and elsewhere, speaking of the Frankfurt National Assembly, Marx used the Assembly's verbatim reports, which were later published in book form under the heading *Stenographischer Bericht über die Verhandlungen der deutschen constituirenden Nationalversammlung zu Frankfurt am Main*, Frankfurt am Main, 1848-1849.   p. 103

94 On August 26, 1848 Denmark and Prussia concluded an armistice in Malmö which nullified the revolutionary and democratic gains of the peoples of Schleswig and Holstein and virtually sanctioned the continuance of Danish rule there. On September 16, 1848 the Frankfurt National Assembly ratified the armistice. This decision caused an outburst of indignation in Germany's democratic circles. On September 17, 1848 a mass meeting held in the Pfingstweide meadow in the northeast suburb of Frankfurt am Main adopted a resolution demanding that the deputies who had voted for ratification should be declared traitors and urging the Left deputies to walk out of the Assembly (*Stenographischer Bericht...*, Bd. 3, S. 2184). While some extreme Left deputies complied with these demands, Karl Vogt came out against them. On September 18 the popular movement in Frankfurt against the ratification of the Malmö armistice developed into an uprising which was brutally suppressed by government troops.   p. 103

95 On October 9, 1848 the Frankfurt National Assembly adopted a "Law for the Protection of the Constituent National Assembly and of the Officials of the Central Authority" ("Gesetz betreffend den Schutz der Konstituierenden Reichsversammlung und der Beamten der Zentralgewalt", *Stenographischer Bericht...*, Bd. 4, S. 2528-29). Under this law, insulting a deputy of the Assembly or a representative of the central authority (an Imperial Regent, a minister or any other official) was punishable by imprisonment. This was one of the repressive measures against the people introduced after the September uprising in Frankfurt.   p. 103

96 The *Central March Association*, thus named after the March 1848 revolution in Germany, was founded in Frankfurt am Main at the end of November 1848 by Left-wing deputies to the Frankfurt National Assembly and had branches in various towns in Germany. Fröbel, Simon, Ruge, Vogt and other petty-bourgeois democratic leaders of the March associations confined themselves to revolutionary phrase-mongering and showed indecision and inconsistency in the struggle against counter-revolutionaries, for which Marx and Engels sharply criticised them (e.g., in the article "Ein Aktenstück des Märzvereins", *Neue Rheinische Zeitung*, No. 181, December 29, 1848).   p. 103

97 See Engels' works "Elberfeld" and *The Campaign for the German Imperial Constitution* (present edition, Vols. 9 and 10).   p. 105

98 In November and early December 1848 a coup d'état took place in Prussia

which led to the establishment of the arch-reactionary Brandenburg-Manteuffel
Ministry and the dissolution of the National Assembly.   p. 105

99 See Note 70.   p. 106

100 At the elections to the Frankfurt National Assembly in May 1848, the Silesian
district of Striegau (Strzegom) elected Wilhelm Wolff to deputise when
necessary for the liberal deputy Stenzel, who obtained a majority vote. When
Stenzel and a group of other liberal deputies walked out of the Assembly in
May 1849, his seat went to Wolff.

"...the Frankfurt Assembly, which was 'in the process of dissolution'"—
Marx ironically quotes the statement in which the liberals in question
announced their withdrawal from the Assembly (*Stenographischer Bericht...*,
Bd. 9, S. 6746).   p. 106

101 The proclamation "The German National Assembly to the German Nation"
("Die deutsche Nationalversammlung an das deutsche Volk") drawn up by the
poet J. L. Uhland on behalf of the moderate democrats was dictated by the
latter's desire for a political rapprochement with the liberal bourgeoisie. It
offered no concrete programme of action and boiled down to an impotent
appeal to the German nation to press for the introduction of the Imperial
Constitution.

The other proclamation, stemming from the Committee of Thirty,
contained an equally ineffectual call to the armies of those German states which
refused to recognise the National Assembly, to swear allegiance to the Imperial
Constitution.

The Committee of Thirty was set up by the Frankfurt National Assembly on
April 11, 1849 to devise steps conducive to the implementation of the Imperial
Constitution in view of the ambiguous stand of Frederick William IV, King of
Prussia, on the Assembly's offer of the Imperial Crown. Originally Frederick
William IV made his acceptance contingent on the attitude of the other
German princes, but on April 28, 1849 he rejected the Imperial Constitution
and the Imperial Crown.   p. 106

102 In early May 1849 Middle Franconia (part of Bavaria) was swept by a wave of
protests against the rejection of the Imperial Constitution by the Bavarian
Government. The movement culminated in a mass rally in Nuremberg on May
13 attended by 50,000 people. In his address Karl Vogt, under cover of
pseudo-revolutionary phrases, urged the people to abstain from resolute action.

"Wailers" (Heuler)—the name the republican democrats in Germany applied
to the moderate constitutionalists in 1848 and 1849. The latter, in turn, called
their opponents "agitators" *(Wühler)*.   p. 109

103 An ironic reference to Louis Bonaparte, who was brought up in the Swiss
canton of Thurgau. In 1832 he became a citizen of that canton and in 1833 an
honorary citizen of the Swiss Republic.   p. 111

104 The *Great Exhibition in London,* from May to October 1851, was the first world
trade and industrial exhibition.   p. 113

105 This refers to Heinrich Heine's political articles for the Augsburg *Allgemeine
Zeitung* from Paris in the 1830s and 1840s and to the essays published in the
same newspaper by the German Orientalist Jakob Philipp Fallmerayer in the
early 1840s. Heine published most of the articles in question in book form

under the titles *Französische Zustände* (1832) and *Lutetia* (1854). Fallmerayer's essays appeared in a two-volume edition under the title *Fragmente aus dem Orient* in 1845.   p. 114

[106] "Bas Empire" (Lower Empire) is the name sometimes given to the Byzantine Empire and also to the late Roman Empire in historical literature. It came to be applied to any state in decline or disintegration.   p. 115

[107] At the beginning of April 1859 Vogt sent Freiligrath and others his political "Programme" calling on the states of the German Confederation to maintain neutrality in the war France and Piedmont were preparing against Austria. Vogt urged political leaders to support his "Programme" in the press. (See Vogt, *Mein Prozess...*, Dokumente, S. 33.)   p. 115

[108] In this footnote Marx outlines the history of the publication of his exposé *Lord Palmerston* (see present edition, Vol. 12). It was conceived as a series of articles for the *New-York Daily Tribune*, but not all of the articles were published there. Between October 1853 and January 1854 four instalments appeared as anonymous leading articles, externally unconnected and under different titles.

Simultaneously, betweeen October 22 and December 24, 1853, the Chartist *People's Paper* published eight articles under the common title *Lord Palmerston* with the editorial note: "Written for the *New-York Tribune* by Dr. Marx, and communicated by him to us."

The pamhlet against Palmerston was widely circulated. On November 26, 1853 the *Glasgow Sentinel* reprinted from the *Tribune* the third article of the series under the title "Lord Palmerston and Russia". In December of the same year the London publisher Tucker put out this article in pamphlet form. In early February 1854 a second edition of the pamphlet appeared with Marx's participation, now under the heading *Palmerston and Poland.* Somewhat later Tucker published another pamphlet, *Palmerston and the Treaty of Unkiar Skelessi* (the heading on the title page was: *Palmerston, What Has He Done?*), which reproduced, with a number of alterations, the text of the fourth and fifth articles in the series.

Between December 1855 and February 1856 all eight articles were reprinted in *The Free Press*, organ of the London Urquhartists, and, as a separate edition, in No. 5 of *The Free Press Serials*. At about the same time individual articles of the series appeared in the Urquhartist *Sheffield Free Press* and later in a number of other newspapers.   p. 116

[109] The *Foreign Affairs Committees* were public organisations set up by the Urquhartists in a number of English cities between the 1840s and 1860s, mainly with the aim of opposing Palmerston's policy.   p. 117

[110] This refers to Marx's unfinished introduction to a work he proposed to write on the history of British and Russian diplomacy in the eighteenth century. The introduction was first published under the title *Revelations of the Diplomatic History of the 18th Century* in the *Sheffield Free Press* and the London *Free Press* between June 1856 and April 1857. In 1899 Eleanor Aveling, Marx's daughter, published it in London in book form under the heading *Secret Diplomatic History of the Eighteenth Century.*   p. 117

[111] The *Manchester School*—a trend in economic thought reflecting the interests of the industrial bourgeoisie. It advocated Free Trade and non-interference by the state in economic affairs. In the 1840s and 1850s the Free Traders were an

independent political group; later they constituted the Left wing of the Liberal Party.   p. 117

112 *Mormons*—members of a religious sect founded in the United States in 1830 by Joseph Smith (1805-1844) who wrote the *Book of Mormon* (1830) on the basis of alleged divine revelations. In the name of the prophet Mormon the book tells of the migration of the Israelite tribes to America which, it claims, took place in antiquity.   p. 118

113 This refers to *La question romaine,* a pamphlet by E. About published in Brussels in 1859. A supplement to the *Schweizer Handels-Courier,* No. 150, June 2, 1859 published an article "Die römische Frage (von E. About. Fortsetzung). Pius IX".   p. 118

114 These words are not from Müllner but from Franz Grillparzer's play *Die Ahnfrau* (Act III).   p. 120

115 On June 7, 1859 the *Allgemeine Zeitung* (No. 158) carried an article under the editorial heading "Venedey über die Stellung Deutschlands und Preussens zur italienischen Frage" ("Venedey on the Position of Germany and Prussia on the Italian Question") including a letter by Venedey to a friend of his in Prussia which was originally published in the *Zeitung für Norddeutschland.* Among other things, the letter exposed Vogt's ties with Prince Joseph Napoleon.   p. 120

116 Marx ironically calls Vogt a "diminisher of the Empire" (*Mindrer des Reichs*) by contrast to "Augmenter of the Empire" (*Mehrer des Reichs*), a title given to German emperors in the Middle Ages. See also p. 166 of this volume.

The *"Little Germany" press*—the press favouring a "Little Germany", i.e. the unification of Germany under Prussia's supremacy without Austria.   p. 122

117 A copy of the letters by Liebknecht and Blind (of September 8, 1860) is contained in Marx's notebook for 1860. The originals have not been found. The italics are presumably Marx's.   p. 122

118 *Eisele* and *Beisele* were a pair of ridiculously stupid characters in the humorous weekly *Fliegende Blätter* started in 1844. They were also the heroes of Johann Wilhelm Christern's anonymously published story *Doktor Eisele's und Baron von Beisele's Landtagsreise im April 1847.*   p. 131

119 *Sine studio* means here "without favour". It is part of the phrase "sine ira et studio" ("without anger and prejudice") with which Tacitus declared his intention to write an unbiased history (*Annales,* Liber primus, I).

Marx's use of the phrase with reference to Vogt's *Studien* is clearly ironic.
                                                                          p. 133

120 This refers to the series of pro-Bonapartist pamphlets put out by the Dentu publishing house in Paris in 1859 and 1860.   p. 135

121 *Théâtre de la Porte Saint-Martin*—a theatre company in Paris that catered to low tastes during the Second Empire.   p. 135

122 The *Seven Years' War* (1756-63)—a European war in which England and Prussia fought against the coalition of Austria, France, Russia, Saxony and Sweden. In 1756-57, the Prussian troops of Frederick II won a number of victories over the Austrian and French armies; however, the success of the Russian forces in Prussia (1757-60) put Frederick II in a critical position,

nullifying the results of his victories. The war ended with France having to cede some of her colonies (including Canada and almost all of her possessions in the East Indies) to Britain, while Prussia, Austria and Saxony had to recognise the pre-war frontiers.   p. 135

123 The *Treaty of Basle* was concluded separately by the French Republic and Prussia, a member of the European Coalition, on April 5, 1795. Prussia was forced to sign it in view of the successes of the French army and the growing differences between the coalition members, above all between Prussia and Austria. Its conclusion marked the beginning of the coalition's disintegration. On July 22, 1795 Spain also signed a separate peace treaty with France in Basle.   p. 135

124 The treaty was designed to prevent the seizure by Prussia of the King of Saxony's possessions and the annexation by Russia of all the lands of the former Duchy of Warsaw.   p. 135

125 The agreement, concluded in October 1821 during King George IV's visit to Hanover, was directed against Russia's policy on the Greek question.
                                                                                         p. 135

126 On July 8, 1859 the emperors of France and Austria held a separate meeting—without the King of Piedmont, France's ally in the war against Austria (see Note 13)—in Villafranca, at which they reached an agreement on an armistice. The meeting was held on the initiative of Napoleon III, who feared that the protracted war might give a fresh impulse to the revolutionary and national liberation movement in Italy and other European states. On July 11 France and Austria signed a preliminary peace treaty under which Austria was to cede to France its rights to Lombardy and France was to transfer this territory to Piedmont. Venetia was to remain under Austrian supremacy (despite the terms of the Plombières agreement, see Note 159) and the princes of the Central Italian states were to be restored to their thrones. A confederation of Italian states was to be formed under the honorary chairmanship of the Pope.

The Villafranca agreements formed the basis of the peace treaty France, Austria and Piedmont concluded in Zurich on November 10, 1859 (see Marx's articles "What Has Italy Gained?", "The Peace" and "The Treaty of Villafranca" in Vol. 16 of the present edition and Engels' letter to Marx of July 14, 1859, present edition, Vol. 40).   p. 136

127 This refers to the peace treaty concluded by the Habsburgs and representatives of the Hungarian nobility at Szatmar, Hungary, in April 1711, following the defeat of the national liberation movement in Hungary. Under the peace treaty, Hungary became part of the Habsburg Empire. During the liberation war in Hungary British diplomacy sought to secure an early termination of the hostilities and preserve the integrity of the Habsburg Empire, Britain's ally in the War of the Spanish Succession.   p. 136

128 The reference is to the London Convention of July 15, 1840 between Britain, Russia, Austria and Prussia on supporting the Turkish Sultan against the Egyptian ruler Mehemet Ali. France, which supported Mehemet Ali, did not participate. The threat of an anti-French coalition made France withdraw her support for the Egyptian ruler.   p. 137

19*

129 Under a treaty concluded in 1816 by Britain and the Kingdom of the Two
Sicilies (the Kingdom of Naples) the latter undertook not to grant commercial
privileges to third countries prejudicial to Britain's interests. In 1838 the King
of Naples granted a French company the monopoly right to mine sulphur in
Sicily, which evoked a sharp protest from Britain. To make the King of Naples
rescind his decision the British Government in 1840 ordered its navy in the
Mediterranean to open hostilities. Naples was forced to comply with Britain's
demands.   p. 137

130 In 1797 the British Government issued a special *Bank Restriction Act* making
banknotes legal tender and suspending the payment of gold for them. To all
intents and purposes convertibility was not reintroduced until 1821. The return
to convertibility was made possible by a law passed in 1819.   p. 138

131 In August 1858 Russia and Piedmont concluded an agreement granting the
Russian Steamship and Trading Company the temporary right to use the
eastern part of the Villafranca harbour, near Nice, for mooring, refuelling and
repairing its ships.
    In 1853 Prussia bought from the Duchy of Oldenburg a strip of the shore
in the Jade Bay to set up a naval base there. It was built between 1855 and
1869 and named Wilhelmshaven.   p. 138

132 This refers to the repercussions of the uprising in the free city of Cracow (the
Cracow Republic), which, by decision of the Congress of Vienna, had been
placed under the joint control of Austria, Prussia and Russia. On February 22,
1846 the insurgents seized power in Cracow, established a National Government and issued a manifesto abolishing feudal services. The uprising was
suppressed at the beginning of March. In November 1846 Austria, Prussia and
Russia signed a treaty incorporating Cracow into the Austrian Empire.

                                                                            p. 139

133 This refers to the decree of November 20 (8), 1847, signed by Nicholas I,
allowing serfs to buy themselves off, together with their land, when their
landlords' estates were put under distraint. (For details see Marx's article "The
Emancipation Question", present edition, Vol. 16.)   p. 140

134 To strengthen its influence in the Balkans, Russia supported the national
liberation movement of the Balkan peoples against Turkish domination.
Together with France, which likewise sought to consolidate its influence in the
area, Russia backed the striving of Moldavia and Wallachia to unite and form
a Romanian state. With French and Russian support Colonel Alexandru
Cuza was elected hospodar (ruler) of Moldavia in January 1859 and of
Wallachia in early February 1859. A united Romanian state was set up
in 1862.   p. 141

135 The memorandum was printed in the *Preussisches Wochenblatt zur Besprechung
politischer Tagesfragen*, Nos. 23, 24 and 25 of June 9, 16 and 23, 1855. The
source of its origin was not indicated. On July 13, 1859 it was reprinted in *The
Free Press* under the heading "Memoir on Russia, for the Instruction of the
Present Emperor. Drawn up by the Cabinet in 1837". Marx used the document
in one of his reports for the *New-York Daily Tribune* (see present edition, Vol.
16). The memorandum attracted his attention in connection with the
aggravation of the struggle over the question of German and Italian unification
and the fight against Bonapartism. In a letter to Engels of July 19, 1859 Marx
wrote that he intended to sum up Russia's role in this tragicomedy and at the

same time expose Bonaparte's intrigues. After familiarising themselves with this document Marx and Engels expressed doubts about the authenticity of certain passages (see Engels' letter to Marx of June 18, 1859 and Marx's letter to Engels of July 19, 1859, present edition, Vol. 40).

Bismarck in his reminiscences (*Gedanken und Erinnerungen von Otto Fürst von Bismarck,* Stuttgart, 1898, Bd. 1, S. 111-12) says that the memorandum was a falsification.

p. 141

[136] The *Congress of Nemirov*—the peace talks held by Russia, Austria and Turkey in the Ukrainian town of Nemirov between August and November 1737. The congress was convened on Turkey's initiative during the Russo-Turkish war of 1735-39, which Austria entered, on the side of Russia, in 1737. The peace terms put forward by Russia called, among other things, for granting Moldavia and Wallachia the status of independent principalities under Russian protection. Turkey declared most of the terms unacceptable and resumed hostilities.

The *Congress of Focșani* was held at the Romanian town of Focșani in July and August 1772 with a view to ending the Russo-Turkish war started by Turkey in 1768. The Russian delegation proposed, in particular, that Wallachia and Moldavia should be granted independence under the joint protection of the European powers. Turkey rejected Russia's proposals. No agreement was reached and the hostilities were resumed.

p. 142

[137] The *Peace of Bucharest,* concluded on May 28 (16), 1812, put an end to the Russo-Turkish war of 1806-12. Under its terms, Russia got Bessarabia and certain areas in Transcaucasia. Turkey was to grant internal autonomy to Serbia and confirm its earlier agreements with Russia extending a measure of autonomy to Moldavia and Wallachia.

p. 142

[138] *Règlement organique* (1831-32)—constitutional acts laying down the socio-political system of the Danubian Principalities (Wallachia and Moldavia) after the Russo-Turkish war of 1828-29. The *Règlement,* based on a draft framed by P. D. Kiselev, head of the Russian administration, was adopted by an assembly of boyars and clergymen. Legislative power in each of the Principalities was vested in an assembly elected by the big landowners. Executive power was wielded by the hospodars, rulers elected for life by representatives of the landowners, the clergy and the towns. The *Règlement* envisaged a number of bourgeois reforms: abolition of internal customs duties, introduction of free trade, and the right of peasants to move from one owner to another. However, in view of the preservation of serfdom and concentration of political power in the hands of the big landowners and boyars, the progressive forces in the Principalities regarded the *Règlement* as a symbol of feudal stagnation. It was repealed during the 1848 revolution.

p. 142

[139] The *Hetairia* (full name: *Philike Hetairia*) was a Greek secret organisation founded in Odessa in 1814. It moved its headquarters to Constantinople in 1818 and soon won a nation-wide following. In 1821 the Hetairia prepared a national liberation uprising in Greece, after the beginning of which it was disbanded.

p. 143

[140] At its congress in Verona (October to December 1822) the Holy Alliance decided to launch an armed intervention against revolutionary Spain. In 1823 French troops invaded Spain and restored the absolute power of Ferdinand VII. They stayed in the country until 1828.

p. 143

[141] At *Navarino* (a port in Greece) on October 20, 1827 the Turko-Egyptian navy clashed with the British, French and Russian squadrons sent into Greek waters for armed mediation in the war between Turkey and the Greek insurgents. The battle was fought after the Turkish command had refused to end the massacre of the Greek population. The forces of the three European powers, commanded by the British Vice-Admiral Edward Codrington, routed the Turko-Egyptian fleet. This facilitated the national liberation struggle of the Greeks and Russia's success in its war against Turkey in 1828 and 1829.

p. 143

[142] *Young Italy* (Giovine Italia) was a secret organisation of Italian revolutionaries (1831-48) founded by Mazzini. It fought for national independence and a united Italian republic.   p. 144

[143] In October 1850 Emperor Nicholas I of Russia, Emperor Francis Joseph of Austria and Count Frederick William von Brandenburg, the head of the Prussian Government, met in Warsaw. The conference was held on the initiative of Nicholas I in connection with the sharpening struggle between Austria and Prussia for supremacy in Germany. The Russian Tsar, acting as arbiter, used his influence to make Prussia abandon its attempts to form a political confederation of German states under Prussia's aegis. The dispute was settled when the heads of the Austrian and Prussian governments signed an agreement in Olmütz (Olomouc) on November 29, 1850 under which Prussia renounced its claims to supremacy in Germany and yielded on the issues of Schleswig-Holstein and Hesse-Cassel. As a result of the agreement an Austrian army corps was sent to Holstein.   p. 145

[144] Pozzo di Borgo, Russia's Ambassador to Paris, sent the dispatch in question to Count Nesselrode, the Russian Chancellor, on October 16 (4), 1825 in reply to the latter's circular letter of August 18 (6), 1825. The circular, drawn up at the instructions of Alexander I, asked the Russian Ambassadors abroad for their opinion about the Western Powers' policy vis-à-vis Russia in connection with the Eastern question. Pozzo di Borgo suggested in his dispatch that Russia should resort to armed force in dealing with Turkey. The dispatch was published in *Recueil des documents pour la plupart secrets et inédits et d'autres pièces historiques utiles à consulter dans la crise actuelle (juillet 1853)*, Paris. Marx used the second (1854) edition of the book.   p. 145

[145] *Finis Poloniae!*—a phrase attributed—without sufficient grounds—to Tadeusz Kościuszko, the leader of the national liberation movement in Poland in 1794. He is supposed to have uttered it after the defeat of the insurgent army at the battle of Maciejowice (October 10, 1794) when he was taken prisoner.

p. 148

[146] Marx is referring to the map of Slav lands compiled by the Czech Slavonic scholar Pavel Josef Šafařík for his book *Slovanský národopis (Slavonic Ethnography)* published in 1842.   p. 151

[147] *The Lay of Ludwig (Das Ludwigslied)* was written in the Frankish dialect by an anonymous poet in the late ninth century. It is a panegyric of the West Frankish King Louis III, celebrating his victory over the Normans at Sancourt in 881 (*Hausschatz der Volkspoesie*, Leipzig, 1846).   p. 154

[148] On June 11, 1849 Ledru-Rollin, the leader of the petty-bourgeois democrats, tabled a motion in the Legislative Assembly calling for the impeachment of President Louis Bonaparte and the government for violating the Constitution by sending French troops to crush the Roman Republic and restore the temporal power of the Pope. After it had been voted down by the conservative majority of the Assembly the petty-bourgeois democrats tried to organise a mass protest demonstration on June 13, which was dispersed by government troops. The leaders of the Montagne, the petty-bourgeois faction in the Assembly, were stripped of their powers as deputies and persecuted. Some of them were forced to emigrate. The June 13 events revealed the Montagne leaders' indecision and inability to head the revolutionary movement of the masses (see Marx's *The Class Struggles in France, 1848 to 1850*, present edition, Vol. 10, pp. 101-07).

p. 155

[149] *Napoléon le Petit* (Napoleon the Little)—the nickname given to Louis Bonaparte by Victor Hugo in a speech he made to the French Legislative Assembly in 1851. It gained wide currency after the publication in 1852 of Hugo's *Napoléon le Petit*.

p. 156

[150] Here Marx uses the words "ein Ende mit Schrecken", apparently an allusion to the dictum "Lieber ein Ende mit Schrecken als ein Schrecken ohne Ende" ("A dreadful end is better than dread without end"). It is attributed to Ferdinand Schill, commander of volunteer units that fought against Napoleon's troops in 1806-07. Schill is believed to have uttered these words in a speech he made in the market-place of Arneburg on the Elbe on May 12, 1809 when he urged Prussia to fight France.

p. 156

[151] In the early 1850s the French Government drew up a plan for the import of African Negroes, including inhabitants of Portugal's African colonies, for work on plantations in France's West Indian colonies. The implementation of the plan was tantamount to a revival of the slave trade and led to a conflict between France and Portugal.

p. 157

[152] This refers to the abortive attempt by the Italian revolutionaries Orsini and Pieri to assassinate Napoleon III on January 14, 1858. Marx refers to it in several of his articles, e.g. "The War Prospect in France" and "Quid pro Quo" (see present edition, Vol. 16).

p. 157

[153] By the *Lois de sûreté publique* (laws on social security) Marx means the *Loi des suspects* (law on suspects) adopted by the Corps Législatif on February 19, 1858. It granted the government and the Emperor the unlimited right to deport persons suspected of hostility towards the regime of the Second Empire to various places in France and Algeria and even to banish them from French territory.

p. 157

[154] By the decree of January 27, 1858 the territory of the Second Empire was divided into five General Captaincies headed by marshals. This was done on the pattern of Spain, where the captain generals (commanders of military districts) wielded full power.

The decree on the regency and the establishment of the Privy Council was issued on February 1, 1858, soon after Orsini's attempt on the life of Napoleon III. Pélissier was a member of the Council, which was to become the Regency Council if the Emperor's son, a minor, acceded to the throne.

p. 157

155 Napoleon III was the son of Napoleon I's brother Louis Bonaparte, King of Holland from 1806 to 1810. By calling Napoleon III the "nephew of the battle of Austerlitz" Marx alludes to the fact that the coup d'état of December 2, 1851 was timed to coincide with the anniversary of the battle of Austerlitz (December 2, 1805) at which Napoleon I defeated the allied Russian and Austrian forces.   p. 157

156 At the end of 1858 the French journalist Montalembert was put on trial for writing an article condemning the regime of the Second Empire ("Un débat sur l'Inde au parlement anglais", Le Correspondant, nouvelle série, V. IX, octobre 1858). He was pardoned by Napoleon III but rejected the pardon and demanded his acquittal. Marx ironically draws a parallel between this trial and that of John Hampden, a prominent figure in the English seventeenth-century revolution, who in 1636 refused to pay "ship money", a royal tax not authorised by the House of Commons. The Hampden trial increased the opposition to absolutism in England.

   In his pamphlet De la Justice poursuivie par l'Eglise (Brussels, 1858) Proudhon compares the Bonaparte and Orléans dynasties and gives preference to the principles of government proclaimed by the latter, but makes reservations concerning the need for certain democratic reforms. Marx ironically compares these reservations with the Acte additionel, the constitutional regulations introduced by Napoleon I in France in 1815 upon his return from Elba.
                                                                        p. 157

157 This refers to the abortive republican uprising of troops in Chalon-sur-Saône on March 6, 1858 (see Marx's article "Portents of the Day", present edition, Vol. 15).   p. 157

158 On January 20, 1858 Count Walewski, the French Minister of Foreign Affairs, sent a Note to the British Government expressing dissatisfaction with Britain's granting asylum to political refugees. In this connection Palmerston tabled the Conspiracy to Murder Bill in the House of Commons on February 8. During its second reading Milner Gibson proposed an amendment censuring the Palmerston Government for not giving an appropriate reply to the Note. The amendment, adopted by the majority of the House, amounted to a vote of no-confidence in the Government and forced it to resign.   p. 158

159 On July 21, 1858, at Plombières, Napoleon III and Prime Minister Cavour of the Kingdom of Sardinia (Piedmont) reached a secret agreement envisaging Franco-Sardinian military co-operation against Austria, the abolition of Austrian rule in Lombardy and Venetia and their union with Piedmont, the establishment of a North Italian state to be ruled by the Savoy dynasty, and the cession by Piedmont of Savoy and Nice to France. The agreement was formalised by a Franco-Sardinian treaty concluded in Turin in January 1859. During the Plombières meeting the question of a Franco-Sardinian war against Austria was decided. It started in April 1859.

   In the autumn of 1858, Palmerston, then head of the Whig opposition to the Derby-Disraeli Tory Cabinet, was invited by Napoleon III to Compiègne to clarify his position on the impending Franco-Austrian war. At the meeting Palmerston did not object to the Austrians being driven out of Italy, but in his speech at the opening of Parliament on February 3, 1859 he condemned France's action.   p. 159

[160] On October 10, 1850 Louis Bonaparte, then President of the French Republic, held a general review of troops on the plain of Satory (near Versailles). During the review Bonaparte, who was preparing a coup d'état, treated the soldiers and officers to sausages in order to win their support.   p. 163

[161] At the Congress of Paris on March 30, 1856 France, Britain, Austria, Sardinia, Prussia and Turkey, on the one hand, and Russia, on the other, signed a peace treaty that concluded the Crimean War (1853-56). Russia, defeated in the war, was forced to cede the estuary of the Danube and part of South Bessarabia, renounce its protection of the Danubian Principalities, and agree to the neutralisation of the Black Sea, which involved the closure of the Straits to foreign warships and a ban on the maintenance by Russia and Turkey of naval arsenals and navies in the Black Sea. In exchange for Sevastopol and the other Crimean towns seized by the Allies, Russia was to return Kars to Turkey. France refused to support Britain's demand for the severance of the Caucasus from Russia and Austria's demand for the incorporation of Bessarabia into Turkey. The Congress marked the beginning of a Franco-Russian rapprochement.   p. 163

[162] The *Thirty Years' War* (1618-48)—a European war in which the Pope, the Spanish and Austrian Habsburgs and the Catholic German princes, rallied under the banner of Catholicism, fought the Protestant countries: Bohemia, Denmark, Sweden, the Republic of the Netherlands and a number of Protestant German states. The rulers of Catholic France—rivals of the Habsburgs—supported the Protestant camp. Germany was the principal battle area and the main object of plunder and territorial claims. The Treaty of Westphalia (1648) sealed the political dismemberment of Germany.   p. 168

[163] During the Irish uprising of 1798 the town of Kilkenny was occupied by Hessian mercenaries serving in the British army, who used to amuse themselves by watching fights between cats with their tails tied together. One day, a soldier, seeing an officer approaching, cut off the cats' tails with his sword and the cats ran away. The officer was told that the cats had eaten each other and only their tails remained.   p. 170

[164] The *Treaty of Campoformio,* signed on October 17, 1797, concluded the victorious war of the French Republic against Austria, a member of the first anti-French coalition. Under the treaty, France got Belgium, the Ionian Islands and part of Albania. Austria was to help France annex the left bank of the Rhine, and relinquished its former possessions in Northern Italy. Together with part of the abolished Venetian Republic, these constituted the Cisalpine Republic, a new state under French protection. A big portion of the Venetian Republic, including Venice, and also Istria and Dalmatia, were given to Austria in exchange for concessions made to France on the Rhine frontier.   p. 171

[165] The *Council of States*—one of the two houses of Switzerland's Federal Assembly (Parliament). The other house is called the National Council.   p. 175

[166] *Vallée des Dappes*—a mountain valley on the border of the Swiss Canton of Vaud and France. The Congress of Vienna (1814-15) ruled it to be Swiss territory; however France later refused to recognise this decision. Because of its strategic importance the Vallée des Dappes remained a bone of contention

between the two states until Switzerland ceded part of it to France in exchange
for territorial compensation in 1862.   p. 175

167 In the autumn of 1856 a conflict developed between Prussia and Switzerland
over the events in Neuchâtel (in German: Neuenburg). From 1707 to 1806 the
principality of Neuchâtel was a dwarf state under Prussian rule. In 1815, by
decision of the Vienna Congress, it was incorporated into the Swiss
Confederation as its 21st canton, at the same time remaining a vassal of Prussia.
In February 1848 a bourgeois revolution in Neuchâtel put an end to Prussian
rule and a republic was proclaimed. In 1852 Britain, France and Russia signed
a protocol in London which re-affirmed the Prussian King's rights to
Neuchâtel. The Prusso-Swiss conflict flared up with fresh violence in
September 1856 when the Swiss authorities arrested the participants in an
abortive monarchist putsch in Neuchâtel who had the support of the Prussian
King. The Swiss Government demanded that Prussia should renounce all its
claims to the canton. The conflict was settled in the spring of 1857 thanks to
the diplomatic intervention of other powers, notably France. The Prussian King
had to waive his claim to Neuchâtel, while the Swiss Government released the
arrested royalists.   p. 175

168 The *Sonderbund*—a separatist union of the seven economically backward
Catholic cantons of Switzerland formed in 1843 to resist progressive bourgeois
reforms and to defend the privileges of the Church and the Jesuits. The decree
of the Swiss Diet of July 1847 dissolving the Sonderbund was used by the latter
as a pretext for starting hostilities against the other cantons early in November.
On November 23, 1847 the Sonderbund army was defeated by the federal
forces. Attempts by Austria and Prussia to interfere in Swiss affairs in support
of the Sonderbund failed. Louis Philippe's Government virtually sided with
these powers in protecting the Sonderbund.   p. 176

169 In this Note, directed to a number of states, the Federal Council declared that
in the event of war in Italy, Switzerland would defend its neutrality and
territorial integrity and would, in keeping with the resolutions of the Congress
of Vienna, occupy the neutralised area of Savoy (Northern Savoy).
The Congress had proclaimed the "perpetual neutrality" of Switzerland
and, in its Final Act, adopted on June 9, 1815, declared Chablais and Faucigny,
the provinces of Northern Savoy, a neutralised territory and authorised
Switzerland, in the event of war or the threat of war between the neighbouring
states, to occupy these provinces, at the same time enjoining the Kingdom of
Sardinia to withdraw its troops from there.   p. 176

170 Marx quotes from *Klage (Lament)*, an anonymous twelfth-century German
poem. It is a kind of supplement to the *Nibelungenlied* (or *Der Nibelunge Not*).
Marx probably used the 1826 edition by Karl Lachmann *Der Nibelungen Not mit
der Klage*. He quotes from an entry in his notebook of 1860.
Iwein, oder der Ritter mit dem Löwen (Ywain, or the Knight of the Lion) is a
narrative poem by the medieval German poet Hartmann von Aue. Its central
idea is the sacrifice of happiness for the sake of honour. The poem is an
adaptation of the novel *Yvain ou le Chevalier au Lion* by the French
twelfth-century writer Chrétien de Troyes. Marx presumably used the edition,
Hartmann von Aue, *Iwein, Eine Erzählung* (Mit Anmerkungen von G. F.
Benecke und K. Lachmann), Berlin, 1843.   p. 184

171 *Die Kaiserchronik*—a German epic of the twelfth century telling in semi-legendary form the history of the Roman and German emperors from Caesar to 1147. The extant version is attributed to the twelfth-century German poet Konrad. Marx probably used the edition prepared by Heinrich Kurz, *Geschichte der deutschen Literatur,* Leipzig, 1857.   p. 185

172 Prince Napoleon commanded a division in the Crimea in 1854. Lacking military talent and unpopular with the army, he feigned ill health to stay away from directing military operations and later returned to Paris without official permission.   p. 189

173 An allusion to Napoleon III's rumoured illegitimacy. Officially he was the son of King Louis Bonaparte of Holland, a brother of Napoleon I.   p. 190

174 See Note 70.   p. 190

175 See Note 165.   p. 192

176 See Note 159.   p. 192

177 *Corybants*—attendants of the goddess Cybele who were supposed to accompany her with wild dances and music; also priests of Cybele who acted as Corybants with orgiastic processions and rites.   p. 194

178 The *Crédit Mobilier (Société général du Crédit Mobilier)* was a French joint-stock bank founded in 1852 by the Péreire brothers. Closely connected with and protected by the Government of Napoleon III, it engaged in large-scale speculation. The bank was involved, in particular, in the railway-building business. It went bankrupt in 1867 and was liquidated in 1871.   p. 198

179 *Helvetia*—a Swiss student association which in 1859-60 opposed Napoleon III's plans for the annexation of Savoy to France.   p. 201

180 See Note 45.   p. 204

181 The *Fusionists* advocated fusion of the Legitimists (the supporters of the elder branch of the French Bourbon dynasty) and the Orleanists (the adherents of the younger branch).
Collège de France—one of France's oldest higher educational establishments (founded 1530 in Paris).
L'Institut de France—France's highest scientific and art centre. It comprises a number of leading academies, including the Académie Française.   p. 207

182 This refers to the committee of the party of Order, which sat in the *rue de Poitiers.* The party of Order formed in 1848 was a coalition of monarchist groups: the Legitimists (supporters of the Bourbon dynasty), the Orleanists (supporters of the Orleans dynasty) and the Bonapartists. It was the party of the conservative big bourgeoisie. From 1849 until the coup d'état of December 2, 1851 it held sway in the Legislative Assembly of the Second Republic.
                                                                          p. 208

183 An allusion to the shrine of the three Magi in Cologne Cathedral (cf. Heinrich Heine, *Deutschland, ein Wintermärchen,* Chapter VII).   p. 210

184 Marx is referring to Vogt's speech in the Frankfurt National Assembly on April 24, 1849 *(Stenographischer Bericht über die Verhandlungen der deutschen constituiren-*

den Nationalversammlung zu Frankfurt am Main). An excerpt from Vogt's speech was published in the *Neue Rheinische Zeitung,* No. 283, April 27, 1849 and is contained in Marx's notebook. p. 211

185 *Mouse Tower*—a tower built on a rock in the middle of the Rhine below the town of Bingen. Hemmed in by rocks, this section of the river is called the Binger Loch (Bingen Hole). According to one version, the name of the tower is associated with Archbishop Hatto II of Mayence. Legend has it that he ordered a number of starving people to be burnt in a barn. When their screams were heard, he jokingly told the bystanders that these were the cries of the mice who had caused the food shortage. This earned him the disfavour of mice, to avoid which he had a tower built for him on a rock in the Binger Loch. However the mice found him out there and devoured him. p. 212

186 An allusion to Vogt's participation in the Genevan joint-stock company La Cimentaire (see this volume, p. 327). p. 212

187 An allusion to the prolonged resistance that the garrison of Komárom fortress, commanded by General Klapka, offered to the besieging Austrian army and the Russian troops sent by Tsar Nicholas I. The fortress held out until the end of September 1849. The defence of Komárom was the closing act of the Hungarian revolution of 1848-49. p. 214

188 This refers to the rising in Milan on February 6, 1853 organised by the followers of the Italian revolutionary Mazzini and supported by Hungarian revolutionary refugees. The aim of the insurgents, mostly Italian patriotic workers, was to overthrow Austrian rule in Italy. However, the leaders' conspiratorial tactics and failure to take into account the actual situation led to the rapid defeat of the insurgents. Marx analysed the rising in a number of articles (see present edition, Vol. 11, pp. 508-09, 513-16 and 535-37). p. 217

189 Speaking of manifestos issued by Kossuth and Mazzini, Marx based himself on the article "Data by Which to Judge of Kossuth" (*The Free Press,* No. 5, May 27, 1859), which mentioned a manifesto issued by Kossuth in 1855 and added: "The names associated in this with Kossuth were Ledru-Rollin and Mazzini."

The *Central Committee of European Democracy,* set up in London in June 1850 on Mazzini's initiative, was an organisation of bourgeois and petty-bourgeois refugees from different countries. Kossuth played an important part in it, as well as Mazzini, Ledru-Rollin and Ruge. The Committee's Inaugural Manifesto, "Aux peuples!", of July 22, 1850 (*Le Proscrit,* No. 2, August 6, 1850) was criticised by Marx and Engels in their international review for May to October 1850 published in the autumn of that year in the *Neue Rheinische Zeitung. Politisch-ökonomische Revue* (see present edition, Vol. 10, pp. 529-32). Extremely heterogeneous in composition and ideological principles, the Committee virtually disintegrated in March 1852 because of the strained relations between the Italian and French democratic refugees. p. 218

190 Kossuth's lectures of 1858 and a number of his articles were published in Brussels in 1859 under the title: Kossuth L., *L'Europe, l'Autriche et la Hongrie.*

The *Concordats* are agreements between the Pope and the governments of individual countries on the status and privileges of the Catholic Church in these countries. Under the Concordat of 1855 concluded by the Holy See and Vienna, the Catholic Church in Austria was to enjoy autonomy, the right of direct communication with Rome and the right to own property. It was to act as supreme spiritual censor and wield a vast influence on the schools.

p. 221

191 The facts Marx presents here and further on (p. 222) concerning Kossuth's meeting with Napoleon III and financial dealings with the Bonapartists were related to him by Szemere (see Marx's letter to Engels of September 28, 1859). He also used them in his article "Kossuth and Louis Napoleon", published in the *New-York Daily Tribune*, No. 5748, September 24, 1859 (see present edition, Vol. 16). The article caused considerable repercussions among Hungarian refugees in the United States. "Hungarians in New York, Chicago, New Orleans, etc., have held meetings at which they resolved to send Kossuth a letter challenging him to justify himself with respect to my article in the *New-York Tribune*," Marx wrote to Engels on November 19, 1859 (present edition, Vol. 40).

A version of this article, headlined "Particulars of Kossuth's Transactions with Louis Napoleon" was published in *The Free Press*, No. 10, September 28, 1859. On October 8, 1859 Marx wrote to Szemere that "the *Free Press* report was reprinted in English, Scottish and Irish provincial newspapers". A German version of the article appeared in the supplement to the *Allgemeine Zeitung*, No. 276, October 3, 1859. On October 10 Marx informed Engels that it had also been reprinted by the *Weser-Zeitung*. p. 221

192 This refers to Emperor Francis Joseph's diploma of October 20, 1860 (das Kaiserliche Diplom vom 20. Oktober 1860) which granted a measure of autonomy to the non-German parts of the Austrian Empire. It was a half-measure designed to placate the advocates of federalism, particularly the Hungarians. (Engels analysed it in his article "Austria—Progress of the Revolution", see this volume, pp. 499-500.) However the October diploma was rescinded a few months later by the Patent of February 26, 1861, which reintroduced the centralist system in the Austrian Empire. p. 225

193 *In usum Delphini*—literally: "for the use of the Dauphin", in a figurative sense: "with omissions", "bowdlerised". The phrase gained currency after 1668 when the works of ancient classics were published for the son of Louis XIV, the heir to the French throne (the Dauphin), expurgated of all "objectionable" passages. p. 225

194 On August 13, 1849, at Világos, the Hungarian army commanded by Görgey surrendered to the Tsarist troops sent to help the Habsburgs suppress the revolution in Hungary. Although the Hungarian army possessed considerable resources and was able to continue the struggle, Görgey treasonably capitulated to meet the wishes of the conservative nobility who were opposed to a spread of the revolution. p. 226

195 The *ultramontane party* in Switzerland was formed in the 1840s on the initiative of the reactionary Catholic circles in connection with the intensified opposition of the economically backward cantons to the liberal-democratic reforms carried out by the bourgeoisie. This opposition led to the establishment of the Sonderbund (see Note 168) and a civil war in Switzerland. p. 228

196 This refers to one of the charitable educational institutions run by the Herrnhut communities. The first of these communities was set up in Herrnhut, Saxony, in 1722 by followers of a religious fraternity originally known as the Moravian

Brethren. There were a number of Herrnhut communities in Germany, America and South Africa.   p. 231

197 *"Laissez aller et laissez faire"* was the formula of the advocates of free trade and non-intervention of the state in economic relations.   p. 231

198 This refers to the street riots in Geneva in October 1846 caused by differences between bourgeois radicals and Rightists over the attitude to ♭℮ adopted towards the Sonderbund and democratic reforms in the administration of the canton of Geneva.   p. 231

199 See Note 168.   p. 231

200 In January 1849 Mazzini and J. Ph. Becker advanced a plan for establishing a volunteer German-Helvetian republican legion to support the revolutionary movement in Sicily. The Swiss Federal Council banned propaganda of the plan in the Swiss press as prejudicial to Switzerland's neutrality. Becker's attempts to organise the shipment to Italy of the 2,500 volunteers assembled in Marseilles failed because of a ban imposed by the French authorities, who were preparing an intervention against the Roman Republic.   p. 232

201 See Note 178.   p. 234

202 See Marx's article "The Berlin *National-Zeitung* to the Primary Electors" (present edition, Vol. 8, p. 271).

Schilda—the name of a town whose inhabitants, portrayed in *Die Schildbürger,* a German popular satirical book of the late 16th century, have come to be regarded as epitomes of philistine narrow-mindedness and obtuseness.   p. 236

203 The original has "denkende Leser" ("thinking readers") here. This ironic reference to the readers of the *National-Zeitung* seems to be an allusion to the title of K. Rotteck's well-known book *Allgemeine Geschichte vom Anfang der historischen Kenntniß bis auf unsere Zeiten; für denkende Geschichtsfreunde (Universal History from the Beginnings of Historical Knowledge to Modern Times; for Thinking Friends of History),* Freiburg und Konstanz, 1813-1818.   p. 236

204 These lines (Marx quotes in English and gives the German translation in a footnote) are from Alexander Pope's *The Dunciad. An Heroic Poem,* Book I, written between 1728 and 1743. Pope gives a satirical portrayal of his literary adversaries, relegating them to the realm of Dulness.   p. 237

205 The *Neue Oder-Zeitung* was a German bourgeois-democratic daily published under this title in Breslau (Wrocław) from 1849 to 1855.

It started publication in March 1849 following a split in the editorial board of the oppositional Catholic *Allgemeine Oder-Zeitung,* which appeared from 1846. The *Neue Oder-Zeitung* was the most radical newspaper in Germany in the 1850s, and the object of government persecution. Its editorial board was headed by the bourgeois democrats Temme, Stein and Elsner. The last named became Editor-in-Chief in September 1855. In 1855 Marx contributed to the *Neue Oder-Zeitung* as its London correspondent. In view of the almost complete absence of a working-class press in the years of reaction Marx and Engels considered it essential to use the bourgeois-democratic press in the struggle against the reactionary forces.   p. 238

206 See present edition, Vol. 8, pp. 390-91 ("Stein"). The italics in this passage were partly changed by Marx.

Agreers Assembly (*Vereinbarer-Versammlung*) was Marx's and Engels' ironic way of referring to the Prussian National Assembly, which was guided by the "theory of agreement". Convened in Berlin in May 1848, it was to draw up a Constitution not on the basis of sovereign and constituent rights but "by agreement with the Crown" (the principle formulated by the Camphausen-Hansemann Government and adopted by the majority of the Assembly). The Crown used the theory of agreement to camouflage its preparations for a counter-revolutionary coup d'état. On December 5, 1848 the Prussian National Assembly was disbanded.

The *imposed Constitution* was made public on the same day. It introduced a two-chamber parliament in Prussia. By the imposition of age and property qualifications the First Chamber was made a privileged chamber of the gentry. Under the electoral law of December 6, 1848, the right to vote in the two-stage elections to the Second Chamber was granted only to "independent Prussians". The two Chambers first met on February 26, 1849. However, the Branden-burg-Manteuffel government, displeased with the position of the Left-wing deputies of the Second Chamber, though their opposition was rather moderate, dissolved it on April 27. The pretext for the dissolution was the approval by the Second Chamber of the Imperial Constitution drawn up by the Frankfurt National Assembly. Subsequently, the imposed Constitution was repeatedly revised, on the initiative of the ruling circles of Prussia, in a still more anti-democratic spirit.   p. 238

207 The Corn Laws were repealed in June 1846. They imposed high import duties on agricultural produce in the interests of the landowners, in order to maintain high prices on the home market. The repeal of the Corn Laws marked a victory for the industrial bourgeoisie, who opposed them under the slogan of free trade.   p. 239

208 The First Democratic Congress, held in Frankfurt am Main from June 14 to June 17, 1848 and attended by delegates of 89 democratic and workers' organisations from different German cities, decided to unite all democratic associations and set up district committees and a Central Committee of German Democrats. The latter had its headquarters in Berlin.   p. 239

209 See Note 203.   p. 242

210 *Septembrists* was the name given to the Jacobins by their enemies who slanderously accused them of wanton brutality in *September* 1792, during the French Revolution.   p. 243

211 *Levites*—Hebrew priests in the service of the Temple of Jerusalem for whose benefit tithes were collected (see *Numbers* 3:39).   p. 245

212 The friend in question was Ferdinand Lassalle (see Marx's letters to him of February 23 and March 3, 1860). In reply to Marx's request Lassalle answered that no one in Berlin knew of any *Daily Telegraph* correspondent (Lassalle's

letter to Marx of March 11, 1860, in: Fr. Mehring, *Briefe von Ferdinand Lassalle.—Aus dem literarischen Nachlass von Karl Marx, Friedrich Engels und Ferdinand Lassalle*, 4. Bd., Stuttgart, 1902).

The acquaintance mentioned further in the text was presumably Eduard Fischel. An entry in Marx's notebook for 1860 mentions the dispatch of a letter to him (it has not been found). Marx learned the name of the *Daily Telegraph* correspondent from Fischel's letter of May 30, 1860.   p. 246

213 *Magistrat* in German means municipal or city council.   p. 247

214 The *Echternach procession* (or leaping procession) has been held annually in the Luxemburg town of Echternach at Whitsun since the Middle Ages in gratitude for the termination of an epidemic of St. Vitus's dance (chorea) which raged in the town in 1374. The participants in the procession perform complicated forward and backward movements.   p. 247

215 An allusion to the speculative activities of the Crédit Mobilier bank founded by the Péreire Brothers (see Note 178).   p. 249

216 Marx calls Vincke a *knight of the joyful countenance* by analogy with the Knight of the Doleful Countenance (Don Quixote).
Chevalier sans peur et sans reproche (knight without fear or reproach)—appellation of the medieval knight Pierre du Terrail seigneur de Bayard. It is used with reference to other people too, both in its literal sense and ironically.
                    p. 250

217 The conservative deputies of the Frankfurt National Assembly arranged a banquet in honour of the Regent of the Empire, Archduke John, who arrived in Frankfurt am Main on July 11, 1848. Vincke was present too. The reference is to his speech at the sitting of July 15, 1848 (*Deutsche Reichstags-Zeitung*, No. 49, July 16, 1848).
The couplet quoted lower in the text is from an eighteenth-century student song.   p. 251

218 The *Corpus juris civilis*, compiled in the sixth century under the Emperor Justinian, was a code of law regulating property relations in Rome's slave-owning society. It was applied in part in Germany from the fifteenth to the nineteenth century.   p. 251

219 An allusion to Benda's challenging Vincke to a duel for his provocative anti-Jewish remarks which Benda took as a personal insult. Vincke refused to fight. The *Neue Rheinische Zeitung* wrote about the incident in its issue No. 184, January 1, 1849.
The *United Diet*, convened by Frederick William IV in Berlin in April 1847, was an assembly of Prussia's eight provincial diets and, like these, was based on the principle of social estates. Its terms of reference were limited to the endorsement of new taxes and loans, a deliberative vote in the discussions of draft laws and the right to petition the king. The first United Diet was dissolved because of its refusal to approve a new loan.   p. 251

220 Here and below Marx used the reports on the session of the Frankfurt National Assembly published in the *Neue Rheinische Zeitung*.

An account of Vincke's speech appeared in the *Neue Rheinische Zeitung*, No. 126, October 26, 1848.   p. 252

221 This refers to the counter-revolutionary stand of the German and Austrian bourgeoisie during the Vienna uprising in October 1848. It was manifest, in particular, in the actions of the majority of the Frankfurt National Assembly and the central authority which, posing as mediator, virtually sabotaged aid to revolutionary Vienna. Vincke actively supported this attitude (*Neue Rheinische Zeitung*, No. 126, October 26, 1848).   p. 254

222 The Fata Morgana of *Little Germany*—a plan for the unification of Germany from above under Prussia's aegis and excluding Austria. Supported by the majority of the bourgeoisie, it reflected the struggle between Austria and Prussia for supremacy in Germany after unification.   p. 254

223 Here Marx summarises Vincke's speeches in the Prussian United Diet on December 29, 1848 and January 3, 1849 (*Neue Rheinische Zeitung*, Nos. 184 and 185, January 1 and 3, 1849).   p. 255

224 *Daimios*—powerful feudal barons in medieval Japan.   p. 255

225 The *Ministry of Action* (Ministerium der That) was the name given during the 1848-49 revolution to Prussia's Auerswald-Hansemann government (June-September 1848) (see Engels' article "The Fall of the Government of Action", present edition, Vol. 7, pp. 417-19).   p. 256

226 These words were spoken by Count von Brandenburg, the Prussian Prime Minister, at a sitting of the Lower Chamber of the Prussian Diet on April 20, 1849 in connection with the proposal to adopt the Imperial Constitution (*Neue Rheinische Zeitung*, No. 280, April 24, 1849).   p. 257

227 See Note 193.   p. 259

228 This refers to the *Democratic Association* founded in Brussels in the autumn of 1847. It consisted of proletarian revolutionaries, mainly German revolutionary refugees, and radical bourgeois and petty-bourgeois democrats. Marx and Engels took an active part in setting up the Association. On November 15, 1847 Marx was elected its Vice-President (the President was Lucien Jottrand, a Belgian democrat), and under his influence the Association became a leading centre of the international democratic movement. During the February 1848 revolution in France, the proletarian wing of the Association pressed for the armament of Belgian workers and an intensification of the struggle for a democratic republic. However after Marx's expulsion from Brussels in early March 1848 and the suppression of the revolutionary elements by the Belgian authorities, the Association's activities assumed a narrower, purely local character and virtually ceased in 1849.   p. 264

229 The *Labour Parliament* met in Manchester from March 6 to 18, 1854. It had been called in connection with the rise of the strike movement in Britain in 1853 on the initiative of a group of Chartists headed by Ernest Jones. As early as the end of 1853 (Marx mistakenly gives this as the date of the Labour Parliament's meeting) this group proposed setting up a broad working-class

organisation called The Mass Movement which was to bring together the trade
unions and the unorganised workers with a view to co-ordinating strikes in
different parts of the country. The organisation was to be headed by a
periodically convened Labour Parliament consisting of delegates elected by
meetings of unorganised workers and the trade unions affiliated with The Mass
Movement. The Labour Parliament adopted the programme of The Mass
Movement and formed a five-member executive committee. Marx, elected an
honorary delegate to the Parliament, sent a letter which was read out on March
10 (see present edition, Vol. 13, pp. 57-58). In it he put forward the task of
establishing an independent mass working-class party in Britain.

However, the attempt to set up The Mass Movement failed because most
trade union leaders rejected political struggle and refused to support the idea
of forming a united mass working-class organisation. The decline of the strike
movement in the summer of 1854 was a contributing factor. The Labour
Parliament did not meet after March 1854.   p. 265

230 Marx intended to write a pamphlet entitled *On Prussian Justice* (see his letters
to Engels of October 25, 1860 and to Lassalle of October 2, 1860, present
edition, Vol. 41). The plan did not materialise.   p. 271

231 *Code civil (Code Napoléon)*—French Civil Code published in 1804. It was
introduced by Napoleon in the conquered regions of West and Southwest
Germany and remained in force in the Rhine Province after its incorporation
into Prussia in 1815.   p. 271

232 The *Patriots* was a republican society of German refugees in London in the
1850s and 60s. Its members included Blind, Freiligrath and Hollinger.

The *National Association (Deutscher National-Verein)* was a party of the
German liberal bourgeoisie which advocated the unification of Germany
(without Austria) in a strong centralised state under the aegis of the Prussian
monarchy. Its inaugural congress was held in Frankfurt in September 1859.

The open letter of the Patriots to the National Association was published in
a number of German newspapers in November 1859. It contained a vaguely
formulated plan for the dynastic unification of Germany under Prussia's aegis.
                                                                     p. 274

233 *Quirites*—the citizens of Ancient Rome in their civil capacity.   p. 293

234 Schily's letter to Marx is not dated. Presumably it was written at the end of
June 1860. It deals with the fate of German refugees, participants in the
revolution of 1848-49, who were not members of the Frankfurt National
Assembly.   p. 296

235 The *Grand Councils* in Switzerland were the legislatures of the city cantons set
up under the Constitution of 1803.

The *National Council*—one of the two chambers of the Swiss Federal Assembly
formed under the Constitution of 1848 (the other chamber was the Council of
States).

The *Federal Council* was the supreme federal executive body, formed under
the 1848 Constitution. Its chairman was the president of the republic.

The *Council of States*—see Note 165.   p. 297

[236] See Note 17.

p. 299

[237] *Vae victis!* (woe to the vanquished!). Defeated by the Gauls at Allia in 390 the Romans had to pay a ransom of a thousand pounds of gold. When the Romans complained that the weights used by the victors were too heavy, the Gauls' king Brennus exclaimed "Vae victis!" and threw his big sword on the scales too. (Titus Livius, V, 48).

p. 301

[238] Marx's assumption that Vogt, as the Berne correspondent of the *Frankfurter Journal,* was the author of the articles in question has not been proved.

p. 302

[239] A reference to the Biblical "fleshpots" of Egypt. During the Jews' exodus from Egypt, the fainthearts among them, depressed by the hardships of the march and by hunger, recalled with longing the days of captivity when they at least had enough to eat.

p. 302

[240] The protest in question was quoted in Schily's letter to Marx (written after March 6, 1860).

p. 303

[241] See Note 75.

p. 307

[242] See Note 59.

p. 308

[243] See Note 66.

p. 311

[244] This refers to the book *Die Communisten-Verschwörungen des neunzehnten Jahrhunderts,* Berlin, Erster Theil 1853, Zweiter Theil 1854, compiled by the police officers Wermuth and Stieber. The appendices to the first volume, a "history" of the working-class movement written for the information of the police, contained some documents of the Communist League. The second volume was a blacklist of persons associated with the working-class and democratic movement, complete with biographical data.

p. 311

[245] See Note 87.

p. 314

[246] On May 15, 1848 workers led by Blanqui and Barbès staged a revolutionary uprising against the anti-labour and anti-democratic policy of the bourgeois Constituent Assembly, which met on May 4. Participants in the popular demonstration forced their way into its premises and demanded the formation of a Ministry of Labour and a number of other measures. An attempt was made to set up a revolutionary government. However, National Guards from the bourgeois districts and units of the regular army helped restore the Assembly to power. The leaders of the movement were arrested and put on trial.

p. 321

[247] The New York journal *Putnam's Monthly* published Engels' survey *The Armies of Europe* (see present edition, Vol. 14). It had been written at the request of Marx, who received an order for it through Charles Dana, editor of the *New-York Daily Tribune.* Marx helped Engels in writing the survey by supplying him material from the British Museum.

p. 323

248 The Order of St. Gregory the Great was founded by Pope Gregory XVI in 1831.   p. 324

249 The meeting of the Russian and Austrian emperors and the Prince Regent of Prussia took place in Warsaw. The attempted rapprochement between Austria, Prussia and Russia was motivated by a desire to prevent the unification of Italy and counteract the foreign policy of Napoleon III, who supported Victor Emmanuel II of Sardinia.   p. 324

250 *Maronites*—members of the Maronite Christian Church, chiefly in Lebanon. The reference here is to the clashes between Maronite peasants and townspeople, on the one hand, and their feudal lords belonging to the Druse Moslem sect, on the other. Externally a religious conflict between Christians and Moslems, it was essentially a class conflict. See also Note 316.   p. 325

251 An allusion to Louis Bonaparte's financial claims on the National Assembly at the time of his Presidency (1848-52).
Clichy, in Paris, was a debtors' prison from 1826 to 1867.   p. 327

252 The memorandum was sent to Marx by Bertalan Szemere. The covering letter has not been found. It was presumably written in February 1860. The memorandum is an account of a conversation Kossuth had with the British MP Sandford on May 30, 1854. Szemere learned of this conversation from a letter he had received from Richard Cobden, leader of the British Free Traders.
                                                                          p. 328

253 In July 1848 the Austrian Government asked Hungary to provide troops for the suppression of the liberation struggle in Italy. Kossuth readily supported this request and urged the State Assembly to grant it. After winning a victory at Custozza on July 25 Austria consolidated its positions in Italy and threw all its forces against the liberation struggle in Hungary.   p. 328

254 According to verified data, the right to raise tithes was first relinquished by Doroczy Zsigmond, the representative of the bishopric of Pecs, who made a statement to this effect in the Lower Chamber. The representatives of other bishoprics followed his example.   p. 328

255 On June 16 and 17, 1860, at Baden-Baden, Napoleon III met the Prince Regent William of Prussia, and the princes of other German states. Hoping to realise his ambition of annexing the German lands on the left bank of the Rhine, he sought a deal with Prussia at the expense of the small German states. The meeting ended in failure for Napoleon and helped Prussia secure a key role in Germany's foreign policy.   p. 329

256 This article was written by Marx for the *New-York Daily Tribune* to which he contributed from August 1851 to March 1862. On Marx's request many of the articles were written by Engels (see notes 273, 302, 314). By agreement with the *New-York Daily Tribune* editors Marx wrote on some of his articles dealing with different European countries "Paris", "Berlin" or "Vienna" respectively. (See Marx's letters to Engels of November 10, 1858, December 16, 1858 and January 13 and 15, 1859 and also Marx's letter to F. Lassalle of March 28, 1859; present edition, Vol. 40).

The articles which Marx and Engels contributed to the *New-York Daily Tribune* mainly dealt with the most important questions of foreign and home policy, the working-class movement, the economic development of the major European countries, colonial expansion and the national liberation movement in the oppressed and dependent countries. They immediately attracted attention by their profundity, political insight and literary merit. Many of Marx's and Engels' contributions were reprinted in special issues of the *New-York Daily Tribune*—the *New-York Weekly Tribune* and *Semi-Weekly Tribune*—and some of them also in the Chartist *People's Paper.* Other papers, in particular the *New-York Times,* quoted passages from Marx's and Engels' articles.

On many occasions the *New-York Daily Tribune* editors treated these articles quite arbitrarily; they printed them unsigned, as editorials, made insertions and introduced new passages which sometimes ran contrary to what Marx and Engels wanted to say. Marx repeatedly protested against those practices. From the autumn of 1857, when the financial position of the *New-York Daily Tribune* deteriorated due to the economic crisis that gripped the USA, Marx had to reduce the number of his contributions to the paper, and during the American Civil War he stopped sending them altogether, mainly because the *Tribune* had come under the sway of people advocating a compromise with the slave-owning states.

p. 330

257 *Quakers* (or *Society of Friends*)—a religious sect founded in England during the seventeenth-century revolution and later widespread in North America. They rejected the Established Church with its rites and preached pacifist ideas.

p. 330

258 The reference is to *Société générale du Crédit Mobilier*—see Note 178.

Crédit Foncier, a French joint-stock bank, set up in 1852, granted short- and long-term loans on the security of immovable property. Between 1854 and 1859 it granted loans totalling 2,000 million francs to the government of Napoleon III.

By referring to the banks of Napoleonic France as *Crédits ambulants* (travelling credits) Marx emphasised their instability.

p. 330

259 Rich gold deposits were discovered in California in 1848 and Australia in 1851. Apart from their great importance for the commercial and industrial development of Europe and America, these discoveries whipped up stock-exchange speculation in the capitalist countries.

The *Tuileries*—the royal palace in Paris, residence of Napoleon III.

p. 331

260 A reference to an imperial decree of Napoleon III on grain reserves of November 16, 1858 (*Le Moniteur universel,* No. 322, November 18, 1858). See Marx's article "Project for the Regulation of the Price of Bread in France", present edition, Vol. 16, and Marx's letter to Lassalle of February 4, 1859, Vol. 40.

p. 332

261 *Droit d'octroi*—a right, originating from feudal times, of cities to levy tolls on imported consumer goods. It was repealed in 1791 during the French Revolution, but later reintroduced on some foodstuffs (salt, wine, fish, etc.). These tolls varied from town to town.

p. 334

262 A reference to the preparations for an Opium War against China conducted by the British and French governments in early 1860. The war was unleashed in the

summer of the same year with the aim of imposing onerous new terms upon China.

The Anglo-French commercial treaty, signed on January 23, 1860, signified a triumph for the advocates of free trade in both countries and served the interests of the British industrial bourgeoisie (for details see this volume, pp. 341-44).

Marx is referring to the movement for the national unification of Italy, which gained momentum during and after the Austro-Italo-French War of 1859 (see Note 13) and was opposed by a number of European countries. In the spring and summer of 1859 popular insurrections flared up in Tuscany, Modena, Parma and Romagna. The members of the ruling dynasties there fled from their duchies to seek the protection of the Austrian army. The national assemblies set up as the result of the insurrections declared that the population of the duchies wished to be incorporated in Piedmont. This question was finally settled in March 1860 by a plebiscite.   p. 335

263 This refers to the second Opium War, waged by Britain and France against China in 1856-60.   p. 335

264 The object of the Anglo-Persian War of 1856-57 was to establish British influence in Persia, pave the way for further colonial expansion in the Middle East and Central Asia and prevent the Shah of Persia from establishing his power over the independent principality of Herat. When Persian troops occupied Herat in October 1856 Britain used this as a pretext to open hostilities. The war took an unfavourable turn for Persia. However, the national liberation uprising that flared up in India in 1857 and continued up to 1859 compelled Britain to conclude a peace treaty with Persia in all haste. Under the terms of the treaty signed in Paris in March 1857, Persia repudiated its claims to Herat, which, in 1863, was incorporated into the possessions of the Afghan Emir.   p. 336

265 Britain interfered in the civil war in Portugal (1828-34) waged by the liberal nobility, bourgeoisie and intelligentsia, which were supported by the anti-feudal section of the peasantry and fought for the preservation of the constitutional monarchy and against the feudal aristocracy, which sought to restore absolute monarchy and was backed up by the clergy and reaction-influenced peasants in some districts of Spain. The absolutists were led by Dom Miguel, a pretender to the Portuguese throne. In an attempt to consolidate their influence in the Iberian Peninsula and weaken the positions of Austria, which supported the absolutists, the British and French governments sent a fleet to the Portuguese coast (in 1831) to blockade the Tagus and Douro rivers, thus facilitating the victory of the constitutionalists.

The Anglo-Greek conflict referred to occurred in June 1850. When the British Government presented Greece with an ultimatum and sent ships to blockade Piraeus, using as a pretext the burning (in Athens in 1847) of the house of a Portuguese merchant, Pacifico, who was a British subject. The real object of this move, however, was to make Greece surrender several strategically important islands in the Aegean Sea.

The war against Afghanistan was instigated by the British Government in 1838. British troops invaded Afghanistan, but British rule was short-lived. In November 1841 a popular insurrection broke out and the occupying troops were defeated. In 1842 Britain made another attempt to conquer Afghanistan, but this also ended in total failure.   p. 338

266 The Anglo-Chinese Treaty, signed on October 8, 1843, supplemented the Treaty of Nanking (1842), which was concluded after the Anglo-Chinese War of 1840-42 (known as the first Opium War) and was the first of a series of unequal treaties imposed by the Western powers on China and reducing it to the status of a semi-colony.

Under the supplementary treaty of 1843 the British secured further concessions from China, including the right to have special settlements for foreign citizens in the open ports, the right of exterritoriality and most-favoured-nation treatment.   p. 338

267 A reference to the Tientsin Russo-Chinese Treaty signed on June 13 (1), 1858. It stipulated among other things that Russian envoys going to Peking could sail up the Peiho River via Daga.   p. 338

268 The seizure of a British ship carrying contraband opium by the Chinese authorities in October 1856, followed by the savage bombardment of Canton by the British Navy, served as a pretext for the second Opium War.   p. 338

269 A reference to the struggle for power in Ancient Rome waged by the Roman general Lucius Cornelius Sulla supported by the nobility and army veterans. It resulted in the establishment of Sulla's dictatorship in 82 B. C. Here, Marx has in mind Napoleon III.   p. 339

270 See Note 262.   p. 341

271 Marx is referring to the Anglo-French Commercial Treaty of 1860, a source of intricate political intrigues in the relations between the two countries. He compares this treaty with the "sweet changeling" (Puck) of Oberon, king of the farries, and his wife Titania (Shakespeare, A Midsummer Night's Dream, Act II, Scene 1), Puck being the cause of Oberon's wicked tricks.   p. 341

272 See Note 207.   p. 342

273 The subject of this and several other articles was suggested to Engels by Marx who wrote in his letter of November 3, 1859: "Coudn't you do me an article on the recent changes in the Prussian army?" (see present edition, Vol. 40). The Prussian military reform is also described in the article "Preparations for War in Prussia" (see this volume, pp. 493-96) and in Engels' "The War Question in Prussia and the German Workers' Party" (present edition, Vol. 20).   p. 345

274 See Note 13.

The Crimean War (1853-56), or the Eastern war, was waged by Russia against the allied forces of Britain, France and Turkey for supremacy in the Middle East and ended with the signing of the Paris Peace Treaty (1856). The war is described by Marx and Engels in the articles included in volumes 13-15 of the present edition.   p. 345

275 A reference to the colonial war in Algeria, launched by the French Government in 1830. The Algerian people put up a stubborn resistance to the French colonialists; it took them 40 years to turn Algeria into a French colony.
                                   p. 345

276 These battles took place during the Austro-Italo-French War between the Kingdom of Sardinia (Piedmont) and France on the one hand, and Austria on the other (see Note 13). In the battle at *Magenta* (June 4, 1859) the Austrian army was defeated by the French (see Engels' articles "A Chapter of History" and "The Austrian Defeat", present edition, Vol. 16). At *Solferino* (June 24, 1859) the Austrians were again defeated by the French and Piedmontese forces (see Engels' articles "The Battle at Solferino" and "Historical Justice", present edition, Vol. 16).   p. 346

277 See Note 76.   p. 348

278 The *battle of Austerlitz* between the Russo-Austrian and the French armies on December 2, 1805, ended in victory for the French commanded by Napoleon I.
    At the *battle of Jena* on October 14, 1806, the Prussian troops were defeated by Napoleon's army. This resulted in Prussia's capitulation.
    At the *battle of Wagram* on July 5-6, 1809, Napoleon defeated the Austrian army commanded by Archduke Charles.   p. 349

279 This refers to Marx's articles dealing with the budget proposed by Gladstone: among them are "Feargus O'Connor.—Ministerial Defeats.—The Budget", "L.S.D., or Class Budgets, and Who's Relieved by Them", "Riot at Constantinople.—German Table Moving.—The Budget", "Soap for the People, a Sop for *The Times*.—The Coalition Budget" (see present edition, Vol. 12).

                                                                        p. 351

280 A reference to the "liberal course" proclaimed by Prince William of Prussia (King of Prussia from 1861) in October 1858, when he took up the regency. In the bourgeois press this course was described as a "new era". Actually he did not carry out any of the reforms expected by the bourgeoisie; but in 1860 a previously prepared military reform was effected which abolished the remnants of democratism still surviving in the Prussian army after the national liberation war against Napoleon I in 1813-15. This reform stipulated that henceforth the Landwehr would be used only for garrison duties, and it considerably increased the strength of the army in peacetime.   p. 367

281 See notes 13 and 126.
    A reference to the diplomatic documents of the Austro-Italo-French War of 1859, published by the Prussian Government in the *Neue Preussische Zeitung*, Nos. 170, 171, 173 and 174 (July 24, 26, 28 and 29, 1859) and in the *Allgemeine Zeitung*, No. 211 (July 30, 1859). For details see Marx's article "Quid pro Quo" in Volume 16 of the present edition.   p. 368

282 See notes 123 and 278.   p. 368

283 The meeting between Alexander II and William, Prince Regent of Prussia, took place in October 1859 in Breslau (Wrocław). Although no political objects of the meeting were officially mentioned either in Prussia or in Russia, the press of both countries stressed its great political importance for consolidating the alliance of the two sovereigns.   p. 368

284 See Note 278.   p. 369

[285] See notes 65 and 59.   p. 369

[286] *Siculi*—one of the ancient tribes in Sicily.   p. 370

[287] A reference to a popular rising in Sicily against the French Anjou dynasty, which conquered Southern Italy and Sicily in 1267. On the evening of March 31, 1282, the population of Palermo took the chimes for vespers as a signal to massacre several thousand French knights and soldiers. As a result, the whole of Sicily was freed from French domination and came under the King of Aragon.   p. 371

[288] Popular unrest in Sicily against Francis II of Naples and his hirelings began in the autumn of 1859. The uprising that broke out in October was suppressed, but in the spring of 1860 disturbances broke out again. The Palermo uprising in May 1860 was again crushed by the royal forces. Peasant guerrilla units were operating all over the island, however, and they joined Garibaldi after he landed in Sicily with his "Thousand" volunteers.   p. 372

[289] *Bullier's Correspondance*, a Paris news agency founded in the 1850s and later amalgamated with *Havas*.   p. 373

[290] The *Zollverein*, a union of German states which established a common customs frontier, was set up in 1834 under the aegis of Prussia. Brought into being by the need to create an all-German market, the Customs Union subsequently embraced all the German states except Austria and a few of the smaller states.
                                                                                          p. 373

[291] A reference to the Paris peace treaties of 1814 and 1815 signed by France and the main participants of the sixth and seventh anti-French coalitions (Russia, Britain, Austria and Prussia) that defeated Napoleon. Under the terms of the first treaty, signed on May 30, 1814, France lost all the territories won by her in the 1792-1814 wars, with the exception of several border fortresses and Western Savoy. Under the provisions of the second Paris treaty the territory of France was limited by the 1790 borders and she was deprived of strategically important points on her Eastern frontier, including the fortress of Landau.
                                                                                          p. 374

[292] See Note 280.   p. 375

[293] A reference to the treaty of alliance and mutual guarantees between Russia and Prussia (Traité d'alliance et de garantie mutuelle conclu à St. Petersbourg entre la Russie et la Prusse) concluded in June 1714 during the Northern War between Russia and Sweden (1700-21) when Russia sought to win Prussia over to her side by promising to divide Swedish possessions in Germany. Under the treaty Prussia was guaranteed the possession of Eastern Pomerania with the town of Stettin (Szczecin).   p. 377

[294] On the *Seven Years' War* (1756-63) see Note 122.
     The death of Empress Elisabeth on January 5, 1762 (December 25, 1761) led to a sudden change in Russia's foreign policy. Her successor, Peter III, concluded a peace treaty with Prussia thereby giving the latter an opportunity to sign, in 1763, the Hubertusburg peace treaty with Austria and Saxony and retain the possession of Silesia.   p. 377

295 The three partitions of Poland (by Austria, Prussia and Russia) took place at
    the end of the eighteenth century (1772, 1793, 1795).
        Russia gained Lithuanian, Byelorussian and Ukrainian territories; Polish
    land, including Pomorze, Great Poland, and part of Mazovia with Warsaw,
    went over to Prussia; and Austria received the Western Ukraine and part of
    Smaller Poland. As a result of the third partition Poland ceased to exist as a
    state.   p. 377

296 The *Congress of Vienna* was held by European monarchs and their ministers in
    1814-15. They established the borders and status of the European states after
    the victory over Napoleonic France and sanctioned, contrary to the national
    interests and will of the peoples, the reshaping of Europe's political map and
    the restoration of the "legitimate" dynasties. By decision of the Congress of
    Vienna, territories along the right and left banks of the Rhine, as well as
    Northern Saxony, were incorporated into Prussia, notwithstanding the opposi-
    tion of Britain, Austria and France.   p. 377

297 See Note 283.   p. 377

298 A reference to the claims of Napoleon III to the left bank of the Rhine, which
    the French ruling circles had considered France's "natural frontier" in the east
    ever since the seventeenth century. For details see Engels' articles "Po and
    Rhine" and "Savoy, Nice and the Rhine" (present edition Vol. 16).   p. 378

299 The *Olmütz agreement*—see Note 143.
    The *Federal Diet*—see Note 77.   p. 379

300 In the letter which William, Prince Regent of Prussia, sent to Albert, Prince
    Consort of England in February 1860, he expressed his readiness to accept
    Britain's proposal concerning the alliance between Britain, Austria and Prussia,
    into which he hoped to draw Russia as well. This proposal was called forth by
    the increasingly aggressive tendencies of the government of Napoleon III with
    regard to the German lands on the left bank of the Rhine and by France's
    annexation of Savoy and Nice.   p. 382

301 In the spring of 1833 Russian troops were landed at Unkiar-Skelessi, near the
    Bosporus, to render assistance to the Turkish Sultan against the army of the
    insurgent Egyptian ruler Mehemet Ali. In May 1833 the Porte, with the
    mediation of Britain and France, signed a peace treaty with Mehemet Ali,
    ceding him Syria and Palestine. However, Russian diplomats took advantage of
    the strained situation and the presence of Russian troops in Turkey and
    prevailed upon the Porte to sign, on July 8, 1833, the Unkiar-Skelessi Treaty
    for a defensive alliance with Russia. On the insistence of Russia a secret clause
    was included in the treaty prohibiting all foreign warships, except those of
    Russia, to pass through the Dardanelles. This circumstance greatly aggravated
    the relations between Russia and the West-European countries and, during a
    new Turko-Egyptian crisis (1839-41), the tsarist government had to comply
    with their demand that in peacetime the straits should be closed to the warships
    of all foreign states without exception.   p. 382

302 The subject of this article was suggested by Marx who wrote to Engels on June

2, 1860 asking him to write a small article about "the Garibaldi's affair" (see present edition, Vol. 41). p. 386

303 A reference to the defence of the Roman Republic which was virtually directed by Garibaldi from April to July 1849. In April 1849, President Louis Bonaparte and the French Government sent an expeditionary corps to Italy under General Oudinot to intervene against the Roman Republic proclaimed on February 9, 1849, and to restore the secular power of the Pope. On April 30, 1849, the French troops were driven back from Rome. The main blow was dealt by Garibaldi's volunteer corps. Oudinot violated the terms of the armistice signed by the French, however, and on June 3 started a new offensive against the Roman Republic, which had just completed a military campaign against Neapolitan troops in the south and was engaged in rebuffing the Austrians in the north. After a month of heroic defence, Rome was captured by the interventionists and the Roman Republic ceased to exist. p. 387

304 This item and the next one ("Interesting from Prussia") were directed against the Bonapartist agents among the European democrats and exposed the chauvinist nature of About's pamphlet (see this volume, pp. 400-01, as well as Marx's letters to Engels of June 16, 1860 and December 26, 1860, and Marx's letter to J. Ph. Becker of June 23, 1860, present edition, Vol. 41), the publication of which was connected with the forthcoming meeting between Napoleon III and William, Prince Regent of Prussia (see Note 255). Marx used quotations from About's pamphlet to unmask the activity of the Prussian police agents among European democrats. In Herr Vogt Marx revealed the connection between About's ideas and Vogt's activity as a secret agent in the pay of Napoleon III (see this volume, pp. 183, 328-29). At Marx's suggestion, Sigismund Borkheim, one of the German democrats, wrote a pamphlet entitled Napoleon III und Preussen. Antwort eines deutschen Flüchtlings auf "Preussen in 1860" von Edmond About, London, 1860.

Marx must have used the proofs of About's pamphlet supplied to him by Borkheim, since in both his articles and in the Notebook for 1860 containing passages from About's pamphlet he gives its original title Napoleon III et la Prusse (see also this volume, pp. 328-29).

The extracts given by Marx in this article were checked against About's pamphlet. Marx's text is set in large type. While quoting from the pamphlet, Marx often changed punctuation and paragraphs; sometimes, instead of direct quotations, he gave a précis of the text in which case the editors of this volume have omitted quotation marks; omissions in quotations are indicated by omission marks in square brackets. p. 391

305 See Note 190. p. 392

306 See Note 255. p. 397

307 The governments of Britain and the Kingdom of Sardinia flirted with Napoleon III in an effort to secure an exclusive alliance with France. p. 399

308 Alexander II and Napoleon III met in Stuttgart on September 25, 1857. Their meeting testified to the emerging rapprochement between France and Russia after the Crimean War. p. 399

309 The Rhenish Confederation (Rheinbund) of the states of Western and Southern Germany was founded in 1806 under the protectorate of Napoleon. These

states officially broke with the Holy Roman Empire of the German nation, which ceased to exist shortly afterwards. When Napoleon lost the military campaign of 1813 the confederation fell apart.   p. 399

310 Speaking of the *Dutch savior of society* Marx has in mind Napoleon III, who was a son of Louis Bonaparte (brother of Napoleon I), King of Holland in 1806-10. On the Congress of Vienna, see Note 296.

The Congresses of the Holy Alliance (an association of European monarchs founded in September 1815, on the initiative of the Russian Tsar Alexander I and the Austrian Chancellor Metternich to suppress revolutionary movements and preserve feudal monarchies in European countries) took place in Aix-la-Chapelle (1818), in Troppau (Opava) and Laibach (Ljubljana) (1820-21), and in Verona (1822). The Laibach Congress proclaimed the principle of interference by the Holy Alliance members in the internal affairs of other countries with the aim of maintaining monarchies there; and adopted a decision on sending the Austrian army to Italy to suppress the revolutionary and national liberation movement in that country. The Verona Congress sanctioned French armed intervention against Spain.   p. 400

311 In 1857-59 India was the scene of a big popular uprising against the British. It flared up in the spring of 1857 among the Sepoy units of the Bengal army and spread to large areas in Northern and Central India. Its main strength was in the peasants and the poor urban artisans. Directed by local feudal lords it was put down owing to the country's disunity, religious and caste differences and also because of the military and technical superiority of the British.   p. 407

312 The letter which Garibaldi sent in the summer of 1860 to Mr. Green, an English acquaintance of Marx, shows that Garibaldi wanted the struggle waged by the Italian people for the national unification of the country and its liberation from foreign rule to be independent of Napoleon III's policy. Marx is referring to this in his letters to Engels of July 9 and to Lassalle of September 15, 1860 (see present edition, Vol. 41).   p. 421

313 A reference to the *Società Nazionale Italiana,* a political organisation of a liberal monarchist trend founded in 1856 in Turin and other towns by G. Pallavicino, an Italian political figure, and La Farina, an agent in the pay of Cavour. Its aim was to popularise the ideas of Italy's unification under the aegis of the Savoy dynasty and to enlist the country's national forces for this cause. Garibaldi was an active member of this association and represented its revolutionary wing, but the decisive role in the organisation was played by Cavour's accomplices.   p. 423

314 The subject of this and several other articles was suggested by Marx who wrote to Engels on June 25: "I would be grateful if by Friday or Saturday you could write an article for the *Tribune* either on the defences of England, or on Garibaldi, or on the Indian trade" (see present edition, Vol. 41). On July 25 Marx informed Engels that he had received his article "British Defenses" and promised to send him the *Report of the Commissioners Appointed to Consider the Defences of the United Kingdom; together with the Minutes of Evidence and Appendix,* London, 1860. Concerning British defences Engels wrote one more article (end of July 1860) entitled "Could the French Sack London?" (this volume, pp. 434-38).

The article "Garibaldi's Movements" was written by Engels on August 8 (this volume, pp. 449-52).
As is evident from Engels' letter of July 26, 1860 (see present edition, Vol. 41) an article on Indian commerce was not written. Marx devoted a few lines to this question in his article "British Commerce" (this volume, pp. 406-09).

p. 425

315 During the Crimean War of 1853-56 Sevastopol was besieged by the British, French, Turkish and Sardinian troops. In the course of the fighting, Sevastopol was badly damaged.   p. 426

316 In 1859 Northern Lebanon was the scene of an anti-feudal rebellion started by the Maronite peasants (see Note 250); disturbances spread to the centre of Lebanon and in the spring of 1860 fierce clashes took place between Druses and Maronites. This was largely due to British and French policy. Britain gave support to the Druse feudalists, whereas the Maronite feudal lords and the clergy were backed by France. British and French emissaries incited enmity between rival Druse and Maronite feudal groups and fanned religious strife between Moslems and Christians. The Turkish authorities also played a provocative part. Napoleon III used the massacre of May-June 1860 as a pretext for sending an expeditionary corps to Lebanon. The agreement between Britain, Austria, Russia, France, Prussia and Turkey provided for setting up an international commission and specified the term during which the French troops were to stay in Lebanon. Under pressure from Britain and Austria, the French forces were withdrawn from that country in 1861.

p. 429

317 The conflict was caused by La Guéronnière's pamphlet Le Pape et le Congrès, which appeared in France at the close of December 1859 and was inspired by Napoleon III. The clericals saw in it an attempt on the part of the emperor to restrict the secular power of Pius IX. The higher Catholic clergy of France started a campaign against Napoleon III after Pius IX strongly denounced the pamphlet in an Encyclical early in 1860.   p. 430

318 A reference to the monarchist parties of Legitimists and Orleanists that formed in the early half of the nineteenth century. The Legitimist Party stood for the big landowners and the restoration of the Bourbons. The Orleanist Party, that ruled during the July monarchy, represented the interests of big financial and industrial capital and supported the restoration of the Orleans, that is, the younger branch of the Bourbons.   p. 431

319 See Note 232.   p. 431

320 Francis Joseph of Austria, and William, Prince Regent of Prussia, met on July 26, 1860 in Teplitz (Teplice). The Austrian emperor sought Prussia's support in case of a war with France and Sardinia.   p. 431

321 In the early 1840s, under pressure from France and Britain, Turkey had to reorganise the administration of Lebanon, which was divided into two sectors. The northern sector, with a Maronite population, was administered by a governor from among the Maronite feudal lords connected with France, while the southern sector, populated by Maronites and Druse Moslems, was ruled by

a governor from among the Druse feudal lords connected with Britain. While remaining within the framework of the Turkish Empire, Lebanon received a certain degree of autonomy in the sphere of judiciary, finance, etc. Seeking to increase their political influence in Lebanon and win the Lebanese market, the European powers fanned religious strife between Maronites and Druses.

p. 431

322 A reference to the revolution of 1688-89, after which constitutional monarchy was consolidated in England on the basis of a compromise between the landed aristocracy and the bourgeoisie. The 1689 Bill of Rights and other acts limited the rights of the king still further and extended the rights of Parliament.

p. 432

323 Under the Act for the Better Government of India, adopted by the British Parliament on August 2, 1858, India passed under the control of the British crown and the East India Company was liquidated. The Act also provided for the formation of the Indian Council as an advisory body of the Board of Control for India. The Governor-General of India became known as the Viceroy, though he remained virtually functionary of the Secretary of State for India in London.   p. 432

324 In a letter to Persigny, the French Ambassador in London, written on July 25, 1860, and published in French papers (*Le Constitutionnel*, "Paris le I^e août", No. 215, August 2, 1860), Napoleon III denied a hostile attitude to Britain and sought to dispel suspicion and distrust, prevalent in Britain at the time, of his foreign policy (see this volume, p. 446).   p. 439

325 The *will of Peter the Great*—a spurious document circulated by enemies of Russia. The idea of the existence of the "will" was advanced in the West as early as 1797. In 1812 Ch. L. Lesur described the contents of this pseudo-will in his book *Des progrès de la puissance russe, depuis son origine jusqu'au commencement du XIXe siècle*, and in 1836 it was reproduced as a document in T. F. Gaillardet's book *Mémoires du Chevalier d'Eon*. In Marx's and Engels' lifetime many people in Western Europe regarded this document as authentic.

p. 440

326 A reference to the *Rhine-song* ("Der deutsche Rhein")—a poem by Nicolaus Becker which was widely used by nationalists in their own interests. It was written in 1840 and set to music by several composers.   p. 440

327 The *Liberal Party* was formed in Britain in the late 1850s and early 1860s. It united in its ranks the Whigs, the Manchester men (representatives of the industrial bourgeoisie) and the Peelites (moderate Tories). In the British two-party system the Liberal Party's counterpart was the emerging party of Conservatives (former Tories).   p. 444

328 At *St. Stephen's Chapel* (in Westminster Palace) the British House of Commons held its sessions from the sixteenth century to the nineteenth.   p. 445

329 A reference to a Bill passed in August 1860. Under the Act for the Reorganisation of the Indian Army, the European contingent of the Indian Army, formerly at the disposal of the East India Company, became part of the British royal armed forces, and the number of British soldiers in the Indian army increased sharply. Adopted after the suppression of the Indian uprising

of 1857-59 (see Note 311) the Act was one of the measures the British
Government resorted to in an effort to consolidate British rule in India.

p. 445

330 See Note 323.   p. 446

331 See Note 316.   p. 446

332 *Robert Macaire*—a social comedy staged by the famous French actor Frédérick
Lemaître in collaboration with the playwrights Antier and Saint-Amand. Marx
is referring to Macaire's words "Foi d'honnête homme ... pas de bêtises!" (Acte
II, III tableau, scène VIII). The character of Robert Macaire, portraying a
clever swindler, was a biting satire on the domination of the financial
aristocracy under the July monarchy. Marx alluded to this character on several
occasions. See, for example, *The Class Struggles in France, 1848 to 1850* (present
edition, Vol. 10, p. 50).   p. 447

333 A reference to Lombardy, which France ceded to Piedmont under the
Villafranca Peace Treaty (see Note 126), as well as to Romagna and the duchies
of Parma, Modena and Tuscany, which were incorporated into Piedmont
following the plebiscite of March 1860.   p. 453

334 *Partant pour la Syrie* (Departing for Syria)—the opening words of a song sung
at the festivities arranged by Napoleon III at the time of the Second Empire.
Marx is alluding to the Syrian expedition.   p. 455

335 See notes 255 and 320.   p. 457

336 The *assemblée des notables*—a consultative body irregularly convened by French
kings from the fourteenth century to the eighteenth. It consisted of
representatives of the higher clergy and court nobility, and also of mayors of
the cities. In 1787, on the eve of the French Revolution, it voted down the
government's tax bill and met for the last time in 1788 to discuss the
composition of, and elections to, the States General.
    The *States General*—a body representing the social estates in medieval
France. It consisted of clergymen, nobles and burghers. Convened in May
1789, after a 175-year interval, at a time when the bourgeois revolution was
maturing in France, the States General were on June 17 transformed by the
decision of the deputies of the third estate into the National Assembly, which
on July 9 proclaimed itself the Constituent Assembly and became the supreme
organ of revolutionary France.   p. 459

337 *Mark Lane*—the grain stock exchange in London.   p. 461

338 In 1860 France put forth a project which acknowledged Spain as a great
power. Owing to Britain's opposition, the project did not materialise.

p. 464

339 See Note 324.   p. 464

340 Marx is quoting from "The Oriental Question", an article published in the
Russky Invalid, Nos. 164 and 165 on July 31 and August 2, 1860, making some
changes in the text of the journal. Apparently, he was using a version of this

article printed in the European press. The most important divergences are
indicated in the footnotes.   p. 467

341 After the defeat of the Roman Republic in 1849 the French interventionist
troops did not leave Rome until 1870.   p. 471

342 *"Brown Bess"*—the name used by British soldiers in the eighteenth and early
nineteenth centuries for a flint-lock musket with a brown walnut stock.
                                                                 p. 477

343 See notes 232 and 249.   p. 484

344 On March 3 (February 19), 1859, Russia and France concluded in Paris a secret
agreement under which Russia undertook to adopt a "political and military
stand which most easily proves its favourable neutrality towards France"
(Article 1) and to make no objection to the Kingdom of Sardinia being enlarged
in the event of a war between France and Sardinia on the one hand and
Austria on the other. France undertook to raise the question of revising those
articles of the Paris Peace Treaty of 1856 which restricted Russia's rights in the
Black Sea area and robbed her of a part of Bessarabia.   p. 486

345 On June 26, 1849, the liberal deputies of the Frankfurt National Assembly,
who had walked out after the Prussian King's refusal to accept the Imperial
Crown, met in Gotha for a three-day conference which resulted in the
formation of the Gotha party. It expressed the interests of the pro-Prussian
German bourgeoisie and supported the policy of Prussian ruling circles aimed
at uniting Germany under the hegemony of Hohenzollern Prussia.   p. 486

346 See Note 281.   p. 489

347 *Via sacra* (sacred road)—in Ancient Rome victorious troops marched in
triumph along this highway. The expression "via sacra" is also used to describe
a victorious campaign.
Here an allusion to an appeal sent by Napoleon III to his army from Genoa
on May 12, 1859, when he became the commander-in-chief. The appeal said, in
part: "Dans la voie sacrée de l'ancienne Rome les inscriptions se pressaient sur
le marbre pour rappeler au peuple ses hauts faits: de même aujourd'hui, en
passant par Mondovi, Marengo, Lodi, Castiglione, Arcole, Rivoli, vous
marcherez dans une autre voie sacrée, au milieu de ces glorieux souvenirs"
("Along the sacred road of Ancient Rome inscriptions were carved on marble
to commemorate the people's feats. Today likewise, passing through Mondovi,
Marengo, Lodi, Castiglione, Arcole and Rivoli, you will march along another
sacred road, amidst these glorious memories").   p. 489

348 *Quirinal*—one of the seven hills on which Rome is situated. p. 490

349 See notes 53 and 259.   p. 490

350 This refers to the commercial treaty between Prussia and Austria, concluded in
Berlin on February 19, 1853. It eliminated many of the customs barriers that

obstructed the development of trade between the two countries. (See Marx, "Kossuth and Mazzini.—Intrigues of the Prussian Government.—Austro-Prussian Commercial Treaty.— *The Times* and the Refugees", present edition, Vol. 11.)

Concerning the *Zollverein* see Note 290.   p. 492

351 See Note 192.   p. 493

352 An allusion to the Constitution of the Austrian monarchy (Gesamtmonarchie) introduced by Francis Joseph on *March 4, 1849* (Reichsverfassung für das Kaiserthum Oesterreich. Olmütz, 4 März 1849. In: *Wiener Zeitung*, No. 57, March 8, 1849). Despite the promises of autonomy to the lands inhabited by non-Austrians, the imposed Constitution was conceived in an anti-democratic spirit of centralised bureaucracy and anti-democratic government (the Emperor and his Ministers were to enjoy full powers). The Constitution of March 4 was a step towards restoring absolutism in Austria. Nevertheless the Constitution limited the Emperor's power and it was abrogated by the imperial patent of December 31, 1851. (Concerning the Constitution of March 4, 1849, see F. Engels' articles "The War in Italy and Hungary", "From the Theatre of War.—Windischgrätz's Comments on the Imposed Constitution", present edition, Vol. 9, pp. 148, 261-64, and "Letters from Germany", Vol. 10, p. 11.)   p. 493

353 The reference is to Hungary's unwritten constitution which was the oldest in Europe and based on ancient traditions and legislative acts of the Kingdom. The independence of the Diet was guaranteed in the interests of the Hungarian nobility, as also was the Diet's right to decide the most important state questions, including financial credits and army recruitment.   p. 493

354 Lord Strafford, Charles I's favourite and an ardent champion of absolutism, was accused of high treason and executed in 1641 by demand of Parliament supported by the people of London and the suburbs.   p. 495

355 An Act to Regulate the Issue of Banknotes, and for Giving to the Governor and Company of the Bank of England Certain Privileges for a Limited Period was introduced by Robert Peel on July 19, 1844. It envisaged the division of the Bank of England into two completely independent departments, each with its own cash account—the Banking Department, dealing exclusively with credit operations and the Issue Department, issuing banknotes.

The Act limited the number of banknotes in circulation and guaranteed them with definite gold and silver reserves which could not be used for the credit operations of the Banking Department. Further issues of banknotes were allowed only in the event of a corresponding increase in the precious metal reserves.

Marx analysed the Act of 1844 and its significance in a number of articles for the *New-York Daily Tribune*: "The Vienna Note.—The United States and Europe.—Letters from Shumla.—Peel's Bank Act" (see present edition, Vol. 12), "The English Bank Act of 1844 and the Monetary Crisis in Britain", "The British Revulsion" (Vol. 15) and "The English Bank Act of 1844" (Vol. 16). A detailed description of the Act was given by Marx later, in *Capital,* Vol. III, Chapter XXXIV.   p. 498

356 See Note 192.   p. 499

357 The reference is to Austria's provincial constitutions published as a continua
tion of the "October Diploma" (Der Kaiserliche Diplom von 20. Oktober
1860)—"Landes-Ordnung und Landtags-Wahlordnung für das Herzogthum
Steiermark", "Landes-Ordnung und Landtags-Wahlordnung für das Herzogthum Kärnthen", "Landes-Ordnung und Landtags-Wahlordnung für das
Herzogthum Salzburg", "Landes-Ordnung und Landtags-Wahlordnung für die
gefürstete Grafschaft Tirol", Verfassung der Oesterreichische Monarchie, Wien,
1861. p. 499

358 The county assemblies, based on the estate principle, were a form of
self-government in Hungary. In 1848, as a result of the revolutionary changes
in the country, representatives of the entire population without any estate
distinctions were allowed to sit in these assemblies. After the defeat of the
1848-49 revolution the county assemblies were disbanded, and the comitatus as
an administrative unit was abolished. p. 500

359 This is Marx's synopsis of Imre Szabó's two-volume study, The State Policy of
Modern Europe, from the Beginning of the Sixteenth Century to the Present Time,
which was published anonymously in London in May-June 1857. Szabó's work,
written in English, is a summary of inter-state relations in Europe from the
Italian wars of the early 16th century to the Paris Congress of 1856. It reflects
the influence of David Urquhart's views. Marx compiled his synopsis in the first
half of June 1860 in connection with his work on Herr Vogt. He needed this
historical investigation to expose the counter-revolutionary nature of Napoleon
III's policy. In taking notes he concentrated on the events and fully ignored
Szabó's interpretation of them. Some notes refer to events not mentioned in
Szabó's work and are probably based on other sources. In the present edition
these insertions and Marx's conclusions are set in large type. The names of
persons and geographical names are reproduced in Marx's transcription, with
their present spelling given in footnotes. Obvious mistakes have been silently
corrected.
    Marx drew on these notes above all in the chapter "Dâ-Dâ Vogt and His
Studies" (see this volume, pp. 133-83). p. 505

360 The Union of Calmar (1397-1523) included Denmark, Norway (with Iceland)
and Sweden (with Finland) under the sovereignty of the Danish kings. Sweden
virtually broke away in 1449. The attempt of the Danish King Christian II to
bring it back into the union by staging a bloodbath in Stockholm led to a final
rupture and the restoration of Swedish statehood (1523). p. 505

361 This refers to the League of Cognac formed on May 22, 1526. p. 505

362 Traité des dames—an ironic designation of the Peace of Cambray (August 1529),
which was concluded with the active co-operation of Louise of Savoy (Francis
I's mother) and Margaret (Charles V's aunt). p. 506

363 This refers to the rejection by Charles V and the Augsburg Imperial Diet in
1530 of the Confession of Augsburg, which laid down the principles of
Lutheranism and established the ritual aspect. p. 506

364 The League of Schmalkalden (February 27, 1531), named after the town in
Thuringia where it was formed, was a union of Protestant princes and a
number of Imperial towns for the protection of the Reformation against the

Catholic princes headed by Emperor Charles V. From 1546 to 1548 the League and the Emperor were engaged in a war which ended in the latter's victory and the disintegration of the League.   p. 506

365 In 1534 Henry VIII broke off relations with the Pope and was proclaimed Head of the Anglican Church by Parliament (Act of Supremacy).   p. 506

366 The Augsburg *Interim* was a treaty between the German Catholics and Protestants adopted by the Imperial Diet in Augsburg after the Protestants' defeat in the Schmalkalden War. A compromise that satisfied neither party, it was superseded by the Religious Peace of Augsburg (1555).   p. 506

367 The *Treaty of Cateau-Cambrésis* (1559) put an end to the Italian Wars (1494-1559). It consisted of two treaties: one between France and England and another between France and Spain. France renounced all claims to possessions in Italy. The Savoy Duchy, captured by Francis I in 1536, was restored and given part of Piedmont.   p. 506

368 Marx is obviously referring to an international treaty proposed in *Mémoires des sages et royales économies d'Estat, domestiques, politiques et militaires de Henry le Grand*, a book by Sully, Counsellor to Henry IV, published in 1638. Drawn up by Sully (even though he attributes it to Henry IV) at the height of the Thirty Years' War, it was anti-Habsburg in character and advocated the expulsion of the Turks and Tatars from Europe and the establishment of a conglomerate of Christian states under the nominal supremacy of the Pope, but actually led by France. The plan was patently unrealistic.   .p. 509

369 From 1604 to 1606 Hungary, Hungarian-ruled Slovakia and Transylvania were the scene of an anti-Habsburg liberation movement led by the Hungarian feudal lord Istvan Bocskai. The anti-feudal demands of the peasants taking part in the movement made its leaders accept a compromise with the Habsburgs. The treaty signed by Bocskai and Rudolph II in Vienna in 1606 restored Transylvania's independence, granted religious freedom to the Protestants and replaced a number of the Emperor's counsellors by members of the Hungarian nobility.   p. 510

370 The Thirty Years' War (see Note 162) was sparked off by an anti-Habsburg uprising in Bohemia which lasted from 1618 to 1620. The Bohemians were supported by Gábor Bethlen, leader of a similar uprising in Hungary. The insurgents suffered a decisive defeat at Bílá Hora on November 8, 1620.

p. 510

371 The anti-Habsburg movement in Hungary led by Gábor Bethlen (1619-26) was one aspect of the Thirty Years' War and ended in the signing of the Pozsony (Bratislava) Peace on December 20, 1626.   p. 510

372 The *Edict of Restitution* (1629) provided for the restoration of secularised church land to the German Catholic princes. It was the result of the successes achieved by the Habsburg-Catholic camp in the early stage of the Thirty Years' War. The Edict was officially revoked by the Peace Treaty of Westphalia (October 24, 1648).   p. 510

373 The *Truce of Altmark* was concluded by Poland and Sweden with French

mediation for six years on September 26, 1629. It enabled Sweden to open hostilities against the Habsburgs.   p. 510

374 This refers to the war of the Mantuan Succession (1628-31), which formed the third stage of the Thirty Years' War.   p. 510

375 The *Peace of Prague* was concluded by the German Protestant princes with the Emperor on May 30, 1635.   p. 510

376 *Anne of Austria*, consort of Louis XIII of France, was the daughter of Philip III of Spain and tried to pursue a pro-Spanish policy at the time of her regency (1643-61), during the minority of her son Louis XIV. France's virtual ruler at that time was Mazarin.   p. 511

377 The *Peace of Westphalia*, signed in Münster on October 24, 1648, consisted of two interlinked peace treaties: the Osnabrück Treaty (between the Holy Roman Emperor and his allies, on the one hand, and Sweden and its allies, on the other) and the Münster Treaty (between the Emperor and France with its allies). Peace negotiations had been under way from 1645. The Peace of Westphalia virtually sealed Germany's political fragmentation (see also Note 162).   p. 511

378 This refers to Spain's separate treaty with Holland (one of the series of Westphalian treaties).   p. 511

379 Bohemia formed part of the Habsburg Empire (1526-1918).
    Speaking of the *amnesty* Marx means the promises Britain, France, Sweden, Denmark and other states made to Bohemia during the Thirty Years' War when it fought on the side of the anti-Habsburg coalition. Under the Peace of Westphalia, the Bohemian lands, the scene of military operations throughout the Thirty Years' War, remained under Habsburg rule.   p. 511

380 This refers to the Westminster Peace Treaty of April 14, 1654, which concluded the first Anglo-Dutch war (1652-54). It was waged for mastery of the seas and ended in defeat for Holland. The latter was forced to reconcile itself to the English Navigation Act of 1651, which was directed against the Dutch carrying trade.   p. 511

381 After the Peace of Westphalia (1648) France continued its war against Spain. It was concluded by the Treaty of the Pyrenees, signed on Fezan Island on Bidasoa River on November 7, 1659. As a result, hegemony in Western Europe passed from Spain to France.   p. 512

382 This refers to the terms of the Peace of Roeskilde concluded on February 26, 1658, which ended the Danish-Swedish War of 1657-58.
    Sound duties—the money toll exacted from 1425 onwards by Denmark from foreign ships passing through the Sound.   p. 512

383 The *Peace of Oliva*, signed on May 3, 1660, by Sweden, on the one hand, and Poland, Emperor Leopold I and Elector Frederick-William of Brandenburg, on the other, was one of the series of treaties that ended the Northern War (1655-60).   p. 512

384 The *jus devolutionis* was a legal principle in some of the Netherland provinces under which, in the event of a second marriage of the father, his land passed to his children by the first marriage. It served as a basis for Louis XIV, married to Maria Theresa, daughter of Philip IV of Spain by his first marriage, to launch a war for the Spanish Netherlands (the War of Devolution, 1667-68) against Charles II, King of Spain, son of Philip IV of second marriage. Philip IV died in 1668.   p. 512

385 This refers to the Peace of Nijmegen, concluded by France and Sweden with Emperor Leopold I on February 5, 1679. It confirmed the terms of the Peace of Westphalia and was one of the Nijmegen treaties of 1678-79 which ended the war of 1672-78 waged by a coalition of states headed by France against a coalition under the Netherlands.   p. 513

386 The *Chambres de réunion* were set up by Louis XIV at the municipal council of Breisach and the Parliaments of Metz and Besançon in 1679-80 to provide legal justification for France's claims to territories in Alsace, Western Lorraine and some other areas.   p. 513

387 The Peace of Ryswik (or Rijswijk) concluded the 1688-97 war between France and the Augsburg League (the Netherlands, England, Spain, the German Empire, Savoy, Sweden, and a number of German and Italian principalities). It confirmed, with certain alterations, the pre-war frontiers of the states involved. France was forced to recognise William of Orange as King of Great Britain and Ireland and thus reconcile itself to the coup d'état of 1688-89.   p. 513

388 The Grand Alliance—the anti-French coalition formed on September 7, 1701 in The Hague by Emperor Leopold I, Britain and the Netherlands on the eve of the War of the Spanish Succession. Prussia, Denmark, Portugal and several other states joined the alliance later. By calling it the second Grand Alliance, Szabó treats the anti-French coalition of 1688 as the first.   p. 514

389 What is meant here is the beginning of the War of the Spanish Succession, in which the first action was the dispatch in 1701 of Imperial troops under Eugene of Savoy to Italy to prevent the capture of the Duchy of Milan by the French. War was officially declared on Louis XIV in 1702.   p. 514

390 This refers to the anti-Habsburg liberation movement in Hungary (1703-11) led by Ferenc II Rákóczy. An active part in it, particularly in the early period, was played by the peasants, who put forward anti-feudal demands. The movement ended in the signing of the Treaty of Szatmar (1711) (see Note 127) and the surrender of the insurgent army. Hungary was incorporated into the Habsburg Empire. Rákóczy regarded the Szatmar treaty as a betrayal and refused to recognise it.   p. 514

391 The *Aaland Congress* (1718-19)—preliminary peace talks between representatives of Russia and Sweden during the Great Northern War (1700-21). The parties failed to reach agreement.   p. 515

392 The *Great Northern War* (1700-21) was concluded by a series of peace treaties: the *Treaty of Stockholm* (*November 9, 1719*) between Sweden and Britain (Hanover); the *Treaty of Stockholm* (*January 21, 1720*) between Sweden and

Prussia; the treaty between Sweden and Denmark (July 3, 1720) and the Treaty of Nystadt (September 10/August 30, 1721) between Russia and Sweden. Marx gives the wrong date, November 1, when referring to the Treaty of Stockholm between Sweden and Britain. p. 515

393 *Quadruple Alliance* (1718)—the alliance formed by France and Britain and later joined by Austria (the Netherlands was expected to join too) to uphold the terms of the Peace of Utrecht in the face of Spain's attempts to recover its possessions in Italy turned over to Austria under the Utrecht peace agreements. The conflict took the form of a war by France and Britain against Spain which ended in Spain's defeat and accession (1720) to the Quadruple Alliance. p. 515

394 This refers to the Hanoverian Alliance formed by France, Britain and Prussia on September 3, 1725 and joined by the Netherlands in 1726 and Denmark and Sweden in 1727. It was directed against Spain and Austria. p. 516

395 The *Pragmatic Sanction* was a law on succession to the throne issued by Charles VI of Habsburg in 1713. It decreed the indivisibility of the Habsburgs' hereditary lands and envisaged the possibility of the Crown of the Austrian Empire passing to Maria Theresa, Charles VI's daughter. p. 516

396 This refers to the treaties (including the Peace of Utrecht and the Peace of Rastatt) concluded between 1713 and 1715 by France and Spain with the members of the anti-French coalition (Britain, the Netherlands, Portugal, Prussia, Savoy and the Austrian Habsburgs) to end the long War of the Spanish Succession. Their major provision was the retention of the Spanish throne by Philip Bourbon, grandson of Louis XIV, but the King of France was forced to renounce his plans for merging the French and Spanish monarchies. A number of French and Spanish colonies in the West Indies and North America, and also Gibraltar and the port of Mahón on Minorca Island were turned over to Britain. It also secured the *asiento,* a monopoly right to import African slaves into the Spanish dominions in America. p. 518

397 A mistake in Szabó's book: the Hanovero-Hessian troops were beaten by a French army under Marshal L. Ch. d'Estrées. Marshal L. F. Richelieu assumed command of this army in 1758. p. 518

398 This refers to the Battle of Leiten (Lutynia) in Silesia on December 5, 1757 at which Frederick II defeated the Austrians and secured the capture of Silesia by Prussia. p. 518

399 An allusion to the fact that one of the main causes of the Seven Years' War (see Note 122) was Anglo-French rivalry over colonies. p. 518

400 The *Hubertusburg Peace,* signed by Austria and Saxony with Prussia on February 15, 1763, was made possible by Peter III, who not only stopped all hostilities against Prussia but pledged himself to Frederick II to use whatever influence Russia could exert on Austria to end the Seven Years' War (1756-63). Under the Hubertusburg Peace, Prussia recovered all the territories it had lost during the war. p. 519

[401] This refers to the benefits Sweden gained under the Peace of Westphalia, which gave it control of the main harbours on the Baltic and the North Sea (see also Note 162).   p. 519

[402] An allusion to the *liberum veto*, the right of every member of the Diet to veto its decisions; introduced in 1652, it aggravated feudal anarchy in Poland. p. 519

[403] *Stamp duty*—the duty imposed in North America on commercial and judicial documents and periodicals. It was introduced by the Stamp Act, endorsed by the British Parliament on March 22, 1765.   p. 520

[404] *Potato War*—ironic name given to the War of the Bavarian Succession (1778-79), waged by Prussia and Saxony against Austria.   p. 520

[405] The Armed Neutrality, a policy directed against Britain, was based on five principles of international law put forward in 1778 in connection with problems of navigation in the Sound. The Armed Neutrality was also acceded to by Denmark, Sweden and Prussia.   p. 520

[406] In June and July 1790 representatives of Austria, Prussia, Poland, Britain and the Netherlands conferred in the Silesian town of Reichenbach. Worried by Russia's successes in the Russo-Turkish War (1787-91), they obliged Austria to make peace with Turkey (see Note 408).   p. 520

[407] The *Peace of Värälä*, signed on August 14, 1790, ended the Russo-Swedish War of 1788-90. Russia recognised the new Swedish Constitution, which curtailed the rights of the Riksdag, strengthened the King's authority and confirmed the privileges of the nobility. The peace treaty recognised Russia's right to the territories it has obtained under the Nystadt and Abo treaties (see this volume, pp. 515, 517).   p. 520

[408] On August 4, 1791 Austria and Turkey signed a *peace treaty at Sistova*, Bulgaria, terminating the Austro-Turkish War of 1788-90 on the basis of the *status quo ante bellum*. Austria obtained Stara Orsova, but without the right to erect fortifications there.   p. 520

[409] The *Treaty of Jassy*, signed on December 29, 1791 (January 9, 1792), ended the Russo-Turkish War of 1787-91. It confirmed the annexation of the Crimea to Russia and laid down the Russo-Turkish frontier along the Dniester.   p. 520

[410] In his synopsis of Volume II of Szabó's book, Marx adds the letter "a" to the numbers of chapters: Ia, IIa, etc.   p. 520

[411] Under the separate *Treaty of Basle* (July 22, 1795) concluded by France and Spain, the former obtained the Spanish (eastern) part of Haiti. The western part of the island, called Santo Domingo from 1697 to 1803, was owned by France under the Ryswick peace treaty of 1697 (see Note 387). In the nineteenth century the whole of Haiti was sometimes referred to as Santo Domingo.   p. 522

[412] This refers to the treaty between France and the Batavian Republic, which was formed on the territory of the Dutch Kingdom following the entry of French republican troops into the country and a rising of the local population

(January-March 1795) against the reactionary regime of Stadtholder William V. Signed in May 1795, the treaty provided for the transfer of part of the republic's territory to France. In 1806 Napoleon I transformed the Batavian Republic into the Kingdom of Holland. p. 522

413 See Note 164. p. 522

414 This refers to the negotiations to settle the territorial disputes involving the Holy Roman Empire held by representatives of France, Austria, Prussia and a number of other German states in Rastatt from December 9, 1797. In March 1798 the Imperial delegation approved the transfer of the left bank of the Rhine to France (this seems to be the event Marx had in mind in recording the date in question), and on April 23, 1799 the congress closed because of the outbreak of hostilities between the second coalition and France. p. 522

415 The *Parthenopaean Republic* was proclaimed on the territory of the Kingdom of the Two Sicilies on January 22, 1799 by Neapolitan republicans backed by the troops of the French Directory. It only survived until June 23, 1799 when the power of the Bourbons (Ferdinand IV) was restored with British help.
p. 522

416 This refers to the Federal Diet, an assembly of representatives of the German states which formed the German Confederation (see Note 76) at the Congress of Vienna on June 8, 1815. p. 524

417 The *Wartburg Festival* was held on the initiative of Jena University students on October 18, 1817 to commemorate the tercentenary of the Reformation and the fourth anniversary of the Battle of Leipzig. The Festival was a demonstration of the students' opposition to the Metternich regime.

The *Burschenschaften* were German student organisations formed during the liberation struggle against Napoleon. They advocated the unification of Germany and combined progressive ideas with extreme nationalism. Szabó mistakenly associates the rise of these organisations with the Wartburg Festival.
p. 525

418 Marx refers to the Constitution adopted by the Cortes in Cadiz on March 18, 1812, in the course of the Spanish revolution of 1808-14. It envisaged a series of bourgeois-democratic reforms and was repealed by Ferdinand VII on May 4, 1814. Reintroduced by Riego during the Spanish revolution of 1820-23, it was again repealed on October 1, 1823 by Ferdinand VII, who had earlier sworn allegiance to it. It was again introduced on August 12, 1836 and remained in force until June 18, 1837. p. 525

419 This refers to the Central Commission of Investigation set up at Mainz on August 31, 1819 at a conference of ministers of Austria, Prussia, Bavaria, Saxony and other member states of the German Confederation to combat the liberal and revolutionary opposition in Germany. p. 525

420 At an early stage of their activity in the nineteenth century the Carbonari headed the anti-French movement in the Kingdom of Naples (against Murat) and helped Ferdinand I and his son Francis I recover the crown of the Kingdom of the Two Sicilies. The source used by Marx mistakenly calls Francis an emperor. p. 525

421 I.e., the Constitution of Cadiz (see Note 418).   p. 525

422 The Ulema were Moslem doctors of divine law and theology who controlled the judiciary and the religious institutions and schools in Moslem countries. They enjoyed high prestige in the political life of the Ottoman Empire.   p. 525

423 Hetairia—see Note 139.   p. 525

424 An allusion to the fact that before entering the Russian diplomatic service in 1809 G. Capo d'Istria held a number of posts in the Republic of the Seven United Islands set up on the Ionian Islands under the Russo-Turkish convention of 1800.   p. 525

425 See Note 301.   p. 526

426 This refers to the Convention on the Iberian Peninsula signed by the four powers in London on April 22, 1834 (see Note 265).   p. 526

427 See Note 128.   p. 526

428 See Note 168.   p. 526

429 At the beginning of his pontificate (1846), Pope Pius IX announced a programme of moderate liberal-bourgeois reforms (establishment of a commission on the administrative reorganisation of the Papal States, limited political amnesty and other measures).   p. 527

430 From here on Marx's notes follow not the text of Volume II of Szabó's book but the chronological table appended to it (*State Policy...*, Vol. II, pp. 389-91).
                                                                        p. 527

NAME INDEX

A

Abbas I (1571-1629)—Shah of Persia (1587-1629).—510

Abd-el-Kader (c. 1808-1883)—Emir of Algeria; a leader of the Arabs in the 1832-47 national liberation war in Algeria and Morocco against the French; prisoner of war in France (1847-52); set free and granted a pension by the French Government; later lived in Damascus.—443

Abdul Mejid (1823-1861)—Sultan of Turkey (1839-61).—468

Abel, Karl (b. 1837)—German philologist and journalist, Berlin correspondent of *The Daily Telegraph.*—246-50

Aberdeen, George Hamilton Gordon, Earl of (1784-1860)—British Tory statesman; leader of the Peelites from 1850; Foreign Secretary (1828-30, 1841-46); Prime Minister of the Coalition Government (1852-55).—383

About, Edmond François Valentin (1828-1885)—French journalist, Bonapartist.—118, 162, 182, 183, 186, 206, 212, 271, 324, 325, 328, 329, 391, 392, 393-96, 400, 431, 439

Abt—German journalist, petty-bourgeois democrat; emigrated to Geneva in the early 1850s; expelled from the local German Workers' Association for slander.—38, 39, 41, 44, 47

Adolf (1817-1905)—Duke of Nassau (1839-66), Grand Duke of Luxembourg (1890-1905).—398

Adolphus Frederick (1710-1771)—King of Sweden (1751-71) from the Holstein-Gottorp House.—517

Aeschylus (525-456 B.C.)—Greek dramatist.—299

Agassiz, Louis Jean Rodolphe (1807-1873)—Swiss-born American naturalist, opponent of Darwinism.—45

Alberoni, Giulio (1664-1752)—Spanish statesman, cardinal; First Minister of King Philip V (from 1717 to 1719).—224, 515

Albert, Prince Consort of Queen Victoria of Great Britain (1819-1861).—382, 383, 397

Alberts—secretary of Prussian Embassy in London in the 1850s.—305

Alexander I (1777-1825)—Emperor of Russia (1801-25).—138, 140, 142, 143, 147, 153, 377, 485, 522, 524, 525, 526

Alexander II (1818-1881)—Emperor of Russia (1855-81).—138-42, 144-47, 150, 153, 154, 165, 166, 171, 336, 368, 377, 399, 430, 431, 485

Alexander of Macedon (*Alexander the Great*) (356-323 B.C.)—general and statesman.—190

Ali (*Ali Pasha*) (1741-1822)—actual ruler of the Albanian and Greek lands belonging to Turkey (1788-1822).—526

Altenhöfer, August Joseph (1804-1876)—German journalist, an editor of the

Augsburg *Allgemeine Zeitung.*—112

Alvensleben, Gustav von (1803-1881)— Prussian general, confidant of the Prince Regent of Prussia who became King William I in 1861.—216, 397

Amarante—see *Chaves, Manoel de Silveira*

Angoulême, Charles de Valois, Duke of (1573-1650)—Charles IX's natural son; served in the army of Louis XIII.—510

Anne (1601-1666)—Consort of Louis XIII of France from 1615; Regent (1643-61) for her son Louis XIV; daughter of Philip III of Spain.— 510, 511

Anne (1665-1714)—Queen of Great Britain and Ireland (1702-14).—514

Anne (*Anna*) (1693-1740)—Empress of Russia (1730-40).—142, 516, 517

Anne (*Anna Petrovna*) (1708-1728)— daughter of Peter I of Russia; married Charles I, the Duke of Holstein-Gottorp, in 1725, mother of Peter III.—515

Anson, George, Baron (1697-1762)— British admiral, First Lord of the Admiralty (1751-56, 1757-62); took part in the war of the Austrian Succession (1740-48); carried out reforms in the British navy.—517

Apollonius of Rhodes (*Rhodius*) (3rd cent. B.C.)—Greek poet and grammarian, author of the epic *Argonautica.*—199

Aragon, House of (11th-15th cent.).— 371

Argyll, Archibald Campbell, Earl of (1629-1685)—Scottish aristocrat; headed the rebellion against James II in May and June 1685; executed after the defeat of the rebellion.—73

Armstrong, William George, Baron Armstrong of Cragside from 1887 (1810-1900)—English inventor and industrialist; noted for his invention of a special type of rifled cannon.—361-65

Arndt, Ernst Moritz (1769-1860)— German writer, historian and philologist; took part in the struggle against Napoleonic rule; deputy to the Frankfurt National Assembly

(Right Centre) in 1848-49.—134

Arnim, Harry, Count von (1824-1881)— German conservative diplomat, Bismarck's opponent, envoy (1871) and Ambassador (1872-74) to Paris; arrested for appropriating diplomatic documents (1874) and expelled from the country.—307

Arnim-Boitzenburg, Adolf Heinrich, Count von (1803-1868)—Prussian statesman; Minister of the Interior (1842-45) and Prime Minister (March 19-29, 1848); deputy to the Frankfurt National Assembly (Right wing) in 1849.—252

Assermann, Ferenc (1821-1893)—Hungarian army officer, took part in the revolution of 1848-49 in Hungary.— 225-26

August (*us*) *II* (*the Strong*) (1670-1733)— King of Poland (1697-1706, 1709-33) and Elector of Saxony as Frederick Augustus I (1694-1733).—515, 516

August (*us*) *III* (1696-1763)—King of Poland (1734-63) and Elector of Saxony (from 1733) as Frederick Augustus II; son of Augustus II.—516, 517, 519

B

Babst, Ivan Kondratyevich (1824-1881)— Russian economist, historian and writer; professor of political economy at the universities of Kazan (from 1851) and Moscow (from 1857); gave public lectures on political economy in the early 1860s.—42

Badel, Marguerite (*Rigolboche*) (born c. 1842)—French dancer.—326

Badinguet—see *Napoleon III*

Baerensprung, von—chief of the Prussian police in Posen in the late 1850s.—394, 395

Baker, Robert—British official, factory inspector in the 1850s and 1860s.— 410, 416-18, 419, 420

Balzac, Honoré de (1799-1850)—French novelist.—36, 266

Bamberger, Ludwig (1823-1899)— German democratic journalist; took

and in the 1848-49 revolution; commanded the Baden people's militia during the 1849 Baden-Palatinate uprising; prominent figure in the First International in the 1860s, delegate to all its congresses; friend and associate of Marx and Engels.—51, 60, 61, 62, 63, 77, 82, 228, 230-33, 235, 250, 262, 267, 299, 304, 310, 327

Becker, Max Joseph (d. 1896)—German engineer, democrat; took part in the 1849 Baden-Palatinate uprising; after its defeat emigrated first to Switzerland and then to the USA.—30, 32

Becker, Nicolaus (1809-1845)—German poet, author of the song "Der deutsche Rhein".—440

Beckmann—Prussian police spy in Paris in the early 1850s, Paris correspondent of the Kölnische Zeitung.—56, 307

Belle-Isle, Charles Louis Auguste Fouquet, duc de (1684-1761)—French military leader and diplomat, Marshal of France (from 1741), War Minister from 1750 (with intervals); fought in the war of the Austrian Succession (1740-48).—517

Benda, Robert von (1816-1899)—German liberal politician, member of the Prussian Chamber of Deputies from 1859; member of the Imperial Diet from 1867; a National-Liberal.—251

Bernadotte, Jean Baptiste Jules (c. 1763-1844)—Marshal of France; was adopted by Charles XIII of Sweden (1810) and became heir to the Swedish throne; fought in the war against Napoleon I (1813); King of Sweden and Norway as Charles XIV John (1818-44).—524

Bernis, François Joachim Pierre de (1715-1794)—French statesman, diplomat and writer; cardinal from 1758; Foreign Minister (1757-58).—518

Berry, Charles Ferdinand (1686-1714)—grandson of Louis XIV; married (1710) Marie Louise, daughter of Philippe of Orleans.—514

Berryer, Pierre Antoine (1790-1868)—French lawyer and politician, deputy to the Constituent and Legislative Assemblies during the Second Republic, Legitimist.—157

Berwick, James Fitzjames, Duke of (1670-1734)—Marshal of France, natural son of James II of Great Britain; fought in the wars of the Spanish (1701-14) and the Polish (1733-35) Succession.—516

Bethell, Richard, 1st Lord Westbury (1800-1873)—British lawyer and liberal statesman; Attorney General (1856-59, 1860-61) and Lord Chancellor (1861-65).—445

Bethlen, Gábor (1580-1629)—leader of the anti-Habsburg movement in the Kingdom of Hungary (1619-26), Prince of Transylvania (1613-29) and King of Hungary (1620-21).—510

Beust, Friedrich von (1817-1899)—former Prussian army officer; committee member of the Cologne Workers' Association (1848); an editor of the Neue Kölnische Zeitung (September 1848-February 1849); took part in the 1849 Baden-Palatinate uprising; emigrated to Switzerland; professor of pedagogy.—76

Biedermann, Friedrich Karl (1812-1901)—German historian and writer, liberal; deputy to the Frankfurt National Assembly (Centre) in 1848; later a National-Liberal.—302

Biscamp, Elard—German democratic journalist; took part in the 1848-49 revolution in Germany; emigrated after the defeat of the revolution; member of the editorial board of Das Volk, organ of the German refugees in London published with Marx's collaboration.—17, 117-18, 127, 240, 261, 263, 265, 273, 275, 277, 286, 289, 296-301

Bixio, Girolamo (Nino) (1821-1873)—Italian democrat; took part in the 1848-49 national liberation war, the defence of the Roman Republic (April-July 1849) and Garibaldi's revolutionary campaign in Southern Italy (1860); became general of the Italian army in 1862; commanded the detachment of Garibaldians that captured Rome (1870).—473, 477

Blanc, Jean Joseph Louis (1811-1882)—French petty-bourgeois socialist, historian; member of the Provisional Government and President of the Luxembourg Commission (1848); pursued a policy of conciliation with the bourgeoisie; emigrated to England (August 1848) and became a leader of the petty-bourgeois refugees in London.—69, 265

Blanchenay, Louis (1800-1881)—Swiss politician, deputy to the National Council (1848-60); customs director (1861-73).—198

Blanqui, Louis Auguste (1805-1881)—French revolutionary, utopian communist; organised several secret societies and plots; adhered to the extreme Left of the democratic and proletarian movement during the 1848 revolution.—69

Blind, Karl (1826-1907)—German democratic journalist; took part in the Baden revolutionary movement in 1848-49; a leader of the German petty-bourgeois refugees in London in the 1850s; National-Liberal in the 1860s.—3, 4, 7-11, 13, 16, 17, 116-18, 119, 122-32, 186, 240, 263, 267, 273, 275-78, 283-86, 289, 315-19

Blondin (pseudonym of Jean François Gravelet) (1824-1897)—famous French tightrope walker.—225

Bloomfield, John Arthur Douglas, Baron Bloomfield of Oakhampton and Redwood (1802-1879)—British diplomat, envoy to Berlin (1851-60) and Ambassador to Vienna (1860-71).—383

Blum, Robert (1807-1848)—German democratic journalist; leader of the Left in the Frankfurt National Assembly; took part in the defence of Vienna in October 1848; court-martialled and executed after the fall of the city.—39, 71, 73, 74, 192, 243

Bluntschli, Johann Caspar (1808-1881)—Swiss lawyer and politician.—79

Bobzin, Friedrich Heinrich Karl (b. 1826)—German artisan, member of the German Workers' Association in

Brussels (1847); took part in the 1849 Baden-Palatinate uprising; together with Gustav Struve headed the democratic Association of German Emigrants in London.—33

Boiardo (Bojardo), Matteo Maria (c. 1441-1494)—Italian poet of the Renaissance, author of L'Orlando innamorato.—313

Boichot, Jean Baptiste (1820-1889)—French republican; deputy to the Legislative Assembly (1849); took part in the demonstration of June 13, 1849; later an émigré and one of the leaders of the French emigrant society in London; returned to Paris (1854) where he was again persecuted by the police and imprisoned; amnestied in 1859.—53

Bolivar y Ponte, Simon (1783-1830)—South American politician, one of the chief leaders of the South American Spanish colonies in their war of independence; President of the Republic of Colombia (1819-30).—219, 328

Bonaparte—imperial dynasty in France (1804-14, 1815 and 1852-70).—175, 188, 194

Bonaparte, Jérôme Napoléon Joseph Charles Paul (1784-1860)—youngest brother of Napoleon I; King of Westphalia (1807-13), Marshal of France from 1850.—170

Bonaparte, Louis (1778-1846)—brother of Napoleon I; King of Holland (1806-10); father of Napoleon III.—189-90

Bonaparte, Louis—see Napoleon III

Bonaparte, Prince Napoléon Joseph Charles Paul (Plon-Plon) (1822-1891)—son of Jérôme Bonaparte, cousin of Napoleon III; adopted the name of Jérôme after the death of his elder brother (1847); deputy to the Constituent and Legislative Assemblies during the Second Republic; commanded a division in the Crimea (1854) and a corps in the Austro-Italo-French war (1859); went by the name of Plon-Plon and the Red Prince.—40, 49, 58, 60, 116, 123,

148, 170, 187-90, 193, 197-99, 205, 206, 211-12, 221, 222, 225, 258, 316

Bonerius (Boner), Ulrich (1324-1349)— German poet and preaching monk; author of a collection of fables, *Der Edel Stein*, based on Latin sources.— 193

Boniface, Louis (b. 1796)—French journalist, Bonapartist.— 186, 211

Bónis, Samu (Samuel) (1810-1879)— Hungarian lawyer and politician; took part in the 1848-49 revolution; supported Kossuth.— 328

Bonnivet, Guillaume Gouffier, seigneur de (1488-1525)—French admiral; commanded the French troops (1523-25) during the Italian war; killed in the battle of Pavia.— 505

Borchardt, Louis—German physician, one of Engels' acquaintances in Manchester.— 119

Borkheim, Sigismund Ludwig (1825-1885)—German democratic journalist; took part in the 1849 Baden-Palatinate uprising; emigrated after its defeat; London merchant from 1851; was on friendly terms with Marx and Engels.— 29, 30, 31, 32, 41, 42, 61, 329

Borkmann—private secretary of William, Prince Regent of Prussia.— 397

Bosco—Neapolitan general; fought against Garibaldi's revolutionary detachments in South Italy (1860).— 475

Bougeant, Guillaume Hyacinthe (1690-1743)—French historian and man of letters, Jesuit; his best known works are on the history of the Thirty Years' War (1618-48) and the Peace of Westphalia.— 511

Bourbon, Charles, duc de (1490-1527)— commander-in-chief of the French army under Francis I; later went over to the side of Charles V; defeated the French troops in the battle of Pavia (1525).— 505

Bourbons—royal dynasty in France (1589-1792, 1814-15, 1815-30), Spain (1700-1808, 1814-68, 1874-1931 and since 1975), and some of the Italian states.— 371, 459, 460, 472, 518, 521, 523

Brandenburg, Friedrich Wilhelm, Count of (1792-1850)—Prussian general and statesman; headed the counter-revolutionary Ministry (November 1848-November 1850).— 255

Brass, August (1818-1876)—German journalist; took part in the 1848-49 revolution in Germany; emigrated to Switzerland after its defeat; editor-in-chief of the *Neue Schweizer Zeitung* (1859-60).— 187, 188

Braun, Karl Johann von Braunthal (Jean Charles) (1802-1866)—German novelist.— 242

Brentano, Lorenz Peter (1813-1891)— Baden democrat, lawyer, deputy to the Frankfurt National Assembly (Left wing) in 1848; headed the Baden Provisional Government (1849); after the defeat of the Baden-Palatinate uprising emigrated to Switzerland and later to the USA.— 51, 254

Brézé, Urbain de Maillé, marquis de (1597-1650)—French military leader and diplomat; fought in the Thirty Years' War (1618-48); Marshal of France from 1632.— 510

Briganti (d. 1860)—Neapolitan general; fought against Garibaldi's revolutionary detachments in South Italy and was killed by the insurgent Neapolitan soldiers (1860).— 474, 478

Brillat-Savarin, Anthelme (1755-1826)— French lawyer and writer.— 197

Brunnow, Filipp Ivanovich (1797-1875)—Russian diplomat; took part in the Troppau, Laibach and Verona Congresses of the Holy Alliance; envoy (1840-54, 1858-60) and Ambassador (1860-74) to London.— 146

Brunswick, Karl Wilhelm Ferdinand, Duke of (1735-1806)—commander-in-chief of the Austro-Prussian army fighting against revolutionary France (1792).— 521

Bucher, Lothar (1817-1892)—Prussian official and journalist; deputy to the Prussian National Assembly (Left Centre) in 1848; refugee in London and correspondent of the Berlin *National-Zeitung*; subsequently a National-Liberal.—88, 115

Büchner, *Ludwig* (1824-1899) —German physiologist and vulgar materialist philosopher.—72, 106, 190

Bullier—French journalist, Bonapartist.—186

Bunsen, *Christian Karl Josias, Baron von* (1791-1860)—Prussian diplomat, writer and theologian; Ambassador to London (1842-54).—310

Bürgers, *Heinrich* (1820-1878)—German journalist, contributor to the *Rheinische Zeitung* (1842-43); member of the Cologne community of the Communist League (1848); one of the *Neue Rheinische Zeitung* editors; subsequently a liberal.—262

Burgoyne, *Sir John Fox, Baronet* (1782-1871)—British military engineer, general, field marshal from 1868; military adviser and chief of the engineers in the Crimea (1854-55).—438

Buss, *Franz Joseph von* (1803-1878)—German lawyer and politician; opposed Prussia's hegemony.—107

Bute, *John Stuart, Earl of* (1713-1792)—British Tory statesman, Prime Minister (1762-63).—135, 518

Butenev, *Appollinary Petrovich* (1787-1866)—Russian diplomat, Ambassador to Turkey (1830-40); envoy to Rome (1843-56) and to Turkey (1856-58).—144, 219-20

Butler, *Samuel* (1612-1680)—English satirical poet, author of the poem *Hudibras.*—190

Byron, *George Gordon Noel, Lord* (1788-1824)—English poet.—78, 243

C

Cabet, *Étienne* (1788-1856)—French writer, utopian communist, author of *Voyage en Icarie.*—88, 89

Cagliostro, *Alessandro, Count (Giuseppe Balsamo)* (1743-1795)—Italian impostor.—334

Cairns, *Hugh McCalmont* (1819-1885)—British lawyer and statesman, Tory and later (from the 1860s) a Conservative; Lord Justice of Appeal (from 1858), Lord Chancellor (1868, 1874-80), M.P.—445

Calderón *de la Barca, Pedro* (1600-1681)—Spanish dramatist and poet. —28, 251

Cambacérès, *Jean Jacques Régis, duc de* (1753-1824)—French lawyer and statesman; President of the Convention (1794-95), then consul; counsellor of Napoleon I, one of the compilers of the *Code civil.*—197

Cambridge, *George William Frederick Charles, Duke of* (1819-1904)—British general, commander-in-chief of the British army (1856-95).—432

Cammarano, *Salvatore* (1801-1852)—Italian dramatist, author of several opera libretti.—77

Camoens *(Camões), Luis Vaz de* (c. 1524-1580)—Portuguese poet, author of the epic poem *Os Lusiadas.*—99, 190

Canning, *Charles John* (1812-1862)—British statesman, Tory and subsequently Peelite; Postmaster General (1853-55), Governor-General of India (1856-62).—480

Canning, *George* (1770-1827)—British Tory statesman and diplomat, Foreign Secretary (1807-09, 1822-27), Prime Minister (1827).—337, 525-26

Capo d'Istria, *Giovanni Antonio (Joannes), Count* (1776-1831)—Greek statesman and diplomat; was in the Russian service (1809-22), Second Secretary of State for Foreign Affairs in Russia (1815-22); President of Greece (1827-31).—143, 525-26

Carlier, *Pierre Charles Joseph* (1799-1858)—Prefect of the Paris police (1849-51), Bonapartist.—55

Castella—Swiss radical politician, member of the government of the Freiburg (Fribourg) Canton (1847-56). —53

Castlereagh, *Robert Stewart, Marquis of Londonderry, Viscount* (1769-1822)—British Tory statesman, brutally suppressed the uprising in Ireland (1798); Chief Secretary for Ireland

Charles (Karl Ludwig)—(1771-1847)—Archduke of Austria; general and writer on military science; fought in the wars against Napoleonic France (1792-1809).—524

Chateaubriand, François René, vicomte de (1768-1848)—French writer, statesman and diplomat; supported the policy of the Holy Alliance; Foreign Minister (1822-24).—143

Châtillon—see *Coligny, Gaspard de*

Chaves, Manoel de Silveira, Pinto de Fonseca, marquis de, Count of Amarante (1784-1830)—Portuguese general and politician, supporter of the absolute monarchy, a leader of the revolt that sparked off the Miguelist wars (1823-34).—525

Chelsea, Viscount—British diplomat, secretary at the British Embassy in Paris (1859).—160

Chenu, Adolphe (born c. 1817)—member of secret revolutionary societies in France during the July monarchy, agent-provocateur of the secret police.—73

Cherval, Julien (real name *Joseph Cramer*)—Prussian police spy who had gained entry into the Communist League and led one of the Paris communities belonging to the sectarian Willich-Schapper group; accused of complicity in the so-called Franco-German plot in Paris in February 1852; escaped from prison with the connivance of the police; agent-provocateur in Switzerland under the name of Nugent (1853-54).—44, 55, 56, 57, 58, 59, 60, 118, 180, 261, 262, 266-67, 276, 278-80, 283, 285, 304-05, 308-09, 311

Chevalier, Michel (1806-1879)—French engineer, economist and writer, follower of Saint-Simon; championed Napoleon III's economic policy; contributed to the *Journal des Débats*.—341-42

Choiseul, Étienne François, duc de, comte de Stainville (1719-1785)—French statesman and military leader; Foreign Minister (1758-70), and at the same time War and Naval Minister (1761-66).—518

Christern, Johann Wilhelm—author of the anonymously published satirical pamphlet *Doctor Eisele's und Baron von Beisele's Landtagsreise im April 1847.*—131, 274

Christian IV (1577-1648)—King of Denmark and Norway (1588-1648).—510

Christina (1626-1689)—Queen of Sweden (1632-44).—512

Cialdini, Enrico, Duke of Gaeta (1811-1892)—Italian general; commanded a brigade of the Sardinian corps in the Crimea (1855).—489

Cicero (Marcus Tullius Cicero) (106-43 B.C.)—Roman statesman, orator and philosopher.—68, 70-71, 297, 371

Cincinnatus (Lucius Quinctius Cincinnatus) (c. 519-c. 438 B.C.)—Roman politician, patrician; a model of simplicity and valour.—257

Clairville, Louis François (Nicolaie, dit) (1811-1879)—French dramatist and journalist.—324

Claudius, Matthias (pseudonyms *Asmus* or *der Wandsbecker Bote*) (1740-1815)—German poet and writer, published *Der Wandsbecker Bote* in 1771-75.—242

Clement VII (Giulio de Medici) (1478-1534)—Pope (1523-34).—491, 506

Clossmann, A. von (d. 1871)—German army officer, petty-bourgeois democrat; took part in the 1849 Baden-Palatinate uprising; later emigrated to Switzerland.—188

Clothilde of Savoy (1843-1911)—Princess of Savoy, daughter of Victor Emmanuel II of Sardinia, wife of Prince Napoleon (Plon-Plon) from 1859.—212

Cluss, Adolph (1825-1905)—German engineer, member of the Communist League; secretary of the Workers' Educational Association in Mainz (1848); emigrated to the USA (1848) where, in the 1850s, he was active in the German-American workers' organisations; one of the first propagators of scientific communism in America.—309

Cobden, Richard (1804-1865)—English

Ducommun, Elie (1833-1906)—Swiss radical statesman and journalist, editor of the *Revue de Genève* from 1855.—200

Dufaure, Jules Armand Stanislas (1798-1881)—French lawyer and politician, Orleanist; deputy to the Constituent Assembly (1848); Minister of the Interior in the Cavaignac Government (October-December 1848); inspired the suppression of the Paris Commune.—157

Dulon, Rudolph (1807-1870)—German pastor; emigrated to the USA in 1853.—87

Dumont (Du Mont), Joseph (1811-1861)—German journalist, moderate liberal; publisher of the *Kölnische Zeitung* from 1831; changed his name to Del Monte (Delmonte).—5, 6, 242

Dunne—British army officer; took part in Garibaldi's revolutionary campaign in South Italy (1860).—451

Duns Scotus, John (c. 1265-1308)—Scottish scholastic theologian.—251, 255

Dupin, André Marie Jean Jacques (1783-1865)—French lawyer and politician, Orleanist, deputy to the Constituent Assembly (1848-49) and President of the Legislative Assembly (1849-51); subsequently a Bonapartist.—228

Dupont, Emile (b. 1821)—French public figure, member of the co-operative society in Valenciennes; editor of a number of journals, including *La voix du proscrit;* author of articles on the position of the miners.—36

Dušek, František (1797-1873)—Hungarian statesman of Bohemian descent; Minister of Finance in the Szemere Government during the 1848-49 revolution.—223

E

Éber, Nándor (1825-1885)—Hungarian journalist; took part in the 1848-49 revolutionary movement and in Garibaldi's revolutionary campaign in South Italy (1860).—473

Eichhoff, Karl Wilhelm (1833-1895)—German socialist journalist; in the late 1850s exposed Stieber as a police spy in the press and was brought to trial for this; refugee in London (1861-66); member of the First International from 1868, and one of its first historians; member of the German Social-Democratic Workers' Party from 1869.—65

Eisenmann, Johann Gottfried (1795-1867)—German physician and writer; deputy to the Frankfurt National Assembly (Centre, later Left wing) in 1848-49.—103

Eleanor of Austria (1498-1558)—sister of Charles V, the Holy Roman Emperor; wife of Manuel I of Portugal and from 1530, of Francis I of France.—506

Eleonora of Portugal—see *Eleanor of Austria*

Elizabeth I (1533-1603)—Queen of England (1558-1603).—506, 509

Elizabeth of Parma—see *Farnese, Elizabeth*

Elizabeth of Valois (1545-1568)—daughter of Henry II of France; wife of Philip II of Spain from 1559.—506

Elizabeth (Elizaveta Petrovna) (1709-1761)—Empress of Russia (1741-61).—517, 518

Elsner, Karl Friedrich Moritz (1809-1894)—Silesian radical journalist; deputy to the Prussian National Assembly (Left wing) in 1848; an editor of the *Neue Oder Zeitung* in the 1850s.—263

Emmermann, Karl—chief forester from the Rhine Province; commanded an infantry unit of the Baden-Palatinate insurgent army in 1849; emigrated to Switzerland.—76, 77

Enfantin, Barthélemy Prosper (1796-1864)—French utopian socialist, a disciple of Saint-Simon; held leading posts in a number of capitalist enterprises from the mid-1840s.—341

Engels, Frederick (1820-1895).—6, 33, 40, 79, 81, 84-86, 88-90, 96-97, 101,

24, 449-52, 458, 460, 464, 471-78, 490-91

Gebert, August—Mecklenburg joiner; member of the Communist League in Switzerland and later in London; after the split in 1850 belonged to the sectarian Willich-Schapper group. —52

George I (1660-1727)—King of Great Britain and Ireland (1714-27), Elector of Hanover (1698-1714).—515

George III (1738-1820)—King of Great Britain and Ireland (1760-1820).— 411

George V (1819-1878)—King of Hanover (1851-66).—398

Gerlach, Ernst Ludwig von (1795-1877)—Prussian lawyer, reactionary politician, one of the founders of the *Neue Preussische Zeitung.*—247

Gibson, Thomas Milner (1806-1884)— British politician and statesman, Free Trader, President of the Board of Trade (1859-65, 1865-66).—409, 444

Gipperich, Joseph—German tailor; member of a Paris community of the Communist League supporting the sectarian Willich-Schapper group after the split in the League in 1850; became a secret agent of the Prussian police; one of the accused at the trial of the so-called Franco-German plot in Paris in February 1852; escaped from prison with the aid of the police; emigrated to England in 1852.—308

Girardin, Delphine de (1804-1855)— French authoress; wife of Émile de Girardin.—37

Girardin, Émile de (1806-1881)— French journalist and politician; editor of *La Presse* (the 1830s-60s, with intervals); moderate republican, later Bonapartist.—207

Giusti, Giuseppe (1809-1850)—Italian satirical poet.—203

Gladstone, William Ewart (1809-1898)— British statesman, Tory and later Peelite, leader of the Liberal Party in the latter half of the century; Chancellor of the Exchequer (1852-55, 1859-66), Prime Minister (1868-74,

1880-85, 1886, 1892-94).—336, 341, 350, 351, 353, 444

Gneisenau, August Wilhelm Anton Neithardt von (1760-1831)—Prussian field marshal-general; one of the organisers of the liberation struggle against Napoleonic rule.—146

Goegg, Amand (1820-1897)—German journalist, democrat; member of the Baden Provisional Government (1849); emigrated after the revolution; member of the First International; joined the German Social-Democrats in the 1870s.—98-99, 313

Goethe, Johann Wolfgang von (1749-1832)—German poet.—71, 74, 91, 183, 251

Goldheim—Prussian police officer; a secret agent of the Prussian police in London in the early 1850s.—58, 310-12

Golitsin, Alexander Mikhailovich, Prince (1718-1783)—Russian diplomat, Ambassador to London (1755-62), Vice-Chancellor (1762-75).—135, 518

Goluchowski, Agenor, Count (1812-1875)—Polish aristocrat, Austrian conservative statesman; Viceroy of Galicia (1849-59, 1866-67, 1871-75); Austrian Minister of the Interior (1859-60).—501

Gorchakoff (*Gorchakov*), *Alexander Mikhailovich, Prince* (1788-1883)—Russian statesman and diplomat, Ambassador to Vienna (1854-56), Foreign Minister (1856-82), State Chancellor (1867-82).—368, 375, 429, 491

Görgey (*Görgei*), *Arthur* (1818-1916)— military leader of the 1848-49 revolution in Hungary; commander-in-chief of the Hungarian army (April-June 1849); voiced the conservative sentiments of the nobility; advocated agreement with the Habsburgs and, later, capitulation; War Minister from May 1849.—148, 214, 215, 226-27

Gottfried von Strassburg (late 12th-early 13th cent.)—German poet, author of *Tristan und Isolde.*—156

Götze—Prussian lawyer; Vice-President

of the Prussian High Court in the 1850s.—270

Grabbe, Pavel Khristoforovich, Count (1789-1875)—Russian military leader and statesman; took part in suppressing the Polish insurrection of 1830-31 and in the Tsarist troops' intervention against revolutionary Hungary in 1849.—227

Grandguillot, Alcide Pierre (1829-1891)—French journalist, Bonapartist; editor-in-chief of *Le Constitutionnel* from 1859; editor-in-chief of *Le Pays* (1863-65).—176, 186, 324, 325

Granier de Cassagnac, Bernard Adolphe (1806-1880)—French journalist, Orleanist before the 1848 revolution, later Bonapartist; deputy to the Corps Législatif (1852-70); contributed to *Le Constitutionnel.*—36, 186, 211

Granville, George Leveson-Gower, Earl of (1815-1891)—British statesman, Whig and later Liberal, Foreign Secretary (1851-52, 1870-74, 1880-85), President of the Council (1852-54, 1855-58, 1859-65), Secretary of State for the Colonies (1868-70, 1886).—339

Grégoire (Georgi Petrovich Postnikov) (1784-1860)—Russian theologian, Metropolitan of St. Petersburg and Novgorod from 1855.—441

Gregory XVI (Bartolommeo Alberto, otherwise Mauro Cappellari) (1765-1846)—Pope (1831-46).—144

Greif—Prussian police officer; one of the chiefs of the Prussian secret service in London in the early 1850s.—55, 57, 305, 306-10

Greiner, Theodor Ludwig—German lawyer, petty-bourgeois democrat; member of the Palatinate revolutionary Provisional Government (1849); emigrated first to Switzerland and then to the USA after the defeat of the revolution.—100-01, 110

Grey, Sir Henry George, Earl of from 1845 (1802-1894)—British statesman, Whig; Secretary at War (1835-39), Colonial Secretary (1846-52).—194, 335-40

Griscelli, Jacques François—Corsican-born Bonapartist police agent.—421, 422, 424, 490

Grün, Karl (1817-1887)—German writer, member of the Prussian National Assembly during the 1848-49 revolution.—199

Grunich—German democrat; refugee in London in the early 1850s.—33

Guébriant, Jean Baptiste Budes, comte de (1602-1643)—Marshal of France; fought in the Thirty Years' War (1618-48).—510

Guise, Duke of—see *Henry II of Lorraine*

Guizot, François Pierre Guillaume (1787-1874)—French historian and statesman; virtually directed France's foreign and domestic policy from 1840 to the February 1848 revolution; expressed the interests of the financial bourgeoisie.—36, 79, 263

Gumpert, Eduard (d. 1893)—German physician resident in Manchester, a friend of Marx and Engels.—119

Gustav(us) I (Gustavus Vasa) (1496-1560)—King of Sweden (1523-60).—505

Gustav(us) II (Adolphus) (1594-1632)—King of Sweden (1611-32).—509, 510, 511

Guthschmidt—Prussian judicial official.—283, 290, 291

Guyon, Richard Debaufre (1803-1856)—British army officer, general of the Hungarian revolutionary army; served in the Turkish army under the name of Khourschid Pasha after the defeat of the Hungarian revolution; commanded Turkish troops in the Caucasus (1853).—214

H

Habsburgs (or *Hapsburgs*)—dynasty of emperors of the Holy Roman Empire (1273-1806, intermittently), of Austria (from 1804) and of Austria-Hungary (1867-1918).—108, 149, 254, 274, 371, 374, 376, 379-80, 487, 494, 506, 509, 512, 517, 524, 527

Hackländer, Friedrich Wilhelm von (1816-1877)—German writer.—183

daughter of Philip IV of Spain.—511-12

Maria Theres(i)a (Marie Therese) (1717-1780)—Archduchess of Austria (1740-80); Holy Roman Empress (1745-80).—222, 516-19

Marie de Medicis (1573-1642)—wife of Henry IV of France.—510

Marilley, Étienne (1804-1889)—Bishop of Freiburg (1846-79); inspired the anti-democratic revolt in Freiburg (Fribourg) on December 24, 1848.—235

Mario, Alberto (1825-1883)—Italian politician and writer; took part in Garibaldi's revolutionary campaign in South Italy (1860).—424

Marlborough, John Churchill, Duke of (1650-1722)—British general; commander-in-chief of the British troops (1702-11) in the war of the Spanish Succession.—514

Martin—French journalist, contributor to *Le Constitutionnel*; Bonapartist.—186

Marx, Jenny (née *von Westphalen*) (1814-1881)—wife of Karl Marx.—73, 264, 322

Marx, Karl (1818-1883).—3, 4, 5, 6, 7, 8, 11, 12, 14, 15, 16, 17, 19, 20, 25, 26, 27, 28, 29, 32, 33, 39, 40, 41, 42, 43-49, 50, 51, 54, 55, 57-61, 67, 69, 111, 113-25, 127-31, 133-39, 141-55, 156-69, 173, 187, 189, 191-204, 205, 207-13, 214, 216-20, 225, 228, 236, 237, 242, 244, 246, 259-95, 296, 303-05, 309-10, 319-20, 321-24, 326, 328, 335, 350, 385

Maupas, Charlemagne Émile de (1818-1888)—French lawyer, Bonapartist; Prefect of the Paris police (1851); an organiser of the coup d'état of December 2, 1851; Minister of Police (1852-53).—307

Maurice Saxe, von (1521-1553)—Elector of Saxony from 1547; Duke from 1541; commander-in-chief of the Imperial troops in the Smalkald war (1546-48).—506

Maurice Saxe, comte de (1696-1750)—Marshal of France; fought in the war of the Austrian Succession (1741-48);

writer on military science.—517

Maximilian I (1459-1519)—Holy Roman Emperor (1493-1519).—505

Maximilian I (1573-1651)—Duke of Bavaria from 1597 and Elector (1623).—510

Maximilian II (1811-1864)—King of Bavaria (1848-64).—397

Maximilian III Josef (1727-1777)—Elector of Bavaria (1745-77).—517, 520

Mayer, Karl (1819-1889)—German petty-bourgeois democrat; deputy to the Frankfurt National Assembly (1848-49); emigrated to Switzerland after the defeat of the revolution; editor of the Stuttgart newspaper *Beobachter* in the 1860s.—120, 204-05

Mazarin, Jules (1602-1661)—French cardinal and statesman; Prime Minister, virtual ruler of France from 1643 (under Louis XIV).—511-12

Mazzini, Giuseppe (1805-1872)—Italian revolutionary, democrat; head of the Provisional Government of the Roman Republic (1849); an organiser of the Central Committee of European Democracy in London (1850); sought for support among the Bonapartists (the early 1850s); subsequently opposed Bonapartism.—153, 180-81, 217, 218, 221, 232, 395, 423, 489, 490

Medici del Vacello, Giacomo (1817-1882)—Italian general; fought in the national liberation war of 1848-49 and defended the Roman Republic in April-July 1849; took part in Garibaldi's revolutionary campaign in South Italy (1860).—421, 449, 473, 477

Melendez—Neapolitan general; fought against Garibaldi's revolutionary detachments in South Italy (1860).—474, 478

Mellinet, François Aimé (1768-1852)—Belgian general; took part in the democratic movement and the 1830 revolution in Belgium; Honorary President of the Brussels Democratic Association; one of the accused at the Risquons Tout trial.—264

Mendes de Haro, Luiz, Count (1598-

1661)—Spanish statesman and diplomat; First Minister of Spain from 1643.—511

Meszlenyi, Zsuzsánna (née *Kossuth*) (1806-1856)—sister of Lajos Kossuth; inspector of hospitals during the 1848-49 revolution in Hungary.—222

Metternich-Winneburg, Clemens Wenzel Lothar, Prince von (1773-1859)—Austrian statesman and diplomat; Foreign Minister (1809-21) and Chancellor (1821-48); one of the founders of the Holy Alliance.—135, 148, 399, 525-26

Meyen, Eduard (1812-1870)—German writer, Young Hegelian; emigrated to England after the defeat of the 1848-49 revolution.—4-7, 18, 97, 239-42, 308

Miguel Maria Evaristo (*Dom Miguel*) (1802-1866)—King of Portugal (1828-34).—143, 337, 525, 526

Mikhail Fyodorovich (1596-1645)—first tsar (1613-45) of the Russian Romanov dynasty (1613-1917).—509

Minié, Claude Étienne (1804-1879)—French colonel, inventor of a new type of rifle adopted by the French army in 1852.—348

Miskowsky, Henryk Ludvic (d. 1854)—Polish army officer; took part in the 1848-49 revolution in Hungary; emigrated first to Turkey and then to London after the defeat of the revolution.—84-85

Missori, Giuseppe (1829-1911)—Italian army officer; took part in the national liberation movement in Italy; fought in Garibaldi's revolutionary detachments in the 1860s.—473, 477

Mohammed (or *Muhammad, Mahomet*) (c. 570-632)—founder of Islam.—40

Mohammed Ali (or *Mehemet Ali*) (1769-1849)—Viceroy of Egypt (1805-48).—526

Molé, Louis Mathieu, comte (1781-1855)—French statesman, Orleanist; Prime Minister (1836-37, 1837-39); deputy to the Constituent and Legislative Assemblies during the Second Republic.—146

Moll, Joseph (1813-1849)—German watchmaker; prominent figure in the German and international working-class movement; a leader of the League of the Just; member of the Central Authority of the Communist League; President of the Cologne Workers' Assosiation and member of the Rhenish District Committee of Democrats (July-September 1848); killed in battle during the Baden-Palatinate uprising in 1849.—79

Monroe, James (1758-1831)—American statesman; President of the USA (1817-25); issued a declaration (1823) formulating the principles of US foreign policy, known as the Monroe doctrine.—143, 525

Montalembert, Charles Forbes René de Tryon, comte de (1810-1870)—French politician and writer; deputy to the Constituent and Legislative Assemblies (1848-51); Orleanist, leader of the Catholic party; supported Louis Bonaparte during the coup d'état of December 2, 1851, but soon afterwards joined the opposition.—157

Morny, Charles Auguste Louis Joseph, duc de (1811-1865)—French politician, Bonapartist, half-brother of Napoleon III; deputy to the Legislative Assembly (1849-51); an organiser of the coup d'état of December 2, 1851; Minister of the Interior (December 1851-January 1852); President of the *Corps Législatif* (1854-56, 1857-65).—36, 159

Mozart, Wolfgang Amadeus (1756-1791)—Austrian composer.—40

Mucius Scaevola—Roman lawyer.—293

Müller, Georg—German refugee in London in 1860, Chairman of the German Workers' Educational Society.—264

Müllner, Amandus Gottfried Adolf (1774-1829)—German poet and literary critic.—120

Münnich (*Munich*), *Khristofor Antonovich, Count* (1683-1767)—Russian military leader and statesman, field marshal-general, engineer; commanded Russian troops in the Crimea and in

Carbonari and commanded the army of the rebels during the 1820-21 Neapolitan revolution; took part in the 1848-49 revolution in Italy.— 525

Perczel, Mór (Moritz) (1811-1899)— Hungarian general; took part in the 1848-49 revolution in Hungary; emigrated to Turkey after the defeat of the revolution and, in 1851, to England.— 149, 224

Péreire, Isaac (1806-1880)—French banker, Bonapartist, deputy to the Corps Législatif; founded the joint-stock bank Crédit Mobilier together with his brother Émile (1852); author of works on credit.—248, 341

Perponcher-Sedlnitzki, Wilhelm, Count von (1819-1893)—Prussian diplomat; envoy to Naples in the early 1860s.— 488

Perrée, Jean Baptiste Emmanuel (1761-1800)— French naval officer, rear admiral (1798); fought in Napoleon I's campaigns in Venice and Toulon (1796-98); commanded the French fleet in the Adriatic.— 163

Perrier, John—Swiss radical politician, member of the Grand Council (1852, 1856-60), Fazy's supporter.— 196, 199-201

Persigny, Jean Gilbert Victor Fialin, comte (1808-1872)—French statesman, Bonapartist, deputy to the Legislative Assembly (1849-51); an organiser of the coup d'état of December 2, 1851; Minister of the Interior (1852-54, 1860-63); Ambassador to London (1855-58, 1859-60).— 174, 383, 447

Persius (Aulus Persius Flaccus) (34-62)— Roman satirist.— 243, 245

Peter I ("the Great") (1672-1725)—Tsar of Russia (1682-1721), Emperor of Russia (1721-25).— 117, 142, 513-16

Peter the Hermit (c. 1050-1115)— French monk and preacher; a leader of the peasant volunteer corps in the first crusade (1096-99).— 440

Peter III (1728-1762)— Emperor of Russia (1761-62).— 518

Petétin, Anselme (1807-1873)— French writer; at first republican and later

Bonapartist; Prefect of Savoy (1860-61).— 193

Pfuel, Ernst Heinrich Adolf von (1779-1866)— Prussian general; Prime Minister and War Minister (September-October 1848).—256

Philip (1720-1765)—Duke of Parma (1748-65).— 518

Philip II (or Philip Augustus) (1165-1223)— King of France (1180-1223); a leader of the third crusade (1189-91).—440

Philip II (1527-1598)— King of Spain (1556-98).— 506, 509

Philip III (1578-1621)— King of Spain (1598-1621).— 509, 510

Philip IV (1605-1665)—King of Spain (1621-65).— 510

Philip V (1683-1746)— King of Spain (1700-24, 1724-46), Duke of Anjou.— 513-15, 517

Philippe of Orléans (1674-1723)—Duke of Chartres; Regent of France (1715-23) during the infancy of Louis XV.— 514, 515

Philipson, Grigory Ivanovich (1809-1883)— Russian general; fought in the war in the Caucasus (1835-49).— 220-21

Piat, Jean Pierre (1774-1862)—French general, Bonapartist; organised and headed the Society of December 10.— 34

Pietri, Pierre Marie (1809-1864)— French politician, Bonapartist, Prefect of the Paris police (1852-58).— 49

Pindar, Peter—see Wolcot, John

Pitt, William ("the Younger") (1759-1806)—British statesman, Tory; Prime Minister (1783-1801, 1804-06).— 59, 135, 338, 521, 523

Pitt, William, Earl of Chatham (1708-1778)— British statesman, Whig; Foreign Secretary and Secretary of State for War (1756-61); Prime Minister (1766-68).— 518

Pius VII (Gregorio Luigi Barnaba Chiaramonti) (1742-1823)— Pope (1800-23).— 523, 525

Pius IX (Giovanni Maria Mastai-Ferretti) (1792-1878)— Pope (1846-78).— 141,

154, 430, 458, 460, 485, 526-27
Plautus, Titus (Titus Maccius Plautus)
(c. 254-184 B.C.)—Roman dramatist.—112
Plümicke, F.C.—German army officer,
author of Handbuch für die Königlich
Preussischen Artillerie-Offiziere.—65
Poniatowski—see Stanislaus II
Pope, Alexander (1688-1744)—English
poet.—237, 247, 250, 327
Post—Prussian police officer.—394-95
Pourtalès, Albert (1812-1861)—Prussian
diplomat; envoy to Constantinople
(1850) and Paris (1859).—373
Pozzo di Borgo, Karl Osipovich, Count
(1764-1842)—Russian diplomat of
Corsican descent; envoy to Paris
(1814-21); Ambassador to Paris
(1821-35) and to London (1835-
39).—145, 524, 526
Prince of Prussia—see William I
Prince Regent—see William I
Proudhon, Pierre Joseph (1809-1865)—
French writer, economist and sociologist; a founder of anarchism;
deputy to the Constituent Assembly
(1848).—90, 157
Pückler, Erdmann, Count von (b. 1792)—
Prussian Minister of Agriculture
from 1858.—397
Pulszky, Ferenc (1814-1897)—Hungarian
politician, writer and archaeologist of
Polish descent; took part in the
1848-49 revolution in Hungary;
emigrated after its defeat; contributed to the New-York Daily Tribune
in the 1850s; returned to Hungary in
1867 after an amnesty; deputy to the
Diet (1867-76, 1884-97).—224
Puttkammer—Oberpräsident of the
Prussian province of Posen (1851-
60).—395
Pyat, Félix (1810-1889)—French journalist, dramatist and politician, petty-
bourgeois democrat; took part in the
1848 revolution; opposed an independent working-class movement;
fought against Marx and the First
International for a number of
years.—395
Pythagoras (c. 571-c. 497 B.C.)—Greek
philosopher and mathematician.—
239, 295

R

Rademacher, Johann Gottfried (1772-
1849)—German physician famous
for his peculiar classification of diseases according to remedies.—33
Radetzky, Joseph, Count of Radetz (1766-
1858)—Austrian field marshal; commanded the Austrian forces in North
Italy from 1831; suppressed the national liberation movement in Italy
(1848-49); Governor-General of the
Kingdom of Lombardy and Venice
(1850-56).—136
Radowitz, Joseph Maria von (1797-
1853)—Prussian general and statesman; a leader of the Right wing in
the Frankfurt National Assembly
(1848-49).—251-53
Raisin, Pierre (1820-1870)—Swiss lawyer and politician, member of the
Grand Council.—297
Rákóczy, Ferenc (1676-1735)—leader of
the Hungarian national liberation
movement against the Habsburgs
(early 18th cent.).—225
Rákóczy, György I (1593-1648)—Prince
of Transylvania; fought against the
Habsburgs and the Ottoman Empire
for the unification of all Hungarian
lands; acted in league with Sweden
during the Thirty Years' War.—510
Rákóczy, György II (1621-1660)—Prince
of Transylvania (1648-60).—511
Rákóczy, Jozsef (1700-1738)—one of the
last representatives of the ancient
Hungarian family of Transylvanian
princes; lived in Turkey from 1736;
died during the military expedition
to Moldavia.—516
Ranickel—German bookbinder, petty-
bourgeois democrat; took part in the
1848-49 revolution in Germany;
emigrated to Switzerland after its
defeat.—39, 40, 41, 44, 45, 55, 63,
76, 77, 78, 118, 120, 193, 205-06,
250, 299
Raspail, François Vincent (1794-1878)—
French naturalist, sociologist and writer close to the revolutionary proletariat; took part in the revolutions
of 1830 and 1848; deputy to the
Constituent Assembly (1869).—69

Raveaux, Franz (1810-1851)—German politician; deputy to the Frankfurt National Assembly (Left Centre) in 1848-49; imperial commissioner in Switzerland and one of the five imperial regents in June 1849; member of the Baden Provisional Government; emigrated after the revolution.— 210, 253

Rechberg and Rothenlöwen, Johann Bernhard, Count von (1806-1899)— Austrian statesman and diplomat; Prime Minister (1859-60); Foreign Minister (1859-64).— 368, 491

Redgrave, Alexander—English inspector of factories.— 410, 414, 416

Reh, Theodore—German lawyer; deputy to the Frankfurt National Assembly (1848-49).— 106-08

Reichardt, Joseph Martin (1803-1872)— German lawyer, democrat; deputy to the Frankfurt National Assembly; member of the Palatinate revolutionary Provisional Government (1849); emigrated to the USA after the defeat of the revolution.— 255

Reichenbach, Georg von (1772-1826)— Bavarian army officer and inventor.— 356

Reichenbach, Oskar, Count (b. 1815)— Silesian landowner, democrat; deputy to the Frankfurt National Assembly (1848-49); emigrated to England (1850) and later to the USA.— 315

Reinach, Arnold (c. 1820-1870)— German petty-bourgeois democrat; took part in the 1848-49 revolution in Germany; afterwards emigrated to Switzerland.— 120, 299

Rémusat, Charles François Marie, comte de (1797-1875)—French statesman and writer, Orleanist; Minister of the Interior (1840); deputy to the Constituent and Legislative Assemblies during the Second Republic.— 56

Repnin, Nikolai Vasilyevich, Prince (1734-1801)—Russian military leader and diplomat; field marshal-general from 1796; took part in the Seven Years' War (1756-63); Ambassador to Poland (1763-69); fought in the Russo-Turkish wars (1768-74, 1787-91).— 519

Reshid Pasha Mustafa Mehemed (1802-1858)—Turkish statesman; repeatedly held the posts of Grand Vizier and Foreign Minister (May 1853-May 1855, with intervals).— 149, 218, 382

Reuter, Max—Prussian police agent in London in the early 1850s.— 307

Reuter, Paul Julius, Baron (1816-1899)— founder of the Reuter telegraph agency in London (1851); German by birth.— 277, 307

Rewitt—London Refugee Committee emissary to Posen.— 395

Rheinländer, Georg Friedrich—German revolutionary, member of the Paris Outlaws' League, later refugee in London.— 60, 228

Richelieu, Armand Emmanuel du Plessis, duc de (1766-1822)—French statesman; emigrated to Russia on the outbreak of the French Revolution; returned to France in 1813; Prime Minister and Minister of Foreign Affairs (1815-18, 1820-21).— 143

Richelieu, Armand Jean du Plessis, duc de (1585-1642)—French cardinal and statesman.— 510, 511

Richelieu, Louis François Armand du Plessis, duc de (1696-1788)—French military leader and diplomat; Marshal of France from 1748; fought in the wars of the Spanish, Polish and Austrian Succession and in the Seven Years' War.— 518

Riesser, Gabriel (1806-1863)—German lawyer and politician; deputy to the Frankfurt National Assembly (first Right Centre and then, from September 1848, Left Centre) in 1848-49.— 109

Rigolboche—see Badel, Marguerite.

Rincon, Antonio—Italian-born French diplomat, envoy to Constantinople; assassinated in Italy on Charles V's order (1530).— 506

Rings, L.W.—member of the Communist League; refugee in London in the early 1850s; supporter of Marx and Engels.— 309

Roesler, Gustav Adolf (1818-1855)—

German teacher and journalist; member of the Left wing in the Frankfurt National Assembly (1848-49); emigrated to the USA in 1850.—98

Rogier, Charles Latour (1800-1885)—Belgian statesman, Minister of the Interior (1848-52).—263

Romanoffs (Romanovs)—dynasty of Russian tsars and emperors (1613-1917).—401

Roon, Albrecht Theodor Emil, Count von (1803-1879)—Prussian statesman and military leader; field marshal-general from 1873; War Minister (1859-73) and Naval Minister (1861-71); reorganised the Prussian army.—252

Rosenblum, Eduard—German student; took part in the 1849 Baden-Palatinate uprising; emigrated after its defeat.—30-32

Röser, Peter Gerhard (1814-1865)—cigarmaker; prominent figure in the German working-class movement; Vice-President of the Cologne Workers' Association (1848-49); member of the Communist League; one of the accused at the Cologne Communist trial (1852); sentenced to six years' imprisonment; later sided with the Lassalleans.—309

Rotteck, Karl Wenzeslaus Rodecker von (1775-1840)—German historian and liberal politician.—236

Rouher, Eugène (1814-1884)—French statesman, Bonapartist; deputy to the Constituent and Legislative Assemblies during the Second Republic; Minister of Justice (1849-52 with intervals); held a number of government posts during the Second Empire.—341

Rousseau, Jean Jacques (1712-1778)—French philosopher and writer of the Enlightenment.—232, 401

Rudolph II (1552-1612)—Holy Roman Emperor (1576-1612).—509

Ruge, Arnold (1802-1880)—German radical journalist and Young Hegelian philosopher; deputy to the Frankfurt National Assembly (Left wing) in 1848; a leader of the German petty-bourgeois refugees in England in the 1850s.—4, 87, 97-99, 308

Russell, John Russell, Earl (1792-1878)—British statesman, Whig leader; Prime Minister (1846-52, 1865-66); Foreign Secretary (1852-53, 1859-65).—53, 177, 193, 194, 195, 196, 368, 373, 375, 378, 383, 439

Ruyter or Ruiter, Michiel Adriaanzoon de (1607-1676)—Dutch admiral, commander-in-chief of the fleet of the States-General of the Netherlands during the second and third Anglo-Dutch wars (1665-67, 1672-74); chief admiral-lieutenant of the Netherlands from 1673.—512

S

Sacchi, Gaetano (1824-1886)—Italian army officer; took part in Garibaldi's campaigns in South Italy; general from 1862.—450

Saedt, Otto Joseph Arnold (1816-1886)—Prussian judicial official; Public Prosecutor in Cologne from 1848; prosecutor at the Cologne Communist trial (1852).—66-67

Šafařík, Pavel Josef (1795-1861)—Slovak philologist, historian and archaeologist, representative of the liberal wing in the national movement.—151

Saint-Simon, Claude Henri de Rouvroy, comte de (1760-1825)—French utopian socialist.—88

Sandford, William—British radical parliamentary leader.—328

Sauernheimer—German brushmaker; refugee in Switzerland and Chairman of the German Workers' Association in Geneva in the early 1850s.—39, 44

Saussure, Théodore de (1824-1903)—Swiss statesman, writer and artist; leader of the opposition aristocratic party; member of the Grand Council (1854-56, 1858-72).—199

Savoy, dynasty of—Italian dynasty ruling in the Sardinian Kingdom (1720-1861) and in the united Italian Kingdom (1861-1946).—423

Sazonov, Nikolai Ivanovich (1815-1862)—Russian journalist; emigrated in the early 1840s and contributed to various journals and newspapers.— 41-42

Schabelitz, Jacob (1827-1899)—Swiss publisher and bookseller; member of the Fraternal Democrats society from 1846, member of the Communist League; maintained contact with Marx and Engels in the late 1840s and the early 1850s.—57, 65

Schaible, Karl Heinrich (1824-1899)— German physician and writer; took part in the 1849 Baden-Palatinate uprising; afterwards emigrated to England.—130-32, 213, 267, 283, 285

Schaller, Julien (1807-1871)—Swiss statesman; head of the government of the Freiburg (Fribourg) Canton (1848-56).—53

Schapper, Karl (c. 1812-1870)— prominent figure in the German and international working-class movement, a leader of the League of the Just, member of the Central Authority of the Communist League; took part in the 1848-49 revolution; after the revolution, a leader of the sectarian group that split away from the Communist League in 1850; later a member of the General Council of the First International.—50, 80, 266, 307

Scherzer, Andreas (1807-1879)—German tailor; member of one of the Paris communities, which joined the Willich-Schapper sectarian group after the split in the Communist League, one of the accused in the case of the so-called Franco-German conspiracy in Paris in February 1852; subsequently emigrated to England and became a leader of the German Workers' Educational Society in London, publisher of *Die Neue Zeit* and contributor to *Das Volk.*—117, 118, 316, 317

Schiess, Johann Ulrich (1813-1883)— Swiss politician and diplomat, Chancellor of the Confederation (1848-81).—179, 193

Schiller, Johann Christoph Friedrich von (1759-1805)—German poet, dramatist, historian and philosopher.—8, 35, 39, 40, 48, 65, 71, 101, 187, 192, 258

Schily, Victor (1810-1875)—German lawyer, democrat; took part in the 1849 Baden-Palatinate uprising; emigrated to France; member of the First International.—39-46, 51, 76, 77, 101, 296-301

Schimmelpfennig, Alexander (1824-1865)—Prussian army officer, democrat; took part in the 1849 Baden-Palatinate uprising; emigrated to the USA; adhered to the Willich-Schapper sectarian group; fought in the American Civil War on the side of the Union.—75-76, 84-88, 91, 93, 97, 99

Schleinitz, Alexander Gustav Adolf, Baron von (1807-1885)—Prussian statesman, Foreign Minister (June 1848, 1849-50, 1858-61).—248, 368, 375, 376-79, 382, 383, 398, 489, 491

Schlickmann—Prussian judicial official.—294, 295

Schlöffel, Friedrich Wilhelm (1800-1870)—Silesian factory owner, democrat; deputy to the Frankfurt National Assembly (Left wing) in 1848.—107

Schlöffel, Gustav Adolph (c. 1828-1849)—German student and journalist; took part in the 1848-49 revolution in Germany and Hungary; correspondent of the *Neue Rheinische Zeitung* in the Frankfurt National Assembly.—102, 105, 107

Schmerling, Anton von (1805-1893)— Austrian statesman, liberal; deputy to the Frankfurt National Assembly (Right Centre) in 1848-49; Minister of the Interior (July-September 1848), Prime Minister and Minister of Foreign Affairs (September 1848). —254, 501

Schneider II, Karl—German lawyer, democrat; President of the Cologne Democratic Society and member of the Rhenish District Committee of Democrats; defended Marx and Engels at the trial of the *Neue Rheinische*

Zeitung on February 7, 1849; counsel for the defence at the Cologne Communist trial (1852).—57, 262, 267

Schramm, Konrad (c. 1822-1858)— German proletarian revolutionary, member of the Communist League; emigrated to London in 1849; responsible editor of the *Neue Rheinische Zeitung* and *Politisch-ökonomische Revue;* friend and associate of Marx and Engels.—83-86, 285

Schulenburg, Friedrich Wilhelm, Count von der (1742-1815)—Prussian statesman, Governor of Berlin (1806).—67

Schüler, Ernst (1807-1881)—German politician and writer, democrat; emigrated to Switzerland in 1833 and became a teacher; published the newspaper *Schweizer Handels-Courier* from 1853; disseminated Bonapartist ideas in the 1850s and 1860s.—119

Schüler, Friedrich (1791-1873)—deputy to the Frankfurt National Assembly (1848); elected one of the five Imperial Regents in June 1849; emigrated after the suppression of the Baden-Palatinate uprising.—210

Schultze—Prussian judicial official.— 283, 290, 291

Schurz, Karl (1829-1906)—German petty-bourgeois democrat; took part in the 1849 Baden-Palatinate uprising; emigrated to Switzerland; later US statesman.—87, 88, 97, 99

Schwarck—Chief Public Prosecutor of the Prussian Court of Appeal.—19, 268-69

Schwarzenberg, Felix Ludwig Johann Friedrich, Prince zu (1800-1852)— Austrian conservative statesman and diplomat; envoy to Turin (1838-46) and to Naples (1846-48); after the suppression of the Vienna uprising in October 1848 Prime Minister and Minister of Foreign Affairs (November 1848-1852).—379

Schwerin, Maximilian Heinrich Karl, Count (1804-1872)—Prussian statesman, Minister of Religious Worship, Public Education and Medicine (March-June 1848); deputy to the

Frankfurt National Assembly (Right wing); Minister of the Interior (1859-62); National-Liberal.—238, 395

Scitovszky, János (b. 1785)—Primate of Hungary.—501

Scott, Sir Walter (1771-1832)—Scottish poet and novelist.—97

Seckendorf, August Heinrich Eduard Friedrich, Baron von (1807-1885)— Prussian legal official; member of the Second Chamber (Centre) in 1849; public prosecutor at the Cologne Communist trial (1852).—309

Seidensticker, Georg Friedrich Karl Theodor (1797-1862)—German lawyer and politician; sentenced to imprisonment for participation in the 1831 Göttingen riot; emigrated to the USA in 1845 and became a journalist there.—97

Semrau, August (1816-1893)—German journalist and poet.—238

Seneca, Lucius Annaeus (c. 4 B.C.-A.D. 65)—Roman stoic philosopher.—299

Sepher Pasha—Circassian prince; served the Turks and took part in the Russo-Turkish war (1826-28); directed the Circassians' military operations against Russia (1855-59).—219

Sforza—see *Francesco II Sforza*

Shakespeare, William (1564-1616)— English dramatist and poet.—29, 35, 38, 40, 46, 47, 48, 55, 59, 116, 128, 190, 244-45, 378

Sigel, Albert (1827-1884)—Baden army officer, journalist; took part in the Baden revolutionary movement (1848-49); emigrated to the USA in 1853; fought in the American Civil War on the side of the Union.—96, 97

Sigel, Franz (1824-1902)—Baden army officer, democrat, one of the military leaders of the 1849 Baden-Palatinate uprising; refugee in Switzerland, England and (from 1852) in the USA; fought in the American Civil War on the side of the Union.—96, 97

Simon, Édouard (1824-1897)—Berlin-born French journalist, Bonapartist spy.—42, 93-94, 112-13, 206-11, 236, 240, 245

(1810-12, 1825-28, 1841-58).—429

Struve, Amalie (d. 1862)—wife of Gustav Struve; took part in the democratic movement in Germany in 1848-49.—232

Struve, Gustav von (1805-1870)—German journalist, democrat; a leader of the Baden uprisings in April and September 1848, of the Baden-Palatinate uprising in 1849 and later of the German petty-bourgeois refugees in England; fought in the American Civil War on the side of the Union.—32, 33, 51, 53, 232

Stuarts (also *Steuarts, Stewarts*)—royal dynasty in Scotland from 1371 and England (1603-49 and 1660-1714).—514, 518

Sue, Eugène Marie Joseph (1804-1857)—French writer, author of sentimental novels dealing with social problems.—306

Sulla (*Lucius Cornelius Sulla*) (138-78 B.C.)—Roman general and statesman; consul (88 B.C.); dictator (82-79 B.C.).—339

Suvorov, Alexander Arkadyevich, Count Suvorov Rimniksky, Prince Italysky (1804-1882)—Russian military leader and statesman; fought in the Russo-Turkish wars (1826-28, 1828-29); took part in the suppression of the 1830-31 uprising in Poland; Governor-General of the Baltic provinces (1848-61).—384

Suvorov, Alexander Vasilyevich, Count Suvorov Rimniksby, Prince Italysky (1729-1800)—Russian field marshal—521

Szabó, Imre von (1820-1865)—Hungarian army officer; took part in the 1848-49 revolution in Hungary; member of the first Hungarian revolutionary government (March-September 1848) and deputy to the State Assembly in Debrecen (1849); after the defeat of the revolution, emigrated to Paris and later to London.—505

Szécsen, Antal, Count (1819-1896)—Hungarian statesman, conservative;

supported the Austrian monarchy during the 1848-49 revolution in Hungary; took part in elaborating the 1860 October diploma.—501

Szemere, Bartholomäus (*Bertalan*) (1812-1869)—Hungarian politician and writer; Minister of the Interior and head of the revolutionary government (1849); emigrated after the defeat of the revolution.—43, 149, 219, 224, 225, 328, 501

Szirmay, Pál, Count (1804-1883)—Hungarian politician; member of the Chamber of Deputies (1848); after the defeat of the revolution refugee and Lajos Kossuth's emissary in Paris; was amnestied in 1855 and returned to Hungary.—217

T

Tacitus, Publius Cornelius (c. 55-c. 120)—Roman historian and orator.—156, 285, 300

Tamisier, François Laurent Alphonse (1809-1880)—French army officer, military inventor and politician.—357

Tausenau, Karl (1808-1873)—Austrian politician, democrat; head of the Central Committee of the Vienna Democratic Societies during the 1848 revolution; emigrated to London in 1849.—97-98

Taylor, Tom (1817-1880)—English dramatist and journalist; contributed to several periodicals.—404, 437

Techow, Gustav Adolf (1813-1893)—Prussian army officer, petty-bourgeois democrat; took part in the 1848 revolutionary events in Berlin; Chief of the General Staff of the Palatinate revolutionary army; emigrated to Switzerland after the defeat of the 1849 Baden-Palatinate uprising and became a leader of the refugee organisation Revolutionary Centralisation; left for Australia in 1852.—75-77, 83-86, 88-99, 241, 260-61, 283, 285, 287, 291

Teleki, László (*Ladislaus*)*, Count* (1811-1861)—Hungarian politician and writer; represented the Hungarian Republic in France during the 1848-49 revolution in Hungary; remained in France after the defeat of the revolution.—221

Temme, Jodocus Donatus Hubertus (1798-1881)—German lawyer, democrat; deputy to the Prussian National Assembly (Left wing) in 1848; deputy to the Frankfurt National Assembly in 1849.—256

Thouvenel, Édouard Antoine (1818-1866)—French statesman and diplomat, Bonapartist; envoy to Athens (1848-50) and to Munich (1850-51); Ambassador to Constantinople (1855-60); Foreign Minister (1852, 1860-62).—175, 194-96, 197, 399

Totti—Bonapartist police spy, Corsican by birth.—421, 422, 424, 490

Tourte, Abraham Louis (1818-1863)—Swiss statesman and diplomat, envoy to Turin from 1860.—53-54, 235, 297, 298, 299

Treuille de Beaulieu, Antoine Hector Thésee, baron (1809-1886)—French general, military inventor.—357

Trog, Johann von Olten (1807-1867)—Swiss lawyer; deputy to the National Council for Solothurn Canton (1848-57); Federal Commissar (1852-56).—232, 297, 302

Tromp, Cornelis (1629-1691)—Dutch admiral; fought in the second and third Anglo-Dutch wars (1665-67, 1672-74); commander-in-chief of the Dutch fleet from 1676.—512

Tucker—London publisher.—116

Turenne, Henri de la Tour d'Auvergne, vicomte de (1611-1675)—French general, Marshal of France from 1643; commander-in-chief of the French army in Germany during the Thirty Years' War (1618-48); fought in the wars of the Fronde and in the Devolution War (1667-68); author of memoirs.—510, 512

Türr, István (Achmed Kiamil Bey) (1825-1908)—Hungarian army officer; took part in the 1848-49 revolution in Italy and Germany; emigrated to Turkey; fought in the Cri-

mean war on the side of the Allies; joined Garibaldi's revolutionary campaign in South Italy (1860); general of the Italian army from 1861.—219, 473, 490, 491

Tzschirner, Samuel Erdmann (c. 1812-1870)—German lawyer; leader of the extreme Left in the Saxon Diet during the 1848-49 revolution; one of the leaders of the May 1849 uprising in Dresden; participant in the 1849 Baden-Palatinate uprising; emigrated to Switzerland after the defeat of the revolution and became a member of the Central Committee of the refugee organisation Revolutionary Centralisation; later emigrated to England.—94

U

Uhland, Ludwig (1787-1862)—German romantic poet; deputy to the Frankfurt National Assembly (Left Centre) in 1848-49.—106-08, 392

Ulloa, Girolamo (1810-1891)—Neapolitan general; took part in the national liberation and revolutionary movements in Italy in 1848-49; emigrated to France after the defeat of the revolution; commanded the Tuscan army in the Austro-Italo-French war of 1859.—40

Ulmer, Johann—member of the Communist League; refugee in London in the early 1850s; supported Marx and Engels during the split in the Communist League.—309

Ulpianus (Ulpian), Domitius (c. 170-228)—Roman lawyer and statesman.—293

Ulrich (1487-1550)—Duke of Württemberg from 1498; expelled in 1519; tried to use the peasant movement of 1525 to restore his power; re-established himself on the Württemberg throne in 1534.—204

Urquhart, David (1805-1877)—British diplomat, writer and politician, Turkophile; went on diplomatic missions to Turkey in the 1830s; Tory M.P. (1847-52); opposed Palmerston's policy; founder and editor of *The Free Press* (1855-77), which appeared under the heading *Diplomatic Review* from 1866.—5-6, 8, 116, 118, 148, 150, 214-18

V

Varnhagen von Ense, Karl August (1785-1858)—German novelist and literary critic of a liberal trend.—369

Varus, Publius Quintilius (d. A.D. 9)—Roman politician and general; ruled Germania (6-9); killed in battle in the Teutoburger Wald during the uprising of the German tribes.—251

Vay, Miklos, Baron (1802-1894)—Hungarian statesman, conservative; government commissioner in Transylvania (1848); pursued the policy of compromise with the Austrian monarchy.—501

Vegezzi-Ruscalla, Giovenale—Italian writer of the midnineteenth century, author of the pamphlet *La nazionalità di Nizza.*—198

Venedey, Jakob (1805-1871)—German radical journalist; deputy to the Frankfurt National Assembly (Left wing) in 1848-49; liberal after the 1848-49 revolution.—69, 103, 109, 120, 251

Véron, Louis Désiré (1798-1867)—French journalist and politician, Orleanist till 1848 and afterwards Bonapartist; owner and publisher of *Le Constitutionnel* (1844-52).—36

Vespasian (*Titus Flavius Sabinus Vespasianus*) (9-79)—Roman Emperor (69-79).—249

Viale—Neapolitan general; fought against Garibaldi's revolutionary detachments in South Italy in 1860.—474, 478

Victor Amadeus I (1587-1637)—Duke of Savoy from 1630.—510

Victor Amadeus II (1666-1732)—Duke of Savoy (1675-1730); King of Sicily (1713-18); first King of Sardinia (1720-30).—513-14

Victor Emmanuel II (1820-1878)—Duke of Savoy; King of Sardinia (1848-61);

King of Italy (1861-78).—173-74, 200, 212, 382, 392, 399

Victoria (1819-1901)—Queen of Great Britain and Ireland (1837-1901).—335, 399

Vidocq, François Eugène (1775-1857)—French secret police agent; chief of the secret criminal police (*La Sûreté*) (1812-27); his name was used to denote any cunning sleuth and rogue.—395

Villars, Claude Louis Hector, prince de Martignes (1653-1734)—French general, Marshal of France from 1702; fought in the wars of the Spanish (1701-14) and the Polish (1733-36) Succession.—516

Vincenzo II Gonzaga (1594-1627)—the last of the Gonzaga dukes of Mantua (1626-27); cardinal from 1615.—510

Vincke, Georg Ernst Friedrich, Baron von (1811-1875)—Prussian politician; a leader of the Right wing in the Frankfurt National Assembly (1848-49); deputy to the Second Chamber (Right wing) in 1849; elected to the Chamber of Deputies of the Prussian Diet in the 1850s and 1860s; moderate liberal.—61, 102, 250-58, 393

Virgil (*Publius Vergilius Maro*) (70-19 B.C.)—Roman poet.—46, 78, 239, 282, 303

Visconti, Valentina (1366-1408)—Duchess, grandmother of Louis XII, came from a noble Milan family.—505

Vladimirescu, Tudor (c. 1780-1821)—leader of the 1821 Wallachian popular uprising against rich landowners and the Turkish yoke.—143

Vögele, A.—German refugee in London, compositor in Hollinger's printshop in 1859.—3, 10, 11, 119, 123-31, 267, 275, 276, 283-85, 319-20

Vogt, Adolf (b. 1823)—Swiss doctor, Karl Vogt's brother.—203

Vogt, Emil (1820-1883)—Swiss lawyer, Karl Vogt's brother.—203

Vogt, Gustav (1829-1901)—Swiss lawyer, writer and radical politician; director of the statistical bureau

(1860-62); Karl Vogt's brother.—201, 203

Vogt, Karl (1817-1895)—German naturalist, petty-bourgeois democrat; deputy to the Frankfurt National Assembly (Left wing) in 1848-49; one of the five Imperial Regents in June 1849; emigrated in 1849; subsequently was subsidised by Napoleon III; slandered Marx and Engels.—4, 9, 10, 11, 25-29, 32, 33, 38, 39, 40-49, 51, 52, 53-78, 86, 100, 102, 103-05, 108, 122, 123-30, 131-42, 145, 147, 148-51, 154-56, 159, 161, 163, 165, 166-67, 170-83, 184-88, 189-93, 195-98, 200-01, 203-06, 208, 212, 214, 225, 228, 235, 238-42, 246, 250-52, 258-61, 264-69, 273-84, 299-302, 304, 313, 316, 317, 318, 327, 328, 329

Vogt, Philipp Friedrich Wilhelm (1786-1861)—German doctor; lived in Switzerland from the early 1830s; professor of medicine in the Berne Higher School from 1835; an adherent of the liberals; Karl Vogt's father.—64, 203

W

Wahrendorff, Martin, Baron von (1789-1861)—Swedish manufacturer and military inventor.—357

Walewski, Alexandre Florian Joseph Colonna, comte (1810-1868)—French diplomat and statesman, son of Napoleon I and the Polish Countess Marie Walewska; took part in the 1830-31 Polish insurrection; emigrated to France after its defeat; French Foreign Minister (1855-60).—193

Wallenstein, Albrecht Wenzel Eusebius von, Duke of Friedland and Mecklenburg, Prince of Sagan (1583-1634)—general of the Holy Roman Empire, commander-in-chief during the Thirty Years' War (1618-48); Bohemian by birth.—510

Walther von der Vogelweide (c. 1170-c. 1230)—German minnesinger.—108

Wanner—Swiss consul in Le Havre.—300

Warren, Sir Peter (1703-1752)—British admiral of Irish descent; fought in the war of the Austrian Succession (1740-48); M.P.—517

Warwick, Richard Neville, Earl of Warwick and Salisbury ("the Kingmaker") (1428-1471)—English feudal lord; fought in the Wars of the Roses (1455-85).—256

Weber—Prussian lawyer, Marx's counsel in the trial against the Berlin *National-Zeitung* in 1860.—19, 25, 261, 262, 264, 268, 283, 293-95

Weerth, Georg Ludwig (1822-1856)—German poet and journalist, member of the Communist League, a founder of proletarian poetry in Germany; an editor of the *Neue Rheinische Zeitung* in 1848-49.—320

Weitling, Wilhelm Christian (1808-1871)—German tailor; one of the early leaders of the working-class movement in Germany and a theoretician of utopian egalitarian communism.—79

Wellington, Arthur Wellesley, Duke of (1769-1852)—British general and statesman, Tory; Prime Minister (1828-30), Foreign Secretary (1834-35).—352

Wermuth—police director in Hanover; an organiser of and witness for the prosecution at the Cologne Communist trial (1852); collaborated with Stieber on the book *Die Kommunisten-Verschwörungen des neunzehnten Jahrhunderts.*—58

Wesendonck, Hugo—Düsseldorf lawyer; deputy to the Frankfurt National Assembly (Left wing) in 1848-49; deputy to the Second Chamber (extreme Left wing) in 1849.—106

Westphalen, Ferdinand Otto Wilhelm Henning von (1799-1876)—Prussian statesman; Minister of the Interior (1850-58); stepbrother of Jenny Marx, Karl Marx's wife.—73

Weydemeyer, Joseph (1818-1866)—prominent figure in the German and American working-class movement;

Wrangel, Friedrich Heinrich Ernst, Count
von (1784-1877)—Prussian general;
took part in the counter-revolutionary coup d'état in Berlin and
in the dissolution of the Prussian National Assembly in November 1848.
—255

Würth—German politician, deputy to
the Frankfurt National Assembly.—
109

Wyss—barrister in Berne in the
1850s.—300, 301

Y

Ypsilanti, Alexander (1792-1828)—
prominent figure in the Greek national liberation movement; major-
general of the Russian army, participant in the 1812 war; raised a
revolt in Moldavia (1821); fled to
Austria after its defeat, was arrested
and kept in prison up to 1827;
released as a result of Russia's inter-
cession.—143, 526

Z

Zabel, Friedrich (1802-1875)—German
liberal journalist, editor of the Berlin

National-Zeitung (1848-75).—19, 20,
236, 246-47, 259-79, 281-95, 308,
324, 327

Zachariä, Heinrich Albert (1806-1875)—
German lawyer; deputy to the Frank-
furt National Assembly (Right
Centre) in 1848-49.—103, 108

Zápolya, Janos (Johann) (1487-1540)—
Transylvanian voivode; suppressed
the 1514 peasant uprising in Hungary; King of Hungary (1526-40).—
506

Zerfy, Gustav (real name Hirsch) (born
c. 1820)—Hungarian journalist; took
part in the 1848-49 revolution in
Hungary; emigrated to Paris in 1852
and to London in early 1853; maintained contact with Marx in the early
1850s; later supported Kinkel.—219

Zimmermann, Ernst Wilhelm Eduard
(1807-1878)—German historian,demo-
crat; took part in the 1848-49 revolution; deputy to the Frankfurt National Assembly (Left wing).—103,
109

Zitz, Franz Heinrich (1803-1877)—
German lawyer, democrat; deputy to
the Frankfurt National Assembly
(Left wing) in 1848; took part in the
1849 Baden-Palatinate uprising;
emigrated to the USA.—98

INDEX OF LITERARY AND MYTHOLOGICAL NAMES

Abel (Bib.)—the second son of Adam,
slain by his elder brother Cain.—247

Abigail (Bib.).—247

Aeolus (Gr. Myth.)—the god of the
winds; hence Aeolian harp—stringed
instrument producing musical sounds
on exposure to wind.—225

Ahasuerus or The Wandering Jew—the
subject of a medieval legend, condemned to wander until the Day of
Judgment for having mocked Christ
on the day of Crucifixion.—376

Aladdin—a character in the Arabian
Nights, owner of a magic lamp.—467

Argonauts (Gr. Myth.)—heroes who
sailed with Jason, on the ship Argo,
to Colchis for the golden fleece,

which was guarded by a dragon. The
poet and musician Orpheus partici-
pated in this feat, which was described in the 3rd century B.C. by
Apollonius of Rhodes in his poem
Argonautica.—199-201

Bacchus (Dionysus)—the Greek and
Roman god of wine and mirth.—190,
205

Beisele—see Eisele

Bottom—a character in Shakespeare's
comedy A Midsummer Night's
Dream.—35

Cain (Bib.)—the eldest son of Adam,
who killed his brother Abel out of
jealousy.—247

Cassandra (Gr. Myth.)—a daughter of Priam, King of Troy, endowed with the gift of prophecy.—470

Ceres (Rom. Myth.)—see Demeter

Cipriano—a character in Calderón's play El Mágico prodigioso, an image close to Faust.—251

Clarin—a character in Calderón's play El Mágico prodigioso.—28

Crevel—a character in Balzac's novel La Cousine Bette, a parvenu, money-grubber and profligate.—36

Demeter (Gr. Myth.)—goddess of agriculture, fertility and marriage.—370

Don Quixote—the title character in Cervantes' novel.—190

Dunce I and Dunce II—characters in Alexander Pope's poem The Dunciad.—237, 275

Egeria (Rom. Myth.)—a prophetic nymph.—189, 197, 198

Eisele and Beisele—main characters in an anonymously published satirical pamphlet by J. W. Christern Doctor Eisele's und Baron von Beisele's Landtagsreise im April 1847.—131, 274

Falstaff, Sir John—a fat, merry, ribald and boastful knight in Shakespeare's Merry Wives of Windsor and King Henry IV.—29, 33, 38, 40, 46, 48, 57, 59, 69, 70, 74, 101, 148, 197, 203, 251, 258

Faunus (Rom. Myth.)—the god of nature and fertility, worshipped by shepherds and farmers.—257

Faust—the title character of Goethe's tragedy.—71, 251

Fleur de Marie—the heroine of Eugène Sue's novel Les Mystères de Paris, a girl who grows up amidst criminals but preserves her natural nobility and purity of soul. The author gave her the name of a lily that grows in swamps but has snow-white petals.—306

George, Saint—the mythological dragon slayer.—255

Gorgellantua—the main character in Johann Fischart's adaptation of Rabelais' Gargantua et Pantagruel.—33

Guillery—the title character of Edmond About's comedy.—325, 328-29

Gurgelgrosslinger—see Gorgellantua

Habakkuk (Bib.)—a prophet.—243

Hamlet—the title character of Shakespeare's tragedy.—116, 190, 245

Harlequin—a character in the commedia dell'arte, a servant in love who often finds himself in a tight corner but knows how to get out of it.—102, 103, 251

Henry IV—the title character of Shakespeare's drama.—49, 55, 74

Henry Percy (called Hotspur)—a character in Shakespeare's drama King Henry IV, a gay, jesting, fiery-tempered soldier.—86

Hesperides (Gr. Myth.)—nymphs, daughters of Hesperus, who watched with a dragon over the garden of golden apples in the Isles of the Blest. —443

Hudibras—the title character of Samuel Butler's satirical poem, a man inclined to meaningless arguments and debates and capable of proving the most absurd propositions by means of syllogisms.—190

Iphigenia (Gr. Myth.)—the daughter of Clytemnestra and Agamemnon, offered as a sacrifice to Artemis to enable the Greek fleet to sail to Troy; title character of Euripides' tragedy.—212

Janus (Rom. Myth.)—god represented with two faces looking in opposite directions.—190

Jaromir—the main character in Grillparzer's tragedy Die Ahnfrau.—120

Jeremiah—a prophet who bewails the destruction of Jerusalem.—105

John—see Falstaff

John Bull—the title character in John Arbuthnot's book The History of John Bull (18th cent.). His name is often used to personify England.—344, 439

Jupiter (Jove)—the supreme god of the Romans, corresponding to the Greek Zeus.—244

Kobes I—the title hero of Heinrich Heine's satirical poem; Jakob Venedey's nickname.—69, 109
Künigunde (Cunégonde)—the heroine of Voltaire's philosophical novel Candide.—208, 329

Lazarillo—the hero of the anonymous Spanish story, Lazarillo de Tormes (mid-16th cent.), a smart fellow.—183
Leporello—a character in Mozart's opera Don Giovanni, Don Juan's servant.—40, 199

Mephistopheles—the Devil in Goethe's tragedy Faust.—227
Moscon—a character in Calderón's play El Mágico prodigioso.—251
Moses (Bib.).—245, 247
Munchausen—an extravagantly mendacious story-teller.—309

Oedipus (Gr. Myth.)—the King of Thebes, who solved the riddle of the Sphinx and saved Thebes from the monster; hero of Sophocles' tragedy Oedipus Rex.—199
Ophelia—a character in Shakespeare's tragedy Hamlet.—245
Orlando—the hero of Boiardo's poem Orlando innamorato and Ariosto's L'Orlando furioso.—313
Orpheus (Gr. Myth.)—the Thracian poet and musician whose singing tamed wild beasts and even charmed stones; took part in the Argonauts' expedition in quest of the golden fleece.—199

Pantaloon (Ital. Pantalone)—a character in the commedia dell'arte; a rich but miserly Venetian merchant, a foolish old man.—251
Parolles—a character in Shakespeare's comedy All's Well That Ends Well.—40

Paul (Bib.)—one of Christ's twelve apostles, originally called "Saul of Tarsus".—77
Pecksniff—a character in Charles Dickens' novel Martin Chuzzlewit, an unctuous hypocrite talking much of benevolence and other kindly virtues.—174
Polonius—a character in Shakespeare's tragedy Hamlet, a garrulous courtier.—66, 177
Polyphemus (Gr. Myth.)—a Cyclops who lived in a Sicilian cavern and devoured human beings.—370
Posa, Marquis—a character in Schiller's tragedy Don Carlos, a noble-minded and freethinking courtier who tried to influence the despotic king.—188
Prometheus (Gr. Myth.)—a Titan who stole fire from the gods and gave it to men; was chained by Zeus to a rock. The main character of Aeschylus' tragedy Prometheus Bound.—299
Prudhomme, Joseph—a character of a complacent and narrow-minded philistine created by Henri Monnier.—206
Puck (Robin Goodfellow)—a character in Shakespeare's play A Midsummer Night's Dream.—341
Punch—the principal character in the English comic puppet-show Punch and Judy, a quarrelsome hook-nosed humpback.—239
Punchinello—a character in the commedia dell'arte, a short, stout buffoon.—102

Quasimodo—a character in Hugo's novel Notre Dame de Paris; his name came to personify ugliness.—210, 221

Richmond—a character in Shakespeare's drama King Richard III.—39

Schufterle and Spiegelberg—characters in Schiller's drama Die Räuber, robbers and murderers lacking any moral principles.—35
Sikes, Bill—a character in Charles Dick-

INDEX OF QUOTED
AND MENTIONED LITERATURE

WORKS BY KARL MARX AND FREDERICK ENGELS

Marx, Karl

The Berlin "National-Zeitung" to the Primary Electors (present edition, Vol. 8)
— Die Berliner Nationalzeitung an die Urwähler. In: *Neue Rheinische Zeitung,*
Nr. 205, 207 (Zweite Ausgabe), 26., 28. Januar 1849.—236

British Commerce (this volume). In: *New-York Daily Tribune,* No. 5998, July 16,
1860.—432, 463, 479—80

The Class Struggles in France, 1848 to 1850 (present edition, Vol. 10)
— Die Klassenkampfe in Frankreich 1848 bis 1850 (published in 1850 under
the title *1848 bis 1849*). In: *Neue Rheinische Zeitung. Politisch-ökonomische
Revue,* Nr. 1, 2, 3, 5-6, Januar, Februar, März, Mai bis Oktober 1850.—90

A Contribution to the Critique of Political Economy (present edition, Vol. 30)
— Zur Kritik der Politischen Oekonomie, Erstes Heft, Berlin, 1859.—42

A Curious Piece of History. In: *New-York Daily Tribune,* No. 5352, June 16,
1858.—220

Declaration (this volume)
— Erklärung. In: *Allgemeine Zeitung,* Nr. 325, 21. November 1859. See also:
C. Vogt, *Mein Prozess gegen die Allgemeine Zeitung,* Genf, 1859.—16, 126

Declaration (this volume)
— Erklärung. In: *Allgemeine Zeitung,* Nr. 336, 1. Dezember 1860, Beilage.—25,
275

The Eighteenth Brumaire of Louis Bonaparte (present edition, Vol. 11)
— Der 18te Brumaire des Louis Napoleon. In: *Die Revolution. Eine Zeitschrift
in zwanglosen Heften.* New York, 1852, H. 1.—5, 34-37
— Der achtzehnte Brumaire des Louis Bonaparte. New York, 1852.—34

The Emperor Napoleon III and Prussia (this volume). In: *New-York Daily Tribune,* No.
5986, June 30, 1860.—400

[*Events in Syria.—Session of the British Parliament.—The State of British Commerce*]
(this volume). In: *New-York Daily Tribune,* No. 6021, August 11, 1860.—439

[*To the Editor of "The Daily Telegraph"*] (this volume).—128

To the Editors of the "Volks-Zeitung". Declaration (this volume)
— Offener Brief in Sachen Vogt und Berliner "National-Zeitung". An die Redaktion der "Volks-Zeitung". Erklärung. In: *Volks-Zeitung,* Nr. 35, 10. Februar 1860. See also: *Kölnische Zeitung,* Nr. 41, 10. Februar 1860, Beilage; *Die Reform,* Nr. 18, 11. Februar 1860; *Allgemeine Zeitung,* Nr. 48, 17. Februar 1860, Beilage (distorted) and other German newspapers.—14, 17, 19, 25

A Traitor in Circassia. In: *The Free Press,* No. 34, April 1, 1857.—219

The Trial of the Rhenish District Committee of Democrats [*Speech by Karl Marx*] (present edition, Vol. 8)
— Der Prozess gegen den Rheinischen Kreisausschuss der Demokraten. In: *Zwei politische Prozesse.* Verhandelt vor den Februar-Assisen zu Köln. Köln, 1849. Verlag der Expedition der "Neuen Rheinischen Zeitung".—91

Trouble in Germany (present edition, Vol. 16). In: *New-York Daily Tribune,* No. 5807, December 2, 1859.—378

The War Prospect in Prussia (present edition, Vol. 16). In: *New-York Daily Tribune,* No. 5598, March 31, 1859.—114

Engels, Frederick

The Armies of Europe (present edition, Vol. 14). In: *Putnam's Monthly,* Nos. 32, 33, and 36, August, September and December 1855.—323

The Campaign for the German Imperial Constitution (present edition, Vol. 10)
— Die deutsche Reichsverfassungskampagne. In: *Neue Rheinische Zeitung. Politisch-ökonomische Revue,* Nr. 1, 2, 3, Januar, Februar, März 1850.—79-81, 96, 101, 249

The Condition of the Working-Class in England. From Personal Observation and Authentic Sources (present edition, Vol. 4)
— Die Lage der arbeitenden Klasse in England. Nach eigner Anschauung und authentischen Quellen. Leipzig, 1845.—90

The Frankfurt Assembly Debates the Polish Question (present edition, Vol. 7)
— Die Polendebatte in Frankfurt. In: *Neue Rheinische Zeitung,* Nr. 70, 73, 81, 82, 86, 90, 91, 93, 96, 9., 12., 20., 22., 26., 31. August; 1., 3., 7. September 1848.—87

The History of the Rifle, I-VIII (present edition, Vol. 18). In: *The Volunteer Journal, for Lancashire and Cheshire,* Nos. 9, 11, 14, 15, 17, 18, 19 and 20, November 3 and 17, December 8, 15 and 29, 1860, January 5, 12 and 19, 1861.—348

WORKS BY DIFFERENT AUTHORS

[About, E.] *Compère Guillery.*—329
— *La Prusse en 1860*, Paris, 1860.—119, 162, 182, 183, 212, 328-39, 391-96, 400
— *Die römische Frage (von E. About. Fortsetzung).* Pius IX. In: *Schweizer Handels-Courier*, Nr. 150, 2. Juni 1859, Beilage.—118
— *La Syrie et l'alliance russe*, Paris, Dentu, 1860.—439

Abt. *Carl Vogt und Carl Marx oder die Bürstenheimer.* In: *Stimmen der Zeit. Wochenschrift für Politik und Literatur*, Nr. 39, Winter 1861, Beilage.—39, 44-45

Aischylos. *Prometheus vinctus.*—299

Alexandre I. [Manifesto of December 11, 1814.] In: D'Angeberg, *Recueil des traités, conventions et actes diplomatiques concernant la Pologne. 1762-1862*, Paris, 1862.—142

Alvensleben. L. *Kossuth nach der Capitulation von Vilagos*, Weimar, 1852.—216

Apollonius. *Argonautica.*—199

Бабст, И. [A course of public lectures on political economy, January 1860.] In: *Московскія вѣдомости*, № 19, январь 24, 1860 (lst lecture). In: *Вѣстникъ промышлѣнности*, январь 1860 (9 lectures).—42

Balzac, H. de. *La Cousine Bette.*—36
— *Illusions perdues.*—266

Bamberger, L. *Juchhe nach Italia!* Bern und Genf, 1859.—249

Bassermann, F. D. [Speech in the Frankfurt National Assembly on April 25, 1848.] In: *Stenographischer Bericht über die Verhandlungen der deutschen constituirenden Nationalversammlung zu Frankfurt am Main*, Bd. 8, Frankfurt am Main, 1849.—105

Bazancourt, [C.-L.]. *L'Expédition de Crimée jusqu'à la prise de Sébastopol. Chroniques de la guerre de l'Orient*, 5e éd., t. I-II, Paris, 1857.—164

Becker, N. *Der deutsche Rhein.* In: *Gedichte von Nicolaus Becker*, Köln, 1841.—440

Beckmann. [A notice on Cherval's conspiracy.] In: *Kölnische Zeitung*, 25. Februar 1852.—56-57

Bethell, R. [Speech in the House of Commons on August 6, 1860.] In: *The Times*, No. 23692, August 7, 1860.—445

Bible
  The Old Testament
    Genesis.—131
    Numbers.—72, 244-45
    Psalms.—44, 238, 298
  The New Testament
    Matthew.—36, 44, 46, 238
    Luke.—238
    The Acts of the Apostles.—77

Butler, S. *Hudibras, a Poem Written in the Time of the Civil War*, Vols. 1-3, London, 1757.—190

Byron, G. *Don Juan.*—78
— *Epitaph.*—243

Cabet, E. *Voyage en Icarie*, Paris, 1840.—88, 89

Cairns, H. [Speech in the House of Commons on August 6, 1860.] In: *The Times*, No. 23692, August 7, 1860.—445

Calderón, P. de la Barca. *El Mágico prodigioso.*—28, 251

Camoens, Luis de. *Os Lusiadas.*—99, 190

Cervantes Saavedra, M. de. *Vida y hechos del ingenioso Hidalgo Don Quixote de la Mancha.*—100, 190, 258

Chateaubriand, F.-R. *Congrès de Vérone*, Paris, 1838.—143

Châtelet, C. *Crimes et délits de l'Angleterre contre la France, ou l'Angleterre jugée par elle-même*, Lyon, 1860.—324, 325

Chenu, A. *Les conspirateurs. Les sociétés secrètes. La préfecture de police sous Caussidière. Les corps francs*, Paris, 1850.—73

Christern, J. W. *Doctor Eisele's und Baron von Beisele's Landtagsreise im April 1847.*—131, 274

Cicero, M[arcus] Tullius. *De haruspicum responso.*—297
— *De natura deorum.*—295
— *Orationes in Catilinam.*—68

Colins, J. G. *L'économie politique. Sources des révolutions et des utopies prétendues socialistes*, v. I-III, Paris, 1856-57.—331
— *Science sociale*, Paris, 1857.—331

Cowley, H. [Speech in the House of Lords on April 23, 1860.] In: *The Times*, No. 23602, April 24, 1860.—196

Cuvier, G. *Discours sur les révolutions du globe. Recherches sur les Ossements fossiles*, Paris, 1821-24.—73

Dante. *La divina comedia.*—50, 75, 209, 279
— *Die göttliche Komödie des Dante Alighieri. Aus dem Italienischen übersetzt und erklärt von Karl Ludwig Kannegiesser*, Leipzig, 1843.—74, 100

Demosphenes, *Olynthiacae.*—68

Derby, E. [Speech in the House of Lords on January 24, 1860.] In: *The Times*, No. 23525, January 25, 1860.—339-40

Dickens, Ch. *The Adventures of Oliver Twist.*—70
— *The Life and Adventures of Martin Chuzzlewit (1843-44).*—174

Disraeli, B. [Speech in the House of Commons on January 24, 1860.] In: *The Times*, No. 23525, January 25, 1860.—344

Dolgoroukow, P. *La vérité sur la Russie*, Paris, 1860.—141, 429

Donizetti, G. *Belisario*. Opera. Libretto by S. Cammarano.—77

Douglas, H. *A Treatise on Naval Gunnery. Dedicated by Special Permission to the Lords Commissioners of the Admiralty*, 3rd ed., London, Murray, 1851.—360, 363

Dréolle, E. *Paris, 10 juillet.* In: *Le Constitutionnel*, No. 193, 11 juillet 1860.—430

Dupont, É. *Chronique de l'intérieur.* In: *La voix du proscrit*, No. 8, 15 décembre 1850.—36

[Eichhoff, W.] [Erklärung vor dem Criminalgericht 8.-15. Mai 1860.] In: *Königlich privilegirte Berlinische Zeitung*, Nr. 108, 9. Mai 1860, Beilage.—65
— *Stieber.* In: *Hermann*, 10., 17., 24. September; 8., 22., 29. Oktober 1859.—65

Eisenmann, G. [Speech in the Frankfurt National Assembly on October 11, 1848.] In: *Stenographischer Bericht über die Verhandlungen der deutschen constituirenden Nationalversammlung zu Frankfurt am Main*, Frankfurt am Main, 1848-49.—103

Epigram (anon.). In: *Anthologia Graeca*, XI, 203, vers. 7, 8.—245

L'Europe en 1860 [Paris, 1859] (a description of the map). In: *The Times*, Nos. 23228 and 23229, February 12 and 14, 1859.—137

Fallmerayer, J. Ph. *Fragmente aus dem Orient*, Bd. I-II, Stuttgart und Tübingen, 1845.—114

Favre, J. [Speech in the Legislative Assembly on July 13, 1860.] In: *Le Moniteur universel*, No. 195, 15 juillet 1860.—455

Fazy, J. J. [Speech at the meeting on the premises of the *Club populaire* on February 3, 1860.] In: *Revue de Genève*, No. 29, 5 février 1860, Appendice.—196-97

Fischart, J. *Affentheurliche, Naupengeheurliche Geschichtklitterung: von Thaten und Rahten der vor kurtzen langen und je weilen vollennwolbeschreyten Helden und Herrn: Grandgoschier, Gorgellantua und Pantagruel. Königen inn Utopien, Ledewelt und Nienenreich, Soldan der Neuen Kannarrien und Oudyssen Inseln: auch Grossfürsten im Nubel Nibel Nebelland, Erbvögt auff Nichilburg, und Niderherren zu Nullibingen, Nullenstein und Niergendheym Etwan von M. Franz Rabelais Französisch entworffen*, Achte Ausgabe, 1617.—28, 33, 70, 118, 252, 254

La foi des traités les puissances signataires et l'empereur Napoléon III, Paris, Dentu, 1859.—140, 172, 431

Fourier, Ch. *Théorie de l'unité universelle.* In: *Œuvres complètes de Ch. Fourier*, v. 2, Paris, 1843; v. 5, Paris, 1841.—38

Garibaldi, G. [Address to the people of Palermo on September 10, 1860.] In: *L'Indépendance belge*, No. 261, 17 septembre 1860.—490
— [Address to Victor Emmanuel, May 1860.] In: *Allgemeine Zeitung*, Nr. 143, 22. Mai 1860.—382

Gladstone, W. E. [Speeches in the House of Commons]
— April 18, 1853. In: *The Times*, No. 21406, April 19, 1853.—351
— May 8, 1854. In: *The Times*, No. 21736, May 9, 1854.—351
— January 25, 1860. In: *The Times*, No. 23526, January 26, 1860.—341

— February 10, 1860. In: *The Times*, No. 23540, February 11, 1860.—350, 351, 352, 353

— August 6, 1860. In: *The Times*, No. 23692, August 7, 1860.—444

Goethe, J. W. von. *Faust.*—71, 91, 311
— *Wilhelm Meisters Lehrjahre.*—74

Görgei, A. *Mein Leben und Wirken in Ungarn in den Jahren 1848 und 1849*, Bd. 1-2, Leipzig, 1852.—226

Gottfried von Strassburg. *Tristan und Isolde.*—136

Granville. [Speech in the House of Lords on January 24, 1860.] In: *The Times*, No. 23525, January 25, 1860.—339

[Greiner, Th. L.] *Der flüchtige Reichsregent Vogt mit seinem Anhange und die deutsche Monatsschrift von Adolf Kolatschek*, 1850.—101

Grey, G. [Speech in the House of Lords on January 24, 1860.] In: *The Times*, No. 23525, January 25, 1860.—335, 336

Grillparzer, F. *Die Ahnfrau.*—120

Grün, K. *Louis Bonaparte, die Sphinx auf dem französischen Kaiserthron*, Hamburg, 1860.—199

Häfner, L. [The character sketch of Marx.] In: *Hamburger Nachrichten*, 28. Februar 1851.—99

Hartmann von Aue. *Iwein. Eine Erzählung*, Berlin, 1843.—184

Haxthausen, A. *Studien über die innern Zustände des Volkslebens, und insbesondere die ländlichen Einrichtungen Russlands*, Bd. 1-3, Hannover-Berlin, 1847-52.—146

Hegel, G. W. F. *Die Wissenschaft der Logik*, Berlin, 1833-34.—6

Heine, H. *Französische Zustände.*—114
— *Die Heimkehr.*—235
— *Kobes I.*—69, 108
— *Lutetia.*—114
— *Reisebilder.*—181

Herbert, S. [Speeches in the House of Commons]
— February 17, 1860. In: *The Times*, No. 23546, February 18, 1860.—363
— June 26, 1860. In: *The Times*, No. 23657, June 27, 1860.—404, 436

Hermann, K. [Speech in the District Court in Augsburg on October 24, 1859.] In: C. Vogt, *Mein Prozess gegen die Allgemeine Zeitung*, Genf, 1859.—28, 33

[Hirsch, W.] *Die Opfer der Moucharderie, Rechtfertigungsschrift von Wilhelm Hirsch*. In: *Belletristisches Journal und New-Yorker Criminal Zeitung*, 1., 8., 15., 22. April 1853.—305, 311

Horace (Quintus Horatius Flaccus). *Epistolae.*—214
— *Satirae.*—26, 136, 247

Horsman, E. [Speech in the House of Commons on July 26, 1860.] In: *The Times*, No. 23683, July 27, 1860.—432

Hugo, V. *Napoléon le Petit*, Londres, 1852.—189

[Humboldt, A.] *Briefe von Alexander von Humboldt an Varnhagen von Ense aus den Jahren 1827 bis 1858*. Aufl. 4, Leipzig, 1860.—369

Joinville, F. F. *De l'État des forces navales de la France. Avec l'appendice et les notes*, Francfort s/M., 1844.—434

Jourdan, L. *Les frontières naturelles*. In: *Le Siècle*, 31 mai 1860.—206

Juvenal (Decimus Junius Juvenalis). *Satirae*, Liber I.—44

Die Kaiserchronik. In: *Geschichte der deutschen Literatur*, Leipzig, 1857.—185

Карамзинъ, Н. М. *Исторія Государства Россійскаго*, Т. XI, Санктпетербургъ, 1824, стр. 23.—141, 485

Kinglake, A. W. [Speech in the House of Commons on July 12, 1860.] In: *The Times*, No. 23671, July 13, 1860.—172, 208

[Kinkel, G.] *Brief des Herausgebers an einen Freund in Amerika*. In: *Hermann*, Nr. 12, 26. März 1859.—314
— *Denkschrift über das deutsche Nationalanlehn zur Förderung der Revolution, d. d. Elmira im Staate New York, 22. Febr. 1852*. In: *New-Yorker Staats-Zeitung*, 2. März 1852.—314
— *Vertheidigungsrede des Dr. G. Kinkel vor dem preussischen Kriegsgericht zu Rastatt am 4. August 1849*. In: *Abend-Post*, Nr. 78, 79, 5., 6. April 1850.—6, 95-96

Die Klage. In: *Der Nibelunge Noth mit der Klage. In der ältesten Gestalt. Mit den Abweichungen der gemeinen Lesart*, Berlin, 1826.—184

[Klapka, G.] *Memoiren. April bis October 1849*, Leipzig, 1850.—226

Kolatschek, A. *Die Juchheisten*. In: *Stimmen der Zeit*, Oktober 1860.—327

[Kossuth, L.] *Authentic Life of His Excellency Louis Kossuth...*, London, 1851.—216, 223
— *L'Europe, l'Autriche et la Hongrie*, 2ᵉ éd. augmentée, Bruxelles, 1859.—165, 223
— *In the Name of the Hungarian Nation. To the Soldiers Quartered in Italy. February, 1853*. In: *The Times*, No. 21348, February 10, 1853. In the article: *M. Kossuth and the Insurrection in Lombardy*.—217
— [Letter to McAdam in Glasgow. London, September 26, 1859.] In: *The Times*, No. 23428, October 4, 1859.—224
— *Meine Schriften aus der Emigration*, Bd. I-III.—224

La Farina, Giuseppe. *Storia d'Italia dal 1815 al 1850*, v. I-V, Torino, 1851-52.—423

La Guéronnière, Arthur. *L'empereur Napoléon III et l'Italie*, Paris, Dentu, 1859.—182, 373
— *Napoléon III, portrait politique*, Paris, 1853.—182
— *Portrait politique de l'empereur Napoléon III*, trad. en arabe par M. Rochaid Dahdah, Paris, 1860.—182

Lapinski, Th. *Feldzug der Ungarischen Hauptarmee im Jahre 1849*, Hamburg, 1850.—148, 214, 215, 226, 227

Las Cases, E. *Mémorial de Sainte-Hélène, ou journal où se trouve consigné, jour par jour, ce qu'a dit et fait Napoléon durant dix-huit mois,* t. 2, Paris, 1824.—143

[Lassalle, F.] *Der italienische Krieg und die Aufgabe Preussens. Eine Stimme aus der Demokratie,* Berlin, 1859.—27

[Lévy, A.] *L'empereur Napoléon III et les principautés roumaines.* Nouvelle éd., Paris, 1858.—182

Lichnowski, F. [Speech in the Frankfurt National Assembly on July 25, 1848.] In: *Neue Rheinische Zeitung,* 1. September 1848.—87

Liebig, Justus von. *Die Chemie in ihrer Anwendung auf Agricultur und Physiologie,* Braunschweig, 1840.—243

Liebknecht, W. [An die Redaction der "Allgemeine Zeitung", Augsburg.] London, 19. Oktober 1859. In: *Allgemeine Zeitung,* Nr. 300, 27. Oktober 1859.—240

[Lommel, G.] *Das Centralfest der Deutschen Arbeiterbildungsvereine in der Westschweiz (Lausanne, 1859),* Genf, 1859.—68, 69, 71, 185, 190, 191
— *Die Schiller-Feier in Genf. Nebst einem Nachtrag enthaltend die diesjährige Todtenfeier für Robert Blum,* Genf. 1859.—71, 72, 74

Longinus. *On the Sublime.*—120

Das Ludwigslied. In: *Hausschatz der Volkspoesie. Sammlung der vorzüglichsten und eigenthümlichsten Volkslieder aller Länder und Zeiten,* Leipzig, 1846.—154, 159

[McAdam.] [Statement.] In: *The Times,* No. 23431, October 7, 1859.—224

Das Mähre von Weinschwelg (a thirteenth-century German comic poem).—52

De Maistre, X. *Voyage autour de ma chambre.* In: *Œuvres complètes,* Paris, 1847.—247

Malmesbury, J. [Statement in the House of Lords on April 23, 1860.] In: *The Times,* No. 23602, April 24, 1860.—178, 179, 181

Mazzini, G. *La Guerra.* In: *Pensiero ed Azione,* No. 17, 2-16 maggio 1859.—153, 180, 500

[Meyen, E.] *Carl Vogts Kampf gegen die Augsburger Allgem. Zeitung und die Marxianer.* In: *Der Freischütz,* Nr. 17, 18, 19, 20, 21, 9., 11., 14., 16., 18. Februar 1860.—18, 240
— *Der Process Carl Vogt's gegen die Augsburger Allg. Ztg.* In: *Der Freischütz,* Nr. 132, 3. November 1859. In the section: *Aus der Tagesgeschichte.*—4

Morny, Ch. *Discours prononcé par M. le comte de Morny, président du Corps législatif le 8 février 1859 à l'ouverture de la session législative de 1859.* In: *Le Moniteur universel,* No. 40, 9 février 1859.—159

Mozart, W. A. *Don Giovanni.* Opera. Libretto by Lorenzo da Ponte.—40

Napoléon III et la question roumaine, Paris, 1859.—162, 429

Newcastle. [Speech in the House of Lords on January 24, 1860.] In: *The Times,* No. 23525, January 25, 1860.—337

Niegolewscki. [Speech in the Chamber of Deputies on May 12, 1860.] In: *Allgemeine Zeitung*, Nr. 136, 15. Mai 1860.—394-95, 400

Oliphant, L. *Universal Suffrage and Napoleon III*, London, 1860.—180

Olivier. [Speech in the *Corps Législatif* on June 26, 1860.] In: *Le Moniteur universel*, No. 180, 28 juin 1860.—430-31

Orges, H. *Erklärung*. In: *Allgemeine Zeitung*, Nr. 12, 12. Januar 1860.—263, 317

Palmerston, H. J. T. [Speeches in the House of Commons]
— July 21, 1849. In: *The Times*, No. 20235, July 23, 1849.—136
— January 25, 1860. In: *The Times*, No. 23526, January 26, 1860.—339

Persius, Flaccus. *Satirae.*—213, 243, 245

Petétin, A. *De l'annexion de la Savoie*, Paris, 1859.—193

[Pindar, P.] *The Lousiad. The Works of Peter Pindar, Esq. [John Wolcot]*. In 3 vols., Vol. I, London, 1797.—99

Plautus. *Poenulus.*—112

Plümicke, J. C. *Handbuch für die Königlich Preussischen Artillerie-Offiziere. Entworfen.* Th. I. *Das Materielle der Artillerie*, Berlin, 1820.—65

La politique anglaise, Paris, Dentu, 1860.—174

Pope, A. *The Dunciad. An Heroic Poem*, London, 1728.—237, 247, 250

Proudhon, P.-J. *De la justice poursuivie par l'église*, Bruxelles, 1858.—157

Rademacher, J. G. *Rechtfertigung der von den Gelehrten misskannten, verstandesrechten Erfahrungsheillehre der alten scheidekünstigen Geheimärzte und treue Mittheilung des Ergebnisses einer 25-jährigen Erprobung dieser Lehre am Krankenbette*, 2. Ausg., Bd. 1, Berlin, 1846.—33

Radowitz, J. [Speech in the Frankfurt National Assembly on August 12, 1848.] In: *Neue Rheinische Zeitung*, Nr. 76, 15. August 1848.—253

Raveaux, F. [Speech in the Frankfurt National Assembly on September 16, 1848.] In: *Stenographischer Bericht über die Verhandlungen der deutschen constituirenden Nationalversammlung zu Frankfurt am Main*, Frankfurt am Main, 1848.—253

Reichenbach, O. *Lithographierte Erklärung*, 28. Oktober 1852.—315

Rotteck, K. *Allgemeine Geschichte vom Anfang der historischen Kenntniss bis auf unsere Zeiten; für denkende Geschichtsfreunde*, Freiburg und Konstanz, 1813-18.—236, 242

Rousseau, J.-J. *Le contrat social ou principes du droit politique*, v. 5, Londres, 1782.—401

Ruge, A. *Enthüllungen*. September 1853. In: *Herold des Westens*, 11. September 1853.—87

Russell, J. [Speech in the House of Commons on March 26, 1860.] In: *The Times*, No. 23578, March 27, 1860.—383

[Šafařík, P. J.] *Slovanský zeměvid*. In: P. J. Šafařík, *Slovanský národopis*, 1842.—151

Saint-Amand (Jean-Armand Lacoste), Antier et F. Lemaître. *Robert Macaire*, pièce, Paris, 1834.—447

Schaible, Ch. *The Vogt Pamphlet. To the Editor of "The Daily Telegraph"*, London, Febr. 14. In: *The Daily Telegraph*, February 15, 1860.—130

Schiller, J. Ch. F. von. *Don Carlos. Infant von Spanien.*—258
— *Der Jüngling am Bache.*—187
— *Die Räuber.*—35
— *Wallenstein Tod.*—8
— *Wilhelm Tell.*—40, 48, 101

Schleinitz. [Speech in the Prussian Diet on April 20, 1860.] In: *Stenographische Berichte über die Verhandlungen des Preussischen Hauses der Abgeordneten*, Bd. 2, Berlin, 1860.—379

Schlöffel, F. W. [Speech in the Frankfurt National Assembly on April 25, 1849.] In: · *Stenographischer Bericht über die Verhandlungen der deutschen constituirenden Nationalversammlung zu Frankfurt am Main*, Bd. 8, Frankfurt am Main, 1848.—107

Schulenburg, F. W. [Address to the People of Berlin on October 17, 1806.] In: *Le Moniteur universel*, No. 304, 31 octobre 1806.—67

Scott, Sir Walter. *Waverley.*—97

Senecae, L. Annaeus. *Medea.*—299

Shakespeare. W. *All's Well That Ends Well.*—40
— *The Comedy of Errors.*—260
— *Hamlet, Prince of Denmark.*—116, 190, 245
— *King Henry IV.*—29, 38, 40, 46, 47, 48, 55, 59, 128
— *King Richard II.*—86
— *King Richard III.*—38
— *Love's Labour's Lost.*—272
— *Macbeth.*—40
— *The Merchant of Venice.*—245
— *Midsummer Night's Dream.*—35
— *Romeo and Juliet.*—378

Simon, E. *Un tableau de moeurs politiques en Allemagne. Le procès de M. Vogt avec la gazette d'Augsbourg.* In: *Revue contemporaine*, 9e année, 2e série, t. 13, Paris, 1860.—42, 93, 112, 113, 209

Smith, J. *Book of Mormon*, 1830.—118

Sterne, L. *The Life and Opinions of Tristram Shandy. Gent.*—245, 246

Stratford de Redcliffe. [Interpellation respecting the Syrian affairs in the House of Lords on August 3, 1860.] In: *The Times*, No. 23690, August 4, 1860,—429

[Szabó, I.] *The State Policy of Modern Europe, from the Beginning of the Sixteenth Century to the Present Time.* In two volumes, London, 1857.—505-27

Szemere, B. *Hungary, from 1848 to 1860*, London, 1860.—149, 225

Tacitus. *Annales.*—133
— *Vita Julii Agricolae.*—285

Turquan, J. *Une illuminée au XIXe siècle (la baronne de Krüdener), 1766-1824*, Paris, s.a.—138

Uhland, L. *Die deutsche Nationalversammlung an das deutsche Volk.* In: *Stenographischer Bericht über die Verhandlungen der deutschen constituirenden Nationalversammlung zu Frankfurt am Main,* Bd. 9, Frankfurt am Main, 1849.—106

Des Sängers Fluch.—108

Urquhart, D. *The Crisis. France in Face of the Four Powers,* Paris, 1840.—147
— *Diplomatic Transactions in Central Asia from 1834 to 1839,* London, 1841.—116-17
— *England, France, Russia and Turkey.* In: E. Tucker, *Political Fly-Sheets,* No. 3, 1835.—116
— *The New Hope for Poland,* London, 1855.—148
— *Progress of Russia in the West, North, and South, by Opening the Sources of Opinion and Appropriating the Channels of Wealth and Power,* London, 1853.—116-17
— [Speech at a meeting in London on May 9, 1859.] In: *The Free Press,* No. 5, May 27, 1859. In the article: *Mr. Urquhart's Address on Neutrality.*—117
— *Visit to the Hungarian Exiles at Kutayah, etc. Appendix. Correspondence of Kossuth,* London [1853].—214-18

Vegezzi-Ruscalla. *La nazionalità di Nizza,* 3 ed., Nizza, 1860.—198

Venedey, J. *Pro domo und pro patria gegen Karl Vogt,* Hannover, F. Brecke, 1860.—69, 109, 120, 121
— [Speech in the Frankfurt National Assembly on September 19, 1848.] In: *Neue Rheinische Zeitung,* Nr. 109, 22. September 1848. In the section: *Deutschland. 22. September 1848.*—103
— [To the editors of the *Allgemeine Zeitung.*] In: *Allgemeine Zeitung,* Nr. 158, 7. Juni 1859.—120-21

Vincke, G. [Speeches in the Frankfurt National Assembly]
— June 21, 1848. In: *Neue Rheinische Zeitung,* Nr. 25, 25. Juni 1848.—251, 254
— July 15, 1848. In: *Deutsche Reichstags-Zeitung,* Nr. 49, 16. Juli 1848.—251
— August 8, 1848. In: *Neue Rheinische Zeitung,* Nr. 72, 11. August 1848.—254
— September 16, 1848. In: *Neue Rheinische Zeitung,* Nr. 106, 19. September 1848.—252
— October 23, 1848. In: *Neue Rheinische Zeitung,* Nr. 126, 26. Oktober 1848.—254
— October 24, 1848. In: *Stenographischer Bericht über die Verhandlungen der deutschen constituirenden Nationalversammlung zu Frankfurt am Main,* Frankfurt am Main, 1848.—254
— November 14, 1848. In: *Neue Rheinische Zeitung,* Nr. 145, 17. November 1848.—255
— December 12, 1848. In: *Neue Rheinische Zeitung,* Nr. 169, 15. Dezember 1848.—255
— [Speech in the Prussian National Assembly on December 13, 1848.] In: *Neue Rheinische Zeitung,* Nr. 196, 16. Januar 1849.—256
— [Speech in the Prussian United Diet on December 28, 1848.] In: *Neue Rheinische Zeitung,* Nr. 184, 1. Januar 1849.—256
— [Speech in the Prussian United Diet.] In: *Neue Rheinische Zeitung,* Nr. 185, 3. Januar 1849.—256
— [Speech in the Second Chamber of the Prussian National Assembly on March 22, 1849.] In: *Neue Rheinische Zeitung,* Nr. 255, 25. März 1849.—257

— *Zur Warnung.* In: *Das Volk,* Nr. 6, 11. Juni 1859.—38, 119

La vraie question. France-Italie-Autriche, Paris, Dentu, 1859.—139, 162, 172, 431

Walther von der Vogelweide. *Die Gedichte....* Hrsg. von K. Lachmann, Berlin, 1827.—108

Wermouth-Stieber. *Die Communisten-Verschwörungen des neunzehnten Jahrhunderts,* Bd. 1-2, Berlin, 1853.—312-13

Wesendonk. *Erklärung,* Düsseldorf, 8. Februar 1849. In: *Neue Rheinische Zeitung,* Nr. 219, 11. Februar 1849, Beilage.—106

Weydemeyer, J., Cluss, A., Jacoby, A. *An die Redaction der New-Yorker Criminal-Zeitung,* 7. November 1853. In: *Belletristisches Journal und New-Yorker Criminal-Zeitung,* Nr. 37, 25. November 1853.—313

Willich, A. *Doctor Karl Marx und seine Enthüllungen.* In: *Belletristisches Journal und New-Yorker Criminal-Zeitung,* 28. Oktober, 4. November 1853.—65

Wolff, W. *Erklärung,* Manchester, 6. Februar 1860. In: *Die Reform.* 11. Februar 1860; *Volks-Zeitung,* 24. Februar 1860; *Allgemeine Zeitung,* Nr. 44, 13. Februar 1860, Beilage.—73
— *Nachträgliches aus dem Reich.* In: *Neue Rheinische Zeitung. Politisch-ökonomische Revue,* April 1850.—109, 115
— [Speech in the Frankfurt National Assembly on May 26, 1849.] In: *Stenographischer Bericht über die Verhandlungen der deutschen constituirenden Nationalversammlung zu Frankfurt am Main,* Bd. 9, Frankfurt am Main, 1849.—106

Wolfram von Eschenbach. *Parzival.*—213

Wood, Ch. [Resolution in the House of Commons on August 13, 1860.] In: *The Times,* No. 23698, August 14, 1860.—456

[Zabel, F.] *Karl Vogt und die Allgemeine Zeitung.* In: *National-Zeitung,* Nr. 37, 22. Januar 1860.—12, 14, 25, 127, 359
— *Wie man radikale Flugblätter macht.* In: *National-Zeitung,* Nr. 41, 25. Januar 1860.—12, 14, 25, 72, 127, 259, 276-77

Zachariae, H. A. [Speech in the Frankfurt National Assembly on September 19, 1848.] In: *Stenographischer Bericht über die Verhandlungen der deutschen constituirenden Nationalversammlung zu Frankfurt am Main,* Frankfurt am Main, 1848-49.—103

Zimmermann, E. [Speech in the Frankfurt National Assembly on October 10, 1848.] In: *Stenographischer Bericht über die Verhandlungen der deutschen constituirenden Nationalversammlung zu Frankfurt am Main,* Bd. 4, Frankfurt am Main, 1848.—103

DOCUMENTS

An Act for the better Government of India. August 2, 1858.—432, 445-46

An Act for the preservation of the Health and Morals of Apprentices and others employed in cotton and other mills, and cotton and other factories (1802).—411

An Act to regulate the issue of bank notes and for giving to the governor and company of the Bank of England certain privileges for a limited period. July 19, 1844. In: *The Statutes of the United Kingdom of Great Britain and Ireland, 7&8 Victoria, 1844,* London, 1844.—498

An Act to regulate the Issue of Bank Notes in Ireland, and to regulate the Repayment of certain sums advanced by the Governor and Company of the Bank of Ireland for the Public service (21 July 1845).—498

Aufruf an das deutsche Volk, 26. Mai 1849. In: *Stenographischer Bericht über die Verhandlungen der deutschen constituirenden Nationalversammlung zu Frankfurt am Main,* Bd. 9, Frankfurt am Main, 1849.—106

Aux démocrates de toutes les nations. In: *Le Constitutionnel,* 18 novembre 1850.—81

Bonaparte, L.-N. *Au nom du peuple français.* In: *Le Moniteur universel,* No. 15, 15 janvier 1852.—330
— *Discours de Bordeaux,* 9 octobre 1852.—334

Bloomfield. J. [Dispatch to Lord John Russell, January 14, 1860.] In: *L'Indépendance belge,* No. 73, 13 mars 1860.—383

Code Napoléon, Paris und Leipzig, 1808.—271

Confession of Bangya Before the Council of War. In: *The Free Press,* No. 16, May 12, 1858.—220

Corpus juris civilis. Hrsg. von C. Otto, Bd. I, Leipzig, 1830.—251

Correspondence relative to the Affairs of Hungary. 1847-1849. Presented to both Houses of Parliament by Command of Her Majesty, August 15, 1850, London, 1850.—215

Correspondence respecting the Affairs of Italy. January to May 1859. London, 1859:
— Chelsea to Malmesbury, March 5, 1859.—160
— Cowley to Malmesbury, April 10, 1859 (extract).—134, 158
— Harris to Malmesbury, March 24, 1859.—177

Correspondence respecting the Affairs of Italy from the Signing of Preliminaries of Villafranca to the Postponement of the Congress, London, 1860.—378

Correspondence respecting the proposed annexation of Savoy and Nice to France. Presented to the House of Commons by Command of Her Majesty, in pursuance of their Address dated February 28, 1860, London, 1860:
— Cowley to Russell, received February 8, 1860.—194
— Cowley to Russell, received July 5, 1860.—193
— Grey to Russell, received January 10, 1860.—194
— Harris to Russell, received January 25, 1860.—176-77, 195
— Harris to Russell, received February 6, 1860.—195

656 Index of Quoted and Mentioned Literature

— Harris to Russell, received February 9, 1860.—196
— Hudson to Russell, received February 16, 1860.—53, 195

[Debates in the *Corps Législatif* on the new loan.] In: *Le Moniteur universel,* No. 117, 27 avril 1859.—455

[Debates in the Frankfurt National Assembly on the Polish elections, June 5, 1848.] In: *Neue Rheinische Zeitung,* Nr. 10, 10. Juni 1848.—253

[Debates in the House of Commons on May 31 and June 1, 1860.] In: *The Times,* No. 23635, June 1, 1860.—434

[Debates in the House of Commons on fortification, July 23, 1860.] In: *The Times,* No. 23680, July 24, 1860.—446

[Debates in the Prussian Diet on April 21, 1860.] In: *The Times,* No. 23604, April 26, 1860.—379

[Debates in the Prussian Diet on the military expenses, February 10, 1860.] In: *Stenographische Berichte über die Verhandlungen des Preussischen Hauses der Abgeordneten,* Bd. 1, Berlin, 1860.—495

[Declaration of the German Workers' Educational Association in West Switzerland, August 1859.] In: *Allgemeine Zeitung,* Nr. 235, 23. August 1859.—39

[Decree on the customs duties on grain and flour, August 18, 1860.] In: *Le Moniteur universel,* No. 235, 23 août 1860.—465

Extract from the Minutes of the Council of War, held at Aderbi, Circassia, on Mehemed Bey alias Jean Bangya d'Hlosfaloa. In: *The Free Press,* No. 16, May 12, 1858.—220

Firmàn réglant la condition des sujets chrétiens de la Porte Ottomane, 18 février 1856.—468

Frederick William IV. [Address to the Berlin population on March 19, 1848.] In: *Allgemeine Preussische Zeitung,* Nr. 80, 20. März 1848.—367

George III R. *Message respecting Vessels captured by Spain at Nootka Sound. 1790. 5 May.* In: *The Parliamentary History of England from the Earliest Period to the Year 1803,* London, 1816, Vol. 28.—337

George IV R. [Message respecting Portugal, 11 December, 1826.] In: *Hansard's Parliamentary Debates,* London, 1827, Vol. 16.—337

Gesetz, betreffend die Dienstvergehen der Richter und die unfreiwillige Versetzung derselben auf eine andere Stelle oder in den Ruhestand. Vom 7. Mai 1851. In: *Gesetz-Sammlung für die Königlichen Preussischen Staaten 1851,* Berlin.—271

Gesetz über die Einführung des Strafgesetzbuchs für die Preussischen Staaten. Vom 14. April 1851. In: *Gesetz-Sammlung für die Königlichen Preussischen Staaten 1851.*—268

Gortschakoff, A. M. [Circular of May 20, 1860 to Russian Embassies in foreign countries.] In: *Allgemeine Zeitung,* Nr. 165, 13. Juni 1860.—429

— *Circularschreiben an die russischen Gesandtschaften vom 15. (27.) Mai 1859.* In: *Allgemeine Zeitung*, Nr. 167, 16. Juni 1859.—375

Das Kaiserliche Diplom vom 20. Oktober 1860.... In: *Verfassung der Oesterreichischen Monarchie...*, Wien, 1861.—225, 493, 499, 500

Loi relative à l'importation et à l'exportation des céréales [le 15 avril 1832]. In: *Le Moniteur universel,* No. 109, 18 avril 1832.—465

Napoléon Bonaparte. *Correspondance inédite, officielle et confidentielle de Napoléon Bonaparte. Avec les cours étrangères, les princes, les ministres, et les généraux français et etrangers, en Italie, en Allemagne et en Egypte,* Paris, 1819, v. 1-7.—163
— *A la municipalité de Venise. Montebello, le 7 prairial, an 5 (26 mai 1797).*—162
— *Au chef de division commandant la marine française dans le golfe Adriatique. Montebello, le 25 prairial, an 5 (13 juin 1797).*—163
— *Au quartier-général à Montebello, le 30 floréal, an 5 (19 mai 1797.) Au Directoire executif.*—163

[Napoleon I.] *Proclamation Addressed to the Hungarians by Napoleon I. From Schoenbrunn, in May, 1809.* In: B. Szemere, *Hungary, from 1848 to 1860,* London, 1860.—162

Napoleon III. [Decree on the granaries of November 16, 1858.] In: *Le Moniteur universel,* No. 322, le 18 novembre 1858.—157
— [Letter to Mr. Fould, Minister of State, of January 5, 1860.] In: *Le Moniteur universel,* No. 15, 15 janvier 1860.—330-34
— [Letter to Persigny of July 25, 1860.] In: *Le Constitutionnel,* No. 215, 2 août 1860; *The Times,* Nos. 23687 and 23688, August 1 and 2, 1860.—439, 447

Note adressée par le conseil fédéral de la Suisse aux diverses puissances, pour exposer l'attitude que la Suisse se propose de prendre dans l'éventualité d'une guerre en Italie. Bern, 14 mars [1859]. In: D'Angeberg, *Recueil des traités, conventions et actes diplomatiques concernant l'Autriche et l'Italie,* Paris, 1859.—176, 178

Papers, 1858-1860, respecting past or apprehended Disturbances in Syria, 4 parts, London, 1860.—429

Pozzo di Borgo, K. *Dépêche réservée du général Pozzo di Borgo en date de Paris du 4/16 octobre 1825.* In: *Recueil de documents relatifs à la Russie pour la plupart secrets et inédits utiles à consulter dans la crise actuelle,* Paris, 1854.—145

Règlement organique de la principauté de Moldavie, New York, s.a.—142, 165

Reichs-Verfassung für das Kaiserthum Österreich, Olmütz, 4. März 1849. In: *Wiener Zeitung,* Nr. 57, 8. März 1849.—493, 501

Report of the Commissioners appointed to consider the Defences of the United Kingdom; together with the Minutes of Evidence and Appendix; also Correspondence relative to a Site for an internal Arsenal. Presented to both Houses of Parliament by Command of Her Majesty, London, 1860.—425, 434

[Report on the debates in the British Parliament on the plan for the national defence.] In: *The Times,* No. 23680, July 24, 1860.—425

[Report on "Prozess Vogt gegen die Redaction der Allgemeinen Zeitung".] In: *Allgemeine Zeitung,* Nr. 300, 301, 27, 28. Oktober 1859.—125

Reports of the Inspectors of Factories to Her Majesty's Principal Secretary of State for the Home Department, for the Half Year ending 30th April 1860, London, 1860.—410-12, 413-16, 417-20

[Resolution on the abolition of the English army in India, June 12, 1860.] In: *The Times,* No. 23645, June 13, 1860.—432

Schleinitz, A. [Dispatch of May 26, 1859 to General F. A. Willisen in Vienna concerning the mediation in the Italian war.] In: *Allgemeine Zeitung,* Nr. 211, 30. Juli 1859.—368, 489
— [Dispatch to K. Werther, Prussian Ambassador in Vienna, of June 14, 1859.] In: *Neue Preussische Zeitung,* Nr. 174, 29. Juli 1859.—368, 489
— [Circular to the Prussian representatives at German Courts of June 24, 1859.] In: *Neue Preussische Zeitung,* Nr. 171, 26. Juli 1859.—316, 489
— [Dispatch to the Prussian representatives in London and St. Petersburg of June 24, 1859.] In: *Neue Preussische Zeitung,* Nr. 170, 24. Juli 1859.—316, 489
— [Circular to Bismarck, Prussian representative in St. Petersburg, of June 26, 1859.] In: *Neue Preussische Zeitung,* Nr. 171, 26. Juli 1859.—317, 489
— [Dispatch to Count Bernstorf, Prussian representative in London, of June 27, 1859.] In: *Neue Preussische Zeitung,* Nr. 171, 26. Juli 1859.—316, 489
— [Dispatch to K. Werther, Prussian Ambassador in Vienna, of July 5, 1859.] In: *Neue Preussische Zeitung,* Nr. 174, 29. Juli 1859.—316, 489
— [Dispatch to the Prussian representatives at German Courts of July 11, 1859.] In: *Neue Preussische Zeitung,* Nr. 173, 28. Juli 1859.—316, 489
— [Dispatch to the Prussian representatives at German Courts of July 21, 1859.] In: *Neue Preussische Zeitung,* Nr. 170, 24. Juli 1859.—316, 489
— [Dispatch to K. Werther, Prussian Ambassador in Vienna, of July 23, 1859.] In: *Neue Preussische Zeitung,* Nr. 174, 29. Juli 1859.—316, 489
— *Preussische Circulardepesche. 6. Juni 1860.* In: *Allgemeine Zeitung,* Nr. 261, ·17. September 1860.—398

Thouvenel, E. A. [Circular of the French Ministry for Foreign Affairs to the Embassies.] In: *Le Moniteur universel,* No. 82, 22 mars 1860.—194, 195

Treaties (chronologically):
— *Traité conclu à Schwedt entre la Russie et la Prusse, relatif à la remise en séquestre au roi de Prusse des Villes de Stettin, Stralsund et Wismar, 1713, 6 octobre.*—377
— *Traité d'alliance et de garantie mutuelle conclu à St. Pétersbourg entre la Russie et la Prusse* [1 (2) juin 1714].—377
— *Traité de paix entre Sa Majesté le roi de Prusse et la République française conclu et signé à Bâle, le 5 avril 1795.*—135, 368
— *Traité entre la France et la république de Venise, signé à Milan, le 16 mai 1797.*—162-63
— *Traité de paix signé à Paris. 1814, 30 mai.*—374

— *Traité secret d'alliance défensive, conclu à Vienne entre l'Autriche, la Grande-Bretagne et la France, contre la Russie et la Prusse, le 3 janvier 1815.*—135, 374
— *Traité de paix signé à Paris, suivi d'un article additionnel. 1815, 20 novembre.*—374
— *Traité d'Unkiar-Iskelessi entre la Russie et la Porte Ottomane, signé à Constantinople, le 8 juillet 1833.*—382
— *Traité supplementaire entre S. M. la reine du Royaume-Uni de la Grande-Bretagne et d'Irlande et l'empereur de Chine, signé à Houmon-Schai, le 8 octobre 1843.*—338
— *Traité de commerce entre la Prusse et l'Autriche et de douanes, signé à Berlin, suivi d'articles séparés, d'un protocole, de deux tarifs, d'un cartel douanier et d'un cartel monétaire. 1853, 19 février.*—491
— *Traité d'amitié entre la Russie et la Chine, signé à Tian-Tsin, le 13 juin 1858.*—338
— *Treaty of Commerce between Her Majesty and the Emperor of the French. Signed at Paris. January 23, 1860.*—335, 341, 350, 373, 481

Verfassungsurkunde für Kurhessen. Vom 5. Januar 1831. In: *Geschichte der kurhessischen Landtage von 1830-1835.* Dargestellt von Ferdinand Gössel. Cassel, 1837.—379

Verfassungsurkunde für den Preussischen Staat. Vom 5. Dezember 1848. In: *Gesetz-Sammlung für die Königlichen Preussischen Staaten,* Berlin, 1848.—376

Verfassungsurkunde für den Preussischen Staat. Vom 31. Januar 1850. In: *Gesetz-Sammlung für die Königlichen Preussischen Staaten,* Berlin, 1850.—295

Verordnung, betreffend die Dienstvergehen der Richter und die unfreiwillige Versetzung derselben auf eine andere Stelle oder in den Ruhestand. Vom 10. Juli 1849. In: *Gesetz-Sammlung für die Königlichen Preussischen Staaten, 1849,* Berlin.—271

[Victoria R.] *The Queen's Speech. The Address. 1860, 24 January.* In: *The Times,* No. 23525, January 25, 1860.—335

Wilhelm I. [The speech from the throne at the opening of the Prussian Diet on May 23, 1860.] In: *Königlich privilegirte Berlinische Zeitung von Staats- und gelehrten Sachen,* Nr. 120, 24. Mai 1860.—383

ANONYMOUS ARTICLES AND REPORTS PUBLISHED
IN PERIODIC EDITIONS

Allgemeine Zeitung, Nr. 215, 3. August 1859, Beilage: *Das Centralfest der deutschen Arbeiterbildungsvereine in der Westschweiz zu Lausanne 1859.*—39

Baltische Monatsschrift, Oktober 1859, Bd. I, H. I.: *Acht Monate des Jahres 1859.*—384

Der Bund, Nr. 71, 12. März 1860: *Pro domo.*—179

Le Constitutionnel, No. 193, 11 juillet 1860: *Paris, 10 juillet.*—430
— No. 198, 16 juillet 1860: *Affaires des deux Siciles.*—421

— No. 23637, June 4, 1860: *London, Monday, June 4, 1860.*—435
— No. 23653, June 22, 1860: *London, Friday, June 22, 1860.*—404
— No. 23654, June 23, 1860: *London, Saturday, June 23, 1860.*—435
— No. 23655, June 25, 1860: *London, Monday, June 25, 1860.*—403
— No. 23658, June 28, 1860: *London, Thursday, June 28, 1860.*—404
— No. 23679, July 23, 1860 (telegram).—421
— No. 23698, August 14, 1860: *The Corn Trade.*—461
— No. 23703, August 20, 1860: *Ireland (From our own correspondent). The Harvest.*—462
— No. 23704, August 21, 1860: *The Corn Trade.*—461
— No. 23728, September 18, 1860.—490

Das Volk, Nr. 2, 14. Mai 1859: *Der Reichsregent.*—118
— Nr. 5, 4. Juni 1859: *Mazzini und Monsieur Bonaparte.*—180

Volksblatt, 7. November 1859: [An article on Marx.]—208-09

INDEX OF PERIODICALS

works by Marx.—5, 6, 8, 10, 116, 123, 124, 128, 150, 218, 219-20, 223, 267, 317

Der Freischütz—a German newspaper on literature and art, published in Hamburg from 1825 to 1878.—4, 18, 240-42

Galignani's Messenger—an English-language newspaper published in Paris from 1814; at first, three times weekly and then daily; it mostly reprinted excerpts from major English, American and French papers.—173

Gardeners' Chronicle and Agricultural Gazette—an agricultural weekly published in London since 1841.—462

La Gazette du Nord—a weekly founded in Paris in 1859.—42

The Glasgow Sentinel—a Scottish weekly newspaper, organ of the Tories, published in Glasgow from 1850 to 1877.—116, 221

Hamburger Nachrichten—a German newspaper published until 1868.—99

Handels-Courier—see *Schweizer Handels-Courier*

Hermann. Deutsches Wochenblatt aus London—a German-language weekly for the petty-bourgeois refugees published in London from January 1859; from January to July 1859, it was published and edited by Gottfried Kinkel.—6, 117, 314

Herold des Westens—a German-language weekly published in Louisville (USA) in 1853 and edited by Karl Heinzen.—87

Die Hornisse—A German newspaper published in Cassel in 1848-50 by the petty-bourgeois democrats Heise and Kellner; Biscamp was a contributor in 1848-49.—118

L'Indépendance belge. Journal mondial d'informations politiques et littéraires—a liberal daily founded in Brussels in 1831.—206, 211, 320-21, 383, 490

L'Indépendant—a Swiss democratic weekly published in Geneva in 1851-52.—54, 297

La Jeune Italie—a French-language paper published in Paris in 1843 by Mazzini's supporters.—144

Journal de Constantinople—a Turkish newspaper published in French from 1848. Subsidised by the Turkish Government as an official organ, it was actually a vehicle for French influence; appeared 6 times a month.—220

Journal des Débats politiques et littéraires—a French daily published in Paris from 1789 to 1944; after the 1851 coup d'état, an organ of the moderate Orleanist opposition.—207

Journal de Genève—a Swiss conservative daily founded in 1826.—302

Journal du tir fédéral—a Swiss newspaper published by the Shooting Society in French and German.—298

Kladderadatsch—an illustrated satirical weekly of liberal and, later, nationalist-liberal trend, published in Berlin from 1848.—239, 290

Kölnische Zeitung—a German daily published in Cologne from 1802 to 1945; during the 1848-49 revolution and the subsequent period of political reaction, it represented the interests of the Prussian liberal bourgeoisie.—5, 17, 56, 127, 128, 242, 243, 248, 306, 311, 321

Königlich privilegirte Berlinische Zeitung von Staats- und gelehrten Sachen—a German moderate liberal newspaper published from 1785; known also as *Vossische Zeitung* after its owner Christian Friedrich Voss.—65, 378, 383

Kreuz-Zeitung—see *Neue Preussische Zeitung*

Lithographierte Correspondenz—a German-language daily published in Paris from 1845 to 1849.—186

Mainzer Zeitung—a German newspaper published from 1802; in 1848 it was edited by Ludwig Bamberger.—248

The Manchester Guardian—a daily founded in 1821; organ of the Free Traders and, from the mid-nineteenth century, of the Liberal Party.—326-27

Le Messager du Léman—a Swiss democratic daily published in Geneva in French from 1853.—62

Monatsschrift—see *Deutsche Monatsschrift für Politik, Wissenschaft, Kunst und Leben*

Le Moniteur universel—a daily published in Paris from 1789 to 1901; appeared under this title after 1811; from 1799 to 1868—an official government publication.—134, 154, 159-62, 183, 195, 325, 330, 431, 455, 465

Morgenblatt für gebildete Leser—a German literary daily published in Stuttgart and Tübingen from 1807 to 1865; carried a number of reports by Engels in 1840-41.—113

The Morning Chronicle—a daily published in London from 1770 to 1862; in the 1840s, organ of the Whigs; in the early 1850s, organ of the Peelites and later of the Conservatives.—211

The Morning Star—an English daily published by the Free Traders from 1856 to 1869; had a regular evening edition, *The Evening Star.*—117

La Nation Suisse—a radical daily published in Geneva from 1860 to 1866.—206

Le National—a French moderate republican daily published in Paris from 1830 to 1851.—231

National-Zeitung—a daily published in Berlin from 1848 to 1915; expressed liberal views in the 1850s.—12, 25, 26, 72, 81, 115, 125, 127, 128, 130, 236, 237, 246, 259, 260, 264, 265, 268, 271, 277, 282, 283, 285, 289, 291, 292, 293, 294, 302, 326, 373

Les Nationalités Messager des intérêts, nouveaux, quotidien, politique et littéraire—a French-language daily influenced by Cavour; published in 1860 in both Paris and Turin.—211

Neue Deutsche Zeitung—a democratic daily published in Darmstadt from July 1, 1848 to April 1, 1849 and in Frankfurt am Main until it was suppressed on December 14, 1850. One of its editors was Joseph Weydemeyer, a member of the Communist League.—96

Neue Hannoversche Zeitung—a German conservative monarchist daily published from 1857 to 1883.—274

Neue Oder-Zeitung—a German daily published under this title in Breslau (Wrocław) from 1849 to 1855; in the 1850s it was the most radical of German papers and was persecuted by the Government authorities; in 1855 Marx was its London correspondent.—238, 263

Neue Preussische Zeitung—a conservative daily published in Berlin from June 1848 to 1939; mouthpiece of the Prussian junkers and Court circles; known also as the *Kreuz-Zeitung*, because its heading included a cross bearing the motto "Forward with God for King and Fatherland!"—73, 257

Neue Rheinische Zeitung. Organ der Demokratie—a German daily newspaper, organ of the revolutionary proletarian democrats during the German revolution of 1848-49; published in Cologne under Marx's editorship from June 1, 1848 to May 19, 1849 (with an interval from September 27 to October 12, 1848).—29, 41, 55, 73, 102, 103, 104-05, 106, 155, 236, 237, 238, 242, 250, 251, 260, 264, 272, 276, 281, 288, 291, 321

Neue Rheinische Zeitung. Politisch-ökonomische Revue—a theoretical and political journal published by Marx and Engels from December 1849 to November 1850 as the organ of the Communist League after the *Neue Rheinische Zeitung* which they published in Cologne during the 1848-49 revolution.—81, 90-92, 96, 101, 109, 115

Neue Schweizer Zeitung—a radical weekly published in Geneva from 1859 to 1860 by the German refugee August Brass.—187, 188

Neue Zeit—a German petty-bourgeois weekly published in New York from 1855 to 1857.—85

Die Neue Zeit—the organ of the German refugees published in London between June 1858 and April 1859.—85, 117

Neue Zürcher-Zeitung—a Swiss liberal newspaper first published in 1780; in the 1850-60s, expressed Bonapartist views.—198

New-York Daily Tribune—a daily published from 1841 to 1924; spoke for the Left wing of the American Whigs until the mid-1850s and subsequently for the Republican Party, held progressive views and denounced slavery. Marx and Engels contributed to it from August 1851 to March 1862. The newspaper brought out a number of special issues including the *New-York Semi-Weekly Tribune* and the *New-York Weekly Tribune*.—4, 5, 114, 116, 153, 217, 220, 223, 265, 323-24, 407, 409, 421, 479

New-York Semi-Weekly Tribune—a special issue of the *New-York Daily Tribune*, appearing on Tuesdays and Fridays.—361, 464

The New-York Times—a Republican daily founded in 1851.—5

New-York Weekly Tribune—a special issue of the *New-York Daily Tribune* published every Saturday.—464

New-Yorker Criminal-Zeitung—see *Belletristisches Journal und New-Yorker Criminal-Zeitung*

New-Yorker Humorist—a German-language comic journal published in New-York.—32